# MAY YOU LIVE IN INTERESTING TIMES

Lao Dee

MINERVA PRESS
LONDON
ATLANTA MONTREUX SYDNEY

MAY YOU LIVE IN INTERESTING TIMES


ISBN 075410 285 8

First published 1998 by
MINERVA PRESS
195 Knightsbridge
London SW7 1RE

Printed in Great Britain for Minerva Press

# MAY YOU LIVE IN INTERESTING TIMES

a clear conscience without bitterness

# *Chapter One*

Carefully, slowly, push by push Lilian opened the door of her parents' hovel in the narrow, unpaved alley which was musky and deserted at this time of the night.

She was late again, indecently late for an eighteen-year-old Chinese girl to come home. She was a coffee shop waitress in the posh, new hotel for foreigners and her evening shift finished at eleven o'clock, in time for her to catch the last bus of the day back to its depot not far from where she lived with her parents.

Twelve o'clock was therefore a normal hour to be back, however, during the past few months it had been more often than not past one o'clock, if not later.

If that old hag Hu Guoshang, who lived across the alley from her parents, heard the creaking door she would come out of her filthy, dark and bare shack, yelling and screaming her hatred for modern youth in their colourful Western clothes, embittered as she was by her own lost youth and betrayed ideals as one of Uncle Mao's former Red Guards. Old Turtle, as former Leader Hu was now called behind her back by all who hated and feared her meddling and harangues, would wake up the whole neighbourhood with her squawking. She would call Lilian the most terrible names which the other old women in the alley would, with unholy glee, pretend to believe.

Su Ping, Lilian's sweet and shy mother, would again cry her eyes out for days. Her mother had suffered so much during Leader Hu's five years of total power in the late Sixties and early Seventies for no other reason than that she had been the only woman in the district with a higher education.

And, of course, also for having married Li Kunlen, the man Hu had wanted for herself.

Kunlen, Lilian's witless father, would creep even deeper in his dark corner in the tiny kitchen where he had lived a life of his own since they had dumped him in front of the house now twelve years ago already. He still cringed at the sound of the voice that had sentenced him to twenty years' hard labour as punishment for making his wife pregnant in spite of the Leader Hu's repeated rejection of his request for permission to have a child.

Lilian had been six years old when she had seen two military men in a jeep stop in front of her house and had heard them ask the neighbours whether this was the house where former renegade Li Kunlen used to live. When the neighbours said it was, the soldiers had pulled a blue and green bundle from the back seat of the jeep and had dumped it against the front door of the house.

Then they had driven away, in a cloud of dust, crushing one of Auntie Liu's chickens and nearly missing another one.

Auntie Liu, after all these years, still nourished her grudge against the whole People's Liberation Army for refusing to pay for the dead bird when she had brought it to the neighbourhood command post.

Since then Auntie Liu had performed her daily show of defiance and contempt for authority by crossing the main street at the corner of the alley, stepping in front of the traffic just when the militiaman turned to give the way free.

In the middle of the street, with cars, buses, trucks and bikes horning and ringing on all sides, Auntie Liu, at the top of her voice, would scold the militiaman for failing to protect the working people. The young militiamen did not like to be made fools of and they were angry with the commandant for his standing order to let the old woman have her way, which they knew was not out of compassion but out of sheer bourgeois greed.

The commandant was an inveterate gambler and every day, half an hour or so before Auntie Liu usually would come waddling out of the alley for her show, he could be seen sneaking out of his office and into the meatshop at the corner where bets up to ten yuan could be placed on whether she would be knocked down that day or not, either by a vehicle or by an angry militiaman on duty.

The commandant made out very nicely by betting against this happening.

Little Lilian was still staring at what appeared to be an old man in a filthy, dark blue jacket and baggy green trousers, who was blowing in his cupped, bony hands to warm them in spite of the humid summer heat, when she heard a sob and a stifled scream behind her.

Her mother had rushed past her to pull the old man to his feet and hustle him inside, kicking the door shut with her heel in Lilian's face.

Lilian had sat for hours on the tiny stool beside the front door, vaguely aware of the monotonously mumbling man's voice that droned on and on and on in spite of Mother's hushed cries and whispers.

At twilight Auntie Liu had brought her a bowl of noodle soup with a chicken wing and had waited while she finished slurping the soup, not saying a word but glaring at Leader Hu who had come out of her hole to see what was going on.

Auntie Liu had stood like a sentry until finally the door of Lilian's house had opened just wide enough for her to be pulled inside by her mother. Mother had hugged and kissed her and her face had become all wet with her mother's tears.

Finally Mother had calmed down a bit and, taking Lilian by one hand, she had urged her close to the man huddled in the corner and who was still mumbling and making low, groaning sounds in his hands cupped over his mouth.

Still holding Lilian by one hand Mother had taken her other hand and had put it on the man's coarse, lustreless hair.

'This is Li Kunlen,' she had said. 'He was the most handsome man in town, always laughing, always singing, always happy, no mountain too high, no lake too deep, no river too wild, no task too heavy for him.

'He loved me. He is your father and he would have loved you too, taking you on his shoulders to show you the world. You are the crime they punished him for. His mind wanders in an unhappy world, but one day it will find its way back to this house and we must be there so that he can see you.

'Every morning you will wash his face and feed him his gruel so that you will be the first person he sees when he wakes up.'

And so it had been.

First through primary school, then middle school until she had been assigned her first job, she had prepared, first thing in the morning, her father's gruel, with boiled chicken or salted pork, had spooned it into his slack mouth while watching that big, bony prominence in his throat hop up and down after every spoonful and adroitly forestalling occasional eruptions from soiling his undershirt.

She only vaguely remembered those first few nights when Mother had tried to make him sleep with her.

He had screamed, arms flailing, legs kicking, and Mother had given up.

Mother had then made a kind of plank bed beside the coalstove in the kitchen's darkest corner and that had been his place ever since. During the day he sat with his back against the wall, knees drawn up under his chin, always blowing and mumbling in his cupped hands which seemed cold forever.

After evening rice Mother would change him into his nightdress and help him lie down under his quilt.

Lilian had never felt part of what must surely pass between her father and mother. Nor did she ever feel any stirrings inside her, whether from pity or love, for that whimpering and slavering, helpless child-man. She also had never felt any jealousy when Mother sat beside him on the plank bed, holding his head against her breast and stroking his hair while gently rocking and softly crooning old songs. She had quietly sat in her own chair, staring at the two strangers who were reliving some past life of their own in which she had had no part.

Without question or protest she had done her filial duty during all those years since he had first appeared.

Every day she had washed his face, cleaned his ears and nostrils, fed him his gruel and walked him up and down the alley, which took them more than half an hour because of Father shuffling ever so slowly and because of the five-minute stop they had to make, on Mother's orders, in front of Leader Hu's shack.

The first week or so the neighbours had come outside to watch them while Father stood there, trembling and shaking over his whole body as if sensing with his dim mind some kind of evil vibration emanating from behind the closed door and the grime-covered window of Hu's hovel.

But it had remained deadly silent inside though everybody knew Hu was there.

And so it had gone on, for twelve years. A ritual, a drama in which Lilian had no part and in which the neighbours quickly lost interest, or so it seemed.

So it seemed indeed, nine months ago, when Lilian had come home after her third day in her job. She had seen a crowd in front of Auntie Liu's house trying to catch a glimpse of the programme on Auntie's new television set which had been installed that very morning.

When Lilian had also tried to get a look, Old Yang had cackled that she should go inside since she had contributed more than anybody else to the set.

At her question what he meant by that, Lao Yang had told her how during twelve years nearly everybody in the neighbourhood, including the militia post commandant, had participated in Auntie Liu's lottery by predicting when Old Turtle would crack in Lilian's mother's psychological war.

Ten fen per day had been the rate to be paid into the pool for every day until the predicted day.

If the day passed without Old Turtle having cracked the money was forfeited.

Auntie Liu had been the only one to predict that Hu would not crack before Lilian's last walk with her father, which, as she had subtly wheedled

Lilian's mother into telling her long ago, would be on Lilian's first day as a worker.

Lao Yang had already calculated that Auntie Liu's winnings after twelve years amounted to at least four thousand yuan, enough to pay for the TV set and new furniture.

Lilian had burst into laughter and when she had said that Auntie Liu had been the cleverest of them all, everybody had laughed also and they had pushed her through the crowd to the open window to see Auntie Liu leaning back in a new easy chair, legs wide, flipping her sandals with her bare feet, while watching the announcer in Beijing castigate the evils of capitalism.

At first Mother had been angry when Lilian had told her the story, however, that hadn't lasted long for that same evening Auntie Liu had come to see them, bringing freshly cooked chicken rice and good-luck cookies for all of them, a portable Japanese radio for Mother and a red envelope with twenty, new, ten yuan notes for Lilian.

For Father she had brought a pair of new shoes. It was the first time since Father had come back home that there had been laughter and jokes in Lilian's house.

Since that day the atmosphere at home had been much lighter and Father had seemed to be very happy with the furry little brown puppy Lilian had bought for him the next day, for five yuan, from the meat shop tenant.

Ciaokeli, as Mother and Lilian had called the little dog, licked Father's face and hands, which kept him clean and made him apparently very happy since he kept hugging the little mongrel with a vague, beatific smile.

When they had let Auntie out that fine evening, Auntie had picked up a basket she had put on the floor beside the front door and, pulling back the cloth cover, had shown them its contents: a beautiful fat chicken, already plucked and cleaned, and three oranges.

'For former Leader Hu,' Auntie Liu had said and Mother had nodded her approval.

It was proper for Auntie Liu to show gratitude for her luck; it had nothing to do with Old Turtle herself, although she could take it as a gesture of peace if she so chose. Auntie Liu had put the basket down in front of Hu's front door and had knocked three times. Without waiting for Hu to open the door Auntie had gone back to her own house.

The following morning she had found the basket back on her own doorstep, still containing the chicken and the oranges, however, not three but four, meaning death, and on top of them a huge, dark brown human turd.

With that very rude gesture Old Turtle had placed herself for good outside the neighbourhood community.

Just to be on the safe side, however, people kept on enquiring politely after her health and asking whether she had eaten her rice already when they passed her in the alley. Before you kick a dog be sure you know who its master is and for the moment people didn't know who former Leader Hu's master was or would be some unfortunate day.

Lilian, of all people, could also not afford to ignore the sour, ugly old woman, were it only for her parents' sake, who had suffered enough already because of Hu's animosity.

She had always been Hu's favourite victim, even as a small girl when Hu wilfully bumped against her to make her fall in the mud. Lately she had become the subject of Hu's anti-decadence harangues because of her Western-style clothes, make-up and permed hair. Lilian had often wondered why she and everybody else always thought of Hu as old. Hu had been after her father so she couldn't be much older than Mother who was only forty-six and still very good-looking.

Lilian knew that she took after her mother and she felt flattered when at times a young man, overcoming his shyness and forgetting Chinese socialist morals, whispered, in passing her, that she was beautiful. However, she was only eighteen and had still eight years to decide on a man.

The thought made her shiver with an almost fearful aversion. Since her assignment as a waitress to the foreign guests only Golden Flower Hotel, she had come to see Chinese men, notably young men her own age, as awkward, ill-mannered, impolite and ignorant louts, who lacked the most elementary courtesy towards women.

Besides that, they didn't take care of themselves either. Their fingernails were dirty, their teeth had brown stains from smoking too much and greenish-grey muck because they didn't brush them. Their hair was unwashed and unkempt. Their clothes were either too tight or too wide and their shirt collars were filthy and too wide around their scrawny, grubby chicken necks.

They talked too loudly, thinking very highly of themselves, and threw cigarettes at each other across the table or even across the whole room, all swagger and bluster and no substance. They snickered and laughed like the braying asses they were when they played their silly games of seeing who could drink the most bottles of beer. Or when slamming their cards down on the table during the endless, noisy card games. Or when blocking the sidewalks with their rickety billiard tables and crooked cues.

Sometimes the foreigners brought a group of Chinese into the hotel where otherwise they were not allowed in because they couldn't pay in foreign exchange certificates. The Chinese would have lunch or dinner with the foreigners to celebrate something or other.

Terrible. All the girls were so ashamed to serve at their table. They would pull matchsticks to decide who would serve the dishes and who would clean up afterwards.

The worst was when the Chinese wanted Western food.

They didn't know how to handle the food with knife and fork so they skewered the steak on their fork and tore the pieces off with their teeth, which was difficult because the meat was tough, and then they spat the gristle and bones back on their plate. They spat out the salad because they didn't like the raw vegetables and the sauce.

They slurped, with their lips like trumpets, the yolks of the fried eggs from their plate. They made room for more food, or the next course, by pushing the offal on to the table or on to the floor. They spilled half of the bottle of beer on the table when trying to fill their hosts' glasses and staggered around the table to make a toast with their hosts or friends or with whoever happened to be sitting at neighbouring tables.

They shouted all at the same time while their faces grew redder and redder. Finally, while one of the foreigners paid the bill, they all staggered off to the toilets where they made another terrible mess.

Unfamiliar with the Western-style toilets, they would try to stand or squat on the rim and, of course, fall off or miss the hole and soil themselves when pulling up their trousers.

At long last, under loud laughter and shoulder slapping, they would stumble through the lobby and into the waiting van whose driver would bring them back to their office or dump them near the place where they lived.

Foreigners, for the first time in China, would stay behind stunned by what they had just witnessed, now and then muttering some comment that made them laugh nervously. Others, who had apparently seen it all before, walked off with their guests, helped them in the toilets pretending they needed to relieve themselves as well, then guided them through the lobby and into their van and waved goodbye until the van had turned the corner and disappeared.

Then they went straight to their rooms.

Their leader would come down later to sign the bill and to give each of the girls in the restaurant two or three FEC for all the trouble and the extra cleaning work.

How different they were, the foreigners, Lilian thought. Westerners, Japanese, even the overseas Chinese from Hong Kong or Singapore or wherever, they were all clean, with nice clothes; even their working clothes were nice.

They were almost always in a good mood but even if they were not, they were always polite, saying please and thank you for every small matter you did for them. Ten weeks ago a group of twelve foreign engineers had arrived. They were from Germany and Holland and would stay for several months.

One of the Holland-people was their leader. He was older than the others and could speak good standard Chinese and also Cantonese dialect. He lived in Hong Kong and had spent much time in China already. His Chinese name was Dee Huilin but the Chinese who had accompanied his group the day they had checked in, called him Lao Dee, which was a familiar yet respectful form of address.

Lao Dee had requested twelve rooms on the same floor and the whole group was now staying on the seventeenth floor. Shen Beiyuen, Auntie Liu's seventh niece who worked in housekeeping, had promised Lilian to show her one day their rooms and the strange things and books and magazines they left lying around in the room.

The things Beiyuen had told her about those magazines had made her blush and giggle convulsively and Beiyuen had made her swear never to tell the other girls. Lilian couldn't wait to see those things for herself. The German and Dutch people were very nice, especially the Dutch who were all young, in their late twenties she guessed, fun-loving and handsome. They were so carefree, so self-assured and happy-go-lucky.

Soon everybody in the hotel, personnel and other guests alike, liked them and smiled at them or reciprocated their joking remarks when, in the morning, after breakfast, they waited in the lobby for the van the city had assigned to them to transport them to the construction site and back to the hotel at the end of the afternoon. They were working on a big project some twenty kilometres north of the city and would be staying for at least four or five months, maybe longer.

Still others would come at a later date, Lao Dee had told her, when they were going to start up the new factory.

Lilian was very happy because they had chosen her corner of the coffee shop as their fixed place where they wanted to have their breakfast and dinner every day and also their lunch on Sundays when they had the day off. She would always keep the same three tables free for them and when they came into the restaurant they would quickly push the tables together to make one long one and sit all twelve of them around it. Lao Dee always sat at one end, with his back to the wall and the kitchen door, and Gert, the oldest of the German engineers, a nice man who always smiled but hardly ever spoke, sat at the other end. Only Lilian and her good friend Zing Neiping served them. When Lilian had the evening shift, Neiping had the morning shift and vice versa.

Roger Wu, the Hong Kong Chinese staff-training manager, had made that arrangement when the foreigners had started to leave small FEC on the table, as a tip, after they had signed the bill. They were happy, they said, because Lilian and Neiping spoke good English and had a sense of humour. They were always joking and teasing each other as well as the girls. Not always very refined perhaps, but Lilian and Neiping found it all in good nature so they laughed and giggled and even joked back.

Roger took twenty-five per cent of the tips, which he shared with Vice-Manager Zhou, or so he said. Lilian and Neiping shared another twenty-five per cent while the remaining fifty per cent was divided equally amongst the other waiters and waitresses and the cooks and kitchen personnel. That way there was no need for the others to be jealous and everybody co-operated smoothly to give the foreigners satisfaction, which was not always that easy.

Now they wanted big steaks with a special kind of fried potatoes the cooks didn't know how to prepare so the Dutchmen showed them, then again they fancied cheese and bread with butter with their beer. But always they wanted thousand island dressing. Not in the small bowls it was normally served in, no! They wanted it in the big salad bowls. Apart from in their coffee and beer, they put the pinkish goo on and in everything else.

Within two weeks after their arrival the hotel had run out of its stock of tomato ketchup, so no more thousand island dressing. This had caused an uproar, much to the merriment of the other foreigners in the restaurant who had enthusiastically joined in the protest, drumming with forks and knives and spoons on the plates and the tables, while chanting: 'We want thousand island! We want thousand island!'

Roger Wu had finally climbed on top of a table and, arms lifted high beating a tray with a ladle, had shouted at the top of his voice, 'Shut up! Shut up! Shut up!' until the din had died down and everybody had looked up at him. Roger had explained that in two weeks the hotel's whole five-year plan's allocation of tomato ketchup had been consumed and that extraordinary measures would have to be taken to get approval from the city's economic planning committee for a new allocation.

In the meantime he would ask Lao Dee, who he knew would go to Hong Kong for the weekend, to bring four hundred bottles of ketchup from his, Roger's, cousin who happened to be the distributor of the stuff there.

Cousin Wu would pack the bottles neatly for air transport and deliver the package at the check-in counter of Lao Dee's return flight.

Payment would be made in renmenbi to Cousin Wu's chicken farm in Guangdong Province, where he needed the Chinese money anyway to pay the workers and the farmers. Rather than changing good Hong Kong dollars, which Cousin Wu earned with the export of chicken feet, at the government's lousy exchange rate, he could earn renmenbi this way.

So everybody benefited and next week there would again be lakes and rivers of thousand island dressing.

Jan, the tall Dutch engineer, had lifted Roger on his shoulders and, to loud applause, had galloped between the tables, neighing like a horse while Roger beat the tray with the ladle. The other foreigners, Westerners, overseas Chinese and Japanese alike, had then all followed Jan and Roger, holding each other by the waist, snaking their way through the coffee shop, through the lobby, up the stairs to the mezzanine floor, around the mezzanine, down the stairs again and back to the coffee shop, all the while chanting, 'lakes and rivers, rivers and lakes, lakes and rivers.'

The Chinese personnel couldn't believe their eyes and ears. They had never seen a scene like that and they stood in the lobby, their mouths agape.

Lilian had seen Vice-Manager Zhou slip out through the lobby doors and ride off on his bicycle, probably to the security police to complain about the crazy foreigners before one of the informers amongst his personnel would report the matter and he, Zhou, would be accused of tolerating or, worse, encouraging mayhem and hooliganism in his hotel.

The following evening Lilian had spotted the security men, in civil suits, in the lobby and she had quietly whispered the fact in Lao Dee's ear when he and his men came into the coffee shop for their usual tea and beer before going up to their rooms to wash up and change before dinner.

Lao Dee had smiled and winked at her and had said a few words to his men who later, when they went up to their room, stopped on the way out of the coffee shop at the other tables to warn the other foreigners.

It had been the quietest evening Lilian could remember. The foreigners were really nice people who didn't want to cause trouble for the hotel's personnel.

After dinner that evening the Japanese had come to Lao Dee's table and, after a slight bow, invited him and his men to the new CAAC hotel where the manager had appointed a karaoke bar.

Lao Dee had quickly explained to his men what a karaoke bar was and when they had nodded enthusiastically that they would like to go, Lao Dee had stood up and, bowing equally politely, had told the Japanese that he and his men were delighted and honoured.

Since then they went there almost every night and soon the other foreigners, tempted by the shows, joined them and beer sales in the bar on the mezzanine floor dropped to almost zero. The occasional foreigners who stayed only one or two nights in the hotel wondered where the heck everybody was.

When they had gone to their rooms, after dinner, the coffee shop had been full with a cheerful crowd and when they came down half an hour later for a drink in the bar the whole place was deserted.

Lilian, from her place in the corner of the coffee shop could just see them sitting in the bar on the mezzanine floor above the other end of the lobby, lonely and bored, staring at their beer or whisky, probably despairing of accomplishing anything that might make head office happy.

Her shift finished at eleven o'clock; however, after ten, with everybody gone and the tables set for the following day's breakfast, she had nothing more to do than wait her time out, changing her mind a thousand times about whether to join Jan and his mates in the karaoke bar as he had asked her a few times, or not. He had even given her ten FEC for a taxi.

Then, three weeks ago she had suddenly made up her mind and had gone to the CAAC hotel and up to the top floor where the karaoke bar had been installed by breaking out the separating walls between six adjacent rooms of which two were corner rooms. An interior decoration company from Hong Kong had done the rest, including the installation of the sound system and the giant TV screen.

The hotel manager could be proud of a beautifully appointed L-shaped bar that earned the hotel a lot of foreign currency. He had been with an investigation delegation to Japan and there he got the idea for the bar. He had pushed it through against the opposition of the hotel's Party secretary who said that a bar like that was decadent and bad for morale and that such permissiveness would inevitably corrupt Chinese youth.

Finally the city's vice-mayor and the vice-director of the local CAAC office had approved the plan, provided only foreign exchange certificates were accepted and no local Chinese people were allowed in unless accompanied by foreigners who would pay for them the twenty FEC cover charge and their drinks. Local Chinese were to be strictly prohibited from singing, however.

Consequently, that first time three weeks ago, the hotel's security guard had refused to let Lilian in since she was unaccompanied and had not enough FEC to pay the cover charge. After a lot of arguing the guard had finally pocketed the five FEC she had left after having paid the taxi and he had agreed to look inside the bar for the tall, white-haired foreigner with hair growing on his arms and coming out of his open-necked shirt.

After a short while the guard had returned with Jan, who had been delighted to see her.

He had paid the cover charge and given another five FEC to the guard.

Later that night Lilian, pretending she had to go the washroom, had asked for her own money back from the guard, arguing that it was unreasonable to be paid twice for the same service.

The guard had argued that Lilian had paid him to show willingness to go looking for the foreigner and that the foreigner had then paid him for actually finding him so that the ten FEC were well deserved.

Lilian had then wondered aloud whether the other workers in the hotel would not like to have the same tip-sharing system as in her hotel and that she actually could suggest the idea to the bar-waitresses inside. The guard had given this a few seconds of deep thought and then he had said that it was still too early to introduce such sophisticated ideas as profit-sharing in a Chinese hotel.

On the one hand the workers in his hotel were still very ignorant about such things, he said, and on the other hand the hotel's Party secretary was a bit rigid in his views about people making honest money over and above their lousy salaries.

Besides, the secretary was still sore about his loss of face. Lilian and he, on the contrary, were well ahead of their fellow workers in such matters, thanks to their close and frequent contacts with the foreign friends whose weakness and carelessness with money could be exploited to their mutual advantage, the guard had reasoned.

It would therefore be reasonable to return two FEC fifty fen to Lilian to seal their deal for future co-operation.

While she put the money back in her purse, Lilian had decided to give it a try. She had suggested that the guard have a talk with the taxi drivers who usually waited in front of the hotel until the bar's closing-time to bring the foreigners back to their own hotel. Instead of charging five FEC for the trip they should charge two FEC for each passenger after midnight, she had said.

The foreigners always climbed with five, or even six, into one taxi when they had had too much to drink and the least drunk of them was almost always the same person and he always paid the five FEC and never got his friends' share back.

They simply forgot to pay him back and he was embarrassed to ask them the next day for such a small amount of less than one FEC.

As Lilian saw it everybody would benefit from the new scheme.

The foreigner who always paid could either collect the two FEC fare from each of his friends before they began their binge or he could collect such a nice, round sum the next day without appearing to be stingy. The drivers could keep fifty per cent of the money over the regular fare of five FEC and Lilian and the guard could share the other fifty per cent for having thought out this new profit scheme.

Comrade Du, as the guard then solemnly introduced himself to Lilian, commended himself for his correct evaluation of the possibilities of their partnership and Lilian went back into the bar.

Since that first night three weeks ago Lilian had been back six times already and so far so good. Old Turtle had not once caught her coming home late. A few times she had come waddling out of her shack just when Lilian pulled the door behind her and set out to her evening shift.

As she followed Lilian to the corner of the alley she made loud and snide remarks about whoring coming back in fashion and that a crackdown by the Party was inevitable to protect the people's morals. On that glorious day she, Leader Hu, would personally wipe the muck off the faces of shameless girls such as that no-good daughter of that arrogant intellectual slut Su Ping, who thought herself to be superior to the ordinary working people.

However, Lilian had ignored her and Auntie Liu had put a halt to Hu's harassment by appearing in her doorway when Lilian was about to pass by her house.

Auntie had made it a habit to walk Lilian to the corner of the alley and Lilian had learned that there was usually a hidden meaning behind Auntie's seemingly casual remarks. Like the other day when she told Lilian that she had heard rumours about people getting caught changing foreigners' money in the street for renmenbi.

It was said that there were Party members and informers amongst the money changers.

Such a pity, Auntie Liu had mused, if only those people who had got caught with foreigners' money had known her, Liu Meiling, they would not only have got a good rate but been safe as well. Of course, the rate would not be as high as the one on the street; however, it would still be a much better one than the official rate the foreigners got at the Bank of China counter in their hotel.

There would be a small commission for her, Liu Meiling, and for her friend the militia commandant, who had ways to reintroduce the foreigners' money legally back into the official circuit through his cousin who worked in the CAAC office where the foreigners paid for their plane tickets in cash. Furthermore, the commandant's sister worked in the local Bank of China branch office where she was in charge of foreign cash deposits. Her manager was besotted with her and never checked her accounts for fear of being denounced by her to the bank's Party secretary for pinching her buttocks when she stood next to him behind his desk, waiting for him to sign the daily cash register.

Lilian had given much thought to Auntie Liu's remarks and she saw the advantages of such a convoluted chain of actions in which she could not be directly implicated and she appreciated the fact that this would cost a few renmenbi per FEC; that was only fair.

She decided to try it out with a small amount, say fifty FEC, and see how it went.

She was doing well these past few weeks.

Her share of the coffee shop tips and the taxi-drivers' scheme, together with the FEC Jan pushed into her apron pocket almost every other day now and which she need not share with others, amounted to about eighty, sometimes even as much as one hundred FEC per week.

That was a lot of renmenbi, even at Auntie Liu's exchange rate.

She thought she could even do better, but she would have to talk to Lao Dee first and she wasn't sure whether he was ripe for a little deal as yet, though he would also benefit.

The trouble was, Lilian mused, that he didn't really need the money so why would he bother?

Lao Dee was entitled to a white card issued by the government allowing him to pay for certain Chinese products in renmenbi. So far he had not bothered to use the card, Lilian knew, because he saw no real advantage as he had to change first his dollars for FEC at the hotel's counter of the Bank of China, at the official low rate, a blatant theft Lao Dee said, and then again, at the same counter, change his FEC for renmenbi at two renmenbi for one FEC, another rip-off, Lao Dee said.

The difference in buying and selling rates in this official rip-off process made the Chinese products actually more expensive for him in renmenbi than were he to pay directly in FEC.

However, if Lilian offered him four renmenbi for one FEC and she got herself six from Auntie Liu, who herself would get six fifty, or perhaps even seven, from the commandant, everybody would benefit. She decided to give herself a week to see how Lao Dee would react to a few stories she would tell him about ordinary Chinese trying to make a bit of extra money.

She would, casually of course, mention a few times how well everybody thought he knew China and the Chinese way of doing things and then she would make her proposal.

Or not. It would be nice though if he were amenable.

She would also try to find out more about Jan. She was sure that he liked her, that he was perhaps even in love with her, what with the way he looked at her and all the extra money he gave her.

She knew from the hotel security, where they kept copies of his visa application, that he was not married. He had a girlfriend, however, for she had seen a girl's picture in his wallet when, one evening during dinner, Lao Dee had given his men their pocket money for the next week. Jokingly she had grabbed the wallet and made off with it to show the picture to the other girls.

They had giggled convulsively with little shrieks of feigned outrage at each other's remarks about the foreign girl's long nose and big tits hanging loose, like watermelons, in her T-shirt. Finally, she had given the wallet back and Jan had acted awkwardly, not quite decided whether to be angry or to take the joke in good spirits.

She had told him that all the girls thought his girlfriend was very beautiful with such a long nose so unlike and so much more attractive than Chinese girls' snub noses.

The big tits she hadn't mentioned yet.

Jan had looked a bit dubious about the compliments and had punched Heinz who had made a remark and a gesture Lilian had learned meant something obscene.

A few days later, when Jan had paid in the karaoke bar, she had looked sideways in his wallet and had noticed that the girl's picture was no longer there.

## *Chapter Two*

Lilian had finally managed to open the door of her house wide enough for her to slip inside and with a sigh of relief she softly closed the door behind her. Again she had been able to avoid trouble with Old Turtle, however, it might well be the last time after what had happened tonight in the karaoke bar.

Usually the foreigners; Japanese, overseas Chinese and Westerners alike, had great fun singing to the music that came from the big loudspeakers in every corner and to the text of the songs which appeared on the huge television screen below the film scenes. They would egg each other on and cheer at ever more daring and provocative stints with the microphone in the changing colours of the spotlight directed on the small, round, slightly elevated platform where the singer did his act.

As the night wore on and the Westerners and overseas Chinese drank their tenth or so can of beer and the Japanese were on their eighth shared bottle of whisky, matters sometimes got out of hand and they did silly things.

But always there was this one Dutchman or German who, in accordance with Lao Dee's rules of behaviour, stayed reasonably sober to call people to order before things became really out of control and the hotel security would have to call in the police, something nobody wanted since it could mean the closure of the bar.

Tonight, however, Lao Dee had not shown up for dinner and had also not joined his men afterwards. Already dinner had been a rowdy affair with everybody toasting everybody else in the coffee shop and when they finally got up from their tables it was close to ten thirty and they had each had at least six cans of beer.

Just before eleven Lao Dee had come down to the coffee shop and had asked her whether she would be going to the CAAC hotel. When she had said she would, he had asked her to call him in his room, by phone, if things turned bad and he would come straightaway.

When she had entered the lobby of the CAAC hotel, Comrade Du, the security guard, had caught up with her before she could get into the elevator. Du had been frightened and he had abandoned his post at the bar's entrance to wait for her downstairs. He had told her that everybody in the bar had gone crazy and that he would have to report the matter to the police, to protect himself.

She had given him five one-dollar bills and had told him not to call the police unless she told him so. Should he cheat her and call the police he wouldn't be able to explain the dollars and that would make whatever he said suspect.

When she entered the bar the racket was incredible.

Frank, one of the Dutch engineers, stood on the small singer's platform and held his portable radio against the microphone while it played a really gross tape of a man and a woman groaning and gasping and crying in love making.

The Japanese had gone completely crazy and one of them stood on his chair, swaying his erect, dripping member from left to right, his hands behind his back, to the cheers of his friends.

The waitresses and bar girls were hiding in a corner, behind the heavy curtains, whispering and pushing each other, pretending to ignore what was happening behind their backs.

Three other Dutchmen were acting as barmen.

To Lilian's dismay she saw a number of local Chinese youths, who had apparently been taken out for the night by that group of loud-mouthed Cantonese from Hong Kong who had checked into the hotel that very morning. With red faces from drinking too much the locals were shouting across the bar at each other, annoying the Westerners with their cloying challenges to *ganbei* and their pushy offers of Chinese cigarettes, which, they yelled, were the best cigarettes in the world and fit only for real men like themselves.

They knocked over the foreigners' glasses, fell over the bar stools, vomited in the corners and two stood urinating against a wall.

Jan, his face flushed with anger, had a terrible row with a local boy. The boy had long, greasy hair and wore high-heeled shoes and very tight trousers. Apparently he had spilled his beer down Jan's shirt while trying to kiss him.

Lilian had tried all she could to calm Jan down, shouting in his ear that the young Chinese was the son of the city garrison commander and could therefore make a lot of trouble for everybody.

However, Jan had been too angry to listen to her and he had grabbed the young man by his collar and the bottom of his pants and while Horst, the German of room 1748, had kept the door open, Jan had thrown the boy with such force into the corridor that he had fallen down the stairs opposite the bar door.

Lilian had pushed Jan into the corridor and had shouted at him while slapping his face. 'You stupid, big monkey! You dumb pig! You go shame yourself, making trouble for all the friends!'

Jan had stood there, stricken, mumbling nonsense that she was even more beautiful when she was angry and how he could ever have thought that she was such a fragile little doll.

She had bitten her lower lip and cried a little to re-establish that little doll image and, seeing her tears, he had pulled her against him and had given her a quick hug and a kiss that missed her mouth and landed instead just below her snotty nose.

Jan had wiped his mouth, stared at her and, catching the din on the other side of the door, he had mumbled, 'Jesus Christ, have to stop that madhouse.'

'Call your leader,' she had urged him, 'call Lao Dee, before the boy, Xiao Lu, returns with the police.'

They had both rushed down to the lobby and had got through to their hotel at the first ring. Fortunately the night operator was not asleep yet and he had put her through to Lao Dee's room without asking questions. She had told Lao Dee to come as quickly as he could and then she had passed the telephone to Jan who had done some more explaining while she had gone to look for Comrade Du to tell him the trouble would soon be over.

Comrade Du had been too scared to talk back for he had also recognised the son of the city's military commander hobbling through the lobby, bleeding like a pig from his nose.

Jan had gone back to the bar while Lilian had waited in the lobby for Lao Dee.

She would have to leave immediately for her hotel after having explained to Lao Dee what she had seen and the trouble that could come from it.

Lao Dee didn't need her in the bar and she had her own damage control to do with the night operator of her hotel. She would have to give him money for not logging her call on his nightshift roster which he had to put on Secretary Du's desk every morning when he went off duty at seven o'clock. She would also have to ask the taxi driver to wait for her in the lane behind the hotel's back door and to drive her to the corner of her alley after her talk with the operator.

All that would cost money.

Her part had gone well.

The operator had taken the ten-FEC note and had torn up the roster sheet with the one call that had come in that night; hers. He had taken a blank sheet, written his name and the date on it and had then sat back, watching her with a quizzical smile.

Then in between slurps from his glass of green tea, he had said that he had heard rumours that some of the hotel's workers had become too close to the foreigners and that Secretary Du was trying to find out who those traitors were.

Secretary Du was still very sore at what had happened last week when those terrible Dutch people had managed to put that obscene tape of theirs on the hotel's piped-in music system, the operator had told her. That had caused such an uproar amongst the guests and workers that Vice-Manager Zhou had had to report the matter to the city's security police.

That nice, elderly Dutch engineer who spoke Chinese had apologised to Vice-Manager Zhou and to the security people and they had all celebrated the happy outcome of the misunderstanding about the tape in that expensive seafood restaurant in Hainan Road, not far from where he lived, the operator had told her.

Just when he had been about to leave for work the other night he had seen five taxis waiting in front of the seafood restaurant and he had waited to see who were those rich people that could afford to pay for at least three tables and have their guests driven home in taxis.

To his surprise he had seen Vice-Manager Zhou come staggering out of the restaurant, a bottle of *maotai* in one hand, followed by the hotel's whole security team, twelve people in all, and another twelve people whom he had recognised as policemen, each also with a bottle of famous-brand *maotai*. They had obviously been roaring drunk and had all the time laughed like idiots while toasting each other with their bottles.

Finally a foreigner, whom the operator had recognised as the Dutchman they called Lao Dee, had come out of the restaurant, also not too firm on his legs, and everybody had started to say goodbye to everybody else, which had lasted for more than twenty minutes.

Then Lao Dee had begun to push the others, one by one, into the taxis, six men to one car, and each time he had had a carful the operator had seen him pass a one hundred-FEC note to the driver and had heard him give instructions to drop off each passenger in front of the man's house.

Lao Dee had finally taken the last taxi and back in the hotel he had called room service and ordered a pot of hot Chiu-Chao tea, the best remedy against the after-effects of too much alcohol, the operator had added for Lilian's benefit.

At six o'clock in the morning the operator had logged another call from Lao Dee's room to room service, this time for congee and rice water, a sure sign that Lao Dee was suffering from an upset stomach and loose bowels and the fact he took his breakfast in his room was undoubtedly because he wouldn't be able to stand the sight and smell of the greasy fried eggs his men always ate for breakfast.

The operator had gone on to say that if Lilian knew of a friend being too chummy with the foreigners, she should perhaps caution this friend, especially against associating so openly with those Dutch people that it couldn't escape Secretary Du's attention.

Lilian had thanked the operator for his solicitous concern and had promised him that she would keep a close eye on her friends and if one of them as much as smiled at the Dutch she would immediately warn her against the dire consequences.

The operator had nodded approvingly and, musingly, he had gone on to say that these were troubling and confusing times, what with the Party seemingly incapable of keeping things under control. The leaders were certainly out of touch, if ever they had been in touch, with the young and their aspirations, he had added, as if talking to himself. The young these days mocked the old Party values of sobriety and shared poverty and were becoming increasingly impatient and angry that they had been lied to all these years about life outside China.

Now they saw for themselves what foreigners were like and the freedom they had and the nice things and all that money.

Our young people want the same and they want it now, the operator had said, emerging from his reverie; and looking directly at Lilian, he had added that he had a daughter about Lilian's age and not only did she openly challenge his authority, and that of the neighbourhood Party committee as well, she also wanted, demanded, things he simply hadn't the means to pay for.

Lilian had nodded and hummed knowingly during the operator's monologue and when he fell finally silent she had added the last piece to the delicate structure of their nascent *guanxi* relationship.

'I know,' she had said, 'I am a young woman myself and not a day goes by when I am not tempted by one thing or another, so I understand what your daughter must feel. However, I also know that all these new things cost a lot of money so I also understand how you feel.

'At least your daughter is lucky that she has a father who recognises the cause of the problem and who is in a position to gather information and to render small services which may be of value to certain people with the means to show their appreciation. I wish I had a father like that,' and, smiling wistfully, she had said goodbye to the operator, who kept repeating that she only had to let him know if she needed something.

The taxi driver had fallen asleep and had irritably demanded an additional fifteen FEC to drive her to her lane. It had been a costly evening, yet she was certain that the money had been well spent and that she would reap the benefits. At least, if things turned out all right and for that to happen it was absolutely necessary that the local Chinese, who had made such fools of themselves tonight, didn't boast to their friends about their experiences and start rumours and gossip flying. This would force the police to conduct investigations and find culprits, if only to protect themselves.

Maybe she should go to the hotel early tomorrow morning to speak to Lao Dee before he left for work and suggest that he talk to the Hong Kong Chinese, who, after all, had caused all the trouble with their stupid idea of bringing those local idiots to the bar. Surely those Hong Kong people knew them, or at least a few of them, or else they wouldn't have invited them. Probably they were involved in the same project so the Hong Kongers should have some leverage and be able to keep their local friends from talking their heads off.

The unpleasantness with General Lu's effeminate son was a different matter entirely.

Maybe she needn't be as afraid of the consequences as she had been earlier, now that she saw the whole affair in a more detached frame of mind. Surely General Lu was embarrassed enough as it was because of his son's sexual proclivities and wouldn't exactly be looking forward to an official investigation of what had happened between his son and a foreigner.

Tomorrow morning she would tell Lao Dee to instruct Jan, if ever the police came to interrogate him, to pretend genuine indignation at young Lu's offensively lecherous behaviour, saying however, that as far as he was concerned, the matter was closed. That would leave the police a way out and their confidential report to the city's Party secretary would mention that they had succeeded in convincing the foreigner not to press charges against Xiao Lu for lechery.

The general would read the report with relief and the matter would be hushed up. Satisfaction all around and the foreigners would come out of it smelling of roses.

Happy that she had it all worked out so neatly, Lilian tiptoed into the small living-cum-bedroom and to her relief she heard her mother snoring very softly. Her luck tonight had held, but it was better not to push it too far so she decided to lie down on the couch instead of in bed with Mother and risk waking her and invite questions.

Once, a few weeks ago, she had told Mother not to ask questions if she knew already she wasn't going to like the answers but Mother was still a bit opinionated and insisted she had a right to know what her daughter was doing. She took her shoes off and, groaning contentedly, let herself sink down on to the couch, fully dressed so that the plastic wouldn't stick to her skin so much.

She wondered what it would be like to sleep in those big hotel beds and she couldn't help thinking of Jan and the way he had looked at her that night.

The sensation of warmth that spread from her breasts down her belly and the tingling contractions there made her tense all over. It wasn't the first time her body had tricked her that way and in a self-taught reflex she called up the images of the documentary film she had once seen on the hotel's in-house movie system about that man in his small canoe descending the rapids of a narrow and very wild river, manoeuvring frenetically with his paddle to avoid the rocks, now and then overturning and disappearing completely in the white water.

She saw herself as that man and the furious river as her life.

This was now the fourth time already over the past three weeks or so that these particular images had enabled her to regain control over her body and she wondered fearfully whether it was some kind of foreboding that her life was gaining a momentum she might not be able to control much longer.

In spite of herself she thought of that evening, now seemingly a hundred thousand years ago, when her life had taken that irrevocable turn, whether for better or for worse she wasn't sure, though sometimes she feared the latter.

Auntie Liu had asked her for evening rice and to meet her seventh niece, Shen Beiyuen, who worked at the same hotel Lilian had been assigned to a week earlier. Beiyuen had been with the hotel since its opening a year ago and had heard and seen many strange things. Auntie Liu thought that listening to Beiyuen telling about her experiences might be useful for Lilian.

The memory of that evening made her chuckle. Good grief, as Lao Dee would say, the things she had heard that evening and that had happened since!

How naive she had still been then.

How simple life had still seemed then.

## *Chapter Three*

'Beiyuen is in the kitchen, preparing chicken noodle soup,' Auntie Liu said loudly when she let Lilian in. 'She will come in a moment, when the soup is ready.'

Then, behind her hand, she had whispered in Lilian's ear, 'Be careful what you say in Beiyuen's presence. She is dangerous because she is so guileless it makes you want to cry. She once came running after me into the meat shop to tell me, in front of everybody and all excited, that the chicken I had gone to complain about and had wanted to change free of charge for a fresh one was actually my old hen, the one I had killed three days ago because it no longer laid any eggs but just ate more. The one I had bought from the meat shop yesterday, she had just found in the soup pot and was really quite delicious. Oh, my face was so red as everybody laughed and now the shop tenant, that thieving, gambling good-for-nothing, always sells me the tough meat and the old chicken for the high price because he knows nobody will believe me when I complain.'

Lilian couldn't help laughing and Auntie Liu said, indignantly, 'Yes, you laugh now, but I hope you won't have reason to cry later, like your Vice-Manager Zhou Zouliang, who still cries himself to sleep every night because of what Beiyuen did to his career.

'Vice-Manager Zhou was officially criticised by the city Party committee because of a letter a foreign guest wrote to his host company and which was of course forwarded to the city Party secretary as is the rule for all correspondence from foreigners. The foreigner wrote that when one afternoon he had returned to the hotel earlier than usual to pick up some documents he needed for a meeting, he had found the door of his room blocked by a housekeeping trolley and that the girl had told him,' and here Auntie mimicked Beiyuen's high-pitched voice and staccato way of talking, '"You cannot go in, Mister. Manager Zhou now in bed sleep. He all place piss vomit. He eat, drink too much. When awake I clean first second time already".'

Auntie Liu sighed. 'Very bad, that letter. Very stupid of this guest. He should have demanded another room and talked to Vice-Manager Zhou the next day and got favourable treatment. Now what? Only anger and mistrust and missed chances. Never mention Shen Beiyuen in Vice-Manager Zhou's presence. He is very touchy about her and never even goes near her. Beiyuen thinks that that's because he is secretly in love with her since he ogles her from far and then scuttles off as if he has seen a ghost.'

At that moment Beiyuen came into the room carrying a tray with three bowls of steaming hot soup and a plate of meat dumplings.

'Eat,' she laughed, 'Auntie told me soup enough, keep pork for tomorrow, however, I think Lilian is good friend to make Auntie earn so much money to buy all these wonderful television and new soft chairs, so I also make dumplings.'

Lilian burst out laughing at the sight of Auntie Liu burying her red face in her soup bowl, frantically shovelling the noodles in her mouth with her chopsticks.

'If people would act in accordance with their own good advice to others, they wouldn't be embarrassed so often,' Lilian said laughingly, which caused Auntie to swallow her noodles the wrong way, so that both girls had to beat her on the back to force the food back up.

After a lot of whooping and coughing and slapping the old woman finally breathed normally again. Wiping the tears from her eyes with the sleeve of her jacket Auntie Liu suddenly hiccuped and belched loudly, starting a general hilarity until all three were convulsed with laughter, helpless to stop until Old Yang yelled outside in the alley that Leader Hu might still suffer her fit in a delayed reaction and everybody would claim his money back from Liu Meiling.

'I'll keep a few dumplings for you, envious old man!' Auntie yelled back. 'Now go back to bed and make your old woman laugh for a change!'

Still giggling and chuckling, Auntie and the two girls slurped their soup and ate their dumplings. The food was delicious and Beiyuen turned out to be a very nice person.

She had a round face and her cheeks were as red and shiny as the foreign apples one saw these days in the Friendship Store. Her eyes were so slanted and slitted that one wondered how she managed to see with them.

She had an astonishing voice, tinkling like small porcelain bells brushed by the wind. She had a gurgling laugh that started way down in her belly and then came bubbling all the way up to end on a high, silvery note when it left her lovely, small mouth.

Lilian found her adorable, though she appeared to be a baffling contradiction in every respect. Her remarks and observations were almost shockingly down-to-earth and matter-of-fact and Lilian could well imagine that she made people nervous.

Utterly without malice she couldn't distinguish between things that could be said and those that had better be left unsaid. People with an uneasy conscience would be better off avoiding her.

However, because of her funny face, her tinkling, lilting voice and her maddening laugh one felt helplessly incapable of being angry with her.

It was not difficult to understand Vice-Manager Zhou's reaction to Beiyuen.

Egged on by Auntie Liu's interested though leading questions, Beiyuen talked in her funny, direct manner about the hotel, the leaders, the workers and the many, many things that went wrong in the beginning, after the hotel's soft opening.

The leaders and workers who had been assigned to work in the hotel by the city's Party committee not only knew nothing about the hotel business but most of the workers had just finished middle school or the local language institute and had never worked before.

Those appointed as leaders were people who had good connections in the Party or city committees and they had been given a soft job in return for reporting on the foreigners and for providing favours in the hotel, such as dinners in the hotel's restaurants for their protectors and their friends and relatives, and rooms to spend the night when they were too drunk to stand let alone walk home.

All without paying of course.

Party Secretary Du had been specially selected from the Party's young local cadres because of his visceral hatred for everything foreign, for his zeal in promoting Party discipline and for his obsessive insistence on daily study sessions on Party doctrine and important speeches by the Party's elderly top leaders.

He saw it as his mission to stand as a rock of socialist righteousness between the ideological purity of the hotel's Chinese employees and the upcoming flood tide of foreign evils, most of all the evils of loose morals and individualistic thought and action.

Right from the first day the temporary Hong Kong Chinese staff-training managers had clashed with Secretary Du and the hotel's manager and vice-manager about virtually everything that needed to be done. They found out that they had no authority to give orders, let alone to impose sanctions, and that the hotel's leaders didn't want or dare to exert authority.

The leaders came and went as they pleased and when they were in the hotel they said that they were too busy managing to attend the training sessions and lectures. Besides, they said, they were leaders and therefore they knew all there was to know about how to run a hotel, which was very easy anyhow.

All there was to it, they told the Hong Kongers, was for the guests to observe the rules made by Secretary Du.

These rules had been stencilled, after having been approved by the city's Party committee on discipline, and the stencils had been put in every room's hotel information folder, which was clearly marked: VITALITY INFORMATION STUDY ON ARRIVAL IN ROOM BEFORE OTHER THINGS.

It was the guest's duty to read the rules carefully on arrival and to consult them regularly during his stay to avoid mistakes on his part. The rules anticipated every possibility of misdemeanour and they were also clear on the matter of payment. Restaurant bills, laundry and telephone charges had to be paid immediately, the room charge had to be paid the evening before the day of departure or every three days in case the guest stayed longer.

It was Beiyuen's duty, and that of the other girls of housekeeping, to check every day whether the rules had indeed been removed from the folder by the guest and placed prominently on the room's desk for easy consultation. If still in the folder, probably unseen, or worse, used as a piece of scribbling paper, the girls had to put a new stencil on the guest's pillow and report him to Secretary Du.

That was all there was to running a hotel, Du and the leaders said, so what could be easier than that? All that foreign nonsense about guest satisfaction. If the guest wasn't happy he should pay for his room and leave.

He would find out soon enough that the hotels for local Chinese and the guest houses were far worse than this beautiful new hotel and he would come back, all meek, and make no more trouble.

The Hong Kong training managers also had many problems with the ordinary hotel workers. Not so much because of ill will on the workers' part but because they were not allowed to tell the workers directly what to do and how to do it. They had to ask the worker's section leader to have this or that done and when the leader was in a meeting with Secretary Du, which was almost always the case, nothing could be done.

The rare worker who was willing to do something without actually being told so and did it without clearing his action with his section leader or with

Secretary Du personally, was punished with extra study after working hours or, worse, was transferred to a filthy Chinese hotel or even to a factory. Beiyuen had often noticed how training managers and guests alike were driven to fury and despair by the rules for the workers' own working, resting and meal times.

The first shift began at seven in the morning, however, the workers who had to leave their home before six, which meant everybody, had the right to have breakfast first, in the hotel's canteen; and because the canteen's cooks also began work at seven, nobody was at his or her post before eight. Unfortunately, between seven and eight was also the time that most, if not all, of the guests wanted their breakfast in the coffee shop.

With nobody there to take their orders, let alone to prepare their greasy eggs with bacon and toast and jam, they quickly became impatient and angry.

Roger Wu, the Hong Kong training manager, in his black suit, really tried his best to keep tempers from getting out of hand.

He would run around with the coffee pot and pour and splash both cups and saucers full with the bitter, black stuff that he kept replenishing himself from the large tin of mediocre quality instant coffee and lukewarm water directly from the boiler in the kitchen.

One could immediately single out the guests who had been to China before.

They had brought their own bread and cheese or cereals with instant milk powder and they used the hot water from the room thermos they took down with them to the coffee shop. Many of them even had their own jar of good quality instant coffee. They only used the plates, bowls and cutlery of the coffee shop which had fortunately been put ready on the tables the evening before by the outgoing shift.

They winked knowingly at the harassed Roger and grinned mockingly at their inexperienced fellow guests' vain attempts to get attention and their protests at having coffee splashed over their table, files and trousers.

Beiyuen also merrily recalled the pandemonium on each floor and in the lobby when, at the busiest times of the day and early evening, scores of guests who wanted either to go down for breakfast, lunch or dinner, or go up to their rooms, had to wait twenty minutes or more for a place in the one lift still in service, the other five lifts being blocked on the top floor because the operators were having their meal or a rest period. No amount of protest or abuse by the exasperated guests or of pleading by the despairing Hong Kongers could persuade Secretary Du to change his mind. In his book lifts were machines and machines had operators.

That the lifts, installed by Japan's Three-Leaf Company, were fully automatic and were meant to be operated by the guests themselves, made no difference to Secretary Du. To him that was just another foul capitalist trick to get rid of the working class and in Du's China that was not going to work.

The controversy had lasted three months and the daily angry scenes had finally been reported to the city's vice-mayor. The vice-mayor had apparently managed to prevail over the city's Party secretary since a compromise had been reached. During the operators' mealtimes and rest periods the guests would be permitted to push the buttons themselves.

The words 'operate the lifts themselves' were carefully avoided. At all other times each lift had to have one operator to whom the guests had to indicate their floor of destination, upon which the operator, if awake or if not absorbed in a filthy magazine given to him or her by an overseas Chinese guest, would push the appropriate button and, upon arrival at the designated floor, would announce the floor's number clearly in Chinese and in English, provided his or her mouth wasn't still full with food or if not too absorbed in magazines or nose-picking.

Secretary Du had coached the operating instructions on a sheet of hotel letter paper which he had then glued on the lift's back wall. In a grudging concession to those guests unable to read Chinese he had ordered Lao Dao of the engineering department to make a translation in some foreign dialect or other and to stick it below the Chinese text.

Lao Dao's version, in the English dialect, read: 'Guests are invited to push themselves the button of their respective floors of destination. If, however, the lift operator is present you are kindly requested to allow him or her the courtesy to do this for you since this is the task assigned to him or her.'

It was not an exact translation of Du's terse text, but then one could hardly address the foreign friends in such a peremptory manner, Lao Dao had argued when Du had criticised him for being too polite to those contemptible barbarians.

The guests, though, had never paid much attention to the instructions and the frustrations of the first three months were soon forgotten. These days the guests might just wonder why that same girl, in her rumpled, greasy hotel uniform, was always slumped in the small corner next to the push-button plate, reading a tatty magazine or just staring vacuously at nothing, going up and down, up and down, for hours on end.

If someone had told this observant guest that this same girl would most probably still be there in ten years or even until the end of her working life, unless some day the system would change and allow her to choose her own job, he wouldn't have believed it.

Perhaps if he took the trouble to read Lao Dao's translation he would feel a bit of compassion?

Lilian enjoyed listening to Beiyuen. She could imagine the problems the people, personnel and guests alike, must have had to deal with in the beginning, however, she could also see the humour of it all and she felt a pang of regret that she had not been there in those pioneering times.

Now all but one of the Hong Kong managers had gone back to Hong Kong or maybe to some other joint venture hotel in China.

Only Roger Wu was still there and he would stay at least one more year. The owner of Roger's hotel in Hong Kong was the joint venture partner and he had made a deal with Vice-Manager Zhou. Zhou, when he would be asked by the Chinese partners whether Roger Wu was still needed, would say that one more year of general assistance was advisable. In the event of trouble between the local and foreign partners Wu could be blamed which would offer the others a way out and save face.

Actually Zhou was only the vice-manager while Yu Pufang was the director.

Yu was a high Party member who only showed his face when high-level delegations from abroad were staying in his hotel, with ministers or vice-ministers from Beijing, or with the provincial governor and his staff.

Then, when the important guests were assembled in the lobby to wait for the bus that would take them on a tour or to a meeting, Yu would walk briskly through the lobby with a frown on his face as if he were preoccupied and on his way to a problem situation that needed his expert guidance. Or, when the delegation members were having dinner with the high officials from Beijing and Shenyang, director Yu would stroll casually through the restaurant, nodding and smiling at the usual guests as if he knew them all personally and he would greet the delegates and officials, acting surprised and delighted to see them there also just while he was making his customary inspection round.

He then used to stand for a short while behind the chairs of the highest level officials, with his hands jovially on their shoulders, talking and laughing, to show the foreign dignitaries and the wielders of power from Beijing and Shenyang how close he was to the local Party hierarchy.

He would interrupt this show of camaraderie a few times to dash across the restaurant to give directives to a waitress, one hand pointing and gesticulating, his other arm around her shoulders in a fatherly and reassuring manner.

During Yu's show, Zhou would stay in the background, snorting derisively at his superior's antics while nevertheless nervously watching the officials' faces. If he saw signs of annoyance or embarrassment Zhou would be delighted; if, on the other hand, the big shots seemed amused he would worry and bite the nail of his left thumb.

Other than on those occasions, however, Director Yu never set a foot in the hotel and Vice-Manager Zhou had the responsibility and, of course, the risk of blame when things went wrong.

Like all other vice-positions in China, Vice-Manager Zhou was not a Party member and his fate was blame when things went wrong and credit for his leader, Director Yu, when everything went well. When there was neither blame nor credit, Secretary Du was praised for maintaining discipline and *status quo*.

In fact, Vice-Manager Zhou was in a no-win situation. His only hope was to be admitted as a Party member, however, that was now a somewhat remote prospect because of the unfortunate business with Beiyuen and the irate foreign guest's letter.

Auntie Liu skilfully used this second reference to this particular foreigner to steer Beiyuen away from the subject of the hotel's Chinese staff. She wondered aloud whether the foreigners were always so easy to deal with and whether their finicky habits and hot tempers were also not the cause of a lot of trouble. Beiyuen immediately launched herself in a hilarious though surprisingly accurate description of the different kinds of foreigners and their idiosyncrasies which proved an inexhaustible source of further merriment.

'There are three main groups,' she said, 'each group very different from us Chinese, however, also very different from one another.

'First there are the Hua-Qiao, the overseas Chinese, who are mostly from Hong Kong, however some are also from Singapore and from America. Amongst them they are not so different, except that those from Singapore and America are quiet-like and speak good, standard Chinese. The Hong Kong people speak Canton dialect, very loud and not so refined and I cannot understand what they talk about amongst themselves. Besides, they all talk at the same time and laugh a lot, not paying any attention to other people.

'If the Cantonese enter a lift or sit down in a restaurant they always do so as a group and immediately conversation around them becomes impossible. Often this annoys the other foreigners, who sometimes ostentatiously get up from their table and carry everything to another table as far away as possible from the Cantonese, who don't even notice or, if they do, make some remark, obscene I'm sure, that makes them all roar with laughter.

'If, by exception, you see a Hong Kong Chinese alone he always has a pair of headphones clamped over his ears and a tape player attached to his belt and he hums and sometimes all of a sudden starts to sing the Cantonese song, totally oblivious of whatever is going on around him. However, they normally get on very well with the Westerners though you seldom see them together. I think that the Cantonese simply has the urge to talk all the time and about everything that passes through his mind. This makes the Westerners uneasy, I think.

'On the other hand, the Cantonese is bored by the Westerner's long-winded stories, always about himself and rarely funny, and long silences. So they say "hi" when they come across each other or they exchange a quiet joking remark, however, other than that, they have nothing in common and they avoid each other quite naturally. No bad feelings, though, just too different I guess.

'To us Chinese, the Hong Kong people are always very kind and polite, a bit like indulgent, soft-hearted elder brothers. Secretary Du says that that is because they are afraid of us and want to make a good impression now that Hong Kong will belong to China again soon, in 1997 I believe he said. When I asked Roger Wu once whether this was true he replied that I should make up my own mind and not have it made up for me by others.

'"We are also Chinese what!" Roger said, "and we are embarrassed when we hear the Westerners talk amongst each other about the mainland Chinese, as they call you, and tell anecdotes about how stupid and stubborn and rude you are and that you have no manners and always think that you know everything better than the foreign experts."

'It's true, you know,' Beiyuen continued, 'I always hear our men boast that the foreigners cannot teach them anything and that the way they have always done things is still the best. And while they say that, they just sit there and talk and laugh and smoke and drink tea, all the while mocking the foreigners, yet they never repair the things I have reported broken for more than a month already, or oil the wheels of my trolley which squeal like a lovesick cat, making me feel ashamed when I push the trolley in the corridor.

'The guests were making jokes about me and my trolley. They joked that one Chinese opera on TV in their room is enough, no need for me to sing in the corridor. So shameful.

'I think we should listen to the Hong Kong people who are clever Chinese and who mean well and sincerely try to teach us how to do things in a modern way and we should pay no attention to the hateful instructions of that nasty man Du. Whenever I hear Du laugh, in that mean, snickering way of his, I feel cold all of a sudden and I know that someone is in trouble.'

Beiyuen had actually shivered as she said that and she had shown Lilian the goosebumps on her arms.

'Merely thinking of that man does that to me already,' she had said. 'When he sneaks up on me, while I am doing the rooms, to see whether I am looking in the magazines, I feel my heart sink into my stomach and I have to squeeze my eyes tight to keep the tears inside.

'He has no right to enter the guest rooms, but when I told him so once, he looked at me with those eyes of his, like a dead fish, and he said that I had probably already forgotten that I was Chinese and that my first duty was to the Party who had given me my job.

'He continued to muse that the foreigners had possibly already succeeded in seducing me, what with my foreign hairstyle and the colourful clothes I was wearing outside working hours. Perhaps he should transfer me to a farming commune, he said, to work with the peasants and to learn to be simple again and obedient.

'I was so frightened when he said that. I would die of shame and sorrow if I had to work as a peasant, so what could I do? I let him in. I make the bed and clean the room and all the time watch him from the corners of my eyes as he roams about the room, taking the guest's belongings in his hands, the books, the magazines, even the clothes in the wardrobe to feel in the pockets. He sometimes takes the magazines to his office, saying he will give them back to me later so that I can put them back in the rooms before the guests return. He says that as a Party secretary he makes the rules and regulations for others to obey, not for himself to abide by. It is his duty to check the magazines, he says, to see whether they contain anything bad about China.

'All foreigners are China's enemies, Du says, and the only reason they are now all over China is to spy on us and to steal our secrets. Therefore it is his responsibility and duty towards the Party and China to enter the rooms and find out which secrets the foreigners have already stolen and to expose the foreigners' own secret weapons for destroying China. He frightens me. I think he is really quite mad. Stay away from him, Lilian! He hates us girls because he thinks we are much too friendly with the foreigners.

'In his lectures for the staff and workers he tells us that we should always keep in mind, in dealing with the guests, that they are in fact our enemies, who are only here to rob us of our dignity, and it will be quite natural for us not to smile at them but just confine ourselves to yes and no and to do no more than what is minimally required.

'This makes Roger Wu so angry that he once complained about Du's hatemongering. But what can Zhou do? Nothing! He isn't even a Party member himself, so he has no influence.' Beiyuen fell silent, momentarily troubled by her reminiscences, her pretty pixie face sombre.

Then, suddenly, her face lit up, instantly lifting the gloom that had overtaken the room, and laughingly she lilted, 'Who am I to say that the Cantonese are talkative? I am far worse. My throat is all dry.'

Auntie and Lilian burst out laughing, relieved by the sudden mood change.

Lilian got up from her curled position on the couch and refilled the mugs with hot water from the kettle and checked whether fresh tea leaves were needed. Then the three of them sipped the fresh, hot tea, now and then spitting out a tea-leaf. It was a nice, cosy, companion-like silence and each was lost in her own thoughts.

The older woman was thinking that the evening was turning out much better than she could have hoped for.

She had always known that seventh niece Beiyuen was a sharp girl, however she had always thought her to be somewhat shallow with a flashlight-like intelligence, momentarily blinding both bystander and probably Beiyuen herself as well, and not capable of thinking things through. However, Beiyuen's insight into people's characters and motives really surprised her. This was good, very good.

If her opinion of Lilian turned out to be correct the two girls could well work together.

Lilian in the forefront, her pretty and friendly face and good command of English essential assets in her contact with the foreigners.

Beiyuen in the background to keep an eye and an ear on Du and his schemes.

With her access to the guest rooms, Beiyuen would be in a position to see whether something had been going on that could land the guest in trouble. She could then manipulate her cleaning schedule in such a way that Du would not check that room and she would warn Lilian to put the guest on guard. The grateful guest would reward Lilian, who would share with Beiyuen, who would share with her Auntie Liu.

Everyone would benefit, even China, she chuckled to herself.

Beiyuen's voice woke her from her own schemes and she listened again as Beiyuen went on with her narrative.

'The second distinct group of foreigners is the Japanese,' Beiyuen continued. 'The Japanese are different from everybody else. We Chinese, we don't know what to think of them. We know they have a lot of money and that they make all those beautiful and clever things such as the cars and trucks you see everywhere, the TV sets in all the hotel's rooms and yours as well, Auntie, the cameras and portable tape players the Hua-Qiao and Westerners hang around their neck. However, we do not understand how it is possible that they can do all that. They seem always so confused, so helpless, so humble.

'They always do everything wrong and then they apologise, always they apologise so profusely and so politely that it makes you uneasy because most of the time you don't know what they are apologising for. At other times they thank you just as profusely and you don't know what for, since you don't remember having done anything special.

'They are weird. They seldom speak or understand one word of Chinese, yet in their rooms they have books and magazines with so many Chinese characters. How is that possible? You also never see a Japanese alone, by himself. There are always at least three of them, but mostly they are in groups of six or more and not only the tourists but the businessmen as well. They always want adjacent rooms so that they can walk in and out of each other's rooms in their bathrobe or pyjamas and also come and go together.

'When you see them looking in your direction and talking excitedly amongst themselves you know that they want to ask you something, only they don't know how, so they discuss first. I go about my business, pretending not to notice, until one of them has been commissioned by the others to step forward and address me. He bows, then asks something. I don't understand what he says so I guess and I tell him that their laundry will be back before six o'clock.

'He is very surprised and tells his friends, who wait, smiling and nodding, in the background, what he thinks I have told him and they all look surprised and resume their discussion. Now somebody else steps forward, bows and points to the towels on the trolley, at least that's what I think, so I assume he wants more towels for they bath a lot. I gesture for them to follow me to the floor's storeroom and I give each of them two extra towels.

'They bow and take the towels, but they start to converse again, a bit worriedly I notice, probably about what to do with all the towels for I can see from their gestures and expressions that that was not what they wanted. Then a third one tries and all of a sudden I think that I can distinguish the word "restaurant" so I decide they want to know where the Chinese restaurant is. Relieved, I just about shout at them, "twenty-second floor!" and I gesture, two hands open and closed twice, plus two fingers, and I point up.

'Still they look worried, however resignedly they bow, say "*hai, hai, hai,*" nod vigorously, say something more and "*domo harigato,*" I think, and trot off to the lifts where they take a lift down, not up. I am too exasperated to go after them, glad to be rid of them. However, after a moment I begin to feel sorry for them and angry with myself for not having been more patient. So I go down to the lobby and, peeping out from the lift, I see them gesticulating to the duty manager and to Roger Wu who speaks a little Japanese. All of a sudden Roger sees me and he yells at me. "Beiyuen, come here! Now!"

'As I approach, hesitantly, Roger yells again, "Why did you give these Japanese gentlemen towels and tell them to go down and clean the lobby with their bare hands and the towels? All they wanted to ask you was to allow them to oil the wheels of your trolley for they think that you must be embarrassed by the squealing. And you tell *them* to go and clean the lobby and the poor sods ask *me* where they should start! Beiyuen, you make me feel so embarrassed."'

Auntie and Lilian had smiled and chuckled while Beiyuen told her story, but when she came to the point where she mimicked the indignant Roger Wu and they visualised the Japanese in their business suits, on their knees, cleaning the lobby floor with the bath towels, they couldn't help being convulsed with laughter, tears running down their cheeks.

Wiping the tears from their eyes with the back of their hands and still hiccuping with suppressed laughter, they heard Beiyuen say, 'Yes, you laugh! but I tell you that it is not always fun to have these Japanese on your floor. After dinner they get together in one of their rooms and drink whisky until they are all drunk – stoned even. Then when each goes back to his room they knock on their own door. Of course nobody opens it, however, they knock and knock and yell at each other that nobody is in the room.

'The noise wakes up the guests in the adjacent and opposite rooms who come outside to see what's going on. Terrible the names the other foreigners then call the Japanese. My face is all red to hear such words.

'I don't like the night shift, sitting there all alone behind the floor desk while such things go on. I prefer the day shift, though there is much more work to do and not always pleasant, either. One morning, very early, I had just begun work, and a Western guest calls housekeeping. He sounds very angry. He just about shouts at me over the telephone that when he came out of his room to go down to the coffee shop for breakfast he had stumbled over a Japanese, lying naked in front of his door, sleeping, with shit and vomit all over the carpet and now also on his shoes. He wants me to come immediately and clean up the mess.

'So I hurry to the scene and I can smell the trouble before I see it. Such a bad smell that I nearly gag. However, it is not my duty to clean such things so I knock on the doors of the other Japanese and show them their friend on the floor, like a pig in his own filth. The others become very excited and they gesture for me to open their friend's room with my pass-key.

'They drag him inside and then they start cleaning the carpet with toilet paper, water and soap. Finally they rub the carpet with bath towels and sprinkle after shave lotion to suppress the bad smell as best they can. One of them, on his knees, wipes the Westerner's shoes with a towel. I can see that this embarrasses the Westerner. He taps the Japanese on the shoulder and tells him to stop, that he'll do it himself and he keeps saying that he is sorry to have blown his stack, whatever that means. After the commotion the Japanese lock themselves in their sick friend's room.

'At ten o'clock I see their interpreter, Mr Zing, from the foreign trade office, come out of the lift and hurry through the corridor. I hear him knock in a special way and the Japanese let him in. After two hours, as I am about to stop for lunch, they come out of the room and in unison march towards the storeroom where I am busy. The whole group stops at five paces from where I am and the man who was sick steps forward three more paces and bows. Very deep he bows and he stays like that, bent forward from the waist, looking at the floor. He shouts something, like a dog barking. His five friends shout "Hai!" in unison and bow, not so deep as the first one though.

'Mr Zing steps forward, looking uncomfortable and translates, "Hashimoto-san says that he is deeply ashamed about what happened. It is unforgivable. The other five concur."

'The man he calls Hashimoto-san, still bent at the waist, does some more barking, quite a bit longer this time, like stop-go. When finally he falls silent, the interpreter translates again.

'"Hashimoto-san says that when his friends left his room last night he went to bed and fell asleep. Sometime later he wakes up, feeling sick and in great need to answer the triple call of nature. He gets up, cannot find the light switch, opens what he thinks is the bathroom door. It is not. It is the room door and he has locked himself out. He can no longer hold in the calls of nature and relieves himself, from below and from above. Exhausted and still sick he falls asleep. The next thing he remembers is people staring at him and the Chinese girl of the squealing wheels seeing his nakedness and shame."

'Zing hesitates, falls silent and looks uneasily at Hashimoto-san who keeps staring at the floor, crookedly rigid as if frozen. The five others also stand there, motionless and make no effort to help the interpreter out of what is clearly a predicament. Getting no response from his customers, Zing shrugs his shoulders and continues. "Hashimoto-san insists that he be punished and they have unanimously agreed, in my presence, that he cannot bear the shame to stay here, so he will return to Japan by tonight's plane to Hong Kong. I have reserved his seat already. If the honourable girl of the squealing wheels is not satisfied they beg you to say so now and they will retire, discuss and come forward with a new proposal."

'I feel terribly embarrassed and all I want is for them to leave me alone and go play their silly games elsewhere. So I stamp my foot and tell Zing, "You tell your Hashimoto-san that I don't care and that I don't want him to be punished. It is not fair to ask my approval for this stupid punishment business. How can I approve? What will his Party leaders do to him? Or to his wife and child? I cannot take such responsibility and I refuse to approve or disapprove and that's it. Go away and leave me in peace!"

'Zing, perspiring and clearly uncomfortable, translates my words in a kind of rush. All I can distinguish is *ah-no-ho-hu-sta*, or something like that, over and over again. Hashimoto-san and his friends look crestfallen. However, they bow deeply, take a few steps backwards, bow again, then turn and go back to Hashimoto's room. When I come back from lunch, the interpreter Zing is waiting for me, alone this time.

'He says that to us Chinese, the Japanese may seem crazy, however, that's their business, isn't it? Whatever we may think, Hashimoto-san is desperate and wants the girl of the squealing wheels to approve. The first thing his boss in Japan will ask is whether the offended party, that is I, is satisfied. If I didn't approve that means I am not satisfied and the shame reflects on the boss as well and so on and so forth. Is that what I want? Why not say quickly that I approve and let them stew in their own juice, the idiots?

'So I accompany Zing to Hashimoto-san's room. They all stare at me, except Hashimoto-san, who quickly adopts again the same bowed position as before. I take a deep breath and shout, very loud, "*I approve*" and then I run out of the room, feeling like a fool. Ten minutes later I see them all march through the corridor and push the lift button to go down. I turn my back and pretend to be busy to spare Hashimoto-san the humiliation of a last bow.

'Interpreter Zing stops a moment next to my trolley and stares at me, curiously. "I have one small question, if I may," he says. "Why do the Japanese call you the girl of the squealing wheels?"

'I stare haughtily back at him and without answering I push my trolley to the next room. When I look back over my shoulder, Zing still stands there, grinning. Then he waves at me, turns and quickly joins the Japanese who are about to enter the lift. The last thing I see before the lift door closes is Hashimoto-san bowing in my direction.'

Beiyuen fell silent, clearly still upset at the memory.

Auntie Liu sighed and shook her head.

'Don't take it that hard,' she said, 'I know the Japanese. During the war, in 1938, when I was about your age, they shot dead my two brothers and my father for reasons that didn't even matter enough for them to tell us. They just sent my mother a note to collect the bodies for burial.

'Mother hired a cart and we pushed it to the middle school building where the Japanese had put up their offices, my own former school to boot. Mother had to sign for the bodies as if she was collecting a parcel at the post office, then six soldiers put the bodies in the cart, carefully and neatly straight. That done, the officer in charge saluted my mother, bowed very slightly and asked her, in excellent Chinese, to forgive him that he had not had the opportunity to have the clothes of her husband and her sons washed and ironed. He assured her that they had not suffered for the soldiers had aimed well with steady hands.

'I thought he was very friendly and polite. I was even ashamed that my mother cried all the time and did not answer him equally nicely and politely. Thinking of that moment now, I ask myself what I had wanted my mother to say. Something equally dignified, like: "Thank you, Lieutenant. On behalf of my husband and sons I congratulate you for your men's fine performance in making such neat little holes. Don't worry about the state of their clothes, they can be repaired, unlike the bodies, but that's only a small matter. With your permission I now take leave of you and your fine young men. Give my regards to your dear lady in Japan and perhaps, after the war, you can both come to Shanghai and have tea at my house."

'I am sure that had she said that the Japanese would have taken her wholly seriously. As it was, mother wept all the way home and she wasn't much help pushing the cart. Very Chinese, very un-Japanese, I am afraid. They are weird, the Japanese, and we Chinese will never understand them. But we must always fear them, just as the man with his pet weasel must always fear for his own throat. The question is not if, but when the little vermin bites and how long it will then take before the creepy little beast has bled him to death.

'But enough about the Japanese. Remember though, they are weird, tiring, tiresome, evasive, exasperating; however, in the end they'll have it their way. Always they will succeed in having matters going their way, whatever the issue. Now let's have some more soup and then Beiyuen will tell us about the Westerners and that will be enough for tonight.'

Lilian refilled the bowls and for a while none of them spoke as they slurped the soup, sucked in the noodles and spat out the chicken bones.

The bowls empty, they sat back and gently rubbed their stomach until they belched contentedly.

'That was delicious, Beiyuen,' Auntie said. 'You are a good cook. You should come more often and we'll invite Lilian and I'll teach you that old game of mahjong. Once you know how to play well we'll ask the meat shop tenant and the post commandant to join us and we'll play for money. Both of them still boast how good they used to be at the game so they can't be that good. We'll let them win first and when they're hooked we'll take their money, bit by bit, not all at once. Occasionally we'll have to let them win to maintain the illusion that they can make good their losses.'

Lilian laughed and asked, 'Why are you always thinking about money, Auntie?' adding mockingly, 'The Party says that it's glorious to share each other's poverty.'

'That's right,' Liu Meiling replied, 'if you have nothing it is always glorious to share with others who have something. That finally everybody ends up with nothing; the Party does not say that, does it? Life itself has taught me that there is very little glory in poverty and the Party wigs know that as well.

'Haven't you noticed the difference between what they preach and what they practise for themselves? Watch those mid-level cadres and their relatives and notice how they lead the good life and lack in nothing. They'll go to *any* length, including murder, to keep their privileged positions. They carefully nourish the people's illusion that total power, total domination rather, over country and people resides with the few uncultured old fossils in Beijing, who live their cloistered lives screened off from the toiling masses about whom they care and know nothing. The real power, however, the power that matters, the one of command and control, of punishment and reward, is subtly and jealously exercised by the mid-level puppeteers.

'We all know their puppets, the so-called Party cadres, from bad experiences. They crawl all over the place like vermin, the idlers. Bloated with self-importance and smug with their good fortune they fawn on their superiors. "Yes comrade, no comrade, you are right, comrade, how well you see the needs of the people, comrade; I shall see to it immediately, comrade."

'And always they gather for another of those already countless and endless and pointless meetings, the pathetic clowns, with their black, old ladies' bags full of scribbled pieces of paper from previous meetings and which nobody has ever bothered to read. They talk pompously and ponderously about things they know nothing about. They discuss projects nobody has ever heard of or has any need for. They propose actions so stupid that it makes you want to cry.

And all the while they drink tea, chain-smoke cigarettes and take notes with that pensive air of the great mind at work.

'They take a break for lunch provided by an inwardly contemptuous but outwardly obsequious neighbourhood, followed by a rest of at least two hours, belching and farting like flatulent cows and snoring like pigs. And nobody ever asks or cares what is the use of all those meetings. What are the results? What has been decided? It's nothing but a grotesque, perverse comedy wherein the players select, reward and punish each other. The most coveted reward is additional privileges, the most feared punishment is the revocation of privileges. And then, of course, there always looms the ultimate sanction, the irrevocable disgrace of expulsion from the party, to be sent back to where they came from, back amidst the nameless, faceless and voiceless People.

'Is it because they have failed in their duties or acted against the interests of the motherland that they bring down upon themselves these punitive measures? *How naive*! *People, motherland*, nothing but empty slogans! What counts is the *Party*, the giver and taker of life, that monstrous, cancerous tumour in our collective intestines, feeding on our energy and blood.

'Each Party member, whether high official or lowly cadre, has his role and the prerogatives and privileges that go with it, much like the cells in the tumour have each their specific field of harm caused by defects in their specific genetic code and which are followed rigidly and predictably, even during their wildest proliferation. This is the Party disciplinarians' dream! Unfortunately, however, for those disciplinarians, that is, a member cannot as yet be genetically programmed. He can only be programmed mentally for his role and this, of course, always carries the risk of errors because his emotions, usually the negative ones such as greed and ambition, can never be completely eradicated. So what happens? The member exceeds his authority and encroaches on the grazing rights of his immediate superiors, *the* capital sin for a Communist. This will never be tolerated, forgiven or even forgotten and the trespasser must be punished, immediately and ruthlessly.

'Even in the rare case that the offender is motivated by a positive emotion, such as compassion with us ordinary mortals, and is willing to listen or worse, from the Party's point of view, stands up for our rights, he will be called to order, criticised or even punished, if he persists in his erroneous way. As a lowly cadre, possessing no vital knowledge about Party affairs, he will be expelled; as a high official, knowing too much, he will be relieved of his office and hidden in some faraway, high-security place or put under house arrest on some trumped-up charge or other and quietly killed after a sufficiently long time has passed for people to have forgotten about him. Ninety-five per cent or more of the Chinese people have no say in, and know nothing about, the system that rules them in their own name, the system of the three ruling castes.

'The highest caste is the cruel, power-hungry old men in Beijing, playing their silly but deadly games of back-stabbing and intrigues. However, they are too remote from the ordinary people to make any difference as to who for the moment is on top or who is down. The middle caste consists of the sly and self-seeking profiteers, the ones who occupy every profitable place and position throughout China, wheeling and dealing and purloining their influence, manipulating every situation to their advantage. The lowest caste is made up of the low-level cadres, those uncultured and ignorant morons the ordinary people have to deal with in every aspect of their lives. Incapable of doing an honest job, they lick and fawn upwards for the petty privileges they crave and kick downwards to silence the people who are daily witnesses to their stupidity and incompetence, to stifle every hint of individual thinking, to crush every trace of dissatisfaction.

'The Chinese people, especially the young, like you girls, owe no loyalty to such a system. You owe it nothing, you hear me! *Nothing*! Your only loyalty is to yourself and the very few people you can trust implicitly. Don't be a fool! Beat the system with the same means that it tries to beat you; that is with lies, cheating and hypocrisy. Never refuse a task, an assignment or a job, however, do as little as you can get away with. Never volunteer for anything. Never give the slightest reason to pass the blame for something that went wrong on you. Always have a scapegoat, or an excuse, ready to fall back on, just in case. And all the while you observe and find out what advantage you can get out of any given situation. And never forget, *money* is the biggest advantage there is; it's handy and convenient and it's not traceable if you don't put it in the bank. Remember, the banks belong to the system. Never put your money in the bank. Enjoy the things money can buy for you: nice food, nice clothes, some gold jewellery, make-up and so on. However, don't show off. Never be ostentatious so as not to make people envious.

'Use also some of the money to buy favours, to bind people to you. But again, don't overdo that either, so as not to make people resentful. A packet of cigarettes, a few bottles of beer, a fat chicken, a meal in a good but not too expensive restaurant, some cookies, these kind of small gestures, that's enough. However, be unpredictable with your small favours so that people don't take them for granted.'

Auntie Liu fell silent and smiled at the two girls, a fleeting, strangely sad little smile.

What a strange and complex person she is, Lilian thought to herself, and how wrongly I have judged her all these years. Her air of the simple, folksy old woman is just that, a screen. A simple old woman doesn't know about the things she talked about, certainly not in that manner, as if she spoke from personal experience.

And then the words and expressions she uses. I had difficulty following her sometimes and I have been to middle school. I have to find out about her past. I'm sure Mother knows more about her. I often get the impression that there is some kind of tacit understanding between those two not to let me in on certain things.

Her thoughts were interrupted when Lilian heard Beiyuen say, 'Auntie Meiling, what terrible things you say. It makes me scared, you know. Scared of what they must have done to you to make you so full of anger, so cynical about the Party and our leaders, so materialistic about what matters in life. I have not judged you well, Auntie Meiling. You are fat, you waddle like a goose, you behave as a cantankerous though essentially a good-hearted old woman, however, I can see now that it's only an act. You are, in fact, very smart and wily and calculating.

'Still, you are nevertheless vulnerable because you are emotional and when you are carried away by your emotions you talk too much and you say things in front of people you don't really know well enough to confide in. Mind you, you have nothing to fear from me, nor from Lilian either, because we both know that you mean well. Though I shan't forget your words when I deal with people, I shall deal with them on my own terms first. How can we live together if a priori I have to assume that everybody is either a moron or a greedy profiteer bent on exploiting me?

'I know I don't have your experience in life, I'm only eighteen, but I must say that so far I haven't been treated badly nor have I, as far as I know, wronged others on purpose. Actually, I'm quite happy with my life.'

Beiyuen fell silent and smiled her radiant, guileless smile, that wonderful expression of her whole attitude to life and the people around her.

So much for my judgement of people, Lilian thought wryly. First Auntie Liu has fooled me all these years by her appearance as a quarrelsome and meddlesome, however, basically good-hearted old woman, while, in fact, she is like a smouldering fire barely contained by her intelligence and undoubtedly excellent education, though erupting in flames when fanned by her anger at and contempt for pretentious fools and corrupt profiteers.

And now it appears that I have been completely misled by my superficial first impressions of Beiyuen as well. She is a deep one, Beiyuen is, with a strong character and a good heart, radiating a kind of innate goodness and happiness bound to disarm and mollify, but the basest evildoers.

It didn't surprise Lilian one bit to see Auntie Liu wiping her eyes.

'It's late already,' Auntie said. 'Perhaps we should leave the Westerners for some other time. I don't think I can stomach your stories about those foreign devils on just noodle soup and dumplings. We'll need something more solid in our stomachs and I propose a good, full dinner for our next get-together.'

Lilian and Beiyuen laughed at Auntie's words, relieved that the atmosphere was again as it had been before her outburst.

'Beiyuen, you walk Lilian home,' Auntie added, 'and when you come back I shall be in bed. You can sleep on the couch. No need to wash the bowls tonight. Now go! This old woman is tired, so leave me alone.'

Lilian thanked Auntie for the delicious soup and dumplings and promised that the next time she would prepare the food: spicy, strange-taste chicken with sesame seeds, Sichuan-style. She had learned to prepare that dish well, from her mother, who was from Sichuan Province.

They fixed a date two weeks hence and Beiyuen accompanied Lilian to her home a few houses down the alley. When they passed in front of former Leader Hu's house the old woman came outside and glared at the two girls, muttering all kinds of invectives under her breath. The malevolence emanating from the old woman was nigh palpable and the girls felt suddenly cold.

They shivered as they quickly said goodbye.

## *Chapter Four*

Lying fully dressed on the couch in the tiny room of her parents' house, her mother peacefully asleep in bed, Lilian was thinking how much had happened and how much her life had changed since that first memorable night at Auntie Liu's house, now only nine months back but seemingly ages ago.

She wondered what would have become of her had she not been more or less adopted by Auntie Liu as her granddaughter, what would have happened without Auntie's guidance when things had been difficult and she had been confused about what to do.

She and Beiyuen had become very close friends, almost like twin sisters. However, their friendship had nothing of that overbearing meddlesomeness and possessiveness one sees so often in the relationship between women. Lilian found it so easy to talk and listen to Beiyuen and she always felt better after having spent some time with her.

A wave of warmth and grateful happiness surged suddenly through her body and Lilian could barely suppress the urge to scream as loud as she could, at the very top of her voice, to release the surge of heat. Just in time she stifled her scream that would have woken up and frightened the whole neighbourhood.

The nightmares of the years of the Cultural Revolution when people were dragged off, screaming, in the small hours of the morning to the interrogation centres, remained indelibly printed in people's minds.

Her scream would rekindle those old fears, whatever the Party might now say about it all having been a regrettable and tragic mistake. So Lilian stretched her fingers as wide and as hard as she could to push the tingling sensation out of her body through her fingertips and she tensed all the muscles of her body, taut, tauter, like a cat, until it ached.

She counted to twenty, then suddenly she let go and she felt all the pent-up energy drawn out of her and herself floating in the air and drifting off to sleep.

## *Chapter Five*

Thrice that second get-together had been postponed at Lilian's request and a new date set.

However, when she, for the fourth time, had come up with a last-minute excuse, Auntie had no longer insisted.

Though Lilian dropped in on Auntie Liu quite often, then for this little problem, then for that question, then again for something else still, she didn't fool the old woman one bit: Lilian was in love and apparently deeply troubled by the implications. She was restless and distraught and couldn't stay in one place or keep up a coherent conversation for more than a few minutes at a time.

The reasons she gave for popping in unexpectedly were mere pretexts, Auntie Liu knew. Each time she came to unburden her troubled heart, yet, at the last moment, the vital, often rehearsed words hovering on her lips, she couldn't muster the courage and left after some trivial talk.

Auntie Liu was sure it was that foreign engineer, Jan. Somehow Lilian always managed to slip his name into whatever the conversation was about and in what she herself evidently thought was a casual, offhand manner. Auntie herself became increasingly restless because of her own wavering about whether to intervene or not.

From her own observation long ago and, more recently, from Beiyuen's chit-chat, she knew enough about the foreigners' unconstrained demeanour in matters of relationships between men and women to fear that Lilian was about to make a terrible mistake. A mistake that would inevitably have grave consequences, both for Lilian herself and for her relatives and friends. From the Party's point of view those close to Lilian should either have stopped such an impropriety before it was bound to get out of hand and embarrass not only the Party but every right-thinking Chinese as well, or, failing to do so, should have reported the matter to Lilian's leaders.

The leader would then talk to Lilian quietly, to make her see the error of her way, leaving no doubt about the stern measures the Party would take should she persist in her error. The foreigner would simply be denied re-entry after the expiry of his visa to avoid the uproar that a few earlier cases of deportation, in similar circumstances, had caused in the West. And, of course, Lilian would be transferred to some dingy Chinese hotel or, worse, sent for re-education to some commune or other in one of the poorer, faraway provinces.

Auntie Liu was certain that all these things were incessantly buzzing through Lilian's mind and that that was the only reason for her increasingly restless irritability, an irritability that might very well cause her to act irrationally and defy both Liu Meiling's good advice, if offered unsolicited, and the Party's authority.

The danger of this happening was in fact very real, Auntie Liu feared, since Lilian had begun to ventilate her newfound, undoubtedly foreigner-inspired, alien ideas about freedom of expression and action. On the other hand, the loud-mouthed Dutchman had surely no idea of the anxiety he caused or, more likely, he couldn't care less. His lecherous nature influenced by Lilian's delicate, graceful Chinese femininity, he would touch her playfully in the presence of his friends, totally oblivious to the embarrassment and mental turmoil he caused her by doing that.

Even if one gave him the benefit of the doubt and assumed for one moment that he was serious about Lilian, how did he figure the future with her? In his country full of loons like him? Lilian would never fit in. In China? How pathetically naive. Both the people and the system would drive him out of his mind, supposing he had one.

Auntie felt a deep pity for Lilian, whose attraction to the happy-go-lucky, handsome young foreigner, so different from the unkempt and uncouth Chinese boys, was only normal for a healthy and modern girl of her age and in her position. She imagined Lilian alone, at night, her head reeling from merely thinking about how to find a way out of her dilemma and biting her pillow so as not to cry out her anger and frustration about the unfairness of it all.

When three months after the last postponement of their dinner date Lilian had still not unbosomed herself, Auntie Liu decided to act. She confided her worries to Beiyuen who admitted, relieved, that she had been hesitating for quite some time already about whether to see her elder relative about the matter or not. Beiyuen proposed they go together to see Lao Dao, the head of the hotel's engineering department, who had become quite close to Lao Dee, the leader of the foreign engineers.

Lao Dao had gracefully accepted the bottle of cheap, mauve, chemical wine and, after the preliminary chit-chat, he had listened gravely to the older woman's outpouring of worries about Lilian. He had not once interrupted her, not even when, in her discomfort, she had repeated herself several times. When she had finally fallen silent, exhausted and cursing herself for making such a fuss, he had nodded pensively, cracking his finger joints.

He himself had grown increasingly concerned these past few months, he told Auntie Liu and Beiyuen about the entire goings-on with the foreigners and about how it would inevitably and all of a sudden backfire one day.

The city's Party committee would finally have to do something, even if that meant less hard currency income. It could no longer ignore the hotel unit Party secretary's increasingly vociferous rantings about the foreign devils' unjust influence on the Chinese staff's moral and political rectitude.

Lao Dao had promised he would give the matter very urgent and serious thought to find a face-saving way out for everybody.

'We cannot tell the foreigners in the same blunt way they tell us that we Chinese are all stupid and lazy and backward, that their habits are often shocking to us,' Lao Dao had said. 'We must tell them that we are not yet mature enough for their liberal way of thinking and ask them to show consideration for our old-fashioned prudishness and ignorance. Though I probably sell my friend Lao Dee short when I break the matter to him so circumspectly,' he had added, smiling every so slightly and a bit mockingly.

Two weeks after her talk with Lao Dao, Auntie Liu had noticed an almost overnight change in Lilian's behaviour.

As of old she had greeted Auntie in her friendly, merry way when she came past on her way home or to work and one day she had called out when their next dinner together would be. Relieved, Auntie had shouted back from inside her house that she couldn't wait. During the following days she had begun to toy with the idea of giving the next get-together with the two girls a bit more substance than the mere gossip about foreigners and locals, however much she had enjoyed that the first time, now already more than four months ago.

She ruminated a plan for a kind of informal gathering, every two weeks or so, of a few people who she knew had lived interesting lives and who she might be able to coax, in the relaxed atmosphere after good food and drink enjoyed together, into telling their life story.

She could perhaps even contribute her own story.

Perhaps that man Lao Dee, of whom both Lilian and Lao Dao spoke so highly, could be persuaded to attend the gatherings, provided his Chinese was good enough of course. He could make notes and afterwards decide whether there was stuff for a book, to be published outside China, naturally. The storytellers should have fictive names in the book to make them untraceable for the authorities and Lao Dee should be made to swear never to reveal their true identities.

The more she thought about it the more she liked the idea, were it only to assuage her own, long repressed desire to take her revenge by exposing, through the life stories of a few ordinary people, the corrupt and cruel system, and its perpetrators, that had made China, and herself personally, suffer so much for such a long time now.

It was worth trying and she decided to wait for the right opportunity to take the next step.

Her chance came a few days later, on a beautifully sunny Thursday morning. She knew that Thursday was both girls' day off. She had been waiting in line in front of the bakery shop to buy its weekly speciality, *chiaxiubao*, a kind of steamed dumpling made of white dough with a delicious, sweetish, minced roast pork filling.

This particular bakery's *chiaxiubao* were famous for the purity of the white dough and the richness of the filling and people came from all over town to buy the maximum of six pieces per person. The woman who prepared the *chiaxiu* was originally from Fujian Province and she came only on Thursdays to this neighbourhood bakery and since she made only a limited quantity you had to be early and stand in line before she started sales at eight o'clock.

Auntie Liu had been the second in the queue that morning, right behind Beiyuen, and they had both grinned at Lilian who was number eleven. When Auntie and Beiyuen had been served they had walked over to where Lilian was standing in line and had asked her to stop by at Auntie's on her way home. She had done so and Auntie had proposed dinner together that same evening.

The long-overdue Sichuan food night, Auntie had said.

'In fact, why don't you ask your mother to come as well?' Auntie had added, as if it were just an afterthought. 'Your mother can cook the strange-taste chicken at home and bring it over,' Auntie had continued. 'Beiyuen and I will prepare a beef noodle soup Nanjing-style, and we'll have the *chiaxiubao* for dessert. After dinner you tell us about the Westerners since you seem to have become quite an expert in dealing with the red-haired devils. I'll ask Dao Huimin to come as well. You know him surely, Lilian? Old Uncle Dao, of your hotel's engineering department? He has studied abroad, long ago, and I'm sure he can tell us a lot of things. Now, what do you think?'

Lilian had been hesitant about bringing her mother in on those stories about the Westerners. Auntie Liu had been quite persuasive, however.

'Your mother can use some distraction,' she had said. 'As it is, life passes her by, always alone with that dimwitted father of yours. Twelve years now already. Must be very depressing for her. He doesn't even recognise her, or you, for that matter. She keeps hoping that his mind will come back one day, but that's hopeless, of course, and in her heart she must know that.

'I happen to know the doctor who examines your father occasionally for the evaluation report required by the Party for the pittance they pay him. I asked him once what he thought of Kunlen's condition. He said it's hopeless. That his mind is gone, for good. He pities your mother, he says, for her fixation that Kunlen will be well again one day. Physically Kunlen is as strong as an ox, the doctor said, what with all the gruel you have been feeding him these past twelve years, and he can grow very old, a burden on your mother for the rest of her life.

'In a few years you'll be married, Lilian, and you'll have your own family to take care of and your mother will be all alone, caring for an idiot who most probably will outlive her. So why don't you and your mother start thinking of placing him in a state institute for the mentally handicapped? The State has a very heavy responsibility for all this because it made him the way he is. So let it take care of him and allow your mother to lead her own life. She deserves better than the kind of dog life she is leading now. After all she has gone through it's time for her to enjoy some happiness and possibly go back to Luding, in Sichuan, to live with her parents, your grandparents, Lilian, and get some sunlight on her pretty face.

'She never saw her parents again after Hongbayue in 1966. In 1972 she received word from them that they were back in their old house, in Luding, together with your Uncle Dan whom you have never met. Your mother was so happy and she immediately applied for a travel permit, for you and for herself, to visit her parents. However, Leader Hu rejected her application because she was the wife of renegade Li Kunlen. During the next five years your mother applied every regulatory six months, however, each time she was refused the permit. Then, in 1977, Kunlen was dumped on her and she gave up. Too ashamed to bring him to visit her parents and not prepared to leave him alone at home.

'She never told you all this, eh? I know she didn't because she once told me that she wanted you to grow up unburdened by the old hatreds of a past you had no part in. And you were a strange child, Lilian. You never asked about your grandparents, although you saw that other children your age had grandfathers and grandmothers taking care of them while their own parents worked. I think that somehow you took me for your grandmother in spite of the fact that you called me Auntie. However, you are a big girl now, Lilian, and I think that after all these years of acting as your *de facto* grandmother, I have earned the right to interfere. It's time for you to learn the facts about your mother's past. However, for that we must first bring her back to, and make her accept, the present as it is and what better moment than to begin tonight?'

# *Chapter Six*

To Lilian's surprise, Mother had accepted Auntie's invitation gladly.

Earlier than usual Lilian had fed Father his evening rice gruel while Mother had prepared his plank bed for the night. While she was feeding him his gruel Lilian thought about what Auntie Liu had said that morning and all of a sudden she saw her father with different eyes.

What kind of life is this? she thought. Liquid rice gruel, morning, midday and evening, for twelve years already. When we once tried to feed him a piece of solid food, such a nice morsel of tender chicken, it was a disaster. He choked on it and we had to beat him on his back until it finally shot out of his windpipe. He screamed and cried for hours afterwards because in his dim wits beating is punishment.

He remained upset for days, cowering in his corner on the miserable plank bed whenever Mother or I came near him. What a life! Auntie is right! We simply must find a way out of this dreary, mind and soul-destroying rut. How fortunate we are that Auntie has the guts to say these kind of things.

At six o'clock Mother had installed Father for the night. He had been docile as usual and had obediently closed his eyes when Mother had pulled the quilt up to his chin. Ciaokeli had snuggled up against him and would, as usual, lick up his dribble during the night. If something really unusual happened, like Father getting up or becoming all excited, as he sometimes did, Ciaokeli would bark and they would hear him at Auntie's and be home within a few minutes.

Mother had prepared a wok full of strange-taste chicken, with roasted sesame seeds.

Lilian had gone to see Roger Wu at the hotel and had wheedled him out of two catties of first grade rice, from down south, Guangdong Province probably. She would cook the rice at Auntie's and serve it, steaming hot, with the spicy chicken dish.

Carrying the wok with the strange-taste chicken in between them and the *chiaxiubao* and rice in the other hand, Mother and Lilian arrived at Auntie's.

The delicious smell of Nanjing beef noodle soup wafted past them when Beiyuen let them in.

Beiyuen took the wok and, while Auntie busied herself with Mother, Lilian followed Beiyuen into the kitchen. She washed the rice three times with cold, clean water to remove the traces of flour and then put the rice in a pan and under just the right quantity of water, about three fingers above the rice, to cook the rice perfectly dry and the grains detached. If you didn't wash out the flour the rice would become sticky, if you put in too much water, it would become like a thick porridge. Too little water and it would be cooked off while the rice still had a hard bit inside. To get that right was also difficult so it was best to do it properly the first time.

Beiyuen put Lilian's six pieces of *chiaxiubao* with hers and Auntie's into small, round wicker baskets which she then put on an old rusty riddle placed over a pot with boiling water. The steam would heat the *chiaxiubao* and keep them hot and ever so slightly moist until it was time to eat them for dessert.

While the girls waited for the rice to cook, Beiyuen whispered, 'Don't be shocked. Auntie Meiling has cajoled Lao Dao into inviting Lao Dee as well tonight. They will be here any minute. As well as I know my dear aunt she has something else on her mind than just a nice dinner and a few funny tales. Why else would she want a Westerner in on it?'

Lilian had been shocked nevertheless, dismayed even. How could Auntie Liu do this to her? How could she be expected to talk about her experiences with Westerners in the presence of such a prominent one who, besides, had always been so kind to her and to whom she owed so much of her knowledge?

However, before she could say something or protest to Auntie Liu, Beiyuen said, 'There they are. Let's greet them.'

The girls went back into the front room and joined in the greeting of the two men.

Both Lao Dee and Lao Dao greeted the four women cordially, as good friends, however, in a nice, polite and respectful manner and Lilian felt the heat of her initial temper about Auntie's perfidy drain from her heart and she even managed a smile and said what a nice surprise it was to see her teacher of Western ways.

This made Lao Dee laugh and he said that this time it was he who had come to learn rather than to teach. He was most of all in need to be taught some modesty, he said, a quality he sadly lacked, unlike his young Chinese friends, he added jokingly, amidst general laughter.

Uncle Dao had brought eight big bottles of Bohai beer and a piece of ice in an old jute bag to keep the beer cold. Later they could add small chippings of ice to their glasses of beer and soft drinks, Lao Dao told the girls.

Lao Dee had also brought a present for each of them: a beautiful box of luxury English soap, each piece wrapped in fine, painted paper, for Mother; fine quality Belgian chocolates in a gold paper box for Auntie and a gorgeously coloured silk scarf for both Lilian and Beiyuen.

Mother and Auntie were genuinely pleased with their gifts and the girls were delighted as much with their gifts as with the foretaste of their friends' envy. Lilian was proud and happy to see how well her friend Lao Dee got on with the two older women. She was overjoyed as her mother burst out laughing at the puns Lao Dee and Auntie exchanged at each other's expense. Auntie had clearly found her equal in Lao Dee in that respect and it was obvious she enjoyed it thoroughly.

Dinner was wonderful.

Everybody enjoyed the delicious food and the two men sincerely praised the different cooks of the different dishes.

They all drank beer with crushed ice and laughed and joked at Auntie and Beiyuen's red faces. Lilian had never seen her mother so cheerful, elated almost, and Auntie had winked at her, conspiratorially, and she had been very happy.

After the meal the two girls quickly cleared the table and washed up while the adults talked quietly amongst themselves. Lilian and Beiyuen joined the others, carrying a tray with six mugs and a pot of steaming jasmine tea.

Lilian poured each a mug of tea and for a while they sipped from the fragrant brew, occasionally contributing a remark or comment about one thing or another, until the desultory conversation petered out completely.

Dreamily inhaling the vapour from their mugs they patiently waited for Auntie to say what was on her mind. They were in no hurry and nobody looked in Auntie's direction to somehow signal that they were waiting for her to speak. Auntie needed to collect her thoughts, they knew, and would speak when ready, not before.

Clasping her mug in both hands, gazing through the twirling vapour at nothing in particular, she began to talk, barely audible at first, just rippling the surface of the silence, like the small flute in a frozen-still orchestra starts on its tune in the waiting, deadly silent auditorium.

Her voice is different, like Beiyuen's, it shot through Lilian's mind, before she focused on Auntie's words.

'Four months ago Lilian, Beiyuen and I had our first dinner, here in this room,' Auntie said and, after a short silence, she continued. 'We talked about many things but mostly Beiyuen told us about her early days in the hotel. She told us about the foreigners and we shook our heads in disbelief at their strange habits and we laughed, a bit awkwardly, at their foolish pranks. She told us about the hotel's workers and leaders, our own Chinese people, and we were ashamed at their stupidity, stubbornness and sloppy laziness.

'She told us about Party Secretary Du and his personal hatred for the foreigners and all things foreign, his meanness and stupid Communist rigidity and zealous, hypocritical bigotry and we shivered with fear and shook with impotent anger. Together we talked about money and the advantages and risks of making, saving and spending it and as a result I got carried away and ran off at the mouth about the Party and its leaders and the system they impose on us and that suffocates us. I said things I shouldn't have perhaps, however, was glad I did, after all. The evening ended on a somewhat emotional note and we never got to talk afterwards about the weirdest foreigners of all, the Westerners. From what I have heard people say, Lilian has since become quite an expert in dealing with the Westerners, who all seem to like her very much and one of whom has even become a trusted friend, a counsellor of sorts in worldly affairs.

'Lao Dee, may I call you Lao Dee? We are happy that you deigned to come to this hovel tonight and share our modest meal and put up with our ignorance. Lilian, please tell us about the Westerners so that we may learn from you and adjust our prejudices about those barbarians whose role in the Party's Four Modernisations campaign seems to become more important by the day and who, one day, will influence the daily life of all of us. Perhaps Lao Dee can afterwards put certain matters in the right perspective so that we do not replace our prejudice by another equally unjust one?'

Auntie fell silent and took a good swallow of her tea.

A vague little smile had hovered now and then about Lao Dee's lips during Auntie's monologue and he had laughed outright when she spoke about prejudices.

Serious again though, he replied, 'First of all, Auntie Liu, may I call you Auntie? Allow me to tell you how pleased I am to be here, as your guest and friend, and to be able to share such delicious food with you. I am well aware that I am a privileged person to receive such honour and I am grateful. I shall do all I can to remain worthy of your friendship and trust. These are interesting times and I am sure that all of you have lived interesting lives, of which, in a general sense, nothing is known in the West. Ignorance is the only cause of prejudices and I can tell you that we Westerners have far more of them, and more deep-rooted ones, than you Chinese.

'You invited me here tonight, Liu Meiling, and you and your friends made me feel welcome with their unfeigned and guilelessly folksy warm-heartedness I have come to know as so typical of the Chinese in China. Still, I sense a faint inkling of a motive behind your hospitality, Meiling. It may help you to make up your mind about what I guess you have in mind when I assure you that nothing that has been or still will be said in the cosiness of this small group of friends will be talked about by me in the company of others, unless you ask or allow me to do so.'

Softly blowing in her mug of hot tea, unobtrusively replenished by Lilian, Auntie Liu had been watching Lao Dee, her eyes nearly closed, while he spoke.

When he fell silent, she said, with a hint of a smile, 'You are indeed an astute man, Lao Dee, I take your hint. However, for the time being, let me just say that I would like it very much if we could meet here every other Thursday. That's the best day for the girls, as it is their day off, and I think for you as well, Lao Dee, as I presume you leave on Fridays if and when you go for the weekend to Hong Kong. Each time we can try a few different dishes for dinner. Perhaps Lao Dee can even prepare some Western food for us to try. Beiyuen and I will help you in the kitchen.

'After dinner we talk about whatever comes to mind or about any particular subject one of us may bring up for discussion. That way we old people have something to look forward to, something that'll break the monotony of our lives. Besides that, we who lead such interesting lives, according to you, will hear from you what is really going on in China and in the world. We elderly Chinese see the world only from the bottom of a well, with the Party painting the sky an artificial blue and a carbide lamp for the sun. In return you, Lao Dee, and the girls, may perhaps glean a few usable grains amongst the chaff that remained after the threshing we received during our past lives. What do you think?' Auntie said and ostensibly she spat out a few tea leaves that had got stuck on her tongue.

They all nodded their agreement, mumbling that it was a splendid idea.

Lilian had noticed Lao Dee's wink at Auntie though, and Auntie's slyly mocking smile in reply. What was going on between those two?

They didn't even know each other before today. Was that perhaps what people call a meeting of the minds?

She felt a pang of jealousy. Lao Dee wasn't obviously her discovery alone any more.

'Well, now that we have all agreed, why don't you begin, Lilian, and tell us about your experiences with the invaders from the West, those corrupters of our morals and minds?' Auntie Liu said, laughing. 'Don't mince your words, my dear, now that your friend Lao Dee is present.'

Lilian blushed self-consciously.

However, the others' encouraging smiles and relaxed attitude put her at ease and, hesitantly at first but quickly gaining confidence, she told her story.

## *Chapter Seven*

'When Roger Wu, our staff-training manager from Hong Kong, told me in the second week of last February, after I had been only three weeks in training, that he had assigned me to the coffee shop and in particular to the four tables reserved, or rather requisitioned, by the foreign engineers from Holland and Germany, I was scared,' she began.

'I tried all kinds of excuses to make Roger change his mind,' she continued, already at ease with her audience and herself, 'however, to no avail. He was adamant that I was the only suitable person because I could speak passably good English and was not as timorous as the other girls, who, indeed, never dare to do anything unless it's in their instructions. Anything unusual happens and they just stand there, all red in their face and either start to giggle foolishly, hands clasped over their mouth, or they suddenly run away and cry.

'"Those hairy *guailos* from Holland are very unpredictable and impolite," Roger said. "They treat everything as a joke, though, it's very difficult for us to understand their humour. At other times, a small matter can make them very impatient and angry and they shout at you. So embarrassing. So, to serve those fatheads their greasy eggs and steaks and fries and cans of beer, lots of cans of beer, I need a girl who isn't easily ruffled or bullied or, worse, who runs to Secretary Du to complain.

'"I want no incidents between Du and the foreigners because of somebody trained by me. I'll be on the next plane to Hong Kong and what then? So you, Lilian, and that female ox Zing Neiping who never gets upset at anything, are assigned to those four tables and that's it. Comrade Zing doesn't speak a word of English, and never will I'm afraid, so you do all the talking, Lilian. No more protests from you or I'll have you transferred to the Dong Fang Guest House."

'That threat by Roger did it. I'd rather clean the toilets in our hotel and on my knees, than work in that filthy guest house for low-ranking cadres. So all the girls of Roger's class and Roger himself watched from behind the curtains of the Bank of China office in the lobby when the group of foreigners arrived from the airport by the beer factory's bus that late February afternoon. For the past five days Zhu Xingfa, the vice-director of the beer factory, a clever and fast-talking Shanghainese, had come to the hotel every day, at noon, to make sure the rooms, all on the same floor, the seventeenth, would be available that Friday evening, that the laundry department was well prepared for the huge amount of laundry that had to be washed, ironed and returned to the rooms the same day, and that the coffee shop personnel understood that the foreigners didn't eat from the same dish but that each would order his own food and expect it to be served on his own plate which had to be put in front of himself only and not in the middle of the table.

'Vice-Director Zhu also told us not to show surprise if the foreigners ordered the strangest combinations of food and ate them in the wrong order, or, worse, mixed them on their plate and shovelled the lot, pell-mell, into their mouth with a knife and fork. He had visited the foreigners' countries, Zhu said, as a member of an investigation delegation, to select the equipment for the new factory, and the things he saw there simply baffled description. Zhu said that we, in the hotel, couldn't even begin to understand the way those foreigners lived in their country. So he told us not to be stubborn and argue or follow our own head, but to simply serve them what they ordered even if it made us sick.

'At five o'clock that particular Friday afternoon in February the doorman gave us the pre-arranged sign that the factory bus was arriving and we all rushed to our hiding place to get our first glimpse of the aliens. They were huge in the colourful jackets and brown, fur-lined half-boots as they filed into the lobby. They stood quietly together and watched the leaders of the beer factory carry their bags and suitcases inside, while their own leader, obviously the oldest of them, was checking everybody in, together with Vice-Director Zhu. That took quite some time for, in spite of Zhu's precautions during the previous days, the front office people had nevertheless put the foreigners up in rooms scattered over all floors, except of course on the seventeenth as requested by him. We could hear Vice-Director Zhu arguing loudly with Dong Shenfu, the front office manager.

'Only that very morning Dong had assured him, Zhu shouted, that everything was as agreed. So how was it possible that now, only a few hours later, all the rooms on the seventeenth floor were occupied?

'"They are *not* occupied," I heard Beiyuen say and, clearly indignant, she continued, "I know because my leader and Roger assigned their rooms to me, fourteen in all, for cleaning every day. I have a list with the numbers. That man Dong is deliberately making trouble for Vice-Director Zhu and I know also why: Dong asked Zhu for sixty bottles of beer and transfer of his brother, who is a bottle shop worker in the old factory, to the new factory and in a higher position. Zhu probably gave him less than sixty bottles, stingy Shanghainese as he is, letting Dong feel that his service isn't all that important. And now Dong makes Zhu lose face in front of the foreigners. They will think that Zhu isn't all that important a man in Dalian, that he hasn't really much influence."

'Then we saw the leader of the foreigners intervene in the argument between Dong and Zhu. Dong, embarrassed and red-faced, put a telephone on the counter in front of the foreigner who dialled a number from a business card he had fished out of his wallet. He spoke for a few minutes in the phone and then handed the handset to Dong. Dong, his face redder and redder, listened and nodded several times before putting down the phone. Within five minutes everything was settled and the foreigners trooped to the lifts each with a key for a room on the seventeenth. The factory leaders followed with the luggage in the service lift. One of the front office girls told us later that the foreign leader had asked Dong who was staying in the rooms reserved for them by Vice-Director Zhu, as all the keys were still in the pigeon-holes.

'Dong had replied that the rooms weren't actually taken but that he had to keep the rooms free in case an important Party delegation turned up at the last moment. A standing order for all first class hotels in China, Dong had haughtily told the foreigner. The foreigner had nodded understandingly, yet had asked for a telephone to call his friend Xian Hexia, the city Party secretary, to enquire whether there was a particular Party delegation due that evening. Secretary Xian had yelled so loudly over the phone that Dong had grimacingly removed the phone away from his ear and everybody had been able to hear what Xian said to Dong, which wasn't very nice. Dong had become all meek and obsequious and repeatedly said that it was all a terrible misunderstanding. Two months later Dong was suddenly transferred to the Shuang Menlou Guest House in Nanjing.

'That evening, at seven o'clock, the foreigners came all down together to the coffee shop and Roger led them personally to the four tables in the corner nearest to the kitchen. He told them that those four tables were especially reserved for them and then he called Zing Neiping and me to come forward and he introduced us by our names and told the foreigners that the two of us would be their waitresses during their stay at the hotel. The foreigners smiled and nodded at us, very friendly-like, and their leader thanked Roger for his excellent care. Then, after a very short discussion in their own language, they all sat down and since then they have each always sat in the same place, their leader in the corner, on the bench along the wall, from where he can see the whole coffee shop, the lobby and the bar on the mezzanine floor.

'It was obvious the foreigners had showered or taken a bath. Their hair was combed though still wet and they smelled strongly of soap and lotion. They all wore different shirts and trousers, their leader a white, short-sleeved shirt with breast pockets and a pair of dark blue trousers. It's easy for me to remember as he is always dressed the same, except on Sundays. Even now, as he sits there, he is wearing his eternal white shirt and blue pants.'

Lao Dee burst out laughing and everybody joined in the laughter, even Mother, who at first had looked reproachfully at Lilian, as if she were about to reprimand her for her candour.

Lilian smiled at Lao Dee and said, 'You don't probably know this, Lao Dee, but during the first few weeks everything you and your men did or said or wore was commented on and analysed for some special meaning. After the first month the curiosity lessened and now everybody has accepted you and your men and grown accustomed to your presence. The hotel will seem empty and desolate the day you leave. Especially the girls in the coffee shop, even those who don't serve at your tables, will miss you terribly. For me life will never be the same again. I am so accustomed to seeing you enter the coffee shop in the morning, at a quarter to seven, with your copy of the *China Daily*. You always smile and wish me good morning, "morning love" or "*zou zou wo airen*" and you read the newspaper while I serve you your coffee and cereals and fruit salad. Your men always come rushing in at the last minute and the next five minutes are very hectic, serving everybody his eggs and bacon and toast and coffee before you all rush off to the construction site.

'However, those thirty minutes before your men arrive have become very precious to me. It's still quiet at that hour and you and I talk about all kinds of things. Then we talk in English, then in Chinese, then again in a mixture of the two, whatever suits us or the subject best. You told me not to be shy or self-conscious and just talk about whatever I felt like talking about and never mind mistakes or mispronunciations. You would correct me if they were really important. The same went for your Chinese, you said, and you told me not to be afraid to correct you as well. That's the only way to learn to speak a foreign language, you said. I especially like the Sunday mornings. Sunday is your day off and your men sleep in very late, sometimes as late as twelve o'clock. You always come down to the coffee shop at around eight though, in your Sunday clothes, and you have four or five different newspapers and a few magazines with you. Your company sends them to you from Hong Kong every Friday, you told me, by a special service, DHL you call that. You don't like to stay in your room, you told me, so you come down to the coffee shop to read your papers and magazines while you have first a bigger breakfast than usual during the week and later you order a piece of apple pie and more coffee. You show me the foreign newspapers and magazines and you often read or translate articles for me. The other girls have taken the habit of coming over to our corner as well and you don't mind me discussing with them the things you just told me.

'It is so difficult for us to understand how different your lives are from ours and I doubt whether we will ever fully understand the way you live and work. How you can go wherever you want to whenever you want to and however you want to without having to ask permission from your governments or Party leaders. In fact, you have no Party leaders who can tell you what and what not to do. Imagine, no one to tell you what is best for you, to remind you of your duties, to explain the Party's motives if you feel treated unjustly so you can accept the way things are and not worry. No wonder those foreigners have such terrible mood swings the other girls say. Now they are boisterously happy, now frighteningly angry, then again they are withdrawn and worried. One always has to look at their faces just to see what mood they are in, the girls say. It's true, you know. I also have learned that at certain moments I better keep quiet, serve you your food and withdraw to my corner.' Lilian paused.

'I once told you about the other girls' uneasiness, Lao Dee, and you said that the reason why the Chinese didn't understand the foreigners' unpredictable moods was because they didn't understand that the freedom to make one's own decisions, and to live with the consequences of those decisions, is not always easy to handle. Depending on the outcome of those decisions and the way other people react to them, one can indeed be alternately happy or worried, elated or sad, satisfied or angry, you said. You said also that the foreigners are often exasperated by the Chinese and the circumstances under which they have to work here in China. "We work hard," you said, I remember the exact words, "and we make very long hours to do a perfect job and to finish on time, and though one would assume that that is what the Chinese want, a perfect job on time, they often don't seem to care and are often unwilling to co-operate. It's very frustrating and very difficult for my men to understand that attitude," you told me.'

'That's right,' Lao Dee interrupted Lilian. 'What I didn't tell you at the time was that I had probably made a mistake during the preparation for the job in China. I had lived in Hong Kong for six years already and loved the place so I thought it would be a good idea to have the men spend a few days in Hong Kong before continuing to Dalian, both to get over the jet lag and to prepare them for the shock of living in a totally different culture. They were ravingly enthusiastic about Hong Kong, about the dynamism of the place that gets to you and makes you throb in tune, about the devil-may-care attitude of the people, Chinese and foreigners alike, and how they work together and get things done in a way and at a pace people in Europe can only dream about. I was so pleased with their reaction, because I am so proud of Hong Kong, that for four days I showed them around everywhere and never failed to point out to them how well and how beautifully and, above all, how fast things were done. The evening before our departure for Dalian we had dinner together in a revolving restaurant high above the ocean of lights that is Hong Kong and they also felt the pulsing rhythm in their veins, they assured me.' Lao Dee smiled ruefully.

'It was then that I realised I had made a big mistake and I tried to prepare them for the fact that China wouldn't be at all like that, would in fact be the very opposite. I told them the Chinese of mainland China would come across as uncaring, lazy, rough, with a couldn't care less attitude. That they would be unwilling to take responsibility, would be unco-operative and so heedless of their own work that it would often seem as if they did things wrongly or badly on purpose. That the Chinese managers and leaders have no authority over their workers and would always try to avoid situations in which they would have to give orders or reprimand the workers. That the workers would seize any opportunity to walk away from the job at hand or just to sit down, smoke, spit on the ground and laugh uproariously at some growled comment or other by one of them about whoever or whatever is going on before them. That the directors and managers would promise to arrange things, however, would never deliver. That, instead, they would remain closeted for days on end, in meetings, drinking tea and smoking and posturing with fake accomplishments or boasting of objectives they have neither the means nor the ability to achieve. That, however, they would never come to the shop floor and follow the work in progress and ask the foreigners to explain how the new equipment works.

'I said all these things to them and tried to explain why the mainland Chinese are like that, so different from their fellow Chinese in Hong Kong, however, I didn't get it across. What did I expect? After a delicious, abundant meal from a buffet without equal, drinking their umpteenth glass of perfectly drawn draught beer, smoking a cigar offered and lit by the epitome of the perfect waiter, they weren't in the mood for this kind of depressing talk. *They* patted *me* on my head and told me not to worry, everything would be all right, surely I saw things a bit too negatively? Now they know better and they laugh wryly when I remind them of that night in Hong Kong. However, I try to explain to them that it's not the people, that it's the system that has made the mainland Chinese like that, that has killed their innate zest for work, their basic decency and trustworthiness. It's an inhumane system that encourages deceit and make-believe conformity to its so-called Unified Thought doctrine, that debases people's innate goodness and decency and good manners. All this is, however, difficult to understand for the foreigners,' Lao Dee concluded, 'and there are times when the frustrations simply become too much and the men explode.'

He fell silent and Lilian took over.

'I'll never forget that Friday afternoon in April,' she continued her narrative. 'You remember, Lao Dee?'

Without waiting for Lao Dee's reply she went on, addressing the others.

'Lao Dee and his men came back earlier than usual from work and one of the men slammed the sliding door of their van so hard that we heard it in the coffee shop. They didn't go up to their rooms first, to shower and change as they normally do, but came straight to the coffee shop. We hadn't expected them back that early so their four tables were still occupied by the hotel's Party committee for its daily meeting. The Germans gripped the committee members by their shoulders and told them furiously to get out. Secretary Du's spectacles fell off his nose as he tried to protest, his voice quavering and squeaking like a turkey that's being strangled.' She smiled.

'Vice-Manager Zhou and the security guard, Hu, and Manager Yu grabbed their papers and, stumbling over their chairs in their haste, bolted out of the coffee shop. Secretary Du ran after them, squawking and squealing, trying to prevent his papers from slipping from under one arm while at the same trying to hook his spectacles back behind his ears. He didn't pay attention to where he put his feet and so he missed that fancy little bridge over the goldfish pond between the lobby and the coffee shop and he fell, arms flailing, papers flying, amongst carps and plastic lotuses. He scrambled up and out of the pond and, dripping wet, disappeared through the lobby, leaving his papers and one shoe behind. Everybody saw the big hole in the heel of the gauzy, black sock on his shoeless foot. We were petrified with fright, but the other foreign guests applauded loudly and shouted, "Hooray!"'

Auntie Liu burst out laughing and shouted, 'Hooray!' making the others laugh also.

'Lovely, lovely,' she hiccuped. 'Oh, how I wish I had seen it with my own eyes, though you describe it very well, my love. What a sight that must have been. But go on, Lilian, my love, let's hear the rest of this wonderful story.'

Lilian smiled and continued.

'Lao Dee and his men sat down and they ordered double pepper steaks, French fries and Heineken beer for all. Only Lao Dee ordered Hainan chicken rice and tea. The group of English engineers, who are building that new glass factory, were the first to get up from their tables and stand around their Dutch and German colleagues. The Hong Kong Chinese, who work on all kinds of smaller projects, and the Italians of that new truck factory, followed suit. They all wanted to know what had happened and for a moment everybody talked at the same time. Finally Rene, Lao Dee's assistant, called for silence and he explained.

'It appeared that the Monday before they had found out that Vice-Director Zhu of the new factory had always lied to them when he had assured them that the utilities would be ready in time for them to start the test runs of the new machines. Lao Dee had overheard a dispute between two Chinese engineers. One of them had objected to being forced by Vice-Director Zhu to lie to the foreigners about the state of the work to be done by the Chinese themselves and he had shouted at his colleague, "The foreigners have come much too early, at least six months too early. We haven't even got approval from Beijing to start work on the project. We can't go on lying to the foreigners. Every day they ask me when the work will be started, and say that we'll never be ready on time. And each time I must reply that we will manage, and that they must not worry. I'm making a fool of myself. What must the foreigners think of us, Chinese engineers, if we say such unreasonable things?"

'Lao Dee had immediately stopped all work and called a meeting, ordering Vice-Director Zhu, who was in a meeting in town, by phone to come to the site at once. Both the foreign and Chinese engineers had been present when Lao Dee had confronted Vice-Director Zhu with what he had overheard. Zhu had at first tried to squirm out of the web of lies he had entangled himself in during the past couple of months, however, in the end he had admitted that he had misrepresented the situation when he had sent the fax message to Holland, saying that the foreigners could start their work. It had been his hope that the presence of the foreigners on site would put the pressure on the authorities in Beijing to quickly grant approval for him to start work on the Chinese part of the job, he had told Lao Dee and his men. When the approval kept on being postponed, in spite of several visits by him to the ministries in Beijing, he had become desperate and had told his own engineers to lie to the foreigners if asked when they would start. Lao Dee had angrily told Vice-Director Zhu that in four weeks he would be forced to stop work if by then there was still no water, electricity, cooling, steam and compressed air.

'What did Vice-Director Zhu expect him to do then? Lao Dee had asked angrily. Go back to Europe and come back some other time? Who was going to pay for all the extra costs? And what about the other projects, both in China and elsewhere, he had scheduled already? Vice-Director Zhu had promised immediate and grand-scale action and he had implored Lao Dee to give him one week to show that he was serious. He would put four contractors, with thousands of workers, on the job, night and day, and would begin to supply the utilities one by one, starting in four weeks, to enable the foreign friends to start the test runs of their machines. It would need some improvisation and the situation would not be ideal but at least the friends wouldn't need to go back to Europe. And, in spite of everybody's misgivings, Lao Dee had again given that liar Zhu the benefit of the doubt.

'"How many times did you warn him orally?" Rene asked Lao Dee rhetorically. "How many memos did you send him to tell him that he was far behind the work schedule you had made for him, for his own job to boot, because he wasn't capable of making such a schedule himself? And each time he told you, orally of course, never in writing, 'next week, next week we'll start' though even the biggest jackass could see that even in Europe and under the best of circumstances it would take at least a month to prepare the work and then three months, working in three shifts, to complete such a big installation. And what do you think happened this time?" Rene shouted, looking angrily at the crowd. "The liar didn't turn up the whole week."

'"Every day we asked 'Where's Vice-Director Zhu?' and every day we got the same answer: 'Vice-Director Zhu has a meeting, a very important meeting, with very important leaders from Beijing. And what did that wonderful, capable director and those very important leaders from Beijing do during those very important meetings?" Rene shouted rhetorically.

'"*Nothing! Nothing at all!*" the crowd shouted back in chorus. "*They drank their tea, had a pee and let things be*!"

'By that time the uproar in the coffee shop had drawn the attention of the other guests in the lobby and of the front office staff and they rushed over to the coffee shop to see what was going on. I saw Roger Wu push himself through the crowd to where Lao Dee was sitting, quietly eating his chicken rice. Roger bent over Lao Dee and urgently spoke in his ear. Lao Dee laughed and put down his chopsticks. He sat up straight and, raising his voice only slightly, he said, "Hold your horses! Now!" The din died down quickly, the last of the Cantonese stopped jabbering, Rene sat down again and everybody looked at Lao Dee. Lilian looked at Lao Dee, and began to quote his words said that day.

'"Lo and behold," Lao Dee began, smiling derisively. "Fifteen capable, presumably intelligent but, above all, free people who voluntarily came to China to do a job the Chinese can't do themselves and for which each of them is paid, in salaries and bonuses, more than a Chinese engineer earns in his whole lifetime. Outside their working hours they live in this luxury hotel, each in a comfortable, temperature-controlled room twice the size of their Chinese colleagues' family apartments or hovels, with radio, TV, telephone and minibar and their own bathroom with hot and cold water, fresh, fluffy towels every day, individually packed soap and shampoo and conditioners and shower gel and mouthwash and what have you. Whatever mess they make in their room is quickly and discreetly cleaned up while they are out and their clothes are washed and ironed for them every day. They have their breakfast and dinner served at their table, in this restaurant, by girls who have to work one month for what the foreign friends spend on meals and dinner in one day.

'"In the morning they are picked up in front of the hotel at a time convenient to them and driven to their workplace in an air-conditioned van, the stereo sound system blaring full blast the tapes they brought with them. Though they work undeniably very hard, yet they work a few hours and have coffee in the site office in a relaxed and friendly atmosphere amongst themselves. They work another two hours and have lunch in a special room separate from the Chinese workers' own canteen, the cook specially hired for the duration of their stay from a good restaurant in town. After lunch they work another few hours and are then driven back to their hotel. They bathe and change into clean clothes, have drinks and dinner and spend the rest of the evening as they please, where they please and with whom they please. After three to five months they have finished their jobs and return home to pocket their double salaries and bonuses and all they know about China is the hotel where they stayed, the road from the hotel to the project site and a few hotel bars and how to get there by taxi. From behind the windows of their van or taxi they stare at the scene outside, condescendingly interested at first, however quickly losing interest in what they see as an alien world, full of filth, pollution, poverty, old and ramshackle hovels street after street after street, sombre crowds of people who never seem to lack smelly, patched, dull dark blue, grey or green baggy clothes, endless files of slowly pedalling cyclists, absent-mindedly and continuously ringing their bells, totally oblivious of the world around them, staring ahead with lacklustre eyes into some dark and cold hell. The foreign friends snicker at the few pathetically, pseudo-modernly clad young people in ill-fitting, clashingly coloured clothes and high-heeled shoes, the boys with long, greasy hair, defiance in their smouldering eyes, the girls twittering like starlings, eyes twinkling. They, the foreign friends, never give a thought to the courage it takes for these youngsters, daring to be different, to crawl out of the sucking mud of their joyless, dull and oppressive society.

'"These fifteen free and intelligent people and others like them, in their scores, all over China, never tire of telling each other and their uncomprehending and obligingly snickering friends and relatives back home, the same tired stories and anecdotes, over and over again, all basically true, mind you, about the laziness of the Chinese, their stupidity, their backwardness, their rough and sloppy and to-hell-with-it working habits, their shoddy and always defect tools and equipment, their stubbornness and pig-headedness, their bloody-mindedness. However, very few, if anyone at all, of these privileged foreign friends have taken the trouble of reading up about China and its people and they therefore know next to nothing about its history, its culture and about the oppressive, the inhumane and asinine system that has been imposed on their land and as a result of which the Chinese have become a nation of bloody-minded dodgers, liars and pretenders, not only in dealing with foreigners but also amongst themselves. Look at our friends from Hong Kong. They are also Chinese, however, are they like the mainland Chinese?

'"No! You all cry out indignantly. No! Never! We can't imagine a greater difference! Yes! I reply. Yes! Intrinsically they are the same, all Chinese, however, it's the system that has made them so different.

'"So see what a social system does to make or break a people! Our German friends should know this. They needn't come as far as China to learn this. Each of them has done jobs in the eastern part of their country and they know what the same system did to their fellow Germans. I can understand your anger and frustrations. I am quite a hot-tempered character myself and more often than I care to remember my first reaction was also anger when I was lied to, cheated or taken for a ride. However, I then think: poor bastards, what a rotten life you have. How lucky I am to have been born a Westerner, a free man. Free to live where I want and how I want. Free to work where I want and to do the kind of work I am good at and can feel good about. Free to spend the money I earn on whatever I fancy, answerable to nobody but myself. Free to spend my leisure time as I like. Free to speak my mind, free to choose and read the books and newspapers and magazines I like, free to like and dislike and free from fear of each other as we sit here. Just imagine how different our lives are from those of the poor bastards we are all so worked up about. Ever asked yourself how they feel? Do we know the man or woman who has been assigned to assist us, to work with us, to learn from us? Does it ever occur to us that he or she may have other ambitions?

'"No, it doesn't, and we get angry when he is absent-minded or sullen and makes no effort to understand us when we try to explain something; when she never volunteers for anything; when he comes late and leaves early or disappears all the time to the toilet or the canteen; when she makes the same mistake over and over again. So we become so exasperated that we ignore them and do the work ourselves. Do we ask ourselves why they act that way? Perhaps he would have liked to decide for himself what to do with his life, instead of that being decided for him and with a complete disregard for his own opinion and talents to boot. He hates every minute on the job, however he can't tell us that. Maybe she loves a man and would have liked to have a family. Instead the man she loves has been assigned a job two thousand kilometres away and she sees him only once a year, for one week, and even then they have no right to privacy. A stealthy look, a surreptitious touch, a whispered word of endearment is all they can give each other, surrounded as they are, day and night, by people they cannot trust.

'"Do we ever give a thought to how they feel when they see us leave after work to our luxury hotel, to a shower or bath and clean leisure clothes, to drinks and dinner in a relaxed and convivial atmosphere, to a tranquil night's sleep in a large, clean bed in our air-conditioned room? How does *he* feel when he returns to his crummy little flat or shack, half the size of our room, where he lives with his parents or with his wife, his child and his mother? Perhaps he would also like to decide for himself how to spend his evening. Instead there are vegetables and pork or chicken to buy on the market, every day again, for they have no refrigerator, food to prepare in the cramped mini-kitchen, dishes, pots and pans to clean, clothes to wash and mend and hung to dry outside the window. This finished, there are the neighbourhood struggle meetings to attend for two to three hours every evening, with mandatory community study of yet another important speech by somebody or other in Beijing, with questions to answer, in public, about his behaviour and self-criticism to utter in front of everybody if he has deviated from the Party's guidelines, with denouncements to make of others or to undergo himself.

'"What a life! What a bloody hell of a life! And yet we yell and scream at them, insult and curse them and the poor sods don't even dare to shout back because their leaders have instructed them not to upset the foreign friends. What foreign friends, dammit? Obnoxious, spoilt and unfeeling jerks, that is what we are! And yet, despite everything, there is always that one man, that one girl, who looks up to us, eager for a gesture of friendship, for a bit of affection, beaming when you accept a cigarette he virtually thrusts at you, or a cookie she has baked herself and shyly, blushing, fumbles in your hand hoping the others don't see, happy as an affectionate dog if you don't chase him away but let him just sit there and watch while we are having our coffee break or let him carry our shiny tools or clean the machines. You begin to like him, you share a laugh, he tries your food, you give him a packet of cigarettes or a fake Swiss army knife or her a little scarf you got for free in the plane and you laugh, a bit embarrassed though, at their happy gratitude. You discover that he is intelligent and you teach him how to operate the electric tools, or the computer, or how to read a plan, whatever.

'"And then, suddenly, one day, he doesn't turn up and you get only evasive answers when you ask for him, whether he is sick or on leave. Nobody, not even the leader or the director, knows, or so they say. So you shrug your shoulders. Too bad. You made a mistake. He was after all just another lazy, ungrateful bastard and you'll be damned if you waste your time and good intentions again. That the sneaky Party spy reported him for becoming too chummy with the foreigner and that he was transferred to some crummy, dark and filthy Chinese factory to punish him, re-educate him as they call it, *that* you wouldn't know."'

Lilian fell silent and looked at Lao Dee, waiting for him to say something. He smiled at her but remained silent and she, hesitating briefly, continued her narrative.

'While Lao Dee spoke, by turn sad and angry, emotional and contemptuous, the other foreigners did not interrupt him once. Even the guests who had nothing to do with the matter had stopped eating to better listen to him. Roger Wu kept up a running, whispered, approximate translation for the coffee shop staff who were watching the scene from the corner where they usually idle. When Lao Dee fell silent, the Hong Kong Chinese impulsively thronged around him, patting his back and shoulders, saying how much they agreed with him. I noticed that some of them were moved to tears. People sauntered back to their chairs, softly talking amongst themselves to conceal their embarrassment. Lao Dee's own men ate their cold food and said nothing. Since that Friday evening the long-staying foreign guests, notably the Dutch and Germans, have been remarkably less boisterous and hot-tempered.

'The week after that Friday Lao Dee accompanied Vice-Director Zhu to Beijing. Lao Dee told me the next Sunday morning that Zhu and he had visited together the minister of light industry and finance and had, in three days, obtained all the approvals for Vice-Director Zhu to begin his work. As a special gesture of friendly co-operation the Dutch and German teams offered five modern welding machines to Vice-Director Zhu for him to give on loan to the Ministry of Light Industry's contracting department. Lao Dee promised them that his specialist welders would train the ministries in the operation of the machines and that they would all assist in every possible way to speed up the part of the installation work to be done by the Chinese themselves. A couple of weeks ago Jan told me that most of the backlog had been made good and that the delay won't be more than four or five weeks, not long enough to justify sending back the whole crew. Only the two computer specialists will go back for about two months to complete a small project in Europe, however, they'll be back in August. Most of us in the hotel like the foreigners now that they are no longer so quick-tempered and we are no longer afraid of them and many of us even dare to joke back. Though they often behave outrageously, they are always kind and never mean. Do you remember the name-giving ceremony, Lao Dee?' Lilian asked, laughing.

Lao Dee chuckled and said, 'It was good fun. Quite un-Chinese I'm afraid. But, please tell the others.'

'One day Roger Wu, during one of our training sessions, told us that in Hong Kong many Chinese, whose work involves daily contacts with the foreigners, have adopted a Western name,' Lilian continued. 'Roger said it would be a good idea if we did the same to show that we wholeheartedly embraced the Party's modernisation drive. We all agreed and Roger went to see Vice-Manager Zhou to propose that the staff wear name badges and that everyone should adopt a Western name besides his or her Chinese name, just to make it easy for the stupid foreign devils who always make such gibberish of Chinese names. He told Zhou that a few of his staff were already the victims of misplaced jokes by colleagues because of the wrong pronunciations of their names by the foreigners. Zhou approved despite Secretary Du's protestations that Chinese people should not be called by other names than their honourable Chinese ones and that foreigners who didn't take the trouble to learn how to pronounce them correctly and consequently caused embarrassment to the bearers of those honourable names, had to be reported and be expelled from the country.

'Roger asked us to each draw up a shortlist of five Western names in order of our own preference. He said he would organise an official name-giving ceremony during a friendship party for the long-staying guests. One evening, during dinner, Roger came to the coffee shop to ask Lao Dee and his men what they thought of his idea. They were immediately enthusiastic and suggested that the party be held on a Saturday afternoon around the indoor swimming pool on the top floor. All the foreigners, not only the Dutch and the Germans but also the English, the Italians, the Americans, the Japanese, the Danes and the Hong Kongers, sacrificed two Sundays to build food stalls, barbecues and beer stands around the pool with their own tools and from materials they bought in town with their own money or borrowed from the construction sites.

'The Saturday of the party they all stopped work early and were back at the hotel at two o'clock. They arranged tables and chairs around the pool and at four o'clock the Chinese staff were invited to come to the swimming pool area, in our best clothes, not our hotel uniforms. The English, Americans and Hong Kongers acted as waiters and each of us was led to a chair specially reserved for him or her. The Dutch, Italians and Japanese were the cooks; the Germans and the Danes the barmen. The food was Western: barbecued steaks, French fries and Italian noodles with sausage meat and tomato sauce. We didn't like the food very much, however, the foreigners did their best to make us happy so that we, in turn, did our best to eat their food and drink their beer and Coca-Cola with ice. None of us knew how to use fork and knife and when the Italians and the English showed us how to eat the steak and how to twirl the noodles around the fork, we all laughed and giggled with red faces from the beer and embarrassment. Some of our men just skewered the whole steak on their fork and bit off pieces, spurred on by gales of hilarity from their table companions. It was all so friendly and in such good cheer that we ate all the food and drank all the beer and Coca-Cola.

'When there was nothing left to eat and drink, the foreigners quickly cleared the tables and the name-giving began. The Germans had been busy the Friday night before installing a platform on the diving plank, above the pool, that could hold some ten people. Roger Wu acted as the master of ceremonies and he climbed up the ladder to the platform, followed by three Italians, who would play the guitar and accordion and sing, and by two Danes for the baptisms. We girls shivered in anticipation and to hide our nervousness we pushed each other, giggling and laughing shrilly, a bit hysterically, I'm afraid. Suddenly, three Dutchmen, in swimming trunks, dived into the pool, shouting hallelujah, and positioned themselves in front of the platform, treading water, just in case somebody fell off.

'Roger called the boys first, three at a time, by their full Chinese names. Cheered on and pushed forward by those whose turn was yet to come they awkwardly climbed the short stairs up to the platform, where they were told to stand close to the edge, facing the crowd. Then Roger read their own shortlists of preferred names from which the foreigners had to choose one by lifting their right hand if they approved of the name. There was little variety. The boys' lists read as if they had copied them from each other: Robert, Roger, Michael, Andrew, Kenneth, Leonard, David, an occasional Dennis. The result was three Roberts, four Michaels, two Andrews, two Kenneths, two Leonards, three Davids and one Dennis. Roger Wu would not have another Roger. He was unique, he said. Before it was the girls' turn, the Italians played a few beautiful tunes and Stefano, their leader, sang a few songs.'

'Stefano loves to sing,' Beiyuen interrupted Lilian.

'He has a complete sound system in his room, with four huge loudspeakers, one in each corner. Actually, he has two rooms,' Beiyuen explained, 'with a connecting door. One serves as his office and I am not allowed to dust the special desk since the day I threw away a few crumpled pieces of paper. Even the wastepaper basket I am not allowed to empty since he often crumples a note and throws it in the basket, absent-mindedly or in anger, and later wants it back. He then scatters the contents of the basket on the floor and, on his knees, looks for that particular note. He loves opera music, Western opera that is, not Chinese. He always sings the arias in tune with his tapes or discs, at least when he is happy which is most of the time, fortunately. Sometimes, however, he is very unhappy, usually after a telephone call with his country.

'He telephones every day and shouts in the phone and talks very, very fast. How can they think and talk so fast all at the same time? He always calls between three and four o'clock in the afternoon since then it's morning in Italy and his leader is in the office, Stefano once explained to me. I always do the other rooms first so that by that time I have reached Stefano's. It's very funny to see him hopping up and down behind his desk, gesticulating and yelling at the phone, even when from the squeaking on the phone it's obvious that his leader is yelling at the same time at him. How do they understand each other? And how dare he yell at his leader like that? Those calls always last twenty minutes or more. Such a shame. Guan Shaoxia of accounting told me his telephone bills for one month are more than what she earns in two years. When the call has made him happy, Stefano opens the door of his room and he sings songs with high and low trills. When his leader in Italy says things that make him unhappy, he disappears straight into his bathroom and fills his bath.

'Stefano always takes a hot bath when he is upset and he plays with little plastic toy ducks and a plastic turtle that paddles with its flippers when he winds its mechanism. It makes him laugh and I know already that a few minutes later he'll start to sing, mournfully at first, however, gradually the songs become merrier and when I hear the song called *"funiculi funicula"* I know he's his usual happy self again. All the girls in housekeeping like Stefano. He is always friendly and chats with us when we clean his room or bring his thermos with hot water. His Chinese is also very good. More scholarly than yours, Lao Dee. You speak like the people talk amongst themselves; Stefano talks like in books. He always gives us a handful of the small, round cookies he keeps in a high colourful tin on his desk. I like their strong almond taste. I brought the ones he gave me yesterday for you to try.'

Beiyuen gave each of the others three of the small, round, brownish cookies and gingerly at first they nibbled at a crunchy amaretti. They found it delicious and quickly ate the other two as well.

'Italy is a southern province of Europe, if I remember correctly,' Mother said. 'Perhaps that's why this man Stefano is so different from those Dutchmen and Germans, who are from the northern provinces. In China it's the same, isn't it? The Cantonese are so different from the people in Heilongjiang, Jilin and Liaoning. I am from Sichuan myself and I can tell you it took me some getting used to here in the north. People here are so much more bland, like their food. Perhaps people are what they eat?'

Mother laughed and added, 'Perhaps my daughter could finish her story? I'm enjoying it more than I thought I would. These foreigners are actually quite human, I find, weird but human, nevertheless.'

Lilian smiled at her and picked up where she had been interrupted by Beiyuen.

'The girls' name lists were not much more varied than the boys',' she continued. 'Elisabeth, Olivia, Vanessa, Catherine, Juliana were the favourites. I had chosen Virginia for myself, only Virginia, no other name. Most of the names were shortened by the foreigners and to loud applause Elisabeth became Betty, Betsy and Liz, Catherine became Cathy and Katie and so on. When it was my turn Roger told the crowd that my romanised second and third name, if written as one word in Pinyin, as is now the custom, was exactly like the English girl's name Lilian and he therefore proposed to leave it like that, Lilian being a very pretty name, he said.

'I felt my heart miss a beat when he said that and I had to squeeze my eyes shut to keep tears from rolling down my cheeks. I had so much looked forward to wearing a tag with Virginia on it and the foreigners calling me by that name since none of the other girls had thought of that name and now I would be stuck with my Chinese name. I heard everybody applaud Roger's proposal, muffled as through a thick fog. My friend Zing Neiping, who had been named Olivia, kicked me under the table and then I heard Lao Dee's voice and I forced myself to listen to what he had to say. Lilian was undeniably a beautiful name, I heard him say, however, for a foreigner, it was just a name and it did not say anything about the person I was. I blushed when he went on to say that he would like to propose a name that evoked an image of my cheerful smile and delicacy. Lao Dee said that he personally always thought of me as of that tiny, simple little flower, the daisy, that made people feel good after the long, dark and cold days of winter because it signalled the return of the light and warmth and new life, of spring and summer. He therefore would like to propose that I be named Daisy, an unusual name, but so, in China, were the dimples in my cheeks, he said.

'Before I could say something I felt myself being lifted up and thrown high up in the air and then falling, falling until the cheers and applause were suddenly switched off by the cold water of the pool closing in around me. I can't swim, but I didn't panic as I felt already the grip of one of the Dutchmen pulling me up to the surface. It was my friend Jan and he smiled at me when he pushed me to the pool ladder and helped me find the rungs with my hands and feet. I think it was then that I fell in love with him. It was the feeling of complete security he gave me in a situation where on my own I would have been totally helpless. Dripping wet but very happy I hurried to the changing room to change into my hotel uniform. Ever since that Saturday there is a heart-warming sort of complicity between the foreigners and us Chinese. A smile of recognition, a wink, even a joking remark when coming across each other in the lobby or in the corridors or when standing together in the lift. It made us all feel so good. As if we all belonged to one, big, happy family, Neiping said to me once. Roger Wu asked Lao Dao to make the badges with the names written in stylish roman letters; like real calligraphy. I haven't thanked you yet, Uncle Dao, I know you made it especially beautiful for me,' and on a sudden impulse Lilian gave Lao Dao a quick peck on his cheek which made the old man blush.

'A pretty emotional lot, these Westerners, judging from what you have told us,' Auntie Liu said, 'and contagious at that, seeing as I do a young girl kiss an old man who is not even a relative and that in the presence of her own mother,' she added, smiling.

'Too much emotion is tiring, and often tiresome for others, however, too much secretiveness is also not good,' Auntie continued. 'People can learn so much from each other, especially if we are of different races and cultures; tolerance for each other's differences, for instance, so that we can get along and go about our business as decent human beings. Our friend Lao Dee seems to understand that. He has lived in many different countries and worked with people of different races and cultures and just because of that I'm sure he scoffs at that fashionable but nefarious notion that all people are the same just as, on the other hand, he will have nothing but contempt for those who claim to be superior merely because they are of a different race or culture. Of course, every race, every culture, has its share of superior, mediocre and inferior people, though inferior is a very loaded word, I know. Remarkably though, and regardless of race and culture, those different groups have more or less the same pattern. A small number of people, men as well as women, are superior in one or a few or even, rarely, in many respects, the vast majority are just ordinary, mediocre even perhaps; and finally a small minority are downright inferior or, perhaps, under-performing is a better term. This inequality can be physical as well as intellectual or, more rarely, both.

'That's the way it has always been and will always be and no amount of social engineering or political sophism will ever change that. The tragedies in the past were often the result of the so-called superior specimens behaving like prima donnas and claiming an exulted status with the God-given right to treat their inferiors with contempt and like slaves. The tragedy of the present results from the fact that a few superior specimens have, only for their own glory, seen the potential for power that lies in numbers. They have made the mediocre majority aware of the strength that lies in vast numbers and they now dominate the world. Predictably, mediocre as they are, they have gone for the cheap revenge of oppressing the gifted individuals and denying them the opportunity to exercise their talents. This makes the present tragedy far worse than the past ones because it leads to a standstill in human development followed by an increasingly fast regression until everything finally breaks down and nothing and nobody works any more. Our only hope is a well-understood self-interest, strange as this may sound, which makes us realise that we have all our role to play.

'By well-understood self-interest I mean that both the gifted, talented individuals and the majority of ordinary, mediocre people realise that they need each other to lead a decent life. The talented men and women to invent, develop, discover whatever is necessary for real, honest progress that benefits humanity as a whole and to lead the others to implement, to carry out, to work, to harvest. When this interrelationship is understood by all as the cornerstone for what is generally considered to be a good life, then perhaps, just perhaps, respect and tolerance may slowly take a place next to naked self-interest in human relationships. Respect by all for all, regardless of racial, cultural, physical, intellectual or material differences, simply based on the shared status of *humanness*. Tolerance by all for all simply based on the recognition that not only are all humans *different* in their humanness but also that they have the *right* to be different. With respect and tolerance will grow the realisation that the small minority, who, through no fault of their own, cannot contribute, deserve to be cared for simply because of our common human heritage of which they got an unfair small part.'

Auntie Liu fell silent.

They sat in silence, each thinking about what Auntie had said and how it might apply to their own situation.

Surreptitiously Lilian and Beiyuen looked at each other and then at Lao Dao, who was the oldest person present. It would be unbecoming for them, as the youngest, to comment on Auntie's opinion.

As if on cue Old Dao coughed to indicate he would like to say something and Auntie said, smilingly, 'Go ahead, old friend, say what you have on your mind.'

'Thank you, Meiling,' Lao Dao said, chuckling, 'it's not often that I am asked for my opinion.'

Then, serious again, he continued, 'You have spoken well, Meiling, I know you well and long enough and can therefore rightly say that you are certainly not a fuzzy-brained idealist but rather a hard-nosed realist. It does therefore not surprise me that you make a case for respect and tolerance in our relations with others. I agree with you that a society whose members' only preoccupation is to satisfy their own self-interest is not worthy of human beings. On the other hand, I find that if the majority of the people cannot satisfy their basic needs, or self-interest if you wish to call it that, it is unrealistic to expect them to show respect and tolerance for each other, let alone for the few who can and do look after themselves. Envy, jealousy, hatred even for those who are better off and excel is very much in man's nature, I'm afraid. Several systems of social organisation have been tried and are still being tried out to solve this seeming paradox. No system will ever be perfect. Some systems were and are more imperfect than others and they have all disappeared or will disappear, slowly, through gradual adjustment to changing times and people's expectations and demands, or abruptly, through violent upheaval.

'Though our present system in China has undeniably succeeded in guaranteeing everybody a reasonably decent existence, decent as measured by what life was before 1949, the standards of decency have not evolved with the changing times and the expectations of the people and they no longer suffice today, notably not for the younger generation. Young people everywhere take the purely materialistic standards for food, shelter, elementary health care, selective education, for which their parents fought, often at the cost of their lives, for granted and they now want also such abstract matters as freedom of speech, of travel, of choice of work and place of work, included in their basic rights. The Party Elders will, of course, never agree to that. As a result one hears and sees and feels the signs of restlessness, rebelliousness and discontent everywhere.

'The other night I had a long discussion about the restless stirrings in our society with our friend Lao Dee. He travels to many places in China and everywhere it is the same, he says. Beijing, Nanjing, Shanghai, Chongqing and most restless of all seems to be Guangzhou because of Hong Kong's proximity and influence. People in Guangdong Province watch Hong Kong TV which makes them even more impatient with their present situation. Young people these days are defiant and provocative, Lao Dee says. They break the codes of social conduct, even the law. Students as well as the younger workers accost him in the street, in parks, in trains and buses, in the small restaurants where he has his meals, and draw him into discussion about life in China. They ask him about life in the outside world, how ordinary people live and work there. Defiantly they tell him, sometimes shout at him, that they'll have it all likewise, not at some time in the future, not in five or ten years, *no*! next year! Next month! *Tomorrow*!

'Lao Dee often meets with Party officials, occasionally at a very high level, vice-ministers and ministers and so on, even with Zhao Ziyang twice, and he says that they are all aware of the situation and are deeply worried. Lao Dee says that the seeming lack of response by the Party is not because the leaders are divided or hesitant but because they are merely trying to find a consensus about how to respond and when. Lao Dee says that during his discussions with the young people, which he never seeks – even tries to avoid for fear of agents provocateurs out to frame him for instigation of social unrest – he tries to warn them, to advise them to back off, to go slowly, a little push here, a small pull there, until such time that they themselves will be in a position to influence matters.

'However, they won't listen, Lao Dee says. Some even get angry with him and accuse him of siding with the Party for fear of losing his lucrative contracts. Lao Dee reproaches us, the older generation of non-Party members, that we are too passive, that we just sit there and let the young become reckless. When, not *if* any more, the young commit the ultimate, the unforgivable act of defiance and provoke the Party into reacting before it has its act together, it will be the old hardliners who'll impose their solution to the problem and we, the parent generation, will be to blame for the resulting disaster, Lao Dee says.

'I agree with him, however, I don't know what to do. I have so little influence. The only thing I can think of is to make young people realise how good they have it now, how much better off they are than we were when we were their age. How much has changed already for the better in our society and that this change will unavoidably go even further, slowly perhaps, groping for compromises between the ambitions of the few and the needs of the many, provided the hotheads, the reckless ones, are kept in check. However, how many young people can I reach? One? Two perhaps? And besides, what can I *do* to make them realise the danger they are courting?'

Gesturing helplessly, the old man looked at his friend.

Lao Dee saw that the women watched him closely as well.

How different their characters are, he thought to himself, impenetrable Chinese? My foot! Xu Suping or Madam Li, Lilian's mother, is clearly afraid. What beautiful eyes she has, big almonds filled with glistening, molten chocolate. Tense, however, with almost perfect self-control. She blushes. She *knows* what I am thinking.

Liu Meiling, Auntie Liu, playing, as usual, the teaser, a hint of a sardonic smile hovering about her lips which she wants me to notice, of course, as she tries to hide her deep concern for the two girls and for Lilian's mother. Beiyuen is smiling, as always. I can't see her eyes, too slitted, so I don't know what she is thinking. However, she isn't afraid or even concerned, that's for sure. She would be an ideal missionary.

And then elfin, little Lilian. She is clearly angry. Her eyes, as beautiful as her mother's, are flashing and if looks could kill, Lao Dao and I would be dead by now. She's breathing fast, her cute little nose quivers. What a waste, this girl, in China. I wonder whether I did well to interfere in her affair with Jan. I am sure she could manage on her own in Holland should Jan leave her or she walk out on him. I better say something before she pre-empts me.

Lao Dee cleared his throat.

'It's a delicate matter,' he began, charily. 'I suggested to Huimin that he tell his life story to his children, which he never did, and to his children's children, and now I suggest that he tell us as well, here, tonight, or some other night, whenever he is ready. This will be particularly important for Lilian and Beiyuen.

'Only by comparison with how life was before this time, in the first years after liberation and the subsequent periods of great upheaval, can they learn to understand and, perhaps, appreciate how much has changed already for the better and that it takes time for even a small change to take hold and permeate such a massive society of more than a billion people who have never known anything other than an authoritarian, centralised system of government. They must not yet compare themselves and their lives with the foreigners and the way these people live. Outside China, societies also differ in many respects. Some are very advanced and free and people there seem to have every conceivable luxury, like in most countries of Western Europe and North America. Others are not so advanced and are more restrictive, either politically or religiously.

'However, it took all these societies many generations to evolve into their present state and they coexist, though sometimes uneasily, because their peoples have finally come to realise that destroying other peoples' societies and imposing alien concepts is no longer acceptable. A nation can take another's society as its model, that is of course possible, even desirable perhaps, but it will still have to fashion the model to suit its own character, its culture, its history and keep readjusting and planning for the future. A society with a go-and-do-as-you-please morality is maybe what the Dutch people need since it suits their character and they have the means to pay for it, so far at least.

'Yet such a kind of society isn't everybody's cup of tea, not even in Europe, and it would be utterly unsuitable, disastrous even, for China, apart from the fact that China will never possess the means to offer the same sustainable affluence to its billion or more citizens. Now, one may argue whether it is fair that on this one planet one people seemingly has it all while others have so much less or even lack the most basic things. That is, however, an issue that the next two or three generations will have to debate and try to find a generally acceptable solution for. I very much doubt, though, whether a peaceful solution to the problem of inequality will ever be possible.

'For the time being, however, this is not something China should concern itself with other than in a purely academic manner lest the rich countries conveniently forget that China has a big say in the matter. After all, it represents a quarter of the world's population. What China should concern itself with are the spasms and, after all, still modest ambitions of its own people.'

Lao Dee fell silent and looked a bit uneasily at Lilian, who, more than once, had shown her impatience, only just short of interrupting him.

'You never said such things to me before,' she began hotly.

'It's not fair! You and your men give us a taste of what life can be like, yet we are *not* allowed to eat the dish? From the nodding of all your venerable old heads I see that you are all in complete agreement. What are you old people so afraid of? That we bit off more than we can chew and swallow? Let me tell you, *it has gone too far already*!

'Students of the university have met with us several times already, in parks, on the beach, wherever and whenever we can steal a moment of privacy. It's difficult for them to get into contact with foreigners since they are not allowed into the hotels for foreigners and have no FEC to pay in bars frequented by them. So *we* tell them all we know. We give them the newspapers and magazines and books and brochures we retrieve from the wastepaper baskets in the guest rooms, the double copies of the faxes the foreigners send or receive in the business centre. Everything foreign we can lay our hands on we pass on to the students and we discuss and dream and, above all, plan together for a future when we, too, will have all those things.

'And now you tell us to *back off*? To put all those dreams and plans on ice and wait patiently and obediently for the Party to hand out a small dollop of freedom here, a little bit of luxury there and then be grateful to boot? We are *not stupid*, Lao Dee! From what we have seen we know that whatever the foreigners can do we can do also, perhaps even better because we are *motivated*! Whatever the foreigners teach we can learn, and fast at that, because we are *motivated*!

'And once we have all the knowledge and can do all the things ourselves, then we want the rewards that go with them and we want them *now* and *here* and *not* at some indefinite time in the future.'

Lilian fell silent and looked defiantly, eyes flashing angrily, cheeks burning, at the adults who had been listening with mounting astonishment and alarm.

Her mother was clearly mortified by her tone and words towards a man who could be her grandfather and she was about to stand up and reprimand her daughter when Lao Dao added further to her utter bewilderment.

Chucklingly the old man said, 'Lo and behold, the daring and maturity of our modern youth. Our Chinese Antigone. If what happened to her is anything to go by...! You said in your retort to Lao Dee's wise words that you are not stupid, Lilian. I am sure you are not. However, you are naive and foolhardy and that's a very dangerous mixture. If we two old fools, Lao Dee and I, agree, it is for different reasons.

'What I fear is a backlash from the Party and a throwback to the times of ruthless oppression while what Lao Dee fears is that what you think you know of the foreigner's life is merely the seductively glittering and glamorous, opulent side of it. He knows that you are *not*, *cannot* yet be prepared for the very tough side of it and that the ruthlessness of his society with its fine rewards for success and ugly rejection for failure will simply be too much to cope with if the transition from our protective, uncompetitive Chinese society to his competitive one is as brusque as you crave. Only the very best amongst you would be able to adapt and succeed. The vast majority, however, would not be able to make it and they would fall by the roadside; drop-outs, unable to adapt.

'Success breeds wealth and status which breed pride and greed for more, higher, bigger, which breed irritation and shame for the unsuccessful former comrades who, in turn, will be full of resentment, envy and anger, blaming everything and everyone for their own failure except, of course, themselves as that is the way we have always been conditioned in our Chinese society. So China would end up with the worst excesses of the two systems, a relatively small, successful minority wallowing in wealth and flaunting luxuries, with the unavoidable and despicable hangers-on and a vast, sullen, resentful majority who either fell off the bandwagon or who never had or got a chance in the first place. And isn't that exactly how it all began in the years 1921 to 1949? History all over again, but this time worse, much worse, I'm afraid.'

Lao Dao fell silent and smiled, a bit sadly, at Lilian.

'Don't get me wrong, my love,' he added, 'I don't begrudge you the chance for a better life that was denied to me, as you may have been led to believe. On the contrary, I am so wary and chary, almost to the point of appearing cowardly meek to you, lest at the very moment that conditions are ripe for a gradual change for the better for all of us things go wrong because of the rashness and brusqueness of a bunch of inconsiderate young people.

'And don't think either that I, and I speak for Lao Dee as well, I'm sure, am in any way offended by the tone and words of your retort, as your mother seems to think, judging from her shocked expression. We Chinese have for too long been conditioned, as part of our culture, not to speak our mind or, if absolutely unavoidable, to do so in the most circumspect and indirect way, always courteous, so as not to give offence or cause loss of face. People not familiar with our culture or those who were brought up in a democratic society, wherein everything and everybody can be questioned, often think that we Chinese don't feel strongly about anything, that we are vague, evasive and indecisive.

'Now that China can't live in splendid isolation any more and has more and more dealings with other peoples, cultures and social systems, we must change our ways of talking and discussing lest we be misunderstood and end up holding the wrong end of the stick or are left empty-handed altogether. Your outburst Lilian, was therefore entirely justified and acceptable.'

Lilian, grateful for Lao Dao's graceful and respectful reaction to her intemperateness and also much subdued by his reasoning, replied, 'Thank you, Uncle Dao, for putting me in my place so gently. However, emboldened as I now am by your exhortation to speak our minds, I do have a few questions.

'If the recent past, the years of your youth and early adulthood, was so bad and so terrible that we must do everything in our power, even sacrifice our immediate ideals, to avoid a throwback to it, why is it then that we know *next to nothing* about those years? Why is it that older people are so *evasive* or even shut up entirely when we as much as *allude* to those times? Why was I never told what made my father into the scared half-wit I have dutifully and obediently helped to care for for the past twelve years? What *happened* to him? *Where was he* until those soldiers dumped him in front of me, twelve years ago?

'Why does nobody tell me about my grandparents and a mysterious Uncle Dan whose name I heard for the first time today, from Auntie Liu to boot, not from my own mother? I didn't even know the good man existed. Why do I know nothing about my own mother's past? Apart from her occasional remark that it was "*difficult*" when she scolds me for being an irresponsible, spoilt brat? To me it seems as if all your pasts have at some point in time coalesced into some sort of black hole from which no memory can escape and from which we young people must be kept away at all costs lest we be sucked into it and be crushed out of existence.

'How can you expect us to moderate our expectations and scale down our ambitions if all you do is keep alluding to some mysterious, terrible past which, you all argue so frantically, must never be allowed to repeat itself? Why not explain to us *what* was so terrible and *why* we must fear a repetition so much? Don't you trust our ability to judge for ourselves? I can tell you that we will not let you make up our minds for us. Or is it perhaps that you have always exaggerated the magnitude of the horrors to hide your own failures and inadequacies and are now simply afraid of questions and queries?'

Though she had spoken quietly, there had been a trace of defiance, even arrogance, in Lilian's voice, notably by the end. The adults remained silent, fidgeting with their empty tea mugs, obviously waiting for one of them to speak up.

Finally Auntie Liu spoke, quietly and without her usual, brusque, no-nonsense mannerisms.

'You have made your point, Lilian,' she said, 'and it's a valid one. We, the older people, must tell you what really happened, both for our own sake and yours. Why now all of a sudden? you will ask, why not earlier? Why wait so long? There are several reasons for that, Lilian, and they may be more complicated than you think and different for each of us. Two main reasons, however, will be the same for everyone and those are shame and cowardice.

'Shame about what Chinese did to Chinese. Shame that the instigators of the horrors were not only never made to answer for their crimes but are still in power today. Shame that the perpetrators of the horrors, those contemptible arse-lickers of the instigators, have not only gone unpunished but still show openly, after all these years, their hatred for us, like former Leader Hu Guoshang, Old Turtle, does here every day in our neighbourhood, and millions like her do every day all over China. Shame that we, the people they made to suffer so terribly and unjustly, cower in silence in their presence, obsequiously enquiring about their health, only daring to call them names behind their backs when we're sure they can't hear or identify us. And finally, shame that we are such cowards and don't dare to demand redress for all the wrongs they did to us.

'This collective cowardice has tormented two generations of Chinese, preventing them from speaking up and finding understanding. Yet, we must stop this morbid self-reproach, which earns us no respect. Instead, we must tell about the individual acts of true humaneness, of true heroism, by common people on both sides of China's great divide, that each of us has witnessed or benefited from during those times of tribulations. However, why do I have the gut feeling that your generation is not really interested, Lilian?

'Am I correct in thinking that nowadays unselfishness is something that is scoffed at rather than admired? That sacrifice earns contempt rather than respect? Is your generation still capable of gratitude? Can you still appreciate the true value of a deed that has brought nothing but foreseeable misery, however that was done because it was *the right thing to do*?

'I am asking this, Lilian, because you asked yourself whether the fact that your mother never talked to you about her past wouldn't be perhaps because she wanted to hide her failure. Her failure as what? As a mother? Were it not for her courage to do the right thing, in spite of the threat of misery and suffering, you would not be sitting there challenging her. You see, Lilian, your mother got pregnant with you in spite of Leader Hu's earlier rejection of your parents' application to have a child. By defying Hu's authority your parents defied the Party, a very serious political crime in those times. Your mother confided in me and I, ever the pragmatic one, proposed an abortion before her pregnancy became visible, to avoid punishment for herself and her husband. She refused and here you are, Lilian, challenging her credibility. Her husband, young Li Kunlen, was arrested and, in a mockery of justice, condemned to twenty years of hard labour by a People's Tribunal, composed of unwashed, spiteful dullards who danced to Hu's fiddle.

'For six years Hu Guoshang, that ugly, bitter, hateful failure, appointed by the Party as the leader of the Red Guards in this area, was allowed to terrorise our neighbourhood. Your mother was one of her favourite victims for the sole reason that she was a decent, pretty, well-educated young woman who had the misfortune to fall in love with the dashing but foolhardy and reckless young man Hu had wanted for herself. The madness unleashed by the Party on our poor country gave Hu, and others like her all over China, her chance to vent her anger, rage and hate for all that is decent under the guise of stamping out political dissent. And how she took her revenge on your father. He spent a mere seven of his twenty-year sentence in the prison and labour camps in Shanxi and Gansu, however, it was enough to break the man's spirit and turn him into the slobbering idiot you have to feed every morning. Did you ever feel love for him? I don't think so and even your mother won't reproach you for that, I'm sure. However, perhaps once you know what really happened you will appreciate how much your parents have suffered, and still do, for giving you the life you appear to enjoy so much.'

Liu Meiling fell silent.

Finally, after a long, oppressive silence, Lilian looked up, first at Auntie then at her mother and said, ruefully, 'I'm sorry, really I am. I didn't mean to hurt you, none of you, least of all Mother. Please forgive me if I did. Try to understand, though. I sometimes grieve that part of my mother's life seems to be taboo for me. Most of the time I manage to shrug it off and think that she must have her valid reasons for keeping certain things from me. At other times, however, like tonight, it gets to me and I feel an angry sadness at not being deemed worthy of her trust and, in spite of myself, I say things that must hurt you.'

She paused and, addressing her mother directly, she continued, 'I beg you, Mother, to trust me and let me learn my lessons from what happened to you. Only then can I, from my own conviction, try to influence my friends and help prevent, at least here in Dalian, that which Lao Dao and Lao Dee are so afraid of.'

Hesitating again to collect her thoughts, she added with an ominous foreboding, 'If it's not too late already. Things have gained a momentum that will be very hard to arrest. I'm afraid nobody will want to listen to me because they don't want to hear what I have to say.'

'We may indeed have wasted precious time,' Auntie agreed, 'but at least we can try. It's late so I propose that next Thursday we meet again here for a simple dinner and that afterwards Su Ping will tell us her story. I know it's quite a long story so be prepared for a late night. Then, one week later, our friend Dao Huimin will tell us his life story. I think I speak for all of us if I ask Lao Dee to honour us with his presence.'

Lao Dee waited for the others to nod their assent before he said, 'It is I who is honoured by your trust and friendship and I don't know how to thank you. I assured you earlier this evening that nothing that would be said here would be talked or written about by me unless you allow me to do so. I wonder, however, if you would allow me to record your stories so that I can listen, undistracted, and project myself into your world rather than scribbling notes.

'I could bring a good quality tape recorder and enough tapes and unobtrusively record what is said. You can always order me to stop the recording for a while.

'Furthermore, the tapes won't leave this house unless with your permission, if you decide to give the stories a wider audience. In that case I won't use your real names, of course, and, where necessary, I would change the locations if the real ones would mean trouble for you or for the people living there. However, the book would essentially tell the stories as you told them, stories of ordinary people for ordinary people. People identify with people, with the fortunes and misfortunes and sufferings of those like themselves.'

He paused, watching for signs of hesitation. Seeing none, he continued, 'There is another aspect to the matter of writing about your lives. I will have to do some reconnoitring in the places you are going to talk about. I want to taste the local atmosphere, to walk where you walked, to see what you saw. I am allowed to travel freely in your country and I am sure I can obtain permission for you to accompany me, especially if I guarantee to pay for your expenses. This would allow Lilian to visit the place where her mother spent her youth and to see her grandparents and the mysterious Uncle Dan. Together we could visit all the places of her mother's memories. The same goes for Lao Dao and, of course, for you, Meiling.'

Lao Dee smiled a bit ruefully when he saw the others staring at him.

'I'm not trying to bait you,' he said, chuckling, 'I got a bit carried away by my own enthusiasm. In fact, we could anyhow do a bit of travelling together, book or no book. It would be the perfect way for me to thank you for adopting me as your friend.'

Auntie Liu burst out laughing.

'By all means, bring your recorder and tapes next week,' she exclaimed. 'Whether we decide to use them, we'll discuss that later. Whether I'll drag my old carcass all over China is something that'll depend on a few things I don't care to talk about now. However, for Su Ping and Lilian, for Beiyuen and Lao Dao it is simply a wonderful prospect. Enough for now. It's late. Let's go to bed.'

They took their leave of each other inside so as not to dwell unnecessarily long in front of the house and draw the attention of the neighbours, notably that of Old Turtle.

Once outside and the door closed, Lilian and her mother walked quickly home while Lao Dao and Lao Dee walked back to the hotel talking quietly and contentedly about the way things had gone.

## *Chapter Eight*

Ciaokeli had recognised their footsteps long before Mother opened, carefully, the creaking front door.

They almost stumbled over the affectionate little mongrel as he turned and twisted between their legs, licking their hands as they bent over to caress him and calm him down, depositing little droplets of urine on their shoes and on the floor from sheer joy. Other than excited breathing and snorting, the little dog made no sound; no yapping, no yelping.

The first few nights after Lilian had brought him home as a present for Father, Ciaokeli had still yearned for his mother and he had howled plaintively till daybreak.

The howling had somehow triggered the ghostly fears that had lain buried for so long deep within Father's tormented soul and he had become very agitated.

The trembling puppy had watched from a corner of the kitchen as Mother and Lilian had been up and about the whole night trying to calm Father down with hot tea, hot and cold towels, rubbing oil over him and cooing nonsense talk.

After three nights like this Mother and Lilian had become exhausted and irritable because of lack of sleep.

The fourth night, just when Mother was about to say that she couldn't go on like this and that Lilian would have to return Ciaokeli to the tenant of the meat shop from whom she had bought him for five yuan, the little dog had suddenly crept out of his corner, hesitantly and quiveringly at first, but then, in a rush, he had jumped on Father's chest and licked his face.

Father had stopped his moaning and tossing about and had opened his eyes to stare at the dog's face above him with a look of utter surprise that, but for the slack, open mouth, almost made him look handsome. Hesitantly he had put his arms around the little animal and the dim-witted man and the dog had lain still, softly whimpering together, until they had both fallen asleep.

Since that night Ciaokeli had never yapped, howled, yelped or barked again as if he knew that that would unleash Father's lurking fears. Turning and twisting and rolling on his back, licking and whimpering, leaving tiny puddles of urine in his wake, he showed his intense happiness at seeing Mother or Lilian again, however short their absence had been. With Ciaokeli darting in front of her into the kitchen and on to Father's plank bed, Mother went to make sure that Father was quietly asleep.

Closing the kitchen door softly behind her she whispered, 'It's almost two o'clock already. Try and get some sleep. I'll sit here quietly on the couch and wait for the morning to prepare your tea and congee before you go to work. I won't be able to sleep; too many things on my mind and my turning and tossing about would only keep you awake. Don't worry, one more sleepless night won't hurt.'

Lilian laughed softly and hugged her mother affectionately. Wiping the tears caused by a huge yawn from her eyes, she whispered, chucklingly, 'When you have finished straightening out those things in your mind, you had better begin thinking about the story you're going to tell next week. I want you to impress Lao Dee because I want him to write this book about you and the others so that you and I can accompany him one day to Luding and visit your parents and Uncle Dan. I'm not a little curious, you know.'

Still chuckling she quickly undressed and crept, with only her ungainly underpants and brassiere on, underneath the sheet of the double bed she normally shared with her mother. She stretched and yawned a few times, writhed and wriggled, until a contented groan signalled that she had found the right position.

Within seconds she was fast asleep, like a healthy, contented cat.

Su Ping watched her sleeping daughter and sighed. How little they both knew about each other's lives and innermost feelings, she thought. Twelve years ago, when she had got her husband back, she had lost her daughter, who, young as she was, had nevertheless intuitively felt that she had suddenly become an outsider.

Lilian had seemingly never resented her mother's preoccupation with that wreck of a man that was her father, nor had she ever demanded attention by throwing these childish tantrums children her age are prone to when they feel neglected. On the contrary, it had been she, her mother, who often had resented the child's dutiful but essentially loveless manner of fulfilling her filial duty towards her father. Fortunately there had never been any question of reproach or recriminations by either of them.

During her most impressionable years I have excluded her from my life, Su Ping thought ruefully. How unfair it would be for me to expect her to make me now part of hers.

At first, she had felt sad that Lilian had apparently found in Liu Meiling the mother and grandmother figure every woman-child needs during the often painful process of growing up in a cruel and prejudiced world. Had she, Su Ping, not sought and found comfort and solace with Auntie Liu long ago? When she had been unable to cope with all the problems brought about by a foolhardy, irresponsible husband and an unauthorised pregnancy, compounded by her own status of intellectual, a non-person without rights?

Driven to despair by Leader Hu's personal vendetta against her and her husband, had she not turned to Auntie Liu for help and consolation when her pregnancy had become visible as the flouting of Hu's authority that it, in fact, was?

Hu had had Kunlen arrested, tried and sentenced to twenty years of forced labour and had threatened her with expulsion from her house. Auntie Liu had used her connections to at least prevent the expulsion and had supported her for months when she had lost her job and social assistance because the child she carried was 'unapproved'.

After Lilian's birth, Auntie Liu had used her connections one more time to get her her job back at the community crèche and also to get approved status for Lilian so that she could bring the baby with her to the crèche during her shift. Auntie Liu has been a true and trustworthy companion all these years, both a mother and a friend, Su Ping thought, so what have I to begrudge Lilian for? I should be happy instead!

With a shock she woke up from her reverie and saw Lilian, fully dressed, standing in front of her, laughing merrily.

'I must have fallen asleep,' Su Ping said, embarrassed, 'I'll prepare your breakfast immediately.'

'Don't bother,' Lilian replied, 'it's only five o'clock. I'll leave now. When I check in before six I've the right to have breakfast in the hotel with the outgoing night shift and incoming workers who have to leave their homes before five to be on time. Why don't you stretch out in bed and maybe catch another hour of sleep? Father doesn't need you until seven, you know that. Don't wait up for me tonight, I'll probably be late. See you!' with that she was gone.

Grimacing from her sore muscles, Su Ping fell down on her bed and was asleep almost as soon as her head touched the pillow.

It was past eight when Ciaokeli's cold, little muzzle against her throat woke her up and with a start she dashed after the dog into the kitchen to find her husband lying in his own excrement. It had happened many times, especially in the first few months after his homecoming, before she had been able to condition his bowel and bladder movements to a more or less regular schedule.

However, today was the first time the stench had made her retch with revulsion and she wept, both from shame and relief that she could now, for the first time, admit to herself that Auntie Liu was right and that this ordeal had to end, both for her own and for her daughter's sake. Her relief at this sudden insight and determination was so great that she heaved a long, shuddering sigh which made her laugh in spite of herself.

Wiping the tears from her eyes with the back of her hand, she bent over the human wreck on the plank bed and began to clean up the mess. To keep herself from vomiting, she tried to focus her mind on the long-repressed memories of beautiful, mild Sichuan, on her cosy little home on the hillside above the small town of Luding and the Dada River, on the majestic Gongga Mountains which she had contemplated so often from amongst the flowers of their tiny garden.

'I, we, Lilian and I are going back,' she said aloud to herself. 'Auntie Liu will help me to get Kunlen in a state institution. She wouldn't have suggested such a thing if she didn't think she could be of help to get him admitted. I'll have to ask her though if she's also heard the rumours that the inmates are given a lethal injection if after one year they haven't responded to treatment. If that's true I wouldn't know what to do. Lilian would have to have her say, too. After all, he's her father. Perhaps we could take him back after one year? We'll have been to Sichuan in the meantime and Father and Mother and Uncle Dan will have given their opinion and advice as well. As it is, it becomes more and more important that we get to Luding, Lilian and I. We need Lao Dee for that, for the travel permits and to pay for the expenses. So Lilian was right, though for the wrong reasons, that everything depends on how well I tell my story to impress Lao Dee.'

# *Chapter Nine*

The following Wednesday evening Auntie Liu came to see Su Ping to tell her not to bother buying *chiaxiubao* the next morning for their dinner that Thursday night.

'Lao Dao and Lao Dee came to see me this afternoon,' she told Su Ping. 'They proposed we start early, if possible as early as three o'clock, so that the storytellers have all the time they need and don't feel they have to hurry and consequently tell a kind of shortened version. Lao Dee suggested we don't waste time preparing dinner. He said the manager of the All Under Heaven restaurant, where he often entertains city and Party officials, and leaves big tips, I'm sure, has agreed to deliver as many as six different dishes to my house, provided he can deliver before six o'clock and take the containers back with him immediately. Before I could bring up the matter of cash, Lao Dee said he would of course pay for everything, not only this time but the following times as well.

'He said he would also take care of the beer and wine and soft drinks and would each time bring one or two special teas for us to try. He said it was the least he could do to repay us for our friendship and hospitality and that it wasn't in the least because he doubted our ability to do some fine home cooking which is always superior to restaurant cooking. The flatterer. His only concern was to make us feel relaxed and to avoid long interruptions, he said.

'Then he asked me to select six dishes from the menu he had with him. I noticed he had erased the prices. However, I know what is expensive and what is not so I chose one cheap, four medium and one expensive dish, a double-boiled shark's fin soup, which I haven't tasted since before liberation and, I'm sure, you and the girls haven't ever set eyes on yet. When I heard Lao Dao suck in his breath I knew it was a very expensive choice. However, Lao Dee just laughed and said I had chosen well. A gentleman he is, that Lao Dee, and not stingy at all.'

Auntie Liu fell silent and peered at Su Ping.

'You look different,' she said, 'happier, more relaxed, no more that brooding, remote worriedness draped around you like a cloak. Made up your mind about your dilemma, eh?'

Su Ping laughed and said, 'I'll tell my story first and then we'll see whether Lao Dee still wants to pursue that idea of his to go to Luding. If he does, and if we decide to accompany him, I'll have to make arrangements for Kunlen and Ciaokeli and I'll need your advice and possibly help as well.'

'I'll do what I can to help you, you know that,' Auntie replied. 'As for me travelling to Luding you can forget it,' she snorted derisively.

'Oh yes, Lao Dee showed me his tape-recorder and a small microphone, a directional microphone as he called it,' she said, changing the subject. 'We decided to put the recorder behind the easy chair, in the corner, where he will sit, so that he can easily change the tapes, and rest the microphone on the TV set. When you and Lao Dao tell your stories you won't even notice that you are being recorded, which is important, Lao Dee says.'

The two women chit-chatted for another hour or so about the thousand and one trivial things that make up life in the small world that's a back alley in a provincial Chinese town.

After Auntie had left Su Ping checked on her husband one last time before retiring to bed. She looked at the grown man who fitfully sucked his thumb in his sleep full of demons.

Rather too loudly she said, 'It has been enough, Kunlen! I owe you no more! It's time for me to start living again!'

When Su Ping fell asleep, at ease with her new-found self, Lilian had not come home yet. However, that no longer worried her mother.

# *Chapter Ten*

## Thursday, 7th July, 1988

While they waited for Beiyuen to let them in that Thursday afternoon, Su Ping and Lilian could clearly distinguish the voices of those within, notably Lao Dee's, who, being a foreigner, had the tendency to speak clearly and articulately so as not to be misunderstood.

Once inside, they reciprocated the others' cordial greetings before Su Ping said, 'We must be more careful and not speak too loudly. Our voices can be heard outside in the alley, and someone intent on overhearing what we are talking about could understand most of what we say if he or she were to stand close to the door or the window. I'm sure Old Turtle's curiosity, and Lao Yang's, of course, is already piqued by our comings and goings, particularly Lao Dee's. When later the restaurant people deliver our dinner, they'd die to know what's going on here, in this house. Heaven knows, Hu may even report us to the militia for plotting a counter-revolution.'

'A good point, Su Ping,' Auntie Liu replied gravely. 'We had better have a plausible story ready in case the militia comes knocking at the door or calls any one of us for an interrogation in their office. Any suggestions? The story must of course be the same for each of us.'

Lao Dee hemmed and said, 'I have thought about that eventuality, however, only for myself, for when I would be queried about what I am doing here. I didn't think the same could happen to you, which is unforgivably stupid since it is, of course, much more likely. However, the story I made up could suit you equally well. What I was going to tell the police or militia was that I am gathering material for a book I want to write about Chinese folklore, medicine and cooking. I have persuaded you to tell me stories, anecdotes, legends, old wives' tales, recipes and what have you, for which I pay you in kind, that is, in food. Different dishes from different regions, which I have prepared for us by my good friend Mu Ping, the senior cook of the All Under Heaven Restaurant. Mu Ping'll gladly testify for me when ask him to. If they ask us why we don't eat in the restaurant, we'll say that we want to be free to analyse and criticise the food, which wouldn't be nice in front of other customers. What do you think?' Lao Dee looked expectantly at the others.

'An excellent story,' Lao Dao said, laughingly. 'Everybody in my street, where the All Under Heaven Restaurant is, knows about your friendship with the cook Mu Ping. Mu Ping's from some godforsaken place in Yunnan, I believe, and he's a great talker, like most southerners. Every morning, after he has been to the market for his purchases of the day, and before he has to start preparations for the lunch hour rush, he sits on his heels on the sidewalk in front of the restaurant, smoking that horrible pipe of his, addressing each and every passer-by, asking indiscreet questions or telling them whatever is on his own mind.

'So everybody knows, of course, that you're fond of spicy food, Lao Dee, and that occasionally you bring special ingredients for him from Hong Kong that can't be found here in the north, in exchange for a nice, spicy meal and, naturally, the recipe of some special dish. Those special dishes you prepare yourself, together with Mu Ping, in the restaurant's kitchen. Our own Vice-Manager Zhou told me once that he had tasted a dish prepared by you and that it was excellent. So I don't think we'll have any problem finding witnesses who'll testify as to your interest in Chinese culinary tradition.'

Lao Dee laughed and said that preparing unusual dishes was one of his hobbies and that in whatever place in whatever country he happened to stay, he would always scout for restaurants or food stalls known for some special dish. If he liked the dish and had been a few times back to the restaurant or to the food stall he would befriend the cook or the owner and try to wheedle the recipe out of him.

'So, that's agreed then,' Lao Dee said, 'Su Ping, you choose the food for next Thursday's dinner,' and he handed her the menu. 'There are some Sichuan dishes on the card, not many though, as the local people don't like spicy food so much. It gives them piles, they say. However, if you know some that are not on the menu, write them out and I'm sure Mu Ping can prepare them for us. Tell Lilian your choice by next Wednesday and she'll tell me. I usually eat at the All Under Heaven on Wednesdays, with my Dutch engineers: the Germans don't like Chinese food so much. If you have a very special request Mu Ping and I may even try it out before he prepares it for all of us.'

'I know such a dish,' Su Ping said softly and the others saw that she was suddenly moved.

'It's called "Beggars Chicken" and it evokes very special memories for me, as you'll hear later since it figures so prominently in the part of my story that's set in Luding. Oh, what an incredible coincidence it would be if we could have it for dinner next Thursday, for then, I think, I'll have got as far as that part.'

Su Ping's voice choked from a sudden, overwhelming emotion and tears glistened on her cheeks. Head bent, eyes closed, she sat motionless for a few minutes, her thoughts in some place and time in the past.

The others waited patiently for her to retake control of herself. Suddenly she threw her head back, the mass of her glossy hair for an instant unfurled like the tail of a peacock before it fell smoothly back in its normal place over her right shoulder, and she laughed apologetically.

'I'm sorry,' she said, 'the thought of Beggars Chicken was like a cue. Memories of happy times I had repressed a long time ago flashed through my mind, pell-mell, yet... so vividly that they quite literally took my breath away. I have come to realise these past few days that for too long I have passively and morbidly let sadness, sorrow, bitterness and, to be honest, self-pity govern my life. Cross-grained and morose, I refused to see the good things around me: my healthy, intelligent and pretty daughter; Liu Meiling's friendship and compassion; the privacy in our cosy, little house.

'In my worst moods I even resented the help and guidance Meiling gave me ever since she took pity for the first time on the desperate, helpless, pregnant naive girl I was still then. Discouraging affection and unwilling to show it, I instead turned all my attention to fussing over a hopeless mental case, who doesn't even recognise me, his wife, and who will never know his daughter. Lilian grew up and drifted away from me and it was you, Meiling, who gave her the love, affection and guidance I was too self-absorbed to give. What would have become of me, of Lilian, had you not been there for us when you thought we needed you, even if I was too ornery to ask.

It is for that reason that I think I must first tell you about the part of my life that revolved around the neighbourhood and the role Liu Meiling, Auntie Liu as we affectionately call her now, played in it, rather than begin with the earlier part and events in faraway Sichuan Province. The Xu Suping of that period seems like a stranger to me now that I have been thinking about her again these past few days. When I could no longer fool myself thinking that I could coax Kunlen's mind back from that terrible nether world, I was so ashamed that I closed the door to my past and locked anybody still living there out of both our lives. That by the same token I locked Lilian out as well I did not realise. I fervently hope it isn't too late to let them back into my life.'

Su Ping fell silent, eyes downcast, fingers twining and untwining. Lao Dao, Lao Dee and Beiyuen didn't speak; as strangers it would be inappropriate to give their unsolicited opinion.

Suddenly Lilian stood up from her chair and, kneeling in front of her mother, she said, softly and with such affection that the others were moved, 'You have tormented yourself long enough now, Mother. Father has warped your life ever since you first fell in love with him. It's time to close the door on that episode of your life and let Grandfather and Grandmother and Uncle Dan and myself back in. I know that you love your father and mother and the little I knew, and still know, about you sufficed for me to love you too, despite what you may think. From the way you have changed since last Thursday, I have a pretty good idea of what the real Xu Suping was like and I like her, so I want to know everything about her.'

She rested her head against her mother's and their hands groped, then found each other.

After a few minutes of respectful silence, Auntie Liu cleared her throat and said gently, 'Your life, for the past twelve years or so, has been like a frozen river, Su Ping. A long, severe winter indeed, during which you suffered from one of life's most destructive emotional extremes, morbidity. However, the sun is becoming warmer by the day now and the thaw has finally set in. Water is seeping down, along the edge of the ice, feeding the still sluggish stream of life below, a trickle at first, then stronger and faster until its new-found force shatters the walls of its icy prison and it rushes, unstoppably, towards the boundless freedom of the ocean.

'Goodness is like water. It seeps along the edges into your life, eroding the bonds you imposed on yourself, until the taste of your new-found freedom becomes so strong that you will not rest until you have shattered the last shackles. This process of liberating one's self carries the risk of tilting into another of life's extremes; exuberant, complete selfishness. Your innate decency, your love for Lilian and for your parents; your friendship for us will save you from this extreme though. Extremes, whichever, are all in the end destructive and lead to chaos and misery in one's own and often in other people's lives as well. Knowing when and where to stop, both in yielding and in striving, leads to contentment, which is an enduring emotion, contrary to joy and happiness, which are often short-lived and prone to disappointment, or sorrow and anger, which eat your soul. Knowing the mean, the course of moderation, is knowing contentment. There is no greater misery than not knowing this.'

Auntie Liu fell silent, smiled and said, changing the subject, 'Let us now brew one of Lao Dee's fine, exotic teas and savour its fragrance and taste before Su Ping begins.'

Together they decided on a delicate pek-ho Lao Dee had brought back from Xiamen, in southern Fujian Province, three days ago. Beiyuen, peering into the kettle of water on the stove, gave a running commentary on the art of heating water for brewing tea.

'The water has to be exactly the right temperature when it is poured on to the tea leaves,' she remarked. 'Not warm enough and the fragrance won't be released, too hot and the fragrance will evaporate within seconds and only a bitter taste will remain. You have to observe the small bubbles as they form on the bottom of the kettle. At first they are very small, the size of grains of sand. Then they begin to coalesce and rise to the surface. When they are about the size of the eyes of a small fish the temperature is just right. Now!' and she quickly took the kettle from the oven and slowly poured the water on to the tea leaves in Auntie's best teapot.

'Now the tea must be left for exactly three minutes,' Beiyuen continued. 'That is the extraction or the brewing process, whereby the right ingredients in the right quantities and proportion pass from the leaves into the water. Not long enough and the extraction process is incomplete and the tea tastes and smells weak and watery. Too long and the extraction has gone too far and the tea tastes bitter. Now it's time,' and carefully she poured the golden tea into the translucent, old-fashioned teacups Auntie Liu had taken out of a carton box she kept under her bed.

Reverently they first sniffed the twirling vapour, nostrils quivering, then, eyes closed for greater concentration, they sipped tiny quantities which they moved over and around their tongue to experience every nuance of taste before swallowing.

'Good, very, very good,' Lao Dao pronounced with obvious satisfaction. 'That must have cost you, Lao Dee.'

Lao Dee grinned affectionately at his friend and replied evasively, 'Everything in life has its price, my friend, even the things which initially seem free. The bill may be a little late in coming, but come it will, and you must pay the whole amount due, as with charge cards. You, of all people, should know that. Always one should ask oneself, "Is it worth the price?" And if yes, "Can I afford it?" And if yes, "Am I willing to pay that price? Do I need it?" In this particular case the answers were yes, so enjoy your tea and stop worrying about my thriftlessness.'

Lao Dao grinned and nodded at Beiyuen who was about to replenish the cups while the tea was still not over-brewed.

After another silence, Lao Dee said, thoughtfully, 'besides the price of things, there is also their value, which need not be the same thing at all. Value has sentimental connotations and therefore something may be worthless in terms of price, that is, money, and still have great sentimental value, in fact be priceless, for a particular person. For instance, the value of this tea, enjoyed by us in this particular circumstance, far exceeds the price I paid for it. In other circumstances, hurried and with unappreciative people, it would have been a waste of good money.

'Mood and circumstance determine how we look at things, past and present, and this can make a world of difference. Su Ping will find, I think, that the present atmosphere of warmth, of friendship will take the sharp edges off her bitter experiences and that reliving them will be easier than she thinks now. It'll be a relief, it'll set her free and it'll make her content with her present life.

'Now something completely different. Have you thought about the proposal I made last week, that we, together, after we have heard Su Ping and Huimin's stories, retrace their odyssey?'

Lao Dee fell silent and looked at each of the others in turn.

Their different reactions made him smile. They were so predictable. The two girls, visibly elated by the prospect of the discovery tour, whispered excitedly, their heads close together, occasionally casting furtive, worried glances at their elders whose deliberations they took for a lack of enthusiasm.

Auntie Liu pouted and muttered, 'I would be in your way. I waddle like a fat goose. People will laugh at me and you will be ashamed of me. So you had better count me out.'

Wrinkling her nose, she added, as if it were an afterthought, 'Besides, I haven't any decent clothes and shoes to wear and my hair hasn't been touched by a hairdresser since Jiang Qing imposed the inverted flowerpot style to make every woman as ugly as she was, the snake.'

Lao Dee laughed and said, 'You don't look that bad to me, however, I'll arrange for the hotel's hairdresser, a nice girl, to visit you at home one evening and refashion your hair a bit; black streaked with grey, very distinguished. Su Ping, I think, will gladly take you to the clothes department of the Friendship Store. I'll give you the FEC to pay and you can buy yourselves new clothes and shoes and whatever else women of class need to travel in style'.

The faces of Su Ping and Auntie had lit up in delight and both exclaimed almost in unison, 'That's very kind of you, Lao Dee. Of course we would very much like to make the trip.'

Auntie grinned and added, 'It will be something to see that old scoundrel Chen Dan again after all these years. That face of his when he'll see me.'

Su Ping stared at her in utter astonishment, 'I didn't know you knew Uncle Dan!' she exclaimed. 'You never told me!'

An enigmatic little smile hovered around Auntie's lips as she said, 'All in good time, Su Ping my dear, all in its own good time.'

Relieved, everybody laughed merrily and the girls clapped their hands in delight.

'That's settled then,' Lao Dee said, 'our trip will take four to six weeks and I propose we depart early September. In September and October we'll have good weather, even in north-western Xinjiang where Lao Dao'll take us. Besides, that period would fit in very nicely with my work planning. By mid-August I'll have to stop work on the project to give the Chinese contractors time to catch up with us. I'll send the men home for a short vacation and take a month's leave myself. I'll ask my wife if she would like to accompany us as well, it would be a wonderful experience for her to see rural China. Different from the big cities and Westernised hotels she has been to so far in China. She doesn't understand Chinese, but Lilian will take care of her, I'm sure.

'I have to be back here in Dalian by mid-October, my men at the latest by the end of October, if we want the factory to be in full production by mid-December. That way everybody can be home for Christmas and New Year. I'll be back, with a few automation specialists, in January next year to put the final touches to everything and prepare for the handing over of the installations to the Chinese. If the Chinese drag their feet again while I'm on my trip with you, I'm in serious trouble, even if it means only a two-week additional delay. Later than early November I cannot let the men come back, we won't be able to finish by mid-December and no German or Dutchman will agree to stay here over Christmas and New Year. You see my dilemma? All the problems can be reduced to the same denominator, that is: money!

'Who is going to pay for fifteen extra air fares? Who is going to pay if the Chinese ruin the production in our absence? The Chinese? Never, even if all the delays are demonstrably their fault! Once a budget is fixed, even if it was years ago, they can never get additional funds. Even only applying for additional money would mean the end of their career or of their ambition to become a Party member. So they won't and, honestly, I can't blame them. So is it I who is going to pay? It's not in my budget either and all the built-in contingencies have been used up already a long time ago. Once a project is under way the Chinese always want something more, nicer, bigger, faster or more sophisticated than what they agreed to and paid for during the contract negotiations. They keep pestering and wheedling the foreign friend until he gives in.

However, such presents add up fast and before you realise it you have started eating the few per cent profit that was left when the contract was finally signed, which, in itself, is never less than two years after your final offer. That prices have gone up in the meantime is none of the Chinese's concern they say, capitalist tricks to make huge profits at the expense of China, they say. Apart from the money there is another side to the problem. If we only resume work after New Year, that is our New Year, the plant can't be in full production by Chinese New Year early February, as stated in the contract, so I'll overrun the delivery date. The Chinese will be furious and will put the blame squarely on me. They'll refuse to consider that their own delays caused the whole mess in the first place.

'Instead they'll keep on hammering the fact that we lost more than a month by refusing to work in November and December. What do they care about my money problems? Nothing! What do they care about our family holidays? Not a damn! What goodwill do we get in return for having played Mr Nice Guy all these months, for giving them more than they were entitled to, to do their work for them? Nothing! "It is your duty!" they will say, "for the friendship!" they will say. Always when they begin to talk about "friendship," "friends" and "friendly this and friendly that," I'll prepare myself for another bloodletting. The very concepts mean nothing to a Communist. All he knows and cares about is that those words apparently mellow the foreigner and weaken his position and that is what matters: one-way traffic only.

'The reason why I bother you with my problems is that I ask your understanding if, during our trip, I have to leave you on your own for a few days now and then to show my face on the site to keep the momentum going. Chinese contractors, a misnomer if ever there was one, even if they are under the same ministry, do not co-operate, or co-ordinate their jobs, amongst themselves. If their jobs overlap in a certain area and they happen to be in that area at the same time, they will not sit down and consult together about how to proceed in the best possible way and with the least loss of time. No! They will all stop work and wait for somebody to take responsibility and tell them who should proceed first and what the others should do in the meantime. Usually that's the foreign friend, who doesn't care about blame or loss of face. Their own leaders will waste their time in fruitless meeting after fruitless meeting and not budge an inch while their men sit on their arses, smoke and wait, day after day after day. However, what if the foreign friend is not there to cut the knot for them? So you understand, I hope, that I'll have to be there occasionally.'

Lao Dee finished and shrugged his shoulders. 'Can't be helped,' he added philosophically.

'We understand,' Lao Dao replied. 'Don't worry about us. We'll explore the local scene while you're away. I am sorry, however, about your problems with the Chinese contractors. Perhaps there is a solution. As you know, I only work the night shift at the hotel, have breakfast there and go home for a few hours' sleep. That way my daughter and her husband and child have the bed to themselves during the night, which is important for they work daytime only while the child is in a crèche.

'I could, if that would help you, Lao Dee, spend a few hours every afternoon at the construction site to keep an eye on the Chinese contractors for you to avoid the kind of collision course you're so afraid of. If you tell them nicely and respectfully that my presence is only to improve communications between them and your men, they won't see it as a loss of face and will be glad to accept me. If I report to you every day whatever problems they have or I foresee, you can probably help them out immediately instead of discovering after one week that work hasn't progressed because of some silly dispute they are too pig-headed to solve amongst themselves and too proud to ask you to solve it for them. Over the next six weeks or so, until the time when we go on our trip, this might just make up the difference in time you need to have your men back here by mid-October and finish your job by Christmas. What do think? Perhaps I can even earn my trip that way?'

Lao Dee laughed, then, seriously, said, 'An excellent idea Huimin, I am grateful for your offer and accept gladly. Call me in my room or leave word with the hotel doorman at what time you want to be picked up at home and I'll send the driver with the van. Explain to the driver where you live. I'll clear the matter with Vice-Manager Zhou and with the head engineer of the Bureau of Light Industry.

'So that you know and tell the same story, I'll tell them that it was I who approached you to sound you out about the possibility of familiarising yourself with the drawings, instruction books and operating procedures, which are all in English, so that when the last foreigner has left, the Chinese managers, leaders and operators have somebody to fall back on to translate for them in case of problems. I'll tell them that you agreed, provided you receive no payment and that I accepted your proviso. However, you do not know, I'll tell them, that I intend to reward you by giving you a paid trip through China, as a model worker who unselfishly sacrifices his time for the good of the project and its young leaders. If I put it that way they can hardly refuse my request later to grant you six weeks' unpaid leave. Excellent! I am in your debt, Huimin.'

'How ironic,' Lao Dao sighed, 'thirty-five years ago I was cajoled by the Party into leaving my adoptive country England, and returned to Mother China to do exactly the kind of work I am now so timidly volunteering for, albeit that I was then promised a position similar to the one Lao Dee is holding now. I fell for it and returned, as did thousands of other naives from all over the world. However, we were never given the chance to prove our love and loyalty for China, to which the Party had so persuasively appealed. Instead we were treated as saboteurs, members of some sinister plot to sabotage the proletariat's glorious achievements and its triumphant march towards the future. And now…'

Lao Dao suddenly fell silent, grinned ruefully and said, 'I'm sorry, I digress, it's not my turn yet. I can see that Su Ping is getting impatient with me demanding the limelight. Go ahead, my dear, the floor is all yours,' and with a flourish he gestured Su Ping to begin.

Amused, Su Ping smiled at the kind, old man, cleared her throat and with her usual, serene seriousness she began her narrative.

## *Chapter Eleven*

### August 1966–August 1988

'As I said earlier I shall tell my story in two parts, the last part first. I shall narrate this part in the first person, since I am that person. In the second part I shall tell you about Xu Suping of Luding as if she were another person, somebody I have known intimately, but who, for the time being, is still like a stranger to me. Xu Suping of Luding was a happy-go-lucky, all-things-bright-and-beautiful, elfin-like creature and it's difficult enough for *me* to imagine that she is, in fact, my *alter ego*, let alone for *you*. The events that triggered the metamorphosis have haunted me ever since.'

★

Xu Suping, and the tens of millions of innocent victims like her, were caught in the taifong of Hongbayue, that hurricane of collective madness that wreaked havoc and mayhem all over China, unleashed at its full force in August 1966.

She was torn loose from hearth and house and chased randomly hither and thither, like a dead leaf amongst countless millions. At one time leaf Suping fluttered to the ground momentarily, on a platform of Changsha's railway station, amidst an amorphous mass of thousands of other dead leaves already there, will-lessly waiting for the next gust of wind to sweep them up and blow them to heaven knows where else. Slowly she emerged from her daze and began to notice things around her.

A frail, old man stood near her. He had got there before her with a contingent of enemies of socialism from Guiyang. The white characters on his red armband read, 'feudalist dog Liang from Guiyang'. Hers said 'bourgeois scoundrel Xu Suping'. It appeared that the Red Guards had imposed a discipline of alternating six hours standing and two hours sitting or lying. They were all standing now, I in my first shift, the old man in his third or fifth, heaven knew how long he had been there. Several times I saw him vacillate, however each time he managed to stay on his feet.

Halfway during my second shift though, the old man's knees suddenly buckled and he fell against my legs. I tried to help him up, back on his feet, but the Red Guard with the many pimples on her face had already noticed him and she jumped off the tender from where she had been watching the crowd and came rushing towards us, yelling at me not to dirty my hands with the feudalist dog or else she would have me put on the same armband. The girl kicked the old man in his stomach and ribcage until he managed to scramble up again. Swaying on his feet, staring wide-eyed and unseeing ahead of him, he managed to stay on his feet for the remaining three hours. Indifferent to his suffering the Red Guard had returned to her observation post on top of the tender. The 'bourgeois' on my left and the 'deviationist' on my right whispered, lips barely moving and eyes staring straight ahead, that 'feudalists' and 'traitors' were being sent to forced labour camps in Shanxi and Xinjiang where they were almost certain to die, so they advised me not to provoke the Red Guard again.

When the old man fell again, during my third shift, I also kept staring ahead and made no movement to help. The Red Guard kicked the old man repeatedly, however, this time he only managed to get on his knees and then he toppled slowly sideways, his eyes almost popping out of his head and a thick, greenish stream of vomit gushing out of his gaping mouth. He kept gushing vomit; it was incredible that so much vomit could come out of such a frail, old body. It splashed on my shoes and socks, but I didn't move.

Then the flow stopped suddenly and the old man hiccuped once, flopped once, like a dying fish, and laid still, dead. The vomit smelled very bad, sour and acrid, and I retched at the smell and sight.

The Red Guard ordered two 'traitorous dogs' to carry the body away, but she forbade us to clean up the mess so the people around the puddle of vomit stood and laid there in the stench until finally, twenty-four hours later and four days late, a train pulled in the station alongside our platform.

Screaming, yelling, kicking and beating the Red Guards forced another thousand or so of their herd on board the train already overcrowded with Jiang Qing's hapless victims from down south.

Stumbling and tripping over the mass of inert bodies on the floor of the cattle car, pushed in my back by those scrambling in after me, I got to the far corner where I let myself down on the floor, squeezing myself in between two middle-aged men who were already sitting there, their back against the wall, their knees pulled up to their chin, their eyes dim and unseeing.

They grunted in unwilling protest, like sluggish pigs, yet moved aside a bit to let me settle down.

The stench of rancid, unwashed bodies and urine gripped my throat and I retched violently. The acid eruption of my heaving stomach burned in my throat and I had to swallow desperately to keep it down. Breathing ever so shallowly I forced my mind back in time by concentrating with all my might on the little garden behind our house.

I felt myself drifting off into a soft, warm glow that reminded me of the late afternoon sunlight that suffused the peaceful scene as I sat with my parents, before evening rice, outside in the garden, watching in comfortable silence the cool evening shadows slowly creeping up the slope from way down in the valley to where we were sitting, our minds distractedly yet playfully guessing whose light would pop up next in the small town below. Fully withdrawn in my own innermost world I felt my mother wrap a blanket around me against the breeze that always springs up as soon as the sun disappears behind the mountains of the distant, blue-black range of Daxue Shan.

I think I smiled in my reverie, just as I always smiled at Mother to thank her for caring. I felt the pressure that had clamped my temples like a vice fade away and the relief was exhilarating and almost sensual in its intensity.

I woke up hours, or was it days? later. I didn't know and I didn't care. The scene around me hadn't changed and dreamily I registered the sounds and movements of the train, while instinctively letting my body sway with the irregular jerks. A pang of hunger and the sting of a full bladder brought me suddenly back to reality.

I looked around nervously and I caught the eye of a youngish man two bodies further down the wall. He seemed almost nonchalantly relaxed as he sat there, his back and head leaning against the wall, head slightly rolling to and fro, absent-mindedly watching me through his half-closed eyes each time his head lolled in my direction. I smiled, timidly I think, and was relieved to see him smile back.

'Welcome back into this best of all worlds,' he said, and laughed. 'You have been far away and undoubtedly to a different world judging by the beatific smile that never left your face since you apparently cut down the oxygen supply to your brain two days ago, in Changsha. I couldn't help watching you, you're so pretty. By the way, my name is Wu, Wu Ju, as you can read on my dog tag. I am, or rather was, a medical doctor in Kunming before I was found out as a decadent bourgeois enemy of our beloved motherland. Nice to meet a fellow bourgeois scoundrel,' and laughingly he proffered his hand.

I couldn't help laughing also as I shook his hand and introduced myself.

'Two days, you said?' I asked incredulously, 'Two days and a night I have been dreaming and sleeping? No wonder I'm hungry and feel the call of nature. The most pressing first, how and where am I supposed to relieve myself?'

'If you are in distress you must use the hole in the floor, over there, in the corner nearest to the sliding door,' Wu said. 'Shove the people lying around the hole aside and do whatever you have to do. Do not think about it. Shut all thoughts of shame out of your mind. I'm afraid there is nothing to wipe yourself with though. If you can wait a few hours longer, the train is sure to stop somewhere in the middle of nowhere and, car by car, the prisoners will be allowed to descend for about fifteen minutes, to stretch their legs and relieve themselves. Red Guards will watch your every move though and harass you no end.

'About your hunger, I'm not so certain if they are going to provide us with food.

'The last time they dumped a basket with rice and vegetables in the car was while we were waiting in Guiyang for almost twenty hours, now three days ago, so I could use some food and drink myself. Scraped the last grains of rice out of my pocket yesterday. At whatever station the train stops, the place is in turmoil. There is no organisation, no plan, no authority, nothing. The Red Guards, juvenile scum, scream and yell and order and countermand, however, nobody is in charge. If the local Party structure is still intact and if the secretary is a decent person and if he has been advised of the train's arrival, three very big ifs, it is just possible that there is some food for distribution to the prisoners, if, and that's the fourth big if, the place's own food chain is still operational. Apparently in Changsha either one or all four ifs were unfulfilled since we didn't get anything to eat or to drink.

'One bit of good advice, though. If at the next station they throw a basket with food in the car, forget whatever good manners your parents undoubtedly taught you. Jump over whoever doesn't get up fast enough, shove aside whoever got there before you and start gorging yourself there and then while stuffing your pockets, or whatever, for later.'

He smiled and said apologetically, 'I'm sorry, I talk too much. Go and relieve yourself in the corner over there. I see you squeezing your legs together so you won't be able to keep it up any longer. Don't mind about people watching. The state they are in any impropriety is the last thing on their mind and, speaking for myself, I prefer a more romantic setting.'

My face red hot with embarrassment I stumbled over the bodies on the floor as I made my way to the far corner. Behind me I heard Wu's mocking laughter.

I squatted over the hole and closed my eyes.

Back in my own corner I found my place occupied. Wu smiled up at me and said, 'I have taken the liberty to rearrange the poor bastards a bit to make room for you next to me. No evil intent, I swear. All I want is someone to talk to, to listen to and to take turns sleeping. While one sleeps the other guards our belongings.

'I saw you wear a money belt. Clever girl. I'm wearing one myself and I wouldn't want my throat cut in my sleep by one of those Dai people from southern Yunnan, the ones with the wild eyes against the wall opposite from us. One of them was fingering me in Guiyang while I was busy stuffing my pockets with rice and I'm sure he felt the bulge of my belt. He must have the cleanest fingernails in the whole of China by now as he has been doing nothing but paring them with his big knife, grinning maliciously whenever I happen to look in his direction. He makes me nervous and he knows that, the bastard. So what do you think, Su Ping? Do we join forces?'

In answer to his question I sat down on the floor, next to him, careful not to touch or even brush his arm with my hip and thigh. For a while neither of us spoke; we stared ahead at nothing in particular.

Then, all of a sudden, Wu burst out laughing.

'We're so silly,' he said, chuckling, 'so terribly bourgeois trying not to touch each other lest we give the wrong impression. To whom, for heaven's sake? To those poor bastards lying pell-mell against and almost on top of each other? You think they care? So let's try to be as comfortable as possible under the given circumstances. When you want to try to sleep just say so and rest your head against my shoulder or on my lap instead of against that steel wall and when it's my turn I'll do the same. All right?'

I nodded and suddenly, as in an impulse, I put my hand on his and squeezed his fingers.

'Thank you,' I whispered, 'thank you for your kindness and respect.'

Wu briefly squeezed my hand to confirm his understanding and we both relaxed.

The swarthy Dai, incessantly scraping the palm of his left hand with his knife, now kept staring straight at us and we could no longer pretend not to be aware of him so we stared back. The man grinned and slowly passed the knife over his throat, back and forth, back and forth.

I shivered and I felt Wu tensing his muscles.

'What a nasty, wicked man,' I whispered.

'He hates us Han Chinese,' Wu replied, under his breath, 'most of the minority tribes do since the Han banned their customs as superstitious dribble during the Great Leap Forward. They say that our aim is to sinify them, to destroy their cultures and racial identity by imposing on them our laws, our language and what is left of our culture. We impregnate their women, however, we need not accept responsibility for the consequences.

'In fact, the few decent men amongst us who would are discouraged from doing so and are transferred to other regions leaving the tribe with the half-breeds. From kindergarten through middle school the half-breed children receive favourable treatment and are openly brainwashed as to the superiority of their fathers' race. They are encouraged to marry early, but only with a girl of their own tribe, never with a pure-blooded Han Chinese girl, and they are allowed more children, to dilute the tribe's blood further. On the other hand, the pressure on a Han girl contemplating marriage with a half-breed or a minority tribesman are such that she will never go through with it. The minorities fear that in a few generations there won't be any minority people left, no Dais, no Huis, no Miaos, no Yis, no Manzus, no Zhuangs, no Buyis.

'Perhaps only those of Muslim faith, living in the Western regions, will survive a while longer because of their religious ties with related peoples on the other side of the border. All one grey, amorphous, look-alike, happy Chinese family, staring in curious amazement tinged with revulsion, at the occasional Mendelian freak dancing in a circus. Members of the minorities who try to warn their peoples against this insidious plot by the Han authorities disappear without a trace or end their lives miserably in labour camps. Probably those Dais over there were put aboard the wrong train. Certain is the big man with the knife and wavy hair doesn't like us.'

While Wu talked I gradually regained my composure and I tried to stare the Dai down, unflinchingly.

After a while, frowning uneasily, he lowered his gaze.

I nudged Wu in his ribs and said, 'He's a coward. You see? I have stared him down.'

'Yes,' Wu replied worriedly, 'most of them are and it's when you expose them that they are most dangerous. He's now pondering ways how to get at us indirectly. So beware!'

For a while neither of us spoke and imperceptibly we both drifted off into a somnolence induced by the train's monotonous rumbling and clicking while it meandered its unpredictable, unplanned way into the central and northern provinces.

A change in the train's rhythm woke me from my half-sleep and I realised I had slumped against Wu Ju and that he had put his arm around my shoulders.

I yawned and slowly sat up straight, stretching my sore upper back muscles and rolling my head from left to right and back until I heard the vertebrae in my neck crack and the painful stiffness faded away.

'How long have I been sleeping like that?' I asked Wu. 'You must be aching all over from sitting still so long. I'm so sorry.'

Wu laughed and looked at me, quite affectionately, I thought. 'No reason to be sorry,' he said. 'It was quite an experience to feel you so close to me. So trusting and innocent, what? I have never been married, never even had an intimate relationship with a girlfriend. However, I now begin to understand what the author of one of my psychology handbooks meant when he wrote that in times of great mental stress, in what is felt to be a life-threatening situation, men and women, complete strangers, can become very intimate and do things that under ordinary circumstances would be completely out of character.

'Later, when the situation is back to normal, they are often ashamed of what they did and hide the experience in their subconscious. At the time, as a student, I scoffed at the author's views and thought them to be typical of the lewd Westerner and not valid for us Chinese, with our bred-in sense of propriety. I now realise that we're all the same, all human, and that the need for trust and tenderness, affection and love is in our genes and that it can indeed be triggered by a single event or a concurrence of circumstances, even, I think, in the most depraved and wicked human being. For a while, as you slept with your head on my shoulder and I felt the warmth of your body seep into mine with every slight, pulsating pressure of your breathing, nothing mattered any more. This train, the people lying around us, the abuse I suffered in Kunming, it seemed all so remote, as if it did no longer concern me. Even now that I am back to reality, I still don't seem to care as much as before. Do you understand, Su Ping? Have you heard what I said?'

'I heard and I understand,' I replied. 'My own feelings confuse me at the moment, even frighten me in a sense, however, I do feel better, less anxious and tense, sitting here close to you.'

I didn't withdraw my hand when he took it in his.

We didn't speak for quite a while. I think that we were both afraid to break the fragile spell whereby our thoughts wavered incongruously in a mishmash of fantasy and reality.

Gradually I became aware of his voice, muffled as if we were surrounded by a thick fog, and I realised that he was talking to me, telling me about himself, and I listened, didn't interrupt him once, any comment or commiseration out of place.

He told me about his student years in Chongqing and about his later years, as a young doctor, in Kunming. About his parents, who had both passed away, and about his sister and her husband who had denounced him for being a closet homosexual, which he was not but refused to prove. How, instead, he had accused his interrogators that they and their so-called laws were the abomination, not he, Wu Ju. How they had put him in jail, in a cell with six men of the minority Buyi tribe, who, by order of his jailers, had sodomised him in turns until, after two hellish weeks, bleeding and too sore to sit or stand, he had screamed at the guards that he would sign any confession they wanted. How they had still let him scream for hours before they had suddenly entered the cell and interrupted the goings-on to drag him outside, bleeding, naked and utterly humiliated.

Sobbing he had signed papers without even being given a chance to read whatever he confessed to. They had given him back his clothes and had locked him up in a cell, alone this time.

Utterly exhausted, he had slept for two nights and two days in spite of his soreness.

The third day they had come for him and had ordered him to stand on the platform of a truck holding a white banner with black characters proclaiming his crime, 'Bourgeois lewdster and sodomiser.'

They drove him around Kunming, through sullen crowds who pelted him with rotting vegetables and excrement.

Back in his cell, they refused to let him wash up and for two days he was left without food, filthy and stinking. Finally, on the third day, a female guard whose child he had once delivered couldn't stand it any longer and she had brought him a bucket of water and soap to wash himself. She had given him prison clothes and the next day she had given him back his own clothes, washed and ironed.

He had told her, whisperingly, about the money belt and where he had hidden it in his former house.

Two days later she had given him the belt, surreptitiously, refusing to take even one yuan for herself.

A week later they had kicked him out of his cell and had made him run through the streets of Kunming, with hundreds of other prisoners, like a herd of wildebeest, to the train station. The next day a train, consisting only of freight and cattle cars, had pulled into the station and everyone had been kicked and pushed on board.

After four days and stops in Guiyang, Huaihua and Xiangtan, the train had arrived in Changsha and he had seen me scramble into the car and his heart had made a leap.

I heard him out, at times crying silently, squeezing his hand during the most terrifying episodes. When he finally fell silent we sat huddled together for a long time, holding hands.

Then, as if reliving a dream, I told him about Xu Suping, about her youth, her friends at school, her parents, her happiness in her little house with its small garden on the mountain slope above Luding.

I told him about the two strange guests who popped into Suping's life one day to stay a week or two, but who, to everybody's contentment, stayed on until the upheavals of Hongbayue broke up their cosy life together.

I narrated a few anecdotes that made him smile while he stroked the back of my hand, evidently grateful for my attempt to lighten his mood and distract his thoughts from the nightmare in Kunming.

Slowly, however, I felt myself drifting off to sleep again, my eyelids impossibly heavy. With a conscious effort I shook my head and, breathing deeply, I managed to halt my slide into oblivion and crawl back up the slope to the present.

'Not again,' I said to myself, 'it's his turn now to sleep if he can. What shall I do if his head slides into my lap?'

It was too late already to devise a strategy. From his shallow breathing, occasionally interrupted by a shuddering sigh, I knew he had fallen asleep.

When a few minutes later he turned over on his left side and put his head in the hollow between my thighs and my belly, fumbling to find the right position as if I were a pillow, I didn't mind and I stroked his hair.

An abrupt, violent jerk followed by a succession of smaller ones and the screeching of braking wheels jolted us back into the present.

'We're going to stop somewhere,' Wu said, suddenly wide awake and sitting upright again. 'They must have run out of coal by now so I think it's a station where we're going to stop, possibly Hefei. It will take hours before they even find coal, let alone convince the locals to cede it, for free of course, to that ragtag gang of wild-eyed youths who commandeer this train in the name of the wonderful Cultural Revolution. The only reason they may get what they want is that the people in Hefei want to get rid of this train as quickly as possible. Hopefully they'll think of some food for us as well.'

After much jolting and jerking, screeching and hissing, the train came finally to a total stop.

The sudden silence, broken only and irregularly by a hiss from some part of the train, like the rattle of a dying man, hummed in my ears.

Unwittingly though, I tensed my body as if I expected something untoward to happen at any moment. Still, the piercing sound of a whistle came so sudden that I nearly wet myself.

Scarcely recovered I was assaulted, almost bodily, by a two hundred decibel blast of several loudspeakers blaring martial music. Just as abruptly the music stopped and a strident female voice, screaming at the top of her voice, announced, 'You have arrived in Hefei! Hefei's workers are in the forefront of our beloved Chairman Mao's Great Proletarian Cultural Revolution, fighting his enemies to the death! Long live our beloved Chairman Mao and Comrade Jiang Qing!'

She fell silent and the blaring music took over again.

Numbed, I waited for the racket to stop, shaking my head at Wu who tried to tell me something. I saw his lips moving but I couldn't hear what he said. He shrugged and leaned back against the wall, meekly.

Abruptly the music stopped and I shook my head and pinched my nose to make the eardrums pop and relieve the humming pressure. I noticed that most people had scrambled to a sitting position, others were standing. Everybody was apparently waiting for something to happen, thinking of one thing only: food, drink.

'If that female dragon over the loudspeakers truly reflects the situation here in Hefei then it's bad news, I'm afraid,' Wu whispered in my ear.

'We can forget about food and they'll have rounded up a few thousand renegades of their own, waiting to be herded on board this train. It is possible though that it is a ploy to deflect the attention of roving gangs of Red Guards and if that's the case they may show us some compassion. I fear the first and hope for the latter.'

During the next ten minutes or so there was much yelling, ordering, countermanding and running around outside on the platform with juvenile voices belonging to both boys and girls, by far outnumbering the few, hesitant adult tones.

Suddenly there was an assembly of babble outside our car and then the sliding door rumbled open.

A gust of cool, moist air, carrying the smell of rain on dusty roads, washed though the car, sweeping the sickening staleness and rancid body odours from every nook and cranny. It had apparently been raining and the sky was still grey and overcast which gave the daylight a softness that didn't hurt our eyes after three days and nights of alternating total and semi-darkness.

Through the legs of those standing between me and the door opening I saw what looked like a big, black blob on a carpet of dull blue, green and grey colours.

I rubbed my eyes and looked again. Prisoners, it shot through my mind, rows of prisoners, sitting with bowed heads, like tailors. There must be thousands assembled here in this station, judging from the scores of heads I can see through this door alone.

'No food for us,' I heard Wu mumble beside me, 'only more people. We'll suffocate in this car. Somehow we'll have to make a hole in the front wall of the car to let in fresh air when the train is moving again or else we'll all die of suffocation rather than of starvation.'

About to reply, my breath suddenly caught in my throat and I felt a sense of panic get hold of me. A premonition of impending doom clamped my head and I grabbed Wu's hand, desperate to tell him to get rid of his money belt, however, my words came out in a half-croak, half-whisper.

Wu bent over and asked, 'What is it, my love? Don't worry, we'll manage.' And then he apparently saw also what had caused my panic and I saw him pale in fear.

The Dai was standing outside on the platform, excitedly talking and gesticulating to a group of Red Guards who looked alternately at the Dai and in the direction of our car.

A tall, gangling youth with wild eyes and a long, irregular, red, angry face, probably the leading Red Guard, shouted, 'Get him out!' and the whole gang rushed to the door opening, yelling, 'Wu Ju! Capitalist roader, get out! We'll squash you like a cockroach!'

Trembling, Wu scrambled up, then he bent over and took my face between his hands. 'It is not to be, my love,' he said and his voice strangled on a sob. 'This is the end for me. I loved you at first sight and dreamt about a life with you, in Luding, and that we had a daughter exactly like you. Take care of yourself first and foremost, always.'

Then he kissed me full on my lips wet with tears and snot. Before I could say something, tell him I loved him too, he was dragged backwards to the door opening by two Red Guards, girls, hardly seventeen, their faces contorted by rage and hatred.

I scrambled up, but a scream of triumphant malice froze me halfway in my attempt to follow him outside and, horror-stricken, I watched as the Red Guards held Wu's money belt up in the air for all to see, screaming and hopping up and down like demented demons.

Their leader, the youth with the wild eyes, his balled fists punctuating his every shriek cried, 'This filthy sodomiser has been exposed as a thief as well, stealing from the people, stealing from our beloved Chairman Mao! His punishment is death by the hands of our Chairman Mao's little revolutionary generals, here, on the spot, for all of you to see as a warning that you cannot escape the wrath of the people!'

The gang pushed Wu to the ground and an orgy of kicking and beating began and probably continued long after Wu's last whimper.

I didn't see the end as, mercifully, I fainted.

It must have been hours later that I woke from my stupor and found a woman had taken Wu's place beside me. She had her right arm behind my back and supported my head with her knees which she had pulled up to her chest.

I felt the rumble of the moving train in my ear against her knee and I tried to sit up straight.

As from far away, as through a thick fog, I heard the woman tell me that Wu's broken body had been left lying on the platform until the departure of the train some six hours later. The Red Guards had gouged his eyes and smashed his face and she would never forget his empty eye sockets staring into the car as he had been abandoned there, on the platform, she said.

Probably because of him staring like that, none of the Hefei prisoners had later climbed into the car, which was a good thing, she said, since there was already so little space.

I decided to hate her for her stupid callousness and I made no attempt to look at her or to reply. Instead I sought out the Dai against the opposite wall and when I had eye contact I put all the hatred I could muster in an unflinching gaze until the triumphant sneer faded slowly from around his silly moustache and his eyes shiftily tried to avoid mine. I kept staring at him and slowly, coldly, bit by bit, a plan to destroy him, to avenge the first and only man I truly loved, evolved in my mind.

I had no scruples to carry out my plan. I simply had to wait until the next station.

Throughout the night I kept staring at him, from under my half-closed eyelids and I coldly observed how he became increasingly agitated, which was just what I wanted.

Halfway through the next morning the train came to a stop and from the hollow, reverberating sounds outside I deduced that it was a big station, which was perfect.

Time to carry out my plan.

First I dishevelled my hair. Then I tore my blouse open, leaving the buttons dangling by a few threads only. Next I took off my underpants and smudged them on the dirty plank floor. I closed my eyes, thought of Wu as strongly as I could and bit my lower lip until I tasted blood. I wiped my bleeding lip with the dirty underpants, staining them and streaking my cheeks with blood and dirt.

This done, I jumped up and over the people on the floor and began pounding with my fists on the metal sliding door, screaming hysterically for help. I think everybody was staring at my back, thinking I had gone crazy, however, I kept on pounding and screaming.

After what must have been no more that three or four minutes I heard voices outside, on the platform, and the door rumbled open. All in one glance, which I made as wild-eyed and frantic as possible, I saw the characters Tianjin on the boards hanging from the platform roof beams, the astonished faces of a dozen or so Red Guards and, best of all, the caps of four soldiers. Unseen I dropped my dirty, bloodstained underpants behind the Dai, between the wall and his back, and I screamed, 'Help, I have been raped!' over and over again, until I thought it was time to burst out in a whooping, hysterical sobbing.

One of the soldiers pulled me out of the car and caught me in his arms before I could fall on the platform.

Shaking me to make me stop crying, his red, angry face so close I could smell his breath, he shouted, 'Where is the pig who did this to you?'

'He's not Chinese,' I wailed, 'he was all over me trying to kiss me with that filthy moustache brushing my face, tearing my blouse open and pulling my underpants off, pushing his fingers up in me! You are Chinese, you cannot let a poor Chinese girl be fouled by such an animal!'

The Red Guards were all over each other, clambering into the car, and within seconds they came back, standing in the door opening holding the screaming and kicking Dai in an armlock.

One of the Red Guards, a pretty girl of about sixteen, held up my pants for all to see and shouted, 'The pig still had her underpants. Tried to hide them behind his back. There is dirt from her hands and blood from her on it. This proves he's a rapist!'

The Dai was apoplectic with rage and fright and did what I hoped he would do. He suddenly jerked himself loose, jumped off the car and bolted towards the end of the platform which was stupid as there was no crowd there in which he could lose himself.

The soldiers yelled at the Red Guards not to run after him, then, aiming their rifles, they shouted, 'Stop! Stop! Surrender yourself or we'll shoot!'

The Dai kept on running straight ahead, only once looking back over his shoulder, at me, and I saw the look of fear and defeat in his eyes. Then I heard several shots and I saw him stumble and fall.

Suddenly I felt very tired and listlessly I let myself be taken by my arm and led away from the scene. It was the pretty little Red Guard who took me up.

Full of concern she seated me in the waiting room and while she continued to pat my hand she interrupted her soothing small talk to ask somebody to bring me a mug of hot tea and a bowl of rice with chicken and vegetables.

She stayed with me, looking on with a lovely smile as I slobbered my tea and gobbled my rice, interrupted at odd moments by a sob from deep down in my belly and which was no longer play-acting.

To my own horror I felt soiled, as if I had been raped for real, raped by myself through letting myself be possessed by hatred and, in a sense, cowardice. Cunning deception of others, to have them do the thing you haven't got the guts to do yourself, in this instance taking the life of another human being, is not something to be proud of.

I thanked the girl for her concern and asked her to take me back to the train.

She took me by my arm and together we shuffled to where my train was waiting. We looked like patient and nurse.

'What a silly accusation,' the girl said, frowning her pretty, arching eyebrows as she read my armband. 'Bourgeois scoundrel. What does that mean? We haven't got such a silly category here in Tianjin, not as long as my father is the Party secretary here. What did you do, Su Ping? What was your crime? My name is Xian Shaoxia, by the way.'

I smiled tiredly and replied, 'I committed no crime, Shaoxia. I was an assistant teacher at Middle School Number Three in Luding, Sichuan Province, the same school where my mother taught history and my father mathematics. We never wronged anyone and we were always respectful of the Party and the workers.'

'So unfair!' Shaoxia exclaimed. 'Perhaps I can make good a little bit the wrong done to you. I really would like you to have a good opinion about the Red Guards. Most of us really mean well you know. It is a good thing to wipe clean the slate of the past and start anew. A new, just society wherein everybody is equal, wherein each contributes according to his or her talent and potential and each is rewarded according to his or her needs and nobody is haunted by memories of an unjust past. Don't you think that that is something worth striving and sacrificing for, Su Ping?'

Her voice was lovely, silvery, tinkling, her accent the sing-song of the native mandarin speaker, her naivety so sincere and touching, so I agreed it was worth striving and sacrificing for.

I must have sounded tired and listless though, for she said solicitously, 'You must be very tired, Su Ping, what with the terrible things that happened to you. I heard your train goes all the way to Harbin where the prisoners will be divided over several labour camps. That would be terrible for you for it's very cold in Harbin and the work will be hard.

'I shall go home directly from here and speak to my father. I'll tell him about you and your ordeal and ask him to send a message to my uncle, who is the Party secretary of Dalian city, to take you off the train there and give you something useful to do to help the Cultural Revolution there in Dalian until you can return home after it is over. I promise, Su Ping. My father has never refused me anything if I asked nicely.'

I doubted if ever any man would be able to refuse Shaoxia anything. She laughed merrily, squeezed my arm and surreptitiously fumbled my panties in my hand.

She helped me up in the car and I heard her mumble the number of the car, probably to tell her father and her uncle in Dalian. Once inside the car, I turned to wave goodbye and with her radiant smile still hovering before my eyes and little silver bells tinkling in my ears I sank down on that half a square metre of dirty plank floor where I had fallen in love, known a man's tenderness, mourned the death of my lover, conceived and executed a fiendish plan to murder by proxy the man responsible for the death of my lover and all that in less than a hundred hours. Quietly I looked around the car.

The four other Dais, whom I had hardly noticed the previous days, focused as I was on that one man, were gone as well. Probably taken off the train by the Red Guards and the soldiers and now in prison for complicity.

The rest of the men and women, the same probably, I didn't know for sure, were still there, lying around, sleeping.

Nobody paid any attention to me, no curiosity, nothing.

I looked at the woman beside me, the one who had taken Wu Ju's place. Her armband said her name was Wong Meilin and that she was a 'decadent bourgeois'.

To my surprise I noticed that she was probably only a few years older than myself and quite pretty at that, with short cropped hair. She noticed I was looking at her and she smiled, a friendly smile.

'I used to know Doctor Wu, back in Kunming,' she said, 'he treated me once for an accident I had in my factory'.

She showed me her left hand and I saw that the little finger was missing.

'Crushed in a lathe,' she explained, 'it was the operator's fault. I am now a qualified lathe operator while he tills his commune's rice fields, behind a fellow ox. However, he probably still does, in relative freedom, while I am sitting here in this bloody train on my way to heaven knows where. You know why, Su Ping? Because I refused to become a Party member. Told my unit secretary I had no time for his silly meetings and preferred to spend my spare time my own way. He almost had an apoplexy. One day he ordered me to his office. On his desk were my books, novels, smuggled through Thailand and Burma from Hong Kong. I bought them in Xishuanbanna, at a road stall. My parents live in Xishuanbanna and I was born there.

'I used to visit them twice a year and each time I would buy books. I like to read in my free time, however, not the boring books in stencils with speeches you have to study as a Party member. Anyhow, the comrade secretary said it was obvious to him that no doubt I was a member of an underground network of intellectuals hell-bent on overthrowing the Party. I told him he was a true proletarian arsehole and here I am, me and my big mouth.'

I laughed, in spite of myself. She had a funny way of saying things and a funny accent as well.

Before I could comment, however, Meilin continued, 'I overheard the soldiers say that this train is going to Harbin. Did that pretty Red Guard girl tell you anything?'

I nodded and replied that Shaoxia had indeed mentioned Harbin as the final destination of the train.

'I once read an article in the *People's Daily* about all the machine factories in Harbin,' Meilin said, hopefully. 'Do you think I can get a place as a lathe operator?'

I said I thought she could, but that she would have to make things happen rather than wait passively for the Red Guards in Harbin to send her somewhere or other at their whim, for in that case she would probably end up in a commune near the border with Siberia or, worse, North Korea.

Meilin shivered and said, in a small voice, 'I'm sure I would freeze to death in those places. I can't stand the cold,' and, totally inconsequentially, she added, 'Doctor Wu didn't deserve to die, you know, not now and not in such a horrible way. He treated me well, very caring he was, giving me three weeks' sick leave so I could read a lot to forget my throbbing little finger that was no longer there. Strange you can feel pain in something that doesn't exist. That filthy Dai deserved to die though. Very clever what you did, Su Ping, and very brave too. You gave me some good ideas about how to take care of myself. Men are so stupid, they know nothing about women.'

She fell silent, then added, in a sly, pensive tone, 'When we arrive in Harbin I'll pretend to have some mysterious female sickness. If the train continues like this, like a stuffed snake, and stops in the big cities before Harbin, I'll have my periods when we get to Harbin and I'll pretend a miscarriage. I'll cry and whimper and tell them I was kicked in my belly a few times during the trip all the way from Kunming.

'I'll be in a hospital while the Red Guards send all the others to the communes in Siberia and North Korea as you said. Once everybody's gone I'll tell the doctors I feel better thanks to their good care and our beloved Chairman Mao's thoughts and could I please contribute to this great revolution as a lathe operator in one of their beautiful machine factories. What do you think of this beautiful plan, Xiaoxu?'

Touched by her naivety and familiarity, I told her to be careful about the miscarriage part. Doctors could verify that and find out that it was impossible and then worse would happen to her as she would be punished for trying to deceive high officials.

Meilin laughed heartily and said, chuckling, 'Don't worry, Xiaoxu, I know what you are thinking; stuffy, aren't you? I'm no longer a virgin and once was three weeks overdue. I ate so many pineapples that I got a running diarrhoea, however, my periods came and that was the most important. I suppose they don't grow pineapples in Harbin so I'll have to be more careful. I wonder what women use where there are no pineapples,' she mused.

'I'll have to find out from the older women in the factory or perhaps from a friendly nurse in the hospital. I'll seduce the Party secretary or another high city official, anyhow, somebody with enough influence to send me back to Kunming to eat pineapples to get rid of his implant and save his position and his marriage to that old, smelly dragon. Once back in Kunming I'll go straight to my parents in Xishuanbanna. Perhaps I'll go and live across the border and wait until this crazy Cultural Revolution is over. Perhaps I'll never come back to China.'

She looked at me and said, delighted, 'You see, Xiaoxu? All that I learned from you. Aren't you happy for me?'

I was too flabbergasted to say anything.

While we, or rather Wong Meilin, had been talking, our train had pulled out of Tianjin station and had reached its cruising speed. Our car's continuous, creaking motion and the monotonous rumbling and clickety-clack of its wheels had lulled Meilin to sleep, her head lolling against my left shoulder.

*

Su Ping broke off and looked at her daughter and Beiyuen.

'I now realise how pathetic she was with that mixture of starry-eyed naivety and vulgar slyness so typical of pretty girls who grow up in an environment of earthy, worldly wisdom but who live part-time in the world of unrealistic intrigues of their cheap, thirteen in a dozen, little novels. They mix dream and reality and concoct fantasies, with themselves in the leading role, of course, that are dangerous and inevitably end badly.

'Although at that time I felt instinctively that things would go badly for Wong Meilin in the harsh and cold world of the north I didn't care, at least not enough to bother and try to talk some sense into her head. What had happened to elfin Xiaoxu's compassionate nature? Already then I could fantasise about the sordid details of how I would arrange an accident if I were the man she had compromised. Terrible, isn't it?

'Is then each human being born with a capacity for evil? A kind of dormant, past life, or lives, marked by evil? Or a hereditary, wrong programming of the genes that can be awakened, or triggered, by a traumatic incident such as I had brought upon myself in Tianjin? Have the good and decent people simply been lucky because they never experienced a trauma like that or are they holy heroes who have been able to resist temptations and overcome traumas? Are those who succumb and go astray to blame and to be punished or, on the contrary, are they victims of circumstances, sorry creatures, who should be given help? And what about their victims? Should they be given help or are they to blame as the instrument, willing or unwilling, of their fellow creature's misdeed?' Su Ping shrugged.

'In my opinion people are, in principle, responsible for their own actions and, to a certain extent, also for their fellows' behaviour and, consequently, every human being must abide by a body of impartial, civilised and human laws. If you accept that premise, criminals must be punished, humanely, however, and their ill-gotten gains confiscated and their victims, or their relatives for that matter, must be compensated within reason. Victims who take the law in their own hands are like the criminals who wronged them and must be dealt with as such. However, what if a civilised society breaks down? When its laws are abolished and civilised behaviour is declared counter-revolutionary and punishable, at whim, by self-appointed executioners answerable to no one but themselves?

'This was the case in China at that time so when I was victimised in more than one sense, it was right to defend myself as best I could and even to mete out retribution to a murderer who, in the given circumstances, would not only have escaped punishment but instead would have been feted as a revolutionary hero for denouncing a capitalist roader.

'I have therefore never regretted what I did although at first, immediately after my deed, I felt bad about it.' She collected her thoughts together and continued with her story.

*

I must have fallen asleep as well for the rattle and irregular jerks of the train reducing speed woke me up and I shivered. The air in the car had become much colder, a sign we were now in Liaoning Province.

Daylight, I had no idea of which day, was seeping through the chink between the sliding door and the wall when the train finally came to a halt. Apart from the sighs and groans of the settling train there came no sound from outside so we were either very early or the train had stopped in the countryside waiting for permission to enter the station.

I was glad that the changes in rhythm and the sudden silence hadn't interrupted Meilin's sleep since I wasn't in the mood for her twaddle. I was too busy imagining all kinds of scenarios wherein the pretty little Red Guard Xian Shaoxia's scheme to get me off the train in Dalian wouldn't work.

The always recurring scenario was that the train was standing before the junction at Haicheng and that the Red Guards were quarrelling amongst themselves whether to continue north or to go south again, to Dalian, first. I tried to find arguments in favour of Dalian but couldn't and, masochistically, I conjured up the triumphant faces of the Red Guards in favour of continuing to Anshan, Shenyang and Harbin.

I had no idea how long we had been standing there when, almost imperceptibly, the train began moving again and alternately stopped and inched forward until I heard the telltale sounds of a big railway station.

I braced myself for a similar onslaught of martial music and propaganda as in Hefei and, even worse, the announcement of the name Anshan, when suddenly a clear, matter-of-fact man's voice announced through the loudspeakers that train number 2678 would in a few minutes come to a stop alongside platform number sixteen.

'This is not a regular train,' the voice announced, 'and neither will the passengers on board be allowed off nor will new passengers be taken on board. Train personnel, including Red Guards, may alight, however, they are not permitted to go beyond platform number sixteen. Two tenders with coal are graciously offered by the Dalian City Council to permit train number 2678 to resume its revolutionary journey in exactly half an hour. By order of the stationmaster, Xian Xuexian!'

When I heard the name Dalian my heart jumped in joy that turned to despair almost immediately. Half an hour the train would remain here and nobody would be allowed off or taken on. Shaoxia had failed and I had been a fool to believe it would work. More probably she had forgotten about me as soon as she had turned her back.

A cackle of bickering, juvenile voices outside my car shook me out of my morbid reflections and I heard a deep, male voice say, 'Stop arguing with me! I have signed orders from the city Party secretary, Xian Xuemin, to take this person Xu Suping off the train and to lead her to his representative who is waiting in the stationmaster's office, with further instructions concerning the woman, I suppose. The stationmaster is our Party secretary's brother, by the way. If you want to question the comrade secretary's orders you will have to take it up with him directly and suffer the consequences, for I warn you, Comrade Xian is not an easy man and does not like his orders questioned by minions such as you.'

My heart jumped again, with joy, untainted this time.

Beautiful little Shaoxia had kept word and had indeed managed to persuade her father to intervene for me.

Still, the Red Guards didn't give up that easily and one of them shouted, 'We have *our* orders directly from our beloved Great Leader Chairman Mao and Comrade Jiang Qing and your puny secretary will be squashed if he interferes in our great plan.'

'I'll tell him that,' I heard the man with the deep voice reply in a mocking tone, 'or, rather, why don't you tell him that yourself? I'm sure he will be impressed and let you take, with your prisoner, the next train to catch up with your comrades in Shenyang.'

'I'll report to the leaders in Harbin that you have taken a prisoner off the train against my objections,' I heard the stubborn Red Guard mutter.

'You do that,' the man replied, 'and you may well end up making the full complement of prisoners again. Now, open that door!'

There were no more protests and after the usual fiddling with the padlocks the door was pushed aside.

I saw a group of Red Guards and a tall man in a neat, dark blue suit standing on the platform.

The man stepped close to the door opening and, peering into the rancid gloom inside, he said, in a slightly raised voice, 'Xu Suping? Please come forward and identify yourself!'

While I scrambled up I felt Meilin squeeze my hand.

'Good luck to you,' she whispered. 'I saw in your eyes that you worried about me. Thank you for that. Don't worry, however, I can take care of myself. I know you can too. See you again some day somewhere, perhaps.'

I squeezed her hand and smiled at her upturned face. Her eyes were brimming with tears. Such desperate loneliness I read in them. In a sudden impulse I bent down and kissed her.

'Goodbye little lathe operator,' I whispered, 'don't lose another finger.'

Then I turned brusquely and, gingerly stepping over the other prisoners on the floor, I swiftly reached the door opening. Looking down in the tall man's face I said as clearly as I could, 'I am Xu Suping of Luding and this is my only identification,' and I turned my right arm to show him my armband.

I saw a ghost of a smile flicker over his face as he looked up at me and said, 'that is enough Xu Suping of Luding. Let me help you down,' and he proffered his hand.

I took his hand and jumped down on the platform.

'I thank the pride of our motherland for their graceful co-operation,' the man said, deadly serious, to the Red Guards. 'My leader's letter of appreciation will reach Harbin ahead of you. My advice to you is to remain suitably modest whilst waiting for your own leaders' commendation.'

I couldn't help smiling. What a clever move by this man.

The Red Guards realised also that they had been outmanoeuvred and angrily they pushed the door shut.

The man took my elbow and said, 'Come with me, Xu Suping of Luding, Comrade Guo Chuanxing is waiting for you in the stationmaster's office. Comrade Guo told us that he knows you from his stint as Luding's Party secretary and that he owes you and is prepared to stick his neck out for you. I think you are a lucky person, Xu Suping, with people like Comrade Guo and little Xian Shaoxia prepared to put in a good word for you.

'First little Shaoxia in Tianjin, my secretary's niece, speaking up for you to her father who then contacts his brother here in Dalian. Then, when my secretary discussed his brother's request with us in a meeting, there is Guo who has the guts to say openly that he knew you in Luding and that because of your honesty and righteousness he didn't make a major error of judgement that would have had him expelled from the Party, but just a minor one that earned him a demotion and a probationary period here in Dalian, his hometown. Guo told my secretary that he is prepared to take responsibility for your good behaviour. I am telling you all this, Suping, because I know that Guo himself will never even hint to you that his future now depends on you. Don't let him down!'

I was too emotional for words so I just shook my head vehemently that I wouldn't, ever.

We had reached the stationmaster's office and my guide opened the door for me, announcing, 'Xu Suping of Luding, Comrade Guo.'

As I walked into the office I heard him close the door behind me. I never saw him again, yet I'll never forget his grave, civilised voice and the dignity with which he treated me.

I immediately recognised the man behind the desk. He was much less nervous though than when I first met him in Luding and he had a nice smile when he stood up from his chair and proffered his hand.

'Nice to meet you again, Suping,' he said, 'please sit down,' and he gestured at a chair in front of the desk.

I sat down and nervously babbled the usual nonsense, 'Thank you, Comrade Guo. I am so grateful. I don't deserve that.'

Guo smiled, then he said, seriously, 'Don't be nervous, Suping, and don't thank me. I am merely repaying my moral debt to you and you and I are both fortunate that Secretary Xian understands these things. I told him, as well as the other council members, what you did for me, a nervous, stuck-up, lowly cadre appointed to a position too big for him still at that time, though, vain as I was, I didn't realise that then.

'I told them how you stood up for me with those two horrible scientists out to destroy me and came to see me, in defiance probably of your own intellectual parents, to warn me. That I am now sitting here, have the respect of my superiors and that I shall probably be promoted again, within a year or so, to secretary in a medium-sized city, that I have to thank you for. Secretary Xian and the council members understand that I must pay my debt to you and they gave me full latitude to deal with your case.'

'You are an honourable person, Guo Chuanxing,' I said, my voice quavering from emotion, 'and I am a very lucky person to have met you that day in Luding and to have followed my intuition about you.'

'Thank you, Suping,' Guo replied, 'I cherish your esteem. We live in difficult times these days and it has only just begun. We must be very careful lest the wrong elements, who are unleashing such horrors on our country, destroy all of us. When this madness ends, and end it will, I want to be able to live with myself and to look people in the eyes, not avoid them out of shame for what I did. Now, let's be practical. Take that armband off first and hand it to me.'

With trembling fingers I fumbled with the safety pin until Guo opened it for me and took the armband off to put it in his pocket.

My eyes brimmed with tears.

'Don't cry,' Guo said earnestly, 'keep your poise, be earnest and dignified. I know you have gone through trying times, however, don't be so overly, emotionally grateful each time somebody does you a small favour. It makes people suspicious and wonder what you may be hiding to be so obsequious. They may report you to the Red Guards to earn merit for themselves and once those misguided youths have you in their claws again they'll make you confess to any crime that's in fashion at that time. I won't be able to help you then.

'Now, tell me, when you were sentenced and became convict number so-and-so, did they give you a paper to hand over to the authorities of the place they were sending you to?'

I nodded and took the papers out of my money belt and handed them to him.

Taking the papers Guo said, 'You have money on you, eh? Very sensible, however, do not flaunt it or even use it the first few weeks. Use only the advance on your pay, even if it's not enough. Don't buy things, or more things, than people in your situation can afford. Don't arouse suspicion. Keep a very low profile. Don't draw attention to yourself. Is that clear?'

I nodded.

Guo looked through the papers and said, 'You have been even luckier than you thought, Suping. These papers are addressed to the secretary of Chengdu, by name even, which is a big mistake. The man was murdered, lynched by a mob of Red Guards and hangers-on, for treason, which means that he was in all probability an ordinary, decent man trying to make life a bit more bearable for the unfortunate, innocent people the People's Tribunals had saddled him with. I heard that after they murdered him the Red Guards put all the convicts he had been in charge of on trains to Shanxi and Xinjiang. We heard rumours about beatings and even torture. You were lucky when they either put you on the wrong truck in Luding, or when your truck took a wrong turn somewhere, and you ended up in Changsha.

'They put you on train 2678 without knowing or caring where you would end up and your luck held when the pointsman in Dezhou didn't shunt your train to Shijiazhuang, as he should have done, but to Tianjin instead, where that little elf, Xian Shaoxia happened to be at the station when you denounced that Dai person for raping you.

'I met her once, here in Dalian, when she stayed with her uncle, Secretary Xian. Extraordinary girl. Made me feel uncomfortable. Didn't know I was capable of the feelings she aroused in me. I fantasised about keeping her in a cage, for me alone, to watch her and listen to her for the sheer beauty of her face and her silvery voice. I was glad she went back to Tianjin when she did or I would have lost my head and made a fool of myself. I was smitten with her. Can you believe it, Suping? Me, the earnest Party cadre, in love with a girl ten years my junior?'

Guo stared at me, wonderingly, as if he still couldn't believe it. I smiled at him and said I could, both because I now knew him to be a good-hearted person and because I had met Shaoxia myself and could very well imagine the devastating effect she could have on an innocent man, or on any man for that matter.

'Yes, you're probably right,' Guo mused, 'but it frightened me the way I almost lost my head. Be that as it may, you were fortunate again, Suping, when Shaoxia manipulated her father and her uncle, who are both as wax in her little hands, in taking you off the train and that I happened to be here, owing you a debt I can't possibly wash my hands of. I hope it's your karma, Suping, or else I'm afraid it's too much luck in such a short time and you should be prepared for some bad things later in your life.

'Now, here is your temporary residency permit signed by the vice-mayor and the Party secretary. You must apply for renewal every year, in September. Don't forget! Renewal won't be a problem, provided you have an occupation. However, if you're too late with your application, even if you have a job, rejection is automatic and irrevocable. Any questions so far?'

I took my residency card and put it in my belt.

The questions of where I was going to live and how I would earn my keep were burning on my tongue; however, asking them would mean that I doubted Guo had thought of that as well, so I said I had no questions.

'Very well,' he said. 'Now about your immediate needs. I found you a place to live and to work in a kindergarten near the port. I'm sorry but you'll have to live for a few weeks, two months at the most, in the women's section of the dock workers' dormitory, until a small, single house becomes available. It's quite nice and very quiet, at the dead end of a small lane off the main street and at walking distance from the kindergarten. I'm sure you'll like it.

'The old woman living there now is very sick and cannot be moved. Besides, she has been living there her whole life and it would be cruel to expel her now she is about to die. Her daughter, who is from Shenyang, stays with her and takes care of her. However, the daughter's in-laws all live up north and she wants to go back there as soon as her mother has passed away. I have arranged that the house will be assigned to you. The rent is very little. You will be all right there. Let's go now. I'll accompany you to the kindergarten. The matron will be there. She'll show you your place in the dormitory later.'

Guo got up from his chair and came around the desk to walk me to the door.

Unthinkingly I took his hand and kissed it, tears streaming down my face.

For a moment Guo stood as if petrified, then, suddenly, he stroked the back of my head and said, with such kindness that I felt more tears coming, 'Come on, Suping! Get a hold of yourself. Everything will be all right. Only, please, think before you act. You're much too emotional for your own good.'

Guo and I walked from the station to the port district as it wasn't far.

He introduced me to the elderly woman in charge of the kindergarten and told us to try and work together in good humour. He would follow the developments with the house, he promised me, and would come back to see me as soon as I could move in.

Right from the beginning I got along well with the matron and, after a few days of mutual watchfulness, with the children as well.

The other women in the dormitory, all dock workers, were friendly but they kept to themselves and I had little contact with them. I took my morning and noon rice in the kindergarten's canteen and had dinner in either one of the small restaurants around the port area.

Twice Matron asked me to share dinner with her in her small flat, in the dock workers' quarters, where she lived alone since the accidental death of her husband. Her only daughter lived in Wuhan, with her in-laws, she told me, and their only contact was a card around New Year. I could feel it made her sad and that she was lonely, though she always kept a cheerful appearance.

I settled into a kind of quiet routine and was surprised when, about two months later, Guo came to see me to tell me the old woman had died and that the daughter, after having cleaned the house, had gone back to Shenyang or thereabouts. Guo accompanied me to the small house, the last one in a narrow, unpaved dead-end alley.

Together we inspected the house.

The old woman's rickety furniture was still there; the daughter had left a note on the table saying that the new tenant could do with the furniture as she pleased, keep it or dispose of it, whatever.

I told Guo I didn't want to keep it as I felt queasy about touching chairs or mattresses used by a sick, old person. In spite of the daughter's, apparently half-hearted, efforts to clean the house, there still lingered that peculiar rancid smell so typical of sickly, old people. Apart from that, it was an endearing little house waiting to be turned again into a cosy, little home.

Guo was visibly pleased with my enthusiasm.

When I told him that I had already made a deal with a furniture maker to pay a deposit and twelve monthly instalments for a new bed, four chairs, a table, a wardrobe, a chest and a few other, smaller things to make the house cosy, he laughed outright and said that he should actually frown upon such a capitalist form of consumerism, however, that in my case he would let it pass in the hope that one day I would become a good Communist.

In front of the furniture maker's workshop he took his leave of me. Taking both my hands between his, he said, 'I see that you are doing fine, Suping, and I am glad. I reckon that I have paid my debt to you, so there are no more obligations. For our friendship's sake though, I'll keep an eye on you and I hope you'll know where to find me should you need help. I won't visit you unless there is something really important that I have to tell you. It's not that I am afraid to be seen with you. It's that I would get ideas about you and me that could never work and worrying about that would distract me from my duties to the Party. We are too different. I will always try to be a good Communist while you don't even want to be one. So let's say goodbye now. You owe me nothing, I owe you nothing.'

He then suddenly embraced me, as two good friends would, looked at me one more time, a strange, wistful smile on his face, turned and walked off without looking back once. I never saw him again.

Twice he sent a message, though, with a short, personal letter, very friendly and very concerned about my well-being.

The first note was delivered about a year after we said farewell. After enquiring about my health and how I was getting on, he went on to warn me about the newly appointed neighbourhood community leader, Hu Guoshang, who, Guo said, was the living example of every argument used by counter-revolutionaries and anti-Communists to depict communism as evil and inhuman. Hu hated the very ground an intellectual had walked on, Guo wrote, and he warned me to be very, very careful and not to provoke her in any way.

His second letter was given to me still six months later. In it he warned me quite bluntly against my relationship with Li Kunlen, who, Guo wrote, was an irresponsible and vain person who one day would come to grief and drag me down with him if I continued to associate with him. He went on to say that he wouldn't be able to help me out again, should I land myself in trouble, since he had received his reinstatement as an assistant Party secretary in Urumqi, in Xinjiang Autonomous Region.

By the time I would have received his letter, he would have left for Urumqi already, he wrote. He also asked me to destroy his two letters to me, to protect him, just in case something should happen to me. I should have liked to keep them, as a souvenir of a decent man who had been good to me, however, I burned them then as that was the least I could do for him.

Who told him about Kunlen and me, I don't know, and Guo didn't tell me, of course.

He must have had his spies watching me and though I was sure he meant well I saw it as the typical Communist interference in one's personal life and I stubbornly decided I would marry Kunlen should he ask me.

I sometimes wonder whether my own uneasiness about Kunlen's character would have had the better of me had Guo not warned me against associating with him.

But then, what's the use of such speculation and, besides, I now have my daughter and that's all that counts.

My karma, as Guo would say. Strange Communist he was, to believe in karma. However, I am anticipating events.

The first year passed quietly and relatively quickly. I liked my job, and the matron, and most of the children, and they obviously liked me. I had gone to visit the other inhabitants of the alley to introduce myself and though no real friendship developed, all of them being so much older than I was, everybody spoke well of me and greeted me when I passed by to and from work. I seldom left my little world, except on Sundays, my day off, when I went to the beach, regardless of the weather. I would walk for hours along the shore, the cold foam occasionally splashing my rolled-up trousers.

Halfway, at the point of return, I had discovered a small cove, where I would sit, out of sight, staring out over the sea, absent-mindedly playing with the pebbles and sand, fantasising about the free world beyond. Outside this private little dream world things didn't look so good.

There were rumours about the deteriorating situation in town, about how Party Secretary Xian only just managed to stay in power, battling against the increasingly vitriolic attacks from the younger Party members and the Red Guards. To placate them Xian had to give in more and more often, always managing to choose the lesser of two evils, and gradually terror crept into the daily lives of the people of Dalian, later than elsewhere in China, but still it grew.

Somehow our neighbourhood was spared for more than a year and all of us went about our daily lives as if there was no Cultural Revolution raging in the rest of China. Of course, there were shortages, then of this, then of that, then of something else still, however, we either learned to do without or somebody, with relatives in the countryside, managed to smuggle into our alley more than he needed for himself and shared it with the other inhabitants.

This created a sort of cosy atmosphere of solidarity and complicity.

Then, as predicted by Guo in his letter to me, everything changed with the arrival of Hu Guoshang and her gang of Red Guards and hangers-on.

Though I had been forewarned I couldn't do the same for my neighbours as they might have wondered how I knew about her and possibly made the connection with the preferential treatment I had got from Guo when he had arranged to have my little house assigned to me. I knew others had had designs of their own on the house and that some had been very disappointed and envious, when I, a stranger, and a young, single woman to boot, had moved in. Though the initial gossip and rumour-mongering had died down after a while, people had not forgotten. In fact, people never forget such things and a seemingly innocuous, unconnected event will trigger old memories and the gossip and innuendoes, often more vicious than the first time, will start all over again. So I told nobody about what I knew about Hu lest I cause trouble for Guo and for myself.

I was at the kindergarten when I saw her march by in the street, an ugly, stocky woman of indeterminate age, at the head of a group of about twenty youths carrying red flags and shouting slogans. Hu herself didn't open her mouth, her lips a thin line, her eyes darting left and right, missing nothing, her strides too long for her short, bow-legs.

The first thing she did was to occupy the little school in the main street and to proclaim it the neighbourhood Party centre. The two teachers and forty-two pupils were sent home after an harangue about their revolutionary duties and the reprehensibility of such bourgeois habits as learning.

The same day she put up big-character posters everywhere ordering everybody; child, man or woman, between the ages of five and eighty-five, to gather every evening of the week in the Party centre to participate in mandatory, revolutionary struggle meetings.

That evening more that three hundred people of all ages assembled in the school yard. Except for Lao Yang, who was already old at that time so you can imagine how old he must be now, though he hasn't changed a bit, that cantankerous old blab, everybody from my alley was there. From where I stood, on one side of the yard, I noticed that a few seemed to be just curious, grinning mischievously at each other. Most, however, looked indifferent and a bit defiant, though not defiant enough apparently to dare stay away.

Then I noticed a youngish man, in the front row, tall, erect, hands deep in the pockets of his dark green trousers that appeared to fit him well judging by the way they tightened around his shapely bottom.

I couldn't see his face so I squeezed myself through the crowd to get closer and see what he looked like when suddenly he turned his head to look behind him.

His eyes caught and held mine for a second or two.

It was as if my heart stopped before it started racing like mad. That man and Wu Ju, they were as like as two peas!

I stood there as if petrified, unable to take my eyes off him, his face; as, pushing people unceremoniously out of his way, he came to stand next to me.

Proffering his hand he said, still smiling, 'My name is Li, Li Kunlen, and who are you, if I may ask?'

I mumbled my name which at first he didn't catch so I had to repeat myself twice.

He laughed, a nice, merry laugh, and said, 'It definitely is one of those days today. First I am told this morning that that crummy old workshop where I worked, as a welder, for the past fifteen months, was closing to allow its leaders and workers to heed the call of the goddess Jiang Qing to first destroy and then rebuild the nation in her honour and to her greater glory.

'I am also informed that there is no money left in the till, every fen having been donated to our revolutionary leaders, so I decide to heed the call of my common sense rather than Jiang Qing's and I hurry straight to the labour placement unit farthest away from the filthy, stinking northern part of town, the one near here, in the southern port area. A kind, motherly woman, sitting like a benign little Buddha behind her desk, is the only one left in the office, all the others busily making revolution, she tells me.

'She is surprised, but pleased, that I want to work and she assigns me the job of bicycle-frame welder in the new factory on the beach road where most of the workers have also walked off their jobs, she says. She also arranges a bed and a locker for me in the seamen's house dormitory. Convinced that so much luck cannot last I do indeed find a poster on the dormitory's door ordering every occupant to attend tonight the first struggle meeting in this neighbourhood in the yard of the nearby little school, signed Hu Guoshang, neighbourhood community leader.

'Pondering the freakishness of luck, I stand here waiting for bugbear Hu and what happens? The most lovely girl I have ever seen, staring at me as if she sees a ghost. I didn't know I looked that forbidding to little girls. Perhaps that's why Hu used to like me so much?'

I felt myself blushing hotly, probably as red as a peony, and I stammered, 'I wasn't frightened by you. You gave me a shock because you so closely look like someone dear to me that for one moment I thought that he was standing there. That's why I stared.'

Li Kunlen smiled and said, 'Bad luck again then for me. I envy that lucky man.'

'There is no need to envy him,' I said softly. 'He's dead. Murdered by a gang of Red Guards, in Hefei, last year. For a few hours he and I found comfort in each other's presence, in the prisoners' train, between Changsha and Hefei. I think we were in love.'

Li put a hand on my arm and said, with that exquisite tenderness in his voice I found out later was as fake as Lady Wu's jewels, 'I am so sorry, Su Ping. Forgive me my callousness please.'

'It's nothing,' I replied, laughing, a bit uncertainly, through my tears.

'Now tell me all about your romance with Leader Hu.'

He frowned, momentarily annoyed, I thought, and I was afraid I had said something wrong.

However, in one of those sudden mood swings I learned to dread later, he burst out laughing and exclaimed, 'Romance? Nothing romance! On the contrary. Hu and I are from the same village, Wanfu, about one hundred and fifty kilometres north of Dalian. My father was the village blacksmith and her's the pig breeder on the communal farm. Like his pigs he had a whole litter of young and his sow of a wife reared them likewise.

'Guoshang was the last. You know? The one that can't find a tit and is trampled on by the others? She didn't die though but instead grew up ugly and sullen, given to violent bouts of temper, taking her hatred for her family out on the weak and defenceless. Whenever you heard the animals scream; pigs, goats, chickens, you could be sure Guoshang was busy hurting them. I used to accompany my father to the farm whenever there was a job to be done and I loved to be with the animals, to feed them and to caress them. At first they were afraid and shied away from me but gradually they got accustomed to me and let me come near them and touch them.

'I noticed then that many had traces of blood on them and that the pigs had blue and green spots where Guoshang had beaten or stabbed them, probably with a pitchfork from behind the fence. I hated her though I hardly ever saw her while I was there. Then, one day, my father's job took longer than he had thought and we had to stay overnight at the farm. My father was entitled to a true bed in the main building while I had to sleep in the barn, in the straw. I didn't care. I can sleep anywhere.

'In the middle of the night I felt something snuggling up to me and, not fully awake yet, I felt a wet mouth slobbering all over my face and a hand squeezing my jadestalk. I jumped up, pushed Guoshang, for it was she, off me and ran, as if the devil were on my heels, to the main building. I woke up everybody and told them what had happened. Perhaps I shouldn't have done that, but I was frightened and angry and I wanted to hurt her. My father sent me home straight away, in the middle of the night, and he never took me with him again. He was angry about the way I had behaved, like a coward he said, and he never told me what happened to Guoshang.

'A few months after the incident, when I was just nineteen, I left for Anshan to become a welder. I stayed four years in Anshan and only went back to Wanfu once, after one year, to see my parents. They weren't particularly glad to see me and after a week I went back to Anshan. I haven't seen them since. A year ago a sheet of steel slipped out of its straps, crushing two workers on the shop floor. My leader blamed me for not checking the straps before hoisting the sheet up and, as punishment for my so-called neglect, I was ostracised and sent to that crummy little workshop here in Dalian, the one that closed down this morning. And now I am standing here while Hu Guoshang, of all people, is looking down at me.'

He fell silent and pointed at the open window on the first floor where Hu had appeared, looking down at the crowd in the yard. From the way Li had described her I could guess how she savoured this moment, the power she had over these people, the fear she could read on the hundreds of faces looking up at her.

Suddenly she shouted, 'Long live our beloved Chairman Mao and Comrade Jiang Qing!'

When there was no response from the crowd, she screamed furiously, 'You ungrateful dogs! You owe everything to our two great leaders, the greatest leaders of all times! Repeat after me, seven times! My Red Guards are watching you! Anyone not shouting or not shouting loud enough will be punished!'

And again, at the top of her voice, she shouted her slogan and this time the crowd, including myself and Li, roared back, 'Long live our beloved Chairman Mao and Comrade Jiang Qing!' seven times.

During the next hour or so Hu took us through the whole panoply of party slogans, making us shout each one seven times, at the top of our voices, until most people were so hoarse that they couldn't utter a sound any more.

Hu then embarked on another line.

'This neighbourhood has been lacking severely in revolutionary zeal and ardour!' she yelled, apparently none the worse after an hour of shouting.

'This will change as from today! My leaders have sent me here to impose strict revolutionary discipline and to weed out the enemies of the Party and the People hiding amongst you! I demand fifty volunteers, men and women, to demolish the partition walls between the four classrooms on the ground floor to make it one big hall and as from tomorrow evening I will conduct there revolutionary struggle meetings, every evening! Attendance by all of you is mandatory! Absence will be punished severely!

'My Red Guards will patrol the streets and lanes several times every day and they have my orders to enter any house where they suspect counter-revolutionary propaganda material is hidden, and to arrest, on the spot, any person they suspect of counter-revolutionary activities! Anybody knowing about such things, or even only suspecting them, must come forward during the evening meetings and denounce those enemies of the People! Remember! There will be lenient treatment for those who confess themselves! However, severe punishment awaits those who remain stubborn! Those who denounce others will be rewarded!'

Hu fell silent and let her message of terror sink in. I saw frightened faces all around.

Then Hu shouted, 'Fifty volunteers step forward, now! Everybody else must go home! Tomorrow evening at seven o'clock you must all report for the struggle meeting! Go now!'

Li Kunlen did not step forward to volunteer for Hu's demolition work. I saw him looking contemptuously at the men and women rushing forward to the school's entrance to do Hu's bidding.

'Have you ever seen such a thing?' he sneered. 'Tells you something, what? From now on beware of the people around you, every minute of the day. If they think they can gain merit in Hu's eyes they'll denounce you for everything they can think of will please her. And that ugly sow stands there and yells at us and doesn't even bother to show us her so-called orders. Orders from whom? And none of us has the guts to demand to be shown those orders, myself included. Makes you want to throw up. I'm disgusted with myself.'

Taking my arm, he said dejectedly, 'Come, let's go.'

He accompanied me to my house and we said goodbye, promising to see each other again.

From that day onwards the whole atmosphere in our neighbourhood changed.

Before Hu's arrival people would greet each other amiably or stop for some gossip or small talk when passing each other in the street and alleys, or sit down for a chat with people sitting outside in front of their house on a balmy summer evening. People waiting in line for a shop to open, or for something special on sale, would chat and laugh together while shuffling forward.

All those little things that make life in a small neighbourhood, where everybody knows everybody, so pleasant and cosy and which I had come to like so much, were forgotten after only two days of Hu's new regime.

People became wary of each other, mistrusting, and scurried home from whatever they had been doing, eyes downcast or glancing left, right and back over their shoulder, worriedly and suspiciously.

During the first few weeks Hu's Red Guards ransacked each and every house and hovel for baubles or small valuables deemed unproletarian, for pre-revolution books deemed counter-revolutionary, for possessions other than the most needed were deemed bourgeois, if not worse.

During their search they screamed and yelled at the cowering inhabitants, accusing them of the most ludicrous and far-fetched misdeeds, kicking against the furniture, tearing curtains down, leaving behind a mess, everything damaged and dirty. They forced the unlucky owners to load the confiscated things on a handcart and to push the cart to the school yard where they had to dump them on the ground and stand guard next to their meagre possessions until that night's meeting.

The first thing on Hu's agenda was to harangue them, in her hysterically screaming voice, about their bourgeois capitalist tendencies. Next she gave a sign to her Red Guards who then forced the victims to smash their pitiful belongings with a sledgehammer.

That done the Red Guards pushed and bustled them into the newly made hall, on the ground floor, where, kneeling in front of the crowd, they had to don dunce caps and recant their erroneous beliefs and embrace the new, proletarian, Cultural Revolutionary ideals of total eradication of the past.

On several occasions I had to restrain Kunlen from rushing forward and taking on the Red Guards. He then squeezed my hand so hard it hurt and, breathing heavily, he managed to control himself.

Kunlen and I had continued to see each other regularly and we usually came to the meetings together.

The Red Guards also ransacked my little hovel and, ironically, I got a clean bill of revolutionary health since they couldn't find anything but the barest necessities. The same held for Kunlen when they searched the seamen's house, so neither of us had to go through the recanting ordeal.

The second part of the struggle meetings consisted of political indoctrination, communal recitation of Chairman Mao's thoughts and the chanting of criticism of 'the traitorous dog Lin', 'the feudalistic, reactionary, bourgeois criminal Kung' or of whoever else had fallen from grace at the time.

The third and last part of the meetings was dedicated to self-criticism or denouncements.

People were forced to come to the front and criticise themselves for all kinds of petty, silly sins.

Others, nasty, hateful people with a score to settle in a long-festering feud, came forward of their own to denounce their enemies for whatever crime they had fabricated in their vicious little minds. If it suited Hu the crimes couldn't be so far-fetched or she would pretend to believe them and she would condemn the accused to a grovelling display of remorse and to beg the crowd for forgiveness.

Mind you, not to beg the accuser but the crowd. As there were no such whimsy things as individual rights, a crime against one was a crime against all and pardon or punishment could therefore only be dispensed by the People and thus, by implication, by the Party.

At other times, Hu would pounce on the accuser and, screaming hysterically in his face, she would accuse him in turn of making false denunciations. Her Red Guards would then push the wretch to the ground, pulling his arms high behind his back, until he screamed his confession. Hu would then condemn him or her, for this happened to women as well, to some kind of humiliating community service such as cleaning the communal toilets with bare hands, Hu's favourite punishment.

As she was totally unpredictable, making denouncements, true or false, was a risky business and people much preferred self-criticism.

This went on for six months or so and people got used to the barking and posturing by Hu and her high-strung, thin-skinned goons. We underwent the hullabaloo with that couldn't-care-less-passivity the foreigners seem to think is typically Chinese.

Kunlen and I sought each other's company whenever we had an opportunity and gradually we fell in love; at least I did.

He was handsome, charming and exasperating.

Four months after we first met he asked me to marry him. At first I hesitated for reasons I couldn't, or rather wouldn't, explain. However, he kept asking every other week or more often and I knew I either had to give in or offend him and lose him. Then I got Guo's second letter and his, what I pretended to believe was unfounded, criticism of Kunlen angered me.

Deep in my heart I knew Guo was right though. Kunlen was vain and boastful and sneaky.

I had arranged with Matron to have the Wednesday off, the same day as Kunlen, instead of the Sunday, and together we always went to the beach as he enjoyed that as much as I did. During our long walks he would talk for hours about whatever subjects came to his mind. My role was to listen and to agree and I often kicked at the pebbles in sheer exasperation. He didn't notice. Sitting in my sheltered little cove he would talk about a plan that was gradually taking form in his mind, an outrageous plan to outwit Hu. Again my role was to listen and to agree and I threw pebbles by the handful in the lapping waves, bored and exasperated, but again, he didn't notice.

Whenever I tried to get a word in he either raised his voice a little and spoke a bit faster until I gave up or he told me irritably to stop interrupting him unless I had something worthwhile to add.

Sometimes, however, he would listen to me, with that supercilious and condescending little smile that hurt me even more and that made my eyes burn with tears of disappointment and despair. Afterwards, in bed, I would cry my eyes out, all the time seeing that stupid, complacent smile on his lips, until after a while I no longer cried out of sadness but out of anger.

Anger at my own stupidity, anger at Kunlen's stupidity, anger at the prospect of the bleary, swollen eyes that would stare back at me in the morning, from the little mirror above the kitchen sink, while I prepared my congee.

When I got up, those Thursday mornings, I was always firmly determined not to look. However, hardly in the kitchen, the mirror was like a powerful, irresistible magnet and I would look, first thing. What I saw then made me stamp my feet in anger and on quite a few occasions I smashed a bowl on the floor.

Later, at the kindergarten, Matron would cluck like an old hen on seeing my face and when Kunlen stopped by, on the way to his work, he would laugh, the fool. I think now that it was more the dread to be alone again, without somebody my own age to talk to and to feel secure with, than love that made me decide to say yes the next time Kunlen would ask me to marry him.

Three weeks after I got good-hearted Guo's letter we applied for a wedding permit.

Of course Hu refused.

When Kunlen asked her why she became very angry and told him that she had no reason to give him.

As was the rule we reapplied every month and each time Hu refused. Suddenly, however, after three months, when we submitted our fourth application, she came down from her office on the first floor and told us abruptly that she would sign the permit there and then. She didn't give any explanation for her sudden change of heart, however, we thanked her nevertheless. She didn't acknowledge our expression of gratitude, knowing full well, I'm sure, that we didn't mean it anyway, but told us instead gruffly to get out.

The next Wednesday we went to the city town hall and registered our marriage. Twenty minutes later we were outside again, as Mr and Mrs Li. Kunlen moved in with me the same day. We bought a few more things such as a bigger bed, the same one Lilian and I now share.

We were happy most of the time, the occasional quarrel solved quickly, with Kunlen giving in more often than I, and gracefully at that, so I had high hopes that he had changed somehow for the better.

How wrong I was.

One night, about two months after our marriage, as I was lying in his arms in bed, he told me that he had made up his mind about his plan to defy Hu and the Party and that he would wage his own guerrilla war.

Without talking about it with me first, he had arranged to be assigned permanently to the evening shift in the bicycle factory so that he would both miss the morning propaganda meetings in the factory and Hu's struggle meetings in the evening.

He grinned when he told me how he had tricked his work unit leader into believing that he spent the morning hours meditating on Chairman Mao's thoughts and that, as a result of the spiritual guidance he so derived from the Great Helmsman's all-encompassing wisdom, his hand would be firm and his welding torch unerring and fast so that he could surpass the leader's daily quota of frames.

Only on the Wednesday evenings, on his day off, would he have to attend Hu's meetings, he said.

He was surprised and annoyed when I cried because I would have to attend the other six evenings of the week without him. He turned his back on me and fell asleep as I wept, feeling abandoned and betrayed.

When I got up the next morning, bleary-eyed from crying and lack of sleep he had already prepared congee for both of us. He laughed and joked until I finally couldn't help laughing also. He promised he would clean the house every morning as his shift started at two o'clock only.

The following Wednesday we attended the meeting together. Since a few weeks already the spirit had apparently gone out of Hu and the meetings dragged on and on, with long uninspired silences.

Everyone's baubles and books had been destroyed by then, everybody had already criticised himself more than twice and the denunciations had petered out as well so there was only Hu to harangue and admonish and even for her three hours every evening was too much.

I think that's why she looked relieved and assented readily when Kunlen asked her permission to take the stage.

Again I was flabbergasted.

He had told me nothing about what he intended to do but I knew him too well and was afraid he would deliberately try to provoke Hu and her Red Guards as part of his so-called one-man guerrilla fight. He squeezed my arm and before I could say something he had jumped on the stage, facing the crowd in the hall.

Like a seasoned actor he waited for silence and then a while longer to heighten the tension. Suddenly he raised his right arm and there, in his right hand, was Mao's Little Red Book.

'This book, this precious jewel of wisdom, is all you and I need!' he shouted in a stentorian voice.

'It is not only what you and I need!' he continued in the same tone. 'It is all that *China* needs! All that the *world* needs!'

He fell silent to let his words sink in and to let his eyes roam over the stunned audience. He smiled at Hu and I couldn't believe my eyes when I saw her smiling back at him. Poor sod.

Now that he had the audience's full attention, he didn't need to raise his voice so much, so he continued in much lower, almost conspiratorial tone.

'I have studied this book and all those cases where people performed true miracles by simply following the all-encompassing guidelines of our beloved Chairman Mao, of the greatest Helmsman not only China but all humankind has ever known. My heart leaps with joy now our own dear leader, Comrade Hu here, has given me the opportunity to tell you about my great and abiding love for our Chairman Mao, and to tell you about the men, women and children who let their lives be guided by him.'

A scattering of hesitant applause at first, then faster and louder the whole crowd began to applaud, glad undoubtedly of the distraction, and a few shouted, 'Tell us, Comrade Li! Tell us!'

Kunlen, good actor as he was, seized the mood of the crowd and, as if driven by holy, revolutionary fervour, Mao's Little Red Book in his left hand, his right fist shaking and punctuating his recitation, he read from the booklet, like some kind of preacher. He had done his homework well and at every guideline from the Great Helmsman he roused the crowd with the most incredible feats men, women and children all over China had been able to accomplish by simply practising Chairman Mao's thoughts.

Kunlen was indeed a gifted storyteller and the crowd gasped, sighed, wept and cheered as he spoke, with great emotion, of the heroes of socialist virtue who, armed only with the sacred little book, had stopped swollen rivers from flooding their communes' fields; had arrested billion-ton mudslides that came thundering down mountain slopes, just in time, at the outskirts of their villages, amidst scenes of hysterical gratitude from the idolising villagers; had killed, with their bare hands, bloodthirsty bears and raging, wild boars to protect their singing and unstoppable production brigades in the course of achieving yet another output record; had removed fifty-pound tumours from the bellies of smiling, starry-eyed patients, with a simple kitchen knife, to the cheers of excitedly gesticulating doctors; had saved trustingly smiling children from blazing school buildings; had made the rain stop and the sun shine in times of floods and had made clouds obscure the sun and unleash the rain in times of drought.

I knew that his act was intended as a mockery of such stories spread by the Party's propaganda zealots; however, who would dare challenge him?

Hu? If she were to object against his act and have him removed from the stage, she would in fact challenge the power of Mao's thoughts and she risked being accused of heresy, by Kunlen in the first place, of course.

He was so clever, my handsome but foolhardy husband. Maybe too clever and I feared that, if he continued this way, and I was sure he would, he would come to grief, which was exactly what Guo had warned me about.

Walking home that night, after his performance, Kunlen was exultant.

'Did you see the reaction of the crowd?' he enthused. 'The fools believed every word I said. And Hu? Did you see her face at the end? She wasn't happy at all. She knows I am poking fun at her and her precious, great leader. However, she can't prove it, so she can't stop me. I hope she has an apoplexy one of these evenings.'

He kept talking like that long after we had retired to bed, very much in love with himself rather than with me.

At one time I protested feebly that he couldn't hope to win a one-man crusade against the all-powerful Party.

He laughed mockingly, and said, 'You have seen nothing yet, Su Ping. Wait until I have my new act together in a week or two.'

He refused to tell me what this new act was all about, so I angrily turned my back on him and pretended to sleep.

Two days later, on Friday morning, something happened that would subtly change life in our neighbourhood in the months and years to come and influence my own life in more than one respect.

I still remember the scene as if it happened yesterday.

Matron had told me that morning to take the eldest children, those five and six year old brats who should actually be attending Little School Number Two if Hu hadn't closed it, to a lecture on socialist architecture at the Party's head office a few streets away from our neighbourhood.

With twenty children snaking behind me, holding each other by the tail of their coats, I was just approaching the corner of our alley when a ramshackle, noisy old truck, its roaring engine belching thick, black smoke, came rattling down the main street and stopped at the corner.

A middle-aged woman in a white blouse and black trousers climbed down from the truck's loading platform and then tried to take down two old-fashioned, battered, reed suitcases held together with pink, plastic string. The woman shouted at the truck driver to give her a hand, but he pretended not to hear her and instead kept pressing and releasing the accelerator, which made the engine alternately soar and die down, virtually suffocating the woman with its sooty exhaust while she was struggling with her suitcases.

Yelling above the roar of the engine she ridiculed the driver's physical, mental and sexual capabilities with such rude and descriptive adjectives that I felt my cheeks and ears burning with embarrassment.

When she finally had her suitcases down on the pavement, the woman went to the front of the truck and pulled the driver by his filthy, torn shirt from his seat so that he, too, fell on the pavement. The engine hiccuped a few times, then stalled, while the driver shriekingly called the woman a filthy, reactionary, bourgeois Shanghainese whore.

This was apparently the extent of his vocabulary of expletives since he kept repeating the insult in an increasingly hysterical pitch. A big crowd of pedestrians and cyclists, always in the mood for a good row, had gathered around the scene and mockingly they took sides in the shouting match between the woman and the driver, cheering them on while the cyclists rang their bells in an ear-splitting accompaniment.

I frantically tried to pull my charge of twenty pairs of wide open ears through the crowd to get away from the scene, however, the bicycles blocked our way and I could only return the way I had come, back to the kindergarten. Dragging the children back, almost at a trot, I could imagine what would happen if they remembered the rude words and repeated them at home.

Their parents would complain to the Red Guards and I would be blamed and accused of corrupting the minds of revolutionary socialist youth.

Back at the kindergarten I told Matron what had happened and she told me I had done well to return forthwith.

Together we had the children recite twelve times the 'Missiles and Bombs' song followed by 'The Night-Soil Collectors Coming Down the Mountain.'

Hopefully that would make the little monsters forget what they had heard in the street, Matron said.

However, I wasn't so sure the spoiled brats wouldn't remember a few abusive words and blurt them out during one of the customary tantrums at home.

For the next few weeks I lived in terror at the thought of Leader Hu, at the head of her Red Guards, barging into the classroom, or my house, to take me to the Party centre and make me confess to all sorts of crimes against the State or the People. When I came home that evening I saw that the door of house 383/7 was open.

House 383/7 was a big house, a few houses up the alley. It had been uninhabited for as long as I had lived in the alley so I was surprised to see the open door.

Lao Yang was sitting on his tiny chair in front of his shack and he cackled, 'It's that vulgar woman who came with the truck this morning. I saw you fleeing the scene with the children and it's as well that you did. Such language. Even a Cantonese would have blushed and that from a woman's mouth! It's a shame! I'm sure she has connections high up in the Party or else the municipality would not assign such a big house to her, a single woman.

'I was once inside that house, you know. It has a big kitchen with room enough for a small table and three chairs, and a living room and a separate bedroom. Altogether at least forty square metres, more than three times what a young couple is entitled to. Look at how you have to make do in that small house of yours, you being married and maybe a child in the making, eh?' He cackled mischievously as I blushed and quickly continued on my way home.

A child. That rusty old man had put his finger on another point of contention between Kunlen and I. We had already applied four times to Hu to be allowed to have a child and each time she had rejected our plea.

I suspected her of having approved our marriage so suddenly and unexpectedly only to be able to deny us the joy of a child. She so openly enjoyed our disappointment each time she turned us down.

Kunlen took it very badly and he became irritable and angry with me when I took my precautions each time we made love, which wasn't often, him never being home before eleven at night and with his preoccupation with his Wednesday night performance. However, a month ago, he forced himself in me before I could put the spermicide gel in.

I cried and tried to resist but he came quickly and then fell asleep with his arms around me to prevent me from getting up and rinsing myself with vinegar.

I cried the whole night while he slept with that contented, triumphant little smile on his face I had come to know so well.

When I told him three weeks later that my periods were a week late already and that I felt a bit nauseated in the morning and that my breasts were a bit swollen and painful, he laughed loudly and triumphantly and merely said that that would teach Hu a lesson.

No kiss for me, no concern about how I felt, no sharing of my worries, nothing; only triumph that he had once more managed to defy Hu.

And now old Yang mentioning a child. Had Kunlen bragged about his manly prowess? What would happen once my situation became visible?

I was scared to death thinking about the possible consequences.

The day after the sensational arrival of the new tenant of house 383/7 I saw her outside, painting with deft, elegant strokes her name on the door with white paint, not red as was the official direction.

I stopped and read, 'Liu Meiling'.

The woman stepped back a few paces to admire her work, then smiled at me and said, 'Now you know my name, what is yours, please?'

I introduced myself and pointed out to her where I lived.

'So you're the wife of that handsome young rascal who came home at eleven o'clock last night, singing and whistling and not giving a damn about other people sleeping. He was inside your house before I could grab him by his stiff neck and teach him some manners. You tell him, Su Ping, that I am an old woman and need my sleep.'

I laughed and said I would convey the message, not that it would make any difference, I added. I knew already then that there wouldn't be much love lost between my swaggering husband and this tough, no-nonsense woman.

'Who's that scruffy old man over there, ogling us as if we were a pair of taxi girls?' Madam Liu asked.

'That's Lao Yang,' I replied. 'He lives there, with an old woman people say is not his legal wife. He hears and sees everything that goes on in this alley.'

'And comments on everything as well, no doubt,' Madam Liu said, grimly. 'I know the type. Think their age permits them to say whatever passes through their shrivelled mind.'

'I would think that you won't have much of a problem with that,' I said, smiling, 'the first time he does that to you will also be the last time, I'm sure.'

Madam Liu looked at me searchingly, then, suddenly, she burst out laughing.

'You are a sharp young lady,' she chuckled. 'I think I am going to like you. Whenever you have a spot of trouble and need some advice from a person who has seen and heard it all, or a shoulder to cry on, come and see me, any time. All right?'

'All right, I will,' I said, 'but now I have to be off to my work.'

Over the next few weeks the alley followed with mounting interest the battle of wills between Madam Liu and Leader Hu.

Leader Hu accosted Madam Liu daily and people heard Hu threaten the direst consequences if Madam Liu continued to stay away from the evening struggle meetings.

People commented excitedly on how Madam Liu just looked at Hu, shrugged her shoulders and turned her back on a fuming Hu.

Then, suddenly, one day, Hu stopped her harassment and from that day on she obviously avoided Madam Liu. This meant, of course, a terrible loss of face for Hu and people began whispering.

Who was that enigmatic woman whom nobody dared to call Comrade Liu or just Liu?

She had a way of carrying herself and of looking at people that made the word '*tongzhi*' stick in one's throat. Her *guanxi* had to be very powerful since she not only got the big house assigned to her but also seemed protected by the high political powers.

Likely enough it was a very high-ranking official who either owed her or her family a very big favour or about whom she knew something that could harm him very badly if she leaked it to the Party or, worse, made it public which would embarrass the Party as well.

The other women in the neighbourhood, slighted by Madam Liu's humiliating rejection of their advances and disappointed because they couldn't find out more about her, started gossiping and rumour-mongering. These rumours, feeding on each other, spiralled to outrageous and ludicrous heights, ranging from Yuan Shikai's bastard sister to Pockface Huang's daughter to Zhou Enlai's illegitimate daughter to Mao Zedong's repudiated mistress to Sun Yatsun's former concubine.

Madam Liu was undoubtedly aware of the rumours and mystery surrounding her person, yet she never stooped to challenge the gossips or to deny the rumours.

I spoke up a few times in her defence, scolding the gossips and telling them to mind their own business.

Kunlen mocked the women by spreading the rumour that Madam Liu was actually a reincarnation of Kuan Yin, the goddess of mercy, condemned by the Party for favouritism and sent for re-education among the ordinary people to learn about socialist mercy and about how to distribute other people's property and spend other people's money.

It all ended rather suddenly one day with a public scolding of a group of women arrested by the militia, not the Red Guards of course, for an attempt at housebreaking.

I remember the incident clearly, on a Wednesday it happened, Kunlen's and my day off from work. We had been to the beach as usual and were returning home when we noticed a small group of women from our alley standing at the corner of the alley and the main street.

They nervously looked up and down the street as if at any moment expecting to see a certain person.

'Oh, oh,' Kunlen said. 'The witches are excited and clearly have a bad conscience, the connivers.'

We soon saw the reason why.

A second, smaller group of women had apparently just forced the door of house 383/7 as we saw them trooping inside, all excited.

Kunlen sprinted to Madam Liu's house and pulled the door shut, holding it whilst the women tried, from the inside, to pull it open and flee the scene.

He shouted at me to call the militia. When I returned with the commandant and two of his men, Madam Liu had come home in the meantime.

She shrugged the incident off and asked the commandant to collect money from the women to repair the door and to leave it at that. The commandant was visibly relieved that he wouldn't have to fill out all the forms of an arrest warrant, at least twelve two-page copies for each of the would-be burglars. Because of the bad quality of the paper one couldn't press too hard with the pen so three copies were the most one could make each time without tearing the paper.

He insisted, a bit pompously though, that he would give the women a warning and a public scolding instead. He took the names of the shamefaced women and ordered them to pay two yuan each to Madam Liu to have the lock of the door repaired. He also told them that he would call them on stage that night, before Leader Hu started her struggle meeting, and that he would publicly criticise them for their crime. He told them that they ought to be grateful to Madam Liu for not pressing charges and also to Kunlen for not insisting to officially report them.

That evening the commandant came to the Party centre and called the women on stage.

He told the crowd what the women had been up to and then he called on Madam Liu Meiling to step forward and receive the culprits' apologies.

Madam Liu had not bothered to turn up so the commandant called Kunlen on the stage to receive the apologies instead. He made a bit of a show of it, reprimanding the women for rumour-mongering as that was the main cause of social envy and unproletarian curiosity, the commandant said.

The crowd, except of course the red-faced husbands and children, laughed and cheered and applauded the commandant's wisdom and magnanimity to leave the matter at that.

Later that evening I saw Madam Liu enter the hall, in the middle of Kunlen's act. She remained standing near the door though, and I saw her frowning as she listened to Kunlen. As usual on the Wednesday evening he roused the audience with the audacities of Long Wei, the Revolutionary Socialist Youth Brigade Leader.

Long Wei was Kunlen's most recent creation. Ever since he first introduced Long Wei to the audience I had been apprehensive about the whole idea. Long Wei's adventures and accomplishments, thanks to his unwavering faith in Chairman Mao's thoughts, were even more ludicrous than the tales invented by the Party's own propaganda department.

I repeatedly told Kunlen so after his performances and that I was afraid Leader Hu would make trouble for him and for me as well. She couldn't be that stupid not to see that his whole act was one big mockery.

However, he just laughed at me defiantly and mocked me for my fears.

'You know, Su Ping,' he said. 'I actually *am* Long Wei. Only I gave him qualities which are in every respect the opposite of my own. Where I am a mocker of authority and discipline, Long Wei is the obedient arse-licker. Where I am the malingering dodger of my socialist duties, Long Wei is the holier-than-thou socialist saint. Where I am the great pretender-believer in Mao's humbug, Long Wei is the ultimate, the absolute believer, the idiot who would actually eat Mao's shit and say it tastes like cake.

'When I make Long Wei do things even a *moron*, a non-Communist moron that is, would recognise as fairy tale nonsense, I actually appeal to every normal person's sense of ridicule. Once people start to laugh it will be the beginning of the end of this degrading craze and, hopefully, of that sly, double-dealing, moon-faced, megalomaniac peasant from Hunan. He will be swept away by the roaring gale of laughter from a billion Chinese. By exaggerating Long Wei's exploits I hope to open people's minds when they try to imitate him.

'Last week my friend Chou Weijun asked for a replacement smoked-glass plate for his welding mask. The new Party secretary of our factory unit, a pimply bed-wetter, told Weijun he didn't need a mask if he wholeheartedly followed Mao's thoughts. Weijun is now blind for the rest of his life, the poor devil, and no incantations from the Little Red Book will give him back his eyesight.

'However, Long Wei does not exhort people to do things that make them blind, or deaf, or whatever. On the contrary! He cures the blind and the deaf mute and the lame and the leper, all feats that people can try to emulate. Where Long Wei succeeds though, they won't and I count on it that that'll set them thinking that perhaps those so-called magic 'thoughts' are nothing but a lot of dangerous nonsense.'

I begged Kunlen to stop acting the lone crusader and instead to pretend to go along with the system and its maniacs, if only for my sake and that of his unborn child.

'One man cannot undo the system or even hope to change it,' I said to him.

'Oh yes, he can,' he replied. 'Look at what Mao did. He started it all by himself, with just a gang of illiterate peasants from Hunan. What can be done by one man can also be undone by one man. And Mao knows that and that's why he eliminates all those of his former comrades who he perceives, in his paranoia, as his competitors for power. You know that, Su Ping. Those whom we glorify today, we vilify tomorrow. And the people don't even notice that the names in the slogans have changed, sometimes overnight, let alone ask "*Why*?" or "*How come*?" It drives me mad, Su Ping! I can't stand the fools! The loner who still has his wit and the guts to lift his finger and ask, however timidly, "Can you explain, please?" is silenced, locked up in a cell so small that he can't stretch his arms and legs. Can you imagine the pain, Su Ping? Or he is deported to Shanxi's open coal pits. But whatever, unless he grovels and repents and conforms and never opens his mouth again to question the Party, he'll be out of circulation for good.'

I am quite familiar with my country's history and I knew that Kunlen was right. One man can change it all, only I didn't believe that Li Kunlen was such a man. He didn't have the character, the personality, but how to tell him that?

All throughout our long and turbulent history there has popped up on the scene that single-minded and ruthless individual, local hero or highway brigand, saint or devil, soldier or philosopher, who managed to rally the downtrodden and oppressed behind his banner and to overthrow the reigning power of the moment, usurping, for better or worse, usually worse, power for himself, only to be overthrown again when, in turn, *he* went too far in his abuse of the people.

It's always the same pattern.

The man who assumes power by force becomes automatically the hero, his past sins and execrable misdeeds forgiven but not forgotten.

That's the Chinese way. We Chinese do not resent power, however autocratic, or even despotic; actually we have never known otherwise. What we *do* resent, however, is *abuse* of power, blatant favouritism and corruption.

Reasonable favours for services rendered, in both directions, is acceptable, however. It is even considered the normal way of life. Everybody accepts it and everybody would do the same if he had the power. We are a reasonable people.

But excesses are something different. They are not *reasonable* and when they become too much to bear we rally behind the banner of yet another hero who promises us justice and equality before the law.

However, it was always the *peasants* who rallied, never the city dwellers, and I did not believe Kunlen capable of rallying even *one* peasant behind him. Earthy as they are, they would see through him as the smooth-talking fake he was. He couldn't fool them even for one minute.

They would know instinctively that for Kunlen it was either a game or the vindictiveness of the peeved child and that when the going got rough he would abandon them just like that and hide, probably under the nearest skirt.

Besides, this time it might just be different from all those previous times.

'Power comes out of the barrel of a gun,' Mao always said, 'and the Party holds the gun and will use it,' he could have added. Not that that was necessary. Everybody understood. Just as it was understood that as long as the Party held the gun nobody else did. Many times I argued with Kunlen about these things, whispering in his ear, in the safety of our bed, after his Wednesday night performances.

But he didn't listen. Kunlen never liked to listen to people who didn't agree with him; he was too much in love with himself. I told him about my mother who used to be a teacher of history and culture at a middle school in Luding and who taught me China's real history, in the evening, at home.

During the day, in school, I had of course to learn the Party's revised and sanitised version, from my own mother to boot. Mother taught me how to draw parallels between past and present events and my father, who was a teacher of mathematics at the same school, showed me how to analyse the factors that caused those events, and how, based on that analysis, to make a reasoned prediction of the future.

And now, the first person to whom I explained my theories, my own husband at that, laughed in my face and treated me as if I were a backward peasant girl. As if I were on sufferance in such intellectual company as Li Kunlen's, but barely, and only on condition not to argue.

Oh, he was intelligent, no doubt about that, and I was often surprised at the extent of his knowledge – not at the depth though. Lacking formal education, middle school and higher, he couldn't know that educated people try to reason and to separate fact from fiction, or even from mere assumption. That they put you in your place, gently or rudely, when you get carried away or confuse wistful thinking and proof, so that you learn to be modest and to think before you say something.

I had come to dread those Wednesday nights and not only because I feared for Kunlen's and my own safety.

The morning after that particular Wednesday evening when she had come to listen to Kunlen, Madam Liu stood in front of her house, apparently waiting for me to pass by on my way to work.

She greeted me, very friendly, and invited me to come inside for a moment.

She asked me to sit down and offered me a mug of green tea which I accepted politely, wondering what it was all about. While I sipped my tea, a bit uneasily, Madam Liu watched me pensively over the rim of her own mug.

'I thank you for what you and your husband did yesterday to protect my house,' Madam Liu began, a bit formally I thought. 'Those harpies wouldn't have found what they were looking for, some kind of proof undoubtedly for the ridiculous rumours they have been spreading around about me. I wouldn't be so stupid to keep whatever could incriminate me, or others for that matter, in this hovel here. However, you didn't know that and both of you took a big risk in taking my side. I am therefore in your debt.'

She peremptorily waved aside my protest that it was nothing, really, and she continued.

'Unfortunately I won't be able to do something for your husband when, not *if*, mind you, he gets himself into trouble with those mockeries of his. His act is good, no doubt about that, and his motives are also laudable from his point of view at least. However, he just hasn't the stature to worry the Party. He is just a nuisance, a buzzing, irritating fly that will be squashed as soon as it sits down for a moment. Leader Hu hates him and that not only for mocking her dignity as this neighbourhood's Party leader.

'I found out that Li once mocked her dignity as a woman and rejected her somewhat clumsy advances and boasted about it in public. That was bad and unnecessary. A man can't sometimes help it if he hurts a woman's feelings, however, if he is an understanding and compassionate man, he'll do what he can to be kind and discreet, whoever the woman is, and she will eventually learn to accept and, above all, she will remain grateful for his discretion. Hu has no reason whatsoever to be grateful and she won't spare Li Kunlen, believe me. She just waits for a tangible error on his part to pounce on him and, looking at you, I wonder if he hasn't already committed that error.

'I think that you are pregnant, Su Ping, and, if true, you have defied Hu's authority one time too many, I'm afraid. You blush, Su Ping, so I have guessed right, eh? I can help you, if you want, to get an abortion in a clinic in a different part of town so that Hu won't hear about it. I just mention it. Think about it. Don't be rash but don't be of two minds for too long either.

'I know you are angry that an evil person like Hu can abuse her official power with impunity and make your life miserable just to vent her personal spite upon Kunlen and yourself. There's no justice for people like you, Su Ping, you can go nowhere to find redress for your grievance, you'll even be locked up if you complain too loudly. Because I know a thing or two about a man or two, who wouldn't like what I know become public knowledge I can pull a string now and then or twist an arm here or there so that the Hus leave me in relative peace.

'But those not so lucky can only accept what is decided for them, bow their head and squeeze their eyes so as not to show the tears of helpless rage lest they make a bad situation even worse. However, I tell you, Su Ping, that one day the Party will have done with Hu and her ilk and discard them as the trash they are, even blame them for the present aberrations and mistakes. They'll be shunned by the new hopefuls as the living reminders of shameful deeds the

Party wants buried and forgotten. Shunned by the Party, cast out by society, they'll live their dreary lives in hate and bitterness feeling used and betrayed. You and I will both live to see that happen, Su Ping.'

Madam Liu fell silent, snorted and said, a bit ironically, 'I see wariness in your eyes, Su Ping. You wonder why I say all this to you, eh? A total stranger. The thought has passed your mind that I'm perhaps trying to trick you, to make you confide in me and report you to Hu later.'

Madam Liu smiled and gestured that I need not bother to protest.

'No offence taken,' she said, 'it's better to be cautious. You see, Su Ping, I know who you are and where you're from, I found that out. Why? Sheer curiosity, I'm afraid. I happen to know a few people who are very good friends of one of the two men your parents trusted and sheltered and treated as family when they had been branded social lepers by the Party. I once knew that man, Chen Dan, myself and I owe him. By helping you I can at least repay a small part of my debt to him. However, as I have said already, this has nothing to do with your husband. I simply cannot ask my friends to take risks for Li Kunlen. You will understand once I'm free to tell you who these friends are. For now I suggest that you talk to your husband and try to persuade him to stop playing the hero.'

I remember how I sat there, struggling with conflicting emotions caused by what that strange and enigmatic woman had told me.

On the one hand I knew that she was right about everything she had said. About me expecting, about Kunlen's character and buffoonery and how he put our very lives in jeopardy by his foolhardiness.

On the other hand my heart rebelled at the woman's superior air, at her nonchalant dismissal of Kunlen as too unimportant to bother about and her just as casual assumption that I agreed with that assessment of my husband.

But most of all I was angry because of her unsolicited offer to arrange for me to abort my child.

I knew also that I was being unreasonable, which made it even worse.

Madam Liu was just trying to be helpful and friendly and, after all, I had not wanted to become pregnant, had I? And now this woman knew my secret, all my secrets. It just wasn't fair.

I felt the blood rush to my head and was about to explode when I looked up in to Madam Liu's eyes. The sympathy and compassion I saw in her eyes made the fear and anger flow out of me and I cried and cried, with big heaving sobs and a lot of snot and slobber.

I felt a pair of big, strong arms around me and a hand that stroked the back of my head and kneaded the nape of my neck and after a while I calmed down.

★

Su Ping fell silent and looked at Auntie Liu, her eyes brimming with tears.

Lao Dee saw that the older woman was equally moved by the memories the two of them shared and he felt excluded, like the others, out of place.

Then Auntie Liu laughed and broke the spell.

'For a long time I held that little heap of female misery in my arms,' she said, still moved by the memory.

'I stroked that splendid mass of glossy, flowing long hair and couldn't help smiling at the occasional shudder welling up from all the way down in her belly.'

Lilian bit her lower lip so as not to cry as her mother wiped the tears from her eyes with the back of her right hand.

Su Ping continued with her tale.

★

How long I laid there, on my knees beside the couch, my head in Auntie's lap, I don't know. I felt the anxiety that had been building up all those months since Hongbayue slowly drain away and the relief was almost sensual in its intensity.

I finally woke up from my reverie when Auntie Liu, Madam Liu I should say, shifted her position.

'You have been far away,' Madam Liu said.

'I shall now go and see Matron at the kindergarten and tell her that you are not feeling well and won't be coming in today. Next I shall kick your famous husband out of his nest and tell him to join us here for a light midday meal. Tomorrow he can tell his leader that he was ill and couldn't come to work. The man won't care, shortly nobody will turn up any more, anyhow. Then I shall buy a nice, fat chicken and fresh noodles and you and I will prepare a good, rich chicken and noodle soup for the three of us.

'After our meal you will tell us about yourself and your parents and about what happened to you when Lan Ping, that chicken-brained third-rate so-called artist who got into our Great Helmsman's pants, started her crazy vendetta against whoever she imagined did ever slight her, or her god, in the past. Jiang Qing, the senile old dodderer called her; Jiang Hong or Gou Fuchao would have been more appropriate for that vindictive bitch. You will tell us about your trek after Hongbayue and how you ended up here in this dreary town.

'Talking about this will take that load off your mind that has been weighing you down for the past two years while it will give cocky Kunlen something to think about. Hopefully it will teach him some modesty and make him realise how lucky he is having you as his wife. Now, while I am on my errands, you wash your face and your hair with this nice-smelling soap in this fancy bottle. An alien from a different galaxy and time gave it to me as a present long ago, longer than I care to remember. I'll be back in an hour or so. Be good!' With that Madam Liu Meiling pulled the front door shut behind her.

I had listened absent-mindedly to Auntie Liu's instructions. Vaguely I was aware that I was supposed to wash my hair, eat soup and talk about myself.

The bottle of soap Madam Liu had given me had a strange yet beautiful shape. It had a dark blue and gold label, showing, in profile, a beautiful foreign girl with long, wavy golden hair and a long, straight nose. I chuckled at the thought that the soap might make my hair also golden and my snub-nose long and straight.

Kunlen would like that, I thought, it would give him prestige, that vain peacock. 'Yeeeon! Yeeeon! Look at beautiful me and my pretty foreign hen! Yeeeon! Yeeeon!'

Angrily I went into the wash-house behind the kitchen and bent over the tub. With a saucepan I scooped the water from the tub and poured it over my head. I gasped at the sudden, cold shock and then I laughed at my own silliness.

Happily I put a cupped handful of the fragrant liquid soap on my wet hair and rubbed it in with my fingertips for a few minutes. Then I ladled pan after pan of water over my head to rinse out the soap, eyes closed.

When I opened my eyes to grope for the towel I was struck by the enormous amount of foam already flowing over the rim of the tub, in a thick, greenish, cascading stream on to the wash-house floor.

I stood stock-still. As if mesmerised I stared at the greenish blobs and suddenly a memory washed over me like a wave of putrefaction and I was back in Changsha's train station, the little old man toppled over against my legs, vomiting over my shoes and socks in an endless, greenish, sour stream.

I actually felt the acrid stench burn in my nose and heard the demented screams of the Red Guard, who had kicked the old man to death, inside my head. I retched and vomited and cried, my forehead on the rim of the tub.

Vaguely I heard the front door being opened and closed, then two voices, a man and a woman talking, and suddenly I felt myself being lifted off the ground by two strong arms behind my knees and shoulders and carried out of the wash-house.

I noticed Madam Liu's body odour and breath on my face as she laid me down on a bed.

'Ghosts of the past haunting you, my dear?' I heard her say. 'We'll soon get rid of them. Don't you worry. Breathe deeply and slowly while you stay here in this dark room. I'll call you when the soup is ready. I'll add some fish sauce and fresh ginger, that'll do you good. Now don't worry about a thing and try to sleep a bit.'

I heard Kunlen's voice in the room, asking, 'What's the matter with my wife? Why is she sick here, in your house?'

'We'll soon know,' I heard Madam Liu reply and continue. 'Now get out of here and go clean the chicken for me, behind the kitchen, outside. When you're ready I'll prepare the soup and by then Su Ping will feel much better already. Don't stand there as if you see snot burning. Out! Out!'

I heard the door being closed and footsteps fading away. I must have drifted off to sleep as suddenly I woke up to a delicious smell of chicken soup. I opened my eyes and saw Madam Liu looking down at me, laughing.

'I knew the smell would wake you up,' she said, smiling, 'that's why I opened the door a few minutes ago. No need to shake you. It didn't take two minutes and you started sniffing. Very funny. Now, get up and come with me. Kunlen is waiting, hungry no doubt.'

Quickly I got up and followed Madam Liu into the front room.

I shook my head a few times from left to right and back to relieve the stiffness in my neck and to make my hair fall nicely. It fell supple and loose and it smelled of flowers. Kunlen sat at the table and looked up when I came in. He seemed ill at ease and awkward. He smiled, however, and asked how I felt.

I smiled also and said I felt fine.

'Now, sit down and enjoy the food,' Madam Liu said. 'The chicken was quite expensive so we had better not talk while we eat lest we forget to taste the soup and the fresh noodles. Such a shame that would be. First we eat and then we talk. No, that's not what I meant. First we eat and then *you* talk, Su Ping, while Kunlen and I listen. Take all the time you need, Su Ping. We have the whole afternoon and the evening as well.

'I told Hu that I need both of you here tonight to help me sort out my papers. That'll make her sick with curiosity. Enough talk for now. Let's eat!' And Madam Liu gave the good example by serving herself a very generous portion of noodles and chicken and not too much liquid.

Kunlen and I followed her example and for the next twenty minutes we enjoyed the food. After that we took a short nap.

Madam Liu was the first to wake up and her stretching and groaning woke us up in turn.

'Kunlen, you and I will clean the dishes and the kitchen and prepare hot water in the thermos for tea,' she ordered. 'Su Ping, you clear that table, please, and then sit down to collect your thoughts so that you can tell us a coherent story.'

And so it happened.

Madam Liu put three mugs with green tea leaves on the small, low table and then filled the mugs with steaming hot water from the thermos. Sitting down next to Kunlen, her hands cupped around her mug, she said, 'Any time you're ready you can begin, dear.'

Sipping from the hot, bitter tea, now and then spitting back a leaf that had got stuck between my teeth, I watched Madam Liu and Kunlen through the vapour that twirled around my nose and my eyes.

Slowly they faded into the background as my mind regressed to that one particular scene in our small garden in Luding, when for the first time I had a foreboding of what was going to happen to me, to us, to our poor people. A foreboding of the unimaginably malevolent forces that were going to be unleashed all over China by screaming, raging demons; of upheavals so gigantic that they would spiral completely out of even the instigators' control; of the shattered lives of a whole people.

I shivered as I began to tell my story, a shorter version of what I will tell you later today.

I talked until nine that evening, pausing only once for a bowl of rice with what was left of the soup.

Madam Liu and Kunlen didn't interrupt me with questions or comments. Even during our short break we hardly spoke.

It was past ten o'clock when a very subdued Kunlen and I went finally home. Just before leaving we told Madam Liu that I would keep the baby, come what may.

She said nothing at first, she just embraced me. Then she grumbled over my shoulder at Kunlen, 'You can be proud of your wife, young man. I only hope she can be proud of you as well when the shit hits the fan. Take the blame when Hu confronts you for defying her authority. Tell her you forced your wife and pay the bill, like a man, whatever the price.'

When I turned to look at him I saw tears in his eyes.

In an attempt at levity he said he wouldn't duck the shit.

A month after that memorable day at Madam Liu's, Leader Hu began her reign of real terror. She had been away for ten days and even her Red Guards, who had lost most of their revolutionary zeal by then, didn't know where she had gone or why. Only Lao Yang cackled to whoever would listen that Hu's absence was a bad omen.

The leader of his son's neighbourhood, in the northern part of the city, had also suddenly disappeared. Lao Yang said his son had heard rumours that in other big cities the infamous People's Tribunals, after a year of relative inactivity, had begun their witch-hunt again following a whirlwind tour by Jiang Qing and her courtiers through the country's main cities.

His son had told him, Lao Yang said, that the People's Tribunals had received fixed quotas for condemnations of confessed counter-revolutionary renegades, a certain percentage, he said, of the population over eighteen years old.

Leader Hu had undoubtedly been summoned to Shenyang, Lao Yang said, to receive her instructions on how to blow new life into the sagging Cultural Revolution in her area and to be told her quota of renegades. If for two consecutive months she didn't meet her quota, she herself would be accused of lacking in revolutionary zeal and dedication to Chairman Mao and be sent for re-education to a people's commune, Lao Yang cackled with undisguised glee. I didn't think there was much chance of that ever happening.

Frightened by Lao Yang's dire predictions everybody waited worriedly for Hu's return from her secret mission.

Then, one evening, she was back at the community centre and from the first moment she opened her mouth everybody knew it would be bad, very bad.

People had been trickling into the court of the centre, the former school, and by eight o'clock most of us were there, talking good-naturedly together as had been the case for the past four months or so.

Suddenly the windows on the first floor were thrown open, one pane breaking into smithereens as it banged against the wall, and Hu appeared in the opening. Well orchestrated, her Red Guards, all pumped up again and each armed with a long, wooden truncheon, poured forth from the door of the centre into the yard and took up positions around the crowd.

Everybody fell silent and looked up at Hu in the window apprehensively. All were expecting something bad but she surpassed our worst fears.

Had her harangues in the past always been edifying, in the twisted Communist way of seeing things, exhorting us to show true revolutionary zeal and ardour, she now poured a stream of invective over our heads, in such a hysterically screaming voice that I saw people instinctively pull up their shoulders as if to protect themselves against the verbal assault.

She went on and on, beating the window sill with a short, thick piece of wood, a sort of mallet, during the worst passages of her diatribe, as if she wanted to hammer into our numbed brains our utter worthlessness, our total depravity, our complete humiliation.

She stopped the vituperation as suddenly as she had begun and ordered the Red Guards, in a stern voice, to escort us into the building. Threatening us with their truncheons, actually hitting those in the rear who were not quick enough, the Red Guards herded us into the meeting hall.

I was in the front and as soon as I came into the hall, pushed and shoved in the back by the herd behind me, I recognised the scene.

Just as in Luding, two years ago, I found myself face to face again with a People's Tribunal, not yet as an accused individual but certainly as a faceless member of a collectively guilty crowd.

There she sat, our Leader Hu Guoshang, behind a long, wooden table covered with a piece of overhanging red cloth. On each side of her sat four strangers in rumpled dark blue and dark green suits, four women and four men, in their forties and fifties.

From the shape of their faces, the grubbiness of their whole appearance, the stubble on the men's faces, the lacklustre, unkempt hair of the women, the indifference in their small eyes, I knew these strangers were the worst kind of peasants, the kind from whom no one, however slightly above their status, whether real or in appearance only, could expect the tiniest iota of compassion. Above the heads of the members of the People's Tribunal, against the wall, hung a red banner with big, white characters saying, 'Expose and Eradicate the Enemies of the People'.

On the overhanging flap of the tablecloth, the big characters read, 'Reward For Those Who Denounce Others'.

When everybody was finally inside, the Red Guards closed the doors and took up positions along the walls. Leader Hu stared at the crowd until the last whisper and shuffling of feet had died down. She then hit the table with her mallet and with such force that the elderly woman on her right jumped up in fright.

There were a few giggles in the crowd, mine included, and I saw that Hu was annoyed.

She hawked and harrumphed a few times and then said, loudly, 'I have been appointed by the Party's provincial headquarters in Shenyang as the prosecutor and chief judge of this People's Tribunal. It is my duty to eradicate the counter-revolutionary enemies of the Party and People who are surreptitiously undermining the Great Proletarian Cultural Revolution in this neighbourhood.

'During her recent visit to Shenyang, Comrade Jiang Qing has personally identified the many nests of vipers in Liaoning Province and she has unerringly put her finger on this particular neighbourhood as a hotbed of clandestine agitation against the dictatorship of the proletariat. To make it clear that nothing can be hidden from her, Comrade Jiang Qing even indicated the exact number of traitors of the people's cause and I have been entrusted with the task to find and destroy each and every one of the vermin. Though I know the number of traitors amongst you, thanks to Comrade Jiang Qing's incredible intelligence, I do not know yet who they are, at least not all. But I'll find them, trust me on that count. So unless you can prove your innocence I consider each of you guilty of treason and the only way I see that you can prove your innocence is by denouncing the real traitors amongst you. It's as simple as that.

'Each month I have to expose and condemn ten counter-revolutionary traitors. If the denunciations and the resulting condemnations number less than ten I shall pick at random anyone amongst you and make him, or her, confess. I shall *not* fail the Party and Comrade Jiang Qing. Remember the instruction of our beloved Party "Lenient treatment for those who confess, severe punishment for those who remain stubborn".'

Hu fell silent and let her eyes roam over the stunned and apprehensive crowd.

I had watched the other judges while Hu said those terrible things. The four women had watched the crowd with a baleful look, sneers curling their lips. I was sure that any attempt to defend oneself against the accusations would be taken as a traitorous act in itself by those harpies, as a brazen act of defiance against the authority invested in them by the Party and therefore against the Party itself, by definition a treasonous act.

So each case would be a matter of either guilty by own admission or by implication. There was no escape. Once you were called in front of the bench you were lost. The four male judges had not once shown signs of interest. Two of them had actually had difficulty staying awake during Hu's address, starting up each time their lolling heads almost touched the bench.

It was obvious that Hu and her four witches were going to run the show and that the men were just going to assent to whatever the five women would decree.

They reminded me of a cartoon I once saw. The cartoonist had depicted the Western nations as a pack of drooling, exultant hyenas watching their hapless prey, the Third World in that case, die in agony before they would pounce and tear it to pieces. The abject mortal fear and despair in the wildly rolling eyes of the prey was uncanny and still makes me shiver after all these years.

For a fraction of a second I felt Hu's eyes lock on to mine and the sheer, exultant malice was like a physical blow to my head and I reeled from the impact.

I was the prey and I knew there was no escape.

Numb with fear I heard Hu say, 'The first official session of this People's Tribunal is set for tomorrow morning at ten o'clock. My office will be open as from eight o'clock to receive advance confessions in writing or denunciations. Denunciations must be made in person and must be substantiated by proof or be easily traceable.

'Those making false or unsubstantiated accusations will be considered guilty of an attempt to discredit the Party which carries a mandatory sentence of twenty years' hard labour. During the trials the evening struggle meetings are suspended. Everyone over the age of twelve and falling under the jurisdiction of this People's Tribunal must attend the sessions. Factories and shops will be closed as from tomorrow to allow everybody to attend. Absence is an admission of guilt. You are now dismissed!' With a bang of her mallet Hu punctuated the end of her address, shocking me back into the sordid reality.

The Red Guards opened the door and, like zombies in a horror film, people began to file out of the hall. As I had been in the front row I was among the last to step into the cool night outside.

I saw people glancing at each other furtively, as if they were sizing each other up as possible victims to be sacrificed to save their own skin.

When I came home Kunlen was already there.

Nervously cracking his fingers he said, 'The factory will only work night shifts as of tomorrow. The People's Tribunal ordered the factory to close, however, our factory manager decided to work on night shift only.

'I volunteered and my leader accepted. I don't know how he is going to pay me though. The factory has run out of money. The last few months people haven't paid for the bicycles, they just took them. Our new unit secretary decreed that the factory could no longer demand payment from the people.

'Paying for things is bourgeois, not proletarian, he said, and why would they pay for something that belonged to them already anyway? In a true proletarian society everything belongs to everybody, he said. Everybody either produces things or serves the people according to his abilities and takes according to his needs, so there is no need for money, the moron said.

'The factory's till was empty yesterday, for the first time in its history, so my manager went to see leader Hu today, having heard that she had come back from Shenyang. We went to his house tonight to ask him how his mission went. From far we heard his wife wailing. When we asked her what happened she cried that her husband had been arrested at the Party secretary's behest, for anti-proletarian agitation. His case will probably be the first one on the agenda tomorrow. What can we do, Su Ping? How can we live without money if this craze becomes general policy? Do I have to go out and take, or steal, what we need for our living?'

I told him what Hu had said at the community centre.

When I had finished we just stared at each other wordlessly, too afraid and too worried to find words of comfort.

We slept fitfully that night, lying awake for long periods, staring in the dark, aware the other was awake as well yet not talking, premonitions of impending doom churning in our minds.

The following morning, at nine o'clock, the doors of the court hall, as the meeting place was called henceforth, were opened by the Red Guards and the good people of the neighbourhood trooped inside.

At ten o'clock exactly Chief Judge-cum-Prosecutor Hu Guoshang and her eight judges filed in and took their seats behind the bench. Following a resounding bang with her mallet Hu announced, in a loud voice, 'People's Tribunal Number Four of Dalian south is now in session!'

Her imitation of the inflexions of her Beijing mentors didn't sound at all well in her uncultured voice.

'Leading Red Guard, bring the first accused forward!' Hu intoned and two Red Guards, pushing a man by his shoulders, came through a door at the right of the judges' bench, followed by a tall, gangly youth I had never seen before. Apparently it was the leading Red Guard. He held a whip in his right hand.

'That's my manager, Yang Yikun,' Kunlen whispered in my ear, 'so it's true what his wife told us yesterday.'

Manager Yang was forced to his knees by the two Red Guards, who then stood aside while only the leading Red Guard remained standing behind the defendant, lovingly gliding his whip through his left hand.

'State your name and occupation!' Hu shouted at the prostrated man.

'Yang Yikun, manager of the White Rabbit Bicycle Factory,' Yang replied in a calm and clear voice.

'You are accused of anti-proletarian agitation by the Party secretary of your unit, Comrade Wu Hongmao!' Hu shouted. 'What is your answer to this accusation? Do you confess?'

'I will not dignify such rubbish with a reply, or you for that matter,' Yang said clearly and the audience gasped.

'Five lashes, give him five lashes!' Hu screamed, outraged. 'Five lashes for contempt of the court!'

The Red Guard, a youth probably not yet twenty years old, whipped the grey-haired, elderly man, who could have been his father, with all his might.

I distinctly heard the swishing sound of the thong before it bit into Yang's back with a kind of slurping sound. At the third lash a dark stain appeared in Yang's green jacket. His back had been ripped open in spite of his jacket and he was bleeding.

I heard Kunlen suck in his breath after each lash and, glancing sideways at him, I saw that he was crying.

Yang didn't utter a sound though and when Hu shouted at him, after the Red Guard stood back, panting, 'I repeat my question to you, Yang: do you confess?' he merely shrugged his shoulders.

This horrible drama went on for nearly half an hour and then Yang fainted, while the Red Guard, red-faced and wild-eyed, was administering what must have been the fortieth lash.

The two assistant Red Guards carried the unconscious man into the classroom next door, kicking the door shut behind them.

Yang had never uttered a word or even a groan after his first insult to Hu, which had been a veritable verbal lash for her. The whole case had become a disaster for Hu; she had suffered a terrible loss of face and from her flushed, angry face I knew that she realised this.

The initial whispers in the crowd became an audible murmur and I was sure Kunlen was about to say something loudly when Hu seized the initiative again and shouted, 'The criminal Yang will be interrogated further in closed chambers and sentence will be passed tomorrow! Next case!'

The next case was a man, not from our alley, who had been denounced by his own son of fourteen for complaining about the closure of the schools and universities a year ago and for making the remark that China would become the laughing stock of the world for producing a whole generation of morons. The man was accused of inciting counter-revolution and the audience was forced to shout its support for Hu's wild summing-up of all the misdeeds to which such could lead.

Red Guards posted along the walls were monitoring the ardour of the spectators' acclamations and those thought to be lacking were dragged from where they stood to before the bench and forced down on their knees next to the defendant.

Hu accused them of conspiring with the accused to subvert the dictatorship of the proletariat and ordered their immediate arrest.

We quickly realised that the safest way was to simply stare ahead, unseeing, and shout 'Yeah! Yeah! Yeah!' during Hu's accusations and, better still, to add abuse like 'stinking renegade' or 'dirty traitor,' or 'revisionist dog' when you felt one of the Red Guards was looking in your direction.

It was both terrible and pathetic.

Hu reached her daily quota of three to four condemnations, however, it was such pathetically small stuff that even Hu must have realised that there was little glory to be got for her in this neighbourhood, in spite of Comrade Jiang Qing calling it a hotbed of counter-revolutionary activities.

We were all such ordinary people; simple, unassuming heroes in our own way, who tried to simply ignore Hu's snotty Red Guards and her own increasingly strident and threatening exhortations to denounce neighbours or friends or relatives for whatever anti-socialist act or remark.

We had already gone through all that a year or so ago and people were simply sick and tired of the foolishness of it all.

So there were remarkably few denunciations and I was proud of my neighbourhood.

Hu became, therefore, increasingly dependent on her own inventiveness to find her victims. So she reinstated the nightly struggle meetings with renewed vigour.

People lacking zeal during the loud and rhythmical chanting of the denouncements, vilifications and glorifications, or those who found nothing or not enough to criticise in themselves or in their fellows, or, worse, those who mixed up the names to be vilified and the ones to be glorified, were singled out by the Red Guards, or by Hu herself, and accused of harbouring reactionary, subversive thoughts. The poor devils were not allowed to go home after the meeting but were, instead, psychologically browbeaten and physically abused during the rest of the night, at the centre, the Red Guards and Hu taking turns, until, completely exhausted, they finally confessed to some thought crime or attitude crime or other.

The punishment was heavy though. Five years of re-education in a people's commune was the mildest sentence.

During the third week of her reign as People's Tribunal prosecutor, Hu devised a new method of intimidation and victimisation for the more serious cases.

Those who had been pronounced guilty of whatever misdeed were made to stand, for a day and a night, in front of the community centre, regardless of the weather, with a piece of white cloth around their neck, their crime written on it in big, red characters. The condemned were transported early evening by truck to the city's detention centre from where they were deported, together with the victims of other People's Tribunals, to people's communes for re-education or to labour camps in other, remote provinces.

Hu was determined to best her quota of renegades.

Rumours had it that if she did not meet her quota she would be sent herself to a commune in some godforsaken, remote place, to work in the fields with the production brigade and the peasants, twelve hours a day, seven days a week, followed by four hours every evening of political indoctrination and communal recitation of Chairman Mao's thoughts. That was something to condemn others to, not something she would wish for herself as a refresher course in socialism.

One remarkable fact was that Madam Liu, or Auntie Liu as she had told me to call her, never turned up for any court session or struggle meeting.

Even during those times of fanatical witch-hunting she appeared out of Hu's reach.

Kunlen and I had become much closer since I had poured my heart out at Auntie Liu's. He treated me with respect, even love and care and he had abandoned his boastful, cocky attitude towards other people as well. My pregnancy was now plainly visible and many people had already made good-humoured remarks and still there had been no reaction from Hu.

Against better judgement we let our fears slowly fade into the background of our daily preoccupations.

Then, one night, my whole world fell to pieces.

Heavy pounding on the door woke us with a start. Kunlen switched on the light and I noticed that his face was ashen and that he was perspiring heavily. With trembling hands he put on his trousers as the pounding became louder and louder.

Voices, outside in the alley, shouted his name, ordering him to open the door.

'They have come for me, my love,' he whispered and I could smell his fear. 'Stay here and first thing tomorrow morning go to Madam Liu and ask her for protection. Perhaps she can help me as well.'

Further words were cut off by the noise of the front door being kicked in and a dozen or so Red Guards trooping into our room behind their tall leader.

'Both of you! Get dressed!' he snarled. 'You are under arrest for open rebellion against the Party's explicit orders. You are to come with me to the court hall by order of Chief Judge and Leader Hu. Immediately!'

It was as if all life went out of Kunlen and he didn't protest when the Red Guards remained in our room and rummaged through our affairs while I took off my nightgown and put on my trousers and jacket.

Surrounded by angrily jabbering Red Guards, Kunlen and I were escorted, at a half-trot, to the court hall. People who had been awakened by the noise and gone outside to see what was going on were beaten up by the Red Guards, with their truncheons, and chased back inside their house.

In a flash I saw Auntie Liu wresting the weapon from a guard who was going to beat her and hitting him instead over his head. We were past Auntie's house already but behind me I heard the boy yelp in pain.

The leader turned his head and, without interrupting his trot, he shouted at the hapless guard, 'Leave the old hag alone', 'move, move!'

At the community centre, or court hall, the guards locked us up in two separate rooms on the first floor.

I tried to get Kunlen's attention before they locked the door behind me, hoping fervently for a glance, a gesture, anything that would tell me he was thinking of me, cared about me, but in vain. He was tearfully engrossed in himself, his lips trembling and I could smell the acridness of his wretched fear as the guards shoved him roughly past me into the adjacent room. I was disappointed and embarrassed by his disarray in front of the young Red Guards.

I wasn't surprised though as I had known all along that Kunlen was a hero only to himself, in his dreams and fantasies, not in the real world. Also, I didn't feel alone as for the first time I felt my child clearly.

She, I always thought of the baby as a she, I don't know why, was kicking violently, probably not happy with my early morning run which must have disturbed her own sleep as well. The wall clock showed four o'clock in the morning, and it was still dark outside.

Nobody came to see me and I just sat on the only chair, hands pressed against my belly to offer some resistance to the baby's kicking and to let her know I was there.

I was startled out of my introspection by Leader Hu barging into the room. Imperiously she motioned the Red Guards to stay outside. She slammed the door shut and stared down at me, balefully. I looked up at her, smiled and patiently waited for her to say what she had come to say.

Momentarily disconcerted by my attitude, she quickly regained her composure and, scowling, she snarled, 'You will appear before the People's Tribunal at ten o'clock on charges of aiding and abetting your husband in committing the heinous crime of sedition against the People's government. It is my intention to refer you to the High Tribunal in Shenyang with the recommendation to sentence you to death.'

I couldn't help laughing. 'Sentence me to death for conceiving a child?' I asked, acting incredulous. 'Are you inferring that I raped my husband?'

'We have your man's confession,' Hu exulted, 'a sworn statement that you deliberately misled him into believing that you had taken the usual precautions before intercourse and that he was appalled when you told him six weeks later that you were pregnant.'

It was as if my heart stopped and, eyes stinging with tears, ears ringing, I heard Hu's mocking voice, as through a thick fog, 'Li told me, in front of witnesses, that he wanted to report you immediately for your deliberate disobedience of my interdiction for you to have a child, however, you pleaded with him and promised him you would seek an abortion in the harbour clinic. Three days later you told him you had it done and he believed you. Later, however, he began to wonder how it was that you seem to become fatter by the week and why you were letting up in forcing yourself on him, although he was secretly relieved to be left in peace by you.

'Then one morning, last week, he confronted you when you were unwell in the kitchen and you admitted that you had lied to him and were still with child. He threatened to report you, to the People's Tribunal this time, so that you could be sent for abortion and subsequently be punished and undergo re-education. However, you threatened to kill yourself, Li told us, and he was left in a terrible quandary about what to do. His only crime is that he was weak-hearted and did not resolutely report you immediately as he should have; the resoluteness the Party demands from all of us when we have knowledge of a crime against the State and the Party.

'Today one of my judges, who used to be a midwife before she joined the Party, saw you in the street and immediately knew that you were at least three months pregnant. She asked me whether you had obtained my permission. You transgressed my ruling, so I had both of you arrested. Li is not at peace, having confessed and recognised that he has been amiss in his first duty, which is to the Party and not to you and your unborn child.

'He accepts that he will have to be punished and he begged me to set an example and send him for at least a year to a commune to live among the peasants and learn about the true socialist meaning of life. I will try to make the other judges go along with a ruling somewhat like that. Yours, however, is a different case entirely and no punishment can be severe enough for you.'

At that she left the room without further ado, slamming the door behind her.

I felt sick, my head was reeling and my stomach wanted to throw up, but only a sour liquid came up that burned my throat and nose.

I felt utterly betrayed by Kunlen and was about to throw myself on the floor to cry my heart out when I found that I had no such inclination at all and that instead a hot anger began to suffuse my whole being.

I was not going to let that happen to me.

I would fight and at least I would have the satisfaction of making Kunlen pay for his betrayal, for his cowardice, for his… and I fumed on and on.

I was so engrossed in making up beautiful, resounding sentences which I would pronounce before the court that I was surprised when the door opened brusquely and the leading Red Guard ordered me to stand up and precede him to the court hall.

A glance at the wall clock told me it was past ten o'clock. I got up from my chair, shrugged off the Red Guard's hands and walked determinedly through the corridor to the hall.

When he stepped past me to open the door, I proudly pushed my still only slightly protruding belly forward and entered the hall, walking with steps I made as resounding as possible along the path the buzzing crowd opened in front of me.

I stopped in front of the bench and looked, angrily defiant, around me.

Kunlen was already there, on his knees, in front of the bench. Contemptuously I ignored his timid smile.

I saw Auntie Liu in the front row and I gave her a grim yet grateful smile of recognition.

Then I faced the bench and waited.

The two Red Guards gripped my upper arms and tried to force me down on my knees.

Roughly and contemptuously I shrugged them off and announced clearly and loudly, 'In my position I will not kneel! I beg the court's indulgence. I do not mean to show disrespect!'

I saw Hu hesitate and look in the direction where I knew Auntie Liu was standing behind and to the right of me. Hu nodded at the Red Guards and said, surprisingly quietly, 'The defendant is allowed to remain standing'.

The buzz of the crowd became louder and Hu banged her gavel on the bench.

'Silence!' she shouted angrily. 'The court is in session! The People's Tribunal will now deal with the case of sedition and rebellion against the Party and the State by the criminals Li Kunlen and Li née Xu Suping. This is a very serious case and unless the criminals can prove mitigating circumstances, this court must recommend a mandatory death sentence for either or both of them to the Liaoning Provincial People's Tribunal in Shenyang. So the audience will remain silent and take heart that we have uncovered this heinous crime against our socialist laws!'

At that, Hu let her baleful eyes roam over the crowd until the silence was total.

Then she looked in turn at Kunlen and at me and began her interrogation.

'Li Kunlen and Li Xu Suping,' she began, speaking harshly, 'do you admit that on April 14th, May 15th and June 20th of this year you petitioned me, in my capacity as Party secretary of this neighbourhood, for permission to have a child? Answer yes or no only!'

I heard Kunlen's stammered 'Yes, comrade' beside and below me and I nodded.

'Nodding is *not* enough!' Hu snarled, 'Say loudly yes or no!'

'Yes!' I said loudly.

'What was my answer to each of your requests?' Hu asked.

'Our request was denied each time,' Kunlen answered softly.

'Louder!' Hu shouted. 'The People must hear you!'

'Our request was denied each time!' Kunlen cried.

'And what is your answer?' Hu then shouted at me.

'The same as his,' I replied calmly.

I saw Hu hesitate, however, she let my indirect answer pass.

'And what is your situation now!' Hu continued, looking at me triumphantly.

'I am with child,' I said, as proudly as I could.

The crowd behind me murmured excitedly.

Hu took the time to let my words sink in, then she banged her gavel and shouted, 'Silence! Silence!'

When the murmur had died down, she looked at me again and cried, 'You are with child?' and to emphasise how incredulous she was, she repeated, louder still, 'You are with child?' Then, shrilly, 'Do you mean to say that you deliberately and underhandedly transgressed my explicit order to refrain, for the time being and until such time as the Party sees fit, from having a child? Be careful how you answer,' she warned, in a calmer voice, 'I have here your husband's full confession.'

'I know about his confession, Leader Hu,' I replied indignantly. 'You yourself came to tell me early this morning, in that room where you kept me isolated for six hours, about how he had put the blame on me to get away with a light sentence himself. You know Kunlen, eh? Leader Hu? You know that he is easily scared and will do anything to save his hide. So you made a deal, didn't you?

'A light sentence for him in return for an aggravating accusation against me, because you so desperately need a big case. I refuse to play your game and to dignify both of you with denials and counter-accusations. Explain to the people here how you obtained Kunlen's confession and let him explain how a man can make a child against his will. You know the saying that you can lead a horse to water but that you can't make it drink? Well, with a man it's a bit like that, *you* should know that.'

The audience erupted in a roar of laughter and Hu, her face red with fury, banged her gavel repeatedly on the bench to restore order.

When finally the noise had abated somewhat, she said threateningly, 'You watch your big mouth, Xu! Your innuendoes about my behaviour will be held against you.'

Suddenly I recognised Auntie Liu's voice as she shouted, 'Request permission to speak for the defendant!'

'Permission denied!' Hu shouted back. 'You will remain silent or I'll have you expelled!'

'I will *not* remain silent!' Auntie Liu thundered. 'And you will *not* have me expelled! This is a so-called People's Tribunal and I am one of the People, so you also sit there in my name, to my eternal shame. You constantly exhort the people here to denounce and accuse. Is that our only role in your distorted concept of justice? I, Liu Meiling, now choose to speak up in *defence* of a person accused by you and another member of the people and that is my good right and I dare you to stop me!'

Hu scowled as the hall fell deadly silent.

'You can speak up,' she said reluctantly, 'however, be sure that what you say is pertinent to this case or else I'll have you arrested for contempt of this court.'

'Oh, you won't have that pleasure, I assure you,' Auntie Liu laughed, scornfully, 'not that your court isn't below my contempt though.

'Now then, to the point,' she continued, suddenly deadly serious. 'About six weeks ago, the day after my house was broken into, I had a talk with the defendant Xu Suping, in my house. I told her straightforwardly that I thought she was pregnant, that this was in defiance of your ruling and I asked her whether she wanted for me to arrange an abortion, discreetly of course, so that there would be no loss of face for anybody, including you, Hu.

'The defendant told me that she had felt the child moving in her body and that she could not bring herself to have it killed. That is how she called it:

*killed*! I did not insist. I respect her too much for that. However, I did ask her how it could happen that she, an intelligent girl, had done something that could only cause her trouble.

'She then told me how her husband, the defendant Li Kunlen now before you, had prevented her by force from using the anti-conception gel and had then forced himself in her and, after the short and pleasureless copulation, had again prevented her from rinsing herself with vinegar. If they were not married you could call it rape and I really wonder if you couldn't call it that anyhow. She also told me how hurt she had felt when, four weeks later, when she had told him she was afraid she was pregnant, he had merely laughed triumphantly and cried that that "would teach that sow Hu a lesson".'

I heard the crowd gasp in disbelief and I saw that Hu was close to an apoplexy.

'When later that day Li Kunlen came into my house,' Auntie Liu continued imperturbably, 'I reproached him for his callous behaviour towards his wife and his irresponsible attitude in general.

'Again Li laughed and said he was not going to be pushed around, certainly not by that sow Hu Guoshang, whose only aim was to get even with him for repudiating her advances a few years ago. He said that he knew what he was doing and that he was fully prepared to face the consequences and that his wife need not fear for herself. She was not to blame. Those were his words: *she is not to blame*! Now, from what I understand here, you have coaxed some kind of confession from him wherein he pretends just the opposite of what happened?'

I'll never forget that wicked sneer on Hu's face as she looked in turn at me and, past me, at Auntie Liu.

'I don't know where you get that idea,' she said, mockingly. 'All I told the defendant Xu was that I had Li's full confession. His confession is that he acknowledges his wife's pregnancy, acknowledges that this is against my temporary interdiction for him and his wife to have a child and acknowledges that both of them can be punished for that under the law against sedition and rebellion. That is all he confessed and no force was used to obtain this confession, neither by me nor by my Red Guards.'

My head was reeling, my anger and despair were choking me and, in a strangled voice, I croaked, 'You lied to me, Hu. You are a despicable, wicked person. You told me that Kunlen had portrayed me as a sex-crazed woman who had forced him, time and again, to try and get me with child.

'That when I told him I was pregnant he threatened to report me. That his only crime was that he hadn't done so, firstly because he had foolishly believed me when I had promised him to seek an abortion and later, when he found out I had lied to him, because I had threatened to kill myself if he did. That he had begged you to punish him for failing in his socialist duties. A one-year sentence of re-education in a people's commune you said he had bargained for and you would try to persuade the other judges to go along with that.'

I fell silent, exhausted, angry, confused and, above all, so sorry about what I had done to Kunlen.

'Total nonsense!' Hu shouted. 'You make it all up. I never said those things to you. All I told you when I came to see you in your room, at eight o'clock this morning, was that your husband had confessed to having acted against the wish of the Party and that he was prepared to repeat his confession in front of the People's Tribunal and accept the consequences. I then told you that if you would do the same, I would consider recommending leniency for you as well. And now you make up this cock and bull story of me telling you how Li incriminated you.'

She laughed triumphantly and continued, 'I am sure, however, that the version Liu Meiling gave the court is the correct one and I thank you both for your voluntary denunciation of the criminal Li Kunlen. I declare you, Xu Suping, innocent of the charges of sedition and rebellion, but you are guilty of neglect of your socialist duties to report the rape by your husband and your unwanted pregnancy at a time when an abortion was still possible. I accept, as a mitigating circumstance, that he is, after all, your husband.

'For not applying for an abortion you must be punished. This People's Tribunal decrees therefore that your child will not have recognised status and that consequently you will not qualify for child allowance and free medical care and free schooling for the child. You are now free to go. The court will recess until two o'clock.'

If Auntie Liu had not come forward at that moment and put her arms around me, I'm sure I would have thrown myself at Kunlen and begged him for forgiveness.

As it was, Auntie Liu led me out of the hall and walked me to her house where she put me to bed after making me swallow some sort of bitter concoction she kept in a medicine chest in her bedroom.

I slept for two days and a night and when I woke up Auntie Liu sat there, in a chair, watching me.

She had prepared a hearty meal of chicken rice, beef noodles and green vegetables in oyster sauce and we ate in silence. I was ravenous. When we finally sat down, with a mug of tea, Auntie told me that she had gone back to the court hall that afternoon, while I was soundly asleep, to hear Kunlen's fate.

Hu had asked Kunlen if he had any comments on Liu Meiling's rendition of the events. He had seemed resigned to his fate and had told Hu that it had all gone as told by Liu and that he had given me no chance, that I was not to blame for anything.

Hu had then quickly summarised the case against him and ruled that Kunlen would be transferred to Shenyang's Detention Centre that same afternoon with Hu's recommendation that he be sentenced to twenty-five years' hard labour in some uranium mine or other. Kunlen had made no comment, he had merely shrugged his shoulders and before the Red Guards could intervene, he had turned his face to the people in the hall and had shouted:

'The sow got her revenge after all! Revenge for a personal slight many years ago. She tricked my wife and her friend Liu Meiling into making accusations against me! Let this be a lesson for all of you! *Never ever trust a Communist! Never ever trust the Communist Party!'*

While he was still shouting these warnings, the Red Guards had already jumped on him trying to silence him in a frenzy of kicking and beating.

While they dragged him backwards out of the hall Kunlen had still managed to shout, 'Liu Meiling! Take care of Su Ping! Take care of the child! If it's a boy call him Jian, if it's a girl call her Lilian!'

Hu had hurriedly closed the session and ordered the struggle meeting to begin immediately, probably to prevent the people from discussing the case amongst them by making them chant slogans until they would be too tired to think of anything else but sleep.

When Auntie Liu had finished her report I wept and sobbed that I had betrayed Kunlen. Auntie Liu let me cry for a while and then she said, 'Stop crying, Su Ping! It won't solve anything. Hu tricked you and me as well. Be glad Kunlen wasn't such a coward after all. I don't think I can do something for him, I won't even try. I don't think I can do something about Hu either, not officially at least. It was pure deceit what she did to you and to Kunlen but then that is what the whole Communist Party is about, has always been and will always be.

'I will let my friends know what happened though, let them know my outrage at the way Hu misled me and perverts justice to satisfy her own vindictiveness. They may be willing to influence things a bit, push a bit here, pull a bit there and in the end, in four to eight months' time, Hu may be told to tone down or she may even be transferred altogether. We'll see what happens. In any case, you and I won't attend her silly People's Tribunal sessions any more. For the time being you'll stay with me. We'll pack a few things you need and lock up your house.

'After all, I have a debt of honour to Kunlen. But for my testimony, he would have got off with the year's re-education perhaps. But then you, Su Ping, you would have got the same and that we didn't want, did we? That's why I attended the session this morning, to intervene, if necessary, to get you out of Hu's claws. So, treachery or not by Hu, I'm afraid I would have been forced to do what I did, that is to make Kunlen take the brunt, to make it look like rape.

'I know that's bad, however, that's what it was, wasn't it? That's one of the very few points on which I agree with the Party. Forced sexual intercourse, without the woman's consent, is rape and it doesn't matter whether the man and woman are married or not. Usually, if there are no physical consequences, the matter is glossed over, shrugged off or settled between the two families; about the psychological consequences for the woman nobody cares. However, if there is lasting damage it is now at least possible for the woman to get redress, that I must grant the Communists.'

I gratefully accepted Auntie Liu's offer, or order rather, to stay with her for a while until I felt I could manage on my own again.

Ten days after Kunlen's transfer to Shenyang I received notice from the People's Tribunal that he had been sentenced conform with Hu's recommendation. The notice didn't say where he would have to serve his sentence. I went to see Hu to ask her whether she knew, or could find out for me, so that I could write to him.

She told me rudely and impatiently that he wasn't allowed to receive mail so there was no purpose for me to know where he was. 'You'll have to wait twenty-five years,' she told me, laughing sardonically.

How I hated her for the way she delighted in our misfortune.

I stayed six weeks with Auntie Liu and by then I felt sufficiently in control of myself again to move back into my own house.

I don't know what would have become of me had Auntie not taken pity on me. For one thing, I would have lost my house as well. Two weeks after the notice about Kunlen, Hu served another notice stating that my house would be repossessed and to hand in my residency permit.

Auntie had gone out and I was alone at home when the leading Red Guard made me sign for having been served the notice of eviction.

I was desperate. I was sure Hu was trying to destroy me, to finish the job she had begun with Kunlen. Without a residency permit I was not allowed to stay in Dalian. Where could I go? Five months pregnant at that.

When Auntie came home she found me crying disconsolately. She picked the notice up from the floor, where I had thrown it in my first fit of anger, read it and told me to come with her to my house. There she told me to stay inside and not to open the door for anyone but her. Then she was gone.

She stayed away a long time, more than three hours, and I imagined all kinds of scenarios, each more terrible than the other. Finally I heard Auntie's voice calling to open the door. She gave me back the receipt I had signed for the notice and told me to destroy it. Then she herself tore up the notice in front of my eyes.

'The matter is settled,' she said, gruffly. 'Hu saw the light. At first she didn't want to listen, almost had me thrown out of her office by that snotty Red Guard of hers, the tall one. So I went to see the city's Party secretary, an acquaintance of old, let's say. I explained the matter together with a few more things and he gladly accompanied me back to Hu's office. He stayed inside, alone with Hu, for almost half an hour, while I waited outside.

'Then he asked me to come in and, in front of Hu, subdued looking but inwardly fuming I'm sure, Secretary Xian explained to me that it had all been an unfortunate misunderstanding, a case of mistaken identity and that the easiest way was to give me back the signed receipt and to ask you, Su Ping, to tear it up together with the eviction notice. I said that it was understandable that in an office as busy as Hu's mistakes were bound to be made by those carrying out her orders and that some of them inevitably would slip through. However, everything was settled now and no hard feelings, of course. We shook hands and Xian and I left together.

'I accompanied him to the nearest bus stop and while we were waiting for the bus, not sure whether there would be one in service, Xian told me he thought the worst excesses of the Cultural Revolution might be over. "Excesses will gradually become the exception rather than the rule," he said, and he continued. "With the return of reason comes the delicate task to determine who abused his or her position and power for personal reasons and who committed excesses out of misguided zeal. Both are equally a disgrace to the Party, however, in both categories there are those who are expendable and others who are not for whatever reason.

'"Ways must be found to protect and even clear the latter of wrongdoing at the expense of the former. Show trials will be organised to channel the justified anger of the abused people. However, show trials are risky, very risky business and they must be prepared very carefully to avoid any backlash that could hurt the stayers. This takes time, a lot of time, so we're in this situation for another five or seven years, I guess. So, a good piece of advice, Meiling, keep a low profile and your temper in check and tell your protégé to do the same."

'A bus driver who had actually taken the trouble to go to work and to stop for us, yelled, 'Get on if you want to go somewhere! There won't be another bus today! Everybody is making revolution except me! My wife forbids it! Says revolutions never filled bellies!' and he roared with laughter.

Xian laughed also at the young man's infectious merriment and shouted back, "You have a sensible wife, comrade! More people thinking like her and we wouldn't be in this mess!"

'The driver laughed joyously and, banging the horn with his fist to spur Xian on to jump on board, he let the clutch come up suddenly, forcing Xian to jump on to the moving bus. Xian looked back and waved and I thought I could see him sticking up his thumb. I waved back and stuck up my thumb as well.'

Auntie Liu fell silent, waiting for me to say something. I couldn't. Instead I cried and embraced her.

She held me tight and whispered in my ear, 'About the child's unapproved status. We'll cross that bridge when we come to it. Don't worry.'

Then we cleaned the house while we were there.

'In a month or so you should move back into your own house,' Auntie said, 'not because I don't want you to stay with me but because Hu may have another go at it under the pretext that if you don't live in your house you don't need it either. We can't ask Secretary Xian again to intervene.'

So one month later I moved back into my own house. Since the kindergarten had been closed I had little to do in my small house. I spent most of the day and evening with Auntie Liu, either at my house or at hers.

We were never at a loss for a subject to talk about and the days, weeks and then months passed uneventfully. I never heard from Kunlen.

Ten days or so before my delivery Auntie Liu and I made arrangements with the harbour clinic and on 1st August, 1969 I gave birth to a healthy baby girl.

Auntie Liu assisted with the delivery and through the waves of pain I heard the nurses and the clinic's doctor call her comrade woman doctor.

*

'I never mentioned that to you, Auntie Liu, but I clearly heard it, I'm sure about that.'

Su Ping fell silent and looked expectantly at Liu Meiling as if inviting her to say something, a clarification, perhaps? The older woman merely smiled, however, and remained silent. Su Ping shrugged her shoulders and didn't insist.

'Three days after the childbirth I was discharged from the clinic,' Su Ping continued.

★

Auntie Liu had come to fetch me and the baby. From then on my life changed out and out. I was fully occupied from morning till evening and in the first few weeks during the night as well. Auntie Liu dropped in once or twice every day and when I took the baby for a short walk I usually ended up at her house.

When the baby was three months old I took her to the city hall to register her under the name of Li Lilian.

The elderly man at the register asked me to show him the preliminary registration certificate by the neighbourhood Party secretariat. I told him I didn't have one as my child was unapproved.

He stared at me for a long time without saying a word. I looked back at him, as calmly and dignified as I could manage. Perhaps he heard my pounding heart, though, for he sighed and with slow, deliberate movements changed his fountain pen for a pencil.

Then, equally slowly he wrote after Lilian's name: preliminary certificate number to be supplied.

Without a smile or a sign of nervousness he stood up, nodded deferentially and, very formally, proffered his hand to congratulate me with my daughter.

'Raise her well, Madam Li,' was all he said and he gave me his handkerchief to wipe my eyes brimming with tears from gratitude and relief.

When I came home Auntie Liu was waiting for me with freshly prepared sea cucumber soup. I told her what the kind man at the city hall had done and she was visibly moved.

During the day the neighbours dropped by to admire the baby. While Auntie Liu held Lilian on her lap I served tea and cookies.

Time passed uneventfully and Lilian grew up a lively and friendly child.

The kindergarten reopened when Lilian was about fifteen months old. The whole neighbourhood signed a petition to Hu to give me back my position as assistant matron.

Nobody was really surprised when she refused. Two weeks later, however, Matron sent the children back home with a small note for the parents explaining that at her age she couldn't cope alone and could only take half the number of children every other day. The parents went to see Auntie Liu and together they marched on the community centre.

At first Hu refused to receive them, however, when the group of people blocked the door and refused to disperse, she relented and let them inside to hear their grievances and plea for my reinstatement.

After two hours of haggling Hu finally gave in and Auntie made her sign a declaration that I was reinstated as assistant matron and, oh wonder, that I was allowed to keep Lilian at the kindergarten during my working-hours.

Auntie told me to have Matron sign an attendance slip for Lilian, every day. When I asked her why, she said I would understand later. When I had one hundred slips Auntie told me to give them to her and she went to see Hu.

When she came back Auntie triumphantly showed me a back-dated preliminary registration certificate for Lilian.

'Hu was angry and befuddled when I showed her the attendance slips for Lilian,' Auntie said, grinning mischievously. 'She never expected that, of course. An unapproved child is not allowed to attend kindergarten and school free of charge. When I pointed out to her that she herself had approved Lilian's official status four months ago when she signed your reinstatement, including your right to bring Lilian with you to work, she was furious.

'She argued that being present at the kindergarten passively is not the same as attending; however, she realised she was at fault when I said that Matron had attested that Lilian had indeed participated in the other children's activities. You see, Su Ping, I have watched Hu these past few months. Already at the time she signed your reinstatement she wasn't her usual self, I found; she gave in too easily so I think maybe she is in trouble, eh? That's why I told you to collect those slips signed by Matron, not by you like you do for the other children. From her reaction when I showed her the slips I saw that I had guessed right, this error of hers is probably what her enemies are waiting for.

'So I proposed a deal: a back-dated preliminary certificate against the slips. Hu ranted and fumed and threatened but I didn't budge, just sat there and gazed at her making a fool of herself. In the end she signed, as I knew she would or else she would have called the Red Guards already to throw me out of her office. So here you are, love. Your child is now officially a citizen of the People's Republic of China.'

I laughed and cried and danced with joy and kissed Auntie Liu.

The next morning I went back to the city hall. The same elderly gentleman received me, took the certificate and ponderously erased the pencilled characters he wrote sixteen months ago. Then, with his fountain pen, he wrote the certificate's number after Lilian's name, painstakingly, taking his time, as if he savoured every numeral as a work of art.

He blew on the fresh ink to make it dry a bit before rolling his half-round blotter over the page and, looking up at me, he said, 'It took you some time to find it, Madam Li. Don't forget where you put it this time.'

When he shook my hand there was a glint of a smile, in his eyes more than on his lips.

Impulsively I leant forward and kissed his hand. I felt him freeze and, withdrawing my hand, I turned and walked to the door.

Before closing the door behind me I looked back. He still stood there, staring after me. I waved and, hesitantly, he waved back.

*

Su Ping looked around at them all.

'I never saw him again. If he's still alive he must be way over sixty, now. Perhaps Lilian and I should find out and bring him a box of cookies, perhaps even that colourful round tin with Western cookies, like the one Lilian once got as a present from you, Lao Dee. In his own, dusty way he was a real hero. He took risks, for me, for Lilian, at a time when even such a small act of defiance of authority could have been construed as a misdeed punishable by hard labour. He needed not do it. I'd rather not think about what would have happened if he hadn't. I think we, Lilian and I, owe him our respect and gratitude and that we should show him this. I feel ashamed I didn't think of him earlier. I hope he is still alive. All of a sudden I'm in a hurry to find out and make up. Tomorrow I'll go to the city hall and make enquiries.'

Su Ping fell silent and smiled, a bit ruefully and introspectively. 'Strange things, memories,' she said pensively. 'Do you know? I still can see the brown spots on his pate, through his sparse, wispy white hair and the thick, blue veins on the back of his right hand as he was slowly drawing each numeral.

'We were both holding our breath, he probably because of the enormity of what he was doing, cheating the *State*, the *ultimate authority*, I because I saw the official existence of my daughter taking shape, willing his pen to write faster before disaster could strike at the very last moment. I still remember that I only exhaled in relief when he closed the register and Lilian had become one of the twenty thousand or so number in that volume, existent yet lost and anonymous among the many. The safest status in those times.'

Suddenly Su Ping burst out laughing. 'What am I doing?' she chuckled. 'I have almost finished the first part of my story, you are undoubtedly hungry and impatient for me to finish and for the food to arrive and I lose myself in reminiscences. Let me get back on track.'

*

Lilian grew up a precocious child. At a very early age she spoke like an adult and knew how to draw the basic characters. The schools had reopened by the time she was five years old and she did well in class.

During all those years she asked only once about her father, when she had just turned four. I explained that her father had gone to work in a far-off place and would return one day to play with her on the beach. I can still see her nodding her pretty little head, very seriously, while I spoke to her and when I had finished all she said was, 'I'll wait', and she went to see Auntie Liu.

She never mentioned him again.

When the soldiers dumped a filthy, old dodderer in front of her and I told her later he was the father she had been waiting for, the shock and disappointment must have been terrible. She didn't show it though, her composure, or is it nonchalance, never wavered. Equably she performed her daily filial duties, showing neither disgust for Kunlen's messy, half-witted eating habits nor compassion for the same, let alone love.

During the first few weeks after Kunlen's return I was deeply hurt by what I saw as Lilian's lack of feeling for her father as well as for my predicament. Then came the time that I resented her apparent equanimity in situations where I would have either screamed in frustrated, helpless anger or smothered Kunlen with desperate affection.

It is only when I began to envy her for the cheery detachment that I realised that for a very long time, actually from the first moment I saw Kunlen, I hadn't felt any love for him either. Only my guilt complex had made me deny this and fake a love that wasn't really there.

It was all a show, an exaggerated public display, as it always is in such circumstances I think, to silence that nagging small voice that mockingly reminds you of your real motives.

Unwittingly Lilian, little as she was, saved me from losing my mind.

If she had acted differently, hysterically, as a child sometimes does, whether by rejecting her father in disgust or, quite the contrary, by doting on him, she would have triggered my own sense for the dramatic and I'm sure the whole family Li would have been locked up in an asylum long ago.

As it is, I will now start the proceedings to have Kunlen institutionalised.

Lilian and I cannot go on like this. I think I have paid my debt, if ever there was question of indebtness, and that I should come out of my shell of the past and try and catch up with the life my daughter, all of you, have been leading and see for myself what has been going on all these years.

★

Su Ping fell silent and smiled at her daughter, a melancholic, imploring little smile.

Lilian smiled through her tears, lips quivering, as she got up from her chair and crouched in front of her mother, taking her hands in hers.

Looking up into her mother's face, cheeks glistening, she said lovingly, 'We'll make it, Mother. Together, you and I. You'll be my best friend. I am so proud of you. We're going to be very, very happy together.

'We're also going to visit Grandfather and Grandmother and Uncle Dan and you'll let *me* tell them what happened and why we couldn't go and see them earlier. It'll be much less emotional if I do that. No protestations, no reproaches, they'll just listen and afterwards, alone with you, there'll be only compassion and love and tacit understanding that certain things should remain unsaid. Are you happy now, Mother?'

As an answer Su Ping leaned her forehead against Lilian's and their long, glossy hair mingled and fell like a curtain around them as if to shield their intimacy against all intrusive stares.

Auntie Liu and Beiyuen cried and laughed at the same time, while Lao Dao busied himself with a handkerchief.

Lao Dee felt like the onlooker he was and intended to stay. This is only the first story, he thought to himself, if the others are anything like it and I let myself get emotionally involved each time, I'll lose my objectivity and won't be able to relate on my own terms with the Chinese any more. I can't let that happen. If I give them the impression that I can be emotionally manipulated, their stories won't stay sober and truthful for long and that'll be the end of the whole idea. Everybody loses.

He was relieved when he recognised his friend Mu Ping's voice shouting, outside in the alley, 'Lao Dee, my friend! Where are you? I have your food here! Food worthy of an emperor, prepared by the greatest cook alive today in the Middle People's Republic, sadly wasted on an ignorant barbarian and his plebeian friends. Open the door, you, the resident of this unproletarian house, and stand in awe!'

Auntie Liu burst out laughing. 'The brazen rascal,' she chuckled, 'it's about time we should take each other's measure after all I have heard about him.'

Lao Dee opened the door just when Mu Ping was about to pound on it. Fist still lifted the cheeky little southerner stared back in open-mouthed amazement at the faces of Lilian, Beiyuen and Su Ping who peered over Lao Dee's shoulder at him and his pushcart.

He swallowed and quipped, 'I didn't know you would be entertaining those bewitching houris, Lao Dee. Had you told me I would have prepared an extra dish for you, raw oysters with a fresh ginger and chilli sauce on the side. Nothing like it to make you the unforgettable man in their life.'

Su Ping uttered a few strange sounds the others didn't understand but which made Mu Ping roar with laughter.

Grinning mischievously he croaked something at Su Ping and Lao Dee saw her blush very prettily.

'She called me a dirty-minded rascal, in my own dialect,' Mu Ping said, still grinning. 'I told her a dirty mind is a joy for ever, provided you can give it some substance, with my special medicine, of course. All words and no deeds, a man's bane, a woman's bore, eh? My dear!' And he gave Su Ping a friendly wink.

'From all the hot air coming in through that open door it must be your friend the southerner, Lao Dee!' Auntie shouted from the room.

'What did I hear the mongrel say? All words and no deeds? I thought that was the southerners' trade! Let me taste his food and perhaps I may change my prejudice!'

Mu Ping grinned broadly.

'The lady's from Shanghai, I hear,' he said, loud enough to be heard inside. 'That explains the expensive shark fin's soup. Who would order such an expensive dish but a Shanghainese who knows she need not pay, or share the bill?'

Lao Dee couldn't help laughing and to his relief he heard Auntie Liu chuckle at Mu Ping's tit for tat.

'Come in for a moment, Mu Ping, my friend,' Lao Dee said. 'Lilian and Beiyuen will bring the dishes inside and transfer the food to our own dishes. While they wash up yours so that you can take them back with you we'll have a beer together.'

'No need,' Mu Ping replied, 'you can bring my dishes back tomorrow. The food will suffer if you transfer it just before eating it. Besides you shouldn't wait too long or the dishes will be cold. I'll watch you eat while I have that beer and then I have to go back to my restaurant to throw more pearls before the swine.'

Lilian and Beiyuen quickly set the table while Mu Ping greeted Lao Dao, Auntie Liu and Su Ping as if he had known them all his life.

Everybody took to the little man immediately and the animated talk continued well after Lilian called that food had been served, interrupted only by slurping and smacking and comments about the food, which was really delicious.

Mu Ping was clearly delighted with the praise and expert comments by Auntie Liu and Su Ping. Lao Dee was happy for him and happy that the meal created such a convivial and relaxed atmosphere.

Mu Ping stayed for the whole meal and took himself and his dishes back to his restaurant after a very cordial leave-taking and after they had promised to visit his restaurant for an extensive meal offered by him and Lao Dee.

'An excellent cook and a very nice man,' Auntie Liu commented after Mu Ping had left.

'And an intelligent, shrewd man as well,' Lao Dee said, 'something people may not suspect behind his natural, cheery disposition and talkativeness. I like him. To me he is the quintessential Chinese. The survivor, rolling with the punches and coming out on top; indestructible, always in a good mood, always good for a laugh and a joke, reliable and trustworthy without the showy display and yet a very keen and shrewd observer of his fellow humans.

'I refuse to believe that Hu Guoshang and her ilk represent the true face behind the collective smiles of all is well in this best of all socialist worlds. They are merely the dregs that float to the surface of the stagnant pool, in a bubble of foul-smelling gas, when somebody stirs up the muck on the bottom.

'The law of averages dictates that China has a greater number of these woeful failures than any other country on this planet because of the sheer size of its population. But the phenomenon is the same everywhere. Whether revolution or counter-revolution, demonstrations for or against, whether past or present or future, the leader has his coterie of rabble-rousers to take care of the dirty work by manipulating the basest instincts of society's misfits.

'You had your leader Mao, his rabble-rouser Jiang Qing, her misfit Hu and hundreds of thousands like her. However, watch the paintings of the earliest throes of the French Revolution, the pictures of the Russian and Spanish revolutions, the film of the race riots in America, even those at Kent University, of the fanatical religious demonstrations in the Middle East, of football hooligans on the rampage, of protest demonstrations against whatever ridiculous matter has been made into an issue by manipulative politicians. Is it any different from what you saw in the early stages of the Great Proletarian Cultural Revolution?

'Those men and women, boys and girls *you* saw, are they any different from those on the paintings and in the films? French, Russian, Spanish, Iranian, English, Dutch, German, their balled fists high above their head, their wild eyes full of hate or of gloating, malicious joy, their wide open drooling mouths screaming slogans or invective; are they in any way different from your own misguided Red Guards?

'Those bombastic dispensers of summary popular justice, bloated with self-importance, and their henchmen executioners, their faces flushed with bloodlust, are they different from your own Hu Guoshang and her leading Red Guard? Are they the true faces of the nation? Any nation? No, they are not! They are the dregs of society, mobilised and manipulated to do the dirty handwork to clear the leader's path to power.

'However, once his evil goal is achieved, on the shoulders of the rabble, that same rabble becomes a liability, a constant reminder of the leader's own origin he wants to forget and to be forgotten, an obstacle for gaining the respectability of his peers he craves so much for he knows it is essential for his admittance into that inner circle of bloated, ruthless, power-corrupted murderers, terrorists and ordinary thieves at the top. You see them in the newspaper pictures and on TV, waving from the open door of a special plane, pontificating from behind a lectern, giving rehearsed, inane answers to politically correct questions by smart, self-serving interviewers, stuffing themselves at yet another banquet while their unfortunate unhappy people at home suffer and starve.

'At home a new coterie of profiteers appears on the scene. Slick, sly and ruthless they get rid of the uncouth rabble-rousers first. Paid off or killed or victimised in show trials, whatever serves the new breed of manipulators best. Then the rabble is told to back off, to lie low or else... Grudgingly, ears flat, tail between their legs, they crawl back into the muck, feeling betrayed and forsaken. Throughout the history of every culture and society it's the same drama repeating itself endlessly, only the actors and their supporters change, the ordinary decent people the eternal victims. Whether intellectuals or factory workers or peasants, they are the hostages of their own conscience which demands a reason for them to be stirred into joining some movement or other. The rabble need no reason or justification, they are lead by emotions and blindly follow those who know how to play or manipulate those emotions. Easily divided on whatever the issue of the moment is, the reasonable, decent, ordinary people talk and debate and stand by, helpless and hopeless, as the issue is forced by a manipulative leader.'

Lao Dee fell silent, shrugging his shoulders.

'Why the diatribe, Lao Dee?' Auntie Liu asked. 'Why the generalisation?'

'I sense a tinge of shame when you talk about what happened to you,' Lao Dee answered, 'shame, I think, about what Chinese did to Chinese. As if this was something uniquely Chinese. I want you to know that it is not.

'Ever since man began to stand and walk upright and his brain developed at the expense of his animal instincts, he has killed, murdered, tortured, maimed and oppressed his own kind. At first the only motive was to achieve and then maintain physical domination and its attendant benefits. Soon greed for more benefits than he could possibly enjoy himself, but could bestow on next of kin, friends and supporters to ensure their continuing allegiance, became another powerful motive.

'Inevitably possession of riches, whether to gain or defend, was next as the notion of *power* became understood. Those who lacked the physical prowess to gain the power that comes with material wealth, cleverly developed the idea of spiritual power and declared themselves the go-between in arranging deals with the supernatural and thus religions were born, the biggest single cause of mass killings and oppression, until this very day.

'Spiritual power was declared superior to material power, though the clever religious leaders schemed and intrigued to gain the support of the wealthy worldly powers for their own special version of belief and its attendant hocus-pocus.

'Captives of an unprovable promise of reward or threat of punishment, after death of course so that there can be no witness, the materially powerful but mentally weak did and still do the bidding of the priests and cult leaders who prophesy the idea of superiority and inferiority among competing beliefs and believers, probably the second biggest cause of killing and mayhem. Unavoidably religion became embroiled in politics, a notorious example being the Roman Catholic Church throughout most of its history, and now we see on the world scene religions and cults dominated and used by politicians, governments and politicians dominated and used by their religions and cult leaders and, as an inevitable reaction, purely political cults that have not only forsworn any allegiance to whatever religion but have even condemned religion as a baneful collection of superstitions, as pernicious as addiction to drugs as your own Great Leader Mao proclaimed.

'That he is just as fanatical and intolerant of dissent in imposing his own cult than the popes were in the Spanish and Portuguese colonies or the fundamentalist mullahs are in the Muslim world, that may not be said. We, you and I, as we sit here, and the hundreds of millions like us outside, world-wide, will forever be incapable of stopping that monstrous conspiracy by the corrupt corrupters that transcends the world's artificial state, cultural and racial divides and whose sole aim is *power*: to gain it if they haven't got it yet, to keep it if they have.

'And despite all the rhetoric aimed at one another, however, intended to deceive the gullible ones like us, the corrupt corrupters have their code of dishonour to always stop just short of actually harming each other, physically or each other's vital interests, the ultimate, unforgivable sin by their code.

'Whatever the outcome of their incessant wars, guerrilla terrorist attacks or political slur campaigns they stay in power or, if temporary removal is considered desirable, they retire to a comfortable and pleasant playground or are given a totally useless but always well-paid position until the outcry or scandal about their misdeeds is forgotten and they can safely pop back on the scene. Only those who do not belong to the inner circle of the corrupt corrupters die in the dirty little wars or are sent to prison as war criminals or are otherwise sacrificed on the altar of public indignation.

'Even the complete nutcases of the inner circle, those psychopaths who have totally regressed to the animal stage and actually ate their enemies, like cannibals, have not been put down but continue to live in luxury in the country of an old friend. Those who really go too far in their lying and cheating and stealing are sometimes impeached when there is really no other way out. However, they are simultaneously pardoned and retired to a beautiful estate while retaining their pay and benefits and title. In a supreme manifestation of cynicism and contempt for the ordinary man they even confer on themselves fake doctorates or spurious honorifics like elder statesmen.

'It's unbelievable and makes you want to pull out your hair and cry in despair and disgust. So don't think that whatever you went through, however bad or depraved, has not happened before and elsewhere as well.'

'So why do we tell you our story?' Su Ping asked. 'What's the purpose? Why would people care if it's just another variation on an endlessly repeating universal theme?'

Disheartened she looked at the others, who avoided her eyes and instead looked at Lao Dee questioningly, anxiously.

Lao Dee realised that he shouldn't have let himself get carried away by his own helpless anger at a situation that was as perverted as it was unassailable.

Probably only Lao Dao, and perhaps Liu Meiling, were old and cynical enough to have come to the same conclusion themselves, though the Chinese were generally ignorant and naive about the world outside China and had altogether a much too high opinion about the situation there.

However, he couldn't let Su Ping and the two girls become the victims of his own contemptuous disbelief in the sincerity and competence of politicians and religious leaders, whoever they were.

Carefully choosing his words he said, 'People will care, Su Ping, because your stories are about ordinary men and women in whom they recognise themselves. The things that happened to you could have happened to them, have perhaps even happened to them.

'People cannot grasp the enormity of what has happened in China these past fifty years, and notably during those terrible ten years of the so-called Cultural Revolution. From statistics, it is clear that so many million Chinese died in terrible circumstances. "So what?" the cynics will say, "there are enough of them left, aren't there? And proportionally the figure is less than the number of Jews exterminated by Hitler and his henchmen or than the number of *kulaks* murdered on Stalin's orders, so what's all the fuss?"

'The less cynical, ordinary people cannot grasp such big numbers. Five dying in a car crash, two hundred dying in a plane crash, that they can grasp and they shiver. But five thousand killed in an earthquake, or thirty thousand killed in a civil war, far from their bed as the Dutch say, that is beyond them and they shrug their shoulders and read on or turn to the sports pages.

'However, the personal stirring experiences of a few ordinary men and women, struggling, suffering and surviving during a reign of terror inflicted on them by their own leaders, that will touch every ordinary person and he will ask himself why those terrible crimes committed by the Communists have not been exposed in the news media of his own country. Hopefully he will even question the political leaders of his country, why they ignored what went on for so long in China and why some of them ever preached or still preach Mao's ideas, Maoism they call it, as the ideal recipe for a just and humane society. Do you know that some of these public figures even went as far as to show their support for Mao's variety of the Communist creed by wearing the kind of suit Mao always wore?

'One would laugh at it if it weren't so intensely, sadly naive. Or is it wickedness? The least our now informed ordinary person will do is to write off these so-called leaders as the stupid dupes they are, unfit to have a say in the running of his society. Even these days, when people should already know better, there is a movement in Latin America that calls itself the Shining Path and whose members profess themselves inspired by Mao's thoughts and theories and who, consequently, kill, murder and terrorise the local populations to establish, they say, the Mao type of a just and humane society.

'And would you believe that there are many people in Europe and in the US who actually support those Shining Path criminals and claim that that is what Latin America needs, what the whole world needs? Did they ever ask the ordinary Chinese what he thinks about such naivety or perfidy? No, on the contrary. The very few Chinese who managed to escape from the proletarian paradise and the even fewer among them who dare to speak up and warn against such things are depicted as escaped criminals who have an axe to grind with their righteous and benign leaders at home and whose only aim is to stir up trouble and poison the rest of the world's mind by slandering the great achievements of the Chinese Communist Party and its leaders.

'And your leaders play this craziness, this gullibility, to the hilt by showing the world such a respectable appearance in their confidence-inspiring Western suits and ties, with their benign smiles and sincere-sounding declarations about how much they care about their people, peace and the world. So when they say in interviews with foreign news media, left-leaning, even pro-Communist, most of them, that never anything untoward happened in China, that every Chinese wholeheartedly supports and loves the Communist Party and its leaders, that those few deranged minds the enemies of socialism in the West persistently call dissidents are nothing more or less than common criminals who belong in prison, as is done in every law-abiding country, the people actually believe them, even those who should know better. Why do they believe them? Because it's easier!

'What we now hope to achieve, you by telling me your stories and I by putting them to paper in what I hope will be a readable form, is to shake that complacency, that gullibility and make people see through the lies and deceit and hypocrisy with which the Communists and socialists try to cajole them into bringing them to power there where they can't grab power by force.'

Lao Dee fell silent, looked at the others and concluded, 'I hope I have answered your question, Su Ping, and that I have reassured you that we have still a worth while project.'

'Yes, you have, Lao Dee,' Su Ping replied. 'I, we, didn't know that you have this Communist rot in your society and that it is also your intention to contribute, however little, to stopping this rot by means of our stories. I thought we only wanted people to know what happened in China. So this is even better. But tell me, Lao Dee, how is it possible that a normally intelligent person who understands and enjoys the benefits of freedom in everything he says or does, who enjoys his part of the general prosperity, professes Communist sympathies? Why don't your leaders silence those people?'

Flushed with indignant exasperation Su Ping looked at the others.

Lao Dee chuckled and shook his head.

'To answer your first question, Su Ping. I really don't know. I have often thought about it myself and haven't been able to find a clear-cut answer. Is it stupidity? Is it to show off a differentness? Is it to make themselves look interesting? Is it perversion? Is it simply wickedness? I think it's a bit of everything, a mishmash of all the above tendencies, because what I have found is that those people hardly ever have a character of their own.

'They are often weaklings unable to inspire respect as they really are and therefore they cling to every idea or philosophy that's fashionable at the moment, for instance communism and they profess their sympathies without of course ever even considering to share their relative wealth with the poor. They bleat about the superiority of communism while living in a big luxury house, wearing expensive designer clothes, driving luxury cars and gorging themselves at dinner parties. And you know what's the worst part of it? Not that they show themselves to be the utter fools that they are but that nobody challenges them and exposes their hypocrisy.

'This brings me to your second question which shows me that you, in spite of everything that you have endured and of what has been said, are still a product of your society. Our leader cannot silence these people. As long as you do not commit a crime as a result of or in accordance with what you profess you cannot be arrested let alone condemned or silenced. That is democracy as we in the West understand it. A famous Frenchman once said, "I don't like what you say but I'll fight until I die so that you can say it." And though it is often tempting to say that somebody whose views and maxims go against everything you believe in should be silenced, no true democrat would want the kind of society where that would be possible.

I personally hate what these people say, or pretend they stand for, I even hate them as persons and I won't miss an opportunity to tell them that, to challenge them, to ridicule them, to expose them, however, I *will* stop short of wishing a political system for my world where I could simply denounce them to the authorities and see them arrested and locked up. I think that we, notably in the West, are very complacent about that most precious of all democratic values, that is freedom. It's enough to spend some time of your life in a Communist country to never be complacent again and to be cured, for good, of any silly notion about how desirable the communist system is.

'Unfortunately the sympathisers never bother to check whether their theories and preferences have any base in reality and therefore, I'm afraid, we'll have to put up with them as a constant pain in the neck, bothersome, annoying and equally useless as buzzing flies. However, unlike the venerable Frenchman I won't exert myself to protect their right to make fools of themselves. They fall flat on their face? Even break their thick necks? Fine with me, because, you see, that's also freedom, my freedom to choose not to be my brother's keeper.'

Everybody laughed at this grim, humoristic note.

'Beiyuen, why don't you prepare a fresh mug of tea for all of us?' Auntie Liu asked. 'And then Su Ping can begin the second part of her story.'

Su Ping nodded. 'It's even more important now that I tell it well after what Lao Dee told us,' she said and she settled comfortably back in her chair, closed her eyes and tried to collect her thoughts and go back in time to when and where it had all begun, about twenty-two years ago in Luding, Sichuan Province.

The others sipped their tea and kept silent so as not to disturb her train of thought.

Savouring both the tea and their refound sense of purpose and conviviality they waited contentedly for Su Ping to begin. Emerging from her reverie she said, 'As I said earlier, I shall tell you now the story of Xu Suping of Luding and as if she were another person, which, in fact, I still feel she is. I hope that at some time during our stay with my parents I'll be able to reconnect with her life so that she'll be part of me again. Xu Suping's story would not be complete, however, if I did not include the extraordinary story of an equally extraordinary man called Chen Dan, Uncle Dan as Xu Suping called him and as even I now still think of him. Uncle Dan's influence on Suping at that time, and on me still for that matter, can hardly be overestimated.'

Thoughtfully Su Ping sipped from her tea. She let her thoughts mingle and float with the fragrant vapour twirling around her nose and eyelashes and slowly the others, the room, the present faded from her consciousness as images of the past took form and she saw the familiar, peaceful setting in the small garden behind her house in Luding emerge.

# *Chapter Twelve*

## Different Owner, Same Cook; Different Sauce, Same Dish, Summer 1965

The air was warm and very still and the different sounds of people going about their early evening business in the small town below in the valley carried clearly to where Xu Suping and her parents were sitting, in their small garden overlooking the valley and the river.

Like every fine summer evening the three of them had gathered, after dinner, in the garden to watch the setting sun's kaleidoscopic display of colours on the peaks of the mountains that surrounded the darkening town. The mountains looked liked giant torches in hues of red, gold, pink and, strangely, bright green. The view was breathtakingly beautiful against the distant blue-black background of the Daxue Shan range.

Madam Xu née Liu Guixian and her daughter Suping were quietly and contentedly watching the beautiful and peaceful scenery while now and then drawing each other's attention to something either of them had noticed particularly, but mostly they remained silent, each at peace with herself and the world.

Usually, Xu Ximing enjoyed the relaxed, random chit-chat with his wife and daughter about the trivial little things that had happened during the day, however, these past few days he had not been in the right mood for such trivialities.

Actually, ever since a few weeks ago rumours had begun to seep into this quiet little town about what was happening in Beijing, Shanghai and the other big cities, he had been troubled, even apprehensive and nervous.

He had asked his wife, a teacher of Chinese history and culture at Luding's first middle school, and his daughter, an assistant teacher of Chinese language and calligraphy at the same school, to prepare a summary of comparable past events for him, going as far back as they could, to the founding of China if possible. He himself, the headmaster and teacher of mathematics at Luding's third middle school, would analyse the seeming similarities and try to work out a probable future course of events.

For years he had been playing with the idea that the future, politically speaking, ought to be predictable given the right input of variables derived from a careful analysis of the past. The idea of unpredictability, of chaos, was abhorrent to his mathematical mind and that such could be the case for mankind's evolution was unthinkable.

'God doesn't play dice', Einstein once said and Xu Ximing couldn't agree more. Not that he believed in a God like Einstein had in mind when he said that but he believed in Heaven and Earth and Nature and in a preordained sequence of events. Like Einstein searched for a unified field theory of nature's physical forces, he, Xu Ximing, searched for a unified evolution theory for mankind.

The solution lay in the past, in history and in seeing the similarities. Two weeks ago his wife and daughter had given him the study they had prepared for him and they had even highlighted the similarities they thought were significant in the light of what was happening now. Every free moment he had worked on it and he had become increasingly agitated, Suping thought.

Tonight he had acted totally out of character. During dinner he had been unusually silent and absent-minded and even when they had retired, as they always did, to the garden, he had not said a word, which was stranger still since he never failed to make some philosophical remark or other about the peace and beauty of life in China as compared to the rest of the world and about the privilege of being Chinese.

Not that he would know much about the outside world first-hand since he had never been abroad, but that did not prevent him, like practically all Chinese, to profess with utter and unshakeable conviction, that China and all things Chinese were by far the best in the world.

Instead he had taken the sheaf of papers with him outside and he had continued to fumble with the sheets, going back and forth with his pen over the notes he had made, as if chasing some elusive factor to make everything fall into place.

Suping smiled and winked at her mother, who was just commenting on the unusual great number of trash-burning fires that lit up the lower-lying areas of the town, when they heard Father shift in his chair and harrumph a few times, his usual way to announce that he was about to say something important.

'I am left with a number of factors that I cannot balance with similar ones in the past because I cannot find them,' Xu said, a bit peevishly, Suping thought.

'I can only make approximations and that's not good enough,' Xu continued. 'Therefore I cannot extrapolate and that means that mathematically there's no connection between the present and the future. My conclusion, therefore, is that either present and future are the same, which means no further evolution or revolutions to ruin the sameness, or an unknown and unpredictable event will shatter that sameness at any moment and a new kind of existence without any link with history as we know it, including our present, will come into being.'

Xu looked up from his papers and noticed the puzzled expression on his wife's face.

'I see disbelief and doubt in your eyes, Guixian,' he said reproachfully, 'you probably think that I am being pedantic? In love with my cherished analysis? That I have not taken the perpetually unpredictable human factor into account? But I have! I have! Judge for yourself!

'Allow me to put before the two of you the four factors which I think are without precedent in our history and to set forth my reasoning why they may, no, they *will*, result in the dire consequences I mentioned. I say dire because I think that both unchanging sameness and catastrophic upheaval are equally disastrous for society. I shall ask for your comment on each of those four factors. Please correct me if you think that my reasoning is lacking in rigour. We cannot afford to make mistakes, to overlook even the minutest tendril of faulty logic, since our future depends on the premise that all four factors apply. If only one of them can be refuted my theory does not hold. So let me begin.'

A few times during Xu's discourse, Suping had caught her mother's eye and had seen her smile ever so slightly. Liu Guixian knew her husband was given to pedantry and to pontificating about the obvious, as so many scholars were in the exact sciences. Yes or no, true or false, black or white were their criteria, altogether a bit too simplistic for real life with its subjectivisms and inherent 'maybes', 'probablys', nuances and shades of grey.

She also knew, however, that he was scrupulously honest and that before making a statement, surely one of such magnitude as he had just made, he would have verified and reverified every conceivable argument that might invalidate it. He would never resent it though if others sincerely tried to disprove his arguments and he would reciprocate with equal sincerity.

Because of his one-track mindedness, however, he was incapable of dealing with flippancy or mockingly negative criticism. This would make him angry and he would begin to stutter and completely lose his composure. So Guixian would give him her undivided attention and she nodded at her daughter to do the same.

Xu Ximing had been watching his wife and daughter while they were evidently collecting their thoughts, putting the restful atmosphere and scenery out of their minds with barely concealed regret. Xu thought he was a lucky man.

Though he found their demonstrations of affection embarrassing, especially in the presence of strangers, their affection meant more to him than his introvert and shy character allowed him to show. As a rule, however, he felt awkward in the company of women, especially intelligent women, with a character and opinion of their own.

They were not logical. Their reactions were unpredictable. They jumped to conclusions on the basis of unsubstantiated assumptions, of gut feelings, of intuitive assessments. They cried when one would expect them to laugh and vice versa. Sometimes they cried and laughed at the same time, which always baffled him.

Such behaviour was perhaps typical of uneducated peasant women and very young girls; however, from his wife, a scholar in her own right, and his daughter who also had a very fine mind and, unusually for a woman, a great talent for mathematical thinking, one would not expect such irrationality. And yet they also surprised him often by doing or saying the unexpected when he was least prepared for it, upsetting his nicely ordered train of thought.

Frustrating, neurotic creatures, all of them, he thought, his own womanfolk no exception.

Ruefully he realised that he was being grossly unfair and that, in his heart, he was envious of their perceptiveness and sensitivity for abstract matters that could not be captured in formulas as constants or variables. How conceited of him to say that women were illogical just because they arrived at insight and understanding in a manner he could not fathom.

How often had his wife, or his daughter for that matter, not surprised him with the rationality and logic of her arguments in defence of a conclusion she had arrived at by intuition and which by means of her process of indirect proof had then turned out to be correct.

He hoped with all his heart that his wife and daughter would prove him wrong this time, yet he feared they would not. He consulted one more time his notes and began to argue his thesis.

'I shall be brief. I shall neither belabour the obvious nor expound on facts one can assume to be known by everybody. That would only distract from the essential.'

'Am I too pompous?' he worried. 'Probably yes, judging from that little smile Guixian always wears when I talk like that. Why can't I talk like any ordinary man?

'Of the four factors which I have retained as being without precedent,' Xu continued, 'the first concerns the exercise and maintenance of direct power, the other three concern the indirect means by which an institution maintains itself in power. The first factor is weapons!

'Modern weaponry is completely different from that in the past. Modern weapons can kill great numbers of people in the blink of any eye and from a safe and comfortable distance. Both killers and killed remain anonymous, not like in the past when individuals battled with individuals, often in hand-to-hand combat, with axes, spears and knives, or from a short distance, within eyeshot, with bow and arrow. Even the old-fashioned single-shot rifles and guns had still some of the man-to-man heroism and bravery. Any reasonably competent blacksmith in days of old could forge weapons of good quality. Even improvisations, often made by the warriors themselves from any approximately suitable material at hand, were still sufficiently lethal for the purpose of fighting a battle. Examples abound and everybody knows and enjoys these stories about those heroes of old.

'By contrast, modern weaponry requires sophisticated and complicated machinery to make and highly scientific technology to design. Not only are all these modern weapons in the hands of the Party and its extension, the People's Liberation Army, but also the technology and monopoly of their manufacture are the Party's exclusively.

'We also know that the Party has no scruples or qualms to use the weapons against any perceived threat to its hold on power, including its own people, should they muster the audacity or have the illusion that they can challenge the Party's monopoly on the power over life and death of every Chinese. "Power comes out of the barrel of a gun", is a saying attributed to Mao Zedong and, by implication, he meant that not only does the Party hold the gun and nobody else, but also that the Party will use it if provoked or threatened. Now then, do you agree with my contention that this factor has no precedent?'

Suping and her mother rolled enquiring eyes at each other, then shrugged their shoulders and, turning to face Xu, hands open and palms up, gestured, 'No contest'.

Xu smiled and continued.

'The second factor is social control! The total encompassment and permeation of our society by the Communist social control methods and the fundamental changes the incessant indoctrination and propaganda have caused in the traditional Chinese way of thinking have no equal in the past. The Party is literally everywhere and has pervaded all layers of our society. It controls all aspects of each individual's life, from birth till death. It has arrogated the right to decide whether life will or will not be permitted by allowing or denying married couples the right to have more than one child. Even to have one child official permission from the local Party branch is a prerequisite.

'I am certain that sooner rather than later the Party will also allot an official lifespan to each man and woman on the basis of an average of say eighteen formative years plus forty socially useful years plus a bonus of two leisure years, the latter always at the discretion of the Party and dependent on the incumbent's conduct sheet. Only the Party will have the right to extend or to reduce the number of formative years depending on its assessment of society's requirements for certain categories of people: scientists, engineers, physicians and factory workers will need a different number of formative years.

'Upon completion of one's allotted lifespan one will be expected to take one's own life, voluntarily, as one's duty to society. I foresee official "Life Termination Centres" where this can be done peacefully and in pleasant surroundings while the sound system plays an appropriate socialist battle song and one dies with a last, recorded, "Thank you, dear comrade!' from the Great Helmsman himself in one's ears. Dedicated Party cadres, specialising in various termination techniques, all equally pleasant I am sure, will always be on standby to advise the 'dear leaver' and to help him overcome any last-minute hesitation.

'The Party's pre-eminent tool for exercising such an all-pervasive system of social control is the modern means of communication. Telephone, telex and radio permit both instant feedback from law enforcers in even the remotest regions to provincial control centres or directly to central control at the Party's headquarters in Beijing and, by return, unchallengeable instructions from the Party's top leaders for immediate retribution for any sign of dissent or rebellion. The dispatch of troops to reinforce local militia or army units is only a matter of hours by plane. In the past, reports about dissension or rebellion took days, weeks, even months to reach the central government. By then the local magistrates or provincial governors had either been assassinated long ago or joined the rebels and the revolution was already well under way. I ask you again, do you agree also that this factor is a unique aspect of the present and has no precedent?'

Suping had noticed that her mother had jotted down a few notes during her father's discourse and that she was now about to answer him.

'I grant you, Ximing,' Guixian said, 'that the comprehensiveness of the Communist system we now live under is probably unique, both within the context of our time and when compared to other systems of social control and repression that have been tried out on our people in the past. However, the system itself and its aim, that is the acquisition and subsequent maintenance of power, are of course not new or unique and in that respect the Chinese people have known worse, far worse as you well know.

'For instance, compared to the hideous legalist system of *fa-jia*, initiated by Shang Yang and later perfected by Han Fei, in the state of Qin, the present Communist Party's system of repression and control, of punishment and reward, is the epitome of benevolence and humaneness. Let us learn, however, from what happened more than two thousand years ago to Shang Yang and Han Fei and their system which surely they also thought would last for ever. To begin with those two gruesome monsters themselves died the victims of their own system. The Lord of Shang was caught by his own secret police when, ironically, he tried to escape from the prison state Qin he himself had created. In accordance with his own draconian laws he was condemned to death and torn apart by two pairs of oxen, a form of death penalty he particularly favoured, for others, I'm sure. Han Fei was tricked by Li Xu, an envious competitor for the favours of Ying Zheng, into killing himself.

'If Han Fei had followed his own advice on how to deal with high officials, Li Xu would have died instead. Nevertheless, Ying Zheng was a great admirer of Han Fei's ideas and adopted them as the official state philosophy. He subjugated the six neighbouring states, established the Qin dynasty and henceforth called himself Qin Shi Huang Di, the Yellow Emperor, the first emperor of All Under Heaven, that is, of China. Qin Shi ruled as an absolute despot, a remorseless tyrant who undeniably accomplished incredible feats during his short reign of only eleven years, something that would have been totally impossible though without what is in my opinion the most appallingly repressive system China, and perhaps even the whole world, has ever known.

'After his death, nobles, generals and, for the first time in our history, also the peasants rose in revolt against Li Xu who, as the first minister, tried to continue Qin Shi's terrible oppression under the second emperor as well. Both were lesser men than Qin Shi and so they were killed during an uprising only two years after the first emperor's death.

'Is there not a lesson somewhere here also? A great man succeeded by lesser ones who then can't keep his legacy together? One year after Li Xu's and the second emperor's death, Liu Bang, a peasant turned general, seizes Xiangyang, the capital of Qin Shi's China and the third emperor of the Qin dynasty, also the last as you know, surrenders to Liu. In the next four years Liu Bang eliminates a number of competitors for power and then he establishes what he calls the Han dynasty, named after the river Han near the place where he was born. He changes his name and calls himself henceforth Han Gaoxi, the first emperor of the Han-dynasty, though in fact he was the fourth emperor of China.

'Han Gaoxi, a very pragmatic and down-to-earth man, a true peasant actually, realises that with terror and oppression one does not win the hearts of the people and he abolishes the hated legalist state philosophy. Another lesson here? Instead he adopts Chiu Kung's teachings as the official philosophy of the House of Han and therefore of the State of China. This philosophy, or Confucianism as it is listed among the world's great philosophies, will last throughout the successive dynasties, *and* the republic of China, until the Communists seize power in 1949 and replace it by their own alien system. The point I am trying to make, Ximing, is that terror and repression by the State cannot last.

'The people will revolt and fight, even with their bare hands if they don't have weapons as, according to your theory, they won't, and they will overthrow the hated system and its perpetrators. Of course they will then establish another system which, in its turn, will be overthrown a few years later, or a generation later, or a hundred generations later, when the people can no longer bear the abuse perpetrated in its name. So I say that the Communist system will also not last for ever.'

Guixian fell silent and looked at her husband, waiting for his reaction, a bit defiantly, Suping thought.

Xu had listened to his wife without a sign of impatience and he now looked at her with a slightly quizzical smile.

'That was an admirable synopsis of our early history, Guixian,' he said, 'and equally admirably tied up with the present. However, you left out a troubling yet quintessential fact that would have invalidated the very point you wanted to make in the end. I am a bit puzzled why you did that.

'On the one hand I cannot imagine that the fact has escaped you, on the other hand I refuse to believe that your eagerness to find fault with my reasoning, however understandable, led you to omit it deliberately. That would be unworthy of an academician of your standing. The fact I am referring to is simply this, "*Legalism did not die twenty-two hundred years ago!*" It has been and still is the basis for every type and form of government since Qin Shi Huang Di, only less blatantly so. Communism now and Confucianism before are merely different veneers to fool or charm the superficial people.

You scratch the surface of either philosophy and you find Han Fei's steely eyes looking at you.

'Han Gaoxi, that pragmatic and wily peasant, was experienced enough in dealing with people to know that man's nature is essentially evil and egoistic and that only strict laws and their unrelenting and stern enforcement are *the* indispensable conditions for an orderly society of men. "Put your trust in laws, not in people", is Han Fei's basic rule for enlightened, good government and every emperor, king, president, dictator or Great Helmsman could not agree more. Yet, Han Gaoxi had himself succeeded in overthrowing the Qin dynasty by manipulating and channelling, to his own advantage, the people's outrage at legalism's unnecessarily excessive brutality and cruelty.

So he realised that if his own, still fragile, Han-dynasty were to survive him and last, he would have to find a workable and acceptable balance between what the people need, that is a *stern* government, and what the people want, that is a *benevolent* government. In fact, he needed to find the right balance between the stick and the carrot. Quite a feat, but he managed that very well by dressing the steel structure of legalism in the fancy clothes of Chiu's mumbo-jumbo about filial piety and respect and, not to forget, by giving the people Chiu's silly rules to play their equally silly games by, the so-called Rituals.

Fortunately for Han Gaoxi, Chiu had been conveniently dead for over three hundred and fifty years and, equally conveniently, all the old books about this philosophy had been burned by Qin Shi and Li Xu, often together with the scholars. Those scholars who had not been burned or buried alive were not burdened with too many scruples and were only too eager, I guess, to please Han Gaoxi when he invited them to his court and asked them to "rewrite from memory" Chiu's thoughts and ideas.

'I am sure they enthusiastically accepted Han Gaoxi's offer to refresh and guide their individual and collective memories. I have no doubt that the result of that collective effort of scholars and emperor would have been more to Han Fei's liking than to good old Chiu's. However, be that as it may, it surely was to Han Gaoxi's taste. And then, twenty-two hundred years later, there appears that other pragmatic and wily peasant on the scene.

'He's from Hunan this one, more or less from the same tough soil as the peasant Liu Bang before that one made himself the fourth emperor of China and the first of his own dynasty. To manipulate *his* peasants and to channel *their* outrage at abuse, corruption and extortion, so rife at that time, the peasant Mao Zedong had only an impractical alien philosophy by an irascible, bearded, foreign scholar-devil at his disposal. Very un-Chinese and therefore totally unsuitable to rouse the hundreds of millions of wretched, backward peasants and to persuade them to rally behind him as their leader in what he intends to be the greatest of all revolutions and of all times. Mao knows from the Communists' earlier failures and infighting that with only a few thousand intellectuals familiar with foreign ideas, and factory workers in the cities, one does not make revolution in China, let alone pull it off.

'If he wants to succeed he needs the masses in the country, the wretched and downtrodden peasants, all four hundred million of them, and he won't manage that without an ideal capable of stirring their narrow, backward minds and mistrusting hearts. So Mao must adapt the foreign philosophy of Marx and Engels and Lenin to the Chinese psyche. In short, he must turn it into a Chinese philosophy. Mao also understands though, that he cannot hope to lead such enormous numbers of unruly and opportunistic Chinese to victory without stern discipline and a strict rule of law, let alone to keep them from killing each other in a free-for-all over the spoils of that victory.

'One has to admit, however reluctantly, that because of these insights and, subsequently, for seeking and finding the solution in our own history, the man from Hunan is a genius. In search of a solution to his first problem: that of how to establish a Communist ideology with Chinese characteristics, Mao discovers that twenty-three hundred years before Marx was born there roamed about, in the states of Lu, Chu and Sung, a man called Mo Di, Mo Zi to his disciples and followers. Mo Zi was the champion of the have-nots of that time, of the downtrodden, the oppressed, the lowly and the humble. He called Chiu Kung, who had died a few years before he himself was born, a pompous ass and he scoffed and fulminated against Kung's doctrine and rituals of propriety, human-heartedness and of righteousness from *within*. Mo Zi preached to despise wealth and to condemn gracious living and any form of ostentatiousness, including cleanliness and fragrances. He extolled the virtues of poverty, of hard work and an ascetic life, of body odour and of uniformity.

'He practised in his own community a strict meritocracy in which the individual was totally subordinated to the community's interests. His authority and thought control were absolute and condoned no questioning. He preached the same kind of organisation for states and their governments. He justified double standards about what is just and unjust, notably in wars, and about what is right or wrong in human relationships.

'Mo Zi was a pragmatic man though, who had no illusions about any so-called innate, intrinsic righteousness in man's nature, least of all in the nature of those whose case he championed. Righteousness is the Will of Heaven, he preached, and has to be enforced by law and coercion since it is not in man's nature to be righteous. In fact, Mo Zi was *the* arch-Communist, and a Chinese to boot, in whose life and work Mao found an abundance of typically Chinese folklore, of anecdotes, facts, feats and fiction to serve as the foundation of a communism Chinese-style and thus to satisfy the obsessive preoccupation of the Chinese with their own history.

'The references by Marx and Engels to the circumstances in Western Europe a century ago and by Lenin to the Russian situation under the tsars, which are of course meaningless and of no interest whatsoever to the Chinese, can therefore be omitted from Mao's ideology. For this Mo Zi has earned a place of honour in the Chinese Communist Party's Gallery of Socialist Heroes and we chant his praise in the Party's slogans in schools, workshops and at political meetings. Besides, Mo Zi's principle of law and coercion was *the* solution to Mao's second problem of how to keep the people in line. On how to practise that principle, Mao found his inspiration by studying Shang Yang and Han Fei.

'Let me now point out to you, Guixian, and to you as well, Suping, the similarities between the Party's practices and concepts and the teachings of Han Fei, the arch-legalist. Again Mao had the genius, firstly, to interpret correctly the reasons why legalism in its pure form failed and, secondly, to make the necessary adjustments so that the Party's form of legalism would not fail. Now take good note, you two!

'Han Fei said, "The morality of the state and the ethics of the individual cannot be equalled, in fact, they are incompatible. It is therefore the people's duty to live and work for the state and to carry out every order and decree without fail or criticism. The people must not think or discuss, only obey." The Party says, "It is the people's duty to carry out, faithfully and unfailingly, the instructions of the Central Committee of the Chinese Communist Party under the leadership of Chairman Mao."

'Han Fei taught, "The state must be united under centralised rule, exercised by an unquestionable authority, personified by an aloof, enigmatic, ruthless and remorseless despot, who embodies all wisdom, virtue and courage. This Ruler not only enforces the law, *he is the law*! Holding the two handles of punishment and favour."

'With hindsight we now know that it is in this that Han Fei went wrong. Not in his concept itself, but in his insistence on one-headed rule by a despot. In spite of his genius, Han Fei was still a man of his time and in those ancient times the very notion of collective leadership was unknown, so you can't really call it a failure. It was Mao's genius, however, that he understood that a "one-headed monster" becomes easily the focus of the people's anger and outrage and, hence, a symbol of perceived misrule.

'So Mao proclaims the "dictatorship of the proletariat", a grey, amorphous and faceless "multi million-headed monster". Under such a system everybody is his own and everybody else's dictator so where to focus one's anger and outrage at perceived misrule? Mao put the crown of cynicism on this brilliant move by proclaiming that the Party had the proletariat's mandate to govern the People's Republic of China, thereby equating the people with the proletariat. He further proclaimed that the Central Committee had the Party's mandate to govern the Party and finally, sublimely cynical postulate, that he, Mao Zedong, had the Central Committee's mandate to rule on all and everything for and on its behalf. What a beautiful construction!

'The principle of accountability implied in a mandate becomes so diluted as to be virtually non-existent since there is nobody who can claim to have been elected as the one Mao or the Party should account to. By whom should he have been elected? By himself? To demand an account of his own actions as his own and others' dictator? How absurd the Party would say. How can *one* cell in your body protest against the action of your body as a whole? It would go unnoticed. Not even a hundred thousand protesting cells would be noticed. A hundred million protesting, out-of-line cells would be noticed though and diagnosed as a cancer, to be removed surgically. To be *purged* in the Party's jargon and analogy.

'In case of success all the credit goes to Mao, the final mandatee. In case of failure he only needs to sacrifice a scapegoat from any one of the many intermediate layers of delegated authority to assuage the mob's thirst for revenge, while he himself remains untouched and untouchable. However, let me continue with my case of similarities between Han Fei's *fa-jia* and Mao's *communism*.

'Han Fei first abolished the privileged classes, confiscated their members' private property and possessions and then turned everybody, forcibly, into a peasant or a soldier or, preferably, into both. Twenty-five hundred years later Mao does exactly the same. He abolishes private property, confiscates people's private possessions and decrees that the proletariat, and in particular its peasant and soldier members, is henceforth the dominating class. Those who have some kind of individual worth that cannot be taken away from them are divided into six subclasses of decreasing respectability with the intellectuals as the lowest form of life, the "stinking ninth class".

'Han Fei decreed that people would be held responsible for one another's conduct and that the family, or any other social group of people for that matter, would be punished collectively for the crime of any individual member. He stressed that all bonds of loyalty, of friendship and of filial piety must be uprooted and that people must be forced to spy on one another and to denounce unbelievers and wrongdoers by rewarding those who do and by punishing, swiftly and hideously, those who don't. Now, isn't that exactly what Mao's Party preaches also? Haven't private feelings been declared *unsocial*? Hasn't family loyalty been condemned as *feudalistic* and as a *poisonous element of Confucianism*?

'As a result children spy on their parents and parents on their children and they outdo themselves in denouncing each other for the paltriest of thought crimes. Neighbourhood committees have been made responsible for the conduct of families under their surveillance. Registration of the population is rigorous and every personal detail is recorded, including every social or thought crime you have ever been accused of, whether proven or not, to haunt you until the end of your days.

'To travel you need approval from the local police unit and you must report to the nearest police station upon arrival at destination and account for the time exceeding what is deemed the normal travelling time. No one can live in another neighbourhood let alone in another town without official permission and no one can ever travel abroad privately. The collective comes first and before all else and we now have communal fields and farms, communal crèches, schools and centres, communal political study and indoctrinations and soon we'll have communal life termination centres as well.

'Party cadres are required to suppress feelings of personal affection and to cultivate a "Party nature" instead, the tenor of which is that their life belongs to the Party and has to be sacrificed if duty to the Party demands this. Only where punishment is concerned is the Party less brutal than Han Fei prescribed. The Party prefers brainwashing to brain removal by decapitation. Only when persuasion fails, or for crimes for which there can be no repentance, there is the neat bullet to the back of the head and the bill for one yuan for the bullet to the relatives.

'Han Fei finally decreed that no books other than the one about the *law* are permitted. The law is the sole subject of instruction, Han Fei said, and the officials are the teachers. He ordered all existing books, *and* anyone caught hiding them, to be burned. Substitute Communist ideology for what Han Fei called *the law* and Party cadres for what he called *the officials* and you have the present situation.

'It won't be long before the Party will order the burning of books it does not approve of. Need I elaborate further, Guixian? I don't think so. Legalism, in one form or another, has dominated life in China for more than two thousand years and it is so much part of the Chinese psyche that we, the Chinese people, would not know how to deal with a non-legalist and democratic system. We simply would not be able to function. The Chinese Communist Party understands this and besides, its leaders and cadres *are* Chinese, so what can you expect? Shang Yang and Han Fei have also, like Mo Zi, their seat in the Gallery of Socialist Heroes and we must praise them as the ultimate *materialists* and *leftists* and as Mao's honourable predecessors.

'Even the ultimate practitioner of the legalist philosophy, the first emperor Qin Shi Huang Di, is praised by the Party as the *first progressive unifier* of all China, it being understood that Mao Zedong is the last. Well, now, my dear naive wife and daughter, after this useful digression, shall I return to my argument and my four factors without precedent? Or are you still unconvinced?'

Mother nodded, gloomily Suping thought, that Father had made his point and he went on.

'The third factor is the *dictatorship of the proletariat*! As I already said in my defence of the second factor, this postulate has been a true stroke of genius by Mao Zedong. What is in fact this proletariat?

'In today's China this means about ninety per cent of the population, if not more, so about seven hundred million people and increasing by one hundred thousand per day. They are unlearned and uncultured. All they are interested in and motivated by are life's basic needs and urges, the most important of which is the rice bowl and what's in it, the so-called iron rice bowl, unbreakable and guaranteed full twice a day. We must be honest though and admit that, for the first time in our long history, the lot of these people has indeed improved tremendously, no doubt about that and a good thing of course if it had not to be at the minority's expense.

'So when the Party, with malicious glee, tells these morons that they are henceforth the masters of their own fate, gives them what they crave and warns them that *the others*, their former exploiters, will take it all away from them again if given only the tiniest chance, it, in fact, assigns seven hundred million sentries to watch every move and gesture and overhear every word of those who think that there must be more to life than eating, sleeping, working, playing cards, drab colours and dull uniformity.

'With one and a half billion uncaring, malicious, exultant, defiant and triumphant eyes watching the certified *enemies of the people*, with the Party mandated as it says it is, to act in all matters for and on behalf of those watchful eyes, how can one ever expect either one of the subclasses to dare raise a dissenting voice, let alone to rally the other subclasses and force, or rather induce, the reigning class to throw away its privileges? It's simply inconceivable, so do you concur that also this third factor is without precedent?'

Xu's wife and daughter didn't even need to look at each other for consultation. Miserably they shrugged their shoulders.

'The fourth factor is *thought control*,' Xu continued. 'This phenomenon is so uniquely of our time that the word "unprecedented" needs no arguing, I think. What I mean by thought control is the mass production and dissemination of written and spoken propaganda, of pseudo-science and pseudo-knowledge, ubiquitously and continuously, by newspapers, books, radio, TV, theatre and films, by loudspeakers in workshops, offices, schools and on street corners. The impact of this totally one-sided, unending and relentless onslaught of disinformation and distortion of facts and figures and of untruths about the real life, both in China and abroad, on the senses and thought process of the people is absolutely fantastic.

'Virtually nobody has learned to think independently. Most of us have never travelled outside our region, let alone to other countries. We all lack any standard of reference or of comparison to other forms of human society, so what the Party hammers into our brains becomes the truth, *is the truth*! Within one generation the Party will have succeeded in bullying our wonderful, kind-hearted, hospitable and friendly Chinese people into a numb and amorphous mass of neurotic and paranoid xenophobes, totally alienated from all human interrelationships on this planet. To the other peoples the Chinese have become an alien species, frightening and incomprehensible, hostile and aggressive.

'When one tries to understand why the Party's propaganda is so extraordinary successful, the usual and obvious reasons come to mind first in China's closed society: the constant and unavoidable exposure to indoctrination and propaganda; the complete absence of anything written, spoken or visual that contradicts the Party line and, to a lesser extent; the cloyingly fanatical one-track mindedness of the Party's gospel preachers. Two reasons are always overlooked, however.

'The first is that the Chinese *want* to believe the Party lies and boastful claims of always greater achievements because that suits our natural feelings of racial superiority. The very idea that the Chinese way of doing things could be inferior, that our achievements could be less than those of foreigners or, supreme insult, that we could even learn from the barbarians, is loathsome to us Chinese. The second overlooked, or underestimated, reason is our language. I am proud of our beautiful language and the manner in which the three of us have been debating these varied issues, here in this peaceful, utterly Chinese setting, over the past few months, has been an intellectual delight for me. However, we have to realise that our language is unique. That it is often thought of by foreigners as vague, ambivalent, impalpable and almost impossible to learn and to achieve the same kind of fluency they have in one another's languages. That difficulty is further compounded by our way of writing, which makes the number of foreigners who are really able to communicate fluently with the Chinese too small to be or to cause a threat to the Party's version of the truth.

'On the other hand our language is the perfect barrier, from the Party's point of view, against any contamination of the people's minds by the outside world's communication networks since for all practical purposes the Chinese people cannot understand anything written or spoken in whatever foreign language. Consequently, translation will always be necessary and that, as well as the printing, is and will remain the Party's monopoly.'

Xu fell silent and looked at his wife and daughter. When they remained silent, he resumed, hesitatingly. 'I have finished my dissertation.' And, increasingly emotionally, 'Am I right in my deduction and conclusion that China has no other future than the one decided and planned by the Communist Party and by the Party only and exclusively?

'Am I right when I assert that the three of us, and hundreds of thousands of non-persons like us, as well as the hundreds of millions unlike us, are irrelevant in the Party's scheme? That at best we are tolerated, provided we bow our head and do exactly as we are told, unquestioningly? That we have neither rights nor recourse if and when the Communists decide that we are guilty of something or other they need not even specify let alone prove? That they can have us tried and condemned by what they cynically call a court of justice, to prison, forced labour, re-education, exile or even to death?

'I see fear in your eyes, so you *do* indeed realise that my doomsday vision has a sufficient degree of probability to guide us from now on in the conduct of our lives. If we evaluate realistically the increasingly numerous rumours and true stories that seep even into our quiet, little backwater here, in Sichuan, the conclusion that a political storm is gathering, a *taifong* rather, the like of which China has not seen yet, seems to me inevitable.

'There are clear indications that Mao feels that he is being sidetracked, cleverly elevated as it were to the position of a remote godhead by his more intellectual and pragmatic comrades, notably Liu Shaoqi, who think that "permanent revolution by the masses" and mad, radical policies and stunts are not exactly what China needs after that disastrous so-called Great Leap Forward. That folly, that unmitigated disaster, cost China dearly. It destroyed what was left of our industry and agriculture and caused tens of millions of people to die of starvation and untreated diseases. Liu and Zhou Enlai know very well that Mao himself is a disaster when it comes to ordinary, practical leadership. They cannot eliminate him, however. The man is simply too big a legend with the people and they need his prestige to push their own policies through.

'Mao, in his assumed aloofness but ever the clever and deadly intriguer, is now using Jiang Qing, that horrible, spiteful woman of his, to whip her gang of maniacs, those so-called Red Guards, adolescents bred on hatred, without culture or education and led by neurotic, frigid females in their difficult age, into a frenzy against the last vestiges of what they call the feudal past. These maniacs will swoop down on the country like a swarm of crazed wasps, attacking, without distinction, whatever lives and moves, stinging whatever is without the narrow scope of their conditioned instincts.

'We *must* mentally prepare ourselves for the day that we will hear the distant, ominous and angry buzz grow louder and louder and our sky is suddenly darkened by the swarm of vermin swooping down on us here as well. When that happens our strategy must be to lie low, to keep the lowest possible profile so as not to attract attention, all the while hoping that the lunacy will peter out from sheer exhaustion and that reason will prevail one day, within the Party, in the person of Zhou Enlai.

'Zhou the Mandarin, that arch-Taoist, will ultimately succeed and prevent the total destruction of Chinese society by the Chinese people themselves owing to his uniquely subtle and suggestive ways with Mao, manipulative perhaps, but effective. Jiang Qing hates Zhou with a visceral hatred for his influence on her Master, however, her ravings will run off him like water off a duck's back. She is like a dog, biting whoever and whatever the Master orders her to bite. That leads me to my final recommendations.

'Whatever happens to us, however bad the situation may seem, we must try to guess the Party's objectives and ulterior motives and then try to act in line with them. Whether we like it or not, the Party is here to stay, for good, and when we accept that as a fact we can do nothing about and act accordingly, we can lead a reasonably worth while life, that is to say, for a Chinese who is neither a Party member nor a Communist. This means that we must not envy the foreigners their freedom to say what they want, to do what they want, to go and stay where they want, when they want. Such freedom will never be ours because the Party won't allow it. Period. So acquiesce and we can manage to live without it. Avoid foreigners and you won't be tempted.

'Also, we must keep our temper when the Party minions look over our shoulder and breathe down our neck with every step we take, every book we read, everything we teach or do. They won't understand what it is all about and they will ask stupid questions or they will forbid things in a high-handed and peremptory manner, just to show they have power over us.

'We must never let them feel that they are intellectually inferior to us. We must pretend humbleness and flatter their ego and try to manipulate their bloated vanity to our advantage, very subtly. If we look at it as a game in which we try to outsmart them we may even get some sardonic, intellectual pleasure from it all. It helps if we remind ourselves from time to time, for instance when our sentinels are particularly obnoxious, that those minions are just as irrelevant to the Party as we are, probably even more so because they have already forfeited their soul while ours is still struggling and for that reason we may, just may hold the Party's interest in us. We will get hurt but in rolling with the punches we can minimise the pain.

'How should we see the Party? In its most benevolent mood, it is still like a spoilt and jealous woman, exacting unquestioning love and devotion to all her predictable and unpredictable whims. In its most malevolent, it is like one of those monstrous gods of ancient peoples, exacting sacrifice and even death in the cruellest manner you can imagine. In its usual, indifferent mood, it is like that great shark that devours without recognition, or even awareness, the remora that has just cleaned its teeth.

'Remember these analogies when you have to deal with the Party at the higher echelons of officials: be always careful, take nothing for granted. Tread carefully, as if you're walking on eggs. Remember! Do not presume on the jealous and fickle woman! Remember! Do not provoke or defy the monstrous god! Remember! Do not second-guess the great shark! You are women. Use both your brain and your intuition. Suspect always the worst and do precisely what you are ordered to do, not more, not less, not different. Thus you cannot be blamed.

'For me it will be more difficult. With my kind of face and with my height, humility looks suspicious. Worst of all, I can't bend my figures and formulas to make one plus one equal three. Mathematical logic and Communist logic are incompatible, I'm afraid, and I am too well-known in my profession so that when I make the two compatible by bending the rules, they'll blame me for cheating and if I don't they'll call me a defeatist enemy of socialist progress.

So I am damned if I do and damned if I don't. A no-win situation. All I can hope for is that I'll manage to stay sane.'

Xu Ximing fell silent and smiled at his wife and daughter. Mother and Suping had never heard Father talk at such length and so emotionally and they had shivered in fear of the bleak picture he had painted of how life would be in the future. But his ending on that light, mocking note, so characteristic of his self-deprecating sense of humour, made them smile in spite of their tears.

Conscious all of a sudden of the chilly night air, they shivered and made ready to carry their chairs inside. Suddenly and impulsively they embraced each other, something none of them remembered had ever happened before.

They stood for a while, holding each other, distractedly watching the many trash fires below in the valley, thinking with a sense of foreboding about their future. Then, slowly, almost embarrassedly, they moved apart and went inside.

None of them spoke while Mother heated the soup for a last bowl, as always, before retiring to bed.

They said goodnight with that peculiar self-conscious ordinariness of voice people use to hide their true emotions from each other.

The next day they heard that the fires they had seen the evening before had not been the burning of trash but of 'the poisoned weeds of reactionary culture' by the truth squads of the Communist Party.

These truth squads were sent by Jiang Qing from Beijing throughout the country to preach about revolutionary culture and scientific thought, to burn the old, feudal and bourgeois books they requisitioned from libraries and people's homes and to distribute 'the fragrant flowers of socialist literature and science'.

Every day brought new stories and rumours about outrages committed by the squads, and the officials who accompanied them, against everything that was good and decent and respectable.

## *Chapter Thirteen*

### The Opera Warriors, Autumn 1965–Summer 1966

Life at home was never the same again after that fateful evening.

Father became depressed and stayed home from school more and more often. As he had predicted, his science could not prove the superiority of the socialist system, however, he could calculate the cost to China of the Party's disastrous Great Leap Forward of the previous years.

So the Party officials told him that there was no need for that reactionary, counter-revolutionary and subversive kind of mathematics and since he knew of no other kind, he stayed home, pleading that he needed time to readjust his views and that in the meantime he felt unworthy of teaching the new science of socialist statistics.

Mother had been forbidden to teach from the fourth revised edition since 1950 of China's history, which had only been issued five years earlier. History classes were temporarily suspended and Mother had been ordered to rewrite her papers in accordance with the Party's latest directives.

A whole new list of well-known and not so well-known personalities, from the remote past until yesterday had to be added to the already long list of enemies of the People. While her mother corrected the more scholarly things, Suping helped her by writing out the enemies' names for the appendix to the new lecture papers.

The appendix had been Father's idea.

'It's a lot easier and faster to update than rewriting each time the whole paper,' he had said.

Suping didn't mind writing out the names in chronological order, but she found all those adjectives to be written after each name so silly.

'Slave driver', 'feudal exploiter of the masses', 'barking dog', 'capitalist roader', 'stinking capitalist roader', 'traitor', 'traitorous revisionist' and so on and so forth. What a bore! And you had to be attentive since the adjectives were not interchangeable.

Apparently not anybody qualified as a capitalist roader, let alone as a stinking one.

Even in the Communist hell there is inequality, she thought wryly, so what about their paradise?

Suping, who besides her tasks as an assistant teacher during the day had her duties in the evening as an assistant librarian at Luding's middle school libraries, had been ordered to burn the poisoned weeds and to teach only from the fragrant flowers. She waited for one week to see whether some truth squad man or woman would come to check on her.

Nobody came, however, so she took two or three copies of each book from the libraries and brought them home. There she packed them tightly in oil-paper and buried them under the floor of her bedroom.

Then she made a pile of the remaining books into the school yard and asked a truth squad leader to witness the burning.

He had signed the inventory Suping had made without checking her numbers or else he would have found out that she had cheated by including the number of books buried at home.

Xu Ximing had watched his daughter when she had buried them. 'The saviour of Chinese culture,' he had chuckled, yet the pride in his eyes had belied the slightly mocking tone of his voice.

'If we estimate at ten per cent, at any given time, the number of Chinese proud enough of our cultural heritage to defy the reigning tyranny and bury, during their lifetime, only three of the books ordered to be destroyed, that would make two hundred million books during our time alone.'

Xu grinned and continued. 'Imagine, the average total of all the times such a crime took place would amount to some two billion books, covering twenty-five hundred years of our known history. More, I'm sure, than there have ever been printed but never mind that. From time to time there will be discoveries of buried books and the Party will not even bother to suppress the news. Instead the books will be put on display, probably in a travelling "Exposition of Relics of the Uncivilised Pre-Socialist Past".

'Dedicated guides will recite certain passages from the books and the visitors will stare at each other in mute, shared horror and loathing at the coarseness, the despair, the blood, sweat and tears, the unseemly, obscene exuberance and the ribaldry of life in pre-Party times. Spontaneously some will start shouting at the guides to stop quoting from those works of the devil and others will join, chanting the praise of Unified Socialist Thought and its prophet Mao Zedong, peace be upon him!'

'And his will shall be done, in heaven as well as on earth. Amen!' boomed an unfamiliar voice from the front room. The cackling laugh that followed was so incongruous with the booming voice that Suping was sure there were two men, two strangers, in the house.

Frightened, she looked at her father.

They had been caught in a flagrant act of subversion and her heart sank in her stomach as she thought of what would happen if the two men, who had entered her house without announcing themselves, were Party officials.

The chill of naked fear gripped the nape of her neck.

'Never fear!' shouted the booming voice. 'We came in to ask where Xu Ximing, the great mathematician, lives. Rumours have it that he is working on a new, socialist statistical method and my friend and I thought that maybe we could contribute. But we think that we have found the man, judging by the brilliant summary of China's future culture that we couldn't help overhearing coming from what is presumably the bedroom. Not a promising future, I'm afraid, neither for our culture, nor for the new statistical science of socialist pipe dreams.'

Again there was the cackling laugh.

Somewhat reassured, Father and Suping came out of the bedroom into the living room and there they stood stock still, staring open-mouthed at the two oddest men they had ever seen, one grinning amiably, the other staring gloomily back at them.

Suping would never forget that spectacle and whenever she thought about that moment later, she invariably had a fit of laughter.

One man was short and burly, with a round, red face and incredibly spiky grey hair that stood out like the quills of a porcupine. He had crooked and broken, brownish-yellow teeth bared in a friendly grin and he wore a pair of cheap, steel-rimmed spectacles on his small, bulbous nose. His eyes twinkled mischievously behind the thick glasses.

He wore a kind of round-necked peasant shirt and a pair of too large trousers, held up on his round stomach by a piece of rope as a belt. He had the trousers rolled up to above his knees because of the hot weather and he wore a pair of red, transparent socks in dirty, black shoes. The other, gloomy man was tall, exceptionally tall even. He had a long, sad, lugubrious face, like an old, tired horse, and his heavy-lidded eyes had a look as if he was still recovering from a kick while wary of another one coming.

He wore a dark blue woollen pullover in spite of the heat and a pair of brown trousers, undoubtedly the largest size he had been able to find twenty years ago, yet still they ended halfway between his knees and his ankles. The excess of trouser material on top was unevenly distributed around his meagre waist under a black, plastic belt. His fly lacked several buttons, showing red, woollen underpants. He wore one blue and one brown sock, transparent, with embroidery, and brown, plastic sandals.

Suping wondered whether he had possibly sewn the top part of red underpants on the legs of blue ones since what hung out from under his trousers was dark blue.

She got a second shock when the short man began to speak. His was the deep, sonorous voice, which was unexpected.

'Shame on you, Xu Ximing,' the voice boomed. 'Have you no better way to entertain a lovely young maiden in your bedroom than to batter her ears with academic claptrap? What, indeed, has become of our culture?'

'Shame on *you*, grey-haired man, for your dirty mind. The lovely young maiden happens to be his daughter,' Mother said, disapprovingly. She had come home a few minutes earlier and, unnoticed by the others, had overheard the short man's words.

'Who *are* you two!' she added.

'I am Chen Dan, nicknamed Tall Chen,' the short man boomed, 'professor, or rather ex-professor, of theoretical physics at the University of Chongqing. I was told by the university's commissar, a pimple-faced, bed-watering former clockmaker, that my services were no longer needed and to remove the subversive cloud of my presence from Chongqing's stinking sky. So I decided to return to my village, which is near here, an academic backwater were it not for your illustrious person, Xu.

'My failure to our socialist motherland is that, despite my earnest efforts, I have not been able to make the second law of thermodynamics comply with Communist economical planning. Or vice versa, I forget. That shining intellect the Party appointed as our rector got his position because he promised that energy could be created by waving Mao's book. I failed him and consequently he failed the Party, so I was kicked out while he's still there, beating air with air.'

Chen Dan fell silent, grinned and, pointing at his gloomy, tall friend, he continued the introduction.

'This man here, who looks like a sick horse but who acts like a jackass, is my friend and namesake Chen Juntao, nicknamed Short Chen. No relative, thank God. He is, was rather, professor of astronomy, also at the University of Chongqing. He was also kicked out. His crime was worse than mine. His was abomination! Blasphemy!

'Like that Spanish hero fool Don Quixote, who rather looked like him I think, Ai Chen fought the combined windmills of our new rector and of Chongqing's Party Committee when he stubbornly kept insisting, hence my jackass analogy, that a dying star first becomes a red giant and then a white dwarf. They insisted that Ai Chen teach the reverse, that is that a dark star first becomes a red giant and then a brilliant star. This, they said, would then conform to our Great Helmsman's ascendancy from unknown genius to Red Giant to the future bright, shining star of all mankind.

'A red giant being actually a dying star and, worse, becoming a white dwarf? Intolerable! *Lèse majesté*! Blasphemy! Ai Chen told the morons that the universe does not concern itself with man's futility and that nobody, not even a megalomaniac peasant from Hunan, could change anything whatsoever. The rector waved the book and told the Party geniuses that *he* could and would. Rather stupid of my friend, I think. Does the Party give him the chance to change the cosmic order of things and he botches it. Integrity, he calls it. Typical bourgeois hypocrisy I call it. So here we are, Xu. We had high hopes that you would be willing to put us up for a week or so, while we scout around for a roof of our own.

'As I said before, this *is* my home town, however, my family is minding its own business and not keen, I'm sure, of complicating life by putting up with a social reject like me. Besides, I wasn't exactly the family's favourite offshoot either. Ai Chen's home town is in Heilongjiang where it's much too cold for his bloodless, old carcass, so I have to take care of him as well. In the cosmic order of things he is so adamant he can't change belongs also his inability to look after himself. So what's your verdict, Xu? And Madam Xu, of course,' he added, making a funnily gallant little bow in Mother's direction, which was somehow touchingly pathetic, Suping thought.

On several instances during Gao Chen's story, Suping had barely been able to remain serious, but now, watching his anxious grin and his friend's glum, sad face, she could hold back no longer and she burst into a hiccuping, helpless laughter.

'Your daughter has a great sense of humour, Xu,' Gao Chen said, chucklingly. 'Her merriment about our predicament confirms my opinion that when all reason fails the best thing to do is to laugh. If nothing else, it keeps you sane for better times.'

'We are delighted to offer you our hospitality,' Father said, after Mother had nodded at him.

And so the most unlikely pair of academics Suping had ever seen moved in with them. Together they moved Suping's bed into her parents' bedroom; the two Chens would sleep on mattresses on the floor of her bedroom.

The 'week or so' Gao Chen had said they would like to stay became a month, then two months and before they realised it winter had passed and spring, and then summer was back in the land and the two men were still there and nobody talked any more of 'scouting for a roof of their own'. Right from the start they had got on extraordinary well together.

Without either of them having made a deliberate division of duties, each of the guests had taken on himself certain tasks and so it remained: easygoing, considerate, contented.

Gao Chen cleaned the house, the kitchen and the dishes after the meals, while Ai Chen took care of the small garden as well as the men's laundry as Suping had taught him. Together with Father they went to the market to buy the fresh vegetables and fish or meat or chicken for the day's main meal.

When they were not busy with their household chores they discussed scientific subjects. Mother and Suping usually came home around five in the afternoon and while Suping did the women's laundry and the ironing, Mother prepared the evening meal, which they took together in the front room.

After clearing up they took the three old and the two newly bought wicker chairs outside and quietly talked and discussed until far after dark anything that came to their lively minds. During the winter months it was too cold to sit outside so they stayed inside and talked and discussed and argued until it was time to retire to bed.

One year after having been granted a provisional stay permit by Luding's City and Party Council, the Chens applied for permanent resident status.

Two weeks after having submitted their application a convocation from the recently appointed Party secretary was delivered at home. They had to appear in his office for an interview, mainly to clarify what they had written under 'occupation', the secretary's note said, since it was not quite clear what was meant by 'professor of sciences, temporarily retired to meditate on inadequacy of self, to improve inner self, to better serve the Party's glorious goals in the future, to develop the scientific base for Chairman Mao's Thoughts for the benefit of future generations'.

The two Chens asked Suping to accompany them to the secretary's office, both as a witness and to confirm that the two of them would continue to stay at her parents' house for as long as they had not been allocated a house or flat for themselves. The new secretary appeared to be a nervous, young man, a former primary school teacher, from Dalian, Liaoning Province.

He introduced himself as Guo Chuanxing and acted busy, harassed, probably to hide the fact that he was intimidated by the two scientists' reputation but was shocked by their unlikely appearance.

'I shall approve an extension by six months of your provisional stay permit,' Guo said, staring at the two application forms on his desk before him, 'on condition that you remain within a radius of twenty kilometres of this town. You may not travel and I shall hold this woman Xu Suping and her parents responsible that you do not contravene my order. You must also report regularly, say once a month, on the progress of your study on this scientific base for our Chairman's Thoughts as you have written it here on your application. However, I must report something to my own leaders as well. What can I tell them about that scientific base you are working on? Please speak slowly so that I can write down what you say.'

'Tell your leaders, comrade, that we have begun working on the quantification and qualification of past and present successes of our Chairman Mao's Thoughts,' Gao Chen boomed and Ai Chen cackled.

Startled by the unexpected bassoon sound, Secretary Guo made an involuntary movement and knocked a stack of papers from his table on to the floor.

Hidden underneath the papers was one of those lurid magazines smuggled in from Hong Kong, with pictures of languid Chinese and Japanese girls, with high-heeled shoes on but not much else, sitting on the hood of sleek cars, lying around swimming pools or in huge beds, making silly faces of heavenly delight.

Annoyed and red with embarrassment, Secretary Guo leapt from his chair to snatch the magazine up from the floor.

However, Gao Chen had already picked it up and was looking with a broad grin at the cover page which showed a long-haired girl bending backwards with blank eyes, mouth hanging slack, one hand lifting a big, papaya-shaped breast up to the lapping tongue of a naked man on his knees, while she squeezed the other hand between her crotch.

Suping felt her cheeks burn and she wished she were a thousand miles away from there.

'It's for study!' Secretary Guo shrieked, trying to snatch the magazine out of Gao Chen's hands. 'It's for my paper on "The Five Evil Tactics of Western Subversion"!'

'We understand, Comrade Secretary Guo, we understand,' Ai Chen said soothingly. 'Only when we know evil to be evil can we know what is good. We are pleased and impressed that the comrade secretary lets himself be guided by the wisdom of the Old Master in the performance of his socialist duties to the people. Miss Suping here also understands, I'm sure, how distasteful certain of the comrade secretary's obligations must be to him. She realises, however, that it is all for the greater good if the "Five Evil Tactics" can be recognised before they subvert innocent socialist youth.

'She will agree with my colleague and myself that the comrade secretary deserves our admiration and that we must be discreet and keep this small incident amongst the four of us lest less cultured comrades draw the wrong conclusions. Intelligence has its obligations, has it not? Gao Chen, restrain your vulgar lust and give that piece of capitalist filth back to the comrade secretary!'

With a broad grin and a lewd wink Gao Chen handed the magazine back to Secretary Guo who put it quickly into the drawer of his desk.

'I have just started on my paper,' Guo said, embarrassedly. 'I intend to present it at the Party Congress in March next year. If the leaders approve of my views, I shall ask full powers to implement a crackdown on all elements of the "Five Evil Tactics". However, my research must remain secret so as not to forewarn the enemies of the People and give them time to change their evil tactics.

'I shall therefore be much obliged to you if we can indeed keep this unfortunate incident amongst the four of us. I shall speak well of your study and of Comrade Xu Suping's efforts in destroying the poisonous weeds in her school. Now, can you give me in a few words and slowly, so that I can make notes, what that scientific base for Chairman Mao's Thoughts that you are currently working on comprises?'

Nervously, his pen hovering over a piece of paper, Secretary Guo looked at the two scientists.

Suping wondered what mischief they were up to.

'Tell your leaders first of all that while meditating on our own inadequacy and fallibility, we, my colleague and I, had the first inkling of the immensity of our Chairman Mao's vision,' Ai Chen began, his falsetto voice creaking.

'This insight was probably induced by the rarefied, tranquil atmosphere in Comrade Xu Ximing's garden, which, as the comrade secretary perhaps knows, is situated quite high above the valley and where we often ponder the vagaries of life. A high status often induces light-headedness and euphoria and so it was with us, in that garden.'

Ai Chen fell silent and looked at Gao Chen, who nodded approvingly, rumbling 'teh, teh, teh' in his bassoon voice.

'We saw that it is all a matter of annihilation,' Ai Chen continued, 'annihilation of thesis by anti-thesis, of matter by anti-matter, of reason by unreason, of sense by nonsense. We realised that once we would succeed in synthesising this insight in one unified theory of mutual annihilation, and subsequently proven in an experiment on a world-wide scale, Chairman Mao's vision will have been achieved and there will reign the eternal and universal bliss of communism, a kind of Communist nirvana so to speak, eternal nothingness as it were.'

Secretary Guo was scribbling feverishly to jot down all those beautiful words and when he had finished he looked up with glazed eyes.

'Would you please check what I wrote down?' he asked, hesitantly. 'I'm not sure whether I have all the characters right.'

Suping felt a twang of pity for the earnest young man. He was so eager and naive and not for one moment did he suspect that the two older men with their superior, sardonic minds, were running circles around him.

Guo was going to present the scientists' words in his report, with some comment on how he had managed to coerce them into investigating the annihilation theory of *his*.

His leaders would send his report to their superiors, again with some comment on how right they had been when they had recommended that promising young man for the position of Party secretary of Luding, and so on and so forth, each level eager to claim credit for something they didn't understand.

Until somewhere along the line someone with some common sense left would see through the sham and the mockery and the whole accumulated file would come crashing down through the same channels of communication again, sweeping off their feet all those who thought that some of Guo's glory and credit would rub off on them as well. They would get back at him with a vengeance for causing them to lose face.

They would fabricate a web of lies and conspiracies, entangle him and then have him arrested on some kind or other of trumped-up charge of conspiracy to subvert the Party.

Guo would be condemned to twenty years of forced labour and that would be the end of him.

The two Chens, if ever the matter would be brought back to them, would say that they had been misquoted. That they had in vain tried to make the comrade secretary see the errors in his thinking, but then, in the end, what could they do but to humour the secretary? They were merely two dismissed professors with nothing left after a lifetime of study and hard work but the clothes they were wearing and forced to live off the charity of others.

Suddenly Suping realised that she had just witnessed an act of war.

A war between subtle intelligence and stubborn dogmatic thinking.

'All war is deception,' Sun Tzu said long ago and Suping now saw that the reverse was also true.

All deception is war, she thought wryly, war against trust, against decency, against love and affection and friendship, against all human values. She realised that this was, in fact, the Party's strategy as well.

By practising deception on an unheard-of scale, by sowing fear, mistrust, hatred and uncertainty, by deliberately maintaining a climate of constant and unpredictable political and social changes, the Party kept people at war with one another merely to keep them from uniting against the Party and threatening its monopoly on power.

So the two Chens were actually doing exactly what the Party wanted them to do, in spite of all their intelligence. They were not damaging the Party by destroying its obscure and inexperienced secretary in this small, insignificant town. On the contrary, they were reinforcing the Party's hegemony by engaging in its war of deception.

The Party was smarter than the Chens, smarter than all of them, Suping thought despairingly. Why didn't Uncle Dan and Uncle Juntao see that? What could she *do*?

She was only a girl and they were old men and university professors at that, of much higher intellectual status than she. They would not accept her criticism and Father, despite his respect for her, would side with his peers and reprimand her for presuming too much.

So she decided that later that day she would go back to see Secretary Guo in private. He was only a few years older than she and he would probably accept her advice, if carefully worded, not to try and claim undue credit for something he didn't understand, but instead to send in his report with just a few terse words to the effect that he left it to his superiors to judge the value of the two professors' statements.

If he didn't take sides, there could be no blame. He would get away with an official reprimand for having been too gullible in granting the two men a stay permit.

Suping saw that Ai Chen was reading Guo's notes and that he suggested a few different characters here and there, to make sure that a number of the composite words would be typical of an unscientific mind.

He knows that Guo will pass on the idea as his own, Suping thought, and he'll make sure that Guo will break his neck.

Guo made the changes as Ai Chen suggested.

'I'll make a fair copy later,' he said, 'and include it in my general monthly report to my leaders. Now, let me stamp your stay permits.'

Once he had the stamp, that symbol of petty officialdom's power, in his hovering right hand, Guo stiffened in the exquisite realisation of holding the ultimate power over one's fate.

For a fraction of a second he held his breath, and so, Suping noticed, did Uncle Dan and Uncle Juntao, willing Guo's hand down, then 'bang, bang' and the Chens' sigh of relief at the sight of the red circle with the five-pointed star appearing at the bottom of the permit.

Guo had by then reverted to his earlier attitude as the busy, haughty Party secretary and with a curt 'Report back to me in two months!' he signalled that the interview was over.

None of them spoke while they walked back home.

Many times they had walked the winding, unpaved road together, talking and laughing and Suping joking at the older men's lack of condition as they huffed and puffed up the steeply climbing curves and begged for a short rest to enjoy the beautiful panorama of the foothills and mountains surrounding the town below them.

Now she stared, with unseeing eyes, at the little clouds of dust her feet threw up with each step, paying no attention to the panting men behind her.

Suddenly she halted and turned to look at the two men coming up behind her, their faces red from exertion in trying to keep up with her. Relieved they stopped as well and looked up at her, while wiping the perspiration from their brow with a sleeve of their jackets.

'You just tried to destroy that young man,' she said in a strained voice. 'What is your purpose?'

'Exactly what you said, to destroy him,' Ai Chen replied calmly. 'My learned friend Chen Dan does not agree with me, not yet at least. I'm sure he will, however, and before long.'

Gao Chen sighed and shrugged his shoulders as his friend went on.

'I do not expect ever to be reinstated, however, I do expect that things will become worse, much worse, before there may happen to come a chance, a chance of one in a billion perhaps, that one day somebody with guts and the intelligence to match will stand up for the rights of the few and that the intellectuals will regain their rightful place in society. I'm sure, though, that that will happen long after I'll have departed this sorry world with its upside-down values. For the remainder of my equally sorry life I shall therefore do my best to destroy, in the subtlest possible way and whenever I'll get the chance, those pretentious mediocrities who now dominate our society.

'I am not fooling myself though. I know that what I can do, alone, is petty and pathetic in its utter insignificance. However, if I can inspire only one other person to follow my example and he, or she for that matter, inspires others, then perhaps the people will notice and also see those cadres, like that snotty Guo Chuanxing, as the mediocre, arrogant opportunists they are. I'm afraid your generation won't see that happen, Suping, however, your children might and it'll be your responsibility to prepare them for that so that they won't let the opportunity slip away, through sheer lethargy and cowardice, to restore the right order in our land.'

Suping shrugged her shoulders and in an uneasy silence they walked the last fifty metres to the small lattice-work gate of her tiny front garden.

Xu Ximing had apparently heard them coming up the road for he was waiting for them; voices carried far in the still mountain air and that worried him.

People living along the road could overhear their conversation too, of course, and they might not like what Ai Chen said and report him to the neighbourhood committee. He, his wife and daughter and Gao Chen as well would be guilty by association.

They would have to be more careful, also when they had their evening discussions in the garden.

Fortunately they had always spoken Putonghua in deference to Chen Juntao who was from Heilongjiang and didn't understand their Sichuan dialect. Hopefully the local people hadn't paid much attention therefore to what was being said by Teacher Xu and his friends.

When he had heard them coming up the road, he had carried the chairs outside and had arranged them, as usual, around the small, low table. His wife had put the box with green tea leaves, the mugs and the thermos with hot water on the table and had taken her usual place next to him, waiting for the other three to join them.

The Chens sat down with a sigh of relief and mopped their brow with the moist little towels Mother handed them. Suping put a pinch of tea leaves in each mug, poured hot water on and replaced the lids on the mugs.

Then she sat down as well and for a while the five of them sat in contented silence, enjoying the still warm late afternoon sun. From time to time they took their mug from the table, lifted the lid and sipped from the tea, sniffing its fragrance.

'We got an extension of our stay permit,' Chen Dan said, breaking the convivial silence. 'Suping will tell you how our interview with the new Party secretary went.'

Quietly Suping narrated what had happened in Secretary Guo Chuanxing's office. Father and Mother laughed heartily when she related the incident with the magazine and mimicked Secretary Guo's panicky reaction.

However, when she told them how Uncle Juntao had made Guo write down the quasi-scientific gibberish about the Chens' so-called study of Mao's Thoughts and added her own comment as to what she thought would happen to the secretary's report, Xu had laughed at first but then had looked a bit uneasily at his wife, who was clearly worried.

'You are full of anger, Juntao,' she said softly to Ai Chen. 'Anger and fear are mind killers. They make you say and do things that are not well thought through and which you regret afterwards when it's too late. If you want to wage your own private little war by deception you must be without such emotions lest you lay it on too thick. You must also be patient; the more subtle the tactics the longer they take to work. I think that you do not serve your cause well if in the process you destroy yourself as well. Besides, that would make *us* sad because you are our friend and because we think that some day a different China will need you. Finally, *we* have no wish to be drawn into schemes that may cause us unnecessary harm. So, please, show us the respect that we deserve, as your friends.'

Both during Suping's narrative and Mother's gentle yet firm rebuke of his ill-considered brinkmanship, Ai Chen had been staring at the ground between his feet, elbows on his knees, forehead resting in the palms of his hands.

When Mother fell silent, the others sipped their tea, without comment, patiently waiting for Ai Chen to say something.

'You have spoken well and with unusual perception, Guixian, my friend,' he said, after a long silence. 'I stand corrected,' he continued, 'however, I shall nevertheless carry on my little war, which I believe to be a just one, though never again shall I let anger or arrogance cloud my judgement thereby putting my friends, that most precious of man's possessions, in danger. Please forgive me if because of my egotism I have already made you uncomfortable.'

He fell silent and looked up at Mother with true despair in his eyes.

'That's all right, my friend,' she replied, smiling and mollified. 'However, now that we are on this subject, can't we combine our efforts and try and do something positive and constructive rather than negative and destructive? It all seems so depressing to me if malicious glee is the only thing, the only form of merriment left. Basically I believe my husband's analysis, which he has postulated to us on more than one occasion, to be true. However, it is a mathematician's analysis and it leaves us with no hope because of one factor he did not take into account. The subjective, unpredictable human factor was not given enough credit for its capability to cause change, to *force* change rather.

'You can't blame Ximing for that. He is an objective mathematician, not a psychologist and neither am I. However, since he first exposed his views, I have been very unhappy because of the hopelessness of it all. I felt that we could not let Suping, still so young and yet so intelligent, go off in life on such a negative base, without hope, resigned to a depressing and stifling *status quo* that probably need not be. Can we not, in the time we have left together, look once more at the situation from all possible angles and see whether we can find a ray of hope and if so, how we can contribute, each in our own way, to make that hope come true one day?'

With increasing astonishment Xu Ximing had watched his wife while she spoke her mind.

First she had rebuked Chen Juntao. True, it had been gently and nicely done, but a rebuke it had been nevertheless. And next she had implied that his own analysis might be incomplete. Lacking a crucial factor, she had said.

Finally, to crown it all, she had made a plea for a review of his theory, by all of them.

He felt a whole panoply of feelings rush through him: hurt, anger, shame and the love and respect for his lovely wife. His honesty and respect prevailed, however.

'I had not realised that you had such strong feelings, my love,' he said.

'Apparently I have been a fool for taking your assent, probably my daughter's as well, for granted while I sat there pontificating about my irrefutable arguments in favour of those so-call unprecedented factors. How pathetic, how very typical of the academic mind to relish its own verbal virtuosity, to resent and ignore anything that might upset the beautiful structure of its reasoning, however fallacious.'

Liu Guixian chuckled then burst out laughing at her husband's doleful face.

'No need to feel a fool, my love,' she said. 'It's because you are a man, and a mathematician to boot, that you cannot conceive of another logic than the direct one, the one that says that the shortest distance between two points is a straight line. That need not necessarily be true, you know. At least, for half of China's population, the women that is, it is just one possibility. Perhaps it is a straight line and then, perhaps it is not. Women have a different logic, as you should know by now. Not a very logical logic from your point of view, but still it is a form of logic. And since in our country alone five hundred million females of our species think and act in line with this form of logic you will have to take it into account whether you like it or not.'

Chen Dan, who hadn't said much since his friend Ai Chen had taken the initiative in Secretary Guo's office that afternoon, had listened with mounting admiration, first to Suping and then to her mother.

He had marvelled at the firm yet understanding and gentle way Guixian had put Ai Chen in his place without offending his pride. He had been moved by the loving yet humorous way she had put her pompous husband's rigidity into the much wider perspective of typical male reasoning.

He now laughed loudly, his own gregarious self again.

'What a display of intelligence and of the art of skating on thin ice,' he said.

'If our combined and shining intellects cannot find a solution to China's and mankind's problems, then, pray tell me who can! Xu Ximing, my friend, I have listened to you postulating your theories and I have found them hard to fault. I do agree with your wife though that there is indeed not much in your vision of the future to look forward to. However, being a man, I have considered only two options. Either I resign myself to the seemingly inevitable and surrender, like a dog, belly up and throat exposed, or I defy the system, raise barricades, wave flags, arouse the millions of downtrodden and get shot and be forgotten.

'But now I am told that there is perhaps a third option, the female option. Let's explore it! Ai Chen and myself can also add our ingredients to what has hitherto been the Xu-stew of ideas and philosophies. If Guixian and Suping add a few female flavourings it may become quite a nice, tasty dish. Juntao, my old and dear friend, I know that you have your philosophy all worked out and that you are biting your nails with impatience to impart your views. Pray begin, but be succinct! Don't belabour the obvious, as is your habit. We aren't complete morons and are able to grasp simple truths simply put.'

Ai Chen smiled at his friend's jesting and looked enquiringly at the Xus.

'Please do,' Xu said. 'We shall listen carefully to what the two of you have to say. We are honoured by your trust. Perhaps, just perhaps, we can come up with an idea original enough to catch on with others like us, to fertilise other minds like ours and hence contribute to a better society.'

Guixian and Suping looked at each other when Xu fell silent and smiled.

'There he goes again,' their smiles said, 'never misses an opportunity to see cosmic implications in even the most earthy matter.'

Gao Chen saw their smile and knew what mother and daughter were thinking but could never say of course.

He cleared his throat and said, 'That is beautifully put, Lao Xu. Let us now put our own minds in order first and worry about fertilising other minds later. Lao Chen, the stage is yours!' and he gestured to his friend to begin.

'Firstly, in the most general sense,' Ai Chen began, 'I am of the opinion that the free spirit, the free intellect, must have the first and final say in all matters of life, both in the private, individual sense and within the wider context of the whole society.'

He fell silent and hesitantly looked at the others, who stared back in stony silence.

'Secondly,' he continued, and his falsetto voice betrayed his nervousness, 'secondly, it is my view that superior intelligence capable of abstraction and intellectualisation is very rare in proportion to the sum total of humanity. It is therefore the first and foremost duty of every intellectual to seek out his kindred spirit in others and to do whatever he can to encourage the potential of that spirit, without bias or prejudice of class or race.

'His second duty is to seek to influence or, better still, to control the factors that make a society tick and to make sure that it evolves in a harmonious and balanced manner. This influencing, or controlling, must be done as unostentatiously as possible, regarding both the inner actions and reactions of society itself and its interactions with other, different societies. The guiding principle at all times must be, "*leave well alone*". Whenever possible leave people under the impression that what they are doing is of their own volition, that they can pursue their own ambitions without interference from high quarters. Let them enjoy the small things in life that cost so little but mean so much without some busybody telling them all the time *how* to enjoy or analysing the small things to death so that there is nothing left to enjoy.

'Those who, by virtue of their intelligence and learning, are in a position to influence or to control, must not impose their likes and dislikes but they should instead steer, or rather gently nudge, the vessel of society to remain on course. In dealing with the masses those privileged ones should act as recommended by Meng Zi, in dealing with the individual they should be pragmatic and heed Sun Tzu's words and, finally, in dealing with themselves they should follow Lao Zi. This is what I have to say.'

Ai Chen fell silent, all flustered. 'Very lofty and not of much practical value, I'm afraid,' he added ruefully.

'You have said it,' Gao Chen replied. 'I couldn't have put it as succinctly as that without the fear of offending you. Your philosophy is very commendable for its seeming kind-heartedness, however, it is execrable for its implied elitism, so typical of the superior intellectual of whom you are the stereotype, Juntao, no offence meant, of course.

'I think of myself as a man of learning and knowledge, not as an intellectual. You and Lao Xu, Guixian and Suping, probably take me for an intellectual, even though I do not look like one, however, I assure you that I am not. At least not in the sense that you understand the concept "intellectual".

'Xu Ximing is the descendant of an old and well-to-do Sichuan family and so is Liu Guixian and hence their issue Suping. You, Chen Juntao, are possibly the last in line of an old and venerable Heilongjiang family related to the formerly very wealthy and influential Chens of Shandong. Receiving the best possible education was a matter of course in those circles and a feeling of superiority was bred into you, both by your teachers and by your family elders. That you have not been able to act out that superiority is largely because of what you call the "upside-down values" that prevail in our present society.

'Were it not for the changed circumstances, for those "upside-down values", you would now be part of the elite few, deciding in, for and on behalf of hundreds of millions without even the slightest inclination to ask those plebeians for their opinion. It simply would not occur to you to do that. Out of the superiority of your education and your upbringing you would arrogate what used to be called "Heaven's Mandate" and decide for the lesser ones what is good for them and what they must like and dislike. And I doubt that you and your ilk would feel a strong urge "to seek out kindred spirits" amongst those voiceless hundreds of millions and "to do whatever you can to encourage their potential without bias and prejudice of class or race" as you put it so nicely, Juntao.

'And for me to sit here amongst you and listen to you extolling the superiority of the intellectual spirit and lamenting the loss of privilege that in your ilk's heyday came with rank and status and for you to assume that I share your view and feelings is ironic, to say the least.'

Gao Chen suddenly burst out laughing at the sight of the others' bewildered expressions.

'Never fear,' he chuckled, 'I am not a Communist and I do share most of your feelings. However, I am a realist, not the typical Chinese daydreamer, and my realisation that "the free spirit must have the first and final say" as Juntao so aptly puts it, comes from the other side of the social spectrum and is not, as in your case, simply taken for granted. I *know*, from bitter experience, that it is the only hope for a *humane* society and therefore, though we strive for the same goal, my motivation is that there is *indeed* no alternative, while yours is one of aggrieved paternalism.

'You barely conceal your peeved impatience and you just stop short of saying, irritably yet triumphantly, "We *told* you it wouldn't work. Now move over and let's start again. Let's take it from where we were so rudely interrupted and no more of that nonsense of wanting a say in your own affairs." You see, my friends, if we are going to approach the problem from that angle our efforts are doomed from the very beginning. There *is* no return possible to "where we were so rudely interrupted" as I persiflaged earlier when I mocked your motivation. We *cannot* turn the clock back and pretend that nothing has happened in the meantime.

'Many things have changed. A few for worse, no doubt about that, but by far the most for better and, believe me, when I say that I know it to be true from my own experience. However, I am the first to admit that because of the suppression of the free spirit evolution to an even better form of society has been halted. And that is the reason why I want the intellectuals to be given back the right to contribute and to participate in the running of our society. However, they *must* realise that things will never be the same as before and that if ever they are allowed to participate again it will on the basis of a new set of rules.

'Whether *we*, the five of us, can actually *do* something to make this happen, or even merely to start the stone rolling, I doubt that. I am afraid that it can come about only by way of gradual evolution as tensions, mutual mistrust, antagonisms, animosity and prejudices lessen with time. When the extremes of the social spectrum, left and right politically speaking, have evolved towards some sort of a diffuse centre. A centre of coalescing rather than opposing forces, of switching positions and support depending on what the issues are. All this will take time and, I'm afraid, an outside agent, a catalyst so to speak, to start the process. Let me explain what I mean.

'I am of peasant stock. My parents and their parents before them were landless peasants. Demi-serfs is probably a better word to describe their status, or rather the lack of it. For generations the Chen clan lived in mud and straw huts on the inside of a bend in the Dada River, about fifty kilometres from here. All throughout China's history people like the Chens of Dada He were starving by the millions in times of drought, drowning or dying from diseases in times of floods. And nobody cared.

'They were recruited against their will or killed or raped and plundered by the armies of whatever warlord or general who happened to pass through their part of the country, whether in pursuit of the enemy or in retreat. And nobody cared. They were kicked by left, right and centre and it hurt equally bad. And nobody cared. In their day-to-day struggle to survive there was one and only one preoccupation that dominated everything: their actions, their thoughts, their talk, and that was *food*! Where would the next meal come from, if any.

'If they worked, nothing was less certain than that they would be paid for it and how much. If they were paid they were lucky and if they were decently paid they could deem themselves very, very lucky. If they received nothing they could do nothing about it. Protest? They would be beaten up by their landlord's goons and quite literally kicked off his property; family, children, all of them. I was extraordinary lucky to escape from that sort of existence completely and then to become what I am now, but that is a different story for some other quiet evening, perhaps.

'The role of the peasant, of the ordinary man, that's what my argument is about. Throughout our long and turbulent history it was the peasants and the serfs, those with only duties and no rights, who rallied behind some driven and charismatic revolutionary and overthrew the existing power structure, whose one unforgivable mistake had been to push its abuse of the peasants too far. We Chinese do not resent authoritarian power. We expect and even prefer strict authority because it leaves no room for misunderstanding about who is the boss. What we do resent, however, is *abuse* of power and even then that abuse must be blatant and really deprive us of our most basic needs or else we won't stand up for ourselves and fight.

'We Chinese expect power to be despotic, arbitrary and corrupt and we don't really mind, mostly because we would probably be the same if we were in power. We even respect and admire the ruthless wielder of power as long as his favouritisms and nepotism are not too blatant and the public good he does outweighs his misdeeds.

'However, once we feel the abuse in our guts, our anger starts to build up, oh so slowly because we have a high boiling point and we can take a lot of abuse and for a long time, even to a point that to a foreigner we appear spineless and servile, a whole people in the image of Ah Q. This is because we keep hoping that the powerful will come to their senses so that extreme reactions can be avoided. Yet once we do explode there is no stopping us and frenziedly we destroy and kill every vestige of the abusive system until there is nothing left to destroy.

'Exhausted by the frenzy we install a new power centre. Always a centre, never a structure of consultative government by delegation of powers. Autocratic and centralised absolute power that suits our Chinese character best. But when I say "*we*," I mean my kind of *we*, the peasants because, as Guixian undoubtedly knows well, it was *they* who rebelled and caused the change. Never the city dwellers or, in more recent times, the industrial workers, though their suffering and misery was probably as great, if not greater than the peasants, since they cannot even seek solace for their troubled soul in the beauty and serenity of nature. I'm sure also that their lack of revolutionary zeal is because they don't have the gut feelings that come with living of the land and the fury *we* feel in our gut if we are denied that living.

'The latest but undoubtedly not the last of our great revolutionaries, Mao Zedong, knows his people's history well. His tactic to act in line with our sense of history is admirable. Against the advice of his former Soviet Russian comrades to start his revolution in the cities and amongst the intellectuals, as they had done so successfully before him, he, Mao, went to the poorest of China's poor regions and there he assembled his peasant guerrilla army. The rest of the story is known. And at present four out of five Chinese are better off than before the Communists seized power.

'The rural population can count its blessings. The people eat at least two meals a day and they have a roof over their head. There is work for all, there are schools for the children and care centres for the sick. They have their own peasant militia to ensure security and peace. For the first time in our history one can now travel in complete safety throughout our vast country. Provided one has permission to travel of course, but that's a different matter. The army is a disciplined, well-fed People's Army and raping and looting and plundering gangs of soldiers are for good a thing of the past.

'Taxes are low and, even more importantly, *equitable*, which is also for the first time since throughout our history the government, or rather the scoundrel and his cronies who had arrogated the lucrative governing business, used to sell, as one of their profit schemes, the licence to levy taxes to wealthy landowners and warlords. These local potentates extorted from the people every penny they possessed, three out of every four grains they harvested, quite often and quite literally starving them to death, paid off the government's licence and pocketed the rest. And a very substantial rest it always was. Unimaginable wealth and appalling poverty and nothing in between, that used to be China.

'Nowadays every man, worker and peasant alike, can afford the small luxuries of sharing a bottle of beer with his friends and of smoking a packet of cigarettes a day. Trivial? Prosaic? Perhaps to you but very, very important to them. So what do you expect? That the people will make revolution because they lack intellectual freedom? *Balderdash*! *What* intellectual freedom? That they can't *say* what they want perhaps?

'But they can! They can! They can because *nothing* what those people could ever say constitutes any danger whatsoever for the Party as they know *nothing, nothing at all*, about ideas which the Communists might have reason to fear. If you would only climb down from your intellectual ivory tower once in a while and listen to the things these people talk about and worry about, you would understand what I mean. That they can't *read* what they want, then, perhaps? How would *they* know? They *don't* read and *wouldn't* if you stuck a book on their face. So they don't *miss* your precious books.

'That they can't watch foreign films on television, then, perhaps? What do they *care*? They watch television in their community centre, if it hasn't blown up at least, the TV set I mean. They like traditional opera or the modern socialist variety about the heroic soldier or the model worker rewarded for producing his 6,786th teapot of the year, fourteen per cent over last year's figure, or about the production brigade of tractor factory number six celebrating its thousandth tractor.

'They *smoke* and *laugh* and *applaud* and go home to sleep. Maybe one or two dream of becoming a model worker themselves one day, however, that's about the extent of their life's ambition. That they are still upset by Mao's blunders such as his Great Leap Forward, then, perhaps? Forgiven and probably even forgotten already because the positive far outweighs the negative. Besides, the Communists have admitted that it was all a dreadful mistake. At least, they have admitted it not by saying so but by their omission to talk about it at all because a Communist *never* admits a political mistake and they have backtracked, so what more?

'Our kind of people, or perhaps I should take my distance and say *your* kind of people, always makes the mistake so typical of the naive and egocentric intellectual to think that because *you* are so sensitive about moral justice, ethics, the individual free spirit and other highfalutin ideas, *everybody* feels the same. What a hoot!

'I was born and raised as one of the vaunted and glorious proletariat and I know from experience the unconcern, the indifference, the apathy, the sluggishness, the passiveness, the crude grossness amongst the vast majority of the proletarians and I know only too well the surly, hostile mistrust they evince towards the loner who dares to be different and their unholy gleeful cruelty when they trample the sensitive dreamer in their midst. Save your own skin, avoid trouble, keep out of harm's way, shun people in trouble, roll with the punches and always and only think of yourself first and last. That's about the extent of their social awareness and behavioural code. I'm sure the proletarians the world over are much the same. They may be of different creed or race, however, their attitude and mentality are the same, without a doubt.

'So, what then *does* goad these people to rebel and revolt? I'll tell you what. Only the physical spurs of hunger and pain which they have felt for too long and which were inflicted so arbitrarily and abusively that even they can no longer suppress their anger, fear and despair. However, the Party does not maintain its authority over those who comply willingly or passively by inflicting physical suffering. And spiritual deprivation is not what rouses the people. So what is left? Not much potential to goad these people to rebel and revolt, I'm afraid. And there must be seven hundred million of them by now, I think. But I haven't finished yet. There is more to dampen your naive hopes.

'There are two other sections of the population for whom all that nostalgia for the good old times is nothing but the result of a bad memory. I am referring to the women and the young. Guixian and Suping should know, though perhaps not from own experience, that the Communists have truly liberated the women of China. With a few, rather spectacular exceptions during the course of our history, that anonymous poetess was right when she wrote some eighteen hundred years ago, "how sad it is to be a woman, nothing on earth is held so cheap".

'Chiu Kung, or Master Kung as Suping prefers to call him, I'm sure, was a misogynist, old prude where women were concerned. It was *his* ideas that have determined the female's lot right up to the Communist era. "Women and small men cannot be trusted," the venerable bastard said. "If you give them a hand, they take the arm and will show no respect. However, if you keep them at distance they bear a grudge. It is the woman with no talents who has merit."

'Kung's ideas inspired a book on the training of women that says, "a woman must always be ready to obey commands. If told to come, she must come at once, if told to go she must go quickly. If she does not obey an order, reproach her and beat her. She must work hard and be instructed morning and evening lest she forget her duties. When other people are present she must be modest and express no ideas of her own or opinions different from her husband's or father's or brothers'. When she is sad, she must not weep or scream for this brings bad luck for the family. When she is happy she may not sing for this encourages lewdness."'

Gao Chen burst out laughing at Suping's horrified face.

'You don't like it, young lady?' he asked mockingly. 'Perhaps now you prefer to be called Comrade Suping and be your own boss rather than Lady Suping in the good old times? Because what those males wrote concerned only the ladies, the women whose existence was acknowledged, the daughters of well-to-do families. But what about the girl child of the poor? Of the peasants? Of the serfs and demi-serfs?

'If at birth she wasn't simply drowned, like an unwanted kitten, or knocked with her head against a tree, like a rabbit for dinner, she was to become the slave of her father and her brothers until she was old enough, say twelve, to be sold as a servant or as a bed companion for some senile, old man who hoped to stay young by slobbering over her young body, or as a child prostitute to brothels in a faraway town. Maybe her price would pay for the food to get her family through the winter, or for the next year's rent, or for a new ox, or for the wedding of one of her brothers. The best thing that could happen to her was to be married off to a man of her father's choice, not hers mind you, to establish new family links so very important as a protection against the hostile outside world. Thus, after having been exploited as a domestic servant of her father and brothers, she became the servant of her in-laws, her husband and her own sons. Her only hope was a daughter-in-law of her own one day whom she then could treat as *her* slave.

'All that has completely changed, thanks to the Communists. Now a girl decides for herself whether she will spend her life at home, in a factory or both, as a married female worker. If she is intelligent she has equal chances to go to middle school or university. She can do any job that before was considered the exclusive domain of the man. You now see female engineers, technicians, welders, electricians, masons and what have you, there is no discrimination. She can marry the man of her own choice without all the old-fashioned hullabaloo and the expensive gifts and big feasts that saddled her family and the newly-wed couple with debts for many years. The Chinese woman is now a free person. For the first time in our history, she is a person in her own right and she enjoys it, I'm sure.

'So I ask you again: what do you think? Not a very revolutionary lot either, the women, I'm afraid. Finally there are the young. The Communists gave them freedom from their parents. They are no longer the possession of the family or, as the Communists say, the "family assets". I know, they are now expected to show allegiance to the Party and to the State, however, they do not nearly find that so restrictive as the domination by their family. So the young definitely also like this spin-off of the new social order.

'Apart from that, they wouldn't be good revolutionary material. We Chinese hardly take young people seriously, let alone that older people would follow them in some hare-brained kind of rebellion. Pipe dreams again therefore! So what's left, my friends? A near zero chance to foment a revolution, let alone to pull it off.'

Chen Dan fell silent and stared at the ground between his shuffling feet.

Not once during his monologue, recital almost, had either one of the others made a gesture as if to interrupt him to argue a point. They looked at each other, baffled, like children dumbfounded by the sudden bursting of their colourful balloons.

The man they had considered as one of their own sort had all of a sudden turned out to be an alien from a strange world of primitive needs and urges and ambitions, so utterly unlike their own cosy, neat and civilised little world.

Though friendly and sympathetic, there was no mistaking his mockery of their intellectual conceit and naivety and were it not for his compassion, at the end of his recital, for their evident dejection, they would probably have reacted indignantly to hide the hurt they felt.

Liu Guixian snorted a short, sad and self-deprecating laugh.

'We deserved that, I suppose,' she said, 'so much for our wonderful ideas and theories. For weeks, no, months, we rode our hobby horses, analysing, deducting, drawing conclusions that suited our preconceptions while praising ourselves for our intellectual integrity and objectivity and we never gave a thought to the basic facts of life which motivate the ordinary, the common people and I am aware how condescending that must sound to you, Dan, my friend. How conceited you must find us, to ignore the feelings, needs and hopes of half a billion people in whose midst we live our detached lives.

'We pass them on the road, our eyes meet briefly and we nod or mumble a greeting. They sell us a chicken or vegetables on the market, they repair our shoes, we feel their bodies pressed against ours in the bus or in the queue for a shop and yet we know nothing about them, or they about us for that matter. Why this separation in *us* and *them*? As if it were a matter of course? You reckon yourself amongst whom, Dan? Are you one of us or one of them?'

Guixian fell silent, flustered, and looked at the others almost despairingly.

'Don't go all overboard in your mortification, Guixian,' Gao Chen said laughingly. 'Who, after all, is *not* a victim of the *us and them system*. To everybody his own kind. Even the loner is living an illusion. Family, clan, committee, Party, Chinese, Westerner; one belongs and it's *us* and the others are automatically *them*.

'What is "us" for you, is "them" for somebody else; it's inherent in human nature. You cannot go against your own nature and force yourself to feel one with somebody you have nothing in common with, with whom you can't share your feelings or even one thought. I disagree with those so-called great minds, those starry-eyed visionaries and glassy-eyed dreamers, who claim that all people are equal. Whether equally good or equally bad depends on the great mind's disposition and digestion, however, both role castings are wrong.

'Trying to enforce a society based on either one of these two wrong premises has caused a lot of harm and misery. At least our sly fox Mao Zedong didn't make that mistake. He preaches the inequality of man and makes it the very basis and reason for his class struggle. Though class divisions are not sharply defined and certainly not laid down officially in any government or Party regulation, everyone knows in which class and, within that class, in which category he belongs and he behaves accordingly, knowing *us* from *them*.

'Firstly there is the *proletariat*, the *good people*, which, to Mao, means the poor, both materially and spiritually: the peasants, the workers, the soldiers, the lowest Party cadres, together also known as *the red elements*. Secondly there are the *servants of the proletariat*: the teachers, doctors, managers, technicians, engineers, military officers, shop attendants, militia and the lower and middle Party cadres. Thirdly we have the *bad people* or *the black elements*, a group of people disparagingly called *intellectuals*, such as scientists, professors, poets and writers of non-socialist literature, dissidents and counter-revolutionaries and other, disparate, groups of people such as former landowners, former rich merchants and ordinary criminals.

'The category "ordinary criminals" is somewhat equivocal in China since it comprises also what the Party calls political criminals. It is enough to be suspected of being against the Party and one is automatically a political criminal. It's quite a masterful job actually what the Communists did. First they proclaimed the "dictatorship of the proletariat", then they promoted the proletariat to "the People" and arrogated the mandate to govern in perpetuity for and on behalf of the People. Therefore, anybody who is against the Party is against the People and any overt or covert activity against the People is made a crime punishable by common criminal law. Hence the denomination "political prisoner" is not recognised by the Chinese jurisdiction. There are no political prisoners in China, only common law criminals. This has led to that beautifully crooked logic so typical of Communists in general and of the Chinese variety in particular.

'When Westerners protest against violations of human rights in China, our government rejects these protests with self-righteous outrage. It points out that China is a signatory to the United Nations' Declaration of Human Rights and proclaims, as I said with all the outrage required when the opposite is true, that it scrupulously respects those rights, including the right of its citizens to protection and security and that therefore criminals will be prosecuted and punished as laid down in, and to the full force of, the *law*. Therefore, China in turn lectures the Westerners: *your* protests are against *our* human right to protect our people against the criminals in its midst.

'Crooked logic? Perhaps to the foreigner, however, not to the Chinese. Besides the three classes I mentioned already and far, far above them, we have that one *superclass* consisting of the highest Party cadres, those above rank nine. Privileged, unassailable, unaccountable, self-appointing and self-perpetuating, these present-day mandarins live in luxury. They *and* their families lack nothing. They have their own shops with all the luxury goods and gadgets from the West and Japan. They have domestic servants and gardeners paid for by the party. They ride in chauffeured big, black Red Flag limousines, sitting pontifically in the back seat behind curtained windows, staring straight ahead while they woosh past the plebeian traffic halted in deference for the "great man" along the roadside. For you see, my friends, *they* are the ones who matter and *nobody else, whatever his class*!

'That whole, elaborate machinery of *State–Party–People*, all seven hundred million of "*us*" and regardless of the classes and subdivisions of "*us*", has one and *only one* aim and that is to keep *them* in *their* exalted position, to enable *them* to lead the life *they* lust for and to play the power games *they* crave. The very few of *us* who see through their hoax are expected to play ball and, as a reward, are then permitted to lead a reasonably decent life, by Chinese standards that is. For those amongst *us* who won't play ball and dare to protest, however feebly, life is made pretty miserable. So miserable that in most cases they see the light, repent publicly and shout a confession of their errors and henceforth comply. They still get their reward of a decent life. The Party is magnanimous, you see, however, all the same it keeps a discreet but close watch on these stigmatised people, just to make sure they keep complying. The intellectual in general and the Chinese specimen in particular is not cast for the role of social martyr, I'm afraid. At least, I know that I am *not*.'

'That was a long-winded answer, Guixian, to your simple question of whether I am one of your kind or not, one of *us*, whatever. As I see things, there isn't really much choice, is there? The Party has created and perfected a system, *the system*, by which it rules us and stays in power. *We* cannot fight that system and that's the curse, not only ours in the sense of *us* but for the whole of China and all Chinese, including the exalted ones and, believe me, some of them realise that. However, the system is so totally entrenched and has so permeated every fibre of the fabric of our society that undoing it would unravel that fabric and total chaos would be the result. Our thoughts and actions are conditioned by the system. Who the system wants you to be that is *who* you are. What the systems want you to be that is *what* you are. The system does not permit you to *function* as an *individual*. All but a few have surrendered under the relentless hammering of collectivism, collective action and unified thought. Those few who still fight for their individuality can only do so in silence and by adopting a disguise.

'I am lucky, my disguise is my looks as a proletarian, as a peasant. My refuge is in my mind where I can withdraw, alone, thinking my own thoughts, a blank behind my garrulousness. I am also a poltroon. The mere thought of physical pain inflicted on me by others, of torture if you want to call it that, nauseates me and, as I said earlier already, I shall never be a martyr for whatever cause. I have read Lu Xun's *Quintessence of Worldly Wisdom* and would advise you to do the same. I find his advice very appropriate for the losers that we all are. When I see social injustice, you won't hear me protest lest I be called a reactionary. When I hear somebody slandered or wronged and I know that it is untrue, you won't hear me speak up on his behalf lest I be accused of being in his pay. I don't worry, outwardly at least, about whether what the Party says is right or wrong, straight or crooked, but I smile and try to be friends with everyone. I keep silent and show no sign of what I am really thinking. You find this despicable?

'Sure you do! You prefer the daydreamer who confuses real life and his dreams? I hope you won't find out first-hand that the state's prisons and labour camps are full with these naive simpletons. However, during my spiritual escapes from the dreary daily reality I have my dreams. In my dreams I am free to fantasise that one day, not tomorrow, not next year, probably not even in ten or fifteen years, but simply that one day one or two of the Party's top leaders will find it in themselves to put the interests of the country and of the Chinese people as a whole before their own selfish interests and will permit, even encourage the *gradual* breakdown of the system's stranglehold on our society. Even just one man at the very top could pull that off, provided he has the power, the cogency and, not to forget, the ruthlessness to eliminate his opponents, even his so-called lifelong friends if need be.

'Once the people realise that they can loosen their shackles, that the system can be circumvented because its exponents are no longer all powerful, then the changes, slow and hesitant at first, will finally sweep through all echelons of society. The avowed objective of the changes, reforms is probably a better word, will be to transform China from its present lowly status as a backward and poor Third World country into a modestly modern Second World industrialised state. Once that has been achieved, and that modest aim will be difficult enough already, the country must be developed further, gradually and carefully, so that it can one day join the First World, a position China is entitled to because of the sheer size of the land and its population and because of the culture and age-old civilisation of its intelligent and industrious people. The visionary leader will also be a pragmatic one and he will realise that to achieve those goals in an orderly and controlled manner, he needs the support and co-operation of the despised intellectuals and he will propose a deal.

'The deal will be that in a quid pro quo for their acquiescence that the Party will remain sovereign and will get the credit for every acclaimed achievement and that *they* will take the blame for everything that goes wrong, the intellectuals can have their cherished spiritual freedom, albeit within limits and on tacitly understood conditions. They will be allowed to travel abroad for study and investigation provided the Party can be sure that they return and will not embarrass the Party and its leaders by making critical remarks about the situation in China while abroad. To make sure that they'll behave, their family members and relatives will be held responsible, kept as hostages as it were. They will be allowed to have contacts and exchanges with foreign scientists and to teach true science in our schools and universities. The Party will not question the lists of foreign books and equipment they say they need and they will be allowed to work on true research projects without surveillance by Party nitwits and directives from Chairman Mao.

'Talented and gifted men, women and children will no longer have to hide amongst the masses and pretend to be morons amongst morons. They will be allowed to be themselves, to stand out and develop themselves so that they can contribute to science and to the economy. Perhaps they will even be rewarded for their achievements. Foreign experts will be invited to come to China to teach us modern techniques and technologies. We will be allowed to have contacts with them also outside working hours, in their hotels or even in our home, to exchange ideas and to learn about life abroad. In my fantasies, when I dream about these things, I am there myself when it all happens and I feel like an important man, wallowing in freedom, exhilarated.

'I travel abroad, to America, to Europe, to Japan. I hold modern books of science in my hands and I marvel at the beautiful printing and diagrams and I discuss, on equal footing, with the scientists who understand and can explain all this. I feel with my hands advanced machinery and research equipment and I watch modern computers in operation while friendly, respectful foreign colleagues explain how it all works and then let me do the things. And then, all of a sudden, my heart falls and begins to pound heavily and I feel a chill in the nape of my neck as the nightmare, always the same, shatters my fantasy world. It's the nightmare of the backlash, of a return to a repression worse than the one we are suffering now.

'The reason for the backlash is reckless greed by the relatively few who benefit excessively from the reforms and hateful envy by the vast majority who couldn't make it and who have the old Party machinery on their side. It is inevitable that not everybody will benefit equally from the changes and reforms. Most will either not benefit at all, even lose out possibly, or the benefits will mean nothing to them. Disappointment after the initial, too high and unrealistic hopes will spread, especially when the winners, drunk with their success, become reckless and flaunt their wealth. Incited by this ostentation the masses, in a free-for-all rush and scuffle, will try and grab a part of the wealth and its toys and gadgets. The losers in the scuffle, their ego bruised, angry and envious of the winners, will clamour for the return of "the good, old days when there was still discipline and dignity in shared poverty". The losers amongst the Party's top leaders, who were shunted aside when they opposed the reforms, will seize their chance and return in force. They will purge the Party of every and all reform-minded members, regardless of rank and position, and the intellectuals will pay a terrible price for their support of the revisionists. China will plunge back into the darkness of paranoia and withdrawal, resentful of the whole world and ostracised by the whole world as never before.

'I have looked at this terrible problem from every angle and I have devised many schemes and scenarios by which this nightmare might be prevented, yet none of them stands the test of cold, logical analysis, except one! And that is an alliance, an unholy one perhaps, between the intelligentsia and the Party. We have a lot, if not our lives, at stake and we must be selfish and pragmatic and consequently do what ever we can to keep the reform-minded leaders in power. We must avoid the pitfalls of greed and unholy glee and not be unrealistic and make demands for which the time has not come yet. We must restrain the idealists, the dreamers and the vengeful hotheads amongst us and, if necessary, we must be ruthless enough to denounce them to the authorities.

'We must also restrain the impatient and reckless young, notably the students, from going too fast too soon in their demands for things they know and understand nothing about lest the Party feels threatened by their rash actions and overreacts in trying to re-establish its authority. To remain aloof and neutral, or even to take our distance to such immature people, will *not* be enough to pacify the nervous Party leaders. Though our hearts will bleed and our eyes sting with tears, we *must* denounce these reckless and irresponsible brothers and sisters, expel them from schools, universities and workplaces and openly and unequivocally support the Party's handling of their cases. Even if it comes to an open clash and the Party literally crushes the idealists and opportunists, *we must not be tempted into criticising the Party openly*. Unseen and unheard we can cry our hearts out. This is essential if we want the reforms to continue and to succeed. We must be reliable and trustworthy in the eyes of the Party leaders who gamble their own futures, and probably even their lives, on the success of the reforms. Wife, children, relatives and friends, all those hangers-on who profit from the leader's status, constantly harass him with their question what he has to gain personally and he can't answer them because from a purely materialistic point of view he has indeed nothing to gain and everything to lose.

'So why does he do it? I don't know and I *don't care*! However, what I *do* care about is that the leader is nervous and hypersensitive about signs, real or imagined, of threats to the security of his position and that at the first serious misreading of the situation he may make a U-turn and, in his frantic efforts to save his own skin, do more harm than all the other potentates before him. We must prevent that from happening! However, when I say that we must support the pragmatic, reform-minded leaders I don't mean to say that we have to do so out of loyalty or affection or respect. *No*! *Self-interest* must be the only motive for our support and co-operation! We owe no loyalty to the Party or to any of its leaders, whatever they may say or do that suits us. We must *never ever* trust the Party or the Communists, *any* Communist! Learn! As I did, from what happened to Shen Lishi!

'Lishi was my fellow student in Beijing and my best friend, still is. He fled with his parents in 1949, just before liberation. Via Hong Kong and Taiwan they reached America. His father became a professor of mathematics and his mother got a doctorate in nuclear physics and then became a professor as well, at a very prestigious university I have been told. Lishi became a brilliant physicist in his own right. In 1953 Lishi returned to China following the Party's appeal to Chinese intellectuals living overseas to return and help rebuild the motherland. The idiot! The good, kind, decent, naive idiot!

'First the Communists made him give up his American citizenship in exchange for a Chinese passport. This to give dignity to the motherland, they said. To show the foreigners that China doesn't need their help. Six months later they confiscated his passport and rejected his mandatory application for Party membership. Guess what they stamped on his application form: "Subject's loyalty suspect because of parents in America and relatives in Taiwan."

'Since then, now thirteen years ago, Lishi has been a minor clerk in the statistics department of the Ministry of Light Industry, compiling meaningless lists of Party pleasing figures. He hasn't even the right to travel outside the Beijing municipal area. Friendly, soft-spoken Shen Lishi who doesn't know what evil and malice are, who still believes, after having been betrayed, deceived, lied to, insulted, kicked and kicked around for thirteen years now, that it's all a misunderstanding that will be cleared up soon. He still refuses to believe that he has been betrayed, that the Communists never wanted his contribution but only wanted to deprive America of a great scientist and destroy a hated intellectual as an added bonus. He only wanted to help China and gave up a brilliant career for that, in America, where he could have worked on the most advanced projects and lived in every conceivable luxury.

'He now lives in a twenty-eight square metre apartment with only the most basic, bad quality furniture, a bare concrete floor, no telephone, no television, on the ninth floor, no elevator, twenty stairs to climb and descend, in one of those soul-killing, heart-rendingly monotonous grey blocks in the northern suburbs of Beijing. He earns sixty-five yuan per month, less than half of what that old Party hag, who supervises the communal telephone, earns. Fat, lazy, ugly and abusive, she sits in a concrete shed, operating the only telephone for six blocks of six hundred families each. One telephone for thirty-six hundred families! And when you call and ask her to call your party to the phone, she slams the phone down on you when that person lives higher than the third floor – because the people living on the fourth floor and above are stinking intellectuals and she hates them. And you can do nothing, nothing at all! When in my letters to Lishi I tell him how often I tried to call him, just to talk for a while and hear his voice, he writes back apologetically about that hateful dragon who hates him for everything he represents. Even his meekness enrages her because it prevents her from trampling him if he would ever find the courage in him to complain.

'I must understand, Lishi writes, that her legs are perhaps painful and one cannot expect her to first climb and then descend twenty stairs just to call him. Besides, he lives on the ninth floor, he writes, so he's very low priority. Actually, he is not expected to receive calls, he says. Only to make one now and then and not too often at that, in the shed, while she listens in and cuts him off if she doesn't understand what he's talking about or simply because she thinks he has talked enough. So perhaps I shouldn't try to call him, he says. Just a letter from time to time would make him happy. It makes me want to hit my head against the wall, to kick and kick and hit and hit any Party man or woman until they are dead and can no more yell and abuse and betray good, innocent people like Shen Lishi.'

Suddenly Gao Chen fell silent and he wept. His fists pushed against his eyes, he wept in desperate, impotent anger.

'I, you, we owe no loyalty to a system that betrays and crushes the finest of our people,' he hissed, shaking with anger and emotion.

Guixian gestured for Suping to go inside, whispering, 'Heat the soup and the chicken rice and call us when you're ready.'

Suping was glad she had a reason to leave the others for a while. She felt uneasy when adult men openly displayed such strong emotions.

The bleakness of Father's vision of the future was chilling because of its hopelessness, however, hope for what? Once you had accepted the tenet of Father's vision, that is that your whole life was foreordained, you could acquiesce and live your life, its very predictability and uneventfulness reassuring even.

The cynically manipulative society that Uncle Dan foresaw and seemed even to prefer, was frightening and Suping doubted whether she would be able to play the role he said she had to if she wanted to survive and wait and hope for better times.

Your whole life nothing but pretence? Nobody really being what he seemed? Was Uncle Dan faking his emotions also, perhaps now, this very moment? Was he perhaps trying to trap her parents, herself; to denounce them to advance his own case with the Party?

Who *was* Chen Dan? Was he who and what he said he was?

I'm getting paranoid, crazy even, Suping thought and angrily she slammed a bowl so hard down on the table that it broke into four pieces, which was bad, very bad. Shocked she picked up the pieces, hoping to find a fifth one, were it merely a sliver, however, no such luck.

Worried she began to prepare the food, while straining to hear what the others talked about outside. From the kitchen she could distinguish the men's voices but she could not understand what they said.

There was silence and then her mother's voice took over, clear, lilting, a bit like a soprano singer in an opera, Suping thought.

Maybe it *was* an opera, she thought wryly. All of them just play-acting, using make-believe emotions to hide the petty ordinariness of their trivial real-life characters, so unlike the overrated ones they had created for themselves here, in this puny garden behind their sugar-candy house.

'When I said a while ago,' she heard her mother say, 'that I found Ximing's analysis too mathematical since he didn't take the human factor into account, I hardly expected Dan to base his arguments almost entirely on the predictable unpredictability of that same human factor. Though both of them acknowledged the unchallengeable dominance of the Communist Party as the all-powerful and unaccountable power structure, their vision of the future is as different as their personalities.

'The inevitable conclusion after listening to my dear husband's purely mechanistic arguments is: we have no future. We have irreversibly entered an era of totally controlled and conditioned beehive-like uniformity of thought and action, of life itself, in an unchanging and timeless present conformity, compliance and obedience the only civil criteria by which we are judged. Man's inborn drive to improve his station in life, *the motive* for evolution, deadened, the revolutionary spirit dead, for good. The ironic tenet of Dan's intuitive and experiential arguments, as he develops them in what he calls his fantasies and dreams, is that the very perfecters of *the system*, the *Perfecti* themselves, will initiate the reforms and changes which may very well lead to their own downfall.

'How quintessentially and deliciously human to strive for perfection, the perfection of an absolute power structure in this very instance thereby ruthlessly and indiscriminatingly stamping out risk factors and dissent, and then, once the aim has been achieved and perfection enjoyed for a short while, to get bored by the tediousness of it all and allow, even lure, risk and instability back into the game, just for the thrill. Because that is what it all amounts to, isn't it? A *game*! And we, the erstwhile greatest risk factor, are quite naturally expected to play the game and help our adversaries not to become the losers. How ironic! The Human Comedy! However, I like it better than Ximing's morbid version and I think that I will play ball, as Dan calls it, once the experiments with reforms will start. The idea that it's all a game is somehow reassuring and it can be fun in a way.'

Mother fell silent and Suping was curious how the others would react.

Hurriedly she put five bowls of steaming, hot soup on a tray and carried them outside.

'It's still sticky and warm inside,' she said, 'too hot for heated discussions anyway, so I thought that perhaps you would prefer to eat the soup in the garden.'

The ordinariness of her words after all the verbosity and the smell of the hot soup brought the others back down to earth. Gao Chen laughed, a normal, cordial laugh, not that booming bassoon-like laugh, which somehow had never sounded quite real.

'The earthy sense of humour of you two women never ceases to amaze me,' he said chucklingly. 'With a few words you put all these weighty matters in their right perspective. Guixian summarises in a few easy sentences the quintessence of Ximing's and my own ruminations on the future of our country and then concludes that it's all a game, whereupon her daughter reminds us to eat our soup. Amazing! Why didn't I see it as a game? Too much in love with myself and my hobby horses I'm afraid.

'Guixian, when you chided my gloomy friend Juntao for his crusading and your formalistic husband for his morose doomsaying, you proposed that we find a code of conduct as you called it that would be both positive and fun to live by. You hit the nail on the head. Let us play the game and outsmart the system and outwit the Perfecti as you call the members of the Them Club. The Perfecti! What a splendid find. Even Juntao can play the game. After all, *war is a game less the fun*, for the victims and front-line soldiers at least. I suggest that after our meal Guixian will expound her views as to how to play the game. What do you think?' he asked.

Anxiously, Suping watched her father, then to her relief he smiled broadly.

'Nothing will ever surprise me again where my wife is concerned,' he said laughingly. 'I shall be very happy to trade my gloom-and-doom philosophy for a more light-hearted version. So I concur with Dan. I look forward to what you have to say, my love,' and he smiled at his wife with undisguised pride.

Chen Juntao, who had shed his habitual listless and gloomy air, chuckled, 'From Don Quixote to Di Stefano, I like that.'

'Who the hell is Di Stefano?' Gao Chen asked, his bushy eyebrows raised to touch his porcupine hair.

'A Spanish football player, the best in the world,' his friend answered to everybody's astonishment. 'Don't you read the newspaper? I only read the sports section. It's the only foreign news the Party censors don't bother to cook before consumption, so the journalists can give a free reign to their own imagination for a change. Quite a few amongst them are masters of the *double entendre* and I delight in taking some of their sentences out of their context and replace the name of the losing club, or of the player who was brought down, by the Party or by a particular Party official. Beautiful prose, man, and often quite daring and seditious. You should read it, Dan, and your own verbosity would gain in imagery. You're too pompous. So Guixian taking over the lecturing from you will be quite a relief and a welcome change from that droning of yours.' Ai Chen grinned mockingly at his friend's bewildered expression.

Guixian giggled like a teenager, then, all of a sudden, she said angrily, 'Don't ogle me like that. You make me feel self-conscious and now I think that perhaps I am being too simplistic and already I am searching my mind for longer and bigger words that sound more impressive and I will end up by saying exactly the same things as you did.'

She stamped her feet in exasperation. 'You see? Now already it's all a confused muddle in my head and I don't know any more which are your ideas and which are mine and it's all your fault! Stop talking for a while and eat! I need to think and for that I need silence!'

Like little boys who had been caught with their hands in the cookie jar, the men bashfully cast their eyes down on their soup bowl and for a while they concentrated on the food. To distract their thoughts Suping mentioned a small Hainanese restaurant in town where they served a particularly flavoured chicken rice she would like to learn how to prepare and the others in turn commented on the taste and flavour of dishes they had tasted in their favourite little places.

After the meal Suping cleared the table while the others, yawning and stretching contentedly, watched and listened to the various sights and sounds of town life down below in the valley, occasionally drawing each other's attention to some particular light or noise, guessing at its significance.

When Suping joined them again she brought two big bottles of White Cloud beer for the men to share and a bottle of orange squash for Mother and herself. While they enjoyed their drink, they talked with that mild self-mockery and indulgent humourousness that makes intelligent conversation amongst friends so enjoyable.

Gradually the conversation petered out though and everybody seemed to wait for Mother to start expounding her ideas. Suping saw her mother smile and she was as surprised as the others to hear her say, 'I know that you expect from me a synthesis of our different viewpoints and then some kind of an all-wise, all-practical set of rules by which we can all happily abide. However, I would like to go about it in a different manner, rather like I do it in school, where I prefer to let my students think for themselves and then come up with an answer instead of providing them with a ready-made solution. I have found that people would rather follow their own ideas than those of others and for me that's just fine.

'Let each find the solution to his problem himself and he'll be much prouder and keener to implement that solution than if somebody else has handed a solution to him on a silver platter. Each of you three men has touched on the same, basic points. Even my dear, straight husband talked at one time of it all being a game. However, as if a simple solution were not impressive enough, you drowned the basic tenet again in a lot of extraneous, philosophical claptrap, as Dan would call it, though he himself sinned as well, obfuscating the few and simple factors that motivate people. Since Lao Dan came closest to the point where he could have wrapped up the argument himself but didn't, I would really like him to do that now. Talk plain, simple Chinese and limit yourself to observations that we can all see for ourselves if we would only look for them. Go ahead, Lao Dan, and if you stray from the straight and simple path either one of us will interrupt you and put you back on track.'

Guixian fell silent and smiled mockingly at Gao Chen.

Chucklingly he said, 'That's by far the cleverest ruse I heard so far to get oneself out of a tight spot. All right, I'll try.'

He took his glass of beer from the table and swirled the liquid around to release the gas before taking a sip. His hands around the glass, he pushed himself up with his feet until his chair tipped backwards and he rested with his back against the wall.

'As a child, and later as a student,' he began, 'on the morning of what was going to be a particularly trying day, on my way to an examination or to a first day at work, I looked at an old tree I had passed by so many times before, at a grazing ox in the field beside the road I had walked so often before, at a peasant family planting the paddy, and I found great comfort at the thought that they would all still be there at the end of the day, unchanged and unaffected by the tribulations I would have gone through by then. Why was I comforted by the thought that in spite of all my troubles and fears certain things do not change, will always be there, the same? Because that thought makes your troubles and problems somehow seem less important and therefore less frightening.

'You know that whatever the outcome of your trials, that same old tree will still be there rustling in the wind, that same placid ox will still be chewing his cud, imperturbably, that same peasant family, like every evening, will be trudging back home for a scanty meal after a long day's work, each and all totally unaware of what you went through. And you feel less frightened and you talk to the tree, shout at the ox, wave at the peasants: see you this evening, all of you and you feel a surge of relief and the looming threats are suddenly less intimidating and you feel that you can manage. It is very important, I think, that we have something that is not subject to emotions and tribulations, something that remains always the same. It does not matter what that something is, in fact it will be different for each person, for each of us. An image in his heart, an object she carries on her person or, again, something familiar in his daily environment. Even an inanimate object takes on some kind of sentient life because you confer on it that sentience and you talk to it as if it can hear and understand what you say. But in fact you talk to a calmer and more reasonable projection of yourself and that gives you peace.

'The images that comforted me during my youth and my early adult life have faded away and for many years I had nothing to hang on to. Now, however, I have found myself an image to cherish again and that is this scene here that I will carry in my heart and mind. This house, this lovingly tendered small garden, the setting of the table and the chairs, the view over the valley, the town below, the mountains in the distance, unchanging and unchanged however long our absence will be. And whatever happens to me and wherever I may be, I'll evoke in my mind this setting and in my heart I'll feel its mood and its peacefulness and that'll give me the strength to carry on so that one day I can return.'

Chen Dan fell silent and pensively gazed at the faraway blue-black mountains, seemingly oblivious of the others.

Suping was touched by Gao Chen's words and, looking stealthily at her parents and Ai Chen, she saw that they were also affected by what Gao Chen had said.

She also had her fetish and she blushed at the thought of its silliness. It was the little gate in the fence of the front garden and the little squeak it made when she opened it; for her that squeak signalled that she had come home and had left behind her, for that day at least, what Gao Chen had called the 'tribulations' of the hostile outside world. As soon as she pushed the little gate open and she heard the squeak, all tension flowed out of her and she felt the warm, homey familiarity and peacefulness.

She wondered what kinds of fetishes the others had and if they were as silly as hers.

Nobody said a word, so as not to disturb Gao Chen's train of thought.

Emerging from his reverie, he took a draft of his tepid, flat beer, grimaced and continued his reflective monologue.

'I think that human beings, except probably the freaks, the psychopaths and sociopaths, have basically the same urges, hopes and fears and, as children, have all been afraid of the same bogeyman and in love with the same fairy. I think therefore that it is not a question of *if* but of *when* some of the Party's top leaders will begin to think that perhaps the time has come for a different kind of society. A society wherein people have a say in what they like and don't like. A society that is not kept isolated from the rest of the world. A society that tries to overcome its backwardness and tries to catch up with the other peoples of the world so that it can provide a better life for its own people. A society that dares to take the risk to let its children go to study abroad and return with new ideas, to let the foreigners come in to teach us and help us catch up.

'Herein lie both risk and hope and we must prepare ourselves for both so that we can avoid the risks and realise the hopes. The foreigners don't come to dispense charity and neither do we want that, so there must be mutual benefits. We get modern science, technology and equipment to improve our products so that we can send them abroad and with the money so earned pay for the things we need from them. At first the foreigners will have to live for a while in China to install the modern equipment and to teach us how to operate it, to teach us the modern technologies and computers, efficient working methods and management and so on. Prolonged contacts between those foreigners and our people will be unavoidable and notably our young will watch and listen and they will like not only the new things but also the foreigners themselves, their carefree friendliness and openness because that's how they are, my friend Shen Lishi told me.

'They are not secretive like us Chinese. Aren't we always unwilling to teach others unless we really have to and don't we then teach them as little as possible, and as incompletely as possible at that, lest those others become better than we are and replace us? The foreigner is not like that, Shen says. He is even proud if his pupil becomes better than he, Shen told me. However, the foreigners will not indefinitely put up with the discomforts and inconveniences that are so much part of our life that we don't even feel them any more. After a while they will demand the same standards of comfort they take for granted back home, in their own countries, or else they will leave or refuse to come to China in the first place. The cannot be forced by their governments or parties or companies as people in Communist countries can be forced to do things or to go to places they don't like. So hotels will have to be built to their standards with TV sets that work in each room and programmes they like. In their leisure time they will want to go sightseeing so cars will have to be imported to serve as taxis that don't break down and have to be pushed by the passengers.

'Our people will be struck by their carefree, happy-go-lucky behaviour, by their colourful, stylish clothes, by their modern cameras, by their friendly openness and by how different they are from the ogres as the Party has depicted them. What can we do to first cause the development to start and then to maintain its impetus? When we see the first signs of a change of mood at the Party's top levels we must not overreact and show too much enthusiasm lest the leaders become suspicious. We must always act in accordance with what I would call the Pig Principle.

'As you know, or probably won't now I come to think of it, a pig does always the opposite of what it thinks you want it to do. So the clever peasant beats it at this little game and when he wants the pig to advance he pulls the beast's tail and when he wants it to retreat he pulls it by its ears. Human beings are like pigs in so many respects, the Party leaders no exception. If we wish them to continue on a path of thinking we must show a certain reluctance to make them think that we oppose them for our own, selfish reasons. That will strengthen them in their belief that they are right and they will force ahead. As teachers or professors we must encourage our pupils and students to observe and compare and draw conclusions. As intellectuals we must subtly provoke our fellow citizens to do the same: watch the foreigners, observe what they do, compare their behaviour to that of our own people and draw your own conclusions.

'There are so many opportunities each day to play this little game. Only we must be careful and subtle and always apply the Pig Principle. If a student or trainee talks enthusiastically about the foreigners and their way of working, their equipment and technology, we must seem to belittle his views a bit and downplay a bit his enthusiasm about everything foreign. That both keeps us in good standing with the Party and it enhances our objective. So we must not tell the young people: 'Observe and see for yourselves that everything they have and do is better.' No! We must tell them: 'Observe and see for yourselves that the foreigners' reputation is exaggerated and that our Chinese equipment and way of doing things is just as good or perhaps even better.' That way we stimulate them to be critical and to challenge the foreigners to prove their superiority, which requires a much closer contact between them and our people. Useful for ourselves is that the Party officials see us as the defenders of Chinese knowledge and pride. A drawback for ourselves is that the technocrats amongst the Party officials know of course that the foreign things and methods are better and *they* will see us as envious old dodderers, unwilling to admit our backwardness.

'The foreigners themselves, when they hear about our objections, will speak with contempt of stubborn, old asses stuck in the past, unable to adapt to change, incapable of understanding modern concepts, dangerous old piss-vinegars opposed to change because they can't cope and are afraid of losing their position, and so on and so forth. But, if we are clever, we can even make that drawback work to our advantage by giving the impression that we are not actually *hostile* but merely try to be *objective*, conservative perhaps but objective nevertheless. Party technocrats, students, trainees, managers, foreigners, they will fall over each other in their eagerness to convince us that we have it all wrong. So we will be invited to lectures, to visit new factories, to join investigation delegations sent abroad; all to make us less sceptical, even enthusiastic perhaps.

'Once the whole process is well under way, it will feed on itself. The thirst and hunger for more information, education, goods and a different lifestyle will become ever greater and will no longer be satisfied at the controlled snail's pace the Party had originally in mind. Our young people will become increasingly demanding and impatient and they will want everything and at once and, if they think that it's the only way, they will demand all that by force. That is, of course, a dangerous development and it will force the Party to make a crucial decision. To give in means losing control of the situation and having its power undermined, for good. Not to give in means having to re-establish control by, I'm afraid, very forceful methods and this will inevitably lead to a return of the old, repressive situation. We must *not* allow that to happen!

'So we must temper the young and make them understand that they'll spoil everything for everybody by wanting too much too soon too fast. We can't afford to indulge in unholy glee at the Party's dilemma but instead we must do what we can to avoid that the old Party leaders and the Party itself be embarrassed and lose face. Communists will never give up power voluntarily. Everywhere they are in power, they have taken it by force and the only way to remove them from power is by force as well, by brute force, the kind that comes from the barrel of a gun, the only kind they understand, as you pointed out yourself, Ximing. They do not understand the subtle, pervasive force that a discontented, disillusioned, unwilling and obstructive people represents. You can't shoot people who follow orders, but slowly, oh so slowly. Or who make mistakes because they say they didn't understand the order but seem quite genuine in their expressions of regret. Or who show no initiative and just sit there waiting for orders. Or whose forgetfulness, ignorance or just plain stupidity are just a clever cover for their very subtle little acts of sabotage that underline so many of the breakdowns in our factories.

'Our fellow intellectuals, the engineers and vice-managers, who have to deal every day with these frustrating matters, have a very difficult and risky role. They must gloss over blatant obstruction and gross errors while at the same time, for the Party's benefit and to allay suspicion, they must show concern for the effects of the mistakes, give vague and far-fetched answers when questioned and be zealous to repair the damage or make good the delay. Their seemingly spineless attitude won't make them many friends, I'm afraid. Irritation, annoyance and suspicion from the Party's side, reproaches and contempt from the side of the young workers and students, mockery and disdain from the side of the foreigners. We will disappoint everybody in their hope for our co-operation or guidance or leadership. And yet there is no other way. When, not *if* I hope, twenty-five years from now there will be a shift from this totalitarian one party rule to a more pluralistic society wherein also smaller groups of people with differing views and ideas have no fear to speak up and if such a shift can be achieved without the firing of guns, we will have succeeded. If on the other hand we let ourselves be blinded by apparent achievements and be fooled by a seeming inaction of the Communists and become overconfident and push things too far provoking a backlash by a scared Party, we will have failed. We will have failed not only ourselves, but most of all China's youth and its future and, not to forget, the hopes of the outside world as well.

'Despite all our precautions, however, we must be prepared for a desperate, last-minute attempt by the old Party stalwarts to stop the slide into what they perceive as complete chaos and to reverse the tide. The attendant violence will be of short duration but its toll will be terrible. However, a number of the smartest, younger Party leaders will gamble correctly that the reforms are irreversible and will remain on the side of the reform-minded top leader and a face-saving compromise will be worked out. The reforms will continue, however, at a slower pace and under tight Party control. No such alien nonsense as a fully democratic society Western-style and the human right to make mischief. The intellectuals will remain vulnerable. The old-style Party cadres now suddenly turned reformers to protect themselves know that we have a longer memory than the average person and they will not trust us. True to their nature they will try to make us suspect in the eyes of the people by accusing us of opposing reforms for selfish reasons, of co-operating in the past with anti-reform forces in the Party and so on.

'Perhaps you can't even blame them for that. The whole Party culture is one of mistrust, innuendoes and downright slander and defamation to defend one's own position or to get rid of competitors for better positions. It has been bred into them from the moment they become young pioneers: be vigilant against enemies from within and without, *be vigilant*! No wonder they are all paranoid. They have been brainwashed for too long. I suggest therefore that each of us decides for himself and herself what he or she will do in whatever the circumstances may be, keeping in mind that there will be no credit or glory to be got whatever he or she does. Let us be true unto ourselves in the first place and to our friendship to the extent that this should not require us to sacrifice ourselves. I wouldn't want anyone of you harming him or herself for my sake and neither will I do so for any of you. I am sorry for my emotional outburst earlier this evening. I know it made you uncomfortable, Suping. Please forgive me.'

Gao Chen fell silent but he kept staring in his glass which he continued to swirl though there was no beer left.

Suping hesitated, waiting for Father or Mother to say something; when they remained silent, she said, 'There is nothing to forgive, Uncle Dan. I'm grateful that you have shared your innermost thoughts and feelings with this young and inexperienced female person. I promise you that wherever I shall be and in whatever situation I'll find myself I shall think of you and your advice before I say or do anything whatsoever. You have shown me that I needn't be ashamed if I'm weak and fail my parents or my friends when my instinct for self-preservation is stronger than my feelings for them.'

For the second time that evening Chen Dan was moved to tears, this time, however, not by impotent anger but by relief at Suping's words.

Also for the second time that evening Xu Ximing looked as if he couldn't believe his ears.

First his wife had spoken in a way he had never thought her capable of and now his daughter added insult to injury. She had spoken not only without first asking his permission, no, she had answered Chen directly and in a tone and in a manner that left no doubt that she had made up her mind all for herself and would not give up her opinion even if, he, her father, told her so.

He was in for another shock when Chen spoke directly to his daughter as if she were an equal amongst equals.

'Thank you, *meimei*,' Gao Chen said, calling her little sister, 'thank you for listening to me and thank you for your esteem.'

Xu Ximing was visibly prey to conflicting emotions. Pride and resentment. Pride at his wife and daughter's grace and intelligence and at the respect the two scientists showed them; resentment because none of them had shown him any special consideration. On the contrary, they had dissected his arguments and rejected most of his theories as mere examples of inadequate reasoning. But his honesty and decency won out and, smilingly, he said, 'Lao Dan, my dear friend, I thank you also and my daughter,' (and the slight emphasis on 'my daughter' was not imaginary,) 'has also answered for me and, if I may presume as much, also for my wife judging from her smile. It's getting late and cold. Let's go inside and have some more hot soup.'

They carried the chairs inside and Ai Chen went back one more time to fetch the table and the mugs and glasses.

Xu locked the door and his wife lit a few wax candles, which gave a cosier atmosphere than the single, glaring, white neon tube that hung by two thin chains from the centre of the ceiling. Suping served them a last bowl of the hot, sour and pungent soup that made their noses run.

The last dregs of the soup finished, Ai Chen cleared the table and Xu disappeared into the bedroom, mumbling to no one in particular that a small celebration was in order.

He returned with a bottle of sweet, red wine and the famous red and white porcelain bottle of *maotai*, the fiery one hundred and forty proof spirit made from sorghum or kaoliang.

He took five small tumblers from a drawer of the cupboard and filled them to the rim, red wine for the women, *maotai* for the men. They took their glass and sat down carefully in order not to spill the precious liquor and wine.

Xu remained standing and declared, 'To our friendship! *Ganbei*!'

They lifted their glasses and repeated, 'To our friendship! Bottoms up!'

Xu refilled the glasses. 'To the success of Lao Dan's thoughts! *Ganbei*!'

They lifted their glasses and repeated, 'To the success of Lao Dan's thoughts! Bottoms up!'

Xu refilled the glasses and stated, 'To our motherland, to China! *Ganbei*!'

They lifted their glasses and repeated, 'To our motherland, to China! Bottoms up!' and for the third time they emptied their glasses in one swallow.

Xu refilled the glasses once more and, staring at his own, he said, 'Now that we still have our wits and a bit of fire in our belly on top of the spicy soup that made our noses run, I want us to think just one moment of our immediate future. A political storm is brewing. I feel it, you feel it. The atmosphere is literally crackling. People are nervous and tense and scared. Rumours galore all over China. The most persistent rumour is that Chairman Mao is losing control of the Party and is fighting and scheming for his political life – probably for his physical one as well. The army is divided in its loyalties and will not support him entirely. Mao needs Lin Biao, the bourgeois, but he does not trust him any more than he does his other so-called comrades, least of all Liu.

'Our only hope is Zhou Enlai, however, he is an exponent of Lao Zi's philosophy and consequently he won't act unless he is sure he will succeed.

Jiang Qing hates Zhou because of his culture and decency and not least because of his moderating influence on Mao. I am afraid therefore that she will take the initiative to destroy Mao's real and imaginary enemies. From what I have heard about her, she is a maniac, a fanatic, a hysteric, devoid of compassion and contemptuous of ordinary human decency. Whatever campaign she is about to releash, it will be terrible and on an unprecedented scale. If and how we are going to survive the ordeal, I really don't know, however, what is certain is that we will be uprooted from our sheltered little place here and swept away by the gale and floods of Jiang Qing's wrath, indistinguishable amongst the flotsam of tens, hundreds of millions of our people.

'Our only chance of survival, I see that now very clearly, is to follow Lao Dan's advice to bend with the prevailing wind and to try and stay adrift in the flood waters with the sole objective to stay intact, both physically and functionally. For that we need a dream! A dream shared amongst the five of us! A dream to withdraw into when the world around us has gone crazy and the realisation of our insignificance and helplessness threatens to destroy our last hope. However, this must be a simple idea, not the highfalutin one for the future of China and the world.'

Xu looked up from his glass and lifted it in the others' direction. With a tremor in his voice, both from emotion and a bit from too much liquor as well, he declared, 'To our reunions, here! In this house! In this garden! Every three years until the last one of us comes back here for the last time to die. That is my dream!'

Solemnly they saluted each other with their glasses and repeated, 'That is our dream!' then in perfect unison they threw back their heads and emptied their glasses.

## *Chapter Fourteen*

### Chen Dan's Recipe for Beggars Chicken, August 1966

Suping couldn't remember how or when she had got to bed, but when she woke up the next morning the sun stood already high in the sky.

She had a headache and a foul taste in her mouth.

Father and Mother were still sleeping but judging from the sheets lying on the floor it must have been some night.

Suping blushed and smiled. Good for them, she thought. She wondered what it would be like to make love to a man, to have your body invaded physically.

Respect surely was not enough because the mere thought of such intimacy with Uncle Dan made her shiver and she felt a wave of nausea constrict her throat.

She rushed outside to the toilet shed in the back garden where she retched and vomited.

Relieved but still light-headed she shuffled back to the kitchen where she saw Ai Chen making tea. He looked at her and grinned, gesturing for her to sit down. He handed her a mug of strong, hot tea.

'Sweet and coloured wines and spirits are poisons for the liver and they make you sick,' he said. 'Better to drink a white spirit, like *maotai*, if you have to have alcohol at all. Filthy stuff. Gao Chen has been tossing around in his sleep the whole night. Fighting whole armies of Communists, I think. With him kicking and flailing I couldn't catch any sleep, so I spent the night on the couch in the front room and slept quite well actually.'

Suping sipped the strong, hot tea and was vaguely aware of Ai Chen talking to her. She nodded a few times but had no idea what she was agreeing with.

'It's late already,' she said suddenly. 'Perhaps I had better see a doctor and ask for a few days' sick leave. I'm sick and tired anyhow of the poisonous weeds and fragrant flowers. What a bore! What a waste!' She blew a long breath between pouted lips. 'Pyeeew, to hell with it all!' she exclaimed. 'This is the new Suping speaking. I'm going to watch and second-guess people. I'll play the dumb, silly woman who needs to have everything explained twice and then still does it wrong. Do I look stupid enough like this?' And she let her mouth hang half open and her eyelids droop.

'You rather look like a lovesick Mongol,' her father said behind her. 'Don't play the fool, it doesn't become you. Besides, you can't change from one day to the other, it's just not credible. The new Suping, though deep, acts shallow and dim. She does not display herself nor does she dispute, contend or compete. Thus she will be considered as harmless by the contenders and competitors and go unnoticed and thus she will be able to preserve herself. Try it for a while,' Xu added, chuckling, 'it may even become you. Quite nice for a change, I'm sure.'

Gao Chen and Mother had come into the kitchen and while sipping from the tea Ai Chen had offered them, they had listened to Father's remarks.

They all laughed at Suping's indignant, blushing face and then she saw the humour of it all and she burst out laughing.

Mother heated the rice gruel with salted pork meat left over from the previous morning and gestured for the others to serve themselves. They took some but nobody had much appetite. After a few morsels of the meat Suping put down her bowl and chopsticks.

'My stomach is still a bit upset,' she said, 'I prefer to wait until tonight and in the meantime drink weak, black tea.'

'I'll prepare dinner tonight,' Gao Chen said, 'the authentic Beggars Chicken as prepared by Great-Grandmother Chen more than fifty years ago. Suping, would you like to come with me? First we'll go to the market to buy the ingredients. We'll bring them home so that Ai Chen, Guixian and Ximing can start the preparations while you and I fetch the mud. Clean mud is essential so I'm afraid we'll have to go quite far upstream where the river doesn't yet stink of sewage and chemicals.'

Happy because of the return to the normality of everyday life and at the prospect of a good few hours' walk along the river, Suping quickly made her toilet and got dressed in a comfortable pair of trousers and a wide, raw silk blouse. With her long, glossy hair tied into a ponytail with a red ribbon she looked ravishingly pretty.

Gao Chen, dressed in the same clothes as on the day he had arrived now a year ago already, looked like an old peasant.

Talking animatedly about the effect of various types of mud on the taste of Beggars Chicken and that therefore the taste would differ from place to place and that even in the same place no two preparations would ever be exactly the same, they walked down the road into the valley and crossed the bridge into town.

First they went to the state market where they bought a fat, live chicken for three yuan and twenty fen.

Gao Chen tied the cackling and flapping bird's feet together with a piece of plastic string and hung it, head down, on the thick walking stick he always carried over his shoulder.

'The vegetables and herbs are no good on this market,' he said, 'look at the filth and those miserable, withered vegetables. Terrible. Nobody cares. We'll have to go to the clandestine market downtown. The peasant women unload their best wares there first before they dump the damaged and withered vegetables and the small, worm-eaten fruit on the state market's scale over here. The market supervisor doesn't care about quality and he pays the peasants by weight only. Besides, the women always have a sack with extra good quality wares for him and his two assistants. So, their receipt always shows overweight, more than the quota they have to supply to the State, which keeps them in good standing with the Party.

'The peasants pocket the few yuan the State pays them for their lousy stuff and rush back to the clandestine market where they sell their good stuff to the privileged, mainly Party officials who can afford to pay the higher prices. That's how the system works. Everybody happy, except of course the true proletarians, who have to be content with the rubbish here on this dank and filthy dump they have the gall to call a market. I can't afford to pay the clandestine prices either but I hope that there will be peasants from Dada County and that I can talk to them in their own dialect nobody else understands. I'm sure they'll give us a good discount. Who knows, maybe they even remember Hedgehog Chen who eloped with the Liang girl and Black Dragon Liu and they may give me the few things we need for free.'

Suping clapped her hands and, walking backwards in front of Gao Chen, she exclaimed, her eyes wide open and sparkling with excitement, 'Uncle Dan! What did you say there? You eloped with a beautiful girl! I want to know everything, *everything*! Please Uncle Dan, tell me, tell me! *please*!'

People hurrying past in the street halted and looked curiously at the unlikely pair.

'Tell her, old man!' a few men yelled at them. 'Tell the pretty wench what she wants to know or *we* will *show* her!'

Gao Chen grinned and yelled back with his stentorian voice, 'Go ahead! Give us a surprise! Show the lady what you think she wants to know! But use the sow of this comrade here!' and he pulled the rope from the hands of an old peasant who was walking a monstrous, black and white sow, its tits almost dragging over the ground, to the slaughter section of the market. 'It's more your genre!'

The small crowd that had formed around them roared with laughter, not in the least the two men who had shouted their defiance.

'Now we know what you need that chicken for, old man,' one of the men, a big, jovial fellow, shouted back at Gao Chen. 'Even with its feet bound together it may not feel a thing.' And laughing good-humouredly everybody continued on his or her errand.

'What a vulgar man you can be, Chen Dan,' Suping said with a reproachful sideways look at the still chuckling man beside her who, during the past year had dazzled her with his sardonic, intelligent wit and who now had shocked her with his earthy, rude vulgarity.

'Vulgarity is just one of the many ingredients of the human stew, my love,' Gao Chen said, 'leave out one and the taste is somehow not quite right. Many so-called righteous people are impossible to digest because they lack a sense of humour. They see the mote in other people's eye but not the beam in their own. Don't be a prig or a prude *meimei*. You have a good sense of humour, so use it! One good laugh solves more problems than a thousand piss-vinegars crying foul.'

Suping burst out laughing. 'I believe you are right,' she said. 'I saw that those people were trying to provoke us and make trouble, however, then they laughed at your joke and the momentary tension was defused. No victims, no bullies, no offence, no hurt, just a shared laugh. I'll try and follow your advice, Uncle Dan.' She fell silent, then added, chuckling, 'That makes a lot of advice to follow already.' And, in a gesture of affection, she took the older man by his arm and fell into step with him.

They continued their walk downtown through a warren of narrow, mostly unpaved streets.

They kept to the middle of the street since the sidewalks were full of old people sitting on low stools or on very tiny chairs or just squatting, plucking a chicken, cleaning vegetables, pressing cakes of coal dust and loam, patching a jacket or a pair of trousers, washing dishes in the gutter or merely talking or sleeping or staring ahead at nothing in particular.

Those living at street level had hung their laundry and mattresses, the latter often torn and full of holes, on a couple of chairs or on a rack, outside, on the sidewalk or over a piece of rope strung between the plane trees on either side of the street. Those living on the second floor of the old houses had hung theirs on a pole stuck out of a window or on a rope shared with the neighbours opposite.

Gao Chen and Suping enjoyed the intense humanity of the scene, the peacefulness of ordinary people living their ordinary lives.

'Nothing will ever change these people,' Gao Chen said. 'Emperors, generals, Party leaders, earthquakes or floods destroying half of China or just the village further down the river, they just don't care as long as their own basic needs are not touched. The sameness of their chores, day after day, year after year, of their preoccupations and obligations within the family circle, that's their world and it lies right here, in this warren of streets. What goes on outside does not interest them, not out of deliberate indifference, mind you, but it simply does not occur to them to care about what has no bearing on their basic needs or small worries.

'Bloody-mindedness? Possibly. But then, throughout thousands of years of bad experiences and hardship, we Chinese have discovered the hard way that interfering and meddling in other people's affairs, or even showing mere curiosity, brings nothing but trouble. So, I think it has become part of our genetical make-up to mind our own business and to leave well alone.'

By then Chen Dan and Suping had reached an intersection of six narrow streets forming an irregularly shaped kind of small square. The whole open area was taken up by heaps of cabbages and watermelons and by trestle-tables with the smaller and more delicate fruits, herbs and vegetables.

There were also many wire cages with quails, rabbits, rats, snakes and hairless dogs.

Horse and donkey carts and handcarts stood around the open space, blocking off the streets.

The peasant women and their daughters, wearing a dingy white bonnet, sat on small stools beside their wares, attending to their customers, gruffly, to discourage any attempt at bargaining.

'Let's walk around a bit first,' Gao Chen said. 'I'll listen to what those women talk about amongst themselves and hopefully there'll be a few from Dada County. Then let me do the talking.'

Gao Chen and Suping strolled leisurely amongst the displayed wares, feeling a cabbage here, a watermelon there but buying nothing.

They stopped in front of a trestle-table with all kinds of herbs, garlic, red and green chillies, tomatoes, oozing honeycombs on oil-paper, fresh and preserved eggs, sesame cakes and sweetmeats. Behind the table sat two women, how old was hard to tell, but very old for sure.

Tiny feet in black slippers, crooked little bodies in rust black, quilted pyjamas, shiny and smelly from years of slobber and wiping greasy hands and dripping noses, a black scarf wound around the scrawny necks and wrinkly faces, wisps of grey hair not quite hidden, the two women sat there, motionless, indistinguishable from one another, small monkey faces staring at the passers-by with watery, cloudy slit eyes.

Gao Chen stared at the two crones. Suddenly he said something in a gravelly voice, toneless, almost in a mumble.

Suping didn't understand what he said, however, from the reaction of the two old women it was clear that they surely did. Their eyes and mouth opened wide and they stared back at Gao Chen as if they saw a ghost.

Uttering a kind of hoarse croak, they got up from their stool, gasping and wheezing, and stumbled forward, their grubby little claws stretched out to Gao Chen who took them in his big paws.

Crouching to lower his head to the same height as the old women and holding their hands in his, Gao Chen croaked and grated with apparent delight in answer to what sounded to Suping like two angry turkeys disputing a worm.

This went on for at least five minutes and Suping began to feel uncomfortable with people around them staring at the scene and at her, when Gao Chen looked up at her from his crouched position and said, grinning mischievously, 'Meet Auntie One and Two, the twin sisters Liang. I once lived for two weeks under their bed, in hiding from Chiang Kaishek's gangsters who were after me. As beautiful young women the two sisters fell in love with the same man, however, he loved Auntie Two more than Auntie One.

'Since Auntie Two was three minutes younger than One and since they loved each other too much to cause one another pain, Two told the man that it was either both of them or none and he fled in panic, the coward. He found another woman, fathered her eighteen children in anger who all died in anger, some in establishing the People's Republic, the others in defending the old chaos, likely enough killing each other in the process. One and Two never married, stayed together through bad and good times and now make a living by selling the clandestinely grown produce of the peasants of Dada County. The cakes and cookies they bake themselves though.'

During Gao Chen's introduction the two old women had been staring at Suping, their eyes suddenly sparkling and alive. When he finished, one of them, One probably, according to first birthright, said, in a surprisingly clear voice and in well-modulated Standard Chinese, 'Since this boy here lived in and under our bed for almost two weeks and must have heard quite a lot of yearning women's talk, I wonder whether he became any good at it. We tried to educate him but it was not much use, too regressed still then. Tell me, girl, does he do any better now?'

Suping's face felt like it was on fire.

Gao Chen protested, 'Shame on you two. She is the daughter of my best friend and she calls me uncle. Besides, times are different now as you must be painfully aware of yourselves. So stop the teasing!'

Two cackled, hopping up and down, frighteningly resembling an excited monkey with her crooked legs and her hands touching the ground to keep her balance.

Horrified, Suping looked at the scene. She was no prude, however, the innuendoes and dirty minds of these older people disgusted her and for the first time she realised that the present was a lot healthier, morally at least, than the vaunted past.

First there had been those older men in the street and Uncle Dan's vulgar allusions and now these horrid old harridans. Was that all those people could think about?

How lucky she was to be alive now, to be able to be herself, to move unselfconsciously amongst other people as just another human being, not constantly being reminded of the fact that she was a woman or supposed to behave like one, whatever that meant.

No harassment, no allusions, no innuendoes. For nothing in the world she would have lived in those horrible times. All that hole-and-corner business, the dirty secrets, the cheating and intriguing, bah! What a rotten world! At least the Communists had done a mighty good job to cleanse up those Augean stables.

Whatever her reasons for wanting to change the system, a longing for the former position of the Chinese woman was certainly not one of them.

Her thoughts must have shown explicitly on her face since the bawdy merriment quickly petered out while the two crones shuffled back behind their table and clambered back on to their stools.

Gao Chen quickly relapsed into their ugly, incomprehensible dialect and apparently the conversation was about Beggars Chicken since he was selecting various herbs and spices from the table, handing them one by one to the old hag he had introduced as Auntie Two and who put them into a bag made from a smudged old copy of the *People's Daily*.

When he gestured that he had what he needed, Auntie Two tied a string around the bag while he ostentatiously felt in his pockets for the money to pay.

For the second time the two women got off their stools and, protestingly, pushed the bag into Gao Chen's hands while refusing to take the money he held out to them. This went on for several minutes before it ended as abruptly as it had started.

Gao Chen put a few fen on the table and, taking Suping by her elbow, they went off, turning around every three steps or so to wave at the two women who waved back in perfect unison. Then they turned the corner and were back in the street.

Suping heaved a deep sigh of relief.

Gao Chen looked at her askance.

'Forget it,' he said. 'Those two are relics of a past nobody in his right mind would want to go back to. You can't talk with those people on present-day terms, they just wouldn't understand. They sit there, on their stools, living anachronisms. Don't be too harsh on them, or on me. In my dealings with such people, and with people in general for that matter, I try to adapt to what appeals to them so that they feel at ease with me. This makes it so much easier to communicate and that's what it is all about, isn't it? Communication and interaction.

'I don't make a big deal of anything and I therefore feel equally at ease whether on a market like this or in a tea house or a whorehouse of blessed memory or at a Party meeting or in a high-brow debating society. Sniff, sniff, sniff to know the vibrations, one glance at people's eyes and their posturing and Chen Dan knows whom he is dealing with and he adapts, like a chameleon, to its surroundings. Always adapt, Suping! *Always adapt*! It's *the* secret for survival in all circumstances. See? We got these herbs and spices almost for free. Five fen I paid for what otherwise would have cost us five yuan. And the five fen is just so that they can't say later that I wheedled it out of them for nothing. Honour has its price, my love! Only don't set the price too high so you can't pay it and always make it negotiable.'

Suping laughed. 'You are a complex person, Uncle Dan,' she said, smiling. 'You have a personality for every occasion and thus everybody sees you differently, in his own image as it were, which is only a facet of the whole. I wonder how many facets I haven't seen yet, what kind of surprises you still have up your sleeve. However, don't worry about my tender feelings. I watch and listen and learn. Somehow I have the feeling that your world is more like real life than the cloistered one I have been living in so far with my brainy but naive parents. You popping into our lives is probably the best thing that could have happened to us and just in time at that, what with the turbulent times ahead when personal survival may be all that matters.'

'You'll manage, Xiaoping, you'll manage, don't you worry,' Gao Chen answered. 'You are a likeable person, attractive as a woman, however, not to the extent that other women will be jealous or that men lose their heads. Be flexible and accommodating. In ordinary life there are hardly any issues that are worth arguing about, so don't be sanctimonious but let people have their way. There are also very few principles worth suffering for, let alone dying for, so take it easy and adapt. The world is replete with all kinds of fools. You'll come across them at all levels and stations of life and you'll find that the higher the station the bigger the fool. Don't contend with them but instead humour them or, if you find that too difficult, at least suffer them. Since most fools are men you have an advantage over them as a woman, however, only if you resist the temptation to make them indeed look like the fools they are. Don't embarrass them. But then, the female always did have the gift to let the male posture and preen, did she not? Look at us now! I, pontificating and boasting my worldly wisdom and you just nodding and agreeing, flattering my precious ego.'

They both laughed heartily and in high spirits they crossed the narrow pedestrian cable bridge over the river and climbed the dirt path leading up to the small cluster of houses halfway up the hill where they lived.

Father, Mother and Ai Chen were waiting for them in the garden, sipping from a mug of tea.

'What took you so long?' Mother asked. 'We began to worry that the truth squads had called you up for duty. Look! They are quite busy apparently. She pointed to the town below from where in several places smoke was billowing up into the cloudless sky.

'They don't go where we went,' Gao Chen answered. 'People there would use the fragrant flowers to wipe their arse or to light their cooking fires and that would embarrass the leaders. No, don't worry. There is method in their seeming madness and they do know how to pick their victims. But enough about that. From now on we'll limit ourselves to enjoying the small, ordinary things of life. We have time for a quick mug of tea and then Suping and I have to hurry to fetch the mud and be back before dark.'

Mother poured a mug of hot, green tea for Gao Chen and her daughter and while they all relaxed and contentedly sipped from the tea, Suping told the others about her encounter with Aunties One and Two at the clandestine market and how that had led to her discovery of Gao Chen's excitingly secret past.

'Please, you must also ask him to tell us all about his elopement with the beautiful girl and why he stayed for two weeks under those old aunties' bed,' she pleaded. 'He keeps telling me "some other time, my love," but I want to hear it now.'

Her parents laughed heartily but Ai Chen acted as if he were shocked.

'Why let you slip out those horrid secrets of that dark past of yours?' he said in a plaintive voice. 'You will shock these upright people as you once shocked me. I never got over it you know.' He turned to face Suping.

'This man is a walking and talking wolverine. Don't let him ensnare you with his tales. I tell you, the truth squads are looking in the wrong place for their poisonous weeds.'

Gao Chen grinned. 'Tonight, while the chicken is cooking, I'll tell you my story. At least, if your parents agree.'

Xu and his wife said they would be delighted and Suping clapped her hands in pleasurable anticipation.

Gao Chen nodded and continued, 'While Suping and I fetch the mud my friend Ai Chen will murder and pluck the chicken. Ximing will prepare a very strong, black tea and clean the bird with it, both in and outside. Put the rest of the tea in a pan, Ximing, and let the chicken soak in it until we're back. Guixian will sort the herbs and spices and clean what needs to be cleaned. Then pound the chicken's liver, kidneys, heart and lungs in a mortar with some salt and the chillies to make a smooth paste. By the time you're ready Suping and I will be back and we'll start the cooking. The best place to do that is in the garden. You'll see. If you don't have to do that because you're rich enough to have a kitchen, it's quite amusing. The cooking takes a few hours and needs little supervision. During that time we'll have a beer and I'll tell you the story of my turbulent life. Come on, Suping! Let's get moving!'

For the second time that day Gao Chen and Suping descended the sloping path down to the bridge, but this time they did not cross it into town but turned left to follow the towpath upstream. They walked at a brisk pace, enjoying the soft, fresh wind that followed the course of the river, both water and air channelled by the hills rising steeply on both sides at not more than a hundred metres from the banks.

The wind carried that peculiar smell of wet earth that it picked up from the yellowish-brown water where it foamed and churned around boulders and rocks.

'Smell the air!' Gao Chen exclaimed. 'It's still a bit acrid from the waste the farmers dump into the river. Downstream from the town it's a lot worse though because of the sewage of two hundred thousand people and the waste of the tofu factories. You have to go at least twenty kilometres downstream of the town before the river has cleaned itself sufficiently so that one could bathe in it or use the loam for that matter.

'Here, upstream, we'll find good, clean loam after we have passed the farming area, four or five kilometres at the most. Against the wind you'll notice the clean smell before we reach the fishing area and see the cormorants. Black Dragon Liu taught me how to fish with cormorants. Maybe we can buy a few fish for tomorrow's dinner at a cheap price from the fishermen in the next village. It's very near to where we have to go anyway, for the mud.'

Suping enjoyed herself immensely. What a totally different world this was. So alien and yet its timeless, earthly calm suffused her with such intense feelings of peace and happiness that she had to breathe deeply to stop herself from screaming with pure joy.

The farmers, the fishermen going about their daily chores, imperturbably, and indifferent to the tribulations and upheavals elsewhere, themselves crawling from under the mud and taking up the thread of life again, as before, when some natural or man-made cataclysm had knocked them out temporarily. The sun and the wind, the river and the hills, fathomlessly suffering the whimsical freakishness of nature, totally oblivious of man and his ambitions and restless scheming, ruthless yet neither malevolent nor benevolent.

'It's all so pointless!' she exclaimed suddenly.

'What is pointless?' Gao Chen asked, surprised.

'All that talk. All those deliberations about what do to and what not to do. It all seems so presumptuous, so *futile*! Watch those hills; the river; the farmer over there, behind his ox, ploughing the wetland for this year's second planting of the paddy; the fisherman poling his boat to tonight's catching-place, his cormorants sitting on the board with that ring around their necks, staring ahead, unknowing, uncaring. Close your eyes and feel the wind and the warmth of the sun on your face. Smell the odours of the wetlands, of the river, of the drying freshly mowed grass, subtle yet distinct from one another. Listen and hear the chirring crickets, the rustling reeds, the waves lapping against the bank. All those sights, smells and sounds, the same for ages, past and future.

'That thought gives me such calm, peaceful feelings that I would like to lie down, on my back, in the grass, thinking of nothing, only sensing, aware yet not trying to distinguish and define. Whatever happens to us, to me, one day it will all be nothing but a fading memory of faceless people, of meaningless and forgotten words. However, when I'll recall this moment, these images and these smells and sounds will well up in my soul and it will be as if I am here again and my longing to come back to this place will be as strong as it is now to stay here for ever. A moment fixed in time, forever unchanging. Not a memory but a part of me, for good.'

Gao Chen wiped a tear from his eyes with the back of his right hand.

Suping could barely hear what he said, so softly he spoke, more to himself than to her.

> I cannot come to you. I am afraid.
> I will not come to you. There, I have said it!
> Though all the night I lie awake and know
> That you are lying, waking, even so.
> Though day by day you take the lonely road
> And come at nightfall to a dark abode.
> Yet, if so be you are indeed my friend,
> Then in the end there is one road,
> A road I've never gone,
> And down that road you shall not pass alone.
> And there's one night you'll find me by your side,
> The night that they shall tell me you have died.

'How morbid, Uncle Dan!' Suping cried, eyes brimming with tears. 'What a beautiful poem, but so tragic. Was she your lover, Uncle Dan? Or is she still?'

'It's only a poem,' Gao Chen said softly, 'there is no woman pining and waiting to die to have me come to her side. Sentimental romanticism of older times recited by an old man. Forget it.'

Suping watched him closely. 'I'm not sure I believe you, Uncle Dan,' she said, 'however I won't insist as it will obviously pain you if I do. Look!' she suddenly exclaimed, glad to change the subject. 'Look over there, Uncle Dan! That fisherman! He's waving at us!'

'That's not waving,' Gao Chen said, his old self again, 'he's gesturing for us to wait for him. See? Now he's poling towards this bank. I wonder what he wants.'

The fisherman was near the bank now, about twenty metres upstream and he stood up straight while letting his boat drift with the current to where Suping and Gao Chen stood waiting for him.

Suddenly Gao Chen yelled, 'Monkeyface!' and the fisherman yelled back at him 'Hedgehog!' and he jumped up and down in his boat, frightening his birds who almost strangled themselves on their short leash.

The fisherman called 'Monkeyface' stuck out his pole and Gao Chen slithered down the steep bank to catch it and he pulled the boat alongside the bank.

The fisherman took hold of a cluster of reeds and tied a rope around it, holding his boat in place, and then he jumped ashore. He looked indeed like an ape to Suping yet his face was friendly, all wrinkly smile.

Gao Chen and he embraced affectionately.

'The Liang sisters stopped in our hamlet on their way back home and told everybody that Hedgehog Chen was back,' the man called Monkeyface said laughingly.

'They said you were still as ugly as at the time you hid under their bed, only fatter, and that you had a very pretty girl with you. They gave you herbs for preparing Beggars Chicken, they said, so I guessed immediately that you would go to Willows' Bend for the mud. That's why I was looking for a pretty girl wearing a red scarf and an ugly old dodderer on the towpath and here you are and here I am.'

Gao Chen took him by his elbow and turned to face Suping.

'Monkeyface, this is Xu Suping, the daughter of my best friend, Xu Ximing of Luding. Xiaoping, this is Chen Faxian, my third cousin from my father's side. Faxian always stood by me when the other members of our clan teased me for being different. If Faxian hadn't kicked my father against his shins, which brought him back to his senses, the man might have beaten me to death instead of expelling me from the clan. I have been grateful ever since, both for being still alive and for the expulsion.'

He fell silent and grinning affectionately at his cousin, he said, 'And how has life treated you, Cousin Faxian?'

'I have eight birds now,' Faxian said proudly, pointing at his boat with the cormorants, quieted down again, sitting on their board, ring around their necks and on a short leash. 'The commune never took them away from me since the birds live with me in my house. They are easier and cheaper to keep than a wife and children. I never married, you know. They screech like mad when they have to spend the night outside and no woman would allow them inside because they shit all over the place. The birds, I mean,' he added hastily, seeing Suping's shocked expression.

'The commune leader, Cousin Shaofen, that ugly younger sister of yours, Hedgehog, is disgusted by the way I live my life and she always harangues me during the commune's meeting. But I don't care, Hedgehog! At least it is *my* way of life and not her damned Party's. My hovel, my boat, my birds and the river, that's my life. I catch the fish, keep what I need for myself and for my birds and the rest I give to the commune to do with what they want, I don't care. When I need rice I go to the rice store and ask for it and seventh cousin Yuesheng, Big-Eared Sheng, you remember, who's in charge, gives me what I need and I never pay. So far I have got away with it. It's a good arrangement. They get my fish and I get their bloody rice and no money changes hands.'

Suddenly he burst out laughing. 'I must go now, Cousin Dan,' he said. 'I have run out of kerosene for my fishing lamps and Lao Wong will want to haggle at least half an hour before giving me five litres in advance for the fish I still have to catch tonight. Three *katies* of fish he will ask for one litre of kerosene, the old scoundrel. One *katie* he eats himself and the other two he sells for twice the price of a litre. A good arrangement. From his point of view, that is. Xu Ximing of Luding you said you lived with, Cousin Dan? I'll drop by one of these days and bring you some fish. Keep a few beers in a cold place for me, pretty little apple,' he said, smiling at Suping, 'we have a lot to talk about, Hedgehog and I. You may listen. No vulgarities, I promise.'

He slapped Gao Chen on his back, waved at Suping, slithered down the bank and jumped in his boat. He untied the rope and gave a forceful push with the pole. The boat was caught by the current and within seconds the strange freebooter called Monkeyface Chen was out of sight around the bend. The last they saw of him was a big salute with his left arm.

'A good man, Faxian,' Gao Chen remarked. 'Already as a boy he always did what he believed was right, not what others told him to do. Earned him a lot of beatings, however, they never broke his spirit then and they won't now either, not even the Party.'

He smiled, a bit wistfully Suping thought, and the dreamy look in his eyes told her that his mind was back in the past, probably even in this place where he used to fetch the mud for his grandmother's recipe.

Then he retook control of himself, laughed and, giving Suping a playful push, he exclaimed, 'Come on girl, we're wasting our time. Let's get our mud. It's just around the bend. You see the weeping willows over there? There it is.' He trotted ahead.

Suping followed him and five minutes later she saw a large mudflat glistening in the slanting rays of the afternoon sun.

'When it rains in the mountains the river rises and floods this whole area,' Gao Chen explained. 'Because it is an inside bend the current here is much slower than in the middle of the river and the silt has time to settle. When the water level descends again the river withdraws to its normal course and the area falls dry, though not quite. Below the glistening slicks there are holes that can swallow a man whole within minutes. Now, you stay on the bank, Suping. I know the trick, you'll see.'

Gao Chen selected a long, thick and straight branch amongst the enormous weeping willows and cut it off with his big, old pocket knife.

Quickly he cut off the side branches and he held a stick of about four metres long and fifteen centimetres round.

'The holes are seldom that wide,' he said. 'If I slip into one I'll put the stick across the hole and I'll hang on to it so that I keep my head above the slicks. You go running back and call some people to help you get me out. Don't forget to remind them to bring a rope, but they'll know. They have seen it before. Only people who do dangerous things which they are not well prepared for die. Now, give me a bucket!'

He took off his shoes and socks and Suping handed him one of the two galvanised buckets they had brought with them. Slowly and carefully, bucket in one hand, stick in the other, Gao Chen stepped on to the glistening mudflat.

Testing the consistency of the mud in front of him with the stick before he took the next step, he slowly advanced to a spot about twenty metres from the river bank. There he stopped, put the stick and the bucket down beside him and quickly began to scoop, with both hands, the thick, greyish-blue mud into the bucket.

When it was full he picked up the stick and lifted the bucket and just as gingerly he traced back his steps to the bank. Suping took the full bucket and handed him the empty one.

'Why do you remain so careful?' she asked. 'You know now that there are no holes on that stretch so you can walk much quicker and save us time.'

'The holes move,' Gao Chen said, 'they never stay for more than a few hours in the same place. In a dangerous situation never take anything for granted. Appearances are deceptive. Always check. Always test. Always verify. Don't even trust your own eyes or ears. Verify once, verify twice and then one more time just to make sure.'

With a sudden yell he jumped back on to the bank as, just when he uttered the last words of his admonition, there was a loud, slurping sound and in front of his feet, only half a metre off the bank, there appeared a vortex sucking in the layer of five centimetres or so of water that had been brought to the surface of the mudflat because of his weight.

Gao Chen chuckled at Suping's deadly pale face and frightened eyes.

'*Quod erat demonstrandum*,' he laughed. 'I remained standing for too long in one place. Let's go a bit further down. I can't go back here. My weight may have caused other movements underneath the surface and other holes may suddenly appear on my previous path. No need to tempt fate.'

They walked about fifty metres further upstream and there Gao Chen repeated his manoeuvre. Within five minutes he was back on shore with the second bucketful of mud.

He cleaned his feet and between his toes with tufts of grass, put his socks and shoes back on and said, 'I'll take the two buckets first and we take turns every two hundred metres or so. It's better to carry two heavy objects, one by each hand, than to have the weight of one on one arm only. That makes you walk bent sideways which is tiring and very bad for your spine. It looks polite and civilised to share the burden but actually it's very stupid. So-called civilised behaviour is often contrary to what your intuition and common sense would have you do.'

They walked back along the towpath to Luding, making small talk and stopping for a few seconds every two hundred metres or so to take over the buckets from one another.

It was already past half three when Suping opened the small gate to the back garden. Its squeak made the others look up.

'Shame on you, daughter!' Xu said reproachfully. 'Gao Chen is not your servant. You could at least have carried one of those heavy buckets if two are too heavy for you. Where are the manners your mother and I took so much trouble teaching you? In vain apparently,' he added as an afterthought.

With a deadpan face Suping said, 'I have this afternoon become an adept of a different kind of civilisation than the one you taught me. One which puts the emphasis on intuition and common sense rather than on appearances and so-called polite, good manners. Your standards no longer apply, if they ever did, so your conclusions based on those standards of yours are wrong.'

Suddenly she burst out laughing seeing her father's baffled expression.

'Poor father,' she sniggered, 'just kidding you. Uncle Dan will explain while I fetch him a cold beer. He deserves it. Such a hero!' And still laughing she went inside.

Gao Chen dropped into his old wicker chair and, rubbing his hands to get the cramp out of his fingers, he smiled broadly and told the others about his trip with Suping to Willows' Bend and what had happened on the way, now and then taking a deep swallow from the glass of beer Suping had poured for him.

When he related the episode of the mudflats and his remark about carrying the buckets that had led to Suping's so-called new philosophy about civilisation, Guixian laughed and, looking at her husband, she said, 'Well,

Ximing my love, life is a learning process and on the way one drops the occasional principle that has become obsolete and adopts another that serves its purpose until in turn it has to give way also. It would seem that our daughter learns fast. If only you and I could adapt so easily and without fuss or drama. But perhaps that's the privilege of youth?'

Gao Chen grinned. 'My teacher of life's basic principles, Heilong Liu, used to say that principles are like winds in your belly. You hold them back as long as you can but if you can't stand the cramp any longer, you let them slip out as quietly and as imperceptibly as possible, hoping people won't notice the smell. Now, show me what you have prepared.'

'Everything has been done as ordered by you,' Guixian said. 'Ai Chen took the chicken's life by decapitation and nearly lost a finger in the process. Then he plucked her and together with Ximing washed and bathed her in strong, black tea. There she is now, in the basin, soaking in the tea. I cut and cleaned the herbs and the chillies and made the paste with the chicken's liver, kidneys, heart and lungs. I put the paste ready for you on the kitchen table.

'Fine,' Gao Chen replied, 'well done. Now, Suping, you wash the mud please. Stir it in clean water in the buckets. Let it settle and pour off the dirty water. Repeat that process two more times. Then pour the watery mud on a piece of cloth, fold it and squeeze out as much water as you can. It must have the consistency of moulding clay, neither too wet nor too dry. That'll keep you busy for half an hour.

'Ai Chen, you dig a hole over there, please. In the corner, leewards from where we sit here, so we won't get the smoke in our eyes. About a foot by a foot and half a foot deep will do. Your size fifty foot, I mean. Put the loose earth around the hole so that we can easily shove it back in to cover the chicken in the hot ash. Ximing, you please go and collect a good quantity of dry twigs and other pieces of dry wood you can find. No pine wood please. The resin smell will spoil the chicken. Guixian and I will stuff the chicken with the herbs and the paste and sew it up. Then we smear the rest of the paste on the bird's skin. We forgot to check this morning whether there is enough charcoal left. If not, Suping will have to go quickly to the charcoal seller just across the bridge while we light the fire with the dry wood. Now, let's get started!'

For the next half hour everybody was busy with the assigned tasks. Xu came back with a load of dry twigs and branches and while down the hill he had quickly crossed the bridge and bought for ten fen a bag of nice, light and tinkling pieces of charcoal. He put the wood and charcoal next to Ai Chen's hole.

Guixian carried the stuffed and basted chicken outside, on a plate, and put it also on the ground near the hole.

Gao Chen took charge again.

'Suping and Guixian, please plaster the chicken with an even layer of clay, about one finger thick. Make sure the layer is evenly thick so the chicken won't be too cooked or even burnt in one place and not enough in the other. I myself will now prepare the hot ash oven. It's very important, so watch carefully how it is done.'

Gao Chen took a few handfuls of clay from Suping's stock and smeared it carefully and evenly on the four sides and bottom of the hole Ai Chen had dug out.

'This will bake in the fire and so the walls won't crumble or collapse,' he explained. 'If the ordinary garden soil mixes with the hot ash it can spoil everything by giving the chicken an unpleasant earthy smell.'

Having finished the plastering he loosely balled a few pages of an old *People's Daily* and put the paper on the bottom of the hole. Then he selected the smallest and driest twigs and odd pieces of dry wood and put it all on top of the paper. Finally he lit the paper in a few places with a match. Slowly he first fed all of the wood collected by Ximing in the fire and then the charcoal. Satisfied he watched the almost smokeless fire.

'Very good quality charcoal,' he commented. 'Most people have no idea how important that is. Always check whether the pieces make a nice, tinkling sound when you hit them against one another. Bad quality charcoal or charcoal made from the wrong types of wood doesn't tinkle and it gives off a lot of smoke that spoils the taste of the meat. It may even make you sick. Most types of wood are not even suitable for making charcoal that can be used for roasting or grilling meat. People use ordinary heating charcoal also for roasting and when afterwards they become ill they blame the meat and the butcher.'

Feeding the last pieces of charcoal into the fire, he added, 'We now have to wait until there are no more flames and there remains only a thick layer of glowing, hot ash that looks almost white on the surface. Then we make a shallow hole in the ash, put the chicken in its clay coating into the hole and cover it with hot ash. Finally we cover the lot, first with the rest of Suping's clay and then with the loose earth Ai Chen left around the hole and the cooking begins. It will take about two and a half hours for the chicken to cook in its own juices, so we can dig it out at eight o'clock. Then we have to let it cool off for an hour or so before we can break the mud shell open, so we can have dinner at nine o'clock. Does that suit you, Guixian?'

'Fine with me,' Mother replied. 'In the meantime we can have tea, enjoy the evening calm and listen to your story, Dan.'

Gao Chen nodded. 'We have to wait another twenty minutes before we can put the chicken in the ash. Look, there are still a few flames now and then. In the meantime let's wash up and put on clean clothes. The fire made me hot and dried out so I'll have a mug of hot tea first to bring out the sweat. That'll cool me off a bit before I wash myself with cold water.'

Twenty minutes later everybody was back in the garden, looking refreshed. Mother put a tin of famous brand jasmine tea on the table, for the occasion, and everybody rejoiced in anticipation of its delicate fragrance.

Gao Chen judged the hot ashes to be just right and Suping carefully put the clay ball with the chicken inside into the hollow he had made with an iron ladle in the intensely hot ashes. Then he covered the clay ball with ash, put the rest of the mud on top and finally he shoved the loose earth back on top of everything.

'That's that,' he said, wiping his hands on his socks, oblivious of Mother's disapproving look.

'Let's have a cup of that delicious jasmine tea and then give me some time to collect my thoughts so that I can tell a coherent story with a logical sequence of events. I abhor incoherence. So tiresome.'

Suping put a small amount of jasmine tea in each mug and then poured hot water on top, quickly putting the lid back on the mug as soon as it was three-quarters full in order not to let the fragrance escape.

They sat in silence, each holding the mug clasped in both hands, now and then bringing it close to the nose before lifting the lid just a bit on one side to catch the fragrant vapour in the nostrils and to take a quick sip, which they then rolled over and around their tongue, eyes closed, to try and detect every nuance in taste, before swallowing ever so delicately.

Gao Chen was lost in his thoughts and the others waited patiently and without the usual small talk until he was ready to begin. It was one of those overwhelmingly beautiful and peaceful moments that one wished would last for ever.

The sun was slowly disappearing behind the mountains to the west and while they were still bathed in its light and warmth on their hill slope, the opposite slopes, facing east, and the valley were already swallowed by the advancing twilight. Here and there, in the lowest lying areas, a single light bulb or neon tube lit up.

The neon lights were a harsh, bluish-white and they flickered while the ordinary bulbs spread a soft, even yellowish glow. Suping didn't like neon lights. Their constant hum and irregular flickering were disturbing and one always looked tired and sick when looking at oneself in a mirror.

Perhaps Gao Chen could replace the tube in the living room with a bulb one of these days. She would ask him tomorrow.

There was no wind at all.

Later, the moment the sun would disappear completely behind the mountain, a soft breeze would spring up and rustle the leaves of the trees for a while. It would carry the different smells of cooking fires, trash fires, boiling soup, roasting meat, drying grass and even the musty smell of the river from down below. The breeze would last maybe five or six minutes and then it would die again.

Suping watched the smoke from the small houses and from their small gardens curling up into the still air, straight still, as nature kept its breath. Carried far by the quiet atmosphere the barking of a few dogs, a child's joyous laughter, a woman's voice calling her husband and children for the evening meal were all part of the simple, earthy, timeless peacefulness of the scene.

A wave of contentment and inner peace washed over her. She felt as if every nerve and cell in her body was in perfect and harmonious tune with the earth and the universe beyond the flaming, orange-red mountain peaks.

Through the lashes of her almost closed eyes she watched the full moon and the still, unwavering point of light next to it that was Venus, and she felt all tension flow out of her. She closed her eyes but nothing changed for the scene remained as vivid in every detail, fixed and stored for good in a recess of her mind.

In later years, in times of searing despair and overwhelming, heart-rending sorrow, she would mentally withdraw from her surroundings and let herself slide back into this recess. She would feel herself sucked in faster and faster by a vortex of memories until suddenly everything was back in its place, calm and clear, and she had regressed in time, finding herself again on this hill slope, in this garden, part of the same, forever unchanging scene.

Father, Mother, Uncle Dan, Uncle Juntao, they would all still be there, staring dreamily at the shadows overtaking the mountain peaks, unaware that she had been gone. The chicken would still be baking in its mud shell, the woman would still be calling her family for dinner and the breeze, carrying the familiar, soothing smells and sounds, would not have died down yet.

When then, whether after a few minutes or a few hours, she would have to wake up to the real world again, she would slip away so silently that the others didn't notice, feeling at peace again, her heart no longer heavy and her eyes no longer stinging with tears. Still later, when they had already taken her husband away and she did not know where or how he was, she would regress to her secret world almost every evening and push the ugliness of the day out of her mind and she would fall asleep, feeling at peace with her little daughter Lilian breathing softly against her throat.

From far and yet close she heard her father's voice and slowly she resurfaced in the present.

'Such peace, such tranquil contentment,' she heard him say. 'What is this irresistible, restless, angry urge that makes people kill or destroy, so often in utter despair, that which or those who they love most or what they feel in their soul is good and decent? What is it that drives man, often in spite of the warning voice in his soul, to go further, higher, deeper, to look for something different or for still more of the same? We, my family, we lost all our possessions after liberation and for many years I lamented and resented my loss. Our big house always full of friends and relatives. Our servants, always there to serve a quick bite to eat or a ten-course meal at a moment's notice. The fashionable clothes for every occasion. The trips to Guangzhou, Fuzhou, Suzhou, Hangzhou, Shanghai, Beijing, Wucheng, Hankou, even Kunming. The radio, the gramophone with Western and Chinese records, the beautiful books in my own room.

'And now I sit here, in this tiny garden of a small house I rent from the town council, and to my surprise I realise that I don't miss all those things any longer. I realise that the whining, lamenting and resenting had become a habit, only a habit. I now see that I actually never loved that big house but that I do love this cosy little shack. That I never liked all those bragging and boasting pretentious people but that I do love you and your company. That I never actually tasted all that elaborate food, that I just gobbled, slurped and swallowed, my mind elsewhere, on other pleasures and trivialities, but that I do look forward to enjoy, together with you, that Beggars Chicken I helped prepare myself. I can't help thinking that the Old Master was right after all. If you don't possess anything of value you don't live in fear of losing it either. If you don't strive for success you need not live in fear of failure. If you are moderate and modest in all things people won't envy you and you need not envy them. If you do what you have to do, but no more than that, then you won't crave recognition and praise or feel slighted when it's not given. Lao Zi was probably the most down-to-earth, well-meaning, profound and bondless human being that ever crawled around in the mud on this planet. And the more I listen to your ideas and advice, Chen Dan, the more I watch you going about your business, the more I feel certain that you are in essence a Taoist, a practitioner of the Old Master's way. Am I right, Dan?'

Gao Chen smiled, got up from his chair and, with a piece of wood, scraped a bit of earth and ash from the mud shell to check for cracks and to have a look at the colour and texture of the shell.

'Two hours more for the chicken to become tender,' he said. 'Then another hour for the flavours of the herbs and spices to impregnate the flesh and at the same time for the shell to cool off enough for us to handle it and break it open without the flesh remaining stuck to the inside.'

He returned to his chair, took a sip of his tea, replenished the hot water in his mug, pushed his chair on its hind legs so that he rested with his back against the wall and began.

# *Chapter Fifteen*

## Chen Dan's Story: The Early Years (1915–1932)

I was born in 1915, just three years after the fall of the Manchu dynasty and the Proclamation of the Republic of China.

For the Chen clan of Dada He, however, both events were totally immaterial. They didn't touch them one way or the other. Life was as it had always been and would forever be, a perpetual struggle.

A struggle for food so as to stay alive and a struggle to avoid authority, any authority, so as to stay out of trouble.

I was the fifth son and the last of eight children. If I had been born a girl I would have been drowned at birth, that much I know for sure.

The Chen clan consisted of forty-three families, all in all 266 relatives, living in forty-three hovels built of loam and straw, bamboo lattice-work and bamboo poles. Each hovel had a front and back door, made of rough planks, and three rectangular holes in the walls as windows. There was no glass in those windows, just a piece of oil-paper to prevent people from looking in. It gave the interior a dark, yellowish tinge that was soft on the eyes when coming in from the glaring sun outside. At nightfall mats of plaited bamboo strips were hung on four iron hooks fixed in the mud wall at the four corners of each window.

At the back of the house, on one side of the back door, there was an extension lower than the house itself and with its own sloping roof of short bamboo poles covered with sods.

This was the kitchen. The stove was built of baked loam bricks and there was barely room for one person to move around.

The house itself was actually only one rectangular room with a roof and which was for two-thirds occupied by a kind of platform made of bamboo poles and lattice-work; it was about a foot high.

This platform served at night as the family bed and during the day as a storage place for babies, dirty and washed clothes and the scores of things one uses for a while and then has to put somewhere for the time being.

One corner of the three by four metre structure could be sort of curtained off with bamboo mats hanging from the roof structure. When we children saw Father untying the knots that held the mats rolled up we knew he and Mother had something to discuss that was not for our ears or that they were going to make love, which wasn't often after I was born.

The hamlet of the Chen clan was surrounded on all four sides by a two-metre high fence of bamboo poles tied one against the other by strips of split bamboo.

There was a big front gate, also made of bamboo poles and hinged by means of strops of thick rope. It had to be lifted off the ground to open it in the morning, at five o'clock, and to close it at nightfall. A dirt path led from the gate to the Liang estate.

At the back of the hamlet, facing the River Dada, there was a similar gate in the back wall, only much smaller and it could be opened by one person instead of the four people needed to lift the heavy front gate.

On the outside the paling had been strengthened by stacking big stones and pieces of rock against it and which were held together by hardened loam, like a kind of masonry. The whole wall, both inside and outside, was a thick mass of that terrible morning glory creeper you can't ever get rid of once it has invaded your garden. Some grandmother Chen long dead had thought it a good idea to put some cuttings along the fence because she liked to eat the morning glory as a vegetable in her rice and soup.

Early mornings our hamlet was ringed in blue, late afternoons when the flowers of the day had died, in green.

In the middle of the hamlet stood a magnificent thicket of the green and yellow bamboo; it was at least twelve metres high and some fifty metres around and so dense only a small child could wriggle himself a few metres inside. A dozen wooden benches had been placed around the thicket in a square of twelve by twelve metres for the old people to sit in the shade on hot summer days when the ghosts who lived inside the thicket had retired into the river.

In the evening when, after sunset, the wind came up, the unhappy souls of the Chens who had or had been drowned in the river, moved back into the thicket for the night and during windy nights you could hear them squawking and groaning while the river spirits that haunted them whispered in the rustling leaves.

A dozen or so cats also lived in the thicket to keep it and the hamlet free of mice and rats. Cats that became too fat were killed and cooked in soup and their skins were used to make fur hats for the winter months, when the cold, humid damp of the river seeped through every tear and crack and chilled you to the bone. When the tiny, miauling cries of a litter of just born kittens could be heard, the smallest child was sent into the thick of the bamboo to bring them out. Their eyes still closed, they were skewered alive on sharpened bamboo pins and roasted for the men to eat so as to keep their muscles lean and supple for the hard work they had to do every day.

All around the inside of this paling a width of six metres, divided in two by a half metre wide footpath, was used for growing vegetables such as cabbages, sow cabbages, mustard cabbages, chrysanthemums, lettuce, leeks, chives, taros and so on and so forth, too many to name all. Against the fence facing south tomatoes and chillies were grown, held upright by means of bamboo sticks.

Night-soil was collected every morning by the children over the age of eight and dumped into either one of two deep pits that had been dug outside the fence facing north to prevent the stench from being blown back into the hamlet by the wind.

Dead leaves, vegetable household garbage and offal were also dumped into the pits and from time to time a dozen or so baskets of limy loam from one particular place on the river bank, about one kilometre upstream from the hamlet, were added to the mixture in the pits. When a pit was about two-thirds full, its contents were thoroughly stirred and mixed with long bamboo poles, and then left to ferment and digest for a few weeks.

While one pit was fermenting, the other one was used for dumping. After the fermentation, the digested mixture was smooth and didn't stink at all. It was then taken out of the pit by means of very tightly woven wicker baskets. A big stone was put into the basket to make it sink in the goo and its bail was attached to a rope that could be wound around a horizontal pole resting on two cradles on opposite sides of the pit.

Two strong boys were able to turn the pole and so lift a full basket out of the pit. Two other boys emptied the heavy basket into two smaller ones that were attached with a piece of rope to a bamboo pole that served as a yoke beam. The older men and women carried these baskets back inside the fence and spread the contents over the vegetable garden. Still other men and women worked the fertiliser into the soil with shovels and pointed sticks. The part of the garden that was so fertilised was then left for a week to aerate and then new vegetables were planted.

Some of the vegetables, after harvesting, were dried by spreading them out on bamboo mats, in the sun, chillies and mungo beans notably, others were pickled in big, earthenware pots. When these huge pots were full, a piece of cloth was put on top of the mixture of vegetables, chillies and salt and then a piece of thick plank weighted by means of a big boulder-like stone was put on the cloth to press it all down. The pickled vegetables would be ready for consumption during the winter months.

This whole industry of collecting the night-soil and the collection and sorting of household garbage, the collection of limy loam, the preparation of the fertiliser in the pits and its distribution, the planting, tending, harvesting, cleaning and drying or pickling of the vegetables was the task of the children between five and twelve years old and of the elderly Chens and of those incapable of heavy work on the Liang estate and thus unable to find work elsewhere. Children younger than five were not allowed outside the hamlet. Apart from some light work at home, such as sweeping the dirt floor and around the house or repairing small holes in the walls with a gluey mixture of loam and water, these young children were free to play all day.

The hamlet was our world and it was a peaceful world.

The Chens got on well together and the few hotheads who didn't were made to stay out of each other's way until their frayed tempers had cooled down enough to speak again to each other.

At nightfall, when the last men and women had returned from their work on the estate, the gates were closed and locked for the night until the next morning, five in the summer and half five in the winter.

In the evenings there reigned that feeling of security and cosiness that comes from being with your own kin who care about one another and that makes you feel good and warmly secure inside. In that setting and atmosphere I grew up and contributed to the clan's household as hundreds of Chen children had done before me during the past centuries, two at least, probably even three.

I grew up a sturdy, agile boy with a cheery disposition and I got along well with the other members of the clan.

When I was nine years old I couldn't read, let alone write, and I spoke only the dialect of that area which was even different from the one spoken by the Hu clan on the other side of the river with whom we had no contact anyhow.

The Chens and the Hus were not downright hostile to the point of picking fights but we preferred to ignore each other. The reason for this stand-offishness, I was told, was that a hundred or so years ago a Hu girl had married a Chen boy and then five years later had eloped with a tramp, leaving him with three small children. The Hus had refused to pay damages for the Chen clan's loss of face and ever since no Chen walked where a Hu had walked before and vice versa, of course.

From the age of twelve for the boys and fourteen for the girls every able-bodied Chen worked by tradition on the Liang estate. This was an inviolable tradition for both the Liangs and the Chens since it had been established hundreds of years ago and kept, unbroken, ever since.

The Chen clan was very lucky that the Liang estate was on the same side of the river and that the Liangs were good and decent people. The Chen hamlet was on Liang property and every year the Chens had to supply a hundred manweeks without pay and meals as a kind of rent. Since the clan had usually between forty and sixty men and women working all year round on the estate this arrangement meant that each had to work only a maximum of two weeks free of charge for the Liangs.

It was a good arrangement and everybody was content with it. Three-quarters of the pay consisted of rice, beans, sweet potatoes, tea, watermelons, peaches, kumquats and other fruits and vegetables in season together with fishing rights in the twenty-five kilometres of river bordered by the estate. The remaining quarter was actually calculated in money, however, it wasn't paid out but was chalked up as a credit.

Four times a year the barges of the Liangs descended the river all the way to Chengdu, laden with produce from the estate to be sold to the merchants there. Before each departure the clan's council told the Liang in charge of purchases what things were needed and when the barges had returned from Chengdu the clan was told the cost of each item and the total which was then deducted from the clan's credit. The Liangs even gave us a small interest on the outstanding balance. All very fair and neat.

Since nobody of the clan could write, four or five women had to memorise each a part of the things to be bought and then, in turn, tell the Liang woman in charge of bookkeeping who wrote it all down for her brother or uncle in charge of purchasing.

When I was nearly ten years old I was present one evening when the five women were rehearsing their respective lists of things needed by the clan. After several attempts they still couldn't get it right, probably because the list was unusually long that particular time. Now one then the other forgot a few of the items she had tried so hard to memorise and they were close to tears when the men, who were themselves unable to remember more than five items, got annoyed with them.

Then I stood up and recited all the items without forgetting one and the council decided that my mother would accompany me to the estate and explain to the Liang girl that I was to tell her the things that had to be brought back by the barges. All went smoothly and my mother and the clan were very proud of me.

The Liang girl had laughed and praised my memory. She promised she would write out the list twice and give one copy to me so that I could practise copying the characters. Once I would be able to draw them, she said, she would teach me their meaning and how to read and pronounce them properly.

I think, looking back, that it was at that very moment that my life had turned into a different direction, although for myself it all began nearly three years later when I was just twelve years old.

Liang Ailing, as the girl's name was, kept her promise and when I came to see her again, three months later, to recite the list of purchases for the barges' next trip, she gave me a copy of the previous list and also a pencil. She taught me how to sharpen the pencil and gave me a lot of old, brown paper bags that had holes in them so they couldn't be used any longer for packing rice or beans, to practise my writing.

She gave me a task also: the next time I would come to see her to recite the goods to be purchased I had to be able to write out all the characters and by heart, no copying.

Every day I found time to practise. First I tried with a bamboo stick in fine, dry loam and when I thought I had the knack of it I wrote them down on the brown paper, as often as twenty times for each character until I could do it by heart.

When I went back three months later I first recited the goods requested by the clan and then I waited for her to call me to show her my writing skills. I had to wait a few hours, till noon rice, which she shared with me. Very nice it was, I still remember. Tiny pieces of the white of chicken with rice and chillies fried together in sesame oil and sesame seeds. I had never eaten such food before.

Then it was time to show her my homework and she was delighted that for most of the characters I had even what she called the sequence of strokes right which was unusual she said for somebody unskilled and unschooled who merely copies the characters. She explained the meaning of the words to me and made me repeat the pronunciation and the tone, first in my own dialect, which she spoke as well of course, and then in what she called the tongue of the Han, or *Hanyu* as she told me to call that way of speaking.

She said that saying things in *Hanyu* was necessary or else educated people or people from other parts of Sichuan or China would not understand me. She gave me a copy of the new list I had recited to her and immediately explained the meaning of a new character and its pronunciation and tone.

Again she gave me a task: in three months I should be able to give her a written list since most of the things were always the same; only those items that had not yet been ordered before I could still tell her orally.

Again I practised every day for hours on end, both the writing and the *Hanyu*. People began to call me teasingly the Scholar.

Three months later Ailing was even more delighted and she gave me a brush and an ink stone and real, white paper and she told me to come henceforth every week for one whole afternoon, on the fifth day, and she would teach me calligraphy and many more words.

This went on for almost two and a half years and I learned to read and write and to speak *Hanyu* fluently.

Ailing taught me more than six thousand characters and also the numbers in Western writing so that I could learn calculus, addition, subtraction, multiplication and division.

The second year I spent every day at the Liang manor where I helped Ailing with her paperwork. I also cleaned her workroom and when she had to take stocks in the *godowns* I climbed the piles of bags and bales and counted them behind the first rows and shouted the numbers to her below on the floor to write them down.

The Liang family indulged her unusual friendship for the ugly peasant boy and, apart from the occasional good-humoured teasing by her brothers, they all treated me kindly.

My own clan was not as altruistic and quite a number of my mother's sisters, nieces, aunts and cousins tried to influence my parents to put an end to my learning. When my parents didn't give in the women set their own children against me and gradually I became an outcast in my own clan with only my parents and my third cousin Faxian, who Suping met today, still on my side. Even my own brothers and sisters were against me.

Then, one day, my idyllic little fantasy world crashed around me.

As usual, I had cleaned Ailing's desk and room and had arranged her papers for her. I had put her raincoat and boots ready, for that day we had to go down to the wharf to check the *godowns* and the loading of the barges and it was drizzling.

Then I waited. It was already past ten o'clock when she finally turned up and I saw immediately that there was something terribly wrong.

She had been crying. Her eyes were red and swollen as was her left cheek. Without saying or asking anything I fetched a bowl of cold water and a cloth for her to dab her eyes and then I waited until she would be ready to talk.

Finally she stopped crying, cleaned her face and then gestured for me to come closer for what she was about to tell me had to be whispered.

'You must first promise me never to tell anyone what I am going to tell you now, Xiao Chen,' she whispered, 'you are my only friend and I urgently need your help.'

I swore that I wouldn't tell anyone and told her I would do anything to help her.

She looked at me with those huge almond eyes, always so sparklingly merry that my heart jumped and missed a few beats whenever she looked at me askance from behind those magnificent lashes and now so sombrely sad that my heart felt as heavy as a watermelon.

She hesitated but a fraction of a second, took a deep, shuddering breath and plunged ahead. 'My father has decided that I have to get married,' she whispered, so close to my ear that I felt her warm breath in my ear and on my cheek which gave me goose pimples on my arms and strange stirrings in my belly I had never felt before.

I closed my eyes and clenched my fists and with all my might I concentrated on what she continued to tell me.

'Father has already made all the arrangements for me to marry Yang Zelin of Chengdu, a decrepit, smelly old man, five years older than my own father. A widower with nine children of his own, all older than I am,' she wailed and sobbed.

'Yang has a big estate near Chengdu where he grows white peaches and mulberries and he has his own silk factory. He is very rich and my family would benefit greatly from my marriage with Yang. I was so angry and sad when my father informed me of his plans, decision rather, this morning that I stood up to him and talked back. He slapped my face and ordered me to hold my tongue. I was so terribly disappointed, Xiao Chen, because my sisters and I had always believed our father to be an enlightened man who would allow his daughters a say in their own life. I cried with anger, disappointment and despair and defiantly I blurted out that I was no longer a virgin and that I had been having an affair for the past two years with a man called Liu Longfei. Longfei is a political refugee hiding from both the Nationalists and the Communists and he lives deep in the marshes at the far eastern end of our estate. He is a scholar, Xiao Chen, and a writer as well and he has written in newspapers warning people against Chiang and Sun and Mao, calling them the same devil in different disguises and he openly supported Chen Duxiu who, Longfei says, is the only person with brains and character alive in China today. But never mind all that. You don't understand yet.

'When my father heard me shout at him that I had been the mistress of Heilong Liu, as people call Longfei because of his thick black beard and fierce appearance, he worked himself into a terrible rage and banished me from the manor to the garden house. He forbade my mother and brothers and sisters to talk to me and to give me any money or else he would punish them as well, he threatened. He ordered me to pack one suitcase only and to be out of the manor by nightfall today. Xiao Chen, you must go and tell Longfei what happened and ask him to pick me up at the usual place tonight, after dark. Will you do that for me, Xiao Chen? Please?'

In a sudden impulse and to her utter surprise I planted a thick, sucking kiss on her salty wet cheek and told her, embarrassed by my foolishness, to explain to me where I could find Liu. Ailing smiled at me through her tears and squeezed my arm while she explained how to proceed.

Unnoticed I slipped out of the manor and went down to the river.

Below an overhanging weeping willow, hidden amongst the dense reeds, I found the sturdy raft Liu had made for Ailing. I untied the raft and, kneeling down, I pushed it out of the reeds until the current got hold of it and gently tucked me towards the middle of the stream.

From there I could see the first of the seven poles with the Liang character that Ailing told me I had to pass before I had to start waving a piece of yellow cloth I had found squeezed between the poles of the raft and yell as loudly as I could, '*Heilong*! *Heilong*! *Heilong*!'

If he didn't hear me, Ailing told me, I had to paddle against the current to get back to the left bank before I got too far past the seventh pole. Once back on land I had to find a tree to attach the raft to and then walk into the marshes by the only footpath that led to Liu's shack.

The path was one hundred paces left of the seventh pole, keeping the river at my left, Ailing explained. The path was very narrow and winding, Ailing said, and in several places I might think that it just ended there. Liu had made it deliberately so to confuse eventual pursuers. I simply had to squeeze myself through the reeds to pick up the path again ten or twenty paces further.

Fortunately these emergency measures were not necessary. As my raft drifted and twirled past the sixth pole I saw him already, no mistake possible. A tall man with a thick, black beard stood waist-deep in the river. With a broad swing he threw a net, overhead, into the stream waited for it to sink and then he pulled it back to where he was standing.

When he saw a few, glittering fish he waded back to the bank, opened the net and picked the fish out and threw them higher up, in the grass, where they flip-flopped in the hazy sunlight. I was so concentrated on watching him that I had almost drifted past him already when I hurriedly tore the yellow cloth from between the poles and started waving it, yelling at the top of my voice, '*Heilong*! *Heilong*! *Heilong*!'

Liu looked up, surprised, and when he saw the yellow flag, he shouted, 'Paddle, you stupid turtle! Paddle to get closer to the bank!'

In a few big, splashing steps he got out of the water, scrambled up the steep bank and then ran along the bank to get ahead of me on my raft. When he had gained about twenty metres on me he plunged, head first, into the river and swam with a powerful crawl stroke to meet my raft. He seized it with one hand and with his other arm he swam back to the bank.

He attached the raft to a cluster of tall reeds, lifted me up and carried me on land as if I weighed no more than a few pounds. As he put me down, threw me down rather, he towered over me and looked me over with his glittering eyes as if he were evaluating me for dinner.

Suddenly he burst out laughing, showing large, white teeth in all that black hair on his face. He was a big, broad-shouldered fellow with a very big, longish head, much bigger and very different in shape from my father's.

'You Chen Dan? Xiao Chen as Ailing calls you?' he asked and to my relief his voice was pleasant and reassuring.

As I nodded, he said 'Give me the news, Xiao Chen, bad news first.'

'It's either all bad or all good, depending on what your intentions with Ailing were,' I replied, rather cheekily now I come to think of it.

I shall never forget the way he looked at me, his eyes boring into mine, his teeth in a snarl like a mad dog. He lifted me up with one hand and brought his face so close to mine that I could smell his breath, a fish smell it flashed through my thoughts, rather incongruously, bearing in mind my predicament.

'Speak up, you rascal,' he whispered fiercely, 'speak up or by God and all His saints I'll shake you till all your teeth fall out of that foul, brazen mouth of yours.'

'Ailing has been kicked out of her family by her old man!' I yelled, kicking my feet. 'She refused to marry old Yang Zelin of Chengdu and she told her old man about you! He hit her! Her cheeks are all red and swollen and she cried. I gave her cold water for her eyes. She is now packing her suitcase, only one Liang allowed her. She wants you to pick her up, after dark, at the usual place!'

While I was still yelling those last words he dropped me like an old bag and he laughed and laughed until the tears ran down through his beard.

'I'll pick her up all right,' he finally hiccuped. 'We'll live here in my shack unless the Liangs and their slaves chase us off their property. It'll be some change for Ailing, but she'll manage. At least she'll be *free*! Xiao Chen, come with me. I'll put some dry clothes on and then I'll pull you back, on the raft, to Liang's place, same way I always do with Ailing.'

I followed him as he walked with big strides on the narrow path to what he had called his shack. I found it just beautiful. Entirely built from bamboo poles with a roof at least a foot thick made from reeds, it was three times as big as my family's house. Inside he had covered the bamboo walls with rush mats and he had also made a hanging ceiling of bamboo lattice-work hanging with thick pieces of rope from the bamboo rafters that supported the roof.

He had made easy chairs and a low table, also from bamboo and rushes, and along two walls he had installed shelves, made of rough hewn planks, for his books.

Behind the house he had built cages in which he kept a dozen or so rabbits and ducks. A few hens and a beautiful rooster were scratching the ground for food. Half a dozen geese stood close together, necks stretched straight up, eyeing me suspiciously, gaggling softly amongst them, probably discussing whether the little intruder should be tolerated or screechingly chased off their property.

'My sentinels,' Liu grinned, 'much better than dogs. Better stay away from them or else they'll pull wee willie from your trousers.'

He laughed loudly when instinctively I put my hands over my fly.

'And this is my friend Diaoyu,' he continued, still chuckling, and he stroked the head of a strange, black bird with a long neck and beak. It sat on a small wooden platform, a few feet off the ground, attached by a string and a ring around one of its legs to the short pole that supported the platform.

'It's a cormorant,' Liu said. 'We fish together at night. The small fish I catch with my net are for her and what's left I eat myself, as whitebait. Come and visit us one day, Xiao Chen, and we'll go fishing together. Now come! It's time to go and fetch Ailing.'

I followed him back to the river to where we had left the raft.

'Climb on the raft,' he instructed. 'Kneel with your face towards the bank. I'll walk along the bank and pull you by the rope against the current. Keep the paddle in both hands, one hand high on the handle, one close to the blade. Keep the blade in the water under an open angle to the raft to keep it away from the bank. Don't get entangled in the reeds. Push with the paddle against the reeds or the bank if you get too close. Shout when you can't manage or get tired. Now, move your arse!'

I waded knee-deep through the reeds and climbed on the raft. I untied the rope and threw the loose end to him on the bank. Slowly I drifted out of the reeds and when I was about four metres from the bank Liu started to pull and I manoeuvred with the paddle as he had told me.

After a few trials and errors that made me either almost fall off or made the water rush over the raft, wetting my pants, I got the knack of it and thereafter it was quite easy and fun. For nearly two hours Liu pulled me against the strong current without resting and it was already dark when we reached a huge weeping willow.

There Liu halted and pulled the raft against the bank. With one hand he lifted me off and put me down on land.

'It's here,' he said. 'Ailing will be here any minute now. You can go home now or you can wait to see Ailing one more time. Do as you please.'

'I'll wait,' I said and for about half an hour we sat there, in the grass, without talking, listening for the sound of somebody approaching.

Then we heard footsteps and whispers and Ailing and her youngest brother Yichen were so suddenly upon us that Ailing yelped in fright, like a small dog.

Yichen, who I knew was very close to his sister, was carrying her suitcase. It was clear he had cried for his eyes were all red and almost closed so swollen were his eyelids.

Liu took Ailing in his arms and for a long moment they stood there, wordless, while he gently stroked her beautiful glossy hair. Then Ailing freed herself from Liu's embrace and hugged her brother.

'Thank you for staying with me, Yichen, my little brother,' she said, sobbing. 'Take good care of yourself and don't speak up in my defence when Father works himself into one of his rages. It won't change anything for me but it will make things worse for yourself. One day you'll be your own man and then we'll meet again.'

Her lips quivered and to avoid crying again she quickly turned to me.

'Xiao Chen, thank you for your friendship and for helping me,' she said, her eyes brimming with tears. 'Go home now. It will be very difficult for you to get accepted back into your clan. If it becomes too difficult come back to Longfei and me. You'll at least have a roof over your head and food in your stomach and we'll find something for you to do in return. We'll see what the future brings, one day at a time. You agree, Longfei? Please?' she pleaded.

Longfei nodded, a big grin on his face.

'I'll make him into a real man,' he laughed, 'into the New Age Chinese, who isn't afraid to shake off his shackles and free his mind of old stereotypes. However, the first step is still yours to take, my young friend. Go home and do what your heart tells you to do. Remember! Your heart I say, not your mind. God lives in your heart, the devil in your mind and always they'll pull you in opposite directions. Every choice you make, every decision you take will always be a compromise, neither wholehearted nor wholly rational, so you'll never be completely happy or totally satisfied. Aim for an eighty-twenty trade-off between heart and mind and you'll find out that that's about the best you can do. Now go, Chen Dan! Go!'

I looked at Liu Longfei who already exerted such a strong influence on me, and at Ailing and I saw the worry and tenderness in her eyes, for me.

I felt my knees buckle and everything became unfocused and the nape of my neck felt ice-cold and pricked. I steadied myself against the trunk of the willow and without a word I turned and ran and ran and ran until I found myself leaning against the closed main gate of the Chen hamlet, gasping for breath, heart pounding as if to bust at any moment.

Suddenly the gate swung open and my Uncle Taitung seized my left arm so strongly that I yelped from the pain.

'You miserable little bastard,' he hissed, teeth clenched, lips pulled back. 'You helped that Liang slut get away and now old Liang'll make us pay. His steward will be here tomorrow to take stock of our garden and chickens and ducks and he'll tell us we'll have to work more for free, all because of you and your fancy dreams. I'll make my brother kick you out of the clan or by the river spirit I'll drown you myself to pacify old man Liang!'

Uncle Taitung dragged me to my parents' house and, kicking the front door open, he threw me inside. I stumbled and fell on the floor and before I could scramble up my brothers jumped on me and pinned me down with their knees on my arms and legs.

My father pulled my trousers down over my buttocks and my jacket up to my shoulders and then I heard the swish of his leather belt before I felt the biting, cutting pain, so intense as to be almost exquisite and I screamed and laughed at the same time.

With each lash I shrieked like a pig but then I laughed again, shrieked and laughed, shrieked and laughed until I fainted at last. When I came round I found myself lying on the river bank, the smell of wet grass and earth in my nose, their cool wetness against my burning cheek.

I felt a hand on my shoulder and heard the voice of my cousin Faxian.

'Get up, Hedgehog,' he urged me, in a whisper. 'Get up and away from here before my father finds you here and beats you even more. He's still yelling and screaming that he's going to kill you. I carried you here after you fainted. I had to kick your father against his shins to make him stop lashing you or else he would have beaten you to death. He was completely crazy, out of his mind. Now, try to stand and walk.'

Faxian's urgent whispers got finally through to my feverish brain and I tried to scramble to my feet. I couldn't help yelping from the pain in my legs, bottom and back, however, finally I managed to stand, though with Faxian's help.

For a long moment we stood there, without talking, Faxian's arms around my waist to prevent me from falling. I looked back at the dark and silent hamlet, the small back gate still ajar as left by Faxian.

It was a world lost to me, for good. I felt curiously empty, without emotion, neither sorrow nor anger.

Then, slowly, we turned and hobbled downstream along the river in the direction of Longfei's hiding place.

I never looked back and I have never been back and I have never seen anyone of my family or clan back either, until today when Suping and I met Faxian, or Monkeyface as I used to call him.

I limped away from a different time in a different universe where some freak of a god had put me for a while to observe me in my interactions with the humanoid creatures who lived there. When he had tired of his little game he had simply abandoned me and left me to my fate, like a spoilt child tired of his toy. When the creatures had found out that though outwardly I looked like one of them, inwardly I was totally different they had cast me out of their cage world.

Now I limped back into my own time and universe, into a world where I had been meant to live in in the first place but for that one meddling, freakish god.

It took Faxian and me the whole night to reach the seventh pole with the Liang character.

Here I told Faxian to leave me and to go back to the hamlet before he would be missed and beaten as well for going against the elders' authority. He looked at me, hesitated, then turned and I could hear him running back along the trail.

It took me some trouble to find the footpath alone and then one hour more to reach Longfei's house. The sky was already beginning to lighten when I finally let myself down on the dried sheaves of reed Liu had stacked against the back wall of the house.

Exhausted I fell asleep and even when I felt myself lifted up and carried inside and undressed I didn't wake up entirely. I felt a hand spread a cool, soothing oil on my backside and legs and from that hand's softness and gentleness I dreamily guessed it was Ailing's.

Then I fell asleep again and when I woke up it was dark again outside and I vaguely noticed Longfei and Ailing sitting in the low chairs.

The yellow light of an oil lamp standing behind them, on the low table, cast their huge shadows on the wall next to my bed. I smiled and from the white of their teeth I knew that they smiled back at me and that I was finally back amongst my own species.

Ailing stood up and came to stand next to me. She put her cool hand on my forehead and bent over to whisper, 'Welcome back, Xiaoxing' and from the way she looked at me I knew that she knew that I loved her with that sort of adoring but impossible love only a thirteen year old boy can feel for an older woman who loves already a man her own age. I shot a glance at Longfei and I saw the pity and compassion in his eyes and I knew that he would never mock my love for his Ailing.

'Don't hurt yourself beyond what your heart can bear, Xiaoxing,' he said softly. 'Don't torture yourself. If it becomes too much, you just disappear, without a word. We'll understand and will never think less of you. Until then, if it ever comes to that, you'll live here, with us and do your part of the household chores. We won't treat you as a child but as a younger brother who has been away for some time and who has some catching up to do. We won't teach you so much as letting you share our knowledge whenever you ask for it. But first we'll build a room for you. A room all for yourself, to protect you when you have thoughts you cannot fight and to live your own fantasies. Now, go back to sleep and tomorrow a new life will begin for you, for us.'

*

Gao Chen fell silent. Pensively he continued to stare at the ground, absent-mindedly doodling with a stick in the loose earth, his spirit still in Longfei's house where, long ago, his destiny had begun. His audience remained silent so as not to disturb his train of thought. They had been moved by the story of his early youth and now waited quietly for him to sort out his memories and pick up the thread again.

'And indeed, a new life began, you can say that for sure,' Gao Chen said, more to himself than to the others.

Then, looking up at his friends, he added, 'I had to relate this early part of my life in some detail so that you would understand how a child of landless peasants, serfs rather, was able to escape what seemed to be the fate of his clan.

I didn't do anything deliberate or intentional to break out, things just happened to me. Now let me continue.'

⋆

The next four years with Heilong Liu and Liang Ailing were the most wonderful years of my whole life, even in retrospect. Fortunately for me, and for Ailing as well of course, my love for her turned into a platonic and altruistic kind of love that made me happy, truly happy instead of jealous, when she was happy with her man or sad and upset when I saw that she was.

The Liang family left us alone and they didn't even seem to interfere in a determined way with Yichen's visits every eight weeks or so.

Yichen was Ailing's youngest brother, as I told you earlier. He always brought sweetmeats for Ailing and news about the outside world for Longfei.

Altogether six times during those four years and each time following a visit by Yichen, Longfei left us, always after dark, to return seven or eight days later, just before sunrise. I guess that he travelled by night to avoid his enemies. I was sure that Ailing knew where he went and whom he saw, however, neither he nor she told me and I never asked.

Apart from that one secret they never whispered or spoke softly in my presence or otherwise intimated that I made them feel uncomfortable. Time passed without stress or strain. I had no specific task but I helped out with the many small odd jobs in and around the house.

I got up early every morning, before sunrise, and went down to the river to pull up the bait lines Longfei and I had set out the evening before.

We baited the three or five hooks on each line with the small live white fish we had caught with the cast net that same day. A piece of white-painted wood was attached to the line about four metres from the hooks and a piece of lead was squeezed lightly around the line about forty centimetres from the hooks in order to make the bait wriggle and drag just above the bottom of the river. The other end of the line was attached to a stake driven into the bank.

The big, black eels that lived on the bottom of the river and who scrounged for food during the dark hours of the night would swallow bait and hook and then lie still until morning. At the first glimpse of daylight they would begin to wriggle to free themselves off the hook or, if it was stuck too deep in their guts, they would pull the line, stake and all, into the river. The trick was to pull the line in, slowly and evenly, before the day broke and if there was an eel, still sluggish, on one of the hooks, to quickly manoeuvre the slippery beast into a wicker basket before it went wild.

The first time I pulled an eel on to the bank I was so scared that I stood there as if petrified and it managed to free itself and slither back into the water before I could do something. The second time I brought an eel on dry land I was determined not to be laughed at again by Longfei and Ailing and I threw myself on top of the beast as soon as I had pulled it up in the grass. It was a huge one, more than a metre long and thicker than my arm and impossible to pin down.

With powerful thrusts it managed to free itself and, hissing like a cat, which frightened me because I never thought an eel could make sounds, it slipped from underneath my body and through my arms and hands back into the river.

Longfei and Ailing laughed even louder when I came home, hands, jacket and trousers glistening and stinking with the eel's sticky slime.

Weeks and several thorough washes later I thought I could still smell the fishy odour when I wore those clothes.

The next few days Longfei got up early as well and came with me to pull up the bait lines. Twice he showed me the trick with the wicker basket and then he let me try. I caught the eel the first time I tried and, as Longfei had shown me, I cut the short side line with the hook about ten centimetres from its mouth leaving the hook inside its guts. From that day on I was in charge of the bait lines and the catch of eels.

Once a week we had eel for dinner, and the rest of the week's catch, sometimes as few as four or five, sometimes as many as two dozen, I kept alive in a big, longish wicker basket with a special cover, which I left immersed in the river and attached to a stake in the bank. Every sixth day the owner of a restaurant in Danba would come to collect the basket while returning the empty one of the week before together with the hooks he had recovered from the eels' guts.

The man, Yang Baolin his name was, paid in kind for the eels and for the fish we caught with the cormorant.

Beef, salted pork, salt, sugar, flour, soy sauce, chilli paste, cooking oil, soap, writing paper and ink and pencils, occasionally some piece of clothing or anything else Ailing would order.

He also came after dark, stayed for the evening meal and the night and left after I had caught the eels of the next morning. After dinner Longfei and Yang Baolin went outside, for a quiet smoke or for a walk in the marshes.

Three, sometimes four evenings every week Longfei and I left after sunset and went fishing with Diaoyu the cormorant.

Longfei had built a big raft from six layers of criss-crossed, short and long bamboo poles. It was about four metres long and two wide. In the middle he had cut out a hole of one by one metre wherein we hung a big, long wicker basket and which was then two-thirds immersed in the water. In the basket we kept the fish Diaoyu caught, alive.

Next to the hole he had made a simple plank bench upon which we sat while the cormorant did its job.

At one end of the raft, the stern as we called it grandly, he had made a platform for the bird and a kind of gallows from which he hung the big carbide lamp.

Longfei kept the raft hidden in a narrow and overgrown creek about two hundred metres into the marsh and five hundred metres from the house. The evenings we went to fish Longfei carried Diaoyu to the raft and installed it on its platform. He then attached one end of a very long and thin line to the ring around one of the bird's legs and the other end to the platform's support. Then he adjusted the ring around the cormorant's neck in such a way that it would not be able to swallow a sizeable fish of say half a pound.

These preparations finished, we pushed the raft out of the creek into the river. Slowly the current would pull us downstream and to the middle of the river.

About eight hundred metres from the creek's mouth, in a bend of the river, were the remains of an old, collapsed wooden footbridge, in disuse since many decades. We attached the raft to one of the piers still in reasonably good shape in order to hold it in place against the pull of the current. Then we would wait until it had become completely dark and Longfei would light the carbide lamp.

The glare of the lamp attracted the fish to the surface of the water and, as if hypnotised by the light, they stayed within the circle it made on the surface, an easy prey for the cormorant who slipped soundlessly into and out of the water, each time returning with a fish in its beak.

Longfei would take the fish from Diaoyu's beak and put it in the small basket I held out to him and then I transferred it to the big basket in the hole of the raft.

While we did this routinely and effortlessly we talked about anything that came to our minds.

Longfei did most of the talking, of course and I just listened, absorbing everything he said, like a dry sponge absorbs water. At first I listened without commenting on what Longfei said, however, with time, I also began to advance my own opinion. Longfei encouraged me to be critical and not to accept everything he said at face value.

We talked about the moon, the stars, the sun, the planets and man's role and place in the life of our planet earth.

We talked about the religions and other life philosophies and incidentally I learned that Longfei had been to mission schools in Tianjin and Shanghai where he got a Christian education of course, and also learned to speak and write English.

Through the Christian connection he got a place at the University of Beijing where he boarded for many years with a Christian family of teachers and professors. He had never been a fervent Christian though, and with the years his outlook on life had gradually become that of a freethinker.

We talked about the fish we caught and about the thousands of other kinds of fish in the world's rivers, lakes and oceans. We talked about the cormorant and about the thousands of other species of animals flying in the skies or walking and stalking on the surface of our planet. We discussed the books he gave me to read, the articles he had written himself for *The Weekly Critic* before he had to flee and hide in the marshes. We also talked about the things that cannot be discussed in the presence of a woman, not even in front of Ailing.

I liked talking and listening to Longfei. His stories and anecdotes were always interesting and most of the time amusing and full of humour and many a time we laughed heartily which made Diaoyu nervous.

He himself was genuinely interested in my stories about life in the Chen hamlet and the manners and customs of clan life. I soon learned, however, to avoid one subject, unless he brought it up himself of course, and that was politics.

The wheelings and dealings of China's political scene really upset him. He would become cynical, contemptuous and emotional and raise his voice, frightening the fish away.

Diaoyu would become increasingly nervous, scuttling along the side of the raft, peering into the river, first with one eye, then with the other. Seeing no more fish, she would screech and hop on and off the platform restlessly.

Most of the time I managed to avoid the subject or steer away from it in time, however, now and then and always after one of Yichen's visits or after one of his own trips, he was so full of anger and exasperation that nobody would have been able to stop him talking about it, not even Ailing.

Since I had no experience and little interest, at that time at least, and didn't dare interrupt him, I let him talk until he had exhausted himself. Without actually expecting answers from me, he talked and discussed and argued with me as if I were now one then another of his friends or foes. He would point his finger at me, even grasp me by my jacket in the heat of his argument. At other times he could be remote and contemplative, conciliatory, positive even, deliberating a whole plan for the future of China using me as a sounding board.

I got to hear the names of the prominent people of that time so often that I felt I knew them personally. I particularly remember Sun Wen, better known by his Cantonese name Sun Yatsen, and Chiang Kaishek because Longfei became very emotional when he mentioned these two men. He had been one of Sun's earliest supporters, however, he had become disillusioned, as so many had before and after him, because of Sun's perpetual switches of allegiance, his manipulations and betrayals of his best friends and supporters.

Longfei bristled and snorted with derision as he called Sun a treacherous and vainglorious hypocritical nitwit who thought of himself as his Christian God's greatest gift to China and its downtrodden masses whose case he allegedly championed. The fact that Sun was more or less deified and that a mausoleum would be built for him near Nanjing was the ultimate example of the utter stupidity of those same masses and of the duplicity of their so-called leaders, Longfei said.

Where Sun was not so much an evil as a weak and vain man, Chiang was evil personified according to Longfei. At the mere mention of Chiang, Longfei would rear like a horse and rave on and on about the man's pathological meanness and deviousness, about his alternating arrogance and abject grovelling, about his irascibility and hysterics, his lust for power and glory, his obsession to become the all-time hero of China and how he would destroy and murder anybody who had fallen out of his favour or who had known him in a weak moment or who had been a witness to his duplicity and betrayals.

Longfei said that he had been a witness to so many of Chiang's weak moments, crimes and betrayals that there was no safe place left for him in China, not even in the marshes of faraway Sichuan. The Shanghainese gangsters of Big-Ear Du and Pockface Huang, whom Longfei called Chiang's puppet masters, would get him in the end and murder him in their usual bestial way, Longfei said.

Longfei actually wept, from anger and frustration, when he told me how Mao Zedong and Zhou Enlai had not believed him when he, Longfei, had warned them that Chiang would betray them and have their best people murdered.

'It was like pissing against the wind, Xiao Chen,' Longfei said, 'wetting my pants and shoes and everybody laughing at me. Until there was nobody left to laugh. The idealists, with their precious highfalutin principles, murdered by

Du's Green Gang, the opportunists, with their deep pockets, bought out by Du himself.

'Du, the criminal and opium dealer, who had committed every imaginable and unimaginable crime is now the big man in China and Chiang, who is scared to death of him, who shits in his tight trousers when Du so much as frowns at him, is his frontman, giving Du the legitimacy he needs to get his crooked fingers behind China's banks and government finances. The angels must be weeping when they see the foreigners applauding and hear them singing Du's praise. The very man whose gangsters murdered hundreds of their womenfolk and children, who personally hacked scores of them to pieces or burnt them alive or disembowelled them and then strangled them with their own guts.

'I predicted all that which is happening now, Xiao Chen, everything. I wrote letters to newspapers, even to an American magazine, but they refused to publish them since they are all under Chiang's, or his in-laws', influence. I spoke up during meetings of what was left of our May Fourth Movement, of what was left of the Communist Party, of what was left of the original Nationalist Party, however, people were either too naive or already too scared and they turned their back on me. They actually threw me out in a few instances. And now, Xiao Chen, anybody who is not in the pay or power of Chiang or Du is either dead or on the run or in hiding, Chinese and foreigners alike.

'The last time I saw Yang Baolin he told me that Du's gangsters know already that I am hiding out here. Ailing's scorned lover boy, that fossil Yang Zelin of Chengdu, told Du so himself, Baolin says. Baolin is a Communist, one of the first hour members, one of Chen Duxiu's own men, so he is another good man who won't last long. If Chiang does not have him killed, Mao Zedong will once he has outlived his usefulness for Mao's glory or, more probably, knowing Baolin as I do, when he begins to remind Mao of his earlier promises.

'For the moment all parties leave Yang in peace because the arrangement suits everybody. He runs his inn which is the place where people go when they want something to be known or a message to be passed on. Communists, Nationalists, Du's gangsters, even Chinese-speaking Russians go there and talk loudly, everybody pretending not to listen and not to know who or what the other guests are. Yang tolerates no quarrel in his place and mostly people respect that arrangement, however much they may be provoked by what is said and discussed there. However, it has happened that somebody loses his head and attacks an antagonist. Yang then shoots the attacker with his double-barrelled shotgun before he can blurt out something that may betray whoever or whatever and that's the end of it.

'Yang calls me a cynical bastard with no faith in human goodness but he is also my friend and he is my eyes and ears. As long as Yang remains in place, in his inn, I'm sure I'll have a few hours advance on Du's assassins or Chiang's rabble soldiers when they finally decide to come for me.

'Yang says I should leave now, while it's not too late yet. Join Mao in Hunan, Yang says. For the time being our aims are the same, Yang says. China for the Chinese people and down with its corrupters. Once that has been achieved Mao and I may find some form of accommodation, Yang thinks, but I'm afraid that will not be possible. I know Mao better than most and I tell you he's no different than Du or Chiang. Just as these two scoundrels hijacked the country for their own profit and glory and killed and still kill those who oppose them, so will Mao hijack the minds of the people for his glory and kill or enslave those who oppose or merely disagree with him. But there's no alternative, I'm afraid, so I hesitate while I'm running out of options and of time.'

'One night, nearly three years after I had come to live with Liu Longfei and Liang Ailing, he was unusually quiet, absent-minded rather, leaving me to handle Diaoyu and the fish. Suddenly he said, 'I have made arrangements for you, Xiao Chen, with Yang Baolin. When Ailing and I have to run you must go to Yang; he'll take care of you. Don't worry about money or about who is paying for what; that has all been taken care of. All I want you to concentrate on is to gather knowledge. Read whatever print you can lay your hands on, listen to people who have something worth while to say, watch how the situation in China develops and while you do all that, Xiao Chen, you keep to yourself. Don't espouse any cause, however noble whatever cause may seem to you at any given time. When both the time and you yourself are ripe for that, coincidentally I hope, I'll propose a cause to you myself, which you are then free to embrace or to reject, that'll be up to you. I am prepared to take the risk of rejection.

'Study Old Master Lao's words and follow his way. I tried that and failed, too meddlesome and too emotional, I'm afraid. However, you are a different breed, Chen Dan, and I would at least like you to give it a try. If legends about Lao Zi are anything to go by, you even look like him so perhaps you can be like him in mind as well. Like-minded, as the Communists say. How ironic. Tomorrow we'll start a different way of teaching, a kind of crash course to prepare you for the kind of life Ailing and I think is best suited for you. However, let's be clear about one thing, Dan! You are a free man and you can opt out any time. To opt out on reasoned grounds, however, you must first learn how to reason and what alternative to choose and that is what Ailing and I propose to teach you.

'It will be hard work but there will be plenty of time left to enjoy the kind of life we have led the past three years. Yang Baolin will fake the middle school diplomas for you, but he cannot fake the contests and entrance examinations to enter university for you. So you'll have to possess the knowledge to pass and I want you to pass ahead of everybody. So let's not waste our time, your time rather. It may very well be too late already.'

Longfei had been talking quietly, reflectively almost, and Diaoyu, quieted down by the droning of his voice, had climbed on his knee and made attempts to push its head inside Longfei's open-necked shirt. Absent-mindedly he stroked the bird's long, supple neck and he smiled at me when he said those last words.

*

Chen Dan reflected on these faraway moments for a brief second, glancing at his friends who remained silent though.

'Looking back now, I think that, more than what was said or happened at any other moment in my life, that particular evening, alone with Longfei and Diaoyu, in the dark on that raft, laid the basis for what I am now.

'When I close my eyes and keep still I still hear the sound of the small waves lapping and gurgling against and underneath the raft, the soft creaking of the raft's bamboo structure as it strained against the current on its leash, the occasional splash of a fish trying to jump out of its wicker prison and I can still smell that peculiar odour of rotting vegetation and wetness carried by the wind from the nearby marshes. As they did then, my eyes burn again with tears, my heart pounds and my throat is tight at the memory of my inability to utter the words of love, devotion and gratitude I felt for Longfei and Ailing, the two people who meant everything to me.' He smiled, and once again he was back on that river.

*

We sat there, on the raft, for a long time, without talking, each of us thinking of the things to come and how to act. I decided that I would make Longfei and Ailing proud of me and I said so.

I have never forgotten his smile and the look in his eyes as he said, 'Good on you, little brother. I'll look after you and after those whom you think worthy of your friendship. Go about your way unselfconsciously. Don't make any specific effort to let me know whatever it is that you think I should know. Whatever you do or say will unavoidably affect people around you, whose reaction in turn will affect others until the ripples reach me simply because people know I have an interest in you and because they think that bringing me titbits of information about you may serve their own interest. Through Yang Baolin you'll meet others if and when he sees fit and whom he thinks may be of help to you one way or another.

'But don't forget, Xiao Chen! You can't go on receiving if you have nothing to give. Connections are based on mutual interest, they are never one-sided. You accept a favour and you have created a debt that one day will be called in. So use favours and ask for help very sparingly and only if you can't get out of your fix on your own and even then think twice. However, if you have to ask do it without hesitation and don't bargain and don't belittle the efforts or criticise the results of those you asked for help. That's the way China works, Xiao Chen: good connections based on a proper balance of favours asked for and granted. This also means that you yourself must not grant unasked-for favours or help. This will make people uneasy as they think that you want to make them dependent on you. Try to maintain the balance in your favour, to remain a creditor, you'll feel better!'

At that Longfei stood up and carefully put the sleeping cormorant on its platform. It shifted its position a few times but its eyes remained closed. Do cormorants dream of fish?

It was past one in the morning when we came home.

Ever since that evening the atmosphere at home was subtly different. There was something like an unspoken sense of urgency. The daily routine of household tasks was changed so that I could spend five hours every day on my studies, two in the morning, and three in the afternoon, plus once a week a three-hour test about what I had learned.

Longfei prepared the lessons and the tests for history, geography, arithmetics and, alternately, for mathematics, physics and astronomy. Ailing made me read and interpret classical and contemporary literature and poetry and she taught me the niceties of social intercourse according to Master Kung.

Ailing disapproved of Master Lao and of his philosophy of course and though she usually took Longfei's teasing in good humour, she could react unexpectedly huffily if at a loss for words or a repartee. They both took their assumed task as a teacher very seriously and I did my utmost best to please them.

I didn't realise it at that time but I am now sure I got the best private tuition anyone ever had the good fortune to get. This regime went on for four hundred days and then Longfei and Ailing declared themselves satisfied. They said that at seventeen I had the knowledge of a twenty-one year old university student and the social naivety of a novice nun.

Real life outside the protected and idyllic world I had been living in for the last four years would amply provide me with the kind of education that would turn me into a man of the world, Longfei promised.

How right he was and how soon it came to pass.

★

'Though all this may sound to you as very serious business, the three of us had in fact a wonderful and undemanding life together. The evenings especially were beautiful and peaceful. Ailing had a beautiful voice and she knew many songs; sad ones, gay ones, funny ones and after dinner, when we sat quietly together, she often began to sing, very softly at first as if for herself only, then a bit louder and Longfei would fall in, humming with his baritone voice and I would fetch his mouth organ and softly I would play the melody in support of their voices.

'In many respects our evenings together here remind me of those evening long ago. The same atmosphere of undemanding friendship and trust, the same feeling of shared peace and beauty, accentuated by a similar sense, now as well as then, of impending doom, of the certainty that it can't last.

'Though we knew from what Yang Baolin told us that time was running out for us, the end came nevertheless unexpectedly quick. I shan't ever forget that afternoon of the sixth day of the sixth month of 1932, the day of the second upheaval in my life.' Chen Dan closed his eyes and sighed.

★

Longfei and Ailing were in their room sleeping away the hottest hours of the day while I was dejectedly trying to repair the wicker baskets I used for the eels.

It had been Yang's day to fetch the eels and when I had pulled the basket up on to the bank I had found it empty. The catch of six days, twenty big and medium-sized eels, had escaped because the basket's bottom had fallen out. Yang had been angry when he saw that the cause was a rotten twining and he had scolded me for my neglect. He had left early, not quite over his anger yet, and without his eels. After his departure Longfei went through Yang's reproaches again and quite sternly and I was close to tears.

'Learn your lesson from what happened, Xiaoxing,' Longfei said on a softer tone. 'A disaster is more often than not out of all proportion to its cause, the small things that go wrong when you least expect it and always at the most inconvenient time because you didn't pay attention or postponed their maintenance one time too many.'

He grinned and added, 'Maybe it's a good thing that this happened and that Yang scolded you for your neglect. Life was becoming a bit too easy and this incident brings us back to earth, to the often wicked reality of life outside our protected little world here and where sooner or later you pay for your mistakes, always. So repair the basket and tonight set out more bait lines to make up for the shortfall. Ailing ordered quite a lot of things last week and Yang won't give them to us free of charge because you let his eels escape.'

Laughing loudly Longfei went inside and closed the door in my face.

Dejectedly I went about my task. The humidity must have been close to a hundred per cent and the heat was oppressive and I had trouble staying awake. I must have actually dozed off since I hadn't heard Yang Baolin coming through the reeds until he was upon me, completely out of breath.

'Call Longfei!' he gasped. 'Call Longfei! Quick! There's no time to lose!'

Sensing the urgency I went straight inside and pounded on Longfei's room to wake him and Ailing. From the expression on my face they must have seen that something was very wrong so they wasted no words asking me what it was all about and followed me outside.

Yang had got his breath back somewhat and without preliminaries he rushed into his story.

'I was back in Danba earlier than usual this morning because I was still angry with Xiao Chen and because I had no eels to carry so I walked faster. And a good thing it was, though it doesn't make you any less stupid, Chen Dan,' and he shot me a venomous look in spite of his excitement. 'When I entered the street where I live,' he continued, 'I saw from afar a hundred or so soldiers milling around my inn and about to go inside. Had I been ten minutes later I would have come face to face with them when opening the door. With a feeling of foreboding I approached the inn unnoticed and I listened outside the open window to what was going on inside.

'I heard the officer in charge give orders to form ten search parties to comb the marshes for Liu Longfei and his woman and the boy who lives with them. I hear him cursing that I'm not there to guide the whole group straight to your place, Longfei, as that will make him lose time and the effect of surprise his commanding officer had counted on. The lieutenant orders my wife and her younger brother to prepare food baskets for them while they will wait two hours more for Yang Baolin to return home before they will set off for the marshes on their own. I had heard enough and I slipped out of town, unnoticed I think, and then ran all the way back to warn you, Longfei.'

'Thank you Baolin, my friend,' Longfei answered crisply. 'We knew this moment would come so now that it has let's not waste our time with lamentations. We have about four, maybe five hours before the search parties will get too close, so let's get moving and not in each other's way.'

He grinned and I'm still sure today that he actually enjoyed himself.

'Don't sit there as if you have lost your last penny,' he teased. 'Baolin, help me pack my books and documents in oilcloth and wicker baskets. Years ago, in anticipation of this very moment, I dug a hole underneath the plank floor of the big room. We'll bury the books in that hole and cover them with earth and sods. Ailing, pack only the minimum of clothes for both of us in the duffel bag and put on a pair of trousers and boots suitable for a very long trip. Xiao Chen, pack what you cherish most in a rucksack so that you can move fast through the reeds and bushes using both hands. Find someplace to stay for about a week and then come back here to see what the soldiers did here and report to Yang in Danba. When we have finished packing we'll set fire to the house. My books and documents should be safe from the fire in that hole wrapped in oilcloth and covered by earth.

'The fire and smoke will draw the soldiers' attention away from us while we flee the scene and they won't suspect the hidden treasure under the rubbish. They'll think I lit the fire to burn incriminating evidence, incriminating for others that is, big shots they're after. Xiao Chen, you haven't much packing to do. When you have finished set the rabbits free and chase the chickens and geese and the turkey into the marshes. Ailing and I will take Diaoyu with us. She can catch fish for us as long as we live on the raft. Once we have to abandon the raft we'll set her free as well and she'll have forgotten all about us as soon as we're out of sight, bless her simple soul. Now, move your arse, Chen! Don't stand there like a lovesick dog. We have known for a long time that it would come to this so let's not get sentimental.'

In silence we went about our assigned tasks.

Heart heavy, hands sweaty, eyes stinging with as yet unshed tears I went through my few belongings.

There was nothing left of my clan life. Everything I could call mine had been given to me by Longfei and Ailing and I cherished each and every item, most of all my test papers with Longfei's or Ailing's notes and their often humorous remarks in their own distinctive calligraphy.

Oblivious of what went on around me I leafed through the papers, staring bleary-eyed at what I and they had written. A period of my life, the happiest and most significant period, was about to end, for good.

My sadness and sorrow were overwhelming and I felt nauseated and sweaty and cold, all at once. I hardly noticed that the papers were taken from my limp hands and that my leaden arms were lifted up and put on somebody's shoulders, Ailing's shoulders, as I felt her soft cheek against mine, wetness against wetness.

I smelled her hair and felt her warm breath in my ear as she whispered, 'Xiaoxing, my love, take heart from the good times we had together, from the love and mutual respect that grew between us since that moment seven years ago when you first cited that shopping list to me. So much has happened since then and still we have so much to say and to do together, so this can't be the end. It's only temporary. Keep that in your mind, Xiaoxing, just like I do, just as Longfei does.

'Look at it as if we have temporarily something else to do and while we're at it we'll keep ourselves in good shape, physically and mentally, for the day we'll be together again. If you think that way, you have something to live for, something to look forward to, a purpose. Without such a purpose everything will be frightening. You'll be like a drowning man, flailing in panic to keep his head above the water, gasping for breath, choking on the very waves he makes himself.'

As she spoke I felt the despair, the sorrow and self-pity drain away, all the way down through my queasy guts and weak legs and out through my clammy feet into the ground. I put my forehead against hers and saw her eyes blurred through the tears in my own.

'I love you, Ailing,' I managed to say, my voice choking with emotion. 'I owe you my life and what I am. Whatever good I will be able to accomplish in my future life will be in your honour.'

'Take good care of yourself, Xiaoxing,' Ailing answered, 'that's all I ask of you.'

She took my hand and led me to the bench in the shade of the thicket of shrubbery at the edge of the swamp. We sat down and still holding my hand she said, 'When we'll have finished here Longfei and I will take the big fishing raft and follow the stream as far as we can. We'll abandon and destroy the raft before we reach Chongqing so as not to attract people's attention. Then we'll see. Longfei thinks we can reach Mao's hideout in Hunan in four to six weeks from today. Somehow we'll let Yang Baolin know when we have arrived there; he'll tell you.

'We want you to go to my family's mansion, Xiaoxing. Here's a letter for Yichen. Wait until dark, then slip inside through the small back door of the servants' quarters, the one with the broken lock, you remember? I'm sure it hasn't been repaired yet. Be careful, don't let the servants see you. You know where Yichen's room is. If he isn't in his room, put the letter in his headrest. Hide in one of the *godowns* and keep trying to find Yichen when he's alone. He'll have read my letter by then and he'll hide you in his room and give you food and drink until it'll be safe for you to go back here and then on to Yang Baolin's place in Danba.

'Don't be shy with Baolin. He owes Longfei so many favours that he can't ever hope to repay his debt, financial as well as moral, even if he made you the new emperor of China. However, Yang's a bully, as you have noticed this morning, so he'll try to impress on you that *he* is doing *you* a favour. Don't protest too much or too loudly. Let him have face with his wife and relatives. However, that does *not* mean that you have to accept everything he tells you. If necessary, let him know that you know and he'll tone down. Basically he's a good man, Baolin is. He won't ever betray you and he knows that the deal Longfei made with him about you is very much to his own advantage as well. Now, let's go and see what Longfei and Baolin have been doing, and no more tears. As from today you are a man, Chen Dan, and I count on you to behave like one I can be proud of.'

I laughed through my tears and wiped the snot from my nose and upper lip with a sleeve of my jacket.

Ailing laughed also, took my face between her hands and kissed me on my quivering lips. That was the very first time a woman had kissed me.

I quickly packed my papers and writing material in a piece of oil-paper and put them, with my clothes, in the rucksack Ailing had ordered for me, from Yang, a few months before.

Then I set the rabbits free and chased them together with the chickens, the geese, the ducks and the beautiful rooster into the wetlands. The funny little black and white pig with its wrinkly snub snout refused to be chased off, however. Screaming and squalling it dashed left and right and each time it raced back, sometimes between my legs, to the small enclosure behind the house where we had kept it for the past two years.

Longfei, worried by the racket, came out of the house and then burst out laughing when he saw my red, congested face.

'Make it think you're pulling its tail!' he shouted. 'Attach a stone or something else heavy to its tail and it'll run as fast as it can, straight into the wetlands. You'll see!'

I managed to catch the squealing little animal and put it back in its pen. It snorted happily, like a small child that has had its way, tantrum forgotten already. I filled one of Longfei's old socks with pebbles and attached it with a sliding knot to the small pig's tail. Then I lifted it out of its pen again and put it down in the clearance behind the house, its head turned towards the wetlands. I gave it a good, slapping whack on its round little rump and there it bolted, like lightning. The last thing I saw was Longfei's black sock, bumping up and down and then it was gone.

I went inside and helped Longfei and Yang shovel the last layer of loose soil into the hole on top of the wrapped books and documents. Then we put the floorboards back in place. Next we carried Longfei and Ailing's duffel bags to the big raft and attached them securely to the bench I had sat on so many nights, listening and talking to Longfei.

Again I felt that my emotions were about to get the better of me and I breathed deeply to get a grip on myself. Everything I looked at, everything I touched set off a chain of memories. How was I ever to dull the sharp edges of the feelings of loss and loneliness I now already experienced while Longfei and Ailing weren't even gone yet?

Finally everything was ready for our evacuation and we poured out the cans of paraffin Ailing used to keep in the kitchen for her cooking stove. We poured the bluish, smelly liquid over the furniture, the beds, the floor and against the walls.

I saw that Ailing cried but before I could reach her and console her Longfei put his arm around her shoulders and together, Ailing's head against his shoulder, they walked off without looking back once, to the creek. Yang followed them and I came behind, feeling terribly alone already.

Hundreds of big bluebottle flies, disturbed in their digestion of Diaoyu's droppings and the shrivelled morsels of fish on its platform, buzzed angrily around us while we pushed the raft through the creek to the river. I had never noticed the flies in the evening, they were probably only there during the day.

While Yang held the rope to keep the raft against the bank, first Longfei and then Ailing gave me a last, strong hug, without saying a word, before stepping on to the raft.

Longfei caught the rope Yang threw after him and wound it neatly around Diaoyu's platform.

Yang and I stood there, watching, as both Longfei and Ailing were busy manoeuvring the raft through the reeds and into the current. Once the current got hold of the raft it accelerated quickly towards the middle of the river and they looked up, in our direction.

They both waved cheerfully and we waved back, hesitantly at first, then almost frenetically with both arms though by then Longfei and Ailing were already too busy to notice our impulsiveness, preoccupied as they both were with manoeuvring the big raft around the broken footbridge. Ailing had just the time for a last, quick wave before the raft disappeared out of sight around the bend.

Yang Baolin put his hand on my shoulder and squeezed it in a gesture of affection.

'Come on, Xiao Chen, my friend!' he said, uncommonly gentle. 'You and I have still business to finish here and then we both go our separate ways, for the time being, that is. You go and do whatever Ailing asked you to do for her and you be careful and secretive about it. I expect to see you in two or three weeks.'

Shaking off any further reminiscences we quickly returned to the house.

Yang gave me a box of matches. 'Here, you light the fire!' he said gruffly. 'Burn the past and the memories will haunt you less. Look at the flames consuming your material attachments, then turn around and don't look back! The soldiers will see the smoke and they will all converge here. That'll give us the time to get away. Now, do it man!'

Without further ado I lit the paraffin in every room and I watched, mesmerised, as the slow, blue flames crept over the chairs and tables, over the beds and up the walls. The blackening and crackling of the bamboo surrendering to the flames shook me out of my torpor and quickly I opened the doors and window shutter to let in the wind to feed the fire and I went outside.

Yang was watching the scene from the edge of the clearance and he beckoned me to join him.

'A fire is always the cleanest way to cut the bonds with the past,' he said. 'A fire sets the spirit free. Symbols, tokens, monuments, they inspire nothing but morbidity, shackling you to the past, shutting you off from the present and the future. That was also Longfei's opinion. Good man, good friend Longfei was, is I should say, of course. Ailing mellowed him quite a bit which is so much the better for him, for everybody. They'll manage. People like those two don't just fade from your life. They gave the best of themselves to you Chen Dan. I envy you. Don't ever shame them! Now let's go! Before you come to me in Danba pass by here to see whether Chiang's rabble found Longfei's books and papers. I'm sure they won't but Longfei wants to be sure! That was one shackle, hopefully the only one apart from Ailing and you, that he wasn't able to break loose from.'

He burst out laughing and joyously he slapped my back. Suddenly he growled and snarled like an angry dog and I jumped in fright.

He laughed loudly and shouted, 'Bite man! Bite! That's life! Dog bites dog bites dog!' and he was gone.

Quickly I put my rucksack over my shoulders, looked at the flames one more time, turned and, without looking back as Baolin had said, I took the path leading to the river.

For the first time in four years I went back to the Liang manor.

*

For the second time during his narration Gao Chen fell silent.

'End of the second instalment,' he laughed. 'I'm afraid I got carried away by my memories of what I still feel has been the most significant part of my life. My whole life so far has been like that: abrupt endings and totally new beginnings. Nothing like the gradual evolution of life, the standard pattern for a mature and balanced personality, which society finds so conveniently predictable and socially acceptable. But let's see whether our Beggars Chicken is behaving equally predictably.'

The others burst out laughing. They had been spellbound by Gao Chen's story but were momentarily relieved to stand up and stretch their legs and arms and to yawn until their jaw muscles ached with tension.

They sauntered after Gao Chen and looked on while he brushed the earth and ash aside with a leafy branch to uncover the clay ball that contained the chicken. He took his pocket knife and poked at the mud shell until a small piece fell out.

He lowered himself on his knees and brought his nose close to the small hole in the chicken's shell, sniffing ever so delicately.

He looked up at his friends.

'Very nice smell,' he exclaimed, smiling delightedly, 'very nice indeed! Smell yourself!' and he motioned the others to follow his example.

Each knelt in turn and, after sniffing at the small hole, confirmed Gao Chen's finding that the odour was indeed delicious.

'We can dig it out of the ash now,' he said, 'and let it cool so that we can later remove the shell easily. That'll take another two hours or so, time for me to finish my story. Unless you have had enough,' he added, pretending to be busy digging out the clay ball.

'No, no! Don't stop now, Uncle Dan, please!' Suping exclaimed. 'We want to hear the rest of your story also. Don't we?' she added anxiously, looking at her parents and at Ai Chen.

'Yes, Dan,' her mother said, 'we really want to hear the rest. It's a fascinating story. So unusual and so unexpected. I mean, it's so different from what you would expect,' she finished, a bit lamely and blushing.

'That is indeed the definition of the unexpected, dear,' her husband said, smiling mockingly, 'that something is different from what you would expect. What you meant to say is that such a common man as Chen Dan from his appearance would seem to be is not supposed to have led such an out of the ordinary life. Ugly people lead ugly lives and beautiful people lead beautiful lives. Isn't that it? How naive and how unjust. The eternal prejudice,' he added wryly.

His wife blushed an even deeper red and she twitched nervously with her fingers, like a little girl caught doing something shameful.

Gao Chen, without looking up from his ado with the Beggars Chicken, said, 'Don't do that to your wife, Ximing! She doesn't deserve it and you know that. Guixian is a good person and the last thing she wants is to hurt people, least of all probably me. Only the seemingly flawless, beautiful people hurt others intentionally. It's their right, they think. Actually, I think that it is a reaction against the too high expectations ordinary people have of them. Nobody is perfect and having to maintain such a pretence must be terribly stressful and, in the end, of course, impossible. You know what, Ximing? I am quite *happy* with my ordinariness, my ugliness. People I don't know, and don't *want* to know, never give me a second glance or bother me with their attention. So I am a relatively free man. I need not pretend. I only take the trouble to prove myself when I feel like it. Remaining unnoticed when I felt no inclination to be noticed has served me well.

'And let me tell you one more thing,' he added, looking up at them, sitting up straight, on his heels, knees on the ground, and grinning mischievously, 'it's quite amusing to see people change their mind about you when you let on casually that you're not quite the moron they took you for.'

He fell silent and busied himself with the piping hot clay ball and how to manoeuvre it out of the blistering hot ash pit into the cool grass without burning his fingers. When he finally succeeded he straightened up, groaning and grimacing from the heat and pain in his lower back.

'I'll leave it here for now,' he said, wiping the perspiration from his forehead with the sleeves of his jacket. 'Guixian, my dear, if you would refill my tea mug I'll wipe my face and wash my hands in the meantime. Then, if you're ready, I'll tell you the rest of my life story, that is until I ended up here under your roof. Will there be a final part? Before the curtain falls for good?'

At that he disappeared into the kitchen and the others heard him splashing himself with water.

Xu Ximing looked at his wife and daughter. Wonderingly he said, 'What a dull and uneventful life I have led compared to Gao Chen's. I never seem to have done or experienced anything noteworthy. Something deliberate I mean, on an impulse, my own impulse that is. Things just happened and I never gave them much thought. Even the Communists taking power in 1949 and subsequently the confiscation of all our possessions I didn't experience as traumatic. Just a tiresome incident. Now I recall, even marrying you, Guixian, was *your* decision and initiative, as was the initiation of Suping. How exciting that must all have been for you, my love,' he said in a self-mocking tone. "What a bore!" as my daughter would probably say,' he added ruefully.

Guixian laughed and looking fondly at her husband, she said, 'The price of security and stability is monotony, even boredom from time to time, my dear, however, it is a price every married woman is gladly prepared to pay. Lives like our friend Dan's one reads about in novels and then fantasises about in the privacy of one's dreams. However, real, everyday life must be familiar and predictable, reassuring because of its very day-to-day sameness and the closeness of other boring, predictable people one knows one can trust. And that my dear friend, lover and husband, you have provided amply. I fervently hope that Suping will one day fall for an amiable, stuffy but malleable plodder like you. That she won't be swept off her feet by a dashing, bright-eyed "know-all do-all" who gets his nose bloodied time and again and nothing but misery for the poor wife who, of course, will always be blamed for the great man's failings.'

Ai Chen chuckled and said, 'Malleable, Suping, *malleable*, that's the keyword! You see, I am an amiable, stuffy plodder but I am *not malleable* and that is a recipe for the kind of boredom that drives a woman up the wall and out of her mind if she hasn't quit before it's too late. I know! It happened to me. My wife left me when after having been married to me for three years I still had no idea of her feelings and needs and probably also never would. She eloped with the skipper of one of those barges that ply the Grand Canal between Beijing and Hangzhou, a primitive, near-human creature, without a forehead, whose male instincts react to the female's smell. At first I thought that it was just a fling and that she would come back but when after three months she still had not I went to Suzhou to wait for that barge. They lived on board, you see.

'During the unloading of their cargo I observed them from behind a pile of sacks on the quay. She worked with her skipper and his men, carrying baskets of cabbages on land and bags of rice back on board. They passed close to where I was hiding and the whiffs of stale sweat that wafted in their wake, my wife's no exception, made me sick. She seemed happy and she laughed a lot at the men's bawdy jokes and lewd remarks. Her skipper punched her when one of the dock workers grabbed her under her skirt and she squealed with pleasure. She hit him back, yelling and making explicitly obscene gestures at him which made everybody roar with laughter. What a totally different world she was living in. I had no idea that such things existed. I went back to Shanghai. They never saw me then and I never saw her again. It's been twenty years now. Before liberation all this happened. I don't know whether a marriage can be dissolved by default of one of the partners and, if so, after how many years. If not, then I am still a married man, or a widower for that matter. I don't know.

'Six months after she left me, I had not one piece of clean clothing left, not one sock without holes as big as a fist and I hadn't eaten a decent meal for weeks. Most students stayed away from my lectures. A few kept coming but they sat on the back benches of the amphitheatre. I wondered why, so I raised my voice to make myself heard. One day a colleague put his head around the door of my classroom and suggested I use a radio transmitter to give my message to the aliens instead of shouting it at them. My course was astronomy, you see, and his was mathematics in the room next to me. With my loud voice I had been disturbing his course for quite some time already so he came to see what was going on. Having made his joking remark my colleague sniffed and said, 'It stinks in here, there must be a dead rat somewhere.'

He came into the classroom to look for the dead rat, sniffing and following his nose as the smell became stronger.

When he was close to where I was standing, in front of the blackboard, he suddenly looked at me, eyes narrowing and said, 'Can I see you for a moment, Chen? Outside? In the corridor, please? I have an idea about that dead rat.' I followed him outside and closing the classroom door behind me he said, 'Here's the key to my house, Chen. You know where I live. Tell my housekeeper to prepare a bath for you and to give you lots of tar soap. Tell him also to give you some of my clothes and to prepare a room for you to stay. You are going to stay with me. We'll share the rent. You can't take care of yourself, Chen.'

'I didn't know where he lived but I didn't dare tell him that. I would ask others. Still confused by this unexpected turn of events I heard my colleague add, 'I'll tell your few heroic students to come back tomorrow when the cleaners will have had the dead rat removed and the classroom disinfected. They won't believe it but that doesn't matter as long as you don't lose face.'

That colleague was Chen Dan as you will have guessed already. We have stayed together since that day. Without him I would have perished in my own filth.'

Ai Chen fell silent and looked at his friend with great fondness, adoration even, one could say.

'Those were about the only events in *my* life worth telling you,' he said, smiling self-deprecatingly. Now Dan can take centre stage again as he likes to do so much. Go on, my friend,' he chuckled, 'be brief if you know what that word means. You shouldn't have made us smell your chicken for now I am looking forward already to the end of your story.'

'I wish that wild, vixen wife of yours had not eloped with her caveman,' Gao Chen growled, 'now I can't embellish the part of my story after you intruded in my life. It will be like a fart after all the initial thunder though its smell will still be better than yours at that time.'

Everybody burst out laughing, relieved by the good-natured mockery. Suping suspected that Chen Juntao was like the circus clown who makes people laugh though his own heart cries out for a bit of love and compassion, his self-mockery merely a front behind which he hides his true self, just another delusion. She busied herself with the tea mugs, rinsing the spent leaves out with a bit of water before putting in fresh leaves and topping the mugs with scaldingly hot water.

When she handed Ai Chen his mug his eyes caught hers and she shivered at the despair she saw in their depths. The despair of the over-intelligent but hopelessly impractical man who knows he can't survive in the humdrum of everyday life without someone telling him at every turn and twist what to do.

How scared he must be of a life without his friend and protector, Gao Chen, she thought and she felt an overwhelming pity for this awkward, gangling, good-hearted soul.

Intuitively she looked askance at Gao Chen who was watching her ministrations to his friend's tea mug. Almost imperceptibly he nodded, signalling that he knew what she was thinking.

'My only consolation is the certainty that I'll outlive you, Juntao,' he said, grinning mischievously at his friend. 'So when you finally quit on me I can still concoct a grand finale without having to fear your accusation that I merely indulge in self-aggrandisation.'

Suping saw Ai Chen straighten his back and he took the mug from her, smiling broadly. She was grateful for Gao Chen's understanding and compassion for his awkward friend.

Gao Chen installed himself comfortably, took the mug she offered him, folded his hands around it, for the evening had become a bit chilly, and continued his story.

# *Chapter Sixteen*

## Chen Dan's Story: The Years of Living Dangerously (1932–1966)

The sun was setting when I came within sight of the Liangs' manor. I would have to wait at least two hours before the night would be dark enough for me to sneak up, unseen, to the back door of the servants' quarters.

I decided to bide my time in the garden house. Ailing had told me, long ago, when we were friends already, that her father's second and third wives used to live in that house. Her father had been considerably older than her mother when they had got married and after only five years or so First Lady Liang had to accept that the old man took first one and soon afterwards a second, very much younger wife to keep him youthful and healthy. She had, however, refused to share the main house with the other two wives and thus old Liang had a small though very pretty house built in the garden a hundred metres or so behind the main house.

Apart from his seven children, six boys and the girl Ailing, with his stately first wife, old Liang had sired two children with his second wife, twin girls, but none with his third wife. His second wife had died during childbirth and Third Lady had been charged with the care of the two baby girls.

Eight years later still Third Lady had been pronounced barren by First Lady's doctor and consequently had been demoted to lady-in-waiting, a kind of first servant to the First Lady and her children. Since her duties required her to be on call twenty-four hours a day, it was not convenient for her to stay in the garden house, so she had moved into the annexe to the kitchen, a kind of storeroom for household articles, with sleeping and toilet facilities.

The most important fixture though was the voice-duct to First Lady's quarters and to her eldest son, Yibang's, room. By merely raising their voice in their room they could call former Third Lady.

The twins, having much lower status than Liang's children with First Lady, even less than Ailing though she was four years younger than the twins, had nevertheless been given a nice, big room in the left wing of the main house. First Lady had put her foot down when the old man wanted to send the twins to school, like his other children. She had consented, however, that a retired primary school teacher should come a few hours every week to teach them reading and writing and spoken *Hanyu*. Apart from that one favour, the girls had to learn housework and help the servants.

Ailing had instructed me to call them Auntie One and Auntie Two as she herself and her younger brother Yichen did also. The other members of the household, servants and family alike, simply called them One and Two though nobody could tell them apart. Nobody also knew their real names and they probably had forgotten themselves.

During the time that I came so often to the manor to work and study with Ailing I preferred to do the homework Ailing gave me in the kitchen annexe rather than in my own home where I was constantly teased and taunted by my relatives.

I became very friendly with former Third Lady, whom I called Taitai, and with the twins. They were a cheerful lot and we had many a good time together, laughing a lot though crying a little from time to time as well. I particularly remember a few months of snot and snivel when the assistant gardener, a dashing young man, fled the scene when both One and Two fell in love with him and actually fought over him.

When he consoled One for her bruises she turned out to be Two and he got his own face scratched for saying the right words to the wrong girl. When that happened one time too many he took off, never to be seen again on the estate. The twins were disconsolate for a few weeks, ignoring each other, but then they forgot him and life went on as before though they played pranks on me more and more often.

Sneaking up to the garden house, I was wondering how they were doing.

I saw that it had fallen into serious disrepair since I had been there for the last time four years ago.

About to open the back door I heard voices inside. Quickly I withdrew and hid under the bushes that grew up to the window sill of the living room's side window. One of the glass panes was broken four years ago already and I rightly guessed that it wouldn't have been repaired since. I could easily overhear what was said in the room.

I recognised Yibang's voice as he was talking to his younger brother Yichen whose whining voice I had heard so often during the period when he still came to see Ailing from time to time. It was apparent that Yibang was angry and Yichen frightened.

'The lieutenant and his soldiers will come back here when they don't find that Chen bastard in his clan,' I heard Yibang say with barely controlled anger. The lieutenant thinks that Chen has a letter for you, Yichen, from Ailing, in which she tells you where she and Heilong Liu are fleeing to. He knows that you visited Ailing in the past and he thinks that she probably already told you then where they would go in the event they had to flee. He will have his men torture you, Yichen, to make you talk unless you tell them or, better still, give him Ailing's letter. They may kill us all and burn the house and the warehouses if you don't.

You must tell them, Yichen! You *must*, do you hear me! To protect yourself and the family. If that Hedgehog Chen brings you a letter you *must* give it to the officer so that he and his rabble will leave us in peace. Will you do that, Yichen, little brother?'

Yichen, as usual, sobbed and snivelled and whined. 'I don't want those soldiers to hurt me, *Gege*, I'm so afraid of pain. But I don't want to betray *meimei*!' he wailed.

I had heard enough. Yichen would give in to Yibang or, if not to him, then surely to the lieutenant once the soldiers tickled his tight arse with a red-hot poker, their favourite tool to make people, talk Yang Baolin once told me.

I had a plan but I needed a place where I would be safe for a few hours to work on it. The only place I could think of was Taitai's scullery so I stole to the kitchen's back door and knocked softly. Auntie One, or Two perhaps, opened the door and her mouth fell open in utter astonishment when she recognised me.

I signalled her to keep silent and gestured that I wanted to come inside.

She let me in and I followed her into the kitchen. Taitai and the other half of the twins were equally astonished at first but then delighted to see me again, which was a good omen, for I needed their help for my plan.

I pointed at the opening of the voice duct and motioned for them to come with me into the larder. Taitai lit a candle and closed the larder door behind us.

First of all we embraced affectionately while the three women talked excitedly and asked questions all at the same time.

I didn't reply at all and finally, Taitai first, they got the message and fell silent, Two last as always, which was the only way to know which one she was.

I told them I would tell them the whole story about Ailing, Heilong Liu and myself once they had helped me with a difficult and urgent problem. Briefly I told them what I had by chance overheard outside the garden house and then I showed them the letter Ailing had asked me to get to Yichen.

They agreed with me that Ailing, naive and trusting as she had always been towards her brothers, notably Yichen, had surely revealed Longfei's plans in that letter.

I told them my plan to save everybody from a very bad time. I would steam the envelope open and rewrite Ailing's letter, giving a lot of false information that would throw Chiang's soldiers off their track and keep them busy for weeks following the false lead.

In fact, the soldiers would most probably never discover that they had been misled. They would leave the estate satisfied with the letter Yichen would hand over as soon as he would see them putting the poker in the fire. The women thought it was a beautiful plan and they eagerly agreed to help me to carry it out.

Back in the kitchen Taitai put a kettle on the fire to make the steam for opening the envelope while One went stealthily to the bookkeeper's office to filch a few sheets of ordinary notepaper and a pencil. Since I had to reuse the envelope I fervently hoped that nobody would notice or find it strange that Ailing had written her brother's name on the envelope with a writing brush and ink and subsequently the letter itself with a pencil.

I was able to copy Ailing's calligraphy with a pencil but not with a brush because of the different pressures she and I applied when making the strokes; hers were thinner and more graceful, notably at the starting points.

The risk, however, was a minor one and besides, I had no choice.

The envelope unglued easily when I held it above the steaming kettle spout and I removed Ailing's letter to read it. I felt embarrassed, but again I told myself I had no choice since I had to copy her style and choice of characters. I had guessed rightly.

The letter was written lovingly and trustingly, giving the full details of Liu's plan of escape and their final destination in Hunan. She had also written that I was going to stay for at least a few months in Danba, with Yang Baolin the innkeeper, before moving on to either Beijing or Shanghai depending on the arrangements Yang would be able to make for me. Finally she asked Yichen to give in future any messages for her to Yang who would know how to forward them to her.

I both marvelled and shivered at such naivety. What an unmitigated disaster, if that letter had fallen into the lieutenant's hands. Somehow, and the sooner the better, I would have to let Ailing know that her brothers, including her beloved little brother Yichen, I was sure, could not be trusted and would gladly deliver her to the devil himself if they could save their own arses that way.

I began to rewrite the letter, taking as many characters as possible from those used by Ailing for authenticity. After the preliminaries and endearments, which I left unchanged, I wrote:

*Longfei has decided to travel by night and to rest during daytime. During the first part of our trip we'll hide the raft in the reeds or in a creek at dawn and continue our voyage after sunset. Later, once we have abandoned the raft and set Diaoyu free, we'll hide and rest in safe houses until we reach Wuhan in about three weeks from now.*
*In Wuhan a barge is waiting for us and in another five or six weeks we'll be in Shanghai. I'll write you another letter from there.*

This lie would give me two months to get a letter to Ailing myself to tell her to write a second letter to Yichen with such disinformation as Longfei would judge necessary at that time. I also wrote about Yang Baolin:

*Longfei is now absolutely convinced that Yang Baolin is a Nationalist informer, perhaps even very high up in their secret organisation.*

*You do remember Yang, don't you, Yichen? The innkeeper from Danba, the one with the big mouth? You once met him at our house. He supposedly came to buy eels and fish from us for his restaurant but actually he came to spy on us, Longfei says. This morning Longfei came back from a four-day meeting in Guanxian. He thought it would be a good idea to pass by Danba to see Yang so as not to rouse the man's suspicion that he, Longfei, is on to him.*

*When he was about to enter the inn he heard Yang scolding his wife for not having told the lieutenant to wait for him so that he could have led him and his soldiers directly to our house instead of wasting the lieutenant's time in having him organise a search.*

*What would the Generalissimo think of him, Yang Baolin, if the lieutenant reported the case, Yang wailed.*

*Longfei came running all the way home and we immediately packed the most essential things and set off on the raft. Longfei told Xiao Chen to set fire to the house and make sure all Longfei's belongings, notably his books and papers, were burning well before fleeing himself.*

*The fire will attract the soldiers to the house which will give us and Xiao Chen the time to get away. I gave Xiao Chen this letter for you, my dear little brother. I trust him to deliver it to you when he reaches the manor. I beg you to hide him a few days in your room until the soldiers will have left the area.*

*Please, Yichen. Keep a look out for him and tell him when the coast is clear.*

*Xiao Chen knows how to travel to join us in either Wuhan or, if we have moved on by then, in Jiujiang.*

This was enough disinformation I thought, no need to put it on with a trowel, and I finished the letter copying literally again, Ailing's loving words of goodbye.

I felt a bit sick when I wrote them out.

I folded the letter and put it back into the envelope, glued it and gave it to One, or Two, and told her to go to Yichen's room, to make sure he wasn't in his room and then to put it into his headrest. She was back within minutes.

Then, together, we discussed what best to do about myself. Firstly I needed to know whether my ruse had worked and secondly I had to be sure the soldiers had left the area before I could go back to the house, as Longfei had ordered me, and then on to Danba. This last bit of information I didn't give Taitai and the twins though.

They had tried to read Ailing's letter, upside down, while they had watched me writing the fake letter, but I had shielded both letters off from their prying eyes with my left arm.

Better for them, for me, for all of us, that they didn't know. They didn't owe me anything. On the contrary! I owed them for the help they had already given me, so how could I expect them to suffer pain, or worse, for my sake, if the soldiers tortured them just to see whether they knew something?

Still I needed one more, big favour from them – a place to hide. One and Two simultaneously suggested that I hide in their room, under their bed. Nobody would dare look there for me and they could keep me informed of what was happening. So it was decided and that was the reason I spent two weeks under and, I have to admit shamefully, in the pretty aunties' huge bed.

The lieutenant and his soldiers came back the next morning. I heard them entering the main yard of the manor and I watched the scene below through a split between the drawn curtains of the twins' room on the first floor.

I opened the window slightly to hear what was said outside.

I saw Yibang and Yichen come running out of the front door to meet the troops and I heard Yibang clamour, 'I have very good news for you, Lieutenant! My brother Yichen received a letter from our sister as I told you yesterday he would. In the letter she tells exactly where Heilong Liu and she will be going. Yichen! Give the officer the letter!'

Smiling broadly Yichen handed the letter to the lieutenant, an ascetic and forbidding-looking man in his late twenties, I guessed. The officer read the letter and without a word put it in his breast pocket.

'Chen Dan gave you the letter,' I heard him say to Yichen. 'Where is he now? He has a lot of information I need.'

'I don't know,' Yichen replied, stammering nervously, 'he put the letter in my headrest while we were having dinner, I guess, and then he must have left and hid somewhere, not sure I would indeed hide him as my sister asked me to do.'

This was exactly what I had done so it shouldn't sound too improbable to the lieutenant, yet from the way I saw him staring at Yichen I knew this was going to end badly for young Liang and that it was in fact my fault.

That whole part of him hiding me and so on I should have simply left it out of the letter, an unnecessary embellishment that was going to have terrible consequences which, had I shown a bit more modesty and restraint instead of getting carried away by my beautiful plan, could have been avoided.

This realisation of my stupidity passed like a flash through my head as I heard the officer say, 'You are lying, Liang Yichen! Why would your sister's gigolo leave without even seeing you? I tell you what happened! *You* told Chen that you would have to hand over the letter to me and that he had better hide elsewhere to stay out of my hands. Seize him and make him talk!' he ordered his men.

Yichen fainted and Yibang fell on his knees, begging the lieutenant to believe them, that neither Yichen nor he knew where Chen had gone and why.

'Shoot him!' the officer ordered the soldiers, pointing at Yibang. 'An older brother ought to have better control over the younger one. Shoot him in the stomach and let him die slowly. Make the youngster look and then start on him.'

I shall spare you the goriest details but I swear that I have never forgotten what I saw and heard that day and for many years my worst nightmare was that they would do to me what they did to those poor boys, such *agony*. I am sure my terror of physical pain has everything to do with what I saw that day.

As if petrified I stayed where I was, behind the curtains, on my knees, just able to peep over the window sill.

I saw the soldiers drag a screaming and struggling Yibang to the front gate and tie his wrists to the forged iron spikes on top of the gate doors, forcing him to stand up in his full length, on his toes almost. Then two soldiers cocked their rifles and while two others forced a hysterical Yichen to look on, they shot Yibang twice in his stomach and in his genitals.

They laughed while they did that and one of them made a remark I couldn't hear that made the others roar with laughter. They then left Yibang, hanging by the wrists, writhing and suffering terribly. I saw old Liang come hobbling and stumbling out of the house, staggering towards his dying son.

One of the soldiers tripped the old man and hit him with the butt of his rifle on the head, twice, till he lay still. Four other soldiers tied a noose around Yichen's neck and threw the other end of the rope over a branch of the big peach tree in the yard. Then they pulled the rope until Yichen stood only on the tip of his toes, blue and gurgling, eyes bulging, his fingers desperately trying to widen the noose.

I saw he lost control of his bladder and sphincter, urine and shit streaming down his bare legs in a puddle around his toes. The soldiers pinched their noses and roared with laughter. Now and then they let go off the rope a bit so that Yichen got back on his feet, whoopingly gulping for air. Each time they asked him something, about me no doubt, but each time Yichen's answer seemed to displease them and they pulled him up again.

After what seemed an eternity, mesmerised as I was by what went on, but what must have been close to half an hour, the soldiers tired of their cruel game and apparently still not satisfied, they untied Yichen and dragged him behind the house, out of my sight, to administer horror of another kind, no doubt.

I came out of my trance as it were and nauseated to the point of vomiting I turned away from the window, the scene below etched for ever on my mind: Yibang, unconscious or dead, hanging on the gate, jacket and trousers dark and glistening wet with blood and gore; old Liang, dead or unconscious, crumpled on the ground, face down in the loam dark with his blood; the ascetic young officer sitting quietly on one of the small pillars of the front terrace, absorbed in what he thought was Ailing's letter, absent-mindedly scratching his chin with the obscenely long nail of his left little finger. Not once had he looked up when his men shot Yibang, clobbered Lao Liang and tortured Yichen.

Can we call such creatures human? I think they are evil spirits in human disguise and as such untouchable. They can't be destroyed. If you kill them or if they are legally executed the evil spirit that inhabits the human-like shell merely moves into another carrier body and continues the wickedness. They will be with us for eternity and move amongst us and woe befalls the unfortunate who crosses their path or catches their fancy.

Slowly and rhythmically I breathed through my nose, focusing my mind on breathing and counting: inhaling 'twenty-one', exhaling 'twenty-two', inhaling 'twenty-three' and so on to slow down my pounding heart and suppress the waves of nausea. Just when I began to get myself back under control a shriek, utterly inhuman, piercing and ululating like a siren gone wild shattered my still fragile composure.

Yang Baolin's words 'red-hot poker up his arsehole' flashed through my mind together with a horribly vivid image of Yichen on his knees, a poker sticking out of his behind, mouth wide open in that terrible scream, eyes popping literally out of his distorted face. I felt the blood drain from my head and I became ice-cold. Then I fainted.

As in a haze I felt I was being pulled over the floor and in utter panic that the soldiers were going to grill me I struggled and tried to scream but I couldn't. Something wet and warm was clamped over my mouth. Nearly crazy with terror I opened my eyes and looked up into the pale, frightened faces of Taitai and the twins. Taitai held her hand over my mouth while the girls were fanning my face to give me air. Shudderingly I came to and nodded at Taitai signalling to her that I wouldn't scream. She took her hand off my mouth and helped me on my feet.

Still dizzy I sat down on the bed and the twins sat down beside me, one on either side, each wiping my neck and face with a damp cloth. Taitai pulled up a chair and sat down in front of me, taking my hands in hers.

'The soldiers dragged Yichen into the kitchen,' she whispered, her face so close to mine I could feel her breath. 'They made me heat the poker in the hearth. I thought they just wanted to frighten him or at worst tickle the soles of his feet a bit, like the highway bandits used to do long ago when they wanted their victims to reveal where they hid their money. When they pulled Yichen's trousers down and made him kneel down on the floor, however, I realised what they were going to do to him and I screamed and nearly fainted. One of them hit me on the head and I fell down. In spite of the daze I was in the stench of burnt flesh made my eyes water, but it was that terrible, inhuman shriek that made me hot and cold all at once and every hair in my neck prickled as if I had been lashed with stinging nettles. That shriek will reverberate through my mind for the rest of my life and I'm sure that that's what made you faint as well, Xiao Chen. You have been out for hours.

'It was horrible, no human being should have to suffer and die in such a cruel way as Yichen and Yibang did this morning. They are not human, those monsters of Chiang Kaishek. They are worse than animals, no beast would do such a thing to another beast. Yichen is dead, lucky him. Yibang is dead, lucky him too. The old master has lost his mind, crazy for good, eating his own excrement like some demented child. First Lady just sits there, surrounded and patted by her sobbing remaining children. She stares at something only she can see, head cocked to one side as if listening and she keeps repeating,

"How beautifully Yichen always sings for me, thrilling like a lark. Listen! Isn't it beautiful?" The children cry for her but for the time being it is best that her mind is gone. When Yichen was left dead on the kitchen floor the officer all of a sudden was in a hurry to leave. I don't know where they went, however, I'm sure they'll be back during or after the funerals, to search the house for you, Xiao Chen, so you must stay here, in this room!

'Two people died because of you. Two have lost their mind because of you. We have all suffered because of you. You *must* avenge this, Chen Dan. You *must*! It's your *duty*! The twins and I will take care of you until it is safe for you to leave and go wherever you have to go to carry out this duty. You must join whoever wants to destroy those monsters and their monstrously evil leader, even if for that you have to make a pact with the Communists. Promise me that, Chen Dan, *now*! *Promise*!'

And I promised.

Taitai stood up from her chair.

'I have to take my former place as Third Lady again and do what I have to do,' she said firmly. 'I have to take care of the master and First Lady, and also of the children and the business, until Yicheng, the second son, will be ready to take charge. One and Two, you take care of Xiao Chen until it's safe for him to leave. In the meantime, make a man of him! We can't have a child, a *virgin*, fighting our war, now can we?'

On these words she left the room to take up her new, self-assigned station in life. What a *lady*!

The aunties took their mission very seriously, that's the least one can say.

During the day either one of them was always with me and during the night the two of them squeezed whatever energy I still had left out of me, literally, until I fell asleep, utterly exhausted, one young woman on either side of me, if not exhausted then at least satisfied, I hoped.

We had a deep affection for each other but fortunately no love. I say fortunately because love would have spoilt the fun. Love is too demanding and often too self-centred for love-play since it is always accompanied by jealousy. Always there have to be assurances of uniqueness and fidelity, yet never fully believed, of course. And then *what*? Tantrums and recriminations! Such a pity!

I didn't see much of Taitai. The care for the family and the preparations for the funerals took up all of her time those first few days since, because of the hot weather, the bodies of Yibang and Yichen had to be buried within three days at the most.

Then came the day of the funeral. Taitai had hired a big orchestra in Luding, every member dressed in blue and white. They began arriving at seven o'clock in the morning and were first given a hearty breakfast. At eight o'clock they began to play the mournful, melancholy slow-march music, the same four pieces over and over again, though the funeral procession would start from the courtyard at ten thirty only.

From behind the drawn curtains of my room I watched the preparations and goings-on down below in the yard. I recognised eight of my uncles as the pall-bearers, four for each coffin, blue scarves wound around their head. The coffins had been placed on a dais erected in front of the big stairs leading to the front door of the manor. Old Master Liang, dressed by Taitai in his best suit, sat on a high, straight-backed chair to the right of the dais and First Lady, in a long, white gown, on a slightly lower chair to the left. I couldn't see their faces, only their backs and bowed heads, but I don't think either of them was fully aware of what was going on. The other four children were standing behind the dais.

I saw my whole clan filing past the coffins, one by one, each putting a flower, a fruit or a vegetable on the dais in front of the coffins, in addition to the fake money the adults put in a special, big, earthenware jar. The Chen clan had constructed two beautiful life-size horses and two carriages, from bamboo and paper, painted red and gold, which stood assembled next to the dais.

Many other people I didn't know came into the courtyard, paid their respect to the family and the dead and then withdrew into the shade of the house where chairs and benches had been arranged against the wall for the elderly and the pregnant women.

One and Two were serving hot tea. Taitai was supervising everything from the front door, like a general taking the salute of the troops.

A few minutes before ten the music stopped and in the silence that followed four Buddhist monks performed some rites while the musicians took up their positions at the front gate to lead the procession to the Liang cemetery on the Western slope of the highest hill of the range that enclosed the estate on those sides at a distance of about one kilometre.

My uncles took up their positions behind the orchestra, four by four, carrying the coffins on their shoulders. Behind them came the remaining four Liang brothers, carrying an ornate couch on their shoulders on which Master Liang and First Lady were sitting. Something must have gotten through to First Lady for I saw that she was holding her husband's left hand in hers in her lap. Old Liang's head lolled on her shoulders, from one side to the other because of the movements of the couch. He had probably fallen asleep.

Taitai, in a long, white gown that asserted her status as Third Lady, stood behind the four brothers with Aiping, Ailing's elder sister, or cousin, I never knew for sure, and One and Two, all three in blue robes. Behind them followed other relatives, whom I had never seen before, and finally the personnel of the estate.

The cortège was closed by the members of the Chen clan who had been put in charge of the money jar and the bamboo and paper horses and carriages which were to be burnt on the graves to serve the dead in the hereafter, the fake money to pay the lower spirits for their goodwill in guiding them, the horses and carriages for their transport.

I remembered how Longfei had once spoken mockingly of those superstitions. At that time I had laughed and, of course, agreed with him. Now, confronted with such things first hand and feeling guilty as I did, I thought it wasn't probably such a bad idea after all to take one's precautions. One never knows, does one?

At a sign from Taitai the music started again and the orchestra moved forward in cadence, the two huge drums in front: bong! bong! bong! bong!

The procession followed, stretching out like an accordion and winding like a snake along the dirt road.

It took almost twenty minutes before the last two Chens left the courtyard and closed the big gate behind them. I was now alone in the big house, unbeknownst to all but Taitai and the twins, waiting with a pounding heart and sweaty hands for the soldiers to come back as Taitai had said they would.

I withdrew from the window and sat down on the big bed, eyes closed, concentrating on the scores of small noises made by a big, old, mostly wooden house. Then I noticed the odd ones, the creaking of stairs, the groaning of doors being opened and closed ever so softly. Without thinking, as if in a reflex, I slid underneath the bed and squeezed myself between the wall and the big, wooden trunk in which the girls kept their clothes for the winter.

I rolled myself, foetus-like, knees pulled up to my chin, and breathed as softly and as superficially as I could manage. I broke out in a clammy, cold sweat when I suddenly realised that I had left the window ajar; there was no time to close it. I put my thumb in my mouth and sucked it to suppress my rising panic.

Then I heard the door of the room being opened ever so carefully and apparently two people entered for I heard them whisper and open and close the wardrobe doors. Suddenly daylight flooded the space under the bed; apparently one of them had lifted the overhanging bedcover and was now probably peering under the bed. I held my breath for several seconds and almost panicked at the sound of my pounding heart, then semi-darkness engulfed me again. The soldier hadn't seen me behind the trunk.

I heard them say, in a half-whisper, that *he* was apparently not in this room either and then they closed the door. I decided to stay where I was, without moving, for fear that the soldiers might come back a second time.

How lucky I was that I did that, since a long time later, twenty minutes surely, I suddenly heard the scraping sound of a chair being pushed back and somebody walking. The door opened and closed and all was silent again. Only one of them had left the room the first time, not both as I had assumed, and one had stayed behind, motionless, to see whether I would sneak back into this room after their search. Clever. Very clever!

And I had escaped only by luck, not because of me outwitting them.

Though I was certain they had now left for good, I nevertheless stayed in my hiding place until the girls came back from the funeral about an hour later and told me they saw the soldiers on the road going in the direction of Danba.

The girls changed into their working clothes for they had to help Taitai and the other servants with serving food and drinks to all those who had returned to the manor after the funeral. It was already dark when the last guests left, drunk apparently, as I heard them slur their farewells to Taitai and the Liang children. Once the front gate was closed behind them they began to sing in their drunken voices to give them courage on the dark road and to chase the evil spirits away.

Slowly the singing faded into the distance.

I was writing in my diary when Taitai and the girls entered the room. I told them about the soldiers searching the house and how they had tried to trick me. Taitai turned white as a bed sheet at the thought of how she and the girls would have been punished by the soldiers had I indeed been found in the girls' room.

We decided that I would hide one more week in the room and then quietly slip out during the darkest hours of the night.

Taitai would get some of Yibang's clothes for me. He had been about my size and his clothes were certainly better made and more fashionable than my own so that at least I wouldn't draw people's attention because of my boorish outfit. More importantly of all she gave me Yibang's pocket watch so that I would know the time of day and night.

I still use it. Never had a different one.

I decided that since I had the time now I would write a letter to Ailing and Longfei. Yang Baolin would get it to them through his connections. It was a difficult letter. Not only would Ailing have to bear the shock of her brothers' betrayal of her trust in them but also the horror of their death because of my stupidity.

But could I really have foreseen the lieutenant's duplicity and paranoia?

Perhaps at the age of eighteen one is simply too young to know what makes people act the way they do and the perverse delusions they are capable of. To avoid any future misunderstandings and recriminations about who said what and when, I began my letter by copying the text of her own letter to Yichen. Next I told her, in my own style and writing, what I had overheard during the discussion between Yibang and Yichen in the garden house and that subsequently, being practically certain that she had told Yichen about Longfei's plans, I had decided to open her letter and fake another one to throw Chiang Kaishek's men off their trail.

I then wrote down, from memory, the text of that fake letter. Finally I told her, as soberly and dispassionately as I could manage, what had happened when Yibang and Yichen had handed the fake letter they thought was their sister's to the lieutenant, sparing her, however, the gruesome details of her brothers' death. I also told her that the shock of the boys' death had been too great for her father and mother and that, as a consequence, they had temporarily lost their mind.

In a postscript, as if it were an afterthought, I told her that Taitai had taken charge of the household and the day-to-day running of the family business until her brother Yicheng would be old enough to take over. I also mentioned the great help her stepsisters One and Two had given me, and Taitai of course.

In a second postscript I gave her the day and date I would report to Yang Baolin and promised I would write another letter as soon as I had more news.

I then read and reread the letter and made changes in the text until I was satisfied it was a coherent story, factual and to the point. I rewrote the letter twice, one copy for Ailing and one to keep myself just to avoid any misunderstandings the day I would meet again with her and Longfei.

Three nights later I slipped out of the girls' room and the manor's back door. It was two o'clock in the morning, the time people's sleep is deepest.

The evening before my departure I said farewell to Taitai and thanked her for her help and trust. She embraced and kissed me and I still remember vividly how at that moment I longed to have a mother like her. She gave me a letter for Ailing.

'Don't open this one,' she laughed through her tears, 'it's just women's talk.'

From the way she said that and avoided looking at me I knew that my exploits with the twins were the mainstay of that 'talk', were it only to cheer Ailing up a bit. I felt ashamed. What would Ailing think of me? In my imagination I could hear Longfei's thunderous laugh and instinctively I pulled up my shoulders as if in anticipation of his slap on my back and bawdy, roaring comment.

The girls had their period, which suited me fine. I would need all my wits and strength in the coming hours and our usual romping through half of the night would have sapped me.

Snot, slobber and tears by the three of us and then I tiptoed down the stairs, through the corridor and out through the back door Taitai had left ajar for me. I didn't see a living soul and within minutes I had reached the river bank. I followed the river and, making good time, it was only six o'clock on Yibang's watch when I reached what was left of the place where I had spent the four happiest consecutive years of my life.

The fire had destroyed the house completely. The charred, big bamboo poles had been scattered all over the place by the soldiers searching for loot and clues as to our whereabouts. I found a shovel, its handle burnt and charred, and scraped the badly burnt planking under which we had buried Longfei's books and documents clear of debris.

I lifted two planks and saw that the soil underneath had not been disturbed since the small pebbles we had mixed with the soil, as indicators, were still as we had left them. I put the planks back in place and scattered the debris over them as natural looking as possible. Then I left.

I looked back one more time before taking the path through the marshes to Danba. The whole place shimmered with an eeriness that made me shiver. The silence was total, which was weird in itself, because when we still lived there, there had been the thousand and one little sounds one gets so accustomed to that you only notice them when actually they are no longer there. The twittering of birds, the chirping of crickets, the rustling of leaves in the wind, the clucking of the chickens, the occasional creaking of the house's structure.

Now nothing. Only the acrid smell of burnt wood and scorched earth.

It was eerie and I felt a prickling in my neck. Quickly I turned around and at a half-trot I covered the first two kilometres in less than ten minutes before I slowed down to a normal walking pace.

During the remainder of the way to Danba I made up a credible story in which I would tell Yang Baolin and rehearsed it so often that if questioned on any particular detail I could answer offhandedly, almost unthinkingly. I would tell Yang that Longfei's books and papers had apparently been found by the soldiers and taken away, since I hadn't seen a single shred of paper, burnt or torn, on the premises.

I realised that Yang would report that to Longfei as well, however, I thought it might even be better for Longfei to believe that his compromising writings were in the hands of his enemies until he had had the time to settle in his new situation and evaluate his new and former friends. Later, when he would know who he could trust and who not, I would somehow find a way to let him know the truth and maybe we could even go back together to our place in the marshes and dig up the documents.

I was surprised at my cool and dispassionate reasoning and at the fact that I no longer trusted appearances and seeming demonstrations of friendship. I decided that I would never lie when the truth was plain or easily checked out; however, when I was the only one to know I would not volunteer the information but keep quiet instead to see what people would actually *like* to believe. Friendly but wary would be my attitude towards Yang and towards others I would meet, whether through him or on my own.

I decided I would let Yang read my letter to Ailing though and to give him orally the details I had left out for her sake. When I approached Danba's main street, which ran along the river, I had my philosophy all worked out and I was quite pleased with myself.

It was almost midday on my watch and I found Yang's place without difficulty. Cautiously I walked around the farmlike building, trying to peer through the grimy windows to see whether there was anybody in the taproom. I saw Yang standing beside a table, talking and gesticulating to three men sitting at the table and apparently having their noon meal.

They were laughing at what Yang was telling them and looked all right, so I decided to go inside and I pushed the door open. I saw Yang's mouth fall open in amazement, and before he could utter something stupid, I exclaimed, in my best imitation of the Beijing drawl Longfei had often practised with me, as a joke, 'You must be my Uncle Baolin, my dear mother's brother! How are you, Uncle? I am your nephew, Li Pei, from Beijing and my dear mother sends you her compliments. She begs you to give me some small job in your inn, Uncle, just enough to earn my own upkeep, as she can no longer feed me, widow as she is, poor soul. With five younger children still depending on her.'

Then I staggered a bit, swayed on my feet and toppled over in a simulated faint.

Yang caught on immediately and yelled, at his wife apparently, 'Lingling! Come over here! Quick! Nephew Li Pei from Beijing is here and he just passed out from hunger and weakness!'

He lifted me up, grasping my jacket under my armpits, while his wife Lingling took my ankles and together they carried me out of the taproom, my bottom dragging over the floor.

Through my half-closed eyes I saw the three guests Yang had been talking to watching the scene, mouths open in amazement. I was dragged through a corridor, Yang's wife quickstepping backwards, opening a door at the end of the corridor by bumping against it with her bottom.

While Yang kicked the door shut behind him, they dumped me unceremoniously on the floor. I scrambled to my feet and sat down on a couch. Yang and his wife, never taking their eyes off me, pulled a chair each near the couch and sat down, without a word.

We stared at one another and I was about to say something when suddenly Madam Yang, or Lingling as I'll call her henceforth, began to giggle, her hand over her mouth to stifle the sound. Yang bit his lower lip, trying to keep his face straight but then it split in an ear-to-ear grin.

Relieved, I grinned back and all of a sudden we were on our feet and embraced each other like long-lost relatives.

After quite a while we sat down again and Yang said, 'We were convinced you were dead, Xiao Chen. The soldiers came back here after their search and some of them got quite drunk. They bragged about what they had done at Liang's place. About how they killed Yichen and Yibang and beat up Lao Liang and the mistress.

'Obliquely I asked them whether they had found you and they told me you had escaped to Wuhan but had been caught in the meantime by the army units and killed. The story has been *the* big news in Danba for the past two weeks. Fortunately nobody here knows you by sight so it was really a stroke of genius that you announced yourself as my nephew Li Pei from Beijing. As long as you'll be staying here with us, a few months at the most I guess, you'll be Li Pei. When people ask you questions about life in the capital, make up your story, you're good at that I'm sure, however, don't forget to tell me and Lingling how you gull the poor sods so that we won't be caught saying different things.

'This room here will be yours for as long as you stay with us. We get up at five in the morning and we expect you to give a hand with whatever there is to do in the inn and in the house. After evening rice you may go to your room to study or whatever, or you can keep us company until bedtime, up to you. We close for the day at nine and retire to bed at nine thirty, after finishing our accounts. Before I forget, I have books about Beijing, even some old copies of Beijing's newspapers with articles on life in the capital, and a city plan as well, I believe. Study them so that you won't talk nonsense! As far as I know nobody from Danba has ever been to Beijing and couldn't care less, I'm sure; however, some of the people who pass through here and stay a night or two with us may know their way around there and wish to reminisce with you. All I ask is that you be very careful. These are dangerous and uncertain times.'

Yang fell silent and I nodded my agreement and promised him that I would do my utmost best to stay out of trouble.

At that both of them stood up, smiled, and left the room, leaving me to myself.

At the door Lingling looked back, and I caught her look, curious yet appraising, and I felt queasy in my belly and my heart missed a beat.

I knew then that before long there would be trouble with pretty little Lingling, that was as sure as it would be unavoidable one way or another. Lingling was the kind of woman who, wittingly or unwittingly, rouses the stirrings of even the most suppressed or forgotten lust in a man, probably even in a starving Buddhist hermit. She was small and very slender, with the fresh, pretty looks of a seventeen year old girl.

She had incredibly beautiful almond-shaped eyes, the colour of molten dark chocolate, laughing and sparkling. Her hair was short and straight but very glossy and thick. Her smile was wide, with beautifully regular, immaculately white, small teeth. Her skin had that smooth, creamy texture of polished ivory that incites a craving to bite and chew and taste its juice as if it were a ripe, white Sichuan peach.

While Yang had been doing all the talking, Lingling had been smiling and smiling, the tip of her glistening little red tongue darting along her upper teeth and lip, her tiny hand squeezing my arm to underscore a remark by her husband. I shivered at the memory of her fingers on my arm and the goose pimples returned momentarily.

Slowly I unpacked my rucksack and put the clothes Taitai had given me, Yibang's clothes, in a small wardrobe. The shirts and trousers were awfully crumpled as I had just rolled them tightly to cram them into the rucksack. I would have to iron them first so I went to look for Lingling to ask her for an iron.

I guessed I would probably find her in the kitchen and, following my nose, I found the place by the smells of cooking. It was a huge kitchen and at a glance I noticed the many big larders, the stoves, the huge, round table with as many as twelve chairs arranged around it, and the pans, woks and kettles hanging from hooks on the walls.

At first I didn't notice Lingling as the place was quite dark but suddenly she was there, in front of me and almost against me. She laughed and I felt already weak in my stomach.

'What are you looking for, Xiao Dan?' she asked, a bit mockingly I thought. 'Hungry already?'

I stammered that I would like to use her iron, which was true, however, in spite of that simple truth and of myself, there must have transpired some kind of innuendo in my voice and demeanour, a meaning hidden as yet from my own consciousness but evidently clear to her that I was indeed hungry, though not for food.

She took my two hands in hers and said, in a half-whisper, 'Go back to your room, Xiao Dan. Baolin has closed early today for there are no staying guests and he is preparing to leave for one of those secret meeting places where he spends more time than at home. He'll be away for more than a week, as usual. Before he leaves he will ask you to tell him everything that happened at the Liang manor and what you found this morning at Liu Longfei's place. Baolin has to make his report and the people he'll meet will see to it that Longfei and Ailing are informed about what happened. He also needs to know what Longfei's plans are with you now that you have escaped and are safe.

'So get your thoughts in order, Xiao Dan, and tell Baolin the true facts. Don't hide anything, don't embellish, don't downplay. The smallest detail may be important, if not now then perhaps later. Your story will reach the people in the highest positions and a whole chain of actions and reactions will be set in motion, all based upon what you tell Baolin. As I said, no embellishments, no exaggerations and resist the temptation to play the young hero. Older people dislike young heroes, they don't trust them and their judgements. Now go, and when you have finished with Baolin I'll iron your clothes for you.'

Laughing, she playfully pushed me out of the kitchen and I stumbled through the darkish corridor back to my room.

While waiting for Yang I decided I would write everything down in chronological order and in short, terse sentences. This would be a great help, both for me when telling my story to Baolin, and for him when relating it later to others.

I would write it out twice and then sign both papers and ask Yang to sign them also before I would give him one copy. This would protect not only myself but Yang as well. He might have his own reasons to add or leave out a few things here and there, while others, at their turn, might see an interest in making some alterations here and there. My copy, signed by both of us, would later serve to keep the records straight.

If Yang so wished I could write it out a third time for him to keep as his own copy, however, that could be done after his return. I had hardly begun my memorandum when Lingling came into the room, carrying a pot of tea and a mug which she put on the table in front of me.

She asked what I was doing and I told her. While I was talking to her I felt her hand knead my neck and I smelled her body-odour. It took all my self-restraint to finish my summary though I heard my own voice falter a few times. Lingling smiled admiringly and said it was a splendid idea. After a last scratch with her nails at the nape of my neck she left the room, leaving me in a state and with goose-flesh on my arms.

Breathing deeply I regained control of my nerves and for more than two hours I wrote down everything that had happened since Yang and I had gone our separate ways three weeks earlier. When I was finally satisfied that the report was coherent, factual, dispassionate and in the right order, I took new sheets of paper and, without any further rethinking or last-minute changes, I wrote the whole report twice, neatly and properly.

Each copy covered four sheets of neat and dense but colloquial-style writing and I put the two characters of my name at the bottom of each sheet and also after the full stop of the last sentence of the report. Satisfied with myself and my work I leaned back on my chair and while I was sipping from my mug of tea the door opened and Yang came in.

'Lingling told me what you were doing,' he said, 'a very good idea it is indeed. I see that Longfei's teachings haven't been wasted on you. Now, give me my copy and while I follow your report with my eyes, my ears want to hear you tell your story in your own words, also the things you left out for the sake of terseness or for whatever other reason. There is always the *untold* story, you know, *always*! Now begin! I listen.'

So I told him. Everything, almost. Just in time I checked myself when I got to my amorous feats with the twins. That was none of his business, I thought, and besides, he might get the wrong ideas about my conduct with his wife during his absence. More probably the right ideas, I thought guiltily.

To my relief he didn't seem to notice that I was a bit quiet and superficial in passing over that period and he apparently saw nothing unusual in the situation of a healthy, seventeen year old male hiding for two weeks under the bed of two equally healthy and pretty females in their early thirties. To my own ears my voice sounded creaky and unnatural when I glossed over that time but that was probably my own guilty conscience hinting that before long I would be in his bed with his wife.

I also stuck to my earlier decision and told him that the soldiers had apparently discovered Longfei's books and papers in their hiding place under the floor and had taken the whole lot with them since I had not found a single piece or shred of paper around the totally burnt-out house.

I was surprised and, to my shame, delighted that I found it so easy to lie without a tremor in my voice or a feeling of remorse towards Yang. Finally I handed him my letter to Ailing, which contained both Ailing's own writing to her brother Yichen and the text I faked.

Yang read and reread the letter, looking increasingly preoccupied. For quite some time he just sat there, in his chair, staring at the wall, undoubtedly reliving in his mind everything he had just heard and read. I waited patiently for his reaction.

Finally he looked up at me and I saw respect and admiration in his eyes.

'You have acted correctly and with great perspicacity, Xiao Chen,' he said. 'There is no reason whatsoever for self-reproach. If it weren't for your version of Ailing's letter you deliberately played into the lieutenant's hands, Lingling and I would be dead now and I shiver at the thought of how that monster would have dealt with us. We owe you our lives and I'll tell Lingling before I leave tonight. That'll make her see that you are not the naive, little boy she seems to take you for.'

I marvelled at Yang's own naivety. Or was it his own single-minded preoccupation with his own goals and ideals that made him blind to the secretive little games his wife was playing? He was obviously much older than Lingling and had probably married her in a moment of absent-mindedness, in between two political meetings I guessed, and subsequently her physical needs had not been very prominent on his agenda, if at all.

Longfei had more than once warned me about people like Yang and told me to be always wary of them. Narrow-mindedly and single-mindedly tackling something they believe in, they tolerate no dissenting views, no other needs than those directly associated with the pursuit of their idea. They have no other interests but the one, all-encompassing interest of fulfilling their dream and everything else is subordinate at best, totally ignored at worst. People around them are merely sycophantic voices, barely acknowledged shadows at the rim of their consciousness, drifting to the foreground when summoned, fading into the background when dismissed.

Fortunately Yang Baolin was not that far gone yet. He was earthy, worldly, tough and sly but already he had that gleam in his eyes, that impatience with differing views and opinions and that indifference, if not contempt, for such frivolous needs as love and tenderness his wife might have. I would soon find out, and with that beautiful intellectualisation of the state of the Yang household I had already conveniently eliminated the scruples I had at first felt at Lingling's suggestive flirting.

With that execrable self-complacency of the intellectual who has just analysed a complex relationship and reduced it to a few, simple, entirely self-serving factors, I decided that I would do Yang the favour of administering to his wife the human warmth he wasn't capable of himself and that I so abundantly possessed.

I might even prevent their marriage from breaking up, I told myself smugly. Chen Dan, the great healer of tormented, lonely souls.

Yang left at dark, still preoccupied with an unspoken piece of trouble I had unwittingly given him and without embracing his wife, I noticed complacently.

A few instructions to her as to the running of the business, a few reminders to me as to my role-playing as Nephew Li Pei from Beijing and he was gone.

Lingling and I became so enamoured with each other, so besotted with our lovemaking, that we continued, unashamedly, after Yang's return ten days later, to make love several times a day, wherever we came across each other, accidentally or premeditatedly, in the house or in the barns.

The thrill of the danger of being caught *in flagrante delicto* was merely added spice. We were exhilarated, triumphant even, that Baolin was so pleased that Lingling and I got along so well together. We laughed at the poor sod's naivety.

As Li Pei I was popular with the locals who came more and more to Yang's inn for a pot of tea or a light meal in the hope I would serve them and entertain them with stories and anecdotes about life in Beijing. At first Yang worried that I would entangle myself in the web of fiction I was weaving around the person Li Pei, however, all went well.

Towards visitors in general and those from Beijing, easily recognisable by their peculiar reflective *r*, in particular I behaved naturally, though I was mindful to let them do most of the talking and to merely repeat, in different words, what they had already said earlier themselves.

Three months passed without anything noteworthy happening other than that my infatuation with Lingling subsided somewhat after the first five or six exhausting weeks and fortunately hers with me as well.

We were both secretly relieved, I think, that the mutual feelings of intense lust for each other no longer dominated our every glance, gesture and stolen moment together. Without indulging in psychoanalysis in an attempt to find excuses for our conduct we both realised, I think, that the increasingly bad, guilty feelings afterwards were becoming too strong to be ignored any longer.

We were also tired, both mentally and physically, because of the alternating highs and lows of adrenaline in our system. Tired because of the guilty conscience that makes you read an innuendo in every word spoken, in every glance or gesture by others, most of all by the one you deceive. Tired because of the constant fear of being overheard, of approaching footsteps, of the door being suddenly opened, of the unexplainable.

Tired because of the ever-present and increasingly strong feelings of shame and remorse as it gradually dawns on you that your reckless egoism and obsession, if discovered, will so deeply hurt the one you deceive and whom you respect, even love probably, that you shiver at the consequences. Lingling and I never actually spoke about these things nor did we make any decisions or good resolutions.

We, at least I, had no regrets, merely a vague feeling of unease, but we knew from tacit mutual understanding that we had to stop before irreparable damage would be done. So we stopped. Or rather we let opportunities pass.

By no means did we try to avoid each other, however, we no longer sought the other by every means and ruse as we had done in the past. I felt as if liberated and from her attitude I knew that Lingling felt the same way. Smirks became smiles, innuendoes merely ordinary remarks or little jokes.

Until today I am not absolutely certain whether Yang ever knew of our fooling around or not. I think, hope rather, that he did not, however, if he did I owe him an even greater respect than I did show him after my initial contemptible glee of cuckolding him.

I think sometimes that Yang may indeed have been capable of subordinating petty personal emotions to what he saw as his duty and mission in life. Yang was a true Communist who lived according to his belief, effacing himself and his private feelings and needs for what he saw as the greater good of the whole.

On the eighty-eighth day of my stay with the Yangs, a good omen, Yang told me that he had received word that three professors from Beijing's higher learning institute would shortly come to see me to test my level of knowledge. If satisfactory they would next arrange for me to sit for the entrance examinations. One of the professors had even offered for me to stay with him and his family during the contest which would take at least three weeks. If I passed there would be no time for me to return to Danba as the university courses would start on 2nd October.

During the days before the learned men's arrival I went, as often as I could manage, to a small island in the middle of the river about two miles upstream from Danba. The island was actually nothing more than a strip of higher ground and gravel, overgrown with bamboo, shrubs and mulberry trees, which split the stream in half over a length of about six hundred metres.

A small congregation of twenty-one Buddhist monks lived on the tiny island, in a common longhouse, near a small temple. Both the house and the temple had been built by themselves many years ago from materials they had got by begging from peasants and townsfolk alike.

Yang the Communist had contributed generously; the four dragons on the temple's roof had been both donated and installed by him. Years earlier he had recovered the dragons from a temple destroyed by marauding gangs of so-called soldiers and he had kept them in the big barn, hidden under a stack of mouldy, old jute bags. Even a convinced Communist, a Chinese Communist that is, will not forgo an opportunity to keep more than one iron in the fire. One never knows, does one?

The monks had also built two jetties, one on the mainland and one on the islet, leaving a gap of about twenty metres between them. In normal times a rope ferry, made of bamboo and planks, was attached to either jetty, depending on whether a few of the monks had gone to the mainland to beg for food or whether they were all on the islet.

A big piece of bamboo hung by a piece of rope from a sort of gallows on the mainland jetty and one signalled one's presence and intention to cross over by hitting the bamboo with a mallet that hung next to it.

People the monks had come to know and trust had been given a certain code for hitting the primitive gong and when that happened two monks would appear reasonably quickly to pull the ferry across and back. People without a code depended entirely on the monks' mood and more often than not they were simply ignored.

In times of turbulence and distress the rope ferry was detached and poled out of sight into one of the many overgrown creeks of the islet. Yang, as a venerated benefactor, had of course been given a code and one that made not two but four monks come running up the jetty to ferry him over.

One day, about four weeks after my arrival at his inn, he had taken me to the islet and had introduced me to the abbot and his monks.

Right from that first visit I got along well with them and I went back to see them several times and each time I brought a bag of rice, a few dried fish and a jar of pickled vegetables with chillies which they accepted without thanks or even the slightest attempt at graciousness.

At first I found them a weird bunch of undisciplined and often rude people with no morality or saving grace to speak of. When I once asked them what their philosophy was I got a rude answer and a few even tried to kick my arse. They laughed uproariously at my indignant protest and shouted remarks that were neither here nor there, utter nonsense actually.

During my following visits I was careful not to ask probing questions but to observe them casually instead as they went about whatever they were doing which, however, didn't seem to me to make much sense either. Nevertheless, a few things struck me after a while.

Though they could all of a sudden start yelling and shouting at each other or simply at nobody or nothing in particular, they were never moody. For them, every morning seemed to be a good morning, every day a fine day, however hot, cold, stormy or rainy the weather. It gradually dawned on me that these monks came as close to being free as one can conceive intellectually of the concept freedom.

They were as free as the birds flying, or as the fish swimming, or as the flowers blooming, lacking any particular intention of doing this or that, just as the bird is not consciously performing the act of flying, the fish of swimming or the flower of blooming.

I tried to provoke them by bragging about my outrageous behaviour with Lingling, but I couldn't trick them into making a judgement.

They merely laughed and the abbot bellowed, 'The monkey is a monkey all the time and is not aware of being a monkey fucking his mate while she continues to eat the nut she just found also unaware of being a monkey being fucked while eating a nut. When the monkey's life comes to an end he just expires; he does not lament his fate, he has no regrets, no hopes, no aspirations, simply because he is not conscious of his Buddha nature. He lives just the same, however, he does not live by *Chan*.'

Mockingly the abbot said, 'How can one be called Chen and nevertheless be like a monkey without a Buddha nature?' He deliberately pronounced my name with the wrong tone to make it sound like their creed of Buddhism.

I think that more than any preaching or moralising could have achieved, these mocking words made me conscious of *just a small matter* as the abbot called it when I had asked him once what the difference was between man and animal.

When next I asked him what that 'small matter' was he, for once, had been gracious and said that it was in my mind all the time, but that so far I had failed to recognise it. This 'small matter', however, proved to be a 'great matter' when I came to realise that it is cognisance of our being that makes us human. That realisation has since affected the whole tenor of my life.

You have a *different* consciousness if you do realise that 'there is nothing special, it's all the same' whether you see the things 'before' or 'after', whether you discuss the merits of communism or legalism, feudalism or democracy, whether you contemplate the misty rain on the mountain today or next year, whether you listen to the lapping waves of the river tomorrow or two thousand years hence.

Personal experience and personal contact is what matters, it is *all* that matters. Concepts and ideas, as creations of the mind, have of course their role to play in *how* we experience, however, their role is *to be tools* and ours to be the *masters*, not the other way around. The mistake most people make is that they take concepts for realities, thoughts for experience and a system, whichever, for life itself.

This is wrong. Past, present and future, it is all the same, so it is no use to dwell in the past or to preoccupy oneself with the future. To live in the present and to take things as they are and as you see them, without giving them too much importance or analysing them to death, is not only enough, it is *all* that matters.

It took time for me to realise this. It didn't come as some blinding, sudden insight. However, ever since I have been living in that spirit I have been a contented person. Contentment is so much more satisfying than happiness. Contentment is both a state of the heart and of the mind and therefore it suffuses your whole being. It is achieved from within, not induced from without as happiness is.

Therefore, once you have experienced contentment it is there to stay. There is no fear of losing it since it does not depend on outside factors as the often fleeting feeling of happiness does. Happiness and unhappiness are like laughing and crying, so close together. Contentment is on its own and allows for good and bad to happen to you without either affecting you to the point of euphoria or of despair.

Contentment makes you take whatever happens as it happens, with a smile or a chuckle or a shrug. It liberates you from passions, ambitions and other strong emotions such as love, hate, jealousy, fear and the like, which only upset your biological rhythm and shorten your life. I had already more or less an *inkling of the truth*, as the abbot called it, when I went to visit him a few days before my meeting with the men from Beijing, hoping for some kind of advice or guidance from him.

I told the abbot I was worried that I didn't learn enough in the past and therefore wouldn't pass the examination in Beijing.

'My future depends on passing that examination,' I lamented. 'I have no idea what I shall do should I fail. Besides, all those who have done so much for me will be very disappointed,' I moaned.

The abbot didn't reply but instead pointed at a bird on a branch of a nearby tree.

'What is that?' he asked.

'That is a bird, master,' I replied.

The abbot clapped his hands and the bird flew away.

'Where is the bird now?' he asked.

'It's gone,' I answered, a bit exasperated by this silliness, whereupon the abbot twisted my nose violently.

I cried out in pain and surprised anger, however, the abbot left me no time to react and shouted, 'Is it really gone!'

'I don't care! I don't know! But what I do know is that my nose hurts!' I shouted angrily back at him.

'You have indeed a deep insight in what matters at this very moment,' the abbot said, smiling.

I stared at him, baffled at first by his absurd and flippant remark and then I suddenly realised what he meant. The feelings of tension induced by alternately ruminating over past failures and anguishing about things yet to happen drained out of me while I became *aware*.

Aware of the play of shadows and sunlight on the ground; aware of the soft caress of the wind on my face; aware of the mélange of smells emanating from the river, from the cut and uncut grass I was sitting on, from the cooking fire, from the abbot's body; aware of the medley of sounds, none dominating yet each distinguishable, of chirruping birds and crickets, of rustling leaves, of the river gurgling around the supports of the nearby jetty, of the monks' voices in the background.

In short, I became aware of that *other* life around me that is the *present* and I laughed, spontaneously and unrestrainedly. The abbot burst out laughing also and we slapped each other on the back, unable to stop laughing.

The monks came to see what all the merriment was about and joined in the laughter when they saw the abbot and me dancing like a couple of circus bears. Finally, exhausted, I threw myself on the ground, on my back, spread-eagled, and watched the white clouds alternately coalesce and disintegrate in the intensely blue sky.

I had never experienced such bliss. I couldn't get enough of it and had I died there and then I would have found my life fulfilled. Since that day I live the present to the fullest, untroubled by the past, unconcerned about the future.

I never went back to visit the abbot and his monks. They would have found it strange had I done so since the shackles the master had liberated me from included those of sentimentality. I had become a free man and amongst free people there are no obligations and no pretences, only voluntary acts.

A few days after that memorable last visit to the islet the three people from Beijing arrived at the inn, two elderly men and one woman in her late thirties I guessed.

The men were friendly and introduced themselves as Ma Xiyao, professor of mathematics, and Gao Sheng, professor of physics, at Beijing Daxue, or Beida as they themselves called their university.

The woman didn't introduce herself and also never said a word other than some non-committal and curt reply when Yang or Lingling asked her about her preference for food or drink. I wondered whether she actually tasted let alone enjoyed what she was eating or drinking or whether she simply conducted an unfortunate biological necessity she would rather have dispensed with. However, she was always there during the talks the two professors had with me and I was never allowed to see either of them alone.

Had it not been for my newly found peace of mind I would have been very unsettled, I'm sure. On the contrary, I was completely relaxed, to the point of unconcern, and I contributed freely and unselfconsciously to whatever discussion was going on, always provided, of course, I thought I had something worth while to contribute.

If I thought I didn't or if I knew nothing about the subject they were discussing, I merely listened and when asked for my opinion I honestly said I hadn't any or knew too little about the subject to comment.

The second night of their stay, I must have been asleep for at least an hour already, I woke up when I felt somebody slip next to me under my bedcover.

It was Lingling. I knew her smell so well.

She giggled and whispered, 'Don't worry, Xiao Dan, I am not going to rape you. Baolin sent me to talk to you. He is still discussing with those Beijing people. That woman does all the talking all of a sudden. Baolin slipped out of the taproom for a minute to tell me to go to your room and warn you against her. Her name is Qian Muhua. She is a very important member of the Communist Party who reports directly to Mao Zedong. She thinks that Liu Longfei is bad news for Mao and the Party and that anybody as close to Liu as you are must be his spy and bound to have the same ideas. Baolin says that your individualistic attitude and joviality has strengthened Qian's suspicions that you are not a serious person and that your attitude will have a bad influence on the students at Beida and that as a result the Communist agents will find it more difficult to make recruits for the Party.

'The plan, Qian says, is to build a secret base of Party members all over the country and that the students are very important material for future cadres when the Party will have seized power. People like you, she argues, carry with them the disease of individualism and dissent which will prove to be fatal to the *cause*. Baolin is already blue in the face from arguing with her that you are still malleable and that, once converted, you will be a great asset for the Party. Baolin urges you to hint during the next days that you sympathise with the Communist cause, but that you doubt that Mao is right to be betting the success of the revolution entirely on the peasants and rural masses.

'Baolin says that you must mention your own peasant descent more often and that you know all too well from your own experience that one has to be subtle to manipulate the peasants and have them do what one wants them to do. Baolin says that Qian secretly despises what she calls the proletariat and that in her opinion the revolution will never succeed without the support of the intellectuals. That's why she's so keen to spread Communist ideology in the universities and to recruit students for the Party, Baolin says. He begs you, Xiao Dan, to play-act a bit, for your own sake. Will you do that, Xiao Dan? Please? For me? I am proud to be your friend and I want you to become an important person.' Lingling fell silent and nibbled on my ear.

I laughed and promised her that I would do my best to charm Comrade Qian into changing her mind about me.

'Why don't you charm her into your bed?' Lingling said, giggling and snuggling up to me, deliberately breathing against my throat. 'That would solve your problem with her and her problem with herself,' she continued, mockingly. 'From the way that woman looks at me and then sniffs as if she smells a dead rat I can tell that she never had a man. Married to her highfalutin ideas, she is. Give her some of the medicine you have been so stingy with these past six weeks, Chen. I won't be jealous, I promise.'

The squeeze she gave me where it hurts most told me enough about her professed unselfishness and that she had to be handled with great care. Little elfin Lingling could be a real tigress.

I groaned from the pain and almost out of breath, I hissed, 'You squeezing my balls, the abbot twisting my nose, all for the sake of making me see the truth. It hurts and I am not going to get entangled with another woman, even if that would solve my problem with Comrade Qian in the short term. Nothing but trouble though, in the long term. I shall use only the honeybrush, the jade stem is not for her.'

Lingling breathed in my ear, 'You are very wise, Chen. You really owe that filthy, smelly abbot a big favour for I would have scratched your eyes out should you as much as have thought of giving that woman a snotty nose. Now, I just felt a moment ago that you have been hoarding too much of the precious medicine Baolin doesn't seem to produce any more. So give it to me, my love, I'm all wet.'

And my body had the better of my mind one more time. The very last time it was, with Lingling at least, I thought.

How very wrong I was.

I have to make a jump in time now so that you understand.

Exactly eleven years later, to the day and date, Tuesday, 20th September, 1943, I was a full professor at Fudan University in Shanghai at the time, my manservant interrupted my preparation for my next day's lecture on the relativity of time and space. How ironic!

He told me that there was an apparently very sick woman at the door with a message from nephew Li Pei of Beijing. I rushed past the astonished elderly servant and saw a woman lying, all crumpled up, on the doorstep, in the driving rain. I bent over her and though I knew from the reference to Li Pei that she could be no other than Lingling I did not at first recognise her.

Thin, pale, hollow cheeks, slick wet and dull hair, shivering, however, when she opened her eyes and smiled up at me, the past came rushing at me like the sea coming in after low tide, crashing over me in a cascade of memories.

My servant and I carried her inside and into the kitchen and then I told the old man to leave me and to go home for the day. Without further ado I simply ripped the filthy, torn clothes from her body and silently I wept at the sight of the cold, bluish, white body that had once delighted me so much. Tied to the small of her back she carried a small, oblong parcel of oil-paper. I didn't open it but locked it away in a drawer of my desk.

I bathed her and dressed her in an undervest and underpants of my own, but she kept shivering, teeth chattering. Then I heated the soup my servant had prepared for me, as usual, and I fed her, spoon by spoon, until she had swallowed two whole bowls of the pungent sour-spicy stuff.

She still shivered though.

Still without saying a word I carried her into my room and put her in my bed. I undressed to my underwear and laid down next to her, taking her in my arms and pulling the covers up to our chin. Then I laid still, just holding her. Slowly the shivering subsided and her breathing slowed down and became less superficial. I didn't dare to move for fear of waking her.

When day broke she was still sleeping. Cramped and tired but very, very happy, I disentangled myself and carefully slipped out of bed to prepare myself for the day.

My servant had brought his wife with him and I told her to watch Lingling and to feed her hot soup each time she woke up. She slept and ate soup for four days and nights.

We still didn't talk, only a smile, a caress, an asking how she felt but more mimicked than actually asked with so many words. Then, one late afternoon, I came home from college and found her sitting in the living room, freshly bathed, hair washed and combed, wearing a dress that must have belonged to one of my servant's daughters.

She smiled at me and suddenly the Lingling of old was back. I was so happy and so much in love again that I didn't notice the grooves that ran from her nose to the corners of her mouth and the dark shadows under her eyes.

I only saw those eyes, those beautiful pools of molten chocolate, and I took her in my arms and we just stood there, holding each other, her head against my chest.

That evening she told me her story.

Two years after my departure for Beijing Yang Baolin received warning that Chiang's soldiers were on the way to Danba to arrest him. He and Lingling fled, carrying with them only the most necessary things.

They slept by day and travelled, on foot, by night until they finally reached Mao's forces in the mountains near Qingchuan, on their march to Yan'an.

Yang was made a commissar in Mao's army and gradually, over the years, he earned Mao's trust which meant direct access to Mao himself and his closest comrades. Finally Yang became a member of the so-called inner circle.

Lingling was assigned to the Party section in charge of recruiting and propaganda. There were times when she didn't see Yang for months.

After the Japanese invasion of China in 1937 Yang was given the ungrateful task to liaise with Chiang's Nationalists to co-ordinate the fight against the common enemy. During seven years as the Communists' liaison officer Yang did his utmost to make the unholy alliance with Chiang's Nationalist forces work.

However, when the Japanese, with Chiang's collusion, wiped out a whole division of the People's Liberation Army, Yang was arrested on charges of treason, tried by a small committee of Mao's friends and of course found guilty. When a week-long and terrible torture to make him confess and name other traitors failed he was summarily executed.

Liu Longfei and Ailing, who both held important positions within the Party's upper echelon, had come to see Lingling in secret and had broken the news of Baolin's death to her. They had urged her to flee before the secret police would arrest her as well on charges of complicity.

Longfei had asked Lingling whether Yang had ever entrusted any notes to her and when she had answered that he had, but that she had never read them, Longfei had urged her to take those notes with her.

He had then produced a letter he had written beforehand and he had told Lingling to copy it in her own handwriting. The letter, purportedly written by Lingling, was addressed to Mao Zedong, Zhou Enlai and Li Xiannian and said that she, Wu Lingling, knew from what her husband had told her who the real traitors were and that she had Yang Baolin's private notes, covering a period of seven years, to prove this.

The letter further said that she would leave the notes, in a sealed parcel, with someone she trusted totally and with the instruction to send them to magazines and newspapers abroad should she happen to die of unnatural causes.

She did as Longfei told her, signed and sealed the letter and left it on the kitchen table. With Ailing's help she attached the parcel containing Yang's notes to the small of her back and fled. Longfei had given her a few hundred yuan in small notes, a password and a list with the locations of a number of safe houses between Yan'an and Shanghai. He had told her to learn the locations and the password by heart and to destroy the list.

The people she would meet in the safe houses, he said, would ask no questions but would provide her, free of charge, with food, drink and a bed for two or three nights. When those people would tell her that it was time to move on, she would have to obey, without asking why, Longfei told her.

Longfei had finally instructed her that once in Shanghai she had to find the house of Professor Chen Dan who would do whatever needed to be done, both for her and with Yang's notes.

Since she knew Chen Dan she would figure out her own password to meet him, Longfei had observed dryly.

It had taken Lingling eight weeks to reach Hefei.

There had only been five safe houses between Yan'an and Hefei where she had spent altogether fifteen days and nights to recover her strength and to get information about Japanese troop movements ahead.

The rest of the time she had travelled by night, on foot mainly, occasionally making good time and catching some sleep at the same time by hiding on a goods train, and had slept during daytime, in barns, in dry, overgrown ditches and sometimes in small hostels or with a peasant family. When asked who she was she said she was a Communist resistance fighter on the run from the Japanese.

When she had reached Hefei she had found the safe house on fire. Five men and three women, the occupants of the house undoubtedly, had been hanging, head down, on stakes driven into the unpaved road in front of the house. They had been skinned alive and one of the men, not dead yet, had been shrieking eerily.

Japanese soldiers were still herding the tenants of the other houses in the narrow lane towards an empty plot of land, at the end of the lane, from where Lingling heard the occasional burst of machine-gun fire and the single, cracking shots of pistols.

She fled the scene and, afraid that the safe houses between Hefei and Shanghai had also been compromised and that people would report a fugitive woman to the Japanese or to the Nationalists, she tried to catch some sleep during daytime in barns and abandoned warehouses while travelling on foot after nightfall, stealing an egg here or a turnip there to still the pangs of hunger, drinking from ditches and ponds when thirsty.

Exhausted from lack of sleep and food and from a terrible diarrhoea she had reached the outskirts of Shanghai after twenty frightful days and nights. A railwayman on his night shift, shunting vans for the early morning goods train, had discovered her in one of the vans, too exhausted to flee.

'Fudan University' was all she had been able to say and the railwayman had merely nodded, not saying a word, carrying on with his job.

It was still dark when he had come back, with his bicycle. He had gestured for her to sit on the carrier, one leg on each side, and to put her arms around his waist. The man had taken unlit streets and roads, circumventing the more densely populated suburbs of Shanghai and he had reached the university grounds at around eight o'clock in the morning. Nobody had paid them any particular attention; a man with his sick wife on a bicycle on his way to a doctor perhaps, nothing unusual in wartime Shanghai.

The man had stopped next to a bench in the garden behind one of the lesser buildings and had gestured for Lingling to get off his bike and to sit down on the bench.

'Fudan', was all he had said and then he had pedalled off without another word.

The old gardener had discovered her later, asleep on the bench, and had woken her up. He had asked Lingling what she was doing there and she had merely mentioned my name, Professor Chen Dan.

Without further questions he had led her to a tool shed in the back of the garden and had told her to lie down on his old winter coat he kept in there. He would come back after dark, he said, to bring her to Professor Chen's quarters. And that is what he did and, after a few knocks on the door, he had left her there and then, in the rain.

We were married two months later, in Kunshan, a small town not far from Shanghai.

The rector acted as my witness and my housekeeper's wife as Lingling's.

The mayor of Kunshan was a former study mate of mine and he registered Lingling as one Gao Yaping, a woman who had been missing since those terrible early days of the war when the Japanese had slaughtered thousands of men, women and children in Kunshan alone, then six years ago.

Gao Yaping's parents and relatives had all been killed and accounted for, however, Yaping had never been officially registered as deceased, only as 'missing'.

My friend erased the word 'missing' in the civil records and wrote down 30th November, 1943 as the date of her wedding to one Chen Dan from Dada County, Sichuan Province. Our wedding certificate also gave her name as Gao Yaping.

Two months later Lingling told me that she was expecting and we were completely happy in our small, cloistered academic world.

We had been married four months when for the first time Lingling asked me whether we shouldn't read the notes Yang had left her. I had all but forgotten about those famous notes. They were still in the drawer of my desk where I had locked them away the night of Lingling's arrival.

It took us a week to decipher Yang's sometimes almost illegibly scribbled notes. He must have written most of them in secret, furtively watching those whose words and deeds he recorded, with date, time and place, often relating their words verbatim.

Lingling and I were horror-stricken by what we read. The enormity of it was inconceivable and we looked at each other, appalled and scared to death. We realised that we were too small fry and would never be able to make use of that kind of information. The consequences were too awful to contemplate and we would simply be crushed by the conflicting forces.

Besides, Chiang and his Nationalists, who, as a result of us making the notes public would undoubtedly gain a decisive political victory over the Communists, were probably much worse for China.

Hence we decided to do nothing.

However, we could not destroy the notes. Yang had lived in terror for years to compile them and had died a horrible death just to protect Lingling from their discovery in her possession. So we wrapped them again in oil-paper and hid them inside our mattress.

In tacit mutual understanding we avoided any mention of the notes and their possible implications and after a few weeks we had indeed forgotten about them, happy as we were with each other and with our cloistered life, hardly aware of the turbulence and upheavals taking place in the outside world.

Four months later, two months before our child was due, the world came crashing down on me and I closed, for good, the earlier chapters of my life's story.

I shall never forget that moment, a horror picture for ever frozen in time, when at the end of August 1944 I was interrupted during my lecture on the mathematical concept of infinity by a knock on the door of the lecture room. A student in the front row opened the door and there stood my housekeeper and his wife, eyes downcast, he fiddling with his cap and she with her skirt, both crying silently.

As if in a dream I descended from the dais in front of the blackboard with my formulae scribbled all over it and I went home, the housekeeper and his wife on my heels, crying and wringing their hands, my students following in a silent throng at a discreet distance.

There she was lying, my Lingling, in a pool of blood, her throat cut from ear to ear, the bloody knife put back on the kitchen table before she had crumpled, her right forefingers stiffened on the last stroke of the characters 'eternal silence' written in her blood on the floor tiles.

Suicide in a moment of temporary insanity was the verdict. As in a haze I went through the formalities, wordlessly shaking hands with people I didn't recognise, first at home, then at the mortuary, then at the cemetery until I was finally back in my lifeless home, alone, and could weep and weep for my Lingling whom I had failed by neglecting to protect her.

You see, Lingling was left-handed and in primary school her teacher had been enlightened enough to let the bright little girl use her left hand in writing as well.

The monstrous, power mad criminals who still govern us today, had simply not thought of this little detail when they ordered Lingling's silken throat cut and made it look like a suicide. Or maybe they *had* and was I the only one meant to understand the subtlety of the message 'eternal silence' written with the *wrong* finger in her own blood.

*

Gao Chen fell silent and his friends sat there looking at him as if petrified, afraid and too deeply moved to disturb his train of thoughts and memories.

He heaved a deep sigh and smiled at them through his tears.

'In retrospect it often seems to me as if the periods of my life before and after Lingling are so dull, so listless and devoid of zest compared to the two periods, much too short each of them, during which she so completely dominated my every thought and emotion. First during the interlude in Danba when she was still another man's wife and then during the ten months in Shanghai when we so intensely enjoyed each other's closeness that we forgot about the dark forces that conspired against us in the world around us.

'Lingling and I were soulmates, you see, and we both knew, without ever having to say it with so many words, that everything that had kept us apart: husband, work, life itself, age even perhaps, had been a tragic error. When we said goodbye in Danba three weeks after our last quick lovemaking, we both had the premonition that somehow, some time, some place, fate would throw us together again one last time to make good the waste it had made of our lives.

'I now realise that for what we call *fate* the whole concept of time is meaningless, that it is more a loop than the straight arrow from past to future we think it is and that it makes therefore no sense to lament about the *unfairness* of the length of the eleven years fate kept us apart or about the shortness of the ten months it finally accorded us. For all fate cares it might have been the other way round or both periods might have lasted the time of a hasty kiss only. I shall therefore quickly return to Danba and connect the rest of my story to the Shanghai interlude; one never knows.'

★

As Lingling had suggested, I managed to turn Comrade Qian Muhua around with clever talk before she and the two professors returned to Beijing.

She promised to support my case.

Two weeks later Professor Ma Xiyao was back in Danba to tell me that I had been allowed to sit for the examinations and also that his wife would be very glad to have me living with them for as long as I would stay in Beijing. I needn't worry about the costs, he said, that was all taken care of. Besides, they never had a son, or a child for that matter, much to his wife's sorrow, so Madam Ma was looking forward to have me staying with them.

The good man asked me, with a shy little smile, to indulge his wife should her motherly instincts get the better of her.

I passed my examinations and spent in all eight uneventful years in Beijing, five as a student and three as an assistant lecturer after my graduation in mathematics and physics. I didn't engage in any political or even social activities and I had no real friends, just acquaintances.

Twice Liu Longfei came to visit me. He had become an important man in Mao's Party organisation and his visits took place in the utmost secrecy for Chiang Kaishek would have given a fortune to lay his hands on him and make him talk.

The first time Longfei came to see me was three years after we had said goodbye in what for both of us had been a different life.

I told him what had happened to the Liang family and he took it well: there had been no love lost between the Liangs and him.

I also confessed that his books and papers had not been found by the soldiers as I had told Yang Baolin and were most probably still where we had buried them, under the floor of what had been his and Ailing's bedroom.

He stared at me and I knew from his moving jaw muscles that he was fighting intense and conflicting emotions. Then, suddenly, he relaxed and burst into a roaring laughter.

'For three years since Yang got word to me that my papers were stolen by Chiang's scum you made me live in fear of blackmail, you son of a bastard,' he laughed, apparently too relieved to be angry.

'I realise that you meant well and perhaps, with hindsight and all things considered, you did well by lying to Yang. He is waging his own little war to get Mao's attention and I wouldn't put it beyond him to pull a rabbit out of his hat and expose his old friend Liu Longfei, opportunist as he is all the same. So maybe I do owe you my life, Chen Dan. If I ever underestimated you, little brother, I promise you I won't make that mistake again. Now, give me your copies of the letter, Ailing's own and the one you faked so that we can destroy them. That'll be one worry less, they might still fall in the wrong hands if something untoward happens to you, Xiao Dan.'

I ignored his outstretched hand and for the second time in only a few minutes he had to struggle with his hot temper when I told him I would give those letters only to Ailing personally. However, his decency and friendship won out and he slapped me on my shoulder.

'Right you are, my friend,' he said, smiling broadly. 'Expect Ailing one of these days. You, be good to her. No need for the gory details.'

I promised him that I would tell her the truth, but would spare her what he called the gory details unless she herself asked for them.

He nodded and, standing in the open door of my room, he said, 'I want you to get your doctorate from Beida, Xiao Dan. Once you have that I'll see you again to discuss where to go from there. Be good! Don't do things I wouldn't do,' and at that he was gone.

Three months later, coming home from my course, I found Ailing in the living room talking to Madam Ma, my landlady. With unfeigned joy she leapt at me and fondly embraced and kissed me, to Madam Ma's apparent astonishment, for Ailing was a very pretty as well as a very important person, as the good lady undoubtedly knew.

Ailing and I withdrew to my room where we talked for hours. I told her everything, without leaving anything out. I couldn't, not with Ailing. She would have known immediately if I was holding out on her. She was emotionally strong enough to hear me out when I related, with the gory details, what had happened to her family, though she wept, silently, when I described how her brothers Yichen and Yibang had died and why.

She told me I had acted correctly under the circumstances and she put the letters I gave her in her bag. It had been a terrible shock, she told me, when she had received my letter, through Yang Baolin, three years ago and read how her naivety had brought ruin to her family and nearly had me killed as well, which would have been even more unbearable than her brothers' betrayal of her trust.

She asked me to forgive her and suddenly she threw her arms around me and we sat there, on my bed, for a long time, silently holding each other, each of us finally coming to terms with a terrible episode in our past.

We were woken from our reverie by a knock on the door and Madam Ma coming in carrying a tray with two bowls of hot soup and a big bowl of noodles and vegetables.

She showed no surprise seeing us sitting so close together on my bed. Putting the tray on the table she said, without looking at us, 'You must have a lot to tell each other, things that hurt and cause strong emotions. So tiring but also such a relief, provided there is mutual understanding and forgiveness. I can see that the worst part is behind you now so it's time for a bowl of hot, hearty soup to lift the spirits. Eat first and then tell each other the nicer things which I am sure there must be as well. There always are, life is never all misery. Digest the bad things and try to see them in the right perspective and, above all, in proportion to the whole. It helps and makes you appreciate that which you have. I know!'

Upon these words she smiled at us and the kind and wise Madam Ma closed the door softly behind her.

Ailing and I ate our soup and noodles with vegetables and we felt much better.

With forced cheer, to hide my embarrassment, I told Ailing about my adventures with the twins and several times she burst out laughing. Her sense of humour made me feel less awkward and I could actually joke about the things the girls and I did.

However, when I came to the time I spent in Danba with Yang Baolin and his wife and I told her about my affair with Lingling, the tone of my voice must have changed, the light-heartedness gone, imperceptible to myself but not to Ailing.

She became serious, pensive even and she took my hands in hers. When I told her about my dabbling in Buddhist philosophy and my new-found perception of the true value of life and our subsequent changed attitude towards each other, Ailing smiled, a bit sadly and compassionately.

'Don't fool yourself, Xiaoxing,' she said, 'you love her and from what I see in Lingling's eyes when we meet now and then at Party meetings and she mentions your name, and she always manages to bring your name into whatever the conversation is about, she loves you too. However, there are both circumstances and people in your way and if you lose your head, or Lingling hers for that matter, there will be losers and victims all around, including both of you in the end as well. Neither of you will be able to live with the shame and the hurt you have caused in your folly. Nevertheless, I have a foreboding of an impending tragedy now that I see that same remote look in your eyes when you mention her name. Please don't lose your head, Xiaoxing! Please?'

It was strange that Ailing should mention her foreboding for I had experienced the same feeling of doom myself on more than one occasion. It would pounce on me unexpectedly, like some beast of prey that had crept closer and closer, unnoticed, and then, suddenly, it would be upon me.

Merely thinking of that happening made my heart sink in the pit of my stomach and my knees feel weak and wobbly, an icy chill gripping me by the neck, respiration fast and superficial.

I tried to laugh and my voice sounded to my ears like the bleating of a goat. I promised Ailing I wouldn't do anything stupid.

It must have been close to midnight when she made ready to leave.

'Continue to keep a low profile, Xiao Dan,' she urged. 'The situation in China is bad, very bad. We have reliable information that Japan is preparing for war and we expect the Japanese will attack and invade China. Perhaps next year, perhaps in two years, however, it is inevitable, Mao says, just as inevitable as Japan's defeat in the end. The snake will choke on the rabbit it swallows whole, Mao says. However, before that happens our country and our people will suffer unspeakably and not only our people. Millions of people will have to die atrociously all over Asia before the arrogant ruling clique in Japan will be brought to their knees. Even the Japanese themselves will suffer terribly before it's all over, the stupid ants blinded by their faith in their godhead they call *tenno*.

'In the meantime do *not* take sides, Dan! Stay away from politics. You *must* achieve academic status before China becomes Communist so that they *need* you to build Xinhua, the New China, and to give *them* face in the eyes of the world. You understand, Xiao Dan? Promise?'

I promised.

A last hug and kiss and she was gone.

Five years later I was promoted a doctor in mathematics and physics and lost my cosy position as an assistant lecturer, all on the same day. Overqualified, the board of governors said when I asked them why. A full professorship was out of the question at Beida. Too young and inexperienced and too little status the board of governors said when I asked them why.

So there I sat, that evening, on my bed, the proud but jobless owner of a beautiful certificate with a red lacquer seal. The dean gave me a week to sort out my personal papers and to clear my office for the new incumbent.

On the last night of that week I had my evening meal together with Professor and Madam Ma and our mood alternated between cheery reminiscences and gloomy silences.

The Mas had said that I could stay as long as I liked. They had come to consider me as their son, they said, and the house would be cheerless and empty without me around and Madam Ma wept silently now and then at the prospect.

I had learned to love these two decent and good-hearted people, however, the thought of hanging about in that small house, without something to do, made me almost suffocate.

But where could I go? I belonged nowhere.

After dinner I retired to my room and had just decided I might as well go to bed and try to get some rest after the past couple of sleepless nights when Madam Ma knocked and opened the door at the same time.

'Liu Longfei and Liang Ailing are downstairs to see you, Dan,' she said and her voice trembled as she continued, 'There is a person with them who says he is from Shanghai. His name is Wong Zelin and he is the administrator of Fudan University, he says. I think he has come to offer you a job. I am of course happy for you but my heart is so heavy, Dan. It'll be so silent and lonely in the house without you. Only myself and my learned husband to cook for and he only eating like a bird, noodles and vegetables, vegetables and noodles, every day, not tasting anything with his head full of formulas. Who will now eat my fried pork noodles? My beef noodle soup?' she wailed.

I kissed her and rushed downstairs to meet Longfei, Ailing and the man from Shanghai.

I burst into the living room and saw Ailing, beautiful and radiant as ever, with two men and Professor Ma.

Ailing and the tallest of the two strangers got up from their chairs and came towards me, arms stretched out and smiling delightedly, exclaiming my name. From his voice I recognised Longfei. He had shaved his beard off and his hair had turned a dull grey. His face was deeply lined and he had lost a lot of weight.

He looked a different man entirely.

We embraced as heartily as always and my eyes met Ailing's. She shook her head almost imperceptibly and I affected not to notice any change in Longfei's appearance.

Both congratulated me on my promotion and repeatedly proclaimed to be very proud of me. They then introduced me to Mr Wong, who had a nice smile, showing good, white teeth which made me a bit self-conscious about my own.

We finally sat down and engaged in the usual small talk while enjoying Madam Ma's freshly made green tea. After thirty minutes or so I looked significantly at Ailing, who got the message, for after a few more minutes she gently proposed that we go up to my room and leave Professor and Madam Ma in peace to prepare for the night.

Once in my room, with a fresh pot of tea hastily brewed by Madam Ma after Ailing's words, Longfei came to the point without further ado.

'Dan,' he said, 'I can be candid with you. Wong Zelin and I have been the best of friends for more than twenty-five years. Zelin is the sort of Communist who has great moral but little practical value for the struggle since he strongly believes in humaneness and individual rights. Hence his post as administrator of Fudan, as far away from the bleak Communist world in Shanxi as possible. Zelin's secret task, assigned to him by the Party, has been and still is to spot potential cadres amongst the students and to bring this "malleable material" to the attention of the Shanghai Party cell's secretary, who will then send, eventually, recruiters to approach them. Unfortunately Zelin's criteria of suitability are not what Mao approves of and the number of drop-outs has been far too high for too long already.

'Even more unfortunately there is a faction in the top of the Party hierarchy that is of the opinion that those drop-outs constitute a security risk as long as the Party is not yet in total control of the country and that therefore they must be eliminated before they can do irreparable damage to the cause. Mao pretends not to know of this despicable practice but I know he bloody well does know and so does Zelin. For those of us who believe that communism should not be the final goal for China, let alone that it justifies every means, but that it should merely be a *necessary* interim stage to a more just and democratic society, the physical elimination of so many promising young people is intolerable and that not merely for humane reasons. We need as many well-educated and intelligent men and women as possible to help build a truly democratic China once communism has served its purpose and has become obsolete.

'Now, here is where you come in, Chen Dan! Once you have settled into your position as a member of the Fudan faculty, you will do the spotting of talent. Not the talent Mao is looking for, not the half-cooked idealists Zelin here feels attracted to, *no*! the talent *we* are looking for, the talent China needs for the post-Communist era. You will know one day who, besides Ailing and I, are the people I call *we*. You will observe, test and when you are sure of the correctness of your judgement you will approach the young men and women of your choice and very cautiously feel them out about their political inclination, about their ideas about the future of China and whether they see a role for themselves in that future. Only when their response convinces you that they are the right stuff, that they are capable of both the moral strength and the machiavellian mental duplicity to present the front of and act like a Communist zealot while actually working for the post-Communist future and only *then* do you explain to them the true plan.

'You must explain further that you will have to bring them to the notice of the Party to get them into the circuit and that once they have been approached by the Party recruiters they are on their own. Your own position is certainly not without danger, Dan. If one of your recruits turns deceiver and betrays you to the Party your fate will not be an enviable one. The only self-protection *we* allow you to use is that you may also tell your recruits that you are bound to give their names and particulars to the *Elders*, whom they do not know of course and probably never will, but who will, in due course, reward those who play their role well by manoeuvring them into important positions, first under the Communist system which is the purpose of the whole exercise, and later, of course, in the new society as well. On the other hand they must realise that the Elders are just as capable to make them regret any attempt at double-dealing or downright betrayal.'

Here Longfei paused, for more dramatic effect I suppose, and then he went on. 'I must now *formally* ask you, Chen Dan, with Ailing and Zelin as our witnesses, whether you accept this task.'

He fell silent and looked at me gravely, without a trace of his usual overconfidence.

I stared back at him and, from one blink to the next, the room, Ailing, Zelin and the past nine years vanished and I sat opposite the bearded Longfei of old, on our fishing raft. He was stroking Diaoyu's slender neck, his thoughts elsewhere, and I shivered because of the chilly night air and in the silence after Longfei's monologue I became aware of the smells and sounds of the river and the soft, rolling motion of the raft.

His last words still echoed through my mind. 'When both the time and you will be ripe, coincidentally I hope, I'll propose a cause to you, which you may of course reject. I am prepared to take that risk.'

I must have wrinkled my nose, in that little room in Beijing, as I always seem to do, unwittingly, when seeing, or even thinking of something distasteful, for I heard a loud 'hem' and the spell broke.

The river scene faded and the room and the others swam back into focus.

My eyes registered the moving mouth of the beardless Longfei, however, my mind must have switched back on again a fraction of a second later for I had apparently missed his first words as I heard him say, 'Manipulated, Dan? That all along Ailing and I had this plan in mind while feigning our affection for you? Betraying yours for us? Don't think like that, Dan. Don't do that to yourself, to us, to our friendship! When Ailing and I took little Hedgehog Chen into our life, closed him into our hearts, twelve years ago, we had no ulterior motives, only compassion and, in Ailing's case, genuine affection, love even. You had been living with us about three years when a plan gradually took shape in my mind.

'Ever since my flight from Shanghai, even before that, I had been desperate for an idea of what I could do for China. The ideas I had played with were either too complicated or too fantastic, but always unrealistic because they had in them a fundamental flaw. That flaw was my own *vanity*. I, Liu Longfei, wanted success and recognition for *my idea* in my lifetime! A scenario without Liu Longfei in a major, if not *the* leading role didn't even occur to me. I became dejected by my own powerlessness and insignificance. I was in that state of mind when Ailing and you, Dan, came to live with me. If not for that I would have turned into an eccentric, a lunatic probably, alternately wallowing in self-aggrandisement and self-pity.

'Apart from the love Ailing gave me, it was above all her common sense, her sense of humour and perspective and her realism that brought me back form the brink of megalomania. I realised that my ideas had been too grandiose, that something much simpler and covering a much longer time-span, with myself in the inglorious role of initiator and stimulator, might actually work and ultimately have a chance of success, though that would most probably be long after my own demise. Once I had accepted that premise the idea itself just happened when one day Ailing and I were commenting on your progress, Dan, and I made the remark, "Why are we doing all this, Ailing? Is it for Dan's good? Or is it to satisfy our own intellectual vanity? Wouldn't it be better for him, ultimately, if we did not teach him all these things and how to reason for himself but let nature take its course and hope, for him, that he'll become a conformist, a follower rather than a leader and a critic of other people's ideas? It will all be so much easier for him to accept oppression and tyranny, whether by Communists or by Nationalists, which seems to me to be China's fate, as it has always been and as generations of people like the Chens have meekly done before him."

'I have never forgotten and won't ever forget either Ailing's anger when she replied, "Animals are like that, Longfei! They accept their fate but are not consciously aware that they do this. They meekly accept the kick of a human or his knife that slaughters them or they expose their throat or belly to the leader of their pack to show their submissiveness. They have no hopes, no aspirations because they have no faculty. They have only instincts. Do you want our Dan to be like that, Longfei? His only reason being that of how to adapt and accept without ever knowing that he may have a choice? I know you don't, Longfei! You were merely asking a rhetorical question, weren't you, Longfei? For you have an idea and you just want to be sure it will be workable. I see from your expression that I have hit the nail right on its head, haven't I? Explain yourself, Heilong Liu!"

'It was the first and only time she called me Heilong to my face. So I explained my idea to her. I so vividly recall that moment that I can even repeat every word I said at this time, and I see from Ailing's smile that she does as well.

'What I said was: "When the day comes that you and I have to leave this place, we will join Mao Zedong and his Communists in Hunan. Yang Baolin will see to it that we are expected. I have met Mao a few times, however, I don't know him that well. I found him a bit remote and arrogant, not what you would call a warm and charismatic person. But there are others, Zhou Enlai, Deng Xiaoping, Hu Yaobang to name but a few, who are decent people with an ideal. Probably there are many more like them. I think I can find a common cause with them, that is 'a civilised China respected amongst other civilised nations'. A decent, tolerant and compassionate China where respect for individual human rights is not only embodied in its constitution but is also practised in everyday life and taught in its schools and universities so that once again being Chinese is synonymous with being civilised, decent, tolerant and compassionate.

'"I am convinced that among the Communists there are many men and women whose ideal is just that but who are also aware that a fundamental change, not only in our society as a whole but, to begin with, in the moral make-up of the average Chinese, is an absolute must, a *conditio sine qua non.* Communism can affect such a fundamental change, however, for me and my like-minded communism is *not* the ultimate goal. It is merely a necessary interim stage before we can evolve into a truly democratic society. I am also totally convinced that the Nationalists have nothing to offer. Opportunism, greed, corruption, lust for personal power, those are the elements of the Nationalist creed. The worst that can happen to China is that those criminals, Chiang Kaishek being the worst of the lot, are allowed to continue to exploit

China as their personal property and the Chinese as their slaves, to be used or disposed of according to their whimsical notions of usefulness.

'"My plan is to form, slowly, cautiously and gradually, a circle, or rather a kind of secret society of like-minded men and women who can guide China, first to achieve communism, next through the Communist interlude and finally into the truly democratic era. This will be a long, a very long process and the ultimate goal may very well not be achievable in our lifetime. Besides, the risk that our lifetime will be shortened when the true Communists find out about us is not at all imaginary. You know them when you see them, the true believers. They have that flinty gleam in their eyes and that humourless, grim set mouth. They have that same contempt for the individual needs of our people as the Nationalists have. They are probably worse than the Nationalists who at least notice you as an individual, albeit only in terms of your usefulness. The true Communist can't even conceive of individualism as a human trait. It is clear that we can't achieve our first goal, that of establishing communism throughout China, without these zealots. We need them and we'll have to accept that for a certain time after completing that first step they call the shots, however much we abhor their methods to establish the new order and maintain control. After a while, however, these die-hards of the first hour will have outlived their usefulness, will even become a liability and they will have to be eased out, preferably voluntarily, forcefully if need be.

'"Two sorts of people will be quintessential for this process of mellowing the system, the second step in the evolution of China. First and foremost a change in thinking amongst the top leaders will be necessary and this I see as the vital task, probably the only one, of the members of that secret society I was speaking of earlier. *They* must initiate and then nourish this necessarily gradual and slow change in thinking, *they* are the first of the two sorts of people I was referring to and to describe their *modus operandi* there are only two words and those are *subtleness* and *wariness*. They will have to bide their time and even when that time has come they will find themselves skating on very thin ice. Besides, as I said before, most of these unavoidably *few* men and women, these *Elders* as I will call them from now on, will either be too old or dead already by the time the inherent inefficiency and ineffectiveness of communism can no longer be hidden from even its most zealous disciples. However, that doesn't mean that these zealots will give up their position voluntarily, without a fight, and let others, more moderate and better educated people, take over in a peaceful manner. *No Communist will ever give up power voluntarily*! *He must be forced out*! If the willingness to remove these people by force is lacking then the evolution will *fail*! This is the most critical point of the evolution I have in mind and the balance may very well tip to the side of total suppression of all dissenters, of a ruthless tyranny.

'"This tipping of the balance to the wrong side is a foregone conclusion if those moderate, better educated people are not available. It will be clear, however, that such people are not simply there when you need them, like pushing a button and hey presto there they are. How many do you need, sir? Ten thousand specimens? All right, here you are sir, ten thousand as ordered. Oh, was it a hundred thousand you said, sir? Sorry, I misunderstood. One hundred thousand it is. Anything else, sir? That's not the way it works. Such things need careful and long-term planning and exhaustive selection and testing procedures. I am of course referring to that second sort of people I mentioned earlier. It will take a very long time, at least twenty years, if not longer, to forge a sufficiently large group of people who share a common cause and ideal, who are all of approximately the same age and will be in their prime in twenty to twenty-five years and, equally important, who will occupy important and influential positions at that time. The mental strength of the candidates is most important as well. They must be able to live under the stress of the constant fear of being found out. They must have the patience and self-effacement to be able to wait in vain for many years, perhaps their whole working life for the call that may never come, for the moment to come out of the closet and take charge in their immediate environment during the social upheavals that will inevitably proceed the transition, firstly from the suppressive, authoritarian Communist system to a period of reforms and trials and errors and secondly to a free, more or less democratic society.

'"You can't simply pick such people at random in the street, on the workshop floor or in the field. Only relatively few people qualify for such demands and therefore we have to start as early as possible with the selection and recruitment of suitable candidates. It is obvious that the Elders, and I reckon myself and you, Ailing, as members of that remote, small and exclusive body of men and women of the first hour, will *not* be in a position to make converts. Quite to the contrary! That would be far too dangerous since we can't afford the slightest trace of mistrust by Mao Zedong and his arch-Communist disciples like Chen Yun and Yang Shangkun. Hence the need for people who by the very nature of their position have daily business with young men and women as the Elders' agents in the field. I am of course thinking of teachers and professors. They are indeed in a privileged position to spot potential candidates and to test and observe them, unbeknownst to them of course, until they are practically sure of a correct judgement. The agent will tentatively approach those thought to be suitable to feel them out and see how they react. If their reaction is encouraging the agent may take the decisive step and propose to them to become what is, I believe, called a mole or a sleeper.

'"At this point the agent has irrevocably exposed himself to the candidate so nobody can blame him if he wants to be absolutely sure in his own mind that he has made the right choice and that, if he has the slightest doubt, he prefers to err on the side of caution. Once the die is cast, however, the agent must, of course with the full knowledge and collusion of the candidate, propose him to the local Party cell as a suitable future young cadre. The local Party cell may or may not react; if it does it will alert its own recruiters who will investigate the man or woman proposed by the agent and he or she may still be found wanting and all has been for nothing. However, if the Party recruiters report favourably the agent's candidate-mole or candidate-sleeper will still have to go through the normal process of becoming a Party member. This is the tricky part for the candidate. He or she must have a double moral standard and be equally capable of defending either one. If he fails somewhere along the line, he is in trouble. At best he will be expelled and that's the end of the story and of himself, socially that is. At worst he will be eliminated.

'"If he becomes a turncoat, our agent will be in big trouble. In some way or other, how I have not worked out yet, the agent must also signal the candidate to the Elders. This will be all the more difficult because, for obvious reasons, neither the agent nor the candidate is permitted to know who these elusive Elders are. This for our protection as well as for their own. I'll find a way how this can be done. Once the candidate has become a Party member he will gradually be manoeuvred into a position from which he can be useful to the Plan once the time is judged ripe to set things in motion. The manoeuvring may involve promotion from one position to another, higher one or just the opposite and the mole or sleeper may remain marooned as it were in the same position during his whole working life. This can, of course, be very frustrating. He *must* be able to endure this. The Elders are the sole judges of such things.

'"Until the time of action, and again solely the Elders will decide when this is, the best among the chosen ones will act as moles and provide the Elders with useful information, perhaps even commit, from time to time, some subtle form of sabotage of selected Party programmes. The majority, however, will just pass their time as sleepers, acting the exemplary but dull Communist cadre and wait for the wake-up call which may never come. For now all this is merely a dream and it may very well turn out to be an utopian scheme. But we *must try*, Ailing! We *must have a purpose to live for*! Now, I am well aware that we must begin in a small way. The first thing to do is to start evaluating people *we* know now already, and subsequently everybody we'll meet later, for the role of what I call our agents. I am also well aware that should I, or you for that matter, Ailing, be able to win over one or some of Mao's inner circle for my plan, he or she won't be of much practical value at first. He will be vague and evasive and will certainly not compromise himself by starting to recruit agents. At best he may give a hint, however, don't count on that either. The onus for the dangerous initial spadework will be on me, or you, perhaps on Yang Baolin, though I'm not so sure of him, and on his wife Lingling and on a few others I have in mind.

'"We need not wait until we will be back in the mainstream, however. We can already begin right here at home with our own little hedgehog here. We shall teach Chen Dan all the factual knowledge we have but, above all, we'll teach him to use man's, his, innate faculty of reason to chose what, or what not, to do in whatever the circumstances are. At the time he will have become a teacher or, even better, a professor, which is my fervent hope for him and for us, either one or both of us will approach him with our proposal to become an agent, provided my plan isn't moribund by then. But if he accepts it must be of his own free will, not because of any sort of coercion on our part or because he feels obligated to us for what we have done for him."'

Longfei fell silent and looked me straight in the eye.

'This is the background of my proposal to you, Xiao Dan,' he said. 'Twelve years ago Ailing thought that my plan was workable, that it had a reasonable chance of success and thus we have been working at it ever since. We have been successful so far, more so than we had ever expected and we have been able to form a group of Elders with names and influential positions beyond our wildest dreams. We have also already four hundred agents in place, all over China. Teachers, professors, factory leaders, officers in Chiang's army, civil servants and even a few medical doctors. Their number is steadily growing. It's too early yet to expect them to be fully organised and effective but quite a few have already been busy and this very moment we have four moles and some twenty sleepers within the Party hierarchy in the three big cities Beijing, Nanjing and Shanghai. I now ask you again, Chen Dan: do you agree to be an agent? It's your choice. No obligation. No hard feelings if you say no.'

'I am sorry if at first I gave you the wrong impression, Longfei,' I replied. 'It must have been the fishy smell of our raft that I remember so well that must have, unwittingly, made me wrinkle my nose. Not the idea of having been manipulated by you and Ailing, as you apparently assumed. I remember vividly that night, nine years ago, when you first spoke to me about making me a proposal when both the time and I would be ripe. If you now reckon that I am ripe I should be picked, shouldn't I? Or else I may rot. You continue to look solemn, Longfei, so I guess that I am being flippant and that joking is inappropriate among the good Communists we pretend to be, eh, Longfei? Always keep up the appearances, eh? Life is a deadly serious business, quite deadly sometimes. So, wholly in style, I now declare solemnly, Ailing and Mr Wong being my witnesses, that I agree to be an agent in your plan.'

We all shook hands, embraced, kissed and hugged and then talked some more until the three of them left at three o'clock in the morning in order to be out of the city before daybreak.

Two weeks later I arrived in Shanghai to take up a full professorate at Fudan University. It took me three weeks to settle in and be accepted by the other members of the faculty and another two months to spot my first potential candidate.

# *Chapter Seventeen*

## Chen Dan's Story: Mission Accomplished (August 1966)

By the time Lingling burst back into my life, two years after that memorable evening in Beijing with Longfei, Ailing and Wong Zelin, I had referred only five candidate members to the Shanghai Party secretary, four of whom failed their tests miserably.

I must admit that in spite of Longfei and Ailing's seriousness I didn't take their Plan and their Elders very seriously.

It took Lingling and all she had to give, including her life, to change that as she changed so many other things in my life and in the way I saw myself.

Firstly there were Yang Baolin's notes she brought me and which we read together in the secrecy of our bedroom, making us shiver from the icy dread that gripped us in spite of the warmth of our huddled bodies under the blanket.

Secondly there were our whispered discussions about the terrible secrets Yang revealed in his notes and her own comments on the intrigues and infighting amongst the opportunistic traitors, most of whom she knew or had met personally and which only added to my dread about our future should these evil men ever usurp power.

Thirdly and above all, however, there was that terrible thing they, possibly our future leaders, did to her to keep their dirty secrets from becoming known to the Chinese people and the world at large.

After the initial shock waves of grief and self-reproach following Lingling's death, the horror, the cold-blooded, vicious evil of those responsible for her brutal execution triggered in me such bouts of anger and fury that afterwards, sapped by the consuming rages, I feared for my own sanity.

Revenge was all I wanted, immediate, irreparably destructive revenge for the evil they had done to my Lingling and myself, and Yang's notes were the tool to expose and destroy the monsters who could conceive of such cold-blooded wickedness as the wanton destruction of an innocent, beautiful woman merely as a warning to me.

Had there been an immediate possibility to get the notes into the hands of people with the authority and power to destroy those I wanted hurt and destroyed, I am convinced I would have done that and God knows what would have happened then.

My unworldliness in such things though, combined with my peasantly mistrust that such powerful people would use the notes for their own interests and crush me, Chen Dan, as a bothersome, buzzing fly, provided the necessary time for me to calm down and look at every aspect of the matter in a level-headed manner.

I came to the conclusion that my best chance to exact my revenge laid in Longfei's Plan. Suddenly I saw the insidious, exquisite perfidy of the whole set-up, like a cancer spreading unnoticed throughout the body of the Communist Party, erupting when it's too late, and for the first time after Lingling's death I laughed.

I would be a virulent agent and cause the destruction of the murderers of my wife.

Longfei's Plan would merely be a pretext, a means to realise my own, private plan and all the other agents, moles and sleepers would merely serve *my* purpose, mere proliferating cancer cells of the tumour in the Communist's body that was I and to hell with Longfei's and Ailing's highfalutin ideas for the greater good of China and the world.

I admit, a bit shamefully, that much of my activity as an agent for Longfei's Plan in the first couple of years was inspired by those personal feelings of revenge. Gradually, however, I realised that hate and anger are strongly negative forces and hence sap your vital energy instead of feeding it like joy and contentment do. My frenetic, feverish bitterness left me often exhausted and curiously unable to sleep, what with all the negative thoughts swirling through my head while tossing about, alone, in my bed. It was during one of those sleepless nights, though maybe I was asleep or in some state of mental exhaustion and did I dream it all, that I saw and even felt Lingling.

She wept when she told me that she couldn't find peace where she was because of the web of negative forces that emanated from me and kept her entangled.

'Please let go, let me free and free yourself at the same time, my love,' she sobbed. 'Rediscover the contentment and the small joys of daily life you found in Danba, on the islet with the monks and with me.'

We made love, so slowly and intensely I had never felt before and I came and came, filling her up as she took it all, the radiance on her face indescribable and utterly moving.

I woke up, in a delicious, dreamy kind of contented lassitude as I groped for Lingling to take her in my arms again as before. I found but emptiness beside me, Lingling was gone, again.

Until today I am absolutely certain she was there that night, physically. I never found any stain or wetness on the mattress, you see, though from the tenderness in my loins I knew they should have been there, to be hidden from my housekeeper's wife when she made my bed.

That was the last and final turn Lingling gave to my life. I freed her from my obsessions and she gave me back my decency and contentment.

⋆

Gao Chen fell silent.

Slowly he emerged from his reverie and memories and he looked up, his head bent far backwards, at the velvety black sky and the myriads of flickering stars.

'She is there, roaming free and boundless as I eventually will. True love is letting the loved ones free, not bounding them.'

He sighed deeply and, letting his chair fall back on its four legs, he looked at his friends who hadn't moved, afraid as they were to break the spell.

'For the past twenty-two years it has been my first priority to work for Longfei's Plan,' Gao Chen continued. 'I owed that to Lingling. I must be one of Longfei's most prolific agents with sixty-two moles and more than six hundred sleepers in place at his latest count about a year ago. He didn't give me their names and locations though. Of course I kept a list of the names of the people I recruited, however, I don't know who ultimately became a mole or a sleeper and who remained just an ordinary Party member. I took my friend Chen Juntao in my confidence two years after he so odoriferously stumbled into my life. His opinion about my secrets has been invaluable and undoubtedly contributed to my success rate.'

He hesitated just a fraction of a second, took a deep breath and said, 'And now I should be proud and happy if I could put the crown on my work.'

Looking at Suping and her mother, he asked solemnly, 'Xu Suping, Liu Guixian, would you two do me the honour of allowing me to submit your names to Longfei directly? Bypassing the local Party secretary and therefore the need for you to become Party members first, which in your case is nigh impossible anyhow.'

In the silence that followed Gao Chen's request the three Xus; father, mother and daughter, looked at each other incredulously, completely taken by surprise.

It was one thing to *listen* to the kind of story as told by Gao Chen, to laugh, shiver and weep with him in shared, though safely remote, emotions, however, it was quite another thing to be *part* of such a life.

Gao Chen sensed their fear for the unknown, for becoming a small cog in the giant machinery of a nationwide, underground conspiracy that would turn them, as from the very moment they said yes to Gao Chen's request, into an active enemy of the established order.

In an attempt to allay their apprehension he said, 'I have always found that doing what you consider the right thing to do in the knowledge that there is a certain risk, a certain danger even, involved, gives a zest to your life which otherwise may be a tedious routine. It enhances your awareness of everything you see, smell, taste and feel. However, you may ask: how do you know that which you do is the right thing to do? I myself have but one criterion which is that I must feel good about it, not momentarily, no, all the time. No nagging feelings of guilt or remorse or occasional doubt. No! Only a sense of accomplishing something, of contributing to something you believe in. The feeling is quite exhilarating and even addictive in a pleasurable way, I tell you. I can't deny that there is a certain risk in what I ask from you but then, what price do you put on your own dignity?

'I am not asking from you that you become a mole who actually spies for and collaborates with those whom the Communists rightly consider, from their point of view that is, as reactionary enemies of the State. If found out or betrayed these moles are on their own and you had better not think about what their fate will be then. I am not even asking from you to become a sleeper who may at any given moment be woken up and ordered to commit some form of sabotage, either subtle and over a long period of time or a spectacular and one-off deed. They also may not survive. No! nothing of that heroic stuff! What I am asking from you is that you permit me to inform the Elders about your sympathy for their aims and your willingness to help with the clean-up and turnaround after a corrupt system has been brought down and I personally am thinking of the role you could play in the necessary re-education of our people whose views, opinions and morals have been completely distorted and corrupted by the relentless Communist propaganda.

'If you say yes to that I shall, somehow, convey your names and profiles to Liu Longfei and Liang Ailing in Beijing. They're both old now but still very much with it. I'll also let them know that with both of you won over for the

Plan I consider my part in building its structure as accomplished. I'll remain available, however, no longer in an active role. Now, what do you say?'

During Gao Chen's plea Suping and her mother had looked at Xu and momentarily raised their eyebrows. In silent answer Xu had raised his and both his wife and daughter had nodded, quickly and simultaneously.

Xu had then hesitated for just a fraction of a second before nodding his assent.

Ai Chen, who had watched the mime, marvelled at their mutual understanding.

'Suping and I are deeply honoured by your trust and esteem, Chen Dan, our friend,' Guixian said. 'You may tell Longfei and Ailing, whom, we feel, we know almost personally and intimately after all you have told us. We are proud that we are deemed worthy of playing a modest part in their Plan. I also feel unspeakably relieved that all these years there have been so many people who have apparently neither resignedly nor cowardly bowed to oppression and blatant disregard for human values and dignity. People who were and still are prepared to die a horrible death for the idea of a China that one day will have her rightful place amongst the civilised nations of the world.

'China has no business to be the leader of the so-called Third World. When I see the pictures in the *People's Daily* of these leaders shaking hands with our leaders in Beijing I am so deeply ashamed. They all look like gangsters and most probably are, with their black, reflecting sunglasses they don't even take off when they talk to our leaders; with the moustaches and beards and crowds of creepy so-called secretaries and counsellors who, I have heard, ogle our Chinese women ever so shamelessly. And when I read all that hate language in the joint press release about the rest of the world, I feel like crying out of anger, shame and despair. China has no business with that kind of lowly people. I can't understand how Mao Zedong and Zhou Enlai, especially Zhou, a cultured man, can stoop so low. Oh, I am so ashamed. Our leaders have no class! I wish the Plan would begin tomorrow. I really would like that!'

Guixian fell silent, startled by her own outburst.

'Millions of decent people all over China, even amongst the uneducated who have undoubtedly greatly benefited from the Communist regime, think like you, Guixian,' Gao Chen replied. 'However, they don't speak up, not yet at least. Many don't know how to put into words what they instinctively and uneasily feel is wrong. Many more are afraid of the consequences if they would speak their mind, so they bow their head and mind their own business. Others again, who can or probably would speak their mind, don't know to whom and what's the use anyway, they say to themselves and shrug their shoulders. The Elders, who conceived the Plan, are well aware of this and will, when the time is judged to be ripe, provide the leaders to rally all those millions and they themselves will assume overall leadership. I hope I will still be around when that happens. But you will Guixian, and Suping of course.

'Tomorrow I shall give you Yang Baolin's notes to read. I have carried them around with me since the day Lingling was murdered and I have added to them, in my own writing and from my own observations and from what Longfei and Ailing have told me over the years. They have copied Yang's notes but I have kept the originals in the same state as when Lingling gave them to me. They still have her smell. Only one other person, a woman, the young woman doctor who was to deliver Lingling's baby, our son, has a copy. She became Lingling's best friend in Shanghai and she found the notes under our mattress when she cleaned our bed after Lingling nearly had a miscarriage in her fifth month. Lingling told her everything. It seems a woman needs a woman friend, however much she loves her man. She made a copy of Yang's notes and gave it to the lady doctor as a sign of their friendship and to serve as her protection.

'I only met that woman four or five times. Her family name was Liu, though no relative of Longfei. I didn't feel comfortable in her presence. She had such a fiery temper and she would almost chase me out of my own room when she came to examine Lingling. I'll never forget her rage when I had to tell her Lingling was dead. She didn't need my clever deduction about Lingling's left-handedness to conclude it was murder. She blamed me, in harsh words, for not having provided proper protection for Lingling. She shouted that she hoped I wouldn't be able to live with the guilt of my negligence and die of remorse. I never saw her again.

'Be that as it may, those named and exposed in the notes know for sure that those notes exist, however, they probably think that I alone have them and have hidden them somewhere with my instructions that they be made public should I die, before my time, of suspect and unnatural causes. So they think it is in their interest to see to it that I stay alive and I am sure that word has gone out to that effect. It won't protect me from the turbulence that is about to rock our country but at least I can be sure that in the background there is a watchful eye to see to it that I won't be affected fatally. I'll let it be known, subtly, that I expect the same consideration for those I call my closest and dearest friends, that is the four of you. They will do that, not out of love for me or for you, but out of pure self-interest which is of course the prime mover and spur of man's behaviour.'

Gao Chen grinned his infectious grin and added, 'At this very moment my prime mover is hunger, so back it is to the present and our Beggars Chicken.

They all burst out laughing, relieved that apparently their strange friend did not expect them to comment. He had told them his life's story because they had asked him to, not because he had touted it.

Any comment would have been inappropriate and hopelessly inadequate, if not spurious.

# *Chapter Eighteen*

## The Last Supper, 7th August, 1966

Wonderingly Suping had watched the man she called Uncle Dan and whose unabashed description of his nightly romps with the pretty, voluptuous aunties and his romance with Lingling had caused her such strange, and at times pleasurable, stirrings and constrictions in heart and belly.

She was certain that Mother had noticed her inner turmoil. Their eyes had met a few times when she glanced ever so furtively in Mother's direction during a particularly risqué part of Gao Chen's story. The blush of her own throat and her quickened breathing had betrayed Mother's feelings as well.

Neither Ai Chen nor Father had noticed their arousal though, Suping was sure of that, just as she was sure that Gao Chen had. He was that kind of man. Right from the first day that he had burst into their lives, she and Mother had felt comfortable with him. He radiated a warm aura of sympathy and empathy, without any innuendo of ulterior motives.

He made you feel appreciated and respected, as a woman, the tinge of open admiration stimulating a tingling and proud awareness of your womanly identity, a desire to please him as well as an urge to mother him. The eternal, joyous and reckless boy, belying his disguise as a learned, old and ugly man.

Suping smiled as she watched him, sitting on his heels, knocking and peeling off the chicken's clay shell with the same joyful anticipation as a boy unwrapping his birthday present.

'Suping! Set the table! The baby is almost there!' he called over his shoulder. 'Guixian! The rice! Ximing! The beer! Ai Chen, hand me a large plate! Now! Quick!'

Suddenly everybody was busy with preparations for the evening meal, the delicious smell of the Beggars Chicken spurring them on.

'I propose that we eat in the garden,' Suping said, to no one in particular. 'It's such a beautiful night, everything looks so clear in the moonlight, as if bathed in liquid silver. The darkness, inside, scares me all of a sudden.'

The others didn't bother to answer or argue as it seemed such a good idea and Father and Ai Chen carried the kitchen table outside.

Mother put the large, brown, earthenware bowl, filled with steaming, fragrant rice, on the table while Suping arranged the individual bowls, plates, chopsticks and the small saucers with salty soy sauce, vinegar and freshly grated ginger.

By then Gao Chen had removed the last bits and pieces of clay from the skin of the chicken and slowly he carried the large plate with the still sewn-up fowl to the table. Solemnly he showed the plate around, urging each of them in turn to sniff a waft of the deliciously pungent aroma. Finally he put the plate in the middle of the table.

The others sat down and looked on, mesmerised, as Gao Chen, still standing, cut the piece of string and removed the herbs from the chicken's inside.

'We keep the herbs, in a pan,' he said, 'and after dinner we add the leftovers of the chicken, some water, fish sauce and we put the pan in the hot ash and leave it overnight. Tomorrow I'll strain the stock and use it to cook the noodles for our noon meal. That way nothing is lost. Now, I'll taste the chicken.'

Carefully he pulled a piece of flesh from the carcass with his chopsticks. It came off very easily and, after examining and sniffing the whitish flesh, he put it in his mouth and tasted it thoughtfully, eyes closed, chopsticks lifted up in the air, in his right hand, like a conductor concentrating before striking the orchestra into its piece of music.

The others watched him in rapt attention, their chopsticks hovering over the chicken, ready to strike and rip off the meat at his first sign.

A heavenly smile spread over Gao Chen's face and while he was still halfway through the word 'perfect,' his friends were already munching their first piece of succulent meat. None of them, except Gao Chen himself perhaps, had ever eaten such a deliciously cooked chicken.

Certain things are simply too good for words; any comment, even praise simply detracting from their goodness. So they ate without the usual chit-chat.

After the copious meal they sat back in wordless contentment, a picture of cosy homeliness that would remain engraved in Suping's mind. She woke up from her repose and with the awareness of her contentment came, as always, the dreaded pangs of anguish that it wouldn't last.

Breathing deeply into her cupped hands, which she held over her nose and eyes, she focused her mind on the velvety black spot that drifted within her eyes to block those hateful thoughts.

Immersing herself in the warm, total blackness, she felt the wave of acute sadness that had so suddenly engulfed her recede and the pounding of her heart slow down.

Hovering at the edge of consciousness, unthinking and oblivious of her surroundings, she had no idea how long she had been sitting there like that when a gently kneading of her neck brought her back to the surface.

Rested, relaxed and again in control of herself Suping looked up at Gao Chen standing beside her and she smiled appreciatively.

'That feels good, Uncle Dan,' she said, 'don't stop yet. I feel the heaviness in my head disappear. Such a relief!'

'That was a good trick you did there, half an hour ago,' Gao Chen said, 'I mean putting your cupped hands over your eyes and nose and, breathing slowly and deeply, letting yourself drift off into nowhere. Did you manage to hold on to the black spot you saw, with your mind, floating before your eyes and make it larger and larger until you felt yourself floating too, in total blackness? It's as close as one can get to nirvana while still part of this world, the venerable abbot told me long ago, when he taught me the trick of how to attain *wuxi*. That simple exercise has helped me through many a moment of depression, of anguish, of despair and fear. How is it that *you* know about it?'

'When I have the morning classes there is always that old man who lives near the school with his son and daughter-in-law, doing his *taiqiquan* exercises in the school yard,' Suping replied.

'He leads a neighbourhood class of a dozen or so old men and women. He's over ninety but still looks very young, younger than Father, I think. He is always in a good mood, smiling and wishing me a good day. One day he came to see me, after classes, in the classroom. He said he had observed me, during the pupils' recreation time, and thought that I looked ill and tired. He was right. I had my period, which is always painful, and the children had been unruly and tiresome because of the hot weather and the thunderstorm that was brewing.

'So he told me to sit down, beside him, and he taught me the trick, as you call it, Uncle Dan, how to relax completely. He even gave me what he called a secret word that I had to recite, in a kind of undertone, over and over again, until I would slip into a semi-conscious state. It was a meaningless word, actually more a pleasant, low, humming sound than a word. He warned me not to mention that word to somebody else or it would lose its soporific and hypnotic power, for me that is, while on the other hand that other person could gain influence over my mind. I have used the trick quite often, however, I have never been able to attain total wuxi.

'Tonight I couldn't help thinking of the uncertainties that lie ahead and when I saw us sitting here in this small garden behind our cosy little house, so peaceful and content, I suddenly had the foreboding that it would be the last time we would ever be together like that and then my heart sank and I felt so miserable, Uncle Dan. So I used the trick to suppress those sad thoughts.'

Suping looked up at Gao Chen, her eyes glistening with tears.

'Yes, my love,' he answered, his voice quivering with hardly concealed emotion, 'I had the same foreboding. But we are prepared, aren't we?' and he looked questioningly at his friends.

They nodded gravely and Xu Ximing said, 'Let come what may. We'll drift with the currents and let the future take care of itself. As we promised each other, we'll try to meet each other at least every five years, here in this house if it's still there and provided the people who live here then aren't hostile. Now, do you see that big walnut tree over there, on that steep part of the slope?'

They nodded that they knew it was there.

'It has a large hollow in the trunk, about two metres from the ground,' Xu continued. 'From the outside you see only a small hole. I accidentally discovered it when I saw a squirrel race up the trunk and disappear suddenly. If you stand on a big stone on the higher part of the slope and lean against the tree you can reach the hold and put your hand into the hollow inside the trunk. I propose that whenever one of us happens to be in the neighbourhood he put a message in that hollow. That way we can stay informed about one another. Be sure the squirrel isn't home though. He'll bite you as he bit me, the little scoundrel.'

Xu laughed and showed them an old, small scar on the ball of his right-hand thumb.

'What do you think of my idea?' he asked, hesitantly. 'Is it all too melodramatic?'

'It's a perfect idea, Ximing,' Gao Chen said, admiringly. 'In fact, it's an eminently suitable and practical idea. So much so that I'll hide Yang's notes there now, at this very moment. You'll read them later, Suping, and Guixian, and Ximing of course as well, whenever there is a suitable moment. After reading, you'll put them back in the hollow please. Make sure nobody sees you.'

The Xus nodded and silently they looked on as Gao Chen disappeared inside the house and reappeared a few minutes later, a packet in his hand.

Without comment from any of them, Gao Chen disappeared in the dark, uphill.

Ten minutes later the small squeaks of the gate signalled his return.

'There was nobody home,' he grinned.

'It's late. Let's clean up the garden tomorrow,' he added and suddenly the good cheer was gone.

They mumbled their goodnights and hardly five minutes later the house was dark and they were all asleep.

Or were they really? Suping thought as she herself tossed and tossed around unable to fall asleep.

She finally fell asleep at dawn of the eighth day of the eighth month of 1966, the day the tidal wave of collective madness washed over Luding, leaving nothing but upheaval and human misery in its wake.

# *Chapter Nineteen*

## Hong Bayue: Full of Sound and Fury, Heralding Misery

'Suping! Suping! Wake up! Wake up!'

Her sleep-muddled brain vaguely registered her mother's voice and the tugs at her shoulders. Yawning and stretching she mumbled, 'What's the matter? I'm not hungry. Lemme sleep, please.'

'You *must* get up!' her mother's voice urged whisperingly in her ear. 'We are all up already. Father, Gao Chen and Ai Chen are in the front room, waiting for you and me. We have visitors from downtown, six people. One of them I know quite well, he's the Party secretary of my school. They marched straight into our house and sat down on the couch and the chairs without waiting for Father's invitation to sit down. One of them is a woman. I've seen her somewhere, Suping. Only I can't remember where or on what occasion. She is the one who does the talking though, barking rather. The five men haven't said a word yet. They merely look around as if they are taking inventory and they spit on the ground all the time.

'Gao Chen is working himself into a rage, I can see that. Get dressed quickly, Suping, and join us in the front room before Gao Chen says or does something we'll all live to regret. I must go back to them now before those bumpkins get even more impatient.'

Without further ado Suping got out of bed, washed her face quickly with the cold water in the basin on the dressing table, rubbed her teeth with a forefinger, gargled and rinsed her mouth, combed her long, glossy hair to fall over her right shoulder and put on her raw silk blouse and comfortable slacks.

After one last look at herself in the mirror above the dressing table and liking what she saw, she entered the living room, closing the bedroom door behind her.

Her greeting smile vanished and a surge of anger at the scene flushed her face. Three young men, sprawling on the couch, looked up at her entrance with defiant, sneering faces. The two men who occupied the chairs, their legs stretched awkwardly in front of them, their hands in their trouser pockets, were looking sullenly at the ceiling.

The young woman sat on the only remaining chair, like some evil, minor goddess, ready to jump on her victim. She stared at Suping with a palpable hatred.

Father, Mother and the two Chens were standing behind the table in varying states of emotional turmoil at the deliberate rudeness of the intruders but still managing to hold their tempers.

'I see that we have here a true nest of decadent so-called intellectuals,' the woman hissed, her upper lip pulled up in a sneer that showed her clenched teeth, which were surprisingly even and white for such an otherwise coarse person, Suping thought inconsequentially.

'It's ten o'clock in the morning and there they are, still in their nests while the true proletarians have already been toiling in the fields and factories for hours. We'll let these cows have a taste of the true proletarian life.'

Suddenly she jumped up from the chair and, waving the Little Red Book with Mao's quotations, she shouted, 'Long live the Great Proletarian Cultural Revolution! Long live our Great Leader Chairman Mao!'

The five men, caught off guard by the woman's sudden fervour, scrambled to their feet and frantically searched their pockets for their copy of the little book.

Having found it, they excitedly waved them at the flabbergasted Xus and Chens and shouted, comically pell-mell, 'Long live our Great Leader Chairman Mao!'

Suping burst out laughing at the comic sight of six adults shouting slogans at the top of their voices while waving a ridiculously little book under the noses of four bemused though indignant other adults.

Xu Ximing cast a stern look at his daughter and said, addressing himself to the young woman, 'My daughter appears to be amused. However, I fail to see the humour of this situation and, as the head of this household, I demand to know by what authority you can walk into my house without announcing or introducing yourselves and then add insult to injury by calling us *decadent cows*. Speak up, woman!'

Xu narrowed his eyes and looked closer at the speechless woman who in turn stared at him, open-mouthed.

'I somehow seem to remember you,' Xu continued. 'Didn't you fail the entrance examination at my school some five or six years ago and didn't you then shout at me that you would get me for that because *my* note for your mathematics test was the reason you failed?'

The woman, her face now distorted with rage and hatred, yelled at Xu, 'You haven't forgotten, eh, you pig? Neither have I! We have been sent here, to what you mistakenly call *your* house, by the committee in charge of carrying out the Great Proletarian Cultural Revolution in Luding and in Dada County and I especially.volunteered to reform and re-educate *you*, Xu, you and your cows, Liu Guixian and Suping!'

Calmed down somewhat, she added, indicating the two older men in the chairs, 'These two comrades are from Chongqing. They will guide the revolution here in Chairman Mao's spirit. Despite their status as our leaders they have come today, with us, to this house because they used to know the counter-revolutionaries, Chen Dan and Chen Juntao, who you have been hiding under your roof, Xu, enabling them, with your connivance, to continue to plot against the Party and the proletariat as they have done their whole life. The three young comrades are members of the Luding Labour Union. Satisfied, Xu?' she asked him sneeringly. 'Because it's the last time you will be asked for your opinion. When I will be through with you, the only opinion you'll have is the one of the proletariat or else you will be dead.'

Xu Ximing seemed to grow ten feet tall as he straightened to his full length, his right arm stretched, forefinger pointing at the front door, and he thundered, 'Out! You scum! Out! Out! Out!' And with his left hand he grabbed the woman by her neck and pushed her towards the door.

She stumbled forward and Xu, overtaking her, opened the door wide and shoved her out into the front garden.

'All of you! get out!' he shouted, his voice leaping an octave in hot temper.

Like meek sheep the five men stumbled out after the woman, utter bafflement on their faces at this totally unexpected turn of events. Xu slammed the door shut and turned, heaving, to look at his wife and daughter and his two friends who all stared back at him in complete surprise.

'I got carried away somewhat, I'm afraid,' he said shyly. 'I'm sorry if I shocked you. It won't do us much good, I'm afraid. But then, on the other hand, it can't get much worse that what that woman has in store for us. So what the hell!' and he laughed heartily.

His wife and daughter had never heard him laugh like that before and they rushed past the two flabbergasted Chens and embraced and kissed him.

'Father, we are so proud of you!' they exclaimed in unison. 'How you scared them! They scurried off like a pack of scavenger dogs. Oh, it was wonderful!'

The Chens, recovered from their surprise, laughingly slapped Xu on his back and said they had enjoyed themselves immensely.

Xu was the first to get back to reality.

'What now?' he asked, a bit anxiously, more like the man they used to know. 'I'm afraid they'll be back in force and in no time, perhaps even with the militia or, worse, with a swarm of those horrible Red Guards. What shall we do?'

Before anyone could answer there sounded a hurried ruffle of knocks on the front door.

Startled they looked at one another and Guixian nodded at her daughter to open the door.

The man stood with his back against the door, looking down the path towards the town, however, he turned around when he felt the door being opened behind him. They recognised one of the 'two comrades from Chongqing'.

'May I come in for a moment?' he asked in a polite and cultured tone.

Suping motioned him to come in and then closed the door behind her, leaning with her back against it.

The man, looking at Xu, said, 'I wish to apologise for the unforgivably rude behaviour of the company I was in a few minutes ago. We got the treatment we deserved. I am speaking only on my own behalf though since I am afraid that my *comrades* don't share my view.'

The mocking irony in his voice when he said the word 'comrades' was unmistakable.

'I am also afraid,' the man continued, 'that the powers that be, for the moment and for a long, long time to come, also have a different opinion about what constitutes good manners, if they know at all what that word means. However, to the point. You must be Professor Chen Dan.' He looked at Gao Chen.

Without waiting for confirmation, the man continued, 'We haven't got much time so let me do the talking and don't ask questions unless absolutely necessary. I am very close to Liu Longfei and his wife Liang Ailing who you know so well, Chen. They managed to have me posted in Chongqing four months ago, both to keep me out of Jiang Qing's way, who doesn't like me, and to keep an eye on you to try and limit the inevitable damage to you and your friends during the coming upheaval. Professor Xu's show a few moments ago makes it imperative to keep all of you out of Comrade Qian Weiying's claws. She can drink your blood, Xu.

'I shall use my authority as the comrade leader from the big city committee of Chongqing and declare your reform and re-education outside the competence of the local committee. I don't think that Chongqing is a good alternative though. Our two learned friends here have not exactly endeared themselves to the Communist authorities there during their tenure at the university. So I think that I shall have you deported to Chengdu and ask Chengdu's committee of the Great Proletarian Cultural Revolution to take responsibility for your re-education. The committee chairman is related to an important member of the Politburo and, though a tough Communist, he has a certain wry sense of humour, not too refined perhaps but sure enough for a Communist. You will be out of my reach there, but I'll let Liu Longfei know where you are.

'Perhaps there is someone else to keep track of you. Don't count on it though and, above all, do not expect miracles. Even the most powerful and for the time being still unsuspected comrade of the first hour will be too preoccupied with watching his own steps to care much about small fry like you. Chairman Mao and Jiang Qing, that female hyena, have dug up the old slogan of the 1957 Anti-Rightist Campaign and you, intellectuals of bourgeois origin, are once again called "cow's demon and snake spirit", the evil spirits disguised as humans. Hence Comrade Qian's earlier allusion to you as *cows*.

'Now to the point. I am a member of the People's Tribunal of Luding and I shall try to use my influence with the other members to get you off with a relatively light sentence, to be served in Sichuan, probably in one of the smaller communes that fall under the jurisdiction of Chengdu. Until you are summoned to appear before the People's Tribunal do not go into town. Stay in or near your house. If those loony Red Guards get their claws in you there is nothing I can do for you then; *meiyou futse*. Hide whatever you can't or won't destroy but hide it well! The rest you destroy. It's that simple. Any questions?' He looked in turn at each of them.

'What's your precious name, friend?' Gao Chen asked.

'That's not important,' the man from Chongqing replied. 'However, you may refer to me and call me Li. Not Comrade Li or Leader Li. Just Li. However, do *not* forget: knowing Li, or Liu, or Deng, or even Mao may get you out of trouble today but land you in trouble tomorrow. Fortunes wax and wane very quickly these days, there is simply no way of knowing whether the one in favour today will still be tomorrow, let alone next week. So keep quiet and keep a low profile. There will be more than enough crazy accusations levelled against you as it is – don't advertise opinions or say things that may be used against you. You will find out soon enough that they distort anything you say to suit their purpose and when I say *anything* I mean that literally, so watch every word you say.

'One last warning.

'Courtesy and politeness have been abolished. The concepts have been declared bourgeois and therefore unproletarian. The very words of polite social intercourse are now being purged from our language and therefore using them immediately betrays your bourgeois origin and you will be condemned as an enemy of the People. So heed my words, Professor!' and with a mocking bow in Xu's direction Li opened the door and was gone.

In the sudden silence that followed Li's departure the Xus and the Chens stared at one another, dumbfounded and flabbergasted by the strange turn of events.

'Well, well, well,' Gao Chen said, chuckling, 'we now know at least that Longfei's Plan seems to be working. 'A bit scary though,' he added thoughtfully, 'to find out that you have been watched all this time and that the debris of your blunders has been cleared from your path and all that unbeknownst to yourself. It suits us now, but I'm not so sure I would want to live that way my whole life. Now back to the sordid reality of today,' he added briskly.

'Let's dispense with sentimentality and get our act together. We have today and perhaps, if we're lucky, tomorrow morning to get ready, provided our friend Li has no other cats to whip or gets whipped himself when he gets back to town. So let's try to finish our business here by tonight. We need a simple plan, simple to carry out. Any suggestions?'

'I propose that you tell us what to do, Lao Dan,' Guixian said. 'We have no experience with these kind of emergencies and would most probably waste our time on trivialities and impractical ideas. What do you say?' Questioningly she looked at her husband and daughter.

Xu nodded and said, 'You are so right, Guixian. I wouldn't know where and with what to start'.

Ai Chen said gloomily, 'I have nothing that wouldn't fit into a pocket with a hole in it, but I shall of course be glad to help. Unless Dan thinks I'll be in your way,' he added ruefully.

Suping merely nodded. She felt lethargic and knew that without Gao Chen's prodding she would probably just sit there for hours, mulling over alternatives while, in the end, she would have no energy left to do anything whatsoever.

Gao Chen, watching her out of the corner of his eyes, recognised the symptoms and he knew that he had to shake her out of her apathy quickly or else she would become indifferent and tiresomely argumentative, wasting everybody's precious time.

'First of all let's deal with the money problem,' he said. 'Too much of it and you'll behave in a circumspect way and your fellow renegades will either rob you and probably kill you in the process or denounce you to earn merit and then the guards will confiscate everything and brandish you an inveterate capitalist. Too little is also inconvenient since a bit of fragrant oil can get you a small favour now and then from a guard. So let's put on the table all the money we have and divide it in five equal parts.

'Suping will cut from the grey curtains in her bedroom five strips of fifteen centimetres wide and sew them double to make five belts, one for each of us. Make them long enough so that we can knot them over our belly, purportedly to keep our trousers up. Suping and Guixian will also wear trousers; skirts or dresses will be too inconvenient in the kind of company and situations they'll find themselves. In each belt Suping will stuff one part of the money in such a way that they don't look bulky. Put also a good length of sewing thread and a needle inside each belt and then stitch them closed. Whenever you need some money, go to the toilet, or in bed at night, unravel the stitches, take what you need and sew it closed again. Is this clear so far?'

They nodded in unison and Gao Chen saw with satisfaction that Suping grinningly made the mock gesture of encircling his waist as if measuring the length of the belt for him.

He gave her a wink and continued his instructions. 'Secondly we must decide what we'll take with us. Have no illusions though. The guards will confiscate everything which in their eyes is superfluous or unnecessary and they'll abuse us, verbally or even physically, for remaining attached to our possessions. Besides, the more things we drag along with us, the more we'll worry about losing them. I propose therefore that we take with us only a few spare pieces of clothing and some toiletries, though even that may earn us scorn and abuse. Cleanliness is also unproletarian, though Li forgot to mention that.

'Books are out of the question. Only one book suffices in China these days and that's Mao's collection of recipes for disaster. Be assured they'll give us the red booklet first thing as part of our re-education plan. They'll expect you to study it whenever you have a free moment and to recite from it at the oddest moments. Let's also each take a few pencils, an eraser, a small notebook and the smallest knife we can find lest they accuse us of plotting to assassinate the Great Leader.

'Suping will make five simple little bags from the other curtains. Sew a strip of material on each side of the bag, Suping, so that we can tie the bag to our belly or back, under our shirt or blouse. That way we have our hands free for pushing and shoving during the distribution of food or to get a good place on the lorry or train during the kind of cattle transport that'll be our lot the coming days, or weeks or even months. When we're allowed to sleep we can untie the bag and use it as a headrest so that we'll wake up when our fellow prisoners try to steal it. Finally we'll make a few more and bigger bags for certain books any of us wants to keep, for later. Juntao will rub these bags on the outside with a mixture of cooking oil and ash to make them a bit waterproof and vermin resistant.

'Tonight, after dark, Ximing and Suping will hide those bags inside the hollow walnut tree where I put Yang's notes yesterday evening. There's still a lot of room. Juntao will burn the rest of the books and papers in the stove while Guixian prepares all the food she can and we'll eat until we're completely stuffed. That way at least we won't go hungry the first couple of days. I'm afraid that feeding us won't be the guards' first priority. Any questions? No questions! So get moving!'

The others got up wearily and awkwardly tried to adopt an attitude of purposefulness, frightened as they were, in spite of Gao Chen's skilfully played casualness, by the finality of what they were about to do.

It was indeed one thing to discuss such matters in the safety of your home, Suping thought, and in the company of equally verbose friends, however, it was quite another matter to cut the links with your past for good and to prepare yourself for a future full of unknown terrors, each act as final as it seemed pathetically inadequate.

With a heavy heart and without the usual banter they went about their assigned tasks and it was past eight in the evening when they finally sat together around the dining table.

Guixian had done her best to cook one good last meal from the rests of the Beggars Chicken and all the rice that was left over while Ai Chen, slowly and morosely, fed the fire in the stove with the books Suping had hidden under her bed more than a year ago, on the day he and Gao Chen had blundered into the life of the Xus.

If it hadn't been so sad, Guixian would have burst out laughing at Ai Chen's gloomy face as he leafed through the various books, reading a passage here and there, before tearing them up and slowly feeding them into the fire with heart-rending sighs.

None of them had much appetite though and they merely toyed with their chopsticks and dawdled over the food with gloomy faces.

'I don't think that this doom-and-gloom attitude will do us much good,' Gao Chen said suddenly, breaking the mournful silence. 'We have seen nothing yet and our adversaries have already beaten us before the real fight begins. This is not what I expected after all our discussions and analyses and action plans of the last few months. It's unworthy of us, don't you think so?

'Do you know what the peasants say about those they call the scholars? That is, about people like us, who can read and write and like to act the pompous erudite? That they are nothing but vain cowards, without merit or mettle, forever busy devising plans, each more grandiose and impractical than the rest. Would we be true to that scholar stereotype? Can't we do better than that and show that rabble, aroused by a few deranged minds in Beijing, that we *do* have mettle? Therefore, Ximing, if there is anything left in those bottles of *maotai* and wine let's drink to ourselves and to hell with the loonies!'

They laughed, a bit glumly at first but quickly they shed their gloom and laughed until the tears ran down their cheeks. Merriment? Despair? Who knows but the clowns themselves. They joked and ate every last morsel of meat and grain of rice and drank everything pell-mell until all the bottles were empty. They laughed and laughed and finally stumbled to their beds, still making fun of themselves and of the Great Jester in faraway Beijing until they fell asleep.

Suping dreamed that Jiang Qing was washing the dishes while Gao Chen, in red and blue underpants, was quoting from Mao's little booklet.

Suping woke early the next morning, a bit light-headed because of the alcohol she drank the evening before but otherwise feeling all right.

Her parents' bed was empty so they must have got up before her. She wrinkled her nose when she saw she was still wearing the clothes of the evening before. Quickly she splashed cold water on her face from the basin on the dressing table and groped for the small towel that hung on a nail in the side of the table.

Still combing her hair she went outside where she found her parents and the two Chens in the front garden, apparently enjoying the coolness of the morning air and the magnificent display of shifting red and pink colours on the mountain peaks by the rising yet still invisible sun.

'Good morning, daughter,' Xu said, smilingly, 'we have been sitting here since five o'clock to seek peace and rest for our troubled hearts. Come and join us for a while; it may well be our last time together for a long, long time. You may also get some comfort and inspiration, as we did, from the immutability and predictability of nature's course.'

Hesitatingly and embarrassed by the intimacy of his gesture he took Suping's hand and, pointing at the mountains, he continued, 'See how the light conquers darkness, Suping, how it floods down the mountains in fireworks of red, pink and yellow hues, chasing the night out of every crook and cranny and the fear of darkness out of every heart and soul, man and beast's alike. Listen, Suping, how the birds greet the return of the sun and its light and warmth for yet another of the countless numbers of days yet to come. So immutable and so reassuringly predictable, day after night after day after night, until the end of time.

'Nobody can change that, not even the gods or those who like to think of themselves as gods. How powerless we, and they, are in this natural sequence of events. Yet how much better off *we* are when this very powerlessness comforts and reassures *us*, while it enrages the loonies in Beijing in their anarchistic craze. *We* smile, content in our insignificance, while *they* dementedly rage and scream against their own futility until they collapse and die of sheer exhaustion. Behind their rage and hatred for everything they can't destroy looms the despair at their own insignificance and incompetence in the face of the ultimate imperturbability of nature's complete indifference.

'Throughout the history of man there have been the likes of Mao Zedong and Jiang Qing and their crazy followers, idiots full of sound and fury, signifying nothing, to quote, with some liberty, a great Western poet. How lucky we are that we understand and accept this so that their sound and fury run off our backs like water off a duck's.'

Xu fell silent and then he laughed, good-humouredly and relaxed.

'Straw dogs, we are all sacrificial straw dogs, to quote our own incomparable sage Lao Zi,' he added, with evident satisfaction. 'Only the fools, who for the moment seem to call the shots, don't know that, the sods.'

Gao Chen looked at Xu with obvious affection.

'Our situation in a nutshell, Ximing,' he said, 'and a timely reminder to mind our own business, as Lao Zi did, for if I am not mistaken, there they come, the little revolutionary generals,' he added mockingly.

The others heard it also, the jabber of excited voices carried uphill by the still morning air, faint and distant but rapidly increasing in volume and clearly heading their way.

'Good luck, my friends,' Ximing said, resignedly, 'remember, in five years or less, when we'll meet again, here, in this garden, the mountains will still be there and the sun will again warm our hearts. Now, let's go inside and let events take their course.'

Without further ado they went inside and Suping, being last, closed the door behind her.

While they were still arranging and tying their money belts and belly bags, there was a furious pounding of many fists on the front door and near-hysterical voices yelled, 'Open the door! Open the door, you lazy cows!' while still others shouted slogans.

A big stone shattered the glass of the living room window and bounced on the floor close to where Suping was standing. Some of the gang outside had just begun to kick against the door when Xu, outwardly calm, opened the door.

He was roughly pushed aside as the door was slammed against the wall and about two dozen dishevelled and wild-eyed boys and girls, aged between fifteen and twenty, stampeded inside, pushing and being pushed, the first three or four stumbling and almost falling on their faces as Xu had opened the door quite suddenly.

It was a comical sight and Suping couldn't help laughing. It was all so silly, so asinine, so undignified, she thought. Two men, considerably older, and the woman Qian Weiying, she incessantly gliding a whip through her left hand, came in last.

They all wore the armbands of the Red Guards.

Qian, eyes angry, hit the table top with her whip in a whizzing cracking blow and screamed in Suping's face, 'Why are you laughing, cow? We are here in the name of our Great Leader Chairman Mao to take revolutionary action against you and you laugh? *Bow your head in submission*!' Turning suddenly towards Xu, his wife and the Chens she screamed hysterically, '*Bow your heads, all of you bow your heads or I'll make you suffer here already before we drag you in front of the People's Tribunal*!'

Panting she stood there, eyes blazing, spit dribbling from the corners of her mouth and down her chin.

One of the older men, dressed in the coarse, lustreless dark blue of the peasant, took Suping and Guixian by the elbow and said, in a surprisingly mild voice, 'You and your men, go outside while we search the house for counter-revolutionary propaganda material,' and he gently but firmly pushed them out of the door, followed by Xu and the Chens.

'Stay here,' he said, 'don't interfere, don't try to escape. You can't go anywhere and you can't do anything about whatever will happen to you from now on.' Smiling a bit derisively he added, 'When Comrade Qian is around you had better bow your heads. She is vicious and mean. Don't provoke her!'

Looking over his shoulder at the half-open door, he added quickly, 'My daughter was a pupil of yours, Madam Xu, and she always spoke fondly of you. I am a member of the People's Tribunal that will judge you and your family and friends.'

Without another word he turned around and went back inside the house.

For over half an hour they stood there, silently, in the garden, listening to the sounds of glass and pottery breaking, of fabric being torn and ripped, of wood cracking and splintering, of heavy feet stamping and thudding, of angry voices yelling and screaming in frustration and dispute.

Xu smiled at his wife's despairing and frightened face and said, 'As long as it is not our flesh and bones being torn and broken, my love, I think we can live with a few broken pieces of pottery, can't we? Let them exhaust their fury and smash everything inside. People may not be so easily tempted to move into our house and we'll have a better chance of finding it unoccupied when we return here. In fact, those loonies may well be doing us a favour.'

His wife laughed through her tears at him. 'I am so proud of you,' she said, 'you are so wonderfully brave and relaxed. At least I know that I need not worry about you.'

'If ever I misjudged a person it was you, Ximing,' Gao Chen said, looking at Xu as if he couldn't believe his ears.

'I thought that I was the poised, worldly man, but whereas my self-possession was cultivated, yours comes naturally. Juntao once prophesied that I would meet my master when I would least expect it and the person I would least expect that to be. He was right. I met him. He also said then that if *he* were to meet that other person, and a friend at that, my spell over him would be broken as well. I can see in his eyes that he remembers and that already he sees me with different eyes, sparkling eyes. We have now become friends, true friends, none depending on the other and that includes you Xu, you Guixian and you Suping. Each of us can take care of himself and herself.

'We no longer need the symbolism of ever-present mountains, of cosy garden settings, of ploughing peasants in the rice fields or whatever fetish we did cultivate in our hearts and minds in the past. Of course we will try to see each other again, as we said we would, but the urgency has gone. The very idea, religious belief almost, that that was the only thing that mattered to keep us alive and sane has suddenly lost its ominous overtones of fate.

'What a relief it is to be free to act from now on, in whatever circumstance one finds oneself, in one's own interest, without the burden of worry about others, or of despair about a promise that cannot be kept lest one hurts oneself or somebody else who in the meantime has become close and dear and is in greater need of one's presence. Ximing, you have shown us how to be free people.'

Without the usual quaver in his voice Ai Chen said quietly, 'I thank you for everything you have done for me, Dan, my friend, including that last little push. My awe for you prevented me from seeing my own potential as an individual. I see that now and also that I have to thank Ximing for that. I admire and love all of you, but no longer at the exclusion of my own pride and dignity. Do not worry about me. I have nothing to lose but the dignity I just found and it's too precious a feeling already to let those lunatics take it away from me. I'll manage and, believe me, I am actually looking forward to getting the better of them,' and Ai Chen laughed, a carefree laugh that lit up his whole face.

He's actually quite attractive, Suping thought, surprised.

'You are a different person entirely when you laugh like that, Uncle Juntao,' she said, using for the first time and quite unconsciously the address of respect and endearment. 'However, keep your usual lugubrious expression to hide behind. It's the perfect disguise of somebody already beaten by fate.'

Ai Chen laughed heartily. 'You are right, Suping, my dear,' he said. 'It may very well fool those loonies, just as it fooled myself, and all of you for that matter, all these years. Dan, my dearest friend, just when I have found myself I am about to lose you. How ironic, or would it be your good fate? You have always been the leading clown in the Chen-and-Chen act, so sharing the public's applause might have been too difficult for you.'

Smiling affectionately at his friend, he added, a bit emotionally nevertheless, 'I am only teasing you, Dan. You have been and will always remain the single most important person in my life and my vocabulary is inadequate to tell you how grateful I am to you for having taken care of me all these years. Thanks to you I have been accepted by Ximing, Guixian and Suping and I have become their trusted friend as well. If it needed a Great Proletarian Cultural Revolution to bring this about then at least there is one person in China who gained by it.'

They smiled and affectionately shook hands all around and the men slapped each other's shoulders while Mother and Suping hugged.

They were brutally brought back to reality by a sudden fracas from the house as the front door was kicked from its hinges and four or five youths rushed out in front of an hysterically triumphant Qian who was frantically waving a sheaf of papers.

'Reactionaries! Traitors! Class enemies!' she raved. 'We have found proof of your betrayal of our true socialist State and our Great Leader Chairman Mao!' Wide-eyed, in malevolent exultation she shook the papers in her victims' faces, actually slapping Suping's.

'Tonight you will stand trial and be condemned to death for *treason*!' she screamed, spit and foam in the corners of her mouth. 'That will take the smirk off your faces,' she exulted and sneeringly she ordered, 'bow your head and put your hands on your neck!'

Suddenly calmed down, Qian added in a normal tone, 'Comrade Zhang will march you off to the Detention House. I'll stay here to search for more proof of subversion and counter-revolutionary activities.'

Comrade Zhang turned out to be the elderly peasant and his face was grave as he said, 'Do as Comrade Qian says. Bow your head, clasp your hands on your neck and walk in front of me to the road and downhill into town and to the Detention House. You are not allowed to talk amongst you. You may only talk when a Red Guard orders you to and then only to confess your crime. Confession means that you admit being guilty of the crime you are accused of and you may be given the opportunity to repent and be reformed through working and living with the peasants. If you remain silent you also admit being guilty but unrepentant and in your case that means the death sentence for treason.'

He was interrupted by a furious Qian.

'You talk too much to these traitorous cows and snakes, Zhang!' she shouted angrily. 'If you are not more careful I will accuse you of conniving with these criminals against the Party and our Great Leader. Remember what happened to the other connivers I exposed, Zhang!' she added ominously.

Zhang, flushed with anger, replied bitingly, 'Don't you threaten me, Qian! I need not prove my status as a red element, unlike *you*! You are but an intellectual *manqué*. I shall have you disciplined, Qian!'

Seeing the indecisive and furtive glances of the other Red Guards, Zhang immediately seized the initiative and, stretching his hand out in a peremptory manner, he said loudly, 'Give me those papers, Qian! As a member of the People's Tribunal I need them to prepare the case against these people. We have all heard your accusations based on your perfunctory reading of those papers. Should they appear to be groundless I'll have *you* standing trial for confusing the People's minds with the aim to deceive for personal gain of power and for self-glorification at the expense of our Chairman who is the sole person to decide in such very serious matters.'

Deadly pale and trembling with barely concealed fear Qian handed the papers to Zhang, thereby irrevocably losing face with the other Red Guards.

Zhang, putting the sheaf of papers in the pocket of his jacket, addressed a Red Guard, a gangling youth of about twenty years old, and ordered, 'Put the door back on its hinges and order those vandals inside to stop breaking things. Make a Big Character Poster from one of the white bed sheets and write "Bourgeois Intellectuals" on it with the red paint you must have brought with you. Then nail the sheet against the front of the house before you return to the Detention House. There you wait until you and your group will be called as witnesses in this important case against the bourgeois intellectuals.

'You are now the leader of this group, Du! Behave as one and you will be given other important tasks in the service of our Glorious Leader Chairman Mao who will not fail to notice the orderly way we fulfil our revolutionary duties in Luding.'

The youth beamed with pride and with a triumphant smirk at the snubbed and deflated Qian, he shouted, 'Yes Comrade Leader Zhang! We will do as you order and I will report to you shortly at the Detention House!'

The much subdued Red Guards trooped back into the house, Qian the last to enter and already ignored by the others.

Zhang, turning back to his prisoners, said, not unkindly, 'Take your hands from your neck and start walking normally. The bowed heads can come later, if and when you are found guilty.'

'Thank you, Leader Zhang,' Gao Chen said, 'allow me to bow my head though, in respect for your fairness and dignity. I am afraid you made yourself a nasty enemy on our behalf.'

Zhang snorted, shrugged his shoulders and said tersely, 'Not all peasants are morons, Chen, as you of all people should know, so don't bow your head but rather show respect by your general attitude. Furthermore, if I made an enemy in Comrade Qian it was not on your behalf but on my own. Whether this Great Proletarian Cultural Revolution is necessary is not for me to judge, however, as long as I have a role to play, in my own insignificantly small way, I will not be manipulated for personal gain or vengeance by some vindictive manipulator of a gang of snotty noses yelling all kinds of crazy accusations against completely normal and ordinary people.

'However, do *not* misunderstand me, Chen. If you and your friends are indeed proven to be guilty of treason or sedition, as Qian appears to have concluded already, then you will get the mandatory sentence for that. Our present leaders affirm that a general cleansing of our society is necessary, so dust and now and then some really big pieces of dirt *must* be found to prove them right. Normally people like you make for excellent dust and it doesn't really matter what silly crime you are accused of and whether you confess and repent or not. You are guilty because it is required that you are and because you are foreordained anyway.

'This, however, is true for what I call the silly crimes. Treason is a completely different matter entirely though, which I shall not take lightly, neither the accusation nor the defence. So, if treason does not apply in your case, my advice to you is: confess, repent and accept the sentence without protest. Your punishment will be the same anyway, that of re-education and reforms through labouring with the peasants in the communes. Protesting your innocence is futile and makes matters only worse for you, in every respect: longer and more degrading sessions in the tribunal because your protests irritate the judges, long and more severe sentences, possibly even hard labour in real hardship places like Xinjiang or Gansu or Shanxi, for your effrontery in challenging the judgement of the People and so on.

'I do hope, for you that is, that you understand what I try to say with so many words. What I also hope is that you can explain these papers which would seem to make you into those occasional big pieces of dirt I spoke of earlier. I wouldn't like Qian to be right after all, also for my own sake. What are these papers about anyway? Would you care to answer me now? Madam Xu perhaps?'

Zhang had talked all the way downhill as he walked beside Guixian and Suping and behind Xu and the Chens.

While they were crossing the bridge into town Guixian answered his question.

'They are nothing but our draft papers for *The Revised History of the People's Republic of China* I was ordered to work on by Party Secretary Guo and my headmaster Yang,' she said. 'It was to be part of a nationwide compilation for the Ministry of Education. My husband Ximing and my daughter Suping assisted me in the arduous task by writing out all the names of people and places and the dates of the events.'

Zhang laughed mirthlessly and said, 'The minister of education, Xia Ziyun, is in jail, or perhaps dead already, for opposing Jiang Qing's order to burn down the Beijing Municipal Library; Secretary Guo has been removed from his position and sent back to his province in the north somewhere because of various errors of judgement committed by him and Yang leapt to his death last night from the third floor of your former school, Madam Xu. Master Yang was abused and beaten by Qian Weiying and her gang. They took turns for two days and one night and Lao Yang was not allowed to sleep or to eat and drink, not even to sit down.

'When Qian finally wanted to force a dunce cap over his head and make him run like that through all the streets of the town, Lao Yang apparently jumped off the dais in front of the classroom and straight through the window. He broke his back but bled to death; a shard of glass had pierced the artery in his groin. The crime they wanted the old man to confess to was connivance with the traitor Xia Ziyun in opposing the will of the People by whitewashing the crimes of feudal class enemies. That is what Qian meant she had in store for me when she threatened me a while ago in your house.'

Zhang fell silent and grinned sardonically at Guixian's horrified expression.

'Reputations and positions wax and wane rapidly these days,' he continued thoughtfully, 'sometimes even overnight and I am afraid that many of the adjectives you were ordered to use for our past and present national figures no longer apply. When Qian scrutinises those papers and she finds even one wrong adjective or epitaph attached to the wrong name, she will accuse you of plotting against the State by smearing the name of a meritorious revolutionary, even if he has been dead for over two thousand years, which makes you indeed theoretically guilty of treason.'

Looking quickly up and down the street, he motioned them to follow him into a narrow, dark lane.

'I see from the expression on your faces that you have got the point of what I mean,' he continued in a hushed tone.

'We must be pragmatic and not let a pretence of delicacy and sense of honour towards the dead and the disgraced prevent us from doing what is best for ourselves, that is, *you* must get yourselves out of a quagmire and I must get rid of Comrade Qian. We haven't got much time because we must get to the Detention House before Qian does so listen carefully and don't interrupt me.'

He looked over his shoulder to the lane's exit into the main street and, satisfied that nobody seemed to have noticed them, he bent his head close to the others' and continued in a half-whisper. 'At the start of the session you must ask the court's permission to make a statement. I shall then grant you five minutes to explain your position. Madam Xu must then complain, in a suitable mixture of indignation and mortification, how she has been misled and deceived by Minister Xia Ziyun, Secretary Guo Chuanxing and Yang Wenzhong when they ordered you to write a revised history of our beloved socialist motherland and how guilty you feel towards our Great Leader

Chairman Mao of having been so gullible to believe that something of such importance could be ordered by anybody but himself.

'The court knows, or else I'll point this out, that you cannot possibly know that Xia has been arrested for treason, that Guo has been demoted and transferred and that Yang has killed himself. I shall apprise you of these facts in my sternest voice. You will then react with intense relief and joy and you will praise our Great Leader Chairman Mao for his wisdom and you will repeatedly state how grateful you are that the criminals have been exposed so quickly and before they could do even more damage. Finally you will lament once more your own gullibility and humbly request the People's Tribunal to punish you for your neglect. I shall thereupon propose to the other judges to allow you to publicly repent and criticise your political immaturity. I shall recommend that you be sent for reform and re-education to the people's commune of Taihezhen which is not far from Chengdu, together with your accomplices.

'That will be the best thing that can happen to you under the circumstances. There will be a transport to Chengdu the day after tomorrow and I shall try to get you on it. That is as far as you are concerned. Now my own case against Qian Weiying. Qian knew about Minister Xia's arrest, about Guo's demotion and about Yang's suicide, of course, since she was the one who pushed the old man to it. Many people, some openly, condemn Qian's excessive behaviour. One of Qian's accusations against Yang was that he had ordered historian Liu Guixian, wife of mathematician Xu Ximing, to rewrite the history of China, a project which is now being condemned as revisionist since it did not have Chairman Mao's prior approval. A very serious crime indeed.

'Now, tell me, how can she, on the one hand, accuse Yang of revisionism by ordering you, Madam Xu, to rewrite the history, thereby implying that you were just following orders from your superior, and, on the other, accuse you of treason, thereby implying that *you* were the initiator of the project and a member of the revisionist clique? Since Yang can no longer defend himself we'll explain his suicide as a confession of guilt, leaving you, Madam Xu, and your husband and daughter who assisted you occasionally, merely guilty of gullibility and political immaturity for not questioning whether the work was duly authorised.

'Qian, on the contrary, is deliberately distorting the course of proletarian justice with the aim of taking revenge for not having been admitted to the bourgeois intellectual class when she failed her examination before mathematician Xu. Qian thereby not only puts private interest before public interest but also shows contempt for the proletarian class since apparently, for her, belonging to the bourgeois class is something worth striving for. I shall request the judges to declare her unworthy of being a Red Guard, of being called a little revolutionary general in our Great Proletarian Cultural Revolution and to condemn her to re-education and reform by hard labour in Jilin where she intended to send Lao Yang. A nice, poetic justice. Lao Yang was my daughter's godfather, you see, and this way I can at least avenge his unnecessary suffering and death and at the same time get Qian out of my hair. Is this all clear?' Zhang asked, sharply watching the others' faces for signs of incomprehension or hesitation.

A smile hovered on Xu Ximing's lips as he answered, 'It's very clear, Zhang. This political intriguing is all very new to us, however, answering for myself, I must admit that I quite enjoy it. You are an accomplished politician, Zhang, and I hope that you will get far since I think that you are also an intelligent and basically fair man. Now, I think I can also answer for my wife and daughter, as well as for my friends. We shall do as you say and perform our act most convincingly. Avoiding jail or worse, a bullet in the back of our head, is a very forceful incentive.'

Xu fell silent and chuckled.

'I know that you intended to pay me a sincere compliment, Xu, when you called me a fair man,' Zhang answered, smiling sardonically, 'however, let me dissuade you from that illusion. I am a *pragmatic* man who has suffered a worse than fair share of life's bitterer experiences and who now feels that enough is enough. I have higher ambitions than staying here, in this backwater, as a fourth grade Party secretary. First I want Guo Chuanxing's job as a stepping-stone to more rewarding places and positions. People like Qian are a constant danger to my plans, an ever-present threat hanging over me like some dark cloud from which rain or hailstones can fall at any moment and will, of course, at the worst possible time.

'In this instance I see an opportunity to eliminate that danger and I fully intend to seize it. Only I need your co-operation and why should you give that to me if I weren't in a position to help you as well? Self-interest, my friends, self-interest, the strongest incentive as Xu realises so well.'

Zhang grinned, hesitated for a moment and continued. 'Perhaps I talk too much, however, I think I can risk telling you that I have known Li, whom you also know, during the time he was posted in Chongqing and that I sympathise with his views, insofar as they suit my own plans for myself, that is. You are simply lucky that in your case your fate suits my plans and that it happens to be your *good* fate. I wouldn't have acted otherwise had it been your *ill* fate, so don't thank me. You owe me nothing. I owe you nothing. Now, let's get out of this stinking place and quick march to the Detention House. Let's hope Qian isn't there yet.'

Back in the main street Zhang ordered them to clasp their hands on their neck, as a sign that they had been arrested by the Red Guards, and to walk in the middle of the street as the sidewalks were too crowded with curious onlookers and with Red Guards entering and exiting houses and shops while shouting slogans. Many of them were carrying goods expropriated in the name of the proletariat. Taking revolutionary action against defenceless people can be a lucrative business. Besides their small group there were other groups in a similar predicament, hands clasped in their neck and prodded into a half-trot by slogan-yelling Red Guards armed with whips, sticks and the ubiquitous Little Red Book from which they quoted at the oddest moments and at the top of their voices.

Now and then, on some crazy impulse, a Red Guard grasped in the crowd on the sidewalk and pulled some hapless man or woman on the street. Kicking and hitting he then forced the poor creature to join his group of enemies of the People and on they went.

Why? For what reason? Nobody would ever know, probably not even the Red Guard, crazed and drunk with his unchallengeable power of the moment. Nobody cared either besides the victims and least of all the youth for whom the destruction of a human life or the squashing of a bug was all the same, a thoughtless, indifferent and inconsequential act.

Finally the chaotic cattle drive reached the small square in front of the Detention House. Some five hundred people or so were already gathered there, sitting cross-legged, head bowed, hands clasped in the necks, in rows of forty.

Red Guards, strutting between the rows and along the sides, incessantly shouted invectives and orders to sit upright, often accompanied by a lash of the whip or a blow of the stick on the back or shoulders of their hapless victims.

Zhang's small group came to a halt and appalled, the Xus and the Chens stared at the scene and at each other.

'Can't be helped,' Zhang said with a shrug. 'It's part of the show and any preferential treatment will be very counter-productive. So why don't you just close your mind and blend in with your fellow class enemies. You learned how to do that, Chen Dan, long ago, in Danba, from your friend the abbot.

And you, Miss Xu, the *taiqiquan* master, Zhang, my own father to boot, taught you the trick, didn't he?'

He laughed sardonically at their horrified expressions and chuckled, 'Your evening sessions in the garden were good entertainment. My younger brother is your next-door neighbour, Xu, and from the back of his garden, where he dumps and burns his garbage behind the hedge that separates his and your garden, one can hear practically everything that is said on your side, even in your house if you leave the windows open as you often did. At one time, months ago, when I visited my brother I helped him bring the garbage out after dinner and I heard you talking in your garden.

'I couldn't help but overhear what you said Chen about the *us* and *them* clubs and about your friend Shen Lishi in Beijing. You got carried away by your emotion and you talked loudly. What you said, however, was very interesting, illuminating is a better word, for a small, provincial cadre like myself. Ever since that evening I have been sitting there practically every evening following your discussions and stories. My brother wasn't interested. He's a dimwit and hardly understands standard Chinese.

'It was your stories, Chen, that opened my eyes about the Party and its propaganda and it was there, in that garden, that it dawned on me to look after myself first and foremost. Don't worry! I won't betray you. I see no advantage for me, on the contrary rather. I will have to relate what I heard and somebody, always there will be somebody, may insinuate that I may have been contaminated and need re-education and reform. Don't hand your enemies the stick to beat you with, eh Chen? Maybe one day you will prepare another Beggars Chicken and invite me for the feast, Chen? I left my post in the garden early that evening, the smell made me hungry and the tenor of your conversations had deteriorated because of the alcohol. Allow me to say to all of you, however, that you scholars are so arrogant in your naivety. Incredible! The stupidest peasant wouldn't talk about such things like that, openly, without checking whether he could be overheard.'

Zhang fell silent and shook his head, still incredulous.

'Now, don't shake like that, girl!' he added, in a softer tone and he put his hand on Suping's trembling arm. 'Do as Uncle Zhang says and you'll be out of here in no time at all. I shall propose to the other members of the People's Tribunal that your case be heard first. I'm sure Li will agree and support my proposal. Now, you all sit down here, in the last row, near the door of the Detention House. A bit of advice though. When you are called to appear before the Tribunal you will go inside, one after the other, looking suitably guilty and downcast. You will *not*, and I repeat, *you will not* oppose or resist the

Red Guards who will escort you, whatever they say or do to you. Is that absolutely clear?' he asked in a loud and harsh voice, evidently to impress the Red Guards who had begun to show signs of impatience and suspicion at what looked to them like some hushed conference. Though relieved by Zhang's earlier mockingly friendly tone the Xus and the Chens needed no special reminder to look downcast.

How naive and careless they had been these past few months, indeed, how arrogantly naive as Zhang had said.

Avoiding each other's eyes they sat down on the cobblestones and pulled their heels into their crotch to keep their balance. Before clasping her hands in her neck Suping looked up at the dial clock in the front of the Detention House: it was only half past nine and the sun shone already hot in a cloudless, pale blue sky.

Sighing she let her chin fall on her chest and closed her eyes.

As time passed the almost unbearable shooting pain in her buttocks, thighs, arms and shoulders gradually became more like a throbbing, painful numbness as a burning thirst pushed all other feelings into the background of her awareness.

During the first hour she had tried a few times to shift her position to relieve the stinging stabs of pain somewhat but each time the Red Guard behind her row had yelled at her to sit still and had kicked her in her lower back.

The Red Guard, a girl of seventeen something as Suping had observed from the corner of her eyes, fortunately wore green canvas sneakers so her kicks didn't hurt much, however, on the other hand one couldn't hear her walking either so surreptitiously changing position was risky.

Gradually, however, Suping's awareness of things outside her field of vision, already limited by having to look down all the time, diminished and her initial anguish about her parents and the Chens dimmed to a vague wondering how they were coping with the thirst and the cramps and then, suddenly, even that remnant of feeling ceased entirely, like a light bulb already dim, finally giving out.

Her mind, feverish, hallucinating, began to play tricks on her as she saw the rivulets of sweat in the wrinkly, scrawny neck of the old man in the row in front of her swell in size and coalesce into a swollen river, its banks calving great chunks of reddish soil which toppled into the churning and foamy water. The river's reddish-brown waves washed over the bucking raft she was holding on to while a boy with buck teeth and spiky hair and a bearded man desperately manoeuvred with long bamboo poles to keep the raft in the middle of the stream. Opposite her sat a woman on a bench. She had a black, long-necked bird on her lap and softly crooned old folk songs as she stroked the bird's neck and back. Suping noticed that the woman was young and pretty and had unusually long hands. Suddenly the bird began to screech at her, its beak clapping right in front of Suping's face, the breath smelling foul of rotting fish.

The bird's beady eyes became larger and larger, like pools of darkness, and the foul smell made her feel sick. Instinctively, stomach heaving, she pulled her head back which broke the spell and bird's head dissolved into the blurred face of a girl.

Suping vaguely recognised the Red Guard whose face almost touched hers as she was yelling something. Wrinkling her nose at the sour, foul smell and the spittle that flew out of her mouth, Suping tried to focus her eyes and to urge her feverish, sluggish brain back to the present. Slowly the shouted order to stand up broke through her numbed consciousness yet her muscles refused to obey.

The Red Guard pulled and shoved and kicked and finally Suping managed to roll over, on her knees, and she tried to push herself up.

Her bloodless hands and arms weighed a ton. Her lifeless legs buckled in several unsuccessful attempts before she at last got to her feet, groaning because of the piercing bolts of pain in her lower back and the thousands of needles in her fingers and feet.

She saw her parents and the Chens writhing in a similar situation and she grimaced at them, a mocking, painful grin to signal that she could manage.

Five Red Guards came rushing out of the Detention House and began to push and shove the stumbling and staggering Xus and Chens towards the entrance of the ugly grey and squat building. Another Red Guard was shouting through a loud hailer that the daily session of the People's Tribunal of Luding was about to begin at two o'clock and that the first case was that of the Proletariat versus the bourgeois enemies of the People, Xu Ximing, Liu Guixian, Xu Suping, Chen Dan and Chen Juntao, all five of them so-called scholars and guilty of intellectual arrogance and contempt for the People's Republic of China.

Having made this announcement the youth raised his left arm with Mao's Little Red Book and shouted at the top of his voice:

'Long live our Great Leader Chairman Mao! Long live the Great Proletarian Cultural Revolution! Down with the class enemies!'

The Red Guards in the square raised their left arm in unison with the youth with the loud hailer and screamed the same slogans. Behind her back Suping heard the spectators, several hundred men and women, join the chorus, though somewhat belatedly and discordantly. Not exactly overenthusiastic, she thought wryly, as she entered the building behind the Chens and her parents.

A Red Guard stood halfway up the stairs leading to the first floor. To her surprise Suping recognised the kind, elderly woman of the state market who had sold her and Gao Chen the fat chicken only a few days ago.

She smiled at the woman and tried to make eye contact, thinking of the joke and laughter they had shared about Gao Chen's girth.

But the woman's eyes were like those of a dead fish now and surlily she pointed upwards. 'Up! Quick!' she snarled and they stumbled upstairs, incessantly pushed from behind by the Red Guards detailed to bring them to the People's Tribunal in session.

The stairs gave directly on a large hall, lined on three sides by Red Guards, members of the militia and ordinary men and women in dull blue or green baggy trousers and sloppy jackets. At the far end of the hall, opposite the stairs, stood a long trestle-table under a gigantic portrait of a smiling, moon-faced Mao Zedong that hung on the back wall above a red banner with big, white characters that proclaimed:

*LENIENT TREATMENT FOR THOSE WHO CONFESS.*
*SEVERE PUNISHMENT FOR THOSE WHO REMAIN STUBBORN.*
*REWARD FOR THOSE WHO DENOUNCE OTHERS.*

A second red banner was nailed to the table top over its entire length and hanging down to the floor. The big, white characters on this banner proclaimed:

*WHEN THE ENEMIES WITH GUNS ARE ANNIHILATED,*
*THE ENEMIES WITHOUT GUNS STILL REMAIN.*
*WE MUST NOT UNDERESTIMATE THESE ENEMIES.*

Behind the table sat five men and four women, all dressed in the ubiquitous dull, dark blue, sloppy jackets which they had buttoned up to the throat in spite of the heat in the hall.

The nine judges were staring surlily at the stumbling group of people now approaching the bench, immobile but for the slow to and fro movement of their left hand fanning their face with a piece of cardboard.

The movement was, by chance, perfectly in cadence and the effect was so comical that Suping felt an almost irresistible urge to laugh loudly. Fortunately she managed to control herself just in time.

To her relief she saw that Qian Weiying was not amongst the Red Guards and that Zhang and the man she knew as Li were flanking a man sitting in the middle of the group of nine judges. This man, a caricature of the typical Chinese peasant, was apparently the presiding judge of the People's Tribunal of Luding. His unkempt, lustreless, spiky grey-black hair topped a bony, irregular head with a dark brown, grimy, leathery skin and flap ears.

His eyelids drooped over slightly bulging, mud-brown eyes and his mouth hung slackly open showing irregular, tobacco-stained buck teeth. A tiny trickle of brownish spit ran from the left corner of his mouth to form an increasingly heavy drop at the point of his stubbly chin, which he wiped off with the back of his right hand, mechanically and unconsciously, just when it was about to fall.

They have whisked him from behind his ox and plough and told him to sit behind this bench, Suping thought. The man has no idea what he is doing here and what is going on. They probably told him that he is an important man, a true representative of the proletariat, and that he has been appointed chief judge of the People's Tribunal and that all he has to do is to say the word 'guilty' each time the men on either side of him prod him with their elbow.

I wonder how long it took him to learn how to pronounce the word correctly in Putonghua, she thought contemptuously.

She noticed how Zhang, sitting at the chief judge's left, nudged him with his right elbow to wake him up from his worried misgivings, about his wife probably, who was neglecting her homework what with all those commune meetings these days.

When they had approached the judges' bench and were about three metres away, the prisoners were roughly lined up by the stick-wielding Red Guards to face the judges.

'*Kneel down*!' the leading Red Guard shouted and simultaneously the other guards hit them with the stick in the hollow of their knees, which made them buckle and, pushed down by their shoulders, they fell on their knees on to the bare concrete floor.

'Hands on your back and keep your head down when answering questions from the judges!' he shouted.

Suping had recognised him as the gangling youth who had been promoted that morning by Zhang to take over from that tempestuous woman Qian Weiying. The youth had apparently lost no time in asserting himself in his new capacity which was additional proof that Qian had not been able to regain control and that Zhang had had the upper hand in the struggle for power.

Suping hoped that her parents and the Chens had also noticed Qian's absence and that they would henceforth do as they were told by Zhang early that morning.

'Do you admit guilt?' a gravelly, uncultured voice said in barely comprehensible Putonghua. The voice came from somewhere in front and above their heads.

The president of the court speaks, Suping thought wryly. From the corner of her downcast eyes she saw her father shifting position on his knees and she heard him scrape his throat. She knew that that was usually a prelude to some important statement or to point out a fallacy in an interlocutor's reasoning.

She saw him grimace with exasperation as he said, in his pedantic, mockingly sarcastic way, 'To admit guilt one would normally expect to be informed first what one is accused of, unless, of course, under the proletariat's dictatorship confession precedes the crime.'

Suping heard the leading Red Guard's sharp intake of breath and instinctively she pulled up her shoulders against the expected blow. Fortunately, however, before anybody could say or do something, she heard the mild voice she recognised as Zhang's say, 'This People's Tribunal has reason to believe that Liu Guixian, with the help of her sharp-tongued and arrogant husband Xu Ximing and her pretentious daughter Suping, was preparing a revised edition of the history of our motherland and this with the objective to confuse and deceive the people's minds and so to undermine the authority of our Great Leader Chairman Mao who is the sole person to decide what was, is and will be for the good of China and, on the other hand, what was, is and will be bad.

'Now hear! The People's Tribunal of the town of Luding demands that you make a full and frank confession of your criminal intentions. Speak up!'

To her left Suping heard her mother answer, without hesitation, Zhang's accusation, 'I, Liu Guixian, admit being guilty of *negligence* insofar that I did *not* ask Party Secretary Guo Chuanxing and Headmaster Yang Wenzhong whether they acted on instructions from the minister of education, Xia Ziyun, when they both ordered me to start working on the fourth revised edition of *The History of the People's Republic of China*. I did not question Comrade Guo and Comrade Yang's authority to give me such orders since they are my *leaders*.

Realising the amount of work involved in this glorious task and the urgency of the matter, as emphasised by the leaders Guo and Yang, I asked my husband Ximing and my daughter Suping for help in writing out the names of our past and present national figures, with the appropriate qualification in each case as indicated by Secretary Guo and Headmaster Yang, while I myself would write the main body of the new text. Neither my husband nor my daughter asked me to produce proof that I had been officially commissioned by leaders Guo and Yang, they simply took this for granted.

'Ever since your stern reproaches this morning we have agonised over our lack of revolutionary awareness and we unreservedly admit to being guilty of *negligence* and of *political immaturity* in that we did not foresee the consequences should our papers have fallen in less revolutionary experienced hands than those of the leading Red Guard here present. I shiver at the thought that they could have fallen into the hands of the enemies of our glorious socialist motherland and of our Great Leader Chairman Mao.

'We hope that the comrade judges, in their wisdom, will believe me when I say that we never intended to confuse and deceive the Chinese people, though we shudder at our recklessness. We therefore beg the comrade judges to set an exemplary yet compassionate punishment that will help and encourage us in our endeavours to become politically more mature and to fully embrace and implement the teachings of our Great Leader Chairman Mao.'

Liu Guixian fell silent and knocked her forehead three times on the floor as she knew had been the custom in the pre-liberation magistrates' courts.

With difficulty Suping suppressed a giggle at such a feudal gesture in a Communist People's Tribunal but then those morons would probably be flattered by Mother's show of humility. She imagined how the onlookers were staring, agape, at the scene and she wondered how many amongst them really understood what was going on and how they were being mocked, not only by her mother but also by their own leaders.

In the silence that followed her mother's confession (she really put it on with a trowel, Suping thought a bit worriedly), one could hear the whispered consultation amongst the judges. They seemed to agree quite rapidly since Suping heard again Zhang's voice as he said, 'The People's Tribunal of the town of Luding unanimously agrees to accept your collective plea of guilt to the lesser charge of gross negligence and political immaturity which could have had disastrous consequences for the security and stability of the People's Republic of China, our motherland. Consequently it now lays down the following sentences:

'You, Liu Guixian, are hereby sentenced to five years of reform and re-education through labour and political awareness sessions in a people's commune under the guidance of Secretary Deng Xiaotian of Chengdu. Xu Ximing and Xu Suping, you are hereby sentenced to four years of reform and re-education in a people's commune, also under the guidance of Secretary Deng. The People's Tribunal will request Secretary Deng to have you serve your sentences in different communes so as to avoid any possibility of counter-revolutionary conspiracies amongst the three of you.

'You shall immerse yourselves completely in the life of the peasant class and attend and participate in all political struggle and awareness meetings; the communes' leaders will keep a record of your zeal and attitude. If satisfactory, your sentence may be abrogated after three years, if not satisfactory the original sentence will be extended by three years. You will now sign a written statement of your confessions and your grateful acceptance of the magnanimous proletarian justice rendered by this court.'

Zhang fell silent to let his words sink in, while Li was busily writing, probably the only one, apart from Zhang, able to.

Suping moaned softly.

A wave of nausea had swept from her stomach to her head, back and forth, as she grasped the enormity of the sentences and, dizzily swaying on her hurting knees, she had heard Zhang's words, deadened as if he were speaking from somewhere outside the thick fog that was choking her.

Anger, rage, despair and helplessness in turn fought for control of her mind and soul. Four years of her life taken away from her like that, with a snap of the fingers. Had they told her which *law* she had broken? No! No, because there was no such law that made the copying of names a criminal offence. Had they respected her right to defend herself? No! No, because they knew they had no leg to stand on, legally.

This whole show of so-called proletarian justice for crimes against the proletariat was a farce played by a bunch of farceurs, like Zhang and Li, for the Great Joker, that moon-faced, crazy megalomaniac who was staring down from the wall on her bowed head and in whose name and on whose orders millions of innocent, decent, educated people were denied every and all human rights by the dull blue and green plebs with their inbred hatred for what was civilised, refined and cultured.

Straw dogs they were, all of them, sacrificial straw dogs thrown before that billion-headed Beast he called the proletariat and whose base instinct for random, thoughtless, malevolent violence he was manipulating against the foes he was seeing everywhere around him in his paranoid fear of losing the power he had become addicted to.

Millions of innocent people were being sacrificed to satisfy the Beast's hunger lest it turned against The Great Leader himself, against his insane puppet mistress Jiang Qing and their henchmen like Zhang and Li.

These henchmen were little more than straw dogs themselves, bound to be devoured if they didn't keep up with the Beast's indiscriminate feeding frenzy.

Suping felt herself being pulled up by the sleeve of her blouse and she struggled to her feet trying with all her might to kindle the last flickering embers of anger and hatred inside her so as not to slide down into that pit of despair where she knew she would die miserably.

The sight of the bowed, grey heads of the Chens still on their knees beside her fanned the embers into flames again.

Angry and defiantly she looked at the judges behind their bench, those self-appointed representatives of a society that had elevated a collection of moronic thoughts to its official creed and the nut who spewed them to its god, a god who exulted in the humiliation of such brilliant, decent and harmless men as she had come to know Chen Dan and Chen Juntao, for the sole reason that they had dared to be different, dared to believe in the beauty of understanding things through reason and logic rather than accepting the god's crazy definitions.

About to make a sneering retort the man called Zhang caught her eye for only a fraction of a second, long enough though for her to catch the warning in his glance, as clear as if he had shouted it in her ear, 'Shut up! Shut up or else you spoil everything for all of you, not only for yourself!'

Instead he said, in a loud voice, 'Step forward, one by one, to sign your confession and acceptance of the verdict. Convict number 000221, Liu Guixian! Step forward! Sign here!'

Breathing sharply through her nose to control her emotions, Suping saw her mother approach the bench and sign the two papers Zhang put in front of her. After that she stepped backwards, deadly pale.

'Convict number 000222, Xu Ximing! Step forward! Sign here!'

Father stepped forward, signed and retook his place, a mocking quizzical smile hovering on his lips.

'Convict number 000223, Xu Suping! Step forward! Sign here!'

Suping stepped forward, head high, locking her eyes with Zhang's and wishing looks could indeed kill. All she saw in his eyes was an amused, mocking smile accentuated by the merest of a wink and in turn flushed and livid with rage she jotted down the three characters of her name, the last stroke so forceful that she tore the paper.

'Tsh, tsh,' Zhang grumbled and, grinning sardonically, he added, 'another year perhaps my lady, for damaging state property?'

Then, sternly, 'Now stand back the three of you, and listen carefully! You will be provided with a piece of white cloth and a safety pin. With a brush and ink provided for that purpose you will write clearly and in Western figures the number I just gave you as well as the characters "bourgeois scoundrel" and your family name, your second and third names are not necessary. Henceforth you'll wear this cloth, as an armband, around your left arm. You have to memorise your number and you are obligated to respond if you are called by this number instead of by your name. Losing or destroying your armband will be considered as an act of sabotage of the judiciary system and will be punished severely, at least by doubling your initial sentence. Is that clear?'

They nodded dumbly, however, that was clearly not enough for Zhang ordered them to shout, in unison and as loud as they could, 'That is clear!'

Satisfied Zhang nodded and continued.

'The reason why this People's Tribunal has dropped the serious charge of sedition against you is that thanks to the never-weakening vigilance of our Chairman Mao's comrade-in-arms, Vice-Supreme Commander Lin Biao, former minister of education, Xia Ziyun, has been exposed as a traitor to the policies of our Great Leader Chairman Mao and to the Great Proletarian Cultural Revolution. Xia was arrested and, after his full confession, he has been executed because of the extreme seriousness of his crimes. One of these crimes was the unauthorised instruction to rewrite the history of the People's Republic of China with the avowed intention to cause confusion and dissent amongst the People.

'In his magnanimity and love for his people, our Great Leader Chairman Mao has instructed all the People's Tribunals to show leniency to those working on the revision before the arrest of the traitor Xia was proclaimed. Those who are found to have been working on the revision after they can be assumed to know of the traitor Xia's arrest are to be condemned as collaborators and put to death. The People's Tribunal of the town of Luding has examined your papers, Liu Guixian, and found that your last entry was more than a week ago and since the traitor Xia was exposed only three days ago you therefore fall under our Chairman Mao's decree of leniency.'

Zhang fell silent and looked around the deadly silent hall as everybody already seemed to anticipate what he was going to say next.

'This People's Tribunal, as a true instrument of proletarian justice, is not afraid to expose a rotting ulcer amongst the pure, young people who, as Red Guards, as little revolutionary generals as the Party lovingly calls them, carry out our Great Leader Chairman Mao's policies. The unworthy person known as Qian Weiying, the self-appointed leader of our town's Red Guards, knew about the traitor Xia's execution yet she drove Comrade Headmaster Yang Wenzhong to suicide only yesterday evening with her accusation of treason in spite of the fact that she knew of our Chairman Mao's decree and that Comrade Yang's last entries for the revision were made two weeks ago, as he repeatedly stated in his refutal of her accusation. Again, this morning, at the home of convict Xu Ximing, she levelled accusations of treason at Xu and his wife and daughter without first verifying the date of their last entries.

'This court has therefore decided that Qian acted deliberately against our Great Leader Chairman Mao's orders for reasons of seeking personal revenge for having been thwarted by Xu in her attempts to be admitted into the clique of Luding's so-called intellectuals. For openly disobeying our Chairman Mao and for her contempt for the workers' class by aspiring to become a member of the stinking ninth category, this People's Tribunal has condemned Qian, during a closed session this morning, to twenty-five years of hard labour in the most extreme conditions at the discretion of the Ministry of Mining.

'Qian is now in solitary confinement awaiting instructions from Beijing concerning her transport. Qian's family, to the second degree, has been found guilty of lacking in revolutionary vigilance for not correcting or reporting Qian's excessive tendencies. Consequently they have been condemned to pay a lifelong stipend of thirty yuan per month to the widow of Comrade Headmaster Yang Wenzhong and also to pay for his funeral.'

Zhang fell silent and looked around the hall to allow the audience to digest his words and the Red Guards the hidden meaning behind them that as long as he, Zhang Yizhong, would be in charge of the Great Proletarian Revolution in the town of Luding they had better toe the line, that is, his, Zhang's line.

Suping shivered.

Qian was an evil and vindictive person who had openly threatened to destroy her but still she didn't deserve to be so wantonly sent to a slow and horrible death by a bunch of morons manipulated by two clever opportunists. Suping could guess what the expression 'hard labour in the most extreme conditions and at the discretion of the Ministry of Mining' meant. Qian would be sent to the uranium mines in northern Xinjiang Autonomous Region where she would die of radiation sickness after a year at the most.

Hardly twenty minutes ago Suping had thought that she would exult at the destruction of even a small part of the Beast. Now already she found it difficult to rejoice at the wanton destruction of a fellow human being, however much that person had been an exponent of the despicable system that had created the Beast.

How devilishly clever also to put the blame for Qian's mistake on her relatives.

The system and its Great Leader, who were responsible in the first place for instigating and encouraging behaviour like Qian's, could of course never be at fault.

'The steely eyes of Han Fei are watching all of us all of the time,' her father had once said, and how true that now turned out to be.

Suping noticed that the man called Li, just Li as he had told them himself, acknowledged a signal by Zhang who rounded off his part in the farcical show by addressing her and her parents again. 'Convicts 000221, 222 and 223 will now stand aside and watch the court deal with the case against their friends, the prisoners Chen Dan and Chen Juntao. Comrade Li, the second vice-president of this People's Tribunal, will be their interrogator. The convicts are not allowed to interfere by word or by gesture. Leading Red Guard Du will be held responsible for their good behaviour until such time that they will have boarded their transport to Chengdu.'

Zhang fell silent and gestured for Leading Red Guard Du to usher his charges into the corner of the hall to the right of the judges' bench.

This done to his satisfaction he sat down and signalled Li to proceed.

Li didn't bother to stand up when he began his case against the Chens.

'Chen Dan, investigations by the People's Tribunal have shown that since your arrival in Luding and during the time you stayed in convict 000222's house, you did not engage in political or hostile activities against the Party or the State. Therefore your misdemeanour is basically still the same as the one for which you were dismissed from the University of Chongqing and expelled from that city, that is to say, for your attempt to ridicule the Party's fourth economic five-year plan by saying, openly and in public, that it went against the laws of nature and by qualifying as fools your colleagues who earnestly and wholeheartedly co-operated with the Party in its endeavours to give the five-year plan a scientific base.

'You can deem yourself lucky, Chen, that when the university was closed indefinitely following our Great Leader Chairman Mao's instruction to destroy all vestiges of the old culture so as to build the one, true proletarian society, your successor, Comrade Hu Liyun, had not yet succeeded in eliminating the basic flaw in what you call the laws of nature, although, according to his latest report, he was very close indeed to a breakthrough that would have heralded the beginning of the triumph of socialism over nature. Be that as it may, all that matters no longer since our Great Leader Chairman Mao, tired of the procrastination of the so-called scientists, has simply and masterfully abolished all laws, whether nature's or man-made, and replaced them with only one law, that is 'the Guiding Principle of Unified Thought' conceived by our Great Leader himself.

'The People's Tribunal of the town of Luding has therefore decided to give you the opportunity to realise your error in clinging to old-fashioned values by experiencing first hand the power and simplicity of our Great Leader's Unified Thought Principle. The court orders you, Chen Dan, to serve as the keeper of records in the Model People's Communes under the leadership of Secretary Deng Xiaotian of Chengdu. As the Keeper of Records you must assist wholeheartedly, and sparing no effort, the production brigades of the model communes in meeting their targets following the Unified Thought Principle. Failure to meet the targets will result in blame for the commune's leader, the production brigades' leaders and, of course, for the Keeper of Records. This, I'm sure, will enhance unified thought amongst all leaders and workers in their endeavours to live up to the guiding principle.'

Looking at Gao Chen with what Suping thought was very much a sardonic grin, Li continued, 'You will now stand up and step forward, Chen Dan, and sign this statement of voluntary acceptance of the task given you by this court.'

Gao Chen struggled to his feet and grimacing from pain – or was it in mocking reply to Li – he stumbled forward and, holding on to the judges' table with his left hand, he signed the statement.

Li took the signed document, examined Gao Chen's grass-script characters and, apparently satisfied, he handed the paper to the presiding judge who, in turn, passed it on without as much as a glance, to one of the woman judges who acted as the court's clerk.

Taking one more paper from his bag, Li motioned Gao Chen to approach the table once more and said, 'This is a copy of the declaration you just signed. Sign this one also! Since you are an academic from Chongqing I have to send this copy to my leaders in Beijing.'

Suping couldn't help but marvel at the casual self-confidence with which Li fooled everybody in the hall, except perhaps Zhang who had his own cats to whip and couldn't care less probably about what would happen to all of them as long as everything went his way.

When Gao Chen had also signed the second paper Li took it, folded it and put it away in the breast pocket of his jacket.

'Step aside, Chen Dan,' he said and added, 'since you are strictly speaking not a convict you are not given a number and will not have to wear an armband. You may stay here, with the public, to witness the rest of today's trials or you may return to the house of convict 000222. You are required, however, to report every morning at the Detention House until you have been assigned to a transport to Chengdu. Failure to report for your appointed transport or, subsequently, for your duties at Secretary Deng's office, will be considered as sabotage of our orders and an arrest warrant will be issued for you. The minimum penalty for such an act of sabotage is ten years of hard labour. Now stand aside or leave the hall.'

Slowly Gao Chen walked to the corner where his friends were standing under the surveillance of Leading Red Guard Du. Du scowled at him, however, some kind of intuition must have told him that he had better not interfere and Gao Chen went to stand as close as possible to his friends.

He didn't look at them though as he kept staring at the lonely figure still on his knees in front of the judges' table.

Suping, watching him from aside, saw pity and anguish in his eyes. Her heart missed a beat. Was there something she had missed that Gao Chen hadn't? Was something bad going to happen to Ai Chen?

That would seem unthinkable. Impractical, clumsy, meek, good-hearted, old Uncle Juntao was so utterly harmless. What threat could he possible be to the Party and its Great Leader?

But why then did Uncle Dan look so anguished, almost as if he were going to cry? Apprehensively she watched as Li was consulting a sheaf of papers.

Finally, looking up from his papers and directly at Ai Chen, Li said in a normal, not unfriendly voice, 'The person known as Guo Chuanxing was demoted three days ago from Party secretary of Luding to ordinary Party member with a five-year probationary period and sent back to Dalian. Did you know that, Chen?'

Ai Chen shook his head and answered, 'I did not.'

'There were several reasons for the Party to be dissatisfied with Guo's performance here in Luding,' Li continued in the same bantering tone, 'however, none was so serious that a severe reprimand would not have sufficed, but for one reason. Have you any idea what that reason could be, Chen?'

Again Ai Chen shook his head and replied, 'I have not.'

Li, looking around the silent hall, let his eyes linger for a second on the small group in the corner at his left and Suping thought she saw something like a plea for understanding in his eyes. Then he looked back at Ai Chen and continued in a tone that had suddenly changed from friendly banter to sneering contempt.

'The reason I am referring to, Chen, is the unforgivable error, for a Party secretary, of failing to see an enemy of the People, of the Party, of our Great Leader Chairman Mao himself and all he stands for, when this enemy presents himself in his office in the guise of a meek, old, bumbling, pompous ex-professor. Have you got any idea which ex-professor I am referring to, Chen?'

Suping's heart missed another beat as she heard Ai Chen chuckle before he replied, mockingly, 'From the adjectives you used, Li, I get somehow the impression that you are talking about me, though I fail to see how anybody in his right mind can see in me the devious enemy you described. But perhaps I give you too much credit when I speak of a right mind, Li?'

The audience gasped and the Red Guard standing behind Ai Chen lifted his stick, but with one gesture Li stopped him before he could strike at the old man and continued, imperturbably, 'I have a report that Guo sent to the Sichuan Provincial Security Affairs Commission. It is about a meeting he had in his office with the ex-professors Chen Juntao and Chen Dan and a person called Xu Suping, now known as convict number 000223 and present here in this hall.

'According to Guo the two ex-professors were applying for resident status for Luding and the person Xu Suping was accompanying them in a capacity of guarantor of shelter and of good behaviour. As it behoves a Party secretary Guo queried the two former academics about their stated occupation, which they described, amongst some mockingly humble claptrap, as, and I quote, "To develop the scientific base for Chairman Mao's Guiding Principle of Unified Thought for the benefit of future generations." Do you recall having written that, Chen?'

Awkwardly, because of his arms behind his back, Ai Chen shrugged his shoulders and answered, 'I do. So what? I had to write down something and at that time I thought that the secretary might like that kind of claptrap as you call it, Li.'

Suping held her breath, like everybody else in the audience, however, Li still seemed unperturbed when he continued, 'Good, Chen, very good. At least you are honest. Now let us take a look at the wording of your statement, Chen. You say, and I quote again, "for Chairman Mao's Thoughts", not "for *our* Chairman Mao's thoughts". By deliberately omitting the word "our" you cunningly imply that Chairman Mao is not *your* Great Leader and Chairman. You distance yourself from China's Great Leader and Saviour. This is only the first indication that you are at least a dissenter, even probably a reactionary revisionist, Chen. But there is worse to come so I continue.

'Guo, naive and gullible, traits unbecoming for a Party secretary, even for one as young as he, failed to see your cunning deviousness and instead of exposing you there and then as the enemy of communism that you are, Chen, he decided to encourage you to continue with your so-called scientific project which he asked you to summarise for him for his report to his leaders. The following parts of his report are your words, Chen, even the vulgarised ones, since Guo's background was insufficient to know about the things he wrote, so you must have dictated the words to him.

'I quote, "it is all a matter of annihilation, annihilation of thesis by anti-thesis, of matter by anti-matter, of reason by unreason, of sense by nonsense. When this insight will have been synthesised in one unified theory of mutual annihilation and subsequently proven in an experiment on a world-wide scale, then Chairman Mao's cosmic vision will have been achieved and there will be the eternal and universal bliss of communism, a kind of Communist nirvana so to speak, eternal nothingness as it were." Are these your words, Chen?'

'Does it matter what I say, Li?' Ai Chen replied, laughing mockingly. 'But I understand, Li,' he continued, grinning. 'In this travesty of justice I was already guilty of whatever ludicrous crime you are bound to find culprits for before I was even dragged in here. My sentence has undoubtedly also already been fixed so all you need is a full and frank confession, to use your own jargon, so that you can tidy up your case.

'I always wondered why, in this proletarian paradise of yours, people like you are so hell-bent on *confessions* from those you have earmarked for the role of culprits? They must confess! Always they must *confess*! Why don't you just lock them up or shoot them or dispense with them in any of the many other charming ways you have at your disposal? Is it to pacify the inconvenient pangs of bourgeois conscience that always lurk there, below the Communist self-righteousness? If I don't confess you will be in trouble, won't you, Li? But I want to play my part in your burlesque to the full, Li, and therefore I won't confess just yet. Lead me to it, Li, step by step. If your analysis is scientifically correct I shall answer truthfully. And, perhaps, you would consent to let me look at you while you try to trick me and possibly also to stretch my rheumatic, old legs a bit? Don't worry, Li! I won't threaten the dictatorship of the proletariat by jumping out of the window like old Yang did.'

Ai Chen fell silent and, looking up at the judges, he grinned mischievously at Li.

The audience erupted in an uproar. Though nobody had probably understood a word of what had been said, they recognised defiance when they saw it.

Some shouted, 'Beat him! Beat the pride out of him!'

One group of peasants, looking at the scene from along the wall where they had been lined up, their eyes glazed in total incomprehension, were prodded by the militia to surge forward, towards where Ai Chen was lying on his knees, to show their righteous proletarian outrage at the accused's mocking defiance.

Li waited until the last moment before he lifted his hand whereupon the militia immediately began to push the peasants back while a photographer took pictures of the mêlée.

Ai Chen, sitting upright on his heels, had watched the whole scene with a mocking grin, apparently enjoying himself thoroughly.

'Perfect crowd control, Li,' he taunted, 'well rehearsed, well timed. My compliments. Must have been difficult to teach those morons to dance to your piping. But, pray, continue to amaze me, Li.'

Suping couldn't believe her ears and eyes. Was that man the meek, shy Uncle Juntao she thought she knew? Who she thought would be unable to defend himself against the bullies of this world?

She was so proud of him now that she felt like rushing to him and hug him. Her feelings must have shown on her face for she felt a restraining hand on her arm and, looking aside, she saw her mother shake her head almost imperceptibly.

She also saw her mother smile through her tears and Suping heard her whisper, 'So proud of him. What an inspiration for all of us.'

She looked at Gao Chen and saw that he was smiling sadly. What was *he* thinking?

Li had by then re-established order in the hall and, as if nothing had happened, he said, watching Ai Chen curiously and with unmistakable respect, 'You want some fun, eh, Chen? So let's have fun and see whether you can fool this People's Tribunal as you fooled poor Comrade Guo. By the way, you may remain seated as you are or stand up, as you wish, however, you must stay in your place. Now, let us continue our analysis. The word annihilation, does it mean "to destroy completely", even "to put out of existence"?'

Ai Chen nodded and said, 'It does.'

'The word "thesis" does it mean "a phase of development in dialectic thought"? A premise as it were for developing a philosophy?'

Ai Chen burst out laughing and said, 'I see what you are leading up to, Li. Very clever. But have it your way. Yes, it can mean those things.'

Li, finishing a note on the paper in front of him, continued.

'The word "matter" is that not a synonym for "material" and thus, by implication, for "materialism" when one postulates that material is the only reality as opposed to spiritual things?'

'I see that the reputation for crooked logic, for which you Communists are so notorious, has in you a worthy proponent, Li,' Ai Chen replied in mock admiration. 'But again, I promised to answer you truthfully as long as your deductions are not wholly false, twisted as they may be though. So my answer is still yes.'

'Thank you,' Li said and he made a last note.

He put down his pen and, cracking his fingers one by one, he stared at the wall at the end of the hall, over Ai Chen's shoulder, and said pensively, 'So Chen Juntao, when I rephrase your pseudo-scientific gobbledegook I get the following reactionary, counter-revolutionary and dissenting declaration, "the whole thing is to destroy completely, stronger, to put out of existence the development of dialectic thought, the very premise of a philosophy, so that spiritualism can eradicate materialism and the end of all things material is achieved and nothing remains."

'I now put it to you, Chen, that by "dialectic thought" you mean our Great Leader Chairman Mao's Guiding Principle of Unified Thought, that by "philosophy" you refer to Our Chairman's materialistic, socialist philosophy and that by "spiritualism" you mean religion in all its pernicious forms. In short, Chen, you declare, unintelligibly for the masses but clear as crystal for the despicable elitist enemies of the masses, your intention to wage total war on our Great Leader Chairman Mao, on his thoughts and policies, on his creation, the People's Republic of China, until nothing is left.

'This sums up the People's case against you, Chen Juntao. Now, you have already conceded that my analysis of and deductions from your statements to Guo were correct so I have your confession on record. The People's Republic of China is a legal and legalist State and confessions are an indispensable part of a legal process, so much so that there can be no conviction without prior confession. Sometimes criminals do not understand this logic and consequently they must be *persuaded* to confess or else our whole society would grind to a halt.

'So it is not because of an obsession with the last vestiges of a bourgeois conscience as you implied earlier, but because of our obsession with a logical order of things that we insist on a confession. Be that as it may, it is clear to me, to all of us judges and to those who trust our judgement that you are a most dangerous enemy of the People for whom there can be no leniency. I grant you, however, one last statement, also for the records, but be forewarned that I shall order the Red Guards to stop you in case your words can be construed as inflammatory or seditious or offensive to the Party and to our Great Leader Chairman Mao.'

Li fell silent and his fellow judges as well as the audience seemed to be holding their breath.

Desperately Suping looked in turn at her parents and at Gao Chen but they stared, horror-stricken, at the man called Li.

Tears were running down Gao Chen's cheeks and the veins on his temples stood out, pulsating, like big, blue eels.

Frightened by the fury in his eyes and by the convulsive opening and closing of his hands she rushed over to him, ignoring Leading Red Guard Du, and grasping his hands, she implored, 'Don't, Uncle Dan! Please don't! Please! Please?'

Sobbing, she continued, 'We need you, Uncle Dan! Father, Mother and I, we need you. We love you. Please don't do anything that will bring harm to you, to us. Look at Uncle Juntao! He is going to say something! Let us listen to him, Uncle Dan. Please? Will you keep quiet?'

Gao Chen's head slumped on his chest as he wept openly, the savageness of a moment ago draining out of him.

'Oh my dear, dear friend. My dear, brave, foolish friend, what have you got yourself into,' he sobbed. 'It was not necessary to prove yourself. We, your friends, knew that you are a decent and brave man.'

'Shut up!' Leading Red Guard Du shouted furiously. 'Why do you cry for the criminal? Were you perhaps in league with him? Was he your secret leader? I shall report you to the interrogator so that he can undo your sentences and condemn all of you to death, like that criminal Chen Juntao. You got off much too lightly. Everybody thinks so.'

Roughly he pulled Suping away from Gao Chen and shoved her back into the corner with her parents.

The commotion had not gone unnoticed and Ai Chen was also looking in their direction.

Suping saw that he smiled and made eye contact with his friend Gao Chen, shaking his head ever so slightly and blinking a few times in rapid succession.

Apparently the message got through to his friend since Gao Chen relaxed visibly.

Standing up to his full height Ai Chen looked at the impassive faces of the judges.

Slowly he turned around, looking at the sullen, baleful crowd along the walls of the court hall.

The contempt in his eyes was unmistakable.

Having turned a full circle, he gave one more look at his friends, smiled and winked and then addressed himself to his interrogator, to the man called Li.

'One of the basic tenets of my acquired life philosophy,' Ai Chen began and he smiled in self-mockery as he continued, 'is that although the individual member of what is now called the proletariat may perhaps be able to think for himself in some sort of dim-witted way that is predominately centred on his basic physical urges and needs, much like an animal, a *group* of proletarians exceeding three in number is *not* capable of concerted thought, let alone of a synergic thought process. Whereas the individual proletarian can still, by means of constant minding, prodding and nudging, be made to act in a more or less civilised manner, the group on the other hand can almost exclusively be motivated by things uncivilised and brutal and the bigger the group the greater its capacity, and need, for brutality and savagery.

'The prophets of good have never succeeded. They have all been torn to pieces by the masses they tried to inspire to do good and if their creeds survived it was always in a distorted form, catering to the need to oppress or kill those who think differently. Those who continue to preach the creeds are either intolerant, mentally ill zealots or ruthless opportunists who deftly play to the masses' basest instincts so as to preserve their own position of power. All religions are either dead or teetering examples of this tenet. The prophets of evil have always succeeded though, and in those instances that their creeds or movements did not survive them either, this was not because they mellowed and became more moderate. On the contrary, it was because they became paranoid and, having run out of outside enemies, began to eliminate imaginary enemies within their own supporting structure. Much like a dog gnaws away its own rotting limb or flesh in an instinctive attempt to save its main body, the masses tear to pieces their leaders gone mad.

'Our poor, long-suffering motherland has known many such tyrants in its long and bloody history and it has now reached once more the stage that its most recent, so-called Great Leader has gone the same, apparently foreordained way. What we are witnessing these terrible days is the beginning of the end for your evil god and his frantic, zealous acolytes like you, Li. You called me a most dangerous enemy of the People. In the context that you meant that, I am indeed proud to say that I am, because in your jargon people means system means Communist Party. But then you don't care, do you, Li? You don't care whether the enemies you hunt down are real or imagined. All you care about is to get the number of condemnations you have been set by your own so-called leaders. It's a matter of survival for you and your fellow judges, isn't it? If you fail to meet your target you'll find yourself here, in my place.

'I don't hate you personally, Li, but how I do hate the system and its tyrant you have to serve and keep happy in his thirst for blood and revenge. I don't hate your so-called comrades, behind that table or here in the hall or outside, personally, but I do hate their dumb and blind servility to the system and its tyrant, who merely uses them and their gratuitous, gleeful brutality towards those who are deemed unfit to belong. This is what I wanted to say, Li. Thank you for letting me finish though I am afraid that the reason for your indulgence does not bode well for me. So let me have it, Li. Tell me the sovereign judgement of the People.'

Ai Chen fell silent and smiled at Li who looked pale, Suping thought.

'Don't make it too hard on yourself, Li,' Ai Chen added, without his earlier sarcasm, 'you have your job to do and serve a greater purpose, so get it over with. "If it's to be done, it better be done quick" as another of history's great megalomaniacs once was supposed to have said, though that one had definitely more class than our peasant from Hunan.'

The hall waited in a hush. A few earlier, half-hearted shouts of 'traitor', 'criminal', had quickly petered out when the militia had made no effort to spur the crowd on.

Everybody stared at the lonely man in front of the bench who had dared to defy the almighty, to speak the unspeakable. Instinctively they felt that that tall, shabby man was of a different class, his quiet and fearless dignity instilling that awkward, mixed feeling of self-conscious uneasiness and reluctant respect that inevitably deflates the contrived spontaneous indignation of the masses.

It was that psychologically critical moment so feared by the professional agent provocateur when he feels his grip slip and has to watch helplessly as the crowd disintegrates into heedlessly milling small groups and individuals.

Suping felt the palpable indecision of the crowd and she was convinced that Li deliberately let the moment to seize back control pass.

It suits his purpose to make the Red Guards and the militia feel guilty, she thought, it enforces his hold over them. He'll need that; and Ai Chen's condemnation, to stifle the insinuations about his treatment of Uncle Dan.

She caught Gao Chen's eye and saw his anguished, pleading look for understanding and forgiveness, his open hands miming helplessness.

He suffers terribly, Suping thought, he suffers because the forces that protect him will have to throw his friend before the wolf pack and there is nothing he can do about it. Longfei's Plan works and therefore Ai Chen must be sacrificed so that Gao Chen can be saved, in the first place for his own sake of course but also probably to keep an eye on Mother and myself since both of us are now also part of the equation as Li undoubtedly has guessed already.

Besides, there are still and always Yang Baolin's notes, that powerful incentive for many in the Party top to keep Chen Dan alive. I'm sure that even if Uncle Dan were to accuse himself of the most heinous crimes against the People, Li would laugh it off as an attempt by Uncle Dan to martyr himself.

The Party does not want to make martyrs or political prisoners of its opponents, it wants convicted common law criminals.

She smiled at Gao Chen and mouthed, 'I understand. We understand.'

Gao Chen nodded, grateful for her sympathy and he straightened up, bracing himself for what was to come.

The judges of the People's Tribunal of the town of Luding had finished their deliberations and were leaning back in their chair, watching Ai Chen with glazed eyes, like toads watching a bug they are about to swallow.

Li handed a piece of paper to the president but crabbily the man shoved it back over the table at him, crossly gesturing with his other hand for Li to go ahead.

He doesn't know what's going on, Suping said to herself, and he doesn't care either. Back home he probably used to eat something at this time of the day and have some tea and he is crabby because nobody brings him anything. I am sure that in another ten or fifteen minutes he'll simply walk out to get himself some food, human drama or not.

Li must have sensed the president's mood for he stood up and, reading from the paper he held in his hands just so that he need not look at Ai Chen, he said, with a slight tremor in his voice nevertheless, 'Chen Juntao, the People's Tribunal of the town of Luding has unanimously found you guilty of treason, open dissension, counter-revolutionary heresy as well as of ridiculing and plotting to overthrow the dictatorship of the proletariat. In accordance with the instructions of our Great Leader Chairman Mao concerning the mandatory punishment for these crimes and as mandated by the Sichuan

Provincial People's Tribunal in Chengdu in cases of extreme gravity and urgency, this court hereby condemns you to death by means of a bullet to the back of your head.

'Your execution will take place tomorrow morning at ten o'clock in the People's Sports and Joyful Events Stadium, together with two murderers, four swindlers of state property, one rapist and three saboteurs of state production equipment. You will be driven to the stadium in an open truck and you will carry a banner stating your crimes for the people of Luding to see. You will spend your last hours in solitary confinement and you are not allowed to receive visitors. You may write one last letter which you will have to hand to the prison guard who will pass it on to the Party secretary for his perusal. The secretary will decide whether the letter will be forwarded to the addressee or not.

'Now, is there anybody who can and will claim your body and pay the bill for the bullet? If not, your body will be buried in an unmarked grave in the cemetery for criminals outside the city limits and the possessions you have on you will become the property of the State.'

When Li had pronounced the words 'death by a bullet to the back of your head' Suping had felt all the blood drain from her head and an ice-cold wave of nausea had swept over her. Moaning softly like a frightened puppy her knees had buckled and had her father not seized her upper arm in an iron grip so strong that the pain made her yelp, she would have fainted. She retched and the bitter taste of bile made her shudder.

As if dampened by a thick fog she heard Ai Chen's voice, calm, pleasant, without histrionics, answer Li's question, 'With the judges' permission, my friend, Professor Chen Dan, will collect my body and pay the bill, of one yuan I believe, for the bullet. I also beg the People's Tribunal, as the only favour to this person, to allow my friend to bury my body on the hill, in a plot of fallow land, not far from the house where I spent the happiest year of my life.'

Ai Chen fell silent and Suping, through a haze of tears, saw him making a slight bow in the direction of the judges.

Li, visibly relieved by the calm ordinariness of Ai Chen's reaction, said unhesitatingly and without consulting his fellow judges first, 'Both requests are hereby granted.'

Careful not to let emotion transpire in his voice Li continued matter-of-factly, 'The convict, henceforth to be known as 1/11, will now take off his belt and remove his shoelaces and hand these objects over to his friends while he takes his leave of them. He is allowed five minutes to say his farewells. The court will not allow any scenes or histrionics. Leading Red Guard Du will assign three guards to escort the convicts 000221, 222 and 223 to cell number twenty-one where they will stay until their transport to Chengdu has been arranged.

'Comrade Du will himself escort convict 1/11 to cell number forty-four. He will refrain from any conversation with or intimidation of the convict. He will stand guard outside the convict's cell until the arrival of the truck that will bring the convict to the place of his execution. Comrade Du will be held personally responsible if the convict commits suicide which, I remind him, is a crime against the dictatorship of the proletariat carrying a heavy penalty for those who fail to prevent it. After their farewells to convict 1/11, Chen Dan and the convicts 000221, 222 and 223 will report to me, here behind the table, to receive the written permit to collect the body and have it buried on the hill near their house as well as to sign for receipt of 1/11's property.

'The People's Tribunal of the town of Luding will reconvene tomorrow morning at ten o'clock in the People's Sports and Joyful Events Stadium to witness the execution of the eleven criminals. The trials will continue at two o'clock tomorrow afternoon. As from tomorrow Comrade Secretary Zhang will be the sole interrogator for this tribunal since I have been recalled to Chongqing for urgent business. This session is now adjourned!'

The judges, except Zhang and Li, got up from their chairs and, without a further glance at their victims, stumbled hastily towards the door that led to the canteen for higher officials, the only thing on their mind to get to the chicken and vegetables before the militia would rush in.

The Red Guards raced downstairs to get to the ground floor canteen for lower officials, fearing their comrades on duty outside would have finished already the best morsels when they got there.

Leading Red Guard Du and the three Red Guards appointed by him to escort Suping and her parents looked enviously at the backs of their disappearing comrades, torn between the pangs of hunger and the honour of special revolutionary duty.

Zhang, noticing their predicament, smiled and said, 'I'll watch the convicts for you, Du. Go quickly to the canteen on this floor and get yourself a bowl of chicken rice and vegetables. If anybody tells you that you are not allowed in tell that person that I gave you permission. Now, go and be back in twenty minutes!'

Du and his men rushed off, revolutionary zeal forgotten. Zhang laughed mockingly and said, 'You were right, Chen Juntao, when you said in your diatribe that the proletarians are only motivated by the physical needs, principally the needs of their stomach, I would add. Once those are satisfied they follow their penis, the men at least, for the women I wouldn't know what comes second.

'Look how they rush to the trough. You can hear them grunt and slurp, the pigs. Not worth dying for *that* lot. Fortunately for you, you have your own ideal, Juntao, though I wonder whether there exists any ideal worth dying for.'

'There isn't,' Ai Chen answered, getting up from pulling the laces out of his shoes, 'but then I wasn't given much choice in the matter, was I? The choice was made for me by our friend Li here and all I could do to give both him and me face was to fabricate myself some sort of reason. Now, if you don't mind, let me say farewell to my real friends.'

Holding up his trousers with one hand, his belt hanging over his shoulder, Ai Chen shuffled in his laceless shoes over to where his friends were standing, a smile on his face. Wordlessly they gripped his one free arm and hand and pulled him close to them.

'I can feel your love and strength flow into me,' he said, 'and that's all I need to face down the rabble and its rousers. What a way to depart from this sorry Kingdom of the Morons where the Jester has appointed himself King. With a bang I shall go, quite literally, and, mind you, as a hero much feared. I, Chen Juntao, the timorous, the anti-hero, the bungler, the cuckold, an enemy of the State to The People, a hero to some. What a laugh!'

His friends smiled through their tears, in spite of themselves.

'We love you, Juntao, our good, decent and brave friend,' Guixian said. 'You will remain an inspiration to me, to all of us, in the difficult times ahead.'

'My quiet hero,' Suping said, her voice breaking from emotion and, impulsively, she embraced the awkward man she had come to respect so much.

'I'll miss you, Juntao,' Ximing said, 'however, thanks to you I'll survive to see reason triumph in the end.'

'Thank you, brother,' Gao Chen said finally, holding his friend's hand between his, their foreheads touching.

'Thank you for putting the zest back in my life after Lingling's death. You will see her soon. Give her my love and be good to her while I still crawl a bit longer in the mud here down below. I'll be there tomorrow morning and bring you back to our hill. I'll prepare a place for you under the walnut tree so that you can keep an eye on our house and guard our secrets in the tree while the four of us are wholeheartedly trying to become exemplary socialist revolutionaries. I'll ask Zhang to persuade his half-wit brother from next door to keep your place clean for you and to light a candle on the appropriate days. The brother will remember the old custom, his mind being too small for the Party to bother. I'll give him the money that you put in your belt yesterday, if you don't mind.'

Wiping the tears from his eyes with the back of his right hand, Gao Chen looked his friend in the eyes, his lips quivering.

Ai Chen left his trousers, for what they were, and embraced his friend.

'Thank you, brother,' he said, his voice soft but clear. 'Thank you for everything you did for me and for giving some direction and sense to my life. I don't function very well when the whole world around me is in some sort of crazy flux and the ground under my feet seems to be shifting like on those mudflats in the river you told us about. So, I am not sorry I have to go, it saves both of us a lot of worry. I am sorry, though, to steal the show from you at the last moment but for once I can from now on keep an eye on *you*.'

Pulling his short friend against his chest and caressing his spiky hair, Ai Chen added, teasingly, 'If in the future you get these sudden cold shivers, it'll be I trying to tell you to keep your big mouth shut, for your own good. You'll keep me quite busy, I'm sure.'

Looking over Gao Chen's shoulder at Suping, Ai Chen said, 'You, Suping, and other intelligent young people like you, are the only hope for a future, civilised China. If you can't achieve that in your lifetime, instil the basic values of tolerance, decency and humaneness in your children so that that hope does not die with you, just as because of you my hope will not die with my body tomorrow. Intelligence and knowledge, Suping, and knowledge above all other things, will be the cornerstone of the society of the future and a *conditio sine qua non* for anybody who wants to play a role in it. Without true knowledge there is no future for China.

'The Communists are now frantically trying to destroy the treasure of knowledge gathered over more than two thousand years by our intelligent people and to impose their own travesty of knowledge instead. They have shut China off from the free world and its free flow of ideas and instead hobnob with their ilk, those wicked lunatics of the so-called socialist brotherhood. But they will not succeed, Suping! They will do a lot of damage, and some of it irreparable, before their mad system will unavoidably collapse on itself, but they won't succeed in destroying people's dreams and ideas. It is *your* task, and your *children's*, to build a new China on the ruins left by Mao and his ilk. Take good care of yourself, first and foremost Suping, my love.'

Ai Chen fell silent, then added before anybody could say something, 'There is no need to say more. Words are inadequate in situations like this. I see my guardian, Comrade Du, coming our way, replenished I'm sure and full of revolutionary ardour again. I shall go with him now and I shall not look back.'

Turning towards the bench, he shouted, 'Li! Since you put me in this unenviable situation will you do me the favour of making sure that the soldier tomorrow has a steady hand?'

One last hug for Gao Chen, one last wave at the Xus, one last mocking bow at Li and Zhang, and Chen Juntao, affectionately known as Ai Chen and now as convict 1/11, shuffled through the door held open for him by Leading Red Guard Du.

The poignancy of that moment, the dignity of the man in his shabby clothes, head held high, pathetically trying to walk straight-backed in spite of his sagging trousers and slopping, laceless shoes, would remain for ever imprinted on Suping's mind.

It was the last she saw of Chen Juntao.

The silent emptiness in the hall lasted for several minutes, each adult engrossed in his own thoughts, the three adolescents called little revolutionary generals looking uneasily at each other and at their leaders Zhang and Li, who seemed to ignore their presence.

The Red Guards, children still, sensed a kind of unspoken understanding and sympathy amongst the adults, convicts and Communist leaders alike, which they could not fathom. It made them uneasy and restless.

It was Li who finally broke the silence.

'Quite a character, our friend Chen Juntao,' he said to no one in particular.

'If that's the way you treat your friends, Li, I wonder how you deal with your enemies,' Gao Chen sneered.

'*My* enemies need not worry whether *my* hand is steady,' Li replied grimly and he continued. 'I have my instructions and a lot of leeway to decide how to achieve my objectives. Or should I say *our* objectives, Chen Dan? I once read that somewhere in South America there is a river full of voracious small fish that can devour a man or an ox whole, in minutes. Have your heard that story too, Chen?'

'Yes,' Gao Chen answered, 'piranhas those small fish are called. What do they have to do with the way you treated my friend?'

'The story also said,' Li continued imperturbably, 'that when a herd of cattle has to cross the river on its way to better pastures, the cattle drivers select an old, or sick and useless animal and drive it into the river, downstream from the place where they want to cross with the herd. While the piranhas are busy devouring the useless animal, the valuable animals and, of course, the cattle drivers themselves, get safely to the other side. You see the metaphor in what took place here, Chen?

'The useless animal, the valuable small herd, the piranhas, the cattle drivers, they are all *here*, Chen. Don't you see? I would have preferred the old Roman tactic of bread-and-games for the *vulgus mobile* while we, the elite, play our own silly little games. But that doesn't work any more, Chen. The *vulgus* today is more bloodthirsty than ever. The people lack the boisterous vulgarity of the roman masses. They are too *serious*; all work and revolution and no play, hence my piranha analogy.

'A word of warning for Suping. Your Uncle Juntao told you that knowledge is the power of the future. That is simplistic intellectualism so typical of the ineffectual scholar. Knowledge *per se* does *not* equal power. What he forgot to say, or probably never thought of, is that knowledge is power *provided you use it* and that that takes guts, even ruthlessness. If you lack those qualities, guts and ruthlessness, your knowledge and you yourself remain insignificant. An irritant, yes, shrugged off at best, eliminated at worst. Chen Juntao was himself the quintessential example of the knowledgeable person who was either too ethical or too cowardly to *use* his knowledge. To *your* benefit, Chen Dan, I should add.

'I am sure that during the twenty-two years he lived with you he gathered enough knowledge about you to turn the tables on you, if he had wanted or dared to, and *you* would have had your brains blown out tomorrow and *he* would be keeping records in some unrealistic production scheme or other. As it is, with all the knowledge he possessed he could not even save his own life. Now, is that *power* I ask you?

'So *you*, Suping, who I saw listening so rapturously to the man dispensing his useless wisdom, you had better be a bit more critical and sceptical when people are volunteering their advice. "Possess the *right* kind of knowledge", your venerated Uncle Juntao advised you, eh Suping? Now you know that his advice was incomplete. He should have added "and use it to your advantage", isn't that right, Suping?'

Li fell silent, then he grinned sardonically and added, 'From the pained look in your father's eyes I see that he has got the message though he still finds it ethically objectionable. He'll get over that threshold soon enough, I'll promise him that. A few days in prison will take care of his ethics. Your foxy Uncle Dan, that scholar-in-peasant's disguise knew all this all along, eh Dan, my friend? Never underestimate the peasants, Suping. They may lack formal knowledge, but they know the *facts of life*. They are *sly* and *ruthless*. Don't forget that while you live amongst them.

'Comrade Zhang here is another apt case of the clever peasant-intellectual. Like your Uncle Dan, Suping, but in a much different way. He is ambitious, Comrade Zhang is, and he has his course to power all charted out. Fortunately it suits his own plans for himself to let me have my way with you. If not, we would all be keeping comrade Qian Weiying company, on our way to the mines, eh Zhang?'

Despite her earlier emotions and revulsion and Li's handling of Ai Chen's case, Suping felt a strange fascination for the man. He emanated self-confidence and power and a male magnetism that made her feel all fluttery.

She knew she would do will-lessly whatever he would tell her to do and the very prospect of that she felt alluring. How much more *man* he was than Father, or Uncle Juntao, or even Uncle Dan.

She had noticed clearly that Gao Chen had been at a loss for a retort when Li had teased him.

Gao Chen had found his master and she had been mischievously amused to see him fidget and hear him mutter his feeble protests. She had suddenly realised that Gao Chen was not controlling anything at all, that he was *being* controlled and *used*, much like everybody else, by forces and interests far out of his league and that she had just seen a glimpse of those forces in the person of Li.

Even Zhang, though still to a much lesser extent than Li, was way ahead of Gao Chen, she thought. Deceptively mild and friendly, Zhang was single-mindedly purposeful and he would never have any qualms about using his knowledge to his, and solely his, advantage.

Suping heard Zhang laugh at Li's dig at his machiavellianism. He laughed a lot, Zhang did, she thought. Clever! Angry or indignant denial would have made him vulnerable and incredible and, consequently, subject to follow-up attacks.

A laugh, though, was neither dissenting nor assenting and therefore usually would be the end of the matter.

'There is room for both of us in China, Li,' Zhang said, laughingly. 'I can be a useful man, to *your* master as well. Now, let's get back to the matters at hand,' he continued, matter-of-factly.

'Chen, you need some kind of vehicle to get your friend from the stadium to that hill of yours. My brother has a side car for his bicycle. I think it can take Juntao's body, provided you fasten it somehow. I'll give you a note for my brother asking him to lend you the bike with sidecar. I'll also ask him to keep

Juntao's grave clean as I heard you mention that to Juntao. After the execution come to see me in the stadium's locker room. I'll have the papers for collection of the body and the bill for the bullet ready for you. It'll be one yuan for the bullet and fifty fen for the papers. I'll give you a receipt. I'll arrange also for a burial permit. Please give me a small sketch of the site and the position of the grave in relation to the path so that I can attach it to the burial permit and stamp it for approval. It's a bit unusual since it's outside cemetery grounds, however, the vice-mayor owes me a favour or two. I'll put enough stamps and illegible signatures on it to take a lifetime for some fussy cadre to trace them back in case he would want to contest the permit's validity.

'Now, if you have no questions you had better go, Chen. No need for extensive farewells to your friends here. I'll give instructions to the prison guards to let you visit the prisoners for thirty minutes each day until they leave for Chengdu. I can't put you on the same truck since they are convicts and you are not. I see that our little generals are getting restless so please step forward, Chen Dan, and sign here for receipt of convict 1/11's belt and shoelaces.'

Gao Chen stepped forward and signed.

'Please leave now, Chen,' Zhang added, 'I'll see you tomorrow morning at about ten thirty.'

Gao Chen, uncharacteristically subdued, smiled uncertainly at his friends and said, 'I'll see you tomorrow afternoon. I'll dig Juntao's grave this evening. On the way home I'll order a simple coffin and have it delivered early tomorrow morning so that the coffin maker can help me put it in the grave. Juntao I'll handle by myself. Don't worry about me. I'll manage. Somehow Li's words had a sobering effect on all of us, I think. Emotional tantrums would be out of place, wouldn't they? See you tomorrow.' With a wave, he turned and walked out of the hall, down the stairs and into a hostile, indifferent world.

A different man, a lonely man. Nobody to care for him, nobody to care for.

'Poor Gao Chen,' Suping heard her mother say, 'the small, soap-bubble world we had created and lived in for the past year has blown up. For us it's the first time our world has gone to pieces, but for Gao Chen it must be the third or fourth time already. I wonder whether he has the resilience to pick himself up from the ruins one more time?'

'Oh, he will, no doubt about that,' Li answered. 'People like Chen Dan never have the *best* of all worlds, they lack the character for that. They *let* things happen rather than *make* them happen. But somehow they always survive. As a record-keeper he will learn to fiddle and juggle his figures and people who depend on those fake figures will owe him and make it possible for him to lead a reasonably happy life. He could have been a big man a long time ago had he chosen to *use* people.'

Li fell silent, thoughtful for a moment, then he added, 'I won't see you again. You'll be outside the *taifong*'s path. Keep your own counsel. Let things happen as they come. Don't anticipate. Follow the way of least resistance and you'll survive as well. As things are now you cannot expect intervention or protection again unless your life is in real danger perhaps. I don't know. You are on your own from now on. You owe me nothing. You do not know me. I have already forgotten everything about the few insignificant cases that came before the People's Tribunal during my short stay in Luding. Red Guards! Lead these three convicts to their cell!'

Li turned his back on them and that was the last Suping was to see of him. Or so she thought.

# *Chapter Twenty*

## Convicts

The prison guard leading the way, the three Red Guards following behind them, Xu Ximing, his wife Liu Guixian, and his daughter Suping walked through the dimly lit, drab and damp corridor of Luding's Detention House.

On both sides of the corridor were heavy, steel doors, fastened with padlocks.

The prison guard, a fat, bow-legged woman with small, slit eyes and greasy, short, straight hair, halted in front of a door with the number twenty-one in big, red, irregularly painted figures.

Laboriously she selected a key from amongst a hundred or so on a big, steel ring hanging from a belt, unlocked the padlock and opened the door.

'Get in!' she ordered gruffly.

Pushed roughly between their shoulder blades by the Red Guards, the Xus stumbled forward and into the cell and, before they could have asked or said something, the door was slammed shut and they heard the padlock being replaced and clicked.

Suping looked around in the semi-darkness and her heart sank. Cobwebs, black and heavy with soot and dust, dangled from the ceiling in the corners. The walls, once whitewashed, long ago, probably for the first and only time when the building had been constructed forty or so years ago, were cracked and covered with damp, crumbling, yellowish saltpetre, like a leper oozing from his sores. From the ceiling hung a single, naked bulb, its light barely able to get through the coat of grime and dust, giving the cell a ghostly gloominess.

The floor was bare concrete, black with dampness.

In one corner stood a cement bucket. From the shreds of dried, yellowish-brown old newspaper that still stuck to its rim Suping guessed that the bucket was the cell's toilet.

Next to the bucket, at the end of a piece of steel pipe, fixed to the wall with a few bent, rusty nails and a piece of plank, was a dripping, corroded valve above an open drain. The only furniture consisted of three dust-covered plank beds, stacked one on top of the other against a side wall.

High on the back wall was a small, barred window whose glass pane was so covered with grime that it was nothing more than a slightly lighter patch on the dark wall.

The air was dank and musty. Suping had never in her life been in such a filthy place. Despairingly she stared at her parents, on the verge of tears.

'It's only for a couple of days,' her father said hesitantly. 'We should be glad that we're still together, so let's not complain lest they separate us here already. In the communes we'll have plenty of fresh air, I suppose. Think of poor Ai Chen, his cell is certainly worse than this one and that for the last night of his life.'

Xu was interrupted by a small shutter in the door being opened and the guard peering inside.

'Have you got any money on you?' she asked bluntly.

'For what?' Xu asked, in turn.

'For toilet paper and blankets,' the guard answered irritably. 'You are not entitled to those things, however, if you give me three yuan I'll give you a few old newspapers to wipe your arse with and three blankets, dirty ones. For six yuan I can get you real toilet paper and clean blankets and one towel for the three of you. Now, make up your mind, what do you want?'

'Yes! We'll pay you,' Guixian replied calmly. 'Please get us the paper, the blankets and the towel and we'll have the money for you when you return.'

The guard slammed the shutter and they heard her shuffling away in the corridor.

'Bless Gao Chen and his foresight,' Xu chuckled. 'Quick, Suping, cut your belt and take six yuan out before the old hag returns and sees where we have hidden our money. Mother and I'll give you back four yuan tonight, when nobody observes us.'

From the bag she had tied to her belly, under her blouse, Suping took the small knife she used to use for peeling onions and quickly cut the stitches of her belt. She removed seven yuan and handed the grubby notes to her father.

With the needle and threat that Gao Chen had instructed her to hide in the belt she quickly stitched the belt again and tied it back around her waist. The whole operation had not even taken five minutes.

They smiled triumphantly at each other. It was their first small victory over the system and as such a very important one for their morale.

Guixian blew the dust from the bottom plank bed and gingerly they sat down, closely together, heaving a sigh of relief.

Twenty minutes passed in silence before they heard the shuffling gait of the guard approaching in the corridor.

The shutter opened and they saw the old woman's face in the small opening.

'Stay where you are, on that bed,' she grumbled. 'I have to come inside to put your things on the floor, next to the door.'

They heard her fumbling with the keys and the padlock and then the door swung creakingly open.

The woman came in, breathing heavily, and, while keeping her eyes on her prisoners, she put three folded blankets, a towel, a roll of coarse, greyish toilet paper and a plastic basin on the floor. She fumbled in the pocket of her jacket and produced a piece of soap which she put in the basin.

'The basin and the soap are my own,' she said, straightening up with more heavy breathing. 'There's no charge for that. I know your kind of people like to wash yourself every day. Hide the basin and the soap under the lower bed so that the Red Guards can't see them should they suddenly come in.'

She hesitated, clearly upset by something, then she blurted, 'Thirty years I did my job here. Never missed a day. My leaders never complained and now a bunch of wild-eyed snots yell at me, "Come here! Go there! Do this! Do that!" I told them they couldn't have their interrogation sessions in the cells. That's for the interrogator, I told them. They were so angry they nearly hit me with their sticks.

'They shouted that all old people are reactionaries and should be killed. Only the Red Guards are the true revolutionaries, they screamed, spitting in my face. Only the Red Guards can expose and weed out the real enemies of the People, they holler, the interrogators are much too weak they claim. But for themselves, *everybody* is guilty of many more crimes than the interrogators find out and therefore they *must* have their own interrogation sessions, they say, to discover the hidden crimes and demand heavier sentences. *Not* in my prison, I told them. *Not* as long as I am the guard, I said.

'They all left, very angry. Only Du Zhimin is still there. He brought in a category one prisoner just before you people came in. Maybe you saw him. Tall, shabby man with a lugubrious face. Not a criminal if you ask me. It's not their looks, you know. Some look like angels but are worse than demons. It's their *smell*. Criminals have a peculiar *smell* I would know anywhere. Now Du just sits there, staring at his own prisoner, proud and afraid at the same time.

'The cells in block forty have grated doors so the prisoners can be watched all the time. Some of them try to commit suicide by banging their head against the night-soil bucket or by swallowing their tongue. It's a crime to evade the people's justice by committing suicide and the guard who fails to prevent it is punished. So Du watches his man, number eleven, all the time. Eleven of them there are. Going to be shot tomorrow morning I have been told. I need to know, you see, because no morning rice for them on the day of their execution. Save the rice for the living. Besides, most of them foul their pants when they are made to kneel down to receive the bullet in the back of the head. More rice, more shit. That'll be six yuan.' And the ungainly old woman stretched out her hand.

Xu stood up and took the few steps, slowly, to where she was standing and handed the money to her.

She counted the notes before putting them in the pocket of her trousers.

'We thank you for the soap and the basin,' Xu said, 'though it's your kindness that counts most.'

The guard looked at him and past him at Guixian and Suping.

'You are decent people,' she said brusquely, 'I can tell. Many of those yellers with their red armbands should be here instead of you, like that rabid bitch Qian in cell thirty-nine. They had to tie her to her bed, trying as she did to bite a Red Guard's throat when they brought her in this morning. She bangs her head against the bed planks, foam at her mouth. Terrible. I won't go near her, even tied up as she is.

'Now, you are entitled to a bowl of plain rice for your evening meal. It's five fen for a helping of vegetables, ten fen more for a few pieces of chicken. Tell me what you want. I have to tell the kitchen before five o'clock. The struggle meeting starts at six every evening, until nine. Told them my whole life had been a struggle but they didn't understand. Told me mine was the wrong kind of struggle, theirs the right one, to unify our thoughts. Made me laugh.'

She sighed sadly, 'What a life! Get up at four in the morning just to catch the bus at four thirty to arrive here at ten to six. Day shift from six to six. Struggle meetings from six to nine. Bus back home at nine fifteen, the last one of the day. If I miss it I have to spend the night here, in an empty cell. If I catch it I'm home at eleven. Some housework and it's midnight when I'm finally in bed. Damn their struggle meetings. What do *they* know about struggle. About tired, old bodies who only want to be left in peace. You didn't tell me what you wanted.' She finished her tiredly angry tirade, abruptly and somewhat petulantly, Suping thought.

'We would like some vegetables and a few pieces of chicken with our rice,' Guixian said. 'Ximing, give madam one yuan. Perhaps we could have some tea also? Also tomorrow morning, with our morning rice?'

The guard took the yuan note and, walking backwards out of the door, she mumbled, 'I'll see what I can do,' and she closed the door and the padlock.

They had just washed up a bit and each put a blanket on their beds when they heard loud, quarrelling, juvenile voices in the corridor and coming to a halt in front of their cell.

The shutter in the door opened once more and the guard, squeezing her whole face in the opening, said loudly, 'The convicts must sit down on their bare beds and not move, I repeat *not move*, while I open the door and put the bowls with their rice on the floor!' Then she closed the shutter again, slowly and deliberately.

Hurriedly Guixian pulled the blankets off the beds and pushed them as far as she could underneath the bottom one. Then they sat down rigidly while the fumbling with the keys was still going on outside, taking much longer than before.

'She wants to give us time,' Guixian whispered. 'Suping, quick! Put the soap in your pocket and push the basin under the bed as far as you can!'

'Hurry up! You old sow!' an angry girl's voice shouted. 'You are too slow for the job! Tomorrow all the cells will be full. How will you cope? You are useless!'

Finally the door swung open and five Red Guards, all girls of about seventeen, rushed in, past the old guard who was carrying three bowls of plain rice on a tray.

'Stand up, cows!' the girls screamed, pell-mell, at the Xus. The tallest girl, her pretty features distorted by near-hysterical anger, pushed Xu repeatedly against his chest, yelling, 'Did you order vegetables and chicken? Answer me, cow! Did you?'

Xu had momentarily caught the old woman's eye. She nodded once, then shook her head almost imperceptibly.

'Yes, we did,' Xu answered calmly, 'we knew that that was permitted.'

'*We* determine here what is permitted!' the girl shouted back. 'No more ordering by your kind! You are cows and snakes, enemies of the People! You will all be destroyed! No more vegetables and meat for your kind! Those are for the workers! Did you give that old sow money?' she asked suddenly, in a normal tone and pointing at the old guard.

'*No*! We did not!' Xu replied, 'we would have paid later since we have no money on us at present.'

'They used soap!' another of the girls shrieked, in the corner, where the water tap was. 'I smell it! I smell it! And there is foam in the drain!'

The tall girl brought her face close to Suping's and sniffed.

'Who gave you the soap, cow?' she hissed. 'Don't you know that washing your body with perfumed soap is bourgeois decadence?'

'This is *my* soap,' Suping answered with an indifferent shrug, 'nobody gave it to me,' she added, taking the bar of soap out of her pocket.

The Red Guard snatched the piece of soap from Suping's hand and threw it on the floor.

'Crush it!' she screamed at Suping, 'Crush it, cow, or we'll crush *you*!'

Suping, shoved forward roughly by the girl, stumbled to where the bar of soap had slithered on the floor and she was about to step on it when she heard a man's voice ask, 'What's going on here?'

It was Zhang, standing in the open door, looking at the scene inside.

Suping saw the tall Red Guard go pale as she looked at the other girls who were clearly frightened.

'I dropped my bar of soap,' Suping replied, calmly. 'The Red Guard here ordered me to pick it up. She admonished me to use it sparingly as I would probably not get another piece soon.'

'Soap is subsidised produce and therefore state property,' Zhang said, straight-faced. 'We all have to be careful with state property,' he continued. 'You were quite right to point this out to the prisoner, comrade.' Zhang looked at the tall girl.

'I may add that the wilful destruction of state property, as well the instigation to commit such acts of sabotage, are serious crimes punishable by long prison sentences. The death penalty may even be given in certain instances.'

Zhang fell silent and, after a few uncomfortable seconds, he continued, addressing himself to the five Red Guards, 'Now, go to the canteen and prepare yourselves for the struggle meeting. Comrade Prison Guard Lo will *not* attend the meeting tonight as she will have to be present, as a witness, during my final interrogation of these prisoners here in this cell. Now go!'

Deflated the girls shuffled out of the cell, the tall one last. At the door she turned her head and looked for a second at Suping, quizzically. Then she too disappeared into the dark corridor.

'That was very wise what you did, Suping,' Zhang said smilingly. 'If you handle every difficult situation that delicately and diplomatically you'll get through very well, I'm sure.'

Turning towards the glum-looking prison guard he said, kindly, 'Fetch some vegetables and chicken from the kitchen, Auntie Lo, please. Tell them it is for the comrade interrogator. Then go home. I'll close the cell door padlock for you when I'll have finished with my interrogation here.'

Lo looked up at Zhang and, smiling fleetingly, she said, 'Thank you, Yizhong. You have become a big man in this brave new world of yours. I cannot adapt, Yizhong. I'm too old and tired and I don't care any more. Get me an early retirement, Yizhong. I am sure the vice-mayor owes you a couple of favours like every important person in this county owes you. Cash in one for me, Yizhong. You owe me one.'

Zhang laughed heartily and said, 'I'll think about it, Auntie Lo. I can't promise anything but I'll see what I can do for you. Now, fetch us the vegetables and chicken before they close the kitchen for the struggle meeting at six o'clock.'

Turning to Xu, Zhang added, 'Let's take the top bed down and put it against this wall here. It'll be easier for you to get in and out of bed and for now I can sit on it while we have a few words after you have eaten your rice.'

Without further ado Xu and Zhang lifted the top bed up and carried it across the cell where they put it down on the floor against the opposite wall. Zhang sat down on the bed and gestured for the Xus to sit down on the lower bed opposite him.

'Madam Lo has been my parents' neighbour for over forty years,' he explained. 'I used to see her practically every day until I was twenty and left our village to work and live in a foundry near Emei. We, my brother and I, used to call her Auntie Lo although she is no relative. I always got on very well with her and when I came to visit my parents, twice a year, I always dropped by Auntie Lo's house, to pay my respects and have a bit of gossip. One night, her husband, a cormorant fisherman, drowned while trying to free his bird from a net it had got entangled in. They had no children to support her so Auntie Lo had to find a job. She got herself appointed as a junior guard in the Detention House and she is still here, after all these years.

'The Japanese during the war, the foreigners after the war, the Nationalists, the Communists, the civil war, the massacre of the Communists on the bridge near here, liberation, all the campaigns, Auntie Lo survived them all, unconcerned, indifferent, doing her job every day, a prison fixture. But now it's different apparently. She's clearly upset by the way things are going. In the past, Nationalists, Japanese, foreigners, Communists, they all brought their prisoners in and took them out and Madam Lo was just taken for granted. Her opinion didn't matter. She was the guard and that was just fine with her. She observed, kept her own counsel and her mouth shut.

'But these days, those young Red Guards see her as a relic of the detested past, as an obstacle to the glorious Cultural Revolution unimpressed by their god and heroes. I'm afraid that one of these days she'll become so fed up with their meddling in her business that she'll put the hotheads in their place. They won't take that, of course, and they are crazy enough to force a dunce cap over her head and chase her around town until she drops dead.'

Zhang fell silent, then continued pensively, more talking to himself than to the others, 'I'll have a word with the vice-mayor next week, after my confirmation as the new city Party secretary. I'll propose Leading Red Guard Du for the job. He has been making remarks behind my back about what he considers misplaced leniency towards you and Chen Dan. As the guard in this dump he'll be completely out of the main flow of events and the beauty of it is that he won't realise until it's too late and he'll be marooned here for the rest of his life. The fool may even think at first that it's a promotion.'

Zhang laughed heartily at the prospect of outfoxing yet another nuisance on his path to greater glory.

At that moment Madam Lo returned, carrying a tray with a large, steaming bowl. Suping stood up quickly and took the tray from her.

'Thank you, child,' Madam Lo said, 'your rice has become cold, I'm afraid, however, the chicken and vegetables are still steaming hot so that'll do. Eat before everything becomes cold in the dankness. Thank you also for protecting me against those furies.'

Addressing herself to Zhang, she added, 'I'll go home now, Yizhong. For once I'll be early so that I can catch a good night's sleep. Don't forget to close the padlock and to pull the front door behind you until you hear it click. Those at the struggle meeting always leave by the back door.'

Turning again to her charges she said, 'I'll wake you up at five to six. You have fifteen minutes to make your toilet, after that one of you has to shout "report!" and I'll bring you two pails for you must slop out the night-soil and dump it into the pit in the yard. You will get your morning rice a bit after seven o'clock only since the kitchen personnel eat first and most of them only arrive at around seven. If there are no Red Guards at that time I'll tell the cook to put in a few pieces of chicken, otherwise it'll be just plain rice and I'll give you back your one yuan. Have you any questions?'

They shook their head. It was all depressingly clear.

'Don't forget what I asked you, Yizhong,' Madam Lo added and then she turned and left without a further word or glance, closing the door behind her.

'Eat first,' Zhang said, 'in the meantime I'll do some thinking.'

It was their first meal since the previous afternoon and the Xus ate with gusto.

The rice was third grade and mostly broken grains so, cooked probably the day before, it was doughy and cold. The vegetables and chicken, however, were surprisingly tasty, as the cook had added some oyster sauce, and hot.

All things considered, it was not a bad meal at all and within five minutes everything was finished and Suping washed the bowl and chopsticks under the spraying and splashing tap, wetting her feet and trouser legs. She put the utensils back on the tray and next to the door.

Then she sat down, between her father and mother, waiting for Zhang to say what he thought he had to say.

'I bet that Beggars Chicken tasted much better,' Zhang said, grinning mischievously. 'Good grief, my mouth was watering that night, sitting there behind that hedge without food and drink, for hours. My ears full of Chen Dan's story, my nose quivering with the smell of his chicken, my mouth watering but my stomach empty. I thought the story would never end, interesting as it was though. It made me change my outlook on my own life, as it did for you as well, I'm sure. And that is the main reason why I am here now.'

Zhang fell silent, stood up and pushed the cell door open. He picked up the tray and went into the dark corridor.

He came back almost immediately, without the tray, and pulling the door behind him, he said, smiling wryly, 'I put the things on the floor, a few paces into the corridor. If anybody thinks to be smart and listen to what I say here, he'll trip over the tray and break the bowls, I hope. The noise'll warn us and I'll slam him, or her, with an accusation of wanton destruction of state property.'

He laughed and, lowering himself on the single bed, he said, 'Machiavellianism was the word I heard you use to describe those tricks. I asked late Headmaster Yang what that word meant and I remember how curiously he watched me before he said that he found it kind of strange that I should ask that since I could pass for the Chinese reincarnation of that Italian prince Niccolò Machiavelli, the sly counsellor to his king.'

Xu laughed because of Zhang's funny pronunciation of the foreign name.

'Why do you laugh, Xu?' Zhang asked, good-humouredly.

'Because of the way you pronounce that name,' Xu answered, chuckling. 'In the dialect I used to speak, as a child, the way you pronounced it means something like "you fall for it, prune smells good, rotten inside". How appropriate.'

Zhang smiled. 'Yes, how appropriate,' he said. 'Italians must be a tricky nation. They could teach us Chinese a trick or two, I'm sure.'

'The criminal organisation that ruled China before liberation couldn't have agreed more,' Xu said, serious now. 'However, discussing the similarities between Chinese and Italian culture is not what you are here for, I'm sure, so what *is* on your mind, Zhang Yizhong?'

Zhang, watching the Xu family, eyes half-closed, head leaning back against the wall, said slowly, 'No! You're right, Xu, that is not why I came back to see you. I had better be frank with you. I want to be part of that scheme Chen Dan spoke about that evening you had that Beggars Chicken. I want to play in the same league as Li. I want to know more about those notes, those Yang Baolin notes as I heard you call them. I missed that part of Chen's story because I had to pee. I could hardly do that where I was, you would have heard it, or smelled it, whatever. So I sneaked off for maybe ten minutes, peed, had a mug of tea and came back. All very quick but long enough apparently to miss the important part about those notes.

'What's in those notes, Xu? Why are they so important that Chen Dan, who has them in his possession or has hidden them somewhere, cannot be touched and a big Party shot like Li comes all the way from Chongqing to play the interrogator for him and without hesitation sends a harmless man like Chen Juntao to his death for the sole purpose of taking the heat away from him, Li, as he practically lets Dan go free. If I can use your answers to these questions I will owe you and your family, Xu, and you can call on me for favours in the future, provided I will then still be in a position to dispense favours rather than needing them myself.'

Zhang fell silent but continued to watch them, relaxed, his back against the wall.

Xu looked at his wife and daughter, apparently at a loss what to say.

Guixian nodded and, heaving a big sigh, she looked at Zhang and said, 'I think we owe you for not reporting us to the State Security Bureau. However, we also realise that it is now too late for you to do so since you already gave us such a relatively low sentence despite the fact that you knew all those incriminatory things about us. Reporting us now would probably be the end of Zhang Yizhong's political life, if not of his physical one as well.

'Be that as it may, you already know as much about what Chen Dan calls 'the Plan' as we do since you heard everything we did. You know therefore also that my daughter Suping and I have been or will be proposed by Chen for some minor role or other in the future context of the Plan, some indefinite future if ever there was one. Apart from that we know nothing more than you do. If you want to be part of the Plan, Yizhong, I suggest that you talk to Chen Dan directly, preferably before he leaves for Chengdu as well.

'Now about the so-called Yang Baolin notes. From the early part of Chen Dan's story you remember who Yang Baolin was. The part of Chen's story that I can think of you missed, was about how Yang, over a period of seven years, secretly recorded how some of Mao's closest comrades, those of the very first hour and most of whom still seem to be in power, betrayed him and the Communist cause by conspiring with the Japanese and the Nationalists alike. Yang was tortured to death for refusing to divulge where he kept those notes or whom they were about.

'Yang's widow, Lingling, fled Yan'an with the notes. Lingling managed to reach Shanghai, after terrible hardships, where she found Chen Dan, at that time a professor at Fudan University. They married in secret but Lingling was found murdered seven months later; her throat had been slit. The whole house had been ransacked but nothing of value was stolen. Whether the murderers were burglars turned killers when they were surprised by Lingling's unexpectedly early return while they were searching for the notes or were simply hired killers to intimidate Chen to keep quiet about the notes when they couldn't find them, that much was not clear from Chen Dan's story that evening. I myself intended to ask him about that later, however, the tribulations of the past few days made that hardly relevant any more.

'Whether he has hidden the notes somewhere or carries them with him, on his person, I also don't know, but whatever the case, it seems that he has deposited copies somewhere, or with somebody unknown to me but whom he must trust totally, with the instruction to send the notes to certain foreign magazines and newspapers should he, Chen Dan, or certain close friends of his, including us apparently, die from unnatural causes or as a victim of China's penitentiary system. The damage to the Party as a whole would be enormous, not to speak of those now in power and who are implicated in the notes. Hence the concern of all those in the know, whether crooked or straight, to keep Chen Dan in reasonably good physical shape so that he can die someday of natural causes. I doubt whether you can profit from this knowledge, Yizhong. It might very well prove to be a very dangerous kind of knowledge as long as Chen hasn't made it known that your name be included on the list of those close friends whose demise would set the whole circus in motion. Remember Lingling! Her throat was slit before Chen Dan made those precautionary arrangements. Chen undoubtedly has his reasons for not having avenged Lingling's death, at that time or later, by authorising the publication of the notes. Don't play with fire, Zhang!'

Guixian fell silent and they waited patiently for Zhang's reaction.

After a few minutes of reflection Zhang looked up at Guixian and said, 'You have spoken wisely, Guixian. I shall heed your advice about those notes. I shall, however, speak to Chen Dan about the Plan. There are too many things happening these days that I can't stomach any more. But then I realise that I am between a rock and a hard place. With my high profile I can't possibly withdraw. That would make me suspect and I would end up in a labour camp or worse. On the other hand, continuing as I have done so far with nothing but my own self-promotion to motivate me becomes more and more disgusting. If my self-promotion could fit in with something more worth while, well, that would be the best of all worlds for me, wouldn't it? At the same time the danger of being found out would add a bit of spice as well.'

Zhang fell silent, hesitated for a second, then continued, 'I would like to ask your advice about still another matter that may have some relevance for Chen Dan. Let me explain first. Last week a man was condemned to death by Luding's regular court of justice, so not by those clowns of the so-called People's Tribunal, for murdering seven people. However, since the victims were Red Guards and a commune leader, the murderer's own cousin to boot, the People's Tribunal has arrogated the case under the pretext that the murders were politically inspired. Frankly, I was the one behind the arrogation. You probably know that the People's Tribunals are given quotas of political cases in different categories of gravity. They are bound to find the accused, that's to say the victims, to fill these quotas or else they will be investigated for lack of political ardour and vigilance.

'The highest percentages are in the relatively benign penalty categories, such as re-education and reform through communal service, labour camps and hard labour of up to ten years. For the Tribunals in the smaller towns these are the only categories they are allowed to deal with. The People's Tribunals in the larger towns receive also quotas for hard labour up to twenty-five years, hard labour with extreme prejudice and even straightforward death sentences. Though Luding is not big enough to qualify for such extreme cases, the town has a place in the history of the Communists' Long March and therefore, as a special tribute, its People's Tribunal has been given quotas for all categories. You will understand that even in these days candidates for the death penalty are not so easy to come by, hence my effort to arrogate those cases of the regular court of justice that even remotely smack of politics.

'Of the eleven death sentences to be carried out tomorrow only one, your friend Chen Juntao, was passed by the People's Tribunal, a shortfall of three on our quota for this month. With the arrogation of the Red Guards' murder case and the sabotage and swindling cases, the Tribunal has now nine death sentence cases, one more than its quota for two months. I thought that that would make me shine in the eyes of my leaders.

'Don't stare at me like that, Suping!' Zhang exclaimed suddenly. 'As if I am some kind of horrible monster. Can't you understand that the drive to survive makes you do things that, in retrospect, are not so nice? But who is to judge but oneself?' I told you that I am getting fed up with the whole rigmarole and that I wanted to talk to Chen Dan, didn't I? So hear me out, will you?'

Zhang fell silent, visibly trying to get himself back in control. After a while, he said, barely audible, 'I'm sorry, Suping. I shouldn't have yelled at you. I'm nervous and irritable and not at all happy with myself.'

'Suping has already learned more than I like about life's less pleasant aspects these past few days,' Guixian interrupted calmly. 'However, she hasn't become a complete cynic yet and certain acts of callousness still horrify her. May that remain so I hope, as her mother. But continue, Zhang! Something about that Red Guards' murder case is bothering you specifically and it has something to do with our friend Chen Dan, so what is it? Tell us!'

'The murderer's name is Chen Faxian,' Zhang answered, tonelessly. 'Thinking this afternoon of Chen Dan's life story I suddenly remembered why the murderer's name rang a bell. Chen Faxian is Chen Dan's cousin, the one who protected him that night when he, Dan, was beaten so terribly by his own father for having helped Liang Ailing escape. Faxian later that night helped Dan to reach Liu Longfei's place in the marshes. Do you remember now?'

'Monkeyface!' Suping exclaimed suddenly.

Zhang stared at her, utterly bewildered.

'Monkeyface, Uncle Dan called him,' Suping went on, excitedly. 'We met him the day Uncle Dan and I went to fetch the mud for the Beggars Chicken. He's a fisherman and he was on his boat on the river that day looking for Uncle Dan whom he called "Hedgehog" because of his spiky hair. Those two old women we met at the market earlier that morning, Aunties One and Two, you remember, Mother? they told Chen Faxian that Uncle Dan was back in the neighbourhood.

'Uncle Dan and his cousin Faxian were very happy to see each other again after all those years and Monkeyface Chen was very proud of his boat and his cormorants. He was a free man, he said, and he had a special deal with the commune that was to everybody's advantage. He talked about his cormorants as if they were his wife and children. I remember that so well because at first I didn't understand that he meant his birds and I was shocked by what he said but then we had a good laugh. And now you say that this man is a murderer?

Impossible! There must be some mistake. He seemed such a happy-go-lucky man.'

'That's the trouble with those so-called happy-go-lucky people,' Zhang sighed. 'Because they seem always to be happy and to love the whole world they think the whole world loves them too and they don't understand when a bunch of nasties comes down on them like a ton of bricks and smashes their happy world to smithereens. Most of them become heartbroken, some of them go berserk and that's what Monkeyface did. He went berserk and killed his tormentors, six Red Guards, all in their late teens, and his own cousin, a woman called Chen Neiping, probably Chen Dan's sister, now I come to think of it. She was the commune leader and she was the one who had asked the Red Guards to come to Dada County's commune number four to spread the Cultural Revolution and to cleanse the commune of its counter-revolutionaries. A nasty, ugly woman she was, I heard, full of spite and hate. She denounced her own cousin, Faxian, to the Red Guards as a capitalist exploiter of the commune's workers because he owned a boat and eight cormorants and wanted to be paid for the fish he caught.

'Chen Faxian refused to confess. So they tied him up, beat him, forced excrement in his mouth, smashed his boat to pieces and cut the throats of his birds, before his face, splashing him with their blood. That must have driven him temporarily insane. The Red Guards left him tied to the gate of the hamlet while they gathered for evening rice and a meeting with the commune leader in the community centre, an all-wood construction hardly bigger than the other hovels. Somehow Chen Faxian managed to free himself.

'He beat the old shopkeeper Wong unconscious with a piece of pipe and took all the cans of kerosene, two hundred litres in all, and carried them near the community centre. He blocked the door by pushing wedges underneath it and splashed all two hundred litres of naphtha against the walls and the door and on the thatched roof. That done, he set fire to the hovel. Those inside never had a chance to get out alive and those who tried to get out through the one window had their throat cut. People who tried to put out the fire were chased off by Chen wielding his piece of pipe. They said he was dancing and cheering at the screams of his victims. He didn't try to flee the scene afterwards. The militia found him, weeping and hugging his dead birds.

'During his trial, when asked by the judge whether he had any regrets he said he had only one and that was that he had killed only six Red Guards. They should all be killed, he said, like the rabid dogs they are, and he, Faxian, would do just that given half the chance.'

Zhang fell silent and, shifting uncomfortably under the shocked stares of the Xus, he said, 'I'm worried that tomorrow, when Dan sees, beside his friend Juntao, also his cousin Faxian on the truck amongst the condemned, it'll be a bit too much and that he will do something reckless that may upset the whole, neat arrangement Li and I have made. Somehow I feel that he should be told beforehand and also the true circumstances, not the distorted and exaggerated stories he is bound to hear from the onlookers in the street. What do you think?' He looked at the Xus.

'I most certainly think that he must be told,' Guixian said firmly, 'and since you are going to see him tonight about your song and dance with the Plan, you can tell him about Faxian and about his sister as well.'

Looking at Zhang with a glimpse of a smile, she added, with a hint of mockery in her voice, 'I would tell Chen Dan about his cousin and his sister first if I were you, Yizhong, and, depending on his reaction, connect that with your rather sudden longing to be part of the Plan. That might work better than the other way round.'

'That's another piece of good advice, Liu Guixian,' Zhang said and, relieved, he stood up from the bed.

'I'll go and see Chen now. While I'm there I'll introduce him to my brother and we'll talk about the things Chen wants my brother to do. He's a bit special, my brother is, and Chen might hit the wrong note by himself.'

He took a few steps towards the door, hesitated, then turned and said, 'Chen will want to visit you tomorrow afternoon. I'll write out a visitor's pass for him for between four and five o'clock. I'll drop by tomorrow morning and tell Auntie Lo to put the prisoners, who will begin to pour in after the tribunal will have resumed its sessions at two o'clock, in the other cells first. Ten to twelve prisoners to one cell. Anyhow, there won't be enough beds.

'I'm the interrogator so I'll adjourn the session at six o'clock and order a struggle meeting for seven so as to limit the number of cases tomorrow to a hundred or so. That way Lo can manage to let you have your last night here by yourself, that is, if the trucks for your transport do indeed turn up the day after tomorrow. If they don't, I'm afraid you'll have to share your cell with other prisoners until your transport has been arranged.'

'What about those poor people in the square?' Guixian interrupted. 'There were already close to five hundred when we got there this morning and I suppose that those dreadful Red Guards are herding in more all the time. Today you handled only six cases, ours, those of the two Chens and Qian Weiying's. Tomorrow only a hundred, or so you say. Does that mean that those who haven't been tried yet have to stay there in that square? In the open air sitting on those cobblestones with their hands on their neck during the heat of the day and the cold of the night probably with very little food or drink if anything at all? Have you thought about these things? Have you foreseen that those poor people will get hungry and thirsty and probably need to relieve themselves? Where are they going to do that? It's inhuman, Zhang! It's monstrous!'

Guixian had difficulty keeping her voice down. Suping saw she was crying.

Suping wondered whether she ought to be ashamed of herself for not having thought, even fleetingly, of the unfortunates outside.

Strangely enough she didn't feel anything; no pity, no indignation, nothing, just sheer indifference.

She even chuckled, secretly, when she heard Zhang giving her mother a dressing down.

'So what would you like me to do, Madam Xu?' he sneered. 'Do you perhaps want me to try forty cases more tomorrow so that Lo has to cram ten more people in your cell? You won't be able to talk freely amongst yourselves and with your friend Chen Dan, with all those people around. Are you ready to fight with the others over your beds and blankets and accept to lie on the bare floor, if you lose? Ten more people, Madam Xu, touching you, pushing you, assaulting your senses with their smells, their sniffing, whining and sobbing, their farting, coughing and expectorating. Ten more people you have never met to shit and urinate in the same bucket as you, openly, just as you will have to relieve yourself in front of all of them. Are you ready to slop out all that shit and urine in the morning?

'You see, Madam Xu, it's much easier for me to let that happen than to go to all the trouble of sparing you such a situation. What's the price of your moral outrage, Madam Xu? Forty poor bastards less in the square or your relative comfort and privacy for the next two days and nights? Tell me, Guixian!'

By using her first name Zhang had softened his dressing down a bit at the last moment but he had made his point and Guixian, her head bowed in shame, replied in a small voice, 'Of course, you are right, Yizhong, and you did well to make me see my own hypocrisy. Please do as you said before. We are very grateful for what you do for us.'

'That's all right, Guixian,' Zhang replied and, smilingly, he added, 'You forgot for a moment that you are no longer sitting in your ivory tower, pontificating from a safe distance and in comfort about moral and ethical issues. The mere fact to have to defend oneself in the pigsty of true proletarian life usually changes one's ethical principles pretty fast. To safeguard your own morale in a situation such as the one wherein you find yourself now, you cannot afford your principles of morality, Guixian.

'Keep that in mind, the three of you, and stop wrestling with your consciences. Survival is the name of the game from now on! Go about it single-mindedly and ruthlessly. If need be, at the expense of others.'

Zhang had opened the door while he said those last words.

Turning in the door opening he added, 'If it makes you feel a bit better, Guixian, I'll talk to the vice-mayor tomorrow and ask him to see whether the school buildings, now that they have all been closed, can't be used as temporary detention centres for those awaiting trial. A group of bourgeois scoundrels under the supervision of former students, now playing revolutionary heroes, could even be sent out into the countryside to fetch bales of rice straw and spread the straw on the classroom floors. A nice, first lesson in proletarian solidarity, if such a thing exists at all.

'Now, try to get some sleep. I won't come to see you tomorrow, however, I'll be here the next day when you will board your truck. I'll hand you your transport and assignment documents myself.'

One last nod and Zhang closed the door behind him. They heard the padlock click shut and then the sound of his firm steps faded quickly in the corridor.

In the sudden silence the dripping of the tap in the drain sounded like the ticking of a large clock.

Absent-mindedly they kept shuffling their feet to keep the mosquitoes from settling down on their ankles, occasionally slapping their ears or neck when they heard that exasperating whine around their head.

'You got an earful and you deserved it, Guixian, my love,' Xu said, adding a bit peevishly, 'If you ever feel any more of those moral urgings coming try to think of the consequences first before you speak up. I'm not in the mood to suffer unnecessary hardship as a result of your moral outrage and neither is Suping, I'm sure. We should indeed have studied Lu Xun's *Quintessence of Worldly Wisdom* as Gao Chen once recommended. I'm sure we can use a bit of worldly wisdom in the days ahead. Now, if anybody is going to ask me to say one more profound word, I'm going to scream instead. Let's try to get some sleep. I'll take the top bed, Guixian, you the bottom one and our daughter, who is busily scratching her ankles to bleeding, the single bed opposite.'

At this Xu climbed on to the top bed and with a sigh he stretched himself.

'I'm sorry, Ximing,' his wife said in a small voice. 'I love you both and I promise I won't make trouble again.'

Vainly shifting and turning to find a position on the planks that didn't hurt their sore muscles and equally vainly trying to cover both head and feet with the musty-smelling blanket against the bloodthirsty mosquitoes and the damp, chilly air, they only slept in fits and starts.

Still, the pounding on the door and the stentorian voice of prison guard Lo shouting, 'Wake up! Wake up to another glorious day of the Great Proletarian Cultural Revolution! Long live our Great Leader Chairman Mao!' shocked them back into the sorry reality of Luding's Detention House.

'Night-soil collection in fifteen minutes!' Lo shouted, followed by several loud curses and the sounds of breaking pottery. Madam Lo had just stumbled over Zhang's trap for eavesdroppers, destroying valuable state property.

Ximing laughed loudly.

'Day two of the Xu convicts' life has just begun, 1,459 more to go for me and Suping and another 365 for you, my love,' and with a sob, barely able to suppress his emotion, he embraced and kissed his wife.

Suping joined them and hugged both of them.

'At least *we* have life to look forward to,' she said, sobbing. 'Whatever it may have in store for us, it will always be preferable to death. Poor, poor Uncle Juntao, he will be dead four hours from now. Did he sleep? What is he thinking about now, at this moment? Is he afraid to die? Nobody to talk to. Nobody to hold him and give him courage. Only goggle-eyed Leading Red Guard Du glaring at him through the bars of his cell door.

'Is he listening for the sound of sliding bolts on the death row door?

'Does he fear the crowd along the streets, taunting, jeering and spitting at him? Does he fear the twenty thousand pairs of eyes, in the stadium, watching gloatingly while he is being led to his place, forced to kneel and to bow his head to receive the bullet? Is he afraid it will hurt? Does he hope there will be a last-minute reprieve? So many questions and no answers. I am so sad, Mother, so terribly, terribly sad and scared for him.'

They held each other tightly, Mother and Suping weeping openly and Father fighting to keep his tears back.

Suddenly the shutter in the cell door opened and Madam Lo peered inside.

'It's ten past six,' she grumbled. 'You were supposed to shout "Report!" five minutes ago to signal that you are ready to clean out the night-soil bucket.'

'We have no night-soil, Madam Lo,' Xu said. 'We were thinking of our dear friend in cell forty-four who is going to die in a few hours' time. Have you seen him, Madam Lo? How is he? Tell us, please?'

Madam Lo opened the door and came into the cell without all the precautions of the previous day.

'Your friend is all right,' she said, gruffly. 'He has been talking the whole night to Leading Red Guard Du, who, by order of the People's Tribunal, was not allowed to talk back, not even to tell Chen to shut up. When I came in to relieve Du for a few minutes so that he could go to the toilet, he was mumbling some very nasty words to himself which, I think, he should not repeat in front of his comrades or else I'll see him shortly on the wrong side of a cell door. A really dangerous counter-revolutionary your friend Chen Juntao is, corrupting the mind of a Red Guard as he seems to have done.'

While talking, Madam Lo had shuffled over to the toilet bucket and peered inside.

'You have done nothing,' she said, frowning reproachfully. 'You must be less self-conscious and not care about your own or other people's sensitivities. Holding in your bladder and bowel contents is very bad for your health. Your tongue will become furred, your breath smelly, your skin sweaty with rashes and soon you'll be ill with all the rubbish accumulating and concentrating inside you.'

Shaking her head pityingly, Madam Lo added, 'You *must* get used to sharing your toilet with many people. In the countryside it's like that. Just a shack, in a public place or along the road, one side for men, one side for women, separated only by a small, three foot high wall in the middle. An open drain on each side of the small wall and you just squat above it and let go. You close your mind for the sounds and smells and people around you and let your body take over. Try to think of something pleasant or simply don't think at all. Nobody cares.'

'Thank you, Madam Lo,' Xu said, moved by the ungainly, old woman's gruffly kind attempts to be helpful.

'As you rightly guessed, we are not used to such things. Though our own small house was far from luxuriously appointed, the toilet was the one place where one had the luxury of privacy. Now, it appears, they have even taken that away.'

'I suppose that by "they" you mean the Communists,' Madam Lo replied. 'You are wrong, Xu. It has always been like that in the small towns, the villages and hamlets. Even those big apartment blocks in the cities have communal toilets. I have never known otherwise. Whether your stint amongst the peasants and workers will teach you people anything at all I wouldn't know but it will for certain give you an idea of how privileged you have been all your life.'

Madam Lo fell silent and, reverting to her role as a prison guard, she ordered sternly, 'Xu! Pick up the empty pail and make the movement of slopping out the toilet bucket!'

Xu, shrugging his shoulders, did as told, feeling ridiculous.

'Now pick up the other pail, Xu, fill it with water from the tap and slosh out the toilet bucket with *half* of the water!'

Again Xu complied docilely.

'Topple the toilet bucket into the drain and slosh the rest of the water down the drain as well,' Madam Lo continued.

'Be careful!' she added, sharply. 'You may only use one pail of water so make sure you use it well. If remnants of night-soil remain stuck in the drain it will stink the whole day and night and the next morning it'll be hard to remove. If you take more than one pail of water the other prisoners will report you to the guard so that you will be punished with two days' additional night-soil duty. Don't look so shocked, Xu!' the old woman said gruffly.

'Are you that naive? Your fellow prisoners are *not* your friends, Xu! They will rat on you just for a tiny advantage, to alleviate their own miserable lives. Whether you are punished, live or die doesn't mean a thing to them. Nobody gives a damn about you, Xu. They would kill you if they thought it would benefit them.

'Now, take the pail that's supposed to be full with night-soil and stand next to the door and shout, as loudly as you can, "Report!". Sooner or later the guard will turn up and let you out of the cell. You follow the guard like you are now going to follow me, to the prison yard, so that you understand what I am trying to teach you. In the yard you join the queue of the other prisoners on night-soil duty and when it's your turn you empty your pail in the cesspit. After that you fall in line with the others to rinse the empty pail under the tap in the yard. That finished you put the pail back in the storage shed. Finally you line up with the other prisoners in the yard and wait until you are escorted back to your cell. That may take time, depending on the guard's mood or on the number of prisoners. It happens often that you will not be back in your cell when your morning rice is distributed.

'If you haven't made a deal yet with one of your fellow prisoners to claim your portion for you and actually keep it for you and not eat it himself, you will go hungry until evening rice since no noon rice is served. Have you got all this, Xu? And you, Madam Xu, and your daughter as well. Just because you are women does not mean that you are exempt from night-soil duty.'

They nodded glumly.

'One more thing,' Madam Lo continued. 'At no time may you speak to another prisoner. If you do that and you are caught the guard may order you to remain standing in the yard for as long as he wants, even until he finishes his shift, even overnight. Now, walk in front of me, Xu, I'll give you directions. Later you explain to your wife and daughter. As from tomorrow you *must* know all this. If you make a mistake or ask a question, even of the guard, you will be punished. One day extra night-soil duty for each error.'

At that Xu, shoulders slumping, shuffled out of the door, followed by Lo who slammed the door shut behind her.

Suping and her mother looked at each other in despair.

'Terrible,' Guixian mumbled, half crying. 'Terrible, terrible. I feel so hopeless, so... so humiliated. I'm sure I'll vomit if I have to clean out that horrible bucket full of other people's excrements. I can't take it any more,' and sobbing she sat down on Suping's bed.

Suping felt her eyes stinging with tears, the hot tears of anger, not of self-pity, like her mother's.

'Don't cry like that, Mother!' she exclaimed, angrily stamping her feet. 'Don't let them get at you. If that is the way they say they live and how they want *us* to live as well, then let's show them our contempt by doing as they do, however, without losing our own identity and without sighing and whining. We must show them that we can live like them, like unwashed and uncultured plebs, however, they know that they will never be able to live like we used to.

'Don't give them the gloating satisfaction of seeing you miserable because of the filthy things they make you do. Our dignity must be visible in our eyes and bearing, not in the clothes they'll force us to wear or the things they'll force us to do.'

Taking her mother's tear-streaked face between her hands, Suping added, kindly but firmly, 'Now, stop snivelling and let's wash our face with Madam Lo's scented soap before Father returns.'

They had just finished washing up when the cell door opened again and Xu came in, followed by Madam Lo who carried a basket with bowls and chopsticks in one hand and an insulated container with hot rice in the other.

She in turn was followed by a Red Guard, a young girl of about sixteen with a friendly, pixie face, who carried a basket with mugs and a kettle of hot water.

'Morning rice,' Madam Lo grumbled, 'plain, third-grade rice and hot water, the proletarian breakfast for the spoiled bourgeois,' she added, probably for the Red Guard's benefit.

Madam Lo filled three bowls with sodden lumps of rice, stuck two chopsticks in each and put them down on the single plank bed.

The Red Guard placed three mugs beside the bowls, hesitated, then suddenly she fumbled in a pocket of her jacket and brought out a handful of green tea leaves which she divided over the three mugs. Eyes downcast she then filled the mugs to the rim with hot water.

Madam Lo's beady eyes hadn't missed a thing. She made no comment though.

'Speak up, girl!' she said instead. 'What were Party Secretary Zhang's instructions to you this morning regarding these three convicts?'

The girl took a deep breath, stared fixedly at a point on the wall and began to speak in a high, fast monotone. 'I shall come to your cell at ten o'clock this morning. I shall bring you your armbands, a brush and ink and our Great Leader Chairman Mao's Little Red Book, one for each of you. You must prepare your armbands as instructed by Comrade Zhang yesterday and put them on. You must then learn the first chapter of our Great Leader Mao's Teachings by heart. I shall come back at three o'clock this afternoon to hear you recite from memory the text you have studied. Every day you must learn one chapter by heart until you will be able to quote from the teachings on whatever subject.'

The girl fell silent, blushing and breathing out deeply, visibly relieved that she had been able to finish without error. Then she added, rather comically, 'I shall not fail in my duties because of my love for our Great Leader Chairman Mao.'

'We shall follow your instructions to the letter, Comrade Red Guard Pan,' Xu said, solemnly, 'so that you can report favourably to Party Secretary Zhang on how we fulfil our revolutionary duties wholeheartedly.'

The girl smiled delightedly and said, 'Thank you Academician Xu, and you also, Teacher Liu, for your dedication to reforming your thoughts. Before I became a Red Guard I used to attend your classes and you gave me good notes for what I now realise was worthless bourgeois teaching. I did not know that at that time since I was then still under the pernicious influence of bourgeois, feudalistic ideas. But now I know better, thanks to the struggle meetings I attend. Only by constantly repeating for myself the works of our Great Leader Chairman Mao will I be able to gradually forget what you taught me.

'My leaders have told me that they are satisfied that I shall succeed in eliminating all traces of your wrongful teaching. My leaders will be very pleased when I report on your resolute and wholehearted efforts to fully embrace our Great Leader Chairman Mao's Thoughts. One day, very soon, you and I and Comrade Guard Lo and everybody, we will all think in unified thought conforming with the wishes of our Chairman Mao.'

She nodded brightly at the four incredulous adults, turned and daintily tripped out of the cell, her ponytail dancing from shoulder to shoulder.

'They give me headaches,' the old guard grumbled, 'it's not normal. Nice children like her shouldn't talk that way.'

Looking directly at Xu she added, however, 'Don't make fun of her when she comes to see you, Xu. It's a small matter for you to do what she asks of you. Anyway, she won't understand your irony. Now, eat your rice and drink your tea before everything gets cold. Or rather, comrade Red Guard Pan Lanhua's tea I should say, offered to you with all the unselfish love of her compassionate little heart.'

At that Madam Lo fumbled in her pocket and produced a one-yuan note.

'Here's your money back,' she said, 'no chicken today, not now, not tonight. The revolutionary strugglers last night filched what was left and there won't be any delivery today, the cook told me. Everybody wants to be out in the streets to take revolutionary action against the class enemies. Revolutionary action?' she snorted derisively. 'My arse! Plain looting it is, nothing else. Much more profitable than delivering chicken and vegetables. We are very angry with our comrades as we too had only plain rice for breakfast this morning. So much for proletarian solidarity. Let *me* say that before *you* rub it in Xu,' and grumpily she slammed the door shut behind her.

They trifled with the lukewarm, sodden, tasteless lumpy rice, sipping from the green tea after each bit to rinse their mouth.

When they had finally finished Suping collected the bowls, mugs and chopsticks and rinsed them under the tap.

Then, following her parents' example, she lay down on her bed, on her back, hands behind her head and stared at the ceiling, thinking of nothing in particular, waiting for nothing in particular.

One hour passed like that in total silence, then, all of a sudden, the rumble of a truck engine and the intermittent roar of a crowd, muffled by the walls and the distance to the square in front of the Detention House, shook her out of her indolence and she looked at her watch.

'Nine o'clock,' she announced dreamily. 'Uncle Juntao is about to begin his last voyage on earth.'

'Spare us the imagery of your lively fantasy, Suping,' her father interrupted her quickly.

Chidingly he continued, 'You are always carried away by your imagination and emotions because you ascribe to others feelings you think you would experience yourself under the circumstances. You agonise, suffer or rejoice, as the case may be, because the other person is supposedly agonising, suffering or rejoicing. When you find out later that the other was not as much affected as your empathy made you believe, you feel let down. Your empathy may even prevent you from doing what your reason tells you you should do, for your own sake, for fear of causing hurt. This morning you were all upset, and made us so, because your imagination would have Ai Chen agonising the whole night about unanswerable questions and it appeared that all he did was to sow the seed of counter-revolutionary rebellion in poor Leading Red Guard Du's mind. With wicked glee to boot, I bet.'

Xu fell silent, then continued, chuckling, 'As far as I have been able to gauge Chen Juntao, he may even enjoy the whole circus around his person now that he has accepted his lot. I even think that he is enjoying himself for the first time in his life. I really think that, you know. In *my* imagination I see him, sitting on that truck, watching the crowd with that detached, scientific mind of his, like a biologist would watch a swarm of some sort of bug or other. He may even taunt them just to see how they react and then laugh, amusedly, at their confusion, anger or outrage.

'In the stadium he may even try to embarrass those dour morons of the People's Tribunal, either by doing something irreverent himself or by inciting that volatile character Chen Faxian, Gao Chen's cousin, to do something crazy. What he will certainly *not* do, however, is to let his head hang down or to struggle with the Red Guards, screaming for mercy. His attitude will be one of contemptuous, bored dignity.'

'Your father is right, Suping,' Guixian fell in with her husband. 'That's how we must remember Chen Juntao. He deserves that and it's easier on us as well. Be that as it may, we'll hear from Gao Chen this afternoon how it went. Let's now wait for Comrade Red Guard Pan Lanhua and her message about the virtues of socialist thought reform.'

Suping laughed. 'I'm glad you got over your depression so quickly, Mother,' she said. 'These mood swings are wearing me out though and I shall really do my best to control and then get rid of them completely. Father is right, I shouldn't let myself get carried away by my imagination. From now on I'll do exactly as ordered, speak only when spoken to and never ever volunteer for anything. That way there can be no blame. I'll try to be indifferent to other people's misery or sufferings. I'll just pay no attention, that's all. When things happen around me that do not concern me, I'll stand, sit or squat somewhere away from the goings-on and I'll study my fingernails, my thoughts elsewhere and nowhere, the very image of bored indifference.'

She chuckled and added, 'I really like the idea, you know. Perhaps I should even start smoking cigarettes so that I have something to do with my hands and can literally hide behind a smokescreen. What do you think?'

'Excellent, apart from the smoking,' Xu replied, smiling.

'I am afraid, though, that your eyes will always give you away. Anger, sadness, joy, fear, pity; all these emotions will be reflected in your eyes, Suping. Your eyes have always been the mirrors of your soul, betraying your deepest emotions. So avert your eyes or, better still, close them if you don't want others to see what you are really feeling.'

Their banter was interrupted by Madam Lo opening the shutter in the cell door.

Peering inside, she muttered, 'Red Guard Pan is here to see you. I'll have to lock her in with you. Stay where you are, on your beds, and don't move.'

She withdrew her head and opened the door.

Red Guard Pan came dancing in, a radiant smile on her pert little face.

'Are you all right?' she tinkled. 'Are you ready for your first revolutionary instruction?'

'We are ready, Comrade Red Guard Pan,' Xu replied solemnly.

The girl gave each of them a piece of white cloth and a safety pin and in turn they prepared their armbands, writing with Pan Lanhua's brush and ink their numbers and underneath the three characters of their names followed by 'bourgeois scoundrel'.

This finished, the girl gave them each a copy of Mao's Little Red Book and told them to write their names on the inside of its cover.

'From now on this is the only literature you need,' she trilled, clapping her tiny hands in real delight.

'The Little Red Book contains in condensed form all the accumulated wisdom of humanity as interpreted by our Great Leader Chairman Mao who we must love, venerate and obey. Nothing else matters. Nothing can be more important. Nothing can take precedence. That makes life very, very simple. Do you accept this wholeheartedly and without reservations?'

'We accept that, Comrade Red Guard,' Xu assured her.

'Very well then,' the girl replied happily and she continued.

'Comrade Party Secretary Zhang Yizhong has assigned me to the Detention House to welcome the self-confessed bourgeois intellectual reactionaries and to introduce them to our Great Leader Chairman Mao's Little Red Book. Comrade Zhang says that a ray of sunshine gladdens the heart when the sky is black and heavy with storm clouds and that it is important that those still ignorant of our Chairman's Thoughts begin the long process of reform with a heart full of hope rather than filled with despair. Comrade Zhang says that I am qualified to make those poor people see the light in the darkness of their ignorance because I have so fully and wholeheartedly embraced our Chairman Mao's doctrine.

'I was very nervous and scared when Comrade Zhang gave me that task because all those intellectual reactionaries are so much older than I am and you, Academician Xu and Teacher Liu, have even been my teachers before I became a Young Pioneer and, later, a Red Guard. But Comrade Zhang said that once one has accepted our Great Leader Chairman Mao's doctrine all one's fears simply evaporate. The second most important thing for me, Comrade Zhang says, is to be myself. Everybody will then accept the Little Red Book and promise me to study it carefully and wholeheartedly.'

Comrade Red Guard Pan Lanhua laughed her tinkling, silvery laugh and clapped her hands delightedly.

'I am so happy to see that Comrade Zhang is right,' she added joyfully, 'he is such a good leader. Now, you must all keep the Little Red Book on your person all the time and study it during every spare moment and discuss it with your fellow convicts so as to complete your reform quickly and get your sentences reviewed and reduced to three years. I would be so happy to see you back soon in Luding and teaching our Chairman's Doctrine in the new, revolutionary schools. Comrade Zhang said this morning that I need not come back to see you this afternoon for the rehearsal of the Little Red Book's first chapter since you will leave tomorrow for Chengdu. So I wish you all the best.'

'We wish you all the best as well, Xiao Hua,' Guixian said, clearly moved by the kind-hearted girl.

'We shall do our best to finish our re-education as quickly as possible and when we'll be back here, in our house, we hope that you will come and see us often.'

In a sudden impulse Guixian embraced the pretty little Red Guard, whose eyes suddenly brimmed with tears.

'Remain as you are, Little Orchid,' Guixian whispered, 'seldom a woman had a more appropriate name. True purity, unsullied by the filth of the swamp, a ray of hope for those struggling for breath in the dark, stinking water. How wise of the Party Secretary to assign you here.'

Xu and Suping stood up from their plank bed and took turns to embrace the girl.

'Please be careful,' she whispered, 'there are good and evil people everywhere, even close to our Beloved Chairman Mao. The evil ones always clamour the loudest for the most extreme actions, like former Red Guard Qian Weiying. Avoid their attention. Say nothing in their presence. Bow your head and continue with what you were doing or, if at all possible, slip away and out of their sight.'

Red Guard Pan fell silent, wiped her eyes with the back of her hand, turned and knocked on the door.

Lo must have been waiting in the corridor for the door opened almost immediately and, turning in the doorway, Pan Lanhua waved and with a last 'goodbye now' she was gone.

Madam Lo looked at the Xus and said, chucklingly, 'The new Party Secretary of Luding is a very clever man and also a good man. He knows that, however bad the circumstances are, people can still be made to feel good about something. The girl Pan Lanhua is his secret weapon. Impossible to remain angry with her around. So why don't you study Mao's Little Red Book as I am sure you promised Lanhua you would? There'll be no noon meal and your friend won't be here before four o'clock so you have all that time.'

The door clanged shut and they were alone again.

'I think we might as well study it a bit,' Guixian said, 'were it only to be able to quote from it when it suits our purpose. We have nothing else to do so let's browse through it. I'm not in the mood for philosophical discussions though, until we have heard from Gao Chen this afternoon.'

They lay down on their beds and casually leafed through the book that was to become the inspiration for the greatest mass hysteria mankind has ever known.

People of all walks of life and status were brainwashed with the psychobabble and pseudo-wisdom of a psychopath into believing themselves invulnerable, infallible or omnipotent and died, or caused others to die. People burnt to death, drowned, were crushed or smashed or were operated on, without anaesthetic, by total incompetents and, if not yet dead, died in excruciating pain when left without care or medicine.

All that suffering and misery because the crazy so-called Thoughts of a megalomaniacal, grudging peasant failed miserably when invoked to extinguish fires, to stop floods, to halt avalanches, to give an illiterate peasant the skills of a surgeon, to cure the injured or seriously ill.

Time passed slowly, the only sounds the rustling of paper, an amused chuckle, a derisive grunt.

Their initial interest waned to a bored, annoyed leafing until suddenly Xu exclaimed, 'What a load of superficial claptrap! How is it possible that people don't see the shallowness, the slickness, the utter nonsense. Tells you more about the intellectual mediocrity of those now in charge of our country than anything else.'

'I fear that as long as we stay in the pond, we had better croak with the frogs so as to distract the heron,' Guixian said. 'Besides, the slickness and lack of depth you mentioned correctly can also be used by social malingerers like us to justify whatever we do or fail to do and to outwit the zealots and our reformers.'

'That may be so,' Xu replied, 'but I can't help feeling sorry for Xiao Pan and the hundreds of thousands of starry-eyed naives like her. The day they find out the hard way that their god with the high, tinny voice is nothing more than a fake and a manipulator, the shock may be too great for many and bitterness about a lost youth and wasted opportunities will spoil the rest of their lives. Such a criminal waste. All that enthusiasm and dedication wasted on a cause that was doomed the very moment it was proclaimed as the proletariat's exclusivity. A proletarian society is not viable, it can't even function, because it treats genius, knowledge, new ideas, drive and daring as hostile and undermining. The so-called proletarians, short-sighted by their very nature and blinded by their hatred for the gifted and outstanding, do not realise that for their own good and continuity of their society, they must not only tolerate the bright and exceptionally bright but actually encourage them to come up with new ideas and allow them to improve their lives.

'If, as is now the case in our country, ruthless and opportunist leaders play on those proletarian sentiments to oppress and persecute those who rise above the grey uniformity, it means the beginning of the end and society, their society, will disintegrate in a very short time. It is the masses, the actual proletarians, who will be the victims, not their so-called leaders. Immoral opportunists as they all are, they will have stolen and stashed away enough money to enable them and their families to continue to live the good life. This will be China's tragedy.'

Xu fell silent and neither his wife nor his daughter had the spunk to deny or disagree.

No longer in the mood for Mao's Little Red Book, they lay there in silence, staring at the ceiling into an ominous future.

They must have fallen asleep somehow since they woke up with a start when the shutter in the door was suddenly opened and Madam Lo announced in her usual gruff manner, 'Your friend Chen Dan to see you! Stay where you are!'

The shutter was slammed shut and, after an unusual long fumble with the padlock, the cell door opened and Madam Lo came inside, followed by Gao Chen.

'You have one hour!' she said in a loud voice, then, softer, 'Take your time until I come back with the evening rice.'

Softly this time she closed the door behind her.

The Xus got up from their bed and stood staring, wordlessly, at their friend.

Gao Chen shivered in the chilly, musty atmosphere while his eyes adjusted from the glare outside to the gloom inside the cell. He stepped forward, arms stretched out, and wordlessly they embraced. Arms around one another, their heads against each other, they stood in silence, staring at the floor, trying to control their emotions.

'Ai Chen sends you his love,' Gao Chen finally managed to say, voice breaking. 'He died a brave man, a hero, our hero.'

'Let's pull the beds against each other and sit close together,' Guixian said. 'Then you tell us everything, Brother Dan.'

Suping distributed pieces of toilet paper and they wiped their nose and eyes.

Then they pushed Suping's bed next to Guixian's and sat down in a small circle, the blankets wrapped around them for warmth and a bit of closeness.

Gao Chen pulled a few sheets of paper from the inside pocket of his jacket and arranged them on his knees. Silently he read them for himself first while the others waited patiently for him to collect his thoughts and begin.

'I found this letter in Juntao's jacket when I tidied him up for burial this afternoon,' Gao Chen began his story. 'It is a farewell letter, to the four of us. I shall read it to you now.

*My dearest friends, brothers and sisters.*

*It is six o'clock in the morning and in four hours from now I shall be dead. My heart pounds, my hands are wet and cold with sweat, my head feels light and dizzy, breathing is fast and shallow, cramps trigger my bowels and I have to squeeze my buttocks together so as not to soil myself. This is fear, I guess, the naked, uncushioned fear of a violent death, unavoidably closing in on me, so close already that I can smell him. I* must *do something or else I'll suffocate or do something shameful like crying or screaming. So I write, while my heart cries out for you Dan, for you Guixian, for you Ximing and for you Suping. I pronounce your names again and again while I write the characters stroke for stroke so that I feel closer to you.*

*With Lo's arrival this morning, Red Guard Du's momentary absence to relieve himself and the paling of the grimy little window by the new day, my last one, came the sudden, shocking realisation that I am all alone and that I have* not *been able to stop the time as my mind, yesterday afternoon, tricked me into believing I could if only I could keep talking and role-playing and pretending the whole matter did not concern me.*

*At first, yesterday afternoon, after the verdict, I postured as Chen Juntao the Disdainful and I relished the effect on you, on Li and Zhang and on the rabble in the courtroom. Then, in my cage, my mind created the next scenario, this time for Chen Juntao the Subverter and I relished the way I gradually managed to corrupt Leading Red Guard Du's socialist morals and how he just left his post, disillusioned, a danger unto himself.*

*With Du absent and day breaking my mind has run out of scenarios, its defence mechanism has collapsed and body chemistry has taken over, releasing the triggers of fear and anguish into my bloodstream.*

*I* must *pull myself together or else I shall disgrace myself. I must force my mind to conjure up one more role model, my last one, and it must do so convincingly to stop my body from exposing the real Chen Juntao, the spineless, characterless, cowardly bungler who used to try and solve his problems either by ignoring them or by saddling others with them, like I so often did to you, Dan, during these past twenty-three years.*

*Now, for the first and, ironically, the last time I can neither ignore the fact that I am trapped nor can I depend on you to find a way out since there is no way out other than the one arranged for me by Li and his scam People's Tribunal.*

*I begin to feel the first stirrings of anger, of a cold, though impotent rage at their arbitrariness, at their smug and total disregard for the law that requires them to prove their accusations, to allow me legal assistance, to allow me to produce witnesses who will testify as to my innocence.*

*Unaccountable and unchallengeable they have disdainfully swept the laws aside, those scornful and aloof self-appointed so-called representatives of the People, dispensing oppression and death if and when it suits their purpose and self-serving reasons. If they need a conviction for whatever crime happens to be the flavour of the month, they find a criminal to suit, if they need three convictions they find three criminals, if they need ten thousand convictions they find ten thousand criminals.*

*Were it not that the execution ritual has the distinct advantages of intimidating as well as entertaining the rabble, the dispensers of death might even push their contempt for their victims to the point of foregoing the execution altogether.*

*They have made their point, the condemned totally irrelevant and already forgotten.*

*As you will have noticed by now I have managed to work up a rage good enough, I hope, to sustain a certain dignity up to and including the moment when the soldier pulls the trigger. At least, for now, the debilitating fear I felt earlier has gone. How I shall posture myself during the truck ride to the stadium, and in the stadium during the preparations for my final stand, I don't know. Probably the crowd won't even notice me because of the big attraction in the cage next to mine.*

*He at least* did *rock the system by killing six Red Guards and a commune leader, his own cousin to boot.*

*I heard him tell Comrade Du that his only regrets are that he didn't kill more and try to escape. He could have made a new kind of highway bandit, he said, killing Red Guards and commune leaders like the rabid dogs they are. That is what the rabble understands, raw violence and retribution; the political flimflam of my case doesn't interest them.*

*My dear, beloved brothers and sisters, I shall soon find out whether there is such a thing as life after death and if so, what role will be assigned to my spirit. If I have a say in the matter I shall request to be allowed to look after you until you join me. In the meantime don't count too much on my effectiveness in protecting you and look after yourselves first and foremost.*

*When you read this I'll be beyond anger and hurt, so don't mourn for me.*

*One thing I would like to ask you and that is 'Don't give up on China', whatever happens. The innate goodness, decency and intelligence of the vast majority of its people, our people, will ultimately prevail and the present tribulations instigated by the preachers of hate will be forgotten and relegated to the trash bin of history like other crazes and maniacs before.*

*Remain, each of you, a beacon of sanity during the upheavals that lie ahead of you.*

*With all my love and respect.*
*Your brother Chen Juntao.*

Gao Chen fell silent and slowly folded the sheets of paper. Putting the letter back in his breast pocket, he looked up at his friends with a tired, sad smile.

'Juntao was right,' he said, 'nobody noticed him. It was my cousin's show from start to finish. However, I think Juntao enjoyed the show and that, in a sense, Faxian made it easier for the other condemned men since his clowning must have distracted their thoughts from their own ordeal. People had turned up *en masse* to see the "Monster of Dada County" as his banner and the fliers handed out in the streets by the Red Guards called him. "The vicious, counter-revolutionary killer of six pure, innocent, revolutionary youths and a commune leader, the exemplary, idealistic fighter for the People's Cause, Chen Neiping", so the fliers read. Faxian gave them value for their trouble to come from far and near to attend his execution.

'During the truck ride to the stadium he made obscene gestures to the people lining the streets while shouting abuse at them as well as at the soldiers riding on the back of the truck as guards. The soldiers let him, strangely enough, and didn't react either, even when he pretended to wipe his arse with the banner that proclaimed his crimes and which he was supposed to hold above his head all the time. They didn't interfere and the people laughed and cheered. In the stadium, while the condemned stood in line facing the members of the People's Tribunal and the mayor and vice-mayor, all in their seats of honour, Faxian suddenly opened his trousers and peed in their direction in quite a forceful stream.

'The crowd roared with laughter and actually applauded wildly when the officials stood up from their seats and gesticulated furiously to the soldiers to make Faxian kneel and he, slipping through the hands of the soldiers, dropped his trousers entirely to his ankles and kneeled with his bare arse up in the air towards the officials. What a humiliation for the dignitaries, and Faxian added insult to injury when they finally grabbed him and were about to shoot him. Faxian, even while still a child, could fart when he wanted to and he did that often to embarrass or annoy people or to make them recoil in disgust so that he could snatch the best morsels of food. Now, about to be shot in the suddenly, expectantly silent stadium, he forced out a fart so loud that the young soldier with the pistol staggered back, pulled the trigger in a reflex and missed. Faxian rolled over and over on the ground, pretending to have been hit and in great pain while the crowd cheered him and whistled and booed the soldiers when they struggled to pin him down on the ground and finally, one of them managed to kill him off.'

Gao Chen laughed at the recollection and the others couldn't help but laugh as well.

'The other executions were a hurried affair that went almost unnoticed in the pandemonium by all but myself. Juntao was the last one and then the bodies were dragged in a hurry off the field. What a terrible loss of face for those puffed-up toads. Their authority is in shambles. People smirk and snicker behind their backs. And oh what a clever bastard Zhang Yizhong is. He must have had a premonition that something would go wrong for he stayed below, in the locker room area, while the other members of the tribunal sat in their seats of honour ready to bask in the glory of the people's wrath. Instead of wrath for the condemned it became a hoot for their own, inflated egos.

'When I went to see Zhang to collect Juntao's body, he was almost ebullient. In one move he can now rid himself of Luding's leading Party figures for reasons of grave incompetence in the execution of their revolutionary duties. He told me, with unashamed glee, that he is going to charge the tribunal's most prominent member, after himself that is, with causing ridicule to Chairman Mao's leadership. She happens to be Dong Xifang, the chairwoman of the Party's Disciplinary Commission of Luding, Zhang's personal enemy. She is that sour woman with the dull, short hair who sat next to Li yesterday. It was she who demanded twelve years of hard labour for you, Guixian, and ten years each for Ximing and Suping. She threatened to denounce Zhang for favouritism towards intellectuals when he proposed only three and two years of re-education. Zhang had to settle for five and four years to safeguard his seat on the People's Tribunal and his forthcoming confirmation as Luding's Party secretary.

'Zhang is going to squash Dong, undoubtedly in the same secretively expedient way as he did with Qian Weiying. Before the good proletarians of Luding realise Dong will be on her way to Shanxi or Xinjiang, never to be heard of again. With Dong eliminated and the other Party members and judges cowed and dependent on his goodwill, Zhang can virtually do as he pleases which means that a lot of people can breathe a lot easier.'

Gao Chen fell silent and looked at Guixian.

'Zhang asked me to tell you that he is going to requisition all schools and enough straw from the farming communes to cover the classroom floors,' he continued, smiling at Guixian. 'He will also call a halt to all arbitrary arrests and will order all those already arrested to be transferred from the square to the schools where they will be allowed to lie down in the straw. He said he will also require the Red Guards to bring themselves the charges against those arrested by them and if those charges would be found to be far-fetched, trumped up or altogether unfounded the Red Guards in question will be prosecuted for abuse of authority. He thinks that in the present turmoil it will take months, if not years, before eventual complaints about his moderation will trickle through to Beijing and that by that time the excesses during the early stages of the Cultural Revolution will have become an embarrassment to the more level-headed people in the Party hierarchy and that those people will then actually be grateful to those who did show a bit more restraint. He said he had decided to bet his own future on that premise.'

Smiling ruefully Gao Chen added, 'It is unfortunate, to say the least, that we were amongst the first arrested at a time when Zhang was still feeling his way, uncertain of himself. Only two days later and Juntao might have got off with a much lighter sentence and the three of you might have escaped conviction entirely. But then, on reflection, things might not have gone the way they have now if Zhang had not talked to us, if Juntao's drama had not taken place. Who can tell? Probably even Zhang himself won't be able to answer that question.

'Somehow I think that we, Juntao included, have been like a catalyst for the change in Zhang's thinking, which started way back already, and that the actual reaction took place these past forty-eight hours. If that is so we can take some credit for the better deal a lot of people will get from the Party and the People's Tribunal here in Luding in the months and years to come. I would like you to take some heart from this and accept things as they are since you have served a purpose. Let's try to make the best of the situation we find ourselves in now. What do you think?' Gao Chen looked a bit anxiously at his friends.

'I agree with you, Dan,' Xu replied. 'Belabouring the "if only" scenarios will merely cause more distress and remorse, especially if you couldn't have done anything yourself to change the unfortunate course of events.'

His wife and daughter nodded their agreement and Xu continued, 'You have lifted our spirits with your story about your cousin. What a swashbuckler he must have been. In similar circumstances but different times he might have roused the populace, overthrown the established order, proclaimed himself king or emperor and founded his own dynasty. It has happened before, many times, but, as we concluded earlier, it can't happen again.

The folk hero Chen Faxian has been dispatched, together with the anti-hero Chen Juntao, because neither of them did fit the socialist model Mao has in mind for China. In a way it is *not* a compliment for us that we are thought to be reformable and capable of being remodelled. But enough of those philosophies. Tell us, Gao Chen, what you have been doing since we last saw you yesterday afternoon.'

'On my way home I stopped at the coffin maker's workshop to order a simple, cheap coffin for Juntao,' Gao Chen began his account. 'The man was very busy, anticipating many orders and, as a dedicated Communist, he had upped his prices considerably. When I protested his price of fifty yuan for the simplest pine box he told me haughtily to take it or to leave it, so I took it, inwardly fuming. I had hardly any choice. I don't know any other coffin maker and besides, if I did, he would be as rapacious a capitalist as the first.

'I am afraid that it is typically Chinese to make the most of a given situation or to take advantage of any opportunity to make some money. Perhaps that will be the main reason why Mao is going to fail. Be that as it may, I paid the fifty yuan up front and bargained for delivery to our house either late that night or early the next morning. I told the man why and he was very sympathetic once I had paid him.

'Then I went straight home where I cleaned up the mess the Red Guards had left behind. I'm afraid, Guixian, that we need new furniture and new pottery and glassware. Everything has been smashed. At about half past eight Zhang Yizhong came to see me, with a bottle of *maotai* and two glasses. He told me he had spoken to you about his plans and that you had advised him to go and see me. From what he told me and from the way he brought it I became convinced that he will become my most valuable recruit.

'Unencumbered by idealism, our friend Yizhong is a totally practical man, who is absolutely convinced that communism in China is nothing more than a passing, ill-conceived and ill-conducted experiment in social engineering that will one day, in the not too distant future, crash around the experimenters. He thinks that it is in his best interest to join those who think the same *now* rather than *later*, however, he has no qualms whatsoever to get the best for himself out of the present conditions.

'As I said, a truly pragmatic and realistic man. I have made my plans already how to let Liu Longfei know about Zhang Yizhong, apart from what I told Li. Li came to see me very early this morning, before six it was. He wanted to make sure, he said, that we had understood the crucial importance, for us as well as for our friends, of playing the game and also that I had no ill feelings towards him about Juntao.

'We talked for more than an hour and he fully agreed with my opinion about Zhang. We agreed that we would, each of us, recommend him to Liu Longfei. The coffin maker and his son came at seven o'clock to deliver Juntao's coffin and help me dig his grave. Very kind, they were. Zhang and his brother Yimin had seen the coffin maker's cart arrive and they came to help with the digging of the grave. It's a pity I couldn't tell Juntao. He would have appreciated the joke of Party Secretary Zhang and mysterious Li shovelling and sweating in his grave.

'Then all of us had morning rice and tea in Zhang Yimin's house. His wife is very friendly and even pretty in a coarse way. At half past eight I rode down the hill on Yimin's tricycle, with Li in the carrier. It must have been quite a sight. I dropped Li at the bus station where he was going to catch the bus to Chongqing and I continued to the Detention House. I was just in time to see the condemned climb on the back of an old truck. Juntao was the last to climb aboard. He had to be pushed up by a couple of soldiers, his legs too stiff and his arms too weak to pull himself up. All the condemned wore dark green peasants' trousers and smock frocks.

'Poor Juntao. The soldiers gave him a banner and told him to hold it up, above his head. It was sad, laughable and pathetic all at the same time. He saw me and laughed, pointing at the tricycle. "A bit small for my carcass!" he shouted. "Be careful not to let me fall off, I don't trust your driving skills!"

'I laughed but my eyes stung and my heart cried out for him. While my cousin Faxian was busily rousing the crowd in the square with his histrionics, first when the soldiers urged him to climb on the truck, then when he argued with them about where he should stand on the platform, Juntao made his own pathetic little gesture of defiance by raising his banner upside down. Nobody noticed or cared and I really wept. He was so brave in his own unassuming way that it broke my heart. I followed the truck on my tricycle, amongst hundreds of other people on bicycles ringing their bells and waving to the crowd lining the streets. It was like a circus procession, the rout surging on to the pavement, pounding on the sideboards of the truck, throwing trash and even excrement at the prisoners, yelling and jeering at Faxian's taunts and antics. I was lucky to have a tricycle or else I would also have been overturned like many of those on ordinary bicycles. They fell and started to fight with the crowd.

'I saw Juntao laughing loudly at the scene of falling and fighting people and at Faxian's theatrics. I pedalled and pedalled and was proud of Juntao. It was already past ten o'clock when the truck finally came to a halt in front of the stadium's entrance gate. While the condemned were disembarking and being escorted into the stadium I managed to push my carrier cycle into the corridor underneath the stands. I found the locker room and saw that Zhang was there, sitting behind a trestle-table, writing.

'He motioned for me to come in and he gave me the signed and stamped inhumation permit and a bill for one yuan for the bullet and another receipt for fifty fen for the permit. I paid him one yuan fifty. He asked whether I wanted to see the show, as he called it, or preferred to wait inside. I told him I wanted to watch and he gave me permission to go and sit on the special bench for team coaches in front of and under the main stand. I told you already about Faxian's show, because that's what it was and I think that that's why Zhang used the word, he anticipated that, I'm sure. Juntao really laughed at Faxian's burlesque and he remained very dignified when the soldiers started shooting, first Faxian, then the others, finally him. Just before it was his turn he looked in my direction, smiled and quickly kneeled down.

'The soldier made no mistake. It was over in less than three seconds and I was probably the only one in the stadium, apart from the soldier who shot him, to see him die. The people jeered and booed and whistled and, feeling protected by the anonymity of the crowd, they dared to shout abuse at the officials who I saw slinking off with long faces. The lieutenant in charge of the executions made me sign for receipt of Juntao's body and ordered a soldier to help me carry it to my tricycle. It was difficult to make Juntao fit into the small carrier but the soldier and I finally managed to get him in, in a sitting position, his knees pulled up to his chin. With a piece of rope we tied him to the cycle frame to prevent him from toppling over and falling out of the carrier. I pushed the tricycle out of the corridor and into the street and then I rode home, following outlying streets to avoid marauding gangs of Red Guards.

'Zhang Yimin was waiting for me, the good-hearted soul, squatting beside the path at the foot of our hill. He helped me push the tricycle uphill to Juntao's grave under the walnut tree. Yimin's wife had been to see the coffin maker hoping he would still have some hell-money left over from the past. He had and she bought for five yuan five hundred notes of one hundred yuan each, enough for Juntao to pay his first expenses in the nether world, she said, so as to get out of there as quickly as possible. She had also prepared a bit of food for him for the first day or two, until he would know his way around. So much for Communist atheistic propaganda.

'The three of us managed to get Juntao out of the carrier and into the coffin which we had placed in the grave that morning. He was too long or the coffin was too short, whatever. When we pulled up his knees a bit to make him fit in, we couldn't close the lid, so I decided to remove the footboard of the coffin. Then Juntao's feet stuck out which we agreed looked undignified. Madam Zhang suggested we put his feet into one of the broken night stands and then wrapped the plastic seat cover of the settee around the end of the coffin and the night stand to make it look a bit better and also to prevent the soil from slipping in through the gap between coffin and night stand. So we did and we then apologised to Juntao for all the messing around with his old carcass. We put the money and the food into the coffin, closed the lid and filled the grave with the loose earth. Yimin and I rolled eight big boulders that lie around on the hilltop downhill and placed them on the grave.

'While Yimin planted hibiscus cuttings around the grave in the fresh earth I painted, with white paint I found in Yimin's garden shed, on the boulders, one character per boulder:

*Chen Juntao, unshackled in life and death*

'By then it was half past two already and I had just the time to wash up and rest a bit before coming down to see you. Tonight I'll have evening rice with Yimin and his kindly wife. Perhaps Yizhong will join us, I don't know. He may be too busy preparing his moves against Dong. Perhaps he will even be too busy to make arrangements for me to start serving my sentence. He has more important things on his mind than this worthless and irrelevant person. I'll see what happens, one day at a time.'

Gao Chen fell silent and looked up from staring at the floor between his feet.

Suping had at first been moved by Ai Chen's letter. She had sensed how he had had to force himself to appear brave and she had felt in her own gut his terrible loneliness. But as Gao Chen's story progressed she had at times barely been able to suppress a laugh as her lively imagination pictured the scenes described by Gao Chen.

In the silence that followed Gao Chen's narrative she imagined burly Uncle Dan in his funny trousers, rolled up to above his knees because of the heat, pedalling a tricycle with a lolling, oversized body in the carrier and then pushing it uphill, panting and gasping for breath, together with Zhang Yimin, and the comics of it all became too much and she exploded into laughter.

Wiping the tears of laughter from her eyes with the back of her hand, she hiccuped, 'I'm sorry, Uncle Dan, but it's so funny. First, you on that tricycle with Uncle Juntao in the carrier, his knees up to his chin, and then he in the coffin with his legs too long and you pushing the lid down and his legs popping out from the coffin and you pushing them back in and so on. It's hilarious,' and again she broke into laughter.

The others, despite themselves, couldn't help laughing as well.

'Remember the first day Ai Chen and I came to your house?' Gao Chen chuckled. 'You laughed, Suping, at our appearances, if I remember correctly, and that broke the awkwardness of the moment. I said then that your sense of humour would be your saving grace during difficult times. I was right, wasn't I?'

'Let's keep up the light-hearted mood,' Xu said, 'and as you said it just now, Gao Chen, let's live life one day at a time. So what did Zhang tell you about tomorrow, if anything?'

'He asked me to tell you that your transport to Chengdu has been arranged for tomorrow morning,' Gao Chen replied. 'Zhang expects the trucks to be here around eight o'clock since they will leave Kanding, where the convoy stays overnight, at six in the morning.

'There will be six trucks, he told me, three from Jinchuan, Danba and Qianning joining with two from Litang, Yajiang and Kanding and one from Jiulong. Two trucks will join the convoy here, in Luding, and others will join in Ya'an, Hongye, Meishan and Xinjin. In all there are twenty trucks, about five hundred convicts, Zhang estimates, most of them bound for the communes around Chengdu. They are all light cases, like yours.

'You will arrive in Chengdu the day after tomorrow, late in the evening. You will be put up for a few days in former military barracks while Party Secretary Deng decides on the allocation of the convicts to the various communes and arranges for transport of the different groups. Zhang will give me a letter for Deng tonight or else he'll give it to you himself tomorrow morning. I'll be there to see you off as well. It won't be long before we see each other again when I make my rounds around the communes as the keeper of records.'

Gao Chen was interrupted by the opening of the shutter in the door.

Lo peered inside and grumbled, 'Visitor Chen's time is up. What was all the laughing about a few moments ago? I won't ever understand your kind of people. They just shot your best friend and you dragged his carcass around town and buried him, Chen, and you laugh! I thought I would see you snivelling together. Tell me what's so funny. Perhaps I can laugh also. I haven't had much reason to laugh for a long time.'

Gao Chen smiled at her and said, 'Can you give me five minutes more, Madam Lo, please? I'm almost finished here. I'll knock on the door when I'm ready to leave.'

The old woman snorted and slammed the shutter.

Lowering his voice Gao Chen said, 'Zhang is going to retire her in a few days, as she asked him, so he told me. He found out from her medical records that she has some kind of brain tumour which gives her a permanent headache, sometimes very bad, so she can hardly see. That makes her so grumpy, Zhang says. She doesn't know, or doesn't want to know, that she has no more than two or three years left, provided they don't operate on her with a hacksaw in one hand and Mao's Little Red Book in the other. Zhang suggested to me that he would assign our house to her. Ostensibly because the mountain air would alleviate her headaches and also, of course, to reward her for so many years of dedicated service because it is so much more pleasant in the hills than in those gloomy apartment blocks where she lives now.

'The other reason Zhang can't of course admit is that such an arrangement would free the house again at about the time Ximing and Suping will have served their sentences so that they could move back into our own house. If, on the other hand, the town council would assign the house to a young family it's pretty sure they will still be living there when you are released and as ex-convicts you can hardly expect the council to expel those young people for your benefit. Besides, Zhang says, if I come back earlier I could move in with Madam Lo, as a boarder. In the meantime, he says, he will pay half of her rent as ten yuan per month might be a bit steep for her. The arrangement would benefit everybody, Zhang says.

'What do you think?' Gao Chen asked, a bit anxiously.

'It sounds a bit callous to count on Madam Lo to conveniently die in the near future,' Guixian replied, 'but I think it is a very good plan. Gao Chen, please tell Zhang Yizhong to go ahead and thank him for his consideration. We won't forget his kindness. Whatever he may say about himself, that he does everything for self-serving motives and so on, yet he makes these kind gestures which are of no benefit to him, on the contrary, which could even be construed against him if his luck turns. So, to me, he is a kind and considerate man even if he pretends to be only a mercenary. I sincerely hope that Liu Longfei and Liang Ailing will have a place for him in their Plan. He would do them proud and it would be a blessing for the people who would be under his authority.'

Xu and Suping nodded their agreement, apparently very satisfied also, and Gao Chen, much relieved, said, 'All right, that's arranged then. I'll tell Zhang to go ahead. Don't mention anything to Madam Lo though. Zhang still has to find a replacement for her. He told me he has his doubts now whether the leading Red Guard is still suitable for the post. Du appears to have shouted some very rebellious things this morning as reported by the other Red Guards. Juntao's first and only potential recruit and compromised already the moment he opens his mouth. Oh well, you can't win them all.'

He laughed and, knocking on the door to signal Madam Lo, he said, 'I'll see you tomorrow morning without fail. Try to get some sleep tonight. You don't know how it will be tomorrow night. They may not even let you get off the truck. I'll give Zhang Yimin's wife some money and ask her to cook sticky rice with small pieces of chicken tonight. Tomorrow I'll make small lumps and wrap them individually in pieces of toilet paper for you so that you have something to eat whenever you feel a bit weak during the trip. I haven't much confidence in your Red Guard's logistics or, for that matter, in their concern for your well-being.'

He smiled and, waving goodbye, he turned and walked out of the door.

Madam Lo came in with the evening rice and, while filling up the bowls, she said, 'Not much of a meal, I'm afraid. Still no chicken or vegetables. I'll give them a piece of my mind at their struggle meeting tonight. Nothing but big talk about solidarity amongst the workers, sharing poverty and so on, but in practice they rob and cheat each other whenever they can, the hypocrites. Stealing all the chicken and vegetables yesterday evening, the bastards. Tell me about solidarity from my own kind. All the kindness I ever got was from people I am supposed to hate.'

She put the rice container down and poured hot water from a thermos in the three mugs.

'No tea either tonight,' she grumbled. 'Xiao Pan went to see the executions with that tall, pimple-faced Red Guard, the one yelling at you yesterday about the foam in the drain. Pimple-Face was all flushed and excited but she told me that Xiao Pan had run off, to her house, crying. Couldn't stand it. I was worried when she didn't turn up to help me with the distribution of evening rice but her brother came with the message that his little sister had come home, very upset, and had locked herself in the bedroom. They could hear her sobbing but she refused to open the door or answer her mother's questions. Poor child. I hope her god fell from his pedestal and broke his thick, fat neck.'

Breathing heavily she bent to pick up the rice container and then shuffled to the door. Turning in the door opening she said, 'Eat your rice nevertheless, you may not get much to eat tomorrow. Zhang sent word that you must be ready to leave your cell at half past seven tomorrow morning. To Chengdu you go, I heard. Better for you, I'm sure. Can hardly be worse than here. At least you'll be in the open air. Even working in the field, with the peasants, may not be all that bad. Try to make them like you and the experience may even do you some good. At least the food will be better than this gooey stuff.

'Now, eat and try to sleep. Tomorrow morning you must try to move your bowels or else you'll have a lot of trouble on those ramshackle old trucks. The drivers are like madmen and they'll drive through all the potholes, deliberately. The shocks will trigger your bowels but there won't be any sanitary stops. I'll wake you up at a quarter to six.'

For a while they just sat on their beds, staring absent-mindedly at the soggy, greyish lumps of rice and the wisps of vapour rising from the mugs of hot water.

'I think we should indeed eat our rice,' Xu said and his voice sounded tired all of a sudden. 'I am mentally tired and I'm sure you don't feel much better. Let's leave the beds as they are and we'll lie on the lower ones so we can be closer together. Don't say a word any more about the Zhangs, the Lis, the Chens, the future and what have you or I'll start screaming. I have had it for the time being and for quite some time to come, I'm afraid.'

His wife and daughter nodded and Suping suddenly yawned. She felt tired, exhausted even.

Their meal finished, they lay back on their beds and drifted off to sleep.

It was five o'clock on Xu's watch when he woke up, with a start. Slowly he raised himself from the plank bed, trying not to disturb his wife and daughter.

Carefully he groped his way in the darkness to where the toilet bucket stood. With a sigh he sat down on the clammy, rough concrete rim and tried to focus his thoughts on something pleasant, as Madam Lo had told them, and to let his body take over.

It wasn't easy at first, especially the pleasant thoughts bit, as he tried not to sit with his full weight on the rim, but then suddenly he let go and things went all by themselves.

Much relieved he found the water tap and he began to wash down under the irregular, splashing stream of water. From the movement of the air around him he knew that his wife and daughter were up and probably taking turns on the toilet bucket.

'Just think of nothing and let go,' he said, 'Madam Lo was right. Don't be self-conscious.'

He heard Suping chuckle. 'I'm sitting on the back of my hands,' she laughed, 'that rim is too cold and rough for my tender skin, but apart from that it's all right. I'm moving, as Madam Lo would say. Do you think she wants to check our produce as she did yesterday morning?'

Both Xu and Guixian burst out laughing and then the light came on and they looked owlishly at each other in the gloomy, yellowish light.

'Madam Lo has arrived and pushed the main switch,' Guixian said. 'Suping and I will wash ourselves quickly so that you can slop the toilet, Ximing. In twenty minutes you must report for night-soil duty.'

Xu got dressed and then slopped and rinsed the bucket as if he had done so all his life.

He had finished by the time Madam Lo pounded on the door and shouted '*Wake up! It's ten to six! Report in fifteen minutes!*'

With a stentorian voice Xu replied immediately, '*Report!*'

Madam Lo opened the shutter and peered inside, surprised.

'Finished already?' she asked. 'How did you manage, in the dark?' Then anxiously, 'Did you move?'

'We did,' Guixian replied gravely and behind her she could hear Suping trying to stifle a laugh.

Madam Lo opened the door and shuffled immediately to the toilet bucket for inspection.

Surprised, she looked up. 'It's clean,' she said, 'you slopped it out already. Let me see the slop bucket.'

Apparently satisfied with the Xus' production, she looked at Xu and said, 'You are the first, Xu. Go quickly to the yard, you know the way. Empty the slop bucket in the cesspit, rinse it, stow it and come back here immediately. I won't close the padlock so you can go in by yourself. The tall, pimple-faced girl is in charge this morning. Avoid her, Xu! She is looking for trouble that one.'

Xu did as he was told and he was back within fifteen minutes.

'There are a lot of prisoners now,' he told his wife and daughter. 'Fortunately I was the first and knew what to do, thanks to Madam Lo, bless her simple soul. I didn't speak to anybody and got out of there as fast as I could. The other poor devils are running helter-skelter though, with their buckets, Red Guards yelling and screaming and cracking their whips. Complete pandemonium, nobody knows what to do first or last. I got away before the Red Guards noticed me. As Madam Lo said, that tall girl is in charge. What a fishwife. Am I glad that we'll be out of here today.'

He laughed and said, 'We must have slept like logs that we didn't hear all those prisoners arrive. We even have neighbours in the cells next and opposite ours. On my way back I saw people being ordered out, with the slop buckets, by that Red Guard you protected against Zhang's wrath, Suping, the one who ordered you to squash the soap on the floor. She saw me coming back already and she looked surprised as I was without escort and much too early, of course. She just stared at me, though, and didn't say anything when I let myself into our cell. When I glanced at her, over my shoulder, she even smiled and tried to wink or perhaps I just imagined that since she almost immediately continued to hurry the men with their buckets down the corridor.'

Around half past six Madam Lo arrived with the rice container and the thermos.

'Ah, you are back already, Xu,' she said, apparently satisfied. 'Your morning rice,' she growled, 'same swill as last night, only now it's cold to boot. The cooks refuse to boil new rice. They are angry with the Red Guards. They can't work without a proper morning meal they say. I can't blame them. The morning meal is part of our pay. Last week we haven't been paid our wages. They were our wholehearted and enthusiastic contribution to the Great Proletarian Cultural Revolution. Orders from Beijing, the officials say. All over China people fall over themselves and each other in their enthusiasm to contribute a week's wages, *they* say. My arse! I say.

'I wonder what they do with our money since they don't even pay for their own ten-course meals and drinks in the restaurants. They eat and drink and smoke and laugh their heads off while we have our struggle meetings on an empty stomach. When they are given the bill one or other of them signs it airily and they just walk off, laughing and belching and farting, the pigs. When, the next day, the restaurant manager shows the bills to the Party secretariat, the cadres there just shrug their shoulders and say they have no instructions or authority to pay, apart from the fact that there isn't any money in the till. I know all that because I live next door to a big restaurant where the bigwigs like to hold their dinner meetings as they call their orgies.

'The manager takes the same bus in the morning as I do since he has to be early on the state market for his purchases. The market manager refuses to give him credit any longer if he doesn't pay his outstanding debt first. There's another big party in his restaurant tonight he told me this morning, the whole People's Tribunal will eat there, and he hasn't got any merchandise left and no money to pay for new provisions.'

Madam Lo fell silent and glowered at Xu.

'Tell me, Xu!' she almost shouted at him. 'You are a learned man! Am I that stupid when I say that things can't work that way? They close the schools and universities because education is unnecessary and counter-revolutionary, they say. The youngsters who should be studying things that matter waste their time on our Chairman Mao's drivel and run around like mad beating up their elders. Our so-called leaders waste their time in political meetings and on farcical People's Tribunals, sending everybody who's not a Party member to prison or labour camps. The peasant communes receive no pay for their produce so they now refuse to sell for worthless bonds and hoard instead, waiting for better times and to hell with everybody else.

'However, they run out of seeds and fertiliser and thus their production slows to a halt and in the end *everybody* starves, including the peasants themselves, albeit as the last ones. Is that the way it will all end, Xu?' Madam Lo wailed.

Xu watched the simple, old woman with undisguised respect.

'It will come to that, no doubt about that,' he replied gravely, 'unless people who have the common sense to see the absurdity of what is happening now can muster the courage to say the things you yourself just said, Madam Lo. However, they must ask these questions loudly so that others endowed with less perception also start to think and ask questions. As I said, however, this takes great courage since the risk of being severely punished for such common-sense thoughts is very great. Counter-revolutionary, the madmen call these thoughts. Our hope lies with leaders like Zhang Yizhong, and I am sure that there are many like him, who will need the support of people like you.

'However, that is for later, much later. For the time being even people like Zhang, and others still higher up than he, can do nothing, or almost nothing, to stop the approaching *taifong*. And so far we have seen nothing yet, Madam Lo. What we are experiencing now are still only the high winds that precede the *taifong*. People, like you and us, can but bend with the wind, like the grass and the bamboo, and hope to survive to pick up the pieces of our shattered lives when the *taifong* has raged itself out. The Zhangs and the Lis of this world will then need our support to build a new society on the ruins of the present one. The wreakers and the wreckers, who now hold sway, will have no place or role in that new society, if that is any consolation to you.'

Xu fell silent and smiled fondly at the old woman.

'Try not to protest too much about small matters,' he added, 'lest you irritate the mad dogs. Their feverish, feeble brains have lost the last vestiges of restraint. On the other hand, have your feelers out for truly like-minded people and talk about your thoughts as you did to us. It is all you can do but it is important, very important! The voices of reason must *not* be silenced.'

'I think you are right, Xu,' Madam Lo said, 'I'll keep in mind what you said. I might as well try and give some meaning to my life, for what it's worth and left of it.'

She fell silent, then, abruptly, 'Be ready in half an hour. I'll fetch you and escort you outside.'

'How extraordinary,' Xu mused, watching Madam Lo pull the door behind her.

'Here is this old woman, who has no formal education to speak of and who spent practically her whole working life, like a mole, here in this dungeon, and *she* sees the fallacies and absurdities in the Communist system while seemingly the Great Leader does not. I have the feeling that even Chen Dan, Zhang, Li and probably Liu Longfei and his ilk, with their fixation on moles and sleepers, underestimate the intelligence and perception of the ordinary men and women and how much they will need the support of those common people if they want their new society to succeed.

'Until I met Zhang Yizhong and this Madam Lo, I too, like Ai Chen and the so-called intellectuals, have been stroking my vanity as I equated education with intelligence thereby implying arrogantly that those who have no formal education are by definition incapable of thinking intelligently. How patronising! Only Gao Chen knew better and told us so. And yet I am surprised by Madam Lo's perception. She makes no attempt at intellectualism and therefore her observations are simple and straightforward and she sees the connection between abuse of power and economic mismanagement in a small town and the state our country as a whole must be in and that frightens her and she says so. Life in a small community is but a reflection of life in society as a whole, human nature being the same, everywhere, always, in everybody, whether minister or village carpenter, whether local cadre or leader or Great Leader.

'Madam Lo knows this as a matter of fact and makes no fuss about it. We have forgotten how to think *small* and we think that for things to be important they must at least be *big*, or, better still, *grandiose*. In fact, what Madam Lo taught us, whether by her musings about the state of affairs in Luding or by her instructions and observations about slopping toilet buckets and prison life, is that upbringing and education often obfuscate the really important things in life, the things that *matter* and therefore do not prepare us for *life as it is*, certainly not for *survival* in extreme situations. The implication is that when we find ourselves in such extreme situations we must forget about upbringing and education and let our basic human nature guide us, at least then will we have an equal chance. Lesson: *don't think too much, just do* what your initial impulse was. Thank you, Madam Lo, for your lessons in realism.' And with self-mockery Xu bowed in the direction of the door.

His wife and daughter were eating the cold, soggy rice and didn't bother to comment. Instead Guixian said, 'Eat your rice, Ximing! This qualifies as an extreme situation so don't think too much, just do as Suping and I do which, according to your theory on human nature, is what you have to do. So eat!'

With a sigh Xu sat down on his bed and began trifling with his rice.

A few minutes before eight o'clock Madam Lo opened the door and announced, 'The trucks with convicts from Jinchuan, Litang and Jiulong have arrived. The leading Red Guards in charge of the transports are clamouring for food in the kitchen which, of course, we can't give them so they are angry. Zhang Yizhong hasn't arrived yet and I am scared because of what is happening in the square. His orders were for me to have you and the other convicts bound for Chengdu outside at eight o'clock so that's what I do. By the way, your friend Chen is waiting outside. He gave me these small parcels for you. There's sticky rice with minced chicken in them. He gave me a parcel as well. Very kind of him. I'll eat it later. Put the parcels in your pockets and when you eat from them, on the trucks, do it discreetly or else the other convicts will snatch them from you or report you to the Red Guards, which is worse. Now follow me!'

Suping was the first out of the cell and, still fumbling with the paper-wrapped sticky rice, she followed Madam Lo through the corridor.

The instant she exited through the front door, the sudden, intense glare of the sun which had just cleared the hilltops to the east of Luding made her eyes water and everything became blurred. She closed her eyes and lifted her face up to the sun. Oblivious to what went on around her, she let the sun's warmth suffuse her whole being and the intense pleasure she felt made her shiver.

Breathing deeply she both smelled and tasted the warm, tangy summer air, cherishing as one would a precious wine, the many different nuances of smell and taste. She bit her lower lip to stifle a scream of joy, the musty, chilly gloom of the past forty-eight hours already nothing more than a bad dream.

I'll do whatever it takes but I'll never, ever give *them* a reason to lock *me* up again, she thought. I shall *not* play the heroine! Too bad for Uncle Dan and his grandiose design for China, too bad if he, or Father, thinks less of me but I shall keep bending with the wind, literally, from whatever direction it will blow. Let them all fight their own little wars in whatever way they please. I'll stay out of their silly little games and intrigues and *out of jail, whatever it takes*.

Triggered by the light and warmth of the sun, those unique conditions for *all life*, it had been more a sudden insight into her real *self* than a reasoned train of thoughts and she had become a different person when she opened her eyes and looked at the scene around her.

She saw her parents standing next to the front door, shading their eyes with their hand while watching the scene in front of the Detention House with obvious worry.

Still more convicts bound for Chengdu came stumbling out through the front door to mill around the entrance like frightened sheep.

Suping made no effort to go and stand closer to her parents, her new self wary already that they might drag her along into a situation she no longer wanted to be in. Instead her eyes followed her parents' look and suddenly she caught her breath.

Two thousand or so men, women and children were lying pell-mell on the cobblestones of the square, apparently so exhausted that they didn't react any more to the raging and raving Red Guards who frantically but vainly tried to kick and beat them back into a sitting position.

The women tried to protect their children with their upper bodies, the men merely covered their head with their arms and didn't move, beyond caring.

The Red Guards from the other towns stood next to the trucks with convicts, laughing and shouting mocking comments about the ineptitude of their Luding peers.

Horror-stricken, in spite of her newly adopted detachment, Suping remembered the gory drawings in her history book of Japanese soldiers, faces gloating and sneering in devilish exultation, whipping and bayoneting helpless Chinese, the women wringing their hands, begging in vain for mercy for their children, the men dying with contorted faces while clutching the bayonets that pierced their hearts and bellies.

That was *war* and barbarous Japanese did those horrible things to defenceless Chinese, but this here, in Luding, was *no war*!

Those Red Guards were *Chinese children beating and kicking their own people, probably even their own relatives, in a kind of craze as if they had all collectively gone berserk*.

Despairingly she looked around for Zhang Yizhong. Where was Zhang? Why didn't he put an end to this atrocity? Had he not promised he would do something for these poor people, alleviate their suffering?

Suddenly she noticed Gao Chen looking at her fixedly. When he saw he had caught her eye he put a finger to his lips and shook his head. Then he mouthed the word 'wait'.

Dully she nodded and was about to avert her eyes when she saw Gao Chen point to something to her right. She turned and saw two trucks coming out of one of the streets opening on to the square.

About twenty armed militiamen were standing on the back of each truck.

The trucks came to a screeching halt in front of the Detention House and immediately the militiamen jumped off the trucks and in less than a minute they had encircled the square, one man every ten paces or so, rifle unslung, ready to nip any revolt in the bud.

Five persons, at first hidden from sight by the militiamen standing around them, had stayed behind on the platform of the lead truck, four in a sitting position, their heads between their pulled-up knees, their hands clasped in their necks, and one standing with his back against the truck's cabin, a loud hailer in his right hand.

With a shock Suping recognised Zhang as the man raised the loud hailer to his mouth and bellowed, '*Silence! Stand to attention all Red Guards, as you are!*'

In the sudden silence that followed Zhang's order, Suping's attention wandered as she watched a flight of sparrows taking off from the roof of one of the houses on the other side of the square and disappear in the distance from where she heard the far-off barking of two dogs, one high, one low.

Sparrows, dogs, sun, wind, clouds, oh how she longed to soar into the air and fly away into an unthinking oneness with nature, indifferent, uncaring, unafraid, free.

The blubbering sniffle of the man beside her shocked her back into the filthy sleaze of her real world and a feeling of hopelessness, of powerlessness drained her will to survive. Dully she stared at Zhang on his truck, resigned, uninterested. Zhang was watching the scrappy crowd for signs of unrest. Slowly he turned his gaze around the square and over the people standing behind him in front of the Detention House.

For a fraction of a second Suping was aware of his eyes locking on to hers and she thought she saw the faintest of smiles before he disengaged to complete his turn.

Certain he held everybody's attention Zhang lifted his loud hailer to his mouth again and began his announcement.

'For some time already I have been getting hints from Beijing and other big cities that a conspiracy is brewing to undermine the authority of the Party and its Chairman, our Great and Beloved Leader Mao Zedong. The hints also said that the conspirators would not be outsiders for a chance, but insiders, Party members, Party officials even, who, tired of serving the People, would seize power to serve their own, and only their own, personal interests. I knew therefore that I need not look for the usual methods of rebellion and dissent but for something far more subtle. I suddenly realised that if the conspirators were high Party officials who wanted to get rid of their comrade officials who they thought would remain loyal to our Chairman Mao, the method they would chose would be to make the loyalists appear inept, incompetent. And how better to do that than in public, during an occasion where a great many people would be gathered in one place. Suddenly I knew what that occasion would be and I also knew who the conspirators were.

'The occasion they had chosen to attack the loyalists was the mass execution of the criminals in the stadium yesterday and the conspirators were the five officials who had constantly and vehemently opposed my proposal to have the executions carried out one by one, on alternate days, in the prison courtyard and only in the presence of the judicial court and the People's Tribunal. An execution is *not* a matter of public amusement, I argued. Most of my comrade officials agreed with me, only five disagreed and the most prominent amongst them was Dong Xifang, the chairwoman of the Party's Disciplinary Commission. She was the one who insisted that all nine executions be carried out at the same time and in the stadium and that the people's attendance be compulsory. At that time Dong Xifang was still the highest official in Luding after Secretary Guo's departure and my own appointment as Party Secretary was not yet confirmed, so I had to concede.

'I decided, however, that I would *not* sit with the other judges to witness the execution, both as a protest against Dong's decision and because I knew what was going to happen. You all know what happened. It was disgraceful and degrading and the officials sat there and were ridiculed. *However, that was exactly what Dong and her satellites intended. Dong's intention was to dismiss and arrest me, the Party secretary, for reasons of gross incompetence thereby causing ridicule to the Party, and to appoint her closest associate, Wu Hongmao, in my place!*'

Zhang fell silent, to let his words sink in.

After sweeping his gaze over the crowd and apparently satisfied that he had everybody's attention, even that of the wretches lying in the square, he continued in a normal tone.

'Dong was enraged when she saw I had stayed below and therefore didn't lose face. That night one of her co-conspirators, sick with worry and remorse, came to see me at my house to confess everything. I cannot mention his name as I promised him I would appeal to the Disciplinary Commission in Chongqing to show leniency because of his repentance. With his signed confession, in which he named the four other conspirators as Dong Xifang, Lu Huiqin, Xian Zulie and Hu Baozhi, I went to the militia and the commandant agreed with me that the four criminals should be arrested immediately. We found all four of them at Dong Xifang's house preparing their escape to Beijing where it seems Dong has friends in high places.

'The People's Tribunal of Luding is not competent to deal with treason of this sort and I shall report the matter to Interrogator Li in Chongqing. Pending his return to Luding the four traitors will be incarcerated and kept in solitary confinement at the prison.'

Zhang fell silent and, pointing down at the four people at his feet, he went on, bellowing through his loud hailer, 'Stand up, you miserable traitors and show your faces to the outraged people of Luding!' and he pulled Dong Xifang up by the collar of her jacket. The three others scrambled up as well.

Trembling, Dong with rage, the three others probably with fear, they stood there, on the back of the truck, facing the sullen crowd.

'*Down with the traitors*!' Zhang shouted.

Hesitantly and scattered at first the crowd responded, then, conditioned to know what was expected on such occasions, more and more people joined until everybody roared, '*Down with the traitors Dong, Lu, Xian and Hu*!' *Down with the traitors Dong, Lu, Xian and Hu*!'

On and on it went, until Zhang bellowed, '*Long live our Glorious Chairman Mao for ever and ever*!' and obediently the crowd followed.

Zhang let them go on for five minutes or so. Then, imperiously, he signalled, like a conductor in front of a mass chorus, for silence and but for a few trickling 'Long lives' that died away quickly enough also, he again got the crowd's attention.

'Everything ordered by Dong Xifang during the past two months is hereby revoked. Disciplinary action against Party members is annulled, appointments recommended by Dong or made by her personally are also annulled and the appointees will be investigated for collusion with Dong in the matter of overthrowing the local Party structures for personal gain. Dong's former gang member says in his confession that Dong had ordered the arrest of as many people as possible, under the guise of obstruction of the Great Proletarian Cultural Revolution, so that, after taking power, she and her gang could expropriate all these people's belongings and keep anything valuable for themselves, to enrich themselves beyond imagination. I therefore disband the Red Guards in their present set-up and order them to present themselves for reappointment the day after tomorrow. I shall personally make the appointments.

'In the meantime *no further arrests will be made*! Those arrested and not yet tried by the People's Tribunal will be allowed to return home. Reprisals against the former Red Guards will be punished. People who feel they have been unfairly or badly treated by the former Red Guards can lodge an official complaint. A special complaints commission will be appointed by the People's Tribunal who will receive written and signed complaints every day of the week only for a period of three weeks as from next Monday. The campaign against enemies of the People, bourgeois decadents and adversaries of the Great Proletarian Cultural Revolution will continue unabatedly, however, and arrests will be made by a special investigator accompanied by a group of five or more Red Guards.

'The People's Tribunal of Luding will be in session every day from nine till twelve and from two till five o'clock and will handle not more than ten cases per day. Those bound for trial will not be held for more than forty-eight hours in detention before their trial starts. Those denouncing others for crimes that subsequently lead to arrest and detention must furnish proof of their accusations during the People's Tribunal's dealing with the case. If no or insufficient proof can be furnished the denouncers will be arrested and condemned for false accusations in the pursuit of personal gain or revenge. The penalty will be five to ten years of forced labour. The former Red Guards will now deposit their whips, sticks and red armbands on the ground in front the nearest militiaman. *This concludes my announcement*!'

Stunned the crowd watched as Party Secretary Zhang Yizhong ordered the four accused to climb down from the truck. Still from his position on the truck he called forward four militiamen, gave them instructions whereupon they marched the four accused off to the prison, three streets away.

Astounded the crowd watched as the red-faced Red Guards delivered up the whips and sticks and took off their armbands as their victims, slowly and unbelieving at first, began to scramble to their feet.

Then a murmur started that soon swelled to a loud buzzing. A few random shouts of 'Long live our Party Secretary' were followed by more and within minutes about three thousand people were shouting, in chorus, while clapping their hands rhythmically, 'Long Live Zhang Yizhong our Party Secretary!'

Flabbergasted by the turn of events Suping looked on with still unbelieving eyes as Zhang raised his arm once more and waited until the last cheers had petered out.

Through his loud hailer he said, 'I thank the people of Luding for their trust and support. This afternoon the names of the nine new judges of the People's Tribunal will be posted in several locations throughout the town. Objections against any or all of the appointees can be made, in writing, at the Party secretariat. Objections deemed serious enough to invalidate the appointments will be called to publicly defend their complaints. Objections found to be malicious or slanderous will be held against the complainants and they will be prosecuted for maligning the Party. The penalty will be five to ten years forced labour. *There will be law, order and justice in Luding*!' Now go home, all of you and let events take their just course. Also refrain from further demonstrations.'

Turning around to face the convicts in front of the Detention House, Zhang added, 'The convicts bound for Chengdu will now board these two trucks. Their sentences will be reviewed one year from today and may be remitted, in part or in full, depending on the reports I will receive from Secretary Deng of Chengdu.'

Zhang fell silent and jumped off the truck.

He caught Suping's eye and grinned at her stupefied expression. He walked up to her and said, 'I don't think this development could have been foreseen three days ago, at the time of your arrest, or even a short time ago as yesterday morning. Everything came to a head during and immediately after those executions in the stadium and I simply seized the momentum. I don't think either that you and your parents, and certainly not the Chens, can say that you have been unlucky in that you were arrested and tried before. I think that your cases were the catalyst for Dong's decision to bring things to a head and seize power. It is *not* something I invented. Similar attacks on the established Party hierarchy are taking place all over China and the instigation comes from very high up, from Chairman Mao's own inner circle.

'The instigators' aim is to create total chaos by destroying every and all vestiges of the past, even the recent, Communist past, including those in power at present, and to found, on the rubble, a new brand of total communism à la Mo Zi that no human society can afford, the ants and the bees perhaps, but not the human species. So we must all hope that the level-headed comrades at the top, like Zhou Enlai, Deng Xiaoping and others, will prevail and that the cadres loyal to them, like myself, can maintain this position while riding out the storm. The front-line soldiers of the so-called new order are the Red Guards. Break them and the battle is half won.

'I shall appoint a new batch of Red Guards here in Luding so as not to draw too much attention, however, these will be Red Guards loyal to *me* and not to some power-crazy person in Beijing who for the moment seems to have charmed our Chairman Mao himself. For our Chairman's own interest we *must* withstand this person even if this person and her followers accuse us of disloyalty or even betrayal of the Chairman. This is what I wanted you to know. I saw Chen Dan talking to your parents a moment ago. He must have told them the same things. He knows. I spoke to him last night before I went to see the militia. It was *his* suggestion.'

Zhang had spoken softly, for her ears only, but now he laughed loudly, seeing Suping's stunned expression.

'Good luck,' he said laughingly. 'In a year or two you'll be back, if the rational faction of the Party prevails that is, so pray for us. In the meantime the exercise may well do you some good. I'll send your and your parents' papers to Secretary Deng, hand carried by your good, old Uncle Dan the day after tomorrow. Now go!' and he patted Suping on her shoulder.

'Your parents are already on board the lead truck,' he called after her, 'but that truck is full so board the second one, it's the same convoy anyhow!' And with those words Zhang Yizhong unwittingly changed Suping's life, for good and totally.

## *Chapter Twenty-One*

### Like a Dead Leaf

Still dumbfounded by everything she had seen and heard during the past hour, Suping climbed on board the second truck and found herself a place against the back side board.

With a sigh of relief she sat down on the platform floor and pulled up her knees, leaning her back against the board. Suddenly she noticed Gao Chen's face peering over the board beside her, motioning her to bow her head close to his.

'Don't look so meek,' he hissed, 'you'll be all right. Things are looking much better now that Zhang is completely in charge. He told me he will try to make a deal with Secretary Deng of Chengdu in a couple of weeks from now, at the most in a month or two, to get certain people from Luding reassigned here as soon as he can come forward with a worthwhile project of public interest for which he can claim penal labour with a certain educational background. He can't make it too obvious that he is doing that for you and your parents so he must submit a request for a dozen or more people. Also he cannot ask for people by name and that's why he has to make a deal with Deng.

'He gave me also a small note for Secretary Deng asking him to assign you and your parents to the same commune so you'll be able to see each other every day. I will come and see you at least once a week and if we all look at things in a positive way time will pass very quickly and we may even have a lot of experiences to reminisce and laugh about later when we're all back home on our hill. So cheer up, old girl!'

Suping laughed and cried at the same time and suddenly she bent down and kissed him on his bulbous nose.

'Thank you, Uncle Dan, for cheering me up,' she said, laughing through her tears. 'I'll do my best and I am happy that we shall stay all more or less together. That'll make it a lot easier. It's perhaps an idea to suggest to Zhang to start thinking about a camp for children whose parents have been sent to labour camps. A camp like that needs educators and administrators. We could all play a role there. Will you do that, Uncle Dan?'

'That's the spirit!' Gao Chen exclaimed. 'Of course I will do that. Before you know it we'll all be back here. Now, I see Zhang talking to the leading Red Guards of the other trucks, probably to take charge of the trucks from Luding as well now that he has disbanded the Red Guards here. I see them all nodding quite deferentially so I think I guessed rightly. Yes, Zhang is giving them a sign to get moving and they are climbing aboard their trucks. Here come the drivers of our trucks now. Take care of yourself and maybe, at the next stop, you can change place with somebody on the other truck and join your parents. Good luck and I'll see you in two or three days.'

Gao Chen stepped back and waved as the truck's engine started and in a cloud of black smoke, in fits and starts, the truck began to move.

They drove around the square to catch up with the others and in a convoy of five they took the main street leading to the river and to the road out of town.

Suping's truck was the last one to turn into the street and holding the side board with one hand to steady herself on the jolting truck she turned on her knees to catch one last glance of Gao Chen in the middle of the square, his hand raised high above his head. Just as she raised her arm the driver changed gears too quickly and Gao Chen was obscured by an immense cloud of black smoke.

It was the last memory Suping would have of him, a tiny, waving figure disappearing behind a cloud of black smoke.

Within minutes the convoy had left Luding behind on its way to Chengdu via Tianquan, Ya'an, Hongya, Meishan and Xinjin. More trucks would join them in those places and together they would cover the last stretch from Xinjin to Chengdu.

Suping hoped the Red Guards wouldn't wait too long before making a sanitary stop. The jolts and jerks of the truck at its maximum speed now were having their effect already on her bowels full of doughy rice and she grimaced at the occasional cramps.

Breathing as shallowly as possible so as not to inhale too much soot from the smoke-belching trucks in front and wondering vaguely whether she would have an opportunity to clean up a bit before she would report to Secretary Deng, she dozed off.

The convoy didn't stop in Tianquan. There was no truck with convicts waiting to join and apart from a few people walking along the road and who didn't even look up when the convoy rode past, the place seemed deserted.

The situation in Ya'an was different. The convoy was stopped by Red Guards and the drivers were told to park the trucks along the road near the main intersection and the bridge over the Minjiang.

Two Red Guards were posted beside each truck. Timid requests by the convicts, mainly the women, to be allowed off the trucks to relieve themselves down the river bank were rudely denied. One woman on Suping's truck stood up and raised her voice saying she couldn't keep up any longer. One of the Red Guards, a youth in his early twenties, climbed on board and hit her with his stick, without a word, his face expressionless, until the woman sat down again, sobbing. Suping saw a slow stream of yellow urine spreading from where the woman sat. It trickled through a crack between the planks on to the road before it could reach Suping's place.

The man next to her was not so lucky though. Suping noticed how the wetness stained his trouser legs but he didn't seem to notice since he kept staring dully ahead, at nothing.

After more than an hour of waiting in the hot sun Suping heard the rumble of an approaching truck and the discordant shouts of a number of people. She scrambled to her feet and, upright, she saw an old truck loaded with dejected-looking people slowly coming towards the waiting convoy.

A small, ragbag group of people strolled behind and beside the truck, shouting insults and obscenities at the people on the truck. Four Red Guards, looking just as shabby and recognisable only because of their whips and red armbands, tried in vain to spur the shouters to greater revolutionary fervour.

It was pathetic and Suping felt a growing contempt and irritation with the whole so-called Cultural Revolution and with her own meekness in letting herself be pushed around by those half-baked snots and their bloated leaders.

It was all so silly, too silly and crazy for words.

'Why in heaven's name do those people, do *we* let ourselves be pushed around like that? Why do we accept, meekly and crying, that these arseholes beat us, kick us, scream at us, insult us, uproot us and drag us all over China, on ramshackle old trucks? Why do we piss in our trousers when a moronic snot screamingly denies our request to relieve ourselves in the proper way? Why? Why? What kind of society is this that allows such things, encourages such things? I spit on China and the Chinese and as from this moment I owe them nothing, not to the country, my so-called motherland, what a sick joke that is, and not to its people. I would let everything and everybody go to hell and not lift a finger even if it wouldn't cost me one fen!'

Angrily she stamped her foot and climbed down the truck.

'Hey, you! Bourgeois slut!' one of the Red Guards, a feverish-looking boy of perhaps seventeen, shouted, lifting his stick threateningly. 'Get back on the truck! Who gave you permission to get off?'

'I don't need permission, certainly not from a snot like you, when I, a woman, need to relieve myself,' Suping said, quietly but clearly. 'Now get out of my way so that I can go near the river bank!' and she pushed the flabbergasted youth aside and let herself slide down the bank, in the rushes.

The others on the truck had witnessed the scene and when they saw that the Red Guard didn't react, they all scrambled up and climbed or jumped off the truck and rushed down the bank to seek a moment of privacy amongst the rushes.

As soon as the people on the other four trucks saw what happened they rushed to follow the example and so three minutes after Suping's act of rebellion all hundred and fifty or so convicts were urinating or defecating along the river, leaving the twenty Red Guards speechless and helpless and totally outnumbered.

Taking advantage of the momentary confusion amongst the Red Guards the convicts stretched and walked a few paces up and down the river bank before climbing back, without haste, on board of the trucks.

Many smiled and nodded at Suping and people from the other trucks waved at her. She saw her father stick up his thumb and mouth, 'Proud of you, love you' and she felt much better.

She was the last one to get back on her truck. People smiled up at her and she was momentarily touched when she saw that one man had taken off his jacket and folded it, as a cushion, on her spot.

She found him with her eyes and smiled her thanks. He smiled back at her and blushed way down his milky-white, hairless chest when she sat down on his jacket.

The Red Guards who had flocked together during the quiet rebellion of their charges, pretending to discuss something important to save their face, now began to disperse and, trotting along the line of trucks, they banged on the cabin doors and side boards with their sticks, shouting, 'Everybody on board! Everybody on board!' as if they had given permission to get off in the first place.

The man who gave Suping his jacket snickered and said, in a surprisingly cultured voice and in standard Chinese, 'The despicable wretches. I heard you call them snots. That's exactly what they are, hysterical snots who blindly follow that hatemongering slut in Beijing. If somebody with dignity calls their bluff they shrivel, yet apart from Secretary Zhang, and you just now, nobody dares to stare them down. So, we are probably just as despicable, aren't we?'

He smiled, and holding out his hand, he said, 'By the way, my name is Sun Taiwen. I am, was rather, a teacher at the fifth elementary school in Kunming Street. I once saw you at one of those "poisoned weeds fragrant flowers" meetings for school teachers. We didn't meet though.'

Suping smiled and they shook hands. 'My name's Xu Suping and I feel embarrassed to sit on your jacket,' she said, 'it was very kind of you but there's no need.'

'Please let me,' Sun said, 'it's such a small matter. A small token of my respect.'

Suping was about to reply and make some more small talk with the friendly young man when suddenly the truck's engine roared to life and the black smoke from their own as well as from the other trucks smothered any attempt at talking.

Slowly, the tired, old engine roaring in fits and starts and belching smoke like a locomotive, the truck pulled away from the road side and gathered speed.

Everybody was coughing and scraping his throat and spitting out mucus in cupped hands to inspect, with bleary eyes, for particles of snot and traces of blood before wiping them on trousers or socks.

Sun was in a bad way. He was almost choking as if he had the whooping cough.

'Asthma,' he wheezed in answer to the worried look in Suping's eyes.

As the speed of the trucks increased their exhausts became less dense and also the wind drove them sideways and the people recovered slowly.

'These old ramshackle trucks are like the Chinese economy,' Sun said, smiling weakly. 'Wasteful, polluting, on the verge of total collapse, going in fits and starts, with jolts and jerks. And then, one day, they break down, in one last belch of poisoned smoke and no more, nothing! And we, the passengers, some just sit and die, others jump off the wagon, forage for the last morsels and die a bit later. But we all die, except our beloved leaders who'll last a bit longer because of what they stole and hid away. Just in time, for themselves that is, not for us, they'll invite the overseas Chinese to come back and rebuild the nation. That'll be the end of the Communist's pipedreams. Unfortunately the common people, you and I, won't see that new beginning. For us there's only the unhappy ending.'

'I don't intend to die,' Suping said indignantly. 'I can take care of myself. I won't give *them* the satisfaction seeing *me* die. And I want to be there when the overseas Chinese rebuild the nation, as you call it. And you had better pull yourself together and think positively, as I do, or otherwise you won't even survive this transport.'

'You are the combative type,' Sun laughed. 'Now I understand why Secretary Zhang talked to you this morning. I couldn't hear what he said to you but it must have been important, what with his serious face and gesticulating hands. He reckons that you'll be back soon, of course.'

Suping laughed but didn't comment as Sun was obviously fishing for confidences.

For a while neither of them spoke. They both knew that the next stage in their developing acquaintanceship would require more intimate, personal details and neither was in the mood for that yet, the prospect boring and purposeless.

So they pretended to doze off in their own thoughts.

It was past midday when the convoy rode, without stopping, through Hongya.

It was a hot, windless day and there was nobody to be seen along the road and its side streets.

'The good people of Hongya know their priorities,' Sun snickered. 'There is a time for revolution and a time for eating and taking the afternoon nap. Talking about eating, I'm hungry. I wonder what the pride of the nation has in store for us.'

'Not much, I'm afraid,' Suping replied. 'I was forewarned by Secretary Zhang so our friend brought some sticky rice this morning for on the way. Please share with me,' and she took the small packages with sticky rice and minced chicken from her pockets.

'I don't mind if I do,' Sun said and carefully he removed the toilet paper wrappings from the first of the three packages Suping had given him.

'That tastes good,' he said, his mouth full, 'my first decent food in three days. That prison fodder was terrible.'

They became aware of the people around them staring at them.

'I'm so sorry,' Suping stammered, blushing deeply, 'we should have been more discreet since I haven't enough to share with everybody. I'm sure they'll give us all something to eat in Meishan tonight.'

'No need to apologise, girl,' the old man next to her squeaked. 'Eat your sticky rice,' he continued, cackling, 'you'll need your strength, I'm sure. Thanks to you I could empty my bowels a while ago, in the river and not in my pants which was what was about to happen, so I shouldn't begrudge you your little snack, now, should I? That you chose to share with that young man is only natural, cruel but natural, but then youth is cruel, of course.'

He cackled, then added, 'Just joking, don't mind my silly talk.'

Suddenly he sat up straight and, pointing to the left behind the speeding truck, he squeaked excitedly, 'There! We just passed the turn off to Meishan, on our left. And there go the other five trucks, over there, on the road to Meishan! Do you see them? Only one truck missed the turn-off. We are on our way to Jiajiang! I know! I am from here!'

Out of breath the old man fell silent, gesticulating still wildly.

Worried Suping looked at Sun. 'What's going on?' she asked anxiously. 'Why did our truck leave the convoy? What are we doing here alone? Why is the truck speeding like that? The driver has gone crazy!'

Before Sun could answer, the old man rattled on. 'You'll see! Those three hell-hounds in the cabin with the driver are going to dump us at the railway station and put us on some train or other, heaven knows to where. Once rid of us they'll keep the truck for themselves and join other marauding gangs to steal themselves rich. With a truck to transport the goodies they'll be rich quick. They'll bury the things somewhere secret, abandon the truck and disappear for a few years, waiting for better times.'

Seeing Suping's and Sun's unbelieving stares, he exclaimed, 'It's true! I heard those four scoundrels whisper together while I was shitting in the rushes. They didn't see me, down below where they stood on the bank. I couldn't hear what they said but I'm sure I'm right. You'll see.'

He fell silent and stared morosely down on his hands. 'You'll see, you'll see,' they heard him mutter defiantly.

'You have it all figured out already, eh Lao Wu?' Sun said, teasingly. 'What were you in your younger days? Some sort of highway bandit, perhaps?'

'Stop joking!' Suping said irritably. 'I'm worried. My parents are on the other truck from Luding and that one went to Meishan as planned. Now I come to think of it, why did the driver of our truck let the truck from Ya'an go in front of him instead of behind, as the last of the convoy? Because *he* wanted to stay as last so that he could take the other road at the intersection without the others noticing. I agree with Lao Wu that there must be a plot between the three Red Guards and the driver. Taiwen, please, bang on the cabin to make them stop!'

Without further argument Sun crept over and around the other people sitting and lying pell-mell on the jolting platform floor to the front and started pounding with his fist on the cabin roof.

The truck suddenly swerved to the left of the road then to the right again as the startled driver retook control of the truck.

People screamed out of fright at the sudden manoeuvre and one man pulled Sun down by his jacket, shouting, 'You want to kill us all, arsehole? Go back to your place or I'll throw you off the truck!'

'I want them to stop!' Sun cried, 'We have taken the wrong road! Don't you see?'

'What do I care where they take us as long as I stay alive!' the man yelled back at Sun. 'And if you frighten that driver one more time I'll kill you!'

Meekly Sun crawled back to where Suping and Lao Wu had watched the scene.

'Nothing doing,' he muttered, 'that man is crazy but much stronger than I am. I suggest we just wait and see what happens in Jiajiang. Lao Wu may be wrong and this truck has been ordered to pick up somebody in Jiajiang and then go to Meishan from there so we'll get to Meishan one or two hours later than the others who'll wait for us there.'

Suping and Lao Wu nodded, not convinced and worried.

As it was Lao Wu was right, at least as far as the train part was concerned.

The part of the three Red Guards and the driver being in league and so on was perhaps a figment of the old man's fertile imagination, from reading too many old stories. But then, perhaps it was not. Who would ever know but the four musketeers themselves?

The wall clock above the entrance of Jiajiang's railway station indicated four o'clock when the truck came to a jolting, screeching halt.

The door of the cabin opened creakingly and a Red Guard, a tall, youngish man in his mid-twenties probably, stood on the footboard and cast his glance over the people on the back of the truck.

'There has been a change of plan,' he said in a quiet yet commanding voice.

'This truck has been commandeered by the Party secretary of Jiajiang and I have been ordered to report to him. You will take the train here, for Chengdu. The leading Red Guard of the other five trucks will inform Secretary Deng and he will send people to the railway station in Chengdu to pick you up. Now, you will remain seated on this truck until I come to fetch you with Secretary Yang who will decide where you will have to wait for the train, together with the other convicts over there,' and he pointed over their heads to the square in front of the station.

Suping turned her head to look in the direction indicated by the quiet Red Guard and she changed colour: hundreds of people, probably close to a thousand, were standing silently, abreast in rows of twenty and facing the station in the square. Red Guards, in units of two, continuously and in cadence sliding their whips through the fingers of one hand, walked up and down the four sides of the block of people.

Occasionally one of them stepped between the rows of people, dealt a blow to some unfortunate or other judging from a short, stifled scream and stepped out of the block again to rejoin his comrade who had been waiting quietly and together they resumed their pacing. Not a word was said, nothing. Silence.

Suping shivered in spite of the stifling afternoon heat.

'Not very reassuring,' Sun mumbled close to her ear. 'Still, I am sure we are going to Chengdu after all. This scene here, in the square, reminds me of a book I once read: *Nineteen Eighty-Four* it was called, by an English author, Orwell his name is, or was. Ghoulish, gave me the creeps. Look at those poor people, they look like zombies, the living dead. Charming person Comrade Secretary Yang must be to like this kind of thing.'

'Have no illusion,' Lao Wu whispered. 'I told you, did I not, that I was from Daxiang County near Emei? I am sure now that I recognise that Red Guard who just spoke to us. I can't recall his name right now, it's on the tip of my tongue. It must be seven years or so ago that the police found stolen gold jewellery on his person during a routine identity check. The jewellery was identified as old Madam Hou's who had been found murdered a few days earlier. The boy was only seventeen so he was sentenced to twelve years in a correctional institute also because Madam Hou was the wife of former landowner Hou and her jewellery was the ill-gotten wealth of an exploiter of the working class. There was quite a lot of talk about the case at that time, only locally of course. They must have released him because of the Cultural Revolution. He's probably even a hero in his comrades' eyes for having killed an exploiter of the masses.'

The old man grinned mischievously, 'Once a crook, always a crook though, so our friend smells great prospects. The secretary's name, Yang, also rings a bell. Around the same time as the Hou case there was talk of one of the Yang brothers, the one who had joined Mao's army as a boy when the Communists passed through here on their way up north, having been dismissed from the PLA because of irregularities. It was never explained what those irregularities were so people whispered, they always do. Murder, theft, nepotism, all rumours, probably true, perhaps one, perhaps all.

'Anyhow, one day, the Yang brother turned up in Emei to live with his family. The last thing I remember before I was relocated to Luding as the administrator of an agricultural commune, was Yang marrying the daughter of Jiajiang's Party secretary. I shouldn't be surprised at all if the comrade secretary died a premature death and his grieving son-in-law was appointed his successor, what with all the nasty secrets he must have known about by then. Judging by those Red Guards acting like little soldiers I'm sure Yang is the boss here now.'

Lao Wu fell silent, then suddenly he slammed his left fist in the palm of his right hand and exclaimed, 'Ah, I now remember that Red Guard's name. It's also Yang! Yang Changren. I wouldn't be surprised if he were related to the secretary, a nephew or something. Yang and Yang. What a team! I am now absolutely sure of this game's scenario!'

'And what might that scenario be, convict number 317?' a quiet voice from behind the truck asked.

Suping saw all the colour and vigour drain from Lao Wu's face as he turned slowly in the voice's direction.

Suping and Sun followed his look and saw the Red Guard they knew already standing next to a exceptionally tall man, impeccably dressed in a grey Mao suit.

He had a long, angular face as if chiselled from a block of pale marble and just as motionless. Had that face ever cracked in a laugh or even only a smile? Suping thought irrelevantly. Probably not, judging from his eyes, terribly lifeless eyes, like those of the giant wall-eye she had once seen lying in the fish market.

As from far she heard Lao Wu mumble, in an equally lifeless voice, 'Nothing Secretary Yang. I was just joking, seeing you and Comrade Red Guard Yang have the same name and are probably related, both of you being so tall and handsome.'

'Now we both also like a good joke, don't we, Nephew,' Secretary Yang said, 'so why don't you tell us the joke in the cellar of my office. It's a quiet, private place so only my nephew and I will enjoy your joke. Did you share your joke already with any of your friends here, Wu?'

'It's not like that, Secretary Yang!' Wu cried out. 'I was just babbling to myself in my excitement that I had recognised you and Comrade Red Guard Yang! The others didn't listen! They don't like me! They told me to shut up and called me an old blabbering fossil a while ago when we missed the turn-off in Hongya!'

'I'm afraid that's exactly what you should have done, Wu,' Secretary Yang said, 'however, now we want to keep the joke to ourselves, don't we? So get off the truck and follow the Red Guard!'

Red Guard Yang lifted the hooks of the back board and grabbed Old Wu's ankles. While being pulled to the edge of the loading platform the old man put his hands on Suping and Sun's legs and squeezed. A reassurance? A farewell? Suping caught his eyes as he half jumped, half tumbled off the truck. She saw naked, desperate fear.

Red Guard Yang grabbed old Wu's shoulder to steady him on his wobbly legs and ordered, in the same measured, emotionless voice as his uncle's, 'Walk old man, straight ahead! I will follow and give you directions.'

Secretary Yang looked them over with his cold stare before he said, minutes later, 'You will climb down from the truck in an orderly manner when I tell you to. I'll assign your group a place next to the other convicts, in the square. There you wait until you are called to board the train for Chengdu. You are not permitted to talk and to look around. You stand with your hands on your back and look straight ahead. Is that clear?'

Nobody answered so Yang ordered, 'Get off the trucks, now!'

Sun and Suping were among the first to line up beside the truck and Suping, being closest to Yang, asked timidly, 'Will there be any food or drink for us, Comrade Secretary Yang? We only had a bit of boiled rice this morning, in Luding before we left. And can we go to the toilet please?'

Yang had heard her out without a flicker of emotion, neither impatience nor anger nor compassion.

In the same even tone as before he said, 'I once stood for sixty hours in the snow, without food or drink or permission to relieve myself. I think *you* can hold out another few hours. You have a lot to learn, Xu Suping. Don't waste your breath and my time with silly, decadent questions. Now, follow me, all of you!'

At least he has noticed my name on my armband, Suping thought, trying to keep up with Yang's long paces.

The Luding convicts were lined up with the two front rows of the Jiajiang block with a paced-off gap of five between the two groups.

Suping put her hands on the small of her back and stared in front of her, at the entrance door of the railway station, resigned to keep as low a profile as possible. Both Uncle and Nephew Yang scared her; so cold, so emotionless, so remote. Psychopaths probably, both of them.

'Psst, Suping,' she heard a whisper at her right.

Sun, she thought. Why doesn't he keep his mouth shut? Wait until we are in the train? Then he can talk his head off if he wants to. But now it's dangerous, not only for him but for me as well.

However, Sun had evidently not got Yang's message, nor her silent one for that matter, since he continued in a whisper, 'Lao Wu, one hell of a brave man. They're going to kill him because he knows too much. Wu realises that, that's why he covered for us. But first they are going to torture him, more for fun than to hear how much he knows. They are psychopaths, those two Yangs. Let's hope he can hold out until you and I are on board that bloody train. If he tells those two that he told us about them, and *tell he will*, I'm absolutely certain, and we are not yet on that train then we are in deep trouble, Suping. We'll spend the last few very unpleasant hours of our life in that quiet, private cellar with Uncle and Nephew Yang.

'So pray girl, pray that they're not in a hurry and that Wu's pain threshold is high enough to keep them busy for a couple of hours, long enough for us to hide under Secretary Deng's wings.'

Sun's half-whisper was suddenly interrupted by a high-pitched scream. Frightened, Suping turned her head and saw a Red Guard standing in front of Sun, whose left eye, nose and lips were bleeding.

The Red Guard had his whip ready for a second strike as Sun cowered behind his arms.

The Red Guard, a handsome youth of about Suping's age, said, 'You were forbidden to speak by Comrade Secretary Yang. Take two steps forward, convict 267, then stand to attention and do *not* move while I report your disobedience to Leading Red Guard Yang.' Again the same unemotional monotone.

Sun stepped forward and, like a soldier, stood to attention, his arms stiffly pointing down his legs.

Suping saw him tremble as he licked his burst lips, moaning softly.

She felt a wave of pity and anger wash over her and she had to close her eyes and force her thoughts back in time to the scenery from her garden in Luding just so she didn't step up to Sun and wipe his bloody face.

Therefore she didn't see Leading Red Guard Yang approach together with the Red Guard who had hit Sun. She opened her eyes in horror as she heard the younger Yang's voice order his underling, 'Take him to Secretary Yang's office and lock him in the cellar next to the old man's. My uncle and I will take care of those two tonight once the trains with the convicts will have left.'

'Yes, Comrade Yang, at your orders,' the younger Red Guard replied, and then, evenly, 'Walk convict 267! Straight ahead! I am right behind you so don't try to run. You have no chance.'

Without once looking back and without a word Sun began walking towards the road in front of the station, the Red Guard only three steps behind him.

With all her will-power Suping tried to remain impassive as she felt the leading Red Guard's eyes on her, searching her face for tell-tale signs of fear or worry.

'Did you hear what he said, Suping?' She heard him say, softly, his head close to hers. 'Did he talk to you, Suping?'

'I don't know whether he talked to me Red Guard Yang,' she heard herself say, afraid he might hear the tremble in her voice. 'I didn't listen. It passed my mind that he might be praying as I once overheard him mention to that old man that he was a Christian.'

Coward, coward! Coward! she heard an inner voice shout inside her head.

'A Christian, eh?' Yang said, 'We'll see what he's made of when—'

He didn't finish his sentence as he whirled around at the sound of shouts and screeching brakes.

Horrified Suping saw Sun running towards a fast approaching truck that came speeding up the road in front of the station.

The driver had seen him and braked with all his might but in vain. The old truck skidded and swerved and hit Sun with full force, hurling his body against a lamp-post, like a rag doll. He must have died instantly.

Suping was shaking uncontrollably. She felt two hands grip her upper arm and Yang's warm breath as he snarled, 'Stop screaming, you silly woman. He killed himself because he knew he was guilty of maliciously slandering a high Party official. He managed to escape his rightful punishment by the people of Jiajiang. He was a coward! Do you hear me! He was a coward! Say after me, Suping: he was a coward!'

To her horror, she heard herself say after him, 'He was a coward.'

Loathing herself for what she did, she nevertheless took hold of herself and said, 'You are right, Comrade Yang. He shouldn't have done that! It's a crime to take your life to escape the People's justice. I am sorry for my unrevolutionary behaviour. It was the shock, nothing more. I never saw somebody dying before. I am all right now. Thank you for your concern, Comrade.'

She looked at him, outwardly in control of herself, inwardly loathing herself for her cringing.

Leading Red Guard Yang's searching eyes tried to stare her down, to make her flinch but she managed to keep her face innocently straight and after a couple of minutes he shrugged his shoulders, apparently satisfied that she was just an empty-headed, emotional female, and turned away from her to look at the scene in front of the station. The driver of the truck that had killed Sun and the Red Guard who had been ordered by Yang to escort Sun were arguing loudly while Sun was still lying, unattended, on the pavement, his upper torso forming an impossible angle with his pelvis.

'Your train will be here in another hour or two,' Yang said, over his shoulder and then, all of a sudden, he whirled around to face her one last time to see whether, unobserved, her expression had changed.

Impassively she looked back at him and reassured this time she knew nothing, he turned and walked, with measured steps, towards the quarrelling driver and Red Guard.

With a single gesture he put a halt to the argument and apparently ordered them to get rid of Sun's body for Suping saw the two men pick Sun up by his arms and legs and dump him unceremoniously in the back of the truck.

The driver climbed into the cabin, started the engine and drove off in a cloud of black smoke, deliberately making the engine backfire, like a big gun, to show everybody his anger and contempt.

I will not let complete strangers sneak up to me again and entice me into becoming friendly with them, Suping thought, sad, angry and disgusted with herself. It hurts to see them suffer and you can't help them, or even have to deny them, to save your own skin.

From now on I'll keep to myself and that's *definite* this time. I escaped only by the skin of my teeth a moment ago and hated myself because of Sun Taiwen, a man I have known for two hours at the most. Should I have stood up for him heroically and then found myself in a cell, with Lao Wu, only to be tortured to death? For a complete stranger?

If I hadn't let myself be taken in by his gesture to let me sit on his jacket but had given it back to him and refused to talk instead of sharing my sticky rice with him and if I would have turned my back on that garrulous old man Wu so that he wouldn't have run off at the mouth, both might have thought me a disagreeable, stuffy prude, however, both of them would almost certainly have stayed unnoticed and *alive*!

Now, one is already dead and the other will die, horribly, in a few hours. Is that my fault? Must I blame myself for *their* stupidity? Is it fair that their fate should make me loathe myself just for trying to survive? Am I responsible for the mistakes and posturing of people who are nothing to me, just casual acquaintances who happen to be sympathetic?

No! I am not! And I refuse to feel guilty! I am *not* my brother's keeper and I expect others to think the same.

She breathed deeply, stood up straight and stared ahead, defiantly.

The sun had gone down and with the fast falling darkness came a black cloud of bats flitting in from the river on the other side of the railway.

The creepy little beasts must have heard the whining and buzzing of the mosquitoes and flies above this smelly crowd, Suping thought and involuntarily she contracted the muscles in her back and neck, expecting at any moment that one of the little monsters would get entangled in her hair as she sensed them dive to barely a few centimetres from her head.

'Don't panic,' she mumbled to herself, 'don't panic. They won't touch me. Stay calm.' She hummed to drown out the dancing mosquitoes' whine above her head.

Suddenly, in one swoop, the bats disappeared over the station in the direction of the river and almost at the same time she heard the whistle of an approaching train.

Relieved she let out her breath in a deep sigh and relaxed her tense muscles.

From the corner of her right eye she saw Party Secretary Yang approaching, followed by his nephew, Leading Red Guard Yang.

'The convicts from Luding, ten paces forward!' Red Guard Yang said, hardly raising his voice above normal conversational tone.

The twenty-eight remaining convicts from Luding stepped forward, counting to ten and remained standing to attention.

'Right turn and march and follow me!' Yang ordered.

It mustn't have been an impressive sight, the tired and scared men and women stumbling to keep pace with Red Guard Yang, for Suping saw a momentary flicker of disgust passing over Secretary Yang's face as she passed near him, trying to keep in step with his nephew, her head high.

She felt his eyes pricking between her shoulder blades and she was glad when Yang the Younger turned left and marched towards the side entrance to the station's platform.

Yang marched his charges to the end of the platform where he ordered them to turn, facing the railway, and to remain standing to attention while he would go back for a second contingent.

Slowly the old locomotive, humming and screeching, passed in front of Suping's group followed by the first three of a seemingly endless train of freight vans. The train came to a halt, with jerks and jolts, the sliding door of the fourth van just in front of Suping.

Leading Red Guard Yang and two railway workers squeezed themselves between Suping and the van and Yang opened the padlock on the main bolt of the van's door. The two workers pushed and the door rumbled open.

'Get in!' Yang shouted. 'Twenty people only! The others join the next group for van number five!'

Suping was the first to climb on to the footboard and, grasping the door with her left hand, she pulled herself up and, pushed from behind by those following her, she stumbled into the acrid, humid, warm semi-darkness of the van.

Trying to regain her balance she stepped on something soft and a woman's voice cried out in pain.

In a reflex Suping pulled back her foot and pushed by the scrambling people behind her she fell full length on top of what she realised to her horror were people lying pell-mell on the van's floor.

Muttering panicky apologies she scrambled up and her eyes, adjusted to the gloomy semi-darkness, saw a few empty spots against the front wall of the van. In a few, short leaps over the bodies on the floor she reached a place in the corner, between an elderly man and a young woman.

With a sigh of relief and a mumbled apology to her left and right Suping let herself down, her back against the steel wall. Neither the man nor the woman had reacted to her squeezing herself into the narrow space between them, not even a small shifting out of her way to make it easier for her.

Damn them, Suping thought and defiantly she bumped her bottom first against the woman then against the man to create more space for herself. Grumbling like lazy, somnolent pigs they shifted a bit and Suping was satisfied with the space she had created for herself. She let her chin fall on her chest and, arms around her pulled-up knees, she closed her eyes, ignoring the ongoing scuffle near the door and elsewhere in the van.

She must have dozed off for suddenly she shot upright as the sliding door rumbled shut and the van's interior became pitch dark. She heard several people shouting outside and then a whistle sounded followed by a series of violent jerks and jolts.

The train had left Jiajiang's station. Soon she would be in Chengdu and tomorrow she would see her parents again and perhaps even Uncle Dan with a new supply of sticky rice with minced chicken.

Smiling contentedly at the happy prospect she fell asleep, her forehead resting on her arms and knees.

She woke up with a start as something moved against her head.

Slowly she opened her eyes and saw light filtering through the chinks around the van door, daylight she realised. She became aware of the vibration of the floor against her right hip and the clinks and clanks of the train. The rapid clickety-clack of the wheels on the rails told her the train was moving fast.

Again she felt the movement against her cheek and suddenly she realised she was lying with her head on somebody's legs and she shot up, utterly embarrassed. She heard the man beside her chuckle and she felt herself blushing, hot, and to the roots of her hair, as she rushed her apologies.

'Don't apologise,' the man said in a friendly tone. 'You must have been tired. You fell asleep almost immediately after we left Jiajiang and after an hour or so you sagged against me and in your sleep you shifted and shifted until you felt finally comfortable and that happened to be with your head on my legs. I am sorry I woke you up but my legs became numb and I had to move them a bit.'

In the semi-darkness Suping saw that he smiled, a friendly smile, and he asked, to help her over her embarrassment, 'Where are you from, if I may ask?'

'From Luding,' Suping answered. 'I am so very sorry to have been such a nuisance. I was indeed very tired. We got up at five o'clock yesterday morning in the Detention House, then we had to wait until nine before we finally boarded the trucks for Chengdu. Then our truck missed the turn-off in Hongya for Meishan and Chengdu and we ended up in Jiajiang. There, in Jiajiang they made us stand to attention for three hours before they finally put us on board this train for Chengdu.'

Suddenly a feeling of foreboding dawned on her and she asked, in near panic, 'It's the following day already. Why is the train still going and so fast? We should have been in Chengdu a long time ago? Did I sleep past Chengdu? Say something, please?' She ended in a wail.

The man put his hand on her knee and said softly, 'I am afraid they put you in the wrong train, girl. I, we, the people you found in this van yesterday evening, are from Chengdu and this train is bound for Kunming and perhaps even further, I don't know. I have no idea where I am going. I saw a whole bunch of Red Guards board this train in Chengdu, fed up undoubtedly with Secretary Deng's tight reign there and they literally hijacked this train before Secretary Deng arrived at the station with food and water for the convicts and a schedule for the train and for us. They are totally unpredictable and I really don't know where they will unload us. More than half the vans are still empty, that's why the train is going so fast. I expect we'll be in Kunming by midday.'

The kindly man's voice had become a drone in Suping's ear as she realised Secretary Yang's duplicity. He had never intended the convicts from Luding to go to Chengdu to tell the story of the diverted truck to other convicts and risk the rumours reaching the ears of Secretary Deng, who would, of course, investigate the matter and discover the plans for the scheming Yangs.

She wouldn't see her parents and Uncle Dan, not today, not next week, not next year, if ever.

She felt despair grip her heart and suddenly she wept, silently, her hot tears seeping between the fingers of her hands as she covered her face in shame.

The man beside her didn't say a word. What could he have said that would have made any sense in this mad and wicked world of theirs? Offered any consolation that wouldn't have sounded cheap and futile?

So he remained silent until the girl would have regained her composure.

Perhaps she would tell him why it made such a difference whether she ended up in Chengdu or in Kunming or wherever and then, maybe she would not. He would wait and then, perhaps, he would have to tell her anyhow to keep her story for herself, what with all the ears around them eager to pick up a morsel of information that might bring in a small advantage when reported to a Red Guard.

It took a while but finally the man noticed that her sobbing had stopped and that she was now breathing more regularly with only sporadically a deep, shuddering sigh.

It took a lot longer but, in the end, she took her hands away from her face and wiped them dry on the legs of her trousers before wiping her face with the sleeves of her jacket.

'I am sorry,' she said, without looking at the man.

'It was silly and childish of me to let myself go like that. At first I wept because I felt so terribly sad, then I continued weeping because I felt so sorry for myself and in the end I wept because I was angry and hated the whole world, myself not in the least. And now I feel empty and drained. I have no emotion left and I don't care. Here I am, in this train as it snakes across the country on some crazy, spasmodic and unpredictable trek to nowhere. Like some witless, voracious snake-god it swallows and disgorges hapless, haggard victims wherever its crazy charmers force it to stop.

'I close my eyes and imagine I am an autumn leaf, blown hither and thither, amongst millions of other whirling leaves, by that *taifong* of depraved madness that is devastating the country. And finally, the *taifong* exhausted, the leaves will float down to earth somewhere but to rot and nobody remembers or cares. And you know what should frighten me but doesn't? I don't care myself, not any more!'

'Oh, but you *do*,' the man said, smiling amusedly, 'you *do* care about yourself or else you wouldn't bother to express your thoughts with such beautiful imagery as you did just now, the meaning and tone of each word like a harmonious musical poem, to be savoured like tiny morsels of an exquisite dish.'

Suping grinned and said, 'The last exquisite dish this poetess partook of was Beggars Chicken prepared on a balmy summer evening in her garden, set in what now seems a different universe and time, and by a kind, wise, old alien, her adopted uncle, friend and mentor, called Chen Dan. Her next meal was the typical kind of nourishment the proletariat seems to thrive on, lumps of cold, soggy, third-grade rice dished out and commented upon by a kind, old woman prison guard in the Detention House yesterday morning at seven o'clock. Since then the proletariat, who deprived her of her parents, friends, shelter and freedom and sent her for re-education and reform to a place she is now heading *away* from, has not deemed her worthy of further physical nourishment.

'So she now feels the pangs of hunger and she wonders what kind of proletarian delicacies, if any, will be waiting for her in Kunming. The tiny voice of her earlier high-mindedness, naivety her cynical friends called it, which whispers there *is* still hope, is all but drowned out by the stentorian voice of her newly acquired cynical personality which booms there is none; no hope, no food, no nothing. Just a stop, it booms, for the snake charmer to pee, eat and drink and quarrel about what to feed the snake and onwards we go. We are mere fodder for the snakes. Fodder doesn't eat, it *is* eaten.'

Suping fell silent, grimaced irritably, and said wonderingly, 'Now *why* would I talk to you, a complete stranger, like that? Only yesterday evening, two men, strangers like you until, for no longer than an hour, they became no more than superficial acquaintances, died horribly, one by committing suicide, one by torture while I slept, merely because they talked to me like I now talk to you. So I swore I would keep to myself and no longer relate to anybody, mainly to avoid trouble for myself but also to avoid trouble for others.'

Suping heard the man laugh softly and then he said, 'You can no more change your character than you can make water flow uphill, Xu Suping. Whatever little games you play with yourself in your mind; Suping the Indifferent, Suping the Inaccessible, Suping the Haughty, Suping the Remote, they are just that, games, *mind games*! However, while you are fantasising, your aura and body language radiate a friendly, open, kind-hearted person so people talk to you and you respond, instinctively, until you suddenly remember that you shouldn't and you are so engaging that you even blurt *that* out.

'You're funny, Suping. I hope you don't mind me calling you Suping. I read your name on your armband. My name is Pan Chun by the way. Where was I? Oh yes, what I mean to say, Suping, is that you are who you are. In your case one glance, a first casual encounter, and people feel intuitively what kind of person you are. With others it's more difficult, it takes time to find out their true character. While you were ruminating the death of those two strangers yesterday and blaming yourself for it, did you ask yourself why it was only *they* who died and why not *you* also? They talked to you, you said, however, I'm sure you talked to them as well, so why did the Red Guards pick on *them* and not on *you*? I'll tell you why, Suping. Because the Red Guards, and perhaps even the Party secretary if he was involved as well, were *men,* weren't they? Men, unless they are psychopaths, are incapable of causing *you*, Suping, serious harm. You have that effect on them. You touch in them some remnant of decency, of tenderness, they themselves may have forgotten is there or have suppressed for a long, long time, but nevertheless with you, *vis-à-vis* you I should say, they behave differently.

'Reversely, however, there is a certain type of *woman* who hates, instinctively, *women* like you. Unfortunately, this so-called Great Proletarian Cultural Revolution is *the* dreamt of opportunity for that type of woman to vent her rage and frustrations and complexes as she is whipped up by that hysterical arch female demon in Beijing. So my advice to you, Suping, is to make yourself invisible or, at most, to keep the lowest possible profile, when female Red Guards and female Party officials are around. You are their dreamt of type of victim because you allow them to exult both in your own, obvious, suffering and, almost equally important, in the uneasiness or silent disapproval of their male colleagues. Directly or indirectly, trouble in your future life will be caused by nasty women. Beware!'

'You are very perspicacious, Mr Pan,' Suping said, chuckling, 'and you mean well, I'm sure. Still, I think that you make the error so typical of men to think that just because a woman is pretty, elfin-like, with little spontaneous, or so you think, mannerisms, shiny eyes that easily brim with tears, a quick smile with lips that easily quiver on the verge of weeping, she is vulnerable and loveable and that the only thing a true man can do, must do, is to protect her, preferably by pulling her against his broad chest and by stroking her hair, all the while crooning inanities like 'teh, teh, calm down, I'll take care of you' or 'sorry, sorry, sorry, I didn't mean what I said, can you forgive me?'

'There are women who are genuinely like that and who deserve all that empathy and sympathy, however, most of that type are just little manipulators of the man's ego and lack of understanding of the female psyche. I don't think of myself as a manipulator, although *every* woman manipulates occasionally to have things go her way, but I am certainly not the vulnerable, breakable little creature you seem to think I am. I can be very nasty and unpleasant and, for their own sake, men would do well to treat me as one of their own and not give me any special favours. Uncle Dan and Party Secretary Zhang Yizhong of Luding were quick to realise that when the going got tough. Are you disappointed, Mr Pan?'

Pan burst out laughing, genuinely amused, and said, 'Had you not asked the last question and in the tone you asked it, which made the music, I would have believed you and wondered where I had gone wrong in my analysis. Now I believe both you *and* my analysis and regret, deeply, that I'm not thirty years younger. Be that as it may, I will behave and I shall adjust my attitude so don't hesitate to fall asleep again and use me as a pillow.'

Pan fell silent, chuckled, and said, 'I think that as long as we can still joust and joke like we did in spite of all the chaos around us, the hubristic, humourless lunatics who have now, temporarily, the upper hand, won't succeed in bringing us to heel, ever. The day we lose our sense of humour and proportion we will be truly lost.'

By midday the train began to slow down, irregularly, in fits and starts, until finally, after a whole series of violent jolts, it came to a complete stop.

Outside, the station was complete pandemonium with at least four loudspeakers blaring, pell-mell, incomprehensible orders and announcements, abruptly interrupted at the oddest moments by ear-shattering martial music followed by slogans.

Nothing happened for an hour and a half and the heat inside the van became almost unbearable when suddenly there were shouts outside and the sliding door rumbled open.

Four Red Guards put their head inside the van, shouting orders to get out and assemble on the platform. The din, the heat and the harsh sunlight took the convicts' breath away as they stumbled and staggered to avoid the Red Guards' whips and sticks.

It took them almost an hour to get the five hundred or so convicts in some semblance of a line-up that seemed to satisfy an elderly man in a neat, grey Mao suit who had been looking at the confusion, without comment, for the last fifteen minutes, which had made the Red Guards even more nervous.

Finally the man called one of the Red Guards, a tall, skinny girl of about twenty, over to where he was standing and gave her a brief order.

The girl nodded emphatically, tried to salute and turn around at the same time, got her feet entangled and fell in her full length at the man's feet. With a ghost of a smile he turned and walked off towards the station's main building.

'At least he has a sense of humour,' Suping heard Pan whisper beside her, 'perhaps that improves our chance to get something to eat and drink.'

The girl was still scrambling to her feet as she screechingly ordered the other Red Guards to march the convicts off to *godown* number three.

*Godown* number three was the last in a row of long, low buildings with brick walls and a roofing of rusty, corrugated sheets.

Four Red Guards ran ahead of the shuffling, dispirited throng of prisoners to open the large, wooden doors and a gust of hot air, loaded with the smell of urine and excrement, washed over the convicts as they were herded inside.

At least a thousand people were already there, lying or squatting on the unpaved, yellowish dusty soil. They didn't react as the newcomers stumbled and nearly trampled them under foot.

The Red Guards yelled and screamed instructions as they herded their charges to the far end of the *godown* where a place of about twenty by thirty metres was still unoccupied.

The reason was obvious; the area along the back wall was apparently where the other prisoners had relieved themselves (for how long already?) and the stench was indescribable. People around Suping retched and threw up and she thought she was going to faint as she felt somebody grab her upper arm and pull her away and out of her group. Will-lessly she let herself be dragged over the people lying on the floor until she was pushed down in a spot against a steel column and the side wall where a few resourceful young men had removed a few bricks, near the ground, as breathing holes.

'I saw the light coming in when none of you moved,' she heard Pan say, 'you should be more careful, but for us your carelessness came as a godsend.'

Reluctantly the three men moved aside to let Pan and Suping squeeze themselves between them, hiding the hole in the wall behind their backs.

'Poor devils,' the young man next to Suping mumbled, nodding in the direction of her group of fellow convicts huddled together, standing, afraid to sit or lie down.

'Many of them will have no choice but to lie down in our shit but now we also have a problem. Where to pee and shit from now on?'

'I propose that when the Red Guards are gone we loosen a few more bricks,' Pan said, 'and take them out only when one of us five needs to relieve himself. One at a time and very, very carefully so that the others don't notice or else we'll have a stampede all over us and before you know it our little game will be over. What do you think?'

'A truly wicked proposal,' the young man said, grinning, 'but justified under the circumstances. My friends and I approve.'

It turned out that the young man, who introduced himself as Song Ge, and his two taciturn, morose friends had been languishing in the *godown* for five days already, still waiting for transport to an as yet undetermined place.

He told Suping and Pan that the Red Guards came once a day, around noon, with a truck, to distribute food, mainly rice with cooked slaughterhouse offal and plain water, sometimes weak, green tea.

That day the guards had made their round already so the newcomers would have to wait until the following day. Song showed them how he had folded a banana palm leaf into a makeshift mug for the water or tea.

'Take two leaves tomorrow from the truck,' he told them, 'one for the food and one you fold as I showed you for the water. They don't give you a plate and chopsticks or a mug. You have to eat with your fingers. Drink as much as you can right where they ladle the water in your holder because you can't carry both the leaf with the rice and the leaf with the water back to your place. The water leaks out anyway. We also must take turns to go, two of us at a time, while the other three defend our place here.'

That evening, after dark, two of them took turns to remove sixteen bricks more to create an opening large enough for Pan to crawl through. It was an easy job as the mortar between the bricks was very pliable because of age and poor quality. Then they put the bricks back in place except one behind each of them as a breathing hole once they would lie down to sleep.

But for an occasional remark, mostly by friendly helpful Song, not much was said as time went by.

As Song had told them would be the case a truck drove up and stopped outside the warehouse door at about noon the next day.

As soon as he heard the truck Song grabbed Suping's arm and pulled her to her feet. 'Follow me!' he hissed, 'before the whole crowd rushes to the door. Your friend will go with Ai and Li when we'll be back.'

Song and Suping reached the door just when it swung open, each large, heavy door lifted up from the ground by four Red Guards.

An old, military truck stood outside, its platform towards the door.

Quickly Song grabbed four leaves from the pile on the back of the truck and hastily folded one for Suping, then for himself. Then he pushed Suping to the side of the truck where a Red Guard, a girl not older than fifteen, stood on the truck platform beside an oil drum with water. Surprised she looked down on Suping, hesitated, then, carefully, she poured a ladle of water in the makeshift mug Suping held up to her. Greedily Suping drank the tepid water, her first liquid intake in more than forty-eight hours. Twice more she held up the holder before she felt as if she would burst.

Song had been watching her impatiently and as soon as she had finished her third drink he pushed her around the front of the truck to the other side.

A Red Guard indifferently ladled a heap of rice with small chunks that looked like meat on the banana leaf they held up and open to him and off they went, pushing through the crowd back to their place.

Immediately Pan and the other two young men, Ai and Li as Song had called them, scrambled up and towards the door.

'Don't try to find out what it is they mixed with the rice,' Song mumbled, his mouth already full. 'Just hold the leaf up with your left hand and knead small lumps with the thumb and the two first fingers of your right hand, like this,' and he showed her. 'Then put the lump in your mouth, chew and swallow. Think of something nice. Once it's in your stomach you won't throw up any more and it does its job to fill you up. That's all you want, isn't it? Not to be hungry and weak.'

Suping did as she was told. She began to like Song for his no-nonsense attitude and his helpfulness.

She and Song had finished by the time the other three came back.

She showed Pan how to handle the leaf and the rice and told him what Song had said about eating the food. Pan laughed and said that Song reminded him of a weasel, so quick and darting and so well capable of taking care of himself, a true survivor, Pan said.

Song laughed and said that though he had no formal education to speak of he never forgot anything he heard or saw and that whatever he saw other people doing he could do after them. He also needed only one look at people to know what their weakness was, he said, and added that he was constantly observing those in power at the moment to pounce, like a weasel he grinned, not to kill though but to ingratiate himself and get out of this predicament.

'In a month at the most I'll be giving orders,' he boasted, 'instead of being ordered around by those snots of Red Guards. I have to get out of Kunming though,' he grinned, 'that's why I wait so patiently here in this hell-hole. Those party arseholes know me too well here, especially Secretary Yuan. You must have seen him yesterday when you arrived. Tall, trim man, always in a Mao suit, one day grey, the next day blue. He's a northerner, Yuan is, from Harbin or some godforsaken icy place like that. He's just about as lively as those ice statues they make there. Probably is one himself, heat-resistant. He hates southerners, friend Yuan does. Says we're like pigs and should be treated as such. That's why he has locked us up here, to wallow in our own shit, and feeds us the swill you just ate. The chance that pigs will fly is greater than that I would succeed to get into that man's good graces. He says I'm a thief and a corrupter of people's morals, so he gave me twelve years of re-education amongst the nation's purest, somewhere in Hunan, a place called Lantian or Lianyuan or something like that.

'And why? Because I made a couple of yuan on the side, in the state vegetable market, by wrapping the vegetables for certain customers in picture magazines I got from Burma. The pictures were obscene, Yuan and that horrible wife of his say. She is in charge of party discipline and a judge in the People's Tribunal. She promised me a reduction of my sentence to five years if I mentioned the customers I made the special wrapping for. I refused so she gave me twelve years instead of the ten she earlier gave me. But, what the hell. Five years, ten years, twelve years, what's the difference if you only want to serve a month anyway. One day I'll be back in Kunming to rake in the favours I did my customers and if Yuan's wife is then still there I'll have her killed by my Burmese friends. And maybe Yuan himself as well.'

Suping shivered and was about to say something when she felt Pan squeeze her arm so she kept silent.

She hardly listened to the light chit-chat between Pan and Song as she became more and more preoccupied by the growing pressure in her bladder.

At long last darkness fell and she could take out the bricks and crawl outside to relieve herself in the bushes between the *godown*'s back wall and the talus of the railway.

Her business finished she stood for a long time, her back against the wall, looking at the full moon and millions of stars and savouring the air that smelled of flowers and dry grass. A feeling of immense loneliness gripped her heart and she was about to cry when a hand grabbed her ankle and, looking down, she saw Song's head sticking out through the hole in the wall, looking up at her.

'Hey Suping,' he hissed, 'come back. I'm bursting.'

In spite of herself she giggled and crawled back inside.

She slept well that night, her head against the wall where her hole was so that she breathed the pure, cool night air.

During the next day's food and water distribution Suping could manage by herself as she followed Song.

The same girl was on duty at the water drum and she smiled when it was Suping's turn.

Filling Suping's leaf mug she suddenly bent down and pushed a blue peasant's canteen under her arm.

'For you,' she whispered. 'I filled it with tea. Drink it slowly. Tomorrow I'll exchange it for a full one.'

Suping smiled up at the girl, her eyes brimming with tears.

'Thank you,' she whispered, 'may heaven bless your kind little heart.'

The girl winked, stood up and called, matter-of-factly, 'Move on, next one!'

Her four friends marvelled at her luck and gratefully shared the fragrant tea with her, sipping and savouring in turn and from time to time only to make the canteen last as long as possible. Suping had the last sip at eight in the evening just before settling for the night.

Three days passed like that and the heat and stench inside the *godown* became unbearable.

The prisoners from Kunming hadn't washed for a week and they stank; sour, rancid, nauseatingly.

The fourth day, during the food distribution, Pan spoke to the leading Red Guard in charge of the distribution. He told the boy the situation was grave and if the Party secretary wanted to avoid an outbreak of typhoid, or worse, the plague, he should arrange for the prisoners to bathe, wash their clothes and clean out the *godown*.

The boy listened but didn't reply and the truck left as usual.

Nothing happened that day.

Suddenly the next morning, at seven o'clock, they heard several trucks driving up to the *godown* and stop outside. The doors swung open and the same leading Red Guard stood in the door opening with a loud hailer.

'Everybody outside!' he shouted. 'Assemble in groups of twenty and board the trucks! There are ten trucks so two hundred people at a time! The others stay here and clean out the *godown* until the trucks return! You will all be driven to the hot springs where you will bathe and wash your underwear. There will be Red Guards on duty over there and everybody will be given a packet with scouring soap and disinfectant!'

Suping and her friends were outside within seconds and the first to climb on the lead truck. Barely five minutes later a hundred people or so had scrambled on board the trucks and they rode off, past the station, through the southern outskirts of the town and up the winding road to Anning.

Half an hour later the trucks stopped near a place that said 'hot springs' and the Red Guards ordered them to get off the trucks and line up in an orderly manner.

About twenty other Red Guards filed out of the entrance gate to the springs each carrying a wicker basket with packets made of old newspapers.

Each of the prisoners received two packets, one with scouring soap as used by workers in machine shops to remove oil and grease from their hands and one with a whitish powder the Red Guards explained was a disinfectant to be rubbed in their hair, head, armpits and pubic area alike.

Suping was relieved and glad to see the little girl Red Guard coming towards her, gesturing to follow her away from the male prisoners.

There were about thirty women and five female Red Guards had been assigned to lead them down a footpath of slippery flagstones to a kind of concrete pool overflowing with steaming, hot water.

The friendly girl walked beside Suping and said quietly, 'My name is Fei Lilan. I told my sister about you. She used to be a school teacher before they closed the schools. She now takes care of my father since I am too busy with my duties as a Red Guard. Lilian, that's my sister, doesn't want to be a Red Guard. I told Lilian you also looked like a teacher so she gave me a piece of scented soap for you and clean underwear that you may keep if it fits you.'

Suping was too moved for words so she took the girl's hand and brought it to her lips.

Little Fei Lilan didn't pull her hand back and together, hand in hand, they slithered down the steep footpath.

Quickly the women took off their upper clothes and, in their underwear, they cautiously stepped into the pool to feel the temperature. Judging the temperature just right, not too hot, probably around forty degrees, Suping let herself slide into the water, heaving a deep sigh of relief.

For fifteen glorious minutes the world beyond the whirling steam around her head ceased to exist and she let herself float, arms and legs stretched out wide, bobbing softly on the wavelets the other women made.

She lost track of the time, unthinking, until a slight tug at her hair brought her back from nirvana. Through her half-open eyes she saw Xiao Fei squatting on the edge of the pool gesturing that she should start to wash herself.

Languorously she took off her underpants and bra and handed them to the girl who, in turn, gave her the piece of scented soap. Slowly and thoroughly she cleaned herself while savouring the pleasant, flowery scent of the soap.

Xiao Fei gave Suping's underwear a good rubbing with the scouring soap on the flagstones and then she gestured for Suping to get out of the pool.

Quickly Suping slipped out and wrapped herself in the flimsy towel Xiao Fei gave her. Still with the towel around her she tried on Fei Lilan's underpants and bra and both fitted perfectly.

She gave Xiao Fei a wink, who winked in return and both burst out laughing.

'Lilian says winking is unwomanly,' Xiao Fei giggled. 'I think she says that because she can't wink herself. When she tries she squeezes both eyes shut and chases after me when I laugh at her. You are very beautiful, Suping. Do you think one day I shall be as beautiful as you?'

Moved by the girl's ingeniousness Suping embraced her and said, 'You will be far more beautiful, Lilan. Your beauty is both from within and without and that's true beauty. Mine is merely on the outside. I have let my inside become spoilt by what has happened to me. Thanks to you I realise that that is wrong and that not all is rotten. Thank also your sister Lilian for me, will you?'

Xiao Fei nodded. 'I will,' she said, her lips quivering. 'Please come and visit us when you're free again, Suping, will you?'

'I will,' Suping said, 'I certainly will.'

She put on her trousers and jacket, rubbed them clean with the damp towel, rolled her own underwear tightly into the towel and followed Fei Lilan up the footpath back to where the trucks were waiting.

She felt as if she could take on the whole world.

Pan, Song, Ai and Li were already standing beside the lead truck, looking fresh and cheerful. They waved at Suping who suddenly hurried to join them.

'Your scouring soap must have been of a different quality than ours,' Song laughed, 'you smell like a houri. Be careful, body odours like sweat and unwashed private parts are in these days, decadent bourgeois smells, like yours, are definitely out of favour. Aiee!' he suddenly groaned as Suping hit backwards with her right elbow full in his stomach.

'You are a she-devil,' he gasped. 'Tonight we'll fight it out, in the bushes. Only don't squeal when you lose.'

'Not when, if,' Suping laughed, 'and I'm sure you will squeal like the pig you are.' They all laughed.

All the prisoners had lined up by then, in groups of twenty, next to the same truck they had arrived with. The Red Guards seemed to be waiting though and didn't order them to board the trucks yet.

Suddenly a black limousine appeared around the bend coming from the direction of Kunming and stopped on the other side of the road.

The same tall man, this time in a blue Mao suit, got out from the back seat and crossed the road to where the prisoners were standing.

The tall, skinny Red Guard, the girl who had fallen over her own feet the day Suping had arrived at Kunming's railway station, got out of the front seat next to the car's driver and trotted after Party Secretary Yuan, carrying a paper bag.

Secretary Yuan let his eyes rove over the five groups of prisoners, without haste, and each of them had the distinct impression that the secretary was specifically looking at him, which wasn't true, of course, Suping thought, but such was the magnetism of that ice man's eyes.

Finally Secretary Yuan spoke, without apparent effort and without raising his voice and yet even those standing farthest away had no difficulty catching every word he said such was the sing-song clarity of his icy voice.

'You will not go back to the *godown*,' Yuan said. 'Train number 2442 will depart from platform two at four o'clock this afternoon. You will board that train. Another group of prisoners from your *godown* will join you when they have taken their bath. Red Guard Tang here will hand each of you a kind of batch, a small piece of cloth rather, which you will put in the top buttonhole of your jacket.

'Those who receive a red piece of cloth will board the first two vans after the tender; they will disembark in Changsha and report to Party Secretary Ye Lisan for further orders as to their destination. Those who receive a blue piece of cloth will board the last two vans of the train; they will disembark in Lianyuan where Party Secretary Yu Peixian will assign them to the communes in the area. Any questions?'

Nobody had a question, even Suping kept silent about the matter of Chengdu. She didn't think she would get a sympathetic hearing from Party Secretary Yuan.

'Convict number 624 step forward!' Yuan continued, raising his voice only slightly.

To her surprise Pan, who stood beside her, muttered below his breath, 'What does he want of me?' Then he stepped out of the ranks and called, 'Convict number 624 at your orders, Comrade Secretary Yuan!'

'This man, Pan Chun is his name, called my attention to the unhygienic conditions you had been living in for the past week and the danger this posed not only to your health but, more importantly, to the health of the revolutionaries who are in daily contact with you. The Red Guards have been remiss in their revolutionary duties by not reporting such an obvious danger to the public's health at a time we cannot afford an epidemic of a contagious disease. I myself have been remiss in my leadership duties by not recognising the danger. I thank Comrade Pan for his timely warning.

'Now I understand that before your arrest for obstructing the course of the Great Proletarian Cultural Revolution, you practised medicine, both Chinese and Western, in Mianyang. Is that so?'

'Yes, Comrade Secretary Yuan, that is so,' Pan replied.

'Then you are hereby appointed as my personal assistant for health matters amongst the convicts of Kunming and those who transit through Kunming. You will serve your sentence in that capacity and report to me only. Is that clear?'

'Yes, Comrade Secretary Yuan. Thank you, Comrade Secretary Yuan,' Pan stammered, totally flabbergasted by the turn of events.

'Good,' Yuan said, 'now come with me, in my car. I have things to discuss with you.'

Yuan fell silent and was about to go back to his car when he said, as an afterthought, 'You have two minutes to take leave of your four friends Pan, notably of convict 223 from Luding for whom you seem to have a particular liking.'

Pan grinned and quickly turned to trot back to his group. He shook hands with Li, Ai and Song to whom he said, grasping both his hands, 'Temper your anger, Song. Don't nourish hatred. It's self-defeating. You will pull through and come back a sane person. All right?'

Song nodded, for once speechless, and he embraced Pan.

Standing in front of Suping, Pan took her in his arms without further ado.

'You became a friend, Suping,' he whispered emotionally. 'Come and see me in Mianyang when things have returned to normal. In the meantime use your sense of proportion and don't get carried away by negative thoughts. Remember the autumn leaf? It doesn't care from what direction the wind blows. It offers no resistance and therefore cannot be destroyed. In the end it will just rot, as you said, but that's what we all will do, won't we?'

Smiling through her tears Suping embraced him and said, 'I'm happy for you, Doctor Pan Chun. Take care and all the best. If ever I come back to Luding I'll come and see you. Mianyang isn't that far. Go now, before Secretary Yuan changes his mind.'

With one last wave, Pan turned and quickly joined Secretary Yuan in his limousine, a 1954 model Pobeda she later learned.

Secretary Yuan must be very sure of his power to use a car and driver, she thought, as she saw the car disappear around the bend back to Kunming.

The Red Guard with the paper bag distributed the badges, a red one for Suping, blue ones for Song, Ai and Li.

'There goes our fight tonight,' Song joked but Suping could hear from the way his voice broke that he wasn't happy about their separate destinations.

They were driven back to the station and, before boarding their respective vans, they took leave of each other.

Ai and Li shook her hand, a bit awkwardly, and wished her all the best.

Song took her hands between his and said, with forced cheerfulness, 'I know it will be difficult for you to take care of yourself without my wise counsel, Suping, but you'll probably manage. I had it all figured out, you know. First you would like me, then, gradually, you would fall in love with me and then I would ask you to marry me and we would flee to Burma and make many little Songs and become rich. I'm afraid it has just been a dream, eh? Take care of yourself love and "God bless" as the Shan people in Burma say.'

Suddenly he took her face between his hands and kissed her gently, then he turned and ran after his two friends who were walking towards the far end of the train.

The last thing she saw of him was a wave as he stood already in the doorway of the van.

She waved back, biting her lower lip to stop the quivering. A feeling of desperate, lonely sadness wrenched her heart with such sudden force that her knees buckled and she toppled over, headlong, into that maelstrom of sorrow that was sucking in her whole world.

She was only half-conscious of a girl's voice calling her name and pulling her by her shoulder out of the whirlpool. Will-lessly she followed the pull on her arm and the same voice telling her to lift her feet to step on the footboard and into the semi-darkness of a freight van.

She stumbled forward, hands stretched out in front of her to feel for obstacles as her eyes were burning and brimming with tears. When she felt the warm metal of the van's wall she let herself down, slowly, on her knees, hesitantly feeling for bodies on each side of her on the wooden floor.

Feeling none she turned her back against the wall, buried her head in her arms on her pulled-up knees and wept.

During the next few hours Suping was vaguely aware of other people climbing into the van and groping for a place on the floor to sit or lie down, occasionally bumping against her.

Daylight was already fading when a group of Red Guards went from van to van to close the sliding doors.

The total blackness that engulfed her was like a balm on her swollen eyelids and with a deep, shuddering sigh she withdrew into herself and tried to recall the images of that last evening at home, a scene that would become her refuge whenever the ugliness around her threatened to engulf and suffocate her.

Breathing slowly and only very superficially she unwittingly enhanced her dreamlike state of mind and, unaware of time and place, she didn't notice the train pulling out of Kunming station and slowly gaining speed on its journey to Guiyang.

The train made only a brief halt in Guiyang.

Suping, slowly emerging from her reverie, listened with half an ear to the shouting match next to her van between a number of local officials and the train driver.

The driver was clearly very angry as he clamoured, at the top of his voice, for a supply of coal which the locals refused, yelling they didn't have any coal. One local, high-pitched hysterical female voice even accused the driver of lack of revolutionary zeal, yelling he had but to chant from his Little Red Book and the train would run without coal, all by itself.

The outraged driver cursed the Little Red Book, its author and his ancestors, the local officials and their ancestors and offspring and, near apoplexy Suping imagined, threw his engine into gear yelling at his fireman to shovel or be strangled.

Slowly the train began to move, the locals trying to keep pace, first walking, then at a trot, all the while screaming and shouting at the driver that they had hundreds of convicts for his train, that they would have him arrested, shot, quartered, exiled for life, to no avail. Slowly the train gained speed and the officials fell behind, their hysterical voices fading into the usual cacophony of screaming juveniles and blaring loudspeakers until that also was suddenly cut off as the train apparently entered a tunnel judging by the heavy rumble.

Suping couldn't help smiling as she pictured the fireman shovelling for his life as the driver, hot-tempered as so many of her countrymen, stood behind him with wide open hands ready to strangle him at the slightest sign of lapse.

Suping spent the next ten hours or so in a state of slumber, her body heaving and swaying with the occasional jerks and jolts of the train as it passed by several small stations and through bends and tunnels. She spoke to no one and no one spoke to her, everybody lost in their own thoughts and preoccupied by their increasing pangs of hunger and thirst and pressure in bladder and bowels.

The pain in her lower belly gradually pushed all other preoccupations out of her mind and Suping was about to throw all prudishness overboard and push the people in the corner next to her aside to relieve herself when she was momentarily distracted by a few jolts followed by a sudden slowing down of the clickety-clack on the tracks below her van.

We are going to stop, it went through her mind, 'try to hold it up.'

The sudden piercing whistle of the locomotive just ahead of her van almost made her lose control of her bladder and in spite of her predicament she smiled wryly.

The engine driver, apparently still angry, kept pulling the whistle lever, with short and long bursts, all the way into Lianyuan's railway station where the train finally came to a full and final stop.

Outside, on the platform, she heard a man's voice shout a few, curt orders and within minutes the door of the van rumbled open and a gust of fresh night air blew away the fetid smell of forty unwashed people locked up together for twenty-four hours in not even eight hundred cubic feet of space.

Suping scrambled to her feet and stumbled to the door opening.

'Toilet, please, *please*!' she wailed.

A group of local officials looked up at her in surprise and one man, short and thickset, said, 'Get down, girl, and follow Red Guard Chu here. Chu, take the girl to the toilet.'

Red Guard Chu turned out to be a woman, in her early thirties probably. She had a thin, hollow face and a harelip that made her squeaky 'come with me' nigh unintelligible.

As Suping, immensely relieved, was escorted back to the station's sole platform she saw the officials standing around the engine driver and his fireman and she heard the driver's angry voice telling the locals that the people in Guiyang had rejected his request for coal and that he had barely been able to get the train to Lianyuan and that as far as he was concerned this was the end of the road and goodbye to all of them and their silly revolution.

At that she saw him trying to shake off the Red Guards who hung on to his arms as he stalked off.

The short man shouted angrily, 'Come back here immediately, driver, or I'll have you shot for obstructing the course of the revolution!' Turning in Suping's direction, he said, in a friendlier tone, 'You there! Girl! Come here!'

Suping approached the group of people, all in grey Mao suits, and the short man said, 'My name is Yu Peixian. I am the Party secretary of Lianyuan. You were in the first van after the locomotive and its tender. Did you hear the engine driver here ask for coal in Guiyang?'

Suping looked at the group of Red Guards who barely managed to restrain the struggling, enraged driver and then she said, looking back at the Party secretary, 'Yes, Comrade Secretary Yu. I heard him ask for coal, however, those he talked to refused. One of them, a woman I think judging by the high voice, yelled at him to chant from our Chairman Mao's Little Red Book instead. This made him so angry that without further ado or argument he drove off without taking in the convicts of Guiyang.'

She saw a ghost of a smile on Secretary Yu's lips as he said, more to himself than to the others, 'Fortunately the hot-tempered scoundrel did that or else we here, in Lianyuan, would now have a thousand hungry people to cope with instead of the one hundred who are supposed to disembark here for the communes in Xinshao and Shangfeng. Still I have to find food and shelter for the three hundred people bound for Changsha as long as that train is marooned here.'

Irritably he turned towards the engine driver and ordered, 'You stay with your train, comrade. Tomorrow I'll give you a thousand people to push the train on a sidetrack, van by van if need be. I don't have any coal here in Lianyuan and I can't have you blocking the tracks for other trains that may come through here or else we will end up with half the south's prisoners in our backyard. As it is I have to find at least ten trucks to get those three hundred people to Changsha. What a mess!'

Impatiently he turned his attention to his Red Guards and ordered, 'Get everybody off this train and march them to Middle School Number One. They'll have to spend the night there. Separate those for Changsha from the others and assign them to the classrooms. There won't be any food tonight. It's too late to organise that, but let them drink water as much as they like. Tomorrow morning at eight o'clock I want to see them all in the courtyard. I'll try to have at least some rice and vegetables for them and tea. By that time I'll know more about the transport of the Changsha people. Now, start moving!'

Secretary Yu signalled his assistants to follow him as he walked off, his angry stride too long for his short legs which was rather comic, Suping thought, and she smiled.

Two hours later she was ushered into one of the school's six classrooms, together with forty fellow convicts. The Red Guards had followed Secretary Yu's orders and after a twenty minute march through Lianyuan's main street the prisoners had been assembled, separated in two groups, in the school yard.

In small groups of ten they had been escorted to the school's toilet shed and next to a water tap where they had been permitted to drink as much as they could. Suping had filled her stomach with water to still her hunger a bit since she knew, from Secretary Yu's earlier remarks, that there would be no food that evening. She withdrew into a corner of the classroom and lay down on the bare wooden floor.

She nodded at the two men already sitting there with their backs against the wall but they didn't acknowledge her greeting which solved her dilemma of whether to make conversation or not.

She lay down, pulled her jacket up, over her eyes, and fled into her dreamland.

The following morning was a repeat of the evening before.

In groups of ten they were escorted to the toilet shed and then to the water tap behind the school building to wash up as best as they could.

At half past seven they all stood lined up in the school yard waiting for Party Secretary Yu and the food he had promised them.

At eight o'clock exactly two trucks came out of the main street and stopped in front of the school. Secretary Yu emerged from the lead truck, followed by three Red Guards. He entered the school yard and walked up to take a position in front of the prisoners.

One of the Red Guards handed him a loud hailer and he addressed the crowd, 'Ten minutes from now the Red Guards will start the distribution of food. You will eat in groups of fifty since we have not enough bowls and chopsticks for all of you. Everybody is entitled to one bowl of rice with vegetables and pork meat. The pork is separate and hasn't touched the rice and vegetables so the Muslims amongst you, if any, need not worry.

'You have five minutes to eat after which you will wash the bowl and chopsticks and hand them back to Red Guard Chu on the food truck. You then return to the classroom where you have spent the night. There you wait for the Red Guards to give each of you a piece of paper with a number from one to six. Those with the numbers one and two will assemble here, in the yard, at noon and board the three trucks who will be waiting in front of the school. They leave for Changsha at one o'clock where they'll arrive between five or six o'clock. The Red Guards in charge of the transport will lead them to Secretary Ye Lisan.

'The numbers three and four will leave tomorrow for Changsha. Together with the numbers five and six they will be marched to the railway station this afternoon where they will push the train on the sidetracks. The numbers five and six will leave the day after tomorrow for Xinshao and Shangfeng. These are my instructions. Food distribution will now begin. Proceed in an orderly manner, row by row.'

Suping was surprised at Secretary Yu's quiet authority and competence. He was neither friendly nor unfriendly, just matter-of-fact. And not once had he alluded to the Great Proletarian Cultural Revolution and its Great Leader Chairman Mao.

Most surprising of all, however, were the Red Guards: quiet, unassuming, little fish following the leader fish.

The food was decent, the pork meat even tasty, and the serving was generous. Within minute Suping had shovelled it all down and while rinsing the bowl and chopsticks she drank two whole bowls of water.

Full up, she got back to the classroom and sat down on the floor, her back against the wall, arms around her pulled-up knees. Dreamily, occasionally even drifting off into a slumber, she watched her fellow prisoners.

Secretary Yu's matter-of-fact manner was even reflected in the prisoners' behaviour. With no meanness by the secretary or outrages by the Red Guards to whisper about or console each other about the convicts were just an amorphous, silent mass of shoddy, unkempt people, each keeping to himself, instinctively avoiding eye and bodily contact.

Suping closed her eyes and let herself drift off.

She was roused out of her reverie by a sudden nudge against her shoulder and, looking up, she saw Red Guard Chu standing over her.

'Your number,' Chu quacked and she handed Suping a small piece of paper with the number four.

'Not a very auspicious number,' Suping sighed but Chu just looked down on her, uncomprehendingly.

'Be in the school yard at two o'clock!' Red Guard Chu squawked. 'You will push the train as ordered by Secretary Yu.'

Suping nodded and Chu moved on to distribute her numbers.

By noontime two Red Guards called the convicts with the numbers one and two to board the trucks for Changsha and Suping counted about a hundred people filing out of the door without so much as a look or a wave to those staying behind.

Numb or just plain stupid, Suping thought, why are people like that? Why am I like that? Why do I not just stand up and walk out of here and return to Luding? I am sure nobody would stop me or even care, probably not even Secretary Zhang Yizhong in Luding. He has had his show and what happens afterwards doesn't concern him.

So why *do* I stay in heaven's name? Why do I behave like a sheep being herded to the slaughterhouse? Why can I intellectualise what I could and should do but then do not act? Is it apathy, the dull fear of risk? Could I snap out of it by myself or would I need somebody else or some sudden violent event or other to stir me into action?

Discouraged and disgusted by her own listlessness she let herself drift off to sleep again.

That afternoon she and about five hundred other convicts were marched off to the railway station to push the train she arrived by the previous evening from the main tracks to the sidetracks.

The bilious engine driver was waiting for them, as disagreeable and irascible as ever probably, to take charge of the job. Irritably he told the Red Guards that bringing five hundred people was no use since they couldn't all find a place around the locomotive or a van to push and to pull whereas to push the whole train at once he would need at least three thousand people.

So he ordered them to divide the five hundred in ten groups of fifty persons and then, under his direction, they uncoupled the locomotive and vans.

Suping dragged her feet to avoid being assigned to the team for the locomotive and tender, suspecting it would not only have the heaviest but also the dirtiest job, what with all the soot and oil and grease.

She grinned as the Red Guards assigned her to the group for the last two cars.

After a lot of shouting, cursing, screaming and yelling they finally managed to rearrange the train on the sidetracks and free the main tracks for through trains and Secretary Yu of his worry for an influx of prisoners in his tidy and quiet little fiefdom.

When they entered the school yard, at six o'clock, Secretary Yu was waiting with two trucks of food and tea. They were entitled to an extra helping of pork meat and the tea was fragrant and strong as a token of Secretary Yu's pleasure.

The following day Suping, together with a hundred or so other convicts, boarded three trucks for Changsha. As her truck turned into the main street she coyly waved at Secretary Yu and Red Guard Chu who stood in front of the school watching the trucks ride off.

Surprised they waved back, hesitantly at first but then quite enthusiastically.

Probably very nice people to know and associate with under normal circumstances, Suping thought. Now there is that terribly contrived chasm between us, that separates us into hostile sides all in the name of an ideology nobody the least bit intelligent believes in. So much sorrow and suffering for an ideology that is already dead, preached by a mad woman in the name of an increasingly senile old dodderer who can't keep his hands off the young girls his entourage supplies him with.

And because of that crazy ideology I am sitting here, on this ramshackle old truck, on my way to Changsha and heaven knows where else, while my parents are probably labouring in a peasant commune worried sick about me. What a waste! What a mess! How I hate this whole, rotten life and those lunatics who made it so.

Daylight was fading when the three trucks stopped in front of Changsha's railway station amidst a milling crowd of shouting Red Guards and groups of people, prisoners no doubt, judging by their haggard, dejected looks, trotting helter-skelter in total confusion.

The Red Guards from Lianyuan, who had accompanied the trucks, tried in vain to get the attention of their harassed yet contemptuous bigger city colleagues.

The appeals for attention quickly degenerated into a shouting and slanging match and at one time Suping saw them slugging one another with their bare fists.

Finally a tall man wearing a red armband with the characters for vice-secretary walked up to the trucks and, with a few curses, stopped the fighting.

One of the Red Guards from Lianyuan wailed, in a nasal voice, because of his bleeding nose, that he had one hundred and five prisoners to deliver to Secretary Ye Lisan and please could they be taken off his hands so that he could go back to Lianyuan.

The tall man had listened with barely concealed impatience and irritation and replied gruffly that Secretary Ye was busy and that anyhow they didn't want any more prisoners in Changsha, that they had enough prisoners of their own to last them a lifetime and who the hell was Secretary Yu of that rathole Lianyuan to think that he could dump his garbage into somebody else's backyard and to move those bloody trucks out of Changsha at the double or else he would call the militia and have them shot, Red Guards as well.

At that the tall man stalked off angrily, watched, mouths agape, by the flabbergasted Red Guards from Lianyuan.

'Move your trucks out of the way!' their Changsha colleagues shouted, mockingly, 'Move! Move!' and they began beating the truck's cabin and side boards with their sticks.

Suping, scared and full of foreboding about what would happen next, the least of which would be ending up in the middle of nowhere when the trucks would have run out of gas, took a sudden decision she often pondered about in later years, wondering what would have become of her life if she hadn't taken and acted on it.

Taking advantage of the total confusion around the trucks she slid over the side board of her truck, and once on the ground, she slipped through the crowding Red Guards and prisoners and, unnoticed, entered the station.

Looking around her, inside the departure hall, undecided what to do next, she suddenly heard her name being called out, loudly, by a woman's voice. Looking in the direction of the voice she saw a thickset woman in a blue jacket and green trousers, motioning imperiously for her to approach.

'Don't you know you are not allowed to leave the platform, prisoner 223?' the woman asked, angrily.

Not waiting for Suping's answer, she looked around and called a Red Guard.

'Escort this prisoner back to platform three immediately!' she ordered the Red Guard and with a last disapproving look she turned her back on Suping and forgot about her.

The Red Guard took her elbow in a firm grip and with a little yelp of pain, Suping let herself be guided through the throngs in the hall and up the stairs of the overhead bridge to platform number three.

The Red Guard pushed her through the crowd of prisoners until she came face to face with a pimply female Red Guard who stood next to a tender, watching the convicts.

'You let this one escape, Loh,' Suping's warder said mockingly. 'Fat Mu caught her while she tried to slip out of the station. Comrade Mu wasn't very happy and she'll get you for your laxness, Loh,' and grinning maliciously the youth gave Suping a push in her back so that she almost collided with the Red Guard called Loh.

Before she could lift her arms to protect herself she felt the sharp pain of the vicious blow Red Guard Loh struck at her head and she fainted.

When she came to, a few minutes or a few hours later she didn't know, Red Guard Loh came running up to her and kicked her in her lower back, screaming at her to get to her feet.

She scrambled up, twice falling back on her knees because of Red Guard Loh's vicious kicks in her loins.

Finally she managed to stand up and still dazed and swaying on her wobbly legs, she heard Loh's crazed voice so close to her face that she retched at the fetid smell of the girl's breath.

'If ever you try to get away again, Su Ping, I'll kill you with my own, bare hands,' Loh screamed. 'Do you hear me, Su Ping? Reply! You bourgeois bastard!'

In a daze Suping mumbled that she had heard, replying for the first time to her name being mispronounced as Su Ping.

Had Loh deemed the Xu character too prestigious, too bourgeois and couldn't she bring herself to pronounce it properly or was the omission deliberate to humiliate Suping even more? Most probably though, Loh, in her fury, had simply not noticed the character in the folds of Suping's jacket sleeve.

Whatever the reason, the screeching mispronunciation of her second name and the nauseating pain caused by her first ever physical beating shattered what was left of her self-image, as Xu Suping of Luding and her second life as Su Ping of nowhere began.

⋆

Su Ping fell silent. She had spoken uninterruptedly for ten straight hours.

Her friends, Lao Dao the old engineer, Lao Dee the Dutchman, Auntie Liu the benefactor and her niece Beiyuen and her own daughter Lilian stared at her wordlessly as she stood up from her chair, groaning and stretching to relieve the stiffness in her bones and muscles.

'I am sorry it took so long,' she mumbled, yawning. 'I am sure you are bored to tears and ready for bed. Look at the time. Three o'clock in the morning. Let's try and catch some sleep before dawn breaks. Come Lilian, we go home and see how your father is doing.'

Without further ado the others got up as well and with a mumbled 'Goodbye. See you all next week', they shuffled out of the door and disappeared into the dark, silent alley.

Only Beiyuen stayed behind. She would spend what was left of the night with her Auntie Liu.

## *Chapter Twenty-Two*

### Breaking Away to Live a Life of Her Own

Su Ping and Lilian walked the short distance to their home, down the alley, in silence.

Still, because of her different stride, more purposeful as it were, Lilian instinctively felt that her mother had become a changed person that evening. Somehow reliving her life must have brought that about.

The air in the house was rank with the smells of excrement and vomit and for the first time in her life Lilian heard her mother, otherwise always so calm and composed, curse, and loudly at that. Already, while she had been listening to her mother telling her life story the way she did, it had gradually dawned on Lilian that a totally different woman was hiding beneath that beautifully flawless, composed exterior her mother wanted the outside world to see.

A girlish, fun-loving woman with a refreshing sense of humour, however, also a woman who could fall a prey to sudden fits of temper when provoked or confronted with trying situations in which she felt helpless.

The strenuous life fate had forced upon her had taught her several small tricks how to control her temper most of the time, but it *was* there, all the time, boiling beneath the surface, ready to erupt if the iron self-control failed but for a fraction of a second.

And what Lilian now witnessed, for the first time in *her* life, was obviously such a breakdown of Su Ping's control system and the emotional, temperamental Xu Suping of old taking over.

And then Lilian realised that that whole dual personality thing, the girlishly naive Xu Suping having changed into the suave Su Ping as a result of traumatic experiences, was just one of those small tricks, perhaps the basic one, with which her mother had tried to shield the vulnerable gullible Suping from the wickedness around her.

However, that elfin, vulnerable little creature, as her mother had described her *alter ego*, was a much tougher lady than given credit for and she had apparently shrugged off the whole Su Ping rigmarole and reasserted herself as the *only* personality to represent, and be known as, Xu Suping.

'Welcome back, Xu Suping of Luding,' Lilian said, grinning mischievously, 'and glad to make your acquaintance. From the beginning of your story I liked you much better than that woman Su Ping who impersonated you as my mother and, as your story unfolded, that liking became stronger and stronger and then, suddenly, I *became* you and, while listening to you, it was I who lived your adventures and tribulations, it was I who did what you did, it was I who laughed when you laughed, who cried when you cried, who suffered when you suffered and I *know*, as sure as I know the sun will rise again in a few hours, that I would have thought and acted exactly as *you* did. I am proud of you, Xu Suping, proud that I am your daughter and I love you.'

Her mother wiped a tear from her eyes with the back of her right hand then, suddenly, she burst out laughing.

'You're right, Lilian! What a stuffy, stuck-up creature that Su Ping woman was. Walking on eggs she was, keeping her arse squeezed tight and her face so serene, the hypocrite, suppressing her feelings and killing those of others. What a bore she must have been all those years. But enough is enough. It's time to have some fun again, to live again! Hooray!'

Laughing joyously she took her daughter's hand and together they made a few dance steps, humming and singing a song from Guilin 'Who can compare with us'.

Like two giggling schoolgirls they let themselves fall on the couch, kicked off their shoes and put their feet on the table. Hands clasped behind their head they stared at the ceiling, dreamily.

'It's time to stand up for ourselves, Lilian,' Suping said. 'Uncle Dan, Auntie Liu. I'm sure they have a favour or two to cash in from those old buggers in Beijing, if they are still alive, that is. I want your father placed in an institution and I want a residence permit for Luding. Not just a visit permit, with our friend Lao Dee, but a residence permit. I don't want to stay here in Dalian. I want to go back to Luding and stay there, live there, work there.

'I'll try to persuade Auntie Liu to go and live there as well. She'll have Uncle Dan and Father and Mother to talk to and, besides, the climate will be much better for her old bones and muscles. I'm sure Uncle Dan can get one of the smaller houses on our hill assigned to her. That way she has her privacy and yet she can have her social contacts with us if she feels like it. And when she'll become too old to take care of herself we, that is Father and Mother and I, can take care of her. It'll be wonderful,' and she laughed happily.

'That's all very well,' Lilian said, a bit sadly, 'but what about me? Where am I going to stay with you and Auntie Liu gone?'

Much sobered by Lilian's small voice, Suping wrinkled her nose and said, ruefully, 'I'm so sorry, my love. I got carried away by my own frivolity. Please forgive me. What about you indeed. Luding is too small a place for a girl with your background and after what you have seen of the foreigners' lives. Perhaps Chengdu would be a good place for you. It's so much nicer than Dalian and also so much closer. You could come to visit us every month in Luding. I'm sure there are hotels for foreigners in Chengdu as well. Probably not businessmen, like here in Dalian, but tourists, from all over the world. We'll ask Lao Dee. He has been to Chengdu already, he told me. If he thinks there's nothing for you there, then I'll stay here in Dalian as well, with you. Only I want Kunlen, your father, in an institution. I can't and won't stand it any more.

'Tomorrow, today rather, I'll go to the town hall and submit my case. I hope you can stand the smell a few hours longer because we are *not* going to clean up his mess. I'll invite the people who decide on such placements to come and visit our house this morning so that they can see and smell for themselves. I'll exaggerate a bit and tell them it's like that every day and has been like that for the past twelve years. I'll tell Auntie Liu to watch for them as they pass by her house and then to drop in here, casually like, and add her bit of melodrama. I want a quick decision about Kunlen. I won't wait for the Beijing connection via Uncle Dan and Auntie Liu. It'll take too long. Only if they won't do anything about it here directly, I'll try that. What do you think?'

Lilian looked at her mother askance and smiled ruefully.

'Xu Suping is back well and good,' she said. 'In all my life I haven't heard you talk so much and so fast, so resolute also and bubbling with ideas. It takes some getting used to. Now, you asked me what I thought of your plans. I think that you should do what your heart tells you to. You have suffered enough and denied yourself long enough not to start all over again because of me. I am *not* Li Kunlen and I don't need you holding my hands for the rest of *my* life. It was silly of me to play-act the dependent little girl a while ago. I am a tough cookie, as Lao Dee would say, just as tough, if not more so, than *you* were when you were my age. Besides, I know much more about certain things of life than you did in your time. so compared to me you were indeed naive, though not in the soft, impressionable way people who met you for the first time probably thought of you.

'So, if you or Lao Dee can get me a proper job in Chengdu I would indeed like to go and live there, and the sooner the better. Jan, the Dutch engineer I talked to you about, is in love with me, I know that for sure, and perhaps I am in love with him too. But I am scared. I heard about a girl who fell in love with a Frenchman and she was arrested and put in jail and he was expelled from China. I don't want to go to jail just because I love a foreigner and I don't want Jan to be expelled and Lao Dee in trouble just because he, Jan, fell in love with a Chinese girl. I'm sure the time will come when our government will have to become less xenophobic, however, I doubt that Jan has the patience to wait for that to happen, especially when, after this project here in Dalian, he'll be back in Holland and his former girlfriend dangles her big tits in front of his eyes and teases him in her shorter than short shorts. Men are like that, Auntie Liu told me, they walk where their penis points to.'

'Besides that, I'm also afraid of living in a foreign country. I don't know whether I'll be able to adapt. So it would be best if I could get away from Jan as soon as possible before I succumb and let him in my pants, something he has been trying so hard to make me do for the past few weeks. If the Party doesn't allow me to move to Chengdu, which is very likely, don't forget that, I'll stay here and somehow I'll manage without you and Auntie Liu. Perhaps I even let Jan have his way and to hell with the consequences. I might even make a case of it and become a world celebrity.'

Lilian laughed loudly and hesitantly at first, then wholeheartedly, her mother joined in.

In spite of her re-found identity, Suping had been shocked nevertheless by her daughter's direct approach of matters she herself had never talked about with her parents, however, her sense of humour had prevailed and, like bosom friends, they sobbed with laughter in each other's arms.

They were shocked out of their cosiness by the soft whimper of Kunlen's little watchdog Ciaokeli who had crept up to them, dragging his filthy little body along the floor, and who was now lying under their legs, ears flat, tail wagging hesitantly, eyes looking up mournfully as if expecting to be punished for failing his duty to keep his charge clean.

'Look at that little heap of misery,' Suping exclaimed, bending forward to pick up the little animal. 'Good grief, you stink,' she cried out, keeping the dog, who tried to lick her hands, at arm's length.

'Kunlen's shit became too much for you as well eh, little bastard?' And then, at Lilian, 'Try to get some sleep, darling, I'll give Ciaokeli a good washing and then keep him here, in this room. Then I'll put a clothes-peg on my nose and feed Kunlen his gruel. Fortunately you have the evening shift today so that you can watch your father while I'm at the town hall. I want to be the first in line and suitably distressed so I'll leave here at eight o'clock. I'll try to be back here around eleven or twelve, with the man or woman in charge of institutionalisations. Is that all right with you?'

Lilian nodded and yawned. 'That's all right with me,' she said, still yawning. 'I'll try to be decent when you arrive with those people.' And without further ado, she took off her blouse and skirt and slipped under the blanket of their bed, sticking out her tongue at her mother before pulling the sheet over her head.

Sighing but with a light heart now she had finally taken the big decision to be free again, Suping washed and shampooed the little dog, with Lilian's foreign shampoo, rubbed it until it was nearly dry and then put it next to her sleeping daughter under the blanket. It snuggled in the hollow of Lilian's knees, licked the back of her thighs a few times, which brought a smile to her daughter's face, Suping noticed jealously, and fell asleep.

Next she prepared her husband's gruel and, retching with disgust, she spooned it into his slack, slavering mouth.

'I have done enough for you, Kunlen,' she mumbled. 'If I had been in your place you would have fled a long, long time ago. I used to know you well enough for that. The only good thing you ever did to me was your two-minute contribution to that child, young woman rather, in my bed over there. Since you made that contribution only to spite that old hag Hu Guoshang and not out of love for me or for the fruit of your passionless little effort, Lilian and I have paid our debt a million times over. It's time for both of us to begin a new, unburdened life. For a start I need your unwitting co-operation so I'll let you wallow in your own filth a few hours more.'

At that she closed the kitchen door behind her.

She undressed, washed up, did her hair in a conservative manner and chose the dullest, oldest clothes and shoes she had for her mission to the town hall.

By then it was six o'clock and she hesitated between stretching out for an hour or so beside Lilian and leaving for a roundabout way to the town hall. She chose the latter; a good, long walk would do her good.

She had calculated the detour well and arrived at the town hall at eight o'clock exactly, the official opening time.

The old guard, sitting next to the closed entrance on a tiny chair, looked up at her with rheumy, blinking eyes and croaked that she was too early. The officials wouldn't begin to arrive until half past eight or thereabouts and the door wouldn't be opened before nine, maybe half past, he wheezed.

'I'll wait,' Suping said cheerfully, looking down in the milky-white ringed, mud-brown eyes of the old man, whose grubby, stubbly face hadn't felt water or soap for days or weeks even.

He spat a stream of brown spit on the flagstone footpath just in front of the entrance door, grinned crookedly at Suping showing his sole remaining, enormous, brown-black front tooth, feeling it with his greyish tongue to make sure it was still hanging there, shrugged and withdrew his tiny head with the too big blue cap between his meagre shoulders in his oversized dull blue smock frock.

Like a four hundred year old tortoise, Suping thought as she stepped gingerly over the old man's latest, still slippery, addition to the hundreds, already dried up, brown tobacco stains in front of the door.

Even from those few paces away she could still smell the old man's acridly sweaty uncleanliness.

She breathed deeply to suppress her rising gorge and, turning her back at that terrible picture of neglect and decrepitness, she watched the endless streams, on both sides of the street, of slowly pedalling, zombie-like men and women on their way to a useless task in some useless office or filthy old factory, filling out useless papers nobody would ever look at or producing shoddy things nobody would ever use.

In her mind she saw them coming out of their small, decrepit shacks or small, unpainted, overcrowded flats in those dead-end, gloomy blocks to face another hopeless and useless day in their hopeless and useless lives.

This is still what China is all about and what Lao Dee and other foreigners like him are never going to change, she thought, sighing.

What they are doing, with their projects, affects only a trivial and utterly tiny minority and that only in certain, designated and privileged regions, while the overwhelming majority remains unaffected at best, more likely worse off because the few who *do* benefit will become greedier with time and increasing wealth and will corrupt the officials.

Once corruption has become a way of life the small people will inevitably suffer since they and their needs have become a nuisance, an irritating waste of time for the corrupt officials too busy looking after themselves.

The trend is ominous, Lao Dee says. When three, four years ago a dinner in an expensive restaurant, a bottle of French brandy, a box of Belgian chocolates, a carton of American cigarettes could still win him the favour of officials, even for important matters, nowadays they unashamedly ask for colour TV sets, sponsoring of trips abroad, all expenses paid, even sponsoring of their sons and daughters to go and study abroad, for years, also all expenses paid.

Were the costs of the earlier, small bribes trivial and out of pocket, the present-day bribes are much too expensive and are therefore routinely included in the foreigners' tenders for projects. The officials not only know that and approve the method, they even give hints to the foreigners who do business in China for the first time.

The approved projects become more and more expensive and therefore cost the country extra money that could otherwise be spent to improve the life of the common people.

In another few years, Lao Dee says, the State will have so many of these hidden costs to pay, with increasing modernisation, that there won't be enough money to continue subsidising all those inefficient, even useless, offices and factories and foreclosures will be the order of the day and people will be out of work.

Since unemployment is not recognised in a Communist state, Lao Dee says, the people suddenly out of work will receive no unemployment benefits as this aspect of the social security system has never been thought of. Though for decades people have been paid for useless work, it was still, officially, payment for *work* they did, even if it was totally inefficient or produced nothing.

Paying people for *not working* is a totally different concept, a totally different aspect of what Lao Dee calls a caring society, that is alien to the Chinese mindset, to the Communist system apart from the fact that there is simply *no money*, certainly not for the huge numbers of people who will be out of work in the coming five to ten years, Lao Dee says.

Suping stamped her feet, annoyed with her thoughts.

And I stand here and lament and condemn the corruption that harms the innocent, defenceless people and look what I am doing myself. With subterfuge and veiled innuendoes about people in high positions, who are supposedly my friends, I am manoeuvring to get the State take over the burden of caring for my husband and I have no clue what the cost to the State, to society, will be and what's more, I *don't care*.

All I am thinking of, and care about, is myself in the first place and Lilian in the second and to hell with society and Kunlen.

I soothe my conscience, or what goes for it, by protesting that I have done enough, that I have suffered enough at the hands of the State, that the State made Kunlen as he is and that it is only just that it accepts its responsibility. But what is the State? In the end it's those people on their bicycles. They don't even know, and care even less, that I *exist*. And I blame *them* for my misfortunes and want *them* to take care of Kunlen, at least *pay* for it, while *others*, not I, for heaven's sake, do the caring.

And do I care what happens to Kunlen? Are they going to kill him immediately, or slowly, to reduce the cost to the institute and thus to society?

Or are they really going to care for him, feed him, clean him, clothe him until he dies a natural death? I don't know and I don't *want* to know.

All I want is my freedom and to remain Madam Li because that sounds respectable. My only consolation is that the way of thinking that underlies what I am about to do is the rule rather than the exception. Lao Dee says that in a materialistic society, whether communist or capitalist, whether the fight to survive or the compulsion to consume is the sole preoccupation, people revert to a pack mentality wherein the law of the strongest prevails and wherein there is no place for the invalid.

Where the herds and packs of beasts expel the sickly and disabled, or even devour them, the human pack, also called *society*, acts in a more refined and civilised manner, a so-called *humane* manner.

The strongest, which has come to mean *economically* rather than *physically* strongest, have conceived the institutionalisation of the invalid and the care for them as *work*. The beauty of this concept is manifold.

Firstly, people are freed from the burden of caring for their disabled or elderly relatives so that they need not worry about sacrificing even the smallest of their small joys in life.

Secondly, the care is provided by strangers who have made their profession out of such service and who are paid out of the pack's general means to which *all* pack members contribute in the form of that uniquely human invention called taxes. There exists therefore a nice and clean business relationship between the invalid's relatives and the care providers, eliminating any mutual obligation.

Thirdly, the relatives can soothe their conscience, if any, by gammoning themselves that their beloveds are so much better off in the institution, what with all the pills and tablets and capsules administered at exactly the right time and in exactly the right doses, with the right diet, with the efficient daily bathing operations, with the communal bingo and card evenings.

And if, after all that rational soothing, remorse is still gnawing a bit one can always visit the beloved invalid at the appropriate time and tell him or her, with all the forced cheer one can muster, that he or she is to be envied, so nice and cosy and with only people of the same age and the same defects who *understand* each other so well.

The invalid and the old father or mother nod and say amen so as not to spoil the atmosphere but in their heart they recognise the forced cheer for the tragicomedy it is, a covering-up by the healthy and young of their uneasiness and disgust for the old and disabled and of their egoism.

Lao Dee is very cynical when he talks about such things and he doesn't spare himself at all. He says he's just like the rest of us egoists. He also has done his utmost, years ago, to convince his elderly parents to move into a home for the elderly. His excuses were his job, which required him to live all over the world, and his parents' deep roots in the far north of his country which made it impossible to dislocate *them*. His brothers and sister had their own reasons for not wanting their parents to move in with them so to the institution they went.

He now visits them once every two or three years and even then he starts shifting in his chair after an hour, trying to think up an excuse to leave earlier than planned. Driving off in his car he waves at the old folks standing staring and waving after him from behind the window of their small room and he feels bad almost to the point of crying, but he continues on his way to more important things. Back in his hotel the first thing he does is call them by phone and tell them, with forced cheer, how nice it was, how well they looked, how much they are to be envied in their cosy, small apartment and so well looked after.

And the old folks hide their despair and disappointment and play the game and lie with desperate cheerfulness; yes it was so nice to see him again, to talk about his interesting life, that they are now already looking forward to his next visit which, they hope, will be sooner than in two or three years' time, and perhaps next time he can take his children along also? Such a pity they can't understand each other but they would be so happy to see them one more time.

So he promises that next time will be much sooner and yes he will bring his children, anything to make them feel good and to make himself feel good. Ringing off he hesitates how to spend the few hours he has managed to fabricate for himself: watch TV in his room? Have a drink in the lobby bar? Go for a walk and a drink in some night-club or other? Go to the cinema? Study his presentation for tomorrow one more time?

Reluctantly he goes down to the lobby bar. But for the barman watching, visibly bored, a small TV screen, there's nobody. He orders a beer, finishes half and goes back to his room where he watches, lying on his bed, all the TV channels from one to twenty and back in endless boredom, feeling worse by the minute, picturing his old parents three hundred kilometres to the north watching, in silence, some utterly silly programme on the TV set he bought for them a few years ago.

Were they thinking of him? Were they sad, hiding their sadness from each other, telling each other what a good son he was, leading such a busy life in all those foreign countries and yet finding the time to visit them and bring those fine chocolates they would give to the nurse as the doctor had forbidden them to eat chocolate?

Sighing he switches off the TV and tries to get some sleep. Will I feel like that about Kunlen? Will I regret what I am about to do?

No! My case is *different*! Kunlen is an idiot and has no such feelings as described so cynically and yet so movingly by Lao Dee.

What I am doing is the best for all of us, even for Kunlen.

Suping's train of thought was suddenly interrupted by the groaning of a door opening behind her back. She turned and saw a short, thickset woman with limp, greasy, greyish hair and a face like a doughy, half-done pancake peering at her with dim, sullen eyes from the doorway.

'Good morning,' Suping said with forced friendliness. 'I have business with the department of prisons and asylums.'

The woman didn't answer but looked down at the old guard instead.

'She is the first,' the old man wheezed, 'been here since eight o'clock.'

Suping was surprised to see at least twenty people, who had apparently been waiting behind the old guard but who were now surging pell-mell towards the open door, trying to get in in front of her.

The woman stepped aside, effectively blocking the entrance for the others while motioning Suping to enter first.

'Upstairs, left, second door on the right,' she grumbled as Suping squeezed past her.

'Thank you, comrade, thank you, madam,' she said, hurriedly, and then she crossed the hall at a trot and ran up the stairs, three steps at a time, to remain ahead of other potential customers for prisons and asylums.

A small, white, wooden signboard beside the second door to her right read 'Correction Department'.

Hesitantly Suping knocked and listened and, since she heard no sign of life at the other side of the door, she knocked again, more forcefully this time and opened the door.

Peering into the semi-darkness she noticed a shiny, balding pate with a few wisps of white hair above a wizened monkey face. The old man's eyes, huge in that small face, shone with a kind of mocking pleasure as he looked at Suping.

'Good morning, Madam Li,' he said in a remarkably clear voice. 'How can I be of service this time?'

Suping was flabbergasted. How did the old official know her name? What did he mean by 'this time'? She had never been to this office before.

And then, in a flash, it all came back to her.

Eighteen years ago this same man had helped her get an official birth certificate for Lilian. And she had never properly thanked him for probably risking his career, perhaps even his life, just to help her.

She hadn't even known his name until ten seconds ago when she had knocked on the door and saw a piece of carton tacked to the door with the name Pan Yuren written on it with a felt pen.

'I see you remember me as well,' Mr Pan said, smiling imperceptibly. 'You kissed my hand the second and last time we met, one of the few remarkable moments in my uneventful life. You haven't changed a bit, Mrs Li. How is your daughter? Lilian her name was, if I remember correctly. Not a very common name, that's why I remember probably. Now, tell me! What can I do for you?'

'It's incredible,' Suping mumbled, 'incredible. Only yesterday I mentioned you, and what you did for me and my daughter, to some friends when I was reminiscing about those terrible times. I suddenly felt ashamed that I had never properly thanked you for your kindness and understanding and I told my daughter that we would find out whether you were still around and I asked my friend, a foreigner, to bring a tin of special cookies from Hong Kong, as a belated present for you from me and Lilian. And now I am standing face to face with you again and I still haven't got a token of appreciation for you. Unforgivable, but how was I to know?' She looked imploringly at the old man.

'It's not important, Mrs Li,' old Mr Pan said and, smiling with fine irony, he added, 'The cookies will undoubtedly be of a better quality than eighteen years ago so perhaps it's just as well that you waited a bit.'

Suping laughed, relieved that the old official took it all so well.

'I still haven't paid my eighteen-year-old debt and I am asking you again for a favour, Mr Pan,' she said, suddenly serious. 'It's about my husband, Li Kunlen, Lilian's father. I need about half an hour to explain the matter to you. Could I prevail on you to grant me that much of your time?'

'I have all the time in the world, Mrs Li, so please, tell me about your problem.'

Suping talked for more than half an hour and not once did Mr Pan interrupt her.

When she had finished, he kept looking at her, his chin resting on his stapled fingers.

Finally he said, 'I believe you, Mrs Li, and I believe you are serious and that you have a case. However, for cases such as yours I need to make a report to the city council, the only authority that can decide on such matters, and that report must be based on factual findings. Therefore, I need to visit the place where you live to see the situation for myself and I also need to interview your husband, which will be difficult if what you tell me is correct, and your nearest neighbours and relatives, in your case your daughter. When would be a convenient time for you?'

Suping almost fell over her own words as she rushed, 'Now please, Mr Pan, this very moment?' And blushingly she added, 'I had hoped for that.' She told him in what condition she had left her husband with the aim to impress on the officials who would accompany her the untenableness of the situation.

Nervously she fiddled with her fingers as she waited for Mr Pan's reply.

'You needed not stage such theatricals, Mrs Li,' he said gravely. 'Fortunately you told me and I know already that you are given to impulsiveness so I won't hold it against you, but had you held out on me and confronted me in your house with that scene I would have walked out on you and you could have forgotten the whole thing. Do never try to trap an official with a situation he is not prepared for. Sleight of hand tricks don't go well with officialdom. Never ever try to be too clever, certainly not cleverer than them. The secret of success in dealing with officials is to give them the impression that they are God Almighty and far superior to you. Is that clear?'

Greatly chastened Suping nodded and asked in a small voice, 'Shall I go home quickly and clean up the mess and Kunlen before you arrive?'

Mr Pan smiled, 'That will not be necessary, Mrs Li,' he said. 'Let's just say that you cleaned up everything before hurrying to the town hall and that on your return, in my company, you found that your husband had dirtied himself again in your absence. So embarrassing but what can you do, eh? So let's go.'

Mr Pan closed and locked the door of his office and together they descended the stairs.

Downstairs he said, 'The vice-mayor is in today. Please wait for me, outside if you prefer, while I inform the vice-mayor I'll be on an inspection visit so that he is prepared.'

Suping nodded and stepped outside, into the hurly-burly of mid-morning street life. She leaned with her back against the warm, rough stones of the outside wall and lifted her face, eyes closed, up to the sun. Shivering with sheer, almost sensual delight, she soaked up the warmth, feeling life flow back into her after the chilly gloominess inside the building.

The buzz of the street faded from her awareness as her thoughts drifted to faraway Sichuan where the summers were long and hot, the afternoons spent dozing in the shade, the evenings outside until bedtime and the winters short and mild and days off spent with long walks along the river and in the green hills.

She didn't belong here, in Liaoning, and the last, lingering traces of doubt about the idea of living again with her parents, in Luding, vanished.

If only old Mr Pan would see things her way. Did he have a price? She would have to be very careful wheedling it out of him, the old man very definitely had his pride.

She came to with a shock as she heard Mr Pan's voice beside her. 'Out of the wind and in the sun it's very pleasant today. The wind is chilly though, especially for my aching old bones, so I put on my padded jacket. Lead the way, Mrs Li.'

During their half-hour walk Suping spoke animatedly about her small group of friends and their plans to visit, together, her parents in Luding, thanks to their foreign friend Lao Dee who had graciously offered to pay for all expenses.

She didn't mention her own secret plan to stay behind there though, not yet at least. That would undoubtedly create the impression in Mr Pan's mind that she was a callous, calculating woman who wanted to get rid of her husband and was just using him, Mr Pan, for her own selfish reasons.

Mr Pan didn't say much, he just nodded and smiled.

When they turned the corner into her alley Suping saw Lilian talking to Auntie Liu in front of her house.

Before Suping could introduce Mr Pan, Lilian exclaimed, blushing, 'Oh, Mother, I am so sorry if I spoilt your scenario. Father dirtied himself again after you left and I simply couldn't stand it any more, the stench, Ciaokeli whimpering, in our room, Father whimpering and agitatedly groping for Ciaokeli, it was too much and my heard bled for Father. I went to see Auntie Liu and told her about your scenario and she came with me and told me it was all right to clean up the mess. Auntie said that no respectable official would judge our case on such superficial evidence, on the contrary probably since the whole scenario exuded a set-up. I hope you are not angry with me, Mother,' she finished, lamely.

Before Suping could say something Mr Pan said gravely, 'Your Auntie Liu is a wise woman and you did well, Lilian. You look surprised that I know your name? Bureaucratically speaking, I am responsible for your official existence, girl, and I am glad to see, after eighteen years, that I need not regret my transgression of administrative rules at that time. Now, let's proceed, Mrs Li, if you don't mind.'

While Suping showed Mr Pan around her small quarters and discussed with him, in the kitchen, about Kunlen who was lying on his plank bed, staring with his usual vacuous idiot's smirk at the ceiling while holding the little mongrel Ciaokeli in his arms, Lilian made a fresh pot of tea and readied their best eggshell cups on a tray.

Just as Suping and Mr Pan joined Lilian in the front room Auntie Liu returned with the tin of fine Danish cookies Lao Dee had presented her with.

Suping introduced Auntie Liu to Mr Pan by her formal name Liu Meiling of Shanghai which Mr Pan acknowledged with a formal little bow of his head, stating that he was honoured. Casting a loving glance at Auntie Liu, Suping explained briefly their relationship, emphasising how at every critical phase of her life since her arrival in Dalian, Madam Liu, whom she and Lilian affectionately called Auntie, had been there, with more than just advice and deed, with more love and caring than ever a father and mother could have provided.

With an enigmatic little smile Mr Pan looked at Auntie Liu, who kept staring at her fingers, and then at Suping as he said, 'A few days before you came to my office, at the register, for the first time, with your baby girl, I was summoned to the office of Mr Xian, the Party secretary of our city at that time. There was a woman with Mr Xian whom he didn't bother to introduce to me with her name, he only said she was a dear friend. They were having tea and Mr Xian offered me a cup, which I accepted. Together we chatted for fifteen minutes or so about sundry and inconsequential small matters. Then Mr Xian asked me to show his dear friend out, making quite a show of his cordial leave-taking.

'I escorted the woman to the city hall's front door and said goodbye, rather puzzled, I must admit, by the whole thing. When I was about to close the door the woman turned to face me and said, with a little smile, "Before I forget, Mr Pan, one of these days a young woman by the name of Mrs Li, née Xu Suping, will come to your office to register her baby girl. This young woman is very dear to me, Mr Pan, and anything you can do for her will be very much appreciated, by me, and will not be forgotten." Before I could ask something she turned and walked off.

'And now I am sitting here, in front of the same woman, and finally learn that her name is Liu Meiling. And I presume that the last words she said to me then still apply today, eighteen years later. Or don't they, Madam Liu?'

'They do, Mr Pan, they do and very much so,' Auntie Liu replied with a smile, 'and I should appreciate it if you and I could have a talk, in my house, after your fact-finding mission here.'

'Gladly, Madam Liu, gladly,' old Mr Pan replied, 'but for now let's deal with the matter for which I am here in the first place.'

Looking in turn at Suping and Lilian he said, 'Madam Li, Lilian, let me say first of all that I am very impressed by the way you two have taken care of Kunlen for the past twelve years. You have done more, and better, than most people would have been capable of, certainly if one takes into account that neither of you is actually *qualified* for this kind of specialised care. Therefore, however much I, as an ordinary human being, admire you for what you have done, as a government official, I cannot approve of this situation and it is my duty to inform you that you are both, though Lilian to a lesser degree, liable to be fined, or even imprisoned, for not having applied for official authorisation to keep Li Kunlen at home. In my report I shall of course strongly recommend that those fines, or imprisonment, be waived in view of a number of attenuating circumstances.

'This is, of course, only my personal finding and to be considered by the city council it needs to be supported by the testimonies of at least two persons who must have witnessed what happened here for not less than eight of the twelve years. I am afraid that I must prevail on Madam Liu Meiling, who has been a witness to what has been going on here for all of those twelve years, to sign a written declaration to the effect that she supports my opinion that Mrs Li, née Xu Suping, and her daughter Li Lilian, are neither qualified nor competent to provide the specialised care needed in the case of Li Kunlen and that therefore the said Li Kunlen should be institutionalised without further delay. I realise that this must be difficult for you, Madam Liu, to do this to your friends, however, I must remind you that it is your duty to be truthful to the State.'

Mr Pan fell silent and looked gravely at Auntie Liu.

'I have never wavered in my dedication to the People's Republic of China, Comrade Pan,' Auntie Liu said, with a deadpan face, 'and I shall not waver now,' she continued. 'You can write out the declaration now, or later in my house, and I shall sign it. I'm sure Madam Li and her daughter will understand.'

Suping nodded, doing her utmost to look crestfallen but inwardly marvelling at the comedy played in front of her by those two dyed-in-the-wool manipulators of the system.

'May I suggest you consider Mrs Li's neighbour opposite, our much respected and beloved leader Hu Guoshang, as your second witness, Comrade Pan?' Auntie Liu said mellifluously.

'She will be a hostile witness though, that is, if you inform her in advance of my support for your opinion, or of your opinion pure and simple, she will proclaim the opposite. She has always been a bit spiteful to put it mildly, a stain on an otherwise wonderful and kind character.'

'Thank you for your kind suggestion, Comrade Liu,' Mr Pan said, with a formal little bow of his head in Auntie's direction.

'I know Comrade Hu's kind well. I shall visit her now and tell her she is the second witness I think will fully support my findings that Mrs Li and her daughter are well capable to continue to take care of their husband and father, a view also fully supported by Madam Liu Meiling, by the way. After my conversation with Comrade Hu I shall drop by your house for a little chat, if that is all right with you.

'Thank you for the cookies, they were delicious. Brought from Hong Kong by one of your foreign friends, I presume? In my situation I have unfortunately no opportunity whatsoever to meet the foreign devils, let alone to hobnob with them and make friends. This is a pity, for I have heard that they can be very understanding and generous. Even our compatriots from Hong Kong are making so many friends amongst our people nowadays, distributing their little capitalist baubles as they do, a bit like the sailors of old did to win, if not always the hearts, at least the favour of the primitive natives. Imagine this primitive native Pan Yuren brought to Hong Kong by the conquering barbarians to have a peek and gape at all those wonderful capitalist marvels before the happy reunion in 1997 when our compatriots will become just a few additional pieces of gristle in the thin and tasteless soup that is the People's Republic.

'But I bore you with my pipedream. Mrs Li, I shall do my best to have my report on the secretary's desk today so that the case can be included in the agenda for next Monday's city council meeting. You will be notified of the council's decision the next day, Tuesday that is, and if the council goes along with my recommendations you must prepare yourself for your husband's institutionalisation before the end of next week. Goodbye,' and, after his customary little bow, Mr Pan walked out of the door Lilian held open for him and crossed the alley to knock on Hu Guoshang's door.

Lilian quickly closed the door and joined her mother and Auntie Liu in the front room.

'Quick! Open the window a crack, Lilian, while your mother and I push the couch against the wall under the window. If we crouch on the couch we can hear what Pan and Old Turtle say for I'm sure she won't let him in,' Auntie said, grinning.

Heads close together just below the crack they heard Pan knock again and again on the front door of Hu's shack. Finally they heard the door being opened and Hu's snarly, 'Don't pound like that on my door, you fool. Who are you? What do you want?'

A bit huffily Mr Pan replied, 'My name is Pan and I am the head of the correction department at the city hall. May I come in for a moment? I have to talk to you.'

'No you may not come in!' Hu snarled. 'Do your talking here, official, and don't waste my time! I have very little time and even less patience with officials of your kind. In my time we didn't ask people for permission to enter their house, we simply entered and nobody in his right mind would protest. These days you people have no authority, no backbone,' and parroting Pan she said mockingly, 'May I come in for a moment?'

'I am sorry, Leader Hu,' Pan said, a tinge of irony in his voice. 'On behalf of the city Party secretary I have to ask for your co-operation in the case of Mrs Li, née Xu Suping, versus my department. My department was only very recently informed, by a concerned Party member I may add, of the fact that the said Mrs Li has for the past twelve years tended her mentally and physically severely deficient husband in her own house, together with her daughter. This is in contravention of the rules and regulations since neither Mrs Li nor her daughter are professionally qualified to administer such specialised care. They have therefore been notified that Mr Li must be institutionalised and that they must answer to the city council for contravening the law. Mrs Li, however, has appealed against my department's ruling, pretending that though she and her daughter do not have the official qualifications as a professional nurse, they can do and have done the job just as well, if not better.

'I have just visited them to inspect the situation first-hand and I tend to agree with Mrs Li and I am seriously considering a proposal to the city council to leave the situation as it is. Madam Liu Meiling, a friend of the family, strongly supports this view. However, I need *two* supporting testimonies for my report and I therefore call on you as well, as Mrs Li's nearest neighbour and a respected former community leader, to sign a declaration to the effect that Mrs Li and her daughter Lilian are, in your well-considered opinion, capable of still tending Mr Li.'

Pan fell silent, out of breath probably, and in the ensuing silence Auntie Liu, Suping and Lilian pictured Hu staring at Pan in utter amazement.

Then, suddenly, they heard the raucous squawking Suping remembered was Hu's way of laughing and then Hu shouting, 'Those three witches with their sweet-talking and tears fooled you, dog official, like they have fooled everybody else for the past twenty odd years, except me of course. But then nobody listens to me any more since you have all gone soft in the head. That hussy woman Su Ping and her dolled-up slut of a daughter are totally incapable of tending that miserable man and the sooner you lock him up in an asylum the better for him and for the neighbourhood. Even in my house, locked and all, I can smell it when he has fouled up the place and that happens almost every day. Today especially was terrible. And then that filthy little dog, yelping and slobbering all over the poor man. It's obscene. *Obscene and repugnant, you hear, dog official*!'

Hu's screaming had apparently drawn the attention of the other neighbours since several other voices were asking what was going on, Lao Yang's voice cackling loudest as he called on Pan to lock up Hu Guoshang with Li Kunlen in the same asylum. 'They'll make a beautiful couple there!' he cried. 'That's what she wanted all along! United at last!'

Pan apparently ignored the taunting for he said to Hu, 'I take it then that you do *not* support my view and that you do *not* wish to sign a declaration. However disappointed I am, it is my duty to ask you to sign instead a declaration to the effect that in your opinion Li Kunlen should be institutionalised.'

'Absolutely right, dog official,' Hu growled, 'and add in that declaration that it is also my opinion that his wife and daughter should be prosecuted for contravening the law.'

'Yes, Leader Hu, I shall write out the declaration here and now and I am afraid that in view of your former status as a community leader your opinion will carry much weight with the members of the city council and that Mrs Li has no chance whatsoever to have her appeal granted. As for the prosecution of Mrs Li and her daughter, I shall have to draw up a separate declaration for you to sign since that is a different matter for a different department. May I please come in now, Leader Hu? For a minute only, just to write out the two statements.'

'Come in,' Hu growled and the door of her house was slammed shut.

Auntie Liu, Suping and Lilian stared at one another, horrified. Though things had gone their way and better even than expected thanks to Mr Pan's expert manipulation of Hu, they were nevertheless frightened by Hu's malice and hatred after all these years.

'She is sick,' Auntie Liu said, 'forget it. We have achieved what you wanted, Suping, and that's what counts. Pan has been clever and I am afraid that he has also mentioned his price: a visit to Hong Kong. He has been kind enough though to leave us a way out, to save face. Pan knows full well that arranging such a trip for him ourselves is totally out of the question. He knows we need our foreign friend Lao Dee to do that for us and that we can blame him if the plan falls through.

'Still, face or no face, we have to take it up with Lao Dee and I hate that, begging all the time, then for this, then for that. But it is important. If Kunlen is not in an asylum by the time Lao Dee wants to take us to Luding, you simply cannot go. So if Lao Dee thinks that that trip is important for him he should do something for Pan Yuren, in appreciation of services rendered. What do you think? And who is going to approach him?'

Auntie Liu fell silent and looked in turn at Suping and Lilian.

'I think *you* should, Auntie Liu,' Lilian said. 'Lao Dee likes you. You have the same kind of sardonic sense of humour and it's better if such things come from an older person than from a young girl like me. Mother is out of the question. She hasn't known Lao Dee long enough and hasn't done anything yet that would give her the right to ask for such a big favour.'

She fell silent and looked at Auntie Liu.

'All right,' Auntie said, 'you are probably right, Lilian. I'll try but I'll do it my way and when I think he's in a receptive mood. It also depends of course on what Pan does. No use to talk to Lao Dee before Kunlen has gone and no reason at all if you remain stuck with him. So wait and see.'

Groaning the old woman got up from the couch and said, 'It's time I'm off to my own house now before good old Pan finishes with Old Turtle. See you later.' She waddled out of the door into the alley.

She had barely gone five minutes when Suping and Lilian heard Mr Pan's voice again as he apparently took his leave from Hu.

'Thank you for your valuable co-operation, Leader Hu,' they heard him say. 'I'll now call on Madam Liu one last time to inform her of your opposition to letting Mr Li stay with his family. Perhaps she will now reconsider her own position.'

A contemptuous snort was Mr Pan's only answer as Hu slammed the door in his face.

On the Tuesday of the week following Mr Pan's visit Suping received an official letter from the city council informing her of the council's decision to have her husband Li Kunlen institutionalised and that a place had been reserved for him in the asylum for mentally handicapped in Lushun. She was requested to have him ready for the transfer the following Thursday at nine o'clock in the morning.

The council was also pleased to inform her that the charges against her and her daughter for keeping and tending her husband at home without official approval had been dropped. Suping kept staring at the letter in her trembling fingers until the characters became a blackish blur on a white background. She bit her lower lip in order not to cry as the realisation that what she had put in motion was now irreversible hit her with a numbing force. Her heart pounded wildly and irregularly and she was about to panic when she felt a hand squeeze the nape of her neck and the letter was taken from her numb, icy cold fingers.

'Calm now, calm now,' she heard Auntie Liu croon near her ear. 'There is no reason to panic nor for self-reproach. You did the right thing; for yourself and for Lilian. For Kunlen it makes no difference. Wouldn't have made a difference a long time ago already. You lost twelve years of your life because of him and your own exaggerated loyalty and sense of duty. Now it's time to think of yourself again and of your daughter. Here, drink this glass of wine I brought for you and stop snivelling.'

Laughing through her tears Suping took the small glass from the older woman's hand and still shuddering now and then with a stray sigh she sipped from the sweet red wine.

'It's called *porto*,' Auntie Liu commented, 'have had it for more years than I care to remember. A suitor tried to seduce me after he gave the bottle to me as a present. Bought it in Macau, he said. He fled when I hit him with the bottle in his tender parts. He never came back and I kept the bottle. Carried it with me everywhere. The wine is very good in real emergencies. Had a few myself over the years.

'Bottle is almost empty now. Had to strain your glass to remove the lees. I think I'll ask Lao Dee to bring me another bottle. I'll pay him of course, though I'm sure he won't take my money. Damn him, he keeps chalking up the favours I owe him already, smiling that mocking little smile of his, I'm sure. "Don't bother, Meiling, it's such a small matter,"' she mimicked Lao Dee's Beijing drawl, 'but all those small matters make one hell of a big matter already. It makes my heart turn when I think what he'll say when I broach the subject of Pan Yuren. I'll never be able to repay him,' she sighed.

Suping, her usual self again because of Auntie Liu's distracting small talk, said pensively, 'I don't think we need worry too much about repaying Lao Dee. Firstly because I have the feeling that Westerners are not so obsessed with who does what for whom and moral debts and so on and secondly because I get the impression, each time we ask him something, that he is genuinely pleased to help out. He seems to know, as no other, the restrictions imposed on us Chinese concerning practically every aspect of our life, from birth to death, and, as I said, he seems to be genuinely happy if he can make things happen for us that would otherwise be out of the question, useless even to think about, pipedreams as old Mr Pan would say.

'So let's not torture ourselves and agonise how we can repay him each time we ask him something. Besides I also think that the foreigners aren't so obsessed with face either so when we ask something that he can't or won't do he will simply say so and not feel embarrassed about it or, worse, make promises he can't keep and then avoid us.

'So I propose that next Thursday, when we all meet again in your house to hear Lao Dao tell his story, we tell everybody about Lao Pan and how he arranged for Kunlen to be placed in an institution, and so fast at that, and how he tricked Old Turtle into supporting us. And then, without hemming and hawing, we tell Lao Dee about Lao Pan's allusion to his dream to visit Hong Kong and ask him whether he sees a possibility to arrange that. Needless to beat around the bush, needless to tell him that Pan knows we could never arrange such a thing ourselves, needless to keep harping about moral debts and such drivel, Lao Dee knows all that inside out and I think he must be thoroughly sick of it by now. If he thinks he can arrange something he will say so, if he can't or won't he will say so too. What do you think, Auntie?'

'I think you are absolutely right,' Liu Meiling said, relieved and pleased. 'Let's do it your way.'

The following Thursday Suping and Lilian had husband and father Kunlen fed and washed by eight o'clock. Suping had shaved him and cut the small hairs in his ears and nostrils, while Lilian had trimmed his finger and toenails.

His bowels had been a bit loose these past few days so they waited until the very last moment to dress him in his clean new clothes.

Lilian had taken a whole bunch of notes from her savings and bought a complete new set of clothes for her father: olive green trousers, dark blue jacket, a dark blue cap and green canvas sneakers, woollen socks, woollen underwear, everything double so that the people in the institute could dress him in a clean set every week, or whatever the change frequency was.

She had taken the clothes to an old woman who earned a few yuan on the side by making small name tags and she had paid five yuan to have her father's name tag sewn into each piece of clothing, a small, rectangular piece of white cotton with the three characters of Father's name embroidered in red. That way there would be no mix-up with the other inmates' clothes.

At a quarter to nine Suping dressed her husband while Lilian made fresh tea and put a dozen cookies on a plate for the ambulance personnel.

A few minutes past nine o'clock they heard Lao Yang shrilling like an angry turkey, 'Ambulance! Ambulance! Out of the way! Out of the way!' and then the sound of an engine approaching.

Suping looked at Lilian, her heart pounding, 'We will not go outside, you and I,' she said. 'I will not have the whole neighbourhood gaping at us. We shall take leave of Father here and no big deal. Look at the poor sod, he has no idea what is going on.'

The small front room darkened as the bulk of the ambulance obscured the window.

The driver had driven down the narrow alley in reverse so that he could drive off and turn into the main street without problem. He stopped the ambulance, its backside aligned with the front door, and two male nurses opened the back doors wide and jumped out.

They pulled out a stretcher and entered through the front door held open by Lilian, followed by the driver. Lilian then closed the door in the gaping faces of most of the neighbours.

They wouldn't miss the distraction for anything, she knew, and wouldn't leave until after the ambulance had gone.

'Do you want me to order those people to disperse, Madam?' Lilian heard the driver ask as she joined the others in the room. 'I have the authority, you know!' he added proudly.

'Thank you, that's very kind of you, Comrade,' Mother said, 'but don't bother. Leave them. It's their only distraction since the army dumped the man you have come for on my doorstep, twelve years ago now, and it will probably have to last them for another twelve years, if not longer. Would you like a fresh mug of tea? My daughter just made it for you. Please sit down.'

The three men sat down awkwardly on the settee and mumbled their thanks as Lilian put a mug of steaming tea and three cookies in front of each of them on the low, small table. She handed her mother a mug as well and sat down with hers as Suping took a sip and gestured for the others to do the same. 'Please drink,' she said, spitting back a leaf in her mug, 'and eat your cookies, they are very nice.'

For the next ten minutes not a word was said as they just sipped and spat and munched avoiding looking at one another.

Finally the driver put down his empty mug and stood up, brushing the cookie crumbs off his jacket and trousers on to the floor, and said, 'Thank you for the tea and the cookies Madam, Miss, they were delicious. Now, please, lead us to the patient. We have to report back in Lushun before noon.'

Suping and Lilian stood up also, looked at each other and, after an almost imperceptible nod from her daughter, Suping said hesitantly, 'There's also the little dog, Ciaokeli we call him. My husband, Mr Li, the patient as you called him just now, is very attached to the little mongrel and he to him, in fact they're inseparable. I'm sure my husband will be very agitated, probably even unmanageable, if he doesn't feel the dog, both during the trip in the ambulance and in the asylum. What shall we do?' Imploringly she looked at the driver and his assistants.

The driver bit his lower lip, clearly at a loss. He looked at the two nurses who merely shrugged their shoulders in reply.

Finally he said, 'Nobody in Lushun said anything about a dog. I don't even know whether dogs are allowed in the institute, I never saw one at least. On the other hand, our instructions are to avoid anything that might upset the patients so I think I'll hide behind that order and let Mr Li take his little dog with him. I'll tell the people there what you told us, Madam Li, and then it's up to them to decide what to do. Is that all right with you?'

Suping and Lilian nodded, relieved and grateful for the driver's kindness.

Dragging a screaming Kunlen out of the house and into the ambulance, in front of the whole neighbourhood, was the last thing they needed. What would happen to Ciaokeli in Lushun was the least of their worries for now, though both felt a pang of pity for the affectionate little dog. Perhaps the nurses there would see the advantage of a docile patient and let him keep his dog.

Suping preceded the three men into the tiny kitchen.

Kunlen sat on his plank bed, in his brand new clothes, Ciaokeli clasped in his arms, his cheek pressed against the little dog's head.

Four sad brown eyes looked up at the intruders, apprehensively, resignedly, as if they knew as cows in the slaughterhouse know.

They both know what's going to happen, flashed through Suping's mind and feelings of guilt and pity washed over her.

I can still stop it and then, mustering all her courage and decency she was about to say *stop it* when she felt a hand on her shoulder and heard Lilian's voice whisper near her ear, 'We must now let these men do their job, Mother. Come with me, in the room, so that they can help Father on to the stretcher and into the ambulance. The sooner it's over the better.'

The decisive moment had passed and will-lessly Suping turned her back on her husband of twenty years and followed her daughter into the living room.

Kindly but resolutely, talking reassuringly, the driver made Kunlen stand up so that his two assistants could sweep him off his feet and stretch him out on the stretcher.

Deftly they fastened the straps over his chest and legs and tucked Ciaokeli under his jacket, his little head peeking out at the strangers. He whimpered softly and plaintively.

'It is better not to say your goodbyes now, Madam, Miss,' the driver said in a kind and sympathetic voice. 'It will surely upset you and very likely your husband as well and it serves no purpose. It is much better that you let us depart very quickly and console yourselves with the thought that in two weeks you will visit him, when he has adjusted to his new environment. He will adjust much better and much quicker if he doesn't leave here burdened with conflicting emotions he doesn't understand and can't assimilate. Do you understand that and can you accept my advice?'

Suping and Lilian nodded wordlessly, grateful to submit to the driver's kind but firm authority.

The driver gave a curt order to his men and, after a last smile and friendly nod at mother and daughter, followed them outside, closing the front door behind him.

Before the crowd outside realised what had happened the men had slid the stretcher on its rails into the ambulance, jumped in and pulled the doors shut behind them.

The driver had climbed into the cabin, started the engine and driven off while his men were still locking the doors. Not even half a minute after picking up Kunlen on his stretcher from the kitchen floor, the ambulance disappeared around the corner of the alley into the main street, direction Lushun.

Inside, in the living room, Suping and Lilian stood close together, arms around each other's shoulders, crying soundlessly.

'What have we done, daughter, what have we done, you and I?' Suping sobbed. 'Shall we ever be able to live with our shame?'

'What rubbish!' said Auntie Liu's voice behind them. 'What utter rubbish! You have done finally what you should have done long ago. Freed yourselves from a hopeless situation which for the past twelve years held you prisoners in an atmosphere of gloom and doom. Now stop weeping and snivelling and breathe! Breathe deeply and stand on the points of your toes and stretch your arms upwards as high as you can, until the muscles in your back ache, and say to each other, "Life begins *now*! Happiness begins *now*!"'

Suping and Lilian had let go of each other and, wiping the tears from their eyes, they did, hesitatingly and giggling self-consciously, as Auntie Liu told them.

'I notice some flab around the midriffs,' Auntie Liu said, chuckling, 'perhaps you two should exercise more, and more often, especially with all that wonderful food we are being fed these days by our generous foreign friend. He sent word, by the way, that he expects us in the All Under Heaven restaurant at half past five. His friend the cook, that scoundrel Mu Ping, will prepare a few dishes that don't travel well so he can't deliver the food to my house as he did last time, he says in his little note. After dinner we'll convene at my house to hear Lao Dao's story, at least the first part of it as it threatens to be long, knowing Lao Dao. I have prepared a light beef noodle soup, quite hearty, so why don't you come with me now and eat a bowlful with me. It'll do you good.

'Clean up your faces and put a serious mien on them, just in case our kindly neighbours are still outside waiting to catch a glimpse of the grief-stricken mother and daughter. At least Old Turtle didn't miss the opportunity to announce to the gathering how she had intimidated that old dog official to remove Kunlen from your care and have him placed in an institution. Everybody is horrified by what that mean old hag says and public opinion is on your side. So behave in a dignified manner and nod, with just a little quiver of your lips, at everybody as you walk past them and ignore Old Turtle, whatever she shouts at you.'

Suping and Lilian laughed in spite of their still lingering uneasiness and went about freshening up.

Ready, they followed Auntie Liu outside, hearts pounding and shifty-eyed from nervousness and guilty consciences.

A number of people were still there, turning away from Old Turtle's harangue when they heard the door of the Li residence open.

'Have courage, Suping!' Lao Yang squawked. 'You'll get Kunlen back. We'll sign a petition if you want!'

The others nodded and murmured their assent.

Everybody ignored the mocking, braying laugh in the background and Old Turtle's maliciously triumphant, 'You'll never get him back, Su Ping, you slut! I won! I won! I *won*!' and braying hysterically she slammed her door shut.

The small crowd watched in stunned silence as Suping, Lilian and Auntie Liu quickly made their way to Auntie's house and disappeared inside.

Slowly and silently they dispersed and went back to their own hovels. Even Lao Yang, for once, had no wherewithal against so much hatred, such sickness of the mind.

In a subdued silence they slurped the hearty soup.

Neither of them felt like talking while Lilian, without asking, refilled the bowls for the third time.

Still, finally, the salty, pungent hotness of the broth had its effect and Suping, leaning back with a contented burp and sigh, said pensively, 'She must be crazy, Hu Guoshang. I see her ending up one day in that same asylum, finally united with Kunlen. What a cruel fate, for both of them, should that ever happen.

'I can't help thinking that I was used, like a blind, will-less instrument, by fate, first to taunt them for their arrogance and then to set in motion the slow process of their destruction by madness and hatred.

'Even my manoeuvring to have Kunlen institutionalised was foreordained and cunningly inspired by fate, at the right moment, to bring Kunlen and that crazy woman finally together when there is nothing left of their lives but to wait for the end, one withdrawn in idiocy, the other in a crazy rage that she still can't reach him. Such irony for the three of us. Mere puppets, playthings, we are discarded once the child has grown weary of its nasty little games. Strange, I have always thought of fate as a child, spoilt, unpredictable and with a mean streak.'

Suping fell silent, shaking her head in wonderment at her sudden insight, smiling sadly at her earlier naivety.

'I can't say whether you are right or wrong,' Auntie Liu said, looking askance at Lilian who seemed crestfallen and on the verge of crying. 'I think nobody can, such ideas as yours, insights you would probably call them, are too personal. If you feel them to be true then they *are* true, for you that is, not necessarily for others. Be that as it may, I must point out though that that nasty spoilt child as you see fate has rewarded you handsomely for your unwitting co-operation.

'You look surprised! Are you surprised, Suping? Would you have had your beautiful, loving and intelligent daughter without fate's interference? Would you have acquired such undemanding and devoted friends as you have over the years in different circumstances? Count your blessings rather than wallowing in pseudo-psychological self-denigration. You are still beautiful and healthy, enjoy it and keep yourself well. You have your daughter; enjoy seeing her grow up into a beautiful healthy and wise young woman like yourself. You have your friends who want only the best for you and Lilian; enjoy their company and undemanding friendship. You have your parents, still well I'm sure, who love you and count the days and hours until your reunion and who wouldn't like anything more than for you to stay and live with them in beautiful Sichuan.

'You have your adopted uncle, Chen Dan, who loves you as if you were his own child and who would like nothing more than for you to stay as well so that the two of you can resume your discussions in the garden or during your walks along the river. The State now looks after your husband and it doesn't cost you a fen and for him it doesn't matter whether you visit him once a month or once a year or never again. Your daughter earns enough money for the two of you to live comfortably so there's no need for you to apply for a job. You truly *are* a lucky person, Xu Suping, so stop whining about your fancied, whimsical troubles.'

Auntie fell silent but kept looking defiantly at Suping, all flushed.

Both Suping and Lilian had been staring at her during the unexpected harangue with round eyes and open mouths.

Now Suping began to giggle, blushing, eyes downcast, then, suddenly, she burst out laughing and hiccuped, 'I deserved that dressing down! Thank you, Auntie, for shaking me up.'

Then, serious all of a sudden she said softly, 'I have indeed a lot, no! *everything* to be grateful for and proud of. There's first of all Lilian, my wonderful daughter and friend as well, then you Liu Meiling, both mother and friend to both of us, our other dear friends, all those good-hearted people who at one time or another over the past twenty-odd years have been kind to me, have helped me, even saved my life probably. I shouldn't forget them, ever.

'And now I am going to see my parents again and show them their granddaughter. How happy and proud they'll be. And good old Uncle Dan. How I look forward to seeing him again and showing off my daughter. He'll want to teach her everything he knows should we stay there, with them, in Luding. And once you have dragged *your* old bones over there, Auntie, and felt the warm sun melt your rheumatism away, you may not want to go back either and stay with us. So many plans! So many wonderful things to look forward to. I can't wait for Lao Dao to tell us his story and then for Lao Dee to fix the date for our trip and get all the approvals.'

Impulsively she embraced and kissed first Lilian, then Auntie Liu, then both of them in turn.

Auntie protested at the exuberance but not too strongly and Lilian laughed delightedly, happy to see her mother in such high spirits.

'I have a suggestion,' she said. 'It's now only half past midday. Auntie, why don't you take a rest, while Mother and I clean up here first and put the chairs and mugs and so on ready for tonight? Then we'll go home, dismantle Father's plank bed; give his mattress, blankets and clothes to Lao Yang and then wash and rub and scrub everything and everywhere inside until it smells nice and clean and fresh; *away with the foul, rancid smell of decay*! When we have finished we'll come back here and we'll walk together to All Under Heaven. What do you think?'

Suping and Auntie Liu thought it was a wonderful plan so Auntie retired to her bedroom and Lilian and Mother washed up and swept the floor and arranged the chairs and mugs and glasses for that night's storytelling session.

Then they left and went home, pace swift and heads high, talking animatedly.

At home Suping put on her oldest blouse and pair of trousers and Lilian wriggled herself into a pair of jeans Jan had bought for her in Hong Kong.

She gasped and puffed and Suping tried in vain to choke down her laughter as she hiccuped, 'His girlfriend in Holland may have bigger boobs than you have but you certainly have a bigger bum. You should let him take your measurements otherwise everything he buys for you will be too large above and too small below the waist. I'm sure he would like that, taking your measurements, I mean,' and she exploded with laughter.

Lilian threw her mother a withering look and said disdainfully, 'These kind of trousers have to be tight. I see that in those Western magazines, the Westerners seem to like that and the shabbier they look the better, the jeans I mean. The other day a German girl who stayed in my hotel – she buys tennis shoes for a Western company, much cheaper in China she says, only you have to check the quality very carefully – but never mind all that, she had holes in her jeans, very ragged and frayed holes. I couldn't believe my eyes when I saw her and couldn't believe my ears when she laughed at my shocked face and said that those holes were made deliberately, often by the manufacturer or the sellers, to make the jeans look old and worn and much used. I told Jan I will not make holes in my jeans and he laughed and said that if I ever should change my mind he would like to make them for me and then one more, he added, the dirty-minded pig.'

Lilian's last remark and the way she said it, so matter-of-factly, gave Suping a fit of the giggles.

Lilian stared at her mother wondering what was so funny, then she, too, couldn't keep a straight face and, convulsed with laughter, pushing and slapping each other on the back, they let themselves fall down on the bed.

Sprawled spread-eagled on their backs, staring up at the ceiling, they hiccuped and each time either of them tried to say something the other got another fit and there they went again, and again. Finally, after more than half an hour of alternating fits and fitful silences they were so exhausted that they dozed off.

Startled by Lilian's whistling snore Suping jumped off the bed and a glance at her watch told her they had slept for more than an hour.

She pulled Lilian by her ankles, dragging her nearly off the bed, crying out, 'Wake up, you lazy bum! We have work to do. It's past two o'clock already!'

For the next hour or so they worked steadily, occasionally consulting together what to do with Father's things. The planks of his plank bed they placed upright in a corner of the kitchen. They would chop them up one by one to serve as firewood.

His old clothes, blankets and quilt they put in three old jute bags which they dragged outside and put upright against the wall of the house. The mattress they carried outside also and stood it against the wall beside the bags.

Then Lilian walked up to old Yang, who had been standing in front of his hovel watching as Lilian and Suping went about their business, and asked him if he wanted her father's things.

He peered at her with his beady, glittering magpie eyes and cackled, 'How much?'

'One yuan,' she replied with a deadpan face.

'The whole lot?'

'The whole lot.'

'Deal.' The old man fumbled in his pocket and produced a filthy, worn, yuan note.

Gingerly she took it from him by the utmost tip of one corner and wrapped it in her handkerchief.

'It's all yours, Lao Yang,' she said, 'take it whenever it suits you,' and without further ado she turned on her heels and walked back home.

The next hour they swept, brushed and washed with soap and water, back and front windows open to let the air pass through, until they were satisfied that every trace of Kunlen's and Ciaokeli's body odour was gone.

They closed the windows, took off their clothes and washed themselves and each other's back thoroughly with the perfumed soap Beiyuen pilfered from the hotel rooms after the guests had checked out.

Pilfered was maybe a bit strong a word, though strictly speaking it was just that. Beiyuen's instructions were to collect the unused, still wrapped pieces of soap after the guests had checked out and hand them in, after her round, to her supervisor which she did, always. The used pieces, however, some of them almost new, had to be collected separately, in a plastic bag, and handed in to the supervisor of the staff washrooms for use by Vice-Manager Zhou and Secretary Du.

Beiyuen had, however, spied on the supervisor and seen how he shared the soap with Secretary Du and how they hid the soap in their bags to take it home, probably to press all the small pieces into bigger blocks and sell them in their neighbourhood.

After that Beiyuen had felt no compunction to take the nicest, almost new pieces for herself and hide them inside her bra to smuggle them past the guards.

Auntie Liu and Lilian had no scruples either to share with Beiyuen, gloating at the thought that they cheated that hypocrite Du and not the hotel after all. At six pieces a day, six days a week, each of them had enough soap to last a long, long time.

At half past four Suping and Lilian knocked on Auntie's door and the three burst out laughing when Lilian sniffed and said, 'Same smell! Same soap?'

Auntie Liu closed the door and together they ambled to the restaurant, relaxedly talking about one thing and another.

Auntie laughed heartily when Suping told her about the jeans, the holes and their fit of giggles.

Fortunately they were momentarily distracted by Beiyuen waving to them from the other side of the street as she approached from the opposite direction or else the three of them would have had another fit right there and then.

Beiyuen crossed the street in a trot and greeted them with her usual exuberance. Together they walked the last hundred metres, Beiyuen doing all the talking, about that day's events at the hotel.

At one time she patted her breasts, grinning mischievously. 'No soap today,' she chuckled, 'something better, shampoo and shower gel. Vice-Manager Zhou has introduced those little plastic bottles with shampoo and shower gel to be placed in the bathrooms of newly arrived guests, one small bottle of each. The guests don't like it, however, and how right they are: the shampoo makes their hair fall out and the gel doesn't foam and makes their skin itch. So they continue to use their own stuff in those big, shiny, plastic flasks. Every three days I am supposed to put out new little bottles, but the other ones aren't empty so I pour out the Chinese stuff and fill them again from the guests' flasks. The guests won't notice, it's only a small quantity after all, and we have good quality Western shampoo and gel. Clever, eh?'

Lilian clapped her hands and agreed it was very clever but Auntie shook her head. 'I don't want to know about your little tricks,' she said. 'You give me those little flasks made in China and, for me, what's inside is Chinese as well. There's bliss in ignorance.' And with those words she pushed the restaurant door and entered, followed by the others, smirking behind her back.

Lao Dee and Lao Dao had arrived already.

Seated at one of the smaller, round tables, in the corner near the kitchen exit door, they were talking animatedly to Mu Ping who was standing next to the table wearing an apron that must have been white and without holes long ago and a whitish cap far too small for his big round head.

They looked up as the four women entered and Lao Dee and Lao Dao stood up to greet them like the good, old friends they had become by now.

Not hindered by modesty or tact Mu Ping took part in the greetings as if he had known them all their lives.

The food was delicious, the presentation of each dish a work of art and Mu Ping, his face beaming like the full moon, visibly revelled in the exclamations of admiration each time he personally showed them the dish before handing it to one of the girl servants who then, reverently, put it in the middle of the table.

Each time he waited, in near rapture, eyes turned upwards towards the kitchen god probably, for their praise after the first tentative bite.

They played the game and were lavish in their praise which Mu acknowledged with repeated bows, in disgustingly feigned modesty, before retiring, backwards, to his kitchen for the following masterpiece.

It was past seven o'clock when they finally, contentedly, sat back in their chairs, softly stroking their stomachs and bellies to release the liberating burp.

Lao Dee got up from his chair and stumbled towards the far corner where he huddled for five minutes with the manager and Mu Ping over the bill.

Finally Lilian saw him pull his wallet from his back pocket and count out eight greyish-blue FEC of one-hundred each and, after an ever so brief hesitation, add one more, in all nine hundred FEC, a small fortune at black market rates.

He paid in FEC though he is allowed to pay in renmenbi, it flashed through her mind, 'and of course he did it at the official rate. A very handsome tip for the manager and Mu Ping and, of course, the girls. No wonder they all have a smile from ear to ear, the obsequious flatterers.'

Lao Dee returned to the table, the manager and Mu Ping in his wake.

'That was a very delicious meal, Mu Ping, old friend,' Lao Dee said, 'you are still the uncontested master of cooking. Thank you for the demonstration. I can see my friends here are impressed. We'll be back, that's for sure, however, I'm afraid we have to go now, we're running behind schedule already, aren't we, my friends?'

The others stood up as well and thanked Mu Ping and the manager for the meal and the service.

'There are two taxis waiting outside,' Lao Dee said, 'Lilian, Beiyuen, Suping and Lao Dao, please take the first one, Meiling and I will follow shortly, when Meiling has collected the boxes with the leftovers.'

Lilian had noticed Auntie Liu talking in a low voice to Lao Dee during the meal and she supposed that Auntie would bring up a few things during the taxi ride while she was alone with him.

I'll watch his face when he alights from the taxi, she thought, a lot depends on his good mood now. He shouldn't have wasted so much money on that Mu Ping circus. It's not worth it. Next time Mother, Beiyuen and I will prepare the food, it'll cost only a fraction of what he paid tonight and save us a lot of time as well. I'm sure Lao Dao won't be able to finish his story tonight, not in the careful way he talks, thinking he must explain everything twice and then once more. I'll propose we'll meet again at Auntie's next week to get that storytelling business over with so that Lao Dee can start thinking seriously about our trip to Luding.

The taxi stopped at the corner of the main street and lane nineteen, their lane.

Lilian paid the driver and slowly they walked down the alley to Auntie Liu's house. Suping had a spare key so they entered and took their seats, the same as last time, and settled down, in relaxed silence, to wait for Auntie Liu and Lao Dee.

'I'll prepare the tea now,' Beiyuen said suddenly, 'so we won't waste any more time when they arrive. As it is it'll be eight o'clock when Lao Dao can finally begin his story. I want to hear everything, Uncle Dao, so don't rush yourself or leave anything out. Stop when you're tired and we'll continue next week, quite simple really.'

Old Dao smiled at the kind girl's caring words and said, 'I'm afraid that won't be enough, Beiyuen. You see, Lao Dee knows quite a lot about my life already, in broad lines, mind you. We spent many a late evening in my little office in the hotel's engineering department, talking about all kinds of things and then the important events in one's life are bound to come up in review, one way or another, more as a reflection in connection with a recent happening than as a structured story. It was enough, however, to give him the idea of writing a book, as he explained a couple of weeks ago, so he won't stand for skipping parts of my story, I know that. So, Lilian, I see you're impatient but you had better prepare yourself for two late nights, this one included.

'If you're worried that our trip to Luding is at stake you can put your mind at ease. Only this afternoon, in the restaurant, before you arrived, Lao Dee told me he had arranged everything already, including your, my and Beiyuen's leave without pay, four weeks he told me, and had paid for our tickets already. Unless there are any unforeseen events, we'll leave for Chengdu, not Chongqing, next Monday in five weeks' time. So I have all the time to dither and babble. But don't let on that I told you. Let Lao Dee tell you himself. All right?'

Suping and the girls nodded, clearly delighted with the news.

Only Lilian seemed a bit embarrassed.

'It's not that I didn't want to hear your whole story, Uncle Dao,' she said, blushing, 'on the contrary. But it passed my mind that you could probably tell it, in part or in whole, when we're in Luding, in the same setting Mother used to like so much and where her Uncle Dan told his story. I'm sure my grandparents and Uncle Dan, as I think of him already, would like that and it would help to pass the evening hours in a pleasant way, don't you think so?'

Expectantly she looked at the old man and then at her mother.

'Not a bad idea,' Lao Dao replied and, careful not to hurt her feelings, he continued; 'but I don't think your arguments will wash with Lao Dee and Meiling, for two reasons, three actually.

'Firstly they want no outside disturbances, such as are so much part of the setting in Luding, like neighbours listening, remember Zhang Yizhong, the sights, smells and sounds around us and so on, they distract both the narrator and the listeners. Secondly, the stories are, in their view, very important, not so much for their content as for establishing the firm ties of friendship and respect without which a long trip, during which we'll be in each other's close company all day, is bound to end in recriminations and quarrelling. They don't want that to happen and I can't blame them.

'Thirdly there's the matter of Lao Dee's planning of his own work and of the arrangements he made with Vice-Manager Zhou and Secretary Du concerning our leave of absence. Especially to get Du's leaders to lean on Du, to twist his arm, to give his consent, however grudgingly, must have cost Lao Dee dearly in terms of favours and he won't like the idea of having to go to them again for a change of dates.

'So forget your idea of going on our trip earlier, Lilian. Besides, I personally think that your grandparents and Chen Dan have so much to talk about with your mother and with yourself that they won't actually be stamping and pawing to spend three whole evenings listening to the reminiscences of a complete stranger. I, for one, would feel very uncomfortable inflicting myself upon them like that and that wouldn't do my narrative much good, now would it? So, as far as I am concerned, forget the whole idea.'

Lao Dao fell silent, then, looking at the door, he added, 'Here they are now. Don't even talk about it. Okay?'

Suping, Beiyuen and Lilian, much chastened, nodded.

# *Chapter Twenty-Three*

## Lao Dao's Story

The door opened and Auntie Liu and Lao Dee came in, still laughing, probably about some joke or remark either of them just made outside.

Thick as thieves, those two, Suping thought, embarrassed by the pang of jealousy she felt. The same quick mind, the same sardonic sense of humour with which they try to cover their compassion and good-heartedness. Rats, both of them, I'm sure.

'Meiling told me about what happened this morning, Suping,' Lao Dee said, smiling sympathetically. 'Quite a story. Fancy meeting that old official Pan again after all these years. You really are in his debt, aren't you? Though I must say that he's very nice and low-key about it, Mr Pan is. Some change I assure you. Reason the more to do something for the old man, eh? I'll see what I can do. There may be a way to make his dream come true and that's what we want, don't we? Making people's dreams come true, I mean.

'Next week I'll drive you and Lilian to Lushun. I have something to do there, a service for an old friend, and in the meantime you can visit Kunlen. I'll buy you a few baubles in Hong Kong this weekend to give to the vice-manager and Kunlen's nurses, as a token of your respect and gratitude as it is only your first visit. You tell them you'll be away for a couple of months, to visit your parents in Sichuan to help you get over your grief. The small presents will have made them sympathetic and they won't expect to see you in the near future. You promise to bring them some nice, juicy white peaches from Chengdu and they'll take good care of Kunlen and of Ciaokeli, that is, if the little mongrel is still there next week. Now, what do you say?'

Suping and Lilian stammered their thanks as Lao Dee continued already, 'It's a small matter. Now, did Lao Dao tell you I managed to make all the arrangements for our trip? No? Well, I did. Vice-Manager Zhou, the greedy scoundrel, and Unit Secretary Du, that piss-vinegar, could be convinced to grant Lao Dao, Lilian and Beiyuen four weeks' leave of absence, without pay, to visit relatives and long-time friends in Sichuan. My good friend Dong, the senior engineer of the Dalian Design Institute, paid off a long-standing debt from the time he was in Holland as a member of the investigation delegation and borrowed some money he couldn't repay of course. He put pressure on his brother-in-law, the city Party secretary, Xian Hexia, to grant all five of you a travel permit for four weeks, by air, to Chengdu and by road to Luding and back of course.

'I'll need a passport picture of each of you, next week. Lilian, I'll put you in charge of that. Hand them to me next Thursday and I'll bring them personally to Dong. I have booked the flight and paid for the plane tickets already. We'll travel on the Monday five weeks from now. Through the CCPIT office in Chengdu I have arranged for a Toyota Hi-Ace bus, with driver, to bring us to Luding. I can keep the little bus for four days, so two days after our arrival in Luding I'll return to Chengdu and then by plane to Guangzhou and Hong Kong. While in Chengdu I'll book the flight back to Dalian and buy the tickets, for the six of us, for I have planned to spend the last five days of your stay with you in Luding, if that's all right with you, of course.

'Suping, please write to your parents and give them the dates. Ask them to book three rooms in a suitable guest house in Luding, for me three nights and for Lao Dao, Beiyuen and Meiling in principle for the whole stay, unless your parents can make other arrangements for them later. In any case they should book three nights for the four of us. Also, the first two days, we shall leave you and Lilian alone with your parents and your Uncle Dan. You'll need that time to get reacquainted and accustom yourself again to the old folks and their ways; we, the four strangers, would make them and you uncomfortable and awkward.

'So I presume that at the end of the afternoon of the second day you'll come and fetch us to introduce us to your parents and Chen Dan. I'll give you money to buy whatever you need for a simple dinner for the nine of us. Perhaps there's a restaurant in Luding that is willing to deliver a few dishes at your parents' home, that'll save you time. You work that out over there. Give the old people a say though, don't railroad them with your big-city manners. Don't forget that you intrude in *their* lives and that *you* must adapt, first and foremost in the beginning. With time they'll relax and become less rigid and let you have things your way, so be patient if you think they're slow or stubborn. You hear me, Lilian? Not every older person is like your Auntie Liu here.'

Laughing he bowed in Auntie's direction who, mockingly, acknowledged the compliment with a nod.

'One last thing while on the subject,' Lao Dee continued. 'Suping, please write down your and Meiling's sizes for clothes and shoes. I'll ask my wife to buy something suitable for both of you to wear during the trip and for Sichuan's climate. I'm sure it'll be cheaper and more fashionable in Hong Kong than here in Dalian, judging by those horrible, red, velvety dresses that seem to pass here for chic. I hope you didn't have those horrors in mind for you to show up in in Luding?'

Suping and Auntie Liu burst out laughing at Lao Dee's expression of disgust.

'It's only here in Dalian that you see those shiny red, velvety dresses and always worn too long,' Auntie said, Chuckling, 'don't ask me why. You'll never see such bad taste in Shanghai and probably never in other big cities. If your wife could buy me a few white, cotton blouses and black, ample trousers with comfortable, open, flat heeled shoes to match that would be wonderful and more than sufficient.

'Suping will have other desires, I'm sure, but that's only normal and none of my business, although I would advise one really nice dress to wear the first day. And the same goes for Lilian. You can change in my room in the guest house, before the driver brings you two to your parents' house. So I suggest you tell them in your letter to wait for you at home so that you can freshen up first, in my room, after the long flight and bus trip. Both of you must be at your very best when you see them after such a long time, and Lilian for the first time to boot.

'But it's still five weeks away so we'll have plenty of time to talk about all that. What I would like to say though, and I'm sure I speak for all of us Chinese here, that we'll always be in your debt, Lao Dee. None of us will ever be able to pay you back for what you are doing for us. It is because I now think I know what kind of person you are that makes it so easy to continue to accept the things you do for us, remarkably and nigh shamelessly easy. We could *never* accept such favours from a Chinese, impossible. But then, of course, a Chinese wouldn't dream of extending such favours. Doing favours without the prospect of at least an equal return on investment? Ridiculous!

'You once said that our friendship and hospitality and trust by telling you our life stories is a more than adequate return on your investment in us. I sometimes wonder whether it will turn out to have been really worth it. But that's for you to decide, of course, and even you won't know that for another year or two or even three. It'll take that much time, perhaps more, to put it all together in a readable way and especially to connect the different stories between them. Be that as it may we can already help you to cut costs by having a simple dinner here, in my house, during a short intermezzo in the ongoing story.

'I saw what you paid in that restaurant tonight. It gives me the shivers, so much money! No amount of food for one meal, no kind of food, however delicious and artistically prepared, is worth that kind of money. So the coming Thursdays we women will prepare the food. A simple dinner of soup, vegetables and one main dish is more than enough. Don't think, Lao Dee, that I didn't appreciate the food tonight, or last time delivered by Mu Ping here; on the contrary it was delicious and we are all grateful for the treat. However, twice is enough and now it's time again for simpler fare. It's healthier and also cheaper, so no more invitations to restaurants.'

Auntie Liu fell silent and the others nodded in agreement. Lao Dee smiled and said, 'No more talk about favours, either. It's all part of our deal and the friendship and cosiness I find with you is an additional bonus that's invaluable in itself, so stop feeling grateful and guilty. As for the price of the dinner tonight, don't make too much of it. As you know, cooking is my hobby, unusual dishes that is, and Mu Ping taught me quite a few exceptional recipes and some very clever kitchen tricks that I won't find in any cookbook. That in itself is worth a lot of money. If you saw the prices certain hotels dare to ask for a series of cooking lessons by one of their cooks you would really get the shivers. And not to mention the prices those hotels charge in their chic restaurants, they would take your breath away and that for portions so small that after dinner you are still hungry. So compared to that tonight's price was very, very modest.

'Besides I had a deal with Mu Ping. I don't pay him for his lessons, I just pay for the ingredients but every now and then I have to throw a party in his restaurant and allow him to steal the show. That's what he likes. Like every great artist Mu Ping is a prima donna and thrives on praise and flattery. Tonight was a good show from his point of view and we were the perfect audience. So I think it was a small price to pay to make him shine and happy and I also think it was worth it. Enough about all that! What about giving the floor to our friend Lao Dao now? Give me two minutes to install my tape recorder.'

The others had relaxed visibly during Lao Dee's easygoing explanation and they now exclaimed for Lao Dao to begin.

'I wouldn't mind a mug of your jasmine tea before I begin, Beiyuen,' the old man said.

Pensively he watched her pouring the tea for him and the others as they settled themselves comfortably.

Beiyuen poured the remnants of the tea into the big thermos, filled it up with hot water and put the thermos on the low table.

'Refill yourselves your mug whenever you like,' she said, 'it won't disturb Lao Dao, I'm sure.'

The old man smiled as he took his mug and clasped his bony, veined hands around it.

With a sigh of pleasure he leaned back in his comfortable chair and said, 'It is often that an idea is born over a cup of tea or a glass of wine and so it was with this idea of my friend Lao Dee to have me tell my life story. I still remember the night, early morning rather, when that happened, as if it were yesterday.

'Vice-manager Zhou had thrown a dinner party that evening to thank Lao Dee and his men for saving the hotel's reputation as well as his own and mine, of course. The steam boiler had broken down and naturally, as Murphy would have said, this happened at the worst possible moment. A blizzard had been raging for hours leaving Dalian under one metre of snow and the temperature outside had dropped to minus twenty-eight. Guests came back to the hotel during the day, often by foot as taxis and buses and the tram didn't run any more, struggling and stumbling backwards against the ice-cold wind, only to find the hotel cold and without hot water.

'There was almost a riot going on in the lobby when Lao Dee and his men entered, stamping the snow from their boots. Vice-Manager Zhou, harassed and surrounded by protesting guests, rushed to meet Lao Dee, shouting, "Please help me, Mister Dee, please help me." He had called me in his office to explain the situation and I had followed him into the lobby when the guests, shouting angrily, began to gather to protest and demand he restore the central heating and the hot water. He now gestured impatiently for me to come forward and explain to the Dutchman what had happened.

'I told him that the automatic burner of the steam boiler did start the firing-up cycles but shut down a few seconds later without firing up. I had tried so many times that now the flue was inundated with oil and I was afraid it would explode if the burner would eventually work again, so I had stopped trying and was at a loss what to do. Lao Dee had listened without comment and when I had finished he just said, "Let's have a look. Lead the way please!"

'His men followed us to the boiler room and within five minutes they had found the cause of the malfunctioning: a printed circuit in the boiler's control box didn't work properly and gave the wrong signal to the burner. Lao Dee keeps a box full of printed circuits in his room for all the automatic equipment he and his men are installing. Once those machines are installed and tested, they remove the printed circuits to be sure that the Chinese workers don't start the machines out of curiosity or to sabotage them as it seems happens all too often. Lao Dee told me that later when we had already become good friends.

'He now asked his electrical engineer to fetch the box and within minutes they had found a circuit that could do the job temporarily. Two of his men had in the meantime cleaned the flue and when he told me to start the burner again it worked beautifully.

'An hour later the central heating was working again and the hot water tank was again at its correct temperature. Everybody was happy again. Lao Dee then ordered by fax two original circuits from the boiler manufacturer's agent in Hong Kong to be sent by special courier to him personally as if they were spares he needed for his own equipment. Two days later he gave them to me and I installed one and now keep the second one as a spare.

'If Vice-Manager Zhou had to order the parts he would have to go through the Bureau of Light Industry and the Foreign Trade Import and Export Corporation, who would then apply with the Bank of China to spend the foreign currency. That already would have taken a year or more. Then there is a big chance that the parcel with the prints would get lost in either one of the ten or so offices it has to go through, for verification and stamping of the documents. If and when the hotel is finally notified that the parts can be picked up at some office or other fifteen to eighteen months have passed. Can you imagine? How can things work that way in our country?

'Lao Dee understands the dilemmas we Chinese face in ordering parts from abroad. The bureaucrats understand nothing about machinery. For them machines have the eternal life and maintenance and spare parts are nothing but a waste of money and a clever trick by the engineers to give themselves an air of importance. And bureaucrats hate that, they hate other people being important. You can't change bureaucracy, Lao Dee once said on a different occasion when he had encountered problems in getting a shipment of spares only through customs. Bureaucrats hate change and they hate nothing more that so-called *innovative* change which is said to produce better results than the old routines. It would make them look inept, wouldn't it, and who enjoys appearing inept?

'Be that as it may, Lao Dee refused to be paid for the two printed circuits. It was the first time I heard him say that something was a small matter. I wasn't familiar with the expression and certainly not with the way he said it, so I asked him about it. He laughed and told me his secretary in Singapore used to say it when he thanked her for some special effort or other. However, she said it in Fujianese and he had translated it literally in standard Chinese knowing as he does that Fujianese is a difficult dialect very few people outside Fujian

Province understand. So Vice-Manager Zhou gave a dinner in the hotel's Chinese restaurant for him and his men. I had a few *maotais* too many since Zhou kept on egging me on to have a *maotai, ganbei*, with each of them.

'After dinner Lao Dee accompanied me to my little office where we had a few small cups of strong, bitter Chiu-Chao tea to clear the foggy brains. We talked some and it was all so cosy and quiet and then, without actually intending to, I told him about my background and how I had gotten to the hotel in the last post of my wasted life. It was four o'clock in the morning when Lao Dee left to catch a few hours' sleep. It was a Sunday and his usual day off so it didn't matter so much I guess. A few nights later he came to see me again and asked me to give serious thought to his request to one day tell him the whole story of my life, in a coherent manner and from the beginning, were it only, he said, to unburden myself and perhaps, in the process of telling and re-evaluating, to rid myself of the nefarious idea that my life had been wasted. He, on the other hand, would gain an insight in that particular period in China's history that interested him so much.

'He said that the best way for ordinary people, like himself, to understand a certain period of the history of a country or a people was *not* to read scientific, historical works about it but to read or hear tell a few stories of everyday life by people who had lived during that particular period. People can identify with people, he said, not with theories and generalities. Those do not touch them, he said, but the fortunes and misfortunes and suffering of people like them do.

'Lao Dee is probably right and perhaps, just perhaps, I can gain something for myself as well, as he said I might, by telling you my story and afterwards hearing your opinion about a few episodes and the things I did then. Whether I was right or wrong, whether I had an alternative when I thought I had none, whether I acted naively or plain stupidly and most importantly, whether the balance is as negative as I now still think it is.

'Since the night Lao Dee made his request I have given a lot of thought to the matter, actually there hasn't been a day that I did *not* think about it, so now that I sit here and see you all waiting for me to finally start, I should at least be able to tell a *coherent* story though perhaps not such an interesting one as you seem to anticipate. As I have structured it in my mind though I won't be able to finish it tonight or even in two nights. So I propose that we don't make it too late, say not later than midnight so that we can all still be rested tomorrow. It doesn't really matter, does it, if the third evening it takes three or four hours for me to finish, that is, if you agree to my proposal, of course.'

Lao Dao fell silent and so as not to disturb his train of thought the others merely nodded their assent.

They looked on in silence as Beiyuen carefully refilled the mug he still held between his hands.

With a smile he acknowledged her caring gesture and, after a few small sips of the fresh tea, began the story of his extraordinary life.

## *Chapter Twenty-Four*

### Betrayal

I was born in 1924, in Shanghai, the first and only child of Dao Zemin and Guan Shaoxia; they gave me the name Huimin.

My father worked for Jameson, a big Hong Kong trading company, a so-called hong, in a high and very confidential position. He enjoyed many privileges and our small family lived a life that couldn't have been further removed from that of the masses had we been living on a different planet.

My father even became a Christian, a Presbyterian, to curry favour with the English bosses and their families, I presume. My mother remained a Buddhist though and she prayed daily, in front of the small altar in our dining room, to the Buddha.

Father had brought back the beautiful, two foot high and heavily gold-plated statue from a trip to Thailand. Mother was very proud of *our* Lord Buddha, as she always referred to Him, and had had Him installed in a specially constructed niche in a corner of our dining room facing east.

There He sat, high above our heads even when my tall father was standing straight, smiling ever so slightly and remotely and ever so enigmatically as the Mona Lisa. The Lord, and she for that matter, must have known something we still don't today.

Be that as it may, Mother prayed to our Lord Buddha several times a day and kept fussing around His altar, lighting a fresh candle, snuffing a nearly finished, crooked one, replacing wilted flowers with freshly picked ones or the day-old oranges with newly polished ones.

That and praying to the whole panoply of lesser Taoist deities kept her busy and our family covered against all forms of bad Chinese luck while Father paid homage, once a week on Sundays, to his Christian God, to make sure we had His protection against evils of foreign origin.

I was brought up to show equal respect to both Mother's and Father's Protectors and six days a week I lit my own candle and joss stick on the Lord Buddha's altar while on Sunday I accompanied Father to church to kneel and pray to his God.

My parents didn't forget my worldly education though and they spared neither money nor effort to make it the best available in Shanghai at that time. Because of my father's position I was allowed to attend the school for the children of high Chinese employees of British companies in the English Concession while three times a week, after school hours, private European teachers came to our house to give me extra lessons in mathematics and physics and English.

My teacher of English was a young man from Cambridge, in England, who had been recruited for a six-year teaching stint in Shanghai at a school for the children of English employees of British, Australian and American companies. He was a very personable and likeable young man of impeccable antecedents of course and his lessons were more like storytelling and debating sessions than rote learning of spelling and grammar.

My parents were very understanding and enlightened for Chinese of that time and they were delighted by the budding friendship between the young foreigner and their only son who was only six years his cadet.

Michael Haythorntwaite, for that was my friend and teacher's unpronounceable name, went back to England in 1939, just before the outbreak of the Second World War. I didn't hear from him until after the war, late 1945 it was, although much later, when I asked why he had never replied to my letters, he maintained to have written several letters and had been equally disappointed by my lack of response as I had apparently been by his.

Be that as it may, in his letter of late 1945 he wrote that he had been demobilised, having been a captain of infantry, in Singapore, after the war and was now back in England, in Manchester, where he had got a job as a lecturer at the technical university. He said that he would like to sponsor me to sit for the entrance examination of the faculty of mechanical engineering and would I be interested?

I wrote back that I was delighted that contact between us had been re-established and that I was grateful for his offer to sponsor me which, however, I regretfully had to decline since my mother and I had no money to pay for my trip and stay in England.

I explained that my father had been arrested by the Japanese in 1941, and that we had never heard from him again. My father's former employers had just moved back into their offices, I told Michael, and my mother had received a letter that very morning to inform her that she was eligible for a small widow's pension since they assumed that my father had died at the hands of the Japanese.

With inflation and all that, the amount was just enough to pay for her daily upkeep and not for mine let alone that she could afford to pay me a ticket to England and subsequently my tuition and upkeep in England.

A few months later a second letter arrived, addressed to both my mother and me.

In it Michael wrote that he had enquired at Jameson's London office and that he had been told that the company would be willing to buy off my mother's pension rights with a lump sum payment. He urged my mother to submit an official request to the company's office in Shanghai and to use part of the money to buy a ticket, by steamer, to England for herself and for me.

The remainder of the money would last longer and buy more there than in post-war China, Michael said, what with the civil war still going on with the inevitable Communist takeover.

He said that we could stay with him and his parents until such time that we would have found a place for ourselves and a job for my mother. I could easily find a part-time job, Michael said, to help pay for my studies.

My mother wasted no time and the following day she went to Jameson's offices to submit her written request to be paid a lump sum in lieu of her widow's pension rights.

Ten days later we got the reply that her request had been granted and that the amount of forty-five thousand pounds sterling would be paid according to her instructions.

We went to see the financial manager of the company and told him about our plans. He suggested we take five thousand pounds in cash to pay for our tickets and first expenses in England and that the remaining forty thousand pounds be remitted into the account she would have to open with a bank in Manchester shortly after our arrival there. We followed the kindly man's advice and arrived in England on 15th April, 1946.

Michael was there, in Southampton, to welcome us.

We moved in with him and his parents and stayed with them for two months. We had a wonderful time together, they were such loveable people.

In June 1946 my mother got a job as an interpreter with a textile company that did a lot of business with the Far East; she would be responsible for the correspondence, by hand and in Chinese, with the many, small, family-owned Chinese companies over there and for the translations.

The pay was good and we could afford to rent an apartment in a middle-class neighbourhood.

At about the same time I got a job for the summer as a waiter in a Chinese restaurant. My mother allowed me to keep all the money which I put in my own bank account, for later, to pay for my studies.

Michael and a few of his friends, also lecturers, steamrollered me through several correspondence courses and a daytime summer course; in the evening I worked as a waiter in the restaurant.

In September I sat for the entrance examination and passed with flying colours.

The Haythorntwaites stayed our best friends and during my years in Manchester we visited each other twice monthly, to talk, play bridge and mahjong and to enjoy each other's food, always simple dishes but always prepared with love.

Mother was successful in her job and her company did well, thanks to her, and in 1952 she married the junior partner in the company, a Chinese from Taiwan who had come to England after his small company had been taken over by Mother's company and he had been made a director on her advice. He was originally from Amoy and had fled to Taiwan after the Communists defeated the Nationalists and seized power on the mainland.

A year to the day after Mother's wedding I graduated, with honours, in mechanical and chemical engineering and on the very day of my graduation I was offered a job with Lever Brothers, a big, international company in the detergent and foodstuff business. I gladly accepted the offer and the future seemed mine, I was on top of the world.

How different it all worked out!

During my student years I had keenly followed the developments in China and had become a sympathiser with the Communist cause. My defence of the Communists during the debating sessions of the student society had not gone unnoticed and I was offered a membership card of the English Communist Party, which I refused, much to Michael's chagrin. Michael was a card-carrying member of the Communist Party and a very active one at that.

Two days after my graduation, while at home packing my suitcase in preparation for my move to London, for my new job, Michael came to see me.

He was accompanied by three Chinese, one of whom I recognised as Sha Jiwen, a counsellor at the embassy of the People's Republic of China in Sweden.

Sha had attended a few times our debating sessions at the university as Michael's guest and, on each occasion, had complimented me on my political vision and acumen. Sha now introduced the other two Chinese as comrades

Lai and Peng from Beijing on a trip through Western Europe and on their way to the United States of America.

I invited them in and offered them a glass of tea, English tea of course, which they politely accepted but did not even once sip from.

To cut a long story short, Lai and Peng were on a recruiting mission to Europe and the US to try and persuade university-trained Chinese to return to China 'to help build the motherland' as they put it, 'the sacred duty of every true Chinese, regardless where or when he or she was born,' they added.

Sha Jiwen had put them on to me and, with Michael's help, they had little trouble convincing me that my future was in China and not in the decadent capitalist West.

My contribution to rebuilding a strong and prosperous China by helping the Communist Party to educate and lead the formerly downtrodden masses and modernise the industry would be invaluable, they assured me. It would earn me the personal appreciation of Mao Zedong and the eternal gratitude of the Chinese people.

They strongly urged me *not* to go and see my mother before my departure for China since she was completely under the influence of her husband, an arch-enemy, a member of the traitorous Guomindang who had fled to Taiwan, who would rather kill me than let me serve the motherland. To that Michael added that there was no need for me to inform Lever Brothers that after all I would not come to work for them since they only thought of exploiting me anyhow.

And so I left, without a word, either to my mother, who loved me and had always given her very best for me, or to the people at Lever Brothers who had trusted me enough to offer me a chance to earn a good living.

But then, I was a good Communist, was I not? And love for an individual, even for a parent, and respect for your employer were merely petty bourgeois sentiments unworthy of a true Communist, were they not?

Sha Jiwen came back to see me the following morning to tell me that he would accompany me to Copenhagen where I was to board a Chinese freighter with destination Shanghai.

I thought it was nice of him to keep me company. Later I understood that he was to keep an eye on me and that he would probably have killed me had I changed my mind at the last moment.

We went by train to Hull and took the ferry to Hook of Holland, where we arrived the next morning. Sha knew his way around and after changing trains in Rotterdam and Amsterdam we arrived in Copenhagen that same evening, in time for me to board a rusty old freighter called *Ningbo* ready to sail for Shanghai.

During the whole two-month long trip neither the officers nor the crew ever spoke to me. Only the ship's political officer, or commissar, came to see me from time to time but not for my company and some friendly talk. No, he just warned me sternly and tersely not to try and engage the crew members in a discussion about life in England or the reason of my presence on board.

The ship had one bunk for every three crew members and we were allowed to sleep two four-hour periods every twenty-four hours. During the two eight-hour periods I had to work in the boiler room, as a coal passer.

The ship docked twice to take in coal, once in Luanda, in Africa, and once in Colombo, on Ceylon, an island off the Indian continent that is now called Sri Lanka.

None of the crew, not even the officers, were allowed off the ship and I noticed that the commissar carried a handgun in a holster during the whole time we spent in port and that during the time a port official came on board, with documents to sign and to collect payment for the coal I presume, he did not budge from the captain's side.

The evening before docking the commissar always held a meeting where everybody had to be present, regardless of rank or duty. The meetings were very brief and no questions were allowed. The commissar merely told us that we would enter for a few hours enemy territory and that it was his duty to defend ship and crew against being overrun by the starving, exploited natives who would rush *en masse* to the port when the rumour spread, in town and hinterland, that a ship from the glorious People's Republic of China would dock.

The most desperate might even try to climb on board to escape the hell they were living in, to achieve their dream of living in the workers' paradise that was China.

'Unfortunately, and for their own future benefit, though they may not understand that now, we Chinese leaders cannot allow that because we need those masses later when secret units of the Chinese Communist Party will lead them to rise against their exploiters and overthrow the capitalist puppet regimes of their country.'

I stood next to the tall boiler operator, the one who I had once overheard referring to me as the biggest, naivest arsehole on the face of our planet, a living disgrace to all decent common-sense Chinese, and I heard him snicker disdainfully as the commissar spoke those words.

How right he was, that operator, about what he called me. Until today I cannot understand that those nine weeks I spend on board that typically average Chinese ship did not open my eyes to the harsh reality of the loveless society I was heading for.

Thinking of it again, now, I still think it was self-delusion pure and simple.

I must somehow have persuaded myself that my surly shipmates were of the sort of people Sha Jiwen had referred to as the formerly downtrodden who needed my teaching and leadership and that their distrust and open dislike of me was only because they had been abused and exploited their whole life and couldn't believe their good fortune now that the Communists ruled China and that young, educated men and women like me were going to lead them into a new kind of society based on comradeship, solidarity, equality and shared ideals under the overall and benevolent leadership of the Communist Party.

Full of enthusiasm I disembarked in Shanghai on 10th October, 1953. The commissar accompanied me to the port's Party secretary's office.

In a few, terse words he explained to the shabbily dressed, unkempt person behind the rickety, cluttered desk who I was and why I was there. Then he left, without a word or even a glance at me.

For almost six hours I sat in that dingy, shabby office. Nobody paid me the slightest attention, let alone offered me a mug of tea or a cigarette.

Nobody made even the slightest pretence of working. People, men and women alike, in drab, filthy and baggy dull dark blue or olive green trousers and jackets sauntered in and out of the office, aimlessly.

Others merely hung about on ungainly, old wooden chairs behind graceless, old wooden tables or desks cluttered with piles of shoddy, yellowing notebooks and wrinkly, overused pieces of bluish carbon paper, glasses with remnants of greenish tea and leaves, chipped and cracked saucers serving as ashtrays overflowing with cigarette butts, dirty bowls and chopsticks, filthy and torn hand towels and what have you.

Some of them made an occasional, desultory remark to nobody in particular and apparently without expecting a reply, again others just slept with their head on their arms on top of a pile of papers. The floor was dirty and dusty and tarnished by dried globs of spit and snot.

For the first time since I had left England I felt a tinge of alarm at what I had got myself into.

Finally, at about four o'clock in the afternoon of my first day in the People's Republic of China, two elderly men, indistinguishable in their drab clothes from each other and, for that matter, from everybody else in that dreary place, came into the office and loudly called my name, not Comrade Dao Huimin, not Mister Dao Huimin, just Dao.

Nobody in the office paid them the slightest attention or woke up or stood up or did whatever one can expect when two people enter a room and suddenly start shouting a name.

So I stood up and said that I was the person called Dao. The oldest of the two men merely motioned me to follow him and his colleague outside.

For half an hour I walked in silence behind them along the deserted quays.

A light drizzling rain driven by gusts of wind soaked my Western suit and I shivered, both from the chilly, cold dampness and from the general air of decay and gloomy, chilling miserableness that soaked into my mind.

Finally the two men halted in front of a gate in a barbed wire fence that surrounded a plot of land on the bank of the Huangpu River. An old, derelict, brick one-storey building stood in the middle of that plot of land. Many of its small, square windows had no panes or only shards of broken glass left, the ones still whole were grimy with dust and soot from the smoke of passing ships and tugboats.

The younger of the two men shook and kicked the gate and cursed when no one turned up.

This went on for nearly fifteen minutes when, finally, the door of the building opened and a man in navy blue trousers and army green jacket came out, jogging because of the rain, to open the gate. He merely shrugged his shoulders, blatantly indifferent to their furious questioning why it had taken him so long.

Once inside, the oldest of my escorts wrote my name and a date, of my arrival apparently, on a blackboard on the wall. With ominous foreboding I saw there were about two dozen other names on the board with dates as far back as six months.

Some of the names had been crossed out. My heart sank when I saw that the last crossed name was dated 15th May.

The young man, apparently a guard of some sorts, looked me over then told me, in a bored though not unfriendly voice, to follow him into what was clearly a storeroom. Against the back wall were open shelves filled with clothes, all blue and green, underwear and green, canvas shoes, pell-mell, without any sense of order or system.

The guard told me to take off my soaking wet clothes and flimsy English shoes and to choose from the shelves whatever fitted me.

With the first flicker of common sense since my temporary insanity in Manchester I chose two pairs of woollen socks, two long, woollen underpants of an horrendous red colour, two woollen undershirts, a dark green army pullover, a dark blue cotton jacket and olive green army trousers. A pair of green canvas shoes completed the outfit and I felt warm but ridiculous with the red legs of my underpants showing from under my trousers.

The guard laughed uproariously at my apparent embarrassment, then, probably taking pity, he told me to pull my socks over the legs of the underpants to hide them from view.

Then, kicking my wet clothes and shoes unceremoniously in a corner, he gestured for me to follow him again through another door into a makeshift dormitory where he assigned a cot and a small, rusty metal locker to me.

Then he left, slamming the door behind him, without another word.

There I stood, awkwardly fumbling with my hands in my pockets to keep my trousers from sagging, uncomfortably staring back at an assortment of twenty something pairs of curious, angry, sullen and mocking eyes.

'Good day,' I said, 'how are you. My name is Dao, Dao Huimin. I am an engineer, from Manchester, England and I—'

'*Was recruited by two elderly comrades from Beijing to help rebuild the motherland!*' my audience shouted back, completing my sentence for me.

'Welcome to our precious motherland, Dao Huimin,' the man stretched out on the cot next to mine said mockingly. 'This place here is *not* some kind of purgatory to expiate your capitalist sins before you are allowed into the workers' paradise' as you may be led to believe. No, my fellow sucker, this is only one of the many waiting rooms, not only here in Shanghai but in the other ports of entry into the motherland as well, where the lesser comrades, who hate you for everything you are here for, suck you dry of all your dreams and idealism until they have broken you and you have become like them: lazy, filthy, uncaring, unloving, sullen: a moron amongst the morons.

'Then, when you are no longer deemed a potential danger to their bloody system of oppression and repression, they'll let you join the faceless masses of non-persons, for ever branded an enemy of the proletariat merely because of your upbringing, education and relatives abroad.'

He grinned sardonically at the others' applause.

'Name is Tan,' he continued, 'Tan Kong Teck, from Jakarta, in newly independent Indonesia, where 120 million skulking natives have transferred their hatred for their former colonial masters, the Dutch, to the local Chinese community. I was recruited by the two elderly comrades from Beijing to become the future chief cardiologist at the People's Hospital Number Six in Beijing. Can't say I haven't been warned. An acupuncturist from Nanjing, on loan to Indonesia's megalomaniac women chaser number one Sukarno from his buddy Mao Zedong, warned me, no *adjured* me, *not* to believe the Pied Pipers from Beijing. He said he was going to shoot himself rather than return to Beijing once his little needles lost their magic on Sukarno's main obsession of how to get his dick to rise to the occasion seven times a day.

'I laughed at him, kissed my father, mother, brothers and sisters, who had apparently used up the complete family stock of common sense leaving me, the youngest, with nothing of the precious stuff, and boarded a floating rust hulk in Tanjung Priok, bound for Shanghai. I bet the crew on your ship never talked to you either, Dao? Everybody present here, regardless where he comes from, went through the same ordeal.

'From the moment you are escorted on board by an initially friendly, even jovial counsellor of the Chinese legation, but who becomes increasingly taciturn to the point of gruffness the nearer you come to the ship, you are a non-person with a contagious disease called "free spirit". Only the political officer of the ship is allowed to talk to you. The ship's crew, ordinary seaman or officer alike, risk their job, ever their life, if they do. Have you been warned, Dao? In England? Or are you merely a victim of your naivety?'

'I was told not to contact my mother and stepfather before my departure,' I replied. 'The man from the embassy said they wouldn't understand my idealism to help my people and my motherland and would probably make a scene to keep me in England to be exploited for the rest of my life. Once in China I could write to them regularly, the man said, and keep them informed about my accomplishments in helping to make China strong and prosperous.'

I fell silent, embarrassed by my naivety and stupidity.

Tan looked pityingly at me and said, 'You can write as many letters as you wish, Dao. They will even encourage you to do so. But none of them will ever reach your relatives. You could be dead for all they'll ever know. But here the secret police will read your letters and compile a file on you that will still be used against you fifty years hence. So take my advice, Dao. Don't write! When they ask you why you don't write any letters tell them you have never been on good terms with your mother since she married your stepfather and that you will write to her once you're settled just to let her know that you're alive and well.

'Just fill in the forms they'll give you, tomorrow or next week or next month and fill them in truthfully. After that they'll need about three or four months to screen you and to determine what to do with you. Stay calm, Dao. Don't throw a tantrum. From time to time ask our guard politely whether there is any progress in your case. His job is to report everything you say or do, even, I think, if and when you fart, so give him something to report from time to time and he'll be nicer to you and won't invent things you said just to cover his own arse.'

Tan fell silent and smiled ruefully.

'I am well placed to give you advice, Dao, as I learned the hard way. I have blown my chance ever to get out of here. Six months I have been here now. In the first couple of weeks I yelled and screamed and shouted abuse at him and the whole rotten system. I'm pretty sure they have classified me by now as an incorrigible anti-Communist. I suppose the reason why they let me live and keep me here is that somehow they think I can still serve a purpose, probably to see whether my anti-propaganda has any influence on the others who pass through here.

'But one day, tomorrow or a year from now, I'll have outlived my usefulness and they'll come and fetch me before dawn and drown me in that filthy, stinking river nearby. "Drowned while attempting to escape" will be the official verdict and that will be the end of Tan Kong Teck, the brilliant cardiologist with the great future.'

The lurking despair in his eyes belied his mocking tone and my own eyes stung with tears.

I felt awkward as I thanked him for his advice but he wasn't listening. He had let himself fall back again on his cot and was lying there, hands clasped behind his head, staring up at the rafters and breathing slowly and deeply to control his raging emotions.

I shall be brief about the time I stayed in that ante-room to the People's republic.

There was nothing to do, nothing to occupy the mind with, no books or magazines or newspapers, no radio, nothing but one's own increasingly morbid thoughts as an irresistible, overwhelming boredom spread, like a malignant cancer, through every cell of one's body.

But for Tan I would have slid from self-pity to despair to a state of forlorn, hopeless apathy and into death itself.

As it was, each time I had slipped into near catalepsy he kicked me out of it, often quite literally, slapping my face and forcing some of the tasteless gruel that was our sole food twice a day into my mouth while pinching my nose to let the involuntary body reflexes take over.

Sometimes I saw two faces, sometimes three, staring down on me as I heavingly struggled for breath and panic drove me momentarily back to an awareness of my surroundings. This went on for two weeks, Tan told me later, and he and my two other cot neighbours had sometimes been close to giving up on me and let me die.

What had saved me, Tan sneered, was not so much their altruism as their selfishness as they realised that keeping themselves busy with me and my tantrums shook them out of their own moroseness and led to interesting discussions and debate.

When, finally, I came to and, with Tan's help, managed to stay conscious, I was utterly exhausted but, in some strange way, I felt at peace with myself and resigned to my fate.

Tan introduced the two men who had helped him in pinning me down as he forced the gruel into my mouth and pinched my nose as one Lam Nan from Kuala Lumpur, professor of economics, and one Lim Chee Meng from Sydney, Australia, ophthalmologist. Lam had his cot to my left, Tan to my right and Lim was Tan's right-hand neighbour.

They drew me into their ongoing and never-ending discussions and gradually I became more or less my former self again. Our discussions and chit-chat were in English since Lim only spoke rudimentary Hokkien, which nobody else understood. He was a second-generation Australian and spoke English with a strong Australian accent even with his parents who still spoke Hokkien between them, hence Lim's rudimentary knowledge.

Time passed and we had not the faintest inkling of what went on in the world outside our dormitory.

Our guard, always the same, was no source of information. He was not unfriendly though so we concluded that he was under orders not to speak to us other than what was absolutely necessary and then only what concerned our immediate duties or needs.

Twice a day, at eight in the morning and at six in the evening he wheeled a ten gallon bucket into the dormitory, put the barrow down, shouted 'food!' and left.

In the morning the bucket invariably contained rice gruel with a few, sparse pieces of boiled chicken, in the evening eight times out of ten the same while the other times there were two smaller buckets, one with steamed rice, one with stir-fried vegetables and pork meat.

For drinking there was tea, nothing else. A ten gallon bucket, with a ladle, stood next to the dormitory door, on the floor. When it was almost empty the guard took it outside, flushed the leaves and dregs out and wheeled it back inside, full. The tea was weak, green and bitter but at least it was hot, that is, the first twenty minutes or so for the winter months are cold and damp in Shanghai.

Since we were south of the Yangzi River, heating of buildings, schools, offices and homes was not allowed, a fate, I found out later, shared by all regions south of the Great River.

Every other Monday morning, an hour or so after breakfast the guard unlocked the door again and shouted 'laundry'. Two at a time we were allowed out and into the storeroom to receive clean underwear and socks in exchange for a dirty set.

They were our only distractions; food twice a day, tea, a few ambling strolls a day to the bucket and back, clean underwear twice a month.

The rest of the time we slept or talked or stared at the rafters.

Occasionally I sauntered over to the other cots to strike up a conversation, especially when newcomers had arrived with recent knowledge about the outside world.

Their despair, anger, perplexity and revolt at the situation were always the same though and after some time I no longer found it worth the trouble to let them first pour out all their emotions for the few snippets of news I could finally drag out of them.

So I stayed on my cot and listened, without comment, as Tan briefed the newcomers just as he had briefed me and Lam and Lim.

If after that they sought our company we made room for them and allowed them to listen in and eventually participate in our discussions, provided they stuck to the subject matter and didn't try to bring their own situation into it.

Few were able to abide by that rule, too preoccupied as they were with their own feelings, and they stayed away from us, marooned on their cot, sliding into the kind of despondency and apathy I had barely escaped from myself and not by my own strength of character.

One day I remarked that I felt sorry for them and had qualms about not helping them.

'For your own good and sanity let them,' Tan replied unemotionally. 'It drags you down and you'll risk your own sanity, again. I'm not so sure I would do it again for you either, Dao. I was almost as exhausted as you were when you finally came to your senses and so were Lam and Lim. It was worth it, in your case, since you are now an esteemed member of our debating club, but I wouldn't want to go through the same emotional roller coaster again. The thought alone already depresses me. But don't let me dissuade you from doing what your Christian morals tell you to. However, don't involve me and don't count on me for succour.'

So we kept to ourselves and even sunk as low as to make bets on when a newcomer would break and cry or fly off in a rage. Not very uplifting, I'm afraid.

Six, or perhaps seven weeks after my arrival the guard gave me a bunch of forms to fill in, which I did to the best of my knowledge and truthfully as Tan told me to. I handed the forms back to the guard the next morning.

The next two months or so passed without a word from the guard about my case.

Finally, on 20th February, 1954, the guard called me in his small office. 'This is the man Dao,' he said to an elderly woman, sixty something I guessed, and two somewhat younger men and at that he flopped down in his chair and began to pick his nose.

The woman introduced herself as Chen, unit Party secretary of the Maling Canning Factory, of Shanghai, and the two men respectively as Mu, the vice-manager, and Wang, the senior engineer.

Her manner was blunt, her voice emotionless, neither friendly nor hostile, and she didn't invite me to sit down. Thinking of Tan's advice not to do anything provocative I remained standing.

Chen continued in the same tone. 'You have been assigned to our famous brand factory as a vice-production engineer and your work starts tonight at ten o'clock. The factory operates in two shifts only, afternoon and night, to save electricity during the morning hours for city use. You work both shifts, seven days a week, one day off per month. The factory Party committee has agreed to my proposal to assign to you a room in the factory apartment building, with use of the communal toilets. For that you will pay a rent of two yuan per month. You will take your meals, three per day, in the factory canteen. The price is fixed, twenty fen per day, whether you take the meals or not. Medical care is provided free of charge in the factory clinic. Your pay will be twenty yuan per month gross, twelve net after deduction of rent and meal costs, with yearly increments of two yuan, provided the factory meets its output targets. Once a year you will receive new working clothes; the cost is one monthly salary, net.'

She fell silent and looked at me, indifferently.

She didn't ask if I had any questions so I thanked her and asked whether I could say goodbye to my friends. She said no, gruffly, stood up from her chair and without even a glance at the guard or at her two companions, she made for the door and left, taking for granted that we would follow and close the door.

I nodded my farewell to the guard who shrugged his shoulders with a disdainful snort. For me? For Chen? Probably for all of us and the whole world to boot.

At a trot I caught up with Chen, Mu and Wang.

Nobody spoke during the half-hour walk to the bus station nor during the near one-hour wait in the draughty, ramshackle shelter. Only during the one-hour ride to the bus stop in front of the factory, Wang, the engineer, remarked hesitantly that it was a cold day.

I was about to assent that I thought so too when I noticed the cold, murderous fury in Chen's eyes as she stared at the poor man.

Wang cringed, muttered some feeble excuse and withdrew in himself. Apparently even such an innocuous comment on the weather was considered to be an oblique doubt of the Party's ability to control all things under heaven.

I would have to watch every word, every facial expression, every gesture if I intended to stay out of trouble. Still, I was glad to be out of purgatory and whether it was heaven or hell waiting for me outside I would soon find out.

The first few days I was upbeat and even happy in my sparsely furnished room: a steel, single bed, a straight-backed wooden chair, a small table and a drawer chest were all the furniture I had been allowed to take from the factory storeroom but nevertheless it was *something*.

It didn't take more than three days though for me to realise that my job was an impossible one, that I was totally powerless and totally unable to make anything happen, whether workwise, organisation-wise, management-wise or otherwise.

The factory was completely politicised and workers and their leaders alike spent four to five hours every day in political awareness meetings, in the canteen, with the factory committee chaired by Comrade Chen, the unit Party secretary, after which it was time for the evening meal and the habitual nap.

By then it was past eight o'clock in the evening and impossible to get the dazed afternoon shift workers to do at least some work, they just slipped away and disappeared.

So I had to fire the boilers myself, start the air compressors, open the steam valves and a hundred and one other things to have the production machinery ready for the evening shift only to discover that many workers simply didn't turn up or were much too late, without any explanation or apology or even the willingness to make up for the lost time by working a bit harder.

Sheer madness, however, was the fact that the next day I was criticised, in front of all the workers, for failing to produce the full day's quota.

After three months of fighting this losing battle I asked for a dispensation to attend the last two hours of the daily meeting so that I could start the boilers earlier and have everything ready for production by eight o'clock and get at least two hours of work out of the afternoon shift.

My request was denied, however, by a furious Secretary Chen and I was given an official reprimand for my lack of political motivation.

I asked to see Vice-Manager Mu but when I explained the problem he told me that the political awareness of the workers of the Maling Canning Factory, achieved under the inspirational guidance of Secretary Chen, was the envy of every factory in the Shanghai region and that the factory counted several model workers and thus it was my fault and my fault alone if the output target couldn't be met.

In despair I went to see the senior engineer, Wang, in his cubicle but when I tried to explain my plan he became all agitated and in a shrill voice told me to get out.

Again nine months later, after one year in function and eighteen hours on the factory floor each and every day, I received an official letter from the Party secretary of Shanghai city wherein he accused me of sabotaging socialist production targets as it had been reported to him that the past year's output had fallen sixty per cent short of its target.

In his letter the secretary ordered me to confess freely and openly during my tender of self-criticism in front of the Party committee and the assembled workers of the factory.

By then I had gone through so many crazy things in that craziest of all crazy systems that I realised there was no escaping the ordeal, however, in a fit of defiance I decided not to cringe in abject self-criticism but, instead, to explain *why* production had fallen short, *why* the official targets were unrealistic under the best of circumstances and, while rejecting personal blame, to offer a plan to improve the situation.

So, on the date set for my public humiliation, I took the stage, erected for the occasion in the canteen, and the loud hailer to help my voice raise above the usual hubbub of the assembled chatting, shouting, sauntering, eating, smoking, belching, farting, in short, totally uninterested workers.

Addressing myself to the sullen Party committee and its visitor for the occasion, the Shanghai city Party secretary, in the first row of chairs and who, like me, tried to ignore the background racket, I began by admitting frankly that the production output had indeed fallen far short of the official target but, in the same breath, I rejected the blame for the shortfall.

Quickly, before they could have me dragged off the stage by the younger committee members, I went on and pointed out that not only was a whole shift lost because of the awareness meetings followed by the two hour meal and rest period but that also the official target itself was wholly unrealistic, even in the best of circumstances, since the old and badly maintained equipment was simply neither capable nor in a state to produce that much.

By then the younger committee members, the senior engineer Wang in the lead, were already pushing and shoving me off the stage, and under the cheers, jeers and applause of the workers I was dragged out of the canteen and into Chen's office.

There, during an emergency session led by the city secretary, I was convicted as a saboteur of socialist production and as a subverter of socialist political doctrine. I was put under immediate house arrest pending the full city committee's decision on my punishment.

One month I stayed confined to my room.

Twice a day a woman from the canteen personnel brought me my meals, congee in the morning and the usual evening meal of rice, chicken and some vegetables.

Once a day a security guard accompanied me to the communal toilets to slop out the bucket that had been placed in my room.

Once a week, on Monday morning, a woman came to collect my underwear for washing which she brought back the same evening. A security guard always stood in the door opening while the women went about their business inside and therefore nobody said a word.

From the sideways glances by the canteen girl I knew that she would have dearly liked to talk to me though, but alas, no such luck.

Once she came back after five minutes, out of breath from rushing up the stairs, alone, since the guard had been too lazy to accompany her up all the stairs for a second time when she told him, as if in panic, that she had forgotten a dirty mess tin in my room.

She told me that in a hasty, hushed voice, before adding, 'The women in the canteen and from the production department asked me to tell you that they wish you luck and all the best. We all think that you were right in what you said about the meetings and the machines and that Secretary Chen and Mu and Wang use you as a scapegoat. Now I have to go. Don't let on tomorrow that I talked to you. Farewell!' Suddenly she took my face between her hands and kissed me. A most unusual gesture in such a loveless society and I was deeply moved. I still am, I realise now.

Before I had recovered my astonishment she had left again and the last I heard of her was the click-clack of her slippers as she rushed down the stairs.

I never saw her again either for the next day they sent an elderly man with the food. Had the guard noticed that she didn't have a mess tin in her hand when she returned and had reported the incident?

Had Secretary Chen called the girl into her office and made her confess to having talked to me, a criminal, despite express orders not to?

Had the ugly, old and spiteful woman Chen decided that the pretty, young and spontaneous girl had been spiritually polluted by the forbidden contact with the Westernised oriental criminal and meted out some crazy punishment?

I would never know and I wept with rage and pity.

During those long and lonely days there were moments that I regretted the frustrations of the shop floor and the hullabaloo of the awareness meetings, at least I had felt *alive* then.

There were even moments that I questioned my own sanity when I had foolishly decided to defy the system.

Finally, after thirty days of bored moroseness, despair and anxiety, a guard came to fetch and escort me to Secretary Chen's office.

Flanked by Vice-Manager Mu and a snickering Wang, she told me that the higher echelon Party committee had decided on a, in her opinion much too light, punishment in that I had been dismissed dishonourably from my position in the Maling Canning Factory and transferred, with immediate effect, to the Snowflake Soap Factory in Meishan, a small town in Anhui Province, where I would occupy the lowly position of assistant steam boiler operator.

Wang laughed sneeringly when Chen said that.

'You have every reason to be grateful for our leaders' magnanimity,' Chen added, 'if I had had it my way you would have spent the next ten years of your miserable life in a labour camp for your arrogance and attempt to discredit my political awareness meetings in the factory. Rest assured, however, that I shall regularly enquire about your political attitude in that soap factory and should you dare to persist in your counter-revolutionary behaviour I shall spare no effort to expose you for what I have never doubted you are, a spy and saboteur sent by your rotten capitalist masters to sabotage our glorious proletarian revolution.

'I have already alerted the Party's disciplinary committee about your three chums from your time in the screening centre and about my suspicion that the fellow Tan is your leader and a mole and that his irreverent and impertinent remarks about our country are part of a plot to remain confined in the centre so that he can continue to make recruits amongst the new arrivals. A very clever plot by the capitalists and the Party has officially commended me for my revolutionary alertness and perspicacity, I am proud to say.

'In your case, Dao, recruitment and indoctrination by Tan were not necessary since you had already been recruited long before, first by that feudal dog, your mother, and then, for the finer details, by that traitor Lee Chok Tong from Taiwan, your so-called stepfather. A perfect brood nest for spies and saboteurs and thanks to my alertness they have been exposed and are now under constant surveillance by security agents from our embassy in Denmark. A person staying with them is a marked person, for ever denied entry into our country. As for your chum Tan Kong Teck he has been removed from the centre and is now awaiting trial in a prison in Beijing. So be warned, Dao, I know what you are and I have much influence. I have written to the Snowflake Soap Factory's Party secretary so that he makes no mistake.

'Here is a ticket for this afternoon's train to Hefei. In Hefei you take the bus for Meishan; you pay for the ticket first and claim the money afterwards from the factory. As soon as you arrive in Meishan you report to the town Party secretary and hand him this letter. You can go now!'

Still reeling from Chen's crazy, paranoid ravings I stumbled out of her office and went back to my room to pack my few belongings in the small cardboard suitcase I had bought a few months earlier to replace the one I had travelled with from England and which had been confiscated by the guard of the screening centre and probably ripped apart to look for secret papers.

I kept exhorting myself that Chen's crazy paranoia was an isolated case, tolerated by her leaders because of certain qualities she probably had, and that generally saner and more level-headed people were running the show.

I had the foreboding, however, that I would soon find out that that also was an illusion, like so many of my earlier expectations and hopes, and that the madness and callousness had already metastasised, like malignant tumours, to the vital organs and tissues of this alien society, alien even for me, a Chinese but brought up abroad and therefore spiritually polluted.

## *Chapter Twenty-Five*

### Exile

After a thirty-six hour journey, during which I had dozed intermittently amongst the dozing, sullen aliens, in train and bus, I finally arrived in Meishan on 1st April, 1955.

The fifth native I asked where I could find the local Party secretariat responded by pointing at a two-storey, dusty, small building just opposite the bus station where I had alighted.

Without a word or further ado she then continued on her way, the other four hadn't even acknowledged me when I addressed them. Charming folk in a charming town in a charming province. Misery, poverty and sullenness was all I had seen and met with so far.

The town's Party secretary proved no different.

A snarling 'Way?' was his only reaction to my introduction of myself so I shrugged my shoulders and handed him Chen's letter.

He ripped the envelope open with the inch-long nail of his right little finger and laboriously read and reread Chen's letter.

Finally he looked up at me from behind his ramshackle, cluttered little desk with glittering, eyelashless sliteyes and growled, gravely, 'Chen says you're a spy and a saboteur and a troublemaker, Dao. I don't give a shit about the spy and saboteur thing, there's nothing to spy about or to sabotage here in Meishan and certainly not at that soap factory, where you'll stay marooned for the remainder of your lousy life.

'What I *do* care about though is that troublemaker business. I have carved out quite a good life for myself here, Dao, as you will soon find out, and I know I'll never get any higher on the ladder. I haven't got the appearance and manners for that. I look and often act stupid, Dao, but I'm *not*, so I shall not let you make trouble here and endanger my position. At your first attempt I'll arrange an accident and let you escape with a few broken bones or ribs. If that's not enough to keep you in line I'll have you killed. Is that clear? I'll have none of that cloak-and-dagger intrigue business with trials and all those outsiders poking their noses in my affairs here in Meishan. Chen, that arrogant Shanghainese bitch, is fond of intrigues and one day she'll find out that one pulls the tiger's tail at one's own peril.

'That's not my style, Dao. Too involved, too dangerous. If there's an obstacle on my path I kick it aside or have it removed. If you are in my way, Dao, I'll have you removed. My wife's brother, a vain windbag if ever there was one, is your factory secretary so I have my eyes in the factory. And don't you dare make a fool of my dear brother-in-law. I don't want him to complain to his sister. Is this all very clear, Dao?'

I nodded, dumbfounded by the man's rough-and-ready outspokenness.

'I hope you *do* understand, Dao,' Secretary Peng Heping said, grinning, 'For your own sake. Now get out of here and report to that gasbag Yao, Director Yao to you of course.'

At that he took a toothpick and, eyes closed, concentrated on removing some bothersome remnant of chicken meat from between his rotten, brown, helter-skelter teeth.

I left his office, still dazed by Peng's totally unexpected personality and reception.

I was lucky, only the third person I accosted to ask for directions to the Snowflake Soap Factory bothered to answer, and nicely at that.

The young woman answered cheerfully that she lived near the factory so would I mind walking the rest of the way with her?

I didn't mind of course so we walked and chatted unpretentiously about the little, sundry commonplaces ordinary little people in trivial little towns all over the world chat about and before I realised she took my arm and said, with a friendly smile, 'Here you are, there's the gate. It was nice talking to you. Try to improve the quality of the soap. It ruins my hands and my clothes, not to speak of my hair. Bye now!' And with a friendly wave she continued on her way home.

A nice, friendly, normal, uncomplicated and unsuspicious person. The first I had come across actually, since my arrival in China now almost one and a half years ago.

Director Yao was walking up and down his small office when I knocked on the open door to announce my presence and pronounced my name.

'Ah, finally, there you are, Dao!' Director Yao cried out in obvious relief.

Hurriedly he came forward and grabbed my hand, which I had not proffered, and asked nervously, 'Why are you so late? Where have you been? Did something untoward happen? Secretary Bo, our factory secretary you know, informed me this morning of your arrival today so I assumed you would arrive here by the two o'clock bus from Hefei. It's already past four now so I got worried.'

'I was told to report to the town secretary first and hand him a letter from the factory secretary, Chen, in Shanghai,' I replied, surprised by Yao's nervousness. 'It took some time for Secretary Peng to explain certain things to me,' I added lamely.

'Ah, I understand,' Yao said, again with obvious relief. 'So there's no need for me to go into all that again, eh? You have seen the right person already. Secretary Peng is very good at explaining things, no second-guessing, eh?'

He was hopping up and down, like a chattering starling, nervous and furtive, and he squeezed both eyes shut as he fell silent momentarily and seemingly looked in my direction.

Was it his way to give me a meaning wink?

I decided not to comment, shrugged my shoulders and replied, non-committally that Party Secretary Peng had indeed been straightforward.

'Ah, I thought so, I thought so,' Yao said, rubbing his hands with obvious though nervous pleasure. 'I still need to give you the rundown about the factory and your duties though,' he continued as he flopped down in his chair behind the desk and nonchalantly gestured for me to take the chair in front of him.

'Secretary Peng wouldn't know about that. And probably couldn't care less either,' Yao added thoughtfully and so comically seriously that I burst out laughing, in spite of myself.

Yao looked up, surprised by my hilarity, and said earnestly, 'You laugh, Dao. You'll soon find out, though, that's no laughing matter here. You see, your immediate leader, the senior boiler operator Bo Dinyi, also happens to be the factory unit Party secretary and, to make things doubly complicated, trebly for you in fact, he also happens to be the eldest of the four younger brothers of Secretary Peng's wife Bo Meilan who, and this I say in absolute confidence, Dao, is the last person in the whole of China you would want to be your enemy, apart from Jiang Qing perhaps. I have heard rumours that even Secretary Peng, her husband, trembles when she throws a tantrum. It is whispered that he sometimes sleeps in his office when he hasn't been quick enough humouring her. But you never heard me say that, eh? Dao?'

I assured him that I had heard nothing.

He nodded and went on.

'Factory Secretary Bo is also a member of the Party committee of Meishan and is therefore a much more important man than the usual unit secretary. He has to attend important meetings with other committees all over Meishan

County, even the two-week long meetings, once a year, in Hefei when the committees from every town and city of Anhui Province present the economic figures of their district. So you understand, Dao, that Secretary Bo has no time to concern himself with the factory proper. It would be very unwise to bother him with problems in the factory. Do you understand that, Dao?'

I assured him I did and he continued his briefing.

'I am doing the factory's administration in such a way that Secretary Bo and Secretary Peng can be proud when they present our figures during the quarterly economic output meetings with the other committees of Meishan County, and most importantly of course, during the yearly meeting in Hefei when they submit their report to First Provincial Secretary Zeng Xisheng. Since we are the only soap factory in the province our figures are included in Anhui's yearly report of industrial output Secretary Zeng has to submit personally, in Beijing, in a meeting of the first secretaries of all provinces with the minister of industry. I have been told that on the last day Chairman Mao himself attends the meeting and that he always requests two or three secretaries to highlight their province's report.

'Imagine Dao, our Chairman Mao listening and nodding approvingly at the figures of the Snowflake Soap Factory and asking the names of its leaders! Secretary Bo! Myself! What an honour, Dao!' And rapturously he looked up at the ceiling as if expecting to see Mao's moon face beaming down on him.

'I am telling you all this, Dao,' he continued in a much calmer tone, 'so that you understand how important it is for you *and* for me to keep Secretary Bo happy. Your career and chances of promotion, perhaps even a transfer to a bigger factory in a better place than Meishan depend on it. So don't be quarrelsome, Dao. Don't think that I don't see the mockery in your eyes and I remember the way you laughed a while ago, so I know that you have a tendency to quarrel. Don't! At least *not* with Secretary Bo. Just do your work and remember, always give Secretary Bo a cheerful reply when he occasionally comes to the factory and asks you if all is well.

'Secretary Bo *always* inspects the factory the day before it is his turn to host the weekly meeting of all the factory secretaries of Meishan County. Though the others must have seen the factory a hundred times if not more, Bo always insists on a tour of the production facilities before they closet themselves in the meeting room. Now you must know that during the tour Bo is always very jovial with the workers. He will probably put his arm around your shoulders and laugh and make jokes and tell the other secretaries that you are the best assistant boiler operator in the whole of China and that thanks to you he can attend all those meetings without worrying about the production.

'You must assume a relaxed but respectful stance, laugh at Secretary Bo's remark about you being the best operator, but not too loudly and then face the other secretaries and say, proudly-like, that you are happy and proud to have earned Secretary Bo's trust. We, at the factory, have never failed our secretary, Dao, never! We have always shown a cheerful attitude to make him happy and help him appear a competent secretary in the eyes of the other secretaries and his brother-in-law.'

Yao fell silent, almost out of breath after his harangue, and looked at me anxiously and a bit doubtfully.

I could see him thinking, 'have I put it on too thickly? Not thick enough perhaps? Has he got the message? Does he mean trouble?'

Inwardly I sighed. Yao was probably not a bad man but he was a shyster and a lickspittle, forever yearning, and probably also forever in vain, for what he called 'a better place than Meishan'.

He was adept at communism's golden rules of cringing flattery and of make-believe to curry favour with the political power in his factory, Factory Secretary Bo Dinyi, who was probably too stupid and vain to see through it, but Bo's brother-in-law, that shameless political animal Peng, was no fool and certainly not bamboozled by Yao's and Bo's tricks.

Had he not called them a gasbag and windbag respectively? And if Peng couldn't be hoodwinked could those at higher levels, in Hefei, or the highest, in Beijing, be duped?

I didn't think so though, of course, for their own sake, they had to pretend to believe the whole Potemkin-like charade or else the whole system would collapse.

Yet, Yao, who was obviously not a Party member and never would be, would for ever be known as a cheat, a cringer, who falsified his figures.

Bo, a lowly factory secretary but nevertheless a member of the Nomenklatura, could never be blamed and might one day even be promoted because of his factory's exemplary results.

I nodded and said I wouldn't fail the secretary.

Yao smiled, pleased with himself that he had brought the most difficult part of our interview to a good end.

'Now for the practical details,' he said, briskly. 'Your working hours will be from five in the morning till five in the afternoon, seven days a week and fifty-one weeks a year. Your pay will be five yuan per week. Since you are an essential worker you must live on the factory premises, in a house we specifically built for that purpose. The rent is fifty fen per week. You may take your meals in the canteen, the cost is fifteen fen per day for three meals, whether you take them or not.

'The factory is too small to have its own clinic. In case of an accident or sudden illness you will be treated in the people's clinic, just two streets away. In other, non-urgent cases you wait for the doctor who is available for consultation every Monday morning from nine to twelve, in Secretary Bo's office. Treatment and medicine are free. Any questions?'

I shook my head and said it was all very clear.

'Good! Now let me show you around quickly and introduce you to your co-workers,' he said, leaping up from his chair and dashing off through the door.

So far my only experience with a Chinese factory and working methods had been with the Maling Canning Factory and I shall never forget how stunned I had been on my first day when the senior engineer Wang had shown me around there. My exclamation of disbelief at the filth and mess everywhere and at the appalling state of the machinery, piping and cabling had earned me Wang's eternal enmity.

I had slowly grown accustomed to the situation and even learned to live with my inability to make even the slightest change for the better.

So one would think that I had become filth and neglect inured. Not so.

What I saw there, in the Snowflake Soap Factory, was worse than my worst expectations. I realised I had seen nothing so far.

Years of accumulated filth, garbage, broken and rusty pieces of equipment disposed of haphazardly everywhere on the slimy wet, potholed, once concreted floor; shredded veils of cobwebs, heavy with greasy soot, hanging down from the rafters and the single light bulbs; shoddy, old-fashioned tanks, vessels and machinery, covered with filth and slime and crusts of caustic and, judging by its disorder, probably installed by the town's mad hatter at full moon before they institutionalised him for good; piping running in helter-skelter disorder and without any alignment, its insulation hanging in tatters, not a single valve or flange that did not leak water, caustic or steam, some steam valves so badly that probably half the boiler's capacity blew off there and opening or closing them meant risking third-degree burns; electrical cables hanging and criss-crossing like lianas and aerial roots in a tropical forest, insulation cut and torn, core wires and copper exposed, contact boxes without cover and pieces of wood stuck between the contacts to prevent tripping; terrible, terrible and still, my own domain, the boiler house, took my breath away.

Director Yao must have noticed the horrified expression on my face and the sharp intake of my breath since he stopped mid-sentence in his incessant trivial babble and said, apologetically, that Secretary Bo had simply no time to do his job as the senior boiler operator.

'The man who was appointed six months ago as Bo's helper comes from a nearby farming commune', Yao explained hesitantly, 'and knows nothing about technical matters, you see. Besides, he is the youngest brother of Secretary Bo's wife, a most unpleasant and quarrelsome woman, so we cannot reprimand the man for his laziness and sleeping on the job lest he complain to his sister. We cannot have that woman turn up here at the factory and make a scene as she once did when she suspected Bo of having an affair with one of the female workers. Terrible that was Dao, the poor woman needed twelve stitches in her cheek and had half her hair torn out and all for nothing since it was not she who had an affair with Bo but her sister who works in the bakery opposite the factory. Secretary Peng had to pay the injured woman off to avoid a political scandal.

'Secretary Peng then told Bo to submit a request with the labour department in Hefei for an assistant boiler operator with good qualifications. Three weeks ago Hefei informed us that a certain Dao Huimin from the Maling Canning Factory in Shanghai had been assigned to our factory. There was a separate, secret letter for Secretary Bo which I was not permitted to read. I heard Bo curse when he read the letter and he stormed out of his office, with the letter, to see Secretary Peng. You haven't done anything wrong, have you, Dao?

'Politically, I mean? You are a qualified engineer, I know, so this must be some sort of punishment, a kind of internal exile, or else you wouldn't be here, in this rat hole and in such a lowly position, now would you, Dao?'

He fell silent and looked at me, more anxiously than inquisitively. I merely shrugged my shoulders which didn't seem to reassure him. He didn't insist though and with a deep sigh he said, 'There's a lot going on that I'm not aware of, Dao, and perhaps it's for the best. I can't worry about what I don't know, now can I, Dao?'

'And you can't be blamed either for what you don't know,' I replied flippantly.

'Ah, and there you are being naive, Dao,' Yao said, seriously. 'Being worried is personal, being blamed is political and has nothing to do with knowing or not knowing. It's like a doctor finding your body harbours a disease your mind isn't aware of, yet, and you are grateful because you can still be treated. In the same way our leaders can perceive that deep inside your mind wrong thoughts are lurking, counter-revolutionary thoughts, waiting to spring forth and cause damage to society. As a true Communist you are abhorred that you harbour such thoughts inside you, unbeknownst still to *you* perhaps, but *not* to the perceptive Party leader who has been trained to detect such things *before* they can cause damage, and you are *grateful*, Dao, for the early diagnosis and you accept the blame *willingly* and the punishment *gladly*. Did you accept your punishment gladly, Dao? Are you here willingly?'

'Everything is pretence in this most wonderful of all worlds, eh Comrade Director Yao?' I said, smiling mockingly. 'So I'll pretend that I'm glad to be here; that the slave labour you expect of me is, in fact, my socialist duty to the motherland; that the sullen bunch of impudent, lazy boors hanging around in this pigsty are, in fact, my cheerful co-workers and comrades in a well-managed factory united in their relentless efforts to achieve the production figures you fake in your reports; that the filthy, bare, mud-walled hovel in that plot of fallow land behind the factory you assigned to me is, in fact, a model socialist worker's castle, where I'll rest in true socialist contentment after having joyously fulfilled my socialist duties.

'In return, Director Yao, you'll pretend that you are glad to see me and do me the small favours I'll occasionally ask of you, as a reward for all that pretending and for keeping Mr and Mrs Bo out of your hair. Now, is that a deal, Yao?'

I had seen him shrink, quite literally, during my mockery and there was nothing left of the bombastic little pigwidgin as he said, tiredly, 'It's a deal, Dao. You scratch my back, I'll scratch yours, isn't that the expression? Come and see me for a chat whenever you feel like it.' And at that he turned and shuffled back to his office, suddenly not so springy any more.

I still stood there, looking after him, when I heard a woman's voice beside me, saying, 'What have you done to our great leader, Director Yao, newcomer? Suddenly the puffed-up little quack shuffles like the toad he is.' And she laughed, a lovely, silvery laugh, joyful and unaffected.

I turned and saw the pretty, pert young woman who had been the only one to nod at me and smile when Director Yao gave me the guided tour and had introduced me to the workers as 'Engineer Dao, Dao Huimin, our new assistant boiler operator'. The other workers hadn't even acknowledged Yao's forcedly cheerful 'hello, hello, comrades, how are you today?'

Pointedly ignoring their populist leader they had merely stared at me, sullenly, and a few had hawked and spat a thick glob of phlegm on the floor just in front of our feet.

I hadn't budged, sensing the challenge, however, Yao had jumped backwards, tripped on a piece of junk and had barely managed to stay on his feet.

The workers had snickered insolently and had brayed with laughter when the young woman had exclaimed, 'Welcome, Dao! Welcome on behalf of the workers of the Snowflake Soap Factory! I hope you know how to make soap, Dao! The muck we make here now takes one's skin off and leaves one's clothes full of holes!'

Before I had had time to answer Director Yao had hurriedly pushed me along.

'Name's Liang,' she said, looking up into my face with a smile that took my breath away. 'Shi Liang. Come to see me and let's talk things over before you do or say stupid things. Because I know you will, do or say stupid things, I mean. Your eyes are different from the other men's, not indifferent and insolent like theirs, more inquisitive-like. You *notice* things and that can be *bad* if you want to *change* things. Okay, Dao?' And playfully she punched my arm, laughed, turned and hopped back to her place in the production line to continue whatever she did there, which was probably nothing most of the time.

To cut a long story short, I was not able to convince Secretary Bo's wife's youngest brother to even pretend to do some work so I resigned myself to having to do everything myself.

I got up at half past four in the morning to fetch the brown coal for the day from the heap in the yard with a wheelbarrow. This took me an hour and at half past five I fired the old steam boiler with a rag dipped first in kerosene, a few pieces of wood and a tree stump.

While the fire was taking hold, I began filling the boiler with water by means of the rusty, old and leaking hand-operated well pump. At half past six I shovelled the first brown coal into the boiler and while the steam pressure slowly mounted I had about half an hour to make my toilet and to have morning rice in the canteen before I had to shovel additional coal on to the fire.

At half seven the boiler had reached its maximum steam pressure of three bar and the valves to the soap kettles could be opened.

When the workers began to arrive at around eight o'clock the kettles were hot and work could begin.

Between four and five o'clock in the afternoon the workers started to walk off their stations, without a word or care whether the daily batch was finished or not.

During my first week on the job I tried, after five o'clock, when I had closed the steam valves, to keep the boiler under pressure until the next morning, to save time and work for myself in the morning and money for the factory. All in vain, however. The steam valves, including the main valve on the boiler, were leaking too badly and the baffles no longer functioned, so before seven o'clock the pressure had dropped to zero and the fire had gone out.

I went to see Director Yao and explained to him the advantages of ordering and installing new valves and baffles.

Though he seemed to understand my point, he nevertheless looked hesitant and doubtful. When I asked him why, he said that Secretary Bo, after all one of the most experienced boiler operators in China before he became a brilliant secretary, had never complained about the valves and baffles.

It would be better to explain my theory to Secretary Bo first and if he also agreed that it was a good idea, to let him do the ordering so that it looked as if the idea came from him in the first place. Perhaps it would even be better if I did the explaining to Secretary Bo rather than he, Yao, a layman in such technical matters.

'Forget it,' I said and as I walked out of his office I clearly heard him sigh with relief.

Again one week later I was back in Yao's office, this time to show him my fingernails and the skin on my face and my hair.

'Do you know why my nails are almost gone? Why the flesh under my nails is red and burning like hell? Why my face is all blotched and my hair is falling out in tufts?' I asked him angrily.

He shifted uncomfortably in his chair and from the way he avoided my angry stare I knew that he knew why.

'It's from using our own soap,' I pressed on angrily, 'and now I know also what that young woman meant, the one who made that remark about the muck that takes your skin off and leaves holes in your clothing. I checked the production,' I continued in a calmer voice, 'and I found that firstly the vat operators use too much lye and secondly that they don't neutralise the excess in the last vat. They told me that they have always done it that way.

'I don't understand, Yao! Four years this has gone on by now. You must have received thousands of complaints since you sold the first batch of this so-called soap. Why wasn't anything done? Two of the vat operators even told me that Secretary Bo himself changed the formula four years ago and gave the order to use that much lye and they said that you knew about it. I simply can't believe that.'

Director Yao made a pitiful attempt to appear angry and I knew he lied when he cried out, his voice cracking, that he knew nothing about a change in the formula, that he had never received any complaints about the quality of his Snowflake Soap and that Secretary Bo used to be one of China's most gifted soap technicians before he became the outstanding Party secretary he was now.

'Forget it,' I said, realising I was on dangerous terrain, and I tried to sound suddenly uninterested, 'perhaps it's the food in Meishan that I have to get accustomed to,' and I left Yao's office, feeling his suspicious eyes between my shoulder blades.

I decided, however, to get to the bottom of it and the following day I accosted the young woman Shi Liang as she was leaving for home after work.

She got a fit of the giggles when I showed her my nails and pulled out a tuft of my once shiny but now coarse, lustreless hair.

'You used Snowflake soap,' she hiccuped, 'nobody does. I told you the first day it was dangerous.' Suddenly serious, 'I saw you talking to those two vat operators, the ones who have worked here a long time, before Secretary Bo's time in fact. Be careful, Dao!'

I looked her over and suddenly, impulsively, I said, 'I have to know why nobody complains, Liang. Will you help me? Please find out what happens to the full drums that leave the factory every Friday afternoon for Hefei.'

She laughed but said neither yes nor no.

Ten days passed and I didn't hear from Yao or Bo, whom I hadn't even met yet, or from Liang other than a wink and a smile when I saw her from far in the canteen or in the factory.

She even seemed to avoid me.

Then, one evening, long after working hours, she suddenly came to see me, in my shack.

She walked in just like that, uninvited, and looked around disapprovingly.

'I saw you sweeping out,' she said, frowning, 'and it still looks like a pigsty to me. How can you live this way, Dao? A pile of filthy straw to sleep in and an old crate to sit on and that's all the furniture you have? A heap of smelly straw and a crate? It's a *shame*! An educated young man like you, talking standard Chinese with a Shanghainese accent. What crime did you commit, Dao Huimin, that they have exiled you here, to this godforsaken place and under Secretary Bo, that thieving and lying shyster?'

Her eyes sparkled with anger and I fell hopelessly in love with her there and then.

She gave me a searching look and chided, 'Don't ogle me like that, Huimin, you look like a sick ox. Now, about the soap,' she went on merrily. 'I did as you asked me to.' And she told me her amazing story.

'I asked the truck driver, who every Friday fetches the full drums, for a ride to Hefei since I urgently needed to consult my sister, who lives in Hefei, about family matters. I have no sister who lives in Hefei but Ma can't know that, of course. Ma is the truck driver, I forgot to tell you that. Driver Ma said he could only give me a ride as far as Lu'an because that was as far as he went. I acted surprised and said I had always assumed that the drums were delivered to Hefei's railway station for further transport by train to wherever the soap's destination was.

'Ma said that I had assumed correctly, however, by order of Secretary Bo a different driver, Secretary Bo's eldest brother-in-law Zheng, who lives in Lu'an, took over from him in Lu'an and drove the truck to Hefei to unload the full drums at the station and to reload the empty drums of a previous transport and then back to Lu'an. Ma says that he always stays with his brother and his family and parents in Lu'an to wait for Zheng's return four days later and then drives the truck back to the factory in Meishan. That had been the routine for the past three and a half years Ma said, and it suited him fine. Nobody had ever asked him to account for his time and each week he had four days off to spend with his relatives, so why would he care? In the beginning he wondered why it took Zheng four days, but he had never asked and Zheng had never volunteered an explanation. So I rode with Ma to Lu'an.

'Zheng was there already, at Ma's relatives' house and I asked him straight away whether I could ride with him to Hefei. To my utter surprise Zheng became very angry and scolded Ma for giving me a ride to Lu'an. He shouted that it was strictly forbidden for truck drivers to give people a lift and should Ma ever break the law again he, Zheng, would report him and me to his brother-in-law Secretary Bo who would take stern disciplinary action against us. So I told Zheng that I was sorry and would simply take the bus to Hefei to see my sister. No need for him to get so upset about such a small matter or to make trouble for driver Ma who had only tried to be friendly, I told him. Ma's brother asked me to stay for lunch but I refused politely and said I preferred to take the first available bus to Hefei.

'Zheng's overreaction had made me suspicious and though I had no idea what to expect or what to do about it I nevertheless decided to hang around a bit longer to see what would happen. Ma had told me that Zheng always invited himself for lunch so I had about half an hour or so to find an observation post. I decided to watch the intersection of the street where Ma's brother lives and the main road from the bus stop where I had to take the bus back to Meishan anyway. Zheng would turn left at the intersection and head for Hefei and that would be it. A bit silly to wait just to see him turn and disappear and I was still deliberating whether to take the next bus and forget the whole thing when I saw the truck approaching the intersection. Zheng had been quicker than I thought.

'To my utter surprise he didn't turn left, direction Hefei, but right, back towards Meishan. Instinctively I ducked behind the bus stop shelter for I realised that I was standing on the wrong side of the road if I was to take the bus to Hefei as I had told Zheng I would and that seeing me there might make him suspicious. He was driving slowly and I soon saw why. After about two hundred metres, just before the bridge over the Li River, Zheng turned left, off the main road, and took the dirt road along the river. My hunch had been correct, something was wrong. Quickly I ran to the bridge and saw the truck, jolting in a cloud of dust, about five hundred metres away. Apart from the truck the dirt road was deserted.

'I decided to follow Zheng; there was no wind and the dust cloud thrown up by the truck settled only very slowly and Zheng wouldn't be able to see me in the rear-view mirror. After about one kilometre I saw the low, dilapidated buildings and dry houses of a brick factory. I counted six men who were slowly stacking bricks in the yard alongside the road. I descended the river bank and out of sight of the six men I passed the factory. After yet another kilometre the river made a sharp bend to the left and the road suddenly ended there, in a shallow, gravely place in the river bedding.

'Slowly I approached the place where the road descended into the river, wondering where the truck had gone when suddenly I saw it standing up to its axles in the river. Zheng and two other men were busy on the loading platform emptying the drums, three at a time, into the river. I watched the scene from behind and below a thicket of dusty, muddy bamboo that covers the bank and the shallow part of the river near the bend. Zheng unscrewed the caps while the other two tilted the drums over the side of the truck to let the viscous liquid glug out into the river; glug-glug, glug-glug, in intermittent gushes. When all thirty-six drums were empty Zheng and his men lifted them off the truck, rolled them up the slope and stacked them, two high, along the road. This done, Zheng drove the truck, in reverse, out of the water and up the slope. The two men jumped into the cabin without waiting for Zheng to stop and he continued, still in reverse, on the narrow road in the direction of the main road two kilometres away.

'I didn't know what to think but that something strange and not entirely kosher was going on, that much was clear to me as I stood there watching the truck disappear in a cloud of dust. Pensively I walked back to the main road trying to make sense of the whole weird business. Fortunately I heard the rhythmic shouting "one-two-*three*", "one-two-*three*" or else I would have walked past the brick factory in full view, lost in thought as I was. In the blink of an eye I slid down the bank again and crept closer to where I could, lying against the bank, peek over the road into the yard of the brick factory. I couldn't believe my eyes.

'Zheng sat quietly on a stack of bricks, smoking a cigarette and watching the six men I had seen earlier load the truck with bricks. Three of the men stood on the truck platform and adroitly caught the bricks the three others threw up to them, three at a time, counting one two and *three* as they threw them. While the men on the ground picked up three new bricks, his mate on the truck stacked the previous three on the platform about twenty or so high I think. They were working fast and the truck would be loaded shortly so I decided to stay where I was. If Zheng was to drive off immediately I wouldn't have the time to reach the main road and he would see me and from my dirty appearance would conclude correctly that I had seen the whole operation. So I waited and watched.

'Ten minutes passed and then I saw the men jump off the truck and put up the side boards as Zheng put out his cigarette and let himself slide down the stack of bricks. He exchanged a few words with the factory workers who kept nodding at what he said. With a shouted "see you tomorrow morning at eight!" Zheng climbed into the truck cabin, started the engine and drove out of the yard in my direction. I slithered down the bank and lay down at its lowest point. I felt the water seep through the right leg of my trousers. Above me, on the road, I heard the truck's engine roar as Zheng drove up the slight gradient to the road and turned right. I heard him change gears as he drove off slowly towards the main road. I stayed where I was for another ten minutes and then I made my own way, down the bank, to the main road.

'I hesitated for a moment wondering whether to go back to Ma's brother's house to clean myself a bit before taking the bus back to Meishan but then I thought that that was probably not such a good idea. Though I was certain that Ma knew nothing about Zheng's illegitimate business I was also certain he would tell Zheng that I had missed the bus to Hefei and had come back covered by dust and dried mud. So I pulled a few tufts of grass out of the bank under the bridge and cleaned my shoes with grass and water. Then I took off my jacket and trousers and slapped them against the pillars of the bridge to get the dust out. Finally I washed my hands and face, put my jacket and trousers back on, climbed up the slope to the road and walked back to the bus stop. The bus arrived two hours later and it cost me my last twenty fen to get back to Meishan. And that is my story.'

Liang fell silent and watched me, her expression grave.

'You don't get it, do you?' she asked me, a bit exasperated. 'It's a very profitable racket and they're all involved, Secretary Bo, his horrible wife's brother Zheng Lifei, the secretary of the brick factory and his men and of course also our Director Yao who is probably too scared to complain about the pittance the others pay him to keep his mouth shut about the truck being away six days out of seven for one simple delivery to Hefei, something that shouldn't take more than one day, two at the most if the people in Hefei are a bit slow. However, they will not be slow since they are of course also on Bo's payroll, and besides, there are no drums to unload. I had the whole plan figured out yesterday evening during the ride back from Lu'an.

'Here's how I see it. First Bo makes the soap unusable by changing the recipe so that it contains far too much lye. Nobody wants our soap any more and our former customers in the neighbouring provinces change to different suppliers. Bo keeps one supplier in the books and on the transport documents, somebody far away, in Hubei or Hunan or Sichuan. Next he offers money to the loaders at Hefei's railway station to stamp our factory's copy of the documents for receipt and forwarding of the drums, thirty-six each week, to Hubei or wherever, and then to destroy the railway's own copies since there are no drums to forward. Then he arranges with his friend, the secretary of the brick factory, that he and his eight man crew increase the brick production but, of course, *not* the fixed number of bricks the factory has to supply to the state warehouse, in Hefei probably. Finally Zheng Lifei, Bo's brother-in-law, who lives in Lu'an, comes into the picture.

'Zheng takes over the truck from our naive driver Ma, dumps the soap into the river, uses the truck during four days to sell the brick factory's overproduction to small buyers who have the money to pay cash and well below the State's price of course, for a few hundred or even a few thousand bricks. He probably even delivers the brick factory's mandatory quota to Hefei, has the soap factory's transport papers stamped at the station and pays off the loaders and the loading master. The brick factory's workers are paid their share, a third probably. I think so since they are important, the more bricks they produce the higher everybody's share will be. The brick factory's secretary, Bo and Zheng share equally the remaining two-thirds and Bo deducts a pittance from his own share to pay Director Yao for keeping his mouth shut and, of course, for faking the production figures to make Bo shine in the eyes of his fellow secretaries.

'The chance that some inspector or other from Hefei or Beijing will come to our factory to check our books is nil and even then there are always the documents, stamped and in order. The chance that then the inspector cross-checks with the customers in Hubei or Sichuan is simply beyond belief. This racket has gone on now for almost three and a half years, Dao, and everybody involved has become accustomed to the nice pay-offs. This is too big for us, Dao, so my advice is that we keep our heads low and our mouths shut and that you don't complain any more about leaking steam valves and baffles and unusable soap or otherwise we'll end up one day in our own vats.'

She fell silent and smiled at me, a warm, friendly smile.

'I see in your eyes that you wonder about me,' she said with a chuckle. 'Perhaps one day I'll tell you about myself. Perhaps the day I'll come back to clean out this shack. Bye-bye now' and she was gone, leaving me in a state of great confusion.

I felt certain that her deductions about Bo and his scheme had been correct and I shivered at the thought that she could have been caught by Zheng or by the brick factory workers.

I reproached myself that I shouldn't have asked her to do such dangerous things while staying myself at the factory like a coward. But then I had to admit that she had handled the matter far better than I would have myself and that her advice to let sleeping dogs lie was a sound one.

It was indeed wholly plausible that Zheng and his mates from the brick factory would kill me in my sleep and dump me in one of the vats with lye, should Bo and Yao think that I had become a risk factor. Such a tragic accident. Slipped while taking the temperature of the vats would be the official reading.

But Liang would know and I wasn't quite sure that she would stay quiet.

It was also conceivable that she might misjudge the situation one day and tell her story to the wrong person and end up in a vat as well.

This idea did it for me. I wouldn't say a word, ever!

The following days I went far more often than necessary to check the temperatures of the vats not so much to see whether Liang was already floating around in one of them but to see her and to see her smile at me which made my heart skip a beat and my legs wobbly.

At night, in my mud hovel, I listened for suspicious sounds, for Bo and Zheng and their murderers sneaking up on me to turn me into unusable soap and to calm my racing heart.

I thought of Liang and fantasised about her and me. I was in love and she probably had guessed it even before I knew it.

Another week passed and then Director Yao sent for me to come and see him in his office. He came from behind his desk and with his arm around my shoulder he led me to the chair in front of his desk and made me sit down.

He poured both of us a mug of tea from the big thermos and flopped down, with a deep sigh, in his chair. He looked at me while drumming with his fingers on his desk, clearly uneasy about what he was going to say.

I kept silent but didn't touch my tea since he hadn't invited me to drink yet and I didn't want to offend him.

He's embarrassed, I thought, he doesn't like what he has to tell me, and all of a sudden I panicked at the thought that I might be transferred again, to an even worse place, far from Liang.

Suddenly Director Yao sniffed, swallowed the snot, hawked and swallowed again and said, 'I have spoken to Secretary Bo about what you told me, about the valves and baffles. I didn't mention what you said about the soap quality, Dao, and, it's fortunate for you that I didn't. As it was, your remarks about the valves and baffles have already gone down the wrong way with Bo. Secretary Bo was enraged, Dao, enraged. He shouted at me as if he blamed *me* for your remarks.

'He shouted that the valves were always perfect and had never leaked before. How else could he show his factory to the other secretaries? With all the valves leaking? What a shame! Secretary Bo shouted that it reeked of sabotage all over again, that he had been forewarned by Secretary Chen of the Maling Factory in Shanghai and that you had apparently learned nothing, nothing at all! He said he would have to report the matter to the provincial authorities, Dao.'

Yao looked at me and I saw compassion in his eyes. He wasn't a bad man, if only he wasn't such a wimp.

'I managed to calm him down', Yao continued, 'and he consented to wait a few weeks with his report to see if you give any more trouble, Dao. The trouble for you, however, is that if Bo really wants to have your arse, he'll turn your own criticism against you, Dao. Bo knows, of course, full well that the valves are leaking and have always been leaking for as long as anybody remembers but everybody will support him if he now says that they began leaking after *you* became the assistant boiler operator, Dao.

'So there you are, Dao. A no-win situation if ever there was one. So my advice to you, Dao, is to keep very, very quiet and not to show any more initiatives to improve things in the factory. Everything you criticise, Bo will turn it around and blame *you* for it, pretending furiously that it all started the day you came here. And it is *he* who will be believed Dao, not *you*. What's the word of a convicted saboteur sent by a foreign power against that of a Party secretary, Dao? You see my point? I did my homework Dao as you can hear. Besides, there are other matters of far greater importance if I am to believe the rumours.

'Do I have to remind you, Dao, that Secretary Bo's approval is required for changes in marital status? To have children?'

Suddenly grinning mischievously he added, 'Is there anything you want to know about Shi Liang that she hasn't already told you herself, Dao?'

I couldn't help bursting out laughing at Yao's humorous warning shot across my bows.

'Who is she?' I asked him, just as directly.

Yao watched me, his eyes screwed up, then, suddenly, he nodded at an apparent decision and said, 'You didn't hear this from me, Dao. If she tells you her story herself you listen as if you heard it for the first time. If somebody else gives you a different lecture, you listen and act as if you heard it for the first time. Okay?'

I nodded and Yao continued.

'What I am going to tell you, Dao, is what Secretary Peng told me, so I can't vouch for the truth. I don't know how Peng got himself the appointment as a town Party secretary; he isn't much of a Communist, Peng, but he likes the power and the privileges. One of those privileges is free food and drink in restaurants and even when he calls on people at home he always does so around dinner time. About three years ago he came to see me, at home, as I said, around dinner time. He told me that he was going to send me a young woman and that I had to find her a job, in the factory. A lowly job it had to be, preferably tough on her hands, with no prospect for promotion. Her name was Shi Liang, Peng told me, and she had arrived in Meishan that previous week, from Wuhan.

'I knew better then already than to ask Peng the why and the how and instead invited him to stay for dinner. I still had a bottle of *maotai* at home and since both my wife and I don't drink alcohol, Peng drank more than half of it. The *maotai* made him garrulous and I did my best to laugh at his jokes and when I laughingly said that washing hands with our soap was probably worse for the hands than whatever job, he became suddenly serious in the pedantic way of the drunk and said, "It is important that this Shi girl doesn't play the violin again, Yao."

'I must have looked very stupid for Peng burst out laughing and said, "This girl and her parents went off their heads when a foreigner, an American I believe, a temporary guest teacher at the Wuhan School of Music, offered to sponsor the girl to continue her violin study in America. The parents were themselves teachers at the Wuhan School of Music, violin and piano, I believe, and they applied, *all three of them*, for passports and exit visas to the US, supported by a letter from the American guest teacher in which he said he would pay for everything.

'"Secretary Li of Wuhan was very angry, Yao. He immediately revoked the American's temporary stay permit and gave him forty-eight hours to leave the country since he was found guilty of trying to sweet talk Chinese into a slave labour contract in the US and at the same time to deprive our motherland of their talents. Secretary Li also wanted to set an example, once and for all, for all talented Chinese not to listen to the siren songs of the sweet talkers. He ordered the dismissal of Shi and his wife from the Wuhan School of Music and their expulsion from Wuhan to Meishan. It could have been to any shit place in China, Yao, but Li decided on Meishan and two weeks ago I received a letter from Secretary Li announcing his decision and ordering me to appoint Shi and his wife to the worst primary school in Meishan or Meishan County, at my discretion, and to find a job for their daughter Liang that would be particularly damaging to her hands so that she would never be able to play the violin again. So you see, Yao," Peng said, "it is now important for me to reply to the big shot secretary in Wuhan that I have obeyed his orders and that I give him a few details."

'The next day Liang showed up and I gave her a job at the drum filling station. I exaggerated the dangers of the job when I went to see Peng the next day and told him there was every possibility she would burn her arms and hands, very badly, third-degree burns, at the slightest mistake. I told Liang to be very, very careful when handling the hose and the filling valve so as not to burn her hands.

'Peng was happy, commended me for my loyalty and patriotism and probably wrote his letter to his crazy, vindictive boss in Wuhan claiming the merit for such a diabolical inventiveness for himself. He never got back to me on the matter. And I'm glad, Dao, that Liang did her job well and that her hands are still beautiful and able to play the violin, not that playing the violin is of much use here in Meishan though.'

Yao fell silent and smiled at me, a sad, resigned little smile.

'Don't waste your time fighting windmills, Dao,' he said softly. 'You can't win, ever! Accept your lot and try to find a bit of happiness, of double happiness.'

In spite of myself I was touched by Yao's kindness and compassion and I was about to return his confidence by telling him what Liang and I had discovered and warn him how dangerous it was what he was doing, when I remembered my promise to Liang to keep my mouth shut and never to confide in anybody I hardly knew. So I merely thanked Yao for his confidence and promised I would follow his advice.

I went back to my boiler to find the fire had gone out and the pressure dropped to zero and that everybody had walked off the job and gone home though it was only two o'clock in the afternoon.

But why should I care? A dozen or so drums less this week to dump in the Li River and it wouldn't affect Yao's production figures anyhow, so indeed why should I care?

I went to my shack thinking of Liang and the wickedness she had been a victim of. How could I keep my promise to Yao and *not* let her know that I *knew*?

For the next three weeks I tossed and turned in my straw bed every night, constructing and rejecting sentences how to tell Liang that I loved her and would she marry me.

I was what one would call a handsome young man, however, my experience with women was very limited, zero actually, and even my mother had been a riddle to me, crying when I thought she would laugh at a remark or joke I made, laughing when I thought she would cry, reacting angrily when I thought that something I said or did would make her happy.

Very spiritual and lively she was but also very unpredictable and I recognised the same kind of character in Liang so I knew that the wrong word at the wrong time or place could spoil everything.

So I wavered and wobbled and would probably have gone on wobbling and wavering long after she had married somebody else had she not solved the problem, *my* problem that is, not *hers* apparently, in her own, bafflingly direct manner.

It was a Saturday evening and I was sitting outside my shack, my back leaning against the warm mud wall, eyes closed, enjoying the last warm rays of the sun when suddenly the warmth was cut off by a shadow.

I opened my eyes and saw Liang smiling down at me.

'We have to talk, Dao Huimin,' she said, 'now! It's important.'

'Go ahead, talk,' I replied, my heart pounding.

'I see you diddle-daddle in your work and loiter around the drum filling station though you have no business there and when I catch your eye and smile you blush all over and scurry for cover. I think you are in love, Dao Huimin, but haven't found the courage yet to tell me, if you'll ever find it.

'Now, I could keep you dangling a while longer to amuse myself a bit and play hard to catch were it not that since last week I notice that horrible coal passer of yours, Secretary Bo's youngest brother-in-law, leer at me, the useless drone. I'm very worried, Huimin, that he won't have your inhibitions and will ask me one of these days to marry him. It will be very hard to refuse, for my parents' sake. Bo's wife will be mad if I reject her little brother and she'll want revenge and Bo will have no choice but to take it out on me and on my parents. I can't have that on my conscience, Dao, they have suffered enough because of me.

'So the only way out is that you ask me, Dao, now, this very moment, to marry you and I'll say yes and we'll go straight to Director Yao's house and tell him the great news. We'll ask him for his preliminary approval and to submit our official request to Secretary Bo first thing Monday morning.'

She fell silent and stood there looking down on me, flushed, defiant, embarrassed, shy, breathing deeply.

How feminine, how beautiful she was.

I laughed loudly and took her in my arms and that was all she needed for an answer.

Director Yao smiled broadly when we told him and insisted we drink a glass of fresh jasmine tea with him and his wife.

He nodded knowingly when Liang said, meaningly, that it was important to secure Secretary Bo's approval as quickly as possible before others might try to influence his decision.

Yao promised it would be the first thing he would push under Bo's nose on Monday morning for his signature amongst the usual documents.

Bo was always in a good mood on Monday mornings and in a hurry to be off to the weekly meeting of secretaries and, more specifically, to see the pretty secretary of Yingshan with whom he had a more than comradely relationship, Yao said with a wink.

On the coming Monday the meeting was in Huoshan, Yao said, so Bo would be in an even jollier mood since he could probably find an excuse to stay the night and discuss Party affairs with the lady secretary into the small hours of Tuesday.

Liang and I left kind, old Yao and his wife and went back to my hovel where she spent the night with me. We made love, talked and made love again and again, helping and guiding each other lovingly and without the slightest trace of awkwardness.

The next Monday morning I saw Bo leave his office, in a rush, at nine o'clock and barely five minutes later Yao sent word through the guard that he wanted to see me and Liang. Proudly he showed us the wedding permit signed and stamped by Secretary Bo.

Secretary Bo had asked him to convey his very best wishes, Director Yao said, clearly pleased, and also his excuses for not handing the permit to us himself. However, he had to attend a very important meeting in Huoshan and he was late already so he had to rush to catch the bus.

He would, however, attend our reception after the official wedding, as would Yao himself and his wife, of course, who had been so impressed with us last Saturday evening.

That same evening Liang presented me to her parents.

They looked older than I had imagined but that was probably because they were so wizened, so small and frail.

They seemed more relieved than happy with their daughter's choice, however, after the first awkward minutes and silences the atmosphere became more relaxed thanks to Liang who happily chatted away and made us all laugh with her imitation of Director Yao when he had told us about Secretary Bo's girlfriend.

We were married one week later, on Tuesday 2nd August, 1955, in the presence of Meishan's Party vice-secretary, the vice-mayor, Liang's parents and Director Yao and his wife as our witnesses. The whole ceremony took no more than five minutes.

Liang's parents gave a reception afterwards, in their own small two-room house in a quiet back lane in Meishan's outskirts.

To my surprise all twenty-two factory workers showed up, washed, kempt and in their best clothes. Even Secretary Bo's brother-in-law, Zheng Benhua, my coal passer, came to offer his best wishes with a box of good-luck cookies. Very graceful, I thought.

Secretary Bo sent his wife with a box of sweetmeats and his apologies; he was very busy with matters of state.

Liang and her mother served tea and platters of sweets and cookies. I had bought ten bottles of Jinling Beer and ten bottles of an orange-coloured soft drink, never thinking that so many people would turn up.

However, everybody was friendly and in a good mood and by mixing the beer and the soft drink everybody had a full glass. There was much hilarity when the foam of the mixture flowed, unstoppable, over the rim of the glasses and splashed over the cookies and sweetmeats.

But, as I said, it was all in good spirits and everybody toasted and cheered when Director Yao said a few kind words and granted Liang and me the next day off.

When all the cookies and sweets and drinks were finished the guests suddenly took their leave and within three minutes they were all gone.

Liang's father, hemming and hawing, proposed that Liang and I move in with them since my mud hut behind the factory was really not suitable for a married couple.

Liang's mother quickly cut in and said we would have our privacy since we could have the bedroom for ourselves. She and her husband would sleep in the living room and we would all use the small kitchen for our meals and normal daily intercourse.

Gratefully Liang and I accepted the kind offer. The only inconvenience, for me at least, was that I would have to walk to and from the factory which would take at least half an hour each way.

In the morning the first bus that passed near the Liang residence was around six o'clock, too late for me, and in the evening the last bus that stopped near the factory was at six also, too early for me. That meant that I would have to get up at four instead of half past four and also that I would be home at half past seven only.

Perhaps I could make a deal with Zheng Benhua the coal passer so that every other week he would fire up the boiler in the morning and shut the boiler and valves after work in the evening. If he agreed I could take the bus together with Liang in the morning and evening. That would be nice.

On the morning, of all days, that I had decided to talk to Zheng about staggering our hours he didn't turn up.

It was my duty, as Zheng's leader, to report his absence to Director Yao before nine o'clock, however, I didn't want to anger Zheng so I waited until eleven before I went to see Yao.

On my way to Yao's office I passed Secretary Bo's office and to my utter surprise I saw my coal passer there, sitting behind a desk, asleep as usual, with his head on his arms. I asked Yao why Zheng now sat sleeping in Bo's office instead of in the boiler room and Yao told me that Zheng had been granted Party membership, a long-pending affair, but that finally Secretary Bo's insistence had paid off.

Secretary Bo's wife, Zheng Zhen, had come, with her younger brother, to see Yao that very morning and told him that the factory urgently needed a vice-factory secretary since her husband was away so often.

Now that he was a Party member, Zheng Zhen had told Yao, her brother would be the right man for the position in view of his leadership qualities, so characteristic of the Zhengs.

And without further ado Madam Bo had told her brother to sit behind the vacant visiting dignitaries' desk in her husband's office, who was away on urgent matters of state, and to behave like the vice-factory secretary he henceforth was. Characteristically he had settled for a good nap as soon as his sister was gone.

Director Yao, not having been deemed worthy of Party membership himself, was wary to take Zheng to task.

Instead, ever since Madam Bo's visit he had been worrying how to tell me the news, he said.

I laughed and told him I would miss such a valuable helper and that I needed of course a substitute for Zheng. Perhaps the comrade director would be willing to consider the young man who had recently been appointed as a drum stacker in the filling station?

Director Yao promised he would clear the matter with the new vice-factory secretary and with Secretary Bo.

Three days later young Ma Jitai reported for work.

Ma was a cheerful youngster who didn't seem to take anything seriously but my impression was that this was merely an attitude because he was far too intelligent for the stupid job assigned to him.

He would do his utmost, he said, to learn everything about how to operate the boiler so that one day he could take over my job when I would be promoted to factory engineer.

I immediately saw my chance. I told him there were a few reasons why I would probably never be a factory engineer so why didn't he try to become one, through the ranks as it were. I would teach him, free of charge, but in return he would take over the early morning and late afternoon hours.

Ma Jitai agreed enthusiastically.

Within a week he knew everything there was to know about the operation of the old boiler.

I had worked out a study programme for him, basic mathematics, physics and mechanics, how to make technical sketches and drawings, welding and metallurgy and so on. Jitai absorbed everything, like dry sand the first rain, and I was pleased, both with his progress and the fact that I now had a goal.

After a few weeks I went to see Director Yao and told him about my plans for Ma Jitai and when Yao seemed genuinely pleased I asked him to assign my former shack behind the factory to Ma.

Ma was very happy that he could move out of his parents' small flat, a forty-two square metre utility affair he shared with his parents and his two elder brothers and their wives.

A month and a half after Jitai's appointment as my assistant we had divided the fourteen working hours between us; Ma took the first four hours, from five to nine in the morning and the last three hours, from four to seven in the afternoon and early evening.

Between nine and four he did his homework. I arrived at eight, together with Liang, and left at five, also together with Liang.

From eight to nine I corrected Ma's homework of the previous day and from four to five I prepared new lessons for him for the next day.

Everything worked out fine, though Yao had explained to me that the arrangement should remain strictly between Ma and myself and that if Secretary Bo or Vice-Secretary Zheng came to know about it and would be difficult about the exchange of labour for knowledge, he, Yao, would pretend to know nothing about the whole affair.

I agreed and promised that if Bo made difficulties I would meekly confess to having made a private arrangement with a fellow worker and to have kept it from Director Yao.

I explained to Ma that he was part of the deal I made with Yao and that he also should never implicate Yao.

He could blame me, I told Ma, call me a sweet-talker and confess that he had fallen for my siren song and had let himself be seduced to take the worst working hours in exchange for a few pitiful bits of capitalist knowledge.

Ma stared at me when I said that. There was no trace of his usual smiling, happy-go-lucky, devil-may-care attitude about him. His face was set, his lips a straight line, his eyes glittering like black opals.

'You finished?' he asked curtly.

I nodded.

'First of all I am not the kind of person who will blame others or circumstances to get myself out of a tight spot, certainly not if finding myself in that tight spot was my own choice or the result of my own choice. So old

Yao has nothing to fear. Secondly, like-minded friend Dao, I will *neither* blame you nor *praise* you for what was basically a quid pro quo deal for you. You needed me for your plan to spend more time with your pretty young wife, however, I lacked the knowledge and practice to stand in for you so you proposed to teach me. That you now teach me more than I need for this humdrum job is my good luck but yours as well since it provides you with a stimulus and some sense of accomplishing at least *something*, things all you intellectuals need or you just wither away.'

Ma burst out laughing when he saw my astonishment.

'You are surprised that I use those difficult words, Teacher Dao?' he chuckled. 'Let me tell you something about myself and then we can continue our excellent relationship, our excellent quid pro quo relationship, on a more equal footing. No awkwardness, no guilty feelings on your part, no undue gratefulness on my part, *our* choice, okay?'

I nodded, even more surprised.

'I was the brightest little boy, first in our alley and then of our neighbourhood,' Ma began. 'My father keeps the books at the small state market, my mother is a nurse in the day clinic in our sector of the town. My father is a dreamer, who smokes a pipe, mind you, and my mother worships him and every word he says. She agrees with everything he says and has never, ever, expressed an own opinion. She probably hasn't any.

'Father was proud, too proud, of his bright little son and fantasised and talked, puff, puff, puff, about the boy's great future and all the wonderful things he would learn and study and do and achieve. He never realised the irritation he caused and the resentment he sowed and kept cultivating amongst those exposed to his dreams. His own job as a pen-pusher does also not make him "one of the guys" in our neighbourhood of collective farm workers and other manual labourers. So, bright little son had a difficult time in primary school because the neighbourhood Party committee put pressure on the teachers to keep him at the same level as the other little morons.

'Father was disappointed but I think he must have understood for at home he taught me how to write beautifully, even with a brush and an ink stone. He also taught me arithmetic, mentally and with an abacus, and the background of things, at least his perception of it, which was always mild and fuzzy and narrow as I now realise. Thanks to him I finished school as the best of my class and this must have angered the neighbourhood Party committee secretary, a woman, who was once told by my mother, at the clinic, that her body odour and lack of personal hygiene in her private parts was probably the cause of her husband's lack of libido at home and lusting after other women on the collective farm. When my father and I applied for my admittance to Meishan's middle school our application was turned down by the town Party secretary at the behest of that vindictive neighbourhood Party secretary and I was assigned to the collective farm as a general handyman.

'Six years I spent there and I became never anything more than a handyman. So I applied for a transfer to a factory and three months ago, one year after my application, I was called to the neighbourhood Party secretariat where they told me I had been assigned to the Snowflake Soap Factory as a handyman. Since I left primary school, however, Father and I kept working at my education as best as we could. I can now write twenty-four thousand characters, with a pencil, with a pen and with a brush, as calligraphy, I can make every calculation with figures, however many, but not with Arabic letters as you are now teaching me, Dao, since Father had no knowledge of algebra as you call it.

'I know everything about China's history, from Father's narrow perspective that is, and I have my dreams about the future, *my* future. One of my philosophies is that only the sun rises for free and everything else must be paid for some way or other or is in exchange for something. The deal between you and me, Dao, is just an example. Another of my self-acquired philosophies is that if a chance to better yourself presents itself, grab it and hold on to it. You and your teachings are such a chance, Dao, and I intend to take full advantage of it.

'I will *not* spend the rest of my life as a manual labourer, Dao! You can't imagine how I hate the obtuse, narrow-minded and hateful morons. I feel sick in their foul-smelling, lumbering presence, so I behave like an idiot, my face muscles aching from that stupid grin I hide behind and dead tired every evening of hearing my own trivial, vapid talk. I don't want to be one of them, Dao, and I will do anything, *anything*, to get out of this mess they dare call a factory, to get out of Meishan, out of Anhui, and, nightly fantasy, out of China. As a special favour, Dao, please teach me enough English words so that I can reply in English once I'm across the border in Hong Kong or Macau. Will you do that for me, Dao?'

I nodded and said, 'I will do that for you, Ma. However, I have a wife to look after now and maybe a family later, so don't let out, not even to your parents, that you have a smattering of English. It would definitely mean the end of my trivial but contented existence here and most probably the end of your dreams as well. Is that clear?'

Ma nodded, deadly serious, and said, 'That is clear. Have no fear, my friend.'

## *Chapter Twenty-Six*

### Acquiescence and Contentment

I know this sounds like the usual platitude from a newly-wed man but Liang *did* change my life and my state of mind completely.

Of course I didn't change from one day to the other. Such takes time and a lot of tears, of hurt, of making up, of relapses into my habitual sarcasm and bitterness and rebelliousness at the way life and the Party had treated me.

Liang was always so quick to forget and forgive, so trusting and so ingenuously affectionate and cheerful that I hated myself when I saw the hurt in her eyes and her lips tremble at yet another, unnecessary, sarcastic remark or comment.

At first I found it difficult, if not impossible, to admit my wrong and say that I was sorry and it was always Liang who snuggled up to me, high in my ivory tower of haughty, sulking silence, and said that *she* was sorry. Sorry for what? It was I who had made the beastly remark, *not* she.

But such was Liang's nature. For her pride and face had nothing to do with trying to maintain or re-establish harmony, on the contrary, such feelings are often the last and most difficult obstacles to remove when seemingly the argument has been settled.

It was this attitude of Liang's that made me see myself as I must have appeared to others, to Liang's parents for instance: a stupid, stubborn malcontent with such a high opinion of himself and low opinion of others that he refuses to believe the world can make out without him and that there may be other ways to be happy in life than those of the achiever.

I realised how fortunate I was and that I risked losing it all because of my boorish, insensible selfishness: the love of my beautiful wife, the understanding affection of her kindly parents, the comfortableness of everyday life, the total absence of worry because there was nothing to worry about, no valuable possessions to lose, no money to hoard, no competitors to fear and to outmanoeuvre, no career to strive for.

This realisation was the last straw to break the stubborn camel's back and I adjusted and became a contented man.

One year to the day after our wedding Liang and I asked and received permission to have a child and again one year later, strangely enough again to the very day, our son Xulun was born on 1st August, 1957.

We gave a small Party when Xulun was three months old and Secretary Bo not only honoured us by attending and bringing a nice present for Xulun but he made us very happy as well when he said he would endorse an application for a bigger house.

Six months later we moved into our new house, a detached two-bedroomed house with a beautiful view on Meishan's lake-sized water reservoir.

When Xulun was four and a half years old we received approval, after a two-year wait, for a second child and on 9th February, 1962 our daughter Xuli was born.

More to please Liang than because of my own filial feelings I sent again a card to my mother in England, just as I had done for our wedding and Xulun's birth.

I had never got an answer to any of my letters, sent once a month in the beginning, ages ago now, then rarer and rarer until seven or eight years ago, I had stopped writing completely.

Now months went by without even a fleeting thought of my former life in an alien land.

We lived our simple and frugal but contented life in our little backwater, blissfully unaware of what was brewing in the big cities and of the incessant and often ruthless power struggles at the top of the Party hierarchy.

We fussed and got excited about such trivial things as the birth of our son, our move into the new house, occasional small indispositions in the family, my promotion to assistant engineer, Ma Jitai's promotion to boiler operator and assistant to the assistant engineer, Secretary Bo's amorous adventures and his wife's tantrums, the birth of our daughter; our life a softly purling stream, soothing in its very ordinariness.

⋆

Lao Dao fell silent and focused his attention on his friends whom he had gripped with his narrative.

'I propose we call it a day,' he said, smiling at his friends. 'It's past eleven o'clock already and tomorrow will be a long day for Lao Dee, what with his evening flight to Hong Kong and the things he has to prepare for over there.

My story has come to a turning point so I might as well begin next week with this new chapter of my life. Is that all right with you?'

Without waiting for the others Beiyuen leapt from her chair, clapped her hands and exclaimed, 'That was a beautiful story, Uncle Dao, so upsetting yet so moving and humorous that sometimes I felt like laughing and crying all at once. Already I am looking forward to the next part. Shall I pour us a fresh mug of tea for the road? Yes?' And when the others nodded smilingly she asked, 'Lilian? Please clean out the mugs and put in fresh tea. I'll quickly boil the water.'

Chatting inconsequentially they sniffed and sipped the invigorating brew.

Five minutes later they quickly took leave of one another and Lao Dao and Lao Dee left together for the hotel, a good, half-hour walk, while Suping and Lilian, arm in arm, whispering so as not to wake the neighbours, walked the thirty metres to their house.

Beiyuen quickly cleaned and arranged the glasses and mugs, peeped around Auntie Liu's bedroom door to check whether she was all right (she was fast asleep already and snoring softly) and, humming, prepared herself a makeshift bed on the couch.

Like every evening she lay on her back for a moment, looking up at the ceiling, hoping to see the floating image of Kuan Yin smiling down on her.

Sometimes Kuan Yin was busy elsewhere but tonight she was at her post and, satisfied she had the kindly goddess's attention, Beiyuen reminded her not to forget to remind Lao Dee to give some money to her as well for new clothes for the trip to Luding.

Everybody had some special business there, in Luding, even Auntie Liu with that Uncle Dan of Lilian's mother, except her, Beiyuen. So she was afraid Lao Dee wouldn't think it necessary for her to appear there in nice clothes, what with all the money they cost him already, there never seemed an end to it, now this, then that, the latest in the row that Pan official.

Pay him a trip to Hong Kong was the idea. How absurd. What did he do to earn such a reward? Oblige a pretty woman in distress, twice? Quite a normal thing for a man to do, especially when it was within his power.

She shook her head and cluck-clucked in exasperation at Kuan Yin who, being a pretty woman herself, nodded in agreement.

Reassured that Lao Dee would be prevented from spending his money on undeserving people Beiyuen happily turned herself on her right side and fell asleep.

## *Chapter Twenty-Seven*

### All in the Name of the Great Leader

The following Thursday they gathered early, at three o'clock in the afternoon.

Suping and Lilian had already prepared a simple Sichuan dish for dinner, diced pork meat sauté in sesame oil with dried red chillies, sweet soy sauce, ginger powder and fresh vegetables. It only needed to be warmed up at six o'clock while Beiyuen would cook the rice.

Lao Dee had brought almond bean curd and a can of mixed fruit from Hong Kong for dessert, and a few paper packs of chrysanthemum tea and thick, syrupy fruit juices for the women.

For himself and Lao Dao he had brought a few cans of foreign beers, San Miguel from Hong Kong and Heineken from Singapore he explained, to accompany the meal and for later, during the evening, to keep Lao Dao's throat lubricated and his narrative lively. Everybody laughed when Lao Dee said that and gave his friend a playful nudge with his elbow.

Especially for Auntie Liu he had brought a beautiful, black bottle of the dark red, sweet wine she liked so much.

Everybody would have a small glass, Auntie exclaimed, blushing and pleased, before dinner, to celebrate the good time they had together, and to help Lao Dao to push, momentarily, his black memories into the background.

Lao Dao smiled and quipped that he then better drink the whole bottle.

While Beiyuen prepared fresh tea and Lilian put the insulated box with the beer, the tea and juices in a cool place in the kitchen, the elders took their usual places, chatting contentedly.

Lao Dao, once settled comfortably, withdrew from the conversation to collect his thoughts and prepare the first few sentences; the rest would follow by itself.

Lilian put a mug in front of each and Beiyuen poured the tea and then the two girls sat down as well.

The conversation died down and they quietly waited for Lao Dao to resume his narration.

*

That terrible typhoon that destroyed the last remnants of our Chinese civilisation, the civilisation I had been proud of and come back for, the civilisation the whole world had admired for centuries, that collective madness and hysteria known as the Great Proletarian Cultural Revolution did, of course, not spare Meishan.

The purling, little stream of our small, ordinary lives became a raging torrent and we, the quiet and contented fishermen, were dragged along and scattered, like flotsam, over the flood-stricken land.

From Hefei they came, one late autumn evening, much like the Mongol hordes in the past. Only this time the marauders did not ride on horseback. In buses and on ramshackle trucks they rode, brandishing and waving banners with slogans and a Little Red Book, shrieking their Great Leader's blood-curdling war cries, their eyes crazed, their faces distorted by hatred and malevolent triumph.

Students they were, mostly, girls leading the more slow-witted boys.

After the burning of the library at Hefei's Institute of Great Learning they had swarmed out, like angry wasps, into the countryside and the smaller towns of Anhui leaving nothing but wreckage in their wake.

They trampled flowers and flowering bushes of other colours than red, dragged from their homes people whose only crime was to have held some position of importance before liberation, or who had relatives abroad, or who had been educated to say 'thank you' and 'please' and read books.

Secretary Bo huddled with Secretary Peng, in Bo's office at the factory, for days on end and the day the hordes descended upon Meishan Bo ordered the factory to close and the workers to join the Red Guards as he called the crazy youths.

Only I was called into his office, alone, and told by both Peng and Bo to stay at home and that in a rough tone as if they were giving me house arrest and were already distancing themselves from me.

As the days passed I became increasingly worried by what passers-by told us was going on in town.

Only a few took the time to stop when I, sitting on the bench in front of our house, hailed them and asked them for news. Most of them, however, merely looked furtively in my direction and hurried on, without a word, as if I had the plague. Some, though, shouted their advice to pack a few things and flee to the mountains, like they were going to do themselves.

On the third day of my confinement my father-in-law persuaded us to let him descend into town to try to find out whether we were in any danger. Liang's parents had been living in with us for the past two years since both were getting on in age and needed Liang to care for them.

I won't ever forget the look of despair in the old man's eyes when he came back that evening, wheezing and gasping for breath after the long and rather steep descent to our house. Liang immediately poured him a mug of fresh tea and wiped his neck and forehead as he tremblingly sipped from his tea.

When he had recovered somewhat and could speak again he said, voice still quavering, 'It's terrible, terrible, *terrible*!' That last 'terrible' came out in a shriek.

'The only way to save the children and Liang will be for us, Liang, Mother and myself, to deny that we knew about your past, Huimin,' he continued, crying. 'Please Huimin, for the sake of your children and your wife you must deride openly our gullibility for having believed your lies about your life before you came to Meishan. And we must feign horror at having been so deceived by you. We may even have to accuse you of terrible things.'

He wiped his eyes and, in a calmer tone, he continued, 'My wife and I are too old to care about our lives but we *must* save the children, they are too young to defend themselves. Can you do that for us, Huimin? Can you bear one more betrayal? This time by the very persons you love so much?'

The old man burst into tears.

I was deeply moved but before I could say something Liang replied quietly, 'It's a good plan, Father, and it just may work. The risk that it won't, however, is too great. I am not exactly known as a gullible person and pretending I did not know about my husband's past is simply not credible. That you and Mother didn't know, that they may well believe, especially when I tell them that, had you known, you would have refused permission for me to marry Huimin and that therefore I persuaded him not to talk about his past in your presence. So I won't play the game proposed by you, Father. If Huimin's past is a reason for the Red Guards to arrest him I can probably deflect their rage from you and Mother and the children by telling them defiantly that I knew all the time but hid the truth from you.'

She fell silent and listened, head tilted upwards, eyes half-closed.

'There they come,' she announced quietly.

We all listened sharply and then I heard the still distant singing and sloganeering by what was apparently a large group of people, young voices mostly, the higher voices of girls dominating.

Pale, her voice quavering slightly, she called the children, 'Xulun, Xuli, you must go outside now, behind the house, and walk all the way down to the lake. There you hide in the bushes. Stay there no matter what you may hear from the direction of the house. You wait patiently until Grandfather or Grandmother comes to fetch you there. If the house has been silent for a long time but nobody comes for you, you must go straight to Uncle Yao's house.

'Uncle Yao and Auntie Mei will take care of you until Grandfather and Grandmother come back. Papa and Mama will stay away a bit longer but we will also come back to take care of you again. In the meantime you stay with Grandfather and Grandmother and be very brave and good. Xulun, you must always take good care of Xuli and comfort her when she cries. Now, can you do all this? Without fail?'

Our two beautiful, lovely children looked at us with solemn little faces and nodded.

I saw Xulun take his little sister's hand and squeeze it softly as he pulled her towards Liang and me.

'Give Papa and Mama a kiss,' he said, 'they will be gone for a little while.'

Liang and I kissed and hugged the children, tears streaming down our cheeks.

The noise of a stone or piece of rock flung against the window shutters shattered our intimacy and we heard the shouting and singing very near the house now.

'Go now, Xulun! Go quickly and do as I told you!' Liang said urgently.

Without a word Xulun took his little sister's hand and together they went outside, without looking back, to the place near the lake where we had played and picnicked so often together.

Old Shi closed the back door Xulun had left open and turned to look at his wife and at Liang and me, in wordless sorrow. I saw the fear behind the sorrow.

A loud pounding on the front door and several voices shouting, 'In the name of our Great Leader Chairman Mao, open the door, you cows and snakes!' pushed the thoughts of our children momentarily out of our minds, reminding us of our own plight.

'We are the Red Guards, our Chairman Mao's little revolutionary generals and we have come to take revolutionary action against you!' several girls' voices shouted, over renewed pounding. A piece of rock shattered the window pane as I opened the door.

About two dozen or so boys and girls, aged between fourteen and twenty something, trooped inside, followed by Vice-Secretary Zheng, a mocking, triumphant sneer on his face.

'That's the foreigner-loving traitor Dao, Comrade Dong!' Zheng shrieked, pointing at me. 'And that's the foreigner-loving whore Shi Liang,' he snarled, grabbing Liang's arm.

Two resounding slaps followed by a shriek like that of a stuck pig and Vice-Secretary Zheng was rolling on the floor, sobbing and shrieking, holding his genitals while blood dripped from an ugly gash in his right cheek and from his nose.

My beautiful wife Liang, eyes flashing, cheeks burning from red-hot anger, spat at the moaning man on the floor and glared at the Red Guards who stared back in stunned disbelief.

'You scum!' she hissed. 'You sorry bunch of clowns! Take me and my husband to your leaders in town! Now, immediately! Bursting in here like a herd of wild boars and insulting us, and that in the name of our Great Leader Chairman Mao? How *dare* you! You have no *right*! So get *out*! *Now*! And take us to your leaders so that I can *complain*!'

At that she strutted out of the door and went up the path that led to the road into town, not looking back once.

I saw the Red Guards looking at each other, undecidedly, still stunned by this totally unexpected turn of events.

Their leader, Comrade Dong as Zheng had called him, a skeletally thin young man with an enormous, bulging blackhead on the tip of his bulbous nose, shrugged his shoulders, ordered two of the older boys to help Zheng up from the floor and trotted after Liang.

The others followed, subdued and awkwardly, Zheng closing the row, hobbling and moaning, one hand pressed against his crotch, the other pinching his bleeding nose.

I couldn't suppress a grin at the débâcle and before following my tempestuous spouse I turned to my parents-in-law, who had remained unnoticed in their corner during the short altercation.

'Liang is leading them away from here,' I whispered hurriedly, 'She is so incredibly brave. You can be so proud of your daughter. After I have left, go down to the lake and fetch the children. Take good care of them and teach them to take care of you as well. Xulun is old enough to help you with the chores in and around the house and Xuli will be in a few years. Don't spoil them and talk often about us if we do *not* come back that is. Always talk about us in the present tense, as if we will be back shortly.

'Do *not*, I repeat *do not* go into town to enquire after us, however long it takes before you hear from us, whatever people may tell you happened to us. Only then is there a chance that the Red Guards will forget about you and the children. Now, is that clear?'

Huddled in their corner, like two frightened rabbits, they nodded, wordlessly.

In an impulse I embraced them, first the old lady, then old Shi, then both of them once more.

With a last smile, which I wanted so much to be reassuring, and with a heavy heart, I closed the door and rushed after my wife and her escort already three hundred metres up the road.

The Red Guards had left their truck at the intersection with the main road, a little more than half a kilometre from our house.

When I saw the tired, ramshackle, old Roman truck I could understand why the driver had undoubtedly told his charges to walk the five hundred metres potholed, dirt road down to the lake.

I caught up with the group just as two of the guards were helping the still whimpering Zheng climb on to the platform. Liang stood already on the truck, her back against the cabin, and I quickly jumped aboard and went to stand beside her.

'You were wonderful,' I whispered in her ear, 'I love you and I am so proud of you. I talked to your parents. Told them *not* to come to town to ask about us, whatever happens. That way these crazy kids may forget all about them. Told them to think of the children only. They understood. Kissed both of them. Told them they could be proud of their daughter.'

Liang squeezed my hand and I saw her eyes well tears.

Everybody had climbed on board by then, I counted twenty-six of them, and Leading Red Guard Dong shouted at the driver to get moving, back to town.

Through the small, paneless, cabin back window I could see the driver's face, brazen, a cigarette dangling from a corner of his mouth, a mocking half-smile, half-sneer on his face as if he couldn't care less about the whole, wide world which he probably didn't and got away with.

He started the engine, revved it up until it roared and spewed out thick, black clouds of sooty smoke which the wind blew in our faces to his hilarious delight, and let go of the clutch so suddenly that Dong and his Red Guards tumbled pell-mell, cursing and yelling abuse at each other and the driver, on the rough, dirty floor planks.

I had anticipated the driver's move and had held on to the dented cabin roof with one arm, the other around Liang's shoulder, pressing her against me. We looked down on the heap of sprawling, thrashing bodies and we laughed with malicious glee.

Bellowing with equally malicious glee and hilarity the driver drove his truck back to town, horn blaring incessantly, forcing people on the road to jump into the ditch on either side or be crushed and us, prisoners and guards alike, to hold on to each other for our dear lives or be hurled off the platform as he slalomed through the curves without reducing speed.

Our stop in front of the town hall, after a half-hour agony, was as abrupt as our departure and our unfortunate guards fell in a heap and with an audible whoosh against the cabin and our legs. The driver laughed uproariously, extracted one, last, rattling roar from the poor engine and then cut it off. He jumped out of the cabin and swaggered off towards a small eating place without a glance at his dishevelled passengers.

Leading Red Guard Dong pulled himself together and ordered everybody off the truck.

Avoiding eye contact, both with us and amongst themselves, out of shame for their loss of face, they hustled us into the town hall and up the stairs into a very large room, a kind of makeshift courtroom apparently, judging by what I saw was going on.

Six men and three women were sitting behind three trestle-tables pushed together to make one, long bench.

Above their heads, against the back wall of the room, hung a large red banner with big, white characters, reading:

*LENIENT TREATMENT FOR THOSE WHO CONFESS.*
*SEVERE PUNISHMENT FOR THOSE WHO REMAIN STUBBORN.*
*REWARD FOR THOSE WHO DENOUNCE ENEMIES OF THE PEOPLE.*
*DEATH FOR TRAITORS OF THE PEOPLE.*
*LONG LIVE OUR VICTORIOUS CHAIRMAN MAO.*

Four Red Guards, spurred on by their leader, Dong, hustled us through the room towards what I guessed was the judges' bench.

On Dong's order they suddenly stopped about three metres in front of the bench.

Dong shoved his underlings roughly aside and took Liang's upper arm, trying to force her on her knees. Before I could restrain her she had turned like a striking cobra and slapped the youth's face, hissing, 'Keep your filthy hands off me, you imbecile!'

In a reflex Dong wiped his nose with the back of his hand and stared, stunned, at the blood and snot and the monstrous blackhead that had squirted out of his nose.

The sight made me gag.

Suddenly he shrieked wildly and from his crazed eyes I saw he was about to go berserk.

I stepped in front of Liang to protect her but, suddenly, a loud, stentorian voice shouted, '*Stop it! Immediately!*'

Dong started backwards a full two metres as if he had stepped on another snake and the crowd of fifty or so men and women in the room stopped their jabber and stared at us, sullen and hostile.

It was not difficult to guess whose was the commanding voice. Flanked on either side by four almost caricature-like representatives of the peasant working class, he was unmistakably a high-class mandarin, notwithstanding the austere, high-buttoned light grey jacket.

As a child I had seen pictures of the likes of him, dressed in colourful ceremonial dress and winged, black skullcap; magistrates administering justice in the Emperor's name.

About forty years old I guessed, face long, sharp-featured and intelligent; eyebrows, thick, black, joining above the straight nose and curving upwards at the temples; hair glossy and combed straight back, he sat there, completely at ease, cracking the knuckles of his extraordinary long fingers alternately with either hand while watching us with his glittering, surprisingly round eyes, a slightly sardonic smile hovering at the corners of his mouth.

When his eyes locked on to mine it felt as if I had been hit, physically, just above my nose where the Indians say we had, once, long ago, a third eye.

When he released me and locked on to Liang I knew, from her sharp intake of breath, that his effect on her had been the same and she also would be no match for him whatever he would do to us.

The man was evidently aware of the power of his eyes over people for after a few seconds he released also Liang and, looking downward at his flexing fingers, he said, in a soft and pleasant voice and speaking a very cultured, almost affected, standard Chinese, 'You are facing the People's Tribunal of the County of Meishan. My name is Song Xisheng and I am one of our Great Leader Chairman Mao's special interrogators sent by him throughout the country and to the farthest outposts to see to it that true proletarian justice is dispensed. For the time being Anhui Province is my responsibility. I have come to Meishan expressly for your case and you are here, today, standing trial before this People's Tribunal, on my express orders. The foreign connotations involved here demand that I try your case personally and report directly to the Party's Central Committee.'

Special Interrogator Song fell silent and looked up at us and again I felt the impact of those extraordinary eyes.

Without any deference to the other judges Song continued his monologue.

'Let me summarise the cases against the two of you. You, Dao Huimin, are accused of being a foreign agent, sent to China in 1953, on October 10th to be precise, with the mission to sabotage, in concert with other saboteurs of Chinese descent, the industrial base of the People's Republic of China. You were recruited by Sha Jiwen, a notorious spy from the traitorous Guomindang clique in Taiwan, who had managed to infiltrate our embassy in Stockholm, Sweden. Ma's territory was the whole of Western Europe but with the emphasis on the hostile colonial power England which for the past hundred and twenty years has occupied a part of the People's Republic of China against the wishes of the oppressed and downtrodden people of what they mockingly and arrogantly call the crown colony of Hong Kong.

'Ma introduced you to Lai Xilian and Peng Bishi of our Party's recruitment office who, in good faith it must be said, arranged your transport to China. Lai and Peng have been instrumental in bringing more than sixty saboteurs like you into China and they have confessed last month to exposing our country to great risk and danger because of their extremely grave lack of political awareness and maturity unforgivable in people of their rank and seniority. Both have been expelled from the Party and subsequently tried and sentenced to death. Both have had their sentences commuted by order of our Great Leader Chairman Mao, in his compassionate wisdom. They are now serving twenty-five years of hard labour in Shanxi and Xinjiang. I am telling you this, Dao, so that you realise the extent and omnipresence of the Party's vigilance.

'We know therefore that right from the day you began your job in the Maling Canning Factory, in Shanghai, you have sabotaged both the machinery and the process of political indoctrination of the factory's workers with the aim to cause food shortages and popular anger and dissatisfaction with the rule of our beloved Party. Though you were reported by your factory unit's Party secretary Chen Jianxiu, as an apolitical troublemaker for whom she requested a transfer to a less sensitive production unit in a strategically less important region, she failed to recognise and expose you as a foreign saboteur, notwithstanding the fact that she *knew* of your formation in a hostile foreign country. Chen Jianxiu was expelled last month from the Party and condemned to ten years of re-education in a people's commune. You were transferred to the Snowflake Soap Factory here in peaceful Meishan and barely a week after your arrival you resumed your saboteur's role.

'The factory unit Party vice-secretary, Zheng, at that time still not a Party member yet showing already the mettle and vigilance expected of a member, discovered your true intentions and reported you to his brother-in-law, the factory Party secretary, Bo Dinyi. Secretary Bo ordered Zheng to keep an eye on you at all times and so as to avoid any suspicion of collusion between you and him, he also told Zheng to act the lazy bum unwilling to do the slightest bit of work. Secretary Bo's suspicions were confirmed when you recruited factory worker Shi Liang, remarkably enough also a person with tainted antecedents. Shi Liang's first mission was to find out the effects of the sabotaged product, Snowflake Liquid Soap, on the local population.

'Even before she reported back to you, Secretary Bo had already discovered the dangerous and demoralising effects his erstwhile wonderful product had on the factory workers and his family members and with the help of his younger brother-in-law Zheng he found out that you added an excessive amount of lye to the kettles, again with the help of your accomplice Shi Liang. Instead of exposing the two of you there and then, Secretary Bo decided to continue watching you in order to discover eventual wider ramifications of your plotting and scheming. So as not to let the contaminated soap enter the official supply lines of the people, Secretary Bo took the responsibility to dump the weekly delivery to Hefei into the Li River near Lu'an, again with the secret help of a brother-in-law and the workers of a brick factory who fully understood their revolutionary duty.

'Secretary Bo is an extraordinary patient man, if patient is the right word for such long-term vigilance, and he let this situation go on for *ten* years before he finally made his conclusive report only *three* days ago when Secretary Peng informed him of my arrival. While you and your accomplice Shi Liang continued to sabotage the production, you, Dao, made another recruit in the person of Ma Jitai. Under the guise of teaching him the job of assistant boiler operator you taught him much more than required for this relatively simple job and more specifically English, the language of the major enemies of the People. Once you had completed your instruction you sent Ma Jitai out of the country, to that bastion of enemy activities against the People's Republic of China, to that spy nest Hong Kong.

'He has teamed up with other counter-revolutionary agitators and contributes a column to a virulently anti-Communist Chinese-language tabloid in which he ridicules the political and economic situation in China as well as our leaders, including our Great Leader Chairman Mao and Comrade Jiang Qing. Ma's parents have been arrested and severely punished for their part in his counter-revolutionary formation, notably his father, who taught him the feudal past of our country and how to express his nefarious thoughts in such convincing, elitist language. All this is of *your* doing, Dao, and although that sabotage business in Shanghai and here, in Meishan, is important, the Party considers the Ma Jitai affair a far greater *political* threat with far-reaching long-term consequences.'

Song fell silent and looked at me over his stapled fingers. Did I see respect in those strange eyes? Pity? I still think so today.

'This concludes the People's case against you, Dao Huimin,' Song said and his voice had changed to a softer tone.

'This People's Tribunal will pass sentence at the start of tomorrow's session, at ten o'clock in the morning. You will not be permitted to speak in defence of yourself or to appoint somebody else to speak for you, assuming such a foolish person can be found. In the meantime you will be tied to a post on the raised platform in front of the town hall and you will hold a banner above your head that proclaims your crimes against the People: "Counter-revolutionary agitator in the pay of foreign powers".'

My ears rang and I felt dizzy and nauseated and in an effort to stay on my wobbly legs I grabbed Liang's arm.

Lovingly she supported me and as from far I heard her whisper that she loved me and always would, whatever they would do to me.

As through a haze I saw Song pounding on the bench with a wooden mallet and I heard him shout, '*Silence*!'

The spectators, who had erupted in an excited jabber after Song's conclusion of my case, fell silent and an expectant hush fell over the courtroom.

'I shall now summarise the People's case against the woman Shi Liang, wife and accessory of the foreign agitator Dao Huimin,' Special Interrogator Song continued. 'From the age that you can be held responsible for your behaviour and acts, Shi Liang, you have shown a marked preference for things foreign combined with an aloof scorn for things Chinese, more precisely for our revolutionary musical culture. You were an acknowledged musical talent at an early age but despite the urging of your local neighbourhood committee in Wuhan to switch to our Chinese instruments and revolutionary musical works, you persisted in playing the violin, a Western instrument, and in studying the works of long-dead, feudal, Western composers. On several occasions you were overheard making derogatory comments about contemporary, revolutionary Chinese composers and their work; bunglers without any talent you called them, who produced worthless trash to please the *nyekulturny* Party morons. And these were only your milder expressions.

'In 1950 you were recruited by an American newspaper correspondent based in Wuhan. We know that this man, Sean O'Shaunnessy, was a CIA agent and a sworn enemy of the Chinese Communist Party. He wrote many derogatory and inflammatory articles about our Chairman Mao, though he wrote in the same style about Chiang Kaishek, calling them both wolves in sheep's clothes. Thanks to the vigilance of the Party secretary of Wuhan the plot to get you and your parents out of the country to continue your agitation against the People's Republic from abroad was discovered, just in time, and you and your parents were actually treated very leniently when you were banned from Wuhan and more or less exiled to Meishan. The thought behind the Party's magnanimity at that time was that the small-town atmosphere in the rural province of Anhui would bring you closer to the people and teach you the value of being Chinese.

'The reports by your neighbourhood committee and your factory unit secretary, Bo Dinyi, were initially favourable until the saboteur Dao Huimin appeared on the scene. Because of him you not only rejected but even ridiculed the advances of Zheng Benhua, an upright aspiring Party member and brother-in-law of Secretary Bo, and you more or less thrust yourself on Dao what was exactly what the conspirator wanted, of course. You willingly became his accessory by spying on Secretary Bo and, having proven your worth to him in his nefarious scheming against the People he took advantage of your besottedness with his foreign background and married you.

'On several occasions after your marriage to Dao you were reprimanded by members of your neighbourhood committee for your lack of revolutionary ardour as well as for your levity and mockery during the neighbourhood political meetings. It was to Secretary Bo's credit that he realised that you were incorrigible and to protect the good people in your neighbourhood against your insidious attempts to corrupt their minds he arranged for you and your family to move to a house near the water reservoir where there were no close neighbours.

'The Party's tolerance, however, for such antisocial behaviour has now reached its limits and this People's Tribunal hereby declares you guilty of trying to corrupt the people's minds by mocking and ridiculing their earnest and wholehearted striving to conform to their beloved Party's directives. You have also been found guilty of criminal neglect by failing to report your husband Dao Huimin's treasonous activities against the State and the Party.

This People's Tribunal will also pass sentence on you tomorrow at ten o'clock. In the meantime you will stand on the platform beside the said Dao Huimin and hold up a banner stating your crimes against the People.'

Special Interrogator Song banged his mallet and the table and shouted, 'Today's session of the People's Tribunal of Meishan is now closed! Red Guard Wan Ziqi is hereby promoted to leading Red Guard and will henceforth take the place of former Leading Red Guard Dong. Red Guard Dong is hereby confined to his house for one week as punishment for his lack of leadership and to attend to his injured nose!'

After one final bang Song stood up from his chair and stalked out of the courtroom through a side door, without a glance at Liang and me or at the spectators.

The judges, simple peasants and workers, were clearly at a loss what to do.

They looked at each other, fumbled with their papers to give themselves face, then, suddenly, they grabbed their bags and, shuffling and stumbling, disappeared through the side door in Song's wake.

As if on cue half a dozen Red Guards rushed in and, egged on by an exultantly grinning Vice-Secretary Zheng, they pushed and shoved us through the milling crowd in the room, down the stairs and out of the front door.

There, in front of the town hall, a kind of dais had been erected, wooden planks on small stacks of bricks, about half a metre above the ground. Zheng shouted at us to stand on the dais and then, at the Red Guards, to fetch two pieces of rope to tie our hands behind our back.

A girl, surely not older than fifteen, came rushing out of the town hall shrieking at the other Red Guards not to tie our hands as we wouldn't be able to hold up the banners she was busy preparing.

In the following confusion newly promoted Leading Red Guard Wan took charge and told Vice-Secretary Zheng to back off and that in no uncertain terms. I was surprised to see Zheng actually squirm and then withdraw into the background, biting his lower lip.

The Red Guards were uncertain how to deal with us and they quarrelled whether we would be allowed to sit or even lie down from time to time. A few thought we should be allowed to sleep during the night since nobody would be there to read the banners and yell insults or throw garbage and excrement at us.

The boys were indecisive, changing their opinion all the time depending on who was arguing the loudest, the girls on the other hand were all in favour of having us tied to the posts in the middle of the platform and forced to hold our banners until the next morning ten o'clock, as ordered by Special Interrogator Song.

Finally Leading Red Guard Wan, visibly annoyed by the bickering and apparently also by the meanness of the girls, told the others to shut up and that he had decided Liang and I should take turns in standing upright holding our banner chest-high instead of above our head and that from ten o'clock until six the next morning both of us could try to catch some sleep.

He also ordered four Red Guards, two boys and two girls, to stand guard at the four corners of the platform and to take turns to escort either of us to the public toilets next to the town hall.

Again I was surprised at his apparent authority over the others and at his reasonableness, kindness even, considering the situation.

I saw Liang smile her gratitude at him and the slight nod with which he acknowledged her. He read the banners the girl held up for his inspection and then ordered her to hand them to us, each our own.

'Hold them up to your chin,' he said. 'The people must be able to read them. When they mock you or insult you, you are not allowed to reply or to react in any way. If they throw garbage at you, or worse, raise the banner a bit to protect your face. Officially it's not allowed and also officially I haven't told you this, however, I won't say anything if the banners are soiled. Whatever happens stay calm. What'll happen to you tomorrow will be much worse, I'm afraid. I'll have to leave now. I have other revolutionary cats to whip.' And with a mocking smile at his own words he turned his back on us and walked off, followed by his band of guards, in search of other criminal elements and enemies of the People.

Liang and I took turns to stand holding our banner and we felt utterly silly.

At first the four Red Guards on sentry duty shouted at us to shut up when Liang and I talked to each other but Liang merely smiled at them, sweetly, and continued to talk to me about whatever came to her mind in an effort to lift my spirits.

After a while the Red Guards gave up and they huddled together in one corner of the platform, giggling and whispering.

No more than a dozen people approached the platform, read the banners and, after a curious, half-pitying glance at us, they went their way, undoubtedly counting themselves lucky to have escaped, so far at least, the Red Guards' attention and deciding that keeping a low profile might be the best way to stay unnoticed.

At ten o'clock the guards suddenly stood up and told us to lie down and sleep. They, too, would take turns to sleep, they said, so trying to escape would be suicidal.

Liang and I took off our shoes and wrapped them in our banners to use them as a pillow.

Unashamedly I kissed my wife, a Western habit she'd loved from our very first kiss eleven years ago. Holding hands we huddled, knees and foreheads touching, and shivering from the cold, humid night air, we tried to fool each other by pretending to have fallen asleep.

From time to time I opened one eye to check whether she was indeed asleep only to find her looking at me, so we smiled and squeezed hands and I kissed her on the tip of her nose.

Still, somehow, we must have fallen asleep since I woke up with a start when somebody shook me by the shoulders. I looked up and into Leading Red Guard Wan's ironic eyes.

'Welcome back from your capitalist dream-world into our proletarian, revolutionary reality,' he said mockingly. 'It's half past six and I would advise you to go to the toilet now. At seven o'clock you have to stand here again, holding your banners, when Special Interrogator Song arrives. He's always early, Song the Aristocrat, always so eager to dance to the piping of his plebeian masters in Beijing. I'll ask him if he can spare a few grains of rice for you and your wife.'

Before I could answer Liang said, 'Thank you, Wan Ziqi. You are a good person which encourages me to think that not all our youth has gone collectively crazy. There might be hope with young people like you keeping a sense of humour and a healthy view of what is going on. But forgive me, your name is not a familiar one, not in this area at least. Who are you? And how is it that you can speak out like you do?'

'My family is originally from Hankou,' Wan said, 'I heard about your case, Shi Liang, from family talk. My father disagreed with Wuhan's Party secretary at the time. He's now a big shot in Hefei, my father is, and his brother an even bigger shot in Beijing. I was a student at Nanjing University when it was closed and we were told to forget everything we had learned.

'I joined the Red Guards to do my father a favour and also to stay out of trouble myself. I'm a coward you see, and I wouldn't want to happen to me what is going to happen to you and people like you. So I'm howling with the wolves. Only I try to be kind to the prey before the pack tears it to pieces. The other Red Guards do as I say, not because they fear me personally but because they fear my influence with the two big, bad wolves in Hefei and Beijing.

Even Song may not think it wise to vex me too much. Nevertheless, I advise you to be respectful to Song and I, too, dare not risk pushing my luck too much so I may have to shout at you, even kick you a little, at times. Don't take it badly.'

At that Leading Red Guard Wan Ziqi sauntered off, giving orders to our four guards to escort us to the toilets.

The stench inside was incredible and literally breathtaking. Obviously the accumulated excrement hadn't been removed and the shed had not been washed out for at least a week, the communal cleaners too busy taking revolutionary action elsewhere, no doubt.

My escort, a peasant youth, didn't seem to notice or care. Unceremoniously he lowered his trousers and, squatting over the gutter, he added his own considerable contribution to the stinking goo.

I gagged and with all my might I tried to evoke the picture of a scenery in the English Lake District that had once, long ago, left such an unforgettable image in my mind: a breathtakingly lovely scene of green meadows twinkling with scarlet poppies, white daisies and yellow buttercups, spread like a blanket over gently sloping hills that seemed to emerge before my eyes from the silvery, rippling expanse of a tranquil lake.

My mind recalled the freshness of the air and the smell of wet grass and my sense thus fooled I was able to empty my bladder and bowels, as if in a dream, no longer conscious of the appalling filth and stench.

The women's side was separated from the men's by a metre-high brick wall so I could see Liang, pale and holding a hand before her mouth, trying with all her might not to vomit. I waited for her outside and together we were ushered back to the platform.

Liang was unusually quiet and I was worried. We took up our banners again and tried to ignore the curious stares of a few passers-by.

It was almost eight o'clock when I noticed Special Interrogator Song emerging from a small street opposite the town hall.

He stood still in the middle of the small square in front of the town hall and looked around him with an impatient, angry frown. Clearly displeased he called Leading Red Guard Wan.

I could not overhear what they said but I saw Song gesticulating angrily both at us on our platform and in the direction of the town.

I saw Wan nodding a few times and then come back, at a trot, to where his Red Guards were loitering around the platform. Ignoring us he curtly summoned his Red Guards to leave whatever they were doing and to follow him. At the double they disappeared into one of the small streets opposite.

Song, without a glance at us, stalked past the platform and disappeared inside the town hall.

'Ominous, ominous,' I mumbled at Liang from the corner of my mouth. She didn't reply.

About half an hour later I heard shouting and yelling, distant at first but approaching rapidly until, suddenly, a small crowd of a few hundred people burst on the scene, spurred on by Leading Red Guard Wan and his boys and girls.

Many were brandishing sticks, others had wilted heads of lettuce and rotten cabbages in their hands, some were even carrying night-soil buckets.

The mob stopped just short of the platform and, screaming hysterically, eyes wild and unfocused, people began to pelt us with their rotten vegetables and to throw the contents of their buckets at us while those with the sticks beat the platform as if in a mad rage, hopping up and down like a tribe of demented chimpanzees.

'*Death to the traitor and his whore*!'

'*Defend the motherland against the foreign spies*!'

The mob yelled, screamed and shrieked.

Instinctively we had lifted our arms to protect our faces and from behind her banner Liang looked at me, her eyes wide and wild with absolute terror.

'*Stay calm*!' I shouted at her. '*They won't kill us*! *It's all staged*! *On Song's orders*!'

The madness went on, crescendo, for about fifteen minutes and then it petered out quite rapidly: people were running out of projectiles and inspiration, I think.

Suddenly the din stopped altogether, but for a few half-hearted shouts at the back of the mob until they also ceased.

In the sudden silence I saw Song descending the few steps of the town hall and, stepping gingerly over the rotten vegetables and excrement, approach the platform.

He jumped on the platform and for a fraction of a second I saw him almost lose his balance as he landed on a slippery lettuce leaf but my hope to see him fall flat on his face vanished as he recovered his balance and raised his arm.

'*Comrades*!' he shouted in his stentorian, beautifully modulated voice. 'I hereby transmit to all of you the profound love of our Great Leader Chairman Mao! I shall report to him how impressed I am by your revolutionary ardour and by your outrage at these two criminals who have betrayed our Chairman Mao's ideals and the Great Proletarian Cultural Revolution which is now taking momentum all over China. Chairman Mao and Comrade Jiang Qing are our inspiration and we must always and at all times demonstrate our loyalty and undying love for them by expressing spontaneously and without restraint our outrage at everything foreign and at these two counter-revolutionaries on the payroll of the foreign devils who think that they can turn back the clock of history in our motherland!'

He fell silent to allow the crowd to applaud him and to cheer and shout after Leading Red Guard Wan who had taken a place beside Song on the platform.

*'Long live our Great Leader Chairman Mao!'*

*'Long live our Beloved Comrade Jiang Qing!'*

*'Long live Special Interrogator Song!'*

*'Death to the enemies of the People!'*

I saw Song smiling contemptuously, triumphantly, as he, in the silly Communist fashion, applauded the crowd in return.

Suddenly, with a wide gesture at Liang and me, taking a step back as if our nearness was abhorrent to him, he shouted, 'Look at these two traitors and saboteurs, they look so normal and innocent, *yet they are the People's worst enemies*! Perhaps *your neighbour* is a spy too, or *your brother*, or *your sister*, or the man or woman now standing next to you, or the model worker in your work-unit! Ask yourself which dark secrets your parents are hiding!

'They are so clever, they look so normal, yet they too could all be spies! Be vigilant, comrades! Trust nobody! Watch everybody! The signs are in their eyes! The *fear* for the *wrath* of the People is in their eyes! Report any suspicious-looking person to the Red Guards. Denounce the enemies of the People! Drag them out of their hiding places! Destroy their ill-gotten possessions! Denounce the enemies of our beloved Party! Denounce! Destroy! *It's your revolutionary duty*!'

The crowd, roused into a frenzy by Song's inflammatory rhetoric, delivered in that beautiful voice, cheered and clapped and chanted, at the top of their voices: *'Destroy the enemies of the People*! *Death to the enemies of the Party*! Over and over and over.

It was truly a frightening spectacle and I saw Liang tremble with fear as she watched the rabble's wide open, screaming mouths and crazed, hateful eyes under the shaking, balled fists and she cringed under wave after wave of sound and fury washing over us.

Then I saw Song signal Leading Red Guard Wan to come closer and I heard him say, *sotto voce*, 'Make the crowd work for you, Wan. Use them all like hounds in your hunt for the enemies of the People. Make them understand that they can make merit for themselves by denouncing counter-revolutionaries and other vermin. Tell them that those who find nobody to denounce will be suspect themselves. Tonight I want to see at least a hundred people arrested, Wan, more tomorrow. Keep your prisoners under guard, here, in this square, squatting, hand on their necks.

'Every morning I want to see and hear hundreds of demonstrators with red flags, denouncing the prisoners and shouting slogans. Detail a few of your Red Guards to lead the chanting with loud hailers. Assign the girls, they are good at that and never tire. When the crowd grows tired of shouting and chanting organise a spontaneous bonfire of the prisoners' possessions. The People's Tribunal will deal with twenty to thirty cases per day, so keep your arrests at the same level and the number of prisoners in the square at about two to three hundred at all times. So get busy, Wan! Do a good job, for your own and for the sake of your father and uncles. Do I make myself clear?'

Wan nodded, pale, lips trembling and stammered, 'Yes, Comrade Special Interrogator Song. It will be done as ordered by you!'

'Good Wan, very good,' Song said, smiling warmly and then, for all to see, he embraced Wan, warmly and comradely.

This would give Wan the authority he dearly needed to control his unstable and volatile Red Guards and to impress on the crowd that he was indeed acting on orders from high.

Just as suddenly Song disentangled himself with a face as if he had bitten into a lemon and Wan scuttled off, red-faced, all pumped up to start his reign of terror.

Dismissing Wan, the crowd and the consequences of the hate campaign he had just started from his mind, Song then turned his attention to us.

'God, you two stink,' he said in a normal and friendly tone, laughingly. 'Throw those banners on the ground, they're full of shit, literally and figuratively. Follow me inside. You can clean up in the washroom. I'll have a Red Guard fetch you some clean clothes. After that you can eat a chicken rice in the canteen. The guard will accompany you. When you're finished he'll escort you to the courtroom. You must be there five minutes before the session starts at ten. Now come!' And without further ado he stalked off.

Liang shuffled in front of me as we followed Song. The way she kept to herself, so disheartened, so... so *dispirited* was a better word in Liang's case, frightened me. Had the sheer malevolence of the crowd, of Song, been too much for her? More than her inherent good-heartedness could bear?

We entered the building and Song said, pointing, 'Over there's the washroom. Not very clean either I'm afraid but better than the toilets outside, I'm sure. Cleanliness is not amongst the proletarians' few virtues as you undoubtedly know. Go and clean yourself. Lock the door. The Red Guard will bang on the door and wait for you to take the clean clothes from him. Get dressed and follow him to the canteen. Eat your chicken rice, drink your tea. Eat and drink a lot is my advice. It may be a long time until your next meal.'

He turned and went up the stairs to the first floor, stately, in full control of himself and the situation as it behoves the emperor's magistrate.

I took Liang's hand and led her to the washroom. I quickly undressed and then I undressed her since she made no attempt herself. I kept our underwear separate and threw the rest of our dirty, smelly clothes in a corner.

Lovingly I washed her beautiful body from top to toe and rinsed her long, glossy hair. Without a word she let me do. I quickly washed myself and since there was no towel I used my undershirt to dry both of us.

When the guard pounded on the door I took the clothes from him, undoubtedly shocking him with my nakedness, and locked the door again. The clothes, army cast-offs probably, fitted me all right but were four sizes too large for Liang. She looked so frail and wan and utterly forlorn in those baggy, olive-green trousers, hanging like a stretched accordion down on to her tiny feet, and jacket, the sleeves a foot too long, that my first impulse to burst out laughing died in my throat.

Instead, my eyes welling tears with sadness and compassion, I took her in my arms and stroked her damp, beautiful hair.

I felt her body tense as a low, shuddering wail welled up from deep inside her, such a pitiful cry of pain and grief that it wrenched my heart and no word of consolation would come out.

Then she started crying, with small whines and heaving sobs and I barely could make out what she said, 'What will they do to us, Huimin? To the children? To Father and Mother? I'm so afraid, Huimin, so terribly afraid. All those people. Why do they hate us so much, Huimin? We never did them any harm. Why Huimin? Why?' she sobbed uncontrollably.

I was feeling desperate. I couldn't handle this, not when time was slipping away so fast.

'Please, my love, please, please pull yourself together,' I whispered in her ears, urgently, desperately.

'In a few minutes they'll come for us and won't let me touch you, hold you, comfort you and I'll go crazy thinking of you in such a state, so desperate, so vulnerable, so alone, without me to hold you and protect you. You are everything to me, Liang, my one and only love. You *must* help me, Liang, you can't leave me like this. I'll go crazy.'

My words seemed to quiet her down a bit and I thought I felt her body's tautness lessen.

Had my tone of desperation struck a cord in the female to protect her child in trouble? She had often teased me for my childishness after she had first helped me and mothered me over some tantrum or other. Probably yes and I should have been content and kept silent and let her find her own way to cope, to create her own illusions, however irrational.

How little did and still do I understand women.

But no, I thought I should be rational and realistic and prepare her for the worst, so I said a lot of things I still think today I shouldn't have said and she would have scrambled back from the brink, on her own, and perhaps have sat here now with me.

So I said, 'I don't know what they are going to do to us my love, or rather what Song has up his sleeve for us, but we better prepare ourselves for the worst. Song dances to the tunes of his masters in Beijing and because of his aristocratic mien he has to leap higher and do more extreme things than his peasant colleagues or else they'll find fault with him and throw him to the wolves. The wolves and sharks tear their own to pieces at the slightest weakness and so does the rabble we saw and heard outside.

'But I am Song's big fish, a foreign traitor, and he'll make the most of it. Perhaps he doesn't care so much about you and even less about the children and your parents. There's no glory for him there. So if it can help you, or the children, you must disavow me, Liang, and howl with the wolves. It won't matter to me. I know why you do that. I'll survive, provided I can think of you as I have always known you, strong and determined, taking care of our children when they'll release you after a while, a short while I'm sure. Do you understand that, Liang, my love?'

Barely audible she whispered, as if speaking more in herself than to me, 'I don't want to live without you, Huimin, without my children. If Song takes them away I'll wither and die. I feel the cold fingers of death already gripping my heart, my head reels and feels like it is clamped in a vice.'

Desperately I shook her like a rag doll, pleading, 'Liang, please, Liang, please, my love don't let yourself go like that! Don't give in to those morbid feelings. I need you, Liang. Xulun and Xuli need you. Please come back! Please!'

It was no use, she was slipping away from me as she herself let slip life away from her.

I was desperate and when the Red Guard pounded on the door to escort us to the canteen I shook my head and mumbled to take us to the courtroom instead. He shrugged his shoulders, unconcerned and uncaring and took me by my shoulder, pushing me in the direction of the stairs.

I screamed at him to leave me in peace and carefully I supported Liang as we shuffled up the stairs, one step at a time. When we entered the courtroom we were apparently not yet expected for Song looked surprised. He was sitting all by himself behind the bench while the other judges stood huddled together near the window talking in low voices.

The room was slowly filling up with people from outside, randomly ordered to attend the session and to cheer and applaud the foregone sentences by the court and to jeer and humiliate the hapless victims.

Song motioned our Red Guard to approach the bench and after some whispering and sidelong glances at us, Song suddenly banged his mallet on the bench and shouted, 'The People's Tribunal will convene half an hour earlier today. Red Guards, close the doors! Comrades, take your seats! Everybody pay attention to the proletarian justice rendered by this court on behalf of our Great Leader Chairman Mao in the case of the traitor Dao Huimin and his accomplice Shi Liang. Defendants! Take your stand in front of the bench!'

I almost had to carry Liang to the place, in front of the judges, where we stood the day before, our dignity still intact. Now I had to support Liang and keep her from falling.

My heart beat wildly and irregularly and at times I felt as if the room and everybody was churning around us. Despair about my little Liang was choking me and the bitter taste of bile made me retch.

As if through a thick fog I heard Song's banging to impose silence and then his voice, as he said, 'The case of the People, the State and the Party against you, Dao Huimin, of Manchester, England, and you Shi Liang, of Wuhan, the People's Republic of China, has been correctly summarised yesterday and this People's Tribunal has unanimously reached the verdict: *guilty as charged*. You, Dao Huimin, are hereby sentenced to death for high treason, which sentence, by the powers invested in me by the Party and our Great Leader Chairman Mao, I hereby commute into a life sentence of hard labour to be served as decided by the military commander of Xinjiang Uygur Zizhiqi in Urumqi. You will be transported today and by truck to Hefei where you will board a special train of convict labour to Urumqi tonight.'

Song fell silent to let his words sink in and I felt my knees buckle as I lost my grip on Liang's elbow.

The Red Guard standing behind me gripped the back of my jacket to keep me on my feet.

Desperately I tried to get a grip on myself, shaking my head to clear my ears of the high, whining buzz that nearly drowned Song's voice as he resumed his sentencing.

'You, Shi Liang, are hereby sentenced to ten years of re-education through peasant labour in the people's communes in Gansu Province. You will be transported by truck to Hefei where you will board the special train to Xi'an and Lanzhou tomorrow. Both of you are hereby deprived of parental control with immediate effect and your two children will be put into the State's custody. You parents will be moved to the institute for the elderly in Hefei. Thus has been the decision of the People's Tribunal of Meishan and transcripts of the sentences will be forwarded to the Central Committee's Disciplinary Department in Beijing today. Red Guards, take the convicts to the Detention House!'

I had groped for Liang's hand as Song pronounced her sentence and she had squeezed my hand only once, with all her remaining strength, as if in a dying spasm. Then, suddenly, her hand lay limp and lifeless in mine.

I heard my own, raw, primeval scream as I took her in my arms, crying out her name and covering her face with kisses, all the while holding off, with elbows and feet, the Red Guards who tried to separate us.

Yet I felt them pry open my hold of Liang and force my arms behind my back.

I kicked and screamed at them to let me help my wife but they dragged me backwards out of the courtroom, down the stairs and out of the building all the way to the Detention House where they locked me into a cell.

The last I saw of Liang, with my crazed eyes, was her deadly pale face and small, limp body lying crumpled on the courtroom floor, like a twisted, broken rag doll, in those pathetic, oversized clothes.

It's the last image I have of her. I never saw her again, I never heard from her again.

*

Lao Dao fell silent, unable to stifle a sob as he relived, for the thousandth time or more, those terrible moments.

Lao Dee had difficulty keeping his own emotions in check and he bit his lower lip when he saw Suping and the two girls crying openly.

Auntie Liu sat staring at Lao Dao, tears streaming down her cheeks, unable to move, to utter a word.

Lao Dao, immobile, unwitting, sat staring at the wall, eyes unfocused and unseeing, immersed in his own private hell. Lao Dee felt an immense pity for his friend, and guilt for stirring up such painful memories.

Why am I doing this, he asked himself, what's in it for these people? Did I promise too much when I told them I would let the world know? Will the world care? Give a damn? And if not, what will I tell them? That nobody really cares what they and millions, tens of millions of other innocent people went through? Suffered? Lost? That the terrible collective madness with which a whole nation turned on itself, incited and spurred on by a bunch of power-crazed demagogues, in an all-out ten-year long destructive rage of young against old, ignorance against culture, prejudice against reason, primitivism against ancient civilisation, evil against goodness, no longer has the capacity to surprise? To baffle? To anger? To scare? To move a world blasé with and numbed by a daily menu on TV and in the newspapers of more of the same? Of violence? Of genocide? Crime? Greed? Corruption? Wars? Fanaticism? Tell me what's new, people will say, shrug their shoulders and go about their business.

Will these simple, naive, kind-hearted people understand when I try to break it gently that nobody cares? Worse even, that they are being tiresome in view of new economic realities? They may not understand but they will resign themselves one more time to their insignificance and thank me for trying.

Lao Dee was woken from his reverie by Lao Dao's gently coughing and he found the others staring at him.

'You were far away, my friend,' Lao Dao said, smiling, 'I just proposed that we have a quick dinner and a drink first, but you didn't hear me. It's a good moment to have a short pause, I think. After dinner I'll continue and I propose to make a jump in time of about ten years to connect the present with the past I just told you about. The interlude plays in an alien world and depicts the life of a stranger, alien unto myself until today. His story will be for next week. What do you say? Are you girls going to prepare me and my friend a drink or do we have to serve ourselves?' And jokingly he poked Lilian in the ribs.

With a squeal she jumped up from her chair and laughingly she told her mother and Beiyuen to give her a hand.

Everybody was happy that the sad, gloomy spell that had gripped them all the last half hour or so had been broken.

Only Lao Dee and Auntie Liu saw the lingering grief in Lao Dao's eyes behind the melancholy small smile.

With tacit accord not to dwell on any particular part of Lao Dao's story, Auntie Liu and Lao Dee chatted quietly about one thing and another, leaving it up to their old friend to join in whenever he felt like it.

When Suping came into the room with the main dish, still in the wok and put it on the table, Lao Dee looked up and said, 'By the way, Suping, next week, Tuesday, I have to be in Lushun to deliver a message from a very dear friend of mine in Hong Kong. Can you be ready at eight o'clock in the morning? I'll pick you up at the corner of the alley and the main street. I'll be in a normal car, a white Santana probably. Lilian can come also, of course, if she can get the day off to visit her father. I'll bring the small presents for the nursing staff with me. You distribute them if and as you see fit. Okay?'

Lilian, who had overheard Lao Dee's last words, said, 'I discussed this business of visiting my father in Lushun with Zing Neiping, my friend in the coffee shop, and she warned me to be very careful. She said she heard a story once about a girl who had visited her grandmother in Lushun and who, a month later, was suddenly transferred from her job in the housekeeping department of the Dong Fang Hotel to the asylum in Lushun, as an assistant nurse in the department of her grandmother. The nurses hate having to clean up after those demented, old people and if they can trap some family member or other who used to care for a parent before he was institutionalised, they will submit a request for additional personnel with a special recommendation to assign such and such a person who already has experience. Neiping says that might happen to me, or even to Mother. So I think I had better not go.

'Mother has the excuse of her family in Luding and the fact that Father was institutionalised precisely because she lacked the official qualifications. I am young enough to learn, they will say, and to clean up the shit of an old dodderer you don't need all that much experience, just a solid stomach, a pair of strong arms and the less brains the better so that the real nurses can exploit you.'

She fell silent, flushed and defiantly she added, 'I won't run the risk of the nursing staff chatting up on me, all friendly-like, and hearing me out how long I took care of my father already and then, a month later, Vice-Manager Zhou calling me in his office to tell me I have been promoted to assistant nurse in Lushun. If that creep Du, our unit secretary, hears about it he will personally escort me to Lushun to make sure I get the dirtiest job there is.'

Lao Dee burst out laughing at Lilian's spirited indignation and soon everybody laughed loudly, including Lilian herself, though she wondered what was so funny.

Finally, Suping still hiccuping, cried out, 'All right, all right, you won't come. What a pity though to throw away such a beautiful career opportunity.' And she had another fit of the giggles.

Lao Dee was relieved to see Lao Dao laughing heartily as well and, exchanging a glance with Auntie Liu, he exclaimed, 'Calm down, calm down everybody. Meiling, won't you come with Suping next Tuesday to keep her company and the well-meaning citizens of Dalian from drawing the wrong conclusions about her and me?'

'Yes,' Auntie Liu said, grinning, 'I'll come with you both and afterwards, on our way back, we pick up Lao Dao and have a seafood dinner together in that new restaurant on the coastal road opposite Bangshui Dao, without those two hussies. It'll be my treat and no protest from you, Lao Dee. Okay? Now, let's eat.'

In the best of spirits they joked and ate and drank and when they relaxed over the last glass of foreign beer and fruit juice Lao Dee pulled a long, aluminium cylinder from the inside pocket of his jacket and said to Lao Dao, 'I heard you mention once that long ago, in England, on the day of your mother's wedding, your stepfather offered you a real Cuban cigar and that the two of you sat there, in silence, for two hours, smoking and sniffing and that after that one cigar you decided to quit smoking since nothing could ever come close. I don't smoke myself, never have as a matter of fact, but I did and still do enjoy the smell of a good cigar. I bought you two Havanas, Davidoffs, in the most expensive tobacco shop in Hong Kong, in the lobby of the Peninsula Hotel, and I would like you to smoke one now, if you feel like it of course.'

At that he handed the aluminium cylinder to Lao Dao.

Moved by his friend's thoughtful gesture Lao Dao took the colourful little tube and gingerly screwed off its cap. Then, with great care he extracted the long, matted gold-brown cigar and passed it under his nose.

Eyes closed he stretched out his hand and Lao Dao passed him a shiny little instrument he had just fetched from his pocket. Delicately Lao Dao clipped a tiny piece from the rounded end of the cigar before putting it between his quivering lips and rolling it softly to and fro.

Leaning back, eyes closed, he then waited while Lao Dee lit a match and held the flame in front of the square end of the cigar. Lao Dao slowly sucked and puffed until the cigar was evenly lit and small, light blue clouds of smoke were drifting up to the ceiling.

With a sigh of utter contentment Lao Dao seemed to close out the surroundings and to let himself drift with the whirling trail of fragrant smoke, back into the past.

The women had been watching the little ritual played out in front of them with mounting amazement.

'That smell brings back memories of the past,' Auntie Liu said, dreamily and more to herself than to the others, who couldn't believe their ears as she continued, 'memories of the only man I have ever loved but couldn't have because he was so much in love with his wife, so besottedly in love that he was oblivious to my feelings for him, also long after she had died. My pride and bad temper prevented me from showing my real feelings and we drifted apart, out of each other's lives and that was the end of it for me. I never married, though my heart and soul yearned for love and children. A wasted woman's life and all because of one man as if he were that special. No man deserves such sacrifice. Do you hear me, Lilian? Beiyuen? No man deserves the sacrifice of a woman's life or happiness.

'If you can't have the man you think is the only one for you, shrug him off and look for the next best, who'll turn out to be just as good, or just as bad, depending on the temptations placed along his life's path. No man can withstand a pair of beguiling eyes and moist, trembling lips set in a cute body even if his own wife's are the wiliest, wettest and cutest. It's in their nature, their genes, they can't help it. Those who seem faithful are so because they are afraid of the consequences, not because of their moral fibre. My eyes weren't beguiling, just ill-tempered, my lips were trembling but always with fury, my body wasn't cute, just average and therefore I had no chance. Mind my words and do better, the three of you. Now let's listen to Lao Dao, who hasn't listened to what I said and Lao Dee only with half an ear. Men have a knack not to hear what they don't want to hear.'

As if on cue Lao Dee said, 'I'm sorry, Meiling, I wasn't listening. What did you say?' He looked at her apologetically. Bewildered he looked around as the four women burst out laughing.

He shook his head in puzzlement and said to his friend, 'Do you hear them laugh, Huimin? I haven't a clue what's so funny. Sometimes women exasperate me. I once heard a Japanese say that women are like air: you can't live without it but normally you're not conscious it's there. He said that was the way it should be. It may be true for Japanese women, I don't know, but it's certainly not true for European women and neither for Chinese, judging by what I see and hear here, in this house. They *never* let me forget they're there. What do *you* say, old friend?'

'I'm sorry, Lao Dee, I wasn't listening. What was it you said about women?' Lao Dao said from behind his smokescreen, which caused another gale of laughter from the women.

'Never mind, old friend, never mind,' Lao Dee said hastily. 'Some other time perhaps. Please continue your story.'

'Right, some other time perhaps,' Lao Dao said, absent-mindedly. 'Now I'll continue the second part of my story. Actually it's the third part as I told you but the story runs better this way.' And at that he began the last leg of his life's story.

# *Chapter Twenty-Eight*

## Adapt, Mr Dao! Adapt!

'When my sentence was remitted on 14th August, 1976, after serving ten years of the life sentence Song gave me, I went back to Meishan in the hope to be reunited with my family. Somehow I never doubted that everybody would be home long before me.

'Every step I took, every move and gesture I made was as I had planned in the fantasy world I had created for myself during those ten years in Xinjiang and in which I immersed myself every night before falling asleep.

'I had refined my secret world, my refuge from the ugly reality of everyday life, to the point that, in my imagination, I actually smelled the flowers and the wafts of stale air rising up from the hot, dusty road that leads to our house after the first, hard drops of a rainstorm; that I actually heard the rustling of the trees on the lake shore in the sudden gusts of wind; that I actually saw the lake darken under the black sky and the ripples, whipped by the wind, become foam-topped, rushing waves; that I actually felt the roughness of the wooden front door of our house as I hit it with my fist in our secret code: tock... tock tock, tock... tock tock, to tell my loved ones it was I, home again, at last.

'And then, inside, I heard the delighted squeals of my children: Papa! Papa! And the lilting, silvery voice of my wife Liang admonishing the children to calm down as she rushed to open the door for me.

'And then I felt her embrace, her loins against mine, her warm breath in my throat, her fragrant hair tickle my nose, her vibrancy arouse me such that it ached and I could think of nothing and nobody else but her and me and I would lift her up and carry her to our bedroom and we would make love. At that moment I usually woke up, tense and almost in tears and I had to help myself to release the tension and fall asleep again.'

Lao Dao fell silent, breathing deeply, stifling a sob.

His friends made no sound and after a while he continued.

⋆

As if nature had conspired to make my fantasies last until the very last moment, a rumbling thunder and strong gusts of wind carrying the first, big drops of an approaching summer rainstorm, made me shiver when I got off the bus, at the corner of the dirt road leading down to our house and the lake.

As I walked the last five hundred metres of my ten-year odyssey down the sloping path, I *did* smell that peculiar odour of rain on a hot, dusty road and I *did* see the white-topped wavelets on the black expanse of the lake down below.

Suddenly I was hit from behind by the full force of the wind and the sudden, ice-cold, pouring rain and I ran, my heart thumping, a terrible premonition of impending disasters invading my mind, sweeping away my carefully tended dream-world. Out of breath and drenched to my skin I reached the house. Already I no longer thought of it as *my* house.

Shivering from the cold wetness and fear I pounded on the door: bong! bong! bong! Too anguished for the carefully rehearsed tock... tock tock of my dreams.

I heard shuffling feet approach and then a gruff man's voice shouting, 'Who's there?'

'My name is Dao, Dao Huimin!' I called back, my mouth close to the chink between door and frame. 'I used to live here and I am looking for my wife and children! Please let me in, Comrade!'

The door opened suddenly and I saw an old man in a filthy, dark blue jacket and dark green trousers staring at me. I stared back at him, not recognising him, and, over his shoulder, at a haggard-looking woman wearing a knitted black vest and grey trousers, her arms stretched sideways as if to hold back two girls in their early twenties with sullen, defiant faces.

Everybody stared at me as if they saw a ghost and suddenly the three long hairs sprouting from a big wart on the man's chin made the connection in my mind and I asked, hesitantly, 'Bo Dinyi, Secretary Bo Dinyi of the Snowflake Soap Factory?'

The man croaked a hoarse, joyless laugh, '*Former* Party Secretary Bo Dinyi you mean, Dao,' he rasped.

'Come in, you are all wet. You can stay with us for a day or two while you try and find out about your family but we can't offer you much to eat as we have barely enough for ourselves.'

His wife was about to protest but with an impatient gesture Bo cut her off and said gruffly, 'Shut up, woman! You and your precious brother caused us enough misery as it is. If I say that Dao can stay here then that's it, you hear? Now go and prepare us some tea! At least *that* we can afford.'

He motioned for me to follow him inside, into the living room where I once had spent so many happy hours and I sat down, gingerly, because of my wet trousers, on the edge of the couch that had once been mine.

Surreptitiously I glanced around and noticed that most of the furniture that had once been the whole family's pride was still there, though badly neglected with the woodwork scratched, the glass panels broken or cracked, the upholstery full of stains and torn in places.

Bo must have noticed the expression of sadness on my face since he remarked, wryly, 'Not like in your days, eh Dao? Wife's not a very good housewife, I'm afraid, if there's anything she is good at except at nagging and talking and boasting about her rotten family. Besides, we have gone through bad times. Not as bad as yours, I'm sure, but bad nevertheless. If it hadn't been for Zheng Benhua, that snake of a brother-in-law of mine, I could well have been a powerful man now, high up in the Party.

'That stupid, good-for-nothing, ungrateful lout thought he could take over my position if I were disgraced, so he went to see your friend, Special Interrogator Song and told him that not *you* but I, *Bo Dinyi*, had sabotaged the soap during all those years and used the factory truck to make money for myself. That mean-spirited, aristocratic bastard Song at first pretended not to believe Benhua and accused him of counter-revolutionary plotting against a loyal Party secretary. Benhua was expelled from the Party and sentenced to hard labour in Shanxi; a twenty-year sentence he got. I haven't seen *him* back yet and never hope to, either. Good riddance.

'Hardly a week after Benhua had left, by truck, to Hefei, Song had *me* arrested, the devil. He had discovered the truth, he said, and he had *me* expelled from the Party as well and sentenced to nine years of peasant labour in a farmers' commune in Yaxian County. The leader of the production brigade was summoned, by that fiend Song, to be present at my sentencing and he was ordered to give me the hardest, lowliest tasks and no days off for rest. The things they made me do, Dao, you have no idea. They made me pull the plough, in team with an ox and whipped *me* instead of that stupid animal. They made me clean out the night-soil and dung the fields from the cesspit.

'Every evening, for nine years, they made me repeat my self-criticism about enriching myself at the proletariat's expense in front of the whole commune, with everybody yelling and spitting at me and pelting me with rotten vegetables from a heap they specially kept for that purpose.

'Nine years I went through hell, Dao! Nine bloody years wasted! And look at me now! A lowly municipal worker, that's what I am now. I sweep the sidewalks and gutters around the Party building in town. I clean out the spittoons and the ashtrays after daily committee meetings. Only one member is brave enough not to ignore or humiliate me. I once endorsed his application for Party membership so he felt he owed me. He managed to have this house here assigned to me. I now grow some vegetables and yams on the land near the lake, there where it's soggy. At least I learned that much during my commune years.'

He sniggered sarcastically and then, suddenly, he bent forwards and, squinting at me, he spat out, 'You must *enjoy* this, Dao! How you must enjoy this after what I did to you, don't you, Dao?'

I sighed and said, 'To be honest, I don't give a damn, Bo. For all I care you could be the Party secretary-general in Beijing or the cleaner of Meishan's public toilets or dying of consumption, Bo. After what I went through I no longer care what happened or happens to others, Bo, and I reserve my hatred for people of a different calibre than you, for Song for instance.

'You must be really stupid to think that your false accusations against me made one iota of a difference for what Song had already decided he would do to me *before* he even came to Meishan. He was only one of Jiang Qing's bloodthirsty witch-hunters, Bo, and I was the big fish, the foreign spy and saboteur. He didn't *need* your accusations and all that you achieved was to make yourself even more contemptible in Song's eyes because he knew all along that it was you and your greedy, vulgar in-laws who misused your position to cheat and rob the State.

'You see, Bo, Song didn't hate me and he certainly had no contempt for me, on the contrary probably. I was his *equal* intellectually and my condemnation was a *political* deed. I was a *political criminal* who had played his game and lost and therefore had to pay the price. It was as simple as that. *You*, on the other hand, Bo, were nothing but a stupid, ordinary thief, a contemptible *common law criminal* without brains in Song's eyes and the viciousness of your sentence was a measure of Song's total contempt for people like you.

'But, as I said before, I don't care, Dinyi. I feel no like or dislike for you, only indifference and don't insult my intelligence by suggesting that I feel glee at your misfortune. All I care about is to find out what happened to Liang, to my children, to my parents-in-law. For ten years I nourished the dream that I would find them here, waiting for me. That was stupid and naive, I must admit that now, though the dream probably helped me to remain sane. However, now that I am here you might as well tell me what you know, if anything.'

Bo had pulled away from me while I threw those uncomplimentary things at him and he glared at me when I fell silent.

Suddenly he burst out laughing, braying like the jackass he was, and exclaimed, 'You really don't know, do you, Dao? They never told you, did they, Dao? They let you believe your wife was still alive, didn't they, Dao? Or perhaps nobody cared, like you now don't give a damn about anything and anybody. Your wife died there and then Dao, in the courtroom, while those horrible Red Guards were still dragging you down the stairs.'

My heart missed a beat, stopped and then resumed, wildly and irregularly.

I stood up from the couch but had to grip the table so as not to fall.

Breathing deeply to regain control of myself I mumbled, 'How do you *know*, Bo? Have you seen her dead body? Tell me but don't mock me, Dinyi.'

I felt him take me by the shoulders and push me down on the couch as he shouted at his wife to bring two mugs of hot tea immediately.

Vaguely, as through a haze, I saw her put the mugs on the table in front of us and then I felt a hot mug being pushed in my hands and Bo folding my clammy, cold fingers around it.

'Drink first,' I heard him say and his concern touched me, in spite of everything and my own carefully cultivated indifference. Gratefully I slurped from the scaldingly hot tea.

'Feel a bit better already?' he asked, gently, and when I nodded he continued, 'I can tell you what happened exactly as I remember it, Huimin,' he began, 'it's still as clear in my mind as if it were yesterday. I was in the courtroom, standing near the stairs, when the Red Guards dragged you downstairs. You were kicking and thrashing and screaming as if you had gone berserk and six Red Guards could barely manage to hold on to you. I didn't follow them downstairs though, however tempted I was to try to get a blow or a kick at you in the general mêlée.

'I had seen Liang faint and Song calling angrily for Wan Ziqi, the leading Red Guard and I wanted to see what would happen. I saw Wan come rushing into the building and up the stairs, three at a time and run to the front of the courtroom, to where Liang was lying on the floor. Song and Wan lifted her up from the floor and between them they carried her through the room and down the stairs and out of the building. As they passed next to where I was standing I clearly saw Liang's face. It was deadly pale and her head was lolling from one side to the other, unnaturally, as if there was no strength in her muscles at all.

'I was convinced she was dead already, though I couldn't know for sure, of course. I followed Song and Wan downstairs, thronging with the other spectators, and was just in time outside to see Song and Wan dump your wife over the side board of that old truck that brought you in the day before. You remember? The one with the crazy driver? I saw Song talk briefly to Wan, who nodded and then jumped into the cabin, pummelling the driver to wake him up. They drove off in an awful hurry, I don't know to where. Song, looking quite worried I thought, ordered all of us standing there, drummed-up spectators, Red Guards, myself, to stay outside but *not* to leave the square and to wait until the next session.

'He then went back into the building, closing the door behind him. I clearly remember his words "*not to leave the square*" as I found that strange at that time, and also because I was miffed in my importance as a Party secretary that I had to stay there, outside, in the rain, with all the other people. I didn't care to go against Song's orders though, so I stayed. It was past noon already when I heard a truck approaching at great speed and then I saw that it was Wan, apparently coming back from wherever he had been.

'The truck came at great speed and it skidded on the cobblestones as the driver braked in front of the town hall. Wan had already leapt out of the cabin before it came to a full standstill, yelling, at the top of his voice, "The prisoner Shi Liang tried to escape and fell from the truck! She is dead! She is dead!"

'Song and his fellow jerks of the People's Tribunal came rushing out of the building and everybody in the square converged around the truck as Wan and Song climbed on the platform. They lowered Liang's body into the arms of a couple of Red Guards and when they trotted off, in the direction of the hospital, I saw Liang's face. There was now brown, congealed blood around her open mouth where there had been none before and I saw that her blouse was torn and streaked with mud and bloodstains. I even thought I saw the imprint of a truck tyre on the front of her blouse. That didn't register as unusual at that time but later, when I thought of it, it struck me as odd.

'Song was still standing on the truck as he announced loudly, "The convict Shi Liang died accidentally when she attempted to escape the People's judgement. No blame attaches to Leading Red Guard Wan Ziqi and the driver. They did what they could to revive the convict Shi Liang. The medical examiner of the hospital of Meishan will certify her death as due to injuries sustained when overrun by a truck.

'"The People's Tribunal of Meishan, in deference to the sorrow of the convict's elderly parents, magnanimously revokes hereby its earlier decision regarding the convict's two children and appoints the grandparents Shi Zelin and his wife Hsu Xulian as the children's guardians. They may also remain, for the time being, in their present residence. The convict Shi Liang will be buried in the section reserved for criminals in Meishan's municipal cemetery. This is the decision of the People's Tribunal of Meishan. Long live our Great Leader Chairman Mao and Comrade Jiang Qing!"

'At that Song began to applaud the crowd and we all clapped and cheered for him and his magnanimous decision. I'm sure you must have heard the clapping and the cheering in your cell, Huimin, since the Detention House is not that far from the square. It's unbelievable actually, all this rigmarole going on not more than two hundred metres from where you were locked up and nobody telling you. But then Wan must have told the guards there to shut up or face Song's wrath and then you were transported to Hefei that same afternoon, if I remember correctly.'

He fell silent, looked at me and, with his usual sensitivity, taking my numbness for acquiescence, he went on, 'I forgot about your wife, Dao, since I became increasingly worried about my brother-in-law Zheng Benhua's scheming and insinuations. Only a few days after the incident with your wife, the idiot boasted, in the presence of quite a number of hangers-on, that he would become the town's next Party secretary to replace Peng since he knew something about Special Interrogator Song that would make Song as wax in his hands and accede to all his demands. The next day he was arrested, tried and sentenced to twenty years' hard labour in Shanxi's mines.

'His crime? Slander and defamation of high Party officials, notably Secretary Bo Dinyi and Party Secretary Peng, with the aim to usurp the power invested by the People in those two outstanding officials. Two days after Zheng Benhua's departure, the mad truck driver was killed when the brakes of his truck failed in a curve near Lu'an, while racing with another truck. The truck shot through the railing of the bridge and plunged into the river below.

'Leading Red Guard Wan, who sat next to the driver, was also killed and four other Red Guards and ten of the twenty prisoners on board were severely injured. On the eve of their funeral I was arrested on charges of corruption. The next day, Song had the People's Tribunal expel me from the Party and condemn me to nine years of re-education.

'There, in that Yaxian commune, I became preoccupied, obsessed rather, with all possible schemes of revenge. Like you, Dao, nourishing your dream about your homecoming, I had my dream about destroying Song whom I saw as the sole cause of my misery. Only I didn't know how. Of course, I could escape, get back to Meishan, ambush him somehow and kill him but that would only land me deeper in the shit as the authorities would put two and two together and start hunting for me. I wouldn't last long, of course, so it had to be more subtle and not involving myself directly. The only problem with that was how to let Song know it was I who was behind his downfall. And then that strange business of your wife's death came back to me.

'Suppose Liang was already dead when Song and Wan dumped her on the truck and that Song then instructed Wan to fake her escape and subsequent accident to hide the fact from the authorities in Beijing that she had died during his, Song's, interrogation session. For some reason Song must have known, or thought, that such an incident would reflect badly on him. Perhaps some people high up would start asking questions and make insinuations, not out of concern for Liang but to get at Song who must have a lot of enemies envious of such an obvious aristocrat's high status. If my supposition were true that would explain the whole charade. First Song's orders for everybody not to leave the square; he needed witnesses, when Wan would come back with his escape and accident story.

'Second my brother-in-law's hasty trial and the much too harsh sentence for what should have been nothing more than a trivial matter of family infighting in Song's eyes, unless of course Benhua had tried to blackmail Song. Perhaps the mad driver had let the cat out of the bag? Or Leading Red Guard Wan Ziqi? Wan was basically a decent boy from a good family and he may have had second thoughts. This would also explain the third oddity, namely the accident with the truck in which both the driver and Wan died. Very convenient for Song, the two only witnesses to what really happened both out of the way, for good.

'I didn't and still don't know what happened to the third, indirect witness to the scam, I mean the doctor of the hospital who signed the death certificate. He must have known that Liang's bruises were inflicted after her death. A medical doctor can see that, I once read in a mystery novel long ago. Perhaps he is still there, at the hospital? Perhaps he also disappeared?'

Bo fell silent, looked at me, saw no reaction and with a tired, melancholy smile he finished his story.

'You know, Dao, for nine years in that commune I nourished my hatred for Song and worked out, then discarded one beautiful plan after the other to get at him and now, already a year after I came back here, I still haven't done a thing. All I do is hang around, quarrel with my wife and my useless, ugly daughters and pretend to work when people look and all the while I nourish my grudge against each and everything and even that has lately become a bore.

'I don't know where Song is now or what he is or how he is and frankly I don't care any more. I am tired pretending I'm a vengeful hero, I'm tired of myself and my life. When you suddenly appeared out of nowhere I had for a moment a flare-up of hope that *you* would go after Song once you heard the truth about Liang's death and that's why I told you the whole thing. But now, I have given up on that also as somehow I don't think you will. I have never known you to be a vengeful person, Dao, and it looks to me as if you lost much of your bravery during those ten years in Xinjiang. I can see that in your dull eyes, Huimin. Am I wrong?'

I didn't reply, even a non-committal answer was too tiresome. Bo didn't insist and remained silent as he stared at the ceiling and absent-mindedly tapped the armrest of his chair with his left little finger. It no longer had that obscene, long nail.

While I listened to Bo rambling on and on I had come to terms with the fact that Liang was dead and that all these years I had simply and against my own better judgement entertained a fiction.

That last glimpse I had of Liang lying there on the floor of that courtroom, so pale and rumpled and lifeless, while the Red Guards dragged me away from her, had been etched in my mind as well as its caption '*she is dead*'.

Yet, at the same time, I had denied that flash of realisation and I kept denying it long enough for the etching and its caption to fade into my subconscious and not to interfere any longer with the self-deceptive images of my dream-world.

Probably my instinct for survival was taking charge already while I was still waiting in that cell in Meishan and that therefore I didn't hear the clapping and cheering Bo had talked about.

Had I kept believing that Liang was dead I would probably have gone insane.

I felt sad and yet strangely relieved as I sat there in our former house and it was as if I heard her lovely voice and laughter around me.

Relieved that she didn't suffer physically as I was convinced that Bo's deductions about her faked accident were correct.

Relieved that she had not had to go through the hell of those faraway communes in Gansu and Qinghai.

I was certain she would have died there of sheer exhaustion and privation amongst the hardened and uncivilised locals and the mere thought of those primitives lusting after her beautiful body and raping her made me cringe.

Was it for that reason that I felt relieved? For selfish reasons? And not because Liang had been spared the pain and humiliation? I shook my head, angry and ashamed at what I had seen and felt during that fraction-of-a-second glimpse at my true self. Was I really such a hypocrite? I was no longer sure that I meant what I said when I finally answered Bo's rhetorical question,

'No, Bo! No, you are *not* wrong. I have no fire in my belly left, no death wish, no lust for revenge on Song or whoever else wronged me, yourself included.

'If Song is still alive I *do* hope he lives in his own little hell, like you do, Bo, but that's about as far as it goes. But tell me, you said that Song, while standing on that rotten truck with my dead wife's body, revoked her sentence of my children and parents-in-law and that he even said they could stay, for the time being, in this house. How is it then that you now live here, Bo? Did they still live here when you got this house assigned to you? What happened to them?'

Bo shook his head and I saw he was surprised by my question.

'That's right,' he said, 'that's what Song said. However, the house was uninhabited when I moved in and now I come to think of it I'm sure it hadn't been lived in for quite a while; there was dust everywhere and that peculiar musty smell of locked, empty rooms. I never even thought about the fact that you had lived here before, let alone asked people around here what happened to your parents-in-law and your children. After all, it was almost ten years ago and I did have my own problems.'

'I understand,' I said, 'no reproach intended. But who do you think could tell me?'

'Ma Renzhi could perhaps find out,' Bo mused. 'Ma is the Party committee member who managed to get this house assigned to me and for a token rent. I couldn't afford the real rent for a house like this, not with the pittance they pay me now. Tomorrow you and I will go and see him. He's a nice young man. If you don't mind sleeping on this couch here, Huimin, you can stay here tonight and we'll take the same bus tomorrow morning. I suppose you have to report to the police and the town council to get a new residency permit, that is, if you wish to stay in Meishan.'

'I have to report to Dalian's shipyard in a week from today,' I replied, 'at least that's what my discharge papers say. So I need only a temporary stay permit, just for the time to find out about my family. Maybe they are no longer in Meishan and I'll have to go somewhere else, so I'll need a new travel permit to go to wherever that somewhere else is. Be that as it may, I am grateful for the hospitality you offered me, Dinyi, and for introducing me to Ma tomorrow.'

Bo shrugged his shoulders and grinned, 'Who would have thought that you and I would one day be in the same deep shit, eh, Huimin? If somebody would have told me so ten years ago I would have had him arrested for trying to undermine the Party.'

I laughed and he called his wife and ordered her to prepare a bowl of noodles and green vegetables for each of us.

She glared at us and was about to protest when I offered her two renmenbi. She snatched the filthy notes from my hands and disappeared into the kitchen, slamming the door shut behind her.

Bo laughed mockingly at the banging of pots and pans on the other side of the door. 'Not a day goes by without a scene or even a fight,' he sighed. 'She blames me for everything and turns into a raging fury when I counter that it's all her precious little brother's fault, that moron. He couldn't even write his own name properly. Good riddance, I shout at her and we don't speak until the next fight.

'What a life, Dao. You shouldn't have given *her* the money, what for? It's *my* food you eat. I could have bought a few cigarettes for myself. Can't remember the last day I had a cigarette. I saw a lot of money in your wallet, Huimin. How did you get it?'

'Fifty yuan and a train ticket to Hefei for ten years of hard labour, Bo, that was what they gave me last week. Some reward!' I snorted. 'How am I going to pay for all my expenses in the coming days? Lodging, food and drink, travel, tea money for people who help me.' I shrugged. 'One day at a time, Dinyi, one day at a time. If I learned one thing it's that.'

Bo had cheered up a bit and said, 'I got nothing, *not a fen* when they kicked me out of that commune. Nothing to show for nine years of work without one single day off, Dao. But I see your point, at least I have a roof over my head, a small plot of land to grow some vegetables and some lousy income. But then I have my wife, that sloth, and two daughters who are even worse, so that cancels out all my advantages and you are still better off, my friend. Now, let's see what the lady of the house cooked up for us,' and I followed him into the kitchen.

I didn't care for Bo calling me his friend but I let it pass. I still needed him and, after all, he had been rather decent to me.

The next morning we went to see Ma Renzhi. Bo showed off his good relationship with Ma and, not hindered by any modesty, he stayed in Ma's office during our conversation.

Ma was indeed a pleasant young man, like Bo told me, and he greeted me and shook my hand without any reserve or prejudice.

I explained the purpose of my visit, which was quite simple really: could he help me in any way in tracing the whereabouts of Shi Zelin, his wife Hsu Xulian and the children Dao Xulun and Dao Xuli, all victims of the Cultural Revolution.

Ma looked pained when I said 'victims of the Cultural Revolution' and replied softly, 'I'll do my best, Comrade Dao. I'll have to ask a few questions though.'

So I quickly summarised for him my own memories of ten years ago and what Bo had told me the previous day.

He nodded pensively while I talked and occasionally I saw him glance at Bo, frowning slightly. I was afraid, for Bo that is, that my story did nothing to improve Ma's regard for him, but I didn't care and Bo didn't notice. He just sat there, leaning back on the small vinyl couch as if he were in his own office again, smiling triumphantly at his friend Ma's kindness to me.

He didn't realise that the Party's attitude towards me, never a Party member and a true victim of one of its worst aberrations, was completely different than towards him, a disgraced former official who had shamed the Party. He would *never* be forgiven and would *always* remain an outcast, whereas I could be accommodated up to a certain point.

Ma promised he would investigate the matter and told me to come back to see him directly and alone, with a slight emphasis on 'alone', at the end of the afternoon.

He suggested that in the meantime I go to the police to report my presence and get a temporary stay permit.

He wrote a small note and told me to hand it to the head of police who was a good friend; it would expedite matters.

The police were friendly after the commandant had read Ma's note and my presence was duly recorded without any questions asked and I was given a stay permit for one week, renewable if necessary, all within fifteen minutes.

That done, I went to the town's small park and pulled a willow sapling, roots and all, from the cluster of weeping willows on the edge of the tiny pond.

I wrapped the roots in a piece of paper I had found on the street and set out for the cemetery. I found Liang's grave, or rather the spot where she had been buried, in the section for criminals as Bo had told me. It was just a slab of concrete, amongst a few dozen similar slabs, green with moss and overgrown by weed. The two characters of her name, Shi Liang, and the date, 1966, 11.30, had been crudely drawn in the concrete while still wet.

I kneeled and wept and prayed to whatever god or spirit might still care, hoping, vaguely and in vain of course, that I would pick up some vibrations from Liang if I concentrated enough on the mental picture I still had of her.

When my knees began to hurt and there was still no message of sorts I scrambled up and with all my might and a lot of puffing and groaning I managed to push the slab about half a metre aside.

I swept the bugs that crawled underneath out of the way and with my bare hands I dug a shallow hole just deep enough to receive the roots of the weeping willow sapling.

I stuffed the moist earth back in firmly and with the bucket I had taken from the cemetery workers' tool shed I fetched a bucketful of water from the cemetery pond and poured it around Liang's spindly little tree.

Then I stood back, bowed my head and closed my eyes and told Liang I loved her and that there would *never* be another woman in my life to take her place.

I promised her I would find our children and tell them about their brave and beautiful mother and to cherish and love her, always and for ever. I asked her to watch the willow grow and one day to pull herself up by its roots and to let herself sway with its branches until she could catch a bird and fly off to find me.

I promised her I would always be on the look-out for that special bird that wouldn't fly away at my approach and I would know it was she and I would take my life and join her.

I kissed the little willow, turned and left, never looking back, never to come back.

I found Bo lethargically sweeping the leaves and litter in the gutter in front of the Party building in small heaps to be shovelled up later and dumped into his two-wheel garbage cart.

He looked pathetic in his baggy, faded, dark blue uniform, green peasant cap, green canvas shoes and with that silly, grimy mask over his nose and mouth as he swept, with slow, apathetic movements the rubbish and smelly, muddy water with his besom.

I invited him for a bowl of noodle soup in a nearby restaurant which made him clearly happy. He dropped his besom where he stood and stuffed his mask in his pocket as we walked together the hundred metres or so to the dingy little restaurant.

I ordered two bowls of beef noodle soup, a plate of stir-fried cabbage and a pot of tea and while we waited for the food to arrive I told him what I had been doing since I had left him earlier.

He listened absent-mindedly, without comment.

We ate in silence and afterwards, sipping our last glass of tea, he said, 'I have been thinking, Huimin. I have to get out of this bloody place or I'll go crazy. I know that if I stay here I'll be sweeping rubbish and cleaning spittoons and shithouses for the rest of my sorry life, not to speak of the daily haggling with that sow of a woman at home. I don't know any particular trade, that's why I became a Party man, but I am physically strong so I could become a construction worker, I think. Carrying cement bags and mixing concrete shouldn't be all that difficult and at least I would be *doing* something, something worthwhile, something constructive.

'When you have settled in Dalian look around, Huimin, and see whether there are big construction works going on. If so, write to me and I'll submit an application to Ma Renzhi to be transferred to Dalian. I won't obtrude myself upon you so don't be afraid I'll bother you there. I'll live on the construction sites, in those hovels the workers always build for themselves, eat the food in the common shed or wherever they feed the workers, screw a female worker now and then and forget my former life.

'Will you do that for me, Huimin? I need to have something to look forward to, something to dream about or else I'll go berserk one day and run amok. Or I might take a swim in the lake behind the house and offer myself as fodder for the eels.'

I laughed and promised I would and I did.

Two years after our little talk in that dingy Meishan restaurant he got his transfer to Dalian's Bureau of Light Industry, Civil Construction Department, thanks to Ma's recommendation and intervention.

He worked as an ordinary worker in a few big construction projects, worked himself up to a qualified mason and as such was part of the crew that built the Fulihua Hotel.

*

Lao Dao broke off his story to elaborate.

'At present he works on Lao Dee's project. I asked Lao Dee about him and he says he's a good man, eh Lao Dee? Making a good job of the complicated foundations for those big tanks of yours. Lao Dee has recommended to the future factory director to keep Bo on after the project as head of the civil maintenance crew and I heard yesterday that the Light Industry Bureau has approved his transfer. Bo himself told me and also that he will be assigned a small flat in the workers' quarters. He's as happy as he can be, Bo Dinyi is. He visits me occasionally, once every three or four months, and always brings a box of cookies because he thinks I like them. We chat for an hour or so and then he leaves, never failing to thank me for saving his life. He never went back to visit his wife and daughters in Meishan, for a very good reason, apart from the fact that he really hated them. He wanted to stay away for the regulatory seven years' separation and then file for divorce.

'He got his divorce last year and now wants to marry again, to the future head of the laboratory of Lao Dee's project. She's a widow he told me, quite a bit younger than he is. She lost her husband because of the Cultural Revolution. Got a heart attack while the Red Guards were beating him up. The man was an engineer and had a few books in German at home which made him a foreign spy, they said. Bo's disgusted by what has become now gradually known, about all the abuses and injustices, and he has become totally apolitical. He has even rejected a suggestion by his work unit secretary to reapply for Party membership. Now back to Meishan.'

⋆

After Bo's outpouring we dozed for an hour or so at our table in the shade of an old plane tree.

At three o'clock I went back to Ma Renzhi's office, without Bo this time.

When I came into his office Ma stood up and came from behind his desk to greet me and to close the door of the office. I knew this was a bad sign.

'Please sit down, Mr Dao,' he said. 'I'm afraid you won't consider it an honour if I call you comrade, so I won't. I understand. I'm afraid the news is not good. I feel so ashamed about what has been done to you and your family in the Party's name. As you know it is not the Party's policy to apologise let alone to make amends for past mistakes so I can only try personally to do my best to help you where and when I can. So let me tell you what I have been able to find out.'

He paused and looked at me. I saw compassion in his eyes.

'Tell me, Mr Ma,' I said, 'and I thank you for your commiseration and for the trouble you have taken for me. Perhaps one day I will feel less hatred for the Party because of you and others like you, decent people.'

'I hope so,' Ma sighed, 'I certainly hope so, also for your own sake. A China without the Communist Party is unthinkable. China *is* the Party and the Party *is* China, whether you like it or not and you had better accept that and live a reasonably decent life than oppose it and spend the rest of your life in one prison after another. Besides, it's what the Christians say about their Church in Rome, the Party is simply too big, it cannot and will not be touched by, or offer apologies for what a few misguided officials did, do or will do in its name. Mistakes have been make, mistakes are being made, now, this very moment, all over China and mistakes will be made, tomorrow, next year, in ten years, a hundred years, but it will *never* lead to the Party's downfall, *never*! So adapt, Mr Dao, adapt!'

He fell silent and looked at me hopefully.

I smiled and said, 'We'll see, Mr Ma, we'll see. For now I hope you're wrong but that's as far as I'll go. I'm not ready yet to *adapt* but I'll follow your advice and *accept*. Your Party need not worry about me preaching revolution. I'll never see the inside of a prison cell again, if I can help it. So tell me what you found out.'

Ma laughed, heartily. 'Forever now the malleable Chinese, eh Mr Dao?' he grinned. 'You ever heard about Ah Q and his worldly wisdom? Oh, well, never mind all that now. You have other fish to fry.

'To begin with I went to the hospital and asked for the records of November and December 1966,' Ma began his story. 'I found that on 1st December, 1966, a certain Shi Zelin and his wife Hsu Xulian came to identify the body of a young woman who had been brought in the day before, on 30th November to be precise.

'The records show that the said Shi and Hsu officially identified the body as that of their daughter Shi Liang and that they accepted the autopsy verdict "death from injuries sustained when run over by a heavy truck". Shi and Hsu signed and thumbprinted the record as did the medical doctor who performed the autopsy. The doctor's name on the record was Ma Guoyang. No relative of mine,' Ma added, as an afterthought.

'In the Party's files here I subsequently found that Dr Ma was arrested on 25th December, 1966, together with a number of other intellectuals, for plotting against the Party. They got unusually long sentences of re-education through peasant labour in communes throughout the provinces of Anhui, Hubei and Henan. Next I went to the town hall, to the registrar's office, to find out more about what happened to the body of your wife and about the whereabouts of your children and parents-in-law.

'To my utter surprise the clerk's name was Ma Guobiao and I asked him whether he was a relative of Dr Ma Guoyang, formerly medical doctor at the hospital. The man was barely civil but he told me that Dr Ma was his father and that his family had lost all trace of him. That they had never had a word from him and he, the son, in his capacity as the registrar's clerk, had filed his father's records in the archives, section "missing, presumed dead". So I'm afraid, Mr Dao, that you have to live with your doubts as to the veracity of Dr Ma's autopsy report.'

Ma fell silent and looked at me, visibly troubled.

I told him that I had no doubt that Dr Ma had been coerced into making a false statement and that his arrest and subsequent disappearance had all been engineered by Song to get rid of the last witness of the real cause of Liang's death.

Ma nodded and continued his narration.

'What I found in the records about your family troubled me even more than Ma's story though. I wrote it down and I read. Shi Zelin's record says, "found dead from drowning on 20th May, 1967: verdict suicide". Hsu Xulian's record states, "left the town of Meishan on or around 25th May, 1967, without permission, destination unknown, probably accompanied by the children Dao Xulun and Dao Xuli, in her tutelage since 29th November, 1966." Investigations as to the whereabouts of the said Hsu Xulian, Dao Xulun and Dao Xuli were closed on 30th May, 1967 by direct order of the militia vice-commander, Chen Qichen. Finally Shi Liang's record says, "buried in plot number 1733, in the criminal section of the municipal cemetery".'

Ma fell silent and I was impressed by the quickness and thoroughness of his investigation. I told him so and I thanked him.

I also told him that I had been to the cemetery and found Liang's plot and mentioned the willow sapling I had planted there. He nodded, full of sympathy, and told me he would issue an order to the cemetery maintenance workers not to remove the sapling. Normally no plants or decorations were allowed in that section, he said, but he would see to it that an exception would be made for plot 1733.

I thanked him again for his concern.

Not knowing what to say next I made ready to get up and take leave of Ma when he said, 'I have a suggestion to make Mr Dao, so hear me out please.'

I sat down again and he continued.

'I suggest that we do the following, Dao. Tomorrow morning you go and ask to see Commander Chen. He's the man you saw this morning for your stay permit. I have already written a letter to him and had it delivered about an hour ago wherein I ask him to tell you all he knows about the death of your father-in-law and about the disappearance of your mother-in-law, Hsu Xulian, and your children. I'm sure he knows a lot more about these two cases.

'Maybe he will give you a hint as to where your family fled and how. I find he closed the case rather quickly, only five days after her disappearance. It looks to me like a cover-up. After you have talked to him, come back to see me and tell me what he told you for, with your permission of course, I propose to continue my investigations regarding the present whereabouts of your family. Chen's information will help me in my search. If I use my position as Meishan's Party committee member and vice-secretary I have ways and means to get things done that you simply don't have, Mr Dao. If you carry out your own investigations you'll find many, if not all official doors closed to you and things may take years, if ever you find out what you want to know.

'So I propose that you leave for Dalian the day after tomorrow and report on time for your new job. That'll make a good impression. As soon as I have the information you need I'll either come to visit you in Dalian to discuss how to proceed next or I'll write to you if no further action is necessary or desirable for the time being. Now, what do you think of my plan?'

I was deeply moved by the young man's kindness and sincere efforts to help me and I said so and added, 'It would seem highly unlikely, Mr Ma, but if ever you think I can do something for you, please find me and I will do my utmost to pay you back in kind.'

Ma smiled and said, 'That's not the reason why I am doing this, Dao Huimin. If I can soften your opinion about the Party and China even a little bit then that's enough reward for me. You see, after you left this morning, Bo Dinyi and I talked for a while and he told me about your past. I am so deeply ashamed about what has been done to you, about the way *you* have been betrayed rather than the other way round, I think that the Party can never make up for that and I'm afraid that nobody actually cares enough to even *try*. I do care enough and I will try. Let that be enough.'

There was nothing more to say so we shook hands and I left.

Outside Bo was waiting for me and he proposed I stay with him for as long as I stayed in Meishan.

I accepted his offer since I had to use my money sparingly. I bought a box of cookies for Bo's wife and daughters and a fat chicken for our evening meal, amounting to four yuan, less than half of what a night in a hostel with dinner and breakfast would have cost me.

The atmosphere that evening was slightly more relaxed and friendly and the women wept a bit when I told them about the tree I had planted on Liang's grave. Bo's wife still remembered Liang; his two daughters didn't and didn't care.

They promised they would water the tree during the dry season and I thanked them, neither of us meaning what we said.

They tried to find out what I discussed with Ma Renzhi and why I was going to see Commander Chen but gave up, annoyed, when I remained vague and evasive.

I slept well that night on the couch. The next morning, at eight o'clock, I was ushered into Commander Chen's office.

Chen was a tall, handsome man with thick, grey hair and penetrating eyes below straight, black eyebrows. His light army-green shirt was actually clean and ironed and the copper of his belt had clearly been polished that morning.

I met his evaluating gaze without shiftiness and, apparently satisfied as to my mental stability, he entered straight away into the subject.

'I have read Vice-Secretary Ma's letter. I have high esteem for his judgement,' and he paused to let me digest the significance of that remark, then continued, 'so I shall tell you what I know about the situation here during the last ten days of May 1967 and which may or may not have a bearing on the circumstances surrounding the death of your father-in-law and the subsequent disappearance of his wife and your two children. Is that correct, Dao? Is that your wish? Do you realise that what I am going to tell you are not facts but merely my own personal suppositions based on my observations and my reasoning but for which I have no *proof*?'

He paused, waiting for my answer.

'Yes to all your questions, Commander,' I answered in the tone and manner I had learned to use with military men.

'Good,' he said with a flicker of a smile that told me I had judged him correctly.

'Amongst the first of the many excesses committed by the Red Guards was the closure of all schools, universities and factories late 1966, early 1967,' Chen began his story. 'So it happened that on 10th May, 1967, the school where your father-in-law was a teacher was closed. The teachers were ordered to confess collectively to the sin of intellectualism and of promoting elitism and therefore division amongst the people. They had to exercise self-criticism every evening, on the platform in front of the town hall while they were being booed and jeered and pelted with rotting vegetables and excrement by a crowd specifically drummed up for that purpose by the Red Guards.

'During the day they were made to carry out all kinds of menial and degrading jobs such as sweeping the streets, cleaning the public latrines, collecting night-soil and so on. Your father-in-law, who had become a withdrawn and bitter man after the death of his daughter, was not well liked by his pupils because of his sudden fits of bad temper. A band of female Red Guards, girls, most of them his former pupils, took their stupid juvenile grudges out on the poor man and made his life hell. You can imagine what that means, Dao. Anyhow, it became apparently too much for him and he drowned himself in the reservoir behind his house, heartbroken, I suppose. His wife spotted him on the morning of 20th May floating too far from the shore to get him out herself so she called the militia.

'It was I, in my capacity as section commander, who directed the body's recovery. A jute bag filled with stones was attached with a piece of rope around his neck so it was clear his death was not accidental. Intestinal gases had already bloated the body and pushed it back to the surface of the lake so I concluded he must have been dead at least eight or ten hours. I interrogated his wife and she told me that the evening before, after a frugal dinner, he had gone outside, behind the house, with a jute bag. She had seen him putting objects in the bag and thought he wanted to bury a few books the Red Guards might find incriminating if ever they came to ransack the house. At about nine o'clock he had come back inside and together they had put the children to bed. She had wondered at his hugging the children, first the girl then the boy, then both. It was out of character, Shi wasn't habitually so effusive. They had gone to bed immediately afterwards and he had held her hand until she had fallen asleep.

'When she woke up at six the next morning he had got up already, but that was not unusual as he always got up before her to prepare tea and congee. When she didn't hear him cluttering about in the kitchen though she had worried and got up to look for him. Not finding him in the house she had a sudden foreboding and had run outside, to the shore of the lake where she saw him floating about twenty metres from the shore. She had rushed back inside, woken the children, told them to remain inside until she came back, dressed and taken the first bus into town. At seven thirty she stumbled into my office, very upset.

'I drove her back in my jeep, with two of my men and at eight fifteen we had recovered the body. Both Madam Shi and the two children wept but otherwise remained composed and dignified. Shi Zelin was buried the next day in the section for suicides in the municipal cemetery. Present were Madam Shi, the two children Dao, the town clerk, to record the burial and mark the grave, and myself in a private capacity and on behalf of my own son and daughter. My children were at one time pupils of teacher Shi and always spoke very highly of him. They are now married and live in Wuhan and Changsha and thus were unable to attend personally.'

Chen fell silent and gazed at me.

I bit my lower lip and closed my eyes to let the wave of helpless rage subside before I spoke. 'The despair to which those ghouls must have driven that dignified and decent old man breaks my heart, Commander Chen. It may be suicide for the records but I chalk up another murder against the Party. That makes two of my loved ones murdered in the Party's name. How many people all over China are grieving like me these days as, gradually, the horrible truth about the past ten years becomes known? Have you any idea, Commander? If it weren't for decent, humane people like Vice-Secretary Ma and yourself I would probably go out of my mind, steal a weapon and kill, kill, kill, at random, before I would kill myself.'

I wept in spite of myself.

Chen poured two mugs of hot tea and urged me to take one.

'Pull yourself together, Dao,' he said, kindly but firmly.

'There has never been a shortage of kindness and humaneness in our people, Dao, and there will never be and that's why we will always survive, our own identity intact, whatever the suffering and hardships inflicted upon us, whether by a misguided bunch of our own people or by aliens. What happened during the past ten, eleven years may well rank amongst the greatest disasters that have befallen our people since Qin Shi Huang Di but we survived, Dao. We lick our wounds, and I admit that some have more wounds to lick than others though *nobody*, I think, remained wholly unscathed, and we try to find the thread of our lives again in the tangled clew that remained. We gingerly untangle it lest it breaks and we go on with it, trying once more our best to make the best of it. Until the next trial, which will come as sure as night follows day follows night.'

Chen snorted and laughed philosophically, then he said, 'Drink your tea, Dao, while I finish my story.'

He paused to make sure I was okay and with him and continued, 'About a week later, on 27th May to be precise, a Red Guard, a girl by the name of Liu Zhen, and a very sweet girl I must add, came to my office to report to me that she had wanted to visit her former schoolmistress, Hsu Xulian, at her home to see whether she needed any help but that she had found the house empty and apparently abandoned. I asked Liu Zhen to accompany me, as well as one confidant, and together we went to the house of Madam Shi.

'The girl Liu Zhen had seen correctly; the house had clearly been abandoned at least three or four days ago judging from the fine layer of dust on the table. The door was closed but unlocked and the key was left in the lock, inside. All the drawers were empty, no clothes, no personal objects. I concluded therefore that Madam Shi had left her house, with the two children, on or around 24th May, 1967, for an unknown destination and that she wanted it that way and also that she intended to stay alive or else she would have killed herself and the two children right there, were it only to make a statement. No use to do such a thing where nobody knows you.

'My man and Liu Zhen agreed and we returned to my office. I wrote a short report, had it countersigned by my confidant and by Liu Zhen as a witness, and filed it where nobody would ever look for it, with the mention, "no further action needed". I asked the other two to keep the whole affair confidential and they haven't broken their promise as far as I know.'

He paused, reflected for a moment on how to say what he was going to say, then continued, 'Their disappearance remained unnoticed. So many people disappeared in those crazy times. Many fled the upheavals and died or were killed or went into hiding somewhere waiting for better times, others were murdered by marauding gangs of Red Guards and were dumped in the woods or mountains or in a river. I don't know for sure where your mother-in-law went, Dao, but if I have to make a guess I would say Wuhan, she probably has relatives there. However, wherever she is her situation is irregular and now that things are slowly getting back to normal she'll have to come out of hiding if only for your children's sake.

'The longer she waits the more difficult it will be to regularise the situation. Now is the best time. With the horrors of the Cultural Revolution still fresh in everybody's mind and the authorities eager to get the situation back to normal they won't ask too many questions. If your mother-in-law chances upon a sympathetic neighbourhood secretary she may get their stay permits without any problem. But somebody has to tell her that and therefore she has to be located first. Perhaps Vice-Secretary Ma Renzhi can help you there.'

I took his last remark as a dismissal and I got up from my chair thanking him sincerely for telling me and for the respect shown to my father-in-law and his understanding in the case of my mother-in-law and my children.

Chen had a firm handshake and, as he opened the door of his office for me, he put a hand on my shoulder and said, 'Take it easy, Dao Huimin. I can understand your anger but try to control yourself. Don't alienate potential friends by talking in season and out of season about the injustices done to you and certainly don't make a nuisance of yourself by demanding compensation or special treatment. If you stay low-key and keep to yourself people in a position to help you by making just a little extra effort may do just that. Do I make myself clear, Dao?'

'Yes Comrade Chen,' I replied calmly, 'loud and clear. Once more, thank you, thank you for everything. Over and out!'

An amused, friendly smile was the last I saw of Chen Qichen, commander of Meishan's militia, a decent and unassumingly courageous man.

I went straight from Chen's office to see Ma to get the whole thing over with as soon as possible. Chen's last words about my mother-in-law's irregular situation and the need for her to come out of hiding as quickly as possible did worry me somehow and I wanted action.

But where to begin? Where to go? Ma was right, of course, I had no chance on my own. I needed his help.

I gave Ma a near verbatim account of my interview with Commander Chen and he nodded emphatically when I came to Chen's remark about the irregularity of my family's situation and the need to regularise it as soon as possible and why.

'The commander is absolutely right,' he said, 'I had better hurry. Next month my leader, Secretary Yu Ning has to attend a meeting in Wuhan. His wife's an invalid so Secretary Yu doesn't like to travel and stay away from home. I'll propose to go in his place. I'm sure he'll agree. Now, the secretaries of Mianyang and Wucheng are of my age and good friends. I'll ask them to make inquiries, discreetly of course. I'll write them a letter telling them I'll come in Secretary Yu's place and how much I look forward to meeting them again. They will know, from my wording, that I need a favour. If they write back saying how pleased they are I'll know that they are willing to do me the favour if they can of course.'

He smiled and said, 'I know it sounds like a roundabout way but it works and nobody can find fault with such a small, friendly note.'

Laughingly he concluded, 'Now, my friend, I suggest you go to Dalian and leave the matter to me. Write me a letter as soon as you are settled in Dalian. I'll lend you fifty yuan since I think you're a bit short of money. You can pay me back in instalments once you get your salary. Is that all right with you?'

For the second time in one hour I thanked, with all my heart, a good and decent man.

The people of Meishan were lucky, very lucky indeed. I wondered how it would be in a big city like Dalian.

# *Chapter Twenty-Nine*

## Talent, a Dangerous Privilege

I arrived in Dalian on the morning of 28th August, 1976, after ninety-six hours of travelling and waiting for different trains in Jinan, Tianjin and Shenyang.

I went straight to the Dalian Shipyard and Shipbuilding Company to report for duty and to get directions where to stay and so on.

The clerk of the personnel department was totally indifferent as to my past and more recent whereabouts but was otherwise friendly and helpful.

With an engaging smile she asked for my particulars one by one which she then wrote down in a huge register that must have contained names and dates as far back as the last empire, so old and well thumbed it looked.

This done, she got up from her chair with a flourish, closed the register with a perky little nod of her pretty head and said, 'Follow me, Comrade Dao. I'll introduce you to your leader.'

I followed the jaunty little bottom she had managed to squeeze that morning into rather daringly tight-fitting trousers and I marvelled at how a certain type of girl radiates a guileless uncomplicated happiness that seems to lighten up even the gloomiest surroundings.

The sky was overcast, the brick pavement sooty and full of potholes, the hangars dark and filthy, the cranes like hovering vultures and yet it was as if the whole wharf lit up as we walked the distance to the biggest of the four hangars.

She asked me to wait outside as she entered a small office just inside the huge, open sliding doors. Through the grimy glass partitioning I saw her talking to an elderly man who nodded occasionally at what she told him.

After a few minutes she opened the door and called me inside. 'Comrade Xu, this is Dao; Dao Huimin, comrade Dao this is Xu Luobao. Engineer Xu is the manager of the machine repair and installation workshop and you have been assigned to his department. Engineer Xu will explain to you your duties and working hours. I asked Manager Xu to allow you off one hour earlier just for today. Come to see me in my office at four o'clock and I shall have all the paperwork ready for you to sign and also the key of your living quarters. I leave you now with Manager Xu.' And with a small wave of her tiny hand she pirouetted and tripped back to her office.

Xu, who hadn't said a word yet, and I followed her with our eyes.

'Like a fire opal amongst the pebbles, Xiao Lu is,' Xu said and I knew I would like the man.

Indeed, right from the start I got on well with Manager Xu. We were of the same age, both born in Shanghai and both mechanical engineers. Engineers are not frivolous prima donnas, they are not interested in politics and politicking. They have their honest machines to look after and talk about and that's about the extent of their world.

My job was to overhaul the diesel engines of ships that came in for repairs.

After observing me for a week or so, quietly and unobtrusively as was his engineer's habit, Xu apparently decided that I was worth his trust since, suddenly, one day, during our tea break, he opened a large drawer of the chest of which only he had the key and took out a thick sheaf of drawings.

He spread them out on the table and said, 'These are the drawings of the extensions of the shipbuilding department. We are going to modernise the installations so that we can also build ships for foreign countries, to earn foreign currency. Our director, Yeh, has great plans.

'Director Yeh told me that I will head the new facilities when the present manager will have reached his retirement age. That'll be in five years from now, early 1981. In the meantime Yeh asked me to work on design drawings for the ships he wants to build for the foreigners, notably ferries for vehicles, trucks and so on. Later Director Yeh wants to build still bigger ships for the transport of luxury cars from Japan to America and Europe. Director Yeh has visited Japan and says that luxury cars are big business in the capitalist world. He has seen things in Japan nobody in China can even begin to comprehend, Director Yeh told me, and therefore it is better to keep quiet but to prepare ourselves for the future.

'Now, I am a good engineer, Dao, as you will have noticed but I have no knowledge of foreign languages or of what the foreigners like and how they think. You do, Dao, and you are also a good engineer as I have noticed. I am therefore going to propose to Yeh that he makes you my assistant also for the new, modern yard and that you prepare the English text for the drawings so that, in time to come, we can discuss them with the foreign engineers who, of course, don't read Chinese. Also all the signs and instruction manuals for the new ships will have to be in English otherwise nobody will buy them. That'll also be your job, Dao. Now, what do you say?'

I thanked Xu for his confidence and told him I would be delighted to act as his assistant, in general and for the foreign content in particular.

He nodded, satisfied and said, 'That's settled then. Director Yeh will be very pleased because I know he was worried about my lack of foreign language skills and exposure. We'll make a good team, you and I, Dao. The fact that you will always be my assistant and always will have to defer to me in meetings and in front of others, notably foreigners, has nothing to do with your capabilities and abilities but everything with your past. I'm sure you understand, Dao, and I think I know you well enough now to be certain that there will be no rancour and envy. As long as you and I get along well and understand each other's positions, we don't care what others think or say. Do you see it also like that?'

I assured him I did and that I was delighted by the challenging new content of our job.

One month after this conversation I was called for a one-to-one meeting with Director Yeh, in his office.

Yeh Peihao was a tall, imposing man with a dark complexion. He looked like and had the bearing of a shogun, a Japanese samurai king of old, like in the pictures in my father's old books. He watched me with his penetrating eyes for what seemed a long time and I saw him weigh his impressions against what he intended to say.

Then, suddenly, he smiled, a smile that lit up his whole face, and he told me to take a seat.

'Xu Luobao told me about you, Dao. He is quite taken with you and thinks you can be very useful to our company. I took the trouble to enquire about you and what I found out about your background would seem to be exactly what both Xu and I need for our future plans: mechanical engineer and foreign trained at that, fluent in English, familiar with the foreigners' way of thinking, ideal one would say, no question about that. What I worry about though, not too much but just enough to feel a bit uneasy, is what I read in the margin, notes by a few officials whose paths you had the misfortune to cross. Now, tell me Dao, how much must I believe of what I read?'

Calmly I met his gaze and said, 'Nothing, Director Yeh, *nothing*, and I don't think I need to elaborate.'

'No, indeed, you need not,' Yeh said smiling ironically, 'but what about your present state of mind, Dao? Feel betrayed? Life and career wasted? Want revenge? Just waiting for an occasion to defect and tell the whole world about evil China? It has crossed your mind, of course, that if my plans are realised you will have frequent contacts with foreigners, will even have to go on board their ships. I can't put a sentry beside you each time you discuss with a foreigner, Dao. Bad publicity. What shall I tell our city's Party secretary to convince him that you will not put the Party to shame and him and me in trouble?'

I sighed and smiled and shrugged my shoulders.

'When I say that you have nothing to fear, that I haven't got the fire in my belly any more, then this may suffice for you, Director Yeh, but it won't probably suffice for the Party secretary. So you need a few arguments, now don't you?

'I won't go out of my way and argue my case as if my life depends on it, it's simply too tiresome and I am simply too tired for that. I would like to do the job because I would like to work with Xu, and I think with you as well, and because it would be nice for a change to do work that's of my intellectual level and that might make a difference for the company and for China. From your enquiries you should know, Director Yeh, that it was for precisely that reason that I came to China in 1953, bursting with energy and enthusiasm for the cause. Maybe my new job would stimulate me to rekindle the embers of that earlier energy and enthusiasm. I think it would, and the fire might flare up again. Who knows, it's worth trying, isn't it?

'About your and the secretary's fear that I might defect if the occasion presents itself I can be brief. I won't! Defect, that is. I have no illusion, Director Yeh, that my knowledge is outdated in the West and that society there has since 1953 evolved in such a manner that I would feel like an alien from a backward planet and that the natives will see me as a curiosity to parade for a while before they tire of me and discard me. Those are the ways of the West. Furthermore I have no relatives but my mother there and she may be dead for all I know, and care, I am tempted to add. On the other hand I probably have my own two children here in China for whom my presence may still be of some consequence.'

I quickly summarised for him what I had found out in Meishan after my release from the Xinjiang *laogai*.

Yeh had listened with genuine interest and had not once interrupted me.

Now, however, sharp as he was, he said, 'How was it, Dao, that you, an ex-convict, was able to find out so much in such a short time? Who did you see? Who told you all that? I see you don't like me asking this but I think you had better tell me. You see, Dao, kindness and helpfulness are not exactly back in fashion yet but people so disposed can be themselves again without incurring the Party's wrath. So whoever was helpful with your search need not fear my retribution. Besides, our city's Party secretary is my friend and kindness and courtesy personified. Now, tell me!'

And suddenly I realised why he was the director. Yeh wouldn't have been out of place in a Western boardroom and I couldn't help laughing when I visualised him in a Western suit and tie.

He watched me quizzically, not seeing any reason for my sudden mirth but he kept quiet.

So I told him about Commander Chen Qichen and Vice-Secretary Ma Renzhi.

He heard me out and then he said, 'Very good, Dao, very good. This Ma connection may very well be the only valid argument capable of convincing my friend Xian, the secretary of Dalian, that you are a risk-free investment for his city of which we, both native sons, are so very proud. How ironic, Dao. After all these years you are finally going to fulfil the mission you came to China for in the first place,' and he burst out laughing as he added, 'some delay! What?'

He offered me a glass of tea and we chatted for another twenty minutes or so before he surprised me by suddenly switching to English. He caught me completely off guard and I had to search for words at first. I complimented him about his fluency and was curious about his American accent.

'Mission school, Dao,' he grinned, 'mission school in Tianjin, before liberation. Even learned how to pray to a God who seems to have given up on us, poor creatures. The only good advice about my relationship to God came from a young missionary, after I had received my diploma.

'"Remember Peihao," he said when I bade him farewell, "God doesn't like whiners. Help thyself and He will help thee." And that is exactly what I have done, Dao.'

We took leave of each other like old friends and I went back to a slightly worried Xu and told him everything would probably be all right.

The following day I wrote a long letter to Vice-Secretary Ma in Meishan. It was then already 10th October, 1976.

I told him about my job and that I was as happy as can be. I told him about Xu and Yeh and the talk I had had with Yeh and that during our conversation I had mentioned how grateful I was for his kindness.

I did not in any way hint at the matter of my children and mother-in-law. I enclosed fifty yuan and thanked him once again for lending the money to me.

Xiao Lu, the pretty little clerk, mailed the letter for me.

Time passed and I grew into my job. I got on well with the other workers and developed an easygoing sort of friendship with Xu and his wife. She worked in the salary department and every two weeks I received my pay from her and signed her register.

There was no envy or competitiveness between Xu and myself. The only problems were machine or work related and we discussed them quietly and unhurriedly, as equals, and always came to a consensus.

When I had been about three months with the company Xu invited me for dinner, one Saturday evening, and he and his wife were apparently just as pleased as I was with the way things went since they invited me that same evening for two weeks hence.

After that it became a pleasant routine, something to look forward to.

Four months passed since I wrote my letter to Ma and there was still no reply from him.

I didn't write a second letter since I felt that that would have been inappropriate and pushy, as if to let him know that I was getting impatient.

Then, one very cold day late February 1977, Xu came to see me in the engine room of a ship where I was testing an engine that had just been overhauled.

'Somebody to see you,' he grumbled. 'He's waiting in our office. Young man. Pleasant and polite, but a Party man. Be careful, Huimin. Don't lose your temper. Take your time. Asked him what it was about but he refused to tell me. Smiled though, so maybe it's good news. Now go; I'll supervise things here for you.'

Nervously asking myself what could have gone wrong again to warrant a visit by what Xu had called a Party man, I hurried to our office.

As soon as I entered my nervous uneasiness turned to utter delight when I saw that my visitor was Vice-Secretary Ma Renzhi.

He jumped up from his chair and came to meet me, hands outstretched. We greeted each other like old friends.

I poured both of us a mug of tea while he explained why he had not written earlier. A meeting of model young cadres had long been in the pipeline, he said, with the most probably venue in Dalian and when the date had suddenly been fixed it was too late for his letter to reach me before his arrival. So he had decided to make it a surprise.

We chatted for a while about one thing and another and he was very happy that I had apparently found my place, finally. Then, suddenly, he changed the subject and came to the point.

Putting his hand on my arm, he said, 'Now it's my turn for some good news, Lao Dao. I have located your mother-in-law and your two children thanks to my friend Hu Xianfu, the Party secretary of Mianyang.'

Suddenly the office was turning like a carousel gone crazy. My ears rang and buzzed and my heart thumped like an engine in overdrive.

Ma's face faded in and out of focus, his lips still moving, but no sound penetrated the ringing and buzzing in my ears. I gestured for him to stop and I stumbled up from my chair and rushed outside, gasping for air.

The bitingly cold air brought me to my senses and I breathed deeply to stop the nauseating light-headedness.

After a few minutes I had sufficiently regained control over myself and I went back into the oppressively hot little office. Our office was probably the only heated one north of the long river by special dispensation from Director Yeh and Dalian's Party secretary, Xian, in deference to Xu's arthritic fingers and only for as long as we would need to prepare the drawings for the extension and the designs for the new type of ships we were going to build, which would be going on forever, of course.

Our office was the envy of the office workers and Xu and I had to be really rude sometimes to prevent them from keeping us from our work as they came in with all kinds of trivial messages and made no attempt to leave as they eyed our thermos with tea and rubbed their blue, ice cold hands above our little coal-stove. Only Xiao Lu could never come too often for us since both of us enjoyed listening with half an ear to her lively chit-chat as we continued our work.

Xiao Lu only needed an occasional grunted assent or an absent-minded 'Is that so?' to keep her going, hovering from subject to subject like a butterfly hovers from flower to flower.

Ma Renzhi had been waiting patiently and discreetly, sipping from his tea, while I got a hold on myself again.

He smiled at me as I sat down again and said, 'It was quite funny actually the way it went, Lao Dao. On the second evening of our conference in Wuhan we had a glass of tea in Hu's room. He obviously wanted to give me the opportunity to bring up the small favour I had alluded to in my letter I needed from him. I asked my friend whether he had clans by the name of Shi or Hsu in his constituency and he said that both families had been living for generations in Mianyang and Honghu County and had always been much respected. Some of his own relatives had married with the Hsu clan he told me and for all these reasons he had found himself in a bit of a quandary for the last couple of months.

'"Is it about a woman named Hsu Xulian and a boy and a girl called Dao?" I asked my friend and it still makes me laugh when I recall his surprise. So I told him the story, your story, and we decided to put the matter before Dong Xitong, the Party secretary of Hubei Province, who hosted the conference.

'Secretary Dong knows what it means to be a victim of circumstances. He himself suffered terribly during the early years of the Cultural Revolution. The Red Guards beat him up for days on end, which left him with a permanent limp because of an unattended and badly healed broken hip. They made him eat his own excrement to make him confess to all sorts of crimes. He was rehabilitated in 1971, after spending four years in solitary confinement in a cell without a light. Zhou Enlai personally intervened for him. Zhou appointed him vice-secretary of Hunan Province and in 1976 he was promoted to secretary of Hubei Province. This conference was Secretary Dong's initiative to discuss past mistakes and to make sure such abominations as the Cultural Revolution never happen again.

'So you see, we had good reasons for thinking Secretary Dong was the right man to seek help from. He was very kind to us and he listened attentively to our story, often interrupting me to ask questions about you and your family, Lao Dao. He promised to investigate the matter and find a satisfactory solution. Two months after the conference I got a letter from my friend Hu Xianfu saying he had some business in Hefei and could I meet him there?

'I went to see him in his hotel in Hefei and he told me that by order of Provincial Secretary Dong a residency permit had been issued to Hsu Xulian and to her grandchildren Dao Xulun and Dao Xuli, backdated on 25th May, 1967. Xianfu also showed me a note signed by Secretary Dong personally and in which he wrote that should Dao Huimin wish to be reunited with his family he would personally give instructions to process and approve his application for residency in Wuhan. Should his family prefer to join him in Dalian he would put in a word for them and Dao with the secretary of Liaoning Province. Secretary Dong also wrote that he personally thinks it would be better for everybody if your family joins you in Dalian.

'My friend has been to see your family, Lao Dao, and they were overjoyed to hear that you are still alive and that their situation has now been regularised. They told Xianfu that they would like most of all to come and live with you here in Dalian. So what do you say, Lao Dao?'

I laughed and wept with joy and told him I would immediately start the procedure to get my family to Dalian. Ma then gave me my family's address, the number of their residency permits and a host of other administrative details that I would have to mention on the application.

He said that if Director Yeh and Manager Xu would be prepared to endorse my application this would help to expedite matters.

To save me the trouble to ask for a day off he had gone to Dalian's town hall and had obtained the application forms for me before coming to my office since it was easy to foresee my reaction, he said laughingly.

'Fill them out, Lao Dao,' he said, 'and get the endorsement of your leaders and of your unit's Party secretary, each with the company stamp, in the next two days if you can. Bring the forms to my hotel the evening before I leave for Hefei, that is the day after tomorrow. My train is in the afternoon so I'll deliver them personally to the town hall in the morning, on my way to the station, and I'll use a bit of *guanxi* to have them processed with priority. After that it's out of my hands and despite the high-level mediation it may still take six months or more before everything is in order.

'Bureaucrats are the same everywhere. You can nudge them a bit but they don't like being pushed, certainly not by people high up on behalf of lowly creatures like you, Lao Dao. Let's not stir up resentment and let them handle the matter in their own traditional way. With all the support you have got they can't *reject* your applications but they can certainly *delay* them, bungle them, lose them, whatever, just to show you who has the real power. It has been such a long time now for you and your family, what's another three or four months? In the meantime you can write each other letters. Do you agree?'

I did and in a sudden impulse of overwhelming gratefulness I embraced that good, decent and kind-hearted young man. I completed the forms and collected all the signatures and stamps within twenty-four hours, with the oral good-luck wishes from Yeh, Xu and the factory secretary, Yu.

I went to Ma's guest house and handed him the papers. He was with several young colleagues and he had unfortunately to decline my invitation to have dinner together, since he had to attend the official conference-closing dinner that evening. We promised to keep in touch.

Three months after Ma's visit I was notified by the Dalian Municipal Administration that my request for family reunion and the subsequent resettlement of Hsu Xulian, Dao Xulun and Dao Xuli in Dalian had been approved.

Again three months later my mother-in-law wrote to me that her application and those of the children to move to Dalian had also been approved and that she had already received the travel permits.

Would it be possible for me to come to Mianyang, she wrote. To meet her family who had been so good to her and to the children? To pay my respects to that nice young man Hu Xianfu, who had been so understanding and helpful? To help her and the children with their luggage during the long train voyage to Dalian?

On 10th September, 1977, I left for Wuhan, my first official leave of ten days after one year with the company and in possession of an official travel permit valid until 20th September.

My friend Xu had suggested I send a cable to my family giving the number and arrival time of the train by which I would arrive in Wuhan on 12th September.

I didn't ask them to meet me upon arrival as Xu had suggested I do. I didn't want to inconvenience my mother-in-law who was too old and my children were undoubtedly still too little. Nevertheless, when my train slowly moved into Wuhan's station, I leaned out of the window like thousands of other passengers, heart pounding, hands wet with perspiration, anxiously watching the faces of the waiting crowd on the platform as the train crept to its final standstill.

Suddenly I saw her, Liang, my wife, standing at the back of the crowd and I shouted like a demented man, '*Liang*! *Liang*! *Liang*!'

She didn't react but kept on watching the passengers hanging out of the windows of the shrieking and jolting cars.

It must have been those jolts that shocked me back into the present and, tears streaming down my face, I croaked, '*Xuli*! *Xuli*!'

In spite of the din she heard my hoarse voice for I saw her looking up, hesitate and then her whole face lit up in that flashing smile I remembered so painfully well.

She hustled through the crowd, pushing and shoving people out of her way, reached up to grasp my hands with one hand while she kept pushing people aside with the other as she trotted beside the still slowly moving car, her beautiful young girl's face, Liang's face, cheeks wet with tears, turned up to look at me. We stared at each other, wordlessly, oblivious of the hustle and bustle around us until a tall young man suddenly appeared beside her and broke the spell. Taking both her and my hand in his, he said, 'Hello, Father! You had better get off now before the new passengers get on with their luggage.'

It was Xulun, my son, practical and even handsomer than I had imagined him to be.

I withdrew back into the car and saw that the joining passengers were already battling for seats. In a sudden panic that I wouldn't be able to get off in time, I got hold of my little suitcase and the heavy jute bag of Liaoning apples and jostling and yelling to let me through I finally tumbled out of the car and on to the platform.

'Welcome to Wuhan,' my son said, grinning, as he helped me up and dust my clothes.

Then we embraced, the three of us, weeping with joy and emotion, oblivious of the jostling crowd around us.

The friendly car superintendent whom I had told about my reunion with my children finally broke our embrace, gently but firmly.

'You block the access to my car,' she said, smiling. 'Pick up these delicious apples before people steal them and go and see the old lady in Mianyang. She must be waiting impatiently.'

I laughed with almost reckless joy. I opened the bag with apples and gave her a few and thanked her for her kind attentions, while my children looked on, smiling.

Affectionately arm in arm we shuffled through the thronging crowd towards our exits, Xuli on my left carrying my small suitcase, Xulun on my right with the bag of apples.

We wrestled through the narrow, one-person-at-a-time turnstile exits, I through the passenger exit with my luggage, ticket between my lips, Xuli and Xulun through theirs.

Finally outside, we clasped one another again, Xulun leading the way towards the bus station opposite the railway station. The bus for Mianyang was there already, still empty, no driver in sight.

'Let's go inside already,' Xulun said. 'The bus is supposed to leave in twenty minutes. It will take two to three hours to Mianyang because of the roadworks.'

We sat down on a seat for two, tightly squeezed against each other, myself in the middle, in the otherwise empty, dusty and ramshackle old bus.

I put my arms around their shoulders and pulled them against me, all of us still too overwhelmed to say more than the odd remark.

Several times either of them, or both at the same time, impulsively kissed the back of my hands or the tips of my fingers and I had to squeeze my eyes shut to stop the welling tears.

I was intensely happy and so, I could feel, were Xulun and Xuli. The time for telling, for talking all at the same time and for sad reminiscences would come later.

Under ordinary circumstances the near three-hour trip to Mianyang would have been a veritable hardship but these were not ordinary circumstances, at least not for the three of us, so we didn't mind the suffocating heat, the throat-parching and nose-clogging dust just as dense inside the bus as it hung, in an impenetrable cloud, over the torn-up road and the nearby fields and hovels.

We hardly noticed the jolts and jerks of the rattling and creaking old vehicle as it swerved from left to right and back to avoid, unsuccessfully, the deepest holes.

We merely breathed as shallowly as possible when the bus had to stop for more than half an hour and the penetrating sweetish smell of boiling tar wafted through the bus in billowing blue-black clouds.

With tearing eyes from the smoke we stared non-committally at a group of road workers who, in front of the bus, fought a hopeless battle to resurface the road.

Women, wearing broad-rimmed hats and a kind of towel as a face mask, were pouring liquid, boiling tar from holed buckets, attached to the end of a six-foot pole, directly on to the laterite ground. When the buckets were empty they refilled them from a drum, cut lengthwise and lying on a wildly flaming and smoking wood fire at the side of the road.

Men were shovelling gravel from a wheelbarrow on to the black goo.

After thirty minutes or so the drum was apparently empty and the workers stood aside watching indifferently as our driver drove the bus straight through the patch of still hot and soft macadam.

I couldn't help snorting at such primitiveness.

'Things are much better organised in Liaoning,' I mumbled in answer to my children's quizzical looks, 'it's green and fresh there. I certainly will be glad to take you out of this stinking primitive place.'

An affectionate squeeze on both sides was my answer.

Finally, after nearly three hours of body-racking and mind-numbing jerks and jolts, the bus came to a halt at what was apparently its final station.

The driver jumped out of his seat and stalked off without a word or a glance at his dozen or so benumbed passengers. He never bothered to collect our fares.

We scrambled to get out ahead of the man with the bunch of live chickens hanging, feet bound together, from a pole. He had boarded the bus in one of the small villages between Wuhan and Mianyang and had managed to hit nearly every passenger in the front seats, either with the pole or with the swaying bunch of cackling chickens as he stumbled through the aisle to the rear of the jolting bus.

'Grandmother keeps repeating how much healthier it will be in Dalian,' Xulun said, smiling, as we dusted each other energetically down on the pavement.

'We are so much looking forward to live there with you, Father,' Xuli said as she carefully cleaned my face of the dust and soot with a small towel she apparently had brought for that purpose.

'Grandmother thinks it will add ten years to her life, the fresh air, the cool summers and crisp winters,' she added, spitting on a clean corner of the towel to better wipe the dust from my eyelids and the grooves on my forehead, as Xulun looked at her ministrations with an affectionate little smile. He loved his little sister, that was clear.

'I'm afraid you will find she has aged a lot, Father,' he said. 'She aged ten years the day she found Grandfather, dead, in the lake. After that she didn't change much though. But don't let it appear if you are a bit shocked when you see her. She is very petite and has little hair left, all white, in a small bun. But otherwise she is as bright and sharp as a magpie and still very good on her legs too.'

He fell silent, smiling fondly, and I felt very proud of my son who had grown into a good and decent young man.

'Grandmother is very strict with me,' Xuli added, laughing, and again I felt my eyes burning as I heard Liang's silver, bubbling laugh.

'She doesn't want me to wear those blue or green trousers and jackets. She says a young girl should wear pretty colours so she buys material and sews blouses and skirts for me. The other girls in the neighbourhood were jealous at first but now their mothers also make colourful clothes for them.'

Laughing, she looked me up and down and said, 'That's better. At least you look presentable now. Not quite the dashing, handsome man Grandmother always boasts about to her sister, Auntie Lili, but that will come when you get over your long train voyage and this terrible bus trip. Let's go home now, it's still about twenty minutes walking.'

Arm in arm we walked, ignoring people's stares as Xulun and Xuli, in turn or sometimes at the same time, briefed me on their grandmother's little mannerisms, Auntie Lili's peculiarities and the way the two twin sisters always seemed to squabble and disagree on everything.

'But don't try to meddle or mediate,' Xulun said, chuckling, 'it's just a game they play, in reality they're as thick as thieves those two magpies, a quarrel with one means a quarrel with both and woe to you then.'

We laughed and I felt proud of my children's sense of humour and real affection for the two old ladies who had brought them up to become good human beings.

'Home' was off the main road, a couple of hundred metres down a small path alongside a canal or canalised little river rather.

Halfway down the path Xuli suddenly urged me forward crying, 'There is Grandmother, coming to meet us. Mami! Here's Father! He's as handsome as you said he would be!'

And then I stood face to face with Madam Shi, née Hsu Xulian and I felt the same awe as on the day, twenty-two years ago, when I had asked her permission, with trembling knees, to marry her daughter. She had looked me over then, from top to toe and back, as she did now with her sharp and inquisitive eyes.

Just like then my knees trembled and buckled.

Just like then she said, her voice a bit reedy now but still strong, 'Young man, what took you so long!'

I laughed and wept and took her in my arms and lifted her up, light and frail as a bird she was, and kissed her on both cheeks. Briefly she put her head on my shoulders, her cheek against mine and I felt the wetness and heard her sniff but then she cried out, 'Put me down, you shameless Western barbarian! What possesses you, kissing me like that, a respectable widow, in front of the whole neighbourhood!'

We all roared with laughter and they almost hustled me inside the neat little cottage and in front of a copy of Mami.

It was almost creepy to see how Mami Lili had aged in exactly the same manner as her twin sister though she had remained unmarried and had not experienced any of the traumas her sister had.

'It's about time you turn up and get your brood out of my hair, young man,' she said in mock severity but I saw her lips tremble and eyes brim with tears.

I embraced her and then the two of them together as I mumbled my thanks for loving and caring for my children.

Time flew. We had so much to talk about and other relatives of Mami and Mami Lili to meet that the three days we could spend together passed as in the blink of an eye.

It was on the day of our departure by the night train from Wuhan that together we went to see Hu Xianfu, Party secretary of Mianyang, to thank him for all he had done for us.

I had brought a bag with tangy and juicy Liaoning apples for him which he accepted with great pleasure.

He insisted we all ate an apple and while we were munching ours he peeled and then cut Mami's in small pieces, joking that it was his job at home to feed his little son and that there wasn't really a big difference between the very young and the very old; they are both headstrong and egoists, he grinned. We all laughed, Mami not the least.

When we told him we would take the train that night to Jinan, he insisted he would arrange for the municipality's official car to bring us to the station in Wuhan.

He advised us to leave an hour earlier and take a different road to Wuhan to avoid the roadworks on the rutted main road.

We protested and said he had done enough already and that we couldn't abuse his kindness but he wouldn't hear of it and he called the driver into his office and told him to pick us up at our house at four o'clock that afternoon.

We took leave of this endearing, kind-hearted young man, urging him to come and visit us if ever he chanced to be in Dalian.

He promised he would and asked us to write him a letter once we had settled to tell him how we had fared.

We went back home and Mami, Xulun and Xuli began their elaborate business of packing their belongings and saying farewell to neighbours and relatives who dropped in for a chat and a mug of tea and a piece of sweetmeat served by Mami Lili.

This went on for the rest of the morning and the early afternoon.

I just sat there, outsider as I was, watching the various scenes of friendly banter and drawn-out emotional farewells. On their way out everybody admonished me to take good care of Mami and the children.

At four o'clock precisely I heard the sound of an approaching car, its engine alternately revving up and dying down, its horn blaring continuously.

I went outside to see what was happening and I saw the car, an old, high-backed Pobeda, coming down the path from the main road in reverse.

Though it showed good thinking by the driver – it would have been impossible to turn the car on the narrow path and driving backwards, up the sloping path, while loaded with people, would have ended up in the canal – he wasn't very adept at driving in reverse.

The car slalomed from one side of the path to the other and several times I rubbed my sweaty hands on my trousers in fear as the driver slowed down and changed direction just in time before toppling over the bank into the canal or crashing into the row of small houses.

The whole neighbourhood had assembled along the path up to Mami Lili's house, watching the car's erratic progress. Finally the driver halted the car, with a final blast of relief on the horn, just in front of our house and cut the engine.

Grinning broadly he got out and shouted, 'I made it despite the loose steering wheel and the wobbly left front wheel. The car needs repairs but we can't get the spare parts.'

Surrounded by at least sixty curious neighbours I loaded the luggage into the boot of the car while Mami and the children made their tearful farewells to Mami Lili. I had to separate them one by one and almost hustle them into the car or otherwise they would still be standing there, hugging and crying.

I closed the rear door, locking them finally inside, took my own leave from Mami Lili with a forceful hug and a kiss and promised that the next summer I would send her the money for a ticket to Dalian to visit us there and stay as long as she liked. We both knew that nothing would come of it but it made leave-taking a lot easier.

I quickly got into the front seat beside the driver and slammed the door shut.

Under the stares and timid waves of the whole neighbourhood we drove off and I praised the driver for his foresight for having backed in the car so that we now could get away quickly. One last wave through the open side windows as the car turned right on to the main road and over the small bridge out of sight.

I heaved a sigh of relief but thought it better not to say anything as I still heard an occasional sniffling behind me. For Mami and the children a chapter of their life had been closed, for good probably, as they left behind a peaceful, friendly and caring rural community.

Primitive though it might have seemed to me, for them it had been their world for the past ten years and now they were heading for an unknown and probably intimidating future in a big, bustling northern city.

There was hardly any traffic on the small, rural road to Wuhan Secretary Hu had told the driver to take.

It took about one and a half hours longer to Wuhan but at least we were spared the ordeal of the rutted, dusty main road and the asphyxiating roadworks.

We got to Wuhan's station with two hours to spare. Mami and the children showed their travel permits to Dalian to the ticket clerk and when her leader and her leader's leader had read and stamped the permits she grudgingly issued the tickets. She never said a word nor even glanced at Mami and the children.

When it was my turn she decided to have some tea and dinner first. Nobody came to relieve her and she returned with her food and drink to her seat behind the counter and for half an hour I had to watch her slurping and smacking as behind me the line of people grew.

Her dinner finished she got up and ambled to the back of the office, listlessly rinsed her bowl and chopsticks in a sink, stopped for a chat with an equally slovenly-looking colleague and finally, after making me and scores of other people wait for almost one hour, she slumped back on her chair and sat, head bent down, without a word, a glance or a gesture that she was ready to resume her work.

The man behind me, seeing me hesitate, tried to squeeze himself in front of me while tending his filthy yuan notes through the small ticket window, yelling, 'Jinan! Jinan!'

I shoved him aside rather roughly and tending my travel permit and money, my whole leave allowance as it was, I raised my voice and asked for a sleeper cabin for four all the way to Dalian.

Without a word she took my papers and money, got up from her chair and shuffled to her leader's desk in the rear of the office.

He read my permit and the attached letter from Dalian's Party secretariat, peered over his glasses at me, mumbled something to the clerk, handed my papers back to her and continued on his register with whatever he was registering. The clerk wrote out the special ticket for the sleeper cabin, underlining the words: *four people*, tore off my regular ticket, counted my money and the change one more time and finally, *finally* shoved the whole lot of papers back through the ticket window.

With a sigh of relief I gathered the lot and squeezed myself through the thronging crowd to where Mami and the children had been waiting with the luggage.

We had used up all but fifteen minutes of the two hours we had been early and actually had to rush to get to the right platform in time.

Behind us there was pandemonium as people realised they would never get their tickets in time.

Before turning through the turnstile I looked back and saw the clerk angrily slam down the shutter of her window and stalk off, actually condemning more than two hundred people to miss their train and to wait for the next day. Her leader and her leader's leader didn't look up, pretending to be busy. They had neither the guts nor probably the authority to call the cantankerous clerk to order.

What a country! What a system! I shivered at the thought that people like that clerk would have had to handle my case.

The car superintendent was the complete opposite of the clerk.

Friendly, polite and caring she preceded us to our sleeper cabin, pulled down the berths and put on the sheets and blankets, explaining that we were lucky since her car would go all the way to Shenyang and we only had to change trains once, for the last leg to Dalian, but that wasn't bad since it was then daytime anyhow.

She brought us fresh green tea leaves and a thermos of hot water, all for ten fen, and told us she would pass every two hours or so to see if we needed anything.

The train voyage was uneventful. We passed the time talking, reminiscing, sleeping and commenting on the scenes and scenery outside our window.

I told them about Dalian and big city life to prepare them for a kind of culture shock but even Mami became increasingly impatient to start a new life.

The car superintendent did us a special favour by knocking on the door when the washroom at the rear end of the car was free and by keeping a watchful eye on other passengers when Mami was inside for her morning ablutions.

She also held a table free for us in the diner for breakfast and dinner.

Thirty-six hours after our departure from Wuhan we arrived in Shenyang, rested and completely at ease with each other. There hadn't been the slightest unpleasantness or even disagreement.

We had to wait two hours for our connecting train to Dalian, an ordinary train without sleeping cabins.

I saw my children observe the other passengers in the car and I heard them whisper that people were so neat and clean and talked so quietly amongst themselves and in Mandarin at that. They were glad that they wouldn't have any difficulty understanding the local people.

We arrived in Dalian in the early afternoon of 18th September. To my utter and pleasant surprise, Xu was waiting for us on the platform.

Our friend Hu Xianfu, Mianyang's Party secretary had sent a cable to Secretary Xian of Dalian, who in turn had advised the factory secretary Yu of our estimated time of arrival and the train number, Xu explained. Xu had been given permission to meet us at the station in company time and to bring us to our new, bigger flat. This was of course the biggest surprise of all.

After my departure Xu's wife had mentioned to her husband that my one-bedroom flat would be much too small for an additional three people, one of them an old lady at that, who needed a bit of privacy.

So she and Xu had gone to see Director Yeh and Secretary Yu who had agreed and had approved an application for a bigger flat made out and signed on my behalf and on the spot by Xu and his wife conditional, of course, upon my own agreement to pay the higher rent.

I was red-faced with shame that I hadn't thought of the problem myself and was effusive in my thanks to Xu. Mami and the children, who had been listening to Xu's explanation, joined me in thanking him which made him blush with embarrassed pleasure.

We went straight to our new flat which looked a bit bare with only my own few belongings and the few pieces of company furniture which Xu had already transferred from my former flat.

He told us that we could choose some additional furniture in the company storeroom that afternoon and probably buy a few new sheets and blankets that afternoon in the company store. The costs could be chalked up and be deducted later from my salary in instalments; his wife had already taken the necessary steps for that, Xu said. I was overwhelmed by my friends' kindness and didn't know how to thank him.

I still had one day left of my leave and I used it to arrange our flat, together with Mami and children, and in the afternoon to show them around Dalian and the countryside.

They were delighted. The children couldn't get enough of criss-crossing the town by tram and Mami loved the bus ride along the coastal road and the sea and the tangy, fresh air. We got out of the bus for a walk along the pebble beach and the children were overwhelmed and overjoyed by the sight and smell of the sea and the islands. They tasted the water and kept shouting at me and at each other that it was salty and so *cold*.

I showed them how to make flat pebbles sail over the water and they cheered as they saw who could make the pebbles flit the most often.

We had freshly steamed shrimps and sea cucumber for dinner in a small roadside restaurant before taking the last bus of the day back to town.

Our new life together had got off to a wonderful start and we were happy.

Mami and the children settled in quickly.

Fortunately Mami had continued to teach the children at home, every day, during the years of the Cultural Revolution so that they were far ahead of most of the young people their age who lost years of basic, formal education. They were allowed to sit for an entrance examination for middle school and did so well that they were both placed in the third year, despite their difference in age.

Two years later they graduated with flying colours.

Thanks to Xu's recommendation, Director Yeh endorsed Xulun's application for admission to the engineering faculty of Shanghai Fudan University and after sitting for an entrance examination he was admitted in September 1979 at the age of twenty-two. His examination results had been so good that he was exempted from contributing to his tuition and boarding costs subject to a yearly review of his achievements.

He graduated as an electrical and mechanical engineer in 1984, with double honours, and again thanks to director Yeh's intervention, Xulun was assigned to our shipyard as Xu's and my understudy.

He followed the evening courses at the institute for foreign languages and became fluent in English, also spoken English which is so often the problem with Chinese, owing to our habit of speaking English at home.

Thanks to Xulun's command of English and his pleasant personality – and his competence of course, our wharf got an order for four so-called roll-on, roll-off ferries from a Belgian shipping company for its ferry service between Belgium and England.

More orders would have followed were it not that in 1986 my leader and friend Xu Luobao died and instead of promoting Xulun to his position, something he had been trained for and deserved more than anybody else, Director Yeh was forced, against his vehement opposition I was told later, to accept the appointment of a man from outside, a man without an engineering degree, without a word of English, but the son of an influential member of Dalian's Open City Economic Commission and a senior Party member. The son himself was also a Party member so Xulun had really no chance and Director Yeh, this brilliant and visionary man, got himself in serious trouble for having opposed the appointment.

Right from the beginning Xulun and I clashed on practically everything with the new manager, Dong Ming. For instance, when we discussed the plans for two new ferries for presentation during the forthcoming visit by a delegation of a Danish shipping company, Dong forbade us to speak English with the Danes and he also had the interpreter tell them that their wish to have the signs and nameplates in English and Danish was not possible.

The Danes were flabbergasted. This was already their fourth visit and this time they had intended to sign the contract and celebrate. They were very upset and angry when all of a sudden Xulun and I, who had got on so well with them during their previous visits and taken them out for dinner so often, speaking and discussing and joking in English, were no longer allowed to speak to them directly but only through an interpreter.

They were so angry that they all crowded around Xulun and myself, pushing and poking us, all the while shouting, '*Why Dao? What the hell is going on here*!

I managed to mumble in English, 'Please, please do not blame us. New boss! Party man! New policies.'

'To *hell* with your new policies!' the Danes shouted. 'Tell your new boss he can stuff them up his arse, the ferries!' And they walked out of the meeting back to their hotel.

I begged Dong to let me go to the hotel to try to calm them down and save the order for the wharf.

He merely looked at me contemptuously and said, 'Let those bloody foreigners get out of our country. We don't need them.' And at that he left for one of those meetings he spent most of his time in.

I wrote immediately a long letter to the Economic Commission explaining what had happened and blaming Dong for losing a valuable order.

Two days later I was called to the mayor's office and without even mentioning my letter or the lost order the vice-mayor offered me the job of chief engineer in the new hotel for foreigners.

My knowledge of English and foreigners made me the ideal candidate for the job, he said.

A nice, cosy job in a quiet place, ideal before retiring in a few years' time, he said. He hoped I would understand. I did, so I accepted and never put a foot back in my department at the wharf.

Xulun had a few miserable months but finally reason and Director Yeh prevailed, apparently, since three months after the incident with the Danes, Dong Ming was transferred to an office job in the Port Authority of Dalian as a vice-unit Party secretary.

Of course they couldn't make Xulun head of the department, not yet at least since that would have meant too much loss of face for Dong Ming's father. So Director Yeh managed to get the head of the drawing room, a gentle old man, two years away from his own retirement, appointed as Xulun's new leader.

He knows absolutely nothing about the construction side of the matter and knows very well why he has been made the leader. He leaves everything to Xulun and in two years' time Xulun will be the boss.

Xulun immediately wrote a long, apologetic letter to the Danes explaining more or less what had happened but that now the situation had returned to normal and would they please forget the whole unfortunate incident. He finished the letter by saying that he realised the wharf had lost their earlier order but that he hoped they could do business again in the future.

He got back a letter by special delivery thanking him for his explanations and assuring him that they understood and would like to pick up the thread again where it had been broken off since they hadn't placed the order with another shipyard yet.

So it looks as if Xulun can save the order for the company.

During those difficult and trying times Xulun's wife was a great support for both Xulun and myself.

The day Xulun came to work for the company he fell head over heels in love with Xiao Lu, the lively and lovely little clerk of the personnel department, as she completed his file and showed him around like she had done for me eight years earlier.

Later she told me she had fallen in love with Xulun that same day when she had chided him for ogling her and he had blushed and acted like a small child caught with his hand in the cookie jar.

They courted for six months and with my blessing and to my utter joy applied for permission to marry in February 1985. Since they were both the right age they received permission to marry, and to have a child, within ten days and they were married on 1st March, 1985.

Director Yeh gave his permission for Xiao Lu to move in with Xulun in our flat since we had a spare room as Xuli had gone to live in Shanghai, for reasons I'll tell you in a moment.

Their little daughter Xulian was born on 31st March, 1986.

Mami was overjoyed with her first and last great-grandchild and that the little girl was named after her.

One month later Mami suddenly died, in her sleep, after almost nine happy years with us. When we found her she still had that contented little smile of hers on her face.

Xuli was granted two days' leave from her school in Shanghai to attend the funeral. Only the three of us accompanied Mami to the cemetery, sad yet glad that she had been so happy during the last years of her life and had died so peacefully.

The rental agreement for the flat was then put in Xulun's name and I got the status of live-in parent. I pay my share of the household costs and the rest of my small salary I save. Who knows? Perhaps one day travel restrictions for ordinary Chinese will be lifted and I can apply for a passport and pay myself a ticket to England and find out whatever became of my mother and my former friends there.

To finish my own story I still have to tell you what happened to my daughter Xuli.

Xuli finished middle school with honours, the same year as Xulun, though she was only seventeen then.

She was very, very pretty, gorgeous as the English would say, but she had only one passion and that was music, classical music. Whatever the costs, whatever the sacrifices, she wanted to be a musician, a violinist.

Mami told me that she had always been like that, even as a little girl. Mami's sister, Mami Lili, still kept Mami's violin hidden under her bedroom floor ever since the day Mami and her husband had been exiled to Meishan.

Every day for four months Mami and Xuli went for a walk in the fields around Mianyang, far away from the nearest farming commune, and there, in a bamboo thicket, Mami took the violin from the jute bag she carried it in so as not to draw people's attention and taught Xuli how to play.

She had such talent that after four months of hiding from people's eyes and ears Mami got all her courage together and went to see the neighbourhood committee's secretary, an elderly woman apparently completely the opposite of your Hu Guoshang or Old Turtle as you call her.

Why the woman and the committee agreed to let Xuli continue her music lessons at home was and probably will always remain an enigma. Playing the violin and Western classical music at that was not and still is not exactly a proletarian pastime. Be that as it may, Xuli became very very good at playing the violin and Xuli wouldn't have been Xuli if after the first few hectic months in Dalian she hadn't begun to try and cajole me into sending money to Mami Lili for a train ticket to Dalian so that she could bring the violin with her.

In the summer of 1978 I sent the money to Mami Lili and one month later there she was, with the violin. Everybody was overjoyed to see her again and Xuli of course to be reunited with her violin.

By that time, and I don't know how, Xuli had already found out about an old Russian émigré, a Jew, who came to Dalian in 1932 as a refugee from Vladivostok where he used to be the director of the local orchestra. He had to flee because of Stalin's pogroms.

In Dalian people still remembered old Shimonov for the violin lessons he gave the Japanese governor during the occupation in exchange apparently for a decent treatment of Dalian's population. When Russia declared war on Japan Shimonov went into hiding, in the countryside where he stayed with relatives of his many grateful Chinese friends.

In 1949, after liberation, the Communists told him he had better go back to Russia but he refused; China had become his country, he said, and strangely enough they left him in peace.

During the first couple of months of the Cultural Revolution the Red Guards had at first tried to arrest him on charges of being a foreign spy and of collaboration with the former occupying enemy Japan but after strong protests from people all over the city they had backed off.

They then began a campaign of harassment but they gave up rather quickly because of Shimonov's violent temper. It seems he walked through the streets, banging pots and pans against each other while shouting expletives and denigrating remarks about the Red Guards, calling them '*nyekulturny schweine*', a double insult by Jewish standards, apparently. Dalian's Party secretary put a stop to the harassment and ordered Shimonov not to leave his neighbourhood or else...

All these anecdotes I found out later, of course, after Mami and Xuli went to see him to ask him whether he would deign to give lessons to my daughter.

He had her play a few notes, then a simple but lovely piece Mami had taught her and accepted her, charging two yuan per lesson.

Six months later I went to see him in secret. Xuli, that little tigress, would have scratched my eyes out had she known, and told the old man that sixteen yuan per month represented a quarter of my salary and was too much money to pour down the drain if Xuli didn't have any talent.

Who was I? What *nyekulturny* barbarian unworthy of such a great talent was I to think that *he, the great master Abraham Jacobovitsch Shimonov would waste his time with a mere fiddler*!

How did I *dare* come to his house and talk about *talent*, something he, *Master Shimonov* had in such abundant supply while I, the greatest cultural nincompoop in the whole of China, no, the whole world, lacked even the very notion since I lived under the same roof as one of the greatest talents he, Shimonov, had ever had the privilege to teach and *I didn't know*! *Had no idea*! Brabbled about *money*! He didn't *want* my money! I could have it *all back*! All the one hundred and four yuan I had paid him so far and not to forget the *fiddle* I had bought for my daughter at some pawnshop or other.

He, Jacobovitsch Shimonov would teach Xuli for free, for *absolutely free*! The fact that he would die in glory, for ever remembered for having discovered and developed her talent would be reward enough for him.

And she would continue to play on *his* violin, the one she had played from the day of her very first lesson, the one he had inherited from his grandfather and which Dao Xuli would inherit in turn, his incomparable, his marvellous Guarneri which Xuli could make laugh and weep and whisper and sing to make the angels weep with joy.

At that he pushed a wooden cigar box in my hands and hustled me out of the door into the street.

The last words I heard Abraham Jacobovitsch Shimonov say were 'undeserving moron who for reasons only known to his inscrutable God had been able to produce such a precious talent'. The cigar box contained exactly one hundred and four yuan in one-yuan notes.

One year later and one week after Xuli got her middle school diploma she came home from Master Shimonov in a state of almost euphoric happiness.

She told me that Shimonov had written to his friend, the director of the Shanghai Conservatory, to ask for an audition for her, Xuli, and that yesterday he had received a reply with a date for the audition.

Shimonov would accompany her, with his precious instrument, and they would stay at his friend's house.

They would leave in two weeks' time and in preparation she would stay with Shimonov and practise every day and the whole day at that.

She passed the audition with flying colours and the conservatory board of directors even gave her the status of live-in student. To pay for her tuition and board, and that until completion of her studies, Master Shimonov donated his precious Guarneri to the State on the sole condition that Xuli would be the only person to play the instrument and that she would be allowed to keep it always with her and eventually travel with it as well.

A week after the audition Xuli came home, only to pack her suitcase and to say goodbye for at least one year.

She began her studies in April 1980.

Two years later, in May 1982, Shimonov died.

His neighbours found him a week later, all shrivelled and smelly, clutching a small newspaper cutting Xuli had sent him in her monthly letter.

Under her picture it said that Dao Xuli had been the soloist during a concert given by the Shanghai Chamber Orchestra in the former French Club for a visiting delegation of officials and scientists from France.

The audience had given a standing ovation to the twenty year old virtuoso for her interpretation of works by Mozart and Saint Saëns, the small article said.

She came over for the funeral of her old teacher and mentor. She was heartbroken. She had really loved the cantankerous, passionate old man without whom she would never have achieved her life's dream.

★

Lao Dao smiled. 'That was seven years ago and she has been abroad several times to play as a soloist with renowned orchestras. She visits us every year around Chinese New Year and then, for a few days, she is our little Xuli again.

'There still doesn't seem to be a man in her life, though Xiao Lu says that during her latest visit she talked a lot about a French pianist she met in Brussels. Xiao Lu is furious with Xulun and me when we say that we hope Xuli won't fall in love with a foreigner. But then Xiao Lu is a woman and not *reasonable* when it's about love.

'Xulun and I know that both Xuli and we ourselves will be in for a lot of trouble if she wants to marry a foreigner. It may very well mean the end of her career, certainly of her international career, and she may end up playing a fiddle, as Shimonov would say, in the lobby of a hotel for foreigners or worse, sent for re-education to a commune. And my own past may catch up with me again if they accuse me of having brought up my daughter in the wrong spirit, with a taste for things foreign. The suspicion may even spill over to Xulun and he may lose his position as they will see his frequent contacts with foreigners as a token of his own personal preference and of his contempt for China and things Chinese.

'You think I am being paranoid? You think that China will be proud of Xuli's fame and Xulun's quiet competence? Forget it! How many people in China have ever heard of Dao Xuli, let alone of Dao Xulun? A few hundred, perhaps? And you think these people care? The authorities would rather send my children to jail, for fifteen or twenty years, than let them contaminate the populace with their foreign influence.

'So you see, my friends, that in spite of all the odds and misfortunes I have been able to contribute my bit to our motherland, yet it is still a very dangerous privilege. The Party can hardly hurt me more than it did already but it's for Xuli and Xulun that I am worried.'

Lao Dao fell silent, sighed, then added, 'That was the first part of my story. I'm sorry if I bored you and I won't blame you in the least if you would tell me to leave that other part for some other time, if ever.'

His friends remained silent for a long time, unable to find something appropriate to say.

Finally Auntie Liu said, 'That was a very moving story, Lao Dao, my friend. What amazes me though is that after all your trials and tribulations you bear no grudges, that instead you seem quite content with life and your status. Intentionally I don't say "with what you made of your life" since from everything you told us, I, at least, get the impression that things happened to you rather than that you *made* them happen. The few good people you met and who did the decent things to do seem to reconcile you to all the vileness that destroyed your career, killed your wife, made you suffer. Because you met these good people when you had given up hope that such people existed after all, you now think that goodness and decency have triumphed after all.

'Well, let me tell you that they haven't and that they won't, ever! Am I being cynical? I don't think so. As long as deeds of civility, of goodness, of decency are being hailed it proves that they are the exception, not the rule. And I am not even thinking of the great malefactors and criminals, not even of the criminals and crooks who strut the world stage disguised as so-called politicians and diplomats lying, cheating, stealing, breaking promises, profiteering and what have you and all for purely selfish motives, no, I am thinking of the obscure ones like that Dong Ming you told us about a moment ago. They are everywhere in our society and probably in other societies as well. Like rampant, ineradicable weeds that strangle and suck life's juices from the plants and flowers that give us health and beauty, they kill the inherent goodness and decency in other people.

'You say they worry you, because of what Dong Ming's manoeuvring behind the scenes through his influential father may do to wreck your son's career and his family life, because of what others like Dong Ming may do to your daughter if she happens to listen to her heart instead of to the chilly reasoning of those who mean well. I got the impression, Lao Dao, that that is the whole tenet of your story and therefore of your life. You told us about your sorrows, apologetically almost, but always in relation to your loved ones, never to yourself. And now you hesitate whether to tell us about the one period of your life that does concern yourself only, those ten years in the *laogai*, postulating we are not interested.

'You are indeed like Ah Q, Lao Dao, my friend. Perhaps I ought to envy you your peace of mind and heart. Or is it that you hide your anger so well? Next week you *are* going to tell us about that other part of your life, Lao Dao. The picture we have of you now is not complete. Like all of us you must have a flaw, perhaps, or probably rather, a flaw that you learned to control but nevertheless a flaw that makes you into an ordinary human being. What do *you* think my friends? Shall we make Lao Dao tell us all so that we can gloat that he *is* human after all?' And smiling mischievously, Liu Meiling looked at the others.

Before they could say something Lao Dao said, smiling good-humouredly, 'I'll humour you, Meiling, like Ah Q would have.' He laughed heartily.

'You are right,' the old man continued, 'I have never been able or even tried to make things happen. It's not my character. I'm a "softy" I'm afraid, yet I do not secretly harbour feelings of anger or hatred and I am not after revenge. Perhaps that is why I am at peace with myself and you are *not*, Meiling. Where you only see and rage about the fields overgrown with weeds, I smell the few flowers that struggle and manage to worship the sun and I marvel at their beauty and strength.

'And so I marvel at the goodness and decency of a few people, not because I am naive as you seem to think, Meiling, but because I think that it *is* marvellous that they *exist* and are *not* afraid to be themselves in spite of the overwhelming numbers of the bad ones who treat the good ones with such contempt and did and still do and will always do everything in their might to destroy humaneness and beauty. Next week I'll tell you the last part of my story, perhaps you'll see my point then.'

Lao Dao fell silent and smiled guilelessly at Auntie Liu.

'You do that,' she grumbled mockingly, 'and I'll owe you big if you manage to convince me and give me some peace of mind in my old age. Now, let's have a last mug of fresh tea and then try to get some sleep. It's past midnight already.'

Pensively they sipped their tea, each lost in his and her own thoughts.

Finally, groaningly, Auntie Liu stood up from her chair, signalling she wanted to retire.

The others quickly took leave of her and of each other and went their different ways.

Lao Dao and Lao Dee walked back to the hotel where Lao Dao began his night shift as Lao Dee arranged the tapes in his suitcase and went to bed for a few hours of restless turning and tossing as for the first time he worried about how to put all the disparate stories together in one comprehensive and readable whole and the time it would take to do so. It would take years, he feared, since he wouldn't be able to make it a full-time job until he would retire in a couple of years.

Until then he would only work on the layout and a preliminary draft during the evenings in his hotel room and every other weekend when he wouldn't go home to Hong Kong.

Satisfied with his decision he finally fell asleep when dawn began to break.

## *Chapter Thirty*

### Hope is but a Dream of Those Awake

Lao Dee arrived early for their next session the following Thursday.

He had to make good his promise to prepare a few Western dishes for dinner and had brought the ingredients as well as a shiny new wok and a Western-style saucepan with cover from his weekend visit to Hong Kong.

Beiyuen quickly called Suping and Lilian to come over for the cooking lesson and the four women admired the beautiful wok.

Lao Dee explained that it was lined with a new kind of material called Teflon which made burning of the food impossible.

He told them never to stir the food with a metal object as that would scratch the lining and defeat its purpose. He showed them a few wooden and Teflon spatulas and told them to use only these when stir-frying or scraping the food from the wok.

Unlike the iron woks made in China, this one had a beautiful reddish-orange enamelled cover which made the wok suitable for more elaborate cooking than just stir-frying, Lao Dee explained.

He then laid out the various ingredients and told them he would prepare three dishes which wouldn't be too alien for the Chinese palate.

As a starter they were going to have a Spanish favourite called *gambas al ayola* or giant prawns deep-fried with lots of garlic with French bread to dip and eat the garlic butter sauce. He had bought the prawns on the fish market that very morning, alive and kicking.

He instructed Beiyuen to peel the garlic and to chop it finely. Between the starter and the main course they would have a lime sherbet to clean the mouth of the strong garlic aftertaste.

He had bought a deep-frozen carton of sherbet from Hong Kong and had arranged with Roger Wu to keep it in the hotel's deep-freeze meat locker until the last moment. The box was still covered with a thick layer of frost so the contents would not melt before they were ready to eat them.

For the main course they would have a southern French dish called *poulet à l'estragon* which he had translated in English and Chinese as Dragon Chicken, a pretty name for Chinese ears.

He showed them and made them smell the small glass containers with the herb called tarragon or dragon and the women agreed that it had indeed a very nice smell. He then asked Lilian to peel and chop the shallots.

He himself would cut the chicken in the right way and in sizeable pieces he said, since the Chinese were not accustomed to that way of cutting up a chicken. They were used to hacking the whole bird indiscriminately in many small pieces with a big chopper. That way every piece, however small, had bones in it which made for messy eating and only possible with chopsticks and not with fork and knife, as is the custom outside China, Lao Dee explained. Steamed rice, though not customary eaten with this dish, would go very well with it and was easy to prepare so he asked Suping to start boiling the rice.

For desert he would prepare a favourite from Thailand, mango with sticky rice and coconut cream.

He had brought fresh Filipino mangoes from Hong Kong, as well as the ready coconut cream in small carton packs and the special kind of rice that becomes glutinous and sticky by boiling.

The women had never seen mangoes before and they were intrigued by the yellowish-orange colour and the strange smell.

'A bit like the stuff I used to clean my furniture with,' Auntie Liu said, sniffing the fruit. 'I forget the name but I wonder how this fruit tastes, smelling as it does like polish.'

Lao Dee laughed and said she was right, that the fruit indeed contained certain compounds similar to those in furniture polish or old-fashioned paint thinner, however, she would find the fruit delicious, he assured her.

Beiyuen had by then finished with the garlic and Lao Dee quickly put a big chunk of Danish butter in the wok and heated it until golden and very hot. He then put the salted fresh prawns in the butter, as they were, with head and feet and everything.

When they were golden brown he added the garlic and let the whole simmer for another ten minutes.

In the meantime he showed the women how to cut and debone the chicken in to manageable pieces.

That ready, he transferred the prawns and garlic butter sauce from the wok into the saucepan, with a wooden spatula and he showed them how easily this type of wok could be cleaned with a bit of hot water and a few drops of detergent and that no trace of the prawns and garlic was left after that.

He then fried the pieces of chicken in the wok, with butter, and when they were golden brown outside and whitish tender inside he added fresh cream from a few small carton packs he had brought from Hong Kong, the chopped shallots, a lot of the dragon and a liberal dose of white pepper.

Finally he put the beautiful cover on the wok, pushed it to a less hot place on the stove and said, 'Let it simmer for another twenty minutes or so. In the meantime I'll prepare the coconut cream and the sticky rice so that they can cool off before we are ready for the dessert. The mangoes I'll peel and cut at the last moment.'

At that moment the door opened and Lao Dao came in, sniffing.

'I merely had to follow my nose from the entrance of the lane,' he said laughingly. 'What delicious smells! Lao Yang is pacing up and down outside your window, Meiling, green with envy. Old Turtle is standing in her doorway and with a face like a thundercloud. For her these smells signal the beginning of the end of China. The invaders from the West have taken over the traditional Chinese kitchen.'

He laughed uproariously and lifted the covers of the wok and the saucepan and sniffed and peered at the contents.

'Good grief,' he remarked, 'even I have never seen such food before. I'm afraid that during those first ten years after the war there wasn't much of fancy food in England and from what I heard then from the occasional foreigner I met the English type of cooking is not renowned with non-Britishers for its refinement and taste. Those fruits I recognise though,' he remarked, 'they are mangoes, aren't they, Lao Dee? I saw them once in the shop-window of a delicatessen shop in London. I remember them because of the outrageous price. Imported mangoes from Jamaica, the tag said, two pounds each. A lot of money then. What a peculiar smell though,' he said wonderingly as he fingered the soft skin of the fruit. 'Like turpentine I would say.'

'That's it!' Auntie Liu exclaimed. 'Now I remember the word, turpentine! What is this foreign devil up to now,' she grumbled jokingly, 'poisoning us while we, naive Chinese, thought we had such a beautiful relationship?'

Everybody laughed and then Lao Dee said, 'Everything is ready. The girls have set the table already so everybody sit down please while I serve the prawns first.

'No need to use the forks and knives I brought or the chopsticks. Just use your fingers and the bread. Afterwards we'll wash our hands and rub them with a few pieces of lemon I brought to remove the strong smell of fried prawns and garlic. Now let's eat. I'll show you how.'

The others watched as Lao Dee took a prawn, removed the head and put the rest in his mouth. They saw him chew and taste and nod approvingly as he broke off a piece of the special bread and wiped part of the garlic butter sauce from his plate with it before biting off the soggy part.

Again he nodded approvingly. 'Good,' he mumbled, his mouth full, 'very good. Try also.'

The others approached their plates, hesitantly at first, but after the first tentative bites they nodded at each other enthusiastically and attacked with gusto.

Within five minutes all the prawns and sauce and butter were gone and they sat back in their chairs, still sucking the last remains of bread and sauce from their fingers.

'That was truly delicious, Lao Dee, my friend,' Auntie Liu said with a contented burp. Beiyuen, did you watch Lao Dee when he did the cooking? I want to eat prawns more often like this. I think you can eat them also with steamed rice instead of with bread. That will be easier for us to get.'

'Oh yes,' Lao Dee replied, 'as a matter of fact I usually eat them with rice at home and then as the main course, with just a green vegetable salad. That's enough. I know you Chinese don't like raw green vegetables with whatever dressing so I didn't bring any. But Westerners like this kind of food with a salad on the side and that's their whole meal. Now let's wash our hands.'

In turn they washed their hands, with soap first, and then rubbed their fingers with a slice of lemon as Lao Dee showed them, and then rinsed and dried their hands on a towel. They all sat down again and watched Lao Dee open the still thawing carton with lime sherbet.

He put two spoons of the greenish water-ice in the teacup in front of each and said, 'Eat the sherbet slowly with the little spoon. Let it melt on your tongue. It's very refreshing and it removes the strong lingering taste of garlic which would spoil the taste of the meat dish.'

They followed his example and again they were delighted.

'What a civilised way of eating,' Auntie Liu said, 'I can imagine that with the proper table setting and utensils it will look very chic.'

'It's a *different* way of eating,' Lao Dee said, 'not better or superior; not inferior, just *different*. It's good to try different kinds of food now and then, to try a greater variety for fun as otherwise eating becomes such a bore, but in general one is best off eating one's own country's or region's food and the simplest dishes are often the best and healthiest.

'When I am in China or in predominantly Chinese countries like Hong Kong or Singapore, I normally eat Chinese food, even at home since that's what the maid is good at preparing. Nothing fancy, just plain, good old-fashioned Chinese dishes with a preference for Cantonese and Sichuan food, two or three dishes at the most for one meal once a day and one of them always steamed or stir-fried leafy green vegetables. It's not only tasty and healthy, it's also good for your wallet since the ingredients and way of cooking are by far the cheapest. Foreign food in foreign restaurants, let alone in chic hotel restaurants, is always obscenely expensive. It's no value for that kind of money and besides, I simply won't pay those prices and feel bad afterwards, morally and physically. I sleep badly after such a meal as it digests very slowly and lies like a stone in my stomach as I toss and turn and curse myself for my stupidity and lax morals.

'Once, long ago, I had a row with the French ambassador in Madagascar when I refused to come to one of his functions because of the price the luxury hotel charged for the food and wine. It represented more than a year's salary of the guard who lived in a hovel in the rear of my garden and who would have to watch over my sleeping children while my wife and I were eating the income for a whole year for him, his wife and their nine children. The ambassador called me a Communist when he asked and I gave him the reason why I refused to come. I called him an arrogant buffoon totally out of touch with the real world outside his little ivory tower. But that was in my firebrand days, when I still thought that such gestures made a difference, had an effect.

'I know now that it didn't, never has and never will. So all I want now is to feel good myself, both mentally, which is not the same as morally, and physically. So I eat Chinese food when in China, Thai when in Thailand, Indonesian when in Indonesia, American country food, not fast food, when in America and European when in Europe. Once every now and then I have some kind or other of exotic food in one of the many little foreign restaurants that pop up all over the world these days or I prepare a few exquisite exotic dishes myself for a social dinner with friends at home and that's fun and everybody enjoys it but it remains the exception and that's how it should be. When we have finished I have still something to add but now let's have the main dish.'

Lilian and her mother put the steamed rice and the wok with the Dragon Chicken in the centre of the table and when Suping lifted the cover off the wok a delicious smell wafted up and tickled their noses and curiosity.

'Let me serve you,' Lao Dee said and suiting action to his words he first put a generous helping of steaming rice on each plate, a bit to the side.

Next he fished six nice, big pieces of chicken meat from the wok and served each a piece, next to the rice. Finally, with a small ladle, he poured some of the greenish-yellow creamy sauce over the rice. The many green bits of dragon and the glazed pieces of shallots made a nice effect on the white rice.

He sat down and said, 'Now watch how Lao Dao and I eat this dish with knife and fork. Don't hesitate to use a spoon if that's easier. Eating must be a joy, not an exercise in legerdemain.'

After a few awkward trials, especially in cutting off a smaller piece of chicken with the knife and fork, the women quickly got the knack of it and relaxed to enjoy the taste and smell of this chic-looking but essentially simple dish.

They loved it and everybody but Lao Dee had second helpings. While the others were busy helping themselves Lao Dee got up and opened a cool box he had brought with him. He took out three bottles of a pinkish white wine, which became immediately wet with condensation.

'I bought this wine in Hong Kong,' he said, 'it's a Californian wine made from the Zinfandel grape. It's light and fruity and in my opinion goes extraordinarily well with this kind of food. We'll try it. If you don't like it, don't drink it. No obligation. Lao Dao and I will finish it later or next time.'

He also took real wine glasses from the box and put one beside each plate on the table.

'Borrowed the glasses from Roger Wu,' he smiled, 'if we do something let's do it well or else let's not do it at all.'

He poured a bit of the ice-cold pinkish wine in Lao Dao's glass and asked him what he thought of it.

Lao Dao took a good draft and let the wine roll around his tongue, his eyes closed.

A slow smile spread over his face and he said, 'Lovely, deliciously fresh and fruity. You may fill my glass, my friend'. Lao Dee grinned as he filled all the glasses.

'To our health and friendship,' he declared, raising his glass.

The others raised their glasses and looking at each other they repeated after Lao Dee, 'To our health and friendship, whatever happens,' and then they sniffed and tasted the wine, carefully, almost hesitantly at first, but then they nodded and smiled and took a good sip.

'My oh my, this is delicious, Lao Dee,' Auntie Liu exclaimed, 'and I bet it's good for our health as well. We should grow the Zinfandel grape in China and then make this type of wine. So light and refreshing, I'm sure it would be a huge success. A few weeks ago I went to the Friendship Store to buy a tin of Danish cookies with the FEC you gave me and there was a stand where they offered the foreign customers a small glass of white wine for tasting, one wine was called Great Wall, the other Dynasty, both produced in China, one in a joint venture with the French, the other with the Australians. I forget which is which. They tasted not bad, rather good even, but by far not as light and refreshing and fruity as this one. Why can't the Americans produce this wine in China as well?'

Lao Dee laughed and said, 'I'm glad you like it. I always drink it with the American type of Mexican food they call Cajun-style food when I'm in Florida or in California. I'll write Mr Mondavi a letter and tell him about your suggestion, Meiling. Who knows? Maybe one day there'll be a Chinese Zinfandel on the market.'

Contentedly they sat for a while, drinking their wine in small, appreciative draughts, talking about one thing and another.

Suping told the others about her visit to Lushun with Lao Dee and Auntie Liu, two days ago.

While Lao Dee had gone about his business there she and Auntie had gone to the asylum to see what had become of Kunlen.

They had been very well received, very cordially in fact, and a nurse had shown them around and explained how they took care of the patients as they call the inmates there. After a few days of observation in a single room Kunlen had been diagnosed as incurable but docile and absolutely non-violent. So they had put him in a special ward with about two dozen men and women like him.

There were a few round tables and chairs so that they could sit in each other's company if they liked and the ward had separate dormitories for the men and women.

Ciaokeli had at first been a bit of a problem since strictly speaking the patients were not allowed to have pets. However, when the doctor and the director had seen for themselves how affectionate the little dog had been, not only with Kunlen but also with the other patients, and how he had even managed to make an old, almost blind woman smile for the first time since she had been admitted more than ten years ago, they had agreed that Ciaokeli could stay.

The doctor had even remarked to the nurse that it might be a good idea to have more pets around. He had said that he was even thinking of writing a paper about the idea as a possible new therapy to be tried out in other asylums as well.

'When we arrived with the nurse at the ward Kunlen wasn't there. He was just having his daily walk in the garden, the ward nurse explained,' Suping said and continued. 'The doctor had found him generally in good health but his legs and back had been weak, too weak, probably from lack of exercise while he had been cared for at home. That's what the nurse told me and the doctor is right, of course. Lilian and I have given him far too little exercise. We were content with him lying there on his plank bed the whole day. That was bad, of course, but I didn't think any further and neither did Lilian. I see now that goodwill and caring aren't enough and that it is a very good thing Kunlen is now getting professional treatment.

'He didn't recognise me when he came back from his walk with a trainee nurse. He didn't even react to my touch and to the sound of my voice when I said loving words to him. He just stood there, smiling that same inane smile I have known so well for the past twelve years. He always smiles like that, the nurse told us. He seems to be happy wherever his mind wanders, she added.

'At that moment Ciaokeli came running up to him, jumping up and down around Kunlen's legs and licking his hands and neither I nor the nurse existed any more for him and the dog. I had seen enough and after the first disappointment I was actually glad. We went to see the director, a very friendly, elderly man, and he told me that unless I have some personal reason to come and see my husband I might as well stay away.

'"He doesn't recognise you, Mrs Li," Director Han said to me. "He doesn't recognise anybody. He's probably just aware of the presence of people moving around him since he doesn't bump into others but evades them if they are in his way. But whether the others register with him as people or just as moving objects we don't know and we can't ask him because he never says a word. He just smiles. So if you agree we'll just let you know by letter if there is anything that requires your presence here but otherwise stay home and spare yourself the trouble and emotional upset."

'I thought that was wise advice so I thanked him and left. Lao Dee was waiting in the car in front of the building and we drove straight back to Dalian. I told Lao Dee what I just told you and he agrees with Director Han and so does Auntie Liu, of course. She always said so. I told Lilian all about it and, pragmatic and down-to-earth as my dear daughter is, she couldn't agree more she said.

'So that's the end of it I think. I'll be a grass widow as long as Kunlen is alive. He may very well outlive me, what with the kind of stressless, wholesome life he is leading there in Lushun. But I have no problem with that,' she added and fell silent.

'You'll have a problem the day you stumble across a nice man your age and of your intellectual level who would like to do more with you than just smart talking,' Auntie Liu grinned. 'I'm not sure whether you could get a divorce if your husband is institutionalised,' she added seriously.

'That's neither here nor there, Auntie Liu!' Suping exclaimed, blushing. 'There's no such man and I wouldn't want to start all over again. Too much trouble and I like my freedom. Lao Dee, please let's have dessert before that old woman makes me all flustered. I'm hungry again. Your food isn't filling enough.'

Everybody laughed and Lao Dee said, 'Okay, I'll peel the mangoes and cut them in stripes. I need a clean plate for that. Lilian, please take the sticky rice and dish out nice, round pieces with the ladle I used for the sauce. Rinse the ladle first. Beiyuen, stir the coconut sauce one last time and pour a spoonful or so over the sticky rice on each plate. Lao Dao, pour us another glass of wine, please.'

Presently Lao Dee showed them the plate with the glistening, juicy, dark orange pieces of mango and then he carefully lifted the pieces from the plate, one by one, and put them next to the sticky rice on each plate.

'Eat it with your spoon,' he said and with a delighted smile he began to eat his own portion.

The others tentatively tasted a small piece of mango and then a tiny spoon tip of sticky rice with coconut cream.

Their eyes widening in surprised appreciation, they nodded at each other and with gusto attacked the remainder on their plate.

'That was very, very good, Lao Dee,' Auntie Liu said, licking her plate, 'what a delicious fruit the mango is. The people in those countries where it grows must be very fond of it.'

'Oh yes, they are,' Lao Dee replied. 'They eat it ripe, just as a fruit, drink it as a creamy juice or in salads while it's still green. There's a variety of mango that stays green and hard and people peel and slice them and crunch them as they dip the slices in a sweet chilli sauce. Very nice. Mangoes are treated with a lot of respect and are never really cheap, even in high season. There are many varieties of mango in the southern Asian countries and the people always think that their country's is the best. I personally like the ones from the Philippines and from Thailand best.'

'If other Thai dishes are as delicious as this dessert, the food there must be wonderful,' Lilian said.

'It is,' Lao Dee answered, 'but I have to qualify that. They have a type of bucolic food that's simply disgusting for the foreign taste, even visually it makes one want to throw up. On the other hand they have what is called royal cuisine and that is simply the most delicious and most refined exotic food there is, refinement on an absolute par with fine Japanese food. If tastiness is important, as it is for me, Thai food is far superior to the bland Japanese type. I have learned to prepare quite a few of such Thai dishes and when I serve them at home, for friends, everybody is always delighted.

'Food and foodstuffs have become quite an industry in Thailand and people like to eat small portions several times a day. The small restaurants are always crowded and every street and road and lane is lined with food stalls where people eat, literally, from early morning till very late at night. Those stalls are nothing more than specially constructed carts, on wheels, with a built-in stove, either gas- or charcoal-fired, and a zinc platform to cut vegetables or meat or to prepare pastry or whatever. A few ramshackle, foldable tables and some stools complete the picture. The stallholders, men or women, hawkers as they are often called, are experts in preparing one or two special dishes and that's what they prepare, one after another, as their customers eat. The prices are often ridiculously low.

'I just love it and I often eat at those stalls. It's delicious, it's fast, it's healthy, it's cheap and it's entertaining to watch the hawker prepare the food and the people ambling past or eating at other tables, served by nearby hawkers. It's local folklore and I think it's a pity that so many young people nowadays tend to flock to the foreign fast food restaurants. Every once in a while it's okay, but as a rule and routine people should eat the food of their country or, in big countries, of their own region and prepared with ingredients that are in season. That's the best way to stay in good health.

'For you Chinese of mainland China, this is no problem since you have no choice, *not yet* I should add. However, if you look around in the other Asian countries and even in Europe and America, the number of unhealthy looking obese people is simply frightening, especially the very young children amongst them. And the reason is food for which their metabolism is unsuited and that is most of the time unhealthy to boot. Too much fat, too much salt, too much sugar, too refined, too much starch, simply too much of everything and add to that too little physical exertion and you have the recipe for a health disaster.

'If you were to eat the kind of food we had for dinner tonight two or three times a week you would be in trouble as well, even the youngsters Lilian and Beiyuen. The Asian digestive system cannot cope with all that alien food and simply turns it into fat. It's a terrible problem and nobody gives a damn. As people become more affluent they also become lazy and egoistic and superficial. It's easier to give money to your children and tell them to get something to eat outside than to prepare the food yourself at home and forgo that special programme on TV or that social gathering with friends or that office party or that reception or that round of golf or whatever people think is important nowadays. And where do the children go after school? Not home, of course, because there's nobody waiting for them there with caringly prepared food or drink.

'No, they flock to one of the many, many fast food restaurants where they gorge on greasy, salty hamburgers with fatty, salty, French fries and thick blobs of mayonnaise, all the while drinking ice-cold sugary chemical concoctions until it's time for the movie and the bags of salty, greasy popcorn. When they finally get home their parents are either in front of the TV set and can't be bothered or are asleep already or are still out with friends. So the children grow up, uncared for and uncaring themselves knowing no better than to repeat the same mistakes with their own children later.

'It's not uncommon to see them having *breakfast* in those very same fast food restaurants before going on to school or wherever. There are fast food chains that play in on this social phenomenon and advertise special breakfast menus. I shudder when I see what is served to those kids. But what do those restaurants care? On the contrary, they encourage those trends and see their profits go up and up and up. Unhealthy food is so much cheaper than healthy food. And why should we care, they say, if even those kids' parents don't?

'It's a terrible problem and nobody is prepared to break the vicious circle because that would mean more *work* and forgoing of easy *pleasures*, in short it would mean *sacrifice*! People refuse sacrifice nowadays, for their elderly, for their young, for their employer unless they are ambitious workaholics, for society, for their immediate environment, let alone when it's far from their bed. People think in terms of immediate pleasures and to hell with the rest and the future, even their own or their own children's. And I see that happening in China as well in the near future. It seems to be an inescapable side effect of progress and modernisation, even in autocratic societies like most of the south-east Asian ones.

'Perhaps the Communist Party with its arbitrary, dictatorial powers will be able to delay the onset for a while longer but it will get the worst of it unless it is prepared to go all the way and return to the dark ages of total oppression. The Party still thinks it can have the cake and eat it and when the leaders realise they can't, it will be too late. With the initiation of the so-called Four Modernisations the Party has dug its own grave. I am sure the cleverest amongst the leaders realise that but ironically enough they also realise that there is no other way. You should watch Gorbachev and what is going to happen in the Soviet Union. That'll be China's fate, in a delayed and slightly diluted version probably, but there will be developments that the Party will *not* like, that the ordinary decent Chinese will *not* like and for once you'll agree with and support the Party. Ironic, isn't it? But then life is one big irony.'

Lao Dee fell silent, then suddenly he laughed and added, 'You see what dinner table conversation can lead to, from the taste of food and wine to the inevitable fate of the world. That's what I like about these eating parties, people diagnose and solve all the world's problems, like that, between dessert and the last swallow of wine. And then everybody goes home and nothing happens and nobody ever changes one iota in his bad, old habits or contributes even a tiny little bit to a better environment or a better world, despite all the lucidity and lofty ideas and strong feelings of the evening before.

'"What can one person do?" they'll ask rhetorically and, providing themselves the easy answer, they'll say, "Nothing! Right?" and they shrug their shoulders helplessly and regretfully and continue to do as they always did.

'They'll continue to vote for the same tired, corrupt old politicians who never had a fresh idea in their lifetime let alone stood up for somebody else's if it didn't serve their own immediate interest. They'll continue to drive, all by themselves, their six cylinder cars on a useless errand where a bicycle or even walking would have been easier and better. They'll continue to cheat the social security provisions while mocking the stupid straights who work and pay the premiums. They'll continue to throw their litter out of the car window or on the street or in the parking place because the nearest litter bin is all of ten metres away.

'They'll continue to gorge on snacks in front of the TV while tut-tutting, their mouths full, at the pictures of starving children, telling each other it's too far from their beds to do something about. They'll continue to turn the other way when they see a gang of muggers beat and rob a defenceless woman or an elderly couple. They'll continue to pretend not to hear the screams as the drunken neighbour beats his wife and children senseless. They'll continue to pretend not to have noticed that the old man or woman living alone two houses further down the street didn't put the garbage outside for the last two weeks.

'They'll continue to pretend that it's none of their business when they see a gang of young louts vandalise a telephone booth, rip plants and flowers out of the beds in public parks, kill the swans in the pond, use a hedgehog as a football, douse a cat with petrol and set it alight, loot shops after their favourite soccer team won, break shop windows and loot after their favourite soccer team lost, damage parked cars, steal parked bicycles, harass and torment defenceless people who happen to have a different skin colour or religion or who wear clothes that set them apart, beat up the tenant of an ice cream parlour and wreck his furniture and equipment simply because the man asked them to pay for their consumptions. And I could continue like that *ad infinitum,* and *ad nauseam.*'

Lao Dee fell silent and shrugged his shoulders.

'I'm sorry if I made you uncomfortable,' he mumbled apologetically.

'You are angry because you feel helpless eh, my friend?' Lao Dao said with great sympathy.

'Yes, I am,' Lao Dee answered, 'but mind you I'm no better myself and *that* is what makes me so angry. Oh, outwardly I am a responsible, educated, civil-minded person. I walk or bike when going by car is not absolutely necessary. I drop my litter in a bin even if I have to keep it in my hand for half a kilometre. I work and try to save enough money so that later, when I retire, I can live from my own savings rather than count on society to pay for my upkeep and pleasures. I pay my taxes and premiums and social contributions on time.

'I regularly donate money to a number of wildlife and environmental conservation programmes. I even donate occasionally to a few religiously-inspired welfare organisations for the so-called Third World. I look after myself, after my loved ones, and after the interests of my few close friends, in that order, and I will *not* steal what I cannot obtain in a normal, legal manner and that's about as far as my social morals go.

'I will not take my vehement criticism of what I see as social ills into the street, the pub, the letters page of newspapers or magazines or to the public forum of a political Party, firstly because I think it's a waste of time and secondly because I fear that repercussions might upset my tranquil, self-centred life. I have never and will never vote for any political Party because my contempt for politicians is only surpassed by my contempt for politicians who I think are, with few exceptions, nothing but rapacious, corrupt, self-seeking mediocrities whose stupid and selfishly motivated wheeling-and-dealing and stirring-up of trouble and stink will inexorably cause the ruin of mankind and this planet.

'I always carry a reasonable amount of cash money in my pocket to hand over in case I'm mugged, hoping the muggers will make off without harming me physically and I will continue on my way without reporting to the police because that's totally useless, they'll merely laugh at me and tell me that it's my own fault, that I shouldn't dress the way I am, that I shouldn't walk the way I do, that I shouldn't have been where I was. They probably stop just short of telling me that I got what I deserved, but even that is not certain these days.

'It's for that same reason that I'll go literally out of my way to avoid getting involved in a brawl, a beating, a harassment, a demonstration, a riot, a looting, a burglary and even an accident. I won't assist the victims and I refuse to be a witness since it'll be I who will end up defending myself against insinuation by the police and its subculture of social workers and psychologists and will be left on my own, unprotected, if the louts or criminals take their revenge on me or on my family.'

'What kind of society is that?' Auntie Liu exclaimed, horrified and indignant. 'Do not the police and your laws protect you in your Western society?'

'No! They don't!' Lao Dee answered categorically. 'Our Western society is more concerned with and interested in the criminal's rights and the psychological reasons for his misdeeds than in the victim's rights and the often lifelong consequences of the violence perpetrated against his person, his family or his property. A whole culture of psychologists, psychiatrists, ethicists and social and legal assistance is slowly but surely strangling the natural human sense for justice and retribution for misdeeds and it is these vague and unworldly people who point the accusing finger, not at the criminal but at his *victim*. It is this culture that has contaminated the thinking of judges, prosecutors and lawyers alike who all bend backwards in trying to find extenuating circumstances for the criminal's behaviour. It's easier and certainly more popular to blame the victim and say that he simply asked to be robbed or attacked or murdered because of his or her provocative or elitist behaviour. Even more popular is to fault the police: illegal proceedings, discrimination, unwarranted brutality are but a few of the standard accusations. Under the circumstances I think it is surprising that there are still men and women prepared to do policework.

'Be that as it may, if you catch a villain in the act of stealing your bicycle, of breaking into your car to steal the radio, of mugging your wife, of spray-painting her fur coat, of robbing your cash register, of burgling your house, you are *not* supposed to defend yourself, your family or your property and all the more so if you possess certain skills in self-defence sports or happen to carry a club or baseball bat or some other instrument that can be construed as a weapon of sorts. If you *do* and the *villain* gets hurt he will lodge a complaint against you and it is *you* who will be condemned for using excessive violence while *he* is being cuddled by a so-called trauma team consisting of a psychologist or psychiatrist, a doctor, and a social worker to help him overcome the shock, all at the expense of society, of course.

'I'm afraid that in terms of money, time and effort spent by society per individual and on the effects this individual's presence and acts have on the world, the criminal is way and way ahead and the disproportion grows with every additional so-called progressive politician joining the ranks of the naive do-gooders and with every additional psychologist and ethicist joining the multitude of these useless and arrogant so-called intellectuals already spawned by the universities.

'For the ordinary man or woman with his or her inborn and inbred sense of justice and injustice, of what is socially responsible and civilised behaviour and what is asocial, criminal and socio-pathological, this situation is incomprehensible, frightening and despairing. Every criminal case, however glaringly clear-cut, is immediately and deliberately muddied by an endless stream of so-called experts spouting their drivel during tendentious interviews on TV and in newspapers and magazines. The ordinary person who wants to see justice done, the criminal punished and the victim indemnified pulls his hair out and bashes his head against the wall in despair.

'And there is *nothing* he can do. The rot cannot be stopped. The damage already caused by the so-called and self-proclaimed humanitarians is incalculable and the final result of their unrealistic ideas will be the total control of every aspect of our daily lives by criminal organisations. And don't think of these organisations as run by the stereotype criminal; thick-necked, cigar-chomping, and crude. Oh no, they are run by businessmen, smooth-talking, elegant, well-educated members of expensive and exclusive golf and country clubs, hobnobbing with government leaders, openly running a multitude of legal businesses from the top floors of towering skyscrapers in the world's most important cities as a cover for the illegal businesses. And there is nothing we can do. The interests are simply too big.'

Lao Dee fell silent as the others watched him with unease.

'Will this happen in China as well?' Suping asked, hesitantly.

'Oh yes,' Lao Dee replied. 'There won't be any impractical and unrealistic humanitarians to pave the way like in the West, no, the criminal organisations will simply buy their way in by bribing the younger generation of leaders who want to lead the good life like their peers in the West and by eliminating the few incorruptible idealists who think they can oppose them. It may take another twenty years but it's unavoidable. There is *nothing* you can do about it. Again, like in the West, the interests are simply too big.'

'If what you say is true and will be China's fate as well, then what did we suffer for all these years? What consolation is there left for us that at least our suffering served some purpose?' Lao Dao asked and his voice quavered with emotion.

'Your suffering, and that of tens of millions like you, was senseless to begin with and most probably will turn out to have served no purpose at all,' Lao Dee replied gravely. 'I'm sorry, my friend, but think about it. Whenever did people, and notably the people's leaders, learn from past mistakes? Don't even think of the rest of the world, but consider only China's past. Apart from a few historians, did anyone see the similarity between the terror you were the victim of and the multitude of reigns of terror unleashed upon the long-suffering Chinese people over the past couple of thousand years? Was there any leader who said, "Hey Mao, what you are about to do now is the same as what Mo Zi did before you and what Han Fei did before Mo Zi and apart from senseless suffering and death for millions of people, they achieved nothing, so stop it, Mao, stop it before it's too late and you too will go down in history as a cruel tyrant!"

'If there was somebody with both the knowledge and the guts to make such a remark, Mao had him undoubtedly eliminated for he went ahead with his crazy campaigns, one more disastrous than the other, with the so-called Great Proletarian Cultural Revolution surpassing them all in terms of craziness, senselessness, the havoc it wreaked on the country as a whole and the sheer, staggering number of people who lost their life or were otherwise victimised, like yourself. And it's the same outside China.

'The Roman Catholic church by order of an old, stubborn pope, still discriminates against women, heretics and non-Catholics; he doesn't order them burned any more as did his predecessors a few hundred years ago but in his heart he must long for those good, old times. The Catholics and Protestants still bomb each other out of existence with the tacit approval of their respective Church Leaders. The Muslim fanatics still dream of conquering the non-Muslim world by fire and by the sword despite several disastrous campaigns in the past.

'The Jews are still persecuted and discriminated against despite the horrors of the Holocaust and several mini-holocausts before and, ironically, have themselves joined the ranks of oppressors. Fifty years after the most disastrous of all wars, sparked off by one crazy megalomaniac, there are still and again groups of people who shave their heads, run around in boots and black shirts brandishing flags with the swastika or some other symbol resembling the Nazi swastika, their faces twitched by hate screams against Jews, gypsies and unfortunate foreigners who have a different skin colour or culture. There are even official political parties whose leaders openly profess their admiration for that crazy megalomaniac Hitler and his ideology of hate and racial superiority and inferiority. If given the chance they would repeat his mistakes all over again.

'There are still seemingly civilised nations who threaten others with war over a piece of disputed territory, over a few insignificant rocks lost in some sea or ocean or other. It is still possible in these days of global interdependence that one nation who prides itself on its language and culture deliberately stirs up trouble in other, friendly nations merely to promote its so-called superior cultural identity and it doesn't shun discrimination, intimidation, coercion and threats to achieve its goals even if those goals fly in the face of all reason and reality. A Greek contemporary of your own, wise old Kung Fu Zi once said that history repeats itself and that sums it all up nicely.'

Lao Dee fell silent and looked at his friends, a sad, mocking little smile on his lips.

'I can anticipate your next question, Lao Dao, and yours as well, Suping,' he continued. '"Why, if all this is true, do we bother to tell our stories? If they won't make any difference as you say, why do we torture ourselves by dragging up all those old, painful memories?" This is what you think, isn't it?'

Lao Dao and Suping nodded, mutely, as Auntie Liu and the girls watched them anxiously.

'Well, the best answer I can give you,' Lao Dee continued, 'is that we don't really *know,* do we? We can't really look into the future, now can we? Maybe, just maybe there is a *chance* that this generation or the next or the one thereafter will be different and *will* learn from the wrongs and mistakes of the past and that they *will* decide to try their best *not* to repeat them. However, if there are no *records*, those wrongs and mistakes will once more fade into oblivion, together with their victims and perpetrators.

'So that is what you are doing here and now, establishing a *record*, in the *hope*, not the *certainty*, that one day people may read them, shake their head in wonder and disgust, add up your experiences and those of other people elsewhere and under different circumstances, and say *enough*! *Enough is enough*! And then, of course, speak about it with others and unite and start to clean out the world's Augean stables, vote the corrupt politicians out of office, restore the rule of law, demand respect for order and civilised behaviour and for each other's rights and duties and racial and cultural differences. If there is no *hope*, there is no *life,* so if you agree, Lao Dao, why don't you continue your story, old friend?'

Lao Dao smiled affectionately at his friend and said, 'So it always boils down to the same age-old dilemma eh, my friend? Hope against one's better judgement. Who did say once, long ago, that hopes are but the dreams of those awake? Perhaps if we old people dream our dreams aloud, our young will turn them into visions. Lilian, Beiyuen, will you hear the rest of my story with that in mind?'

'Oh yes, Uncle Dao,' the two girls replied almost simultaneously. They looked at each other and burst out laughing, making their elders laugh also, hesitantly at first but soon with all their heart, glad to shake off the gloomy seriousness of the past half-hour.

'You two deserve paradise according to the Prophet Muhammad because you made your companions laugh,' Lao Dao said chucklingly. 'You wonder how I know about the Koran, eh? Well let me tell my story and you'll find out. But to begin with let me go back to Meishan, to that fatal date of 30th November, 1966,' Lao Dao began.

# Chapter Thirty-One

## Like Mindless Cattle

The Red Guards dragged me, struggling, kicking and screaming down the stairs, through the hall and into the street and all the way to the Detention House.

They kicked the prison's entrance door open and dragged me inside, through another door held open by a prison guard and dumped me without further ado on the damp floor of a dark, stuffy room. Then they left, in a hurry, slamming the door behind them.

I made no attempt to get up and remained on my back, staring up in the darkness, unable to hold back my tears, tears of rage and sadness at my helplessness, at my failure to be with Liang when she needed me so badly.

I tried to focus my mind on her, excluding all other thoughts, and I prayed to the Christian God to help her. 'Oh God, please help Liang, don't let her suffer pain, please God, please!'

I had never prayed before; neither to the Christian God nor to my mother's panoply of gods and spirits, but that day I prayed and over and over again I beseeched God to have mercy on Liang and not to let her suffer pain at the hands of the Red Guards.

When Bo Dinyi told me ten years later that Liang was already dead when I said those prayers my first reaction was one of scorn for God who had apparently not bothered about her and had ignored my supplications.

But then I thought that maybe He knew what was going to happen, how terrible the Cultural Revolution was going to be and how terribly delicate but quick-tempered people like Liang would be made to suffer, both physically and mentally.

So He had done what I asked and had let her die, there and then, to spare her those sufferings and sorrow. Though it was not what I had meant that day, in that cell, I could see the wisdom of His decision and I felt relieved somehow.

Be that as it may, my praying quietened me down after a while and I scrambled up and looked around in the semi-darkness. I jumped in fright when I saw that I was not alone. Perhaps a dozen other people, all men, young and old, were either sitting or lying on bunks that lined the walls. Those nearest to me stared at me with indifferent eyes, the others were just gazing over my head or staring up at the ceiling.

'How are you?' I asked in a stupid reflex. 'My name is Dao, Dao Huimin,' I added lamely.

There was no reaction at first, then somebody in the far corner chuckled and a cultured voice said mockingly, 'You ask a stupid question and you get a stupid answer, Dao Huimin. We are fine, thank you, and you, Comrade Dao? Are you fine also? Are you here for your pleasure too? Like us? From the way the pride of our nation brought you in here it looked as if you had made other plans for today.'

He chuckled again and added, 'I managed to keep this bunk for myself these past five days, or is it six already? I forget. Never mind though. I'm afraid I'll have to sacrifice my privacy shortly, like everything else, so I might as well offer you to share my berth. That is, provided you don't have lice or fleas or body odour or unnatural preferences like some of our fellow victims have or exude so pronouncedly.'

'I get the gist behind your sarcastic fine talk, Wu!' another voice, angry and hoarse, shouted. 'If you insinuate one more time that I stink I'll beat you up so bad that you would wish you had never come here!'

'I don't need your beating to wish that, Lo,' the man named Wu answered mockingly. 'You hear that, Dao?' he continued. 'Comrade Lo here is the true proletarian. What he doesn't understand he wants to pummel. He should be outside, playing the revolutionary hero, with his like-minded. I have never understood why that rabble insist on calling each other like-minded since most of them don't have one, a mind I mean. What do *you* think, Dao? Speak your mind man, that is if you have one!'

'Knock it off, Wu,' another voice said, tired this one, before I could answer. 'You know Lo can't defend himself against your mockeries. The poor man is here for reasons he can't even pronounce. So leave him alone, Wu, please?'

'All right, all right, Yang, I'll leave your boyfriend alone,' Wu sneered, 'do you accept my offer to share my berth, Dao? Don't be afraid, men are not my taste. I'm bourgeois and decadent in other ways that displease the Party.'

I shuffled towards the corner from where I had heard Wu's voice and felt myself pulled down on a bunk.

'Welcome, Dao,' the man beside me said and I recognised Wu's voice.

'Name's Wu, Wu Fuzhi, medical doctor from Lu'an. The prison was full there so they brought me here. Reading poetry in preference to socialist drivel, and aloud at that, in what I thought was the privacy of my own house, was the crime for which those illiterate peasants who call themselves the People's Tribunal condemned me to nine years of re-education through hard labour. My own daughter, twelve she is, reported me to her class leader. She's now a Red Guard herself, a little revolutionary general. What a joke! What a waste!'

Wu sighed, then asked, 'What are you here for, Dao? What does the rabble have against you?'

I didn't know Wu well enough yet to confide in him and besides I wouldn't gain anything by telling him. He might even be an agent provocateur trying to trick me.

So I said, 'You don't want to know, Wu. Believe me, it's better for both of us. We can be mates while we are together and try to make life a bit easier for one another but I warn you, do *not* try to defend me when those Red Guards start beating me up. It won't do either of us any good.'

Wu didn't answer immediately but after a couple of minutes he said, in a low voice, 'That bad eh, Dao? Thanks for your concern all the same.'

He fell silent and for an hour or so neither of us spoke.

I was thinking of Liang, of the children, my parents-in-law but gradually my thinking became more and more confused as my head became heavier and my ears started buzzing. I started to panic as a wave of nausea made me gag and I tried to get up from the bunk so as not to vomit over myself and Wu. Dizzily, I swayed on my legs.

'Steady,' I heard Wu say, 'breathe through your nose, not too deeply and not too fast. You feel sick because of the poor air and the stench of all those people and our shit in the toilet bucket. There's no ventilation in this cell and there shouldn't be more than four people here. It's a bloody shame. We'll all suffocate for lack of oxygen. I'll give those bastards a piece of my mind.' And suiting the action to the word he jumped off the bunk and made for the door. Pounding the door with both fists he shouted, 'Hey, you bastards! Open the bloody door. We'll all die in here!'

Suddenly the door swung open and an elderly prison guard said, in an urgent, low voice, 'Don't shout like that. The Red Guards will hear you and make you suffer for that. Deliberately they'll cram another dozen or more people into your cell and then what? I'll leave the door ajar as long as I dare, to give you some air, but you *must* keep quiet or else I'll find myself on your side of the door.'

He broke off, listened, then continued hurriedly, 'A while ago the Red Guards assigned to the Detention Hall had a terrible dispute about who would have to accompany a truckload of prisoners to the main intersection to join up with a convoy of trucks from Guangshan, Huangchuan and Gushi bound for Hefei. They all want to go to get out of here but the orders are that only two can go. So I think that you'll leave soon, probably even before dark.'

The old guard fell silent, turning his head, listening. 'There they come,' he said, 'I'm sorry but I'll have to lock the door now. When they're gone I'll open the door again slightly.'

The slight draught of fresh air and the prospect of getting out of that dank, stinking cell soon made me feel a bit better. I thanked Wu for his intervention and he gave me a reassuring squeeze on my arm.

Because of what I had heard the old guard tell Wu, I guessed it was early evening or late afternoon when the door was suddenly thrown wide open and a band of Red Guards came bursting in, shouting, '*Out! Out! You scum!*'

Like a herd of panicking cows we struggled and hustled through the door opening, through the corridor and out of the building, into the street, where a dozen or so other Red Guards joined the stampede down the street towards the square in front of the town hall.

When our group erupted on to the scene in the square I saw hundreds of people milling around a row of six trucks, shouting and jeering and pelting the people jammed on the trucks' platforms with garbage and even stones.

Apparently the trucks from the other three towns had reached the main intersection before Meishan's truck and had turned off the main road into Meishan.

The Red Guards herded us through the jeering crowd towards the already familiar old Roman truck and shouting and screaming made us line up behind the rear end of the truck. Leading Red Guard Wan came struggling through the crowd towards us, his right hand holding a sheaf of paper high above his head.

He ordered us to stand to attention and then called off our names one by one, gave each of us a few sheets of paper, our travelling papers as I saw later, and barked to get on the truck.

I was the first to climb aboard and I sprinted to the front of the platform where I huddled with my back against the driver's cabin. That way I was at least protected from the back against the projectiles this crowd, and probably others along the road to Hefei, would throw at us.

The cabin would also offer shelter against the cold wind once the trucks moved out of town on the open road. I pulled up my knees, crossed my arms over them and rested my head on my forearm to protect my face. Panting, somebody dropped down beside me.

'The rabble has gone crazy,' he gasped and I recognised Wu's voice.

I glanced at him sideways and grinned as I saw him wiping the slimy leaves of rotten cabbages from his face.

'Put your head down, like me,' I said, 'now it's vegetables, in a minute it'll be stones and you can get badly hurt. Now is not the time to get injured. There'll be no medical care for us, not for a long time to come, I'm afraid, so keep yourself whole.'

Our fellow prisoners had by then all scrambled on board and I had to ward off a few who tried to push me from my place. I used my elbows and once I had to lash out with my right leg and kick somebody in his crotch to make him back off. The man doubled up and groaned.

Beside me Wu laughed mockingly and cried out, 'Aiyeeh, poor Yang! Did that nasty man Dao hurt brother Lo's little toy? No more ball games for a while, Lo!'

I nudged him with my right elbow and whispered furiously, 'Keep your mouth shut, Wu. You have enough enemies as it is. Don't be stupid! I'm not going to watch your back for you.'

I saw him nod, ruefully, that he had gotten the message.

A few minutes later I saw Leading Red Guard Wan climb into the cabin, shouting at the driver to start the engine. With a few bangs like gunshots the engine roared to life and thick clouds of acrid, black smoke engulfed us as the driver alternately let the engine roar and die down. I knew what was going to follow so I grasped Wu's arm and shouted above the roar, 'The driver is crazy, I know him. Hold on to me!'

I had barely said that when the driver let go of the clutch and the truck shot forward so suddenly that everybody fell pell-mell over one another. I heard the driver's braying laugh as the crowd scattered out of the way of his vehicle as he tried to crush those who weren't fast enough.

Keeping his thumb on the klaxon he accelerated as he left the square and sped down the main street, followed by the six other trucks from Guangshan, Huangchuan and Gushi, also with their horns blaring.

Before long we turned right on to the main road to Hefei. I looked sideways at Wu and saw that he was laughing at the confusion and frustration of our fellow passengers who held on to each other and the side boards for dear life.

He turned his head to look at me, grinning, and I saw that he was actually enjoying himself.

Five times the convoy stopped to pick up prisoners in the small villages and hamlets too small to have their own truck. At each stop the villagers looked on, sullen and afraid, as a few of their own people were herded towards the trucks by a small gang of screaming Red Guards whose reign of terror had turned their small communities topsy-turvy and set friend against friend, children against parents, pupils against teachers.

Kicked, beaten and shoved in the back by the frenzied Red Guards they scrambled on board the nearest truck.

They looked dazed, scared, haggard and some were clearly near panic as they tried to squeeze themselves in amongst those already there on the platform.

'Look at the poor bastards, Dao,' Wu said, 'they are like cattle headed for the slaughterhouse. They feel in their gut that something bad is going to happen to them but their mind, or what goes for that, can't grasp what so they panic, eyes wild and rolling, mouths dribbling, nostrils glistening with snot yet going where the kicks and proddings urge them to go, mindlessly, uncomprehendingly. You see that, Dao? A few even try to please their tormentors, 'hai, hai, ho, ho, ho! Comrade Red Guard.' See how they trample those in front of them? Cringing toad-eaters, we Chinese, always have been and always will be. Pathetic! Makes one want to cry!'

I didn't bother to answer. He was right of course, it was pathetic. A whole village with age-old customs and interwoven relationships cowering in terror before a few crazy slogan-shouting youths with Little Red Books who were brazenly destroying, killing, terrorising and uprooting in the name of a maniac and his harridan in the big city up north. And nobody dared to stand up to them, myself and Wu included. So what gave us the right to look down on those prisoners and contemptuously compare them with cattle? Were we any better?'

As if he had guessed my thoughts, I heard Wu mumble, 'I know what you are thinking, Dao! We aren't any better, are we? The same kind of cowards.'

Finally, shivering from the cold night air, we arrived at Hefei's railway station. The big clock read eleven thirty. It had taken us almost six hours.

Leading Red Guard Wan jumped out of the truck's cabin and I saw him trot towards a group of men in dark blue smock frocks with red armbands. He talked and gestured in our direction, apparently trying to persuade them to take us off his hands.

Finally one of the men took the sheaf of papers from him and walked towards us, followed by a gesticulating Wan.

The man was short, bow-legged and sickeningly ugly with only a few greenish-brown stubs of teeth left in his half-open, dribbling mouth and dull, lifeless eyes like those of a carp long dead.

He stared at the papers he had taken from Wan and with the obscenely long nail, black with grime, of his left little finger he hesitantly followed what was apparently a list of names for I somehow managed to recognise my name as the man pronounced the characters one by one in a strange, gravely accent.

The idea was of course that we would climb down from the truck one by one as the man read our names but since he didn't say that and because probably most of us didn't understand what he said, nobody moved.

Wan, nervously watching the proceedings at the other trucks where things seemed to be moving, suddenly interrupted the official and shouted at us to get off the truck at the double.

Everybody scrambled up, stiff and groaning from the pain in legs and bottom, and clambered over the side boards to jump on to the pavement.

I saw Wu jump off behind Wan and, pretending to stumble, he shoved Wan in the back of his knees. Wan's knees buckled and, arms flailing wildly as he tried to regain his balance, he fell flat on his face just when a few young men jumped off the truck.

They landed on top of Wan and pretending to have difficulty to maintain their balance they deliberately stamped on his hands and kicked him in his face.

I still see in my mind Wan's face contorted with rage as tears of pain and humiliation streamed down his cheeks as he struggled to get back to his feet.

⋆

Lao Dao paused and smiled at the scene still vivid in his mind after all these years.

Auntie Liu laughed and her eyes sparkled with glee as she said, 'Quite a character, your friend Wu Fuzhi. I think I would have liked him. I wonder what became of him. Did you stay together?'

'Unfortunately for Wu we did,' Lao Dao said and continued, 'his was actually a light case, nine years of re-education only, in a commune, so he shouldn't have been put on that train with me, a criminal case. But they did and afterwards nobody cared.

'There was no one in command at the railway station and confusion reigned everywhere and in everything, pandemonium even at times, with Red Guards milling around, yelling and screaming and shouting slogans and countermanding orders by Party officials and railway officials alike. With the benefit of hindsight I now think we could have disappeared there and then, or got off the train in Xuzhou where it was held up for almost six hours, and gone into hiding during daytime and trek after dark, stealing or begging food until the Cultural Revolution would have petered out.

'But we didn't. Like Wu said, we were like cattle herded to the slaughterhouse, mindless and gutless. I'm sure a Westerner would have tried to escape but we Chinese lack that kind of individuality. We function as part of a whole, for better or for worse.

'Lao Dee says that on the whole the Chinese are poltroons, hereditary and by proclivity. All talk and posturing but no balls and that's why China will never win a war, he says. It will blunder into a war because other countries may just call its bluff but it will pull out after the first bloody nose and blame everybody and everything but its own foolhardiness. But I digress. Let me resume my story.'

⋆

The peasant in his dark blue smock frock and red armband looked at the mêlée without a glimmer in his lifeless eyes and without a glance at the raving and ranting Wan. When he had finally managed to get back on his feet, Wan for a moment glared at our grinning, mocking faces, hesitated, evidently thought better of it and, yelping from the pain in his fingers, wearily hoisted himself into the truck cabin.

Seconds later the engine roared back to life and off they went, Wan and his friend the mad driver, back to Meishan, leaving us in a cloud of thick, black smoke.

I was still listening to the fading blare of the horn when suddenly I heard the peasant official croak something unintelligible. One of the older villagers we had picked up in the last village before Hefei apparently understood the man's dialect for he said that the comrade official wanted us to line up and go through the turnstile and report to the officials on duty on platform one.

Docilely we did as told and lined up behind the row of shuffling people who apathetically and one by one squeezed themselves through the creaking turnstile.

On the other side a dozen or so officials wearing red armbands shouted, '*Travel papers*! *Travel papers*!' and, after a cursory glance at the rumpled pieces of paper held up by the convicts, just shouted a number without as much as looking at the men or women themselves and resumed, *'Travel papers! Travel papers!'*

Wu was immediately behind me as I held up my papers and I heard the official shout, *'Three!'* and then again, *'Three!'* Whether he shouted it twice for my benefit or once for me and once for Wu or whether the official even noticed Wu I don't know, however, be that as it may, Wu was again beside me as we were slowly thronged up the stairs to the overhead bridge to platform three.

'You shouldn't be here!' I yelled in his ear to make myself heard over the din surrounding us. 'I'm going to Urumqi! That's for criminal cases!'

He just snorted, shrugged his shoulders and shouted back, 'What the hell do I care? So don't *you* care for *me*, Dao! You think I ever want to go back to a daughter who got me in this mess and to a wife whose gods, my gods as well, refused to get me out of it? Forget it, Dao! Let's see what happens!'

I didn't quite understand what he meant, so I shrugged and shouted, 'It's your choice, Wu! Don't reproach me later that I didn't warn you!'

'That's exactly *right*, Dao,' he yelled, looking around him exultantly. 'It's my *choice*! Isn't it *wonderful* to have a say in one's own *life*! And that in a *Communist* state!' And he laughed uproariously.

I noticed that people were looking at us and suddenly we had some elbow room as those beside and behind us tried to get away from us. Obviously they thought that we had gone crazy and I couldn't help laughing as well.

Finally we reached platform three and there it was over with our elbow room as we found ourselves in the front row facing the tracks, squeezed left, right and in the back by the ever-increasing number of people.

'If they start surging forward the moment the train comes in we're dead,' I mumbled, more for myself than for Wu and looking sideways I saw him pale as the thought *how* we would die occurred to him.

For the remainder of the two hours we stood there, like sardines in a tin, in the cold drizzle of the first two hours of December 1966.

Wu didn't say a word.

I think he had suddenly realised that he was left without a choice and that life and death now depended on the unpredictable reaction of a sullen, faceless and mindless crowd.

Finally, at two o'clock in the morning by the platform clock, a train pulled into the station and was shunted on to the track alongside our platform.

There was some increased pressure in our backs but we dug our heels in and leaned back and were so able to hold on to our position as first the heat of the hissing, coal-fired locomotive passed dangerously close in front of us, followed by a seemingly endless stream of rumbling and croaking freight cars.

I had counted forty-eight when finally the train came to a stop. I was lucky, the bolted sliding door was just in front of me. I didn't wait for some train official or other to remove the bolt and open the door as I felt the surge in my back and feared I might be pushed in the gap between the car and the platform.

I stepped on the footboard, pulled the bolt out of its holes and let it dangle on its chain and then pushed the sliding door just far enough open to let me through.

It was pitch dark inside the car but from the wave of moist, foul-smelling air that hit my face I knew there were people inside and not a few either. I had no time to take my bearings as already people behind me were shoving me in the back.

Stumbling over the bodies on the floor, trying as best as I could not to step on them, I managed to reach the far corner at the rear of the car and, groping my way on the floor, I found that there was still room to sit with my back against the wall.

Again Wu was close on my heels and he let himself down beside me with a sigh of relief.

'That was very clever of you, Dao, to open that door just a crack and to get in first. Look at what's going on now,' he said.

I saw that the door had been pushed open all the way and against the light of the platform outside I could see what looked like a wave of shadows pouring inside, struggling, shoving, pushing and panting like panicky wildebeest, trampling the shrieking bodies on the floor.

There was no Party or train official or Red Guard in sight and it was a free-for-all stampede.

'There'll be far too many people for this car,' I said, worried. 'We'll be crushed to death in a few minutes or suffocate to death later if we don't stop the flood. Wu, keep my place for me! I'm going to close that door!'

As I jumped up and over the bodies on the floor I made a guess that there must have been at least sixty people already inside, far too many for such a small space.

I reached the door and shouted at the people lying or sitting near it to help me push the door shut. Two got the message immediately and when they joined me to push against the door I saw they were women.

It proved impossible to close the door against the resistance of all the people still trying to get in and I heard the two women yell a few names and call on those people to push back the tide.

From the corner of my eyes I saw a number of people getting up and moving towards the open door and suddenly I heard screams of pain and anger as our newly arrived helpers started to kick indiscriminately at those still trying to get in.

They fell back on the platform and in the few seconds it took them to recover from the surprise the women and I pushed the door shut.

'Hold the door,' I told them, panting from the effort, 'let nobody in any more. There are far too many people inside already as it is. We'll have not enough air to breathe.'

Without waiting for their reaction I went back to my place in the corner and sat down in the space Wu had kept for me.

'Good work,' he said. 'Have you been educated abroad or something? Your decisiveness is unusual, not the usual procrastination of the ordinary Chinese.'

'Shut up, Wu,' I replied, irritably, 'next time there's an emergency you show me you can do more than observe and make grandiloquent comments, okay?'

'Okay!' Wu said and he grinned and punched me in my ribs.

The commotion past, apathy set in again as we sat, back against the wall, arms around pulled-up knees, chin on the chest, eyes closed, mind at zero.

I was vaguely aware that the train began to move and that Wu muttered something under his breath but I couldn't muster the energy to say something or to look at my watch.

I must have fallen asleep somehow since shouts outside and the absence of movement made me come to and I yawned lethargically.

'We are in Bengbu,' Wu said beside me, yawning noisily. 'They are trying to hook up a number of cars from Shanghai and Nanjing to our train. At least that's what I gather from all the yelling and shouting that's going on. It sounds as if the railway people are quarrelling with a bunch of juveniles, Red Guards presumably, about how to go about it. The Red Guards disagree with everything the adults say. They actually threaten each other. What a laugh. We got here at four in the morning and now day's breaking and they've still not finished.'

Indeed, I saw daylight getting through the chinks between the sliding door and the walls and I could distinguish individual people now, not just a dark, amorphous mass like last night.

'I estimate there are about fifty people in this car,' I said to Wu. 'I counted forty-eight cars when this one stopped in front of us in Hefei and there were more. Suppose there were fifty-five and now they are adding cars from Shanghai and Nanjing, say thirty-five in all. That makes ninety cars times fifty people, so there will be about four and a half thousand people on board of this train alone. Probably there are hundreds of trains all over China at this very moment, not every one as long as this one, but take an average of three and a half thousand people per train and say, conservatively, that there are two hundred trains on the move at this very moment, that makes seven hundred thousand people. How are those madmen going to feed all those people? Even providing drinking water will be a major logistic problem. I'm sure nobody thought about that or cared for that matter.'

I saw Wu staring at me, horrified.

'That's terrible,' he cried out. 'You calculate those numbers so off-handedly and your conclusion is so matter-of-fact. Do you realise the implications?'

'I damn well do,' I said grimly, 'I'm hungry and thirsty and I have to relieve myself and that's the most urgent.'

I nudged the man lying on my left and asked him, loudly, 'Where are you from, sir? Did you have something to eat or to drink before we came aboard in Hefei? How does one relieve oneself in this car? Say something, man! Don't lie there like a zombie!'

The man turned his head and looked at me, or at least he looked in the direction of the sound of my voice for I saw that his eyes were black and swollen, almost closed, and that his lips were swollen and had bled. There was dried blood on his chin.

'I'm from Fuzhou,' the man said, talking with difficulty and it was obvious he was in pain. He continued, grimacing, 'We were two hundred when we left Fuzhou four days ago, in eight freight cars, this was the last one. In Nanping they hooked us up to a train from Xiamen and Zhangzhou. In Jingdezhen we waited one whole day and night for a train from Nanchang.

'They opened the door only once to distribute some cold, steamed rice wrapped in a piece of brown paper and to put a few pails of water and one ladle in the car. That was all and this was two days ago.'

He paused, swallowed and added. 'There's a hole in the floor in the opposite corner. When the train's moving you can relieve yourself through that hole. There's no paper though.'

He fell silent and groaningly turned himself on his side.

Just then the train started moving again, finally, and first I then Wu went to look for the hole to relieve ourselves.

When Wu came back and had sat down again he said, sighing, 'These people have no spirit left, Dao. They hardly moved aside as I peed through that hole. I missed the hole a few times because of the jolts of the car and I must have splashed some of them but they didn't budge. At our next stop I'll make a racket so that they'll open the door and I'm going to ask them for food and drink.'

Our next stop was Xuzhou and there was no need for Wu's heroics. The door of our car rumbled open and I saw a truck, rear end turned towards the door opening. Five girls wearing red neckerchiefs stood on the truck's platform watching over two big tubs.

The girls peered into our car and I saw them recoil instinctively when the stench of so many unwashed bodies hit their faces.

One of the girls cried, 'Please come to the door one by one, we have steamed rice with vegetables and fresh water for you!'

I couldn't believe it yet I was the first at the door, closely followed by Wu.

I cast a quick glance up and down the station platform and saw ten or twelve trucks parked like the one in front of our car with girls already busily distributing food and drink.

If the girls on our truck were shocked by my appearance they didn't show it.

Smiling, one of them spooned rice and vegetables from one of the tubs on a piece of brown paper held up by a second girl who in turn passed it on to a third who folded the corners of the paper to close the package before handing it to me with a lovely smile.

'Please go back to your place in the car and eat the rice,' she said, and her voice was like music, 'then come back for fresh water.'

I have never seen fifty hungry, thirsty and dishevelled people behave so well. It was extraordinary.

I ate my rice and vegetables, slowly and thoughtfully, tasting each grain and morsel of vegetables.

From the corner of my eyes I saw Wu wolfing down his portion and I mumbled to him, 'You, a doctor, should know better than to guzzle your food like that on an empty stomach. Before long you'll have cramps.' He didn't hear me or pretended not to. My food finished I went back to the door for my water ration. The same girl who had handed me my rice now held out a ladle with water.

'You can have two,' she said, smiling, 'so don't drink too greedily lest your stomach hurts later.'

She was pretty, very pretty even, with long, shiny hair bound together in a ponytail that swished from shoulder to shoulder as she watched the proceedings of the other girls.

'Who's that man over there, on the platform?' I asked her as I stopped drinking for a moment to breathe, pointing with the ladle at a small, chubby man in a green smock frock with a friendly, round, cherubic face under a dark green cap who was apparently supervising the distribution.

'That's our Party secretary, Li Ju,' she said and the pride in her voice was unmistakable. 'Secretary Li is a very good and a very brave man,' she continued.

'He organised this food and water distribution against the orders of the Red Guards and the interrogator from Beijing. They say that you are criminals and that the people should not waste their time and precious food and drink on you. Secretary Li told us that you are *not* criminals but merely the hapless victims of a bunch of fanatics calling themselves Red Guards and interrogators. He says he can't stop the madness that ravages our country but that he can at least try, with our help, to alleviate the suffering of the innocent victims who pass through his town.

'We all love our secretary and we help him. We are *not* afraid. All the Red Guards in our town are from elsewhere. The people of Xuzhou don't do such bad things,' she finished, indignantly shaking her pretty head.

I watched the man called Li. He must have felt that we were talking about him as he came strolling towards our car.

'Don't talk too much, Meimei,' he said mildly, smiling, 'we have more mouths to feed and we can't hold up the train too long. The Red Guards are getting impatient with our people who are loading coal into the tender, very slowly as I told them.'

Looking up at me in the door opening he added, 'It's still a long long way to Urumqi, my friend, and this may well be the last time you get something to eat and to drink before you get there. Take care of yourself and don't abandon hope. When hope's lost all's lost. This madness can't last, they won't be able to sustain it for long. So just try to survive to tell your story.'

He nodded, smiled and turned to walk off towards a truck whose driver had difficulty in backing up.

Secretary Li Ju, a good, decent man, a quiet hero.

I felt a lump in my throat and my eyes stung. I wonder what has become of him. I sometimes think I should write him a letter, if he's still alive, and tell him how much his kindness and quiet courage meant to me at that moment, that he most probably saved my sanity.

Reluctantly I turned away from the doorway and life outside to go back to my corner and I bumped into Wu who had been standing right behind me.

I saw from the expression on his face that he had overheard what the girl and Secretary Li told me and that he was moved as well.

'Can't let the man down, now can we?' he mumbled as he followed me back to our corner.

It seemed as if the atmosphere in our car had changed, at least for the time being, by that waft of sanity and decency from a world we all thought had gone haywire. People were softly talking amongst themselves and I even heard subdued laughter here and there.

'Thank heavens for Li Ju and his girls,' I said to nobody in particular. 'What a psychological insight the man has. Girls, pretty, fresh, friendly girls to pull us back from the edge of the abyss of despair. As you said, Wu, we can't let the man down. We will survive to tell the world what happened, to shame our so-called leaders who let it happen, who let a few mad dogs do this to us, to China. We must keep the hope that one day tolerance, decency, quiet courage, modesty and friendly kindness as embodied by this obscure little Party secretary and his girls will once again be the hallmarks of China and the essence of being Chinese.'

I fell silent and a quiet resolution suffused my whole being. I felt the sadness, anger and despair that had knotted my stomach like physical pain for the past few days slowly ebb and the same near sensual relief washed over me as when I was still a child and the terrible stomach ache that had me all curled up in bed slowly waned and disappeared.

My mind cleared as if a clamp had suddenly been removed and, for the first time, I saw the people lying and sitting around me quite clearly, as individuals, not as the dark, amorphous tangle of indistinguishable bodies I had stumbled over earlier.

I saw Wu looking at me and I saw what I hadn't noticed before, that he was actually quite a good-looking man with a long face and bright, intelligent eyes.

He smiled and said, 'Glad to meet you too, Dao.'

The man from Fuzhou coughed as he tried to sit up and said, 'Thank you, Mr Dao. I heard this gentleman call you Dao. My name is Tan, Tan Shiwei. I thank you for the things you just said, for rekindling the desire to go on living rather than letting myself slide further and further into that mind-numbing grief for my dead wife, into death itself, to be with her. The Red Guards threw her from the window of her classroom on the fourth floor of the school where both of us were teachers.

'She fell five metres from where they had tied me to a lamp-post and I screamed and screamed and sobbed and pulled at the ropes as if demented until finally I fainted. The tinkle of breaking glass, Meilan's scream, the thud of her little body on the pavement, the blood seeping from her mouth, nose and ears, the rattle of her last breath, these sounds and images have been racing through my mind, like a carousel gone out of control, ever since they untied me the next day. Meilan's body was gone and they laughed and beat me up when I begged them to let me see her. I thought I would go out of my mind but I hung on for the sake of our only son.

'That same day I was herded with hundreds of other victims to the railway station and I saw my son wearing the armband of a Red Guard. He was one of them, driving another group of victims to the station, shouting and kicking and beating the wretches who fell behind. My son, one of those lunatics who killed my wife, his mother. There was no reason for me to continue living and I decided to let myself die. But now you have given me a reason to try to survive so as to tell the world.

'I told you in case I won't survive so that you can tell your children and the world what happened to innocent little Yap Meilan who never wronged anybody. Thrown out of the window of her classroom because she taught the children to be civilised, to say please and thank you and be respectful.'

He paused to wipe the tears from his swollen eyes and continued, forcedly cheerful, 'And now I would like some rice and water, at least if the girls haven't left yet. No, don't bother, Mr Dao,' he added as I made ready to get up and fetch the food for him, 'I'll go myself, thank you.'

He scrambled to his feet, groaning from the pain and stiffness in his back and legs, and staggered towards the sunlit rectangle of the open door.

How symbolic, I thought, as I saw his crooked body outlined against the light.

'Poor man!' I heard the girl with the ponytail exclaim, 'What happened to your face? They beat you, eh? I'll give you two rations of rice. You must be strong. You look so thin. Eat first and I'll fetch a wet towel for you to clean your face.'

Tan came tottering back to our corner with his two parcels of rice clasped against his chest.

'She'll give me a wet towel,' he mumbled as he sat down wearily, 'a wet towel for my face.' And I saw him weep silently.

Secretary Li's men managed to delay the train until the end of the afternoon and twilight was turning to darkness when the sliding doors were closed by several two-men teams of railwaymen. Slowly, very slowly the train gathered speed to about forty kilometres per hour. I calculated the speed from the time it took for the wheels just below me to cover one length of rail, click-clack, click-clack, ten seconds counting from twenty-one to thirty.

For the remainder of our journey the door of our car remained closed.

Perhaps Secretary Li Ju had ordered his men to paint 'full' on our door.

The blaring loudspeakers in the stations where the train stopped for a couple of hours, to load coal I presumed and not to hook up more cars since I didn't feel the tell-tale jolts, informed us, in between socialist martial music, songs and slogans, that the people of Luoyang, Xi'an, Lanzhou, Jiayuguan and Hami were resolutely supporting the Great Proletarian Cultural Revolution under the inspired leadership of their beloved Chairman Mao and were busily crushing and bashing and eradicating and rooting out the bourgeois enemies of the People and their beloved Party.

The revival of our spirits after Xuzhou didn't last. It proved no match for the monotony, the increasingly intense cold as we passed through the mountainous regions after Lanzhou and the mounting apprehension for what was awaiting us at the end of our journey.

The wretchedness of our situation was made worse by the smoke from the locomotive that entered the car through the chinks and fissures and the trellis high in the front wall.

Everybody coughed and spit almost continuously and some so badly that I suspected it was not only from the sooty smoke but that they had caught a bronchitis or worse, pneumonia.

Our clothes were totally unsuitable for the kind of climate and notably the people from the south of Fujian must have suffered terribly. November can still be quite mild over there and I had noticed that Tan didn't wear long underpants or even an undershirt.

He shivered continuously. Poor man, looking so drab with his red-rimmed eyes and black sooty streaks all over his face from constantly wiping his running nose.

I wondered whether I looked any better myself.

# *Chapter Thirty-Two*

## Brother Crab

Four times I saw the shortening day and lengthening night come and go so it must have been one hundred hours and some three and a half thousand kilometres after we left Hefei when at long last the train came to its final stop in Urumqi.

The sudden cessation of the jolting, bumping, rattling and clanking of the past five days did not immediately register with my numbed brain since I continued to feel the tremors of the floor in my legs and buttocks and to hear the rumble in my ears for quite some time afterwards.

Slowly, however, I began to notice the silence broken only by the occasional groan and hiss from the train as it was buffeted by the howling and whistling wind.

Suddenly it dawned on me that there were no blaring loudspeakers and no adolescent voices shouting slogans, orders and counter-orders.

'This must be China's end station,' I heard Wu mutter. 'We must have passed Urumqi and now the train can't go any further. The tracks in Russia are wider, I have heard.'

I laughed and was about to answer when a loud hailer shattered the silence. 'Attention! Attention! All passengers of train number 4578! This is Urumqi! You must now disembark! Listen carefully to your marching orders! Once off the train you must walk straight ahead, away from the train, across an empty plot of land, towards a row of trucks parked along the road in front of you!

'You must line up next to the trucks! The trucks' engines are running and their headlights are on. You cannot miss them! Armed soldiers have orders to shoot anybody who tries to escape!

'Attention! Attention! The car doors will now be opened!'

A moment later the door of our car rumbled open and a gust of wind laden with frozen snow crystals whooshed inside, instantly freezing the hairs in my nostrils as it sliced into my lungs like a knife.

I scrambled up and stepped over my stupefied companions towards the doorway. I peered outside, straight into hell. A near impenetrable white curtain of whirling snow and ice crystals, driven by a howling, gale force wind, raced past an ink-black background, punctuated in the distance by small points of light. The trucks, I thought.

Two shadowy figures beside the tracks, one on each side of the open door, beckoned me to get off. The figure nearest to me struck me a painful blow on my arm just as I was about to grip the steel bar beside the door.

He growled something I didn't understand but got the meaning of instantly. My unprotected hand would have frozen instantaneously to the steel and I shivered and not only from the cold as I thought of how they would have had to free my hand. I jumped off the car and landed painfully on my feet, the shock hurting through my backbone all the way up into my head. I stumbled and fell, face down, in the fine, powdery snow. I scrambled up, hands already numb from the cold.

It was impossible to breathe facing the wind so I turned my back against the wind and shuffled backwards through the shallow snow across the plot of land the loudhailer voice had mentioned to where I had seen the points of light.

From time to time I looked over my shoulder to check my direction. I had barely covered twenty metres and already I could no longer see the train through the whirling snow.

I felt a deep pity for Tan and Wu and the thousands of nameless others but my survival instinct had already taken over and I continued on my own, shutting everything else out of my mind. Walking backwards against a blizzard in unknown terrain isn't easy so not surprisingly I stumbled and nearly fell several times when I stepped into a snow-filled hole or butted against a snow-covered boulder.

Nevertheless I managed to stay on course and glancing for the umpteenth time over my shoulder I saw I was heading for the lead truck of the convoy.

It was then that I heard a booming voice, muffled somewhat by the blizzard, call out, 'You walk like a crab, brother! Though sensible under the circumstances, it is nonconformist and that's what probably got you into this mess in this godforsaken place. You must walk like everybody else in our beloved motherland even if that means you can't breathe, Brother Crab!'

The deep, warm voice and the cheerful laugh that followed the persiflage were so unexpected, so out of place in this desolation, that I felt my heart skip a beat.

I had reached the relative lee behind the truck and turned around to look in the direction I had heard the voice come from. I saw a group of soldiers in dark green overcoats with a brown fur collars. They wore caps with fur ear flaps and a red star on the front. Red and purple long underpants incongruously cascaded from under their quilted trouser legs and over their short boots.

About a dozen un-Chinese faces stared at me without a flicker of sympathy or interest.

Uygurs, I suddenly realised, uncultured barbarians barely able to speak Chinese. So where's the man who had spoken with such beautiful tonal inflexion?

As if guessing my thoughts the voice spoke again, 'I am here, Brother Crab. As I am an exalted Han person you should look for an exalted position amongst these, our less favoured socialist brethren whose brightly coloured underwear still stinks of last month's piss.'

The cabin door of the lead truck opened and a very tall man jumped out, keeping his balance easily as he landed on the snow-covered road.

He was dressed like the others but for the coloured underpants. Erect, unmistakably the commanding officer, he came striding to where I stood and said, 'Kong, *Colonel* Kong, sir for you, Brother Crab.'

He looked at me, closely and appraisingly, eyes narrowed, clearly pondering something.

Then, having made up his mind, he said, 'I don't want to know who you are or what you are here for. You will be known as Brother Crab from now on and you will be my valet. You'll remain my valet until my superiors show mercy and transfer me to a more clement place or until you become irksome, whichever comes first.

'You will make my bed, clean and polish my boots, brush or wash and iron my clothes, prepare my tea, cook my noodles and dumplings, wash the dishes and finally rub the aches out of my shoulders with hot, medicated oil before I retire to bed. If you manage to do all that in less than twenty-four hours you may eat or sleep or do whatever you do with yourself when you are alone. Believe me, Brother Crab, this is the best thing that could happen to you. Now, what do you say?'

'Yes, Colonel Kong, sir!' I stammered, flabbergasted by this totally unexpected turn of events.

'Good!' the colonel replied contentedly, 'Hop! Hop in the truck, before Lieutenant Yu, that shining pride of our People's Army, that piece of shit from shitty Shanghai, sets his feverish socialist eyes on you and deprives me of my feudal pleasures and you of a relatively cosy life. He doesn't wear his rank because he is very egalitarian, our political officer is, but you'll recognise him immediately by the stench of his breath though he'll be altogether too close for your comfort if you can smell him. Always stomach trouble he has, our lieutenant. Indigestion from studying our leaders' speeches, I'm afraid.'

At that he made an about-face and strode off to where a soldier with a loudhailer was unsuccessfully trying to make a huddled mass of people stand in line and to attention on the leeside of the row of trucks.

I saw Colonel Kong take the loudhailer from the soldier and a loud bellow shook the miserable crowd to at least a semblance of attention.

'I am Colonel Kong!' the loudhailer bellowed. 'And this here is our political officer Lieutenant Yu who is in charge of our army's "love the people, hate its enemies" campaign here in Xinjiang. You are here because you are those enemies we hate, hardened saboteurs and subverters of our glorious socialist achievements.

'The best thing for all of us would be for *you* to freeze to death here and now. It's painless and even mildly pleasurable I have been told. *However*, to allow you to expunge your crimes by contributing to the defence of the motherland with all the force that can still be squeezed out of you, we shall have to put you in somewhat better shape first, however much we hate to share with you the food and clothes that have been paid for with the blood, sweat and tears of the very people you have so shamelessly deceived.'

During the colonel's speech I had climbed in the back of his command truck and I was now looking at the ghastly scene outside through the split between the overhanging flaps of the tarpaulin.

It was bitterly cold in the truck but at least I was out of the blizzard and slowly I felt some feeling return to my hands as I squeezed them between my thighs.

How incredibly lucky I had been to have been the first to be noticed by Colonel Kong. Whatever was going to happen later I would worry about then, for the foreseeable future I had it made. I felt good and no remorse whatsoever not to be with my companions outside, in the snow.

⋆

'This may seem callous and unfeeling to you, here in the cosy safety of this room in the company of good friends. However, once you have felt real fear and suffered true physical deprivation, all that matters is the immediate satisfaction of your own needs. What else could *possibly* matter?'

⋆

I counted about thirty trucks by their individual headlights until the lights became blurred in the darkness and the scudding snow. I guessed, hoped rather, that there were more trucks, at least eighty, to transport all those people.

If not, those who would have to stay behind would be dead by the time the trucks returned.

Lieutenant Yu had finally managed to distract the colonel from his satirical address to the assembled prisoners. I saw the tall man bending down, gloved hand over his nose against Yu's putrid breath no doubt, apparently to listen to what Yu had to say.

I saw the colonel nod a few times before he straightened up and, lifting the loudhailer to his mouth, he shouted, 'Oh, you lucky devils! Praise whatever gods or spirits you think are on your side for having blessed you with such a magnanimous political officer as our beloved and respected Lieutenant Yu.

'The lieutenant just suggested to me that you stay the next two weeks in our barracks to attend his lectures on the new course given to our lives by our Great Helmsman Chairman Mao. After these teachings you will see clearly the wrongness of your thoughts and acts and you will be truly grateful for the opportunity to repent by digging trenches for our glorious People's Army in Tacheng whence our heroic Uygur brethren will defend the Han motherland against our criminally misguided socialist brothers from Russia. Now, please keep your enthusiasm in check for a little while longer and try to board the trucks in an orderly manner!'

The colonel lowered the loudhailer and handed it back to a visibly apoplectic Lieutenant Yu.

I was certain that the colonel had twisted the political officer's words and that keeping the prisoners for two weeks in the barracks before transferring them to Tacheng, another six hundred kilometres further north-west, had not at all been Yu's idea.

On the one hand I was glad for the poor bastards to have at least the chance to eat their fill and get appropriate clothing, on the other hand I felt a pang of fear that the colonel would have the opportunity to see more of them and possibly find somebody more suitable to be his valet.

I decided I wouldn't make any effort to find Wu or Tan lest they became jealous and make trouble for me, possibly directing Lieutenant Yu's attention to me.

Tan wouldn't but Wu would try to find me, I was sure of that. If he succeeded I would promise him that I would bring his case to the colonel's attention at the right moment. This could of course take much longer than the two weeks Wu would stay in Urumqi but at least I would have given him hope that I was doing my best to get him out of Tacheng. I was quite happy with myself for having it all worked out so well.

While all this went through my mind the prisoners had apparently managed to get into the trucks for I saw a light code flashing from way back and from truck to truck to Colonel Kong's command truck.

He had been standing for some time beside the truck looking towards the rear of the column and I saw him flash his torch three times in rapid succession and this signal was repeated in turn by the leader of each truck after which I saw them climb into the cabins. I heard the colonel climb into the cabin of our truck and tell the driver to start the engine.

He banged against the metal partitioning and shouted, 'You there, Brother Crab!'

'Yes, Colonel! sir!' I shouted back and so began the undoubtedly strangest three years of hard labour ever served by any convict anywhere in the world.

Three years I served this strange and difficult man, difficult first of all for himself.

Intelligent, erudite and inherently autocratic he couldn't suffer fools and what he called the petty, small-minded souls who dominated every aspect of our society, suffocating every single expression of individuality.

His mood swings were often frightening. Then cold, cynical and contemptuous, then boisterously, pompously sardonic, then again desperately, defiantly rebellious, sometimes all within minutes, he was difficult to predict.

I came to fear his rebellious moods most though for they always ended in a depression that could last for hours. When he was in such a state he expected me to just sit there with him and do or say nothing, just fill space as it were, until he finally mumbled, 'Rub my back, Brother Crab,' and I knew that the worst was over.

At first, at least the first four or five months, he didn't expect me to answer or comment on his rhetorical questions.

During his diatribes he always paced up and down in his quarters, pausing to ask a question which he then answered himself, or to make a point or draw a conclusion after which he resumed his pacing.

Then, one fine evening, late May 1967 it was, he looked at me as he had done hundreds of times before during his monologues, however, this time he actually *saw* me and *watched* me.

'*Answer* my question, Dao!' he said, using my name for the first time.

'Dao Huimin,' he continued, smiling, 'arch criminal, spy and saboteur if I were to believe my former political officer, Lieutenant Yu.'

He burst out laughing at my frightened face.

'Oh, he found out about you, Dao, the bloodthirsty little piranha. You had been here only a few weeks, early January it was, when he came to see me, his dead fish eyes all bulging, stinking one hour before the wind. He poured it all out what he had found out about you. He had gone through your few personal effects and found a letter you never dispatched and your student card of the Manchester Technical University. So careless of you, Dao, to keep those things in your locker. I learned my lesson. Caught him once, red-handed, going through *my* things. He wasn't fazed, refused to apologise. Said it was his job, his duty and his vocation. He demanded you be sent to the uranium mines near Habahe immediately.

'I was in a quandary, Dao, I admit. I outranked Yu by far but my authority is a purely military one while his was political and that's what counts in such matters. When I hesitated he made the mistake to threaten me, by innuendo, and that turned the whole affair into a matter of self-preservation, for me that is. I appeased him and told him I would arrange transport for you for the next morning and that I might have a second candidate for Habahe.

'I explained that I had been watching one of my Uygur sergeants and that I had strong suspicions that he was an agitator for minority rights. To find out for sure I would send out a patrol of Uygurs that same night and suggested that he, Yu, accompany them as an observer. The Uygurs didn't know that he, Yu, spoke their dialect and they would therefore speak freely amongst themselves and he would overhear them and find out whether my suspicions were justified. He fell for it, his zeal his doom.

'I called Sergeant Luen and in Yu's presence gave him instructions to lead a security patrol in the area of Bogda that same night. With his knowledge of local customs and history Yu should have known that the local name for that area is Mat which means death or no return or something similarly sinister, but it escaped his attention. Luen understood though.

'It was a terrible night, fifty degrees below zero and winds up to force ten, from the north-east. I listened to the wind that night as I do often and, as always, I heard the cries and moans of the outcasts our Communist brothers in Moscow dump in their wastelands north of us, just as you and your companions were dumped here in our wastelands, and I knew that I had acted correctly. Yu lost contact with the patrol or the other way round more likely. For three hours they searched for him then gave up and returned to the barracks at seven in the morning. The batteries in their portable radios should have been replaced before the patrol left but the sergeant forgot, or so he said, so they didn't hear Yu's distress calls.

'The sergeant had been delinquent so I gave him ten days' solitary confinement which he spent in his unheated cell wearing full battledress against the cold, so he didn't suffer too much. Anyhow, he must have felt good as he had pleased his vengeful God by killing an infidel and an oppressor of the faith at that.

'A search patrol found Yu late that afternoon, frozen stiff. He had apparently been walking in circles, spirals rather, and away from the camp, until tired he had laid down a moment to rest. That's fatal. Never lie down on frozen snow, Dao! Digging yourself in, in fresh snow, is all right, provided you stay awake. But lying down in frozen snow in the full blast of the wind? It's suicide, even at ten below zero.'

The colonel paused, smiled, then continued, 'You never asked or remarked about Lieutenant Yu's sudden disappearance, Dao. I wonder what you were thinking at that time. Perhaps one day you'll tell me and then, perhaps, you will not. Yu's replacement, Captain Fei, is actually a demoted colonel. Using his influence in return for sexual favours, from male recruits to boot, was his bourgeois sin. Fei is tiresome, moaning and bewailing his lot and talking to me as if we were still equals but he's harmless, so I indulge him and even pretend to sympathise. He's lazy and afraid of mountains and vast, open spaces so he stays in his office and that's just fine with me.

'So, friend Dao, that's why you are still here suffering my ramblings in silence while rubbing the rage out of my system. I'll promote you this instance from sounding board to interlocutor. I'll call you Dao and you'll call me Kong when we're alone. Outside I'll continue to call you Brother Crab and you call me Colonel Kong, *sir*! Like the Americans. I always liked the way you said that, Dao. Where did you learn it?'

'I heard it in a movie once, long ago, in England,' I replied, embarrassed, and then we both burst out laughing.

We became friends, though I never presumed or abused. Perhaps it's because I didn't that we could be friends and at the same time commanding officer and humble valet.

I think the military is the only society where such a double relationship is possible. It is a closed society with a strict discipline and a hierarchy which is neither abused nor resented all the way down the line of command to the lowliest man or woman. Everybody knows his place, his rights and duties precisely circumscribed, a rule for everything and every circumstance; life is reassuringly predictable both in day-to-day affairs and in the long run.

Initiative, innovation, improvements are not only *not* expected, they are frowned upon as abhorrent because they upset the system.

People with a military or bureaucratic mindset *love* an ordered, predictable life. It makes them feel *secure*, whatever their rank or position, however inept they may be. They band together to protect the caste and deal themselves with those who break the code, tolerating no interference by outsiders.

I once said as much to Kong during one of our many discussions. He agreed, sadly, and said that that was precisely the tragedy, not just in the military but of all closed societies that defined their own kind of justice and made their own laws based *not* on respect for the *individual's* rights but on safeguarding the system *against* the individual.

In such societies, Kong said, laws are always on the side of those who have the clout to enforce them and that enforcement is then called justice, however *unjust* it may seem or be from the *victim's* point of view.

'Look at your own case, Dao,' he said. 'Just *one* person, that man Song you told me about, a prosecutor and judge combined in one, handed you a life sentence of hard labour, in fact he condemned you to death and could have had you executed without anybody ever publicly challenging his decision. Maybe within his caste there might have been criticism, maybe even sanctions, but *you* or the public in general would never have heard about it.

'And you? What did you do? Did you appeal his decision? No, you did *not*! Did you contest his competence? No, you did *not*! Did you defend yourself? No, you did *not*! Did the system assign a lawyer to your case? No, it did *not*! Do you think that if the system had done so that lawyer would have challenged the prosecutor-cum-judge? No, you *don't*!

'All you can expect in a society such as ours, Dao, is that the lawyer, for his *own* protection, *begins* by recognising the correctness and justice of the sentence and *then* pleads for a bit of leniency, more as a favour to *him* than to *you*. Do you understand, Dao? Your lawyer, for his own sake, cannot *not* recognise the justice of your sentence. It would mean the end of him. He's part of the system, a system in which the individual has no recourse. Once a decision has been taken or a judgement pronounced and the subsequent events have been set in motion, *nothing can be done*. Mistakes *cannot* be admitted.

'You remember what you told me about that doctor friend of yours? Wu his name was, I believe. That he had been sent here by mistake? You were upset when I said that it was too late for me to do something. I didn't explain why then. I'll explain it now. The final destination, that is which *laogai* and where, for all the prisoners they send to Urumqi, is at the discretion of the commanding officer of the Xinjiang Military Region, that is I. Of course I *cannot* and also *do not* wish to get involved in individual cases. There is only so much misery a person can face and my threshold is low, I know that.

'So I leave the decision, as a matter of course, to my political officer, at that time Lieutenant Yu. Yu enjoyed that. He liked to play God. So when your fellow convicts were sent to Tacheng, it was *Yu's* decision made in and on *my* behalf. Turning that decision back for *one* individual would have meant that I disavowed Yu *and*, by extension, myself. To save face for himself, Yu would have reported me to our political masters for favouritism or for some other sinister intention. I could not have defended myself by pointing out that in Wu's case it had been a mistake that he was sent here in the first place, since mistakes can never be admitted in our system.

'So, Yu's accusation would have stuck and I would have gone the way of Colonel Fei, now Captain Fei, or worse, and Yu would have concocted some kind of plot *why* Wu could have such influence on a senior officer and get him an additional trial and ten or twenty years of hard labour. So do you understand now why I refused to do something for your friend? Both he and I would have lost out and suffered the consequences.

'For you it was different. You were still in transit and I used the privilege of rank and status to appoint you as my valet *before* I announced to the other convicts that they would be sent to Tacheng. Even Yu did not protest. He knew I had the authority to do that. He hated me for what he saw as bourgeois decadence, me having a personal servant, however, as long as I let him play God he wouldn't try anything against me. But have no illusions, Dao. If my successor does not want you or doesn't want a valet *tout court*, he has the discretion to dispatch you wherever he wants in this region and you continue to serve your life sentence.'

He fell silent, waiting for me to say something perhaps?

I said nothing and, after a momentary hesitation, he added, 'Your only hope, and that of all the millions of wretches like you, is that our political leaders, the few at the pinnacle, realise that their monstrous aberration, this so-called Cultural Revolution, will backfire and in the end harm them as well. If and when that happens you may still see the day that your gaolers tell you to sign a paper stating that you voluntarily contributed so and so many years to the construction of the motherland, give you fifty or a hundred yuan for the trouble plus a train ticket back to where you came from. Neither justification nor apology, neither given by them nor demanded by you, that'll be the deal. It was a voluntary contribution, no more, no less.

'"Now shut up and get on with your life," they'll probably say to you. Perhaps, just perhaps, at some time in the far future when the victims will have been all but forgotten, some leader will have the courage *and* the confidence in his own unassailability to admit that it was all a regrettable mistake. But don't count on it and besides, what else than a bitter aftertaste would such an admission leave you? They will *never* compensate you for the suffering and the years and loved ones you lost.'

Kong fell silent and I wept because of the hopelessness of it all. He handed me his face towel and poured me a mug of hot tea from the Russian samovar a visiting Soviet colleague from Frunze had once presented to him, before the confrontation, when they were still brothers in the socialist cause of their respective nations.

He made me rest on his couch and suddenly I felt his hands kneading my neck and he kept kneading until I fell asleep for lack of tears.

The colonel slept on my cot that night.

# *Chapter Thirty-Three*

## No Choice But to Play Ball

Time passed uneventfully.

I had a good life and I was content with the way things were; the food, always enough and reasonably good; the warm clothes for the harsh and long winters; my small but comfortable quarter with kerosene heater, adjoining the colonel's; my evenings with Kong, our discussions, intellectual parrying and games of chess and go; my job that kept me busy and from thinking too much about myself and Liang and the children; the beautiful summer days in the spectacular countryside when Kong ordered me to accompany him on his inspection trips.

As time passed the Cultural Revolution seemed to lose steam since the original stream of convicts wore off to a trickle and finally, during the whole of 1969, not even one short train arrived in Urumqi.

That was also the reason why my nagging fear that one day the good life would come to an end faded gradually from my daily thoughts and weeks passed that I didn't even think of myself as a convict serving a life sentence.

Therefore, the end came all the more unexpectedly.

I remember the day as if it were yesterday, 20th April, 1970, a beautiful, early spring day.

Colonel Kong had been away for a week, to Beijing, for a meeting with other regional commanders and the general staff.

His plane was due to arrive at two o'clock in the afternoon and I had gone to the airport with his driver to welcome him back. As he walked from the plane to the terminal building I saw that he was not alone, two officers of lesser rank were walking beside him.

When Kong saw me he put a finger to his lips to signal that I was to keep quiet.

He formally acknowledged the driver's and my salute and ordered me to collect his and his fellow officers' luggage and to wait for the jeep to come back for me and the suitcases.

I waited with a heavy heart, sensing that something bad was about to happen.

The labels on the two officers' suitcases read Zhang Zhaoxu, Major, and Zhang Zhishan, Captain.

When I finally arrived at the barracks Kong was in his quarters with his two guests and the driver told me that Kong didn't want to be disturbed. So I waited outside.

Finally at six o'clock they came outside and Kong ordered me to fetch his driver with the jeep. He instructed the driver where to drive the two officers and as soon as they had disappeared around the corner he put his arm around my shoulder and said, 'Come with me, my friend. I have bad news for you but then, you expected that already, didn't you?'

I nodded, unable to speak.

Inside he poured us each of mug of tea from the samovar I had filled up with fresh tea that morning. He sat down on his couch and gestured for me to sit down on a chair in front of him.

'One day this had to come, Huimin,' he began, 'however, now that it has I'm not at all sure I like it. I should be glad but I'm not. I feel empty, sort of. Our quiet little life has come to matter a lot to me, our undemanding friendship, our talks, the things we did and enjoyed together, even those bloody winters and our games of chess and go to pass the long evenings. It's over, Huimin, it's over. I have been recalled to Beijing to serve on the staff of General Yang, as a general myself.'

I made a half-hearted gesture as if to get up but he waved me back and continued, 'No need for congratulations. My successor here is Major Zhang and his political officer is Captain Zhang, no relative, Major Zhang Zhaoxu and Captain Zhang Zhishan. Captain Fei has not been able to regain the respect of his fellow Party officers and he will be asked to leave the army. Major Zhang, being still only a major, is not entitled to a valet, apart from the fact that neither he nor you would want to be around each other. Major Zhang's command is also not as extensive as mine, his is only the district of Urumqi. He and the other district commanders will continue to report to me in Beijing.

'The day after tomorrow I shall go on a tour of all the districts to apprise the commanders of the new set-up. The district commander of Karamay, or Kelamayi, is Major Peng Ze. I know him well. He is apolitical but ambitious and it is therefore in his interest to cultivate a good opinion of him with me, his superior, in Beijing. Major Peng is, amongst other things, responsible for a pipeline construction project in his district. It is a job that has gone on for years and will take another hundred years at the present pace of construction. Beijing wants to speed up the project and a labour camp will be built in Tachakou. Major Peng will be given seven years to complete the project and his promotion will depend on his success. He is, however, not a technical man and he will therefore be grateful for any assistance I'll offer him. That is where you come in, Huimin.

'I intend to propose to Peng that you become his technical assistant. With your background as a mechanical engineer it's a job made to order and I'll suggest that Peng puts you in charge both of the technical aspects of the project itself and of the convict labour. Although a convict yourself, you will nevertheless enjoy preferential treatment, such as your own quarters, heated of course in view of the drawing and paperwork you'll have to do, good clothing, double food rations and, of course, dispensation of physical labour in view of your supervisory responsibilities.

'I shall also suggest that you be assigned to him with immediate effect to assist him with the construction of the new *laogai* and with the selection of the labourers from the various camps around Tacheng. There will of course also be a non-convict workforce, welders, crane drivers and so on. I hope you'll be able to assert yourself and become their leader as well. It's a delicate matter. See for yourself how things develop. If Major Peng agrees, and I am certain he will, you will report to him five days from today.'

He fell silent and stood up to pour us another mug of tea, waiting for me to say something.

What was there to say? Oh, I was grateful for what he had done for me, for what he was still going to do for me.

But I felt rejected, much I suppose as a mistress or concubine feels rejected when the man she loves goes back to his wife, for good. Like a mistress I had lived in a make-believe world, fooling myself into believing that I would stay with Kong until, one day, he would intervene and make me a free man again.

Feelings of anger welled after the initial shock and, very unfair of course, I saw his arrangement for me as a buy off, more to make himself feel good than for my benefit.

Kong must have sensed what went through my mind for before I could say or do something stupid he pushed a mug of tea in my hand and said matter-of-factly, 'Don't be stupid, Huimin! We have become friends and that doesn't just end like that! You are probably the only *true* friend I have. If you think reasonably you must admit that what I am proposing is the best I can do for the moment. I cannot, like a magician with a wave of his magic wand, undo your past and make you a free man and neither can I refuse my promotion and transfer.

'What I *can* and *will* do though, is to find a place for you where I still have some control and where you can use your faculties and spend the next seven years reasonably well off. In the meantime I shall follow the developments of that disastrous Cultural Revolution and my new position in Beijing, close to where the puppeteers do their act, is of course ideal to gauge the general mood and which faction will win in the end. From what I heard in Beijing, there are many amongst the top military and even Party leaders who resent Jiang Qing's domination over and manipulation of Chairman Mao and I personally came away with the idea that the whole craze won't last more than another five or seven years.

'I see it as a real possibility that when you'll have finished that pipeline in seven years' time, the revolutionary fuse will have burnt out and I, as a three-star general by then, will be in a position to propose an amnesty for you in reward for your excellent services in finishing that project on time. I will have cultivated the right people by then and they will only be too happy to oblige. You for your part, Huimin, you play the game, do a good job, give due respect and credit to Major Peng, sign the papers on your release stating that you did it all voluntarily and, once back in society a free man, you do *not* exact rehabilitation or compensation from the Party or from the government.

'In the meantime we'll see each other from time to time during my inspection tours of the region. I'll make a special point to check the progress of the pipeline project and to be shown around by the project engineer. And once you'll be a free man again we see where we can meet to reminisce and play chess. Now, what do you say, my friend? Feeling better already?' And laughingly he punched me in my ribs.

By then, my mood had changed completely. I had been childish, indeed, like a fickle mistress.

Kong was sincere and reasonable and our friendship had entered a new phase, we had a deal. I had a *job* to do, for myself but also for *him* for he would lose face, or worse, if I failed.

So I burst out laughing and we hugged each other.

He gave me fifty yuan in one-yuan notes, just in case I would have to grease a few palms, he said.

# *Chapter Thirty-Four*

## Free Men Unto Themselves

Things went as Kong had said they would.

His driver drove me to Karamay and I reported to Major Peng on 27th April, 1970.

Peng was a youngish-looking man, clean and even smartly dressed, not the usual oversized jacket and baggy trousers. I suspected that, like Kong, he had his uniform refitted by a local needlewoman. Also, like Kong, he wore his rank insignia.

Peng was genuinely pleased to see me.

He assigned a room to me in the officers' quarters and told me I could convert it into a bedroom-cum-office and workroom. Once the new camp would be ready I could move to there since I would then be closer to the job, he said.

He told me that the camp should be big enough to accommodate three thousand convict labourers and two hundred specialist workers and that their quarters should be separate.

I told him I needed construction and layout drawings and he said that I would have to go to Tacheng, to the existing convict labour camp there and ask the camp commandant to put them at my disposal for study. Perhaps the commandant would agree to loan them to me for the duration of the construction. He, Peng, would write a small note for the commandant requesting his co-operation and would call him by phone to announce my arrival. He signed a travel permit for five days, assigned a jeep with driver and I went to Tacheng to report to Commandant Hu Sen.

From his name I knew that Hu Sen was not a Han Chinese but I was not prepared for the rest.

Though I was sure that Major Peng had announced my arrival and the purpose of my visit, the guard had clearly received no instructions and I had to wait in the guardhouse until, after two hours, a soldier turned up with the order to escort me to the commandant's office.

Hu Sen didn't return my salute and left me standing in front of his desk while he read and reread Major Peng's note I had handed to him.

He was short and swarthy, sported a moustache, chewed tobacco and smelled of stale sweat.

His glittering, small round eyes didn't miss a thing though for, looking up from Major Peng's note, he sneered and said, 'Where's the star, Dao? You're a convict yourself, eh? You've got influential friends, eh? They sent you here to spy on me and my camp, eh? Study the camp layout and the drawings the note from that shitty Major Peng says. Baloney! I *know* why you're here. They want you to make a report on the conditions in my camp! Too many people die here they say, *Chinese* people that is. The *locals* they don't give a damn about.'

He glared at me and, coming from behind his desk, he stood so close to me that I had to hold my breath in order not to gag. He growled menacingly as he tapped with a short, grubby and hairy forefinger on my chest.

'I warn you, Dao,' he growled, 'you make trouble for me and I guarantee you won't survive the next winter. Never forget that this is *my* country and that all the guards are *my* people and that we *all* hate you Chinese dogs. Accidents happen, do you understand that, convict Dao?'

'I am *not* here to make trouble for you, Commandant,' I replied, trying not to show my revulsion and anger, and I continued. 'As it is I have enough trouble myself, and none of it of my own fault, to last me several lifetimes. However, I'll remember what you said about accidents happening to Chinese people, *my* people, and I'll tell my friends so that they'll know what happened should I meet with an inexplicable accident.

'I may be a dog, a Chinese dog, in your and your people's eyes, Commandant Hu, but we have a saying in Chinese that you may wish to contemplate: before you kick a dog make sure you know who its master is. A few thousand years of experience have taught *us* that kind of worldly wisdom. You say you hate us Chinese. I'm afraid I can't return the compliment. Certain things and people are just not worth such strong feelings. Now, if you allow me, I'll finish my job here as quickly as possible, to our mutual relief, I'm sure.'

Hu Sen had leapt back as if he had stepped on a snake, when I said that I didn't consider him worth of strong feelings, and he was literally spitting his hatred at me as he hissed, 'I may not be able to destroy you, Dao, because I do indeed not know who your master is. So I want you to live, Dao, to live with the feeling of guilt that because of you and of what you just said to me a thousand of your kind will die. Dogs are unclean and those *without* a master must be put down. I hope you'll hear their rattling in your nightmares, Dao!'

He was still choking on his rage as I turned and left his office as fast as I could.

★

Lao Dao paused and looked at Lilian and Beiyuen.

'It was the first time I was confronted with racial and religious hatred,' he said, to the two girls in particular.

'I often thought about it later. It seems to me an intractable problem. It is an intractable fact that people do *not* have equal chances in life and that even *if* they had they simply wouldn't be equally successful. Some will make a success of every chance and consequently lead the good life, many will at least grasp one or two chances and manage to lead a decent life but the great majority, I'm afraid, will miss out on life's chances entirely, either because they're born in the wrong place, or are of the wrong sex, female that is, or are intellectually simply not up to it.

'It is this majority that self-seeking political and religious leaders prey on. The rabble-rousers exploit the frustrations of the unsuccessful and people's natural reluctance to blame their own shortcomings for their failure. The pulpit and the politicians tell the losers that it's not *their fault*, that they are the *victims* of a great world-wide conspiracy against their race, their skin colour, their religion, their creed, their sex, their caste or what have you that differentiates people from each other. Naturally this breeds hatred and resentment and paranoia and even the most innocent look or remark is construed as a racial or religious or sexual or social slight and slur.

'Our own leaders have for too long fanned the fires of discontent and of class, racial and religious hatred elsewhere in the world because it suited their purpose to make trouble there and now they are made to eat a cookie of their own dough as our own minority peoples are told by *their* rousers that the cause of their backwardness is the oppression by the Han Chinese and they are *right*. We Chinese are probably the worst racial supremacists of all people. The students from Africa, sent here by their governments, China's ideological allies in bashing the West, soon find out how bigoted and intolerant we are of customs and appearances un-Chinese.

'The Westerners have known this for a long, long time and it amuses them or at worst it annoys them because they look at it from a superior position but it's the poor Africans who suffer. They are between a rock and a hard place; China would take offence if they complain and vehemently denies the allegations of racism and their own government wouldn't dare or can't afford to take them seriously and offend China. I don't therefore see our leaders dealing wisely with possible future disturbances in trouble spots on China's periphery. People like that camp commandant, Hu Sen, bide their time and in the meantime don't miss a chance to stir up hatred against us.

'I don't envy the Han Chinese who live in those parts of China when people like Hu Sen, or when local politicians manipulating him and his like-minded, think that the time for covert or open revolt has come. It is something we Chinese in China have no experience with and, I'm afraid, will deal with in the wrong way as we always do with unknowns that frighten us. Suppression of the troublemakers will be the predictable overreaction by our leaders.

'I didn't know then and I don't know now what to do. As an individual you can't do anything, that's simply a result of our political system. Anyone drawing attention to a potential political problem, however imminent and dangerous, would be arrested, vilified as a troublemaker himself and thrown in jail, probably for the rest of his life, if he isn't executed in the first place. The reason why I am telling you girls this is that the other day, in the canteen, I heard the girls of the reception make disparaging remarks about the black members of the American trade delegation that was staying in our hotel. A few boys from the coffee shop and girls from housekeeping put in their word and before long silly, off-colour jokes and shrill, affected shrieks of horror went the round.

'Roger Wu came in and stopped the racket. He said that people who work in a hotel shouldn't be prejudiced against guests because of their colour or religion as that *was bad for business*. He didn't say that it is *morally* wrong, only that it's bad for business and that is what worries me, but then Roger is Chinese too, isn't he? Only a bit more worldly and sophisticated but still and always a Chinese. I would like you two to be different, to be an example to others in treating everybody the same, in a natural and guileless manner. Think about it.'

Lao Dao fell silent and when nobody said something, probably because there was little or nothing to add, he shrugged his shoulders and continued with his narrative.

★

The confrontation with Commandant Hu Sen had left me mentally deflated.

I regretted my foolhardiness in standing up to the man. I had gained nothing, on the contrary. Not only could I forget about any co-operation I might need from him but, instead, the man would be hell-bent on making trouble for me. Besides, others would be made to suffer because of my ego trip. I should have cringed and cowered and fawned instead, to give the bastard the feeling of superiority that always appears to elude people like him and that therefore they crave so much.

I found my driver still waiting in the jeep, outside the gate, quietly smoking a cigarette.

Liu was his name, Liu Timo. He was a likeable fellow and he had the cheery, friendly disposition peculiar to the people from Beijing.

During our drive to Tacheng we had talked about all kinds of things as if we had known each other for years so I now told him about my encounter with the commandant and that it had left me with an uneasy foreboding.

He laughed and said I shouldn't worry too much.

'Commandant Hu Sen is a toad,' he said. 'The guards told me that everybody hates him, even the Uygurs, his own people. What amuses them though is that he makes life miserable for Lieutenant Lu, the political officer.'

Liu grinned and continued, 'You should exploit Lieutenant Lu's feelings toward Hu Sen. Invite him for noodles and dumplings tonight, in town. He'll get the drawings for you and sign a permit for you to make your survey of the camp. It's a political matter and therefore Lu's responsibility, not Hu Sen's.'

Liu's common sense had cheered me up and his suggestion to cultivate the political officer was clever. It was my only chance to save my mission and show Major Peng that I was up to the job. Besides, through Lieutenant Lu I might find out whatever happened to Wu and Tan, something that had always been at the back of my mind since I had more or less evaded them in Urumqi now almost three and a half years ago.

Liu must have read my thoughts for he said, 'Let's wait here for the lieutenant. The guards told me that every afternoon he makes his round to inspect the road and defence work along the border and that afterwards he marches the convict labourers back to the camp. It's six o'clock already so they'll be here any moment now. Lu is still quite young the guards told me, so I'm sure he's also still eager to prove himself and I suggest that you tell him that your former commandant, Colonel Kong, now General Kong, and Major Peng especially recommended you see him in view of his authority over the drawings and permission to make a survey of the camp.

'Don't mention anything about your altercation with Hu Sen. Let him find out for himself. Anyhow, Hu Sen's account of what was said and by whom will be different from yours. So when Lu asks you later what happened you shrug your shoulders and tell him, casually, as if it's a small matter not really worth bothering him with. Because of his own experience with Hu Sen, he'll believe you and sympathise with you.'

Liu paused and chuckled, 'As soon as you start building the new camp the Party will send down a political officer to breathe down *your* neck all the time. So if you find that Lu is not such a bad chap after all, why don't you suggest to him that he apply for the job? At least you will know each other already and you can work out a deal that benefits both of you. You'll ask him how he wants his office and meeting room to be arranged and he'll exempt you from attending his propaganda and re-education meetings so you'll have the evenings to yourself. Wouldn't that be nice?'

I burst out laughing and said he should have been a Party member and politician instead of a humble corporal driver.

Liu snorted derisively and said, '*Why* in heaven's name? I have now the best life possible considering my age and background. I am exempted from military exercises other than as the driver of a commanding officer. While even he is then running around getting filthy and tired and making a fool of himself, I wait for him in the field kitchen and have tea and noodles while they're still fresh or I sit quietly in my jeep hidden behind bushes so nobody can see me, camouflaged they call that, and I smoke my cigarette. I don't get dirty, I don't get tired, thirsty or hungry. When there are no exercises, which is most of the time, my only camp duty is to keep my jeep in good order, something nobody else can do or knows an iota about, and to be available when the major needs me to drive him somewhere.

'Nobody orders me around. I get the best pieces of food, even before the major, and besides, he shares the cookies his wife sends him with me. I don't earn much but then I spend nothing either so I save, slowly and surely, for later, for when I find a little house to rent in a small back lane in Beijing and a young, healthy but *plain* woman to look after me. Now, why would I throw away all those advantages and peaceful dreams and become a prostitute and always live in fear of somebody screwing me just a bit too hard and hurting me? Can you give me one good reason, Dao? Just *one*?'

The man was clearly in control of his life and in no need of my silly advice.

'I envy you, Liu,' I told him, 'I envy you for being so content with what you have.'

'It's the only way in this country,' he replied, 'don't *want* too much. Look around you and see what you can get without too much exertion, without making people uneasy or envious and then be happy with that.

'Sometimes I have to drive high-ranking officers who have been abroad on some kind of mission or other or who have the privilege to watch foreign films. I listen when they talk amongst each other about what they have seen and I notice the envy. Foreigners, ordinary people like you and me, Dao, driving their own, private car, having their own house with machines to wash the dishes and the clothes, machines to clean and polish the floors, machines to keep food even for a very long time, and who can fly in aeroplanes wherever they want, on vacation. That is not for us in China, Dao, not *now* and not *ever*!

'I can't go to those foreign countries to live and work there either, so what's the point to think or dream about it? I prefer instead to do the small things that make me happy here and now and to daydream about the things I am going to do later. And while I am doing just that I try to stay out of trouble. That's my recipe for contentment, Dao. Think about it.'

He was right of course and I said so.

In silence, each of us engrossed in his own thoughts, we stared down the narrow dirt road that led from the camp's entrance to the border.

The sun had disappeared behind the mountains of Kazakhstan, their icy peaks a momentary kaleidoscope of red and pink. With twilight came the cold.

I shivered as I saw the icy, cutting wind that swept down from the mountains to the north stir up the dust of the road into a small army of whirling dervishes who, moments later, hurled themselves, howling and crackling, against our jeep. Within seconds everything inside was covered by a thin layer of powdery, reddish-brown dust that parched our throat and clogged our nose.

'There they come,' I heard Liu mumble, 'poor bastards.'

I wiped the dust off the windshield with my glove and I saw a dark huddle coming toward us, one lonely figure, battling the wind on his own, in front.

The guards had abandoned their posts to hide from the dust storm inside the guardhouse and I saw the lone man change into a trot to open the gate himself. He battled with the heavy doors with one hand while holding a piece of cloth over his mouth and nose with the other.

Holding one of the doors open by leaning against it he let the thousand-odd convicts pass, a gaunt, sickly, ragged band of zombies re-entering their graves.

With the sudden realisation of my extraordinary luck came the heart-pounding fear of how little was needed and I would be one of them.

It was a timely reminder of the flimsiness of my own position, a warning to beware of overconfidence. I vowed to be a thousand times more cautious.

The last of the walking dead had by then disappeared inside the camp and the lone man was closing the gate.

'That's Lieutenant Lu Qichen,' Liu said, nudging me with his elbow, 'go and speak to him!'

I got out of the jeep and trotted to where Lu was struggling with the heavy wooden beam used to bolt the gate doors. Without a word I held the doors steady in the wind by pushing one foot underneath, like a wedge, and helped him lift the beam into the hooks.

Once the beam was in place, he looked at me and said, 'Thank you,' then, squinting, 'I haven't seen you before. Who are you?'

'There's my jeep,' I answered, 'please let's get in. It's too cold to talk here. I would like a word with you.'

Hollow eyes in a gaunt face looked at me quizzically and then at the jeep. Shrugging off his initial hesitation he said, 'Okay, let's get in then.'

I opened the door and crept into the narrow back space, beckoning him to take the seat next to Liu.

'What's this all about?' Lu asked, curious but not suspicious, as he turned in his seat to look at me and then at Liu.

'My name is Dao,' I said, 'Dao Huimin. And this is Corporal Driver Liu, Liu Timo. I am from Urumqi, only just transferred to Karamay. Liu is from Karamay, he is Major Peng's driver.

'General Kong and Major Peng send you their regards and request you to kindly use your authority and discretion by helping me in my mission here, that is, to let me study the construction drawings of this camp and to allow me to make a survey of the camp itself. General Kong, on behalf of the Party Central Committee, has put me in charge of the construction of a new labour camp near Karamay and subsequently of the pipeline project. I have been given five years to finish everything.'

Already at the mention of General Kong and Major Peng, Lieutenant Lu had straightened up, looking solemn to hide his obvious pleasure at being known by such high-ranking men, however, when I said the magic words 'Party Central Committee' his eyes glazed over and I saw him swallow an emotional lump before he croaked, 'I will do what I can to help you, Comrade Dao.'

'I am grateful,' I replied. 'Now, Liu and I need a place in town to stay for two or three nights. Could you recommend a guest house? I would be honoured if you agreed to join us for a simple meal tonight. Comrade Liu will of course drive you back to the camp afterwards,' I added hastily when I saw him hesitate.

Lu's face brightened and he said he would be delighted to have dinner with us and to bring us to the town's only hostel. He asked us to give him half an hour to change into clean clothes and to announce in the barracks that the indoctrination meeting planned for that night would be postponed until the next evening.

'The heroes are tired anyway so they won't be too disappointed,' he said with a sudden flash of humour.

We declined his suggestion to wait for him in the guardhouse and told him to take his time while we waited in the jeep. Lu got out and in a trot disappeared through the small, one-man gate into the camp.

Liu chuckled and said, 'You did well, man. Our lieutenant will fall all over himself to please you. The Party Central Committee forsooth!'

*

On the way to town I stayed in the back of the jeep while Lu directed Liu to the hostel.

We stopped in front of a decrepit two-storey building. Liu and I took our kits and joined Lu who was already rattling the steel ring of the door latch.

When after a few minutes still nobody opened we at first took turns to pound on the wooden door until, finally, exasperated, the three of us were all pounding and kicking together.

Suddenly the door swung open and a wave of hot, fetid air struck us in the face.

'Can't you Chinese heathens let a devout Muslim finish his prayers!' an angry mustachioed and bearded face shouted at us.

I saw that Lieutenant Lu was about to react angrily so I stepped forward and said quickly, 'We are sorry if we did disturb you in your prayers, effendi, however, we need your hospitality quite urgently. Would you have a room for two of us for two or three nights?'

Mollified because of my apology and respectful address, the man beckoned us inside.

We hustled through the narrow doorway and, after pushing aside a heavy greasy curtain that smelled of garlic and rancid fat, we found ourselves in a large, overheated room.

There were carpets everywhere, on the floor, on the walls, hanging from the ceiling, however, there were no chairs and only a few small, low tables in the corners. In the middle of the room stood an enormous tiled stove, its large pipe, equipped with a water heater, passing through the back wall. The stove apparently served as the family sleeping place as I saw at least half a dozen pillows scattered on its top surface.

Three women sitting in the farthest corner turned their back on us when the hostel keeper barked something in the local dialect. The man took a register that hung on a piece of string from a nail in the wall next to the curtain and handed it to me.

'You must register and pay up front,' he said sullenly. 'It's two yuan per person per night including towel, soap, hot water and early morning dumplings. The rooms are not heated, so take the dormitory, you are the only guests anyway. The dormitory is warm because of the stove pipe and it has a water heater.'

I opened the book and saw that the last entry was on 20th January, three months ago. Not exactly a popular place, Tacheng.

I entered Liu's and my name and our positions as corporal driver and project manager respectively, both from and returning to Karamay after our sojourn. The man didn't even glance at my entry, let alone ask for our identification which was lucky for me since my piece of identity was a convict card.

He hung the book back on its nail and said he would put our kits in the dormitory for us.

I asked him whether he knew a good place to have dinner.

'If you care for Muslim food you can eat here,' he replied.

'The wife's a very good cook, the best in the area, and we have fresh, suckling lamb. If you prefer your own stuff go to Han's Place. It's three blocks down this street, a two minute walk. The owner's name is Wong, at least I think he's the owner, I'm not sure. He's from Guangzhou, however, he doesn't serve pork or dog because of local sensitivities. His beef noodles and smoked goose are quite tasty though. Go there myself sometimes.'

I thanked him for his explanation and told him we would go to Han's Place that night but would like to try his wife's cooking the following evening.

This apparently pleased him for his face brightened.

'Normally I close for the night at half past nine,' he said, much friendlier all of a sudden. 'Tonight, however, I'll stay open for you until ten, seeing that it is already eight o'clock. You must hurry though since Wong doesn't take orders after eight thirty.'

He glanced surreptitiously over his shoulder toward the women in the far corner before adding in a whisper, 'Be careful how you talk to Wong! Don't take airs and especially *don't* ogle his daughter's tits, though it's very hard to ignore them especially when she takes your order, hanging over the table as she does. Wong'll throw you out, without food or halfway your meal if you upset him.'

He laughed loudly, showing good, strong teeth though stained from chewing tobacco.

He held the curtain open for us and we got out quickly.

Han's Place was easy to find because of the noise of loud voices inside. I pushed the door open and all of a sudden the din was deafening.

It was only a small place with a dozen tables and an open kitchen; the toilets, also open, were at the back.

All the tables were occupied, the diners in various stages of drunkenness, all talking, cheering, toasting, chewing and spitting and pointing their chopsticks at each other at the same time.

One table near the door was nearly finished, judging from the remnants of the meal scattered over the table and on the floor.

Three men were standing, swaying, as they toasted one another with red, flushed faces, while three of their companions were lying with their heads on the table amidst the rubbish, obviously collapsed from too much *maotai*; one man just sat, smiling.

A short, stout man, his moon face shining with sweat under a filthy, whitish cap, shouted and gestured from the kitchen in the back that he would be with us in a moment. I watched Lieutenant Lu and, to my relief, saw that he was smiling.

Liu nudged me in my ribs and shouted in my ear, 'Nice place, Dao! I like it here! You shouldn't have promised that hostel keeper that we would eat at his place tomorrow! You didn't even ask the price! May be very expensive!'

I nodded and shouted back, 'I regret it already! Anyhow, we'll come back here day after tomorrow! And at noon the following day we go back to Karamay! Okay?'

He nodded, beaming and signalled me with his chin to look at Lu.

'Comrade Lu seems to like it too,' he breathed close to my ear. 'Good man! Propose to him your new camp, as I said!'

I nodded that I certainly would.

By then, the rotund little southerner had squeezed himself, with dexterity born of a lifetime's habit, undoubtedly, around the crowded tables and was now talking to the only sober diner sitting at the nearby table.

The man nodded, smiled, and uttered a few words which I didn't understand but which had an immediate, sobering effect on the others who sat down or sat up whatever the case. Another few words by the smiling man and everybody filed out of the door into the cold night.

The man with authority, holding the door open, nodded at us as he said, 'I'll pay you tomorrow, Wong.' And without waiting for an answer he turned and closed the door behind him.

'I'll have the table cleared for you,' Wong said to us. 'It's past eight already so I can only serve you beef noodles in soup, smoked goose with stir-fried noodles and vegetables, salted eggs and dumplings. It's three yuan per person, hot water is free, tea's ten fen per pot for eight, *maotai*'s twenty yuan per bottle.'

'Tea's fine,' I said.

Wong nodded and bellowed over the noise, 'Meimei! Come here!'

A fat girl of about twenty I guessed, Wong's picture to a point, came waddling toward us, left and right bumping her fat arse against tables and diners.

Her breasts were enormous, like watermelons, bumping up and down on her fat, round belly, stretching her sleazy grey pullover near tearing point.

Fortunately our hostel keeper had forewarned us. Wong was watching us, defiantly yet anxiously, for any sign of hilarity. With stony faces we looked around us and watched casually while Meimei first put all the dirty plates and bowls and chopsticks in a pink plastic basin and then, huffing and puffing, swept the rubbish from the table on to the rough, concrete floor with a filthy, wet rag.

Finally she wiped the table surface, as much with her belly and bulging pullover as with the same filthy rag.

Then she stood up and beaming, her unbelievably beautiful, molten chocolate almond eyes laughing and sparkling at us, she gestured for us to take a chair and sit down.

Lieutenant Lu nudged me and pointed with his chin at Liu. I looked and saw Liu staring after the girl with a goggle-eyed expression, mouth wide open.

I burst out laughing as Liu, still staring at father and daughter Wong busying themselves in the kitchen, mumbled, 'That's the girl for me, Dao, the one I have been dreaming about. I knew it the moment I saw her.'

Turning his gaze toward us, he grinned and said, 'If her food is anywhere as good as her looks I'll be back here many times to cultivate her old man and make him ripe for the idea of his Meimei becoming Madam Liu and moving to Beijing with me once I'm out of the army.'

Enthusiastically he punched my shoulder and cried, 'I have it all worked out already, Dao! Her old man can come as well. We'll share the rent for a house in a back lane, near a restaurant on the nearby main street. He and Meimei can work in the restaurant while I stay home to look after our son.

They eat in the restaurant and bring food home for me. That'll be real cheap, Dao. We'll be able to save a lot of money and buy a TV and visit places when they have their week vacation.'

Lu and I laughed heartily and Liu, after a momentary surprise at our hilarity, joined in the laughter.

'What are you three laughing about?' a voice behind us said, suspiciously.

Without even a flicker of hesitation, Lieutenant Lu said, chucklingly, 'Imagine, Wong! My friends here are staying at the hostel a bit further up the street. The keeper proposed we eat at his place. I see us already, sitting on the floor, eating his oily food while his old man and children are sleeping and snoring and farting on the stove. What a difference with your place here!' And anew he burst out laughing.

Relieved and reassured Wong laughed also. 'It's indeed a bit different,' he said, grinning, 'though, mind you, the food is not bad, not bad at all. Su Leima's lady is a good cook. I don't know who she is though. There are three women in that household, Su Leima's wife and his two daughters – or so he says. You only see them from far, scuttling like furtive crabs along the walls of the houses and all wrapped up in kerchiefs. I once had dinner there, with the Party secretary and a few of his men. The same people who had this table when you came in.

'As I said, the food is a bit strange though quite tasty actually. However, Su Leima sits with you, on the floor, and watches you eat with those fierce eyes of his. He doesn't eat himself, just watches and you are afraid to comment lest you say something he might take umbrage at. They are so touchy. You must always praise and praise and praise even if you think the dish isn't really worth all that praise. You hesitate only slightly, you don't cry out with delight after the first bite and he's angry already. Hesitate one more time and he throws a tantrum, yelling it's clear you don't like Muslims since you don't like his food and what not. It puts a strain on you, I think.

'So take my advice if you eat there one evening and I think you'll be forced to, at least if you stay there more than two nights, keep saying, after every mouthful preferably, that it is all very delicious. There's no other conversation possible so you finish quickly, pay his exorbitant price without protest or else he throws a tantrum and you retire to bed fast.'

He paused, then added laughingly, 'The reason why I said that you'll be forced to eat there at least once is that otherwise Su will make life very difficult for you during your last night and when you check out. He'll sing his prayers every two hours for at least half an hour so you won't be able to sleep.

'In the morning he'll put salt in your tea or coffee and when you ask for the bill you'll find that he has put something extra on it. Something or other he broke or damaged himself, probably long ago, but now pretends *you* did or as a pay-off for some affront or other to his womenfolk or for some kind of heathenish behaviour in front of his impressionable, innocent children, or whatever; every outrage has its particular, outrageous price. If you protest he'll go into such a temper that you'll be glad to shell out the money and get out of there.'

'We'll have dinner there tomorrow night,' I said. 'At first, when we saw your place, we regretted that we had promised Su Leima but after what you just told us it's perhaps just as well we did.'

'Yes,' Wong said, 'it's good you did. Tell him to compose the menu for you, that'll make him happy and keep him busy for a while. Then keep telling him it's delicious. Don't mention his wife or the other women and don't look in their direction, that is, if he hasn't locked them up in the kitchen. When he offers you coffee after the meal, accept. It's very strong and you'll have trouble falling asleep but at least you avoid offending him. Now, here's Meimei with your food,' he added, 'don't you dare tell me that it's not good or I'll throw you out.' And roaring with laughter he went back to his kitchen.

The food was very good indeed and we ate with gusto.

Lu and Liu were convivial fellows and, occasionally joined by Wong, we laughed and joked and talked animatedly throughout the meal.

During the smoked goose and stir-fried noodles I made up my mind. Hoping I had judged Lieutenant Lu correctly as a pleasant, fair-minded young man I decided I would not continue our relationship on the basis of deception but that I would tell him who and what I was.

It would be much better that he heard it from me than from Commandant Hu Sen the next morning. That would be a terrible loss of face for him. Unforgivable.

If I had misjudged him he would react badly and that would be the end of it.

Liu and I would return to Karamay the next day. I would explain to Major Peng what had happened and assure him I would be able to build the camp without the drawings of Tacheng. If I had judged Lu correctly though, it would make everything much easier.

So, after our last dumpling, I leaned back on my chair, stroked my stomach, belched contentedly and said, 'I would like to say a few words.'

Lu and Liu stopped their bantering and looked at me. I thought I saw a flicker of apprehension in Liu's eyes but then he looked down on his hands which he opened and closed alternately.

'What I am going to say is at my own risk,' I began, 'so when it turns out badly it is because I misjudged the situation and I'll have only myself to blame.'

The smile had disappeared from Lu's face but apart from that he looked at me, puzzled but not warily.

This gave me hope, so I plunged on.

'You called me Comrade Dao a while ago when we first talked in the jeep, Lieutenant Lu,' I said, looking straight in his eyes.

'I'm afraid I'm *not* your comrade though and perhaps *you* don't *want* to be my comrade once you know who and what I am. You see, Lieutenant, I am a *convict*, serving a life sentence of hard labour.'

I paused to see how Lu would react but he stared back at me without so much as a blink.

I was puzzled and somehow felt at a loss for words.

'Go on, Dao' Lu said, a hint of a mocking smile hovering in the corners of his mouth, 'go on! Tell me how it is possible that I, a lieutenant in the People's Liberation Army and a political officer to boot, am sitting here in a Tacheng municipality restaurant exploited by an unashamedly capitalist Cantonese who only pays half of what he charges to the municipality, enjoying an excellent dinner paid for by a convict in a PLA uniform and accompanied by his own driver. A topsy-turvy world is the least I can think of. I see that the capitalist shark Wong and his sow of a daughter have cleaned the other tables and are about to tell us to pay their wages of sin, so I think you have about twenty minutes to explain yourself, Dao, and it better be good. Go ahead, I won't interrupt you.'

So I took a deep breath and plunged ahead, telling my story in telegraphic style and only the highlights, starting way back in Shanghai, before liberation.

I heard myself talking, monotonous, staccato, like one of those old gramophones, the one with the big horn and the little dog.

I was only vaguely aware that Wong and his daughter Meimei first stood then slowly sat down at our table, listening.

Finally, after almost one hour of non-stop talking, I fell silent and greedily drank the glass of lukewarm tea Liu had poured for me a long time ago.

I avoided the others' eyes, especially Lu's, as I preoccupied myself with taking the tea leaves with my fingers from the tip of my tongue rather than spitting them out on the floor which would have looked a bit too swaggering, I thought.

From the corner of my eye I saw that a few times Wong was about to say something but each time Meimei squeezed his arm and he remained silent. Liu was again staring at his hands.

Obviously they were deferring to Lieutenant Lu.

Suddenly the silence was broken by a short laugh changing to a chuckle as Lu said, 'It would be a shame to break the chain of luck that began for you in Urumqi three and a half years ago, now wouldn't it, Comrade Dao? Perhaps today is *my* lucky day. I think I'll gladly become the political officer in your new *laogai* and look after your political purity.' And playfully he punched me on my shoulder.

With a shout of joy Wong sprang up from his chair.

'A drink! A drink!' he shouted. 'To celebrate the victory of sanity!' And he made for a small wall chest at the back of the restaurant.

We all laughed and slapped one another on the back and I saw Liu taking advantage of the euphoria to plant a smacking kiss on Meimei's blushing cheeks and, when she didn't protest, on her full lips as well.

Wong came back with the famous white and red porcelain bottle and he poured four glasses of the fiery stuff. We downed them and shouted in chorus, 'To the victory of sanity!'

Wong poured another four glasses and, lifting his own, he shouted, 'To everybody his own!' And we emptied our glasses in one gulp and shouted 'To everybody his own!'

Wong refilled our glasses and suddenly speaking in a normal tone, he said as he lifted his glass toward us, 'To peace and tolerance by all for all.'

Our voices a bit quavery, both from emotion and the *maotai*, we replied in unison, 'To peace and tolerance by all for all'.

The bottle empty, I asked for the bill and after noisy refusals by Wong and even noisier attempts by Lu to grab the bill, I finally managed to push thirty-five yuan into Wong's sweaty hand, more than half of the amount Colonel Kong had given me. It was well spent, I thought. I hoped there was enough left to pay Su Leima.

After some more backslapping and laughter and promises to see each other more often, Lu, Liu and I finally managed to close the door behind us.

The cold, pure night air sobered us as by magic and in companionable silence we walked to the jeep in front of our hostel. The wind had died down completely and the silence of the night was total, almost eerie.

I looked up at the sky, at the dazzling expanse of myriads of stars and nebulae and distant galaxies and the exhilaration of being a part, albeit an infinitesimal one, of that whole magnificence was overwhelming.

I insisted on accompanying Lu back to the camp. We talked little during the ride, just an occasional, innocuous remark now and then by either of us acknowledged by the short uh-uh of assent or denial by the others. There was no strain though, we were at ease with each other.

Liu stopped the jeep in front of the camp's gate and Lu, turning in his seat, said, 'I'll see you tomorrow morning at nine, Huimin. My corporal will march the convicts to the border works so I have time to go with you to the Building Registration Office in Tacheng where they keep the drawings of our camp. All right?'

I nodded as Lu got out of the jeep.

'Goodnight you two, and thanks for the dinner and the trust,' he said and slammed the door.

We waited until the guard had unlocked the small gate and Lu, with a last, short wave had disappeared inside the camp.

Liu and I drove back in contented silence.

Innkeeper Su Leima was angry with us as it was already way past ten o'clock but we merely shrugged our shoulders as we walked straight past him into the dormitory.

We slept well, ate a good breakfast of tasty chicken dumplings served by a sullen Su Leima and told him, in a friendly yet matter-of-fact tone, to prepare dinner for three that evening and to choose the dishes himself. This cheered him up a bit and he even made an attempt to bow as he kept the door open for us on our way out.

Lieutenant Lu was waiting for us outside the camp gate. As he climbed in the front seat he grinned at me and said, 'Commandant Hu Sen sends you his cordial curses, Huimin, and his fervent wishes that your black infidel soul may burn in hell for ever. That must have been quite a conversation you had with him. He still breathes fire at the mere mention of your name.'

I laughed and told him about the altercation in Hu Sen's office.

Lu frowned and said, 'He said that about the Chinese, did he? The local people here always seem to simmer with resentment at us Chinese, whom they see as occupiers and suppressers of their language and culture. I'm afraid that one day this whole region will revolt. The tragedy is that I can't report these things. The message is unwelcome so I, as the bringer of bad tidings, will be blamed for inventing problems for my own benefit.'

He sighed, then added, 'So here you have a case where self-preservation must prevail over sense of duty towards the Party and country. Sad but true.'

'I think the phenomenon is universal, Lu,' I said, 'not just Chinese or even Communist, though in totalitarian systems it goes unchecked and unchallenged much longer since there is no recognised opposition whose political duty demands that it brings such unpleasant things to the public's attention. The first sign of alienation of those in power is when they take a dissenting opinion as a personal affront. From the little experience I have in the West this goes also there, both in politics and in big business. Power corrupts and absolute power corrupts absolutely is a saying they have over there and I think it's very true.

'Over there though, such power-mad and power-corrupted people can be removed while here in China they cannot. *If* they are removed here it is by some intrigant who has been manoeuvring behind the scenes to form his own clique of power-hungry friends-for-the-occasion and all the *people* get is more of the same old, corrupt attitudes. Tyranny is the last phase in this process of corruption by power. Tyrants are paranoid, they see enemies everywhere and even the messenger bringing bad news is punished, executed usually, for *daring* to mention that what displeases the great man. Surrounded by fawning sycophants the tyrant's power rests exclusively on a bunch of psychopaths, the so-called secret police, who arbitrarily arrest imaginary enemies of the People, detain them without trial, extort false confessions by torture, set up mock trials that have nothing to do with justice, carry out public executions or secret killings, whatever suits them best, in short who use plain terror and the whole panoply of illegal methods to keep the despot, who feeds them and who allows them to indulge their sick minds, in power.

'I *know*, Lu, because I am such an imaginary enemy of the People and have undergone those illegal methods and still suffer, every minute of every day. Do you realise, Lu, that you are an instrument of the tyranny that did and still does that to me?

'Do you realise that you have absolute power over me? That you could, this very moment, throw in my lot with that of the other convicts in your camp and probably get praised for it? That you could then pick on me, day after day, and drive me to death by suicide or by exhaustion and privation without ever having to answer for it? Perhaps even get rewarded for exemplary revolutionary zeal? That in the event that Liu here would stand up for me you could have him arrested, on the spot, for siding with a convicted enemy of the People, indict him yourself as a counter-revolutionary in aggravating circumstances since he is a soldier and have him shot all in the same day, today if you insist?'

Both Lu and Liu stared at me, clearly horrified by my words. I smiled at them, a sad, tired, weary smile and added, 'On the train that brought me here, Lu, and I dare say on the thousands of trains disgorging men and women like me, there was not *one* person who posed a threat to the Party or to the State. Not *one single person,* Lu!

'Have you ever asked yourself what kind of horrible crimes those people you march every day to and from the border works must have committed to deserve such a lot? I am *sure* you haven't, Lu. You just accept the fact that they are there and that the *why* is not to be queried. You have been conditioned *not* to query the decisions of your political leaders, of the Party. If you ever had done so, even if only *once* in your life, you would not have made it to political officer, *twice* and you would not be a Party member now, *thrice* and you would probably be a convict yourself.

'Such is life under a totalitarian system, Lu. You can *never* be sure. You have *no* control over your own life. Living your quiet little life minding your own business, as our friend Liu is so fond of, is *no* guarantee that you won't be swept up and away by a freak maelstrom of so-called political purges.

'I can do *nothing* to change *my* lot, I have *no* recourse. Only luck can make it bearable as has been the case for me, at least until now. But I realise damned well that my luck can turn at *any* moment and as I said, I'll have no recourse when that happens, no one to turn to for help. My only hope is that some day another clique wrestles the power from the present one and imposes their own version of twisted justice because that is what they always do. In that version they will of course surround themselves with their *own* sycophants and what better candidates than people like *me* and what worse enemies than their predecessor's, people like *you,* Lu!

'You see, Lu, what it all boils down to is that we are *all* victims of the system. Now *you* happen to be on top and in a position to kick *me*, tomorrow it's the reverse. Whether victim or victimiser, we are what we are by whimsical decree, not because of our own design or volition. Once you recognise that you feel a certain relief from the pressure to perform, to impress others: your leaders, your Party, your boss, and instead you start thinking more of your own interest.'

I fell silent as the jeep had reached the outskirts of Tacheng and Liu needed Lu's directions to the Building Registration Office.

When Liu said that the directions were clear and that he wouldn't have a problem to find the place, Lu turned in his seat to look at me and he said, 'I wonder whether it was such a good thing, for me that is, to fall for your easy manners and seemingly trustworthy personality, Dao. Yesterday evening I naively thought so, now I'm not so sure. Damn you, Dao Huimin, you have disturbed my peace of mind with your razzle-dazzle talk!'

'Did I really?' I asked, mockingly. 'Were you really at peace with yourself, Lu Qichen? Or was there a little nagging doubt already there, subconsciously perhaps, but still? And all I did was fan it a bit with my razzle-dazzle, as you call it, so you can't suppress it any longer? And is it that what disturbs you rather than the substance? Be that as it may, Qichen, I think that from now on you will be an ever lousier political officer than before and I propose therefore that we work together to have you appointed commandant of the new camp by Major Peng rather than political officer. That'll be your first step toward regular army service, something you can believe in. Think about it, my friend!'

'Think about this! Think about that! That is all you ever say, Dao, after you have first confused me deeply,' Lu exclaimed suddenly. 'Dammit man, I have not been trained to think as an individual! And besides,' he added, in a mock attempt at angry exasperation, 'why the hell do we do our soul-searching in front of this man Liu! For all I know he may report us for treason or whatever!'

Liu burst out laughing as he stopped the jeep in front of a squat, ugly concrete building with small, grimy windows. Six faded red characters above the entrance, two hanging precariously upside down, said that this was the Tacheng Municipality Building Registration Office.

As he cut the engine, Liu continued mockingly, 'What always surprises me is that people who think of themselves as intellectuals, like you two, invariably suffer from self-doubt. They always seem to need an intellectually acceptable reason for doing or not doing something. Why must everything be explainable and, as a consequence, be explained? Are you scared of feelings, drives, emotions which you cannot describe in beautiful words and then file away in your brain under neatly identifiable headings?

'Whatever happened to your *gut*, your *heart*, your *instinct*? They not only *know* what is waiting for you around the corner but they have also already *decided* what is the proper thing to do and that long before your precious brain has even detected, let alone properly analysed the matter. If you follow your gut feelings, you feel good, if you don't you feel bad, it's as simple as that. So I now go by *my* gut feelings and they tell me to let Lieutenant Lu Qichen solve his own problem. I have only known you less than two days lieutenant, however, I know, in my gut, that I would feel bad if things turned out wrong for you, so don't you worry about *me* doing *you* a bad turn.'

'It's as simple as that,' Lu said, mimicking both Liu's words and tone, good-naturedly though. 'You do the things you feel good about and don't do the things you feel bad about. What a great revelation! Why don't you go to Wong's and ogle Meimei for an hour or so and feel good while we do our tedious jobs and feel bad? Be back here at eleven!'

At that both Lu and I got out of the jeep and cursed Liu as he drove off, grinning in anticipation, with shrieking tires in a cloud of dust.

Although a wooden sign hanging from a nail in the door said that the office was open, the door was locked.

Lu knocked, then, when the door remained closed, he started a pounding that resounded, muffled, inside. At long last the door opened, slowly, creakingly, hesitantly and the simian face of an old man stared up at us, eyes blinking and watering against the glare of daylight.

A cold, musty smell wafted through the crack.

Lu ordered the old man to let us in and we stepped over the threshold into a dank, gloomy atmosphere of decay.

I heard the door being closed and bolted behind us and, when I turned around to ask the old man for directions, he had already slumped down again on his rickety wooden chair and was staring down at his gnarly, intertwined fingers, jaws moving slowly as brownish spit dribbled through the deep furrows at each side of his toothless, sunken mouth.

The old chamber pot next to his chair was nearly overflowing with a foamy, brownish mass, probably the spit of many weeks of guard duty. He apparently lacked precision since the floor around the pot was stained and wet.

At Lu's peremptory question where he could find the drawing section, the old character gestured sideways with his right arm, without looking up and slobberingly mumbled something incomprehensible.

Lu shrugged and, gambling the gesture had been more to the right than to the left, we took the right side of a narrow, dark corridor.

Every four metres or so on our left there was a grimy wooden door once, long ago, painted the kind of green colour that had always made me sick. Thousands of hands had left their greasy marks on the doors as well as on the rough, once whitewashed cement wall.

Small wooden signs, fixed perpendicularly to the lintel of each door, said in small, almost invisible faded red characters what kind of service could be found on the other side of the doors.

Slowly we walked toward the end of the corridor, stopping at each door to decipher the name of the section.

Of course it was the last door.

I knocked and at the same time pushed down the handle, more to verify that the door was indeed locked, which was what I expected, than to open it.

It opened, however, and both Lu and I stood as if frozen. A woman with a round, middle-aged, peasant face, red from congestion and, hopefully, pleasure, her mouth wide open, tongue lolling, stood bent over from the waist and leaning on a desk, her legs as wide as the trousers dropped around her ankles allowed.

A youngish man stood behind her white, naked arse, holding on to the flab of her doughy waist, his trousers on the floor around the grimy ankles of his skinny, white legs. He had obviously arrived at the critical moment for in spite of our stares he continued to pump, pushing and heaving and groaning, his eyes all screwed up.

The woman saw us though and shrieked. In a flash she bent over and pulled up her trousers. Fumbling with her frock smock with one hand while trying to push her undershirt inside her trousers with the other, she made for the doorway, bumping into Lu in her haste to get away from the scene.

The man stood there and stared at us, petrified. His mouth hung open, totally slack. His slimy, already flaccid penis drooped and bumped against his uncontrollably shaking thin thighs. The semen, already too far on its way out to be held back, yet not far enough to be squirted into the woman's innards, dripped uselessly on to the floor and down his knobbly knees.

Beside me I heard Lu breathing heavily and, glancing sideways, I saw him bite his lower lip. Suddenly he burst out laughing and relieved I followed him inside the small office.

Cheerfully Lu slapped the crestfallen man on his shoulder and said, 'That was some coitus interruptus, my friend. Now, pull up your trousers and tell us where we can find the drawings of camp 4369/121 and then leave us. Go and find your woman and tell her we're sorry for the interruption. Quiet her down and assure her there won't be any talk. It's none of our business.'

Mumbling his thanks the man put himself in order. Then, kicking against the bottom one of a stack of several sagging dust-covered cartons he said, 'The drawings are in there. You can take them. There's no register. Nobody cares. Nobody ever comes here.'

Heaving a deep, shuddering sigh as if releasing his pent-up tension, he rushed on. 'My name is Fu, Fu Fusai. You are the first to ask me something since I got this post five years ago. It's the same for Hou Shaoxia, the woman you saw. She has the room opposite mine where the maps of the region are kept. She has been here ten years and has *never* seen a person come to her room. *Never*! Officially there are five other people working in this building, besides old Ma Haozhang, the security guard. I know his name because I looked it up in the duty roster somebody drew up twelve years ago. Ma never speaks, never says a word.

'Every day I say, "Good morning Mr Ma, goodnight Mr Ma, see you tomorrow," but he never replies. I call him Mister Ma, not Comrade Ma, because he's so old. At least I think he's old, he looks old. I never saw the other five people. In all these five years I have *never* even seen them, let alone spoken to them. Shaoxia remembers three who used to come once or twice a week until six or seven years ago they stopped coming.

'Shaoxia and I take our noon meal in a small, private noodle shop next door. The owner is a local. He merely shrugged his shoulders when I asked him a few times, long ago, whether he knew the others. So I stopped asking questions. I don't know where old Ma lives, whether there is anybody who takes care of him, prepares his food, washes his clothes. He is there already when I get here in the morning at eight o'clock and he probably leaves after Shaoxia and I leave at four o'clock, if he leaves at all. He is always dressed the same, always smells the same, tobacco, musty grain, rancid fat. He scares me. Shaoxia thinks he's dead already and that it's his ghost sitting there, on that old chair. She's afraid to go near him.

'We wait for each other in the morning, in front of the door and then I pound on the door until Ma opens and she goes in before me so that I can keep an eye on Ma. Every other Saturday Shaoxia and I go to the town hall to collect our pay. Once, when I had been here one year, I asked the Party secretary what the purpose of my job was since I never did any work and nobody had ever come to ask me something. He told me, angrily, that my job was very important. That I was the guardian of drawings and that all drawings were state property, some of them even state secrets. Some secrets! Look at all the dust! I loathe myself! Nothing to do! Coming to two thousand days shortly and I never even finished the inventory!

'You see that calendar? It's the one of 1962, the year I came here. Each day I wrote "Inventory" and the first carton took me one week, the second three weeks and the fifth, the last of that first stack, more than four months. Then, somehow, I stopped the process of categorisation and I never got round to it again. I just sit here and stare at the cartons and watch them gather dust and sag, sag, sag. They don't sag any more but the dust still builds up. Every year, on Liberation Day, I write my name with my finger in the dust on the top carton of a stack and the characters I wrote five years ago are only barely visible under the dust of four years.

'Shaoxia says I'm a bit mad and perhaps she's right. She dusts her office every other day and afterwards she comes in here to wait for the dust to settle. She's allergic to dust, it makes her sneeze. Three years ago, yes, it must be three years ago by now, she was also waiting in my room for the dust to settle and I went to the latrines. When I came back she was lying on my desk, on her back, her trousers and underpants on the floor. She didn't talk and neither did I and we made love then and ever since, every other day. She's not beautiful and she's much older than I am, forty-two she is, and married. I am not. Girls don't see me. Her husband lost both his legs in a quarry blast that went wrong fifteen years ago, the day after they got married. He's paralysed from the waist down. They never made love as he was too drunk the first night and then he had that accident.

'We were both virgins when we did it for the first time. Her husband moves around the house on a wooden cart with four small steel wheels. The workers of his unit made it for him when he came out of the hospital. He pushes himself with his knuckles, on the floor. He's very strong and always in a bad mood, Shaoxia tells me. She told him about our affair and that she needs the lovemaking. At first, he made terrible scenes, every day when she came home. Finally they made a deal. She would stay with him and take care of him provided he stop his jealous tantrums or else she would divorce him.

'That scared the poor devil. Now they hardly talk. He has made himself a kind of sleeping place in a corner of their room, on the floor, so that he doesn't need her to lift him up on to the bed. He can also take care of his own toilet. Shaoxia washes his clothes and cooks his food and keeps the house clean. What a life! For two years now I have wanted to ask the Party secretary for a transfer to Karamay or Urumqi or, better still, to a place, any place, in China proper.

'However, I haven't the courage. I worry about Shaoxia, I pity her. I'm sure she'll cry when I tell her I'm leaving and I can't stand that. Stupid, I know, but there it is. I stay on and waste the best years of my life because I'm afraid a woman I don't even love and whom I owe nothing is going to cry when I leave her.'

He paused and looked at us, tears and despair in his eyes.

'I'm so sorry to bother you with my silly problems,' he blubbered, 'but I don't know anybody I can talk to. I'm so sick of listening to Shaoxia fantasising about how the two of us could get married if only her man, Ye Guobia his name is, were dead, and we could then request permission to move to Hainan or Yunnan. She's never been to those places but she's convinced it's paradise over there with nice, warm weather all year round. I'm scared to death that one of these days she'll ask me to kill Ye to prove my love for her and that, if I refuse, she'll kill him herself, clumsily, of course, so that the police will know immediately she did it and arrest her. That'll scare her of course and to save herself from the bullet she'll tell the police I put her up to it. What can I do, Officer!' he wailed, clasping Lu's hand.

Lu looked at me. He was clearly embarrassed and didn't know what to say.

I pitied the young man. What a life! Even my own life, as a convict, was preferable to his.

I nodded at Lu who was trying to free his hand from Fu's hand.

'Try to keep going for another three or four months,' I said to Fu. 'I'm in charge of a project near Karamay and I can try to have you assigned to that project as a clerk of works or something like that. That is, if you are interested, of course.'

Fu fell to his knees, sobbing, clasping my legs between his arms, wiping his snotty nose on my trousers.

'Oh, please, comrade, please!' he cried. 'Get me out of here, please!'

'I'll do my best,' I said hurriedly, embarrassed by Fu's emotional behaviour. 'I can't promise I'll succeed but I'll do my best for you. Now, pull yourself together and go and see Shaoxia. Don't mention anything to her though. Don't say anything until the day of your transfer. If you get yourself in trouble I won't remember you and I'll swear I never told or promised you anything. Lieutenant Lu here will testify to that. Leave now and when you come back in say half an hour we'll be gone.'

To my utter embarrassment Fu, still on his knees, kowtowed and knocked his forehead on the floor three times. Then he scrambled up and left the room in a hurry.

'Some kind of recruit you got yourself there,' Lu muttered. 'Now let's find those bloody drawings and get out of here fast. This place gives me the creeps.'

We found the drawings in the carton Fu had kicked against and hurriedly we left the dingy little room.

Old Ma was still sitting on his rickety chair, right leg quivering, head bobbing, jaws moving, slack lips dribbling, dim mind wandering in some obscure world of his own.

We didn't ask him to open the door for us. Instead Lu fumbled with the wooden bar that locked the door on the inside until he found out how it worked and he hastily pulled the door open.

Driver Liu, already waiting in the jeep in front of the building, looked up in surprise when he saw us shooting out through the door like a pair of frightened rabbits.

The intense sunlight and tingling freshness of the air were exhilarating after the musty deadness inside and whooping with relief Lu and I climbed into the jeep.

'Their prank gone awry, the two naughty boys escape,' Liu chuckled, mockingly. 'You should have seen your own faces when you came out of that door, falling over one another in your haste, as if all the damned souls of the nether world were on your heels. Ha, what did I miss?'

On our way back to the camp, through that glorious, sun-splashed country that made the whole story seem unreal, I told him about our brief sojourn in the nether world.

Liu laughed joyously when I described the lewd exertions of Fu and his woman.

However, when I mentioned that I had promised Fu to get him out of there, he frowned and exclaimed, exasperated, 'Why must you always get involved in matters that are none of your business, Dao? What is Fu to you? Nothing! You have never seen the man before! You owe him nothing! He can't possibly do anything for you *ever* that Lieutenant Lu and I cannot do better, easier and as a matter of course. So why the *hell* did you have to create obligations for yourself toward that man Fu?'

'I'm sorry,' I said lamely, 'you are right, of course, but then I pitied the man, that's all.'

'I pitied the man,' Liu repeated after me, mimicking my plaintive voice. 'I pitied the man, that's all.'

He snorted derisively and said, 'Let me tell you, Dao, if you make pity for your fellow human beings the motive for your actions you'll be a very busy man; half a billion Chinese alone qualify already for your good deeds. Be realistic, man! Take care of yourself first and foremost and next select a few deserving friends who may be useful to you one day and let the rest take care of themselves.'

We spent the remainder of the trip back to the camp in silence.

Absent-mindedly I watched the landscape with the bright orange-red poppies and white, pink and mauve cosmos flowers merging in a blur against the blue-black background of the mountains of Kazackskaya.

I tried to see each flower individually, near the roadside, as we drove past, but it made me dizzy and I felt nauseated. As soon as I looked up, however, at the distant fuzzy haze, the discomfort passed almost immediately.

Perhaps I should look at people that way, I thought. See them as a fuzzy mass, not as individuals who can leave a lasting and often disturbing impression.

Fleeting images of Wu and Tan welled up from my subconscious as if to prove the foolishness of such thoughts before, in turn, Liang's image pushed everything else out of my mind.

As always when she visited me I could smell the scent of her body, feel her warm breath against my throat and the tickling caress of her lashes on my cheek and I wept.

Lu and Liu pretended not to notice.

Back in the camp Lu had his own things to do and Liu asked permission to go back to Tacheng to 'further knead the dough of his future life's bread' as he put it. I was sure he didn't mean it entirely metaphorically.

We agreed to meet in front of the gate at six o'clock and have our dinner at Su Leima's guest house together.

Ostensibly carrying and consulting the drawings to give myself an attitude I strolled through the barracks and dependencies, occasionally taking a measurement or looking about pensively.

The barrack walls were made of reddish-grey brick and were only one brick thick. The roof consisted of rafters and corrugated metal sheets. There was no floor, just the bare laterite soil. In the middle of each barrack stood a ten by two metres brick stove, twenty-four bricks high. The bricks showed only faint, old traces of blackening by fire.

In my imagination I heard the wind howling and whistling through the opening between the top of the walls and the roof, chasing the whirling, icy snow crystals until they settled on the huddled, silent figures on the stacked plank beds. I shivered and stamped my feet to break the spell.

The barracks were empty so early in the afternoon, the convicts out in the field building ephemeral fortifications along the border against our revisionist socialist brethren.

I could have dropped the matter there and then as there was nothing for me to learn.

But then it had been a sham anyway, a mere pretext to find out what had become of Wu and Tan.

This had become sort of an obsession with me lately. For the past three years I had hardly had a thought for the two men and suddenly I had this urge to find out what had happened to two people who had been no more than fleeting acquaintances during a few unpleasant days of my life.

Perhaps it was just that, the shared humiliation and helplessness and now that I had a reasonably comfortable life my feelings of guilt about the way I had gone back on them that night in Urumqi were playing up.

The quickest and easiest way would be to ask Lieutenant Lu if he knew about them but then I didn't want to draw too heavily on our still tender friendship.

I decided to give the matter one more day. If by the next evening I hadn't got any further I would return to Karamay and forget about the whole thing.

I killed time ambling from barrack to barrack and became depressed by the dreariness of it all.

One, smaller barrack stood apart from the five bigger ones and had its own guards who refused to let me enter. A corporal told me I needed a special pass, signed by the political officer, to enter the infirmary, for that was what the smaller barrack was.

With a shock I realised that in the new camp too I would have to make provisions for a sickbay, and equipment and qualified personnel, which, somehow, I would have to select from amongst the prisoners.

Having never been sick myself I had simply given no thought to such things, the typical unconcern of the healthy for the sick and needy.

Suddenly I recalled that Wu had at one time mentioned that he was a medical doctor. In a flash it came back to me, the voice in the dark corner of the cell in Meishan's Detention House, 'Name's Wu,' the voice had said, 'Wu Fuzhi, medical doctor. Reading poetry in preference to Party literature was my crime,' or something like that. His own daughter had denounced him, if I remembered correctly.

Perhaps, just perhaps, I might find him in this infirmary so I would have to ask Lu for a permit after all.

I found Liu already waiting outside the gate, staring through the windscreen into a delectable future with fat, sloppy, good-hearted Meimei.

I opened the door and climbed on the back seat.

'From the smirk on your face I gather that your mission was successful,' I said mockingly.

Liu burst out laughing and was about to launch himself into a description of his amorous tactics when fortunately the door opened again and Lieutenant Lu got in and in quite a hurry.

'Get moving!' he ordered Liu curtly even before he had pulled the door shut. 'That animal Hu Sen is about to order a security drill that'll keep me busy the whole night. Just to spite me,' he added as he turned in his seat to look at me while Liu sped the jeep around the curve as fast as he dared.

'I had to sit through three hours of abuse and insinuations all because I had dinner with you two last night at Wong's,' Lu said, obviously very angry. 'I told Hu Sen that it was my business and in my time and then he threatened to report me for saying such counter-revolutionary things. He said that as a political officer I should know that in China there were no such things as own business and own time as all business was Party business and all one's time belonged to the Party. How I hate all this intriguing and circumspection about everything you do and say. I'm sick and tired of it all, Dao. In that new camp of ours we're going to do things differently!'

I laughed and decided that he was in the right mood to bring up the subject of Wu.

'I am thinking that we need a good medical doctor for our camp,' I said, 'somebody who thinks like us and who can actually manage the sickbay and make the best of what we can get as medical supplies, which won't be much, I'm afraid. A friend of mine, from Lu'an near Hefei was arrested at about the same time as I was, for unproletarian behaviour. His daughter had denounced him to the Red Guards for reading classical poetry at night. He was, or is I hope, a medical doctor. Wu's his name. He was on the same train as I, back in December 1966. I was ordered to remain in Urumqi, by General Kong, then still Colonel Kong.

'Wu was put on a military transport that went further west, perhaps as far as Tacheng, I don't know. Anyhow, if he's still alive he would be the right man for the job. Only I wonder where he is now.'

Lu laughed, a short, mirthless, snorting laugh. 'Hoah! I knew it! I knew my luck couldn't last! Your friend Wu, I have the bad feeling that his full name is Wu Fuzhi! Is it, Dao? Tell me it's not true!' And at that Lu gripped my arm and looked at me imploringly.

'I'm afraid it's true,' I said, alarmed, 'what did he do? Why are you so upset?'

'Your man Wu is absolutely allergic to authority, any authority,' Lu answered, shaking his head dejectedly. 'He drives me crazy. If he weren't a doctor and the only one in our camp I would have condemned him to solitary confinement in an unheated cell a long time ago. As it is, he spends most of his off-duty hours in a cell by himself.

'He is incorrigible. When I was assigned here three years ago Hu Sen told me that my predecessor had been transferred and demoted for having failed to discipline a notorious troublemaker called Wu Fuzhi. Short of having him shot or beaten to death Wu had undergone every conceivable punishment but he had always survived, Hu Sen told me. I don't know what to make of what Hu Sen told me next, it's quite a story and, if true, I have reason to be wary of Wu.

'It seems that my predecessor, a certain Captain Zhang, had become obsessed by his inability to break Wu and in an attempt to get at him indirectly he made Wu's only friend, a Fujianese by the name of Tan, stand outside the gate, in the snow at thirty below zero, dressed only in his underwear. Zhang told Wu that Tan would remain standing there unless and until he, Wu, would confess to counter-revolutionary activities and repent in front of all the convicts. At first Wu had fumed and raged, quite unlike his usual haughty and disdainfully mocking attitude, however, finally, he had agreed and Zhang had ordered the whole camp population to stand in the central grounds between the barracks to hear Wu's confession and self-criticism.

'Wu had hardly begun when a guard had come rushing up to Zhang and had whispered something in his ear. Zhang had dismissed the guard and had let Wu continue for another two hours before he had taunted Wu by telling the crowd that Tan had managed to free himself from the fence pole they had shackled him to and had disappeared into the night and the raging snowstorm. Zhang had then refused to organise a search party but had instead dared Wu to go outside by himself to search for his dear friend.

'Wu had gone after his friend, alone, and when he hadn't returned the next morning everybody was convinced he had lost his bearings in the pitch black frozen wasteland and that by then both he and Tan had died. Two days later, however, Wu had suddenly turned up at the gate, more dead than alive and terribly frostbitten, carrying the stiff, dead body of his friend Tan.

'The guard, a Uygur, had been so frightened by the sight of Wu and his burden that he had blurted out that but for Captain Zhang's refusal to let him go after Tan immediately Tan would still be alive. The guard had told Wu that Tan, before fleeing, had knocked on the guardhouse door to draw the guards' attention and when they had opened the door, he had shouted that he would rather die than have his friend Wu compromise his honour for him. What Tan had not counted on, however, was Captain Zhang's duplicity. Hu Sen told me that Zhang had looked on from the watchtower while Wu, all by himself, had hacked a grave for Tan in the frozen graveyard outside the camp's fence and had buried his friend. Afterwards Hu Sen had seen Wu climb up the watchtower and talk to Zhang, very briefly.

'Two months later Zhang was transferred and I arrived two weeks after his departure. At first Hu Sen told me only what I just repeated for you. Much later he told me that Zhang had been transferred to a uranium mining camp which I knew was unusual since those camps don't have political officers for the simple reason that the convicts in those camps are not supposed to survive, at least not in a condition that their political conviction matters a lot. Hu Sen acted secretively as if he were scared of Wu somehow and he advised me to leave Wu alone.

'All this makes me wonder about Wu. What is so special about him? Why is Hu Sen clearly afraid of him? How is it that a ranking Party official like Captain Zhang can be punished for the death of a simple, worthless convict like Tan? So many people die and in far worse circumstances and normally this earns the cadres responsible for those deaths praise, so why not in this case? Is there a connection between Wu and somebody high in the Party's top hierarchy? Is Wu really a prisoner or is he a spy or agent provocateur for the Party's top leaders? What actually do you *know* about Wu, Dao?'

With mounting surprise and, yes, apprehension I had listened to Lu's story.

Indeed, what did I know about Wu? Nothing actually. I had met him in Meishan's Detention House and though his manner of speaking to our fellow convicts had been unnecessarily provocative, I thought, I hadn't noticed any special wariness in the officials' attitude towards him.

Still, what Lu had told me was indeed intriguing.

I decided I would try to find out so I said, a bit lamely, 'I must admit I don't know Wu that well, Lu, however, if what you suspect is true that would be one more good reason to have him on our side so why don't you sign a permit tomorrow morning and let me visit the sickbay and I'll try to find out more about my friend the doctor?'

'I will do that,' Lu replied, 'I'm intrigued, I admit. I even suspect that Commandant Hu Sen has been warned about Wu long ago. He always manages to avoid direct contact with Wu, he even consults a Uygur shaman when he's sick, but he never misses an opportunity to try and set me up against Wu. I am sure Hu Sen provoked Captain Zhang to pick on Wu. Playing Chinese against Chinese and destroying one, or both, in the process, what malicious joy for the Uygur pig.'

Lu breathed deeply, then added, 'If Wu is indeed your man, Huimin, tell him about my change of heart, will you? He won't believe you at first, of course, he'll even think I'm an agent provocateur, but in time he'll realise I'm sincere.'

Driver Liu hadn't said a word during the whole trip to Tacheng but he had apparently got the gist of our discussion about Wu for he said, in a low voice and without a trace of his usual exuberance while he cut the engine in front of our guest house, 'Wu's a member of a secret society. I'm sure! When I was still a young boy I often heard the people in my district gossip mysteriously about the goings-on in Diaoyutai, the place where the Party élite can be found. Most of the people in my neighbourhood have some kind of a job there, as domestic servant, gardener, odd-job man, that sort of thing.

'When they visit their relatives they want to show off and they talk about the important things they witness, about the secrecy surrounding everything in Diaoyutai. How they have been warned sternly to stay away from certain villas. The servants of those villas don't mingle and they speak to nobody. Their masters can only be seen on summer evenings, from afar, as they stroll in their gardens. They never leave their grounds or even the Diaoyutai compound and nobody knows their names or what they look like.

'Still, our top leaders visit them in their villas, even Mao Zedong, Lin Biao, Zhou Enlai and others, and when they return to their own villas it's often already past midnight. Their servants, the ones who are from my neighbourhood, say that after such visits, the leaders look pensive or distraught, or even worried and that for days they are not their usual confident selves. Some of those servants were keen observers and I remember them mentioning that those visits by the leaders always took place when secretive persons from outside the compound had spent the night before in those sequestered villas. These secretive persons always arrived after dark and left before dawn, their heads covered by a dark hood.

'Now, I ask you, who might these persons be? Where did they come from and why did they seem to report to, and probably get their orders from, those equally secretive residents of the villas only our highest leaders may enter? Who else than secret society members are so secretive and so powerful that even China's highest rulers are afraid of them you will answer me, that is, if you know our history well.

'Now, I suspect that Wu Fuzhi is a member of that secret society. Probably not a very high-ranking one or else he wouldn't be in that camp, as a convict, but still a member and therefore the network of fellow members, their spies and agents, will know when he's in real trouble and word will reach the top and the really powerful ones will let it be known: hands off our brothers! Punish those who have gone too far! And that is what happened to your predecessor, Captain Zhang, lieutenant.

'Now, my advice to you, Huimin, is not to be too inquisitive. Don't let Wu guess your suspicions but let *him* assess *you* rather than you him. Greet him as a lost old friend, tell him your story and what you are going to do and then propose to him that you'll try to have him transferred to your new camp. If Wu really wants this and he is what I think he is it'll be a very small matter for him to have your request for his transfer approved. Tell him also about our friend Lieutenant Lu here. Wu'll have him checked out and if Lu is what you and I think he is, that is, a decent, honourable chap, he'll get his transfer as well and as sure as the sun will rise tomorrow. If Lu isn't what we think he is, well, then, perhaps it is as well that he stays with his friend Hu Sen.'

Liu burst out laughing at Lu's bewilderment.

'Not bad reasoning for a simple driver, eh? Comrade Lieutenant Lu?' he chuckled. 'Come, let's try Su Leima's food,' he added cheerfully as he got out of the jeep. 'I wonder whether Su Leima's houris will sing and dance for us.'

He was already banging on the front door when Lu and I caught up with him, Lu still muttering under his breath about sharing food with snakes disguised as asinine corporal drivers and convicts.

Liu and I grinned at each other but said nothing.

Suddenly the door swung open and Su Leima's wild, black eyes, which he vainly tried to focus in a withering stare, peered at us from the mass of unruly hair behind which he hid his weak face, as most bullies do.

A delicious smell of roast meat, onions, garlic and unknown spices wafted past him and we smiled broadly as we lumbered through the door, shoving Su aside and against the wall.

'Don't enter!' he shrieked as Liu pushed the curtain to the main room aside. 'My women are not covered! The food is not yet ready! You are too early!'

Frantically he tried to push past us from behind as we stared, in delighted awe, at three beautiful, bare-breasted women each clad only in a kind of thin, gauze-like sari that hung down from their hips and merely emphasised the curves underneath.

We held our breath in a timeless moment as the women turned their bodies towards us, mockingly inviting little smiles hovering about their lips, and arched their backs so that their breasts pointed straight at us.

Then, as if in slow motion, the eldest, probably the mother, made a languid gesture and suddenly all three turned and disappeared, as in a flash, behind a beautiful carpet that hung from the ceiling all the way to the floor.

The three of us stood there as if petrified, mouths open, eyes bulging, not exactly looking the world's greatest intellects.

Su Leima had finally managed to squeeze himself past us and he burst into the room then stopped suddenly, legs wide, snorting as he moved his lowered head to and fro, like a steer in a bullfight arena looking for its tormentor. Seeing nobody he turned towards us, eyes wild and crazy, spit dribbling through his beard, and shrieked, 'What did you see? Did you see my wife and daughters!'

'Calm down, man,' I said, as firmly as I could manage and speaking softly while I stepped in front of Liu to hide his drooling face. 'We saw nothing, nobody. That delicious smell of your food was just too much for us to think of anything else. We are not accustomed to such overwhelming fragrances, our Chinese food being so bland as you well know. Please forgive us if we behaved rudely and caused offence. It's just that the whole day we have longed for this moment, to taste your food which everybody we met today praised so highly.'

Still breathing heavily but calmed down considerably by my shameless flattery, Su looked at us hesitantly, still undecided whether to trust us or not.

Before he could question us further, however, a woman's voice called something from behind the hanging carpet which appeared to dispel his last, lingering doubts.

He grinned and, looking over his shoulder in the direction of the voice, a bit nervously, I thought, he said, 'That's my wife. She says she has finished the cooking for the infidel dogs, eh honourable guests I mean, and is now ready to serve the first course. So please sit down in the dining area.'

He led us to a white, rectangular kind of tablecloth that had been laid out on the floor and he gestured for us to sit down on the cushions piled on three, small carpets beside the cloth.

We sat down and awkwardly tried to find a comfortable position for our legs.

Su Leima watched our manoeuvring with a sardonic grin, taking his sweet revenge for our earlier affronts to his dignity.

The same woman's voice again called out from behind the carpet curtain and Su Leima, sitting cross-legged on the floor next to it, pulled on a tassel and one lower corner of the carpet was raised exactly halfway and to its middle.

Two small figures appeared in the triangular opening, each carrying a tray. Unmistakably and gracefully feminine in spite of the head-to-toe black robes that left only their huge eyes free, they flowed towards us.

'Roast pieces of suckling lamb in a cinnamon-flavoured shallot and honey sauce,' Su Leima announced from behind the Tanagra figurines who, in a graceful, flowing movement, bent down beside the free side of the cloth and placed the trays in the centre.

There was a moment of tangible tenseness as the girls sat back on their heels and watched us. From the corner of my eyes I saw Su Leima in the background, his white-knuckled fists gripping the tassel, squinting.

Everybody sat completely still and I felt that our first movement would be decisive for some reason or other. Then, suddenly, I remembered and slowly and ostentatiously I put my left hand behind my back and stretched my right arm to pick a morsel of meat from the plate. I let my right hand hover over the dishes for a few seconds, as if hesitating from which dish to take first, hoping that Lu and Liu would get the message.

My eyes met theirs and I nodded almost imperceptibly. My own sigh of relief mingled with that of the girls as I saw my friends stretch their right arm and take from the dishes. I looked up into the girls' liquid eyes that shone like dark, molten chocolate and winked. Their long, curving lashes fluttered and I knew they were smiling behind their veils, relieved that we had passed the test of civilised behaviour.

I heard Su Leima grunt, whether from relief or from disappointment I didn't know and cared even less, utterly happy and excited as I felt because of the sudden stirrings in my loins that told me that after all these years of preoccupation and abstinence I was still a man.

Su Leima didn't partake of the meal but merely pulled or let go of the tassel at the call of his still invisible wife and watched broodingly as his daughters brought in one dish after the other, each one more unusual and delicious than the previous one.

He briefly described each dish while the girls knelt and put it in front of us and neither he nor Lu noticed that with each new dish they knelt a bit closer to Liu and me. After the fourth course I distinctly felt the rounding and warmth of a buttock pressed against my left upper arm.

After the sixth dish I knew it was not a coincidence and when the girl bent a bit forward to remove the empty dishes I surreptitiously passed my left hand from behind under her chador and between her buttocks and I felt her warm, wet nakedness underneath.

For a second or two she stayed bent forward on her knees, immobile, holding her breath, then, with her inner muscles she squeezed the thumb I had thrust up inside her. I made a slight affirmative motion with thumb and middle finger which she acknowledged with another squeeze and a warm wetness flowed in the palm of my hand. I knew she would come and find me that night. Covertly I withdrew my hand and she leaned back on her heels and stood up in one flowing motion.

Opposite me something similar must have happened since I saw Liu glance at me, slightly embarrassedly as it was his right hand which he had had to use for his explorations.

I saw him hesitate then lick his fingers before picking up another morsel of food.

'Indescribably delicious,' he said, smiling and nodding in Su Leima's direction, 'and the best is yet to come, I'm sure.'

Su stared at him and asked querulously, 'What do you mean? You have eaten all the main dishes and there are only the sweets left.'

'That's what I mean,' Liu, that scoundrel, replied with a heavenly smile, 'your delicious sweets and the indelible memories of this unforgettable evening. We will be for ever in your debt, Mr Su for having been allowed a taste of the best you have to offer. You are deservedly blessed with such heavenly cooks as your wife and daughters.'

Su Leima beamed and said we were the first Chinese to so unreservedly appreciate and praise his people's food.

The girls brought the sweets and small cups of strong, black, cloyingly sweet coffee which none of us liked yet which we politely ate and drank. The girls took no further risk and demurely knelt a good distance away from us.

'Raffiah and Sheila are good daughters,' their father said proudly. 'They will be sixteen and eighteen this fall. Next year I'll send them to Qom, in Iran, to study the Koran.'

Taking this as a cue Lu stood up and thanked Su profusely for the wonderful meal adding that if he, Su Leima, needed any help to obtain an exit visa for the two girls he, Lu, would be honoured to oblige.

Liu and I also stood up and thanked Su Leima. Liu proposed to drive Lu quickly back to the camp and Su preceded both of them to the door. I heard him explain to Liu where he could find the key to let himself in as he, Su, had to accompany his wife to a Koran reading session and therefore wouldn't be there to open the door for him on his return.

I could imagine how much in a hurry Liu would be to get rid of Lu and come back for a generous second helping of Su's sweets.

Su almost caught me with that lewd grin of anticipation on my face as he swept the door curtain aside and came back into the room.

'You pay for the meal now,' he said abruptly. 'It's twenty-two yuan. I can't put it on the room bill as that would oblige me to pay half of the amount to this heathen community. The Prophet, peace be upon him, would never forgive me.'

He watched my reaction, suddenly worried, and added, 'We didn't discuss the price beforehand, Dao. I hope I'm not asking too much?'

I immediately reassured him that the meal would have been worth ten times the price to people with the money to pay but that for a poor soldier like myself it was perhaps a bit tough, perhaps ten yuan too high? Besides, my heathen commander, that uncultured, noodle-eating barbarian, would want to know how I was able to spend so much on one single meal at Su Leima's guest house and, sneaky bastard that he was, might enquire with Tacheng community whether the amount had indeed been declared and proper taxes on it paid.

Su scowled, then, suddenly, burst out laughing. 'You are right,' he hollered, 'I forgot that both of us have to account to those sourpusses! Fifteen yuan it is!'

I counted out fifteen notes of one yuan which he folded away, one by one, in a filthy, black, velvet purse while he told me that he would have to go out tonight to a friend's house where his wife and a few other women were rehearsing for a Koran reading contest which would take place that coming September in Druzhba just on the other side of the border.

These contests were held every year, he explained and lasted for ten days. Chinese Muslims were allowed to attend but were not allowed to stay overnight so it took a lot of travelling to and fro each day.

This year for the first time the contestants from China had been promised a ten-day stay permit and his wife, a superb reader, was going to represent the districts of Tacheng and Karamay. He was sure she was going to win as nobody could ululate as beautifully and mournfully as she could.

They would be back at around one o'clock and he would lock up his daughters in the women's quarters so I need not worry about their safety.

I assured him that I was much relieved to hear that and bade him goodnight.

I went to our dormitory and was still busy undressing when Liu came in.

'I saw Su and his wife in the main street walking in the direction I came from,' he said, chuckling.

'He locked his daughters in,' I said, 'lest we worry about their safety. I wonder whether they know how to get out.'

Hardly had I said that when the dormitory door opened slowly and two figures in black robes entered and closed the door softly behind them.

Time stood still as the four of us stood there, staring at each other. Then, as if on cue, the two figures pulled the black chadors over their head and dropped them on the floor.

There they stood, two beautiful, slender, curvaceous girls, their breasts with incredibly large and dark aureoles and long, stiff nipples pointing at us, their lower bellies one mass of curly, black hair so unlike the sparse and lank pubic growth as I remembered Liang had and probably all Chinese women have.

From somewhere came a moan, a growl almost. Perhaps I heard myself since the sound resonated in my ears and, as if in a dream, my eyes riveted on the smallest but hairiest of the two girls, I dropped my clothes on the floor.

I walked towards her, my arms outstretched yet barely longer than the hardest and longest erection I had ever had.

Without a word she took my hands and, walking backwards, her eyes riveted on my erection, she led me to my sleeping mat. Still holding my hands she laid down on her back, legs wide open, pulling me on top of her and straight into her gaping, slimy hot wetness.

The feeling was indescribable. Moaning, her tongue entwining mine in our open, slavering mouths, I sank deeper and deeper into her through quivering, pulling and tucking walls of warmth, into a second, pulsating orifice that squeezed around my near-bursting member and then I came, spurting as if in a whiplash, again and again and again.

I heard the girl shriek as her head fell backwards. In a blur I saw her open mouth, her rolling eyes and I felt her legs squeeze my waist as she pushed her sucking cunt up against my balls and then she, too, came in long, quivering gushes and everything inside her was in turmoil and became incredibly wide.

As if suspended in time and space we pushed and held on to each other, then, suddenly, in unison, we collapsed, completely spent.

I remained on top and inside her as she stretched her legs and nuzzled against my throat. How long we stayed like that I don't know but I came to when I felt the spasms inside her start again, barely perceptible at first but fast growing stronger, provoking my still half-erect member into its second ramrod stiffness.

Slowly she began to move under me, darting her tongue deep into my throat, her hands pushing on my buttocks as if she wanted to swallow me whole.

She came before me in long, gushing jets and the expression on her face made me cry out and I came again and again, her deep-throated gurgle in my ears. Twice more her body demanded satisfaction before it was saturated with my and her own essence. Drained of its last drop my member slipped out of her, small, shrivelled, sticky and numb.

Utterly but deliciously exhausted I rolled off her and turned on my back and for a while we remained like that, her head in the hollow of my left arm. Semi-consciously sounds from the other sleeping mat seeped into our groggy minds telling us that the others had either more energy or were one round behind us.

My girl giggled and then her breathing became faster as she rolled herself on top of me. Slowly, rhythmically, she squeezed me between her velvety thighs while the swollen lips of her cunt nudged and tucked my exhausted member back to life and into her. I felt the erection returning in full force inside her as she lifted her upper body up until my face was between those magnificent breasts. As I sucked the long, stiff nipples I felt the increasing turmoil inside her belly.

Suddenly she sat up straight, lifting both breasts up with her hands, head thrown backwards and moaning and gasping she gushed and gushed down my member while I spurted straight up into the deepest recesses of her womb. With every squirt I arched my back and lifted her up, pushing myself ever deeper into her and I heard her inhale sharply as she felt the hot streams filling her up.

Then, suddenly, I went crazy with possessive lust.

I pulled her down on me, rolled her over on her back while still deeply embedded in her and, my arms behind her knees, I lifted myself on my fists and looked down on all that curly hair, now slick and slimy from our emissions, from which protruded that wide, gaping, pink hole that suckingly held my throbbing member.

As if in a trance I pumped, pulled and thrust, pumped, pulled and thrust, further and further out with each pull, deeper and deeper inside her with each thrust. The sucking sounds drove me wild while she moaned louder and louder and rolled her head from side to side on her glossy mass of hair spread out on the mat. Then, buried balls and all inside her, we came together one last time, ululating like a pair of demented gibbons.

In a daze I pulled my hurting member out of her and, holding her legs up with my shoulders, I buried my whole face in her swollen labia and sucked and licked like a greedy piglet.

Somehow I must have tired and fallen asleep for I never noticed that she left.

We had never said a word, there had been no need, while we literally devoured each other in our mutual lust.

When I came to the next morning I found my clothes neatly folded at the foot end of my sleeping mat and, surprisingly, myself dressed in my underwear.

I felt lethargic yet deliciously empty as I dragged myself to the corner of the dormitory where Su Leima had put the bowls with hot and cold water after his early morning prayers.

Liu was there already, wiping his bleary-eyed face, like a groggy boxer, with a damp, hot cloth.

'Good grief, Dao,' he mumbled, 'I feel like I have been run over by a steamroller. I am all numb down below, it even hurts a bit, and my knees keep buckling. What have we done, Huimin? At times I heard you holler like you were being caned or something.'

'You should have heard yourself,' I replied huffily, 'honking and snorting like a whole herd of hungry hogs, driving my girl out of her mind so that I had to perform beyond even superhuman standards. I doubt very much that your Meimei can match these girls, Liu. She hasn't got that kind of fire in all that belly of hers, I'm sure.'

'Let's not talk about it any more, Dao,' Liu said hurriedly. 'Not to Lieutenant Lu and not between the two of us, even if we think we're alone. That way we won't hurt anybody inadvertently, not these Su girls, not Meimei or your wife if she's still alive that is, not ourselves. What do you think?'

I couldn't agree more and said so and we washed up and dressed as if in a slow-motion film.

We were about to leave the dormitory for our morning dumplings when Su entered, a worried frown on his face.

'You two look drowsy,' he said plaintively. 'I was afraid of that. Don't you notice the strong smell?'

We sniffed carefully, watching each other fearfully, afraid that he meant the smell of our sexual libations.

'Smells like incense, I would say,' I replied hesitantly.

'That's it!' he cried. 'Incense! My daughters burnt incense yesterday night after my wife and I had left. To protect their virtue, being alone with two male strangers under the same roof. During their fervent prayers Raffiah, the youngest, overturned the incense burner. Such a strong smell when my wife and I came home. We had to open all the windows but didn't dare to disturb you.

'Do not blame my girls, I beg you. They are very pious and naive and have been punished enough already, what with the terrible headache they had this morning. Your own drowsiness will pass once you have eaten your dumplings and drunk your tea. Maybe you need something stronger? Coffee perhaps?'

I hurriedly assured him that tea would be fine and that we wouldn't dream of blaming his daughters for what was only an insignificantly small accident.

Su Leima thanked us profusely as Liu and I stumbled to the large pot with dumplings that hung over the wood fire in the dining area.

While we fished the dumplings from the near-boiling water we heard Su, behind the carpet curtain, scold his daughters, in Chinese for our benefit, for having caused the honourable guests a heavy head and weak knees with their silly incense.

'Naive! My foot!' I heard Liu mumble to himself and suddenly I couldn't help but laugh until the tears ran down my cheeks.

'You hear how well the gentlemen take it?' Su cried behind the carpet. 'You should thank them and apologise for thinking them capable of outraging your modesty!'

'This is too much,' Liu whispered, 'let's get out of here, Dao.'

Quickly I put a dozen dumplings in my cap to eat during the drive to the camp and we were about to disappear behind the door curtain when suddenly a woman in a long black robe, without a veil, however, appeared out of nowhere.

Smiling mockingly she said, in a low voice, 'Don't you two scoundrels think that I am as naive as my husband, that gullible big mouth. He has no idea how women feel and I am still amazed that he managed to make me my two beautiful daughters. Used up all his powder with the youngest, I'm afraid. Be that as it may, Su Leima has an ulema meeting tonight, in the mosque.

'You two will be back here by seven at the latest. Tonight it'll be my turn and I'll make those two houris watch while I'll have both of you begging for mercy. Don't be late!' And pulling up her veil, leaving only her laughing eyes free, she turned in a swish and was gone.

'More dumplings, Dao, those few are not enough, man,' Liu growled and he rushed back to the pot and scooped a dozen or so in his own cap.

'We have to eat and rest as much as possible today, Dao,' he mumbled, his mouth full with dumplings, as he caught up with me outside.

'Get your business with Lu and that loony friend of yours out of the way as soon as possible. Tell Lu you haven't slept well, what with all that strange food in your belly, and that you would like to have a late lunch with him at Wong's place instead of dinner and retire to bed early tonight. That way we can have a long and plentiful lunch and a bit of an early dinner to get our strength back. At the same time I can work some more on Meimei and her father and we can still be back at the guest house around six o'clock. What do you think?'

'Fine with me,' I replied. 'Let's go now and not a word to our friend Lu about last night. Can't have him interfere or pass judgement, whatever is worse. Party prejudices about sex will be the hardest for him to shed, I'm afraid.'

'Half an hour with my parents' neighbours who have relatives working in Diaoyutai will cure you of that illusion,' Liu said and laughing loudly he drove off in a cloud of dust and smoke.

'It seems the great man is quite a libidinous character himself,' Liu added, grinning mischievously. 'It's a known fact that he likes to fool around with cute, little girls, the more the merrier, and not only at his home but also when he travels by that special train of his.'

'So, actually, there isn't much difference between him and all those emperors of old whom the Communists tell us to despise for their depraved lifestyles,' I said.

'You said it,' Liu agreed. 'All those in power, whether they lived two thousand years ago or lord over us today, whether rightist, leftist or centrist, they are *all* the same: greedy, corrupt, perverted, incompetent egomaniacs. On stage they are seemingly out for each other's blood but behind the scenes they wheel and deal and protect each other.

'A perpetual show of lower than low moral standards wherein the actors change with time but whose characters as well as the plot will always remain the same. And the audience, you and I and all the ordinary people, watches and pays. Incredible! Makes me sometimes want to hit my head against the wall out of sheer frustration but what's the use? People are stupid, Dao! Have always been and will always be.'

Angrily he accelerated as he turned into the camp's entry, then braked suddenly and stopped so close in front of the guard that the poor man jumped back in fright, dropping his gun as he raised his arms in a reflex parry.

'Oh ye fearless defender of the motherland!' Liu yelled at the frightened man, his head out of the window. 'We seek protection against the evil forces of seduction and depravity! Can you let us in, please!'

Lieutenant Lu had apparently been waiting for us in the guardhouse as I saw him stepping outside to open the gate for us himself.

I saw his grinning face as we drove past him to park the jeep beside the guardhouse.

'Evil forces of seduction, eh?' he sneered. 'Did you spend the night in fright with the covers pulled over your head, perhaps, while the evil forces outraged your manly modesty?'

He burst out laughing at our sheepish faces.

'The speed with which you drove me back to the camp last night, my friend,' he chuckled, slapping Liu on his back, 'all the while sniffing your right hand and humming, you don't think I'm that naive a fool, do you? Who were the first to call for a truce, you or the lovely, rompish girls? You probably. If you want to avoid Mama Su tonight make it a very late dinner at Wong's, otherwise seven or eight is about the time if you feel up to another attack on your male pride.'

He roared with laughter as Liu and I stared at him in stunned disbelief.

'The colonels and generals, while on inspection here, usually cancel their last day's visit to the camp since Su Leima's food didn't become them so well the previous night,' Lu said mockingly.

'Colonels and generals, however, usually travel with aides my age and rank who know better and who gossip, jealous as they are of the good time the old rascals have. This time, however, the girls and their mama are lucky to get two young bulls to romp with.

'What we young officers ask ourselves, however, is whether Su Leima is that naive and dumb that he doesn't know what's going on behind his back or that he simply doesn't care. Some of us think that the women put something in his food and drink that makes him impotent and glad to let them have the occasional fling as long as they keep up appearances. One thing is certain, they don't do it for money. So why? I have always wanted to find out so maybe now's the time?'

I couldn't help laughing out loud and I said, in good grace, 'You are right, Lu. We *did* have a good time last night. I had no idea, however, that this kind of after-dinner service is a regular feature at Su Leima's guest house. Mama has indeed summoned us to the performance tonight where *she* intends to play the leading role, or so she threatened. So, now you *know*, what are we going to do? Liu? What's *your* opinion?'

Liu laughed loudly and said, 'Let's try and pass the second test and become a full member of the Su Ladies Fan Club, like the colonels and generals. I see all kinds of advantages in having at least one thing in common with them, to discuss and compare. A true male comradeship, as it were. So I say, Dao, let's go for it!'

I turned to face Lieutenant Lu and raised my eyebrows in a silent question.

He nodded, more for himself than at us, and said, seriously, 'We have decided to be free persons, at least amongst the three of us, and to respect each other's opinions even if we don't agree personally. We must each live with the consequences of our own actions. Having said this, I am curious and would like to join you tonight, three men against three women, what do you think?'

'Splendid,' I said, 'I look forward to seeing you in action.

'Now, let me find out whether your medic Wu still wants to be my friend and join the club. Whatever the outcome Liu and I return to Karamay tomorrow. I'll leave a small note for Commandant Hu Sen to thank him for his hospitality. That way I don't need to go and see him personally and probably avoid some last-minute unpleasantness. I propose that we go to Wong's place for a late lunch that'll carry over into a very early sort of dinner and that we'll report for duty at Su's around half past six. Is that all right with you?'

Liu and Lu nodded their agreement and Lu gave me the signed permit to visit the camp's sickbay.

We agreed to meet at the guardhouse not later than twelve o'clock. Liu said he would be waiting in the jeep outside the gate as from eleven o'clock just in case we would have to leave in a hurry.

The guard on duty in front of the sickbay inspected my pass and at my question whether Doctor Wu was in he nodded and pointed at a single door at the right side of the barrack. 'Doctor's office,' he said curtly.

The door opened into a narrow corridor with another door at the end and one halfway, in the right wall that had also two windows.

The windows were clean; I could actually see through them into the room beyond.

A man sat behind a desk, his eyes closed, long slender fingers pressed against each other and supporting the head at the bridge of the nose as his elbows rested on the desktop. Apart from his hair, which had become a silvery grey, Wu had not changed. It was Wu Fuzhi all right.

Heart pounding I knocked on the door and I saw him open his eyes and lift his head before I heard his voice call out a clipped 'c'min!'

I opened the door, stepped inside and closed the door behind me. My knees shook and I leaned back against the door so as not to buckle.

'Yes, soldier?' Wu asked, looking sharply at me.

Then his eyes narrowed and he got up from his chair, slowly, hesitantly, as he watched me closely.

'Dao?' he said, hesitantly, 'Dao Huimin? From Meishan? Train number 4578 to Urumqi 1,284 days ago today?'

I nodded, speechless, as tears streamed down my cheeks.

Suddenly, as if in synchronised motion, we embraced and he hugged me so strongly that I exhaled in a whoosh. He laughed and released me, stepping back to look me over, from top to toe and back, his eyes brimming with tears.

'You found me, eh Dao? I knew it, every single day since we lost each other in that snowstorm I have told myself that you would find me, that we would see the end of this madness together, you and I. How happy Tan would have been had he lived to see this moment. Tan's dead, you know, Dao. My fault. Too stubborn, too much pride, too cocky I was to care about him, my only friend all these years in this hell-hole. I'll never forgive myself, Huimin! Never!'

He fell silent and I didn't answer. What could I say?

Then, suddenly, he laughed and pushed me into the chair opposite his desk.

'Sit down, sit down,' he urged me, in nervous anticipation. 'Tell me what happened to you! Why do you wear an army uniform? Don't tell me you have sold your soul to the devil! Wait! Before you begin your story I'll pour us each of mug of tea.'

He fussed with a samovar that stood on a shelf behind him and he poured two mugs of steaming hot tea.

He put one in front of me and sat down again, watching me through the curling, rising vapour, his thin fingers clasped around the hot mug. I noticed that the little finger of his left hand was missing.

'You haven't said a word yet, Huimin,' he said softly. 'Tell me what happened to you after that God-awful evening in Urumqi.'

'I am so very happy to see you again, Fuzhi,' I said. 'We won't lose contact again, I assure you.'

He nodded, clearly moved, as I continued.

'What happened to me after that night is a long, long story, Fuzhi. And so it is with you, I'm sure. In the weeks and months to come we'll see each other every day, that is, if you agree to my plan and provided we can pull it off, so there will be plenty of time to talk. I shall now tell you only the highlights so that you know how and why I got here and finally found you. Later, when we're together and with my two friends who'll become yours as well you must tell your story. I want to hear all about it. You remember what Tan asked us, Fuzhi? In that train? To make our story known so that the world would know what happened to us, what had been done to his wife. I haven't forgotten, Fuzhi.'

Wu nodded and whispered, 'Oh yes. I'll tell you, Huimin, you can count on that. But now tell me about you and your plan.'

So I told him, starting with the night I abandoned him and Tan in that blizzard, at Urumqi's railway station.

He interrupted me only once, to ask a few what I thought were rather probing questions about Colonel Kong, but apart from that he never said a word.

From time to time he stood up to refill our mugs from the samovar then sat down again while I continued talking.

When I finally finished one hour had passed.

Pensively Wu looked at his hands, cracking his long fingers one by one.

I waited for his reaction but when none came I said, awkwardly, 'What happened to your left hand, Fuzhi? I didn't notice before that you missed the little finger.'

'That will be part of my story, Huimin,' he said, 'that and a few other hidden physical and mental souvenirs inflicted by the proletariat's proud defenders. Hidden underneath my clothes and behind my vacuous smile,' he added, smiling mockingly yet mournfully.

'We, that is Shiwei and I, were not as lucky as you have been, Huimin. Don't misunderstand me, though. I am really very happy for you that you did so well for yourself but that fact will make it much more difficult for you to understand the misery and suffering we went through and the things we did, particularly the things I did. You haven't felt the terrible despair we felt, a despair so deep that there were times that we seriously discussed the possibility of helping each other to die as our final escape from the cruelty and madness around us.

'Nor did you ever feel the rage we felt at other times, a rage so hot and consuming that we swore we would do everything, literally *everything*, to survive and avenge all those poor innocent people we saw die a useless and totally undeserved death. When Shiwei died two years ago I envied him, Huimin. I envied him because he himself had chosen the moment of his death, to die for what was in his view a noble reason, that is to spare me, his friend, loss of face. He was a *true* friend, Huimin.'

He paused and stared ahead of him, into a cauldron of hatred and wrath he had been keeping at a boil since the death of his friend, as I was about to discover.

Remotely, more as if he were speaking to himself than to me, he continued, 'I buried him myself. As I looked down on his frozen, withered body in that shallow hole I swore vengeance, the most terrible vengeance possible, on all those who had made him suffer, including those in Fujian province who killed his wife. Since then I have had only that one purpose. The political officer who was directly responsible for his death is either dead already or is still dying a horrible, slow death. Perhaps one day I'll tell you how I arranged that, Huimin, now is not the moment yet.

'Other torturers who came to this infirmary for medical help, soldiers who had kicked him or hit him with their rifle butts, guards who drove him to mental and physical exhaustion, prisoners who told on him and caused him hurt, they all died of complications, of wrong medication, of sudden failure of their kidneys or liver, but always in great pain.

'Oh, I know what you think, Huimin. I see the horror in your eyes. Wu Fuzhi, medical doctor, killing his patients! Criminally insane, that's what the judges would probably say I am and then order my execution, but I don't give a damn. Maybe I can redeem myself a bit though by caring for the innocents beyond the call of normal duty.

'So I sit here and play god, Huimin. I decide who deserves to die and who deserves to live. And now you ask me to follow you to that new *laogai* of yours. I won't know anybody there so what about my oath to Shiwei? Or is it a sign that it has been enough and am I given a last chance to really redeem myself? Maybe I should go with you, Huimin, that is if you still want me after what I told you.'

He fell silent and looked at me, defiantly yet imploringly. The horror he had said earlier he had seen in my eyes was for real.

I had shivered with revulsion during his tale of hatred and revenge and in my imagination I pictured him as the sinister, mad physician bent over his patients' bodies as he subtly manipulated his scalpel or injected his poisonous concoctions causing them to die a horrible, painful death.

My friend Wu Fuzhi was a cold-blooded murderer, a serial killer, a psychopath. Doctors were supposed to cure the sick, not murder them, regardless of who or what they were, however much they deserved to die in terms of emotional human judgement.

True, Wu's victims had directly and with wanton cruelty caused the death, not only of Tan but of countless other innocent people, but could killing those mad fanatics or depraved sadists be justified? Could it be argued that their death saved perhaps hundreds of innocent lives?

What had I got myself into? What if I now rejected him? Would he go completely out of his mind and possible start killing indiscriminately? What if I accepted him? How safe would Lieutenant Lu be if Wu saw him as a representative of the evil forces that made him suffer and that killed his friend? How safe would I be myself if he saw my stroke of luck that night in Urumqi as a betrayal of him and his friend?

On the other hand he might come back to his senses and try to appease his troubled mind and work to redeem himself as he called it.

He must have read my mind as I sat there staring at him, trying to sort out my emotions, for he said, smiling sadly, 'I can imagine what you are thinking, Huimin. Has he gone mad? Will he kill my friends or myself for reasons only an insane mind can conceive? I am *not* mad, Huimin, but every lunatic says that about himself, of course, so you need proof. I can't give you that proof, Huimin. You have to make your own decision. All I can say now is that if you decide to go back on your proposal I will still consider you as my friend and your decision as my fate, as a confirmation that I'll never lead a normal life again.'

His quiet tone and the fact that he didn't aggressively or, worse, self-righteously try to convince me of the rightness of his acts, actually did convince me to stand by my proposal and I said, 'Whether you are mad or not is not for me to judge, Fuzhi. I guess that in some way or other we're all a bit crazy, some more so, and differently, than others.

'Whether you were justified in doing what you did is also not for me to judge. As you said yourself, I can't even begin to imagine what you and Tan Shiwei went through and what that did to you and how you tried to survive and to cope with your memories. You'll have to live with your memories, Fuzhi, and face whoever or whatever you believe you have to account to for what you did during your lifetime. For sure that is not I, but neither am I going to deny you the chance to redeem yourself if you think that that is what you should try to do.

'So I stand by my proposal that I'll try to get you transferred and that you yourself try, by whatever means available to you, to get my request approved. But one thing, Fuzhi, what you have told me remains between the two of us. Others simply would not understand.'

He got up from behind his desk and embraced me. For an instant I held myself rigid and didn't respond, unable to push the thought from my mind that he was a murderer after all. I felt his shoulders sag dejectedly and a wave of pity for this troubled man washed over me and I relaxed and hugged my friend Wu Fuzhi.

Nevertheless that peculiar awkwardness that makes everything one says or does seem artificial would take time to completely go away so I was not entirely unhappy when there was a knock on the door and Wu stepped back, cleared his throat and said, in his normal tone, 'Come in!'

The door opened and in came Lieutenant Lu.

'I saw through the window that you have clearly found each other,' he said cheerfully. 'That's good. I take it that Doctor Wu has agreed to try and get a transfer, Huimin? It's just my luck that I don't seem to be able to escape that troublemaker. I'm only joking, Wu,' he added hastily, seeing Wu's face fall, 'stop being so thin-skinned, man. I am no longer your enemy, if I ever was. I know you see me as a representative of the rotten system that brought you here and caused you so much hurt but please give me the benefit of the doubt.

'Your friend Dao Huimin here has opened my eyes, so to speak, and I am now trying to disentangle myself from the web that very same system has spun around *me*. However, the fly that I am has to go about it very gently so as not to make the web vibrate lest the spider pounce on me and suck me dry. Don't expect me to swipe the web away and kill the spider, Wu, I'm too insignificant for that. However, together with you, Dao and thousands of others like us all over China, I may be able to set in motion a movement that will lead to the collapse of the system. A fly batting its wings in Tacheng causing a hurricane in Beijing. Funny, isn't it? So, Doctor Wu, let's forget our prejudices and old grudges I say.'

Lu fell silent and, afraid that Wu would spoil the atmosphere and kill Lu's enthusiasm with one witheringly cynical remark, I said hastily, 'You're right, Qichen. I'm sure Fuzhi is glad to have a partner, a co-conspirator so to speak, in the coming weeks or months while we wait for your reassignments. You'll have the time to get to know each other better though I would advise you to be careful lest Hu Sen gets wind of our little conspiracy and spoils everything.'

To my relief I saw Wu smile and from his slightly mocking expression when he looked at me I knew that he had got my message.

'Well, well, Lieutenant Lu,' he said with a mocking yet friendly chuckle, 'who would have thought that you and I would ever be partners in the crime of sedition. It'll take some getting used to the idea, for both of us, I'm sure. However, if things are as they now seem to be we should be able to get along, now shouldn't we, Lieutenant Lu? Perhaps a hiccup now and then, a momentary lapse in our new thinking, but apart from that everything should be fine. What do you think?'

The innuendo hadn't been lost on Lu for he answered, smiling with a hint of mockery, 'Yes, I understand, just a hiccup from indigestion. I remember how my father had hiccups sometimes that lasted for days. They stopped just as suddenly as they had started. "No use to go and see a doctor," the old man used to say, "he'll probably kill me just to prove he can stop the bloody hiccup."'

Lu burst out laughing at Wu's quick glance in my direction and said, still grinning, 'No offence meant, doctor, and none taken, I hope.' Then turning to me he added, 'Don't forget our appointment with General Liu at eleven o'clock.' At that he saluted both of us, turned and left.

'Not exactly a pushover, your friend Lu Qichen,' Wu said, laughingly.

'Don't be angry with me, Huimin, if I have my reservations and don't kiss him immediately on both cheeks on your say so. For years the only way to show my loathing for the system was to revolt against its enforcers, political officers like that piece of filth Zhang, who drove Shiwei to his suicide. I didn't bother to make a difference between Zhang and his successor Lu. Why should I? To me they are all the same, rotten Communists for whom their bloody Party is their god, forcing their despicable creed down people's throats until they gag and choke to death.

'I never thought that there might be sceptics amongst them, the occasional man or woman whose innate decency and humaneness hasn't been bred out of them, should I say yet? I didn't want to complicate my life with too much thinking. I liked my straightforward, indiscriminate hatred. So perhaps I did your friend Lu injustice by sweeping him on one heap with all the others. I sincerely hope so since I fear that you have made no secret of your feelings about the Party in his presence. What if he tricked you, Huimin? What if he's a clever provocateur?'

I told Wu that I wasn't worried though it would do no harm to have Lu checked out if he, Wu, had the means to do that.

Then we said goodbye, promising to keep in touch through Lieutenant Lu.

Lu and Liu were waiting for me outside the gate, in the jeep.

I heard the engine start as soon as I came around the last barrack. I hurried through the small gate and was still climbing into the back seat when Liu drove off already.

'Why all the hurry?' I panted as I struggled to close the door.

'I'm afraid Hu Sen will requisition the jeep and Liu to drive him into town,' Lu answered. 'He mentioned he had some local matters to discuss with Su Leima before the ulema meeting tonight. Bullshit, of course. He wants to spy on you and Liu.'

Lu grinned and added, 'I siphoned the petrol from his jeep's tank and the key of the camp's petrol store is in my pocket so he won't be able to go to town today and tomorrow you'll be gone so who cares what he'll find out then from his brother in the faith.'

He laughed, a loud and carefree laugh, and exclaimed, 'Oh, I like this! It's exhilarating, like a game!'

Liu grinned and, addressing me over his left shoulder, said, 'Our political officer suffers the onset of a delayed adolescent syndrome, hence the childish prank. With time his wits will become more refined and rarefied as he'll get accustomed to the new-found freedom of thinking. The poor boy doesn't know what happens to him. True Communists have no sense of humour and don't laugh, at least not wholeheartedly and good-humorously since that liberates the mind, you see.'

Looking ahead again, he continued, mockingly, 'For them no joke, no levity, no self-mockery, no humour! Only deadly, leaden, self-righteous seriousness! Even their Party-approved joy is choreographed with deadly earnestness about deadly earnest matters such as the five thousandth tractor produced by tractor factory number twenty-seven or the 47,388th teapot produced twenty-one days ahead of schedule by the third teapot production brigade of Changsha's twenty-third light industry production unit. It bores me to tears and I'm sure millions with me. We Chinese used to be, and still basically are, I hope, a raucous lot who like a good laugh, even at our expense.

'However, the Party's constant admonishing and exhorting to be serious, to strive, to struggle, to excel, to surpass has made the true believers into completely neurotic and intolerant, humourless humanoids and the rest of our people into a lethargic, sullen lot who couldn't care less about their fellow creatures and the lighter, sunnier side of life. Only if you see this happen all around you and distance yourself from both the Party humanoids and the sullen, morose troglodytes, do you have a chance to survive with your sanity reasonably intact.'

He burst out laughing and, punching Lu in his ribs, he added joyously, 'So have your little jokes and laughs and smiles and grins and chuckles, my friend! It'll keep you sane!'

Glancing sideways at Lu and then over his shoulder at me, he continued, grinning mischievously, 'You should see your faces! As if you heard a monkey recite Lao Zi's wisecracks.

'My former and old teacher at middle school once said that the single most important saying that had shaped his life was that by a French philosopher of hundreds of years ago. "I think therefore I am" that wise man seems to have said and at the time I found that quite profound, still do as a matter of fact. From the Party's point of view those words must be the quintessence of sedition. *Imagine*! *People thinking for themselves*! I propose therefore that we make this very idea the basis of our own co-operation and mutual respect. Let's not make the same mistakes as the Party does and take each other for granted. Okay?'

Lu and I nodded, dumbfounded.

Liu was a remarkable person. He had surprised me before with his wit and wisdom and he would surprise me again, of that I was sure.

I knew that Lu was thinking along the same lines when I heard him say, 'I'm proud that you consider me worthy to be your friend, Liu. Nobody could have said it better and given me a better advice than you just did. Whatever happens there won't be a way back for me. I am afraid, however, that neither Wu Fuzhi nor his high-placed friends will understand the extent of the change that you and Huimin have caused in me. So how will they judge my suitability?'

'I'll take a few minutes this afternoon, at a separate table, and write him a letter,' I said. 'Tomorrow you can give it to him, Qichen. If both of you agree, I'll tell him what we think he is and why Liu's remembrances gave us that idea.

'I'll also tell him that we have nothing like a grand design to undermine the Party let alone to overthrow the existing social system but that we just want to lead a decent life of our own, preferably in the company of a few like-minded men or women, friends perhaps, and do some good if and when the opportunity presents itself. Neither he nor his backers, if any, should get the impression that we are fiery counter-revolutionaries. I at least am not made of that stuff and though I am all for a liberalisation of our society it must be through gradual change and not by violent means. I must have totally misjudged you two if that isn't also your position. Am I right?'

Both Lu and Liu said that they couldn't agree more and that I should make that clear in my letter to Wu to avoid any future misunderstanding.

By then we had arrived at Wong's restaurant.

I won't bore you with another detailed description of our late lunch and early dinner, or, for that matter, of our lascivious rompings later that evening with Mama Su Leima and her lovely daughters.

Wong's food and company were, as expected, excellent and entertaining and we took leave of him and his loveable daughter in the best of spirits and with repeated mutual promises to see each other again soon. This was certainly true for Liu since Wong invited him to stay over a night or two as soon as he had a few days off to discuss his intentions with Meimei and his prospects.

Su Leima had left for his ulema meeting when we arrived at the guest house and Mama Su and her lovely daughters were ready for us.

Mama was a true she-devil. Insatiable in her lust she subsequently tried out then discarded, like so many used rags, Liu and me but then found her match in, of all people, Lu Qichen.

Liu and I were content to spend what was left of our strength after Mama's demands on the same daughter as the previous evening and from my girl's little sighs and mumblings I gathered that the feelings of relief and contentment were mutual.

Lu's beastlike fornicating had apparently been too much for her and in between our own tender romps she watched with a mixture of unholy glee and apprehension the ongoing contest between Lu and her mother as both of them seemed hell-bent on compressing the whole of Empress Wu's libidinous life into one one-night stand.

The women left us at midnight. We were exhausted and Lu, more dead than alive, fell asleep without a thought about how to explain his presence in the dormitory to Su Leima in the morning.

I slept restlessly and was awake when Su brought in the tea at five o'clock the next morning. I told him that Wong's food had ill become Lu so that we had thought it better for him to stay the night with us rather than go back to the camp.

We would pay for him though, I added hastily, when I saw him scowl. He didn't say a word then nor when I paid the bill and signed off the register.

Relieved that we had got away without trouble we drove Lu back to the camp.

Groaning and still wobbly on his feet he got off at the gate and with a mumbled 'see you soon' he shuffled through the small gate, the brown paper parcel with his breakfast dumplings clasped against his chest.

'I'm afraid our friend the political officer-in-name-only Lu Qichen hasn't quite finished surprising us,' Liu mused next to me as we stared after Lu's totteringly retreating figure.

'I only hope that our free thinker to be doesn't go all balmy now that he has had a taste of the forbidden fruit. Such a promising young cadre. Shame on us, Dao!' And laughing uproariously Liu Timo gunned the jeep's engine and drove off, with shrieking tyres and in a cloud of dust, direction Karamay.

Major Peng was genuinely glad to see us back. Proudly he showed me the office-cum-sleeping and living quarters he had arranged for me during my absence, and I thanked him sincerely.

My first priority was to get official approval to form my own project team so I drafted an organisation scheme with myself as the project manager reporting directly to Major Peng, Fu Fusai as draughtsman-cum-clerk of works, Liu Timo as liaison officer, Wu Fuzhi as medical officer and Lu Qichen as overseeing political officer and responsible for all military aspects during the project.

When I submitted my proposal to Major Peng for his signature and forwarding through the appropriate channels he read it several times and then raised his eyes to look at me, quizzically, for quite some time before he said, 'You haven't lost time making friends, Dao. I hope that apart from sharing your views, whatever those may be, they are also capable of getting the job done. It's my neck too, Dao, if you fail.'

'I won't fail, sir,' I replied crisply. 'You get me those people and the tools and materials for which I'll give you the list next week and, besides, you allow Lieutenant Lu to recruit the workers amongst the convicts, the conscripts and the local population and I'll finish that pipeline for you in five years instead of seven years. You and Lieutenant Lu can take all the credit which will earn both of you a nice promotion and a better posting and me a reduction of my sentence, I hope. You will find Lieutenant Lu a capable officer and a true Chinese, Major. He deserves better than perpetual abuse by Commandant Hu Sen, an avowed Chinese hater.

'Wu Fuzhi is a good doctor, I think, and the advantage of him being a convict is that he'll be on permanent duty so to speak. Accidents will inevitably happen during a big project like this one with often round-the-clock work but we can't have people dying on us, certainly not conscripts or locals, for lack of medical care, now can we, sir? It wouldn't look good. So we need a doctor anyhow and Wu won't protest his transfer from Hu Sen's camp, that I know for sure. Not that it would make any difference if he did but we might as well have his wholehearted co-operation. As for Liu Timo, you know him even better than I do so you can easily see how valuable he will be to the project. Fu Fusai is just an acquaintance whom I know to be a suitable man.'

I fell silent and waited for Peng's reaction.

Smiling he said, 'You have a way with words, Dao, if you want something. It has indeed occurred to me that a successful project could enhance my prospects of promotion and transfer out of here. However, on the other hand, failure will undoubtedly mean the end of my hopes for either and both Lu and I will end our days here, probably with our throats slit by the likes of Hu Sen, if not by himself personally. Now, since our mutual friend and mentor General Kong says that you're the expert and, besides, can be trusted, there's no point in me questioning each and every one of your decisions or proposals, so here goes!' And with a flourish he signed my petition.

'I'll ask Liu to find me another driver to replace him,' Peng added. 'Once I'm satisfied with the new man Liu can work for you full-time. Besides, I'll assign a small truck to the project team. I think that'll be more useful than a jeep though Liu will see it as a demotion, I'm afraid, a jeep driver has higher status than a truck driver.' He laughed and added, 'That'll be my sweet revenge for all those times he grinned at me when I came back from manoeuvres cold, tired and hungry while he had his lazy arse glued to the jeep and drank my warm tea and ate my rations. The bastard!'

A week later Major Peng signed, without so much as perusing the lists, my requisition for tools and materials and a separate one for skilled and unskilled labour.

After that I had nothing more to do than to wait for the official approval from Beijing. To kill the time I asked Peng to assign a dozen soldiers to me to make and set out pickets around the perimeter of the new camp and to mark the location of the individual barracks.

That finished we cleared and marked the first ten kilometres of the pipeline trajectory starting from the point where the work had been abandoned four years earlier when work all over China had stopped, at the onset of the Cultural Revolution.

This kept us busy for two weeks and then, one morning, Major Peng came to see me in the field with the news that not only had all my requests and requisitions been approved but that the first convoy of trucks with tools and materials for the new camp was on its way to Karamay, a sure sign of the importance the authorities attached to the project.

Besides, Peng told me, he had been given the authority to requisition locally whatever was needed at short notice.

That same day Peng left for Tacheng to personally present the transfer papers of Lieutenant Lu Qichen and Doctor Wu Fuzhi to Commandant Hu Sen and to be there, and hopefully prevent a row, when Hu Sen would have to announce the transfers to Lu and Wu. Peng would insist on their immediate departure and would bring them back with him, he said.

On his way back he would drop in at the municipality to announce Fu Fusai's reassignment to the mayor and the Party secretary and to give Fu some money for his relocation and transport of himself and his belongings. As an ordinary citizen Fu wasn't entitled to a ride in Major Peng's jeep.

It was a fortunate thing that Peng had mentioned his intention to personally go and see Fu. Imagine, he would have told Fu about his reassignment within earshot of Fu's lover and she would have made a scene in front of the major. What a loss of face!

So I told Peng about Fu's dilemma and why I had promised him a job.

Peng shook his head in disgust and said, 'The things you manage to get yourself embroiled in, Dao Huimin. I can't believe it! Why do you do it, man? If an affair like that backfires you'll be the fall guy blamed by everybody, including Fu himself. You're a fool, Dao! That idiot Fu shits on his own doorstep and you clean it up for him. If that woman turns up here one day don't count on me to get you out of her claws, Dao. What a goddam circus!' And still shaking his head the good major went off to Tacheng.

Two days later his jeep stopped in front of my office and the major jumped out, followed by Lu and Wu.

Liu and I rushed outside to greet them and I noticed Major Peng's surprised look at our mirth.

Lu got his own room and Wu would shack up with me, as would Fu Fusai, who would arrive the next day by bus, Peng told me.

Right from the first day we got along fine with each other, in a relaxed, informal and comradely way.

Fu fitted in well and turned out to be an excellent choice for our team. He was a good draughtsman and had no qualms about helping with whatever odd job needed to be done.

Lu took charge of any military personnel assigned to us and Liu, who had been promoted to the rank of sergeant by Major Peng, acted as Lu's assistant. I made the work planning and Lu and Liu had it carried out. They also had no qualms to actually put their own shoulders to the wheel which earned them the respect of the ordinary soldiers.

We had agreed amongst ourselves that this was the best way to avoid awkward situations which could arise if the soldiers objected to receiving orders from me, or from Wu for that matter, civilians and, worse, convicts as both of us were. As long as there was no sickbay and no patients yet, Wu acted as my assistant.

Like me he wore simple fatigues without the red star or rank insignia.

The soldiers didn't notice or, if they did, didn't let it appear. Perhaps they thought that we were zealous Communist officers who had voluntarily given up their ranks so as to be equal to the ordinary rank and file or, what was most probable, they simply didn't care one way or another.

We took full advantage of the long summer days and often worked up to fifteen hours a day. That rigorous working schedule and the regular, uninterrupted supply of the building materials meant that we finished the new camp within three months.

It had become quite a large camp. Six large barracks, surrounded by a four-metre high fence of barbed wire, for the approximately three thousand convict labour force; three equally large barracks, without fencing though, for the non-convict skilled labour, the contingent of soldiers on rotating guard duty and the truck drivers; four smaller barracks, also unfenced, to serve respectively as kitchen and canteen, as sickbay, as warehouse and as the boiler house.

Furthermore there was a small guardhouse near the main gate, and a truck and local repair shop next to the parking lot for the eighty trucks I had requisitioned for the transport of the labourers between the camp and the work site. Within two years or so the distance would become too great and we would have to relocate the camp.

With that prospect in mind I had given the barracks only the lightest possible foundations, just the footings for the roof support columns, and had chosen a light, all-bolted steel construction for the roof.

The walls were all made of rough wooden planks and the roofing of corrugated galvanised steel sheets which the army supply unit had apparently recovered from former military ammunition warehouses, judging from the code numbers in white paint.

I was well aware that the whole set-up was unsuitable for the severe winters in that region but instead of insulating the roof and walls just enough to maintain a bearable temperature inside I had argued with Major Peng and Wu that it would be faster, easier and cheaper to give the convicts suitable clothes and a spare set they could eventually sleep in together with an extra blanket. An added advantage would be that the successive relocations of the camp to follow the pipeline's progress would also be less time-consuming.

When Wu called me an inhuman bastard Major Peng was convinced that I was right and he, in turn, managed to make the authorities see things my way.

My requisition for convict labour had specified six arrivals in contingents of five hundred each every two weeks, the time needed to erect one large barrack and install the stacked beds and long trestle-tables and banks. That way the workers could immediately be put to work on the assembly and erection of the other barracks.

I had explained to Major Peng and the project team the reason why I was in such a hurry. I told them I wanted to start work on the pipeline well before the onset of the winter since I expected it would take us at least a month to iron out the foul-ups and misunderstandings that always happen at the beginning of a big project.

I had also a secret reason though which I didn't tell them. The first day of October was Liberation Day and I thought it would be excellent propaganda if Major Peng and Lieutenant Lu could officially open the camp and lay the first length of pipe on that date in the presence of local authorities, photographers and reporters of the *People's Daily* and, as a major stunt, General Kong.

Liu had secretly mailed a letter from me to General Kong in which I praised Peng and Lu for their co-operation and dedication to the project and proposed an official opening ceremony on 1st October, 1970.

I wouldn't say anything to Peng and Lu before I got his reply. If Kong declined to come or otherwise rejected the whole idea as so much flimflam it would be a terrible loss of face for them if they had known about and tacitly approved my plan. So I kept quiet.

I hadn't misjudged Kong though for in early September Peng stormed into my office waving an official letter under my nose.

'General Kong will visit the project on Liberation Day!' he stammered. And he requests me and Lu to officially open the new camp and lay the first pipesection in his presence. There will be photographers, the General says, and the pictures will be published in the *PLA* newspaper and in the *People's Daily* and on the billboards in all the big cities to show the people how the *PLA* works for them.'

The good major took a deep breath then added, 'There's a short, separate note in his own writing for you, Huimin. He sends you his best personal regards and says he hopes you can be ready on that auspicious date. Can you, Huimin? Can you!'

I said we could.

What a sly fox Kong was, I thought, and my chuckle made Peng stop in his stride to look at me with narrowed eyes, suspiciously, quizzically.

I grinned at him, like a Cheshire cat.

Early September I diverted half the convict labour force to the pipeline project proper and they began digging the trench from the point where the project had been abandoned four years ago when the tsunami caused by the upheavals in central and eastern China finally reached this Westernmost outpost.

A week before 1st October I began with the training of the crane drivers and their crew of helpers.

Each crew consisted of eight sturdy men who first had to roll a six-metre length of pipe with a diameter of one metre on to two wooden beams, then put a double sling around the pipe so that the crane driver could lift it up, swing it above the trench and then lower it into the trench, guided by the same crew. Down in the trench two welders and their helpers would fit the pipe section into two concrete cradles and align it exactly with the previous section.

Finally I would go down into the trench to check the alignment and give the go-ahead for the welders to make the initial tack welds to keep the pipe in place once the slings were removed.

Two first-class welders would then begin with the definite welding, one outside and one inside the pipe.

I wanted this operation to go like clockwork and after a few days' rehearsing with the same pipe length the men got the knack of it and by the end of September I had the whole exercise down to twelve minutes, including the tack welding.

Fu hadn't budged from my side during the exercises since I wanted him to do the final checking of the pipe alignment, not only before the eyes of the cameras, reporters and General Kong, but also as part of his task in general.

For the trench-digging crews I had tried a staggered working schedule of two hours' hard work followed by two hours' rest rather than have everybody work at the same time and the results were rather spectacular: during the week of pipe-laying exercises the trench, including the preliminary installation of the pipe cradles, had advanced by three hundred metres.

During Kong's visit we could therefore keep up a round-the-clock pipe-laying operation, to impress him and his following.

The day before the general's arrival I asked Peng, Liu and Lu to come to the site to see for themselves one final rehearsal and to be briefed on their own role in the play-acting. I told them where to stand, how to look, what gestures to make, all the while frequently consulting Mao's Little Red Book, to make it look as if the three of them were directing the operation guided by the Thoughts of the Great Leader.

They protested when I insisted we rehearse the final play-acting clamouring that they would look like fools but I convinced them it was for all our and Kong's good so they gave in.

Liu led the men who rolled the pipe sections on to the two beams and put the slings in place, his Little Red Book well in evidence.

Lu sat next to the crane driver, gesticulating with the Little Red Book to guide the pipe above the trench while Peng, on the edge of the trench, and Fu, down in the trench, delightedly nodded at each other, tapping the opened little book with their forefinger, as the pipe was slowly and carefully moved into position.

All three would finally stand on the edge of the trench, looking down excitedly as the sparks of the welders flew and lit up the scene below.

If the photographers were any good the pictures would come out spectacularly.

General Kong arrived in Karamay with a convoy of army vehicles on 29th September.

In the afternoon he came, only accompanied by Major Peng, to our camp in Tachakou.

Our reunion was more than cordial and I gained a lot of face when the general embraced me in front of everybody. He insisted I show him around the camp alone and doing the hour-long tour I gave him we chatted, joked and laughed like of old.

What struck me though was that he made it a point, casually like, to see the infirmary and that when he shook hands with Wu, their handshake was not as perfunctory as one would expect between such a high-ranking official and a non-person like convict Doctor Wu Fuzhi.

Perhaps it was just my imagination but I thought I saw Wu's forefinger tap the back of Kong's hand but then, as I said, I probably saw things that weren't there. Nothing is ever as it seems in this strange, convoluted world of ours.

Kong had a good laugh when I told him about the show I had planned for the next day. He promised to co-operate by insinuating himself in the background each time the photographers took a picture of Peng, Liu and Lu in action.

'You really try to push your friends eh, Huimin?' he said, smiling. 'You may live to regret it man. They may be promoted and transferred long before you have finished the project and you'll find yourself saddled with successors who may be a lot less sympathetic.'

I shrugged and replied, 'They are my friends, that's right and I am proud of that, but first and foremost they are good, capable men and therefore should be given the right position, wherever, whenever. That's more important I think than my own self-interest.'

Kong watched me, his eyes narrowing. Then he suddenly seemed to make up his mind for he said, in a level, no-nonsense tone, 'If I get the tenor of what you say correctly, Huimin, what you imply is that one cannot overestimate the usefulness of the right people in the right positions at the right time. Is my interpretation correct or is my imagination playing tricks on me?'

'No tricks,' I replied, 'that is indeed my opinion.'

'Is there anything in particular I should know?' he asked casually.

I hesitated a fraction of a second but then I decided to plunge ahead and said, 'There is Sergeant Liu Timo. He's from a neighbourhood near Diaoyutai and he knows many people who are employed there as servants, gardeners, maintenance people and the like. Liu told me interesting stories which show a deep insight on his part.

'He would like to be posted near his relatives and bring with him his future wife and her father who at present run a famous restaurant in Tacheng. Wong's his name and his daughter is called Meimei. Perhaps one day they need a good, new cook in Diaoyutai's guest house for visiting high officials or a new head of the guards or both. You may wish to earn the top leaders' gratitude by providing them with such an excellent cook as Wong is, or with a dedicated hard-working kitchen maid as Meimei would be, or with a discreet guard like Liu Timo. On the other hand, Wong, Meimei and Liu would owe you, of course.'

'Of course,' Kong replied in a neutral tone, 'yes, I see, that *would* be interesting, now wouldn't it?'

And, laughing, he added, 'Why don't you tell your friend the sergeant to ask his future father-in-law and Meimei to cook for, say, twelve people on Liberation Day? That is, for you and your project team, including our Doctor Wu, Major Peng, myself and a few officers of my staff? I can't recommend a cook to our country's top leaders if I haven't tasted his food personally first, now can I, Huimin?

'If the sergeant leaves now he can be in Tacheng before midnight, spend the night with his Meimei and drive back tomorrow morning. Perhaps Wong could bring some good, fresh ingredients? I'll pay handsomely and Liu would have a lot of face with Wong and Meimei. What do you think, Huimin?'

I grinned and said it was a wonderful idea and that I would go and see Liu straight away.

Liu slapped my back enthusiastically when I told him about the general's suggestion. I also told him what I had suggested to the general and he thanked me profusely.

I adjured him not to speak to anyone about it though and he, in turn, adjured me not to worry.

Kong and Peng spent almost the entire next day with me discussing my material requirements for 1971 and thereafter, a kind of mini five-year plan that I had prepared for Kong to take with him to Beijing for presentation to the minister involved in the project.

I had used the Western Bill of Materials format and both men praised the comprehensive clarity of my presentation.

I had not gone to the trouble of preparing a budget though, firstly because I hadn't the faintest idea what the cost of things were in China and secondly because the whole idea of budgeting is an alien concept in a Communist society where the state allocates goods and services without the slightest regard for cost-efficiency.

In an attempt to impress Kong and his superiors, however, I had prepared a budget format, without the figures of course. I can still see the smile on Kong's face when he said, after I had explained the purpose of budgeting, 'I'll keep this form for my own instruction and, who knows, for the consideration of the higher authorities in the future, the far future, I'm afraid. For now, however, I won't even show it to the comrade ministers.

'Just imagine some clever little man for reasons of his own putting a price on this project of ours here! The minister might well get a heart attack or cancel the whole project or both. Now, that wouldn't be in our interest, would it? Nor in that of the few thousand poor devils who may now weather the storm here in this little haven of relative comfort and security. We wouldn't want that to happen, now would we? After all the wonderful plans we have worked so hard on?'

Shamefully I had to admit that he was right, of course. Kong laughed at my crestfallen expression and said, chucklingly, 'Don't volunteer information, don't wake up sleeping dogs, don't try to be too clever, all very wise expressions, Huimin. Not observing them brought you to China and in trouble in the first place but you still don't seem to have learned your lesson, my friend,' and playfully he slapped me on my shoulder.

I was angry at myself. That damned Western urge to show off how clever I was. Would I never learn? After all the misery it had brought me?

Liu returned that evening, with a beaming Wong and a self-conscious, timidly smiling Meimei, who, for the occasion, had put on a clean blouse.

With a secretive air and a lot of whispering they unloaded a lot of goodies at the back of the kitchen.

It would be some dinner, I guessed.

Wong and Meimei would spend two nights in Wu's infirmary. Since there were no bedridden patients as yet the twelve beds were empty anyhow.

The Liberation Day show and celebrations went perfectly and as planned.

Everybody, prisoners, non-convict labourers, soldiers and high-ranking visitors were lined up and stood at attention at six o'clock in the morning for the flag-raising ceremony and to the tune of 'The East is Red' from the blaring loudspeakers at the four corners of the parade ground.

Next General Kong gave a short speech which was not foreseen in the programme.

He told the crowd that the project was a very important one and that our Great Leader Chairman Mao had personally accorded it the highest priority.

He further said that Major Peng and lieutenant Lu were deeply committed to finish the project well within the seven years set by the Party and that the convict labour force would receive special commendation for its wholehearted and enthusiastic co-operation and its services to the motherland.

He finally exhorted everybody to give his full support to the project team under the expert leadership of engineer Dao.

When his booming voice, amplified by the loudspeakers, fell silent, Major Peng led the whole assembly in a resounding thrice repeated 'hip, hip hooray!' his right arm shooting up in tune, Little Red Book in his hand, above a sea of rising and descending arms, before he ordered the day shift to board the waiting lined-up trucks.

Peng, Lu, Liu and I rode ahead of the convoy of forty trucks with each forty convicts and five trucks with welders, crane drivers and soldiers to the site.

General Kong would follow one hour later with his retinue of staff officers, reporters and photographers. Everything went according to plan and a lot of pictures were taken.

After the picture-taking the reporters asked Peng and Lu the usual inane questions which they answered graciously and with the required starry eyes when making the obligatory interjections about the Great Leader's infinite wisdom guiding their every action, the Party's love for the common people, the PLA's undying sacrificial love for the common people and the other hypocritical drivel the Communists are so fond of.

Some of the things they said were so ludicrous that I had to bite my lower lip so as not to burst out laughing. I suddenly realised that actually I was a much freer man than my friends since nobody expected me to say such twaddle.

I caught Kong watching me and we grinned at each other.

Dinner that evening was a memorable affair.

Liu had closed off one corner of the canteen, next to the kitchen, with a temporary partitioning of plywood boards and together with a couple of carpenters he had managed to fabricate a round table top, also of plywood, big enough for twelve people to sit around.

Wong had brought the tablecloth, a bit torn here and there but freshly laundered and ironed, and the dining set. The food prepared by Wong, with the help of our own cooks, was delicious and surprisingly varied, given the circumstances.

During the dinner Wong hovered in the space between our table and the kitchen supervising both his assistants in the kitchen and Meimei who served at the table.

I had forewarned Kong and Peng about Meimei's oversized breasts and her father's oversensitiveness and had asked them to brief the other guests and tell them not to stare or snigger or make lewd remarks or tease Liu within earshot of Wong or the girl.

Still, when I led Kong and his five staff members to their seats they suddenly stood as if transfixed at the sight of Meimei standing beside the table, a white apron tied around her big belly, a white cap on her blushing round head, her huge, magnificent, watermelon-like breasts stretching the material of her blouse to near tearing point.

Kong immediately took the initiative, and undoubtedly saved the evening, as he enthused about the stunning table setting and the delectable smells emanating from the kitchen, all the while gesticulating for his men to take their seats.

It was an extraordinary situation. Two convicts, Wu and I, one ordinary citizen, Fu Fusai, one sergeant, Liu Timo, one lieutenant, Lu Qichen, one captain, three majors, one colonel and one major general together enjoying an excellent dinner in an atmosphere of unceremonious mirth and comradeship.

I haven't done military service myself so I can't speak from own experience but I have been told that such is only possible amongst true soldiers and that the morning after the binge everybody is again his normal disciplined and respectful self. None of the presumptuous familiarity civilians of lower rank are given to after a night out with their bosses.

It was past eleven o'clock when General Kong stood up and in a short speech thanked the project team for a wonderful reception and a job well done so far. He thanked Wong and Meimei for the excellent dinner and finally invited everybody to join him in a toast to the project, to each other's future and to China *tout court*, not the People's Republic of China, no, just Zhongguo.

We raised our glasses of *maotai*, shouted '*Ganbei*!' poured the fiery stuff down our throat and thundered, in unison, '*Zhongguo*!'

Then, all of a sudden, everybody was saying goodbye to everybody else, laughing, shaking hands and slapping shoulders. From the corner of my eyes I saw Kong give an envelope to Wong and a smaller one to Meimei who both thanked him profusely.

Kong was the last to walk to his jeep and he gestured for me to follow him out of earshot.

He took both my hands in his and told me I had done well and not to despair; everything would be all right in the end, he said. He would be back for another visit the following spring and would try to make it twice a year.

He released my hands, got in his jeep, gave a short order to his driver and with a last smile at me and a military salute for the others who had walked ahead to salute him as he rode through the gate, my friend was gone.

The next morning Liu drove Wong and Meimei back to Tacheng. From their way with each other it was clear that things had gone well for Liu and that it was now just a matter of practicalities between him and Wong.

We quickly settled into a routine.

Wu's proposals for a division of labour in field and camp duty had been accepted by Peng and myself.

There would be two categories of work in each instance, normal and light, and it was agreed that Wu would have sole responsibility in determining who would be fit or unfit for normal duty.

Normal duty in the field meant eleven hours of physically demanding work and two half-hour rest periods per day six days per week and light duty meant nine hours of odd jobs and three one-hour rest periods per day and that also six days per week.

Normal camp duty consisted of cleaning latrines, laundry service, kitchen work, tending the vegetable garden, repair jobs and the like, for ten hours per day and six days per week. For light camp duty there was no particular work schedule since, in principle, that was only for slightly injured or convalescent people who would be assigned on Wu's orders only. Nobody, not even Lu and Peng, gave a thought to political indoctrination and re-education meetings when we discussed the different time rosters.

It wasn't until six months later, early May 1971 to be exact, that we realised how terribly we had been lacking in our political ardour and only because General Kong, when he advised us of his forthcoming visit to the region and to our project, mentioned in his letter that he would be accompanied by the Party's head of propaganda, Hua Guofeng.

I immediately ordered an assembly of the whole camp population, convicts and non-convicts alike, in the parade grounds, for six o'clock the morning after the reception of Kong's announcement.

I didn't beat about the bush. Counting on the atmosphere of reasonableness, even goodwill, that our project team had managed to establish during the past half year I told the hushed crowd that General Kong would again visit our camp and the fieldworks, however, this time in the company of Comrade Hua Guofeng and that unless everybody co-operated fully with Lieutenant Lu during the two remaining weeks before the high-level visit, not only he but the whole project team and, as a consequence, the whole camp, would be in very serious trouble due to *everybody's* lack of political awareness.

I then handed the microphone to Lu who told the assembly that until the forthcoming visit the number of working hours would be reduced from twelve to nine per day and that there would be political meetings every evening, for two hours, to be attended by the barrack leaders and their deputies together with a group of fifty men from each barrack, a different group every two days, since he estimated that four hours would be enough to bring everybody up to date with the prevailing slogans and the most recent speeches by the country's top leaders.

He would therefore have to conduct six meetings, each consisting of two sessions of two hours, to reach everybody in the camp.

He urged everybody, after completion of his two sessions, to learn the slogans and the names of the top leaders, as well as the significant parts of their speeches, by heart as Comrade Hua Guofeng was well known for his informal walkabouts amongst the people in factories, communes and labour camps during which he chit-chatted and asked seemingly innocuous questions to test their political awareness and correctness.

It would be in everybody's interest, Lu emphasised, that Comrade Hua, after his return to Beijing, would report to our Great Leader Chairman Mao that not only was camp number 272 in Tachakou doing a splendid construction job but, what's more, that the job was done in the correct political spirit.

At the end of his address Lu took a big and unnecessary gamble when he announced that, in spite of the importance of the matter, there would be *no coercion* to participate in the meetings and invited those who did not want to take part to raise their right arm.

I noticed no furtive glances around to see what others were doing, no uneasy shuffling of the feet. Everybody kept looking straight at Lu behind his pulpit and nobody raised his arm.

Everything went well and at the end of the visit Hua Guofeng complimented Lu for the excellent political discipline in the camp.

Apart from this little episode life went on in a monotonous repetitive sequence of six days working followed by one day of rest.

Lu, Liu, Wu and I had agreed to have our day off on the same day during which Fu Fusai did a bit of supervising for each of us both on the site and in the camp.

Since we didn't leave the camp we were there for the calling anyway.

For sentimental reasons I had proposed Sunday as our day off and the others had no objection.

The four of us made it our habit to have our meals together on Sundays and to spend also the remainder of the day in each other's company, discussing, playing go or chess or even bridge. Our initial mutual liking developed into a solid, quiet yet unassuming friendship and we felt comfortable in each other's company.

Sometimes our discussions were quite vehement though and laced with some personal bitterness or grievance about one subject or another. On the whole, however, we were thoughtful and mindful of each other's particular sensitivities.

As always in such situations and I don't know why, each of us, at some time or other, felt he needed to bare his soul and tell his life story.

I have noticed that people, at a certain stage in their relationship to others, always do that. As if they feel that at a certain point in a budding friendship or love further intimacy requires a baring of the soul for the friend's, or lover's, inspection and approval. The more insecure ones are always the most eager in their often pitiful efforts to gain acceptance and it came therefore as no surprise, to me at least, when Lu was the first to volunteer, without our asking or bidding, to tell his story.

To his credit I must say that he was brief and apologetic as he must have realised how bland and unrealistic his life had been, a life so typical of a Communist youth virtually raised by the Party as both his parents had been and still were full-time cadres.

A couple of weeks later it was Liu who thought his time had come.

He told his story with his usual blend of humour and meditative evaluation of his own and other people's motives yet he couldn't disguise, and made no effort to either, I must say, the commonness and dullness of the average man's life in Communist China.

He seemed relieved, however, to have told us and not have fallen in our esteem so we left it at that.

Both Wu and I were more reluctant so the summer and fall of 1971 passed without our contributions.

It was more or less by accident, or chance if you wish, that, after a lively discussion one cold, snowy Sunday during our second winter together, I told the others the story of my life much as I am telling it to you now.

The subject of our discussion had been life outside China, on which I was supposedly the expert, and as I said, in the heat of my arguments in favour of the freedom of choice there, I drifted into comparisons and before I knew it I was well launched into my own experiences abroad and in China.

My friends, and notably Lu, were very upset by the way I had been deceived and betrayed by the Party. If he still needed convincing that communism, in which he had so sincerely believed, was in fact a system rotten to the core and built on lies, duplicity, betrayal and oppression of the very people it pretends to stand for, my story achieved that and more.

Nothing less than the total collapse of the system, as a result of popular revolt led by him and those like-minded, and the punishment of the system's perpetrators, by firing squad preferably, would satisfy him and the people, he exclaimed.

He became impatient, even angry, with me, accusing me of being a dissipated old man, when I tut-tutted at his hotheadedness and reasoned that we shouldn't perhaps hope or work for something so radical as a total collapse but rather for a gradual opening up and liberalisation of the system in China.

China simply didn't have the people with the authority and above all, the knowledge and experience to lead and guide such a huge country like China, from one day to the next into the big alien world of freedom and strange, often ruthless competition.

Nine hundred million hermits, spoken for by a handful of paranoid uneducated farmers, none of them with the faintest idea about life outside, was all China had I taunted him.

Yet, nothing short of a total, bloody counter-revolution would do for Lu Qichen.

I wonder where he is now and what his ideas are now. Has he become more moderate? Has he toned down? Has he learned that in China everything takes time, time and more time and that nothing is ever simple or straightforward? That the simpler things seem the more deceptive they in fact are?

I told him so that day and he became gloomy and despondent and went earlier than usual back to his own quarters.

The whole of the following week he was subdued and listless.

The next Sunday we didn't discuss anything more profound than a go position none of us could solve and what makes somebody a prodigy, which definitely none of us was. For the rest we played bridge and managed to help Lu over his depression by simply not paying attention.

It was three Sundays after our altercation that Wu Fuzhi suddenly made a remark that had us sit up and pay attention.

'I have something to say about what Huimin told us three weeks ago and which upset you so much, Qichen, that you even called him an old, doddering coward if I remember correctly,' he said.

'What I have to say may well help both of you out of your quandary,' he added, as an afterthought.

He rubbed the bridge of his long, straight nose with the forefingers of both hands which he held pressed together over his nose and mouth as he relished the warmth of his breath.

The little kerosene heater did its utmost but with an outside temperature of minus thirty-two, which the force seven wind made seem to be closer to minus fifty-five, it couldn't get the temperature in our room, Lu's as a matter of fact, above minus five, so we sat huddled together, with all our clothes on and our blankets around our shoulders, and waited for Wu to continue.

We watched in silence as he breathed in his slender doctor's hands to get the numbness out. I knew he couldn't talk without gesticulating. I had once asked him why he didn't put on gloves and he had replied, snidely, that he couldn't say anything sensible and worthwhile with his gloves on so we waited until he felt his hands were warm enough to beat the air with.

'My life's story is nothing compared to yours, Huimin,' he began. 'Until the day of my arrest it was pretty much the usual, predictable humdrum life of the bourgeois son of a bourgeois family who had adjusted, with rather bad grace, to our Communist society, except in one respect, which is what I want to talk to you about. First a few details though.

'I was born in Nanfeng on 13th November, 1929, the second child and only son of medical doctor Wu Jianmin and his wife, Yin Shaofen, professor of Chinese architecture at Nanjing University. My father's father and grandfather had both been medical doctors so I was going to be a medical doctor as well. So simple it was. My sister Fuying did have a choice though which she didn't know better than to use to become an architect. Chinese architecture, of course, so original.

'After an uneventful, loveless and passionless youth in Nanjing I was sent to Shanghai, as my father and his father had been before me, to study medicine at Fudan University. By then it was 1949 and the Communists had become the rulers of proletarian China. Strange as it may seem now, that fact had hardly affected my parents and their closeted little life and they, in turn, paid no attention whatsoever to the new order. They were totally apolitical and far above such mundane matters as who ran China and how. In their contemptuous view politics was nothing more than a circus performance by failed would-be intellectuals to keep the plebs occupied and fill their own pockets in the process by abusing their powers and selling their influence.

'On my own, in Shanghai, I attended in the beginning a few student meetings and debating sessions organised by the Communist Youth League but I soon found the whole rigmarole too stupid for words so, after the first couple of months, I stayed away and concentrated on my studies, keeping very much to myself. Time passed uneventfully and I was doing my third year when I first met Wei Qiujou, a student of mathematics. I fell head over heels in love with her and was completely will-less in her presence.

'At first my sheepish adoration seemed to amuse her, however, she never made fun of me or teased me which, I reasoned during my constant, nearly obsessive preoccupation with her, proved that she was a good-hearted girl who took the effects of her womanliness seriously. So, one evening, I gathered all my courage and blurted out that I loved her, with a maddening, almost obsessive passion. She looked at me pensively, a bit worriedly even, but then she took my trembling, clammy hands and told me to take it easy, that I shouldn't worry about there being somebody else in her life so to put my anxiety to rest and that she liked me very much and perhaps would learn to love me too as she gradually would come to know me better. Soon we were inseparable and but for our different faculties, went everywhere together.

'So it happened that one evening she asked me to accompany her to a debating session at the home of her professor of mathematics, a man whom she spoke of so often and so admiringly that each time she mentioned him or quoted him I felt sharp pangs of jealousy. Chen Dan his name was and when Qiujou introduced me to him that evening I could barely keep a straight face as I thought how ludicrous my jealousy had, in fact, been. Professor Chen looked so much a true to life caricature of the eternal Chinese peasant that he was laughable and not on my life could I imagine a woman falling in love with him. How wrong I was, in my arrogance so characteristic of the young male who thinks that all that matters, and, worse, matters for a woman, are handsome looks, I was to find out later.

'What I found out much sooner, in fact that very first evening already, was that from behind that rollicking bucolic facade a brilliantly sharp mind was observing mankind in its vain and pitiful attempts at civilisation. The debating session that evening was extraordinary, as were all the subsequent sessions Qiujou took me to without much urging on her part. Under the guise of repetitions and preparations for examinations Chen and his students debated freely about such things as humanism, religion, political philosophers and ideologies and the good and bad sides of each and every one of them. And always, always Chen hammered on the necessity, the *obligation*, for us to think for ourselves, to make up our own minds, to be critical.

'Soon I began to participate in the debates and I became so fascinated with Professor Chen and his ideas that I even enrolled in his classes of mathematics and physics, as subsidiary subjects, just to see and hear him as often as possible. Also during his official lectures Professor Chen constantly lauded the unlimited possibilities of the human mind, best expressed, he postulated, in the purity and boundlessness of the natural laws of higher mathematics and physics which obeyed no political or religious doctrine. And always he ended his lecture with the same exhortation, to strive for a free spirit and to stand up for intellectual freedom, always and everywhere, whatever the consequences.

'Why he was never arrested for his dissension and subversion of his students' minds I didn't understand and one early spring evening while he, Qiujou and I were strolling on the campus after a particularly lively session at his home, for he lived on the campus, I asked him point-blank why he was apparently untouchable. He burst out laughing and told me to be patient and that perhaps, in a few months' time, I would get an answer to that question and probably to some others, unspoken as yet, as well. Later, with the benefit of hindsight, I realised that from that evening Qiujou began to ask rather probing questions about my political views and about my thoughts on my own role in society. When I sometimes protested, feebly of course, about her intrusiveness she laughed and replied that she wanted to find out everything about me before she would agree to marry me. Mind you, I hadn't even asked her to marry me. It has always been like that between us. Qiujou always answers my questions before I ask them, often even before I realise that I have a question. Sharp and lively mind she had, still has I hope.'

Wu fell silent and surreptitiously wiped his eyes with the back of his right hand. He then cupped his hands over his mouth and breathed noisily, both to warm his numb fingers and to hide his emotion behind the small clouds of vapour.

We waited in silence and without moving and after a while he had collected himself sufficiently to continue his story.

'Four months later, on 2nd August, 1952 to be exact, Professor Chen asked me to come to his house that evening, alone. He received me cordially and, as we savoured a few mugs of very good quality jasmine tea, we talked about small, inconsequential things. After a while the conversation petered out though as Chen seemed to become increasingly distraught and only absent-mindedly responded to what I was saying.

'He frequently consulted his watch as if he were expecting something to happen or someone to knock on the door. I kept my tongue and uneasily waited for him to say something.

Suddenly he said, 'Eight years ago today, probably at this very same hour, my wife, six months pregnant, was murdered in this room because the Party considered her a threat. A happily pregnant, pretty and happy-go-lucky young woman was considered an intolerable threat to the leaders of the Communist Party, most of whom are still the top leaders of the People's Republic of China today, and therefore she had to die. The killers stabbed first our unborn child and then slashed my wife's throat while I was pontificating at a meeting five hundred metres from here.'

'Chen fell silent and wept openly. I shivered and carried by a wave of nausea I reached the bathroom just in time to vomit until my stomach ached and my nose stung from the stinking acidity. I washed my face and saw a stranger looking back at me from the mirror. I didn't recognise myself. Hesitantly I went back into the room. Chen had apparently taken hold of himself for he looked at me as I entered, his eyes red but otherwise calm.

'"My first impulse was revenge," he continued his story, "and in my feverish daydreams I was killing Communists by the scores until my skull felt like it would explode at any moment from so much pent-up rage. Slowly I came to my senses as I realised that the killing of individual Party members, however many before they would finally kill me, was just as immaterial to the Party as the killing of my own wife had been. It's the control over people that is important to the Party, not people themselves. Those who cannot be controlled are a danger to the Party's control over others and they *must* be eliminated. Mostly they simply disappear, never to be seen or heard of again; some are publicly tried on trumped-up charges and condemned to long jail sentences, or even to death, as a reminder to the people to stay in line but then again a few are killed, in as horrible a manner as possible, as a warning to certain particular persons not to interfere. Lingling's murder was such a warning, to me, since those in power in the Party were convinced she had told me her secrets.

'"So I decided to fight back in a different manner, to fight the Party itself and the horrible system it propagates, not the individuals, whatever their personal misdeeds, who at any one time seem to have the upper hand and then disappear again from the scene, for obscure reasons, to be replaced by others who are worse or even more mediocre. I recalled that long ago, in a different life in what then seemed a different universe to me, a very good friend of mine, more a godfather than a friend actually, had foretold that these things would happen and that he had offered me a way to resist and contribute to a future, truly democratic China.

'"I had listened to him and acquiesced, yet, young as I was then, I had never taken his morbid prophecies seriously and consequently I had never made an effort, many years later when I was in a position to do so, to select suitable candidates for his movement as he had asked me to do. It took the personal trauma of my wife's murder to realise that what my friend had prophesied long ago had by then become the terrible reality of everyday life in China.

'"So I re-established contact with my friend, himself a sort of power-broker behind the scenes, and I began to relay to him, via elaborate and secure channels, the names of those young people who I thought were suitable material for his secret society or Brotherhood as he used to call it himself. I knew, and still know, very little myself, both for my own and for the Brotherhood's protection of course. All I know is that in the top of the Party's hierarchy there are men and women who think that the present situation is an aberration yet who for the time being are not in a position to do something about it, to initiate changes and reforms.

'"I have, as I said, a way to channel the names and whereabouts of the young men and women who in my view could be very useful in helping to bring about those reforms and that is the end of it for me. Later, usually months later, I receive a message that such and such of those proposed by me have been screened and selected and please tell them the good news. It is then my task to actually approach the individuals concerned, who are still unaware of the fact that they have been the subjects of a scrutiny by the Brotherhood, and to break the news. You, Wu Fuzhi, have been such a subject for the past couple of months and last week I was told to propose to you to become a mole, since that role seemed to the evaluators to be more in line with your character and your future position as a medical doctor than that of an agent.

'"You know the difference between an agent and a mole? You don't? I'll tell you what I have been told. An agent will from time to time be given a mission to accomplish which may entail great danger to himself. If he is caught he must face the music all alone and be able, both physically and mentally, to withstand extreme duress. Very few are suitable for that role. I wouldn't be for sure. A mole, or sleeper, is a different thing altogether though. The mole waits until he is called upon, which may take years or may even never happen. He simply leads the life that fate dishes out to him, in nothing different from the people around him. The only difference is that in his mind, subconscious even, he knows that the Brotherhood keeps an eye on him and may one day call on him to take certain responsibilities.

'"Now, Wu Fuzhi, do you accept to become such a sleeper? Think about it while I make us some fresh tea."

'I didn't need time to consider so I told Chen that I wanted to be in, preferably even as an agent since I felt I could contribute more and faster. Smiling at my eagerness Chen said, however, that in time I would realise the wisdom of the Brotherhood's decision that I was more suited for the role of a mole so I acquiesced.

'Chen then taught me two tricks, one only to be used in rare and extreme circumstances, to signal to the Brotherhood that I needed help or had something very important to tell them, and one to signal to some other person that I was a member of that secret society. If that other person was a member also he or she would acknowledge my signal; if he wasn't he simply wouldn't recognise the subtle signal and nothing would happen. I felt proud. I was *somebody*. I would play an important role in a future China. If anything, it did a lot for my self-esteem.

'The day after my meeting with Professor Chen I gave the second subtle signal to Qiujou and to my utter joy she acknowledged it with a smile and our first kiss. We felt important. We belonged. We had a purpose!

'We both graduated in the summer of 1954.

'I was assigned as an apprentice doctor to Meishan and Qiujou as an assistant teacher of mathematics to a middle school in Qingdao. After our graduation we had two weeks' vacation which we decided to use to visit our parents together to apprise them of our intention to get married as soon as Qiujou was twenty-six, the age women were allowed to marry. Qiujou's parents were living in Qingdao. Her father was a manager in the beer factory and her mother worked in the administration office of the same factory. They were very friendly and soft-spoken people, very proud of their only daughter and apparently very happy with her choice of her future husband.

'We spent a very pleasant week together and then travelled to Nanjing to visit my parents.

'My father was, as usual, self-centred and self-absorbed, but, nevertheless, he was able to conjure up a last remnant of warmth when he bade goodnight to Qiujou after the first day of her stay. The next day he had already taken her for granted, just as he had always taken me for granted and he ignored her just as he had always ignored me and my sister.

'My mother had apparently read my letter announcing our visit since she remembered Qiujou's qualifications and immediately enlisted her help for her pet project of trying to develop mathematical formulae for the different types of structures in Chinese architecture. She was unable to speak or feel as a woman which was hardly surprising after thirty years of marriage to my father. Qiujou did well though. She indulged my mother and remained respectful to my father in spite of his rudeness.'

'Immediately after my arrival in Meishan I applied for a wedding permit and for Qiujou's transfer to Meishan's middle school. Qiujou did the same in Qingdao. We got permission to marry in March or April 1955 and were informed that Qiujou would be transferred to Meishan in April 1955, after the second semester of the 1954/1955 school year. I travelled to Qingdao on 29th March, 1955 and we were married two days later. The next day we left for Meishan.

'Qiujou was very happy with the small, free-standing house the municipality of Meishan assigned to us. That same night we made our first attempt at having the child we were entitled to and we were apparently successful, which was remarkable considering the clumsy way we fumbled through our first act of love-making. On the first day of January 1956 our daughter Judou was born. It was Judou who denounced me to her Red Guard comrades for reading poetry, which is a crime in Communist China unless it's the drivel produced by our Great Leader.

'Time passed and we were never contacted by the secret sorcerers of the Brotherhood nor did anything happen that warranted a signal from our side. Besides, we cherished the tidy, innocuous routine of our daily life and did our best to grovel ourselves into the good books of the local Party potentates by attending their pathetic struggle meetings at least thrice a week. That and the omnipresence of the Party and its increasingly tight grip on every aspect of people's lives meant that our initial enthusiasm for the Great Cause gradually dwindled until we finally forgot the whole thing. Years later, the evening of our daughter's first day in primary school it was, that's why I remember, the matter slipped into our conversation ever so casual-like and we both laughed, a bit sadly and indulgently, at our own youthful fantasies.

'Open public dissatisfaction with the system? Demonstrations? Unrest? A breakdown of society? The collapse of communism? A takeover by the Brotherhood? A leading role for us and other intellectuals? What balderdash! Professor Chen and his ephemeral, elusive masters had been but a bunch of foolish fantasists probably long gone or marching to the tune themselves by now.

'It wasn't until the day I was arrested that I had a momentary flicker of hope that the gods of my forsaken religion would somehow come to my rescue, at least give a sign of their existence.

'I desperately wore the signal of distress during my trial and I am sure that Qiujou tried every secret channel of contact but to no avail. I was condemned to nine years of hard labour. Nine years of hard labour as punishment for reading poetry after the denunciation by an eleven-year-old child, my own daughter to boot. Man, oh man, I was bitter and I cursed Chen Dan and his fairy tales about the secretive, all-powerful men and women who supposedly kept an eye on me. I cursed my gods and became an agnostic. Then my one and only friend Tan Shiwei died because of me. Seething with a powerless rage I defied the gods and flaunted the signal of distress.

'Nobody contacted me, nobody made even the slightest sign of acknowledgement but I kept wearing it and then, two months later, Tan's murderer, Captain Zhang, was transferred to a death camp where he would inevitably die himself. Even Commandant Hu Sen's sneer was a bit fearful I thought when he said that such a thing had never happened before but then, as long as Chinese killed Chinese, he didn't give a damn, he said.

'So the gods probably existed after all but perhaps their design is so grand and what is at stake so important that they simply can't preoccupy themselves with every inconvenience of each of their disciples. Just a small miracle from time to time and when the need is greatest to keep the faith alive or revive it in the avowed agnostic. Be that as it may, it worked for me and I became a believer again. I only wonder who their agent is or was in the camp. He must have some position there. How else would he and the gods know what I wanted from them? That was my story. I hope I didn't bore you.'

Wu Fuzhi fell silent and blew in his cupped hands.

Nobody said a word at first.

I saw Liu looking at him with a mixture of pity and awe. Lu just sat there, hunched over, staring at the floor.

Suddenly he asked, in a flat monotone, 'Had you checked me out, Fuzhi, as you intimated you would?'

'No! I did *not*,' Wu replied, and he laughed, a bit mockingly I thought.

'I was showing off,' he continued, 'I wouldn't know how to go about it,' and, looking at me directly, he added, 'I got your letter, Huimin, the one you wrote to me the day before your return to Karamay. In it you made altogether too much of my presumed importance. Besides, after my experience I took it that the Brotherhood or Elders, whatever you prefer to call them, would undoubtedly also have their tentacles in your new camp and if Lu were the wrong one they would take care of him as they took care of Captain Zhang.'

Turning his eyes on Lu, he added, grinning, 'Since you are still with us, Qichen, you must be a good one.'

'Is General Kong one of you, Fuzhi?' I asked him, point-blank.

He looked at me, a mocking little smile hovering about his lips.

'You think you noticed something, eh Huimin?' he snorted. 'A peculiar handshake, perhaps? I saw you staring at us the day Kong left. You are right though. I *did* make the signal but Kong didn't acknowledge it. So I don't know. From the way he behaves, however, the things he says and what he has done, for instance for you personally, I would say *yes*, he is one of us, whatever that means nowadays. How else could he get away with such nonconformist behaviour?

'But then, on the other hand, why did he never even touch on such an important matter to you during all those years you were with him? You, with your background and the lousy way the Communists treated you, you must have great value for a secret movement such as Professor Chen Dan described to me. Apparently Kong didn't, judging from the dismayed look in your eyes. It's all a riddle to me.'

'It does make sense though,' I replied, 'if you look at the matter from Kong's point of view, that is,' I went on. 'Take my case for instance, but look at it a bit closer than you just did, Fuzhi. What kind of advantage, need rather, was there for the Elders in enlisting me? Not when I knew I had been betrayed by the Communists the first time, not later when I was betrayed again and again and not now that I am a convict probably for the rest of my life. My only hope was and still is that the existing order be overthrown, then as well as now. Kong knows that so why should he create an unnecessary liability for himself for the movement, when, as a matter of course, they can count on me anyhow should they deem me worthy enough for a place in the new order of things. Logical, isn't it?

'Now look at your own case, Fuzhi. If Kong were one of you he *knows* you are also, from the affair with Tan and Captain Zhang. He didn't need your signal handshake for that and probably didn't like it either. What purpose would be served by making himself known to you as a fellow-traveller? None! He would only increase the danger to himself by entering one more variable in his balancing act, which is, I'm sure, already complicated enough as things are.'

I fell silent and watched Wu as he rubbed the bridge of his nose, a gesture I had come to know as his way to control his volatile temper.

Finally he looked up at me and said, with a rueful little smile, 'I'm sure you are right, Huimin, and I thank you for not rubbing in the fact that I'm not exactly a *predictable* variable. I may even have crossed the line of what the Elders think is permissible when I played the avenging god in my former camp.'

I didn't want him to proffer confidences of that kind since I feared that his self-appointed role of executioner would be too much for Lu and Liu to stomach, so I said hastily, 'Yes, yes, you are right. I didn't see the Tan–Zhang affair as the act of an avenging god but then one could indeed see it as an act of revenge for something terrible done to you personally. The Elders decided to humour you for that once only but may have labelled you afterwards as momentarily unstable, to be watched carefully for a number of years, hence General Kong's snub.

'But enough useless speculation! Let's make some fresh tea and play chess to take our minds off all those depressing subjects. It's too cold to play cards. The chess pieces we can move with our gloves on. Everybody laughed, apparently relieved that the sombre mood was broken.

On 20th January, 1971, the pipe-laying section caught up with the trench diggers.

Trench digging had slowed down to less than half a metre's depth per day because of the rock-hard frozen soil instead of the acquired depth of three metres.

Peng and Lu went along with my proposal to send the non-convict skilled labourers home until 2nd May and to put the convict labour force on a one-shift hacking duty. I had foreseen this and had long ago asked for a diesel generator and air compressors and jackhammers but the equipment was never delivered.

So I had to use pickaxes and even with two men abreast, hacking away for eight hours, seven hundred men in all over a total length of one kilometre and another seven hundred men carrying off the stone-hard clods, I managed only two kilometres of ready trench per month.

By 2nd May, when thaw would allow faster progress again, I would have eight kilometres of trench ready to resume pipe laying.

During the summer and autumn of 1971 the welders and crane drivers would slowly catch up again with the trench diggers until by January 1972 the situation would again be the same.

Peng and Lu were capable of understanding this kind of forward planning, so obvious in Western thinking but so wholly un-Communist.

The idea caught on and they went even one step ahead of me and reduced also the military force by two-thirds.

I told Lu and Liu that they could also take time off, if that is what soldiers can do, but they refused, saying they preferred to stay as they liked our evenings and Sundays together.

On 15th August, 1971, Liu burst into my office, overjoyed yet a bit embarrassed at the same time.

He waved a letter in front of my eyes and told me excitedly that Major Peng had called him that morning and handed him a letter from General Kong announcing Sergeant Liu Timo's transfer to General Kong's staff with effect from 1st October, 1971.

I congratulated him and told him I was happy for him. He thanked me for having spoken to General Kong about his wish to return to Beijing and then we embraced, laughing and crying at the same time.

When we had quietened down a bit I told him it was time to make up his mind about Meimei and her father.

He bit the bullet and barely a month later, on 12th September, Liu and Meimei were married in Tacheng, just in time for him to claim his wife was also subject of his transfer order and would have to follow him to Beijing. Peng, Lu, Wu, Fu and I drove all the way to Tacheng to attend the wedding and the dinner given by Wong.

The ceremony was short and simple but very cordial and the mayor and Party secretary, whom we had met once before, on our first visit to Wong's restaurant long ago, turned out to be really nice men so Wong invited them as well as their closest relatives and staff also for dinner.

It was a wonderful evening. The food was delicious and for the first time Meimei did not serve the guests but had instead the place of honour beside her husband. Her beaming face, her beautiful sparkling eyes and the proud, loving glances she threw at our friend Liu brought the tears to our eyes as we kept toasting the happy couple. There was not one dissonant note during the whole day and evening until the five of us checked in at Su Leima's guest house.

As always the man was furious, this time because we were late, though it was only eleven o'clock, and because we had alcohol on our breath, though none of us was drunk or behaved badly or disrespectfully. Though his scowls and slighting remarks couldn't spoil our good mood, they did dampen our high spirits and we prepared for the night and went to bed without further ado.

★

'I sometimes wonder whether Muslims like Su Leima are ever in a good mood. Do they have a sense of humour? Tolerance for other people's different but harmless sense of fun? I doubt it. They seem always so intense, so resentful, so quick to take offence, sizzling like a drop of water on a hot plate with every innocent, innocuous remark they don't immediately grasp and then, of course, get all wrong.

'Tolerance and a sense of humour are not exactly the hallmark of our Communists and their creed either, but good grief! Compared to life in a society dominated by the likes of Su Leima, ours must look like a true human comedy with its laughs and smiles and tears and undisguised affection between men and women.

'If theirs was the only alternative to ours, you would find me on the barricades waving the red flag and brandishing a gun, of that you can be sure. Lao Dee once said during one of our little talks that there is no greater fanaticism and worse intolerance than those inspired by religions, whatever the variety. And the craziest thing, Lao Dee said, is that the more the situation, whether in the life of an individual or of a nation or of the whole world, would, normally speaking, beg some sort of divine intervention or at least a sign of divine approval or disapproval, the more zealous the believers become if such an intervention or signs do not happen.

'They really march to a different drum, Lao Dee says, one that the ordinary, moderate person cannot hear and they get their marching orders from a different authority, one who has no business with us, ordinary people. For them it's forever "onward Christian soldiers!" or, for that matter, Muslim soldiers or Hindu soldiers or Protestant soldiers or Roman Catholic soldiers. Kill! Kill! Kill! In the name and for the greater glory of God, the Almighty and All Merciful. It must be the saddest, most enduring joke in humanity's long and tragic history. But I ramble. Back now to my story which is nearly finished.'

*

As they did the year before, Wong and Meimei, Madam Liu by now, prepared dinner on Liberation Day, at the same time their farewell dinner.

General Kong had again been able to make it to our outpost and when Wong, in his farewell speech, called him the 'most human and humane of soldiers' he was visibly moved.

In his own speech, Kong praised us for another year of outstanding performance, yet he was less upbeat than the year before.

For the first time he hinted at the uncertain and worrisome times ahead as a result of mounting tensions at the top of the Party hierarchy. Notably the failed *coup* by Marshall Lin Biao only a few weeks earlier had been a terrible blow for the military's prestige and reputation for reliability and the top military leaders were still reeling from the denunciations and accusations by Chairman Mao's wife Jiang Qing, whose evil influence grew by the day.

Fortunately he, Kong, had had no links to Lin Biao and his clique, but still he would have to tread carefully and that therefore we shouldn't be surprised or feel slighted if the next year he would have to cancel his visits in order to keep a close watch on the developments in Beijing.

What he meant but didn't say with so many words was that he probably couldn't afford to be away even for a day since he should be prepared at any moment to switch allegiances, not only to keep his position but simply to survive.

I saw Lu's worried glance in my direction but what could I do but to shrug my shoulders and pull a face at him?

Liu Timo, now a member of General Kong's staff, left us on 2nd October. His wife Meimei and her father would follow him six weeks later, the extra time needed to hand over the restaurant to the new tenant appointed by Tacheng's Party secretary.

The first few weeks we missed Liu terribly. Our evenings and Sundays were no longer the same without his perpetual good mood. Gradually, however, the memory faded as we settled into the rut of winter.

The winter of 1971/1972 was unusually severe and hardly any work was done during January and February.

The camp looked as if deserted. Only at mealtimes the convicts ventured outside, trudging through the knee-high, frozen snow to the canteen and back, pieces of jute bag wrapped around their faces to protect them against the stinging snow crystals swept up by the seemingly perpetual gale force north-east wind.

The rest of the time they spent on their cots, under two covers, with all their clothes on, without speaking, their senses dulled by the howling wind and the creaking of the roofing sheets, motionless lest the intense cold seep under the blankets and suck the last dregs of life's warmth from their tired bones.

Many died or rather ceased to live, going out slowly, like the flickering flame of a candle running out of wick. When their cot neighbours noticed, sometimes days later, they dumped the bodies outside, against the wall exposed to the wind, to be left there, serving as a windbreak, until the first thaw of spring.

The blankets and clothes of the dead were shared out amongst the living, as a matter of fact, without argument or quarrel. Our stocks of practically everything were running low and often out.

I didn't see Major Peng for weeks and even if I had it wouldn't have changed anything; replenishment of our stocks was simply out of the question.

Thaw set in on 20th April but that didn't improve the situation immediately. Instead of the snow it was now melt water that made the unpaved roads impracticable both for the supply trucks from Urumqi and for ourselves.

Finally, early May, the weather changed, almost abruptly, overnight. The temperature shot up into the mid-twenties and within a week the whole world around us exploded into bloom in a riot of colours.

The first thing we did was to dig graves, one individual grave for each of the six hundred and thirty-two men who had died during the long winter, and to plant flowers on top of the mounds of fresh earth as an apology for having used their bodies to build a windbreak.

By mid-May the supply trucks got through to the camp and work on the pipeline could resume.

Major Peng arrived with the first truck from Urumqi on 15th May.

He told me that oil, petrol and food supplies would be much less and often irregularly off and on because of the deteriorating situation everywhere in the country.

We should be glad, he said, that General Kong and the ministries responsible for the project had managed to divert enough goods and materials to us to keep us going at say half-speed until the onset of the next winter. In particular the supply of pipe was worrying him, he said, and working round the clock as we had done before was not only useless but could even be dangerous.

'Who knows what will happen if we have to report work stoppages because we have run out of pipe,' he said. 'If somebody high up in the Party hierarchy stumbles over our report and reads it and, God forbid, orders our camp to be closed and the project to be discontinued, what then? You and your people will again be scattered all over China and everybody will be much worse off than here.

'I suggest, Huimin, that you start thinking about those things and slow down the project to make your stock of pipe last at least another two years. Do *not* report anything to anybody. Don't worry about General Kong. He is too busy dancing musical chairs in Beijing and, besides, he knows you and can guess the reason behind your silence. He may well be grateful that he can conveniently forget about us here and needn't take unpleasant decisions, unpleasant both for him and for us. I'm sure he won't visit us here this year. Can't afford to be away from Beijing even for a day I guess lest he find one of Jiang Qing's puppets behind his desk on his return and he himself accused of all kinds of misdeeds concocted behind his back while he was away visiting his real friends here.'

Peng fell silent and stared at the pickings from his nose under the nail of his forefinger.

I knew him well enough to know that what he had said so far was merely a preliminary to what he really intended to propose so I waited patiently.

After a while he said, musingly, 'Perhaps you should start thinking of diverting part of our workforce to some kind of agricultural project of our own. Instead of depending on outside supplies, haphazard and unreliable in the best of times to come, we could grow our own vegetables and corn and whatever other foodstuff that will grow here. Make a study of the possibilities, Huimin, for your own good.'

I said I would and thanked him for his concern and friendship. Then I asked him whether he had any idea what would happen to him and Lieutenant Lu.

'Stop worrying about others, Huimin,' he replied a bit crabbily. 'Lu and I are soldiers and our life is preordained. Besides, Lu and I are lucky that General Kong trusts us and wants us on his staff. We know that Kong is patiently and slyly building his own little fiefdom, however, we both feel that what the general has in mind will be for the good of China, so we feel honoured by his trust and that he thinks us worthy of a role in his plans and we'll serve him loyally.'

He fell silent, looked at me gravely and added, 'You must reckon with the probability that both Lu and I will be promoted and transferred to Beijing before the end of the year. Though men of my rank have no influence whatsoever on the army's personnel movements I shall hazard the risk of an official reprimand and recommend a friend of mine as my successor here. His name is Shen Guofeng and he has just been promoted to the rank of major. He should have been promoted the same year as I was, four years ago that is, but he was passed over because he spoke his mind too often and too loudly about the Party's political officers whom he despises.

'Shen is a true, no-nonsense soldier from a centuries-old military family tradition and he hates politicking. He learned his lessons the hard way though and realises now that politics is the way of life, also in his beloved army and that he has to adjust and watch and observe and take sides. I talked to him and explained about you and Wu and about your ties with General Kong and about the project.

'He agrees with me that it is in everybody's interest, not in the least his own, that the project here be protracted for say another four or five years and in the lowest possible key at that, to avoid making it a political play ball between opposing factions in Beijing. Lu and I have benefited from the project's original high profile and your excellent performance, Huimin, for which you gave us the credit so we could get our promotion, earlier and bigger, just as you predicted. The situation is different for Shen. He has just been promoted, four years late, and provided he keeps quiet and his big mouth shut, his next promotion will follow automatically in four or five years. No better place than this camp for him to stay out of the limelight. So he, you and Wu and the convicts have a mutual interest in carrying on here quietly and undemandingly.

'Shen is not a very jovial fellow but his one-track mindedness makes dealing with him rather simple. He doesn't understand innuendoes and woolly, roundabout talking irritates him. Talk to him in simple, straightforward Chinese and phrase your questions or requests in such a way that he can answer them with "yes," "no" or "I'll see what I can do". When he asks you something don't look for hidden meanings. Just answer in the same manner, "yes," "no," "I don't know but I'll find out and let you know".

'He also does not disguise his orders as requests. Shen thinks that kind of politeness is hypocritical. If one has the authority to give orders then one should do so, clearly and succinctly, and not beat around the bush ostensibly to spare others' feelings. If Shen gives you an order take the trouble to repeat it, verbally and immediately. He likes that. Not to put you down or to make you feel inferior, that's not Shen's character, but to make sure there's no misunderstanding. Shen hates squabbling after the event. Just keep your relationship with him simple and low-key, Huimin, and you'll get along fine with Major Shen Guofeng.'

'Simple it may be, Peng Ze,' I replied sadly. 'Man, oh man, I'll miss you and Lu Qichen. But don't worry, I'll follow your advice and keep hoping that in four or five years clearer heads will have prevailed in Beijing and innocent victims of the madness like myself will get an amnesty. What else would be the purpose for me?'

My emotion got the better of me and for the first time I wept unashamedly in Peng's presence.

He took my hands in his and his voice shook as he said, 'Lu and I will do everything we possibly can to get you an amnesty, Huimin, and so will General Kong, of that I'm absolutely certain. We won't forget you and won't abandon you, my friend. Have patience! Free you'll be, I promise!'

We hugged each other and then he turned on his heels, got in his jeep and with a brief salute, he drove off.

I discussed Peng's idea of growing our own vegetables and staple food with Lu and Wu and they agreed that it was worth trying.

We changed the camp and project schedules to a one shift on, two shifts off routine and began the selection amongst the convicts of suitable candidates for the agricultural production brigade.

When Fu Fusai preferred to stay on rather than go home, I put him in charge of the farming section.

Through our friend the Party secretary of Tacheng, Fu and Lu managed to get us seedlings, seeds and grains which we planted and sowed in an area of about five hectares around the camp.

By mid-September we were so proud of our neatly tended fields and crops of watermelons, pumpkins, cucumbers, cabbages, wheat and corn that we sent Fu to Tacheng to invite the secretary to see for himself what we had been doing. He was astonished and enthusiastic and he promised his continuing support.

In turn we promised to send him our surplus to supplement his own community's meagre allocations.

Gradually, over the next three years, we extended our fields to cover more than fifty hectares in 1975 and the range of our products to more than twenty, including carrots, tomatoes, capsicums, sweet potatoes and staple products like barley, oats and rye and beans.

We supplied fresh produce to Karamay, the military camp there and to Tacheng.

Wu had started a pickling operation in November 1973 and our pickled vegetables were much in demand during the winter months.

By mid-1975 more than two-thirds of the convict labour force had been permanently assigned to our agricultural and pickling ventures.

But let's go back for a moment to the year 1972.

On 20th October of that year Peng and Lu came to say goodbye to Wu and me and to introduce us to our new commandant, Major Shen Guofeng.

Peng and Lu had received confirmation of their promotion to full colonel and major respectively and had been ordered to report to General Kong's headquarters in Zhangjiakou.

Since we had seen this coming and had said more than once what this meant to the four of us, there was no need now that the moment had come for more displays of emotion, the more so because Major Shen wouldn't have understood, so we took leave of each other with a lot of laughter, backslapping and mutual good wishes.

Major Shen took it all quite naturally and he seemed indeed the quiet, uncomplicated man Peng had told me he was. Together we walked around the camp and our fledgling plantation and then we went to the project site which by then had reached Xinchepaizi; the former commanders Peng and Lu for a last look and to say farewell to a number of people they had learned to know well; the new commandant to get his first impression; Wu and I to show off our organisation.

Everything went well and before the three officers drove off, Shen told us he would visit us on the fifteenth of each month to hear our report and to talk about eventual problems.

His emphasis on the words *hear* and *talk* was not lost on us: Major Shen did not want anything put down in writing unless he and I had discussed the desirability or necessity of a written report first.

There remains one other remarkable thing to relate before my story comes to an end. As you may recall, Wu Fuzhi, Doctor Wu, had been condemned to nine years of hard labour in November 1966 so during the early months of 1975 he began to exhibit the first signs of nervousness.

Had his sentence been duly recorded? Was there somebody in charge of those early records? Where was Special Interrogator Song Xisheng now? Had his files, or he himself for that matter, survived the mayhem of the Cultural Revolution? Should he, Wu, bring the matter of his impending release up for the authorities' attention or would it be better to wait for the authorities to contact him first?

When by the end of July 1975 he had still not received word from whatever authority was dealing with such matters, he asked me to arrange for him to see Major Shen on his forthcoming visit on 15th August.

He asked me to be present during the interview, as a witness. I still recall the conversation word for word.

SHEN: Yes, Doctor, what is this personal matter you wish to see me about?

WU: Major, just in case you do not know this. I was condemned to nine years of re-education through hard labour on 25th November, 1966. Therefore, I shall have served the full sentence on the 25th November next. It is now 15th August and I have had no word from the authorities. My question to you is: should I write a letter, and if yes, to which authority or should I wait until they contact me?

SHEN: You have a copy of your sentence, Doctor Wu?

WU: No, sir.

SHEN: Bad.

WU: Yes, sir.

SHEN: Write a letter to me. Explain your case, briefly, as you just did. Give your full name, the date and place of your trial, the name of the prosecutor. I'll pass your letter on to Colonel Peng and Major Lu. They are in a better position to find out about your case than you or I here. Give me the letter today, before I leave. Saves one month.

WU: Yes, sir. Thank you, sir.

SHEN: No matter. It's my duty.

Watching Wu, he added, ever so softly, 'I'll do my best, Fuzhi.'

On 10th October, ahead of his regular visit, Major Shen came to see me and asked me to call Wu to my office.

Wu, very nervous, presented himself.

Shen came straight to the point. 'Sit down, Doctor Wu, I have bad and good news for you.'

Wu paled and stammered, 'What's the bad news, sir?'

'Colonel Peng and Major Lu were unable to trace your case, Fuzhi,' Shen continued, 'despite enquiring at the Ministry of Justice and at the Party headquarters. Major Lu then went to Meishan to consult the archives there. He found your file but apart from your family's personal dates there was only one addition, that said "deported by truck on 1st December, 1966, to Hefei, further destination unknown". No mention of your trial or your sentence.'

Wu bit his lower lip, then whispered, 'Was there nothing else in my file, sir? About my family?'

Shen looked down on his hands then up at Wu and I saw concern and compassion in his eyes as he said, 'Sooner or later you'll find out anyhow, Fuzhi, so I may as well tell you now, while you're still amongst friends.

'There was a second addition that said, "Wei Qiujou, wife of Wu Fuzhi, registered in Meishan on 1st April, 1955, died by drowning on 4th December, 1966, presumably suicide. Buried in plot 278 of Meishan's municipal cemetery. Wu Judou, daughter of Wu Fuzhi and Wei Qiujou, born in Meishan on 1st January, 1956, died on 4th December, 1966, by drowning, presumably murdered by Wei Qiujou, aforementioned. Buried in plot 278 of Meishan's municipal cemetery."'

Shen fell silent and looked at Wu who had sagged in his chair under the blows of Shen's words. His eyes were closed and his breath came in deep, shuddering heaves.

I sat there, wordless, shocked, and as I looked at Shen I thought I saw tears in his eyes as well.

When there was no immediate reaction from Wu, Shen continued softly, 'Major Lu and Colonel Peng reported their findings to General Kong. General Kong then managed to track down Song Xisheng, the special prosecutor you said in your letter dealt with your case.

'It appears that Song was killed on 25th September, 1970, in Changsha by local Red Guards reportedly after they found him burying the loot he had confiscated from them, ostensibly to give it back to the rightful owners, in the garden of a local accomplice. In his report the militia commandant of Changsha says that the Red Guards forced Song and his accomplice to carry the loot back into the accomplice's house, then locked them into the house with the accomplice's wife and two daughters and their husbands and children after which they set the house on fire. Everybody perished in the fire.

'General Kong thinks that Song travelled with his personal files and that these were also lost in the fire. In a letter I received yesterday from General Kong personally, he says that since there are no official records of your case, you are, as from this moment, a free man. He further instructs me to pay you the amount of two hundred yuan as an advance on your salary owed you by the State for your services as a volunteer camp doctor since 1967. He advises you, Wu, to claim yourself the full amount from the penal labour camp registration department of the Ministry of Justice.'

Shen fell silent. I stared at him, flabbergasted, horrified, and was about to flare up when he pointed with his chin at Wu beside me and glanced at me warningly. I turned to look at Wu and saw that he was weeping, with great, heaving sobs.

Shen got up from his chair and said to me, 'I'll leave you two now. Try to comfort our friend, Dao, and find out from him what he intends to do now that he is free to go. I won't visit you next week, no purpose in that, but I'll expect both of you to come and see me within the next ten days or so when Fuzhi sees things a bit clearer.'

At that Major Shen turned abruptly and left my room without another glance at Wu.

From the rigid way he held himself I knew that the major wasn't his usual imperturbable self either.

I tried to do some paperwork as I left Wu to himself and his grief. What could I say? Sympathy, pity and compassion may well do some good but there is a limit beyond which grief brooks no intrusion and I felt intuitively that Wu's grief was way beyond that limit and that it was up to him to first signal a need for contact.

After a while, more than an hour after Shen had left us, I heard Wu sniff and move in his chair.

I stopped staring at the papers in front of me and looked up and at him.

Bleary-eyed he looked back at me and mumbled, 'Nine years in prison without cause, Huimin. How many millions are there like me? You too, perhaps? My life ruined, my wife the murderess of my daughter to avenge her betrayal of me, her father, and then she kills herself. What a waste! A miserable thief, whose credentials as an interrogator nobody checked, ruined my life and that of countless others, yours included. A society wherein such things can happen is not a civilised society, Huimin. And the so-called leaders of such a society are criminals.

'Even the tyrants of our past and those crazy dictators in Germany and Russia are but small fry compared to our Great Criminal Chairman Mao and his fellow monsters. How I hate them! How I despise them! How I should like to fry them just like the demons they created fried that monster Song!'

Wu had worked himself into a rage and he leapt out of his chair to pound my table with his clenched fists, his eyes bloodshot. I remained silent. Wu wasn't in the mood to listen so I let him rave and spend his rage and fury.

He stopped as suddenly as he had begun, breathing deeply and holding on to the edge of my desk to steady himself, to let the tautness flow out of his body, eyes closed. I saw his body slump, crumple almost, as he turned and shuffled back to his chair.

Groaning to let himself down and looking up at me, he said, smiling sadly, 'Thank you, Huimin, thank you for not saying the usual inane things. I am tired, very tired and I'm afraid I can't make it to my room alone. Would you mind accompanying me, Huimin, and help me give myself a shot of a tranquilliser? I want to sleep, I need to sleep or I'll go crazy. Then, afterwards, I'll decide what I'm going to do with the rest of my life. When I have made my decision, I'll tell you and together we'll tell the good major.'

He slept for two days and three nights and the third day I saw him remove the blanket he had hung, like a curtain, before the window of his room.

He saw me standing in the doorway of my office as I watched him and he waved.

I waved back and went back inside. I was glad to see he was apparently all right but I wasn't going to obtrude myself on him. Whenever he was ready he would come and see me.

I was inspecting the wheat fields two days later when I saw him come walking towards me, quite jauntily I thought. He waved and I waved back and I saw him smiling.

I stood up straight, saluted him the military way and barked, 'Good morning, freeman, sir! Convict number 00743 reporting! The wheat harvest looks promising, sir! Another victory for our socialist production methods freeman, sir!'

Wu grinned and sat down on a small knoll beside the wheat field, carefully choosing a bare spot amongst the poppies and marguerites.

Tapping the ground beside him he said, 'Sit down, Huimin. We need to talk, just you and I. No better place than here with nobody around for miles. I brought a thermos with hot tea and two mugs. Let me pour us one first.'

Quietly we sat there, sipping our tea, enjoying the absence of man-made noise, the rustling of the wheat in the crispy cool breeze, the trills of a pair of skylarks trying to catch the snow-white clouds that drifted southwards in the intensely cobalt blue sky.

'Peaceful contentment, Huimin,' Wu Fuzhi said dreamily, 'I feel that now, in my heart, and my mind is at ease. I slept for two days and three nights, then took a laxative and drank nothing but water for another two days to flush the toxins of anger and hate out of my system. I'm clear-headed now and I have made up my mind. It's time to tell you what I have decided to do. I'm grateful that you didn't ask me the usual inane questions and I'm asking you not to interrupt me while I'm talking. Keep your comments until I have finished. Okay?'

I felt his probing look but I merely nodded as I kept gazing at the undulating wheat rushing like a golden ocean towards the horizon.

'First of all I have decided to stay here with you until they release you. I have no family to go back to and I am not at all in a hurry to find out about my parents or Qiujou's. Besides, I can't leave my patients just like that. Medic Corporal Yu and his men did a good job while I wasn't of this world these past four days but they haven't got the capability to deal with a real emergency.

'Secondly I think we should start the ball rolling and submit a petition for your amnesty. We'll draft the text together and ask Major Shen to endorse it and to add his personal comments. I'm sure he'll agree to forward the petition to our friends Lu Qichen and Peng Ze who will be glad to add their own recommendations before they'll submit it to General Kong. Kong will know who has the authority to stamp "Granted" at the bottom of the bloody paper in exchange for some favour or other. Separate from your petition I'll write a letter myself to the general, offering him my services as his personal physician. I am even prepared to enter the military service and put on a uniform if that is necessary or desirable.

'I have two reasons for my proposal to Kong, which I can't very well put in writing, and I won't insult his intelligence by inventing the usual crap. Kong is clever enough to guess my motives. I'll tell you, however, not because I think you aren't clever enough to guess for yourself, but because I don't *want* you to *guess*. I want you to know for sure because I told you so.

'My first reason is quite honourable. I want Kong to have the best medical care by a *friend* who wants him to survive because he thinks that the general is the only person capable to withstand the pressure from the madmen and criminals at the top of the Party to have the PLA crack down on their opponents. Kong will not let the PLA be used for criminal purposes.

'My second reason is less honourable. I think that as the general's personal physician I'll be in a position to look behind the scenes of power and find out who were responsible for the crimes committed against myself and countless millions of other victims. Once I'll have found out I'll become the perfidious and depraved medicine man playing the avenging god one more time. You know I'm good at that, Huimin.'

He fell silent and I sensed that he had made up his mind and that there was nothing I could do or say that would make him change his plans.

So I replied, 'I know when it's senseless to argue, Fuzhi, so I won't and perhaps I should say "why should I?" I haven't got all that many reasons to take up the cudgels for those you're after, now have I? So I wish you success and I thank you from the bottom of my heart for sticking with me for the time being and for thinking of my future as well.'

'Good,' Wu replied calmly, 'now let's stop thanking each other each and every time we feel the other shows a bit of unselfishness or just an act of ordinary friendship. It's cheap and tiring and undignified. Besides, nothing we do is ever wholly without selfish motives. Even the saints sought their own self-gratification or self-humiliation to get in their gods' good books. The poor wretches who benefited from their so-called goodness were merely a means to help the saintly do-gooder achieve his own selfish goal.

'Man is a selfish beast, genetically so I'm afraid, so there is nothing he can do about it but lie about his true motives. I'm convinced that this built-in selfishness is a prerequisite for the survival of our species, of every species for that matter. Those who pretend differently are either nitwits or hypocrites.'

I laughed and said, 'You're probably right, Fuzhi, certainly where I'm concerned. So, now that we're clear about each other's motives, let's enjoy the sun and the purity of the air *and the silence* for a while longer before we go back to our respective duties and selfish preoccupations.'

We both laughed and, nudging each other playfully with our elbows, we laid down on our back and for the next hour we didn't talk.

He didn't sleep for occasionally I heard him swallow his saliva from chewing on a sour dock and at first I wondered what he was thinking about. Then, suddenly, I realised that I didn't want to know, not cloaked hypocritically as not having the right to intrude, no! Simply that I didn't *want* to share his thoughts and troubles. I didn't care!

What a relief! Contentedly I sighed and wriggled my back against the springy mattress of weeds and flowers and the small bumps of the ground sent sensuous shivers along my spine and for the first time since a long, long time I acutely longed for Liang. A cloud drifting southwards high above me suddenly changed its form and became her face smiling down at me. As I stretched my arms upwards to pull her against me the cloud changed form again and Special Interrogator Song bore down on me.

I panicked and I must have groaned and flailed my arms to push him away from me for suddenly I felt Wu's hand restraining my left arm and his breath near my ear as he whispered, 'Fighting the demons of your past again, eh Huimin? Always ousting the initial pleasant images to torment you, eh? Don't let them, man! Hold on to those first images! Don't let them slip away or disintegrate and in time, the demons will give up and leave you in peace.'

He patted my arm reassuringly as I wept, moved by his caring and ashamed because I hadn't cared for his feelings only a few minutes earlier.

That evening we drafted a petition for my amnesty and a letter to General Kong.

The following day we went to see Major Shen. He read our epistles, suggested a few practical changes here and there and said he would be pleased to endorse both.

He gave us a few sheets of his official stationery for the final drafts, joking that the red star at the top would steer them through the rough seas of the Cultural Revolution's death throes.

'I have been called to Beijing next week,' he told us further, 'and I shall hand both epistles to our friend Major Lu Qichen. That's the best I can do for you. How Lu handles the matter further is up to him. I'll let you know as soon as there is any news.'

## *Chapter Thirty-Five*

### There Will Always be Tomorrow; So Never You Despair!

The autumn and winter of 1975, our sixth together, came and went without any news from Beijing.

Major Shen came to see us routinely on the 15th of every month and gradually our conversations became more general. Both Wu and I were surprised at the extent of his interest and at the depth of his thinking and understanding.

A blizzard and extremely low temperatures left him stranded for three days in our camp after his visit on 15th January, 1976.

As is common amongst men in such circumstances we became even more familiar with each other and on his second day, as we sat huddled together around the small, pot-bellied stove in my room listening distractedly to the raging blizzard outside, he broke the silence and asked us how we had gotten ourselves in this mess.

Both Wu and I told him what had happened to us during those ill-fated last days of November 1966 and, at Wu's insistence, I gave him a summary of my life story.

Shen was deeply shocked and said that if it weren't for our trustworthiness, he would never have believed such terrible things could happen to ordinary people in China. He was absolutely certain, he said, that nobody in the armed forces was even remotely aware of these things. Nobody doubted the Party's version of what went on in China, he said.

We discussed and debated until the small hours of the next day and then slept fitfully, with our clothes on, on the floor, around and almost against the stove, until the dawn's first light which isn't until nine o'clock at that time of the year.

We ate our breakfast in silence and then we dug Shen's jeep out of a metre high snowdrift, still talking very little, just a casual remark now and then about the icy hardness of the snow, about what to do if the engine wouldn't start and about the fact that we perspired in spite of the thermometer still being stuck at minus twenty-eight degrees.

Indeed the wind had died down and the sun, though still low in a cloudless, cobalt blue sky, had enough strength to make us feel uncomfortable as we laboured clumsily in our quilted uniforms to free the jeep. As soon as we stepped in the shade for a moment, however, the perspiration froze instantly on our brows. Finally, by midday, we had the jeep ready and while a couple of jute bags drenched in kerosene burnt under the engine section we had our lunch. Major Shen had become a bit more talkative by that time but I saw that he was still a much troubled man.

The engine started at the third attempt and Wu and I stood gazing after Shen as he drove off.

'There goes a troubled and confused man,' Wu said; 'nothing will ever be the same again for him. He lost the one unshakeable certainty around which he had shaped his life, the moral rightness of the Party of which he saw himself as the standard-bearer and, if need be, the enforcer. And that's our fault, Huimin, yours even more than mine. I wonder whether we should rejoice for having dealt the Party another blow after our friend Lu Qichen's apostasy or feel sorry for our new friend Shen Guofeng, who, I can't help thinking, will find it much harder than Lu to redefine his loyalties. What do you think, Huimin?'

'I think nothing,' I replied curtly, shrugging my shoulders. 'You can afford to indulge such ethical hypocrisy now that you are a free man. I am still a convict and unless men like Shen Guofeng see the terrible unfairness of it all, I'll have wasted my entire life. Since I submitted my petition for amnesty for crimes I never committed, grovelling in fact before the very institution that cheated me and robbed me of my life, I can think of nothing else than what I will do to myself if those despicable, faceless monsters in Beijing reject my plea or, worse, if they don't even deign to answer. So does it surprise you, Fuzhi, that, frankly, I don't give a damn whether Shen Guofeng, *Major* Shen Guofeng of the PLA, enforcer of the Party's rotten philosophy, will or will not be able to redefine his loyalties as you put it?'

I fell silent, choking on my own desperate rage and I rudely shook off Wu's tentative gesture to calm me down as I stalked off to my office and slammed the door shut behind me.

Spring of 1976 came and the planting and sowing of the various crops began.

For almost a year now we had run out of pipe and work on the project had been halted completely. Our camp had turned into a veritable agricultural community.

Shen and I had decided not to renew our requisitions for pipe in order not to draw attention to our situation and to send the skilled, non-convict labour force home. More than half of them asked Shen for permission to stay and to be put to work in the fields instead.

They preferred the quiet tranquillity of life in the camp, they said, with plenty to eat, rather than the uncertainty and shortages, famine even, in their respective towns and villages.

Then, one beautiful Sunday morning in June 1976, the 13th it was, I'll never forget, as Wu and I were strolling through our fields for sheer pleasure, Corporal Yu, Wu's medic, came running up to us, waving his arms to attract our attention, and shouting from far that Major Shen was waiting for us in the camp with an important message.

Hurriedly we returned to the camp, my heart pounding as it swayed between hope and fear.

As we hurried into the entrance I saw Shen standing in front of my office and as soon as he saw us he laughed and waved a paper at us, shouting, '*You are a free man, Huimin!*'

Without even looking at the paper he brandished at me, I pulled him in my arms and hugged and embraced him, tears of joy streaming down my face.

After Shen it was Wu's turn. Both men were truly and deeply moved and they repeatedly hugged me and slapped my shoulders to show how happy they were for my sake.

When I had calmed down a bit we trooped into my office where Shen finally showed me the papers. There were three separate official documents, one for me, one for Wu and one for Major Shen himself.

Shen read mine first. It said that with effect from 26th July, 1976 I would be discharged from penal servitude and that on that date the amount of fifty yuan would be paid to me to cover my expenses until my reporting for duty at the Dalian Shipyard and Shipbuilding Company on 28th August, 1976.

Furthermore, I would be entitled to two free train tickets, from Urumqi to Hefei and from Hefei to Dalian respectively, to be issued at the stations against a copy of the official release paper signed by camp commandant Major Shen Guofeng.

Wu's document said that the authorities recognised a debt to him of 24,000 yuan for ten years of voluntary service as a medical doctor from which amount 23,440 yuan had to be deducted for ten years of food, clothing and shelter, leaving a net amount of 560 yuan to be collected at the Finance Ministry in Beijing, upon presentation of the underlying documents.

Finally, the document addressed to Major Shen ordered him to disband the convict labour force starting 1 August, 1976, and to be completed by 15th August, 1976. The authorities further ordered him to turn over the camp and its inventory as well as the unharvested crops in the field to the Party secretary of Tacheng, Comrade Zhai Siji.

When Major Shen finished reading he looked up at us and we stared at each other in stunned disbelief.

Then, suddenly, Wu burst out laughing and, relieved, Shen joined him. I kept staring at them but slowly the blatant unreality of the terse official prose dawned on me as well and I joined in the merriment.

'Just over five hundred yuan for ten years of work as a doctor!' Wu hiccuped. 'The price of my sacrifice for our glorious and magnanimous socialist motherland!' he shrieked and suddenly he burst into real tears.

'Fifty yuan for ten years of *my* life,' I mumbled disbelievingly. 'You hear that, Guofeng? Fifty yuan and a train ticket to bloody Dalian! How the hell do they expect me to manage with that pittance? Any ideas, Shen? Tell me, I'm all ears!'

'At least you have *something*,' Shen replied, deeply embarrassed, and he continued, rather vehemently. 'What about those poor bastards I'll have to send off in August? It says nothing about send-off money for initial expenses or about a free train ticket to wherever they came from. And the camp won't be the only one that's disbanded. All over China people will be released from camps and communes without a fen in their pockets.

'They'll flood bus and train stations and board any bus or train to get away as fast and as far as possible and that they won't be able to pay for their tickets is nothing compared to what will happen when they grow hungry and thirsty. What a terrible, incredible and dangerous mess that'll create, Huimin!'

He looked at us with despair in his eyes.

Gone was our joy as Shen's words sank in. The prospect of millions of people on the rampage for transport, food and drink was indeed terrifying. Gone was also our own self-pity as we realised our own relative privileged situation.

Wu scraped his throat and said hesitatingly, 'I have an idea. As you know, in the past Party Secretary Zhai always paid a token sum of money for the part of our crops we ceded to him. I know it was just a receipt, a kind of IOU, which we gave back to him a few months later in exchange for fertiliser and new tools. No money changed hands, a mere transaction on paper. But this time we won't need fertiliser so I wonder whether this one time Secretary Zhai wouldn't be willing to pay real money for the last harvest.

'We could divide the amount equally amongst all the prisoners. If only each of them had a few yuan to pay for some food and hot water on the way out of here we probably could avoid food riots already happening here or in Urumqi. That would also be in Secretary Zhai's interest, wouldn't it? What do you think?'

Shen and I thought it an excellent idea and worth proposing to Secretary Zhai.

The three of us drove to Tacheng the next day to see Secretary Zhai. Zhai was surprised and pleased to see us.

Cutting short the usual trivial preliminaries Shen told him we had a serious matter to discuss with him and then handed him the official papers to read for himself first.

I watched Zhai while he read the documents and though at first he showed genuine pleasure at the news about me, I saw him frown and shake his head in disbelief when he had come to the third document about the disbanding of the camp.

Finished his reading he looked up at us, worried.

'I'm very glad for you, Dao, and for you too, Wu,' he said, 'though I'm sorry for the miserly way they have treated you. Both of you deserve better. But knowing you, I'm sure it's not your own problem that you have come to see me about. It's Major Shen's instruction to disband the camp that worries you, eh? Three thousand people let loose without a fen and only their legs to get them to Urumqi and then what? It's inhuman, I know that but that's not what I'm worried about. I foresee trouble, big trouble. Riots, looting, soldiers shooting to kill. I won't have that here in Tacheng and I'm sure I speak for my colleagues in Karamay, Shihezi and Urumqi as well.

'We can't have Chinese killing Chinese, or, worse, Uygur soldiers shooting Chinese civilians. The Muslims will have a field day and throw oil on the fire, sure thing. I beg you Shen, and you as well, Dao and Wu, to keep the matter under wraps until I have talked to my colleagues, though I don't see what we can do.'

Shen looked at me and then at Wu and when we both nodded, he scraped his throat and said, choosing his words carefully, 'We foresaw your reaction, Comrade Secretary Zhai, and before we came to see you we discussed the matter amongst ourselves and we think there is perhaps a way to avoid trouble, at least for the first few days which may be just long enough to maintain calm in this region. What happens later, in the other provinces, is a matter for the authorities there. At least there won't be any gloating Muslim separatists over there to take advantage of the situation.'

Shen fell silent and looked anxiously at Secretary Zhai.

'Continue, Major,' Zhai said, 'I'm listening.'

So Shen told him.

I watched Zhai while Shen talked and I saw him nod a few times, pensively yet approvingly.

When Shen fell silent, Zhai said, 'It's certainly an idea worth considering. I'll have to discuss it with my colleagues though, since there's a lot of money involved, far more than what I can authorise, let alone what I have in cash. Three thousand people times say twenty yuan each, that makes sixty thousand yuan, a considerable sum for which we may even need the approval of First Secretary Sen Pulin. Tomorrow I'll go and see my friends, the secretaries of Shihezi and Karamay. It won't be difficult to convince them we have a serious problem and that we have to try and convince Secretary Jin of Urumqi as well. Jin Zuomin outranks us but the biggest disturbances will be in his city when the ex-convicts will try to board the trains bound for inner China and that will be very bad for Jin's reputation. So I guess he'll be eager to co-operate to get Secretary Sen's attention and approval. Give me a couple of weeks to sort things out.'

Zhai invited us for lunch at Wong's former restaurant.

We found the food to be quite good though not as abundant as in Wong's time.

It was the difference in atmosphere though that struck us most. Where during Wong's time people had been joyful, rowdy, boisterous and, above all, noisy and friendly sociable, they were now very quiet, seemed preoccupied even, paying little or no attention to their chance table companions.

They ate their food, paid and left often without a word or glance at the waitress, who was just as morose.

We had a pleasant time though, talking and laughing as we got to reminiscing about the old days with Wong, Meimei, Liu and Lu and jokingly wondered how Liu was doing in Beijing with his Meimei and her temperamental father.

Our table drew quite a number of curious, distrusting and even hostile glances from the other customers but Zhai didn't seem to care.

After lunch we drove all the way back to our camp. When we passed by Su Leima's hostel I felt butterflies in my belly and imperceptibly looked askance, hoping to catch a glimpse of the voluptuous Madam Su and her beautiful, sensuous daughters.

The window shutters were closed, however, and the place looked deserted.

Quite possibly Su and his womenfolk hadn't returned from some Koran reading contest or other in Iran and was Su now allowed to play the heroic freedom fighter in exile in exchange for the services of his women to his so-called commanders in some movement or other for the liberation of Islamic Xinjiang.

Shen, unaware of what had gone on behind those shutters, drove on, talking animatedly about that nice man Secretary Zhai.

Turning my head away from the hostel's desolate look I caught Wu's mocking half-smile and teasing wink.

Three weeks passed without a word from Secretary Zhai and Major Shen became increasingly worried as August approached.

Then, one afternoon, as Wu and I sat quietly in the shade of the only tree in our camp, a gnarly old mulberry tree, the pride and darling of every one of the men, convict and non-convict alike, we saw Shen turning into the camp entrance with his usual blasts of the horn, one short, one long, one short.

With him were Secretary Zhai and three other men.

Major Shen was in an excellent mood and made light-hearted small talk while Secretary Zhai introduced the three others as Secretary Peng of Shihezi, Secretary Li of Karamay and Secretary Jin of Urumqi.

It was obvious from the others' attitude that Secretary Jin Zuomin was an important man, though Jin himself seemed friendly and unassuming enough.

Wu made fresh hot water and offered cookies all around. The cookies were made of roughly ground oats, barley malt and apple syrup and baked in our camp bakery. Wu and I had experimented with different recipes until we decided on one that produced both nutritious and delicious biscuits that didn't crumble after a few days.

The barley we germinated and then dried ourselves and the syrup we made from the small, sweet apples we had discovered growing in the wild when I was reconnoitring a hilly terrain for the pipeline. On the southerly slopes of the hills the scrawny, small apples were reddish green and sweet and according to Wu full of vitamin C so we harvested them and dried them for the winter months. Everyone in the camp had to eat one apple and two cookies with breakfast every day, and since then the number of Wu's patients with indeterminate complaints had declined spectacularly.

Our guests praised the taste of the cookies and our excellent health care, which was a good sign.

After half an hour of small talk we gave our guests the grand tour around the camp and the fields and they praised the neatness of the camp and the health of our crops which covered already more than a hundred hectares, another good sign judging by Major Shen's broad grins and enthusiastic comments, quite unlike his usual self.

After more hot water and cookies we had a light meal in the canteen at the end of which we toasted each other with a small glass of *maotai* Shen poured ceremoniously from the famous bottle he had brought with him.

Wu then surprised everybody with his own-grown sweet melon and fresh strawberries for dessert.

In a far corner of the camp Wu had his own little garden. Together we had built a closed wooden fence two metres high around a small plot of land of ten by ten metres to protect it from the wind. Inside the fence we had tended sheets of thin transparent plastic to imprison the sun's warmth.

The melon seeds we had got from Wong the day he left but the strawberries Wu had painstakingly cultivated from the grains he had found in a pot of Russian strawberry jam. It had taken him more than a year to grow a few plants in his clinic but now he had already more than a hundred plants bearing fruits.

Our guests were delighted and effusive in their praise.

In an excellent mood we trooped back to my office to hear the real reason for their visit.

Secretary Zhai of Tacheng acted as spokesmen for his colleagues from Shihezi, Karamay and Urumqi.

This was standard procedure. Zhai was the less senior in rank and could therefore be blamed or reprimanded or overruled in case the news he brought was not well received while on the other hand the praise would go to his more senior colleagues, notably Secretary Jin of Urumqi, if the message was popular.

After thanking Wu and me for a wonderful reception and praising us again, officially, for the tidiness of the camp and the fields and, oh miracle, for our private enterprise, he came to the point.

'We have discussed your idea to be paid real money for the camp inventory and the crops now that the camp will be discontinued so that you can use the monies to pay a travel allowance to the prisoners on their discharge. We commend you for the motives behind your idea and recognise the validity of your arguments, however, regretfully, we cannot go along with you in this.'

Zhai fell silent and looked at us over his steel-rimmed, crooked spectacles.

He had apparently expected our astonishment and disappointment after all the earlier good vibrations for he held up his hand to signal us to keep quiet and continued, 'Let me explain the matter as we see it. Our main reason was that the Party, so actually the State, can hardly be expected to pay for what belongs to it already. I am sure I need not remind you of the fact that *all* land within the borders of the People's Republic of China belongs to the People and thus to the Party. Everything built or grown on that land is also owned by the Party or, if you prefer, by the State.

'Did you pay for the materials you used to build the camp, Dao? No! You did not! The State gave them to you so why would we now have to pay for something we own already? Did you pay rent for the land you cultivated? No! you did not! You just took it for granted that you could use it and strictly, very strictly speaking you could because you are of the People.

Furthermore, the State cannot give money to the convicts at the time of their release since until that time they have been fed, clothed and sheltered by the State and their labour is considered in return for that. In conclusion therefore, you cannot sell your produce to the State since both land and labour were, and still are, owed by you to the State.'

Zhai burst out laughing at the expression on our faces.

I looked in despair at Major Shen but he ignored me, scrutinising the palms of his hands as if the solution were written there.

Still smiling, Zhai continued, 'However, let me assure you that we got the point. You were very clever to play on our fear of unrest and riots in your attempt to get your fellow convicts some money. Though for different reasons our concerns coincide and we must co-operate in this matter. As I explained before, we cannot pay the prisoners on the day they are freed since their labours were merely a token repayment for the excellent care the State extended to them over the past ten years.'

Zhai chuckled mockingly and went on. 'However, we, that is the municipalities of Tacheng, Karamay, Shihezi and Urumqi, are prepared to hire the whole bunch of them for ten days of real work and pay them two yuan net per day, with effect from 1st August, the first day of their regained freedom. For that money they will have to clean the camp and the tools and equipment, to harvest the crops still in the field and to train a production brigade from Shihezi to take over the running of the camp. On 11th August they will be free to go with each having twenty yuan of honestly earned money in their pocket.

Major Shen will organise their orderly transport to Urumqi in manageable batches every day from the 11th to the 15th August and Secretary Jin of Urumqi will order the ticket booths at the railway station to be closed on those dates so that the men can board the trains without a boarding ticket. That way we shift the problem of how to make them pay for their seats to the train and car supervisors and that, of course, will be outside our jurisdiction.'

Zhai fell silent and grinned mischievously as Wu and I burst out laughing.

'Now that we have solved our mutual problems to everybody's satisfaction and without loss of face for either party, I have still one last request to make to both Dao Huimin and Wu Fuzhi,' Zhai continued, serious again.

'We, and that includes Major Shen this time, feel that to conduct this whole affair in an orderly fashion your presence is essential. We therefore have to ask you to stay on until the last day, that is until 14th August, and to leave with the last batch of ex-convicts. Do you accept that?'

I looked at Wu, the freeman, and when he nodded at me I replied, 'We accept, Secretary Zhai. I propose, however, that we keep things simple and tell the prisoners that they'll be free as from 11th August and will be paid twenty yuan each for their initial expenses. Furthermore we tell them that there will be daily transports to Urumqi from this date until 15th August where they can board any eastbound train without a boarding ticket. I don't think it will do any good to explain to them your convoluted scheme and that they are actually already free as from 1st August. I foresee a lot of problems, even possibly sabotage, if we do that.'

Everybody agreed and our little machiavellian party broke up with grins, laughter and backslapping all around.

On 31st July I called a general trooping of all prisoners and told them that they would be free men again as from 11th August on which day they could collect a one-time send-off allowance of twenty yuan each.

For a few minutes there reigned a deadly silence as each digested the news for himself. Then a subdued murmur started as the men began talking softly to their neighbours in the ranks.

I saw quite a few who wept openly.

I gave them five minutes to digest the news and regain control of themselves again and then I called them to order and explained the work schedule for their last ten days as convicts.

Everything went without a hitch. Only a few bothered to take leave of Wu and me personally when they collected their money and boarded the trucks. The rest just took the money without a word of thanks or even goodbye, not to me or Wu and not amongst themselves.

They were like cattle, morosely grunting and bumping into each other as they scrambled to board the trucks that would take them to freedom and then to what?

'Ten years have passed and nothing has changed,' Wu remarked as he watched the mêlée.

'People don't really change. So very few have what I call "class", the rest are selfish, ungrateful, ungracious; it's in our genes probably, to ensure the survival of the species. Look how they scramble to get the best seats and then just sit there with those unseeing, bovine eyes while the others, perhaps their buddies for the past ten years, clamber over them to get to the back of the truck. Me, me, me and to hell with the rest. Pathetic! And you and I going out of our way to get them a decent send-off, those arseholes. You think they would be grateful? Say thank you if they knew? Forget it! They don't give a damn, probably think, that is if they are capable of thinking, that *you owe* them the money.

'Why should I care what happens to them? Why of all people should *you* care, Huimin, whether there are riots in bloody Urumqi? Shouldn't you have unholy glee instead? Why are you so *bloody decent*, Dao? We could probably have made a deal with the four Comrade Secretaries and pocketed a nice sum of money ourselves. Why didn't we, for God's sake?'

He looked at me angrily, then, when he saw my mocking smile, he grinned and said, pretending exasperation, 'Okay! Okay! I know! Common decency, wouldn't be able to look me in the face, all that nonsense. Look at those bastards outside, Huimin! They have already forgotten about us, or about the beautiful friendships between them. Most of them would probably kill their best mate if they thought it would give them an advantage during the next couple of days. They don't suffer from scruplemania like we do, Huimin.'

I shrugged my shoulders and didn't comment. It was one of those days for Wu Fuzhi. Probably because he was afraid of his own future and the seemingly stupid resignation of the men outside enraged him.

On 14th August Wu and I took leave of Major Shen in true military fashion, short, clipped, no nonsense, a wonderful way to hide your emotions.

Ours was a through train to Beijing and I had to change trains in Datong and continue to Hefei. Wu would go on to Beijing where he would collect his money before reporting to General Kong's headquarters on 20th August.

We talked little on the train, each of us preoccupied with thoughts about the immediate future. Besides, after so many years of close companionship and even closer friendship there was little left to say, just the occasional desultory remark about the scene outside.

The supervisor of our car was a gentle young woman from Shanghai. We spoke to her in Shanghainese and, after a moment's hesitation, told her who we were.

She never asked us to show her our tickets for our seats and she kept passing with the hot water kettle to replenish our mugs. When our tea leaves were so exhausted that they didn't colour the water any more she gave us a handful of her own free of charge.

We got to Datong in the evening of the third day after our departure from the camp. Wu had an hour before his train would continue for Beijing and my connection to Taiyuan, Shijiazhuang, Jinan, Xuzhou and Hefei was at midnight so we had time for one last meal together.

The station's restaurant was full with people, however, nobody was eating. People looked withdrawn. They hardly talked.

Wu got hold of a filthy food list and tried to order a few dishes.

The unsmiling, listless girl invariably twanged 'meiyou' as she stared at nothing over our heads and even before Wu had pointed the dish out to her. Exasperated we finally settled for a few stale biscuits and a mug of musty smelling tea each.

Wu shrugged his shoulders and grumbled, 'This doesn't exactly cheer me up, Huimin. We may well come to regret our cosy little life in Tachakou. I don't think we missed much fun these past ten years and as far as I can see we are definitely in better physical shape than these people here. They look miserable to me, green even.'

I had noticed the same thing, felt the last traces of my initial good spirits being drained out of me by the atmosphere of gloom and doom.

I was relieved when the loudspeaker announced the imminent departure of the through train to Beijing. Wu paid for the tea and biscuits and I accompanied him to his car.

Wordlessly we embraced, then, brusquely, he disengaged himself and looked at me at arm's length, his eyes brimming with tears.

'Take care of yourself, Huimin,' he whispered, and, in an attempt to lighten the atmosphere, 'you're on your own now! No more Wu Fuzhi to look after you.'

At that he turned and jumped into the slowly accelerating train. The last I saw of him was his sad, tired smile and a small, hesitant gesture of his right hand as if he wanted to grasp at me.

I made a few hesitant, jerky steps as if to catch up with him but then I stood still and, arm still raised halfway up, I stared after Wu's train as it pulled out of the station and disappeared into the night.

'Don't despair! Tomorrow there'll be another train, my friend,' a deep, friendly voice said beside me.

Shocked back into reality I looked up and at the back of a man walking away from me. Over his shoulder he shouted at me cheerfully, 'In fact, there will always be another train, another tomorrow, so never you despair!'

I burst out laughing and shouted back, 'Thank you, my unknown friend! Your reminder was a timely one! Indeed, there will always be *tomorrow*!'

The man waved merrily as he continued walking and then he, too, was gone.

Thirty hours later I got off the train in Hefei. The rest you know. Forgive me if I bored you.

*

The spell they had been under for the past five hours or so broke suddenly with that last apologetic remark by Lao Dao.

Hesitantly at first they shifted their position to relieve the stiffness of the muscles, then, still without speaking, they stretched and groaned and yawned without restraint.

They never cease to amaze me, the Chinese, Lao Dee thought to himself. Despite their eternal fussing about losing face or causing loss of face they can be so rude as to make the angels weep, my Western angels, that is, for it doesn't seem to ruffle Lao Dao's feathers one bit. Look at him now sitting there and literally oozing contentment.

Instead he said, 'I thought I had led an eventful life, however, it has been nothing compared to yours, Huimin. Before you began your story you asked us to tell you afterwards if in our opinion you could have done things differently, if the feelings of guilt you still torture yourself with are justified.

Well, let me tell you that I don't see how you could have acted differently and, to be frank, I am not so sure that I could have managed as well as you did.

'You always made the best of any situation, even as the vilest things happened to you, mostly by bending with the wind but quite often also by acting decisively though always calmly and mildly, whereas, in your place, *my* hot temper would have landed me in even bigger trouble. If I would have survived, a very big *if*, I certainly would not be sitting here now in as good a physical and mental shape as you do and with so many achievements to be proud of.

'Okay, you *did* take the wrong turn in 1953 and that was a mistake, a bad error of judgement rather, however, since then and against all odds you made the best of every situation that was forced upon you. You have known and shown love and friendship and compassion, yet the blind hate and evil and vile wickedness that destroyed millions of your contemporaries never got a hold on you, never sullied you, never provoked you to reciprocate. Even in retrospect, as you let your life unfold before us, you never showed bitterness or anger or rebelliousness towards those who betrayed you and tried to destroy you. Even your hesitant, occasional expressions of regret about the bad things that happened to you were always mild and tempered by your tendency to try and understand what drove those people, to find excuses for their behaviour, to see the shimmering aura of goodness around even the vilest person.

'I envy you for your peace of mind and am astonished, upset even, that you, of all people, think that you should feel guilty about anything you did. You never harmed anybody, on the contrary I would say. Did you ever think of how many people actually owe their life to you? Because of your influence on the running of that *laogai*, I mean, your agricultural venture providing food for everybody whereas elsewhere, in scores of camps all over China, people died of starvation and maltreatment. I am sure that in your camp nobody died through maltreatment or torture or hunger. Through general decrepitude and the terrible cold during the winter months yes, of course, but that wasn't your fault. Hundreds, probably thousands of people ought to be grateful to you. Feeling guilty, my foot!

'Or are you anguishing because you think that you have compromised your precious morality by your amorous rompings with the Su women in Tacheng? Don't tell me that that is the secret reason for your feelings of guilt! That would be so ludicrous! What you did was totally normal and acceptable under the circumstances and after all those years of abstinence. There was no question of love or bonding, no false promises, merely a question of the release of pent-up male and female urges and when it's over it's over. Even Liang, had she lived and had you told her, as you would have knowing you as I do, would have laughed and told you not to be silly to make so much of such an insignificant matter. End of subject she would have added, and I rest my case as well.'

Lao Dee fell silent and looked at his friend with a mixture of mockery and affection.

'Well spoken, Lao Dee,' Auntie Liu said. 'What utter nonsense, Huimin, if what Lao Dee thinks is true. You are an example for all of us, for Lao Dee and me with our bad tempers, for Suping with her pent-up resentments, for Lilian and Beiyuen with their shallow cockiness; we can all learn from you.'

She chuckled and added, 'I see that all this praise makes you uncomfortable eh, dear old friend? So I just want to thank you for sharing your remarkable life story with us. Yours was the last of the series so Lao Dee now has all he needs for his book. Next month he can enjoy the final act as he brings us all together in Luding to meet the people we have come to know so well already from Suping's story.'

Liu Meiling fell silent and made a face at Lao Dee.

The Dutchman chuckled and said, 'I have my own ideas about that reunion, Meiling. I think a few of us are in for a surprise. But we'll see what we'll see, eh Meiling?'

Abandoning his bantering tone, he continued, addressing the others as well, 'Shall we meet again, here, in three weeks from today? I'll have then everything we need for our trip with me, clothes and tickets and so on and we can discuss any last-minute arrangements. What do you think?'

They merely nodded their assent. Now that they no longer had the cosy intimacy of their weekly gatherings to look forward to, something that had come to mean so much to them, they suddenly felt weary of the usual after-session chit-chat.

Lao Dee noticed the almost imperceptible change in atmosphere and the sudden listlessness of his friends and he felt like kicking himself for his unthinking suggestion to meet in three weeks only. As if those Thursday get-togethers had meant nothing to him but for milking them for their most intimate memories.

What a boor I am, he thought, irritated with himself, and backtracking will make things only worse. They will fall all over themselves to tell me that I am imagining things.

Instead he said, hesitatingly as if he were sounding them out, 'This weekend I'll go home to Hong Kong and I have been thinking to ask my wife to come with me next Tuesday for a few days. We could all have dinner together next Thursday at Mu Ping's place and she could make your acquaintance. And for the Sunday I could requisition the project bus and we could all go for a picnic on the beach, you, my engineers, a few managers of the new brewery so that my wife can finally meet everybody she has heard me talking about for so long now already. I would like that and so would she, I'm sure. What do you think of my plan?'

To his relief Lao Dee saw the women's faces light up with pleasure, however, before one of them could say something Lao Dao said, with uncharacteristic eagerness, 'That would be very pleasant, Lao Dee. Do you think I could invite my son Xulun and his wife and my granddaughter as well? Like your wife they also have heard a lot of talk about all of you and I know they are dying to meet my good friends, and the foreigners, of course. Can I ask them to join us for the picnic?'

'Of course you can, my friend, that goes without saying,' Lao Dee replied, laughing. 'Tell them they are most welcome. It's a pity your daughter Xuli can't join us. Perhaps, one day, she would be willing to give a recital in our hotel and I could reserve seats for all of us. Will you mention that to her, Huimin, in your next letter?'

Proudly Lao Dao said he would and, as he got up from his chair, he added, 'Come on, Lao Dee, it's past midnight and time for me to take over the night shift. So far every Thursday the day shift engineer, Zhou Junsheng, has stayed two or three hours later than normal so that I could stay until the end of our evening sessions. He is a nice young man, Zhou is. He told Vice-Manager Zhou, no relation of his, that he will work both shifts while I am away on our trip. Of course, he'll get my salary as well but all the same he refused to claim overtime rates for the hours he does for me so as not to give Secretary Du a reason to refuse my leave or to replace me for good. So you see, Lao Dee, there really *are* nice people, at least they happen to cross *my* path when I need them.' And laughingly he pushed his friend out of the door into the fresh night air.

The two men quickly bade goodbye to their friends and walked to the hotel in easy, companionable silence, each lost in his own thoughts.

While Lilian and Beiyuen washed and arranged the dishes and the beautiful new wok and saucepan, Auntie Liu and Suping talked quietly about the forthcoming trip and how to present the matter in a letter to Suping's parents and Chen Dan.

In particular the presence of so many outsiders, and one of them a foreigner to boot, would require some careful wording.

Suping thought it strange that Auntie made such a point of being referred to in the letter as Auntie Liu and not as Liu Meiling.

'I am an old, cantankerous woman and they are old people as well and we all have our old-fashioned ways,' Auntie muttered gruffly at Suping's quizzical look, 'and now we are at it, I shall introduce myself first to your parents and then to Chen Dan, separately and in private in my room in that guest house with none of you young hussies or those two boyfriends of yours present or I simply won't go.' And at that she got up and huffily disappeared into her bedroom, closing the door behind her with more force than necessary, leaving a puzzled Suping staring after her.

That was how Lilian found her a few minutes later, merely shrugging her shoulders and muttering under her breath when her daughter asked her whether something was the matter.

Making a perplexed face at Beiyuen, Lilian quickly trotted after her mother who was already halfway down the alley to their house.

'Adults,' Beiyuen mumbled to herself as she closed the door, 'how they always manage to complicate things! Life would be so much simpler without them,' and sighing resignedly she lay down on the couch and fell asleep within seconds, as simple as that.

'You didn't have a row with Auntie, now did you, Mother?' Lilian asked as she and her mother were preparing for bed. 'I heard Auntie slam the door of her bedroom and then I found you staring after her as if you had been slapped in the face. Did you offend her or something?'

'Not that I am aware of but then one never knows with that touchy old woman,' Suping replied irritably and continued. 'We were talking calmly about our trip and the letter I would write to my parents and Uncle Dan when all of a sudden she said she didn't want me to mention her full name, only to refer to her as Auntie and then she became all huffy and said she wanted to be alone first with grandfather and grandmother and then with Uncle Dan when she would meet them for the first time, in her room in the guest house she said. I must have looked a bit surprised when she said that and then she suddenly got up and disappeared into her bedroom, slamming the door in my face. It's normal to be surprised when people act like that, no? I can't see anything wrong with looking a bit surprised, now can you?' And indignantly Suping looked at her daughter, adding inconsequentially, 'where did you get that hussy-like underwear? *Open* embroidery *and much too small*! One can see the hair above your crotch and peeking out! Aren't you ashamed of yourself?'

Lilian burst out laughing and retorted, 'Look at yourself in that ugly meal sack you call underpants! You really needn't worry about some nice man getting into *your* pants as Auntie intimated tonight might happen one of these days.'

Grabbing her pillow to defend herself against her mother's flailing fists, she added, yelping with laughter, 'Besides, Auntie was probably thinking of some nice *old* man getting into *her* meal sack when she said that about you. How naive can you be, Mother? Don't you understand at all why Auntie is so upset and nervous at times? Yet it's so obvious. Beiyuen and I have figured out a long time ago why dear old Auntie becomes all flustered and secretive each time somebody mentions our trip to Luding. Now, stop trying to hit me and I'll tell you why! Okay?'

Panting, eyes shooting fire, Suping let her arms drop and cried, 'Okay! you tell me, hussy! You tell your naive, prudish old mother what you and that minx Beiyuen have figured out long ago!'

Grinning, Lilian sat down on the bed and said, in a hushed voice, 'Beiyuen and I are sure that Liu Meiling and your Uncle Dan know each other from the time they both lived in Shanghai. *We* think that Auntie was that irascible woman doctor who treated Chen Dan's wife Lingling while she was pregnant and that she was the one who got hold of Lingling's copy of Yang Baolin's notes and that she still has them. That would explain why Auntie has been untouchable all these years and why she could defy Old Turtle with impunity.'

Seeing her mother staring at her, in surprise, Lilian, smiling a bit pensively, abandoned her flippant tone and added softly, 'Auntie fell in love with Uncle Dan but couldn't show it of course because of Lingling and that is why she was always so brusque with him as he told you and you told us when you narrated his story. Besides, do you remember that Auntie once mentioned how the only man she had ever been in love with had been so smitten with his wife, even after her death, that he had never had eyes for her? So she never told him and never married somebody else. And now we have talked her into accompanying us to Luding where she will see her old love again, old in both senses.

'No wonder that she is nervous and no wonder that she doesn't want him to know that she is coming and no wonder that she doesn't want us around, grinning and gaping and blabbering when she first meets him after so many years and both of them old and no longer attractive. She never thought she would see him again and therefore never took care of herself, of her body I mean, as a woman, to remain attractive and in good shape like you, Mother. And now she regrets it, of course, but it's too late and she is ashamed and afraid Uncle Dan won't be able to hide his shock and disgust. If she is going to cry, whether from sorrow or from joy, she doesn't want us around to see her like that. It's normal, no?'

Suping stared at her daughter, flabbergasted. So young still and yet so perceptive already, she thought, of course she is right, it's indeed so obvious. Why didn't I see it? Have Lao Dao and Lao Dee? No, of course not! They are *men* and wouldn't notice such things even if one wrote it on the wall in big characters.

She sighed and aloud she said, 'Do we have to let Auntie know that we guessed the truth?'

Relieved at her mother's normal tone and that she had obviously accepted her view, Lilian replied, 'No! Of course not! Perhaps that one time when she hinted at her one and only unrequited love she may have half-and-half wished us to push her into telling us her secret but when the moment passed with no reaction from us, I'm sure she was glad we didn't. So we cannot now all of a sudden take her by surprise with our deductions, as if we had been gossiping and poking fun at her behind her back.

'Even in Luding, if everything turns out all right one way or another between her and Uncle Dan we will have to wait whether and until she sees fit to tell us about their past acquaintanceship or friendship or love, whatever she is going to call it, and then we have to pretend to be very surprised, delighted or sad as the case may be. That won't be difficult for Lao Dao, he has no clue anyhow, however, Lao Dee may have an idea of his own. Do you remember what he said tonight? When Auntie said that there still remained the last act of our reunion in Luding?

'He told her, and specifically her, that he had his own ideas about that reunion and that he thought a few of us might be in for a surprise. "We'll see what we'll see, eh Meiling?" were the exact words he said. I remember clearly since Auntie made a face as if she had found a cockroach in her rice. So we have to talk to Lao Dee, you, Beiyuen and I, and then we have to promise each other not to let on. At least that's how I see it,' Lilian ended, shrugging her shoulders.

Her eyes brimming with tears of loving pride, Suping embraced her daughter.

The dinner with Lao Dee and his wife in Mu Ping's All Under Heaven Restaurant was a relaxed and jovial affair without a single false note.

Mrs Dee, a petite and pretty blonde, had an easy laugh and a good sense of humour and she visibly enjoyed the company, the food and the restaurant's raucous atmosphere.

Everybody agreed that the Chinese name, Ah Li, her Chinese painting teacher in Hong Kong had composed for her was an appropriate and auspicious one.

After dinner the two men were told to return to the hotel by themselves as the women would go together to Auntie Liu's place to discuss their outfits for the trip and for Ah Li to take measurements for the ready-to-wear things she would buy in Hong Kong. Afterwards Lilian would accompany Ah Li back to the hotel.

The Sunday outing was a great success.

They were quite a crowd, forty-three to be exact, not counting Mu Ping and his three helpers who went separately by truck with the food and dishes, pots and pans, trestle-tables and firewood to the picnic place on the beach.

The others had all gathered in front of the hotel and punctually at ten o'clock the brewery bus turned up to take them to the beach.

The weather was beautiful though the wind was, as always, a bit chilly.

The Dutch and Germans had brought a number of suitable music tapes for the bus's sound system and before long Jan the engineer, using the microphone with gusto and expertise, had everybody singing and humming along.

Jan had even brought a couple of tapes with Chinese songs by Teresa Teng and, spurred on by Lilian and Beiyuen, the Chinese quickly threw all reservations out of the open windows and sang along lustily, laughing and waving at the people beside the road who stared after the bus with open mouths.

After an hour's drive on the winding coastal road they arrived at the place selected by Lao Dee and everybody got off and clambered down the slope to the beach, the young people shrieking and sliding down, the elders a bit more sedately. Auntie Liu was last, aided by Lao Dao's daughter-in-law who had to take care of her little daughter as well.

Mu Ping had already arrived and was busy with his preparations. Once on the beach everybody but Auntie Liu and Lao Dao took off their upper clothes and an astounding mishmash of long and short underwear, old- and new-fashioned swimming suits and colourful swimming trunks rushed shouting and shrieking through the breakers and headlong into the sea.

Even Lao Dee and his wife Ah Li, admittedly very shy of cold water as a result of their many years in the tropics, frolicked in the clear but ice-cold Bohai Haixia in a hilarious, unruly kind of ball game, men and women indiscriminately yelling, yelping, leaping, diving and splashing after a big multi-coloured plastic ball.

Auntie Liu, sitting cross-legged on a patch of sandy beach cleared of pebbles especially for her, smiled indulgently at the racket all the while keeping one unobtrusive eye on Mu Ping's preparations for the picnic and the other on Lao Dao's granddaughter who seemed mesmerised by the smoke and flying sparks of the fire under the pot with dumplings.

Finally, around noon, at a sign from Mu Ping that the food was ready, Auntie banged with a stick on a rusty, empty oil drum she had found on the beach to summon the others and as one the whole horde left ball and sea for what they were and rushed, screaming in anticipatory delight, out of the water and up the beach towards the trestle-tables and the stacks of bowls and chopsticks.

Lao Dao, forewarned by Lao Dee about this everyone for himself run on the food, had taken up position in front of the tables and, shouting through a loud hailer, he ordered everybody to put on their clothes first so as not to catch cold.

Shrieking that nobody should start eating before everybody was back, the Chinese dispersed all over the stretch of beach, each to his or her small place of hiding to change, rush-rush and teeth chattering, into dry underwear they had brought with them and to put back on their upper clothes.

The Westerners, unconcerned in their free and easy way, took off their bathing trunks and suits, towelled themselves and got dressed in full view.

Even Ah Li, to Auntie's utter amazement, took no notice of all the men around her and made no effort to hide or wrap a towel around her as she changed back into shorts and a T-shirt.

'Never will we Chinese be as carefree as those people,' the old woman mumbled and then her mouth fell open in shock as she saw Lilian and Beiyuen among the barbarians and going about their business, unselfconsciously, as if they already belonged to the tribe.

For better or for worse we appear to have joined the world, she thought and she smiled proudly at the two girls.

Towelling themselves vigorously with the fluffy hotel towels, the girls looked up and caught her smiling. They laughed merrily and waved, free amongst the free.

The picnic was an all-seafood affair, even the dumplings had a shrimp filling, and everybody enjoyed the tangy freshness of Mu Ping's varied concoctions. Beaming with pleasure the little southerner acknowledged the shouts of delight and praise.

After the meal the Chinese, without much ado, found themselves a comfortable position for a nap while the Westerners, restless as is their character, went for a long walk along the beach.

On their return an hour or so later the Chinese were just about to get up from their nap and the Dutch proposed a round robin series of contests between China, Germany and Holland in beach volleyball and badminton doubles.

Cheered on by their non-competing fellow countrymen and women the Chinese won all the badminton matches but were no match for the taller and more experienced Europeans in the two-a-side volleyball contests.

It was past five o'clock when the hills to the west blocked the warmth of the sun and their creeping shadows chilled the enthusiasm of players and supporters alike.

Lao Dao announced the end scores as compiled by Lao Dee and his score keepers: badminton, China first, Germany second and Holland third; volleyball, Holland first, Germany second and China third.

The winning teams got each a voucher for a free meal at Mu Ping's place and the runners-up a case of beer or soft drinks to be picked up in person at the old brewery in town.

Tired but happy everybody clambered back up to the road and on board of the bus. Lao Dee had persuaded the driver to make a grand tour around the city to drop the people off in small groups as near as possible to their homes and it was past eight o'clock when the bus stopped at the corner of their alley and Auntie Liu, Suping, Lilian and Beiyuen got off, the last passengers but for Lao Dee, Ah Li and Lao Dao, who had insisted on staying until the last to bid goodbye to everyone as he or she got off with profuse expressions of gratitude for a wonderful day.

The things, clothes, toiletries and small travel accessories, Ah Li had bought for Auntie Liu, Suping and the two girls in Hong Kong drew forth cries of admiration and delight when Lao Dee unpacked and distributed to every one her due. Everything was tried on and shown off, put on and smelled and for once they completely forgot about dinner.

Lao Dao couldn't hide his emotion when he checked himself in the mirror and saw a dignified Westernised oriental gentleman in his friend's light grey suit, a new, light blue shirt and dark blue tie and comfortable, new, black loafers.

For a moment the women forgot about their own things and stopped their excited babble as they watched him adjust the tie with trembling fingers.

Lao Dee, who had been watching the scene from his easy chair, with an affectionate little smile, winked at Auntie and Suping and motioned them to refrain from comment.

They nodded and instead exclaimed what an impression they were all going to make on the plain folks of Luding as became sophisticated people from the modern open city of Dalian used to entertaining Westerners of high status.

Lao Dee laughed and said, teasingly, 'This Westerner of high status and his friend, the sophisticated gentleman from Dalian, are hungry and would like to take their leave before the kitchen in the hotel refuses to take any more orders. We assume that the sophisticated ladies have some more talking to do and will manage some noodle soup for themselves. We'll see each other next Monday when I'll pick you up at seven in the morning to go to the airport together. Our flight is at ten o'clock but I prefer to have ample time for all the formalities. Please dress sensibly and comfortably for the flight and for the bus ride from Chengdu to Luding.

'In Luding you can change into your fancy dresses for the reunion, okay?'

Now the irreversible moment had finally come they could only nod, their hearts pounding, as they tried to swallow the lump in their throats and say something.

Lao Dee grinned at the croaking sounds and, taking Lao Dao by his elbow, he bowed mockingly at the dumbfounded women and quickly closed the front door behind him.

## *Chapter Thirty-Six*

### The Final Trade-Off

A few minutes before seven o'clock in the morning of Monday, 22nd August, 1988, a Toyota Hi-Ace Lao Dee had borrowed from his Japanese friends reversed into the lane and stopped in front of Madam Liu's house.

Watched by the whole, broodily silent neighbourhood clustered there since Suping and Lilian had locked up their hovel and carried their suitcases over to Auntie's more than an hour earlier, Lao Dee slid open the van's side door and got out, followed by Lao Dao.

While Lao Dao was fumbling to raise the van's rear door, the front door of Auntie's house opened and Lilian and Beiyuen stepped outside, each carrying two suitcases, followed by Suping with two big jute bags of apples.

'Let's get out of here quickly,' Lilian muttered under her breath to Lao Dee, 'I'm sure Old Turtle is watching us from behind that grubby curtain of hers, waiting for this moment to come over and start a row. Lao Yang told me yesterday in confidence that she has been haranguing the neighbours about our get-togethers and our trip and that she's even angrier than usual because she realises she has been tricked into endorsing my father's institutionalisation. People may be apt to follow her rabble-rousing, Lao Yang says, because they feel cheated by what they now see as play-acting and manoeuvring to get rid of my father so as to be free to go on our trip.'

Lao Dee nodded and, loading the last bag of apples, he said over his shoulder, 'Help Auntie into the van! Beiyuen lock the house and get in the van! Huimin, get in last and close the door!'

Without further ado he slammed the hatchback shut and as he stepped to the front of the van he saw Old Turtle come out of her shack in a waddling trot, shaking her right fist with a swinging, pink plastic bag.

No doubt the bag is full of her past few days' shit, he thought and he quickly climbed into the seat beside the driver.

Without waiting for Lao Dee to close the door the driver, who had undoubtedly sensed the urgency and kept the engine running, released the clutch and the van shot forward and out of Old Turtle's reach.

As the van turned left into the main street they had a last glimpse of the scene in the alley, a small crowd staring sullenly at an hysterical woman throwing a bag full of excrement against the door of house 383/7.

Gently pushing an angrily sputtering Auntie Liu back into her seat, Lilian said, 'Take it easy, Auntie. Before long Old Turtle will be scrubbing your door, and probably ours as well. After Lao Yang spoke to me yesterday and warned me she was up to something, I went to see the militia commandant and asked him to keep an eye on our houses. I gave him two hundred yuan, which he took ever so greedily, so I'm sure he'll have a look today, probably even before he goes to his office at eight o'clock. He'll guess, and otherwise Lao Yang'll tell him, who soiled our doors and he'll order Old Turtle to scrub off the shit herself. That'll teach her a lesson, that hateful old hag.'

'Thank you, my dear,' Auntie Liu mumbled, already more dazed than angry. 'I should have thought of enlisting my old friend the commandant myself, but I haven't been quite myself these past few days. I'm sorry,' and uncharacteristically she fell silent, sighing sadly.

'That old hag is a flaming lunatic!' Suping exclaimed, eyes shooting fire. 'She's crazy and ought to be locked up in an asylum!'

Lao Dee turned in his seat and said, chuckling, 'It's quite possible that that's exactly what's going to happen, Suping, perhaps while we're away. Saturday I went to see old Pan Yuren at the town hall to tell him that my friend, the engineer Dong has agreed to add him as a member to the investigation delegation that will visit Hong Kong next month to look at a big public housing estate and its waste water treatment plant in Shatin. One more hanger-on won't matter to the Hong Kongers since they're sure to get the contract for a similar plant in Dalian and maybe Shenyang as well.

'We foreigners know that of the fifteen or even twenty members of such investigation delegations there are perhaps four or five who know the business they're investigating and the rest are just hangers-on, Party members, friends and relatives of Party members and the like, all out for a free ride and the presents at the end of the visit, which they probably have to hand over to their mentors back home though. It's so blatant and sometimes it really is too much, however, as long as we are pretty sure we'll get the contract we don't say anything; the costs for such visits have been included in the project sum anyhow, that is, by those of us who know the game.

'For the smaller companies, however, who have no previous experience in China, the burden can be too heavy and their first contract in China ends often with a loss because of all the unforeseen and unforeseeable costs. Some lick their wounds, fire the overenthusiastic but naive sales engineer who got them into the mess and vow never to do business in China again, others learn from their mistakes and become quite adept at the games the Chinese play and do well, like me and my partners.

'However, be that as it may, Lao Pan was happy and I gave him pocket money for the inevitable little baubles he'll have to buy for his family. The Hong Kongers pay for his trip, lodging and food so I'll get away cheaply. We talked some, Lao Pan and I, and I told him that Madam Huo Guoshang was a bit of a blot on such a nice small neighbourhood as yours. He agreed and told me he had reported to the town council the rude treatment she had given him at the time of his visit to your neighbourhood. The Party secretary had called him in his office, Lao Pan told me, for an oral explanation after which the secretary had said that if one more instance of asocial behaviour came to his ears he would have to take drastic action.

'I'll write a small note at the airport about what I saw this morning and have our driver hand deliver it to Lao Pan. I'll suggest to Lao Pan that he have a talk with the militia commandant now that Lilian has enlisted his help. This morning's event may well be the straw that will break the camel's back.'

Lao Dee burst out laughing at his friends' unbelieving stares and added, chucklingly, 'You see, I have become quite good at solving small problems the indirect way. Chineseness has rubbed off on me, I'm afraid.'

The others laughed, hesitantly at first, then all out, uproariously. Wiping the tears of laughter from her eyes, Auntie Liu said, 'Imagine if they send her back to that hamlet she hails from and have her tend the pigs again. I pity those poor beasts.' And again she burst out laughing.

By then the van had turned right into the access road to the airport and the high-pitched roar of a jet plane about to take off reminded them of what was ahead and all of a sudden everybody quietened down and, nervously twitching their fingers, they watched apprehensively as the van came to a stop in front of the departure hall's glass entrance doors.

'All get out,' Lao Dee announced cheerfully. 'Huimin, you stay with Meiling while Suping, the girls and I carry the luggage to the check-in counter. I'll check quickly whether our flight is still as scheduled and then I'll write the small note for Lao Pan and send the driver back. Then you all wait in the waiting room while I do the checking in, okay?'

They nodded meekly, glancing apprehensively at the hustle and bustle and the many foreigners with their big, unusual suitcases and small, shiny leather attaché cases disgorged by a continuous stream of taxis and limousines.

Most of them seemed to know each other for they shouted greetings and remarks in strange foreign tongues, mostly eliciting bursts of laughter or good-humoured chuckles, sometimes, however, also what left no doubt were angry retorts.

They noticed that many greeted Lao Dee in a respectful manner though and that he had a kind, short remark for everybody and they were proud to be with him.

Half an hour later Lao Dee joined them in the waiting area and told them the luggage had been checked in to Beijing where they would have to change planes to Chengdu.

'We'll have to retrieve our luggage in Beijing and check in again,' he explained. 'They don't check the luggage through to the final destination and perhaps it's better that way. It's a hassle but at least you are sure that your luggage gets there at the same time as you. We have plenty of time in Beijing. If our flight here leaves on time we'll arrive in Beijing at about eleven o'clock and our connection to Chengdu is scheduled at one o'clock, arriving there at three thirty. If all goes well we can be on our way, by the small bus, at about four o'clock and arrive in Luding before eight o'clock tonight. A long, tiring day, I'm afraid, but then it'll be worth it, won't it? Now, let's proceed to the departure lounge.' And he motioned for them to follow him.

Boarding began on time and thanks to Lao Dee's whispered advice they were the last to board the bus and therefore the first to climb up the stairs to the plane's entrance.

Again Lao Dee helped everybody to their seats and to fasten their seat belts.

They had two rows of three seats; Auntie, Lao Dao and Suping the row next to the exit so they had more room for their legs. Lao Dee saw them tense and close their eyes, knuckles white from gripping their armrests, when the plane, an Airbus 310, began taxiing towards the runway and, smiling, he saw their lips move in a mumbled prayer when the plane took its run and finally lifted off.

When the plane settled for the short flight to Beijing and the noise of the engines abated they opened their eyes and looked around furtively, smiling weakly when they caught each other's eyes.

Lao Dee, leaning forward and sideways in his aisle seat, pretended not to have noticed their faces and talked normally, drawing their attention to the clouds outside the windows and the white-crested waves of the sea far below.

A pretty, smiling hostess in an ill-fitting light blue uniform served them a soft drink and a piece of cake from a trolley.

They all relaxed visibly and began to pay attention to what went on around them. Soon they were talking animatedly about all their strange, new experiences and Lao Dee marvelled at their matter-of-fact casualness when the plane began its descent and finally landed in Beijing barely one hour after their departure from Dalian, seasoned air travellers all of them.

The retrieval of their luggage and the check-in for their flight to Chengdu went without a hitch and they had time to have a look around the airport's domestic section.

Behind huge glass partitions they could see the international passengers and they marvelled at the diversity of the foreigners' appearances.

Tall and blond and ponderous, small and swarthy and quirkily gesticulating, sloppily dressed and unkempt, neatly dressed and freshly scrubbed, ludicrously attired and vacuous, they all milled and hung about, oblivious, like fish in an aquarium, to the curious stares and giggles of the Chinese crowding behind the glass wall.

Lao Dee and Lao Dao watched as the women stood with their foreheads against the glass partitions, shading their eyes against the reflection, gigglingly and excitedly commenting and drawing one another's attention to the bizarre crowd on the other side.

'Another couple of years and we Chinese will also start experimenting with dress codes and outward appearances to express our individuality or to defy the Party's dourness,' Lao Dao remarked, more to himself than for his friend's benefit.

Making a doubtful mien Lao Dee said, musingly, 'Probably, but never on such a scale or to such an extreme as in the West. For us Westerners, individualism and personal privacy are the highest good, whereas the Chinese are genetically conformists, conforming to whatever authority decrees what is proper and what is not, whether it's the clan or the association of such-and-such dialect speakers or the Communist Party, the Chinese conform, the rebel the exception. In the outside world, outside China that is, we also have clubs, associations, religious or philosophical sects and social classes who impose their dress and behavioural code on their members and hangers-on, however, always with the aim to *differentiate* themselves from others; uniformity is abhorrent except within the group, of course.

'Most of us go through such a period in our lives, the weaker characters always the most fanatical and tyrannical about the externals that differentiate them from others, but after a few years and sometimes after switching loyalties from one group to another, most of us come to our senses and live our normal, individual lives following our individual taste in what to do and how to appear for work and play, whom to frequent, what to think and generally how to lead our lives.

'I sincerely doubt that the Chinese of mainland China will ever become like that. Even the Chinese born and bred in Western countries never behave in the extravagant or even outrageous manner in showing their individualism as the Americans, Europeans and Australians do. There is always this reticence, this repugnance of vulgarity and flashiness, this uneasiness in dealing with demonstrative behaviour. Generally speaking, the Chinese, and Asians in general, have more class, more dignity than Westerners.'

Lao Dee fell silent, then added, 'We have to go to our gate. I just heard the boarding call for our flight.'

He stood up and called to draw Lilian's attention. Still giggling the women gathered their hand luggage and followed the two men to the gate for the flight to Chengdu.

While they waited for the doors to open Lao Dee explained about flight numbers, boarding calls, departure gates and so on, and that passengers needed to pay attention to such things in order not to miss their flights.

The flight to Chengdu was smooth and pleasant. The plane was less than half full since CAAC had fitted in a Boeing 747, probably for a test flight after maintenance before returning it to the international pool.

They marvelled at the size of the plane, the many lavatories, the galleys, the different classes for the passengers, the huge wings, the enormous engines, the intensely blue expanse above and as far as they could see, the vast fields of clouds, like stately floating mountains of snow-white cotton, below them and, most of all, they wondered what kept such a huge plane aloft in the void.

The flight attendants were friendly and helpful and when the captain stopped for a chat during his stroll through the cabin and smilingly allowed them, one at a time, a peep in the cockpit, their enthusiasm and joy knew no bounds.

Lilian and Beiyuen immediately decided they wanted to become air hostesses as well and they spent the remainder of the flying time with the air hostesses in the galley to get information on how to go about it.

The friendly captain gave them the address of CAAC's personnel department and told them to write a letter with their curriculum vitae.

Time passed quickly and before long they had to take their seats again and fasten their seat belts for the landing at Chengdu Airport.

They were half an hour ahead of schedule because of the big plane's greater speed, yet, when they had collected their luggage and exited the arrival hall, they were, or rather Lao Dee was, greeted by a tall, handsome and cheerful young man who had been waiting for them outside.

Lao Dee and the young man appeared to know each other very well since there was a lot of backslapping and laughter and mutual questions about health, work, projects and family.

This went on for a few minutes and then, finally, Lao Dee turned and introduced his friends from Dalian to Mr Long Wei, manager of CCPIT's Chengdu office.

Everybody immediately took to the friendly and relaxed Long Wei who, neatly dressed in an open-necked, short-sleeved white shirt, khaki slacks and comfortable, brown Timberland shoes, all undoubtedly bought in Hong Kong either by himself or by a foreign friend, was strikingly, pleasantly different from his male contemporaries.

He had a nice smile, showing white, regular teeth, his voice had a pleasant timbre as he spoke standard Chinese with only a hint of an accent, probably somewhere from the south, and he smelled of good soap and a trace of aftershave, in a word a very becoming young man indeed and Lao Dee was secretly amused when he saw Suping eagerly urging her daughter to help Mr Long Wei carry their luggage to the van that had suddenly stopped next to them.

The driver jumped out, greeting Lao Dee with a casual familiarity and the others with a friendly hello, and immediately began loading the luggage into the back of the van.

Then he introduced himself with a cordial handshake as Zee Bin, CCPIT's driver, and suggested they leave immediately to take advantage of their flight's early arrival and arrive in Luding well before dark and allow him to get back to Chengdu before midnight.

Lao Dee saw him looking meaningly at Long Wei when he said that, who caught on immediately as he exclaimed enthusiastically, 'That would be nice indeed for then I can accompany you to Luding and be back in time for tomorrow morning's arrival of a delegation from Hong Kong, people who wish to invest in a luxury hotel for foreigners in Chengdu. Zee Bin and I will show them around and assist them during their talks with the vice-mayor and

Party secretary and people from the Chengdu Import Export Corporation. So let's go!'

Beiyuen took the small seat next to driver Zee Bin, Auntie Liu and Suping the two seats behind the driver. Lao Dee and Lao Dao each had a single seat while the charming Mr Long Wei gently urged Lilian to sit with him in the back seat.

Zee Bin was a good driver and an entertaining tour leader in one as he steered with one hand while gesticulating and pointing with the other at the many pleasant sights of the very pleasant city of Chengdu as he drove the van through the wide, plane tree-lined streets.

The northerners were surprised to see so many people sitting at small tables on the sidewalks in front of the many small restaurants or open shops, whiling away the warm summer afternoon in the shade of the trees having tea or probably also coffee and eating from plates of cut fruit as they played dominoes or checkers or cards.

'No better life than a good life for these southerners, eh?' Auntie Liu grumbled. 'For us in the north it's all work and no play while here it seems to be the other way round. Oh, well, who's right and who's wrong, but after hardly half an hour here I already know what's more pleasant.'

The others burst out laughing and from the back of the van came Long Wei's cheerful voice, exclaiming, 'I am from much further south, from Anning near Kunming. You would love it there, Madam Liu, soaking your painful old bones in the hot springs followed by a gentle beating with a branch of the tea tree, then a nice long nap in the shade and you're all ready for an early dinner and companionable talk until it's time for bed. What a life! We southerners always wonder what makes people want to live in places like Dalian or Shenyang or, worse, Harbin when there are such wonderful places like Yunnan, Guangxi and Sichuan.'

'One is not always the master of one's own life and destiny, Long Wei,' Suping said softly and bending forward toward the driver she asked, 'could you please take the road via Xinjin, Meishan and Hongya, Zee Bin? I'd like to stop, if only for a few minutes, in Hongya, if you and Long Wei don't mind, of course.'

The two friendly young men assured her they didn't mind at all and an hour and a half later Zee Bin, guided by Suping, stopped the van a few kilometres outside Hongya alongside the Min River and near the fork to Jiajiang.

Everybody got out and while the others stretched their legs and made small talk Suping slithered down the river bank and sat down in the grass, her feet just above the softly gurgling small stream.

She gazed at the brownish eddies below her and mesmerised, her mind regressed twenty-two years when for the first time in her life she had stood up against the petty tyranny of a gang of misguided youths and had relieved herself in these very rushes, defying the Red Guards' orders to stay on her truck.

She smiled at the memory of her father and mother sticking up their thumbs at her act of courage and defiance and then she wept as she relived the moment her truck had abandoned the convoy and she had been swept up by the raging taifong of the Cultural Revolution and blown, hither and thither, like a dead autumn leaf, until she had fallen down to earth in Dalian and her life as Su Ping had begun.

As if looking through a kaleidoscope she again saw the faces of those who had briefly touched her life during the early days of her odyssey, drifting into and fading from her field of vision as they had then, yet she shivered when in her mind she heard the scream of young Sun Taiwen and the sickening thud that accompanied the first violent death in her life when Sun had thrown himself, in utter despair, in front of a speeding truck, in a final escape from his torturers, and she groaned and whimpered as she had then.

'You are shivering, Suping and you have goose bumps on your arms, what's the matter dear, you aren't falling ill, now are you?' she heard a voice above her say.

Slowly she came to and bleary-eyed she recognised Lao Dee looking down on her from higher up on the bank, clearly worried.

As she clambered up the bank back to the roadside, the others also gathered around Lao Dee and Lilian, taking her arm to help her to her feet, urged, 'What's wrong, Mother? What happened?'

'Ghosts from the past again! That's what happened,' Auntie Liu's voice answered for her.

'This is the place where your life took the fatal turn, eh Suping? That's why you wanted to stop here, isn't it? Going morbid all over again eh? Don't you think it's time to stop thinking of that moment as the fatal turn of your life but instead to see it as your good fate? If that bloody truck hadn't taken the wrong turn twenty-two years ago you wouldn't be standing here now, surrounded by good and caring friends and a loving daughter worrying about you.

'You would now either be a fussy old spinster teacher living with Mummy and Daddy or you would be married to a dull backwater intellectual who would have made you an even duller small-town bum of a son or a mousy daughter. Be grateful that fate spoilt the cosy little arrangement your Uncle Dan, in co-operation with his selfish buddy, Zhang Yizhong, concocted for you, your parents and himself, of course. I'll give him a piece of my mind, that nosy, interfering old clown!' And snorting indignantly Liu Meiling turned to look at Long Wei who had been making sounds of suppressed laughter.

'What are you laughing about, young man?' Auntie asked, pretending indignation. 'You have no idea what's going on here, of the momentous turn of events this woman, who could be your mother-in-law even, is trying to come to terms with and all you can do is stand there with that silly grin on your face.'

The others burst out laughing, Suping still a bit timidly though, at the sight of Auntie Liu berating a flabbergasted Long Wei.

'Come on, Long Wei, don't mind that cantankerous old woman,' Lilian said laughingly as she took his hand and made him follow her back to the van.

'Let's wait in the van and you can tell me more about life in Chengdu while my mother makes up her mind whether I am the result of bad or good karma on a fateful day now twenty-two years ago when she took the wrong turn and almost never came back.'

Giggling the two young people got back in the van in the back seat.

'And no more worries about that barbarian engineer either,' Auntie grinned, punching Suping in her ribs. 'Fate is indeed treating you kindly, my dear. Now let's continue on our way and no more trips down whatever memory lane we may pass during the remainder of our journey. Okay?' And still chuckling she waddled back to the van and climbed inside noticing *en passant* and with secret pleasure that Long Wei had put his right arm nonchalantly on the back of their seat, behind Lilian's back, as his fingers, with studied absent-mindedness, now and then tapped and then came to rest on her shoulder.

'Maybe, when that young engineer Jan is not absolutely necessary for the remainder of his project, Lao Dee might consider replacing him during the next couple of weeks,' she thought to herself as she took her seat and moving aside a bit to let Suping take hers.

'That would solve a lot of problems, also for Lao Dee himself. It would be an embarrassment for him as well if Lilian tried to elope with that man. I'll bring it up next time I'm alone with him.'

Chuckling inwardly she thought, Who am I to call Chen Dan a nosy, interfering old clown? Look at how I am meddling in other people's business.

But it's for everybody's good, isn't it? That's what all meddlers say, of course. We all mean well. We *may* break people's hearts but we mean well.

Gloomily and not at all proud of herself she stared out of the window, unseeingly, thinking of what was coming her way, of Chen Dan and how they would handle the situation, both of them.

It was a few minutes before seven o'clock when Zee Bin stopped in front of the Shuang Menlou Guest House in Luding.

While Zee Bin, Lilian and Beiyuen unloaded the luggage Lao Dee and Long Wei tried to locate the person supposed to be on duty at the reception desk.

Finally, after almost ten minutes, their desk slapping and shouts of '*Any folk there*?' *Any folk there*!' had apparently convinced the duty manager that ignoring them wouldn't make them go away since they suddenly heard a door slam somewhere on the first floor and then saw a dishevelled young man come stumbling down the stairs all the while fumbling with the buttons of his fly and smock.

'The lout was sleeping in one of the guest rooms, of course,' Long Wei said furiously. 'You know how things are in these godforsaken places, Lao Dee, but what would foreign tourists think of such a lackadaisical attitude? And they may come you know, the tourists I mean, though pilgrims is probably a better description of the morbid hordes that will want to see the bridge here where so many people were killed during Mao's Long March in 1933 or 1934, I forget.'

He fell silent to look contemptuously at the sheepish young man who had finally ended up behind the desk and was now looking at them with a vacuous stare.

'No point giving him a dressing down,' Long Wei mumbled to Lao Dee, 'the man is probably the village idiot but related in some way or other to the mayor so that's why they tucked him away here, in this lousy place. Why you wanted to stay here is a mystery to me, Lao Dee. There's a much better place, the Luding Guest House, a bit further up the road, facing the river. Why don't we just go there? I know the owner, he is a pleasant man and the food at his place is good.'

'I think it was Suping who proposed this place,' Lao Dee replied, 'probably because she remembers it from the time she lived here but never put a foot inside of course and because it's very close to where my friends have most of their business, there, halfway up that hill, on the other side of the river, if I'm correct. Let's ask her whether there is any other, compelling reason for staying here.'

He turned and called Suping to come over to the desk. Ignoring the man behind the desk, who had made no effort so far to enquire what they wanted, Lao Dee said to her, 'Long Wei and I think this is not a good place for us to stay, certainly not for a few weeks as Meiling, Lao Dao and Beiyuen will have to, so he proposes we go to the Luding Guest House a bit further up the road. Is there any special reason why we should stay here? Have your parents any special ties with this place, or your Uncle Dan as far as you know?'

'No, not at all,' Suping replied. 'Auntie and I were just talking what a gloomy, run-down, musty-smelling place this is. I'll be only too glad to go to the other place if Long Wei thinks that that's better. After all, I didn't write and tell my parents where we would be staying, just that you would make the arrangements.'

'Okay, that's solved then,' Lao Dee said cheerfully, 'Long Wei, lead the way, let's get out of here.'

Quickly he told the others what had happened and two minutes later they were on their way again.

Looking over her shoulder as the van turned left and on to the road Lilian saw the man still hanging behind the desk, probably thinking he had imagined it all.

Two kilometres further up the road and upstream from the town proper a freshly painted wooden sign announced the entrance of the Luding Guest House, 'the only place under heaven for the weary traveller'.

'I see your friend the manager has probably followed one of your courses in advertising, Long Wei!' Lao Dee called over his shoulder at the back of the van. 'We have a restaurant called All Under Heaven in Dalian. If the food here is only half as good we're still lucky we took your advice.'

'Let's hope the prices here are not half as outrageous as those of that scoundrel Mu Ping or this whole adventure will bankrupt you, Lao Dee,' Auntie grumbled and they all burst out laughing, even, in the end, Auntie herself.

Zee Bin turned into the entrance and already the first impression was so much more pleasant than at the previous place.

A neat and pretty garden with the type of palm trees one sees everywhere in a Mediterranean-like climate, flowering shrubs, bamboo and a small pond with a fountain, encircled by the guest house's driveway was the first pleasant surprise for the arriving guests.

The second was the freshly whitewashed front wall of the guest house with its cheerful green window frames, clean window panes and, oh wonder, flower boxes with hanging red and pink geraniums on the window ledges.

Still reeling from the impact of all this very un-Chinese cheerfulness and cleanliness, they were in for another surprise when the van stopped in front of the stairs leading to the guest house's entrance and the double glass door with copper locks and push-pull bars was flung open by two young men in white and gold uniform, also clean and crisply ironed, who came rushing down the steps to open the van's doors shouting cheerfully, 'Welcome to Luding! Welcome to the Luding Guest House, the only place under heaven for the weary traveller!'

Even Lao Dee was lost for words as he shook his head in disbelief.

'I'm dreaming,' he finally mumbled, 'I'm dreaming. This place is not *under* heaven, it must *be* heaven.'

Laughing triumphantly Long Wei cried, 'What did I tell you? Wait till you see the rooms, till you meet the manager, till you experience the service, till you taste the food. And you know what? This place is actually *cheaper* than that other place, that horrible Shuang Menlou.

'And you know why? I'll tell you! The Shuang Menlou is owned by the Party and it doesn't care whether it makes or loses money, whether the rooms are occupied or not, whether people come to the restaurant or not. I really think the Party would rather nobody visited because the service there is absent at worst, erratic and unpredictable at best but always very poor, very bad. This guest house though is a joint venture between the Sichuan Foreign Export and Import Corporation and an Australian hotel group. We, the CCPIT offices of Chengdu and Chongqing were involved in the initial negotiations and I suggested at the time that the future manager be given training in the group's hotels in Australia and my leaders followed my advice.

'Mr Lu Yiming, the guest house manager, knows that thanks to my advice he could spend one year abroad and he once told me I could always count on him for any service within the scope of his discretion. I haven't asked for anything so far but now I'm going to ask him to give you the best possible service.'

He fell silent, then added, blushing, 'And perhaps later I'll have a very special request.' And he looked significantly at Lilian and then, as an afterthought, at Beiyuen.

Both girls blushed and suddenly became all flustered about where their suitcases had gone.

As a matter of fact the two bellboys had already put their suitcases and bags with apples together on two trolleys and were now waiting patiently for them to check in.

While Zee Bin went to park the van, they entered the lobby and again were struck by the light, cheerful colours of the paintwork and the colourful wall decorations. Two pretty girls in clean, well-fitting white uniforms greeted them with a genuinely friendly smile from behind the reception desk.

Just when Long Wei was about to explain their business to the girls, the door with a sign that read 'General Manager' in English and Chinese opened and a tall, handsome man in his mid-thirties stepped out.

When he saw Long Wei his face lit up and he came quickly from behind the desk with outstretched hand, exclaiming, 'Long Wei, my friend, what gives me the pleasure of seeing you here? Will you be staying for the night? Are you with this gentleman perhaps?' He nodded at Lao Dee.

Long Wei, visibly pleased by the manager's cordial greeting, introduced Mr Lu Yiming to his friends and explained the purpose of their visit.

Mr Lu shook hands with everybody and told them how pleased he was that they had followed his friend Long Wei's advice to stay in his hotel. Then he took charge of the checking-in formalities and room allocation.

Auntie Liu and Lao Dao each got a double room on the ground floor, with a small terrace opening out on the garden at the back of the hotel and facing south. Lilian and Beiyuen got one double room together on the first floor, also at the back of the hotel.

Lao Dee asked for and got a special price for these three rooms because of the four weeks' occupancy. Suping, who would probably stay only one night, and he himself were shown to rooms on the first floor but at the front of the hotel.

After they had all been given their room keys, Long Wei and Zee Bin took their leave, declining Lao Dee's offer to stay for dinner since they had to get back to Chengdu before midnight to avoid trouble with the police.

Long Wei promised he would be back though and stay for a couple of days which made Lilian blush with pleasure. Zee Bin said, laughing, that he could perhaps drive Long Wei which made Beiyuen blush bright red from the roots of her hair down to the base of her neck.

Long Wei and Zee Bin gone, Lao Dee asked, 'What are your plans, Suping? Are you having dinner with us or are you and Lilian going to see your parents and Chen Dan at once?'

'No, not tonight,' Suping replied, 'besides, they know no better than that we arrive tomorrow, in the course of the morning. When you told us the exact date of our departure, I sent them a cable telling them that we, that is Lilian and I, would come home on Tuesday, around ten in the morning. We thought that would be best, to arrive in the morning, I mean, and not at nine o'clock in the evening. Besides, after twenty-two years we can all wait one more day, now can't we?

'It's not difficult to imagine what will happen. At first, the first hour or so, there will be so much to tell, everybody talking at the same time, trying to get his or her story in, to compress twenty-two years of one's life into a single sentence without pausing for breath and nobody actually listening. Then, suddenly, there will be the awkward silence and fatigue, and sleepiness, and the confusion of who will sleep where followed by a restless, sleepless night for everybody. We can't do that to them and to ourselves either by the way, Lilian and I also gained a lot of first impressions today which we still need to digest and therefore we need a good night's rest.

'I propose therefore that we have a light dinner, it's past eight already, and that we retire early for the night. Tomorrow morning we can have a late breakfast together and afterwards Lilian and I will get dressed properly and go and see the old folks. I'm sure you will know how to spend your time. Still I think that Auntie should stay in her room after her midday nap. I suspect Uncle Dan will get restless after a few hours of Xu family talk and will want to see his old friend, so, if you agree of course, Auntie, I shall suggest that he go and see you by himself, here, in your room.

'It would facilitate things if Lao Dee, Lao Dao and Beiyuen would be out for a walk or something like that after, say, three o'clock. Then we could all meet, here, in the guest house dining room at six and have dinner together. What do you think?' Suping fell silent, a bit embarrassed as she wondered whether the others thought her attitude patronising.

Instead Lao Dee said, 'Very sensible. Seems a good plan to me, Suping. If everybody agrees, let's go to our rooms now and freshen up a bit before we meet in the dining room at say eight thirty for a quick, light dinner. Okay?'

Everybody nodded and Lao Dee added, 'The bell boys will explain the air-conditioning and radio and lights in your room to you. Ask them also to explain the telephone. If you have a problem you can call me through reception. Don't forget to take your keys with you when you leave your rooms. Now, let's go! Follow the bellboys!'

Meekly, like sheep, they trooped after the smiling bellboys.

Dinner was a subdued affair. Everybody was tired and obviously preoccupied by what the following day would bring.

Everybody agreed though, and enthusiastically at that, that their rooms were beautiful and clean and the bathrooms something out of another world.

Lao Dao and Auntie Liu were very happy with the small terrace and the comfortable *chaises longues*. Every afternoon they would take a nap in the sun they said, amid indulgent laughter.

At nine thirty they all bade each other goodnight and withdrew to their respective rooms.

At eight o'clock the next morning everybody showed up for breakfast. Lao Dao and Lao Dee had been up since six o'clock and had just come back from a crisp walk along the river.

Besides them, there were eighteen other guests, two groups of tourists apparently, Spanish and German, Lao Dee explained after listening for a moment to their conversation.

Lao Dee and Lao Dao had an American breakfast, the others preferred Chinese food. The food was freshly prepared and tasty and the service was excellent. The tea and coffee were also freshly brewed and of excellent quality.

'This guest house is smaller but much nicer than our hotel in Dalian,' Lilian said, 'and the whole atmosphere is much more pleasant. Don't you think so too, Beiyuen?'

Beiyuen nodded and said, 'The rooms are also much easier to clean, what with the wooden floor instead of the wall-to-wall carpet we have at the Fulihua Hotel. The rooms smell fresh and I have never seen such white and beautifully starched sheets. We slept like logs, eh Lilian? We didn't use the air-conditioning but opened our window instead. The night air was fresh and it's so quiet here. Almost no traffic noise. How different from Dalian. I wouldn't mind working in this place and spending the rest of my life here.'

'I'm sure that cute little driver Zee Bin wouldn't mind either,' Auntie said laughingly and Beiyuen blushed ever so charmingly.

'Don't be so mean, Auntie,' Lilian said indignantly. 'It *is* nice here, at least what I have seen so far. If the good feeling lasts I'm going to ask Long Wei to put in a word for both of us, Beiyuen and me, I mean, with his friend Mr Lu, the general manger. He, Mr Lu, also looks so much nicer, and *younger*, than Mr Zhou and Mr Yu. I wonder whether they have a Party secretary here. If he's a sourpuss like our Comrade Du that can still spoil everything. But I don't think he's like that. I'm sure he's also a modern and *young* man, or maybe it's a woman. Mr Lu and his staff wouldn't be so genuinely friendly if the secretary was like Du.

'So, perhaps, Auntie, you and Mother's Uncle Dan could use your connections one more time and have us all transferred to Luding? Mother could move in again with Grandfather and Grandmother and perhaps get her former job back at the middle school. Auntie could marry Uncle Dan and get a house assigned to them, preferably on the same hill so that you can all see each other every day and talk. Beiyuen and I could find a job here, in this wonderful guest house, and rent a room together near here.'

Lilian fell silent and burst out laughing at the others' baffled expressions.

'You sly little vixen, you have it all worked out already, eh?' Auntie Liu growled and Lao Dee saw with relief that she only pretended to be angry.

'From the very first time we discussed our little financial deals,' Auntie went on, 'I knew you were way ahead of me and that I should watch out or one day I would end up with you running my life for me. And now you think that day has come, eh? Well, let me tell you, you hussy, you with your calculating little heart all a-flutter for handsome Mr Long Wei, that I will *not* dance to your piping unless it suits *me* and the other old dodderers whose lot you so conveniently throw into the same dirty linen basket as mine. But your opinion has been noted and from now on your keep your nose out of our business, for your own sake as well. Is that understood?'

'Yes, Auntie,' Lilian replied meekly, in a small voice. 'I'm sorry that I got carried away. It won't happen again, I promise.'

The old woman smiled and said, 'I was not joking but I was only pretending to be angry. I love you and I know you mean well. But certain things require patience, can't be forced or the outcome may be the opposite of what you wanted. So let matters take their own course, today especially, but also during the next few days. What will be will be. Isn't that some kind of a song?'

Everybody laughed, relieved that the first potential conflict had been squashed in the butt. Incredible what a sense of humour could do.

'*Que sera, sera*, whatever will be, will be, the future's not ours to see, *que sera sera*,' Lao Dee sang softly and they looked up in surprise as the Spanish tourists at the neighbouring tables applauded and shouted, '*Olé*! *Viva la vida*! *Viva la Cina*!'

Lao Dee smiled in their direction and called back, '*Gracias*! *Viva L'Espagna*!' This elicited more applause and the inevitable questions, shouted by some, asking where he was from and whether it was his first time in China.

Getting up from his chair and motioning his friends to follow his example, Lao Dee laughed and said, in the direction of the Spaniards, 'We are just friends and tourists, Chinese tourists, and we have come all the way to visit memory lane. Ask your tour guide, he'll know where it is.' And at that he led his friends out of the restaurant into the lobby.

After a brief deliberation Auntie Liu decided she would stay in the hotel and relax in the garden, as the weather promised to be warm and sunny, and just wait for things to happen.

Lao Dee, Lao Dao and Beiyuen decided to go out together and stay out for the day. They would consult Mr Lu, the manager, about the things to do, hire a taxi or perhaps a boat for a ride on the river, whatever. They were looking forward to spending a very pleasant day together they said.

Suping and Lilian had of course their own mission.

Agreeing to meet again that evening as from six o'clock in the separate private dining room Lao Dee had booked with Mr Lu personally, they quickly said goodbye and good luck and went their separate ways.

Lao Dee, Lao Dao and Beiyuen were the first to arrive in the dining room.

They had spent a very pleasant day reconnoitring Luding and its surrounds, including a three-hour boat trip downstream, while their taxi followed by road.

Mr Lu had organised the boat for them, a simple fisherman's boat, whose owner or tenant had realised that there was more money in boating a couple of tourists than in fishing. So he fished at night with cormorants and carbide lamps and tied up his boat in front of the guest house during the day, sleeping in the boat and eating in the guest house's kitchen when there were no customers which was still the case most of the time, the area still not the tourist attraction its authorities hoped it would become one day.

Both the boatman and the taxi driver had gladly accepted Lao Dee's invitation to join them for lunch in a small tea garden from where they had a splendid view of Gongga Shan, the towering giant at more than seven thousand metres of the Daxue Shan range.

The eel soup, deep fried eel and steamed river fish with grated ginger, chillies and rice had been delicious. The green tea was freshly brewed from the restaurant's own teabushes.

The fisherman and the driver had been cheerful and knowledgeable and Lao Dao had written down their names just in case he would invite his absent friends and their relatives for the same trip some day during the next week or so.

After lunch the fisherman had gone back alone and the three of them had continued their tour by car.

Lao Dee had told the driver to give them a general tour since they would have enough occasions for more detailed visits later and to drop them back at the guest house around five o'clock.

When they had got out of the car, Mr Lu, who had been hovering in the lobby, apparently waiting for them, came to meet them before they could climb the stairs to the entrance.

In a discreet, low voice he had told them that the old lady of room sixteen, Madam Liu, had a visitor who had arrived at three o'clock, that Mrs Li and her daughter had come back a little more than half an hour ago in the company of an elderly couple, surely Mrs Li's parents as Mr Dee had advised, and that the four of them had gone directly to Mrs Li's room, adjacent to Madam Liu's.

The latest information was that they had stepped out of their rooms into the garden and that Mrs Li had ordered six glasses of a local soft drink which were being served this very moment.

Lao Dee had thanked Mr Lu for the timely information and had complimented him for his discretion which had made him beam with pleasure.

Before retiring discreetly to his office, Mr Lu had added that the private dining room was ready and set for nine people, that he and the cook had composed a dinner of fresh local produce prepared the Sichuan way but not overly spicy, that he had chosen a light, white Australian wine and finally that he had instructed the two girls who would serve at table that night not to greet the guests in the dining room as was the custom in his hotel, but instead, in view of the very private nature of the party as advised by Mr Dee, to wait in the kitchen until they were called by Mr Dee himself.

Without inviting further expressions of appreciation Mr Lu had nodded, smiled and gone back to his office.

Still reeling from so much courtesy and discretion they had at first talked in the same low, almost whispering voice as Mr Lu when they had decided not to disturb the others in the garden but instead to go directly to their rooms, freshen up and change for dinner and meet again at six o'clock sharp in the dining room in order to be there when the others arrived.

Lao Dee had poured a glass of wine for Lao Dao and himself and a soft drink for Beiyuen and, standing together near the potted palm in the far corner, they quietly chit-chatted about the events of the day and commented on the beautiful appointment of the dining room.

The round table had been set for nine and everything looked neat, fresh and meticulously arranged, the beautiful bouquet of wild flowers in the centre of the table lending the whole a cheerful and colourfully festive note.

'Can you imagine our Mr Zhou acting like Mr Lu this afternoon and arranging a dining room like this?' Beiyuen asked, looking at Lao Dao. 'Never in a thousand years, I'm sure,' she answered her own question.

Lao Dao chuckled and said, 'You are of course right, Beiyuen, our Mr Zhou has no notion of these things and if he had it's not in his character to be so obliging, so courteous. But then, comparing Zhou and Lu and their respective situations is not entirely fair to Zhou. Zhou was appointed by the Party to take the blame for everything that goes awry, he probably has no background whatsoever in the hospitality business and the only reluctant training, if you can call it training, he got was from Hong Kongers, Cantonese that is, themselves not exactly shining examples of discretion and politeness.

Mr Lu, on the other hand, was probably selected by Mr Long Wei's CCPIT from many candidates, tested by the Australians and trained for a year in a few of their hotels in Australia. Mr Lu is a professional hotel manager, Mr Zhou is just a boor who had no say in his own appointment. When you take that into account he's not doing too badly, our Mr Zhou.'

Lao Dee laughed and said, 'Ever the apologist, eh, my friend? Always trying to give people a fair hearing, a fair chance. But I think I hear our guests arriving. Beiyuen, why don't you open the door for them.'

The way they came shuffling through the door held open for them by Beiyuen was comically touching.

Incongruously it reminded Lao Dee of a film he had once seen, long ago. The half-shuffling, half-dancing gait of a funeral procession in New Orleans had struck him then as very funny and he nearly burst out laughing again. He checked himself just in time, biting on his lower lip, as he watched his friends approach.

A bit self-conscious, a bit shy also but above all defiantly proud when their eyes locked with his, they slowly shuffled up to where he and Lao Dao were waiting in the far corner.

Auntie was in front, arm in arm with a wizened, old farmer in an outsized, grey, Western suit, pink shirt and green tie. The sparse, spiky white hairs on a liver-spotted, shiny pate, the nose like a small, shrivelled potato but above all the roguish look in the sparkling, intelligent eyes clicked with the picture in Lao Dee's mind and he realised that he finally was about to meet the famous

Chen Dan, ex-professor of mathematics, ex-secret society man in charge of recruiting agents and moles, ex-peasant boy, narrator by proxy of the most extraordinary story of his collection. The defiant pride and protective love in Auntie's eyes as she alternately looked from Lao Dee to the man beside her were unmistakable and touching.

Behind them came Suping, arm in arm, with her ageing *alter idem*, her mother, Xu née Liu Guixian.

Silvery-white hair combed up high in a bun, with wrinkleless, peachlike, delicately small face, Guixian appeared sprightly in her high-collared white blouse and black silk trousers, yet it was the calm, untroubled, slightly curious look in her beautifully shining eyes that struck Lao Dee.

That's how Suping and Lilian will look when old, it flashed through his mind, a reassuring sight for any potential husband.

Lilian was last, beside a tall, erect man with short-cropped shiny grey hair, a pair of rimless glasses on a sharp, straight nose, immaculate in a light grey Mao suit: Xu Ximing the mandarin. His right hand resting lightly on Lilian's right shoulder, her left arm around his waist, he looked at Lao Dee with a mildly surprised look.

Probably surprised the foreign barbarian looks almost human after all, Lao Dee thought, and the insight made him smile a bit ironically.

Lilian, catching his mood and eye shook her head almost imperceptibly, signalling him not to try and make a funny remark.

Auntie, suddenly breaking the silence, began the introductions.

'Dan, my dear, this is Beiyuen, my seventh niece from my mother's side, this is Dao Huimin or Lao Dao as we call him and this, finally, is our friend, counsellor and benefactor Lao Dee to whom we owe this reunion, *our* reunion, and so many other things. Ever since he came into our lives, things have changed, our whole outlook and way of thinking have changed.

'We, his friends from Dalian and you, the three of you, his friends to be, will never be able to repay him and he knows that so he said he might as well cancel any and all debts we owe him, and get on with our new-found lives, the slates clean.'

Everybody burst out laughing which immediately broke the somewhat solemn spell.

Suping introduced her mother, proudly and lovingly and Lilian urged her grandfather forward, taking both his and Lao Dee's hands in hers and, looking up into the two men's faces, she said, voice trembling with emotion, 'Lao Dee has been like a father, an older brother and a friend to me, now I want you two to be friends. I am so proud of both of you.'

Looking down at her eager, upturned face the two men smiled at her and at each other and Xu said, 'With both of us riding so high in this beautiful girl's esteem and our old age precluding rivalry, we could hardly *not* be friends, now could we, Mr Dee? If we were forty years younger it would be a different matter entirely, I'm sure.' And smiling he held out his hand.

Holding Lao Dee's hand between his, Xu said, raising his voice only slightly to silence the babble around, 'Mr Dee, Lao Dee, we three, Chen Dan, my wife Guixian and myself, can now start living the last chapter of our lives and thanks to you it will have a happy ending. With one simple, good-hearted and unselfish gesture you have turned our fears, our feelings of loneliness and unfulfilment into a state of contentment – euphoria is probably a better word. The only thing we can offer you in return and in abundance and that for the remainder of our days is our friendship and hospitality, for you and for those who come recommended by you.'

Xu fell silent and Lao Dee was deeply moved by the dignified old man's sincerity and barely controlled emotion.

Looking around he saw tears in everybody's eyes, even the relative outsiders Lao Dao and Beiyuen were moved to tears as they all applauded discreetly.

Before anybody could speak of his or her special feelings, Lao Dee raised his hands in a defensive gesture and said, affectionately, 'Your obvious joy, the friendship and hospitality proffered to me and, unquestioningly, to those sent by me, cannot be quantified and weighed and neither should you try to quantify and weigh what I, in your eyes, did for you. Everything we did, you and I, and still will do for each other is but a normal consequence of our friendship and our means. No more, no less.

'Having said that we will from now on gracefully and as a matter of course accept what we do for one another without each time feeling obliged to exhaust ourselves in expressions of thanks. We are as we are and we have no hidden motives, neither in asking nor in giving. Do we all agree that that will be the base of our friendship?'

The answer was as spontaneous as it was unexpected in its form when Suping left her mother's side and embraced and kissed the Dutchman on both cheeks and then full on his mouth.

For a second or two Lao Dee held her against him, stroking her glossy, flowing hair, then, releasing her, he said, visibly moved and pleased, 'If that's the way you were going to clean the slate I take back everything I said and will start chalking up debts again right away.'

They all burst out laughing which dispelled the momentary unease of the Ludingers with Suping's utterly un-Chinese move.

Lao Dee immediately took advantage of the light moment and proposed that they moved to the table.

Protesting first, feebly and as a matter of form, he then accepted gracefully the seat of honour between Xu Ximing and his wife Guixian. Suping and Lilian then took the seats besides their father and grandmother respectively while Chen Dan sat beside Lilian with Auntie Liu of course at his side. Lao Dao and Beiyuen, smiling happily, took the remaining two seats.

As if on cue Mr Lu entered at that moment and cordially bade them welcome to his hotel and restaurant. He then looked at Lao Dee who nodded his head and said they were ready to be served.

Mr Lu clapped his hands twice and the two waitresses entered and in turn introduced themselves as Meilan and Meiling, their waitresses for the evening. Both were very pretty with a lovely smile showing beautiful, regular white teeth.

They wore well-tailored white jackets with thin gold braids and, oh wonder, short, black skirts and high-heeled shoes showing off their shapely legs to advantage.

Lao Dee saw Lilian glance at Beiyuen and lean over in front of Uncle Dan and he heard her say, 'And we in Dalian think that *we* are modern. Compared to the way this hotel is run and how these girls are dressed we are but country bumpkins.'

Looking at Lao Dee she said, 'Now I understand why you talked us into these clothes your wife bought for us in Hong Kong. You *knew* that we in Dalian are but old-fashioned backward bumpkins, didn't you, Lao Dee? You were ashamed turning up here with a troop of Liaoning peasants, weren't you?'

Lao Dee grinned and replied, 'You are not far wrong, love. Only it wasn't for me but for you and your mother and Meiling and Beiyuen. I know that for women it can spoil everything if they discover that their local sisters are more fashionable and I saw myself already on an emergency expedition to Hong Kong while you locked yourself in your rooms refusing to see anybody. Couldn't let that happen, now could I? I had been a couple of times to Chengdu and knew people were way ahead of the northerners in fashion and the nicer things in life. So enjoy life while you're here and don't look at me like that, your eyes shooting fire. I'm sure you'll quickly lose your country girl manners and doesn't it give you hope that a local gentleman like Mr Long Wei shares my view?'

Everybody burst out laughing, even, after a short hesitation, Lilian herself though she made a threatening gesture with her balled fist and hissed, 'I'll get you for that! Beware!'

'Anytime my dear, anytime,' Lao Dee chuckled, 'your mother gave you the good example a moment ago.' His comment provoked another burst of laughter.

This light-hearted banter set the tone for the remainder of the evening.

Throughout dinner there was not one awkward silence, only animated light-hearted talk with the occasional *sub voce* exchange of questions and answers, ideas and opinions between neighbours at table, interspersed with delighted remarks and comments on the presentation of the dishes, the taste of the food, the freshness and origin of the ingredients, the fruity freshness of the wine, the friendly and efficient service by Meilan and Meiling.

As if by tacit agreement nobody mentioned the past, not once, nor did whatever other contentious subject slip into the conversation, deliberately or inadvertently, spoiling, as is so often the case, the general atmosphere of *bonhomie*.

Twice Mr Lu came in to enquire whether everything was to their satisfaction, withdrawing, visibly happy, when assured from all sides that things couldn't be better.

During dessert, fresh fruit with almond-taste bean curd, Lao Dee's favourite, Lao Dee stood up and, lightly tapping against his wine glass to ask for attention, he said, 'This was the finest meal in the nicest company for as long as I can recall. I'm sure you enjoyed it as much as I did and I propose a repeat, say next Friday in two weeks time when my wife will be here as well. In the meantime enjoy yourselves and one another's company as you see fit and as you feel comfortable with.

'I will leave tomorrow afternoon for Chongqing for talks about a possible project and on Thursday I'll go to Hong Kong via Guangzhou. The whole of next week I'll be in Dalian, so you can contact me in the hotel if there is anything you want me to do for you there.

'I'll be back here, with my wife, in two weeks from next Thursday and we'll stay of course here in this hotel for two weeks. We all leave together in four weeks from next Friday for Chengdu where my wife will take a flight to Hong Kong and we to Shanghai and Dalian.

'I have arranged with Mr Lu, the hotel manager, that I keep three double rooms here at all times until the day of our departure.

'In principle these rooms are for Lao Dao, Auntie Liu and for Lilian and Beiyuen together but you can change the arrangement when you like as you like. Mr Lu is a modern, Western-educated man who runs a modern hotel in the spirit of our times. I have also arranged with Mr Lu that your laundry, food and drinks will be put on the bill of these three rooms so you need not worry about your cash position. Keep your money for the local expenditures outside the hotel.

'Last but not least, I know that momentous questions will be raised in the days and weeks ahead, requiring from most of you momentous decisions. These questions and decisions regard your private lives and I, as a friend respecting your right to privacy, can of course not interfere and, as a foreigner, I can do very little to help you realise certain decisions.

'Whatever happens we'll remain friends and therefore I now toast to our health and happiness with the excellent brandy and delicious muscat Mr Lu has so graciously offered us.'

At that Lao Dee raised his glass. The others got to their feet as well and raising their glasses to his, they said in chorus, 'to the health and happiness for each and all of us and with our eternal and unrequitable gratitude to you, Dee Huilin.'

They sipped from their glasses, tasted, sniffed then sipped again and then, suddenly, drank the contents in one swallow.

With a contented sigh they put down their glasses and without further ado and within a few minutes everybody had left, Suping with her parents and Chen Dan as she would spend the night with them at home, the others directly to their rooms.

Lao Dee settled the bill with Mr Lu and gave an envelope each to Meilan and Meiling which made them blush with pleasure.

During the next two weeks Lilian called Lao Dee twice in his Dalian hotel room, the first time to say they all had such a wonderful time and that everybody was relaxed and happy, the second time two days before he would return to Luding himself.

Her voice sounded excited when she told him that the momentous decisions he had referred to in his dinner speech had been taken.

She was about to launch herself into a description when probably somebody entered her room for she said, in a much calmer voice, 'Yes, everything is fine and we all look forward to seeing you and Ah Li again next Thursday. Bye for now,' and she had hung up.

Three days later Lao Dee and his wife arrived in Chengdu from Hong Kong.

As arranged by phone Long Wei and Zee Bin were waiting for them at the airport to drive them to Luding but to their surprise Lilian and Beiyuen were there as well.

'Long Wei and Zee Bin came to visit us every weekend while you were away, Lao Dee,' Lilian explained, breathless, excited, eyes sparkling, 'and we have become very good friends, *very* good friends. Last Sunday Long Wei proposed we come with them to Chengdu to meet his and Zee Bin's parents and brother and sister and to stay with them until you and Ah Li arrived. Mother and Auntie had no objection at all, so here we are.' Impulsively both girls embraced him and his wife and, since they were at it, Long Wei and Zee Bin as well.

Ah Li, who had been briefed by Lao Dee on the budding romance between the young people, laughingly took the two girls out of earshot where the three of them started whispering nevertheless, interspersed with the inevitable giggles and little yelps of feigned outrage.

Grinning the three men quickly loaded the luggage in the van and then took their seats to wait patiently for the women to finish their huddled conference.

Vainly trying to stifle their giggling the three women finally clambered on board, stumbled through the aisle pushing and nudging each other like yelping schoolgirls and flopped into the back seat with little squeals of delightful embarrassment.

Questioningly Zee Bin looked at Lao Dee, who shrugged his shoulders and said, 'Don't try to understand, don't pay attention, just drive. In a while, an hour, or two, or three, they'll be so tired that the giggling will stop by itself. Take your time, we're not in a hurry, if we arrive around four at the hotel we have all the time to unpack, freshen up and get ready for dinner. We are all having dinner tonight at the hotel, I hope you two can stay this time to have dinner with us.'

Long Wei said they could and would be very glad to accept Lao Dee's invitation.

That settled, Zee Bin drove off.

It was half past three when the van stopped in front of the guest house and everybody got out, stretching and yawning but for Zee Bin.

The women had quietened down and Lilian and Beiyuen, having slept most of the way, their heads on Ah Li's shoulders, still looked drowsy.

Mr Lu came down the flight of steps to welcome Lao Dee back and to greet Mrs Dee.

Beaming with pleasure he told them that he had assigned them the hotel's only suite, on the second floor, with a view over the whole back garden and facing the mountains in the distance and at the price of a standard double room.

Lao Dee thanked him cordially and told him there would be two more guests for dinner that night, Long Wei and Zee Bin and that he would be delighted if Mr Lu could join the party as well.

Thanking Lao Dee profusely, Mr Lu said he would be equally delighted to accept the kind invitation. Before withdrawing to his office he told Lao Dee that Mr Dao Huimin had left the message that he would like to see Mr Dee before dinner and would come to his suite at six o'clock if that would be convenient.

Lao Dee replied that he would call Mr Dao in his room and tell him to come up when convenient. At that Mr Lu withdrew and Lao Dee and his wife followed the bellboys to their suite while Lilian and Beiyuen, suddenly serious, left with Long Wei and Zee Bin in the van.

'We'll drive up to my grandparents' house,' Lilian had said, 'and we'll come down all together, in the van, and meet the three of you here at six thirty, in the dining room, like last time.'

'What was that all about?' Lao Dee asked his wife as they were unpacking their suitcases. 'All that giggling and secretive ado in Chengdu and in the van and now this sudden seriousness?'

His wife laughed and replied, 'Women's business. I told them those two young men, Long Wei and Zee Bin, would soon want more than just friendly relations, even *very* friendly relations, as Lilian said, and to make up their minds as to how far they would let the men have their way. I also told them that if they thought they had to give in, I would give them each a packet of my pills and supply them more through you.'

Lao Dee stared at his wife in disbelief.

'You told them that? Do you realise that you are undermining their socialist morals, the Party's indoctrination? You could be thrown in jail for that or at least be expelled from the country.'

'Balderdash,' his wife replied cheerfully, eyes twinkling, 'those two healthy young girls are no different from our Western girls. They are the right age, everything is in place and tickles and plays up when nature calls. No apparatchik can change that. Now, before those nice young people get frustrated or into trouble I had better tell them a few things about the how and the what. And you and Lao Dao and the other two old dodderers Xu and Chen Dan, who I haven't met yet, had better stay out of this.' And playfully she unbuttoned his shirt and pressed herself against him.

Satisfied with the response she purred like the coaxing little cat she had never ceased to be.

Lao Dee called Lao Dao in his room at a quarter to six to tell him to come up. Within minutes they greeted each other cordially.

'We all had a great time, thanks to you,' Lao Dao began his report, 'and what you foresaw would happen, did happen. It'll be lonely in Dalian without my friends,' he added ruefully.

'Go on,' Lao Dee said, 'tell me what we can expect over the coming days.'

'Tonight, some time during dinner, Chen Dan or Meiling will announce their plans to get married and settle here in Luding.'

Lao Dao continued, smiling, his momentary ruefulness already forgotten, the happiness of his friends taking precedence.

'Next Suping will announce her decision to move back to Luding and live with and take care of her parents. Once she has settled down she will try to get her former job back, after the necessary retraining of course. She realises her knowledge is a bit rusty and outdated after all these years. What we didn't foresee though is that both Lilian and Beiyuen will want to move to here as well. Both girls think they have found the man of their dreams and both Long Wei and Zee Bin seem to be serious as well.

'Suping and Meiling at first thought it was all a bit sudden and too quick, however, since last week they seem to have acquiesced, at least they didn't object to the girls going to visit the boys' relatives in Chengdu. They only urged them repeatedly to be careful, alluding to you know what.'

'Don't be so prudish, man,' Lao Dee interrupted his friend laughingly, 'my modern-thinking wife here has already briefed the girls and they already made all the arrangements to make it a happy, modern-day courtship. So as far as that aspect is concerned, Suping and Meiling can rest assured, I'm sure my experienced wife will brief them as well and put their minds at ease. Anything else I should know beforehand?'

'No, not specifically,' Lao Dao replied, 'I just wanted you to know what I told you so that you wouldn't be taken by surprise.'

'Don't worry, my friend,' Lao Dee said, chuckling, 'I'm not that easily surprised. Besides, I expected this more or less. Now, if you are ready, we are I think. Aly, are you ready?' he called to his wife who was in the bedroom.

'Coming!' she called back and a moment later they descended the stairs to the lobby and the dining room.

If at all possible the private dining room was even prettier than the last time.

Besides the potted palm in the far corner there was now also a beautiful vase with flowers on an elegant, high-legged stand in two of the other corners of the room.

Meilan and Meiling, dainty in their tight-fitting uniforms were already there, waiting for the guests, each carrying a tray with corsages made up of one beautiful mauve orchid, its stem wrapped in silver paper, for the ladies.

The table was set for twelve this time, with room to spare, and Lao Dee was about to explain the seating arrangement to his wife when the door opened and Mr Lu, bowing slightly from the waist, invited the guests to enter.

Lilian immediately went to stand beside Mrs Dee and introduced to her the other guests, both in English and Chinese.

She had apparently and in secret taught her grandmother to say a few words in English, for to everybody's delighted surprise Mrs Xu Guixian said in a clear voice and with an impeccable accent, 'We thank you for coming, Ah Li, we are honoured by your visit.'

Under applause Mr Lu then took a picture of the two women as they stood hand in hand and smiled into his Japanese camera until the flashlight made them grimace.

'Never take flashlight pictures of blue-eyed people from nearer than three metres,' Lao Dee said to Mr Lu, explaining, 'the reflection off their retinas makes their eyes red in the picture, like devils. If it has to be close, like in this room, take the pictures under a slight angle so that the flash isn't reflected by the eyes. I'm afraid my wife will have you destroy the picture you just took, she wouldn't want herself in the Xus' family album looking like a she-devil. I have often wondered though.'

Everybody laughed at Lao Dee's little joke and still talking amongst each other about what he had just told them they followed his invitation to take their seats as indicated by a small white card with their names, both in characters and in Pinyin spelling.

Mr Lu and the chef had surpassed themselves in the choice, preparation and make-up of the dishes.

Proudly Meilan and Meiling showed the beautifully made up and artistically decorated plates around before putting them on the table.

Dextrously they then cut, divided and distributed the food amongst the twelve bowls or plates, without even once spilling a drop or a morsel on the tablecloth or on their own white gloves.

Mr Lu beamed with pride and pleasure as each following dish elicited new compliments and praise. It could hardly be otherwise then that the conversation and atmosphere matched the food in every respect: animated, lively, cheerful and, at times, serious and erudite.

It was only when Meilan and Meiling had cleared the table for the last course, fresh fruit with almond-flavoured tofu, that Chen Dan stood up from his chair, tapped against his wine glass, scraped his throat and, in a surprisingly clear and resonant voice, asked for everybody's attention.

Looking around the table at his friends' faces, most of them smiling knowingly, he finally directed his attention at Lao Dee and said, 'Lao Dee, my friend, you have been away for two weeks, sixteen days to be precise, and a lot has happened since you left. Some of the lot you may have foreseen, some may even to you come as a surprise, however, whatever it is that happened, it did thanks to your generosity and compassion to bring about this great reunion of relatives and friends new and old. Also on behalf of the others whose life has taken a different course through you I now bring you up to date.

'Claiming the privileges of old age I begin with myself and the person you so affectionately call Auntie Liu. After keeping buried within us, for over forty years, unexpressed feelings of affection, love even, not knowing whether the other was still alive or married to somebody else or even remembered, you brought Liu Meiling and me together again, confident that both she and I would be strong enough to accept the fact that those feelings of old might no longer mean something to either or both of us.

'Right from the moment we set eyes on each other and our hands touched we knew the emotions were there, undiminished. It was just a matter of finding the right word, the right gesture and your uninhibited Western nature also provided us with the means to find them. Liu Meiling and I have decided to get married just as soon as we get our application to wed and for Meiling to move to Luding approved.'

The old savant fell silent and for a moment he was overcome by emotion.

His friends waited in respectful silence, deeply moved as well. When they saw that he was back in control, they applauded and shouted their congratulations, both at him and at the old woman they would always know as Auntie.

Wiping his teary eyes with the back of his hand he smiled lovingly at his future wife and continued, looking again around the circle of friends. 'To remain in the same vein we have also witnessed four cases of blossoming young love. Lilian and Long Wei as well as Beiyuen and Zee Bin have asked me to tell you that they are in love, want to get married as soon as they reach the statutory age and in the meantime will do everything for Lilian and Beiyuen to get approval to move to Luding. They have already been very busy and have succeeded in winding our friend Mr Lu here around their little finger and obtaining his promise that he can guarantee both of them a job here, in this beautiful hotel.'

Everybody burst out laughing and Mr Lu became all flustered by the cheers and salutes.

Chen Dan tapped his glass again, calling for silence and when the noise had abated somewhat he continued, 'Our last case is also a case of love, of filial love, and besides my dear friends Ximing and Guixian as the direct beneficiaries I am also personally very, very happy that Suping has decided to come back to Luding as well, to take care of her parents who are getting on in age and will increasingly need help and care. These are the changes and upheavals you have brought about, Lao Dee. All of us will remain eternally grateful to you.'

Chen Dan fell silent and, after a few seconds of deadly silence, the dining room erupted in cheers and hoorays and everybody trying to grab and pump Lao Dee's hands.

For a few minutes the Dutchman let them do their thing, then he got up from his chair and, brushing the last hands gently but firmly aside, he shouted to make himself heard above the hubbub. 'I have an idea that could be important!'

The noise died down as abruptly as it had erupted and everybody sat down again looking up expectantly at Lao Dee who had remained on his feet.

Looking down at the table in front of him and waiting a few seconds for more effect, he finally said, 'First of all let me tell you how glad I am for you that things have turned out the way they did. That I have been instrumental in bringing this about is yet another reason for me to be glad that we made this trip after all. I'm afraid, however, that for the things you need now, permits to wed, to move from Dalian to Luding, to change jobs, to apply for a house, for I presume that Uncle Dan and Auntie Liu will want a house of their own, I cannot be of any help, except, perhaps, by giving you an idea for a final deal, a final trade-off, to solve all these problems with one master stroke. But before I proceed I have to ask a question and Chen Dan is probably the one who can best answer it,' and looking at Chen Dan, he asked, 'have you any idea where Zhang Yizhong is now and what his position is?'

Chen Dan narrowed his eyes and looked at Lao Dee.

He's speculating, he thinks he knows what I have in mind, Lao Dee thought.

'The shortest answer to your question is: Zhang succeeded!' Chen Dan replied. 'Since through Suping you know about the man, I can add that he contrived to fulfil, as well as have others fulfil for him, all his ambitions but one or two perhaps. He is now in Beijing where he holds vice-ministerial rank and heads some important commission or other, armaments, I believe. You see his name regularly in the newspaper.'

He fell silent, smiled ironically and said, 'That is probably what you wanted to hear, eh? Lao Dee? To develop your idea of the one master stroke during the coming, probably sleepless, night?'

The subtle warning *not* to unfold his idea in front of everybody was not lost on Lao Dee and taking Chen Dan's hint he said, without a flicker of hesitation so as not to give Lu, Long Wei and Zee Bin the feeling that they were being left out, 'Indeed, I now know enough to come up with something that may work. And now something completely different, my wife and I would like to see where you live, on the hill, and also to visit Chen Juntao's grave. Is it all right if we come to see you tomorrow morning, Ximing, say around nine o'clock? Afterwards, if you like that of course, we could make a boat trip together, downstream, and have a leisurely lunch in that small tea garden restaurant in the foothills of Gongga Shan. Lao Dao, Beiyuen and I liked it there very much last time.'

Xu Ximing looked completely nonplussed by the sudden change of subject, so, smiling, his wife replied for him, 'Yes, *of course* you *must* come to see us tomorrow morning. Meiling knows the way, it's a nice walk from the hotel. We shall expect you around nine.'

She also knows what this is all about, it flashed through Lao Dee's mind, that's why she says *Meiling* knows the way, *not* Lilian or Beiyuen. She only wants the principal persons to be there, Chen Dan and Liu Meiling of course since they are the real principals, then she herself, her husband and her daughter.

Oh well, I got out of that hornets' nest by the skin of my teeth. I'll have to apologise tomorrow for my indiscretion. Imagine, talking about blackmailing a high official, the Party itself actually, in the presence of those three nice but young men we still know so little about. What a blunder that would have been, I'm sure though that they have no clue what this was all about, they're bantering amongst themselves and teasing the two girls.

As he sat down again he said quietly, 'That's settled then. Meiling will lead the way tomorrow morning.'

After dessert, Meilan and Meiling served a beautiful golden, sweet muscat for everybody and everybody toasted everybody else and wished the newly betrothed a long and happy life together.

Then, in the best of moods, they bade goodbye and goodnight, promising to see each other the next morning, except for Mr Lu, Long Wei and Zee Bin who had their jobs to do, of course.

Early the next morning Lao Dee called his friend at CITIC in Beijing and through him got the telephone number of Zhang Yizhong's office as well as his direct line and home number.

When Lao Dee and his wife came down to the restaurant for breakfast Auntie Liu, Lao Dao, Lilian and Beiyuen were already there, motioning them to have a seat at their table.

They were in an excellent mood, especially Auntie, who looked a completely different person. Radiating happiness her face no longer had that perpetual frown, sneer rather, she used to show the outside world to keep people at a distance.

While they were eating their breakfast Auntie said, between two slurps from her bowl of congee, 'I told Lao Dao that he is of course included in the party today, that those *in extremis* diversions of yours last night were not meant for him but for Lu and those two young snots who turned my two girls' heads. They just left for Chengdu by the way, after having gorged themselves at your expense, Lao Dee.' She yelped when Lilian, interrupting her translation for Ah Li, pinched her arm.

Lifting a protective arm to keep Lilian away from her, she continued, laughingly, 'I think I know what you have in mind, Lao Dee, you sly machiavellian villain, and I also think it may work.'

'I may still surprise you, Meiling,' Lao Dee replied, smiling, 'let's hear what our friends on the hill have to say when I unfold my proposal. And *of course* my best friend Lao Dao must come as well. What would I do without him!' And affectionately he nudged his friend with his elbow.

A few minutes before nine o'clock the six of them, slightly out of breath after the uphill walk in the sun, already hot at this early hour, arrived at the little gate giving access to the Xu family's little house.

Lao Dee had immediately recognised the place from Suping's story.

The Xus and Chen Dan were sitting behind the house, in the shade, a pot of tea and ten glasses on the low table in front of them.

With a cry of pleasure Suping jumped up from her chair when she heard her friends' voices and rushed to open the gate for them. 'It still creaks,' she laughed as she motioned them to follow her. 'We have borrowed a few chairs from our neighbour, Zhang Yimin,' she continued, 'but there are still not enough so Beiyuen, Lilian and I will sit on the grass. Never mind.'

They all greeted each other cheerfully and Lao Dee saw with pleasure the affectionate hug Lilian gave her mother and her grandparents.

Comfortably seated they talked quietly for a while, inconsequential chit-chat, while sipping from their glasses of tea and enjoying the view on the town and the mountains in the distance, all in a leisurely, distracted sort of way.

Gradually, one after the other, they fell silent, waiting for someone to broach the subject they knew they were all here for.

Fanning herself a bit more vigorously with the pretty, small bamboo and printed silk fan Chen Dan had given her for their betrothal, Auntie Liu finally said, 'Tell us about the final trade-off, Lao Dee, the master stroke you have devised to fulfil our last wishes.'

Lao Dee laughed and looking at his friend Lao Dao, who sat next to his wife, he asked, 'Would you mind translating for my wife, Huimin? Fill her in, briefly, on the background while we discuss the scenario. I never talked to her about the matter. Perhaps you two should sit a bit further away lest your mumbling disturbs us.'

'Okay, okay,' Lao Dao said laughingly, 'I know when I'm not wanted. Come on, dear,' he continued in English, 'let's make ourselves scarce. Your husband asked me to translate and explain for you, however, he doesn't want our mumbling as he calls it to disturb those conspirators as they discuss their tricky business.'

Ah Li laughed and said, 'Oh, I'm used to being sent away when the great minds sit together to change the world. Let's sit over there, out of earshot,' and good-humouredly they carried their chairs a few metres into the garden.

The others had caught the gist of the banter and chuckled as Madam Xu exclaimed, 'You can't chase your wife away like that, Lao Dee, that's *feudal* and feudalism is a crime in this country!'

'Be silent, woman,' her husband growled jokingly. 'If it weren't a crime I would send you and your daughter and those two brats away as well.'

With shrieks of feigned indignation Suping and the two girls flung themselves at the old man demanding an apology, all the while tickling him until he finally begged for mercy.

The others had watched the scene with amusement and they burst out laughing when Xu said, still panting from his ordeal, 'Modern times, bah! The only way I was allowed to approach my grandfather was on my knees, head bowed. Such dignity! And now look what I have become. A plaything for three hussies! Enough! Sit down you three and listen humbly, if you know what that word means, to what we, *men*, will decide for your good.'

Still smiling Lao Dee said, 'You have already more or less guessed what I'm going to propose, so I can be brief. This morning, through a good friend who works for CITIC, in Beijing, I managed to get Zhang Yizhong's direct telephone number at his office as well as his home number. I propose that Uncle Dan call him, at home, tonight, from my hotel room and offer him the two remaining copies of Yang Baolin's notes in return for his guarantee that you will get all the permits you need and within say one month.'

He raised his hand to signal them to hold back a while longer and continued. 'Have no illusions, though. After all these years, sixty almost, the notes will have lost much of their power. Most of the protagonists mentioned by Yang have probably died, those still alive have faded from the scene but for the one, or two perhaps, at the pinnacle of the Party and they won't care any more. My gamble that Zhang, after deliberation with his superiors, will accept the deal, is based on two premises, firstly that the old horses still on top can make use somehow of the revelations, to settle a few personal scores probably, *not* because they are afraid for themselves, and secondly the Party's mania for tidiness, its wish to finally classify the case. Communists hate sensitive papers in non-Communist hands even if they no longer pose a threat. If Zhang accepts your proposal it would be nice if the deal could be done against an appropriate background.

'I suggest therefore that Uncle Dan, after the initial introductory affabilities, should ask Zhang whether he remembers his remark long ago that one day he would like to taste that Beggars Chicken whose smell made his mouth water as he sat there, behind that hedge over there, listening to your stories. When Zhang says that he does remember, Uncle Dan should continue and tell him that next week, Wednesday or Thursday, he will prepare another Beggars Chicken, the one that will beat all previous ones, to celebrate the reunion, after twenty-two years, of Suping with her parents and of himself with a very dear old friend from his Shanghai times, the only one with whom he shared his most precious possession at the time, and that both he and his dear old friend would be honoured and delighted if Zhang could come also to enjoy the chicken and the company and to discuss the conditions for the final closure of a long-standing matter that used to be of great mutual interest.

'Zhang, intelligent and sly as he is, will know immediately what you are referring to and he will say that he will have to confer with others to see whether he can take a few days off at such short notice and that it would be helpful if you could be a bit more specific about those conditions for the closure of that important matter. When he says that there is no point in beating around the bush any longer, so you tell him *exactly* what you want and *when* you want it and you tell him also bluntly that if he can give you a written guarantee or, better still, the permits themselves, he can take the last remaining two copies of the Yang Baolin notes back with him to Beijing.

'So, summarising, you begin with circumspection and when the fish bites you strike and haul him on board, bluntly and decisively, like those big eels you used to catch long ago for the same, good old Yang. It will be the last catch you make for him, Chen Dan.'

Lao Dee fell silent and studied his fingernails as he waited for the others' reaction.

For the first few minutes there was none, the Xus, as if by tacit understanding, deferring to the two main characters in the drama, while for those two consultation by means of eye and facial expressions seemed to suffice.

Finally Chen Dan said, 'An admirable synopsis bearing testimony to a pragmatic, businesslike mind. We, that is Meiling and I, have nothing to add to or to improve on your excellent plan, Lao Dee, the Beggars Chicken part is especially masterly. I shall therefore follow your advice; we have come this far thanks to your guidance so we might as well go all the way. Tonight I'll call Zhang Yizhong at home from your room and we'll see how he reacts.

'Now that we have made our decision I suggest that we put the matter out of our mind until tonight and not waste the precious time we have together with useless speculation. I propose we now visit good old Juntao's grave and tell him that probably within the next six days or so we may relieve him of his sentinel duties regarding what is hidden in the walnut tree above his head. In the meantime we'll put there also, temporarily, the small package Meiling has been hiding under her blouse since she came here this morning.'

Chen Dan chuckled and winked at Meiling as the others applauded and laughed with relief that the serious part was over.

As they got up from their chairs Lao Dee said to Chen Dan, 'I'm sorry about last night. Your warning was timely.'

'No need to apologise,' Chen Dan replied. 'I'm pretty sure there was no risk but then why involve those three young men in this very private affair. Heaven knows what they would think of us, of our wheeling and dealing. Besides, in our society, one has always to be wary of people one hardly knows. Those three seem nice enough young men but only time will tell whether we can trust them. Mr Lu doesn't qualify yet and, to be frank, neither do Long Wei and Zee Bin though Lilian and Beiyuen, with the absolute certitude characteristic of youth, know better, of course. If everything goes according to plan we'll know soon enough who was right, the girls or this suspicious, mistrusting old man. I hope, with all my heart, that I'm wrong and that Lu, Long Wei and Zee Bin keep their promises. But enough about that, let's join the others, they're waiting for us at Juntao's place.'

Lao Dee and his wife, Auntie Liu and Lao Dao had each brought a bouquet of wild flowers and a small woven reed basket with three white peaches which they placed reverently on Juntao's resting place.

The characters *Chen Juantao, unshackled in life and death* had been freshly painted over with glossy, white oil paint only the previous week by Lilian while Suping and Beiyuen had strewn fresh pebble stones between and around the boulders marking the grave.

The day before the three of them and Lao Dao had gone for a long walk upstream to collect a bagful of nice, round, whitish pebbles which they had then soaked in bleach overnight to make them even whiter.

Chen Dan introduced the newcomers from the far north and the two foreign devils to his lifelong friend and then told him about the plan asking him, in the same breath, to make Zhang Yizhong's mind receptive.

Next he stepped on to a big boulder Xu Ximing had rolled for him against the trunk of the old walnut tree and carefully put his hand, holding the package Auntie had handed to him into a hole in the trunk.

Stepping down off the boulder he bowed his head and said, softly, 'Baolin's notes, talisman for his friends, curse for his enemies, bane of my first love, agent of my final love and now, at long last, about to be surrendered to their evil origin after serving us one more and final time to steer our lives in a new direction. Will they fade into oblivion? Be used to wreck a few, nearly finished lives? We will never know and neither is that our business.'

Chen Dan fell silent and, wiping a tear from his eyes, he stepped back amongst his friends.

'I brought something, a present, for you and your friend,' Lao Dee said and he handed Chen Dan a package he had been carrying around since breakfast.

Chen looked at the man who, though an outsider, had had such an impact on their lives, who knew so much about their secret hopes and fears that it made him uneasy, and he was about to say something when he thought better of it and started to unwrap the parcel.

The contents elicited a collective gasp of delighted surprise as Chen bent down and subsequently placed in the centre of Chen Juntao's grave a copper censer and several packages of joss sticks.

Without a word Suping rushed to the small outcrop of silica a few metres further uphill, scooped up the silvery white sand with the empty box that had contained the censer and returned to kneel beside Chen Dan.

Carefully she poured the sand into the censer as Chen sat back on his heels, watching her, holding ten joss sticks, fantail-like, in his hand, ready to push them deep into the sand.

Finally he picked up the box with exceptionally long matches Lao Dee had had the foresight to include in the package and he lit the joss sticks using only two matches. Suping helped him back to his feet and took his arm to support him as his legs were seized with cramps from kneeling down for too long.

The others, but for Lao Dee and his wife, who remained discreetly where they were standing, gathered around Suping and Chen Dan and together, heads bowed, they silently remembered Chen Juntao as the curling wisps of fragrant smoke from the joss sticks wafted up and around them before dissipating in the warm, shimmering air.

They remembered him as they had known him or as they had heard him described, his qualities enhanced and his shortcomings diminished by the time since past and it was probably only Chen Dan who remembered him as the good-hearted, desperately lonely and insecure bumbling soul whose guileless genius had left him defenceless against the malice of mediocrity.

It was Ah Li's wondering voice that finally broke the spell as she said, 'For a while already I have been wondering what is missing, something so familiar that one doesn't notice consciously when it's there but does when it's absent yet can't put a finger on it. But it just came to me, there are no *birds* here! No chirps, no coos, no trills! Where have all the birds gone!'

The others looked up, surprised and uncomprehending, at the outlandish sounds in this most Chinese of Chinese places and circumstances.

Lao Dao smiled and replied in English, 'There are very few birds because they killed most of them, the Red Guards and the people coerced by them, because the Great Harlot and her three gigolos in Beijing had decreed that the little beasts ate the people's grain. That after the mass hunt and mass killing the vermin, without any natural enemies, devoured all the crops was something they had not thought of, the sorry clowns, but by then their feeble, malicious minds were already on to fresh mischief. I'm sure there are other outstanding bills from that period of collective madness that haven't come in yet after all these years and for which Lilian and Beiyuen and probably their children will have to pay.'

He fell silent, then translated quickly for the others what all the talk had been about.

Unable to say something that would make sense to the foreigners they shrugged their shoulders, resignedly, a bit nettled nevertheless and strolled back, in silence, to the house.

'Did I say something wrong? Did I offend them?' Ah Li asked her husband. 'I am right, am I not? There *are* no birds in this land where there seem to be only dull colours all tinged with grey, grey dust probably because that's cheap and everywhere.'

Lao Dee laughed loudly, more in an attempt to lift the momentary gloom than because of his wife's witty perceptiveness and replied, with forced cheer, 'No love, you didn't say something wrong and you didn't offend them. They are just embarrassed and cross with themselves that you noticed something they have even forgotten ever was there. And yes love, everything is hazy here, not only nature and its tinged colours but also the people, their language, their thinking, their signals. But, perhaps, that's why I like it here, why I like *them*.'

Raising his voice he called out, 'It's past eleven already. I ordered two boats for eleven. I'm sure they're waiting for us downhill, near the bridge. Let's go down straight away. It'll take two hours at least to the tea garden and I am hungry already!'

Everybody cheered, relieved that the momentary depression had been blown away and Beiyuen and Lilian ran downhill, shouting they would tell the boatmen to wait, while the others followed at a more sedate pace.

Everybody enjoyed the boat trip, the lunch in the tea garden, the freshly brewed tea, the view, the beautiful warm weather and each other's company.

Before they knew it the two taxis ordered by Lao Dee to fetch them at five o'clock to take them back to the hotel signalled their arrival by horning two long followed by two short blasts from the road down below.

Back at the hotel they bade one another goodbye, agreeing to meet the next morning at the Xus' place for morning tea.

Chen Dan and Auntie Liu withdrew to Auntie's little terrace for a quiet talk before he would call Zhang Yizhong from Lao Dee's room at eight o'clock.

The call to Zhang went even better than expected.

It took Zhang only a few seconds to connect after Chen Dan's preliminary introduction and then he seemed genuinely pleased to hear from his old acquaintance.

The habitual mutual affabilities exhausted there was that usual awkward silence and then Zhang said, 'I don't think that after twenty-two years you suddenly felt an irresistible urge to enquire about my well-being, so what's on your mind, Chen?'

Chen Dan chuckled and replied, 'Haven't changed much, eh Yizhong? Oh well, there goes my well-prepared speech. Straight questions deserve straight answers. Do you remember that evening after Chen Juntao's execution when you came to see me, alone, in Xu's house and we talked about a great plan you wanted to be part of and about certain notes, the Yang Baolin notes, you so very much wanted to lay your hands on? Of course you remember. Do you also remember that when you visited the Xus in their prison cell that afternoon you told them how your mouth watered when you were spying on us telling our stories and eating our Beggars Chicken while you were hiding behind the hedge in your brother's garden? Of course you remember that also because you never forget anything.

'Well, we're planning another Beggars Chicken dinner next week, Wednesday, to celebrate Xu Suping's homecoming for the first time after twenty-two years and that with her beautiful daughter to boot. Suping has been living in Dalian all these years caring for her husband who was dumped on her doorstep by the Party after its little revolutionary generals, as you used to call them, drove him out of his mind and turned him into a certified idiot, a cripple both mentally and physically. Suping made a few very good friends there, in Dalian, and they came with her to Luding to meet her parents.

'Now, imagine my surprise, Yizhong, when one of those friends, actually more a protective grandmother to Suping and her daughter than a mere friend, used to be my first wife's doctor and best friend before your Party's goons slit Lingling's throat as a warning to me. This woman, Liu Meiling is her name as you probably know already, and I renewed our friendship of old and we have even decided to marry and spend the rest of our days together here in Luding, another cause for celebration next week. We, that is the Xus, Suping and I, thought that for old times' sake you might like to join us for that very special dinner in Xu's garden. We would be very pleased and so would Liu Meiling, who has heard so much about you from Suping. Now, apart from this friendly social aspect there is one other thing.'

'There always is, Chen, there always is,' Zhang cut in.

'Yes, you're right, Yizhong, there always is, isn't there?' Chen assented and continued. 'Liu Meiling and I have been talking these past couple of days about those notes Lingling entrusted to us and which have given both of us, and certain people very dear to us, a certain measure of protection and privileges over the past fifty years or so. We both think the time has come to stop playing games and to part with our talisman and we thought you might like to be the go-between and take the credit for finally closing the Yang Baolin case and earn the gratitude of your patrons. Patron saints is the expression that flashed through my mind just now, however, that wouldn't fit their profile, now would it, Yizhong?'

Zhang chuckled and said, 'I can hardly believe that you and that character Liu Meiling have finally realised the errors of your ways and now wish to redeem yourselves, so there must be another reason, something sordidly selfish, no doubt. So tell me, Chen Dan, what's the price this time, this last time if you have it your way?'

'A very small price, Yizhong, insignificant in comparison to what you and the Party and a couple of old stalwarts get in return.' And Chen Dan told him.

Apparently Zhang did not need not take the matter up with his peers or superiors for he said curtly when Chen fell silent, 'I cannot actually give you the *permits*, Dan, that's the authority of the Party's municipal echelons and, like all bureaucrats, they have long, sensitive toes you wouldn't want me to step on on your behalf, certainly not when you no longer have the protection of your talisman.

'What I *can* do, however, is have a friendly letter addressed to the secretaries of Dalian and Luding and signed by someone who will make them sit up straight and fall over themselves to oblige, requesting the personal favour to facilitate the requests that will be submitted presently to their officers by Chen Dan, Liu Meiling, Li née Xu Suping, Li Lilian and Shen Beiyuen. Will that be satisfactory, Dan?'

'That will be satisfactory, Yizhong,' Chen Dan replied and there was no mistaking his emotion.

'See you next week Wednesday then, my friend,' Zhang said, adding, 'I'll find my own way to your place. I'll use the opportunity to visit my brother as well, I have something to discuss with him and his wife, something personal. So goodbye for now.' And at that he hung up.

Chen Dan slowly put down the receiver and looked up at Lao Dee and Auntie Liu.

'I think you more or less got the gist of the conversation,' he said, 'everything went according to plan, we can't go back on our decision now. Zhang will be there Wednesday. We'll need the whole day to prepare everything. I hope everybody will help with the preparations, I'm afraid I'm too old to do more than giving a few directions here and there.'

Lao Dee laughed and told him not to worry, he, Lao Dao, Suping and the two girls would do all the work, including fetching the mud.

'All you have to do, Uncle Dan, is to tell us how to prepare the chicken and for the rest you relax, with Meiling, Ximing and Guixian, enjoy the circus and entertain your friend Zhang with witty conversation,' he added laughingly.

'By the way,' he asked, 'will it be proper for me and my wife to stay for dinner? Zhang may take umbrage at the presence of foreigners, being such a high government official.'

'You and Ah Li stay! Period!' Liu Meiling said, furiously. 'Do you really think that I, and I'm sure I speak for the others as well, that we care a damn about what Comrade Zhang finds, thinks, likes or does not like about you and your wife being there as well? *You* are our friend, not *he* and *never* will he be, let that be clear, however hypocritically we may coo in his face and he knows that and feels the same about us whatever *he* may say or do for us for that matter. Besides, it is *he* who will gain the most by the deal and he'll do *anything*, pretend *anything* to get his crooked, greedy claws on those notes.

'How naive you two are if you really think that he is going to turn those notes over to the secretary-general and his ilk. "Close the case and earn the gratitude of your patrons" I heard you say, Dan. I'm sure he nearly had a fit of laughter when he heard you say that. He knows that the moment he parts with those notes he's a dead man. Gratitude my foot! A knife or a garrotte as he gets out of his car after an unexpected, late night meeting. Why do you think he didn't need to consult anybody before agreeing to come down here and at such short notice to boot?

'No, Comrade Zhang has already one accomplice in mind, probably the one who will sign that letter of recommendation, and to whom he will give one copy while keeping the other copy for himself and together the two schemers will milk the notes for what they're still worth. That's what is going to happen to our talisman, Chen Dan, for the Party and for those still vulnerable nothing will change, a different pair of blackmailers, that's all.'

Liu Meiling fell silent and looked defiantly and mockingly at the two men who had watched her with mounting alarm as she spoke those mocking, cynical words.

'You indeed are a wicked woman to those you hate, Meiling,' Chen Dan sighed, 'the things your cynical mind is capable of conjuring up, they wouldn't occur to me in a thousand lives.'

'Indeed, my dear, learned but naive man,' the old woman said, smiling at him, 'and that's exactly why you need me to protect you for a while longer, just in case.'

She hesitated only a fraction of a second before going on, 'You see, my dear friends, unbeknownst to comrade Zhang there exists a third copy, a true photocopy taken with a camera like Jan the engineer explained to me. Lao Dee can tell you who Jan is if it interests you. Be that as it may, once the decision for our trip to Luding had been taken I started thinking about all the things that could happen and one of those scenarios was what has actually happened. So I saw the need to hedge my bets, only I didn't know how.

'That Sunday, now six weeks ago, when Lao Dee took us all for a picnic it dawned on me when I saw Jan taking pictures with that small camera of his. Through Lao Dao I asked Jan if it was possible to take close-up pictures of a framed diploma. He said it was possible with what he called a wide-angle lens and he explained how it was done. He then wrote his name and Lilian's in the sand with his finger and told me to take a picture. I did and he said I had done it correctly. I then asked him if I could borrow his camera for a few days and he said of course and asked whether I wanted him to put in a new film.

'So the next evening when I was alone at home, Beiyuen having the late shift, I took out the notes, switched off the ceiling lamp in my bedroom and under the light of the reading lamp I took a picture of every page of Yang's notes. I made sure I could read the text through the viewfinder before I pressed the button. I then took out the film and the next day I gave Beiyuen the camera to return to Jan for me. I have carried the film on me ever since that day. You are the first and the only ones to know and I would like to keep it that way.

'You see, if Zhang keeps his word and doesn't cheat us, intentionally or not, we'll never need that film. If he does, however, we have at least the means to ward off the harm, to us, to the Xus, to Suping, to the children if we let it be known that the film exists, outside China. That is, if Lao Dee agrees to keep the film for us, in his safe at home, with a letter signed by both of us, Chen Dan and myself, requesting him to publish the notes in case harm comes to either one or all of us. Will you do that for us, Dee Huilin?'

Initially shocked by the old woman's cynicism and mistrust the two men had next listened to her story, incredulous at first then with unreserved admiration for her almost unbelievable astuteness.

'Of course I will do that for you,' Lao Dee replied, adding ruefully, 'it's about all I can do to regain a bit of self-respect and hopefully your respect as well after the dressing down you just gave us.'

Snorting derisively he continued, 'I don't know how you feel, Dan, but I feel like a very small boy who just found out that, as he was playing his cowboys and Indians game, Mummy was watching over him all the time, unobtrusively, but still manipulating the elements of the game so that he couldn't hurt himself or, inadvertently, others, in the typical foolhardiness of the very young. And now he stands there, confused and hurt, as the magic mirror in which he saw himself as the great, invincible chief, lies in smithereens around him on the ground together with his cocky vanity. You are that mummy, Meiling, because that's how you see yourself, isn't it? Looking at all of us with that half-frown, half-smile, your cocky, foolhardy children playing their silly games.'

Lao Dee fell silent and sighed. 'What about you, Dan?'

'Appropriate imagery, very appropriate and to the point,' Chen Dan replied, 'so to the point in fact that I feel you and I are down and out for the evening. No more posturing for the time being. Have Ah Li massage your ego so that you can sleep. At least you won't have Mummy around you – I think I'll have to suck my thumb.' And with a rueful grin he bade Lao Dee and his wife goodnight.

'Tuck in your baby and croon a lullaby for him, Ah Li!' Auntie Liu growled as she waddled after her man. 'Men!' she added derisively. 'No common sense, too cocky!' And at that she pulled the door shut behind her.

'What did she say?' Aly asked.

'Nothing important, my love,' her husband replied, 'women's talk.'

The next four days passed without stress or strain. They made it a point to see each other once a day, either for lunch or for a late afternoon tea, then in the garden of the hotel then at the Xus' place, but for the remainder of the time they let one another alone.

Lao Dee and his wife spent most of the time in the company of Lao Dao, both because they could converse in English, easily and colloquially, and because they genuinely liked each other.

They made boat trips together as far as Danba, made long walks through the fields, enjoyed simple meals in small, very basic restaurants or sometimes even in farmers' homes when they were invited by the friendly people to join them for their noon or evening rice.

They spent one whole day in Chengdu and loved the relaxed, laid-back atmosphere as they watched the easygoing people from some sidewalk café or other and enjoyed a glass of local tea and a platter of fresh fruit or a simple pork and chilli dish.

Lilian and Beiyuen, who had been told by Suping that their transfer to Luding was now just a matter of time and probably a short time at that, spent most of their time in the hotel making friends with the staff.

Mr Lu had invited them to attend the daily staff meeting if they liked and to feel free to comment or to make suggestions. Their stories about life in their own, big hotel in faraway Dalian, about the foreign guests and their often weird behaviour, about Vice-Manager Zhou and Secretary Du, about the karaoke bar, still an unknown phenomenon in Sichuan let alone in Luding, elicited a lot of laughter and hilarity and Mr Lu secretly praised himself at the prospect of having these two lovely and lively girls on his staff.

With time and the proper training Lilian would become an ideal public and guest relations manager while Beiyuen could probably be trained to run the housekeeping department.

Suping went down to fetch Auntie Liu in the morning at the hotel and walked her back after dinner after a leisurely day at home with the Xus and Chen Dan.

Twice Chen Dan spent the night in Auntie's room and nobody paid any attention.

They were all contented and happy in a relaxed, easygoing manner.

Wednesday came before they realised and preparations for the Beggars Chicken dinner that night started early.

The evening before they had had a light, simple dinner together in the hotel during which Chen Dan had explained where to look for the right mud and how to collect it, which herbs and spices to buy and to look for the right charcoal.

Lao Dee had hired the same boat again, for half a day this time, and ordered the boatman to be in front of the hotel at seven o'clock in the morning to take him, his wife, Lao Dao and the two girls on board. Suping would join them below the bridge and guide them to the place where, twenty-two years ago, she had collected the mud together with Uncle Dan.

At that time the idea of taking a boat for a mission like that would never have occurred to them nor, for that matter, would a boatman have understood or been willing to take them. The idea that one could make some money on the side by doing something different and besides one's job was altogether an alien concept that could even land one in jail.

Times were different now and the idea of making money was now admitted and people were becoming good at it.

Suping and Uncle Dan had walked the whole distance twice that day long ago, in turn carrying the heavy galvanised iron buckets with mud on the way back.

She laughed merrily when she told the others that her father had scolded her when he had seen Uncle Dan carrying the two buckets uphill. It had simply been his turn but her father didn't know that Uncle Dan himself had explained that carrying two buckets at a time was easier on the spine than carrying one bucket each then with one hand, then with the other.

Lao Dee had calculated they needed at least five times as much mud this time and besides he simply was too lazy, he said, to carry those heavy buckets, though they were made of plastic nowadays, over a distance of some ten or twelve kilometres even if they took turns.

So he had hired the boat and it turned out to be a fortunate decision for when they rounded the bend in the river behind which Suping had said were the mudflats she had scooped the mud from the last time, they were shocked to find the place littered with garbage, flotsam from further upstream driven up into this pocket aside from the main stream.

'The usual debris of progress and civilisation,' Lao Dee said sneeringly, 'another two or three generations at the most and there won't be a pristine place left on this planet. Man must be the only animal to foul his own nest. You haven't seen anything yet here in China. Wait until consumerism really takes off. What with the typical Chinese, typical Asian is a better word, attitude of couldn't care less and don't give a damn about anything or anybody that hasn't a direct and on-the-spot bearing on his own personal well-being, China will soon be one huge dump for the jetsam and flotsam of voracious, indifferent consumerism.'

He fell silent, smiled ruefully at his friends and added, 'I'm sorry, these things upset me. Can't stand it if people spoil beautiful things out of sheer indifference. Let's go further upstream to look for a clean place. It's easy with a boat, on foot we would now be in trouble.'

Three kilometres further upstream they finally found the ideal place.

Lilian and Beiyuen had come well prepared for the mud collecting for when they took off their trousers it appeared they wore their swimsuits underneath.

Gingerly they stepped overboard into the clear, knee-deep water, squealing with feigned horror as the soft, muddy bottom squelched between their toes.

They attached one end of a rope around their waists and while Lao Dao and Lao Dee each held the other end, they carefully, small step by small step, ventured up the gently sloping bottom to where it emerged, glistening above the water surface.

They quickly got the hang of it and twenty minutes later the ten buckets were stowed evenly over the length of the boat full to the rim with clean-smelling, greyish-blue mud.

They were back under the bridge at eleven o'clock and Lao Dee paid the boatman the twenty yuan they had agreed on the day before.

'Let's have a cup of coffee or tea first before we buy the other supplies,' he said and taking two buckets he started uphill followed by the others.

Every twenty metres or so they put down the buckets and swayed their arms to restore the blood circulation in their fingers.

The Xus, Chen Dan and Auntie Liu had heard their voices from afar and Guixian had quickly prepared coffee for Lao Dee, Ah Li and Lao Dao and tea for the others while Auntie put the noodle and vegetable soup they would have for lunch on the stove.

As they quietly and contentedly sipped their respective brews, Suping told the others about their expedition to the mudflats.

Chen Dan shook his head in disgust when she told them about the trash and he said, 'It's the pig and chicken farms just outside the city limits, by order of the Party, and the city's own inadequate garbage collection system. People just dump everything in the river rather than see the rubbish pile up on their doorstep. Our friend the boatman the other day complained that there are hardly any fish left from ten kilometres north to twenty kilometres south of the city so he has to go further and further to catch his quota of fish for the state market.

'The price he gets is the same as twenty years ago, however, and where before he could still catch more than his quota to sell on the free market and earn additional income, he now needs at least twelve hours a day five or six days a week to meet his quota. That's why he is so keen on this boat for hire business. Easy, clean money quickly earned. The Party's propaganda can't keep up with the facts of life nowadays and instead of becoming less rigid, of adapting their creed, the zealots become increasingly strident in their condemnation of what they call the loose morals of the people while the pragmatists look the other way but always after what they see as their own interest.'

He fell silent then added, grinning, 'We could ask comrade Zhang tonight what *he* thinks of these things.'

'No way my friend and husband to be!' Auntie Liu exclaimed. 'We agreed to keep the conversation tonight light-hearted and general. Don't you now change the plan and bring politics into it or we'll still be sitting here tomorrow morning and everybody aggravated. There is absolutely nothing to gain from such discussions and everything to lose. We must avoid anything contentious or we may spoil this wonderful chance for a happy ending for all of us. So don't even think about it! Instead let's discuss now our respective tasks for this afternoon. Okay?'

'Well spoken, Meiling,' Lao Dee said, 'I'm looking forward to a nice meal, a new, interesting type of dish, in a relaxed and friendly atmosphere. I'm more than fed up with polemics.

'I think that each and every one of you is about to achieve the best which can reasonably be expected under the circumstances, a peaceful and contented evening of life for Chen Dan and Meiling together and for Ximing and Guixian with their daughter and granddaughter to look after them, for Suping to have her parents and her daughter around and a second chance to make good herself, for Lilian and Beiyuen to have a whole new life to look forward to, so why for heaven's sake would you spoil all that just to make a philosophical point? Be content with what you have, enjoy the love and friendship you have for each other, enjoy your peaceful life here in this quiet, beautiful place far from the hostile world's hubbub and for the rest...' he fell silent and raised his hands in an eloquent gesture of 'none of my business, don't want to know'.

Everybody burst out laughing though the old folks were visibly moved.

'I deserved that dressing down, Lao Dee,' Chen Dan said, 'you are a true friend, always respectful of your friends' idiosyncrasies but not afraid, if the situation calls for it, to put your finger on their fallacies. Thank you, my friend, we'll leave well alone.'

Lao Dee smiled, winked at him and said, 'Now back to our business at hand. Let's plan our time and tasks wisely. Who does what and when? Tell us, Dan, you're the expert.'

His dignity restored, Chen Dan sat up straight and explained his plan of action.

'Lilian and Beiyuen will stay here and wash the mud with clear water to remove all traces of impure smell and taste. As they go along they can help Guixian and Meiling readying the bowls, plates, glasses and what have you. Ximing and I will take turns in digging the hole; four by two by one foot will do, I think.'

He fell silent and nodded at Lao Dao who had raised his hand. 'Yes, what is it, Lao Dao?'

'I remember from Suping's story that when you first prepared your Beggars Chicken you stressed how important it was that the garden soil didn't mix with the ash and that therefore Juntao had to line the walls of the hole with the same mud you used for the chickens' shell,' Lao Dao said. 'This time the hole is much bigger so I propose that we line the wall with bricks. A few hundred bricks will do, I think. What do you think of my idea?'

The others found it an excellent idea and Lao Dee said, 'I'll give you some money, Huimin. Go back to the hotel and ask Mr Lu to call his friend the taxi driver for you. Let him drive you to the nearest brick factory, he'll know where, and load the bricks in the boot of the taxi. Tell him to drive you back here. If the car can't negotiate the slope offer the driver some extra money if he will help you carry the bricks.'

'Excellent, that's another important task taken care of,' Chen Dan took over. 'Now, I have made a list of the ingredients we need. I propose that Lao Dee, Ah Li and Suping go to the market to buy the herbs and spices and the chickens. Ximing and I will buy the charcoal after we'll have finished digging the hole. The charcoal seller lives just at the foot of the hill so it won't be too strenuous for us two old blighters.'

It was past midday when Lao Dee, his wife Ah Li and Suping set about their task.

First they went to the state market to buy the chickens.

Lao Dee chose five fat, healthy birds, one more than Chen Dan had calculated, and, after some haggling, he and the peasant woman agreed on a lump sum price of thirty yuan, including the slaughtering, plucking and cleaning of the chickens. He told the woman they would pick up the chickens on their way back from the free market where they would buy the herbs and spices for Beggars Chicken.

The friendly young woman told him to look for the stall of the Lim sisters from Danba County as they had the freshest herbs and the best dried spices. Not cheap, the sisters' wares, but then somebody who gladly paid ten yuan extra to have his chickens killed and cleaned for him would surely not mind paying a few fen extra for good quality herbs and spices.

Laughingly they took their leave and continued their foraging. On the free market they easily found the Lim sisters' stall on the sidewalk near the town hall entrance.

Suping and Ah Li selected the various herbs from the neat and freshly sprinkled displays while Lao Dee discussed the many varieties of dried spices and prepared pastes with the friendly elderly women.

Laughingly shrugging off his wife's protests he bought a good measure of everything, far more than was needed for that evening's dinner, and on top of it a big piece of honeycomb dripping and oozing with yellowish-brown honey.

As he counted out thirty-six yuan for everything he joked to the small crowd that had gathered around them that his wife's protests were not so much because of him wasting his money on needless things but because she feared the effect all those spices and honey would have on his manly prowess.

Everybody roared with laughter and when his wife understood from Suping's blushing giggle what all the hilarity was about and made as if to hit Lao Dee with her bag, the crowd erupted in a gale of merriment.

Still giggling and laughing the three of them made their way back through the crowded narrow streets to the state market, where the poultry seller had the five chickens ready for them, the innards wrapped separately in several soggy pieces of newspaper.

Fortunately Ah Li had brought a big red, white and blue plastic bag from Hong Kong to carry everything. The two women took turns to help Lao Dee carry the heavy bag through the stiflingly hot narrow streets and up the hill, the afternoon sun like an additional backpack of burning hot coal.

Huffing and puffing and perspiring they finally shuffled into the back garden, dropping the plastic bag there and then for Lilian and Beiyuen to take care of and letting themselves drop, with a sigh of relief, into the wicker chairs.

Greedily they drank the glasses of lukewarm tea Auntie Liu poured and then replenished for them a second and third time before Suping related their exploits to her mother and Auntie Liu while Lao Dee watched Lao Dao stacking the bricks around the walls of the hole under the watchful eyes of Chen Dan and Xu Ximing.

Groaning he heaved himself out of his chair and joined the three men to ask whether he could be of any help just when Lao Dao scrambled up, his handiwork finished.

'Mustard after the meal, my friend,' Lao Dao grunted, slapping Lao Dee on his sweaty wet back. 'We're all set now, I think, for Dan's grand finale. What does the master chef think? Is it to his liking? I hope this one here isn't as difficult to please as your prima donna friend Mu Ping in Dalian, Lao Dee,' he added chucklingly.

Chen Dan laughed and said the pit looked perfect to him. As they stood admiring a job well done they heard Xu's wife Guixian say, 'That must by far be the most expensive hole in the whole world. Two professors of mathematics and two university-schooled engineers to make that hole. Imagine having to pay the fees such specialists command these days.'

Everybody laughed, Ah Li joining in after Lilian had quickly translated her grandmother's joking remark and then she added, 'Men are like children. If they like what they do, however silly in our women's eyes, no effort is too great let alone the time it takes. For over thirty years my clever man has designed and built factories all over the world, never too busy to lend a hand to specialists and workers alike, yet at home I can't even make him change a light bulb or tighten a loose screw. Call the handyman, he says, when I ask him to do such small things meaning, of course, do it yourself.'

'No need to translate, Lilian!' Lao Dee cried but it was too late already and everybody laughed and poked fun at him.

'Enough fooling around,' Chen Dan finally said, serious again, 'there's still work to be done. The women will now prepare the chickens, all five of them. Lao Dee was right to buy one more than I thought we needed. I'm sure Zhang will bring his brother and his brother's wife to the party and even if he didn't we would have to invite them as well, what with all the kindness they showed us these past twenty-odd years.

'Suping and Guixian, just in case you don't remember exactly, pound the herbs and spices with the innards in a mortar to a smooth paste and stuff the chickens with it, after that you stitch them up. I'll show you the right proportions of the herbs and spices. Ah Li, Lilian and Beiyuen, you will mould the clay around the stuffed chickens nicely and evenly. It's better to make the shell a bit too thick than too thin. If it's too thin the mud will crackle, break and the chicken will burn. We have enough mud for the rest of our days so use it liberally.

'Lao Dee and Lao Dao, you're in charge of the charcoal fire. Keep feeding the charcoal into the fire until the hot ash layer is thick enough to bury the five chickens in and cover them completely. That'll take at least an hour. Then the cooking will take another three hours which takes us to six o'clock already. Add another two hours for the cooling off, breaking of the clay shell and removal of what is left of the stuffing and before you know it's eight o'clock before we actually can start eating.

'I propose therefore that we start right away and that as soon as the cooking process is under way, Lao Dee, Ah Li and Lao Dao, and maybe the two girls as well, can go back to the hotel to take a bath and change into clean clothes. If you're back here by six o'clock it's soon enough. We'll ask the Zhangs to come also around that time. It's fun to help with the uncovering of the chickens, to test the cooking and later to break the shells. While all that goes on we can have our pre-dinner drinks and small talk. What do you think?' And the old savant looked at his friends, his eyes sparkling with fun.

The others nodded their assent and set about their assigned tasks.

The women and Chen Dan disappeared into the house to prepare the chickens and Lao Dee and Lao Dao, with the help of Xu, emptied two of the three big jute bags of charcoal into the hole.

Then Lao Dee produced another small marvel of Western ingenuity: small bricks of compressed paraffin to light the fire which he placed here and there amongst and under the charcoal. Nice, big and hot flames began curling around the pieces of charcoal as soon as he touched the little white bricks with a match.

'That'll save us at least half an hour,' Xu said admiringly. 'Dan and I didn't gather much dead wood I'm afraid, because of our sore backs, you see, and besides, it isn't really very dead, the wood I mean, so Dan and I were afraid it would take you a long time to get the fire going, that's why he calculated it would take you one hour.

'But with Lao Dee's system it won't take more than half that time. Wonderful gadgets you have in that world of yours, Lao Dee, the best of all wonderful worlds I think as you must have lots and lots of free time what with all those marvellous time-saving gadgets and devices.'

Lao Dee chuckled as he fanned the roaring flames and said, 'China doesn't have the monopoly of cynical, wise old men, Ximing. The world outside China also produced a few and one of them was Parkinson. Parkinson was a keen observer of human foibles and he noticed that jobs, work or whatever people spend their time on, tend to fill the time made available for them. So if you think that time-saving schemes and gadgets will give people more time to think, to meditate, to read or to do just nothing, you are sadly mistaken and naive. Before you know it they will have invented all kinds of useless, time-consuming things to fill the extra time.

'Parkinson's rules apply for other things as well. The more space you give people the more bric-a-brac they buy to clutter it up, the more people you make available for a job the more are actually needed. Double a team of workers that always managed to do a certain job in eight hours and within less than a week they'll have adapted themselves *and* the job to fill the same eight hours with twice the number of people producing the same end result. My experience over the years has taught me how right he was, good old Parkinson, and I act accordingly. If I think that reasonably speaking a particular job requires three people for eight hours, I assign two and give them six hours, not because I am a heartless slave-driver but because I know those two are ingenious enough to evaluate and divide the workload and come out on top and, what's more, enjoy the challenge.

'Unfortunately this doesn't work in a Communist society which is the confirmation of Parkinson's law *par excellence*. For instance, take the factory I am now building in Dalian. What with all the modern equipment I am installing at the Chinese's own demand, four hundred people in two shifts would be adequate to churn out the maximum production capacity in a year from now. Instead the authorities sent me twelve hundred people, men and women, one year ago already, when all I needed were masons, carpenters, welders and fitters. No prior consultations, nothing. From one day to the next, there they came pouring in through the gate heading straight for the canteen where they have been sitting ever since, every day, smoking, chatting, knitting, sleeping, hanging around bored to tears.

'And now that these days I can give a number of them something to do, cleaning work, helping with the unpacking of small equipment, assisting my foreign specialists and so on, they drag their feet, grumble and disappear after only half an hour or they refuse categorically saying they're for production work only. Do you think that these twelve hundred people will ever be suitable to do a good job? Whatever job? Forget it. I don't envy the Chinese managers who, in the end, will have to carry on with these people. A few of them are aware of the problem and some told me frankly that they are worried. But most of them are cast from the same mould as those so-called workers and couldn't care less either.'

Lao Dee burst out laughing at Xu's perplexed face and added, 'So you see, my friend, you can't win. Better stick to the things you like doing, as my wife said we're so good at, and for the rest don't take life and yourself too seriously.

Look at the beautiful fire we built,' he continued, 'why don't you call Chen Dan and his harem and tell them we're ready to bury the chickens half an hour ahead of schedule, in defiance of Parkinson's law and Communist doctrine.'

Smiling yet shaking his head at the mishmash of mockery and seriousness so typical of the amiable barbarian who had caused such an upset in his well-ordered life, Xu turned and went to tell that other eccentric, Chinese this one, that his foreign compeer had the hot ashes ready for the chickens' burial.

Leading the procession of Guixian, Suping, Ah Li, Lilian and Beiyuen, each carrying a chicken in its still soft clay shell, Chen Dan walked up to where Lao Dee and Lao Dao were kneeling on opposite sides of the hole facing the glowing, whitish ash.

In turn and with great care each woman placed her chicken in Lao Dao's outstretched hands who next put the bluish-grey ball, carefully and gingerly in order not to burn his hands, into the dimples Lao Dee made with a ladle in the intensely hot ashes.

Perspiration was dripping from the two men's faces into the whitish, fluffy heat with small pops and sizzles.

When finally the last bird in its clay shell was lying to Chen Dan's satisfaction, Lao Dee ladled ash from the sides to cover the lot before Lao Dao shoved part of the earth they had dug out of the hole as a bulging cover over the whole.

Groaning, their faces flushed, sweaty and streaked, the two men scrambled back on their feet to a round of applause.

'Come on friend, Ah Li, girls, let's go back to the hotel and freshen up while our friends here attend to their matters,' Lao Dee said. 'We'll be back here by six o'clock, Dan,' he continued, adding *sotto voce* for the old man's ears only. 'Send Suping to meet us if you need more time.'

Chen Dan nodded and squeezed Lao Dee's hands. 'Thank you, my friend,' he mumbled, 'thank you for your understanding and support. Perhaps it is better to wait in the hotel until Suping comes to fetch you. The news she brings you may well influence your choice of drinks for the evening.'

'Right you are old fox, right you are,' Lao Dee agreed, and, grinning, he added, 'we wouldn't want that exemplary proletarian Zhang Yizhong partaking of Mr Lu's better wines and brandy if he has not been as forthcoming as we expect him to be, now would we, old friend? If Suping brings the good news, we shall all drive up here in a taxi and bring adequate and suitable stuff for him and us to imbibe. If on the contrary the news is not good as we expect, I'll send the taxi ahead of us with a few dozen bottles of local soft drinks and turbid beer and we follow on foot looking suitably sombre and morose. What do you think?'

Seeing the old man's lips quiver, the Dutchman realised that for his Chinese friend it was no longer a laughing matter and that all his hope was now staked on the outcome of his meeting with Zhang that afternoon.

Regretting his earlier flippancy, he squeezed the old man's shoulder and said with all the sympathy he felt in his heart, 'Don't worry, Dan. Everything will be fine.'

After their bath and change into freshly laundered and ironed clothes Lao Dee and his wife, Lao Dao and the two girls gathered in the garden behind the hotel to wait for Suping.

The all-seeing and knowing Mr Lu must have noticed them and their subdued manner for barely five minutes after Lilian and Beiyuen had joined their elders, the pretty dining room waitresses Meilan and Meiling appeared, unbidden, pushing a trolley with a tea service and a large plate of multicoloured cookies.

'With Mr Lu's compliments,' Meilan and Meiling tinkled in unison as one poured the tea in real teacups and the other passed the plate with cookies around.

Appreciative of Mr Lu's kind and discreet attention they sipped from the scaldingly hot and fragrant tea and nibbled from a cookie when suddenly Mr Lu erupted from the lobby door and approached briskly.

He was still more than ten metres away when he called out, 'I just saw Madam Li approach on the road. She seems to be in a great hurry but she can't be the bearer of bad news for her face is all smiles and I definitely heard her laugh. Shall I send Meilan and Meiling with more tea and cookies and an additional cup and saucer?'

Slightly out of breath he looked at each of them in turn, a bit apprehensively though for the thought had probably just occurred to him that his concern for these commercially very important guests' well-being might be construed as meddling in their private business and not appreciated.

Relieved he saw their faces light up and the all-important foreigner said, smiling, 'Thank you, Mr Lu. We appreciate your concern. I think an additional cup and saucer and a fresh pot of tea will be in order as we'll all have some more tea while we wait for you to call our usual taxi driver and select twelve bottles of your finest white wine, a bottle of brandy, Remy Martin if you have it, and a bottle of fine port. Call us when you have put all that precious stuff into the boot of the car.'

Mr Lu bowed, turned and hurried back, mentally busily calculating the amount he would add to that weird foreigner's astronomical bill. He shivered, momentarily seized by the panic that lately made him, and more and more often, wake up in cold sweat in the small hours of the night, always after the same dream, nightmare rather, in which an apologetically smiling and shrugging foreigner was surrounded by his crazily jig-jogging Chinese friends jeering in chorus at him, 'Poor Mr Lu! We have no money! Poor Mr Lu!'

'No official policy, use your own judgement and discretion,' the visiting director from head office had said when he had pleaded for a rule to hide behind, a rule that would set a limit over which a guest would be required to settle his bill.

'In China you need official rules to apply and hide behind, not personal judgement and responsibility,' he had argued, 'we Chinese haven't been educated that way.'

'Then you better begin now to educate yourself, mate,' the director had replied and he had gone back to his lucky country where life was so different and so *easy*.

Pulling himself together Mr Lu replaced the worried frown by his customary cheerful smile and held the door for Madam Li. What a lovely woman she is, he thought as she rushed past him, one would never guess she was twelve years his senior. Would she reject him if he were to cultivate her?

Suping burst in on the quiet scene in the garden, jubilating the moment she saw the others. 'The news is good! The news is wonderful! Everybody is already waiting for you to taste the chicken! The Zhangs are already there! Uncle Yizhong is really *nice*! Let's go back quickly, now!'

Out of breath she stopped beside the trolley, her face flushed and radiant, her big almond eyes sparkling as she looked around the circle of friends, literally quivering with joy and impatience.

What a beautiful and lovely woman she is, it flashed through Lao Dee's mind, Jesus, I'll be jealous if she lets a new man into her life. Filthy, smelly, uncultured louts the Chinese men her age. What a waste! But then, that's not the real reason, eh Billy boy, he thought silently.

He blushed when he saw Lao Dao watching him with a sad, compassionate little smile that told him his old friend wasn't duped and had correctly read his feelings.

'No fool like an old fool,' he suddenly shouted and burst out laughing at the others' puzzled stares but also to hide his emotion at the obvious relief on his wife's face. He winked at her with a blurry eye and she winked back, thirty-three years of understanding, tolerance and love confirmed in a timeless flash.

'Give Mr Lu a few minutes to order our taxi and stow the elixirs for this evening's cheer Suping, my dear,' he said, adding, 'you probably didn't notice him in your excitement when you rushed past him just now.'

'As a matter of fact I did notice him,' Suping said, suddenly her usual composed self again, 'I even thought for a moment that he looked worried. Did you do or say something that caused the poor obliging soul to worry?'

'Mr Lu is worried ever since I came back that I won't be able to pay the bill,' Lao Dee said, chuckling. 'The manager in him knows he ought to remind me of the outstanding amount and request payment, the Chinese side fears to cause offence, a dilemma he doesn't know how to handle, so I think I'll relieve his anxiety and tell him to prepare the bill to date, that way there remains only a small amount to pay next week. Wait for me here, I'll call you when we can leave.' And at that Lao Dee got up from his chair, said a few words in Dutch to his wife who nodded, smiling, and started for the lobby entrance just when Mr Lu exited.

'One moment of your time please, Mr Lu,' Lao Dee called, and as he walked towards Mr Lu the others heard him continue, 'I should like to pay my debt, the whole amount up to and including yesterday. How long will it take you to prepare the bill?'

'No time at all, sir, no time at all!' Mr Lu exclaimed, the relief on his face comically obvious and belying the forced insouciance as he added hastily, 'but there is really no need to pay now, sir, it can wait until next Friday when all of you depart.'

'Thank you, Mr Lu, but I think it's better if I pay you now. I'm a businessman like yourself and I don't like it either if my clients hold out on me so let us get this small matter out of the way,' they heard Lao Dee reply as he preceded Mr Lu into the lobby.

His wife, seeing and sensing the others' uneasiness, laughed cheerfully and said, 'Don't think he'll have a heart attack. He knows close to a hundred yuan or so how much it is and only yesterday evening he told me that everything had turned out cheaper than he had budgeted for and that compared to what it would have cost him in Hong Kong the whole show here was a steal. So there's no need for you to feel embarrassed, believe me.'

Lao Dao quickly translated for Suping and Beiyuen and, relieved, they smiled at Ah Li while Lilian poured her mother a cup of tea and passed the cookies around.

Five minutes later Lao Dee called and beckoned them from the lobby entrance.

'Everything is settled,' he said when they joined him in front of the hotel.

'Mr Lu is happy again and I am happy as well, the amount I had to pay was a pleasant surprise and besides the brandy and port I ordered for tonight are offered by Mr Lu and that's not something to be sneezed at, I assure you. Good man that Mr Lu, he knows how to keep his guests happy and all his staff seem to genuinely like him as far as I can see. A rare combination, especially here in China. You can consider yourselves very fortunate, Lilian and Beiyuen, to get Mr Lu as your boss.

'Work hard, be loyal, remain cheerful and he'll look after you also when in a few years' time the big foreign-owned hotels will have heard of him and compete with offers to seduce him. He'll join one of them, of course, the money they'll offer he can never make here in Luding. That is, if he hasn't married a beautiful Luding woman in the meantime, one who doesn't want to leave this beautiful, peaceful place. Not again,' he added as an afterthought.

From the corner of his eye he saw Suping blush or was it his imagination? His heart told him it was not.

'The taxi can't take all six of us,' Lilian said, giggling and prodding her mother playfully. 'Why don't you four old people go ahead. Beiyuen and I can walk.' And laughingly the two girls ran off.

Xu Ximing and Chen Dan were waiting for them when the taxi stopped beside the little gate.

'We heard you coming so Ximing and I came to give you a hand with the bottles,' Chen said as Lao Dee alighted from the car. 'And to tell you what happened away from the Zhangs,' he added.

'Suping told us the good news,' Lao Dee replied, 'now let's unload the bottles first and send the driver on his way before you say another word,' and at that he lifted the cool box Mr Lu had lent him for the evening out of the boot and put it down beside the path with a sigh of relief.

'It's too heavy for you and Ximing, Dan, leave it there,' he puffed as he paid off the driver. 'Huimin and I will carry the box inside as soon as you have told us what happened. I gather everything went as expected?'

'Everything went better than expected, much better,' Chen Dan enthused. 'Yizhong not only gave us the letters but also the cables from both the Party secretary of Dalian and Luding confirming that they expect us shortly in their office to formalise everything. Yizhong spoke to them by telephone to give them orally some kind of explanation everybody can live with and to ask for their co-operation to get the matter over and done with. And that's not all!' And in his excitement the old man grabbed Lao Dee's arm. 'I still can't believe our luck,' he continued emotionally, 'imagine! Yizhong told us that his brother Yimin and his wife Xiaotian will move in with him in his Diaoyutai villa and become the compound's general handyman.

'Yimin's house here will therefore become available and this afternoon Yizhong arranged with Mayor Yu and Party Secretary Lin that the house will be assigned to Meiling and me with effect from the date of our marriage. That way we'll remain as near Ximing and Guixian as we could possibly hope for and Suping can move in with her parents, like before. Isn't that wonderful?' Impulsively Chen Dan embraced Lao Dee and then, in turn, Lao Dao, Suping and a completely flabbergasted Ah Li who had no idea what all the excited gibberish had been about other than that the subject appeared to delight everybody.

Apologetically Chen continued. 'I'm sorry to embarrass you with my emotional behaviour but you understand this means so much to all of us here and I wanted you to know before you meet the Zhangs. Also I wanted to ask you not to mention or allude to any of these matters tonight unless of course Yizhong does so himself. I don't think he will though. After all, it *is* kind of a sensitive matter, a load of dirty linen if you wish, he wouldn't relish washing in public, certainly not with two foreigners present. So let us keep the conversation general, superficial, convivial and relaxed. You remember Meiling said so earlier already and I agree with her. Besides, she quite likes Yizhong and wouldn't want to embarrass or provoke him.

'Of course she at first quarrelled with him, calling him a double-dyed-in-the-wool opportunist and no more a Communist than the president of the United States but when Yizhong burst out laughing instead of reacting angrily and shouted that both he and she had then apparently been tarred with the same brush, she couldn't keep a straight face and they laughed and laughed and slapped each other on the back as the tears streamed down their faces. We had to force a mug of tea on them to make them stop. Now they are as thick as thieves, kindred mischievous characters yet basically good-hearted souls.'

Chen Dan smiled and shook his head in wonder.

'Now let's join them in the garden before Yizhong becomes suspicious,' he continued, 'what with his ilk's ingrained mistrust of people huddling and talking out of earshot. They see plotters and schemers everywhere, no friends, merely temporary allies and potential and real enemies. Even Yizhong may not be able to break a lifelong habit just because this evening's setting differs from that cut-throat jungle he's used to.

'By the way,' he added, 'Xiaotian, Zhang Yimin's wife, told us ever so proudly, bless her simple soul, that Yizhong speaks English quite well, so Lao Dao, beware of how you translate things for Ah Li. Suping, please take Lilian aside as soon as she arrives and tell her to be careful with that pretty little blabbermouth of hers. And that goes for you as well, Lao Dee, no funny deprecating remarks in an aside to your old friend Lao Dao here. We wouldn't want to cause a diplomatic incident with the comrade minister, now would we?' And laughingly he preceded his friends through the creaking little gate, Lao Dee and Lao Dao closing the procession carrying the big, heavy cool box in between them.

The velvety port, ruby-red and sweet, and the white Australian wine, deliciously fresh and deceptively drinkable, quickly levelled the traditional inhibitions of age and status, of gender and culture, easing in, quite naturally, an evening of good-natured banter and artless cheer.

The Zhang brothers volunteered to earn their dinner by retrieving the Beggars Chicken from the still intensely hot ash pit and to much laughter they made quite a show of scooping the heavy clay balls up with a garden shovel and keeping them balanced on the blade as they trotted to a rickety, small wooden table on which they gingerly let the balls roll off.

Next everybody watched with bated breath as Chen Dan tried to steady his trembling hands for the one blow with a small hammer hard enough to crack the shell so that it could be peeled off yet soft enough so as not to crush the mud into the tender flesh beneath.

After the first tentative, glancing blow the second was a firm, decisive hit that split the shell like an overripe watermelon revealing a perfectly cooked, succulent chicken.

With squeals and shouts of delight they sniffed the wafts of delectable, pungent aromas, cheered the chef and egged him on to break the remaining four shells as well.

While still applauding Chen's last successful cracking blow they thronged around the table to watch Lilian and Beiyuen peel off the pieces of baked clay, cut the stitching and remove the slushy stuffing whereafter, one by one, Suping carried the steaming carcasses to the main table.

With joking remarks and feigned protests they all obeyed Auntie Liu's bellowed seat allocation, while Lilian and Beiyuen each put two big bowls of steaming, fragrant rice in the middle of the table in an alternating row with the five chicken dishes and Lao Dee poured everybody a fresh glass of chilled white wine.

Surveying the proceedings from his seat of honour Chen Dan stood up when everybody was finally seated, raised his glass and shouted, his voice still strong though not so booming as Suping remembered, 'To our friendship! *Ganbei*!' at which he took a long, deep sip.

They all raised their glass, shouted, 'To our friendship! *Ganbei*!' and followed his example.

Chen sat down, picked up his chopsticks, looked around the table at the eager, expectant faces, grinned and shouted, '*Chi ba*!' He plunged his chopsticks into the soft flesh and tore off the first piece in the general frenzied attack.

For a while there was only the smacking and grunting of a group of uninhibited Chinese enjoying their food and then it was time for the compliments. Glowing with pride and exuding false modesty Chen Dan acknowledged the others' unanimous praise of the chickens' succulence and flavour.

Nodding and smiling with pleasure Lao Dee listened to his friends' unreserved praise of the rice's flavour, its texture, the size of its firm, detached grains so unlike the bland, small-grained home variety.

Before long the last grain had been picked out of the bowls and not one minute shred of flesh was left on even the smallest gnawed-off bone.

Leaning back against the back of their chair they sighed contentedly and stroked their stomach to release the blocked air in a few rumbling burps.

With glazed eyes they watched absent-mindedly as Beiyuen peered in the teapot, filled it up with fresh, hot water from the big thermos, added a handful of fresh tea leaves and then slowly, lethargically, shuffled around the table to pour everybody a last mug of tea.

In contented, companionable silence they sipped the tea straining the floating leaves with their teeth.

Finally, still without a word, Lao Dee got up and, followed by Lao Dao, disappeared into the house.

A few minutes later they reappeared, Lao Dao carrying, gingerly, a tray with snifters and small elegant cut glass wine glasses borrowed from the ever obliging Mr Lu in exchange for the recipe for Beggars Chicken which, Mr Lu thought, could become a tourist attraction in his restaurant, and Lao Dee with the brandy bottle in one hand and a bottle of Sauternes in the other. His wife had brought two bottles of the golden, sweet wine from home in Hong Kong as her contribution.

Preceded by Lao Dao who put a snifter and a wine glass in front of the men and a wine glass only in front of the women, Lao Dee poured a dash of the brandy in the snifters and filled the glasses with the dessert wine.

The service completed, Lao Dee, standing, lifted his wine glass and said, 'This wonderful evening, full of good cheer, of good food and undemanding friendships, new and old, is at once an end and a beginning. An end to a life we had reconciled ourselves to or taken for granted, a beginning of a new, in any case *different* life.

'For most of us it will indeed be a *new* life in different circumstances and with new opportunities both for better and for worse, for others the difference will merely be in the regret of comfortable companionships or the apprehensive adjustment to new ones. None of us, however, will be unaffected. Indispensable to keep whatever happens in perspective are a sense of humour to laugh at ourselves, the courage to admit we are wrong, the tolerance to accept the other's differentness, the unselfishness to let the other have it his or her way, in short *wisdom*. That we may not be found wanting in critical times! *Ganbei*!' And at that he raised his glass and solemnly pointed it at each of the others who had by then stood up as well to meet his eyes and raise their glasses in his direction.

'*Ganbei*,' they shouted in unison and Argus-eyed they watched him take a small sip and then close his eyes to savour the flavour of the costly wine. Only when they saw him nod as a slow smile lit up his face did they follow his example.

For a brief moment they stood there as in a scene caught in a painting, frozen in time, soaking up the strangely delicious unknown flavour, minds arrested by this one stimulant, then the spell broke and everybody clamoured at once to know everybody else's opinion.

While they savoured their second and very probably last glass of Sauternes of their life, they listened with rapt attention as Lao Dee explained how this very special and unusual wine was produced and they gasped in disbelief when he told them how much one bottle of a certain prestigious origin cost.

Seeing their obvious unease as they fiddled with their glasses he reassured them, laughingly, that the two bottles hadn't cost him anything since a few years ago he and his wife had been given six bottles as a present. It had been his wife's idea, he told them, to bring the last two bottles with her just in case there would come up an occasion to celebrate something very special.

And what could be more special than this very occasion, he added, and relieved everybody applauded and cheered him and his wife.

At the women's behest the men took their snifters and sat down in the easy wicker chairs.

In companionable silence they gazed at the flickering small flames of the fairy lights on the low table and at the light's shifting reflections in the fiery amber spirit as now and then, absent-mindedly, they took a small sip.

As they finished the clearing and cleaning the women, one after the other, sauntered to where the men were sitting and sat down in the grass.

Nobody spoke as the palpable silence wrapped around them like a quilt of rippling silvery moonlight and black shadow that infused their being with the glow of inner peace and bliss.

It was way past midnight when Lao Dee felt a slight squeeze on his ankle and, emerging from his reverie, he caught his wife's eye and nodded imperceptibly.

Putting his left hand lightly on his friend Lao Dao's knee he rose quietly from his chair and said, 'It's time to call it a day. Stay as you are, Lao Dao, my wife and I will find our way.'

Ah Li and Lao Dao had got to their feet as well and followed Lao Dee as he made for the small gate. Smiling, the others stared after them as their silhouettes merged into the darkness.

The following days passed quickly.

Lao Dee, his wife and Lao Dao left their friends to their business and joined them only for a mug of tea or a simple meal in the early evening.

The rest of the time they spent together with short walks along the river or around town trying out some local dish in a small eating place along the way or in the hotel's garden simply enjoying the beautiful warm weather and a book.

Two days after their memorable Beggars Chicken dinner Zhang Yizhong unexpectedly turned up in the coffee shop as they were still having breakfast.

He gracefully accepted Lao Dee's casual invitation to join them and obviously enjoyed the full American breakfast, handling fork and knife with a dexterity that betrayed several trips abroad.

They chit-chatted until, sipping from his last cup of coffee, Zhang told them he was returning to Beijing the next day and would be very pleased if they would have dinner with him, just the three of them, that evening in the hotel's small private dining room.

Lao Dee said they would be delighted and that he would make the arrangements with Mr Lu.

That evening Zhang revealed himself as a great *causeur*, in English to boot in respect for Mrs Dee.

Complimented, in a slightly surprised and enquiring tone though, by Lao Dee on his apparently first-hand knowledge of political and economic affairs in the world outside China, Zhang told them laughingly that many years ago he had been cleared by the Party to receive, weekly and uncensored, *Newsweek*, *Time* and *The Economist* and that he knew probably more about the successes and failures of capitalism and the vicissitudes of Western-style democracy than about the *real* functioning of China's own Communist system.

Probably Lao Dee and Lao Dao were the experts on that matter and could they enlighten him as to how things *really* were, not how the Party portrayed them? In a free-for-all, of course, no holds barred, no offence meant nor taken, no reprisals to be feared, amongst good friends though of different feathers.

It became a long, heated night and only Lao Dao, with a meaningful look and a resigned shrug, acknowledged Ah Li's mounting exasperation and her sudden departure around eleven o'clock when several warning kicks under the table against her husband's shins had produced no results other than that he had finally kicked back and quite painfully at that.

It was past two o'clock in the morning when Lao Dee slipped between the bed sheets, gingerly in order not to wake his wife who had stayed motionless while he had busied himself in the bathroom, careful to make as little noise as possible.

She was awake though, probably hadn't slept yet, for she said in that mockingly disapproving tone he knew so well and with her back turned towards him to further mark her disapproval, 'What were you trying to achieve tonight? Change *China*? *Change* China! Such *hubris*! As if you and that Zhang fellow have any influence, any influence *at all* on how those Communists decide to run their bloody affairs. Ludicrous! You always tell anybody who shows a momentary interest in China how the system stifles every and all kinds of initiative and how careful one has to be about what one can say and do and yet you always launch yourself in heated, futile debates at the slightest provocation. I'll tell you what you *did* achieve though, my dear, tempestuous husband.

'Firstly you ruined a perfectly good dinner for yourself by not paying any attention to what you were swallowing, for me because I worried about you; secondly you made yourself vulnerable, for the umpteenth time, to one more apparatchik who seems to be a bit more worldly than the rest and who pretends to be your friend and interested in your opinion and experience; thirdly you won't be able to catch sleep as you toss about and worry about what you said; fourthly you'll keep me awake as well with your tossing about and pummelling of your pillow and fifthly we'll both have gritty eyes tomorrow, today rather.'

She snorted and tried to punch him in his stomach with her elbow as he snuggled up to her.

'You're so right, my love,' he said ruefully, 'imagine the stupid things I would do if I didn't have you to watch over me.' Playfully he bumped her bottom with his thigh.

She sighed and squeezed his arm. 'You'll never learn,' she muttered. 'Now keep quiet and try to get some sleep.'

They had their last dinner together the evening before their return to Dalian.

Since they had to leave very early the next morning, Ah Li's flight for Guangzhou and Hong Kong leaving at nine thirty and theirs for Shanghai at eleven, Long Wei and Zee Bin had driven up from Chengdu the evening before in time to join them for dinner.

At first the Chinese had proposed to have dinner in the hotel, insisting that this one last time *they* would pay, however both Lao Dee and Ah Li had put their foot down and told them they would *much* prefer to have a quiet, simple, leisurely meal in the garden at the Xus' place and retire early since they had all to get up at three in the morning to be on time at the airport.

And that's how it went.

Auntie Liu briefed the outsiders Lao Dee, Ah Li and Lao Dao and the insiders to be, Long Wei and Zee Bin on the others' exertions with Luding's authorities and how well everything had gone, not in the least of course because Zhang Yizhong had taken the trouble to accompany them during their first and only visit.

Zhang had stayed one day longer expressly for that purpose and though he had presented himself as just an interested friend both the mayor and the Party secretary had received them personally and had instructed the various officials, in their presence, to bring in all the papers, permits and seals for immediate dispatch.

While the officials busied themselves in their respective offices they had had tea and a relaxed, friendly chit-chat with the mayor and the Party secretary who, after the signing and sealing, had personally escorted them outside.

So now there remained the exercise in Dalian which they would tackle first thing next Monday morning, Auntie went on. Zhang had told them to be there at nine o'clock precisely so that he could time his personal phone call to the mayor and Party secretary of Dalian to coincide with their request for an audience.

It would be as good as if he were there in person, Zhang had assured them laughingly.

Once all the papers had been obtained, she and Suping would try and sell their meagre belongings for a few yuan and Lilian and Beiyuen would give notice to Vice-Manager Zhou and Secretary Du.

In all those arrangements would probably not take more than two weeks and then the four of them would pack their suitcases and take the first available flight to Chengdu.

What with the proceeds of the sale of their furniture, kitchenware and TV set and their savings, notably Lilian's, they would have enough money to pay for the tickets and to buy a few necessary new things in Luding or in Chengdu.

While she spoke both she and the others had secretively watched Lao Dee, apprehensive of signs of displeasure now that they had apparently taken the initiative into their own hands, had not even consulted him.

Lao Dee had sensed their mood so when Auntie Liu fell silent he deliberately applauded first her and then all of them and then exclaimed, 'Excellent news and an excellent plan. I must say, you do know how to strike the iron while it's hot. I am proud of you and very happy for you. Coming November, on my next trip to Chongqing, I'll pay you a short visit to see you all well settled in your new lives. But enough about all that. Let's now have that food the smells of which have made my mouth water for the past twenty minutes already.' And laughingly he clapped his hands as he shouted, 'come on, you young people! Show some respect for your hungry elders!'

Everybody laughed, relieved and content.

After dinner and a last, quiet toast with what remained of the brandy and port wine, Lao Dee declined Long Wei's offer to have Zee Bin drive him, his wife and Lao Dao back to the hotel.

'We're not in a hurry,' he told the friendly young man, 'and besides, the walk will do us good. I'm afraid my wife has also eaten too much of the delicious stir-fried kumquat beef.'

He and his wife then said goodbye to Chen Dan, Xu Ximing and his wife Guixian, whose emotions almost got the better of her, and went ahead halfway downhill where they then waited quietly for Lao Dao whose farewells to the three people he had come to love and respect took a bit more time.

'I'm sorry,' the gentle old man said when he finally caught up with them, 'it is a hard wrench to leave this place and these loveable people and return to a humdrum life without the friends to whom I have become more attached than I thought possible. It will be lonely and cold in Dalian without you all. Meiling and Lao Dan said that there will always be a place for me here, in their house and in their hearts but how can I take their place and leave my son and his family in Dalian, assuming that I will ever get permission to leave Dalian? When will I ever see them again? Everything is always so complicated in China, so maddeningly *complicated*!'

Lao Dao fell silent and blew his nose in a handkerchief, a filthy Western habit he had never shed.

Lao Dee put his arm around his friend's shoulders and said, 'Come on, old friend, this talk about a humdrum life is unworthy of you. Tomorrow you'll be glad to see your *family*, you know they love you. And think of your little granddaughter; she probably won't be able to sleep tonight from excitement. You can mean so much to her as she grows up. Imagine the things you can teach her, talk to her about, the cleverest grandfather in all of China!

'You at least still have a *purpose* during the years ahead, something entirely different and more meaningful than sitting here dozing in the sun or blabbing with a few really old people who have nothing but memories and past miseries to talk about and whose opinions no longer matter to anyone. You're still too good for that purposeless kind of life!'

He fell silent and, laughing loudly, he punched his friend on the shoulder.

Lao Dao blew his nose again, laughed quaveringly and said, 'Thank you, William. I deserved that dressing down. You put some heart back into me though.' And straightening his shoulders he took the lead downhill.

For a while they walked in silence, then Lao Dee suddenly held the others back in their stride and as his wife and friend looked at him wonderingly, he said musingly, 'Look at that beautiful half-moon, hanging there so majestically above that peaceful little town, and at those distant, black-on-black mountains jutting up like giant fingers trying to reach for the stars; listen to the silence made even more poignant by the occasional barking of a dog somewhere out there in all that velvety blackness. It's so beautiful, so peaceful, so Chinese, yet why is it that I would never want to live here for good as I would in other beautiful places on earth? Because I would always remain a stranger, an alien in a touchingly, warmly, wonderfully human yet maddeningly alien land.'

Shrugging his shoulders he resumed his walk followed, after a brief hesitation, by his wife and his friend, jogging to catch up with him.

Nobody spoke until they turned from the road into the entrance of the hotel when Lao Dao said softly, without interrupting his stride, 'Yet you did what you did, interfering in an alien culture. However well intentioned, it was *interference* from your point of view, was it not? Life will never be the same again for those you touched here with your alien wand, kindling feelings some never knew they had, rekindling them in others who had learned to live without them, suppressed by the system as you call it, the system we have learned to accept, however alien it must appear to you.

'Will *we* live to regret your interference? Will *you* one day, looking back and from some faraway beautiful place on earth, regret what you did? We'll never know it of each other, will we? For if and when we meet again or if we write each other a letter now and then, we won't mention *that* of course, afraid to appear ungrateful and hurt each other's feelings. So, perhaps, we are all *human* after all.'

CAAC's ground personnel at Shanghai's Domestic Airport, as usual hanging about in small apathetic clusters in their shabby, ill-fitting blue uniforms, indifferently snarled the standard company reply when occasionally a waiting passenger took heart and timidly approached them to ask why the flight was delayed: bad weather in Dalian.

Judging by the eternal delays of CAAC's domestic flights, China's major cities were perpetually afflicted by the world's worst weather.

When they finally landed in Dalian three hours late the weather was sunny and windless and had been so for the past week according to Lao Dao's son who had been waiting at the airport for four hours, with his wife and little daughter, to welcome his father back home. When he had asked why the flight was late he had been told that the weather in Shanghai was bad.

Lao Dao, his granddaughter on his arm, her arms clutched around his neck, her cheek pressed against his, grinned at Lao Dee and shouted, to make himself heard above the din in the arrival hall, 'Welcome back my friend, nothing has changed and nothing ever will!'

Lao Dee laughed and was about to answer when he saw the brewery bus turn off the main road and into the airport driveway.

The bastard didn't forget, it flashed through his mind and, mellowed, irritation forgotten, he smiled affectionately as he saw Zhou, the volatile, temperamental, talkative Shanghainese who was going to be the director of the new plant and who so often infuriated him with his blatant lies and utterly unrealistic promises and demands, sitting next to the driver of the bus, waving.

'Everybody get in the bus,' he shouted, 'Lao Dao, you and your family as well. We'll bring you home first, then Meiling, Suping and the girls and then I get off at my hotel.'

As the others climbed on board with their luggage he stood back with Lao Dao and said, chuckling, 'Look, Vice-Director Zhou helping the ladies with their luggage. I wonder what fantastic tales he has in stock for me this time to explain why no progress was made during my absence. Why we still don't have power or power yes but no steam, or steam yes but no power and no cooling or simply nothing at all. But not to worry! Next week, Friday at five past two, *everything* will be working. He's in a hurry, my friend Zhou is, to get his version of the story to me first, hence his eager beaver behaviour in the bus, before in the hotel my own men, furious of course, brief me on what really is the matter.

'Oh man, do I ever enjoy this! Do you believe me when I say that I'm actually *glad* to be back? Luding was just a dream, an unreal world where nothing ever happens, where people live their insignificant uneventful lives talking or dozing in the sun. Not for us just yet, eh Dao Huimin, my friend? Not as long as there remain battles to be won and wars to be lost here in Dalian, or elsewhere for that matter.'

'What's so funny?' Auntie Liu asked, a bit querulously, as the two men climbed on board, laughing.

'Everything, my dear,' Lao Dee replied, 'everything is funny or nothing is, depends how you look at things,' and chuckling he and Lao Dao took a seat in the back of the bus.

The following Monday morning Auntie Liu, Suping, Lilian and Beiyuen were escorted directly to the mayor's office as soon as the town hall opened at nine o'clock.

City Party Secretary Xian was with Mayor Wu when the porter ushered the four of them into the office and while Xian greeted them cordially and invited them to sit down in the large comfortable chairs, the mayor ordered the porter to bring up fresh tea.

As he shook hands with each of them and enquired after their health Wu told them in the same breath that Vice-Minister Zhang had called him and Xian earlier that morning by phone to brief them personally on the delicate and private nature of the matter at hand and for which he had requested their co-operation and discretion. They had assured the comrade minister that everything would be handled with the greatest expediency and the utmost discretion. The comrade minister had been very pleased and had said many kind words, the mayor told the women beamingly as Secretary Xian nodded approvingly.

At that moment the porter brought in a pot of fresh tea and four additional mugs.

While the mayor personally poured the tea he ordered the porter to fetch a number of documents from various departments and to bring them all at once to his office. As they waited for the porter to return with the papers they sipped from their tea and bantered easily about their visit to Luding and they all agreed that the southern lifestyle was very different from that in the north and that it took some adjusting to.

After some twenty minutes the porter brought in a stack of papers and the mayor told him to see to it that they weren't disturbed for the next hour.

Carefully, in his own handwriting, the mayor then filled out the documents in six-fold for each of them, including a decree nisi of the marriage between Li Kunlen and Xu Suping, a last-minute idea of Auntie Liu, after which he and Secretary Xian signed and stamped each of the copies.

Relaxed and relieved now that everything was irrevocably settled they all had one last mug of tea.

Though the mayor and the secretary seemed in no hurry at all to get rid of them and appeared to be genuinely amused by Lilian's narrative of the Beggars Chicken dinner, Auntie Liu finally gave the signal that it was time to leave.

Each of them shook hands with Mayor Wu and Secretary Xian and thanked the two men for all their kind help and co-operation.

With the promise that if ever they were to visit Luding, perhaps during a pilgrimage to the famous bridge, they would call on them, probably even stay in Lilian and Beiyuen's hotel if they could afford the price, the mayor and the secretary laughingly waved goodbye as the women descended the stairs to the ground floor and went out through the front door.

Lilian and Beiyuen didn't return home with Auntie Liu and Suping but went instead to the hotel and straight to Vice-Manager Zhou's office.

Mr Zhou was flabbergasted by the deadpan announcement that they were resigning, even leaving Dalian for good. However, when he read the city secretary's small personal note, he was gracious and wished them all the best in their new life.

He balked at bit at the girls' request for two weeks' notice, protesting it was too short but he didn't push the matter.

The hotel unit secretary was not graceful when they went to see him. Surly and hostile, Du perused the city secretary's terse official note and all but chased them out of his office.

Roger Wu became emotional almost to the point of tears as at once he bemoaned their departure as a tragic, personal loss and wished them all the success and happiness in the world.

Only a few of their co-workers were sad and told them they would miss them when they heard the news; the others reacted indifferently and shrugged their shoulders. Whether Lilian and Beiyuen were there or not didn't affect them one way or the other, so why the hell would they care?

That Monday evening, in the coffee shop, Lilian's Dutch and German friends, apparently filled in already by Lao Dee, hugged her and told her they would miss her terribly.

Engineer Jan's hug was more than friendly and casual as he almost crushed her against him. Gasping for breath she saw his eyes brimming with tears and his friends busily pretended to consult the menu they knew by heart when he kissed her full on the mouth and whispered he loved her and hoped with all his heart that she would be happy.

Not caring what whoever was watching would think she kissed him also and whispered she would never forget him. When he released her she turned and without looking back she left and went home, too sad and upset to do her work that night.

After a few minutes Jan, in vain trying to get a hold on himself, went up to his room, too sad and upset to have others around.

Two sad, unhappy young people in love with each other, longing for each other from opposing sides of the unbridgeable chasm that separated their politically and culturally antagonistic worlds.

For her last two weeks at the hotel Lilian had the morning shift and didn't serve at table. Roger Wu had arranged it that way and everybody understood why.

After work on their last day Mr Zhou and Roger Wu had organised a small party for Lilian and Beiyuen.

The long-staying guests thought to have a weak spot for either Lilian or Beiyuen or both had found a small note in their room requesting the pleasure of their presence on Friday, 7th October at 1800 hours in the small ballroom for drinks and snacks and to bid farewell to the model workers Li Lilian of the coffee shop and Shen Beiyuen of housekeeping.

Thirty-nine guests and twelve co-workers turned up, all properly dressed, for the occasion.

When Lilian and Beiyuen, escorted by Roger Wu, entered the ballroom at half past six they were greeted with a big round of applause and cheers of hip hip hooray.

The two girls, who had been told that they were expected in Mr Zhou's office where he, Roger Wu and Director Yu would bid farewell to them, were dumbfounded at the sight of the cheering small crowd and they could barely hold back their tears.

Roger pushed a glass of orange juice wrapped in a paper napkin in their clammy trembling hands and then it was Mr Zhou's turn to say a few words.

In his short, kind and candid speech Mr Zhou praised the girls' dedication and cheerful friendliness towards guests and co-workers alike and which was such a far cry from the stereotypical surly indifference of the vast majority of the Chinese workers, Mr Zhou said.

As a Chinese cadre, Mr Zhou continued, one could take heart or at least learn a lesson from the voluntary presence at this occasion of so many foreigners, people who could *not* be coerced to do something they didn't feel like and who had therefore come of their own free will simply because they *liked* Li Lilian and Shen Beiyuen and were *not* indifferent to what happened to them.

At this point Mr Zhou was interrupted by a loud applause and shouts of '*Hear*! *Hear*!' The foreigners applauded because they thought Mr Zhou was being kind to the two girls, Mr Zhou himself and his fellow Chinese applauded to send a message to the two great absentees, Secretary Du and Director Yu who were both too busy enhancing the good of the Chinese working class.

Mr Zhou had pointedly omitted the obligatory excuse for the absence of Party cadres, comrades so and so are very busy but asked me to convey their best wishes, at the beginning of his speech. When the applause died down Mr Zhou called the two girls forward and handed each of them a small red envelope.

With the typical Chinese matter-of-factness in such matters Lilian and Beiyuen opened the envelope and pulled out two notes of one hundred yuan each and showed them to the cheering crowd.

Only Roger Wu knew and Lao Dee guessed that the four hundred yuan, two months' salary, came out of Mr Zhou's own pocket. Both Director Yu and Secretary Du had snorted their disdain for the idea when he had proposed the farewell Party and a small bonus for the girls.

Good man, I'll make it up to him, it flashed, at once yet unbeknownst to each other, through a Dutch and a Chinese mind. After Mr Zhou it was Roger Wu's turn.

Witty yet sensitive he made those present laugh and smile with his anecdotes about the early stages after the hotel's official opening and with typical Cantonese immodesty he called Lilian and Beiyuen the finest examples of his training methods ever and the sole reason why he would persevere with his ungrateful task to separate the few wheat grains from the mountains of chaff.

Perhaps, just perhaps a few grains like these two who would now be transplanted to and germinate in more fertile southern fields, were hidden, waiting to be discovered by him, Roger Wu.

The small ballroom rang with laughter as he called Lilian and Beiyuen forward and also handed them each a red envelope. Like before the girls waved the two notes of a hundred yuan each at the applauding guests.

The leader of the Japanese guests on Beiyuen's floor also said a few words, terse and stammering but very touchingly friendly and a collective gasp escaped from those watching when he presented Beiyuen with three beautifully carved ivory netsuke representing the three wise monkeys. For Lilian he had a graceful ivory statuette of Kuan Yin, the goddess of mercy.

Lilian and Beiyuen were moved to tears. Not in their wildest dreams could they have expected such a beautiful, thoughtful gesture from those awkwardly shy and correct yet sometimes so exasperating little men from those weird and gloomy islands just beyond the horizon. For a minute the two girls stared at the beautiful sculptures, as if irresolutely waiting for inspiration what to do or what to say.

Then suddenly, as if with one accord, they put the expensive baubles in their bag and embraced the stupefied Japanese, one by one, as they stood there lined up behind their spokesman.

Red-faced the men bowed from the waist as they acknowledged the other guests' applause and shouts of 'bravo', 'more, more'.

Lao Dee was the last to speak, both on behalf of his own men and of the other Western guests.

He made it short and to the point. They had not come here, he said, to pay homage to two exemplary hotel employees but rather to say goodbye, all the best and see you some time somewhere. At that he called the girls forward and with a kiss on both cheeks he handed each of them a gift certificate showing a beaming Japanese girl on a feminine model light motorcycle.

'The motorbikes have been paid for by all of us,' he said, 'and are waiting for collection on presentation of these certificates at the dealer's workshop in Chengdu. The machines will give you the freedom to move around at will, use it well,' Lao Dee concluded his speech.

With a last cheer the party was over and as if in a dream Lilian and Beiyuen saw everybody file past them as they stood next to the door. They felt their hands being taken and shaken; they saw the smiles and the moving lips but could not make out the words that were said; they could smell whisky and beer and stale cigarettes as some approached their pouting lips and smacked on or near their cheeks and all the while they repeated after Roger Wu as a prompter right behind them, like a pair of automaton dolls, 'Thank you, thank you so much, *xiexie ni*, *domo harigato*.'

It wasn't until the cold evening air outside brought them back to their senses that they realised that it was over, the end of one life, the beginning of another.

Hesitantly they waved goodbye to Roger Wu who had escorted them outside but who, shivering and suddenly feeling a bit let down, had gone back through the revolving door and was now watching them through the glass partition, alone in the deserted lobby.

He smiled when he saw them regaining their posture and waved back, then, abruptly, he turned and disappeared from sight and out of their life.

With one accord they turned, clutched their bags with the costly presents under their arms and, without looking back, they went home.

The Tuesday after her successful business at the town hall Lao Dao and his son Xulun came to visit Auntie Liu at her home. After a nice, freshly brewed cup of tea and some cheerful banter Lao Dao came straight to the point.

Xulun's small flat was becoming more and more of a problem now that the child was getting bigger and soon would need a separate place to sleep and play. Furthermore Lao Dao couldn't for ever go on or even count on being allowed to work night shifts only so that he could use Xulun and his wife's bed during daytime.

In short, a bigger place was necessary but applying for one in the normal way would be hopeless, it would take years if ever before they would qualify for a bigger apartment.

He had given the matter a lot of thought, Lao Dao said, in fact it was the only thing he had thought about since their return from Luding, and he felt embarrassed and hated it to importune such a good friend as Liu Meiling, but did she think she could still put in a good word for Xulun and for him of course, with her influential friends in the city council and actually have this beautiful house, Meiling's own, assigned to Dao Xulun and his family and his father?

He had said it all in a rush and now he looked at the floor in front of him as he waited for her reply.

'If I am such a good friend as you seem to think I am, why would you hate to importune me. Why *would* you importune me anyway?' Auntie Liu growled, adding, 'what a word "importune", the words you sometimes use, my old friend, to say the obvious, the simple. Tomorrow morning, you, Xulun and I will camp on the town hall's doorstep until the mayor arrives. If my impression of him yesterday is correct he will invite us into his office and there he will offer us a mug of tea and ask what he can do for us.

'We will answer straightforwardly and not beat about the bush, I don't think Mayor Wu is a man who likes beating about bushes. He will tell us he will have to think about it and discuss the matter with the other town council members, which is to say that he will only talk privately with Secretary Xian. If Xian isn't against it, Wu will make the decision there and then and not even put it on the agenda of the council's next meeting.'

It went exactly as Auntie Liu had predicted and two days later she received a hand-written note from the mayor, countersigned by Secretary Xian, that it was in order for her to have Dao Xulun take over the rental agreement of her house 383/7.

She immediately went to the hotel and told Lilian to leave a message for Lao Dao that she needed to see him as soon as convenient.

The next day, Auntie Liu and Suping were still having breakfast together, when Lao Dao, Xulun and his wife came to see her.

'You seem to take for granted that the news is good, turning up here with your whole family at this hour when I'm not even presentable,' Liu Meiling growled, then taking pity on her old friend's crestfallen face, she laughed and said, 'well, the news is good! The mayor wrote me a personal note to tell me that it is okay for me to assign the rental agreement for this house to Xulun. I suppose we just delete my name and personal data and fill in his and then attach the note to prove the changes were legitimate. Now pour yourself a mug of tea and let me finish my breakfast.'

The Daos were overjoyed and when Xiao Lu heard Auntie and Suping discuss how they were going to arrange the sale of their household effects, she took her husband aside and after a few minutes of whispered discussion she announced to Auntie and Suping's surprised delight that she and Xulun would gladly take over everything, the whole kit and caboodle as she called it, provided the price was reasonable of course.

Auntie Liu, feigning outrage, exclaimed growlingly that she wouldn't haggle over a few yuan more or less than two thousand, including the TV set, take it or leave it, and the same went for Suping's things, four hundred yuan, no more, no less.

Lao Dao sputtered and protested that it was practically a give-away at those prices and that he couldn't accept such generosity, however, the three women ignored him and Xulun as they were already discussing busily how to fit in Xiao Lu's own bric-a-brac.

Auntie Liu and Suping also accepted smilingly Xiao Lu's request to pay half the amount on the day the Daos would move in, that is on the day of the others' departure for Luding, and that Lao Dao would bring the other half when he would visit them in Luding, probably during the coming winter months.

Baffled, taken aback, Lao Dao and his son stared at each other as they listened to all these decisions being taken, casually and as a matter of course.

'I often wonder why women bother to put up with us, bumbling slow-witted men,' Lao Dao sighed. 'Why not simply put us down, or eat us like their spider counterparts, once we have done the one thing they can't do themselves. The world might well be a better place.'

'Wrong, Father!' Xulun said. 'Wrong on all counts. Basically females don't like other females, they instinctively distrust each other and each other's motives and without us males to mother, to nag, to push around, they would tear each other's throats out. Besides, there is always that tiny bit of usefulness whenever the need for it arises,' he concluded and both he and his father burst out laughing ignoring, deliberately, the three women's glowering stares.

Suping made one quick day trip to Lushun to see how her husband was doing.

The director received her in his office and told her, very kindly and compassionately, that it would probably be better if she didn't see him. His physical condition had suddenly deteriorated over the past few weeks and he was fed only liquids now, a bit of soup but mostly water to avoid dehydration.

The little dog Ciaokeli had suddenly, three days ago, refused all food and drink and didn't move or sleep as he laid there, on Kunlen's chest, his half-open eyes fixed on Kunlen's slack face.

There were already bets going on amongst the personnel on who would pass away first, Kunlen or Ciaokeli, the kindly doctor said, with a tired indulgent little smile.

Suping thanked him for everything he had done for Kunlen and took her leave.

She didn't notice the jerks and jolts of the old ramshackle bus as she stared with unseeing eyes at the passing, greyish boring landscape.

A human life wasted, she thought as she wiped her eyes with a paper napkin, and nobody cares, not even I. I'm sure the little doctor is going to win the wager, that's probably all *he* cares about.

'Shame on you, Xu Suping of Luding,' she said aloud, 'you are being grossly unfair. He and his nurses were taking care of your idiot husband, something you could no longer bring yourself to do, and while you were gallivanting around in Sichuan. And now you begrudge them their little bit of morbid fun, probably the only kind of fun they know.'

She shrugged her shoulders and stared down the dribbling lewd old man and his ugly hostile wife who sat opposite her.

'They are ugly, hostile and smell bad like Old Turtle, like the lives these people lead,' she mused aloud and, suddenly exultant, 'yet I stared them down! I should have done that years ago with Old Turtle instead of letting her intimidate me and Lilian. Never again. There will be other Old Turtles, probably also in Luding, but I know now how to deal with them. Just ignore them and, if they refuse to be ignored, confront them and stare them down. That'll be my life philosophy from now on, "ignore or, if that doesn't work, confront". I'll tell Lilian.'

At nine o'clock the morning of their departure Lao Dee stopped the van of his Japanese friends in front of house 383/7.

Having passed the Chinese road test years ago he was allowed to drive himself and he did so this Saturday. He helped Lao Dao and Xulun unload the bundles of clothes and cartons with baubles, pots and pans while Xiao Lu, her little daughter tied to her front in a carry bag, went inside.

They would make two more trips that day, after the airport business, to move the remainder of the Dao family possessions. The Daos would not accompany their friends to the airport, it was better for everybody that they stayed in their new home.

Leave-taking was subdued, absent-minded and mercifully quick. Only Lao Yang, standing in the doorway of his hovel, waved goodbye as the van passed, his rheumy eyes watering, or were they tears?

Nobody spoke as Lao Dee drove his friends to the airport. Lost each in her own thoughts, they stared out of the windows at the street scene outside. The sky was overcast and everything looked grey and dusty as people hurried through the dust clouds swept up by a strong, cold north-westerly wind, pieces of cloth pressed over their mouths.

A good day to leave, Lao Dee thought, no regrets for this aspect of Liaoning life.

Beiyuen and Lilian helped Lao Dee drag their suitcases to the front of the line next to their check-in counter and then Lao Dee, abusing his status as a 'foreign friend' squeezed himself in front of the other waiting passengers and checked in for all four of them.

As he busied himself with tickets and boarding passes, a taxi stopped in front of the departure hall and Jan jumped out, leaving the taxi door open. He ran inside, immediately saw Lilian looking in his direction and rushed to meet her as she ran towards him.

They embraced and kissed, then, suddenly, Jan pushed her away from him at arm's length, fumbled in his pocket and slipped something small in the pocket of her jacket. Then he turned and without glancing back he ran out of the hall and jumped into the waiting taxi which drove off while Jan was still pulling the door behind him.

As if in a dream Lilian joined the others who had been looking on at the touching, short interlude.

Wordlessly she showed the others the object Jan had slipped into her pocket, a small, gold pendant in the form of a coin with on the front side the effigy of the Queen of the Netherlands. The back had been filed flat and polished and somebody, probably Jan himself, had engraved, in Dutch, 'I will always love you'.

'What does it say?' Lilian asked, her voice trembling.

'Luck, happiness, long life and prosperity,' Lao Dee lied.

The blaring loudspeaker ordering all passengers for Beijing to board immediately saved him from further embarrassment.

One by one the women embraced and kissed him on both cheeks, turned and filed passed the CAAC girl at the gate door towards the bus that would take them to their plane.

As he drove the van out of the parking lot he saw the elegant shape of the Ilyushin disappear into the racing grey clouds before he heard the roar of its engines.

Too many decibels, he thought incongruously, what a shame, such a beautiful plane. But then, beauty is never perfect, now is it?

# *Epilogue*

Li Lilian and Shen Beiyuen started in their new job on Monday 10th October, 1988.

The first two months they shared a standard room in the hotel, the room which, in all fairness, one couldn't give to a paying guest as it faced the cooling tower with the noisy fan and the deep well with the rattling pump.

Then, after two months of sleepless nights, they were assigned a small, one-room shack at two minutes' walking distance from the hotel. The hotel paid half of the rent of six yuan a month, the other half they shared.

Lilian did a stint in every department before she became Mr Lu's assistant in 1990 and a vice-director in 1991. This latter position entitled her to live in one of the small but very neat management houses on the hotel premises. The other house was occupied by Mr Lu of course.

In 1992 she got permission from the government to follow a six-month management course in Hong Kong.

Barely one month after her return her lover and husband-to-be Long Wei died in a traffic accident when Zee Bin judged wrongly that he could squeeze his van past a truck in a bend just before the top of a hill and collided head-on with a truck coming at full speed from the opposite direction.

Long Wei and a few others, visitors from Beijing, died on the spot. Zee Bin miraculously survived though with a broken pelvis and broken legs.

Mr Lu's fatherly consolations went a bit out of hand and three months later, on January 15th, 1993, he and Lilian got married.

On June 10th of the same year, Lilian gave birth to a son, Lu Wenfu, also to be called William Lu after his godfather Lao Dee.

The hotel's joint venture partners agreed to lease the big former landowner's house about a kilometre downstream from the hotel for the family Lu. They still live there and probably will for the rest of their working lives.

Shen Beiyuen remained faithful to Zee Bin, even when the accident left him jobless and crippled for life. His pelvis had been badly set in the hospital in Chengdu and also his right leg had healed in a strangely crooked way.

Lilian and her husband came to the rescue of their unfortunate friends when a visiting joint venture director agreed to let them hire Zee Bin as a gardener-cum-handyman and to let him have, for five yuan per month, the management house vacated by the Lus themselves, provided Beiyuen were to marry him, of course.

Beiyuen and Zee Bin were married on 20th August, 1993, and their son Zee Ziye, also to be called William Zee after his godfather Lao Dee, was born on 17th June, 1994. They still live there and probably will for the rest of their working lives.

Inspired by Secretary General Deng Xiaoping's hobby, the Lus and the Zees taught themselves how to play bridge and they now spend most of their leisure time together playing cards and playing it very well indeed.

Lilian also convinced her grandparents and her Uncle Dan and Auntie Liu to learn the game. The old people now play every day and enjoy it immensely, especially after Lao Dee brought a special standard for Uncle Dan to put his cards on in front of him so that he no longer drops the cards because of his shaking hands.

Suping moved in with her parents.

From her previous stay she knew that the old folks were still very capable of taking care of themselves and the daily household chores and that for the time being they needed her company more than her care.

She therefore went to see the director of Middle School Number Three to discuss with him her possible reinstatement.

During her chat with Director Yang about her antecedents he mentioned casually that he was a nephew of Suping's former headmaster, Yang, who had committed suicide by jumping out of the window during the first harassing days of the Cultural Revolution.

Suping blanched and told Director Yang about her mother's and, indirectly, her own connections with his uncle and the intrigues that had surrounded his death. She also gave him a brief summary of what had happened to her since those days and how it came that she was now back in Luding.

Director Yang listened without interrupting her even once, nodding, tut-tutting and shaking his head in disbelief.

When she fell silent he sighed and mused that it had been terrible times and that fortunately most things had changed for the better, Suping's own present situation being the best proof, however, that one thing was still the same and would always be and as he said that he handed her a sheaf of papers, stapled together, and remarked, 'Learn by heart what's in these papers, Suping. Party guidelines about what and how to teach the students in middle schools. If you think you can do that you are welcome to start here next month as an assistant teacher, second class. Your performance and attitude will be evaluated on a daily basis by the leaders of your classes, students but also Young Pioneers, who report directly to the school secretary, a full Party member. There will be monthly appraisals and self-criticism sessions. If everything goes well you will be promoted to assistant teacher first class after the first school year. If everything continues to go well you will be appointed as a full-time teacher after two more years. Your starting salary will be thirty-two yuan per month. Do you accept?'

Suping said she did and so she began her second career.

Two months after her arrival in Luding she received a three week old letter from the Lushun Institution advising her that Li Kunlen had died on 15th November, 1988 and would be buried on 16th November in the institution's graveyard.

The envelope was postmarked Lushun, 18th November, 1988, and the letter's ending was: please advise whether you wish to be present for the burial.

Her parents and Uncle Dan dissuaded her, against the mocking encouragement by Auntie Liu, from writing a sarcastic reply, arguing that it would only create trouble and to what end? So instead she wrote a friendly small note thanking the director and his staff for all the care they had given to her husband Li Kunlen.

She signed, Li née Xu Suping and that's how she decided to continue her life, as Mrs Li, widow, after her mother convinced her that people would treat her with more respect than if she were to call herself Xu Suping. They might snigger and think she hadn't been able to catch a husband. That last argument did it of course. So she sent her decree nisi to the mayor of Dalian with a letter of explanation and appreciation for all his help.

She befriended Director Yang's elder brother Peixian, a widower and five years her senior but still in very good shape.

Yang Peixian is the director of the Luding Regional Agricultural Department and his hobby is to compile an inventory of the wild flowers, plants and trees of the Daxue Shan range.

His enthusiasm apparently caught on with Suping for she has become an expert on wild flowers, plants and trees of mountainous regions and she and her friend still spend most of their leisure time working on the inventory at his home or collecting specimens in the mountains.

Secretly bets are being placed with Auntie Liu as to when they will announce plans to get married but for the time being both seem to be content with the present situation which has probably all the conveniences of the marital status and none of the inconveniences.

Perhaps, one day, when Suping's parents will have passed away, she and Peixian may decide to get married were it only to keep the Xu's house on the hill, a bigger and better one than Peixian's which he will have to vacate anyhow the day he will be asked to retire.

Chen Dan had Zhang Yimin's house ready for occupation the day Liu Meiling arrived and they moved in that same day.

The following Monday they went together with the Xus to the town hall to register their marriage, a matter that took no more than five signatures and less than ten minutes.

Dan and Meiling still live there, play bridge with the Xus every day and, without fail, look forward to and enjoy the Sunday lunch with Lilian and Beiyuen and their men. Suping does the shopping, cooking and ironing for them as well as for her parents and Beiyuen takes their laundry to the hotel where she has the privilege to use the big washing machine and drier for herself.

Early morning on 26th May, 1989, Lao Dee received a phone call from Lilian in his hotel room in Nanjing.

She had first called her former hotel in Dalian, however, the operator had told her that Lao Dee had gone to Nanjing for two weeks and that any messages for him had to be forwarded to the hotel there.

At least ten times the cantankerous night shift operator made her repeat the spelling of the foreign name and twice he simply hung up on her in the middle of their shouting match about some letter or other among the general gibberish.

When finally at her third attempt the man deigned to put her through she was already so exasperated that without the customary niceties she shouted, as if she were still dealing with the operator, 'What's going on up there, Lao Dee? The radio says that a few counter-revolutionary elements, students mostly, are fomenting trouble in Beijing and also in Nanjing and Shanghai. But that's not what I hear on the portable radio you gave Auntie. The short wave VOA and BBC speak of massive rallies of students and workers and that there have been clashes with the police and the army. They say Secretary Zhao calls for calm. Uncle Dan is worried, Lao Dee, and he asked me to call you.'

'The situation worries me also,' Lao Dee replied. 'From what I see and hear here I'm sure there will be trouble, big trouble probably. Please don't get involved if ever there are manifestations down there in Luding. Don't take sides and don't translate what you hear on Auntie's radio for people you don't know. Only talk to Uncle Dan, Auntie Liu, your mother and your grandparents about what you hear on the foreign news. Listen only to Uncle Dan's advice, *not* to Auntie's. Tell her to keep her big mouth shut. Tell her I said that.

'I'll call you when I'm back in Dalian. I'll probably come and visit you at the end of next month. Until then stay put and keep a low profile.'

She promised she would heed his advice and rang off.

A few hours later, on his way to the project site on the other side of the river in the brewery director's brand new Pobeda, Lao Dee was stopped as he approached a large traffic circle by a group of excited young people on bicycles who were wearing yellow head and armbands.

A pretty, radiant girl, her face flushed and headband dark with perspiration because of the hot weather, came towards him as he got out of the car and said, in broken English, 'Please you watch what you see, foreign friend, and tell your friends in your country. I give know you that many students and workers, more than sixty ten thousand all, will pass here in demonstration for new freedom we all want in new freedom China. You watch see and listen, understand, foreign friend.'

Noticing his shiny black car she added frowningly, 'Perhaps Comrade Gorbachev sent you in your Soviet car to report about new China glasnost, correct not correct?'

'Not correct,' Lao Dee replied in Chinese, 'I do not report to Comrade Gorbachev but I am stuck in traffic right now so I have no choice but to wait for all of your friends to march by and, having nothing else to do, I'll watch and have my fearful thoughts.' And at that he climbed on the hood of the car and sat down, leaning back against the windshield.

Several people, who had also been stopped by the self-appointed student traffic controllers, had approached during the exchange and they burst out laughing when they saw the girl blush at Lao Dee's wink and broad grin.

A few of the younger men took off their shoes and clambered on to the roof of the sturdy car so as to have a better view of the procession as it filed past. The general mood was relaxed and gay, festive even, as the predominantly young demonstrators waved at the spectators, rang their bicycle bells and brandished their banners.

After a couple of hours and the end of the procession nowhere in sight, the girl and a dozen or so fellow students drifted hesitantly back to where Lao Dee was sitting on his car, struggling to stay awake in the warm sun. The men on the car roof had long since fallen asleep.

'What do you think, foreign friend?' the girl cried as she was still more than ten metres away. 'This is the beginning of a new era in China. We are all united in our demand for democracy. The whole world supports us and is watching our and other demonstrations all over China.'

'That's exactly the problem,' Lao Dee replied, laughing, then he added seriously, 'the outside world supports you all right but only with words as they *watch* and *keep* watching also when, not *if* mind you, your government follows up on its warnings and takes stern action against what it considers a counter-revolution.'

'The government is afraid to take action!' one of the boys shouted. 'It has gone too far, too many people support our case. Even Secretary Zhao Ziyang is on our side!'

Lao Dee saw that quite a crowd of onlookers had gathered around his car, attracted by the exchange between him and the students. Reason told him to back off and not to get involved but then that was not his character and besides he really believed what he wanted to say to these eager young people so he shrugged his shoulders and shouted back, 'I'm afraid that your naivety is only surpassed by your ignorance! I don't know what your field of study is, my foolhardy young friend, but it certainly isn't history, that much is clear.

'Your government, the Party, is *not* afraid as you seem to think, only divided on whether to intervene forthwith or to give you a bit more time to come to your senses of your own accord. *Everybody* in the government, including Secretary Zhao Ziyang, agrees that action *must* and *will* be taken if you don't come to your senses. Maybe there is some disagreement as to how *stern* the action must be with Secretary Zhao Ziyang in favour, for the moment at least, of a softer approach, of *talking* with your leaders and making them see sense. But if that approach fails he'll be just as tough as the others.'

He was interrupted by applause from quite a number of the onlookers, mostly elderly people, while others, the students but also the younger people in the crowd, shouted, '*Wrong*! foreign friend, *wrong*! We must keep the momentum going! We must continue our demonstrations and press our demands! Secretary Zhao Ziyang will listen and the government will listen to Secretary Zhao Ziyang.'

'Secretary Zhao Ziyang will *not* listen!' Lao Dee shouted. 'He has heard enough and he wants *you* to listen to *him* and *my* advice to you is that you *should* as he is probably the only one who wishes you no harm, provided you back off *now*. If you don't, if you let Secretary Zhao Ziyang down and make him lose face, I don't know *what's* going to happen but I fear the worst.

'So I repeat, go back to your kennels. You have made your point. The outside world now knows about you and your dreams. Your own government now realises that it will have to make concessions and some of the Party leaders may even be willing to do so, slowly and gradually, so *don't push your luck*! Go back to your campuses, to your factories and work hard to insinuate yourself into influential positions and *then* work together to change the system from *within*, by dialogue and example, *not* by force.

'No Communist Party has ever given up power *voluntarily* and don't even think of making that happen here in China. You'll need *force* and *arms* to make that happen and you have neither, nor the experience to use them *if* you had. And don't count on the outside world, it may wish you well but it will let you die without lifting a finger. So I repeat one more time, *go home* and, if you know how to do that, *pray* that it isn't too late already!'

Lao Dee fell silent, upset and perspiring and angry with himself that he had let himself be carried away.

This time there was no applause, no shouted arguments for or against. People were looking at each other uneasily and turned their back on the foreigner on his car who said things they all knew were true.

'The foreigner is right,' an elderly man said to no one in particular, 'but then the young won't listen if the truth doesn't suit them, now will they? *We* didn't when we were young so *they* won't now. What has been put in motion will follow its course and whatever will happen will happen. I also fear the worst like our foreign friend here, but then he and I know our history.'

Looking at Lao Dee sliding off the car's hood he added, 'I know you mean well, my friend, however, what you said isn't welcome right now. I therefore think that you should go back to wherever you hail from and stay there for a while to weather the gathering storm.'

'Thank you for your concern, old friend,' Lao Dee replied as he got into his car, 'everybody talks and nobody listens, so sad.' Leaning his head out of the car's side window he added, 'The procession has passed so I'll move on and mind my own business like you will undoubtedly continue to mind yours. Take care!' And with a last wink and a smile and a small wave of his left hand he slowly drove off. In the rear-view mirror he saw the old man staring after the car, oblivious of the milling crowd, his arm raised halfway up, frozen in a hesitant farewell gesture.

On 2nd June Lao Dee called Lilian from his hotel room in Dalian. He told her that everything he heard and saw pointed to an unavoidable clash between the hard-liners in the government and the student movement whose leaders became more strident by the hour as the realisation of what they had unleashed was beginning to sink in and the cold fear of the consequences gripped their hearts. He urged her to stay away from crowds and manifestations.

Three days later he called her again. 'I can't go into details,' he told her curtly, 'the situation, even here in Dalian, is tense and volatile and unpredictable. Ugly things may happen at the slightest provocation. Don't let yourself be drawn into discussions about what you hear and see on Beijing radio or TV. Be very, very careful when you listen to short wave foreign radio stations. Don't talk to strangers, don't talk to foreigners in your hotel about what happened. I'll see you early next month,' and at that he hung up.

He checked into Lilian's hotel on the afternoon of 4th July, 1989.

He had called her two days before, from Hong Kong, to tell her to arrange a simple dinner at her grandparents' home the day of his arrival. He also told her not to invite anybody he had not met before.

When he entered the lobby and walked up to the front desk he saw the receptionist disappear into the front office and barely two seconds later Mr Lu emerged to greet him and take care of his registration.

'Dinner is at six at academician Xu's place,' Lu said *sotto voce*. 'I suggest we, that is you, Lilian, Beiyuen and I leave the hotel at five thirty and walk up there, if that's all right with you, of course.'

Lao Dee nodded and said he just wanted to freshen up a bit first and would come down to the lobby at five fifteen.

If he was surprised that Lu was apparently part of the inner circle of close friends he didn't show it and neither did he mention it to Lilian when she came to his room at four thirty to brief him on the general state of affairs up there, on the hill, the small health problems and shortcomings of old age, the little idiosyncrasies that had developed over time and that had better be ignored when visiting 'the hill' as she, her mother and Beiyuen had come to refer to the old dears.

As if by tacit agreement they didn't mention 'the events' and neither did Mr Lu and Beiyuen during their walk.

Though they were obviously glad to see him again and the girls' chit-chat was cheerful and intimate as ever there was none of the carefree, girlish elation of former times.

He sensed a shimmer of hesitant reticence now and then rather than the erstwhile, sometimes tiresomely, gushing guilelessness and the imperceptible sedateness of their answers and remarks made him bite his lower lip to keep himself from smiling too openly.

They had clearly outgrown girlhood and had become young women, an often emotionally painful process in the best of circumstances and Lao Dee guessed that recent events had left a few additional and unusual emotional scars.

The sound of the creaking little gate brought Suping rushing outside to greet Lao Dee.

'I'm so very happy to see you,' she whispered in his ear as she hugged him, 'so relieved also. Please help us sort ourselves out. Emotions run high and ugly things have been said, especially by Auntie when Uncle Dan and Father tried to reason with her. I'm sure she is sorry for having said things she shouldn't have but you know her, she is so stubborn, too stubborn to apologise. She'll glower at you from her corner when you come in and perhaps say something unpleasant. Don't let on that you notice, please Lao Dee? She doesn't mean it. It's only that she has been so upset, still is as a matter of fact, and thinks that everybody who doesn't march on Beijing to strangle Li Peng and Yang Shangkun and Deng Xiaoping is a coward. She actually told Uncle Dan to give the good example. Can you imagine, the poor dear with his painfully rheumatic legs marching on Beijing to overthrow the government?' And all of a sudden she exploded with hilarious laughter.

'There is no cause for mirth in this country!' Liu Meiling bellowed from inside the house. 'Unless of course this silly old woman is the inspiration for all the hilarity. Only imbeciles, foolish old dodderers and Communists cackle with laughter these days, the spitting image of our beloved Party and government!'

Lao Dee grinned broadly and winked at the others.

'Why do people always say that wisdom comes with the years!' he shouted back in the direction of the house. 'Because they never had the misfortune to cross the path of Liu Meiling of Shanghai, that's why! If they had they would know, as we youngsters all do, that there's no fool like an old fool! Also very appropriate these days, I think!' At that he entered the house, the others, still chuckling, in his wake.

The welcome he got inside was most cordial, even emotional and that was clearly mutual as he first hugged Madam Xu Guixian, prim, lively and lovely as ever, and then made good work of that most formidable of his Chinese friends, the lady Liu Meiling.

As she hugged and embraced him, he noticed she had washed and made up her hair for him, and that she wore the clothes he had bought for her in Hong Kong last year.

'I am so glad to see *you* back, Meiling,' he whispered in her ear, and then louder, for everyone to hear, 'I'm so glad you haven't changed a bit, haven't lost your mettle, fire and folly, aggravating as the combination may be at times. But that's why we all love you.'

He felt the momentary tension flow out of her as she put her chin on his shoulder and addressed the others in the room. 'I'm sorry,' she said tremulously, 'for having been such a pain these past few weeks. A momentary overdose of folly in a normally well-balanced mixture, as this barbarian would probably have diagnosed my state of mind,' and suddenly she burst out laughing, an infectious, liberating hilarity and soon everybody was laughing and chuckling as they all shook hands, hugged and slapped shoulders.

Suping, Lilian, Beiyuen and Mr Lu quickly fetched a table and four chairs from Uncle Dan and Auntie Liu's house next door and they all sat down around the two tables put together.

Gradually the general banter and chit-chat died down and Lao Dee felt their eyes turn towards him, stealthily at first but finally everybody was looking at him and Xu Ximing, the host, said calmly, 'Tell us and show us the facts, Lao Dee. Be succinct. We old people have had enough emotions to last us until our death. As if they matter one way or another. What *does* matter though, for us, is to restore our confidence that the children were somehow *right*, that what they wanted was *decent* and of their *own* volition, not something they were set up to by dubious mischief-makers. You may begin, Lao Dee, we'll listen first and perhaps discuss and debate certain aspects during dinner afterwards.'

Lao Dee nodded and in the silence that followed Xu's words he took from the red, white and blue striped plastic bag he had had with him since his arrival a sheaf of newspaper cuttings, both from English and Chinese-language newspapers, a number of international magazines and the videotape player he always used during his projects for the training sessions.

'We'll look at these later,' he said. 'Let me first give you a summary of my own impressions and of the calmer, more thoughtful considerations abroad. First of all I can put your mind at ease, Ximing; the children as you call them rightly, meant well to begin with and in my opinion they were not set up to it.

'The issue, in the beginning, was also rather straightforward and not political. All the young people asked was that the Party put a stop to the rampant corruption, both within and without the Party, and the matter could have been settled there and then if a few unblemished Party leaders, such as Secretary Zhao Ziyang himself, had invited the most vocal of the student leaders and a few older, critical intellectuals such as Liu Xiaobo, for a kind of round table discussion to come to some sort of action plan. Everybody would have had face and that would have been the end of the whole affair.

'However, as so often in budding conflicts between the very young and the very old, the old Party leaders, the ones who had known the misery in China in the early part of the century, who had teetered on the brink of starvation and freezing death during the long march, who had fought, lost and won during the internal struggles since 1949, were stung by what they considered unseemly impertinence by a bunch of snots who had never known any hardship and had no idea what real suffering meant, who had no appreciation of how much better off they were now as compared to when the old leaders were their age. So any attempts by a few younger Party leaders, like Secretary Zhao Ziyang, to at least listen and make a gesture of accommodation, even if largely symbolic, were brushed off by the likes of Deng Xiaoping, Chun Chen, Yang Shangkun and others. Irritably they must have told Zhao to tell those snots to stop their impertinent yenning or else…!

'So you see, still nothing political, a mere generational conflict between youngsters who ask for something that is basically justified and who can hardly be blamed for having no appreciation of how hard life was before they were born and a number of hard-headed, basically uncultured old men with the typical contempt for intellectual softies. And then, of course, the matter *became* political when the young movement leaders, manipulated or not from behind the scenes by a number of older intellectuals who had had earlier run-ins with authority when they were young and I personally believe they *were,* let's say "encouraged", *demanded* to be heard, *demanded* reforms, *demanded* punishment of corrupt officials. And since a nice umbrella word for all such demands is *democracy* they were, again, "encouraged" to use that word for short and to adopt a token that somehow would *symbolise* democracy.

'And there, before the eyes of an astonished and often gloating world, appeared suddenly the yellow arm and headbands reminiscent of the people's power movement in the Philippines that toppled Marcos the dictator and a Statue of Liberty-like makeshift that was carried around triumphantly, always in full view of eagerly zooming foreign reporters, burned to protest the lack of freedom in China, copied, miniaturised in Hong Kong and distributed by the thousands.

'And then, of course, matters went completely out of hand. Where at first there had been absolutely *no question* of toppling the government, let alone of taking power away from the Communist Party by force, these unspeakable things were suddenly mentioned by increasingly strident voices of often self-appointed leaders for whom the incessant and suggestively obtrusive exposure to the media had become too much. Inexperienced, flushed, dizzy and drunk with self-importance they shouted and yelled things in microphones obligingly thrust in their faces that should *never* have been said.

'Can you imagine what went through the Party leaders' minds when they watched the scenes in the streets of the major cities and in Tienanmen square, and, worst of all, on foreign TV? When they heard the comments and irresponsible speculations by instant China experts on the ravings of a few wanton boys and girls? Everything they fought for, suffered for, the *stability* they had at long last achieved and imposed on China, was all of a sudden under threat, they *themselves* were under threat.

'In nightmarish visions they saw civil war erupting, restive minorities in the peripheral provinces rebelling, Taiwan gloatingly fuelling the unrest, tens of millions of refugees fleeing the country and destabilising neighbouring nations, in short they were convinced the very sacrosanct *stability* of the nation was at stake. Finished were the divisions at the Party top about how to deal with the movement, as one man the leaders stood behind Deng when he removed the compromised Party secretary, not because he suspected Zhao of collusion or disloyalty but because Zhao had lost *face* by not recognising the true danger in time and therefore the authority to deal with the crisis. Deng then summoned the PLA commanders, or went to see them in the province, whatever, and ordered them, or persuaded them, whatever, to put a stop to the movement using every necessary means.

'The military, and that goes for *all* military everywhere, doesn't go for half measures; something is done or not done but not a little bit done as politicians, also *all* politicians everywhere, like so much so that they can keep the problems festering and themselves busy with meddling and muddling. The Party leaders and Communists in general are of course no politicians. The very idea that they would have to beg and flatter and lie and prostitute themselves to con the people into voting for them is alien to the Communists. The Party appoints and dismisses, the people have nothing to do with that.

'Taking these things together and taking into account the sheer magnitude of the consequences of inaction as Deng and his colleagues see them, is it then so surprising that happened what happened? If one thinks, as Deng did, rightly or wrongly, in terms of hundreds of millions of people in upheaval, of the whole country on the brink of chaos, then the elimination of the cause, whether a few hundred, or even a few thousand, instigators, requires no second thoughts, not even a fleeting qualm.

'It's anathema these days, especially in the West, to bring up that aspect of the matter and I must admit that the way the Party followed up on the crackdown with persecution and arbitrary jailing of a number of ineffectual individuals doesn't make it any easier for people, like myself, who try not to run with the howling wolf pack or pass judgement on something we can't comprehend.

'Of course what happened last month was terrible and deplorable and tragic, so many innocent young people died. But the word innocent says it all. They were not only innocent in the sense that they had done no harm and had no evil intentions but they were also innocent in the matter they clamoured; democracy. They didn't and don't know what democracy is! *You* don't know what democracy is as you sit there listening to me. *Nobody* in China knows what the word democracy means, not the people as a whole, not the Party, in essence undemocratic, not even the intellectuals who use the word because it's fashionable. What those hyped youngsters demanded, *instant democracy*, was madness, laughable if it weren't so sad.

'China lacks even the most basic structure for a democracy, it has never had one, nobody knows how to build one. There are no political parties, let alone parties with a programme to administer and to *govern*, with the *people* to implement such a programme if they were given one, with experience in the rule of law, in economics, in international relations. Democracy has to be learned and that takes time, it took us in Western Europe and the United States hundreds of years and still we make mistakes, still we find it difficult sometimes to accept the will of the majority.

'How in the name of all the gods can you have instant democracy in China? The idea alone! Ludicrous! Like building a house on quicksand. Disaster, upheaval, chaos, fighting would have been the inevitable consequences. Though Deng Xiaoping followed a completely different reasoning, his conclusion was the same as mine and as that of many others who know the situation in China. No, the real tragedy is *not* what happened last month. It is the fact that no lessons are learned from it by the Party and its old leaders. They refuse to see that despotic, autocratic systems of government, and of which communism is the worst, are no longer acceptable, not even feasible, in an increasingly open and interdependent world. Instead of clinging to power, rigidly and uncompromisingly, the Party should honestly assess its old role models.

'The inescapable conclusion will be that those models, though perhaps valid at the time of their inception some sixty or seventy years ago, are now hopelessly outdated, superseded by the normal evolution of man and his capabilities and outclassed by the social and intellectual developments in the free societies outside China. The environment wherein man lives is of enormous importance for his evolution, however, it is not *all*-important. Influences from other environments are unavoidable. In free societies those influences, good as well as bad, are literally embraced in man's innate drive to try out anything new and hitherto unknown, discarded after a while or adapted and adopted for better or worse. The choice is man's own, individual one; governments in free societies have little or no influence on that choice. Even if they wanted to, and in the case of bad influences the temptation to intervene may be great, they can't, bound as they are by their society's constitution which precisely guarantees such freedom of choice.

'However, even in tightly controlled and oppressively regulated societies such as Communist or Fascist military dictatorships, outside influences will seep in and contaminate people's minds. Ironically the Communists themselves created the conditions for the contamination by improving the lot of the vast majority of the people. Food is adequate and assured so people need no longer worry about the next meal and therefore they have *time* to think about other, loftier things. The food's better quality combined with the health awareness campaigns and care not only improve the people's physical condition but also their mental capabilities so that they gain the *ability* to think about other, loftier things.

'Finally the *training* in thinking is provided by the education system for the people, the pride of the Communist system and herein lies the irony of it all. The human mind is unique and incomparably more complex than that of life forms lower on the evolutionary ladder or what artificial intelligence will every be. Cetaceans and chimpanzees can be taught tricks that may seem human-like but they are just that, tricks, extremely limited in scope and the creatures unable to make inferences or draw conclusions to apply in new situations presented for their own interpretation. Artificial intelligence is even more limited in scope.

'Humans, however, are always analysing, inferring, deducting and concluding and trying out their conclusions and learning from their experiences. It's innate, in our genes and can't be switched off. It can only be enhanced, improved, by training the brain and it doesn't matter so much how the training is done. Even the most contorted facts, the most ludicrous propaganda fed to the brain is a form of training and if then titbits of different information seep in from outside, contaminating as it were the Communist software, like a computer virus, the inevitable and irrepressible process of analysing, inferring and so on using the new data sets in and there you go: divergent views, dissenting opinions, arguments and debates.

'The only thing the Communists can do, and do, is to try and suppress the arguments and debates and persecute the contenders. The process that has led up to the arguments and debates they can do nothing about, having initiated it themselves by providing education to the people. If the Communists would carry out the suppression and persecution in total secrecy shrouded in total silence they might, just might succeed in containing the process and remain on top.

'However, even Communists are humans after all so they have this irrepressible need, this uniquely *human* flaw, to justify their actions, to convince the people of their correctness and of the dissenters' selfish villainy. The sole result of all these words, and the more strident the more so, is that the *human* minds of the people construe them as counter-arguments, more food for thought, and the process keeps going stimulated by the Communists' own self-righteous garrulousness.

'If now the Communist Party of China would draw the conclusion from recent events that they can no longer contain the evolution of the people's thinking and instead focus on *channelling* the results rather than on *suppressing* them it can still play the major role in China's evolution for a long time to come, one generation at least, probably two, and what is more, the people would be quite content to let it play the major role if they saw the Party make honest efforts to prepare China for a pluralistic form of society, a kind of benevolently paternalistic democracy.

'I don't think that even the most outspoken intellectual critic of the present regime would go any further than that. I even think that that is what the vast majority, if not all of the Chinese would actually *prefer*. They wouldn't feel comfortable in an everything goes and everybody for himself society wherein individual liberties are stretched to excess, wherein a certain measure of restraint for the sake of simple decency is anathema, wherein people refuse to make even a small sacrifice for the common good.

'If such a form of society were to be introduced in China as a result of outside pressures and inside manoeuvring by an infinitesimal minority, it would end in a disaster that could very well engulf the whole of Asia first and, after a while, the rest of the world as well.

'The world cannot afford an unstable China; the number of people affected and driven into a fight for naked survival would be simply too big to be contained.

'Apart from the few blethering muddleheads disgracing their country on the international scene in their arrogated role as the guardians of universal human rights and whose ignorance of what really matters to people in general and to Asians in particular borders on the criminally negligent, the dyed-in-the-wool politicians know very well the crucial importance of a stable and reliable China and they will do everything not to rock the boat, even if the helmsman is Li Peng or Deng Xiaoping or some other diehard Communist, even if the helmsman demands favours such as most favoured nation status, even if at the helmsman's behest they have to disavow, if not in word then certainly in deed, the victims of last month's tragic events.

'I give these politicians the benefit of the doubt, however, and think that they would commit themselves and their countries' co-operation if the Chinese Communist Party was to let them know, discreetly, that it wishes to embark on a gradual, oh so gradual political liberalisation programme following at a prudent distance the ongoing economic liberalisation and to be halted, even reversed temporarily, at the slightest hiccup. If, however, the Party shows no such inclination and persists in the policy of oppression and persecution of those who disagree then so be it. The outside world will *always* accommodate whoever or whatever can keep China in check. The alternative is simply too abhorrent to contemplate.'

Lao Dee fell silent and twiddled his thumbs, waiting for a reaction from the others.

'I'm sorry,' he added ruefully when the others remained silent, 'I probably shouldn't have talked like that, so remote, as if I were debating a matter of academic interest rather than lamenting with you the human tragedy.

'But I can't, I don't have those feelings. Of course I pitied those wild-eyed, frightened children and I couldn't hold back my tears when I saw them and their fantasies crushed by the PLA's tanks, but I also experienced that feeling of cross annoyance I always have when I see self-destructive stupidity in action. Like when I watch a documentary about huge herds of wildebeest drowning and crushing each other to death in their attempts to cross a rain-swollen river. You watch and cry out in helpless exasperation, "How can these stupid animals be so... so... *stupid*! Why don't they wait until the rain stops? Why don't they cross somewhere else where the banks are less steep? They *see* their mates drown and yet they jump! What is there on the other side that makes this massacre worth while?"

'There is an analogy. In China you don't cross the Party, you go with it. You don't try to change its course when it's swollen with conflicting ideas and pressures from inside and outside. You wait until it purls quietly along in its bedding and then you seek out level, common ground to divert its course gently.

'There never will be any change in China unless it is initiated and subsequently controlled by the Party. Both the Chinese and the outside world had better accept that as a fact and live with it and try to make the best of it in everybody's interest, Chinese and non-Chinese alike. This is what I have to say.'

He fell silent, slightly irritated with himself and annoyed with the others, however illogical, that he kept on saying the same thing, kept on flogging a dead horse.

This time, however, there was a reaction, from Xu Ximing, who snorted a mirthless laugh and said, 'My words exactly, only I spoke them almost a generation ago, twenty-four years almost to the date and in precisely this same place. *My* disbelieving listeners at that time were my own wife and daughter, our friend Chen Dan here and Dan's protégé and our dear Chen Juntao, that bumbling, bungling hero over there, under the walnut tree, undoubtedly convulsed with laughter at so much obtuse obstinacy, like bumble-bees buzzing and banging ceaselessly and senselessly against a window pane, denser even than Lao Dee's wildebeest.

'We were only suspected of trying to change the Party's course with idle, ineffectual, intellectual blabber, a crime in itself and yet what a heavy price we paid, especially Juntao, and all to no avail whatsoever. And now another generation is paying for buzzing and banging against the window-pane between China and the outside world. Do you expect me to believe that there won't be a repeat performance in another ten or twenty years? That the bumble-bees and wildebeest will evolve a rudimentary consciousness of what it means to be a bumble-bee or wildebeest and cease to act senselessly? I won't see the day that happens and neither will you, I'm afraid.

'But enough of this imagery. I agree with Lao Dee and say again, as I said before, that political and social change in China and in the way it views the outside world is only possible through the Party and by the Party and, most importantly, only then when it comes to the conclusion that such change is in its own interest and that its total control over every and all aspects is in no danger. *Never ever* will it let pressure or, worse, threats dictate the course and goals and role it has set for itself, least of all if such pressure or threats come from *outsiders* both Chinese and foreign.

'Only *insiders*, that is, high-ranking cadres of proven loyalty to the institution, can nudge the paramount leader towards a willingness to listen to new ideas and try out one or two of the most innocuous, always provided of course they have a scapegoat ready if the trials fail. Let us hope that the new, economic ideas and reforms succeed and that the results are not perceived as a threat by the other top leaders; whether to themselves personally or to the Party as an institution, *the* institution, is irrelevant. Perhaps, just perhaps the economic successes, always provided the unavoidable trappings in their wake remain controllable, will encourage these insiders to start dabbling in some reformist political ideas like for instance a somewhat freer press, a labour union, a few opposition delegates in parliament, appointed at first, elected later if all goes well. Small beer undoubtedly in Western eyes but quite revolutionary for China, as Lao Dee well knows.

'Let us hope also, however, that the West doesn't feel that it needs to *encourage* or, worse, *applaud* and *reward* every small change for the better as it sees it and *frown* upon or, worse, *waggle a warning finger* at the first hiccup or reversal. Even I, an anti-Communist by conviction, would feel offended as a *Chinese* if I were treated like a recalcitrant child, rewarded for "good" behaviour and scolded and punished for "bad" behaviour.

'We are an adult nation with a long and often painful history, longer and more painful than that of most other nations, and we have our pride and dignity, our *Chinese* pride and dignity despite the undoubtedly many shortcomings in the way we run our business. *Our* business I say and that is exactly what I mean. As long as we don't antagonise other nations, and China never will, it's not in our nature, the world has no business lecturing or threatening us. The present state of affairs in our country is of our own doing and so will be the future state of affairs, for better or worse.

'So Lao Dee, my dear friend, you go and tell your story, the stories of ordinary Chinese struggling to survive, for it is the promotion of *understanding* you are after. True understanding engenders *respect* and that is what *we* were after when we told you our stories and let you be part of our lives, what we need even more than sympathy, for respect means that you deem us capable of running our lives, accepting or rejecting as we see fit or achievable, even if you would do things differently or already run your own lives differently. Mutual understanding and respect, the prerequisites for a better world. Add *love* and we have attained wisdom, the requisite for a perfect world. It won't be for tomorrow nor, I'm afraid, for the next century, but one day for sure. Let's not give up hope.'

Xu Ximing fell silent, smiled at his family and friends and, with a wink at Lao Dee, added, 'Now show us the subversive and undoubtedly staged pictures of the horrible mess we supposedly made of our lives, Lao Dee.'

Lao Dee chuckled and said, 'I'm afraid the images have provoked a bit of a setback for your quest for the world's understanding and respect let alone love, Ximing my friend. But then, don't you despair, in a world awash in daily horrors yours will be quickly forgotten, but a wink in your long history of horrors so to speak.

'Besides, a powerful, actually *the* most powerful prerequisite for the world's understanding and respect you are so determined to command is its economic self-interest and *that* a nation the size of China can amply satisfy, regardless of whatever lofty ideal you yourselves may pursue, as long as you consume more than you produce.

'That is the quintessence of the matter, my friend, a healthy imbalance, from the outside world's point of view, between your consumption and production and if your leaders understand that and keep it that way, I'm sure Deng Xiaoping does, the world's political and business leaders will fall all over themselves and each other to pay you homage and show you all the understanding and respect you want. Love not, probably, but then who needs that restrictive commodity if you have the money to buy the non-binding fake?'

For the next hour they bit their lips and wiped their teary eyes as they looked at the pictures in the foreign newspapers and magazines that had shocked the world.

They wept openly when they viewed the video Lao Dee's wife had recorded from Hong Kong television and as one they held their breath, as the whole free world before them, at the scene of that lone young man defying the tanks.

They couldn't get enough of that lonely man's simple, unpretentious bravery and kept urging Lao Dee to rewind the tape and replay that particular passage.

Finally Lao Dee said, as he froze the picture at its most poignant moment, 'I do believe that this ordinary young man and *not* the notorious Ah Q, embodies the true spirit and mettle of the Chinese people and that he has earned you the only kind of respect that matters, that is, the respect for your courage and resilience and, above all, your enduring *humaneness*. Those qualities were the quintessence of every story you told me, which recurred in all of my personal experiences in China and which I'll always remember and cherish and admire you for. I had made a negative of this particular scene you now see on the TV screen and two dozen prints. I thought that you might like to have them.

'Look, I carry one in my wallet myself, to remind me that there *is* an alternative to cringing and fawning on the bullies in our life and that I also may one day have to face the truth about myself: cower or stand up for what I believe in and accept the consequences.'

This time it was Madam Xu who thanked him for his compassionate yet encouraging words testifying to his insight into the particular circumstances of everyday life of the ordinary Chinese.

She thanked him for the pictures and, smiling impishly, for effacing the stigma of Ah Q as the stereotypical Chinese which made everybody laugh, hesitantly at first but quickly changing into a relieved hilarity as the gloominess and depression vanished from their hearts.

Perhaps dinner was not as lively, let alone boisterous, as on previous occasions but it came close enough to say that normality had returned and that they would get on with their lives as best as they could: down-to-earth, pragmatic, cowardly when at risk, brave when not, in short like before and wholly in Ah Q's vein.